W9-BXO-726

DISCARD

The
DAUGHTERS
of
IRELAND

The
DAUGHTERS
of
IRELAND

SANTA
MONTEFIORE

Originally published as *The Daughters of Castle Deverill* in Great Britain in 2016 by Simon & Schuster UK Ltd.

FIRST WILLIAM MORROW EDITION PUBLISHED 2017.

Designed by Diahann Sturge

Library of Congress Cataloging-in-Publication Data has been applied for.

ISBN 978-0-06-245688-5 (paperback)
ISBN 978-0-06-269868-1 (library edition)

17 18 19 20 21   LSC   10 9 8 7 6 5 4 3 2 1

To Sebag
with love and gratitude

Ballinakelly Deverills of Castle Deverill

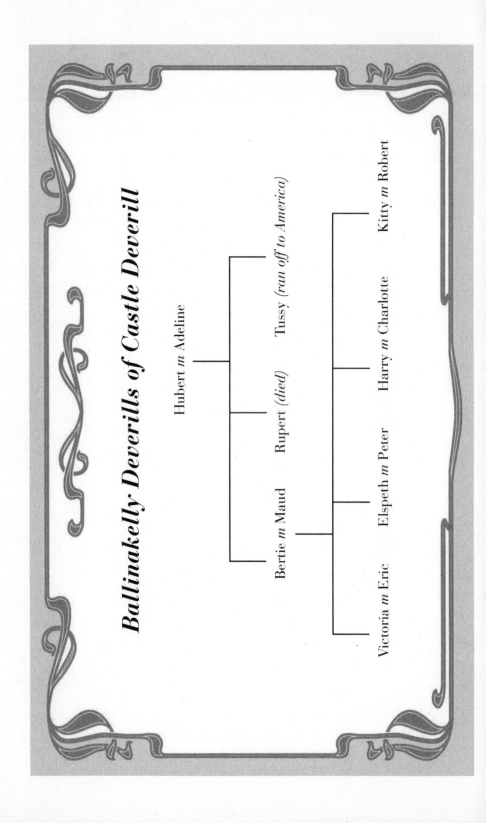

Hubert *m* Adeline

Bertie *m* Maud   Rupert *(died)*   Tussy *(ran off to America)*

Victoria *m* Eric   Elspeth *m* Peter   Harry *m* Charlotte   Kitty *m* Robert

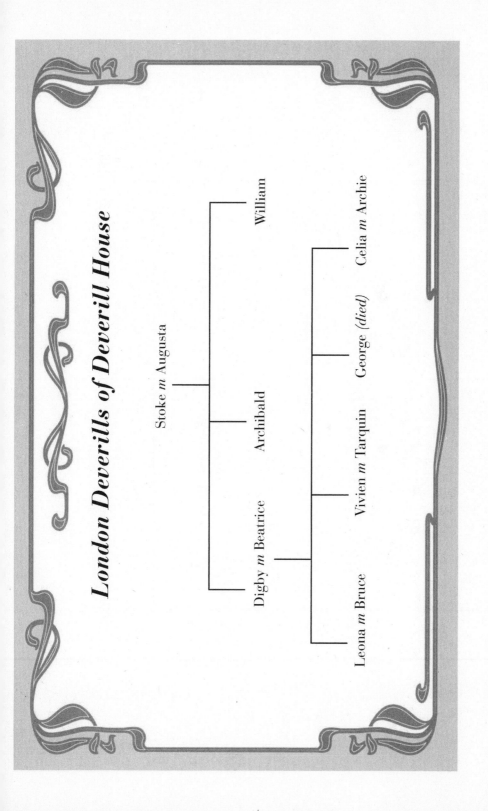

London Deverills of Deverill House

Stoke *m* Augusta

William

Archibald

Digby *m* Beatrice

Leona *m* Bruce

Vivien *m* Tarquin

George *(died)*

Celia *m* Archie

Barton Deverill

A salty wind swept over the white beaches and rocky cliffs of Ballinakelly Bay, carrying on its breath the mournful cry of gulls and the crashing of waves. Gray clouds hung low and a gentle drizzle misted the air. Swathes of green pastures and yellow gorse rendered it hard to believe the violence of Ireland's history, for even in that dull, early spring light, hers was a flawless, innocent beauty. Indeed, in that moment when the seemingly impenetrable canopy above thinned sufficiently to allow a beam of sunlight to filter through it, Barton Deverill, the first Lord Deverill of Ballinakelly, vowed to heal the scars of Cromwell's brutality and bring comfort and prosperity to the people over whom he now presided. Wrapped in a velvet riding cape of the deepest crimson, a wide-brimmed hat with a swirling plume placed at a raffish angle on his head, high leather boots with silver spurs and a sword at his hip, he sat astride his horse and ran his eyes over the vast expanse of land bestowed on him by the recently restored King Charles II in gratitude for his loyalty. Indeed, Barton Deverill had been one of the leading commanders in the fight against Cromwell's conquest of Ireland. After the defeat at Worcester he had fled across the sea with the King and accompanied him during his long exile; a title and land were satisfactory recompense for Cromwell's confiscation of his family's lands in England and the years he had devoted to the Crown. Now he was no longer a young man, thirsty for combat and adventure, but a man in middle age eager to put away his sword and enjoy the fruits of his endeavors. Where better to lay down his roots than here in this startlingly beautiful land?

The castle was taking shape. It was going to be magnificent, overlooking the sea with towers and turrets and high walls thick enough to repel the enemy, although Lord Deverill would have rather seen an end to the violence. Protestant though he was and an Englishman to his marrow, he didn't see why he and the Irish Catholics couldn't respect and tolerate each other. After all, the past lived only in one's memory, whereas the future was forged on the attitudes of today; with understanding and acceptance in the present a peaceful land could surely be attained.

He signaled to his large retinue of attendants and the group continued slowly toward the small hamlet of Ballinakelly. It had rained heavily during the night and the road was thick with mud. The sound of squelching hooves heralded their arrival, striking fear into the hearts of the people who had witnessed too much blood to be complacent about Englishmen on horseback. Men watched them warily, having not until that moment laid eyes upon their new lord and master. Women blanched, hastily sweeping up their children and retreating into their houses and slamming the doors behind them. A few intrepid youngsters remained barefoot in the drizzle like scarecrows, wide-eyed and hungry, as the English gentlemen with fine leather boots and plumes in their hats rode into their midst.

Lord Deverill halted his steed and turned to his friend, Sir Toby Beckwyth-Stubbs, a portly man with a sweeping auburn mustache and long curly hair in the fashionable cut of the Cavaliers. "So this is the heart of my empire," he said, gesticulating with his gloved hand, then added with sarcasm, "I can see that I am well loved here."

"Years of bloodshed have made them wary, Barton," Sir Toby replied. "I'm sure with a little gentle persuasion they can be brought to heel."

"There'll be no persuasion of that nature here, my friend." Barton raised his voice. "I will be a beneficent lord if they'll swear me their allegiance."

Just then, a woman in a long black Bandon cloak stepped into the track. It seemed as if the wind dropped suddenly and a stillness came over the village. The ragged children melted away and only the woman remained, her dress trailing in the mud.

"Who is this?" Lord Deverill demanded.

The estate manager brought his horse alongside his master's. "Maggie O'Leary, milord," he informed him.

"And who is this Maggie O'Leary?"

"Her family owned the land you are building on, milord."

"Ah," said Lord Deverill, rubbing his beard with a gloved hand. "I suppose she wants it back." His joke caused his attendants much amusement and they tossed their heads and laughed. But the young woman stared at them with such boldness the laughter faded into a few nervous chuckles and no one had the courage to outstare her. "I am happy to pay her something," Lord Deverill added.

"She is clearly mad," Sir Toby hissed anxiously. "Let us be rid of her at once."

But Lord Deverill raised his hand. There was something in the confidence of her stance that aroused his curiosity. "No. Let's hear what she has to say."

Maggie O'Leary gave a quiver of her white fingers and, with a movement so light and fluid that her hands might have been a pair of snowy birds, she pulled back her hood. Lord Deverill's breath caught in his chest for he had never before seen such beauty, not even in the French court. Her hair was long and black and shone like the wings of a raven, her face was as pale as moonlight. She curled her lips which were full and red like winterberries. But it was her light green eyes that severed the laughter from their throats and moved the facto-tum to cross himself vigorously and whisper under his breath. "Keep your wits about you, sire, for surely she's a witch."

Maggie O'Leary lifted her chin and settled her gaze on Lord Deverill. Her voice was low and mellifluous, like wind. "*Is mise Peig Ni Laoghaire. A Tiarna Deverill, dhein tú éagóir orm agus ar mo shliocht trín ár dtalamh a thógáil agus ár spiorad a bhriseadh. Go dtí go gceartaíonn tú na h-éagóracha siúd, cuirim malacht ort féin agus d-oidhrí, I dtreo is go mbí sibh gan suaimhneas síoraí I ndomhan na n-anmharbh.*"

Lord Deverill turned to his estate manager. "What did she say?" The old factotum swallowed, afraid to repeat the words.

"Well?" Lord Deverill demanded. "Speak up, man, or have you lost your tongue?"

"Very well, my lord, but God protect us from this witch." He cleared his throat and when he spoke his voice was thin and trembling. "Lord Deverill, you have wronged me and my descendants by taking our land and breaking our spirits. Until you right those wrongs I curse you and your heirs to an eternity of unrest and to the world of the undead." A collective gasp went up behind him and Sir Toby reached for his sword.

Lord Deverill scoffed, turning to his men with an uneasy smile. "Are we to fear the empty words of a peasant woman?" When he looked back she was gone.

PART ONE

Chapter 1

Ballinakelly, 1925

K itty Trench kissed the little boy's soft cheek. As the child returned her smile, her heart flooded with an aching tenderness. "Be good for Miss Elsie, Little Jack," she said softly. She patted his red hair, which was exactly the same shade as hers. "I won't be long." She turned to the nanny, the gentleness in her expression giving way to purpose. "Keep a close eye on him, Elsie. Don't let him out of your sight."

Miss Elsie frowned and wondered whether the anxiety on Mrs. Trench's face had something to do with the strange Irishwoman who had turned up at the house the day before. She had stood on the lawn staring at the child, her expression a mixture of sorrow and longing as if the sight of Little Jack had caused her great anguish. Miss Elsie had approached her and asked if she could help, but the woman had mumbled an excuse and hurriedly bolted for the gate. It was such a peculiar encounter that Miss Elsie had thought to mention it to Mrs. Trench at once. The ferocity of her mistress's reaction had unnerved the nanny. Mrs. Trench had paled and her eyes had filled with fear as if she had, for a long time, dreaded this woman's arrival. She had wrung her hands, not knowing what to do, and she had looked out of the window with her brow drawn into anxious creases. Then, with a sudden burst of resolve, she had run down the garden and disappeared through the gate at the bottom. Miss Elsie didn't know what had passed between the two women, but when Mrs. Trench had returned half an hour later her eyes were red from crying and she was trembling. She had swept the boy into her arms and held him so tightly that Miss Elsie had worried she might smother him. After that, she had taken him upstairs to her bedroom and closed the door behind her, leaving Miss Elsie more curious than ever.

Now the nanny gave her mistress a reassuring smile. "I won't let him out of my sight, Mrs. Trench. I promise," she said, taking the child's hand. "Come, Master Jack, let's go and play with your train."

Kitty went around to the stables and saddled her mare. As she brusquely pulled on the girth and buckled it tightly, she clenched her jaw, replaying the scene from the day before, which had kept her up half the night in fevered arguments and the other half in tormented dreams. The woman was Bridie Doyle, Little Jack's natural mother from a brief and scandalous affair with Kitty's father, Lord Deverill, when she had been Kitty's lady's maid, but she had chosen to abandon the baby boy in a convent in Dublin and run off to America. He had then been taken by someone from the convent and left on Kitty's doorstep with a note requesting that she look after him. What else was she to have done? she argued as she mounted the horse. As far as she could see she had done Bridie a great favor for which Bridie should be eternally grateful. Kitty's father had eventually come to recognize his son, and, together with her husband, Robert, Kitty had raised her half brother as if he were her own child—and loved him just as dearly. There was nothing on earth that could separate her from Little Jack now. Nothing. But Bridie was back and she wanted her son. *I had to leave him once, but I won't do it a second time,* she had said, and the cold hand of fear had squeezed Kitty's heart.

Kitty stifled a sob as she rode out of the stable yard. It wasn't so long ago that she and Bridie had been as close as sisters. When Kitty reflected on everything she had lost, she realized that her friendship with Bridie was one of the most precious. But with the unsolvable problem of Little Jack between them she knew that reconciliation was impossible. She had to accept that the Bridie she had loved was long gone.

Kitty galloped across the fields toward the remains of her once glorious home, now a charred and crumbling ruin inhabited only by rooks and the spirits of the dead. Before the fire four years before, Castle Deverill had stood proud and timeless with its tall windows reflecting the clouds sweeping in over the sea like bright eyes full of dreams. She recalled her grandmother Adeline's little sitting room that smelled of turf fire and lilac and her grandfather Hubert's penchant for firing his gun at Catholics from his dressing-room window. She remembered the musty smell of the library where they'd eat porter cake and play bridge and the small cupboard at the bottom of the servants' staircase where she and Bridie had met secretly as little girls. She smiled at the memory of stealing away from her home in the Hunting Lodge close by to seek entertainment in the affectionate company of her grandparents. In those days the castle had represented a refuge from her uncaring mother and spiteful governess, but now it signified only sorrow and loss and a bygone era that seemed so much more enchanting than the present.

As she galloped across the fields, memories of Castle Deverill in its glory days filled her heart with an intense longing because her father had seen fit to sell it and soon it would belong to somebody else. She thought of Barton Deverill, the first Lord Deverill of Ballinakelly, who had built the castle, and her throat constricted with emotion—nearly three hundred years of family history reduced to ash, and all the male heirs imprisoned within the castle walls for eternity as restless spirits cursed never to find peace. What would become of *them*? It would have been better for her father to have given the ruins to an O'Leary, thus setting them all free and saving himself, but Bertie Deverill didn't believe in curses. Only Kitty and Adeline had had the gift of sight and the misfortune of knowing Bertie's fate. As a child Kitty had found the ghosts amusing; now they just made her sad.

At last the castle came into view. The western tower where her grandmother had set up residence until her death was intact but the rest of it resembled the bones of a great beast gradually decaying into the forest. Ivy and bindweed pulled on the remaining walls, crept in through the empty windows and endeavored to claim every last stone. And yet, for Kitty, the castle still held a mesmeric allure.

She trotted across the ground that had once been the croquet lawn but was now covered in long grasses and weeds. She dismounted and led her horse around to the front, where her cousin was waiting for her beside a shiny black car. Celia Mayberry stood alone, dressed in an elegant cloche hat beneath which her blond hair was tied into a neat chignon, and a long black coat that almost reached the ground. When she saw Kitty her face broke into a wide, excited smile.

"Oh my darling Kitty!" she gushed, striding up and throwing her arms around her. She smelled strongly of tuberose and money and Kitty embraced her fiercely.

"This is a lovely surprise," Kitty exclaimed truthfully, for Celia loved Castle Deverill almost as much as *she* did, having spent every summer of her childhood there with the rest of the "London Deverills," as their English cousins had been known. Kitty felt the need to cling to her with the same ferocity with which she clung to her memories, for Celia was one of the few people in her life who hadn't changed, and as she grew older and further away from the past, Kitty felt ever more grateful for that. "Why didn't you tell me you were coming? You could have stayed with us."

"I wanted to surprise you," said Celia, who looked like a child about to burst with a secret.

"Well, you certainly did that." Kitty looked up at the facade. "It's like a ghost, isn't it? A ghost of our childhood."

"But it will be rebuilt," said Celia firmly.

Kitty looked anxiously at her cousin. "Do you know who bought it? I'm not sure I can bear to know."

Celia laughed. "Me!" she exclaimed. "*I* have bought it. Isn't that wonderful? I'm going to bring back the ghosts of the past and you and I can relive the glorious moments all over again through our children."

"*You*, Celia?" Kitty gasped in astonishment. "*You* bought Castle Deverill?"

"Well, technically Archie bought it. What a generous husband he is!" She beamed with happiness. "Isn't it a riot, Kitty? Well, I'm a Deverill too! I have just as much right as anyone else in the family. Say you're happy, do!"

"Of course I'm happy. I'm relieved it's you and not a stranger, but I admit I'm a little jealous too," Kitty said sheepishly.

Celia flung her arms around her cousin again. "Please don't hate me. I did it for *us*. For the family. The castle couldn't possibly go to a stranger. It would be like giving away one's own child. I couldn't bear to think of someone else building over our memories. This way we can all enjoy it. You can continue to live in the White House, Uncle Bertie in the Hunting Lodge if he so wishes and we can all be terribly happy again. After everything we've suffered we deserve to find happiness, don't you think?"

Kitty laughed affectionately at her cousin's fondness of the dramatic. "You're so right, Celia. It will be wonderful to see the castle brought back to life and by a Deverill no less. It's the way it should be. I only wish it were me."

Celia put a gloved hand on her stomach. "I'm going to have a baby, Kitty," she announced, smiling.

"Goodness, Celia, how many more surprises have you in store for me?"

"Just that and the castle. How about you? Do hurry up. I pray we are both blessed with girls so that they can grow up here at Castle Deverill just like we did." And Kitty realized then that Celia had placed herself here within these castle walls for more than merely the annual month of August. She was one of those shallow people who rewrote their own history and believed in the absolute truth of their version. "Come on," Celia continued, taking Kitty's hand and pulling her through the doorframe into the space where once the great hall had been. "Let's explore. I have grand plans, you know. I want it to be just the same as it was when we were girls, but better. Do you remember the last Summer Ball? Wasn't it marvelous?"

Kitty and Celia waded through the weeds that grew up to their knees, marveling at the small trees that had seeded themselves among the thistles and thorns and stretched their spindly branches toward the light. The ground was soft against their boots as they moved from room to room, disturbing the odd rook and magpie that flew indignantly into the air. Celia chattered on, reliving the past in colorful anecdotes and fond reminiscences, while Kitty was unable to stop the desolation of her ruined home falling upon her like a heavy black veil. With a leaden heart she remembered her grandfather Hubert, killed in the fire, and her grandmother Adeline who had died alone in the western tower only a month ago. She thought of Bridie's brother, Michael Doyle, who had set the castle ablaze, and her own foolish thirst for recrimination, which had only led to her shame in his farmhouse where no one had heard her cries. Her thoughts drifted to her lover, Jack O'Leary, and their meeting at the wall where he had held her tightly and begged her to flee with him to America, then later, on the station platform, when he had been arrested and dragged away. Her head began to spin. Her heart contracted with fear as the monsters of the past were roused from sleep. She left Celia in the remains of the dining room and fled into the library to seek refuge among the more gentle memories of bridge and whist and porter cake.

Kitty leaned back against the wall and closed her eyes with a deep sigh. She realized she was ambivalent about this canary, chattering away about a house whose past she barely understood. Celia's voice receded, overwhelmed by the autumn wind that moaned about the castle walls. But as Kitty shut off her sight, her sixth sense at once became sensitive to the ghosts now gathering around her. The air, already chilly, grew colder still. There was no surer feeling than this to drag her back to her childhood. Gingerly, she opened her eyes. There, standing before her, was her grandmother, as real as if she were made of flesh and blood, only younger than she had been when she had died and dazzlingly bright as if she were standing in a spotlight. Behind her stood Kitty's grandfather, Hubert, Barton Deverill, the first Lord Deverill of Ballinakelly, and other unfortunate Deverill heirs who were bound by Maggie O'Leary's curse to an eternity in limbo, shifting in and out of vision like faces in the prism of a precious stone.

Kitty blinked as Adeline smiled on her tenderly. "You know I'm never far away, my dear," she said and Kitty was so moved by her presence that she barely noticed the hot tears spilling down her cheeks.

"I miss you, Grandma," she whispered.

"Come now, Kitty. You know better than anyone that we are only separated by the boundaries of perception. Love binds us together for eternity. You'll understand eternity when it's your turn. Right now there are more earthly things to discuss."

Kitty wiped her cheeks with her leather glove. "What things?"

"The past," said Adeline, and Kitty knew she meant the prison of the long dead. "The curse *must* be lifted. Perhaps you have the strength to do it; perhaps *only* you."

"But Celia's bought the castle, Grandma."

"Jack O'Leary is the key that will unlock the gates and let them all fly out."

"But I can't have Jack and I don't have the castle." The words gripped her throat like barbed wire. "With all the will in the world I can't make that happen."

"Who are you talking to?" It was Celia. She swept her eyes over the empty room suspiciously and frowned. "You're not speaking to those ghosts of yours, are you? I hope they all go away before Archie and I move in." She laughed nervously. "I was just thinking, I might start a literary salon. I do find literary people so attractive, don't you? Or maybe we'll hire a fashionable spiritualist from London and hold séances. Gosh, that would be amusing. Oliver Cromwell might show up and scare the living daylights out of us all! I've got so many capital ideas. Wouldn't it be a riot to bring back the Summer Ball?" She linked her arm through Kitty's. "Come, let's leave the car here and walk with your horse to the Hunting Lodge. I left Archie to tell Uncle Bertie about us buying the castle. What do you think he'll say?"

Kitty took a deep breath to regain her composure. Those who have suffered develop patience and she had always been good at hiding her pain. "I think he'll be as happy as I am," she said, making her way back through the hall at her cousin's side. "Blood is thicker than water. That's something we Deverills all agree on."

BRIDGET LOCKWOOD SAT at the wooden table in the farmhouse where she had been raised as Bridie Doyle and felt awkwardly out of place. She was too big for the room, as if she had outgrown the furniture, low ceilings and meager windows from where she had once gazed upon the stars and dreamed of a better life. Her clothes were too elegant, her kid gloves and fine hat as incongruous in this house as a circus pony in a cowshed. As Mrs. Lockwood she had become too refined to derive any pleasure from her old simple way of life. Yet the girl in her who had suffered years of clawing homesickness in America longed to savor the familiar comfort of the home for which she had pined. How often had she dreamed of sitting in this very chair, drinking buttermilk, tasting the smoke from the turf fire and the sweet smell of cows from the barn next door? How many times had she craved her feather bed, her father's tread on the stair, her mother's good night kiss and her grandmother's quiet mumbling of the rosary? Too many to count and yet here she was in the middle of all that she had missed. So why did she feel so sad? Because she was no longer that girl. Not a trace of her remained except Little Jack.

The farmhouse had filled with locals keen to welcome Bridie back from America and everyone had commented on her pretty blue tea dress with its beads and tassels and her matching blue T-bar shoes, and the women had rubbed the fabric of her skirt between rough fingers, for only in their dreams would they ever possess such luxuries. There had been dancing, laughter and their neighbor Badger Hanratty's illegal poteen, but Bridie had felt as if she were watching it all from behind a pane of smoked glass, unable to connect with any of the people she had once known and loved so well. She had outgrown them. She had watched Rosetta, her Italian maid and companion whom she had brought back from America, and envied her. The girl had been swung about the room by Bridie's brother Sean, who had clearly lost his heart to her, and by the look on her face she had felt more at home than Bridie had. How Bridie had wished she could kick off her shoes and dance as they did, and yet she couldn't. Her heart was too heavy with grief for her son—and hatred for Kitty Deverill.

Bridie yearned to slip back into the skin she had shed when she had left as a twenty-one-year-old, pregnant and terrified, to hide her secret in Dublin. But the trauma of childbirth, and the wrench of leaving Ireland and her son, had changed Bridie Doyle forever. She had been expecting *one* baby, but was astonished when another, a little girl the nuns had later told her, had arrived, tiny and barely alive, in his wake. They had taken her away to try and revive her, but returned soon after to inform Bridie that the baby had not lived. It was better, they had said, that she nurture the living twin and leave the other to God. Bridie hadn't even been allowed to kiss her daughter's face and say good-bye. Her baby had vanished as if she had never been. Then Lady Rowan-Hampton had persuaded Bridie to leave her son in the care of the nuns and she had been sent off to start a new life in America.

No one who has given away a child can know the bitter desolation and burning guilt of that act. She had already lived more lives than most do in their entire lifetime, and yet to Sean, her mother and her grandmother, she was still their Bridie. They knew nothing of the sorrows she had suffered in America or the anguish she suffered now as she realized her son would never know his mother or the wealth she had, by accident and guile, amassed. They believed she was their Bridie still. She didn't have the heart to tell them that their Bridie was gone.

She reflected on her attempt to buy Castle Deverill, and wondered, if it had succeeded, would she have been willing to stay? Had she tried to buy it as an act of revenge for the wrongs inflicted on her by Bertie and Kitty Deverill, or because of a purer sense of nostalgia? After all, her mother had been the castle's cook and she had grown up running up and down its corridors with Kitty. How would they have reacted on discovering that poor, shoeless Bridie Doyle had become Doyenne of Castle Deverill? The smile that crept across her face confirmed that her intention had been born out of resentment and motivated by a desire to wound. If the opportunity ever arose again, she would take it.

When Sean, Rosetta, Mrs. Doyle and her grandmother Old Mrs. Nagle appeared in the parlor ready for Mass, Bridie asked them all to sit down. She took a deep breath and knitted her fingers. The faces stared anxiously at her. Bridie looked from her mother to her grandmother, then to Rosetta who sat beside Sean, her face flushed with the blossoming of love. "When I was in America I got married," she declared.

Mrs. Doyle and Old Mrs. Nagle looked at her in astonishment. "You're a married woman, Bridie?" said Mrs. Doyle quietly.

"I'm a widow, Mam," Bridie corrected her.

Her grandmother crossed herself. "Married and widowed at twenty-five, God save us! And not chick or child to comfort." Bridie winced but her grandmother did not know the hurt her words had caused.

Mrs. Doyle ran her eyes over her daughter's blue dress and crossed herself as well. "Why aren't you in mourning, Bridie? Any decent widow would wear black to honor her husband."

"I am done with black," Bridie retorted. "Believe me, I have mourned my husband enough."

"Be thankful that your brother Michael isn't here to witness your shame." Mrs. Doyle pressed a handkerchief to her mouth to stifle a sob. "I have worn black since the day your father was taken from us, God rest him, and I will wear it until I join him, God help me."

"Bridie is too young to give up on life, Mam," said Sean gently. "And Michael is in no position to stand in judgment over anybody. I'm sorry, Bridie," he said to his sister, and his voice was heavy with sympathy. "How did he die?"

"A heart attack," Bridie replied.

"Surely he was too young for a heart attack?" said Mrs. Doyle.

Bridie's eyes flicked to Rosetta. She wasn't about to reveal that Mr. Lockwood had been old enough to be her father. "Indeed, it was most unfortunate that he died in his prime. I was planning on bringing him here so that Father Quinn could give us his blessing and you could all meet him . . . but . . ."

"God's will," said Mrs. Doyle tightly, affronted that Bridie hadn't bothered to write and tell them of her marriage. "What was his name?"

"Walter Lockwood and he was a fine man."

"Mrs. Lockwood," said Old Mrs. Nagle thoughtfully. She clearly liked the sound of it.

"We met at Mass," Bridie told them with emphasis, feeling the sudden warmth of approval at the mention of the Church. "He courted me after Mass every Sunday and we grew fond of each other. We were married only seven months, but in those seven months I can honestly say that I have never been so happy. I have much to be grateful for. Although my grief is deep, I am in a position to share my good fortune with my family. He left me broken-hearted but very rich."

"Nothing is more important than your faith, Bridie Doyle," said Old Mrs. Nagle, crossing herself again. "But I'm old enough to remember the Great Famine. Money cannot buy happiness but it can surely save us from starvation and hardship and help us to be miserable in comfort, God help us." Her wrinkled old eyes, as small as raisins, shone in the gloomy light of the room. "The road to sin is paved with gold. But tell me, Bridie, how much are we talking?"

"A cross in this life, a crown in the next," said Mrs. Doyle gravely. "God has seen fit to help us in these hard times, for *that* our hearts must be full of gratitude," she added, suddenly forgetting her daughter's shameful blue dress and the fact that she never wrote to tell them about her marriage. "God bless you, Bridie. I will exchange the washboard for a mangle and thank the Lord for his goodness. Now, to Mass. Let us not forget your brother Michael at Mount Melleray Abbey, Bridie. Let us do another novena to St. Jude that he will be saved from the drink and delivered back to us sober and repentant. Sean, hurry up now, let us not be late."

Bridie sat in the cart in an elegant green coat with fur trimming, alongside her mother and grandmother, wrapped in heavy woolen shawls, and poor Rosetta who was practically falling out of the back, for it was not made for so many. Sean sat above in his Sunday best, driving the donkey who struggled with the weight, until they reached the hill at which point Bridie and Rosetta walked with Sean to lighten the animal's load. A cold wind blew in off the sea, playfully seeking to grab Bridie's hat and carry it away. She held it in place with a firm hand, dismayed to see her fine leather boots sinking into the mud. She resolved to buy her brother a car so that he could drive to Mass, but somehow she knew her grandmother would object to what she considered *"éirí in airde"*—airs and graces. There would be no ostentatious show of wealth in this family as long as she was alive.

Father Quinn had heard of Bridie's triumphant return to Ballinakelly and his greedy eyes settled on her expensive coat and hat and the soft leather gloves on her hands, and knew that she would give generously to the church; after all, there was no family in Ballinakelly more devout than the Doyles. He decided that today's sermon would be about charity and smiled warmly on Bridie Doyle.

Bridie walked down the aisle with her chin up and her shoulders back. She could feel every eye upon her and knew what they were thinking. How far she had come from the ragged and barefooted child she had once been, terrified of Father Quinn's hellfire visions, critical finger-wagging and bullying sermons. She thought of Kitty Deverill with her pretty dresses and silk ribbons in her hair and that fool Celia Deverill who had asked her, "How do you survive in winter without any shoes?" and then the girls at school who had called her a tinker for wearing the dancing shoes Lady Deverill had given her after her father's death, and the seed of resentment that had rooted itself in her heart sprouted yet another shoot to stifle the sweetness there. Her great wealth gave her a heady sense of power. *No one will dare call me a tinker again,* she told herself as she took the place beside her brother, *for I am a lady now and I command their respect.*

It wasn't until she was lighting a candle at the end of Mass that she was struck with a daring yet brilliant idea. If Kitty didn't allow her to see her child she would simply take him. It wouldn't be stealing because you couldn't steal what already belonged to you. *She* was his mother; it was right and natural that he should be with *her*. She would take him to America and start a new life. It was so obvious she couldn't imagine why she hadn't thought of it before. She smiled, blowing out the little flame at the end of the taper. Of course such inspiration had come directly from God. She had been given it at the very moment she had lit the candle for her son. *That* was no coincidence; it was divine intervention, for sure. She silently crossed herself and thanked the Lord for his compassion.

Outside, the locals gathered together on the wet grass as they always did, to greet one another and share the gossip, but today they stood in a semicircle like a herd of timid cows, curious eyes trained on the church door, eagerly awaiting the extravagantly dressed Bridie Doyle to flounce out in her newly acquired finery. In hushed tones they could talk of nothing else: "They say she married a rich old man." "But he died, God rest his soul, and left her a fortune." "He was eighty." "He was ninety, for shame." "She always had ideas above her station, did she not?" "Ah ha, she'll be after another husband now, God save us." "But none of our sons will be good enough for her now." The old people crossed themselves and saw no virtue in her prosperity, for wasn't it written in Matthew that it is easier for a camel to go through the eye of a needle than for a rich man to enter the Kingdom of God? But the young were both resentful and admiring in equal measure and longed with all their hearts to sail as Bridie had done to this land of opportunity and plenty and make fortunes for themselves.

When Bridie stepped out she was startled to find the people of Ballinakelly huddled in a jumble, waiting to see her as if she were royalty. A hush fell about them and no one made a move to meet her. They simply stared and muttered to each other under their breaths. Bridie swept her eyes over the familiar faces of those she had grown up with and found in them a surprising shyness. For a moment she was self-conscious and anxiously looked around for a friend. That was when she saw Jack O'Leary.

He was pushing through the throng, smiling at her reassuringly. His dark brown hair fell over his forehead as it always had, and his pale wintry eyes shone out blue and twinkling with their habitual humor. His lips were curled and Bridie's heart gave a little start at the intimacy in his smile. It took her back to the days when they had been friends. "Jack!" she uttered when he reached her.

He took her arm and walked her across the graveyard to a place far from the crowd where they could speak alone. "Well, would you look at you, Bridie Doyle," he said, shaking his head and rubbing the long bristles on his jaw. "Don't you look like a lady now!"

Bridie basked in his admiration. "I *am* a lady, I'll have you know," she replied and Jack noticed how her Irish vowels had been worn thin in America. "I'm a widow. My husband died," she added and crossed herself. "God rest my husband's soul."

"I'm sorry to hear that, Bridie. You're too young to mourn a husband." He ran his eyes over her coat. "I've got to say that you look grand," he added and as he grinned Bridie noticed that one of his teeth was missing. He looked older too. The lines were deeper around his eyes and mouth, his skin dark and weathered, his gaze deep and full of shadows. Even though his smile remained undimmed, Bridie sensed that he had suffered. He was no longer the insouciant young man with the arrogant gaze, a hawk on his arm, a dog at his heel. There was something touching about him now and she wanted to reach out and run her fingers across his brow.

"Are you back for good?" he asked.

"I don't know, Jack." She turned into the gale and placed her hand on top of her hat to stop it blowing away. Fighting her growing sense of alienation she added, "I don't know where I belong now. I came back expecting everything to be the same, but it is *I* who have changed and that makes everything different." Then aware of sounding vulnerable, she turned back to him and her voice hardened. "I can hardly live the way I used to. I'm accustomed to finer things, you see." Jack arched an eyebrow and Bridie wished she hadn't put on airs in front of him. If there was a man who knew her for what she really was, it was Jack. "Did you marry?" she asked.

"No," he replied. A long silence followed. A silence that resonated with the name Kitty Deverill, as if it came in a whisper on the wind and lingered there between them. "Well, I hope it all turns out well for you, Bridie. It's good to see you home again," he said at last. Bridie was unable to return his smile. Her loathing for her old friend wound around her heart in a twine of thorns. She watched him walk away with that familiar jaunty gait she knew so well and had loved so deeply. It was obvious that, after all these years, he still held out for Kitty Deverill.

Chapter 2

London

"Good God!" Sir Digby Deverill put down the receiver and shook his head. "Well, I'll be damned!" he exclaimed, staring at the telephone as if he wasn't quite able to believe the news it had just delivered to him. He pushed up from his leather chair and went to the drinks tray to pour himself a whiskey from one of the crystal decanters. Holding the glass in his manicured, bejeweled fingers, he gazed out of his study window. He could hear the rattling sound of a car motoring over the leaves on Kensington Palace Gardens, that exclusive, gated street of sumptuous Italianate and Queen Anne mansions built by millionaires, like Digby, who had made their fortunes in the gold mines of Witwatersrand, hence their nickname: Randlords. There he lived in Deverill House, in stately splendor, alongside a fellow Randlord, Sir Abe Bailey, and financier, Lionel Rothschild.

He took a swig, grimacing as the liquid burned a trail down his throat. Instantly he felt fortified. He put down his glass and pulled his gold pocket watch out of his waistcoat by the chain. Deftly, he flicked it open. The shiny face gleamed up at him, giving the time as a quarter to eleven. He strode into the hall, where he was met by a butler in crimson-and-gold livery talking quietly to a footman. When they saw him the footman made a discreet exit while the butler stood to attention awaiting Sir Digby's command. Digby hesitated at the foot of the grand staircase.

He could hear laughter coming from the drawing room upstairs. It sounded like his wife had company. That was not a surprise, she always had company. Beatrice Deverill, exuberant, big-hearted and extravagant, was the most determined socialite in London. Well, it couldn't be helped; he was unable to keep the news to himself a moment longer. He hurried up the stairs, two steps at a time, his white spats revealed beneath his immaculately pressed gray checked trousers with every leap. He hoped to snatch a minute alone with his wife.

When he reached the door he was relieved to find that her guests were only his cousin Bertie's wife, Maud, who was perched stiffly on the edge of the sofa, her severely cut blond bob accentuating the chiseled precision of her cheekbones and the ice-blue of her strikingly beautiful eyes, her eldest daughter, Victoria, who had acquired a certain poise as Countess of Elmrod; and Digby's own mother Augusta, who presided over the group like a fat queen in a Victorian-style black dress with ruffles that frothed about her chins, and a large feathered hat.

As he entered, the four faces looked up at him in surprise. It wasn't usual for Digby to put in an appearance during the day.

He was most often at his gentlemen's club, White's, or tucked away in his study on the telephone to his bankers from Barings or Rothschild, or to Mr. Newcomb, who trained his racehorses in Newmarket, or talking diamonds with his South African cronies. "What is it, Digby?" Beatrice asked, noticing at once his burning cheeks, twitching mustache and the nervous way he played with the large diamond ring that sparkled on the little finger of his right hand. Digby was still a handsome man, with shiny blond hair swept off a wide forehead and bright, intelligent eyes, which now had a look of bewilderment.

He checked himself, suddenly remembering his manners. "Good morning, my dear Maud, Victoria, Mama." He forced a tight smile and bowed, but couldn't hide his impatience to share his news.

"Well, don't stand on ceremony, Digby, what is it?" Augusta demanded stridently.

"Yes, Cousin Digby, we're all frightfully curious," said Victoria, glancing at her mother. Maud looked at Digby expectantly; she loved nothing more than other people's dramas because they gave her a satisfying sense of superiority.

"It's about Castle Deverill," he said, looking directly at Maud, who reddened. "You see, I've just had a telephone call from Bertie."

"What did he want?" Maud asked, putting down her teacup. She hadn't spoken to her husband, Bertie, since he had announced to the entire family at his mother Adeline's funeral that the supposed "foundling," whom their youngest daughter, Kitty, was raising as her own, was, in fact, his illegitimate son. Not only was the news shocking, it was downright humiliating. In fact, she wondered whether she would ever get over the trauma. She had left for London without a word, vowing that she would never speak to him again. She wouldn't set another foot in Ireland, either, and in her opinion the castle could rot into the ground for all the good it had done her. She had never liked the place to begin with.

"Bertie has sold the castle and Celia has bought it," Digby announced and the words rang as clear as shots. The four women stared at him aghast. There was a long silence. Victoria looked nervously at her mother, trying to read her thoughts.

"You mean *Archie* has bought it for her," said Augusta, smiling into the folds of chin that spilled over the ruffles of her dress. "What a devoted husband he has turned out to be."

"Is she mad?" Beatrice gasped. "What on earth is Celia going to do with a ruined castle?"

"Rebuild it?" Victoria suggested with a smirk. Beatrice glanced at her in irritation.

Maud's thin fingers flew to her throat, where they pulled at the skin there, causing it to redden in patches. It was all well and good selling the castle, there was no prestige to be enjoyed from a pile of ruins and a diminishing estate, but she hadn't anticipated a *Deverill* buying it. No, that was much too close for comfort. Better that it had gone to some arriviste American with more money than sense, she mused, than one of the family. It was most unexpected and extremely vexing that it had gone to a Deverill, and to flighty, frivolous and silly Celia of all people! Surely, if it was to remain in the family, it was only right that her son, Harry, the castle's rightful heir, should have it. And why the secrecy? Celia had crawled in like a thief and bought it on the sly. For what? To humiliate *her* and her family no less. Maud narrowed her ice-blue eyes and wondered how she, with her sharp powers of observation, had never noticed the treachery in that dim-witted girl.

"They are both unwise," said Digby. "That place will be the ruin of them. It's the sort of vanity project that will swallow money with little to show for it. I wish they had discussed it with me first." He strode into the room and positioned himself in front of the fire, hooking his thumbs into the pockets of his waistcoat and leaning back on the heels of his debonair wingtip brogues.

"At least it's going to remain in the family," said Victoria. Not that *she* cared one way or the other. She had never liked the damp and cold of Ireland and although her marriage was just as chilly, at least she was Countess of Elmrod living in Broadmere in Kent and a townhouse here in London, where the rooms were warm and the plumbing worked to her satisfaction. She wanted to whisper to her mother that at least Kitty hadn't managed to buy it—*that* would have finished their mother off for good. It would have upset Victoria too. In spite of her own wealth and position in society she was still secretly jealous of her youngest sister.

Augusta settled her imperious gaze on Maud and inhaled loudly up her nose, which signaled an imminent barrage of haughty venom. Digby's mother was not too old to read the unspoken words behind Maud's beautiful but bitter mouth. "How do *you* feel about that, my dear? I imagine it's something of a shock to learn that the estate now passes into the hands of the *London* Deverills. Personally, I congratulate Celia for rescuing the family treasure, because we must all agree that Castle Deverill *is* the jewel in the family crown."

"Oh yes, 'A Deverill's castle is his kingdom'" said Digby,

quoting the family motto that was branded deep into his heart.

"Deverill Rising," Augusta added, referring to Digby's Wilt-shire estate, "is nothing compared to Castle Deverill. I don't know why you didn't buy it yourself, Digby. That sort of money is nothing to you."

Digby puffed out his chest importantly and rocked back and forth on his heels. His mother was not wrong; he could have bought it ten times over. But Digby, for all his extravagance and flamboyance, was a prudent and pragmatic man. "It is not through folly that I have built my fortune, Mother," he retorted. "Your generation remember the days when the British ruled supreme in Ireland and the Anglo-Irish lived like kings, but those days are long gone, as we're all very well aware. The castle was disintegrating long before the rebels burned it to the ground. I wouldn't be so foolish as to entertain ideas of resurrecting something which is well and truly dead. The future's here in England. Ireland is over, as Celia will learn to her cost. The family motto not only refers to bricks and mortar, but to the Deverill spirit, which I carry in my soul. That's *my* castle."

Maud sniffed through dilated nostrils and lifted her delicate chin in a display of self-pitying fortitude. She sighed. "I must admit that this is quite a shock. *Another* shock. As if I haven't had enough shocks to last me a lifetime." She smoothed her silver-blond bob with a tremulous hand. "First, my youngest daughter shames me by insisting on bringing an illegitimate child to London and then my husband announces to the world that the boy is his. And if *that* isn't enough to humiliate me he then decides to sell our son's inheritance . . ." Augusta caught Beatrice's eye. It didn't suit Maud to remember that it was at *her* insistence that her husband had finally agreed to be rid of it. "And now it will belong to Celia. I don't know what to say. I should be happy for her. But I can't be. Poor Harry will be devastated that his home has been snatched from under his nose by his cousin. As for me, it is another cross that I will have to bear."

"Mama, once Papa decided to sell it, it was never going to be Harry's," said Victoria gently. "And I really don't think Harry will mind. He and Celia are practically inseparable and he made it very clear that he didn't want to have anything to do with the place."

Maud shook her head and smiled with studied patience. "My darling, you're missing the point. Had it gone to someone else, *anyone* else, I would not have a problem with it. The problem is that it's gone to a *Deverill*."

Beatrice jumped to her daughter's defense. "Well, it's done now, isn't it? Celia will restore it to its former glory and we shall all enjoy long summers there just like we used to before the war. I'm sure Archie knows what he's doing, darling," she added to Digby. "After all, it's *his* money. Who are we to say how he spends it."

Digby raised a quizzical eyebrow, for one could argue that it wasn't Archie Mayberry's money, but Digby's. No one else in the family knew how much Digby had paid Archie to take Celia back after she had ditched him at their wedding reception and bolted up to Scotland with the best man. In so doing Digby had saved the Mayberry family from financial ruin, and salvaged his daughter's future. "No good will come of it," Digby insisted now with worldly cynicism. "Celia's flighty. She enjoys drama and adventure." He didn't have to convince the present company of *that*. "She'll tire of Ireland when it's finished. She'll crave the excitement of London. Ballinakelly will bore her. Mark my words, once everyone stops talking about her audacity she'll go off in search of something else to entertain herself with and poor Archie will be left with the castle—and most likely an empty bank account—"

"Nonsense," Augusta interrupted, her booming voice smashing through her son's homily like a cannonball. "She'll raise it from the ashes and restore the family's reputation. I just hope I live long enough to see it." She heaved a labored breath. "Although the way I'm going I don't hold out much hope."

Beatrice rolled her eyes with annoyance. Her mother-in-law enjoyed nothing more than talking about her own, always imminent, death. Sometimes she rather wished the Grim Reaper would call her bluff. "Oh, you'll outlive us all, Augusta," she said with forced patience.

Victoria glanced at the clock on the mantelpiece. "I think it's time we left," she said, standing up. "Mama and I are going to look at a house in Chester Square this afternoon," she announced happily. "That will cheer you up, Mother."

Maud pushed herself up from the sofa. "Well, I'll need somewhere to live now we've lost the castle," she replied, smiling on her eldest daughter with gratitude. "At least I have *you*, Victoria, and Harry. Everyone else in my family seems intent on wanting to wound me. I'm afraid I won't come to your Salon tonight, Beatrice. I don't think I'm strong enough." She shook her head as if the weight of the world lay between her ears. "Having the whole of London society talking about me behind my back is another cross I have to bear."

HARRY DEVERILL LAY back against the pillow and took a puff of his cigarette. The sheet was draped across his naked hips, but his stomach and chest were exposed to the breeze that swept in through the open bedroom window. Making love to his wife, Charlotte, was a loathsome duty he endured only because of the mornings he was able to spend with Boysie Bancroft in this nondescript Soho hotel where no one even bothered to question their regular visits. He made his mouth into an O shape and ejected a circle of smoke. If it wasn't for Boysie he didn't think he'd be capable of living such a despicable lie. If it wasn't for Boysie his life wouldn't be worth living because his job selling bonds in the City gave him no pleasure at all. Without Boysie life would have little point.

"My dear fellow, are you going to lie in bed all day?" asked Boysie, wandering into the room from the bathroom. He had put on his underwear and was buttoning up his shirt. His brown hair fell over his forehead in a thick, disheveled fringe, and his petulant lips curled at the corners with amusement.

Harry groaned. "I'm not going in to work today. I find the whole thing a terrific bore. I can't stand it. Besides, I don't want the morning to end."

"Oh, *I* do," said Boysie, tracing with his eyes the large pink scar on Harry's shoulder where he had been shot in the war. "I have lunch at Claridge's with Mama and Aunt Emily, then I shall mosey on down to White's and see who I bump into. Tonight I might pop into your delightful Cousin Beatrice's 'at home.' Last Tuesday her Salon was rather racy with the entire cast of *No, No, Nanette*. All those chorus girls squawking like pretty parrots. It was a 'riot,' as Celia would say. I dare say your Cousin Digby gets a leg over here and there, don't you think?"

"I don't doubt he has a mistress in every corner of London but one can't criticize his devotion as a husband." Harry sighed with frustration and sat up. "I wish I could join you and your mama, but I promised Charlotte I'd take her for lunch at the Ritz. It's her birthday."

"You could always bring her to Claridge's and we could make eyes at each other across the room, perhaps sneak a private moment in the men's room. Nothing beats the thrill of deception."

Harry grinned, his morale restored. "You're wicked, Boysie."

"But that's why you love me." He bent down and kissed him. "You're much too pretty for your own good."

"I'll see you tonight at Cousin Beatrice's then."

Boysie sighed and his heavy eyes settled on Harry's face. "Do you remember the first time I kissed you? That night at Beatrice's?"

"I'll never forget it," said Harry seriously.

"Neither will I." He bent down and kissed him again. "Until tonight, old boy."

Harry walked home through St. James's Park. The light was dull, the bright summer sun having packed up and gone to shine on a more southern shore. Clouds gathered damp and gray and the wind caught the browning leaves and sent them floating to the ground. He pulled his hat firmly onto his head and put his hands in his trouser pockets. Soon it would drizzle and he hadn't bothered to bring a coat. It hadn't looked like rain when he had set out that morning.

When he reached his house in Belgravia Charlotte was waiting for him in the hall. She looked agitated. Guiltily, he panicked that he might have been found out but when he stepped inside she looked so delighted to see him he realized to his relief that he was still above suspicion.

"Thank goodness you're home, darling! I telephoned the office but they said you weren't coming in."

Harry averted his gaze nervously, waiting for her to ask him where he had been. But as he gave his hat to the butler she grabbed his arm. "I've got some news," she blurted.

"Really? Don't keep me in suspense."

"It's about the castle. I know who's bought it."

"You do?" Harry followed her into the sitting room.

"You won't believe it."

"Well, go on!"

"Celia!"

Harry stared at her. "You're joking."

"No, I'm deadly serious. Your cousin Celia has bought it."

"Good Lord. Who told you?"

"Your father telephoned about an hour ago. I didn't know where to reach you. I've been desperate to tell you. You're not angry, are you? You know I adore you with or without a castle and anyway, I wouldn't want to live in Ireland."

"My darling Charlotte, I'm not angry. I'm just rather surprised she didn't tell me herself."

"I'm sure she meant to. Bertie said she'd gone to meet Kitty. I presume she was going to tell her first. You know how close they are."

He sank into a chair and put his elbows on his knees and knitted his fingers. "Well, who'd have thought it, eh? Archie must be mad."

"Madly in love!" Charlotte gushed.

"It'll take a fortune to rebuild it."

"Oh, but Archie's fabulously rich, isn't he?" said Charlotte, not knowing that Archie's fortune came from Digby.

"You never saw Castle Deverill. It's enormous." He felt a sudden, unexpected pain deep inside his chest, as if something were slashing open his heart and releasing memories he hadn't even realized were there.

"Are you all right, darling? You're very flushed." She crouched beside his chair. "You're upset. I can tell. It's only natural. Castle Deverill was your home and your inheritance. But isn't it better that it's gone to someone in the family? It's not lost. You'll still be able to go and visit."

"*Castellum Deverilli est suum regnum*," he said.

"What, darling? Is that Latin?"

He looked at her steadily, feeling like a little boy on the brink of tears. "The family motto. It was written above the front door, that is, before the fire. I didn't think I cared," he told her quietly. "I don't want to live in Ireland, but good Lord, I think I *do* care. I think I care very much. Generations of my family have lived there. One after the other after the other in an unbroken line." He sighed and shook his head. "Papa doesn't speak about it but I know selling it has caused him enormous pain. I can tell by the amount of alcohol he consumes. Happy people don't lose themselves in drink. This has broken the family line which has continued since Barton Deverill was given the land in 1662." He gazed down at his hands. "I'm the broken link."

"Darling, you haven't broken it, your father has," Charlotte reminded him. "And it wasn't his fault the rebels burned it down."

"I know you're right. But still, I feel guilty. Perhaps I should have done more."

"What could you have done? Even *my* money wouldn't be enough to rebuild it. You have to leave it to Celia now and be grateful that it's being kept in the family. I'm sure Barton Deverill would be pleased that his castle is still in the hands of a Deverill."

"Celia will do her best to put it back together again, but it'll never be the same." Charlotte was being so kind but her sweetness curdled. He wished he could share his pain with the man he loved.

Charlotte brushed his cheek with a tender hand. "She will do her best to make it lovely, I'm sure," she said soothingly. "And one day *you* will be Lord Deverill. Give me a son, my darling, and you won't be breaking the family line." She gazed at him with fond eyes, oblivious to the fact that the thought of fathering children turned his stomach. "After all, it's only a house."

Harry looked at her and frowned. Charlotte was his wife and yet she would never understand him. How could she? "No, my darling Charlotte," he said and smiled sadly. "It is so much more than that."

KITTY RETURNED TO the Hunting Lodge, which was a short walk from the castle, with Celia, leading her horse by the reins. She held little affection for this austere, ugly house that had once been her home. It was dark and charmless with small windows and gables that pointed aggressively toward the sky like spears. Although its situation was pretty, it having been built near the river, the water seemed to penetrate the walls and infuse the entire building with a residual damp. Unlike the castle she did not cherish her memories here. She could still feel the sour presence of her Scottish governess in the nursery wing along with the unhappy traces of longing that seemed to linger in the shadows with the damp. Happiness had come naturally for Kitty in the gardens, greenhouses, woodlands and hills, and in the castle, of course, which had always been at the heart of her contentment.

Now she walked her horse around to the stables, where the groom gave it water and hay. Celia chatted excitedly about her plans for the rebuilding. "We're going to put in proper plumbing and electricity. No expense will be spared. Above all, it's going to be much more comfortable than before," she said, taking Kitty by the arm and walking toward the house. "And more beautiful than it ever was. I will hire the finest architect London has to offer and raise this phoenix from the ashes. It's all so thrilling, I can barely breathe!"

They found Kitty's father, Bertie, and Celia's husband, Archie, drinking sherry with Bertie's friend and former lover, Lady Rowan-Hampton, in the drawing room. A turf fire burned weakly in the grate, giving out little heat, and they could barely see one another for the smoke. "Ah, Kitty, what a lovely surprise," said Archie, standing up and kissing her affectionately. "I suppose Celia has told you the good news."

"Yes, she has. I'm still trying to take it in." Kitty resented Archie's enthusiasm. It was all she could do to smile in the wake of such devastating news. "Hello, Papa, hello, Grace." She bent down to kiss her friend Grace Rowan-Hampton and reflected on the miraculous healing power of time. Once, she had despised Grace for her long-standing affair with her father, but now she was grateful to her for her constant loyalty to her former lover, who looked more bloated with booze than ever. Besides Grace, Kitty didn't think her father had many friends left. In his youth Bertie Deverill had been the most dashing man in West Cork, but now he was a wreck, destroyed by whiskey and disillusionment and a nagging sense of his own failings. Even though he had formally recognized Little Jack, the child was a persistent reminder of a shameful moment of weakness.

"My dear Kitty, will you stay for lunch?" Bertie asked. "We must celebrate Celia and Archie's jubilant purchase of the castle."

Kitty thought of Little Jack and her stomach cramped with anxiety. But she dismissed her fears and took off her hat. After all, Miss Elsie had promised not to let him out of her sight. "I'd love to," she replied, sitting down beside Grace.

Grace Rowan-Hampton looked as radiant as a ripe golden plum. Although she was almost fifty, her light brown hair showed only the slightest hint of gray and her molasses-colored eyes were alert and bright and full of her characteristic warmth. Kitty scrutinized her closely and decided that it was the plumpness of her skin and the flawlessness of her complexion that were the key to her beauty; a lifetime of soft rain and gentle sunshine had been kind to her face. "Celia and Archie have taken us all by surprise," Grace said with a smile. "We've been eaten up by curiosity over the last weeks, but now we know we must celebrate. The castle is not lost to the Deverills, after all, but regained. Really, Bertie, I couldn't bear to think of it being bought by someone with no understanding of its history."

"That's what I said to Archie," Celia replied, taking his hand. "I said that it would haunt me for the rest of my days if the place fell into the hands of strangers. I just love the history. All that stuff about Henry VIII or whoever it was. So romantic." Kitty winced. No one with any real connection to the place would get it all so wrong.

"And I decided then that my wife's happiness was more important than anything else in the whole world. We hoped it would make you happy too, Lord Deverill."

Bertie nodded pensively, although Kitty didn't think her father's thoughts contained anything much. He had a distant look in his rheumy eyes, the look of a man to whom little matters beyond the contents of a bottle. "And Celia's having a baby too," Kitty said, changing the subject.

"Yes, as if we didn't have enough to celebrate." Celia beamed, placing a hand on her stomach and sliding her bright eyes to her husband. "We're both very, very happy."

"A baby!" Grace exclaimed. "How very exciting! We must raise our glasses to that too."

"Isn't it wonderful. Everything is just wonderful," said Celia as they lifted their glasses in a toast.

IT WAS LATE afternoon when Kitty rode over the hills to Jack O'Leary's house. The setting sun left a trail of molten gold on the waves as the ocean darkened beneath the pale autumn sky. She had briefly stopped off at home to check on Little Jack, whom she had found happily playing in the nursery with his nanny. Kitty had been relieved to find her husband, Robert, working in his study nearby. He didn't like to be disturbed when he was writing and she was only too happy to leave him and get away. She'd tell him about Celia and the castle later. As she left the White House she was content that Little Jack was safe with Miss Elsie and Robert.

In her haste to see her lover she had forgotten her hat, so that now her long red hair flew out behind her, curling in the gusty wind that swept in off the water. When at last she reached the whitewashed cottage, she hurriedly dismounted and threw herself against the door. "Jack!" she shouted, letting herself in. She sensed at once that he wasn't there. The place felt as quiet and empty as a shell. Then she saw his veterinary bag sitting on the kitchen table and her heart gave a little leap, for he wouldn't have gone visiting without it.

She ran out of the house and hastened down the well-trodden path to the beach, cutting through the wild grasses and heather that eventually gave way to rocks and pale yellow sand. The roar of the sea battled competitively against the bellowing of the gale and Kitty pulled her coat tightly about her and shivered with cold. A moment later she noticed a figure at the other end of the cove. She recognized him immediately, shouted and waved, but her voice was lost in the din of squawking gulls squabbling about the cliffs. She strode on, leaning into the wind, brushing the hair off her face with futile swipes. Jack's dog noticed her first and bounded over the sand to greet her. Her spirits lifted when Jack finally saw her and quickened his pace. The sight of him in his old brown coat, heavy boots and tweed cap was so reassuring that she began to cry, but the wind caught her tears before they could settle and whipped them away.

"What's the matter?" Jack asked, pulling her into his arms. His melodious Irish brogue was like balm to her soul and she rested her cheek against his coat and reminded herself that home was here, in Jack O'Leary's embrace. Their adultery had started as a lightning strike of passion but now had become a way of life—none the less joyful for that. It was the pearl in her oyster.

"Celia has bought Castle Deverill," she told him. She felt him press his bristly face against her head and squeeze her tighter. "I shouldn't mind, but I do."

"Of course you mind, Kitty," he replied with understanding.

"She's going to rebuild it and then she's going to live there and I'm going to be like the poor relation in the White House. Am I being very unworldly?"

"You've suffered worse, Kitty," he reminded her.

"I know. It's only a castle but . . ." She dropped her shoulders and Jack saw the defeat in her eyes.

"It *is* only a castle. But to you, it's always been much more than that, hasn't it?" He kissed her temple, remembering sadly the time he had tried and failed to persuade her to leave it and run off with him to America. Had it been nothing more than a castle they might have been happily married by now, on the other side of the Atlantic.

"And Bridie's back," she added darkly.

"I know. I saw her at Mass this morning, swanking about in her fine clothes and jewelry. Indeed, she found a rich husband in America—and lost him. Word has it she's made a healthy donation to the church. Father Quinn will be delighted."

"She's come back for Little Jack," said Kitty, her stomach clenching again with fear. "She says she had to leave him once and she won't do it again."

"And what did you tell her?"

"That she left him in my safekeeping. But she said it was Michael who left him on my doorstep with the note. She said she's his mother and that he belongs with her. But I've told Little Jack that his mother is in Heaven and that I'll love him and look after him in her stead. I can't now tell him that she's suddenly come back to life."

"She can't have him, Kitty. She would have signed papers in the convent, giving up her right."

Kitty remembered the old Bridie, her dear friend, and her heart buckled for her. "She probably didn't know what she was signing," she said softly.

"Don't feel sorry for her," he reproached. "She's done well for herself, has she not?" He took Kitty's hand and began to walk back up the beach toward his cottage.

"I'm terrified she's going to try and steal him," Kitty confessed with a shy smile. She knew how ridiculous that sounded.

Jack looked down at her and grinned affectionately. "You've always had a fanciful imagination, Kitty Deverill. I don't think Bridie would be foolish enough to attempt kidnap. She'd get as far as Cork and the Garda would be all over her."

"You're right, of course. I'm just being foolish."

He swung her around and kissed her. "What was that for?" she laughed.

"Because I love you." He smiled, revealing the gap where his tooth had been knocked out in prison. He curled a tendril of hair behind her ear and kissed her more ardently. "Forget about the castle and Bridie Doyle. Think about *us*. Concentrate on what's to come, not what has passed. You said this wasn't enough for you anymore. You know it's not enough for me."

"It's not enough, but I don't know how to resolve it."

"Remember I once asked you to come with me to America?"

Kitty's eyes began to sting at the memory. "But they arrested you and you never even knew I had decided to come."

He slipped his fingers around her neck beneath her hair and ran rough thumbs over her jawline. "We could try again. Take Little Jack and start afresh. Perhaps we wouldn't have to go as far as America. Perhaps we could go somewhere else. I understand that you don't want to leave Ireland, but now Celia has bought the castle it's going to be tough living next door, on the estate that once belonged to your father."

Kitty gazed into his pale blue eyes and the sorry sequence of their love story seemed to pass across them like sad clouds. "Let's go to America," she said suddenly, taking Jack by surprise.

"Really?" he gasped.

"Yes. If we go we must go far, far away. It will break Robert's heart. Not only will he lose his wife but he will lose Little Jack, who is like a son to him. He will never forgive me."

"And what about Ireland?"

She put her hands on top of his cold ones and felt the warmth of his Irish vowels wrapping around her like fox's tails. "I'll feel close to Ireland with *you*, Jack. Because every word you speak will bring me back here."

Chapter 3

Bridie heard Rosetta's laughter coming from inside the barn. It was blithe and bubbling like a merry stream. As she approached she realized that in all the months they had known each other, she had never heard Rosetta laugh with such abandon and she suffered a stab of jealousy, for that carefree sound excluded her as surely as the years in America had alienated her from her home. For it came from somewhere warm and intimate, a place Bridie couldn't reach for all her wealth and prestige. Her thoughts turned to Jack O'Leary and the girl in her longed for that innocent time in her life when she had dreamed of laughing so blithely with him, when she had yearned for his arms to hold her and his lips to kiss her; when she had craved his love with every fiber of her being. But Kitty had stolen him as she had later stolen her son. Bridie pushed aside her childhood dreams with a sniff of disdain because she wasn't Bridie Doyle any longer. With a determined hardening of her heart she smothered the tenderness in it that had only brought her unhappiness, and strode into the barn. The laughter stopped at once as the light from outside was thrown across the room. Sean's surprised face appeared from around the back of the hay rick, flushing guiltily. A moment later Rosetta stepped out, the buttons on her blouse half undone and her hair disheveled.

"I need to talk to you, Rosetta," Bridie said stiffly. Then, turning to her brother, she added, "I'm sure there's something you can find to do outside." Sean grinned at Rosetta, whose brown skin was flushed from the roughness of his bristles, and stepped out into the wind, closing the big door behind him. "I see you're already helping on the farm," Bridie said, regretting, even as she spoke, the resentful tone in her voice.

"I would like to be helpful," Rosetta replied. "The country-side here is wild and romantic."

Bridie noticed the dreamy look in her eyes and her jealousy made her mean. "Believe me, there was nothing romantic about my childhood here. Hard winters and poverty are all I remember."

Rosetta's smile faded. "I'm sorry, Bridget." The two women had shared so much, they were more like friends than servant and mistress. Rosetta began to button up her blouse with trembling fingers.

Bridie's heart softened. "Forgive me," she said. "You're right. It *is* romantic and wild here. There was a time when I felt it too. But those days are gone and I can never get them back. I'm leaving, Rosetta. I'm going back to Dublin. Then I'm taking the ship to America. This time for good. I'd like you to come with me, but it's your decision." She sighed, knowing already that their adventure together was to end here. "It's time my brother married. I think he's made his choice." Rosetta blushed, lowering her eyes. "And it's plain that you like him too."

"I do, Bridget," Rosetta replied and Bridie was surprised by the degree of her disappointment and hurt. But her affection for Rosetta overrode her bitterness and she took her friend's hands.

"Has he . . .?"

"Yes, he's asked me to marry him."

"After a fortnight?" said Bridie, astonished.

Rosetta shrugged in that carefree Italian way of hers. "When you know, you know," she said.

Bridie was moved and generosity flowed back into her. Rosetta had always been strong, now she admired her resolve and certainty. "Then you must stay." She embraced Rosetta fiercely, suddenly afraid of setting off on her journey alone. "I'll miss you," she said huskily. "We've been through so much together, you and I. In fact, I realize now that you're my only real friend. It grieves me to lose you." Her voice had suddenly gone as thin as a reed. She cleared her throat and collected herself. "But there's something important I have to do. Something that matters to me more than anything else in the world."

"What will you tell your family?"

"I will write to them from Dublin and explain that I don't belong here anymore. It's like trying to put on an old dress I've grown out of. It no longer fits." She laughed to disguise her tears. "You can tell them I have left for New York. That I couldn't bear to say good-bye. I'll make sure you are all well provided for. Mam can buy her mangle and Sean won't have to worry about the farm any longer. He can buy the land now and repair the house. I doubt he'll be able to do much more than that while Nanna is alive. Write to me, Rosetta." She squeezed her hands.

"How will I know where to find you?"

"I will send you details once I have sorted myself out. It seems that I will require Beaumont Williams's assistance after all," she said, referring to her attorney.

"Are you sure you want to go back to New York?" Rosetta asked.

"Yes, I'll go back and give all those society women something to bitch about! I can count on Mr. Williams to help me. He and his wife, Elaine, were good to me when Mrs. Grimsby died leaving me a fortune. When I knew no one in New York. I know I can rely on them now." She smiled wryly. "Money has a funny way of inspiring loyalty."

"Look after yourself, Bridget."

Bridie gazed at her sadly. "And you look after Sean. He's a good man." She didn't dare mention her other brother, Michael. Rosetta would discover soon enough how very different two brothers could be. It was only a matter of time before Father Quinn released Michael from Mount Melleray.

"Good luck, Bridget. I will pray for you."

"And *I* for *you*. My family will be lucky to have you. They could do with some good Italian cooking." Bridie fought back tears.

"I hope our paths cross again one day."

"So do I, Rosetta. But I don't think they ever will."

A LITTLE LATER Bridie sat in the hackney cab that was to take her to the station in Cork. She knew it would be too dangerous to be seen on the platform in Ballinakelly. She held in her hands the toy bear that she had bought in town and hoped that the boy would like it. She hoped too that once they settled in America he would forget about Ireland and everything he had known here. She looked forward to celebrating his fourth birthday in January and rejoicing in the beginning of a new life together. She'd buy him more presents than he'd ever had. In fact, she'd buy him anything he wanted. Anything to make up for the years they had been apart. Her heart gave a flutter of excitement. If there niggled a shadow of doubt in the bottom of her conscience, she reminded herself that God had thrown light onto the darkness of her despair and inspired her to right this wrong. Little Jack *belonged* to her. As a mother, the Virgin Mary would surely be the first to understand.

Bridie asked the driver to wait in the road a short distance from the entrance to the White House, for she would bring the child through the coppice of trees and not down the main drive for fear of being discovered. She didn't anticipate any obstacles to her plan, so great was her desire that it blinded her to the reality of what she was about to do. All she saw was her son's small hand in hers and the happy-ever-after sunset into which they would surely walk, united and at peace.

It was early afternoon, but the sky was darkened by thick folds of gray cloud so that it seemed much later. The sea was the color of slate, the little boats sailing upon it drab and joyless in the waning light. Even the orange and yellow leaves looked dull in the damp wind that sent them spinning to the earth to collect in piles along the stone wall that encircled the Deverill estate. Bridie hurried down the road, searching for a place in the wall that was low enough to scale. She remembered the times she, Celia and Kitty had met at the wall near the castle to run off and play down by the river with Jack O'Leary, handsome in his jacket and cap, and she had to fight hard to suppress the wistfulness that washed over her in a great wave of regret. The sooner she left Ballinakelly the better, she thought resolutely, for memories were beginning to grow through her carefully constructed defenses like weeds through a crumbling old wall. At last she found a place where the stones had fallen into the decaying bracken behind and she lifted her skirt and nimbly climbed over, taking care not to get the bear wet.

She picked her way through the copse. Her heart was beginning to race and sweat collected on her brow in spite of the cold that was rolling in off the water. She could see the house through the trees. The golden lights in the windows made Bridie feel even more of an outcast, and she resented Kitty for belonging here. Holding the bear tightly she made her way around the back of the house, warily looking out for anyone who might see her.

When she was sure she was quite alone, she edged along the wall, peering in through the windows, searching anxiously. She was beginning to panic that she might never find her son when she spied an open window at the back of the house. Light poured out with laughter she immediately recognized by instinct: the long-lost sound of a child, *her* child.

Her chest constricted with emotion as she crept slowly over the York stone toward the voice that now called to her. In her overanxious imagination the laughter suddenly became the pleading cries of her nightmares, begging for her to find him and bring him home.

She barely dared breathe as she sidled up to the window and peered with one eye through the glass. The cries dissolved and there he was, on the floor with a man she hadn't expected to see, laughing joyously as they played with a brightly painted wooden train set. She balked at the sight of the man, whom she at once recognized as Kitty's old tutor Mr. Trench, now her husband. He was gazing down at the boy with a face full of affection. In fact, he looked quite different from the solemn man who had spent his time teaching Kitty and reading books in the castle. He had always been handsome in a bland, inanimate way, but now his features were brought to life by the laughter in his eyes and the merriment in his wide smile. She clutched the bear to her chest as Mr. Trench pulled Little Jack into his arms and pressed his lips to his face. The child melted against him and giggled. If she hadn't known any better she would have supposed them father and son. Their fondness for each other was natural and real and caused a great swell of jealousy to rise in Bridie's heart. Her eyes filled with tears and she muffled a sob into the bear's soft head.

Just then the woman Bridie had seen on the lawn a fortnight before appeared in the doorway and said something to the man. He released the boy, pushed himself up and reluctantly followed her out of the room. Bridie saw her chance. The window was open. Jack was alone. She knew she only had a few minutes.

Without hesitation she lifted the latch and opened the window wider. Sensing someone behind him, Jack turned around and looked at her in surprise. Bridie leaned in and, smiling encouragingly, held up the bear. The child's eyes settled on the toy and widened with curiosity. To her delight, she watched him jump to his feet and come running with his arms outstretched. For a blessed moment she thought that he was running to *her* and her spirits gave an unexpected leap of joy. But he grabbed the bear and took a step back to look at it. Now she had the opportunity to seize him. She could be quick, in and out in a second. She could lift him into her arms and carry him away and she'd be off into the night before anyone knew what had happened.

"If you come with me, I'll give you another one," she said softly, leaning in through the window. At this the boy's face filled with fear and he dropped the bear as if it had scalded him. His ears flushed scarlet and he burst into tears. His rejection was horrifying and Bridie recoiled as if she had been slapped. She watched helplessly as he stood rooted to the spot, bawling loudly, staring at her as if she were a monster, and the truth finally hit her like a cold slap: Little Jack belonged here. *This* was his home. *These* were his parents. She was nothing more than a stranger, a *threatening* stranger, and her resolve was at once thwarted by compassion and remorse. She put out a hand to comfort him, but the child stared at it in terror and Bridie withdrew it and pressed it hard against her chest.

She stepped back and hid as Mr. Trench and the woman came running into the room. The crying continued but grew quieter as Jack was consoled in the arms of either Mr. Trench or his nanny, Bridie couldn't see from where she stood. She sensed someone at the window and pressed herself flat against the wall, holding her breath and silently praying to the Holy Virgin Mary to protect her. A hand reached out and closed the window, then the curtains were briskly drawn and Bridie was shut out. With her heart now anchored firmly in despair she made her way back through the trees to the waiting cab.

WHEN KITTY RETURNED home, her heart full of hope and dread as she contemplated her future, she found Little Jack in his pajamas, sitting on Robert's knee. Robert's other leg, which did not bend as a result of an illness suffered in childhood, was stretched out in front of him. The boy was listening to a story about a car. He was sucking his thumb and holding his favorite rabbit with the other hand. Engrossed in the story, he didn't lift his head from Robert's shoulder, but remained there sleepy and content. Kitty hovered by the door, forgetting her plan for a moment as she gazed upon the heartwarming scene of her husband and half brother snuggled together in the warm glow of the fire. Robert glanced up at her without interrupting the narrative, and his eyes welcomed her with a smile. Kitty's pleasure was at once marred by her guilt and she retreated from the room, trying without success to picture the same scene replacing Robert with Jack O'Leary.

She found Miss Elsie in the bathroom, tidying up the toy boats Little Jack liked to play with in the bath. "How was your day, Elsie?" she asked, determined to distract herself from the gnawing teeth at her conscience. Even thinking about her flight to America set them on edge.

"Very pleasant, thank you, Mrs. Trench. Little Jack's such a good boy."

"He's tired tonight. He can barely stay awake to listen to the story."

Miss Elsie smiled fondly. "Oh, he is. But he loves his bedtime story and it's a treat to have Mr. Trench reading to him." She turned to face her mistress. From the frown that lined her brow, Kitty could see that something worried her. "He's been very needy tonight, Mrs. Trench," she said.

"Needy?"

"Yes. Something frightened him in the nursery. I don't know what it was. A fox or a bird perhaps at the window. Poor

little mite was sobbing his eyes out. Since then he's been clinging to me or Mr. Trench like a little limpet."

Kitty felt that dreaded cold hand squeezing her heart again.
"Did you see anything at the window?"

"No." Miss Elsie hesitated. She didn't want to admit that she
had broken her promise and let Little Jack out of her sight or
that she had found a strange bear on the floor by the window
and hidden it in the bottom of the toy chest. "Mr. Trench was
with him, but had to leave the room for there was somebody to
see him at the door. I turned my back for only a moment and
that was when he saw it. I'm sure it's nothing but I thought I
should tell you since you might wonder why he's a little unsettled tonight."

"Thank you, Elsie." Kitty hurried back into the bedroom,
where Robert was now lifting the child to his bed. She helped
turn the blankets down so that Robert could slip him beneath.
Then he stroked his red hair off his forehead and planted a kiss
there.

"Good night, sweet boy," he said. But Little Jack was suddenly stirred out of his stupor and grabbed Robert's hand.

"Stay," he whimpered.

Kitty looked at Robert in alarm. "What is it, Jack?" she
asked, kneeling beside his bed. Little Jack sat up and threw his
arms around her, clinging to her as if he was afraid the mattress
might swallow him up.

"The lady might come again."

"What lady?" Kitty looked at Robert in horror because she
knew.

"There *is* no lady, Little Jack. There's only us and Miss Elsie,"
Robert reassured him.

Kitty held him close and stroked his hair. "Where did you see this lady, Little Jack? Can you remember?"

"At the window," he whispered.

"What did she want?"

"She gave me a bear, but I don't want it."

Kitty's stomach plummeted fast and far. "She must have been a tinker, Little Jack," she soothed, struggling to keep the tremor out of her voice. "Nothing to be frightened of, I promise you. She's gone now and she won't be coming back. You're quite safe. We won't let anything bad happen to you, sweetheart. Not ever."

When at last the child had been coaxed back under the bedclothes and stroked to sleep with a gentle hand, Kitty found Robert downstairs in the sitting room, stoking the fire. "Do you think he did see someone at the window?" he asked. Kitty was as pale as ash. "What is it, Kitty?" He put down the poker.

"You know I told you that Little Jack's mother was a maid at the castle?"

"Yes," Robert replied, narrowing his eyes. "Who was she?"

"Bridie Doyle."

Robert stared at her in astonishment. "Bridie Doyle? The plain young woman who worked as your lady's maid?"

"Yes," Kitty replied.

"Good Lord. What was your father thinking?"

"I don't imagine he was thinking at all at that point. Well, after giving birth to him, she disappeared to America and we lost touch. I never thought I'd see her again. But she's come back." Kitty put her hand to her throat. "She's come back for Little Jack."

"How do you know?"

"She turned up here a couple of weeks ago. She told me she

had to leave him once, but she wasn't going to do so a second time. I think it must have been her at the window." The full horror of what might have happened robbed the strength from Kitty's knees and she sank into a chair. "I feared this would happen."

Robert flushed with fury. "How dare she!" He made for the door.

"Where are you going?"

"To tell Miss Doyle that she can't simply march in and steal a child. He doesn't belong to her. The fact that she gave birth to him is of no consequence. She gave him up and that's the end of it. He's Lord Deverill's legitimate son and entrusted into our keeping."

"Oh Robert, you can't just storm into the Doyles' house throwing accusations about. You don't know that she came to steal him. Perhaps she came to give him a present."

He raised an eyebrow cynically. "And you believe that, do you?"

"I want to."

"Then you're a fool, Kitty."

"Robert!"

"Well, I'm not going to give her the benefit of the doubt. This is our boy we're talking about. The child we love more than anything else in the world. You think I'm going to take a risk with him?"

"What are you going to do?"

"I'm going to give her a piece of my mind. I'm going to make sure she never comes near him again."

Kitty had never seen Robert so angry. His fury frightened her. It frightened her because it was fueled by love—and if he loved Little Jack so fiercely, how could she even contemplate taking him off to America?

She thrust her plan to the back of her mind and stood up. "Then I'm coming with you," she announced. "You shouldn't drive with that leg of yours."

"Very well," he replied, walking into the hall. "You can drive, but first go and tell Miss Elsie to keep a close eye on Little Jack."

They hastened down the lanes in silence. The car sped over fallen leaves and twigs swept onto the tracks by relentless winds and autumn rain. The headlights beamed onto the stone walls and hedgerows, exposing for a passing moment a pair of fox's eyes that blazed through the darkness like golden embers. Kitty shivered and gripped the steering wheel with her gloved hands.

At last they began to bump along the stony track that meandered through the valley to the Doyle farmhouse. She slowed down for tonight was not a night to get the car stuck in a pothole or puncture a tire. Kitty's heart began to accelerate as they approached the building where Michael Doyle had violated her, and although she knew Michael wasn't there, the sweat still seeped through her skin because fear does not listen to reason.

Kitty pulled up outside the farmhouse and climbed out. She caught up with Robert and took hold of his hand. "Careful now, Robert," she hissed. "I doubt Bridie's family know about Little Jack."

"I'm not about to set the whole Doyle clan onto our boy, Kitty," he retorted and Kitty felt a surge of confidence at the commanding tone in his voice.

Robert knocked loudly on the door. There was a brief pause before it opened and Sean peered out. He looked surprised and a little apprehensive to see them. Without hesitation he pulled the door wide and invited them in. Inside, Old Mrs. Nagle sat beside the turf fire smoking a clay pipe while Mrs. Doyle rocked on the other side of the hearth, busily darning. A pretty young woman Kitty had never seen before was sitting at the table. Bridie was noticeably absent.

As Kitty and Robert entered, bringing with them a gust of cold wind, four pairs of eyes watched them warily.

"Good evening to you all," said Robert, taking off his hat. "Please forgive our intrusion. We've come to see Miss Doyle."

Mrs. Doyle pursed her lips and put down her sewing.

"She's not here," said Sean, standing in the middle of the room and folding his arms.

"Where is she?" Robert demanded. "It's important."

"She's gone—"

"Gone where?" Kitty interrupted.

"Back to America."

Robert looked at Kitty and she could see the relief sweep across his face like the passing of a storm. "Very well," he said, replacing his hat.

"Can I help you with anything?" Sean asked.

"You just have," Robert replied, making for the door.

Kitty noticed that Mrs. Doyle's cheeks were damp from tears and Old Mrs. Nagle's eyes were brimming with a world-weary blend of sorrow and acceptance. A heaviness pervaded that room which Kitty would have liked to alleviate, but she was keen to be out of there as fast as possible and home, where she felt safe. As she hurried to the car she thought of the loss that poor Mrs. Doyle had suffered and she felt sorry for her.

Kitty started the engine and they set off up the track. As the car drove slowly over the stones Robert reached across the gear stick and put his hand on her leg. He glanced at her, but her features were indiscernible in the darkness. "Are you all right?" he asked.

She took a deep breath. "I am now," she replied.

"You shouldn't have come."

"I wanted to."

He grinned. "Didn't you trust me to do it on my own?"

"I don't trust you at the wheel, no. But I trust you completely in everything else, especially *this*, Robert," she said, turning to look at him. "I felt very sure that whatever happened you'd protect Little Jack; that you'd protect the both of us."

"You know, Kitty, you and Little Jack are the two people I love most in the world. I'd do anything for you."

Kitty turned back to gaze into the road, her guilt slicing a divide through the center of her heart.

BRIDIE STOOD ON the deck of the ship and watched the Irish coastline disappear into the mist. She recalled with bittersweet nostalgia the first time she had left her homeland three years before. She had traveled in steerage then with little more than the clothes on her back and a small bag, full of hope for the future and anguish for the child she was leaving behind, and watched her past grow smaller and smaller until it was gone.

She felt that she had lost Jack not once but twice. She'd had the chance to take him. She'd reached for him but the revelation that the child loved his home had taught her that the fabric of living was as powerful as the lottery of blood, and the very fact that she'd tried to lure the child with a toy shamed her. She'd abandoned him again but this time she'd debased herself in the process.

Now she watched the swirling mist engulf the island she had loved and lost, and knew from the pain in her heart that the wrench was just as severe now as it had been the first time. For in that green land rested the body of her daughter and upon those verdant fields her son would thrive, without a thought for his mother and her longing, without realizing where he really came from. Indeed, he would grow up on the Deverill estate never knowing the simple farmhouse, barely a few miles over the hills, where his roots lay deep and silent.

Tears rolled down her cheeks and she didn't bother to wipe them away. There was a strange pleasure to be found in grief, a certain satisfaction in the aching chest and dull, throbbing head, a sense of triumph in her will to go on living despite the sea below that swelled against the barrel of the boat, inviting her to taste the deadening flavor of oblivion in its wet embrace. She stared now at the black sea and found the rhythm of the waves hypnotic. They called to her in whispers and it would have been so easy to heed their summons and allow them to take away her pain. And yet she didn't. She let grief rattle through her like an old familiar friend, searching the wreckage of her soul for the last remains of sorrow. She knew that, once it had consumed all that she was, there would be nothing left and it would move on. It had done it before and it would do so again.

She closed her eyes and inhaled the damp sea air. She might be leaving her son behind but her daughter, her sweet little girl whom she had not even blessed with a kiss, was with her, for hadn't Kitty taught her that the dead never leave us? That was the only thing of value left of their friendship and she held it close, against her heart.

Chapter 4

Hazel and Laurel, Adeline Deverill's spinster sisters, known as the Shrubs, stood by Adeline's grave and admired the crimson berries they had placed there. They might have been twins, being of the same height, with round, rosy faces, anxious, twitching mouths and graying hair pinned onto the top of their heads. But on closer inspection, Hazel, who was older than her sister by two years, had bright, sky-blue eyes whereas Laurel's were the color of the mist that gathers over the Irish Sea in winter. They had not been beauties in their day, unlike Adeline with her fiery red hair and disarming gaze, but they both possessed a sweetness of nature that showed in the soft contours of their features and in the surprising charm of their smiles. Their need for each other was particularly endearing in two elderly women who seemed to have sacrificed marriage and children to remain together.

"She always loved the color red," said Hazel with a sigh.

"She loved color," Laurel agreed. "*Any* color."

"Except black," Hazel added.

"Black isn't a color, Hazel. It's the *lack* of color."

"Adeline used to say that 'darkness is simply the absence of light.' That it doesn't exist in itself. Do you remember, Laurel?"

"Yes, I do."

"She was so wise. I do miss her." Hazel pressed a crumpled cotton handkerchief to her eye. "She was a reassuring presence during the Troubles."

"Oh, indeed she was," agreed Laurel. "We've lived through turbulent times, but I do feel that peace has descended over Ballinakelly and those beasts who wanted us English out have put away their claws. Don't you think, Hazel?"

"Oh, I do. But how I wish that things hadn't changed. I do so hate change. Nothing was—"

"The same after the fire. I know," said Laurel, finishing the sentence for her sister. "No more games of whist in the library or parties—oh, how I loved the parties."

"No one threw parties like Adeline. No one," said Hazel. "All that's left are the memories. Wonderful, wonderful memories." She sighed sadly at the thought of what had once been. "It won't be the same now Celia's bought the castle."

"No, it won't be the same. It'll be different," agreed Laurel ponderously. "She'll bring it back to life, though, which will be lovely. I do hope she remembers the way it was. Should we advise her, do you think?"

"She'll be grateful for our help, I'm sure. We knew the castle better than anyone else."

"Except possibly Bertie," said Laurel.

"Yes, except Bertie, of course."

"And Kitty, perhaps?" Laurel added.

"Yes, and Kitty," Hazel agreed, a little irritably. "But we know the way *Adeline* would want it to be," said Hazel, gazing upon the damp earth beneath which their sister's body lay buried.

Laurel inhaled deeply. "We're the last of our generation here, you know."

"I'm aware of that, Laurel. One has to look to the younger generation for comfort. I'm very grateful to Elspeth and Kitty. If it wasn't for our great-nieces and their darling children, there'd be no reason to go on. No reason at all."

"Adeline was always certain we'd meet up in the end."

"A load of old rubbish," said Hazel.

Laurel stared at her in surprise. "My dear Hazel, I think that's the first time we've ever disagreed on anything."

"Is it?"

"Yes, it is."

"Well, I hope it doesn't set a precedent," Hazel added anxiously.

"I don't know. It might. Wouldn't that be awful? Suddenly at the grand old age of—"

"Don't say it," Hazel interrupted, putting a hand on her sister's arm.

"At our grand old age then, that we began to disagree."

"We couldn't have that," said Hazel.

"No, we couldn't. It would upset everything."

"Yes, it would. *Everything.*"

"Shall we go home and have a cup of tea?"

"Yes, let's." Hazel smiled with relief. "I'm so happy we agree on that!"

ADELINE WATCHED HER sisters walk out into the street and head off toward home. From her place in Spirit she could see everything that went on in Ballinakelly. Unlike her husband, Hubert, and the other heirs of Castle Deverill who were bound by Maggie O'Leary's curse to remain in the castle until the land was returned to an O'Leary, Adeline was free to come and go as she pleased. Literally a free spirit, she thought with satisfaction. It would have been easy to have left this world altogether; after all, the allure of what human beings call "Heaven" was very strong. But Adeline was bound to Hubert by a more powerful force than curiosity. She had resolved to stay with him because she loved him. She loved Ireland too, and her family who remained here. Only when *their* time ran out would she go home to Heaven; all together, as they had always been.

Adeline was intrigued by the recent comings and goings at the castle. Celia, who was staying at the Hunting Lodge with Bertie, spent a great deal of time exploring the ruins and discussing her plans with Mr. Leclaire, the architect she had brought over from London. Portly like a little toad, with a shiny round face, bald head, fleshy lips and a speech impediment that caused him to spit on his *s*'s, Mr. Kenneth Leclaire was wildly enthusiastic about this ambitious commission. Celia Mayberry was his favorite sort of client: clueless and with a bottomless budget. He had grand ideas and hopped from charred room to charred room behind the dreamy Celia, waving his arms about and describing in lavish superlatives the splendor of those rooms once rebuilt according to his glorious vision. Celia clapped her hands with glee at his every suggestion, squealing encouragement: "Oh, Kenny darling, I just love it! Import it, build it. I want it yesterday!"

Celia wanted Kitty to enjoy the process of restoration as much as she did, and Adeline, so amused by the prancing Mr. Leclaire and Celia's blinkered passion to re-create the past through the rose-tinted hue of her memories, was saddened by the sight of her favorite grandchild, wandering the ruins with her cousin as if she too were a ghost, searching for herself among the ashes.

Kitty cut a lonely, heavyhearted figure. For Kitty, the loss of her home and her beloved grandparents had caused something to shift inside her, subtly like the small movement of a cloud that repositions itself in front of the sun, casting her in shadow. But there was something else. Adeline could intuit that from her vantage point. From where Adeline stood Kitty's soul was laid bare and all the events of her life were revealed to her grandmother like the open pages of a book. Adeline saw the brutal rape in the Doyle farmhouse and the moment on the station platform when Jack O'Leary had been taken from her by the Black and Tans, and she knew that Michael Doyle had not only violated Kitty, but destroyed too her chance of happiness with Jack. His had been the hand that had swiped away her future, and yet, with the same stroke he had brought Little Jack from the convent in Dublin and placed him in Kitty's care. Adeline saw it all with absolute clarity. She also saw the plans Kitty was making to leave for America. She had missed her opportunity once before and was determined not to do it a second time. But Adeline knew that Little Jack didn't belong on the other side of the Atlantic. He was a Deverill and Castle Deverill was where he belonged.

No one had more right to Castle Deverill than Barton Deverill himself, the man who had built it and given it the family motto. Yet he was tired of haunting this accursed place. Adeline had tried to ask him about Maggie O'Leary but, unlike Kitty's, the storybook of Barton's life was closed defiantly shut. There was something in it, she sensed, of which he was greatly ashamed. She could almost see the stain seeping through the paper. Why else would he be so unhappy? Of course it made him desperately sad to see the castle reduced to rubble—it had made them all unhappy to see it so, but the excitement of Celia's plans had cheered them up considerably. Only Barton remained in his mire of misery without any desire to pull himself out and Adeline wondered why.

The curse was constantly on her mind. If it wasn't broken she knew what Bertie and Harry's fate would be. On and on it would continue to punish the Lord Deverills for what the first had done. But what *had* Barton done, exactly? Building a castle on land given to him by Charles II wasn't a crime. Maggie O'Leary had cursed him for what she felt was robbery, but Adeline sensed there was more to it. Perhaps if she could find out what he had *done*, she could figure out a way to *un*do it. When she went to her final resting place she was going to take Hubert, Bertie and Harry with her, come what may.

KITTY RODE OVER the hills above Ballinakelly at a gallop. The wet wind made damp tendrils of her hair and brought the blood to her cheeks. The icy air burned her throat and froze the tip of her nose, and the rhythmic, thunderous sound of hooves on the hard ground took her back to a time of stolen moments with Jack at the Fairy Ring, when the only obstacle to their happiness had been her father's blessing. She laughed bitterly, wishing she could turn back the clock and appreciate how simple life had been back then, before Michael Doyle, the War of Independence and the fire had complicated it beyond anything she could ever have imagined. But now she was leaving it all behind. She would start again from scratch, and forget the past. Together with her two Jacks she would create a future in a new land so that Little Jack could grow out from under the shadow of his family's tragedy. But she couldn't do it alone.

As she had done so many times in the past, she trotted up to Grace Rowan-Hampton's manor and gave her horse to the groom. Once again, Grace was the only person to whom Kitty could turn for help.

Brennan, the supercilious butler, opened the front door and took her coat and gloves. He was not surprised to see Miss Kitty Deverill, as he would always know her even though she was now a married woman. He was used to her turning up without prior warning and striding across the hall, shouting for his mistress. He wondered what it was *this* time.

Grace was in the scullery, making a large flower arrangement for the church, although, at this time of year, there was little in the way of flowers to be found in the garden. She stood in a green dress and teal-colored cardigan with her brown hair pulled back into an untidy bun, leaving stray wisps loose about her hairline and neck. When she saw Kitty she smiled warmly, her brown eyes full of affection. "What a nice surprise," she said, putting down her secateurs. "I need a break from this tedious task. Let's go into the drawing room and have a cup of tea. Brennan has lit a fire in there. My fingers are near falling off they're so cold!"

Kitty followed her into the main part of the house, which was lavishly adorned with Persian rugs and decorated with bright floral wallpapers, wood paneling and gilt-framed portraits of ancestors staring out of the oil with the bulging, watery Rowan-Hampton eyes that had been inherited by their unfortunate descendant Sir Ronald. "Ronald has sent a telegram announcing that he's arriving the day after tomorrow with the boys and their families, so I'm trying to warm up the house," said Grace, treading lightly across the hall. All three of her sons had fought in the Great War and by some miracle survived. Since the Troubles they had preferred to remain in London, where they considered the society more exciting and the streets safer for their children. "I persuaded them all to come home for Christmas this year even though there are few exciting parties to go to. Without the castle the place doesn't feel right anymore. Still, it will be nice to have everyone back in Ballinakelly again. It's lonely here on one's own."

Kitty imagined that Sir Ronald knew all about his wife's infidelity. They clearly adhered to the Edwardian mode of marital conduct: the wife produced an heir and a spare, after which she could make her own arrangements, provided they were discreet. It was a given that men of Sir Ronald's class would take lovers, but Kitty couldn't imagine how the ruddy-faced, barrel-bellied Sir Ronald could appeal to anybody. Truly, the idea was distasteful. Sir Ronald rarely came to Ireland and Grace seemed to have made her own life here without him. Kitty sensed Grace was rather irritated when he showed up. She wondered whether Grace had had other lovers besides her father. Somehow she doubted Grace was ever really on her own.

They sat on opposite sofas and a maid brought in a tray of tea and cake and placed it on the table between them. "I see Celia is plowing ahead with her plans," said Grace. "It must be hard for you and Bertie to watch her and that ridiculous little man she's hired running riot among the ruins of your home. Still, I suppose it's better than the alternative."

"It's better than many alternatives," Kitty replied. She watched Grace pour tea into the china cups. "The Shrubs are driving her to distraction with their suggestions. They think they're being helpful but they don't realize that Celia wants to do it her own way." There was a long silence as Kitty wondered how to begin.

At length Grace smiled knowingly. "What is it, Kitty? I've seen that look in your eyes before. What are you plotting?"

Kitty took a deep breath then plunged in. "I'm leaving for America with Jack O'Leary," she declared. "This time I'm really going and Michael Doyle can't stop me."

At the mention of Michael's name Grace put down the teapot and her smiling eyes turned serious. "Michael is at Mount Melleray, Kitty," she said in a tone that implied Michael had gone to the abbey for pious reasons rather than to be cured of the drink. "I'm sure he regrets many of the things he did during the Troubles, but I've told you before and I'll tell you again, he's not guilty of half the things you accuse him of." She handed Kitty the teacup. "You have to forgive and forget if you ever hope to find happiness."

"There are one or two things I will never forgive him for, Grace," Kitty retorted, but she knew that Grace wouldn't listen to a word against Michael Doyle. She hadn't believed her when Kitty had told her that Michael had been responsible for burning the castle—and Kitty hadn't told her what else Michael had done. She didn't know why, perhaps because of the close roles they had both played during the War of Independence, but

Grace *cared* for Michael. "I'm not here to argue with you," said Kitty. "I need your help."

"I thought so," said Grace, picking up her teacup and settling back into the cushions. "You're sure you want to leave Ballinakelly? You're sure you want to leave Robert?"

Kitty didn't want to think about Robert. The guilt was unbearable. "Jack and I belong together, Grace," she said, angry that she felt she had to argue her case. "Fate has separated us at every turn, but this time nothing can prevent us being together. I need to invent a story so that I can leave with Little Jack without raising suspicion. As you know, Robert writes at home, so he's always in the house. I need you to give me an alibi."

Grace's smile hovered over her teacup. "Considering the alibi you once gave me, it will be my pleasure to repay you in kind."

"So, will you help me?"

"Kitty, my dear, you saved my life after the murder of Colonel Manley. If you hadn't claimed to have had supper with me the night I lured him to his death they would have accused me of being an accomplice in his murder and put me away."

"If they had known half of what you and I got up to during the Troubles they would have put *both* of us away," Kitty added wryly.

"Indeed they would. So helping you now is the very least I can do. But it would be wrong of me, as a friend, not to advise you honestly. Little Jack has two fathers: Bertie, his biological father, and Robert, who is everything a father should be. He has yet to know Bertie, although in time I'm sure he will, but he loves Robert, that's undeniable. Think of *him* when you plot your escape. Is your happiness more important than his? By removing him from everything he knows and loves you will be causing him unknown distress. After all you have been through, surely you can appreciate the importance of firm roots and a loving home with *both* parents." Kitty's face darkened as she was forced to confront the possible consequences of her actions and the shame in building her happiness on the unhappiness of those who loved her. "I'm sorry," Grace continued. "I don't wish to be awkward, but I'm older and wiser than you, and it will be me who is left to pick up the pieces of your desertion. You may not realize it, but your father loves you dearly. He's grown very proud of his illegitimate little son. I can see it in his eyes when he speaks of him. I'm sure that if you give their relationship a chance, Bertie and Little Jack could become great friends."

"Don't forget that my father originally disowned me for taking in Little Jack. He would have preferred that I left him to die on the doorstep."

Grace was shocked. "That's not true," she interjected quickly. "He was horrified at first, of course, but once he had had time to think about it, he changed heart. He realized that nothing in life is more important than family. Didn't he recognize him in front of the whole family? Little Jack is his *son*, Kitty. He's a Deverill."

"I won't be persuaded, Grace. I lost Jack last time because I believed I had a responsibility *here*, but this time I'll take Little Jack with me."

"I don't condone what you are doing, Kitty, but I know that I owe you my life. You can say you're bringing Little Jack to London to stay with me. We'll arrange it after Christmas. I'll help you organize your passage to America and for someone to vouch for you when you get there. God help those you leave behind."

Kitty stood up to go. "Robert will get over me and Papa will survive," she said, making for the door. "After all, he has *you*."

Grace watched her leave. Kitty suspected that Grace's affair with Bertie Deverill had ended the moment Kitty had saved Grace's life. Indeed, Grace had used that as an excuse to end a relationship of which she had grown tired. She had explained to Bertie that she owed Kitty a debt of gratitude which couldn't be paid if she was sleeping with the girl's father. But that was a lie. Only Grace knew the *real* moment it had ended. When, high on the excitement of having played her part in the War of Independence and lured Colonel Manley into the abandoned house on the Dunashee Road so that Michael Doyle and the other rebels could murder him, she and Michael had fallen on each other like wild animals. It had all started then, her affair with Michael Doyle. She went and leaned on the fireplace and gazed into the fire. The flames licked the logs of turf and the smoke was thick and earthy. She wound her hand around the back of her neck and closed her eyes. The heat made her feel drowsy and sensual.

She could see him as clearly as if he were right in front of her, his brooding face close enough to feel his breath on her skin. She could even smell him, that very manly scent which was his alone: sweat, salt, spice and something feral that made her lose control and surrender herself to his every desire. He had taken her then and many times since, and Grace had grown addicted to the pleasure he gave her, for none of her previous lovers could compare to Michael Doyle. He made a mockery of all of them, even Bertie Deverill. There was a vitality about him, an earthiness, a hunger that made her wanton. He handled her roughly, impatiently, and when he was done she pleaded for more. He had reduced her to pulp, but she had never felt more of a woman than when he was inside her.

Now that he was at Mount Melleray she longed for the moment he would return. She fantasized about their reunion. His passion would be all the greater for his having been locked up in an abbey. He would be like a stallion let out into the field at last and she would be waiting for him like an eager mare. She would wait as long as it took. In the meantime, no one else would suffice.

KITTY RETURNED HOME, weary and disgruntled. Grace had been the voice of her conscience and she didn't like it. She knew that what she was planning was selfish and yet, after all she had suffered, didn't she deserve to take something for herself?

. She wanted to ride over to see Jack, but she was careful not to arouse suspicion. The many times she had used her father, her sister Elspeth, who lived close by, and Grace as excuses for her long absences only heightened her chances of getting caught. She had to be discreet. It wouldn't be long before they'd have the rest of their lives to be together. Until that time she'd have to play the good wife.

After going to see Little Jack, who was having his tea, she found Robert in his study, writing. Knowing not to disturb him at his desk she went upstairs and changed out of her riding clothes. When she came down, Robert was in the hall. "Fancy a drink?" he asked, smiling at her. "I could do with one myself. I've been deep in my novel all day. I can barely see the words for the paper." He took off his glasses and rubbed the bridge of his nose. His brown eyes were red-rimmed and bloodshot. "What have you been up to, my darling?"

"I went to see Grace," she replied, stinging with guilt.

"So you did. How is she?"

"Same as always. She's expecting her entire family to descend on her in a couple of days for Christmas." She followed Robert into the drawing room and watched him make for the drinks cabinet.

"What would you like to do for Christmas?" he asked. "I've told my parents we're staying in Ireland this year, considering we've just settled here. Elspeth and Peter have asked us to join them—"

"I know," she interrupted. "But I can't bear their cold house and the chaos. Why don't we ask them and Papa to spend it here with us? After all, Mother will be spending it with Victoria at Broadmere and I doubt Harry will come over. It'll be nice for Little Jack to have his cousins here for a change. We can put up a tree over there," she said, pointing to the far corner, "and he can help decorate it." At the thought of this being Little Jack's last Christmas at the White House her chest tightened and she put a hand against her breast and sat down. The reality of her decision made her appreciate what she had and suddenly everything seemed much dearer to her than she had previously thought. In fact, the idea of losing her home, perhaps forever, made her dizzy with despair.

"Are you all right, darling?" said Robert, handing her a glass of sherry. "You look very pale."

"I'm tired," she replied with a sigh. "I'll go to bed early. That'll put me right."

"Indeed it will. Let's not talk about Christmas."

Just then Little Jack stood in the doorway in his dressing gown with his red hair glistening wet and brushed off his forehead. He was holding a wooden clown puppet on a string. "Look what Robert gave me!"

Kitty looked at her husband. "Did you?"

"I saw it in the window of the toy shop in Ballinakelly and couldn't resist."

"Isn't it fun?" said Little Jack, making it walk across the rug toward Robert.

Kitty watched the child concentrate as he laboriously moved the wooden cross in his hand to lift the clown's big red feet. He reached Robert at last and let him draw him onto his knee, wrapping his arms around his middle and kissing his cheek. "You're so clever, Little Jack. I thought it would take you much longer to make the clown walk." Little Jack beamed a smile at Kitty.

"You *are* clever, darling," she agreed. "How nice of Robert to buy you a present." Little Jack nuzzled against Robert and tears prickled behind Kitty's eyes. Grace's words echoed in her conscience and, with all the will in the world, Kitty was unable to silence them.

Chapter 5

New York, 1925

It's a very great pleasure to see you again, Mrs. Lockwood."
Beaumont L. Williams shook Bridie's hand vigorously. "You
look well, considering you have just endured a long and arduous journey across the sea." He helped her out of her coat, then
gestured to the leather chair in front of the fire and Bridie sat
down, pulling her gloves off finger by finger. She swept her
eyes around Beaumont Williams's office, taking comfort from
the familiar smell of it, for during the three years she had lived
in New York, she had been a regular visitor to these premises.
The aroma of cigar smoke, old leather, dusty books and Mr.
Williams's lime cologne gave her a much-longed-for sense of
home. "I'm sorry the purchase of the castle wasn't a success," he
said, his shrewd eyes twinkling behind his spectacles.

"It was an impulsive idea, Mr. Williams. I saw the article in the newspaper about Lord Deverill selling it and reacted without thinking it through. As it happens, someone else got to it first, but I'm not sorry. I have no desire to live in Ireland."

"I'm very happy to hear that. Elaine and I are the winners then." He settled into the chair opposite and crossed one leg over the other. The shiny buttons on his waistcoat strained over his round belly and he placed his pudgy hands over it, knitting his fingers.

"However," she added ponderously, "continue to keep your ear to the ground. If it ever comes up for sale again, please let me know."

"Of course I will, Mrs. Lockwood. As you are well aware, my ear is always to the ground."

She laughed. "Indeed it is, Mr. Williams. Tell me, how is Elaine? I did miss her," she said, her heart warming at the thought of her old friend.

"Longing to see *you*, Mrs. Lockwood," he replied. "We didn't think you'd be returning."

"I didn't think I would," she replied truthfully. "Those Lockwoods chased me out of Manhattan but I won't be cowed, Mr. Williams. New York is a big enough city for all of us to live together without having to see each other. I considered starting again in a new place, as you once suggested. But New York is all I know outside of Ireland, and I feel at home here. I don't doubt you will find me a nice place to live and that Elaine and I will take up from where we left off and I will soon find friends."

"And a new husband," said Mr. Williams with a smile. "You're young, and if I may say so, Mrs. Lockwood, a fine-looking woman too. You will have all the bachelors of Manhattan howling outside your door like a pack of wolves."

"You make them sound terrifying, Mr. Williams," she said, but her grin told him his flattery had pleased her.

"So, tell me, what made you change your mind and return?"

Bridie sighed, her narrow shoulders and chest rising and falling on her breath. For a moment Mr. Williams glimpsed the lost child beneath the woman's fashionable hat and expensive clothes and he felt a surprising sense of pity, for he was not a man to be easily moved by the pathos of a woman. "Life is strange," she said softly. "I came here as a penniless maid from a small town in the southwest of Ireland, worked for the formidable Mrs. Grimsby, who, by some God-given miracle, chose to leave *me* her fortune when she died, so that I became a very wealthy woman overnight. Then I married a gentleman, a *grand* old gentleman he was indeed, who gave me respectability and companionship. His children might have called me many things, but I am no gold digger, Mr. Williams, and never was. I wanted to be looked after, I wanted to feel safe and I wanted to banish the loneliness forever. Nothing more than that. I was a young girl in a foreign country with no one to look out for me. Indeed I have come a long way." She dropped her gaze into the fire and the warm glow of the flames illuminated for a second a deep regret in her eyes. "I wanted things to return to the way they were, when I was a small, barefooted scarecrow of a girl with a grumbling belly but a home full of love." She smiled wistfully, sinking into her memories while the crackling embers in the grate transported her back to a simpler time. "There was music and laughter and I was as much part of the place as Mam's rocking chair or the big black bastible that hung over the turf fire full of parsnip soup. I'm not so naïve to have forgotten the hardship. The cold, the hunger and the sorrow." She thought of her father then, murdered in broad daylight in the street by a tinker, and her heart contracted with guilt and pain, for if she hadn't been with Kitty and Jack that day and discovered the tinkers poaching on Lord Deverill's land, her father might still be alive, and who knew if she would ever have left Ireland then. "But I'd suffer all that again just for a taste of what it feels like to belong." She dragged her gaze out of the fire and settled it on Mr. Williams who was listening with a grave and compassionate expression on his face. She smiled apologetically. "So, I realized I had to come back to the city that made me."

He nodded and smiled. "This city might have turned you into the fine lady you are today, but you made yourself, Mrs. Lockwood, out of sheer strength of character and courage."

"I've certainly come a long way on my own."

"When you wired to tell me you were on your way I set about finding you somewhere to live. I have an apartment for you to look at, when you feel ready. Elaine will help you put together your household. I understand you returned without Rosetta?"

"Yes, indeed. I need a new maid as soon as possible."

"Let's dine tonight. Elaine is longing to see you. We'll go out, somewhere buzzing. I hope you haven't put away your dancing shoes?"

Bridie laughed, her anxieties about her future falling away in Beaumont Williams's confident and capable hands. "Of course I haven't, Mr. Williams. I will dust them off and take them out and see if they remember the Charleston!"

Bridie spent a fortnight at the Waldorf Astoria Hotel while Beaumont Williams arranged the rental of a spacious apartment on Park Avenue, which was a wide and elegant street a couple of blocks from Central Park, home to New York's richest and most glamorous people. It felt good to be back in Manhattan. She liked the person she was here, in this faraway, vibrant city that seemed to reject the old and embrace the new in a thrilling tide of jazz, bright lights and wild parties. It was the era of Prohibition, all alcohol was banned, and yet you wouldn't have known it. The drinking was just driven underground and it was in these murky speakeasies where bootlegged alcohol was drunk to the music of George Gershwin and Louis Armstrong, Bessie Smith and Duke Ellington that Bridie could forget her past sorrows and dance until the skyline above New York blushed with the pink light of dawn. She could start afresh in the private parties on the Upper East Side where they would consume Orange Blossoms in crystal glasses and sweet-talk in dark corners, and Bridie could reinvent herself yet again, attracting a new crowd of friends who were as full of hedonistic fun as she was. Here, she was Bridget Lockwood, and the noise of the trucks, buses and automobiles, trolley cars, whistles and sirens, hoists and shovels, the clatter of feet treading the sidewalks, the singing in the music halls and the tap dancing in the theaters was so loud as to drown out the little voice that was Bridie Doyle, deep in her soul, calling her home. In the dazzling lights of Times Square she could forge a new happiness, one that came from champagne and shopping, spending money on fashionable clothes and cosmetics, and nights out at the new movie theaters. She embraced New York with a renewed fervor, determined never again to stumble back into her past.

Her apartment was light and airy thanks to its tall ceilings and large windows, and decorated in the opulent and highly fashionable art deco style. Shiny black-and-white marble floors, bold geometric wallpapers, silver and leather furnishings and mirrored surfaces gave the place a feeling of Hollywood glamour that Bridie relished. She felt she was in another world and it suited her perfectly. She gazed out of the window where modest black Fords motored up and down the street beside luxuriously painted Rolls-Royces and Duesenbergs in bright reds and greens, and noticed that there were precious few horses and carts in the city. In Ireland the horse was still the main form of transport and in the countryside very few people had a car. Everything in Manhattan seemed to belong to the future and she was thrilled to be part of this bright new world.

Elaine had found an Ecuadorian couple to work for her. The husband, called Manolo, would be chauffeur, and Imelda, his petite and quiet wife, would be her maid and housekeeper. Mr. Williams had helped her buy a car. She had chosen a sky-blue Winton, with a soft top, which could be pulled back in the summer, and plush leather seats. She was pleased with Manolo and Imelda because neither of them knew where she came from. They took her as they saw her, a wealthy young widow, and she was grateful for that. However, it wasn't long before the infamous Mrs. Lockwood who had graced the society pages of the city's magazines and newspapers only a few months before began to appear once again. But no one wanted to dwell on her past anymore; her rags-to-riches story was old news. They were now interested in the glamour of her clothes and the identity of the lucky men accompanying her out on the town.

"Oh do look, Bridget. There's a photo of you," trilled Elaine one morning, burying her head in the newspaper. "*The delightful Mrs. Lockwood attends Noël Coward's* The Vortex *in a sumptuous mink coat . . .*"

"Don't they have anything better to write about?" Bridie interrupted, secretly thrilled with the attention, for that photograph reinforced her sense of belonging.

"You're a beautiful, rich widow, out on the tiles with a different man every night. You oughtn't to be surprised." Elaine tossed her blond curls and took a long drag on her Lucky Strike cigarette. "I'm glad you wore the dress with the fringe. You look swell, like a real flapper."

"Rather a flapper than a vamp, Elaine," she replied.

Elaine grinned at her over the top of the newspaper. "You're not a vamp, sweetie, you're just having fun. I watch you, being fawned over by the most handsome men in Manhattan, and sometimes wish I wasn't married. Not that Beaumont isn't everything a woman dreams of." She gave a throaty laugh and Bridie laughed with her.

"Mr. Williams is distinguished," Bridie told her, choosing her word carefully because Beaumont Williams was not a handsome man by anyone's standards.

"Sometimes a girl wants a little more dazzle and a little less distinguished, if you know what I mean." Elaine sighed and put down the paper. "A girl needs a bit of adventure, otherwise life can get boring and boredom is the enemy, don't you think?"

"God save us from boredom," Bridie agreed. She brushed a crumb off the lapel of her pink satin dressing gown. "Having nothing to do makes me think and thinking takes me to places I don't want to go. How will we keep ourselves entertained this weekend, Elaine?"

"Beaumont has suggested I take you to Southampton. The Reynoldses are giving a Christmas party on Saturday night that promises to be one of the most lavish of the year. They're very keen for you to come. You add a bit of mystery—"

"And scandal, most likely," Bridie interrupted. "Some people have long memories in this town."

"Not Marigold and Darcy Reynolds. They're great people collectors. Anyone who is anyone will be there, you can be sure of that. We have a modest beach house in Sag Harbor, which we close during the wintertime, but we can stay there." Elaine looked shifty. "Beaumont can't come. Business, you know." She shrugged. "Too bad. We can drive out together, just the two of us. It'll be the bee's knees. What do you say?"

Bridie had inherited Mrs. Grimsby's luxurious pink chateau-style house in the Hamptons, but on the advice of her husband, Walter Lockwood, she had sold it. She hadn't been back since. She remembered gazing out of the window onto the long white beach and the frustration she had felt at not being allowed out to enjoy it. Mrs. Grimsby had been very demanding. Then, after the old woman died, she had finally taken a long walk up the sand. It was on that stroll, with the waves softly lapping at the shore and the glittering light bouncing off the waves, that she had realized she would miss her. She still did sometimes. Mrs. Grimsby's autocracy had given Bridie the greatest sense of security she had had since leaving Ballinakelly pregnant and afraid, and the hard work—and hard it certainly was—had given her a refuge from her pain. "I should like that very much," said Bridie.

On Saturday morning Bridie set off for Southampton in her new blue motor car with Elaine, who had persuaded Bridie that it would be much more fun without Manolo and was sitting confidently behind the wheel. The roof was down and they were wrapped in furs, gloves, hats and scarves to ward off the cold and chatting merrily as they jostled for position among the traffic making its way out of the city for the weekend. It was a crisp winter morning. The sky above Manhattan was a bright cerulean blue, full of optimism and free of cares. The sun hung low over the Hudson, caressing the ripples on the water with fickle kisses, and turning the rising new skyscrapers orange. As they drove over the Brooklyn Bridge Elaine broke into the song "Tea for Two" from the musical *No, No, Nanette,* which had appeared on Broadway that year and got everyone toe-tapping to the catchy tunes. Bridie joined in, although she didn't know all the words, and smiled coyly at the admiring men who glanced at them from the passing cars while their wives weren't looking.

As they left the city giant billboards lined the route, advertising cars, cigarettes and the new Atwater Kent radio set, which Elaine had insisted Bridie buy because it was all the rage. Beautiful faces smiled out from these posters, twenty feet tall, promising pleasure, glamour and happiness, and Bridie, who had bought into that world of material immoderation, delighted at being a part of it. Hers was the pretty smile in the advertisement and hers was the glossy existence behind it. Together, she and Elaine were wild, carefree and liberated, popular, fashionable and blithe.

The highway soon left the city behind and the concrete and brick gave way to fields and woodland, farm buildings and dwellings. Winter had robbed the countryside of its summer foliage and the trees were bare and frozen, their gnarled and twisted branches naked to the winds and rain that swept in off the sea. The young women sang to keep warm, their breath forming icy clouds on the air. It was late afternoon when they reached Elaine's house, which was a white cottage made of clapboard with a weathered gray shingled roof and a veranda overlooking the water. "Beaumont bought this as a young man and even though he has the dough to upgrade, he insists on keeping it. Surprisingly sentimental, don't you think?" said Elaine, drawing up outside.

"I think it's charming," Bridie replied, keen to get inside and warm up.

"Connie should have prepared it for us. Let's go and see." But before she reached the steps up to the front door, a stout little woman no more than five feet tall opened it and the welcoming smell of burning wood greeted them with the promise of hot food and comfort.

Preparing for a party is often more thrilling than the party itself. While one can't predict whether the evening will be a success or a failure, at least one can assure that the two hours or so it takes to get ready are exciting in themselves. With this in mind Elaine and Bridie laced their orange juice with gin, listened to jazz on the gramophone and danced around Elaine's bedroom in satin slips and stockings as they curled their hair and applied their makeup. Connie, who was originally from Mexico, pressed the creases out of their dresses and brushed the scuff from their dancing shoes, muttering to herself in Spanish that no good would come of two young women going off to a party without the presence of men to escort them. But she waved them off with a smile, if not a little warning shake of her head, then retreated inside to tidy up the great mess the two of them had made of the main bedroom.

The Reynoldses' grand Italianate mansion, set in sumptuous grounds overlooking the beach in Southampton, was famous for its spectacular ballroom, baronial-style fireplaces and elaborate gardens. Darcy Reynolds had made his fortune on Wall Street. His motto seemed to be, "No point earning it if you can't show it off." So the mansion, or "summer cottage" as the family referred to it, heaved with entertainments during the summer months and usually fell silent directly after the first frost. This winter, however, was Darcy's fiftieth birthday, and he had decided to celebrate with a lavish Christmas party, the like of which had never been seen on Long Island.

Bridie and Elaine were immediately struck by the lights. It looked like the entire building had been covered in stars, which shone so brightly they almost eclipsed the full moon that glowed like a large silver dollar above the towering ornate chimneys. The central piece of the circular entrance was an impressive gilded staircase that swept up in two curving flights meeting on a landing in front of a wide arched window before parting again. A dazzling crystal chandelier hung above Bridie's head and she couldn't help but remember Castle Deverill and the preparations for the Summer Ball, when the servants would help take down the chandeliers in the ballroom and lay out every little piece of glass on a vast cloth on the floor in order to polish them until they shone like diamonds.

At the far end of the ballroom a jazz band of black musicians led by Fletcher Henderson was positioned on a stage and their energizing music echoed off the walls. The floor was already crowded with fashionable people drinking champagne from crystal flutes and cocktails from slim-stemmed glasses. There were martinis and cosmopolitans and cherries on sticks, and no one gave a thought to Prohibition; if anything, it made the party all the more exiting. Some of the revelers had already begun to dance. Women with feathers and headbands, strings of beads and pearls, fringes and tassels, short dresses, short hair and short attention spans were like exotic birds among the men in bow ties and slicked-back hair. Laughter and conversation rose above the sound of brass and drum and Bridie and Elaine threw themselves into the thick of it. It seemed to Bridie that Elaine knew everyone, but it soon transpired that most people had already heard of the infamous Mrs. Lockwood. It wasn't long before they had glasses of champagne and a crowd around them of admiring suitors all vying for a dance.

"Look, darling, there's Noël Coward talking to Gertrude Lawrence and Constance Carpenter. I wonder what they're plotting?" said Elaine, gazing at the famous English playwright and actresses with curiosity. "Wouldn't you just love to be able to eavesdrop on their conversation?"

"I only have eyes for the luscious Mrs. Lockwood," said a young man who had introduced himself as Frank Linden.

Bridie gave him a quizzical smile. "You're presumptuous," she said tartly.

"How so? Is it so wrong to tell a woman she's a doll?" he replied. He watched her blush, then added, "Dance with me?"

She let her eyes wander over the dancers. Everyone looked as if they were having the most wonderful time. "All right," she replied, handing Elaine her empty champagne flute.

Frank took her hand and threaded through the crowd into the middle of the throng just as the band started to play "Yes, Sir, That's My Baby." A roar went up and a great surge of people flooded the dance floor. Bridie was good at dancing. Ever since she had been swung around the kitchen by her father in Ballinakelly she had loved moving to music. There was nothing more exciting than jazz and she danced energetically while Frank gazed at her with admiration.

Dinner was a banquet of mouthwatering dishes, each one more beautifully presented than the last. Bridie drank more champagne—she had lost count of just how many times her glass had been refilled—and sat down to eat at a round table with Frank, Elaine and a small group of Elaine's friends. She noticed that Elaine was tipsier than usual, flirting outrageously with a young man in a white tuxedo called Donald Shaw, patting his chest with a limp hand and laughing her throaty laugh at everything he said. Her headband had slipped on one side, almost over her left eye, and her kohl had smudged a little, giving her a decadent look. Bridie was glad Mr. Williams was not present to witness it. But she was too drunk on excitement and dizzy with champagne bubbles to worry about Elaine.

It was very hot in the ballroom. The music vibrated in her ears, the alcohol made her drowsy and the sheer delight of being part of such a fashionable crowd gave her a heady sense of omnipotence. So when Frank Linden took her by the hand and led her up the stairs to find a quiet room where they would not be disturbed, she happily obliged. In the darkness of one of the guest bedrooms he pressed her against the wall and kissed her. It felt good to receive the attentions of a man again and she wound her arms around his neck and kissed him back. She closed her eyes and felt the room pleasantly spin.

When she opened them again she was lying on the bed in her underwear and Frank Linden's hand was beneath her slip and caressing her breast. She was too sleepy to do anything about it and besides, the sensual feeling it gave her made her writhe in pleasure like a cat. A low moan escaped her throat and Frank, taking that as a sign of encouragement, slid his hand onto her inner thigh where it lingered for a moment, tentatively teasing. As Bridie didn't protest, rather her staggered breath and soft sighs left him in no doubt that she was willing, he slowly and gently moved his hand north, until it glided over her skin, under her silk panties, and on up her thigh until it could go no farther. Bridie widened her legs with abandon. Her moaning grew into gasps and sighs as she allowed the delicious warmth to spread into her belly.

When she awoke, Frank was lying asleep beside her. She could hear the music coming from downstairs, but it was slow and mellow, and a woman was singing. She climbed off the bed without waking him and fumbled about for her clothes. Once she was dressed she turned the brass doorknob as quietly as she could and slipped into the corridor. As she stepped onto the landing, Elaine was sitting on the top stair, smoking a cigarette. Bridie sat down beside her. "You all right?" she asked.

"Does petting count as infidelity?" Elaine asked in a dull voice.

"I think Mr. Williams would count it."

"Then I've just broken one of the Ten Commandments." She turned to Bridie and her big blue eyes shone. "Didn't I say a girl needs a little adventure from time to time?"

"I think we should go home now," said Bridie.

"You're right. I've had enough adventure for one night." Elaine narrowed her eyes. "Where's Frank?"

"Asleep."

Elaine gasped. "You didn't!"

Chapter 6

Celia and Archie spent Christmas with Sir Digby and Lady Deverill at Deverill Rising, their sumptuous Georgian home in Wiltshire, which Digby had bought and renovated at vast expense with the first fortune he had made in the South African diamond mines. Originally the house had been called Upton Manor, but that wasn't nearly grand enough for the brash and newly rich Digby Deverill. Memories of summers at Castle Deverill inspired him to give his home a name that would last through history and give a sense of dynasty and substance. Therefore he swiftly renamed it Deverill Rising, endowing it with the gravitas of his new status and the weight of his historical name. Their son, George, would have inherited it had his life not been so cruelly cut short in the Great War. This saddened Digby and scoured the gloss from his vision. However, ebullient and always optimistic, Digby endeavored to look for the positive. He filled it with friends at every opportunity and wondered whether a grandson might one day cherish it as he did.

Joining them for the festivities were Celia's older twin sisters, Leona and Vivien, who came with their husbands, Bruce and Tarquin, and their small children. Due to the seven-year age gap between them Celia had never been close to her siblings. The twins were both blond and pretty, with long, aristocratic noses, shallow blue eyes and bland, unremarkable characters. Little could rouse them from passivity. However, ever since Celia had bought the castle and provoked their jealousy, they had shown surprising passion. Neither could believe that flighty Celia, who had shocked London society by bolting from her wedding with the best man, could have snatched the Deverill family seat for herself. It was an outrageous thing to have done and something that infuriated both girls, who lived relatively modestly with their Army husbands. What upset them even more was that their father, in spite of everything Celia had put him through, was inordinately proud of her.

Digby had initially been horrified by Celia's news, but his daughter's excitement and Archie's pride at having made the purchase possible softened his rancor and assuaged Beatrice's reservations. Archie, intent on impressing his father-in-law, told him of the architect's adventurous plans, which, Archie emphasized, included many of his own ideas. Digby requested to meet this Mr. Leclaire at the earliest convenience, for he wanted to make sure that his erratic daughter wasn't being overambitious. It was one thing to restore a castle to its former glory, but quite another to build a palace that wasn't there to begin with. "I will come to Ireland with you in the new year," he declared, his enthusiasm growing at the thought of involving himself. "It'll be good to see Bertie. Tell me, my dear, how is my cousin?"

Celia, riding on the crest of a wonderful wave, was pink in the face with happiness. "Oh Daddy, I'd love you to meet Mr. Leclaire. He's full of ideas. Really, he understands exactly what we want. Everything he suggests I tell him I want it yesterday! It's hilarious. He thinks I'm marvelous."

"You behave as if you have a bottomless pit of money," said Leona sourly.

Celia ignored Leona. "You'll adore him, Papa. We all do. He's a great character!"

"And Cousin Bertie?" prompted her mother gently.

Celia sighed. "He's as well as can be expected, I suppose," she replied, reluctant to divert the conversation away from herself. "Maud has told him that she never wants to return to Ireland and I gather from Harry that she is in the process of buying a house in Chester Square. They will continue to lead separate lives, for I doubt Bertie will ever leave the Hunting Lodge. I told him he can stay there for as long as he wants. It's his home, after all. But he's thrilled I'm rebuilding the castle. Just thrilled. Isn't he, Archie?"

"He's very interested in our plans," Archie agreed.

"I imagine he's putting on a brave face," said Vivien. "I mean how can he possibly enjoy watching someone else rebuilding his home?"

"Celia is hardly 'someone else,' " said Archie.

"Of course he's delighted," Digby interjected.

"I'm so pleased," said Beatrice. "I was worried it would create a rift within the family."

"Oh no, far from it, Mama," Celia gushed. "Everyone is so happy. Kitty especially! Our children will grow up together playing in all the places we used to play. It'll be a riot, history repeating itself. We're going to get into the Irish way of life, aren't we, Archie? Hunting and racing. Archie's going to take the dogs out to shoot snipe just like Cousin Hubert used to do. Oh, it's going to be such fun!" She clapped her hands together without giving another thought to poor Bertie, sinking sorrowfully into his bottles of whiskey.

"I hope you install some heating. As far as I remember, Castle Deverill was uncomfortable, cold and damp," said Leona.

"Oh yes, it was terribly damp," Vivien agreed. "I wore a fur coat in bed to keep warm."

"It's going to have the very best of everything," said Celia firmly.

"Shame you can't spend all that money on improving the weather," said Leona with a chuckle.

Vivien laughed with her. "Goodness, it rains all the time in Ireland, doesn't it?"

"It rains all the time in England too," said Celia, giving her sisters a withering look. "But I always remember the summers in Ballinakelly as being sunny and warm. You know, Archie and I are going to host the Castle Deverill Summer Ball. It'll be just like it used to be. The candlelight, the music, the dancing, and everyone will say that no one throws a party quite like Mrs. Mayberry. Isn't that right, Archie darling?"

Archie Mayberry smiled indulgently at his wife. Buying the castle for Celia had made him feel like a man again and restored him in the eyes of his friends and family. After her bolt from the wedding he worried that her parents might blame him for being too dull to keep her. He feared that he might never regain their esteem and it vexed him that he had been humiliated in front of his friends, but nothing makes people forgive and forget a scandal more surely than money. Digby's bribe, for that is, in essence, what it was, had enabled him not only to pull his family back from the brink of bankruptcy, but to look his own reflection straight in the eye. It was ironic, too, that he had managed to repay his father-in-law's generosity by purchasing the Deverill family seat. Digby Deverill, genial and urbane as he was, was inscrutable in the way that powerful men often are, but from the look on his face, Archie could tell that he had earned his father-in-law's acceptance, which had been his intention all along. As for respect, he hoped he would one day earn that too.

KITTY AND ROBERT had spent Christmas at the White House. Kitty's father, Bertie, had come for Christmas lunch with Elspeth and Peter and the Shrubs. Although Elspeth was seven years older than Kitty the two sisters had grown close ever since Elspeth had married Peter MacCartain and moved into his dank castle a short walk from Castle Deverill, nearly five years before. Little Jack had played with his three cousins and opened his presents with glee. Hazel and Laurel had fussed over the children while Robert and Peter had stood by the fire watching them with amusement. Bertie had put on a good show, not wanting to dampen the festivities, but Kitty could tell that he was deeply depressed. She wondered whether it was the castle he mourned, or his mother Adeline, or perhaps even Grace. She didn't imagine it was Maud.

But Bertie *did* miss his wife. It was one of those ironies of age and marriage: the couple who have bored and betrayed each other in their early years often comfort and sustain each other in their later ones. Bertie had betrayed his wife with his long affair with Grace (and before Grace many other discreet dalliances with pretty girls) but that affair was long over and now he found himself thinking of Maud often. It seemed absurd that after the great freeze that had been their marriage there might be a thawing on his part. He didn't understand it himself. He loved Grace—he would *always* love Grace—but Grace had ended their affair and now they were just friends. The light of desire that had warmed her soft brown eyes had died away and she looked on him with pity—he hated that he had become a man to be pitied. As much as she tried to disguise it, he saw through her. Maud on the other hand didn't pity him, she despised him and there was something rather magnificent about the fury in her—wasn't the opposite of love indifference, after all? Maud was certainly not indifferent. She resented him for *his* affair, but hadn't she been the first to leave the marital bed in favor of his old school chum Eddie Rothmeade's? She thought he didn't know, but he did. She had barely been able to hide her infatuation. But that was long ago and he was ready to forget it. His wife loathed him for his indiscretion with the maid, but hated him even more for having formally recognized the child born of that union. Now she resented him for having sold the castle even though *she* was the one who had encouraged him to do so. He was buying her a house in Belgravia with most of the proceeds, but he knew she wouldn't want him there. Divorce was out of the question for a woman obsessed with society's good opinion, but he wondered whether her head might be turned by another man, one who could give her more than he had been able to. That thought saddened him greatly. When he thought of cold, beautiful Maud, he wondered whether, had he behaved differently (and with less arrogance, perhaps), he might have made her happy. He wondered why, when he tried to *lose* his thoughts in whiskey, he only found them becoming more acute. In the alcohol-induced fog in his mind he saw Maud as she had been when he married her, when her elusive smile had turned on him like the warm rays of dawn. But she'd never smile on him again, he was certain of that. Perhaps the finality of it made him nostalgic for their past. Wasn't that the way of the world? One always wants what one cannot have.

The day after Christmas Kitty heard the news that Liam O'Leary, Jack's father, had died on Christmas Eve. The maid who reported it wasn't sure how he had died, only that the funeral was to take place the following day in the Catholic church of All Saints in Ballinakelly. Kitty wanted to ride over to console Jack, but was fearful that her presence there would arouse suspicion. He was sure to be with his mother and the rest of his family, and there were a good many O'Learys in Ballinakelly, she knew. Instead, she sent the stable boy with a letter of condolence. She was sure that Jack would read between the lines and get word to her as soon as she was able to visit.

The day of the funeral Kitty stood at her bedroom window, gazing out over the sea and biting the dry skin around her thumb with anxiety. She hadn't heard anything from Jack. She wondered whether their plans to depart for America would be delayed—or even canceled. Could he leave his mother so soon after her husband's death? She knew Jack had other siblings and his mother certainly had a sister, because she had heard him speak of her, but she had no idea where they lived, or indeed how intimate they were. Mrs. O'Leary doted on Jack, of that she was sure.

How she would have loved to attend the funeral. But it was impossible. Robert would consider it very strange and the locals would find it odd too, even though, as the local vet, Jack had been coming to Castle Deverill for years to look after the animals. So she waited. What else could she do?

Grace had arranged their departure for the first weekend in February. She wasn't planning on being in London until then and she told Kitty, quite unreservedly, that she hoped the month before leaving would give Kitty time to reconsider. But Kitty was certain that this was what she wanted. Her past had been marred by self-sacrifice. Now was her time and she was determined to take it.

The week before Christmas she had suffered horribly with her menstruation. She had lain in bed with severe abdominal pain and Robert had tactfully slept in his dressing room. But now there was no reason for her to banish her husband to another room, and, surprisingly, she didn't want to. She was about to leave him for the other side of the world. She was on the point of separating him from Little Jack, possibly forever. She hated herself for allowing her passion to make her selfish; after all, Robert had only ever been kind to her. He had only ever loved the two of them. Her sense of guilt was immense and her anticipation of loss drove her deep into his arms. She was like a sea creature clinging to the rock that was her home, while the current swept by to drag her away. As she let him make love to her, she realized, in the light of her imminent departure, that it was possible to love two men at once, in entirely different ways.

At last she received a letter from Jack, asking her to come to his cottage as soon as she was able. Anxious that he was about to postpone their departure she saddled her horse and galloped as fast as the animal could carry her over the hills to his house, which was situated in lonely isolation, overlooking the ocean. She could see a ribbon of smoke floating up from the chimney long before she reached it. A golden glow twinkled in the waning light from one of the downstairs windows. Fog was creeping in off the water and the horizon, usually so clear, was a gray mist in which fishing boats could easily lose themselves. There would be no moon to illuminate the path home, but she was sure she'd find it somehow.

She slipped from her saddle and tied the horse to a fence behind the cottage. She didn't bother to knock, but went straight inside. Jack was sitting at the kitchen table, staring into a half-drunk tankard of stout. When he saw her, he stood up and gathered her into his arms, embracing her fiercely. Her heart buckled at the sight of his grief-stained face and she squeezed him as hard as her arms would allow. Jack cried then. He sobbed into her neck like a little boy and Kitty was reminded of her beloved grandparents and her heart went out to him.

When his pain had passed through him, he returned to his chair and drained his tankard. Kitty put the kettle on the stove and made a pot of tea. He told her that his father had died peacefully in his sleep, but his mother had suffered a very great shock on finding him lying cold and stiff beside her in the morning. "He was a good man," he said quietly. "If it hadn't been for the war, he would have lived a longer life, I'm sure of it. The war was never ours in the first place. He should have done as I did and kept his feet firmly on Irish soil. But we didn't share the same politics. We quarreled over our views and I know he disapproved of my decision not to fight. If he'd only known the half of what I'd got up to during those years he'd have given me more than a clip about the ear. As it was he knew nothing. When he returned from the war something had been extinguished inside him. He never spoke of what he had seen and done but I know it was terrible. It robbed him of his joy. I hope he finds it again, wherever he is."

"He will," said Kitty. "He's home now."

"I love you for your certainty, Kitty." He grinned and watched her bring the pot over to the table and pour two mugs of tea. She sat down opposite and he reached for her hands across the narrow wooden table. "You're either as mad as a March hare or privy to the greatest of all life's mysteries. Whichever it is, I love you all the same."

"And I love you, Jack, in spite of your little faith," she replied with a grin.

"We're going to build a new life in America, you and I and Little Jack. I have dreamed of walking hand in hand with you for all the world to see."

Kitty squeezed his hands hard. "So have I. Life hasn't been kind to us, has it?"

"This time we'll board that boat, whatever life throws at us."

"It'll be exciting for Little Jack. He's never been on a boat."

Jack noticed the disquiet behind her cheerfulness. "I know you worry for him, my darling. But he's a lad. It'll be an adventure." He gazed at her tenderly. "We'll give him brothers and sisters. A big family. He won't have time to remember Ballinakelly."

"I hope you're right."

"He loves you, Kitty, more than anyone in the world. And

he'll grow to love me. I promise you he will. Indeed, I'll be a good father to him."

Kitty's eyes began to sting with tears. "I know you will, Jack. But I'm afraid. I want to do what's best for him, but I have to do what's best for me too. I feel I'm being torn in two. Robert . . ."

Jack's face hardened. "Don't think of Robert, Kitty!" he snapped. "He has no claim on you. You and I are like plants whose roots run very deep and intertwine. We've got a long history together. Shared memories and adventures Robert can never hope to create. He stole you from me. If you hadn't married him you'd have been free to marry me. No, don't argue. You know it's true. If it wasn't for him we'd be together." She nodded and released his hands. Taking up her mug she sipped her tea. "I know you're torn and I appreciate what you're giving up, coming away with me. Don't think I don't understand. But we deserve this, Kitty. There's no other way for us. It's this or nothing. If you can't come with me, I'll go anyway, because a future here without you is impossible."

"I'm coming with you. I promise," she reassured him softly.

He glanced at the window. The fog had gathered around the cottage and darkness had come early. "You'd better ride home now, Kitty, or you'll get lost in the fog."

"I'd know these hills blindfolded," she said, getting up.

"I'll ride with you," he said suddenly, pushing his chair out with a loud scrape.

"You mustn't. If we're seen together we'll ruin everything. I'll be fine. I've ridden these hills all my life."

He pressed his lips to hers and kissed her ardently. "To think there'll soon be a day when I can kiss you from dawn till dusk without interruption."

"Oh Jack, I can't wait. I want you to kiss me now without interruption." She slid her hand between the buttons of his shirt, but he stopped her.

"You have to ride home now, Kitty," he insisted. "If you leave it another moment it'll be totally dark. Please, my darling, you have to go, now."

Reluctantly she slipped into her coat and gloves and pulled her hat down low over her head. She swung herself into the saddle and waved at Jack, who stood forlornly in the doorway. "I long for the day when my home is your home," he said and Kitty blew him a kiss before gently digging her heels into the horse's sides and trotting off along the path that led to the hills.

ROBERT WAS GETTING anxious. It was dark and Kitty was still out with her horse. He didn't understand her need to ride all the time. If she had wanted to go into Ballinakelly she could much more easily have taken the car. He stood at the drawing-room window and stared out into the foggy night. All he could see was his own pale face staring anxiously back at him. He rubbed his chin. No one seemed to know where she had gone. Even the groom hadn't a clue. He had simply shaken his head and told Robert that Mrs. Trench had saddled the mare herself and set off without a word. She had probably just gone for a hack over the hills. But Robert was worried. She would have seen the fog closing in when she set off. Why on earth would she choose a misty afternoon in early January to go hacking over the hills?

He considered going to look for her. What if she had fallen off her horse? What if she had hurt herself? What if she was lying injured in the mud? She'd die of cold out there in the night. His heart was seized with panic. He took a deep breath and tried to think rationally. He'd never find her for a start. Besides, she could be anywhere. He couldn't go walking across the fields on account of his stiff leg, or take the car because those tracks were slippery with mud and he was sure to get stuck, or worse, crash. He felt utterly useless. He could do nothing but wait.

Perhaps she was with her father, he conceded. She had been worrying about him a great deal lately. Bertie was taciturn and melancholy and only Little Jack and his rousing ebullience seemed able to distract him from his woes. But Kitty wouldn't have ridden over the hills if that were the case. She would have cut through the woods and fields, for the Hunting Lodge was only the other side of the estate and she'd surely be home by now. She might have gone to visit Grace. The two of them were as thick as thieves. They seemed closer than sisters even, most notably in the way they spoke to each other, sometimes with impatience, sometimes with affection, but without the reserve that prevailed in most nonfamilial relationships. Indeed, their friendship seemed embedded in depths he would never know. But Grace had a house full of family and no formal invitation had been forthcoming. No, Kitty had not gone to visit Grace, he was sure of that.

When at last the front door opened and Kitty strode in, her face red from the cold and her Titian hair wild and knotted down her back, Robert was at first overcome with relief, then furious that she had caused him such concern. "Where the devil have you been?" he demanded, meeting her in the hall.

Kitty laughed. "You weren't worrying about me in the fog, were you?"

"Of course I was, you silly girl!"

Kitty was affronted by his patronizing tone. "I know those hills better than most shepherds," she retorted crisply. "There was no need for you to worry."

"Where were you?"

She shrugged and pulled off her gloves. "Out riding."

"Where?"

"Why all these questions, Robert? Are you accusing me of having a lover tucked away up there in the hills?"

Robert was stunned. "No," he replied. "That idea hadn't occurred to me. Should it?"

She flushed beneath her weathered complexion. "You're making a mountain out of a molehill. I was simply out riding, as I always do. I wasn't alarmed by the fog."

"I forbid you to ride out like that again. It's dangerous."

Kitty sighed impatiently. "Oh really, Robert. You're sounding like my tutor again!"

"When I was your tutor you were not obliged to obey me. Now I'm your husband, you are."

"I won't be told," she snapped, making for the stairs.

"Yes, you will. You have a little boy who depends on you," he reminded her. "And you have me, for better or for worse. I will not have you rampaging around the countryside in the dark. You have the entire day at your disposal. Please do me the favor of riding during daylight hours. Surely, I'm not asking too much."

Kitty, furious that he was telling her what to do and fired up with guilt about where she had been, was all too quick to inflame the argument. If she was angry with Robert it would make it all the more easy to leave him. She marched up the stairs without looking back. Robert remained in the hall until she had disappeared, then he turned and limped into his study, slamming the door behind him.

Kitty read Little Jack a story and tucked him up in bed. She planted a kiss on his soft forehead and savored for as long as possible the feel of his small arms around her neck, holding her close. Her heart mollified at the sight of him and, when Robert came in to say good night, she found it hard to maintain her sulk. However, she managed to eat her supper in silence. He attempted conversation but she thwarted it with monosyllabic answers until he gave up and only the clinking of cutlery on their plates interrupted the heavily charged silence.

Kitty went to bed alone and turned off the light. Her thoughts shifted to leaving home again and she felt the familiar sense of despair. But just as she closed her eyes she heard the door open and the sound of her husband's shuffling walk as he limped into the bedroom. She wished he would see that she was asleep and leave, but he didn't. He climbed in beside her and wrapped his arms around her, drawing her against him. "I don't want to fight with you, darling," he whispered. "I love you."

His gentle voice lured her out of her brooding and her despair was at once laid aside. She rolled over and kissed him. She kissed him tenderly, and as she did so a tear squeezed through her lashes, for, even as she knew she was betraying Jack, she knew also that she was being guided by a deeper longing. She didn't try to understand it, nor attempt to justify it. But as she undid the buttons of his pajamas and glided her hand over his chest, she knew she was sealing her fate, whichever way it would go; it was in God's hands now.

Chapter 7

After New Year's, Digby Deverill arrived in Ballinakelly with Archie and Celia to stay with his cousin Bertie at the Hunting Lodge. He hadn't been back since Adeline's funeral, when Bertie had announced to the family that he was not only selling the castle but introducing them to his bastard son, Jack Deverill. *That* had been quite a luncheon, Digby mused with a sardonic smile. Maud had stormed out and disappeared to London in a huff, bleating humiliation and hurt. Everyone else had been left speechless, which was quite something for a noisy family such as theirs. Now, a few months later, he was able to reflect on the whole episode with wry amusement.

Digby loved County Cork. He remembered with affection his boyhood summers at Castle Deverill, when he and Bertie and Bertie's younger brother, Rupert, who was later killed in the Great War, had taken the boat out to fish with Cousin Hubert, Bertie's formidable father. Digby was not a natural fisherman, but he had loved the drama of the ocean, the mystery of what lay beneath it, the wide horizon and the sense of being alone in the immense blue. He was fascinated by the local fishermen in their thick sweaters, caps and boots, their craggy faces weathered from years of exposure to the salty winds, their dry hands callused and coarse, and loved to listen to their banter when, at the end of the day, Bertie and Rupert would take him to O'Donovan's in Ballinakelly for a pint of stout. Cousin Hubert had preferred the comfort of his own home—and the security of his own kind. They would find him in the library at the Hunting Lodge (because in those days Bertie's grandparents lived in the castle), eating porter cake in front of the fire with his wolfhounds at his feet, hoping for crumbs. "Anyone for bridge?" he'd ask, and Digby would always be the first to volunteer because there had been something about Cousin Hubert that had made him long for his good opinion.

Now Cousin Hubert was gone, killed in the fire that destroyed the castle. Adeline was gone too. It was a salutary thought and one that reconfirmed Digby's belief that life has to be grabbed by the collar and lived consciously, decisively and courageously, not the way Bertie was living his, drifting rudderless on a current of whiskey and disillusionment. Something had to be done, and soon, or Bertie would be gone too and that would truly be the end of an era.

Digby had come to County Cork to meet Mr. Leclaire, but he had also come with the secret intention of rousing his cousin out of his stupor. He knew he had to await his moment. Bertie had to be in the right frame of mind to hear his advice, for there was always the danger that his cousin would take umbrage, for Bertie was a proud and fragile man, and the consequences could be dire.

While he waited for that elusive moment, Digby threw his enthusiasm into the plans for the castle. He'd seen the ruins the year before but he'd never taken the time to walk among them. Now, with the effervescent Mr. Leclaire leading the way through the rubble (and anticipating, with relish, his enormous bill), Digby wandered slowly from room to room like a dog sniffing for the scent of his past. He found it lingering in the hall where the fireplace still stood, recalling with a wave of nostalgia the Summer Ball when he had stood there with his new wife, Beatrice, who was seeing it for the first time. He remembered her face as clearly as if it had been yesterday. The wonder in it, the joy, the sheer delight at the beauty of the castle, lit up with hundreds of candles and adorned with vast arrangements of flowers.

Mr. Leclaire dragged him out of his reverie by urging him on through the hall into the remains of the drawing room. Shiny black crows hopped about the stones and squabbled among themselves. Mr. Leclaire pointed out the parts of the surviving walls that were still intact and the parts that were simply too weak and would have to be pulled down. He gesticulated extravagantly, waving his arms in the air, while Celia chirped and chattered and thought his every suggestion "marvelous." "I want it yesterday," she said in response to his every suggestion. Archie watched closely for his father-in-law's reaction, hoping that he'd approve, *wanting* him to approve.

"We will use the original stone wherever possible, Sir Digby," said Mr. Leclaire. "But where we are compelled to use new stone we will endeavor to match it as best we can. Mrs.

Mayberry has suggested we buy old stone but I have explained, have I not, Mrs. Mayberry, that the cost will soar considerably. Old stone is very dear."

"I'm sure Mr. Mayberry would like an estimate for both, Mr. Leclaire," said Digby. He smiled at his daughter and Celia slipped her hand around his arm, for she knew from experience what that smile meant: she'd have her old stone one way or another.

As they moved through the ruins toward the surviving western tower where Adeline had set up residence after Hubert was gone, Celia noticed a pair of grubby faces watching them from behind a wall. She nudged Archie. "Look, we're being spied on," she whispered. Archie followed the line of her vision. There, partly hidden among the stones, were two little boys. As soon as they realized they had been spotted their faces disappeared.

"Who are they?" Archie asked.

"Local boys, I imagine. They must be very curious. After all, this castle has dominated Ballinakelly for centuries."

"Don't you think we should say something? They're trespassing. There's a perfectly good sign by the gate telling them this is private property and trespassers will be prosecuted."

"Darling, they don't care about a sign. They're children." She laughed, rummaging in her handbag for some chocolate. Finding a half-eaten bar, she weaved her way through the debris and ash to where the boys were hiding. "Hello, you two monkeys," she said, leaning over with a smile. Startled, they stared up at her with wide, frightened eyes, like a pair of cornered foxes. "Don't be afraid," she said. "I'm not going to be cross. Here, it's hungry work being spies." She held out the chocolate in her gloved hand. They gazed at it warily. "Go on. Aren't you hungry?" The larger of the two boys held out his dirty fingers and took it. "What are your names?" she asked.

The elder boy unwrapped the chocolate and took a bite. "Séamus O'Leary," he replied in a strong Irish brogue. "This is my little brother, Éamon Óg." He elbowed his brother, who was staring at the otherworldly glamour of this English lady with his mouth agape. The diamonds in her ears sparkled like nothing he had ever seen before. As his brother speared him in the ribs he closed his mouth and blinked, but he was unable to tear his gaze away.

"I used to play as a little girl with a boy called O'Leary. Jack O'Leary," said Celia. "He must be related to you."

"He's our cousin," said Séamus. "His da just died," he added, enjoying the taste of chocolate on his tongue.

"I'm sorry to hear that," said Celia.

At that moment, Archie called to her. "Darling, we're going back now to look at the plans."

"You'd better run home before Lord Deverill sees you," she said to the boys. They scurried off without a word, disappearing behind the western tower. Celia returned to Bertie's car, where Mr. Leclaire was standing with Digby, looking up at the front door. "*Castellum Deverilli est suum regnum*," said Mr. Leclaire, reading the inscription still visible in the charred remains of the stone.

"Now it's Celia's kingdom," said Digby.

"I'll be a beneficent landlord," she said, striding over the grass with Archie. "Once the castle is finished I'll throw a small party for the people of Ballinakelly. It will mark a new beginning."

"The people of Ballinakelly have always been loyal to the Deverills," said Digby. "The fire wasn't their doing but the actions of Irish nationalists from other parts of the county, certainly not from here. I'm sure the people of Ballinakelly will be delighted to see it restored to its former splendor. Now, let's go and have a look at those plans, Mr. Leclaire." They climbed into the car, and, with Digby at the wheel, driving much too fast in his usual daredevil manner, they made their way back to the Hunting Lodge.

It wasn't until the last day of Digby's stay that his moment came to talk to Bertie. During the fortnight Digby had watched his cousin closely. He lacked enthusiasm for anything. His heart had been sapped of its juice, his *joie de vivre* turned sour, as if life had disappointed him to the point where he resented fun. He had only gone shooting once and that was because Digby had persuaded him to. They had tramped out with the dogs and shot some snipe, but Bertie had found little enjoyment in the sport he once loved. Pleasure was no longer part of his experience but something enjoyed by other people and he begrudged them for it. The only time he had grown animated was when Kitty had brought his son Little Jack over to see him. The child had the natural charm of the Deverills, Digby thought, and he was certain that Bertie could see himself in the boy, the carefree exuberance that he had lost. Otherwise, his cousin drank too much and oftentimes was so distracted that it was impossible even to converse with him.

As it was Digby's last day in County Cork, Bertie could not deny him an excursion on the boat. The weather was fine, warm even for January, and the sea calm. It was the perfect day to take the boat out, Digby exclaimed heartily, hoping to inject his cousin with enthusiasm. Bertie agreed, reluctantly, and the two of them set off for the harbor where Bertie's boat was moored—Digby in an eye-catching yellow-and-brown Tattersall jacket, waistcoat and breeches, thick yellow socks and matching cap, Bertie in a more discreet tweed suit. Digby waited for the jokes at his expense but Bertie wasn't forthcoming. He had lost his sense of humor too.

Once out on the sea Digby seized his moment. "Now listen here, old chap," he began, and Bertie listened because there was nothing else to do but watch his fishing line and wait for it to tremble. "You've had a tough couple of years, there's no doubt about it," said Digby. "You've suffered terrible losses: the castle, your parents and Maud. But you cannot dwell on the negatives or you'll drown in them. You have to think positively and pull yourself back from the brink. You understand what I'm saying?" Bertie nodded without taking his eyes off the fishing line, or somewhere thereabouts. Digby realized he had made no impression but pressed on valiantly. "What's the core of the problem, Bertie, old chap? It's me, Digby, you're talking to. Eh? Your cousin and friend. I see you're in trouble and I want to help." Still no response. Digby felt his resolve deflate. Like most Englishmen he wasn't good at talking about emotions and rather dreaded having to. But he sensed his cousin's survival depended on him somehow and was determined to press on even though he had rarely felt so uncomfortable. He decided to try another tack. "You remember when we were boys? Your father used to take us out on this very boat and teach us to fish. Of course, he made no headway with me." Digby chuckled joylessly. "I've never been the sporting type."

To his surprise memories began to rouse Bertie from his

languor. The corners of his mouth twitched with the beginnings of a smile. "You were pretty useless on a horse too," he said.

Encouraged, Digby continued to delve into the adventures of their boyhood. "Hubert always claimed to give me a gentle horse, but one look at me and the bloody animal was off. I think he gave me the highly strung ones on purpose."

"If he hadn't, you'd have lagged behind with the old ladies," said Bertie.

"I hate to admit it but those aunts of yours, the Shrubs, were more accomplished in the saddle than I was."

"Do you remember when Rupert scaled down the front of the castle?"

"Adeline nearly had a seizure!"

"So did your mama. I'm sure I remember her fainting flat on her back and someone calling for her smelling salts." The two men laughed. Then Bertie turned serious. "I miss Rupert," he said wistfully.

"He was a good man," said Digby. "If he was here now, and finding solace in whiskey as you do, Bertie, what would you say to him?"

Bertie's face reddened. "I'd tell him to give it up. I'd make him see reason."

"I want *you* to give it up, Bertie," said Digby softly. "It's destroying you and I can't sit back and let you do that to yourself."

There was a long silence as Bertie digested his words. Then he stiffened. "I don't have a problem," he said crisply. "We Irish like our whiskey."

"You're not Irish," Digby retorted. "And you drink too much of it."

"With all due respect, Digby, what business is it of yours?"

"I'm family," he replied with emphasis.

Bertie heaved a sigh. He turned and stared at his cousin with rheumy, bloodshot eyes. "You don't know what it's like. I've lost everything."

"That's no excuse to drown your sorrows in drink."

"Oh, it's easy for you to say, Digby. You with all your millions, a good wife and Deverill Rising that hasn't been burned to the ground by rebels intent on pushing you out of the country your family has lived in for over two hundred and fifty years. You have your parents still. You have the golden touch, Digby. The Devil's luck and probably a blonde in every port. In fact, life is just dandy, isn't it? Well, for some of us it's a struggle. I had a mistress, you know. I loved her. But I lost her too."

Digby was losing patience. "Stop feeling sorry for yourself. The truth is, you're not very attractive when you're drunk—and you seem to be drunk most of the time. She probably got sick of the stench of alcohol on your breath." Digby saw it coming, the punch that would have hit him in the jaw had he not reacted like quicksilver and caught Bertie's arm with surprising strength and agility. Bertie stared at him in bewilderment, breathing heavily like a bull at bay.

Digby bore down on him. "You're a damned idiot, Bertie Deverill. I'm not surprised Maud left you and as for your mistress, well, you've brought it all on yourself, haven't you? Weak, that's what you are, weak. You're not even fit to carry the Deverill name. If your father could see you now he'd probably punch you one himself. As he isn't here, I'm going to do it for him." Digby drew back his fist and landed a blow beneath Bertie's ribs. Bertie bent double and gasped for breath, but managed to swipe at Digby's legs, causing him to reel off balance. The boat rocked from side to side as the two men fought like boys in a playground dispute. But Digby goaded him with every insult he could think of, hoping that Bertie would eventually collapse with exhaustion and see the error of his ways. He didn't collapse, however. He flung himself upon his cousin and they both tumbled over the edge of the boat into the cold sea. A moment later their heads bobbed up, taking in large mouthfuls of salty water and air. Shocked by the cold they were unable to speak.

Digby was the first to make it back. He heaved himself up with difficulty for his clothes were waterlogged and heavy. His boots were like rocks attached to his feet, pulling him down. He flopped onto the bottom of the boat like a fat walrus, fighting for breath. Then he remembered his cousin. He scrambled up and threw himself against the side. Bertie was struggling. His clothes and boots were making it almost impossible for him to tread water. "Do you want to die?" Digby shouted. "Is that what you want? Because if you do, I'll let you go. But if you choose to live you have to give up the drink, Bertie. Do you hear me? It's your choice." Bertie coughed and gagged, sinking suddenly only to propel himself up with a desperate kicking of his legs and flapping of his arms. "What will it be, Bertie?" Digby shouted.

Bertie did not want to die. "Life!" he managed to shout, taking a gulp of salty water and coughing madly. "Please . . . Digby . . . Help . . ."

Digby lifted one of the oars out of its oarlock and carefully held it over the water so that Bertie could grab the blade and haul himself toward the boat. He remained for a moment with his arms flung over the edge, panting. "Come on, old chap.

We've got to get you home before you die of exposure," said Digby gently. He grabbed Bertie's sodden jacket and heaved him over into the body of the boat, where he lay shivering with fear as well as cold.

"You bastard," Bertie gasped, but he was smiling.

"You chose life, Bertie, and I'm going to hold you to it." Digby held out his hand and after a moment's hesitation his cousin took it. Digby pulled him to his feet.

Bertie tottered, then found his balance. "I won't let you down, Digby."

"I know you won't."

The two men embraced, wet and frozen to their bones, but the feeling of camaraderie had never been warmer.

KITTY HADN'T BEEN able to see Jack since their hasty meeting at his cottage after his father's death. He had been staying with his mother, who was inconsolable with grief. They sent each other notes, just as they had done in the old days when they had used the loose stone in the wall in the vegetable garden, but this time Kitty sent the stable boy. They met at the Fairy Ring and snatched stolen kisses, witnessed only by the gulls that wheeled above them like kites on the wind. As the day of their departure loomed Kitty felt it more like the steady approach of an ax, poised to sever her from her home. She dreaded it and longed for it in equal measure. She grew short-tempered with Robert. She snapped at Celia and she cried at the smallest thing.

And then God intervened.

Once she knew her fate a calmness came over her. A resignation that comes from total surrender. It was as if she was letting out a long, slow breath and with it came a sense of peace. She was certain now of what she was going to do. There was no question, no doubt, no indecision, her mind was as clear as crystal. Even the pain of knowing how much hurt she was going to inflict seemed dislocated, belonging to someone else.

The morning before they were due to take the train to Queenstown, Kitty rode over the hills to Jack's cottage. She didn't allow herself to cry. She set her jaw and clenched her teeth and let the cold wind numb her emotions. When she arrived she tied her horse to the fence as usual and pushed open the door. Jack wasn't there, but his bag was packed and ready in the hall. She sat down at the table and waited as the weak winter light retreated slowly across the floorboards.

At last she heard him outside, whistling for his dog. A moment later he opened the door and said her name. "Kitty."

Then he knew. Even before he saw the expression on her face, he knew. This time he didn't sweep her into his arms, promise her he'd wait for her and kiss the pain away. He stared at her in utter disbelief and exasperation, knowing that what she was about to tell him would wound him as surely as a bullet. "Why?" he demanded.

Kitty stared at her fingers, knitted on the table before her. "I'm pregnant," she replied. Jack swayed as if struck. Then she added in a quiet, steady voice, "It's Robert's."

Jack sat down opposite her and put his face in his hands. There ensued a heavy silence. So heavy that Kitty's shoulders dropped beneath the weight and her head began to ache. "Are you sure?" he asked finally.

"I'm sure," she replied.

"How could you?" He looked at her in desperation.

"He's my husband. I couldn't deny him."

"You could have. You could have, Kitty." He raised his voice. "If you had wanted to."

She lifted her chin and dared to look at him. Every twist and turn of their ill-fated love affair seemed to have dulled the light in his eyes a little further and he looked entirely desolate. He shook his head. "So this is it?" he said. "This is what it's come to? After all we've been through. After all the years we've loved each other. This is where we are?"

"I'm sorry," she said.

He banged his fist on the table. "Sorry! You're sorry!"

Kitty's eyes stung with tears. "I *am* sorry."

"Well, sorry doesn't cut it, Kitty Deverill. You're sorry for spilling tea. Sorry for putting mud on the rug. Sorry for every little fecking thing. But sorry isn't a word that even begins to put right the wrong you're doing to me. Do you understand? I've waited for you." His face contorted with disgust. "But I'm done waiting."

A tear splashed onto the table. "There's nothing more I can say."

"Did you ever truly love me, Kitty?"

A flood of emotion filled her chest. She pressed her hand against the pain. "Oh yes, I did, Jack," she gasped. "And I *do*, with all my heart."

"No, you don't. If you loved me you'd be ready to give up everything for me." He stood up and walked to the window, turning his back to her to throw his gaze over the sea. "God knows I've loved you, Kitty Deverill," he said wearily. "God knows too that I'll probably never stop loving you. It'll be a curse I'll just have to live with, but I've survived worse, so I'll survive *this*."

Kitty got up slowly, her body aching. She walked over and slipped her hands around his waist. He said nothing as she rested her forehead between his shoulder blades. She could smell the past on him. The scent of turf fires, hot tea, porter cake and horse sweat. The aroma of damp earth and brine. She closed her eyes and saw themselves as children, balancing on the wall, pottering about the river in search of frogs, kissing at the Fairy Ring, watching the sun sinking into Smuggler's Bay. Then she heard the guns, the cries of men, the shouts of the Black and Tans dragging him off the station platform and she wanted to cling to him and never let him go. He invaded her every sense until she was too overcome to hold back her grief. She held him fiercely, but he remained with his hands on the window frame, gazing stiffly out to sea, and she knew that she had lost him.

She left the cottage. Jack didn't turn around. If he had she might have buckled. She might have run to him; she might even have changed her mind. But he didn't. She mounted her horse and slowly rode back up the path, her heart a boulder in her chest. The wind dried her tears and the sight of those velveteen fields of County Cork soothed her beleaguered spirits as they always had done. Ireland was the one love she could count on.

As she headed for the hills she knew that Jack was right. A pregnancy was the only thing that could keep her from running away with him—and she had known it and allowed it to happen. Fate had played no part nor had Destiny. Kitty had prayed for a child to save her from herself. She knew as surely as she lived and breathed that she belonged here, at Castle Deverill. Not even Jack O'Leary, with the extraordinary power he had over her heart, could tear her from her home.

KITTY'S DESPAIR WAS Adeline's frustration. If Kitty married Jack and somehow returned to claim the castle from Celia, the spirits caught in limbo might at last be released. She watched Kitty ride for home and knew, as well as she knew her own heart, that Kitty's could not be changed. She had chosen Ireland, as she always had.

Adeline stood on the hill overlooking the sea. The wind blew inland off the water in chilly gusts. The waves rose and fell in ever-changing swells and their peaks extended upward as hands reaching toward Heaven. They crashed against the rocks, their efforts reduced to white foam that bubbled and boiled as the water rolled in and out in a rhythm that only God understood. But Adeline heard the melody beneath the roaring and her soul swelled like the sea as she contemplated the land she loved so dearly.

Ireland. Wild, mysterious and deeply beautiful.

"If only Hubert could inhabit these hills as I can," she thought sadly, contemplating the red sky and fiery clouds that seemed to flee the setting sun like sheep with their wool aflame. But instead he had to remain in the castle with the other Lord Deverills and in her opinion the place really wasn't big enough for the lot of them.

Death had changed them little. They were still the people they had been in life, only unencumbered by their earthly bodies. They still grumbled and moaned, argued and complained and generally made a nuisance of themselves. Adeline wondered whether Celia would rue the day she'd decided to rebuild, for Barton's son, Egerton, could be very tiresome when taken by the desire to create mischief. He enjoyed treading heavily down the corridors, making the doors creak and rattling the furniture. It was frustrating not being either on earth or in Heaven, burdened by all the grievances one had in life, only no longer limited in perspective. They had at least gained a little understanding of what their existences had been all about. Life after death was no longer an uncertainty. Time was simply an illusion. Yet, while their souls were drawn to a higher state, they were imprisoned behind bars they could not see, cursed to glimpse the light but remain in shadow, their mortal egos balls and chains about their necks.

Adeline, on the other hand, could go where she pleased. Heaven awaited her with the gates flung wide. Only love tied her to Hubert. While she waited for the curse to be lifted she could see the whole world and as she turned her thoughts to other lands she was once again drawn to the small part of Ireland, and herself, that had strayed across the water . . .

Chapter 8

Connecticut, 1926

Martha Wallace knelt on the window seat and stared in wonder at the snow that fell like fluffy white feathers onto the garden below. Today was her fourth birthday and her English nanny, the kind and gentle Mrs. Goodwin, had told her that God's present for her was snow. The little girl spread her palms against the glass and raised her peat-brown eyes to the sky to see if she could make Him out up there in the clouds, but all she could see were millions of fat flakes, constant and thick and falling fast, and Martha lost herself in the magic of them.

"Right, time to go, dear," said Mrs. Goodwin, walking into Martha's bedroom with the child's crimson coat slung over her arm and her matching hat in her hand. "We don't want to be late for your party. Grandma Wallace has invited all the family to celebrate your big day. It's going to be tremendous fun."

Martha wrenched her eyes away from the mesmerizing whiteness and slid off the window seat. She stood before her nanny. The lady smiled tenderly and crouched down to the child's level. "You look very pretty, my dear," she said, tweaking the blue bows in her dark brown hair and running her gentle eyes over the blue silk dress with its white sash and collar, which she had taken great trouble to press so that not even the smallest crease remained. "I remember when you were a baby. Such a pretty baby you were too. Your mama and papa were so proud they showed you off to everyone. They love you very much, you know. So *you* must be good for *them*."

Martha put her finger across her lips in a well-practiced gesture of conspiracy. "Shhhhh," she hissed through her teeth.

"That's right, my dear." Mrs. Goodwin lowered her voice. "Your secret friends must remain secret," she reminded her firmly, helping her into her coat. "It's not fun if you tell everyone. Then they're not secret any longer, are they?"

"But I can tell *you*, Nanny," Martha whispered, watching as her nanny's fingers deftly fastened the buttons.

"You can tell *me*, but no one else," Mrs. Goodwin confirmed. "You're blessed with a wonderful gift, Martha dear. But not everyone will understand it."

Martha nodded and gazed trustingly at her nanny. Something caught then in Mrs. Goodwin's chest, for when she looked deeply into the child's eyes she was sure she could see the loneliness there. It wasn't that Martha was lacking in love or company but that she seemed to carry an emptiness inside her that nothing was able to fill. She had come into the world with it, this tendency to stare out of the window as if searching for something lost or longing for something only half remembered. She was a melancholy, dreamy, solitary little girl—strange qualities in a child who had every material comfort to please her and drawers of toys to entertain her. Pam Wallace spoiled her only child unashamedly and anything Martha wanted she was given. But Martha didn't want much and little that could be bought attracted her interest. She preferred to sit with her imagination, to watch the clouds float past, to play with insects and flowers, to talk to people no one else could see. In her more fanciful moments Mrs. Goodwin wondered whether Martha could hear the echo of her homeland resonating in her soul or discern the vague memory of having come into the world as *two*, yet set off on her journey as *one*.

Mrs. Goodwin should not have heard Martha's parents discussing the child's origins—and she hadn't intended to. Goodness, if she had known what was to be gleaned, she would rather not have eavesdropped. But as it was, she had heard and there was nothing she could do to *un*hear it now. It had happened when Martha was about two years old. Mr. and Mrs. Wallace's bedroom door had been left ajar and Mrs. Goodwin had chanced to be in the corridor outside, having left the little girl asleep in her bedroom, at the very moment that husband and wife were discussing Martha's obvious loneliness and wondering what to do about it.

"We should have adopted another child," Mrs. Wallace had said to her husband and Mrs. Goodwin had stopped mid-stride as if turned to stone. Barely daring to breathe, she had lingered there, motionless, her curiosity overriding her sense of propriety. "We should have adopted her brother as well," Mrs. Wallace had continued.

"It was you who only wanted one child," Mr. Wallace had

replied. "You said you couldn't cope with more than one. And you wanted a girl."

"That's because a mother never loses a daughter."

"Sister Agatha did try to encourage us to take both babies," he had reminded her. "After all, they were twins. We could always go back to Dublin and see if there are any other babies up for adoption. I'd be very happy to give another orphan a home." An uneasiness had crept over Mrs. Goodwin then as if she had suddenly realized that she was listening to a pair of thieves reviewing a terrible crime.

"If I had known how lonely Martha would turn out to be I would most definitely have taken her brother too," Pam Wallace had conceded.

Stunned and horrified, Mrs. Goodwin had managed to lift her heavy feet off the ground and retreat back down the corridor to the little girl's bedroom. She had leaned over the bed and stared at the child with pity and compassion. Martha had a brother, a *twin* brother, Mrs. Goodwin pondered, gazing at the sleeping toddler. What had become of *him*? she wondered? Did he carry an emptiness in his soul too, as she was sure now that Martha did? Did they both know somehow, subconsciously, that they hadn't always been on their own? And what of their mother? Why had she given up her babies? Mrs. Goodwin was certain that Mr. and Mrs. Wallace would never tell Martha that she was adopted—this was the first Mrs. Goodwin had heard of it and she wondered who else knew. As far as the world outside the Wallace family was concerned, mother and child looked very much alike. Both had dark brown hair, eyes the color of peat and pale Irish skin. There was nothing in their appearance to raise a question about Martha's birth—and Mrs.

Wallace loved Martha, there was no denying that. She loved her dearly. But still, there was something deeply wrong about splitting up twins as they had done—and the thought that Martha might never know where she came from, or indeed that she had a brother, was a very uneasy one.

Mrs. Goodwin took Martha's hand and accompanied her downstairs into the hall where her mother waited, fussing with her handbag. Pam Wallace was as pampered and precious as one would expect the wife of a very rich man to be. Her dark hair was cut into a chic bob that rippled with self-conscious waves, her eyebrows plucked into thin arches that gave her a permanent look of surprise and her small mouth was painted scarlet to match her long fingernails, now hidden in a pair of long white gloves. She was tall and slender with a narrow frame so that the 1920s fashion of dropped-waist dresses and flat chests showed her to her best advantage. In Mrs. Goodwin's day, for she was young at the end of the *previous* century, a woman had to have ample embonpoint, but a voluptuous bosom was no good to anyone nowadays. However, Mrs. Goodwin was no longer interested in men or fashion. After Mr. Goodwin had left her widowed she had given her life to children and she knew from experience that small babies needed something soft to lie against.

Mrs. Wallace turned to watch her daughter walk down the stairs, holding her nanny's hand in case she stumbled, and her scarlet lips spread into a satisfied smile. Martha did her credit, she knew. Her long hair had been brushed until it shone, the ribbons neatly tied into two little bows, her crimson coat done up at the front with shiny red buttons, and her shoes, oh the dainty little blue shoes, dyed to match the dress that peeped out at the bottom of her coat, were as pretty as a doll's. Mrs. Wallace was very pleased. "Well, don't you look a picture, darling," she gushed, holding out her hand. One could only just perceive her Irish accent, concealed beneath her American twang. "You look quite the birthday girl. You will outshine all your cousins!" Martha stepped forward and took her mother's hand. Her chest swelled with pleasure for she liked nothing better than to please her mama.

Mrs. Goodwin was about to put the hat on Martha's head, when a white glove stopped her. "Let's not ruin her hair," said Mrs. Wallace. "You've tied those bows so beautifully, Goodwin. It would be a shame to squash them. We'll hurry out to the car and try not to get wet, won't we, Martha?" Martha nodded, glancing swiftly at her nanny, who smiled at her encouragingly.

Mrs. Goodwin clutched the hat and nodded. "As you wish, Mrs. Wallace."

"Come along now, let's not dawdle. There are presents awaiting you, darling, and cake. Didn't Grandma say that she was going to get Sally to make you the finest chocolate cake you've ever eaten?"

Mrs. Goodwin watched mother and child walk down the steps to the driveway where the chauffeur stood to attention beside the passenger door, his gray cap already thick with snow, his hands probably cold inside his black gloves. She watched her little charge climb onto the leather seat followed by her mother. Then the chauffeur closed the door and a moment later he was behind the wheel, motoring off toward the road, leaving fresh tracks in the snow. Mrs. Goodwin wished the child had worn a hat.

Pam Wallace's mother-in-law's house was a short drive away. Martha enjoyed rides in the car and gazed out of the window at the pretty houses and trees, all covered in white. It looked like a winter wonderland and she was enchanted by it. Pam sat stiffly beside her daughter. She was too consumed by her thoughts to notice the magic of the world outside the car, too anxious about the afternoon ahead to even talk to the child. Her sisters-in-law would be there: Joan, with her four children aged between nine and fourteen, and Dorothy, with her two boys who were ten and twelve. It made Pam bristle with competitiveness just to think of them and she hoped that Martha would impress them with politeness and good manners. If she didn't, they'd simply say that Pam had acted unwisely and bought a child with bad blood.

Ted and Diana Wallace's home was a large red-bricked house with white shutters, a gray-tiled roof and a prestigious-looking porch supported by two sturdy white columns. It was the house in which Larry had grown up and lived with his two elder brothers until he had married Pam at the age of twenty-five. Larry was everything Pam's Irish Catholic parents had wanted for her: old American money, with a fine education and a respectable job in the Foreign Service—well, *almost* everything; Larry Wallace wasn't Catholic. He was well mannered, extremely well connected, impeccably dressed, good at sports, distinguished-looking and, most important, rich, but the problem of his religion was insurmountable to Pam's father, Raymond Tobin, who did not attend the wedding. Having left their home and farm in Clonakilty after their son, Brian, had been murdered by the IRA in 1918 for having fought for the British in the war, Raymond Tobin was not prepared to compromise when it came to religion. "The Tobins have married Catholics for hundreds of years. I will not give Pamela Mary my blessing to go and marry a Protestant," he had said, and he had cut his daughter loose. Hanora, Pam's mother, put aside her reservations for the sake of her youngest daughter, and did her best to accept the man Pam had chosen for love. If losing her son had taught her anything it was that love was the only thing of real value in this world.

Pam had married Larry at the age of twenty-two after a six-month courtship. They had been blissfully happy at the beginning and Pam's efforts to win acceptance from this very East Coast American dynasty, who had also had their reservations about their son marrying a Catholic, had begun to pay off. But after two years of trying unsuccessfully to conceive, Pam's doctor had confirmed her greatest fear: that she would never bear children. The agony of childlessness had propelled her, in desperation, to look into other options.

Adopting a child was most certainly *not* common in the Wallace world. Ted Wallace said that one would never buy a dog without knowing its pedigree so why would one buy a child without knowing exactly where it came from? Diana Wallace worried that it would be hard to love a child who wasn't one's own flesh and blood. But Pam was determined and Larry supported her in the discussions that flared into heated rows around the Wallace dining-room table on Sundays. Pam's father, Raymond Tobin, agreed with Ted Wallace, although the two men had never met. "You won't know what you're getting," he told his daughter. "Buy a son, Pamela Mary, but he won't be a Tobin or a Wallace, whatever name you give him." Her mother, however, understood her daughter's craving for a child and whispered that it would be nice to give a chance to one of those poor Irish babies who were born in convents to unmarried mothers too young to look after them. With her mother's help Pam found an adoption agency in New York that had links with the Convent of Our Lady Queen of Heaven in Dublin. Larry arranged to be sent to Europe to set up and advance diplomatic links with America and they went to live in London for two years—sailing over to Ireland in search of the baby they wanted so badly. Aware that what they were doing was unconventional, they had made every effort to keep it secret. Only Larry's family and Pam's parents knew, for it would have posed too great a challenge to pull off such a deception in families as close as theirs.

Martha was everything a privileged and pampered little girl should be. She was pretty, polite and charming, her features were refined and, in Pam's opinion, aristocratic. Hadn't Sister Agatha said that the baby's mother was well bred? On top of all that, Martha was the apple of Grandma Wallace's eye. This was the first time Diana Wallace had ever thrown any of her grandchildren a birthday party. Pam should have been proud, but she was too worried to enjoy the moment. Joan and Dorothy would be there with their immaculate children, who were small clones of their parents and destined to continue the bloodline, which was so important to Pam's father-in-law, Ted Wallace. Who knew what Martha's bloodline was? Pam turned to her child and there was a warning tone beneath her question. "You're going to be a good girl today, aren't you, Martha?"

"Yes, Mother," Martha replied dutifully. Sensing her mother's nervousness, she began to fidget with her fingers.

When Pam arrived, Joan, who was married to the oldest

Wallace boy, Charles, was already there, perched on the sofa in the drawing room beside Dorothy, who was married to the middle son, Stephen. Their mother-in-law, the formidable Diana Wallace, was holding court in the armchair. Joan's slanting green eyes swiftly assessed the competition, then relaxed into a lazy gaze as she rated herself the better dressed of the three Wallace sisters-in-law. Her short auburn hair curled into her cheekbones like two fish hooks. Her pale lilac-colored dress was fashionably low-waisted and worn beneath a long cardigan in the same color as her hat and adorned with a large knitted flower just below her left shoulder. The impression was one of studied glamour, for even the black shoes, with their T-bar strap, burgundy stockings and the long string of blue beads that dripped down to her waist had been carefully selected according to the trends of the day. Dorothy, who took her lead from Joan in everything, had tried and failed to create the same effect and simply looked dowdy. Pam, whose glamour was as equally contrived as Joan's, only managed to look stiff and plain by comparison.

Grandma Wallace's face lit up when she saw Martha. She held out her arms and the child ran into them, knowing she would always be welcome in Grandma Wallace's embrace. "Well, if it isn't the birthday girl!" said Grandma Wallace. "If I'm not mistaken you've grown again, young lady."

Pam noticed Joan's lips purse at this display of affection between Grandma Wallace and her niece and she allowed herself a moment of pleasure. Joan had relished the fact that Pam was unable to bear children and had enjoyed being the first daughter-in-law to produce grandchildren. Ma and Grumps, as Diana and Ted had soon been called, had doted on those children. Grumps had taken a great interest in the boys' tennis and golf and Ma had read the girls stories and encouraged them to play the piano and paint. Soon after, Dorothy had given birth to boys but Joan hadn't felt threatened by Dorothy; her sister-in-law's admiration for Joan was both eager and blatant and Diana Wallace had always had a special affection for her first son's children. Then Pam and Larry had returned from Europe with a baby.

Pam would never forget the look on Joan's face when she had first laid eyes on Martha. She had peered into the crib and sniffed disdainfully. "The trouble with adopting a child, Pam, is that you don't know what you're getting. Genes are very strong, you know. You might bring her up to be a Wallace, but she'll always be who she really is inside. And what *is* that?" She had shaken her head and pulled a sympathetic face. "Only time will tell." Pam was determined to prove her wrong.

Pam took off Martha's red coat and the little girl stood a moment in her blue silk dress with its white Peter Pan collar and sash. Not even Joan could deny the child's charm and Pam swelled with pleasure because none of Joan or Dorothy's children had ever possessed such heartbreaking sweetness. There was something about Martha that separated her from the rest. She was a swan among geese, Pam thought happily, an orchid among daisies. A moment later the other children appeared, flushed from having been tearing around the house playing hide and seek. A pile of presents had been arranged on the top of the piano and one by one Martha was presented with the shiny packages, tied up with vibrantly colored ribbons and bows. She opened them carefully, with the help of her cousins, and gasped with pleasure when the gifts were revealed. She knew better than to grumble about the ones that didn't appeal to her, and was gracious with her thank-yous, aware all the time of her mother's sharp but satisfied gaze upon her.

Tea was in the conservatory, which had been decorated with pretty paper streamers and brightly colored balloons. The children drank orange juice and ate egg and ham sandwiches and wolfed down the birthday cake, which Mrs. Wallace's cook had made in the shape of a cat. Martha's face, upon seeing the creation ablaze with four candles, had broadened with a captivating smile.

Grandma Wallace could barely take her eyes off her youngest grandchild and seized every opportunity to comment on something amusing that she either said or did. "Why, she's adorable, Pam," Diana Wallace gushed. "She hasn't even got a crumb on that darling dress."

Joan stood in the corner of the conservatory with a cup of tea and bristled with irritation. "It's only because she's adopted," she whispered to Dorothy, knowing she'd find an ally in her. "You see, Ma's overcompensating to make Pam feel better. She's overdoing it, if you ask me, for the girl's an also-ran."

"Oh, I don't think she's an also-ran, Joan," said Dorothy. Then just as Joan was about to take offense at Dorothy's uncharacteristic disagreement, she added, "She's peculiar. My George tells me that Martha has an imaginary grandmother called Adele or Adine or something. An also-ran wouldn't have imaginary grandmothers. If you ask me, I think she's psychic."

Joan narrowed her eyes. "Psychic? Why, whatever do you mean?"

"I think she sees dead people."

"You don't think they're imagined?"

"No, I think she really sees dead people. I read an article in a magazine recently about psychic phenomena. Many small children have imaginary friends who aren't really imaginary. Apparently it's very common."

"Well, none of *my* children had imaginary friends," said Joan.

"Nor mine, thank goodness, and if they had I'd have quickly smacked it out of them! I'm not sure Stephen would approve of such a thing."

"Martha might be cute now," Joan pointed out. "But she could be trouble later. At least we know with our children where their faults come from."

"Oh, we do indeed, Joan."

"Family faults are somehow palatable, but . . ." Joan sighed with ill-concealed schadenfreude. "Martha's faults will always be mystifying."

After tea when the family settled into the drawing room again, Ted Wallace strode into the house with his second son, Stephen, having enjoyed a long lunch at the golf club. Much to Ted's disappointment golf hadn't been possible on account of the thick fleece of snow covering the course. However, both men were in good spirits after eating with friends and finishing off with a game of billiards. Ted was an enthusiast of any pastime that involved a ball and Stephen had inherited not only his father's love of sport but his aptitude for it. They walked in with their bellies full of lunch, laughing as they relived their victory at the billiard table.

The grandchildren stood politely and greeted their grandfather, who was a tall, imposing-looking man with strong shoulders, straight back, thick gray hair swept off a wide, furrowed forehead and a face that, though he was fifty-nine, was still handsome. Ted Wallace was much more interested in the boys, for like him, they were keen games players, but he had a kind word or two for the girls, a comment on their pretty dresses or a question about their pet rabbit or dog. After that, the children ran off and he stood in front of the fireplace to puff on a cigar while Stephen took the place on the sofa beside his wife, lay back against the cushions and stretched out his long legs with a contented sigh.

"It's going to snow all night by the look of things," said Ted. "I wouldn't leave your departure too late. The cars will have trouble in the road with this snow. Not that Diana and I wouldn't be delighted for you all to stay over."

"Dear God, I'm not wearing the right shoes to walk in the snow! If the car gets stuck I'm getting stuck with it," said Joan. "Are you sure it hasn't settled already?" She threw her gaze out of the window apprehensively.

"It'll be good for another hour or so," her father-in-law replied. "And you haven't got far to go." It was true, Ted and Diana Wallace's sons had all managed to find houses within a few miles of their parents, such was the enduring strength of the apron strings.

"I'll call the children," said Dorothy, standing up.

"So, how was the party?" asked Ted through a cloud of cigar smoke.

"Oh, Martha's had such a lovely time," Diana answered. "She's a little treasure."

"It's so nice to see her with her cousins," said Joan. "She's really one of us, isn't she?"

"Of course she is," said Pam, a little too quickly. "It was sweet of you, Ma, to throw her a party. She's loved every minute."

Diana gave a mellifluous laugh. "I'm her *favorite* grand-mother, Pam. I have to do everything I can to remain on top."

"It's hard competing with an imaginary one," Joan said, a devilish smile creeping across her face.

"*Does* she have an imaginary one?" Stephen asked, putting his hands behind his head and yawning.

"Ah, here she is. Why don't we ask her?" said Joan as Martha trailed into the room behind the older children.

"Really, I don't know what Joan's talking about," said Pam uneasily.

"I'm not making it up. Dorothy, what is she called, Martha's imaginary grandmother?" Dorothy blanched in the doorway and looked confused. She clearly didn't want to be seen to be making trouble.

"Help us out, dear," said Joan to the little girl. Martha glanced anxiously at her mother. Joan tapped her long talons on the arm of her chair impatiently. "Well, speak up, dear. What's the name of your imaginary, or perhaps not imaginary, grandmother? We're all longing to hear."

Pam stood up and took her daughter by the hand. "Come along now, darling, we have to get home before we get snowed in." She turned to her sister-in-law and her face hardened. "Sometimes, you can be very unkind, Joan."

Joan laughed, opened her mouth in a silent gasp and pressed her hand against her chest. "Come now, Pam. It was only a bit of fun. You're much too oversensitive. It's one thing for Diana to compete with Grandma Tobin but to compete with a ghost is even beyond the capabilities of Grandma Wallace!" she said.

Diana shook her head. "There's nothing unusual about having imaginary friends. Martha is on her own so much that it's perfectly normal to invent friends to play with. I don't mind you having another grandmother, Martha. So long as she's as nice to you as I am!" Martha smiled, although her eyes glittered with tears.

Mrs. Goodwin noticed that Martha was very subdued when she returned home. Mrs. Wallace told her that the child was simply tired, but later that evening, after Martha had been put to bed, Mrs. Goodwin eavesdropped for the second time. This time she hadn't stumbled across the open door by accident but by design. It wasn't like Martha to be so quiet and solemn, especially after a birthday party. Mr. and Mrs. Wallace were in the drawing room, enjoying a drink before dinner. Mrs. Goodwin hovered outside, ears picking up the relevant snippets of conversation.

"If she were our biological daughter I wouldn't mind her faults, or eccentricities as you call them, because they'd be family faults I'd recognize, but since she comes from we don't know where, I can't help worrying that she's different. I don't want her to be different, Larry. For her to fit into the family, she has to be the same as all the other children. Don't you see?"

"I think you worry too much. She'll grow out of it when she starts going to school and making proper friends."

"I don't want to wait that long. I want to sort it out now."

"And how do you propose to do that?" Larry asked.

"I'll take her to see a doctor."

Larry laughed. "She's not sick, Pam."

"Talking to people we can't see is a kind of sickness, Larry. It's certainly not normal." Pam's voice had now gone up a tone. Mrs. Goodwin put her hand to her throat. What would a doctor make of Martha's "gift" and how would he "cure" it? She heard Mr. Wallace sigh. He didn't have much patience for domestic matters.

"Whatever you think, Pam. If it gives you peace of mind to have some doctor say it's perfectly normal to talk to daisies, be my guest."

"Mary Abercorn has suggested a man in New York who treated her son for anxiety. Bobby is now the most carefree young man you'd ever meet, so he must be good."

"Not a doctor then?"

"No, he's a . . ." She hesitated. "You know, a man who looks after the mind as opposed to the body."

"A quack."

"Really, Larry!"

"All right, a psychiatrist." There was a long pause as Mr. Wallace pondered his wife's suggestion. At last he spoke and there was a conclusiveness in his tone. "As long as he doesn't lay a finger on her," he said firmly.

Mrs. Goodwin had heard enough. She hastened to the stairs and quickly made her way up them, her tread swift and silent on the carpet. When she reached the top, she put her hand on the banister and closed her eyes. She took a deep breath and tried to assuage her fear. Yet, in spite of her efforts it lurked like a heavy shadow in the pit of her belly. She didn't know what this psychiatrist would do, but she knew for certain that no good would come of it.

Chapter 9

Martha lay in bed listening to the familiar sounds of the night: the rustling of people moving about her bedroom, the murmuring of whispered voices, the quiet buzz of activity—although in the darkness she couldn't work out exactly *what* they were doing. She just knew that they were busy, *they* being people but not people like her parents and Mrs. Goodwin; people who she understood instinctively to be not from this world.

These nocturnal goings-on had never frightened Martha because Grandma Adeline had told her that the spirits meant her no harm. "They're just curious," she explained. "This world and the next are much closer than one might imagine." Martha liked Adeline. She had a gentle smile and kind eyes and her laugh was as soft as feathers. With her mother, Martha had to be on best behavior. She had to keep her dresses clean and her shoes shiny. She had to be polite and well mannered. She had to be *good*. Although she was much too young to understand the complex world of adults, she knew intuitively that she had to *win* her mother's affection. She knew that her love was conditional. With Adeline it was different. She sensed Adeline loved her just the way she was. It wasn't anything particular that she said. It was in the tender way she looked at her. She made the child feel cherished.

Mrs. Goodwin had told Martha to keep Adeline secret, but she found it hard when she was as real to her as Grandma Wallace—well, almost. She knew her mother didn't like her to talk about people she referred to as Martha's "imaginary friends." But when Martha did, quite by accident, her mother's face would change. It would grow suddenly hard. She would suck in her affection as if it were a tangible thing, like her grandfather's cigar smoke. One moment it would be filling the space around her and then, with one deep inhalation, it would be gone, pulled out of the air, leaving her cold and isolated and ashamed. During these moments Martha would try very hard to draw it out again. She'd be exceptionally good. By and by this had become a cycle of behavior both mother and daughter had grown accustomed to. Pam withheld her affection in a subconscious bid to assert control while Martha tried so very hard to earn it back. All the while Adeline was there, in the background, reassuring Martha that she was special.

Martha now lay in bed, listening to the noises in her room and finding comfort in them. She didn't realize how tenuous her hold on that world was. She was about to find out.

The following morning Mrs. Goodwin dressed her in a green frock with a matching cardigan and long white socks. She brushed her hair off her face and tied it back with green ribbons. When she was ready she was taken downstairs to the hall where her mother was waiting for her. This time she was going to New York. Mrs. Goodwin had told her how exciting Manhattan was and Martha couldn't wait to see it. She hadn't been anywhere, only as far as Grandma Wallace's house, and the thought of the big city thrilled her.

New York was indeed exciting. Martha pressed her nose to the car window and gazed out onto the tall buildings that had grown higher than trees and onto the sidewalks that were gray with slush. She had never seen so many people and so many cars, all lined up in long rows, some tooting their horns impatiently. It was in front of an elegant brownstone building that the car came to a halt and her mother hooked her handbag over her arm and waited for the chauffeur to open the door for her. As he stood to attention Pam climbed out, then took Martha's hand and led her up the steep steps to the front door.

Martha, who had been chattering happily in the car, suddenly grew quiet. She walked close to her mother and held her hand tightly. There was something oppressive about this place that made her feel afraid. The elevator frightened her too because the door was like an animal cage. It made a rattling noise when it was opened and closed and Martha felt as if she was being imprisoned. She was mightily relieved when her mother pulled it open at the second floor and she was allowed out. A lady with bright red lips and long eyelashes like spider's legs greeted them from behind a desk. Pam said her name and the lady told them to take a seat in the waiting room.

Pam had brought a picture book for Martha to look at while they waited. It was her favorite story about a kitten that gets lost but is later found. The child gazed at the colorful pictures and forgot all about the scary lift. A short while later she was interrupted by a lofty, stiff man in a dark suit and tie towering over her. He had shiny blond hair brushed into a side parting and smooth white skin. "Hello, Martha," he said and the way he articulated her name revealed his foreign origins. He extended his hand and Martha took it and let him shake it. "My name is Mr. Edlund. I'm going to talk to your mother for a moment, then I'm going to ask you to come into my office." Mr. Edlund smiled down at her but Martha was too nervous to smile back. She stared into his big blue eyes, so far away because he really was very tall, and sensed something in his energy that she didn't like. Then he walked away with her mother and disappeared into a room, closing the door behind him. Martha's stomach churned with nerves. She rested the book on her knee but she didn't read it. She just stared at the door, dreading the moment Mr. Edlund would appear and summon her.

After what seemed like a very long time, the door did indeed open and Mr. Edlund called to her. "I'm ready for you now, Martha," he said, and the little girl slipped off the chair and walked anxiously into his room. To her relief she found her mother sitting in front of a wooden desk neatly arranged with papers, books and photographs in frames. There was a chair beside her and Mr. Edlund told Martha to sit in it. She did as she was told and clasped her hands together on her lap. She glanced around the room. There was a medical bed in the corner covered in a white sheet with a standing lamp placed beside it from which a very bright bulb shone out like a demonic eye.

When Mr. Edlund spoke to her, she jumped and wrenched her gaze away from the demonic eye. "Your mother has told me a lot about you, Martha. She says you're a very good girl."

Martha glanced at her mother and saw that she was smiling. This made Martha feel less afraid. "You're an only child and you've just turned four. Is that right?" Martha nodded. "Good. Did you have a nice birthday party?" She nodded again. "Good. I hope you didn't eat too much cake." Martha blushed because she *had* eaten too much cake and had felt a little sick afterward, but she hadn't spilled anything down her dress. She glanced again at her mother, who nodded at her encouragingly.

"Answer Mr. Edlund's questions, Martha. He's a doctor," she said with emphasis. "You can tell him anything." Mr. Edlund did not correct Mrs. Wallace, for although he possessed no qualification, he certainly believed himself to be a doctor of the mind.

"Do you have lots of friends, Martha?" Mr. Edlund asked. Martha didn't know how to reply to this. She didn't really know what friends were. She played with her cousins occasionally, but most of the time she was on her own in the house. Then she thought of Mrs. Goodwin and she nodded. "Who are your friends, Martha?" he asked.

"Mrs. Goodwin," she replied quietly.

"That's the nanny," Pam told him helpfully. She laughed lightly. "She's not a friend, Martha. She's your nanny. That's different."

"Is it true that you have friends other people can't see?" Mr. Edlund continued. Now his face was very serious. Martha squirmed on her chair. Mrs. Goodwin had told her to keep Adeline secret. She looked at her mother, waiting for her to withdraw her affection, but to her bewilderment she was still smiling.

"Darling, you can tell Mr. Edlund anything. You won't be in trouble," she said.

Martha was confused. She didn't understand why she could tell this stranger about Adeline when she wasn't allowed to speak of her at home. "Yes," she said, and her voice was a mere ribbon of sound so that Mr. Edlund had to lean across his desk to hear her.

"Do you have one friend or lots of friends?"

"Lots," she replied.

He nodded. "I see. But your mother tells me you have one special friend."

"Yes," said Martha.

"What is your special friend called?"

"Adeline," said Martha.

"When do you see her?"

"In my bedroom."

"In the night?" Martha nodded. "Is she here now?"

Martha shook her head. "No," she replied.

Mr. Edlund smiled with satisfaction. He leaned back in his chair and knitted his long fingers over his stomach. He looked at Pam, who was so eager for him to cure her daughter of her strange hallucinations that she was ready to believe anything. "This is really very simple," he said, and Pam's whole body seemed to sag with relief.

"Oh, I'm so pleased," she replied.

His eyes fell on the child. "You know that Adeline isn't real, don't you, Martha?" When Martha didn't reply, he added, "She seems real to you, but she's not real. She's like a dream, that's why you see her at night when you're going to sleep. You've made her up because you're lonely and you'd like someone to talk to. Do you understand that Adeline is simply make-believe?"

Martha knew Adeline wasn't made up and she didn't only see her at night when she was going to sleep. But she looked anxiously at her mother. Pam's face was still smiling, but Martha sensed that she was about to suck in her affection and she dreaded the cold feeling of isolation that would follow. She dreaded *that* more than being put on the bed and being stared at by the demonic "eye." So she lied. Mrs. Goodwin had taught her that lying was wrong but she didn't want her mother to withdraw her love and she didn't want Mr. Edlund to ask her any more questions. "Yes," she said and her eyes welled with tears.

Her lie had a surprising effect. Pam turned to her in astonishment. "You see, darling, Adeline is in your head and isn't real at all. I'm not sure why you had to invent a grandmother when you have two perfectly good ones who love you very much." Martha wiped away a tear. Her mother turned back to Mr. Edlund. "How is it possible to invent such a person? She's been consistent about this Adeline woman since she learned to speak."

"The mind is a very complicated thing, Mrs. Wallace. Martha created Adeline out of necessity and now she believes her to be real. Children have especially strong imaginations. It is by no means uncommon. Children generally grow out of these delusions and if they don't—"

"Yes?" Pam asked anxiously.

"There are many avenues we can take. But we don't need to discuss them unless Martha continues to believe she sees people. So, in the meantime, you must make sure she is entertained. She needs friends to play with and she needs to be busy. When she mentions Adeline, gently remind her that the woman is only in her imagination. Remind her regularly because by repeating it you will override the pattern. She is young enough for this to be both efficient and effective."

Pam was very grateful. She left Mr. Edlund's office determined to find Martha little friends to play with and to keep her busy. She would organize violin lessons so that instead of gazing out of the window dreaming the child could practice scales. It was a relief to hear that Martha's fantasies were simply symptomatic of her loneliness. Pam couldn't wait to tell Joan and Dorothy. She'd tell them what Mr. Edlund had said—or rather what *Dr.* Edlund had said; she would lie about that because it sounded better coming from a doctor.

Martha followed her mother down the steps to the car. She didn't speak all the way back, but gazed disconsolately out of the window. Her mother chattered on about how wonderful *Dr.* Edlund was and how sensible his diagnosis was. She didn't realize that he had broken something in Martha: her delight in magic.

Mrs. Goodwin was waiting uneasily in the hall for Martha to return. When the car drew up outside the house it was already getting dark. Snow had begun to fall again. She could see the flakes in the golden auras around the streetlamps. Martha climbed out and walked slowly toward the house. Mrs. Goodwin knew from the way the child carried herself that she was deeply unhappy. Mrs. Wallace held out her hand and Martha took it, allowing herself to be pulled alongside her mother, who was keen to get in out of the snow.

That night when Mrs. Goodwin tucked her into bed she asked about New York. Martha told her nanny that she didn't like Mr. Edlund. "What did he say, dear?"

"Adeline isn't real."

Mrs. Goodwin was about to disagree. She knew that Martha had been born with the gift of second sight, but she didn't want to get the child into trouble. Perhaps it was better that she believed the beings she saw were figments of her imagination. That way she'd be unlikely to slip up and talk about them again. Mrs. Goodwin didn't like to think of the consequences of *that*. What would Mr. Edlund do then? She didn't want Martha to grow up thinking there was something wrong with her. She didn't want Mrs. Wallace thinking there was something wrong with her, either. "My dear, you are a very special child," said Mrs. Goodwin gently. "Sometimes children are so special that adults are incapable of understanding them. Whether or not Adeline is real doesn't matter. She is real to *you*. If she makes you happy there's no harm in that." The child blinked up at Mrs. Goodwin with love and trust. The nanny planted a kiss on her forehead. "Good night and God bless you, dear."

Mrs. Goodwin informed Mrs. Wallace that her daughter was ready for her to say good night. Pam stroked her daughter's hair and kissed her cheek. "You were a very good girl today," she said, and the weight in Martha's heart lightened a little. After she had left the room the child was alone in the darkness. A while later Martha heard the familiar sounds of rustling and shuffling and the hiss of whispers. She pushed herself beneath her blanket and began to sing. She discovered that if she sang she couldn't hear the noises.

Adeline watched her with sadness. She pitied the child's shame and lamented the mother's ignorance. She knew what would happen now, for the same had happened to similar children all through the ages: Martha would lose her gift. She would lose the ability to see the finer vibrations around her and in the process she would lose herself and become just like everyone else. There was nothing Adeline could do about it. She would simply fade like a rainbow when the sun stops shining. "I'll still be with you," she whispered into the darkness beneath the blankets. "I'll always be with you."

The following day Pam presented Martha with a present. Mrs. Goodwin had been very useful in helping her decide what to buy. She needed something for Martha to love. The child wasn't interested in toys and dolls and teddy bears. She loved real creatures like insects, birds and animals. But Mrs. Goodwin had the perfect idea. Martha put the box on the table in front of her and carefully lifted the lid. Inside, two round eyes gazed up at her warily. The child caught her breath. Her face flowered into a wide smile. "It's a kitten!" she exclaimed excitedly. She delved into the box and gently lifted the animal out. The kitten meowed, then snuggled against Martha's warm body as she held it in her arms.

"It's a boy kitten," her mother told her. "So you have to think of a name for him."

"What are you going to call him, dear?" asked Mrs. Goodwin.

Martha thought about it a moment and then a name sprang into her mind. "Little Jack," she said.

Mrs. Wallace was taken aback. She didn't know anyone called Jack. "Whatever made you think of *that* name?" she asked.

"It's a lovely name," said Mrs. Goodwin.

"Well, I'm sure he'll grow into it," said Pam. Martha lowered her head and pressed her lips against the animal's soft head. The two women caught eyes and smiled. Both hoped that, now Martha had a little friend to play with, a *real* little friend, she would no longer be lonely.

"Thank you, Goodwin," said Pam, putting a hand on the older woman's arm.

"My pleasure," said Mrs. Goodwin. "I think Martha and Little Jack were meant for each other."

Chapter 10

Ballinakelly, 1926

Spring smiled on Ballinakelly with the innocent optimism of a child. Radiant sunshine blessed the countryside and scattered the sea with golden kisses. Birds and butterflies took to the air and crickets chirruped happily in the long grasses. Hazel and Laurel made their way to church up the main street, arm in arm. The wind playfully caught the ribbons in their hats and pulled the hems of their dresses, and they responded to its teasing with predictable merriment, trying as best they could to hold on to their hats and their frocks in order to protect their modesty, while still holding on to each other.

At last they reached the church of St. Patrick. Its walls shone orange in the bright light of the sun, and the spire, rising as it did toward Heaven, uplifted the hearts of these two sisters who had suffered terrible fears during the Troubles and were still a little nervous about leaving the safety of their house. They were greeted warmly by Reverend Maddox, whose ruddy face and round belly betrayed his love of fine wine and good food and his inability to indulge in either with any sort of moderation. "My dear Misses Swanton," he said, sandwiching in turn their small hands in his big spongy ones. "Isn't it a beautiful day?" He raised his eyes to the sky in a pious manner, as if he and God were in cahoots, even about the weather.

"Oh, it is indeed," agreed Hazel, almost feeling inclined to thank him. "It is a lovely spring and I'm sure it will be a lovely summer." She sighed heavily. "Adeline would have adored the wildflowers on the hillside."

"Lady Deverill is enjoying the flowers in God's great garden," he reassured her.

"Of course she is," said Laurel.

"Adeline believed she'd be a spirit walking among us," Hazel added. "In which case, she'll be here enjoying it all for herself."

"Oh I'm sure she is," Laurel agreed. "I'm sure she's enjoying God's great garden with poor Reverend Daunt, who was such a good vicar. We are so pleased our humble parish has been sent such a fine replacement."

Reverend Maddox smiled with gratitude and ushered them into the church. "My dear ladies, why don't you step inside and enjoy the music. Mrs. Daunt has been practicing a few new pieces and she'd love you to hear them. Music has been a consolation to her during this difficult time." He watched the two women walk into the church. Two more compatible sisters he had yet to find.

Soon the church was beginning to fill up with the Ascendancy and gentry who had not been chased out of their homes by the rebels during the Troubles, and the working-class Protestants. There was an atmosphere of unity now, a sociability that hadn't existed before. The violence had herded them together in their small minority and they found comfort in each other as if a group of sheep on a windy hillside surrounded on all sides by wolves. Shopkeepers greeted the lords and ladies with sincere smiles and the grandees returned their salutations with equal warmth.

Lord Deverill sat in his usual place in the front row. Kitty was beside him with Robert and JP, as Little Jack was now known, for Kitty had felt that, at four years old, he was too big to be called "little," and considering he was christened Jack Patrick, JP suited him just as well. In truth, the name Jack gave her pain every time she uttered it.

Kitty had noticed a change in her father, subtle like the subliminal shift of a plate beneath the earth's crust. She couldn't say exactly when it had happened, but it was as if he had made a decision to amend the way he saw himself and the world. This deep shift had sent ripples through his being that affected him in so many ways. Gone was the melancholy, the self-pity and the need to drink himself into forgetfulness. He seemed grateful for life, with its small blessings. Most of all he seemed grateful for her and Elspeth, and spent as much time as possible with his little son, JP, who called him "Papa" and enjoyed all the outdoor pursuits that *he* enjoyed. The new clarity in his eyes convinced her that his feelings were genuine, but she couldn't understand what had inspired them. He even supported Celia's renovations of the castle with enthusiasm, wandering around the building site daily, where hundreds of men toiled away like an army of ants on an anthill. She wished she could share his interest in the rebuilding of his old home, but she couldn't; it caused her great anguish.

She didn't want to think of Jack O'Leary either, for that was painful too. He had gone and life had continued. She hadn't believed it possible, but it had happened. Celia had given birth to a baby daughter at the beginning of April, named Constance after her mother-in-law. Kitty's child would arrive in the autumn. Robert was ecstatic. She took his hand now and squeezed it as the jumping chords of Mrs. Daunt's organ playing resounded off the stone walls of the church. Kitty had made her choice; she had now to learn to live with it.

"Who's that man sitting with Grace?" Hazel whispered to Laurel. Laurel leaned forward and looked across the aisle to the other side of the church. There, seated beside Grace Rowan-Hampton, was a man neither Shrub had ever seen before. They both stared, and as they took in his thick silver hair, deep-set brown eyes and tidy white mustache resting above a wide and sensual mouth, time stood still. The chatter around them faded with the organ music and only their hearts, which began to race with an unfamiliar or long-forgotten tempo, resounded in their ears. United as always, the two ladies admired and feared the silver wolf in their midst. Not in the many decades of their dedicated spinsterhood had a man had such power to unbalance them. Suddenly, to their horror, he turned and his eyes met theirs, holding them captive for an excruciating moment. As they were jolted back to their senses with a flush of embarrassment, the music and chatter returned louder than before. He smiled and nodded politely. They tore their gazes away and fanned their flushed faces with their prayer books.

"Lord preserve me," hissed Laurel.

"He must be Grace's father," said Hazel.

"Has he a wife, do you think?" Laurel asked. Then she added hastily, "God forgive me for asking such a thing in His house. Don't answer that, Hazel. I don't know what's got in to me. Must be the heat. It is terribly hot, isn't it?"

"Oh, it is, Laurel. Terribly hot. I didn't see a wife. It appears he's with Grace."

"Look, Reverend Maddox is about to start the service. We must concentrate."

Hazel's fingers fluttered over her mouth. "He smiled at us, Laurel. Did you see?"

Laurel nudged her sister. "Shhh," she hissed. But her lips twitched with excitement.

Reverend Maddox gave a stirring sermon that seemed to go on and on and on. He was well known for enjoying the sound of his own voice to the point of being deaf to anyone else's, but today he was taking more pleasure from it than usual. Perhaps it was due to the sunshine, or maybe to the presence of the distinguished gentleman who was sitting beside Lady Rowan-Hampton whom he felt compelled to impress. Whichever it was, his voice rose and fell in great waves of passion, his sentences elongated like a piece of elastic only to snap back into short, brisk phrases designed to rouse the sleepy faithful.

At last, after he said the closing prayers and the Celtic Blessing he was so fond of, the Shrubs were the first into the aisle to make their escape before this devilishly handsome gentleman was able to see what a pair of quivering fools he had reduced them to.

Grace turned to her father, for indeed it was him. "I'm sorry about the rector, Papa. He mistakes the pulpit for the stage."

Lord Hunt patted his daughter's hand. "My dear, you needn't worry about me. When I am bored, which I often am in church, my mind is inclined to wander. Today, however, it wasn't my mind but my eyes that went wandering." He grinned mischievously.

Grace shook her head. "Papa, you're incorrigible. Mama would turn in her grave to see the way you behave. If you're going to live with me in this small community, you have to conduct yourself with decorum. I warn you, a town like this loves nothing more than to gossip. If you're going to misbehave you have to be discreet."

"I don't know what you're talking about, Grace." He laughed. "I'm a paragon of virtue. Besides, I'm much too old for that sort of thing." He arched a fluffy white eyebrow and smiled a wolf's smile, which told her that he was neither too old nor disinclined to "that sort of thing." Grace smiled too because in her father's lustiness she recognized herself.

They walked out into the sunshine and Grace introduced her father to Bertie and Kitty. The old rogue took Kitty's hand and brought it to his mustache, where the short hairs tickled her skin. "I must say, the women of Ballinakelly are very easy on the eye," he said, his eyes twinkling with mischief.

Kitty laughed. "You're too kind," she said, grinning at Grace, who was shaking her head in mock embarrassment.

"Papa's been here but five minutes and he's already misbehaving," she said.

"A little flirtation is the secret to longevity," said Lord Hunt. "And I intend to live a very long time."

"You must come for dinner," said Bertie cheerfully. "We'd like to welcome you formally."

"That's very kind of you, Lord Deverill. Grace has told me a great deal about your family and I admit that I am intrigued by your history. I was sorry to hear about the fire but curious to learn that the castle is being rebuilt."

"My cousin's daughter has bought it and is in the process of renovating it. Why don't you let me show it to you? It's an ambitious and extravagant project, to say the least, but I believe it's going to be magnificent when it's finished."

"I would like that very much, thank you," said Lord Hunt.

Grace looked at her former lover with tenderness. Recently she had seen glimpses of the carefree Bertie in his smile and in the light in his eyes, which seemed to her like the clear light of a new dawn. There was a fresh look about his clothes too, or perhaps it was the way he held himself in them. His tweed suit no longer looked crumpled and shabby, his hat was restored to its habitual raffish position on his head and his skin ceased to betray an excessive love of alcohol. She had noticed he had stopped drinking whiskey and wine and wondered what had come over him. She had once given him an ultimatum, her or the drink; he had been unable to live without either. Who had succeeded where she had failed?

She climbed behind the wheel of her car and waited for her father to join her. He was enjoying meeting the locals and soaking up the attention the women gave him, for even at seventy-four he was a fine-looking man. Her gaze drifted out of the window. A skinny dog limped along the street on three legs, his sharp nose in the air for he was after a whiff of something savory. Men in caps walked in groups, hands in pockets, eyes still dark with a residual wariness left over from the Troubles. Women stood chatting beneath the clear skies while children played in the road, their laughter bouncing off the walls of the houses. Then she saw Michael Doyle.

She caught her breath. Her heart stalled. The sensation was so acute it was visceral. For a moment she couldn't move. Only her eyes followed him as he ambled nonchalantly up the street with his brother Sean. She blinked, unable to believe what she was seeing, not trusting her sight, for surely, if he was back in Ballinakelly, *she* would have been his first stop? She willed him to look at her, but he didn't even toss her a glance. He strolled on, deep in conversation with his brother. She took in the face she had so often caressed, clear-skinned and glowing now that he was cured of the drink like Bertie. But she wasn't thinking about Bertie. Cast in the shadow of Michael Doyle, Bertie was invisible, as was every other lover she had ever taken. Michael Doyle was back from Mount Melleray and nothing else mattered. He was taller, broader, more rugged and attractive than ever before. A hot, prickling sensation crept over her skin and gathered in her belly. She gripped the steering wheel. He was past her now. She watched his back. Her eyes stung from the staring. How could he not feel her gaze through his jacket? How could he not sense that she was here? Why didn't he turn around? She wanted to run to him; to throw herself at him; to press herself against him and feel his rough hands upon her skin and his hungry mouth upon her lips. But she knew she had to restrain herself. She had to wait. He was only too aware of where she lived. She was certain he would come as soon as he could. Surely, his need for her was as urgent as hers for him?

"That Lord Deverill is a charming young man," said Lord Hunt, climbing stiffly into the passenger seat. He didn't notice his daughter's pale face, or the raw craving in her eyes. "Jolly nice of him to invite me to take a look at the castle. As you know, I have an enormous interest in history."

No sooner had her father closed the door than Grace started the engine and began to drive slowly up the street, her eyes frantically searching. Her father continued to share his thoughts but she wasn't listening. She was determined to see her lover; and for *him* to see *her* and the message in her gaze that told him to come to her. At last, as the car motored toward O'Donovan's, she spotted him. Then she was right beside him. She slowed down, so slow that she was crawling at the same speed as his walking pace. Sean glanced at her, but Michael was so busy talking that he was unaware of the car trailing him and of the desperate woman inside willing him to look at her.

Unable to bear it a moment longer, she tooted the horn. Both men, and the others in the street besides, turned to her in surprise. She leaned out of the window and gave a smile that exposed nothing of the torment beneath it. Desperate she might be, but Grace Rowan-Hampton was a seasoned actress and, when it came to dissembling, no one could surpass her. "Mr. Doyle," she said, without so much as a quiver in her voice.

"Lady Rowan-Hampton." Michael looked astonished to see her there. He doffed his cap and waited to hear what she had to say.

"I'm glad to see you're back. My husband is looking for strong men to clear a copse behind the house. Several trees were brought down in the winter storms. If you and your friends would like some work, will you come up to the house and see me?"

He nodded. "I'll ask in O'Donovan's," he said.

"Thank you," she replied, hoping he was reading the message in her eyes as he always used to. "I will wait for you up at the house. Sir Ronald would like the work to be done as soon as possible. I trust you'll find a few willing volunteers."

She drove on then, for there was nothing else to be said. Her father looked on in bewilderment as she checked her rearview mirror to see if he was watching the car, but he wasn't. He had disappeared inside O'Donovan's and only a cluster of scruffy youths remained in the road, admiring her shiny motor car as it rattled off.

Once home Grace hurried upstairs to change out of her church clothes into a more comfortable dress. She spent a long time at her dressing table arranging her hair, enlivening her cheeks with rouge and applying a little tuberose perfume behind her ears and between her breasts. She was sure that Michael would come.

Ethelred Hunt had claimed for himself a big armchair on the terrace, where, sheltered from the wind and warmed by the sun, he sat with his spectacles on his nose, reading the *Irish Times*. A maid brought him a glass of sherry and he lit a cigarette. He inhaled in a long, satisfying breath before releasing the smoke into the air. He didn't question his daughter's strange behavior outside the pub or the unusually long time she was spending in her bedroom, for Ethelred Hunt was a man whose concern was primarily his own pleasure and right now his attention was focused on those two birdlike ladies who had looked so startled to see him in church. He would have a great deal of fun with those two, he mused. He wasn't known as Ethelred-the-ever-ready for nothing! When at last Grace appeared, her father failed to notice, either, that she was on edge. She waited the rest of the day, but Michael didn't come.

It wasn't until the following morning that Brennan knocked on his mistress's door and announced that there was a group of lads at the front claiming to have come to clear the copse for Sir Ronald. Grace's heart gave a little leap. "Wonderful," she said. "I have told Mr. Tanner to expect them, so would you let him know and he'll look after them." As much as she wanted to run outside she knew that such a public display would be wholly inappropriate and, besides, how long had Michael been in Ballinakelly? She rather relished the idea of making him wait, as he had made *her* wait.

Brennan disappeared to find the head gardener, leaving Grace wringing her hands and pacing the room in agitation. Ethelred had gone off with Bertie to look around the castle and was then going to luncheon at the Hunting Lodge. There was a strong chance he would be gone all afternoon, for Grace suspected that Bertie would want to show him around the whole estate. Her father was a fine horseman and a keen race-goer, and since Bertie was as good as widowed, the two men had much in common. Ronald was in London, where he spent so much of his time these days. She had the house to herself until dark and was determined to make the most of it.

When Michael didn't come to her study window, or stride into her sitting room like he used to do, she began to worry. Had he gone to the copse with the other men in order to be discreet? Surely he could have made something up? She went out onto the terrace and gazed across the lawn. A rustle in the viburnum behind her gave her a start and she spun around, fully expecting to see Michael there with a lusty grin on his face, but it was nothing more than a pair of squabbling pigeons. She heaved a sigh and frowned. Why was he taking so long?

Finally, driven to distraction, she went to find Brennan in the hall. Her butler had seen men come and go over the years and had never so much as raised an eyebrow. Indeed, he had let Michael into the house many times, not bothering to announce him but letting him wander on through the hall as if he belonged there. On one occasion he had even warned him off when Sir Ronald had made an impromptu visit home. Now she asked him if Michael had been with the group of lads. Brennan shook his head. "No, my lady. Michael Doyle was not among them," he told her. Grace's face darkened with fury. How dare he humiliate her?

"Thank you, Brennan. If he does turn up, please tell him I'm indisposed." Then she went upstairs where she fell onto her bed, hugged her pillow and wondered what to do.

That evening her father returned in high spirits, full of talk about the splendid day he had had with Bertie. "Do you know he introduced me to his bastard? A bonny boy he is and as sharp as a tack too. He told me that his wife is so furious she has refused to let him move to London where he has bought her a house in Belgravia. It looks like he's going to be stuck here. I told him he should exchange her for a new one."

"Oh really, Papa," said Grace. "She's not a horse."

"From what I hear about Maud Deverill, Bertie would have had more fun with her if she was." Grace couldn't help but laugh in spite of feeling miserable. At least Lord Hunt was having fun, because *she* wasn't. She had thought of countless reasons why Michael hadn't turned up today but none of them assuaged her disappointment or her fury. His excuse had better be good, *very* good, she told herself, or he would wish himself back at Mount Melleray.

Grace drifted through the week distracted, hiding her frustration beneath a veneer of brittle cheerfulness. It seemed everyone in the county wanted to meet her father. They dined out every night and Ethelred entertained his hosts and their guests with hilarious stories and anecdotes, all exaggerated and embellished and some even totally invented, for Lord Hunt was a man of exceptional imagination. He brought laughter with him wherever he went, but no one was more taken with this witty and charming old wolf than the Shrubs, who, on the following Saturday night, were placed on either side of him at Bertie's dining-room table. They blushed, they stammered and they giggled like schoolgirls as Ethelred ensnared them in the full glare of his attention, rendering them powerless like a pair of guinea fowl, their little hearts aflutter as they had never fluttered before. As was their habit, they were in absolute agreement over the devilishly attractive Lord Hunt, but for the first time in their lives they wished they weren't.

Grace hadn't seen Michael since the Sunday before. She went to church, trying and failing to concentrate on the service, wondering how on earth she was going to seek him out without exposing herself. Her father seemed unconcerned about *his* focus on godly matters and far more interested in finding sport in the poor Shrubs, who sat across the aisle, blushing into their prayer books. As he grinned at the two spinsters and lifted his hand in a small greeting, Grace put her fingers to her lips and scowled into the middle distance.

She knew Michael went to O'Donovan's, but women didn't go to the pub and certainly not women of her class. She knew where he lived, but she couldn't very well turn up at the Doyle farmhouse, asking for him. The old network of note-passing that had worked so efficiently during the War of Independence had long ceased to exist, and even if it had still functioned a note would not bring him to her door. He was avoiding her. For whatever reason—and she convinced herself that there was a very *good* reason—he wasn't coming to see her. So she had no option but to engineer a meeting.

It is a sad fact that, in every affair, one party is keener than the other. Grace knew that only too well. But now *she* was the less desired and she couldn't accept it. Once a lover, man or woman, has given a partner unique delight it's almost impossible to imagine they no longer want it. She would pursue him. She would force him to face her and explain himself.

Her chance came at the Ballinakelly Fair, which took place on the first Friday of May. People had come from all over the county to look at the horses, buy and sell livestock and socialize. The sea breeze swept through the square with playful curiosity, dancing with sunbeams and ladies' hemlines, snatching smoke from the farmers' pipes and the boys' cigarettes. Spirits were high as the men and women flirted and the children played among the chickens and goats, earning a few bob for looking after the cows while the farmers went to the pub. There was music from a band and fortune-telling from tinker women who weaved through the crowd with baskets of heather and holy pictures. Voices rose with the peals of laughter and the mooing of cows and the bleating of sheep. Grace usually enjoyed the fair, but today she was anxious. Nights lying awake in torment had left her nerves frayed. Her father, however, was very excited. He had already met half of Ballinakelly society and was eager to meet the other half. When he bumped into the Shrubs he bowed formally and held out both arms, inviting them to show him around. It was fortunate that he had two arms, for both Laurel and Hazel were determined to take one.

Grace accompanied her father and the Shrubs, commenting on this and that without really listening to the conversation or, indeed, to her own responses. Her eyes scanned the faces for Michael's. She knew he'd be here. As a farmer he made it his business to attend every fair. Perhaps he'd even entered one of his bulls to compete for a prize?

At last she saw him right at the other end of the square: a glimpse of his head, unmistakable with its thick black curls, towering above everyone else's. She quickly left her father and the Shrubs without a word and elbowed her way through the crowd, keeping her head down for fear of getting caught by someone she knew and being compelled to stop and talk. She pushed on, eager to get to him, but it felt like she was wading through the sea, for with every step forward a wave of people came and pushed her back.

At last she lifted her gaze and there he was, right in front of her, gazing back at her with a serious look on his face. His coal-black eyes were the same but the wildness in them had gone. "Top of the morning to you, Lady Rowan-Hampton." The man he had been talking to slipped away and Grace felt as if they were alone on an island in an ocean of people.

"I need to talk to you," she whispered, barely able to restrain herself from placing a trembling hand on his forearm, just to feel him solid beneath her touch. "Why didn't you come and see me? How long have you been back? I've been waiting . . ." She despised the pleading tone in her voice, but she no longer had the will to dissemble.

"I've changed my ways," he replied solemnly, glancing about

him to make sure they weren't being overheard. "I've repented of my sins."

"What are you talking about? You went to be cured of the drink, not to become a monk!"

He lowered his eyes to hide his shame. "I've changed," he repeated, this time with emphasis. "The Michael Doyle you knew is dead. God has cured me of the drink and opened my eyes to the wickedness of my past."

Grace shook her head, unable to comprehend what he was saying. "You're still a man, Michael," she whispered, stepping closer. "God can't change that."

"I will not break His Commandments. You are a married woman, Lady Rowan-Hampton."

"But I *need* you." Even now she wanted to offer herself to him. To taste him, to kiss the sweat off his forehead, and she could scarcely keep her hands from reaching out and stroking him.

"I'm sorry, Grace," he said, this time with more tenderness.

"I waited for you, God damn it. I've waited *months* and *months*." Her voice was pleading, bordering on hysterical. "What am I? A jezebel?"

"Yes," he said with a solemnity that shocked her. "I must never look at a jezebel again. I shall never again visit Babylon."

Michael looked down at this woman who had always been so in control, of herself as well as everybody else. She had been a deadly weapon during the War of Independence, and many a British soldier had lost his life because of her, but here she was standing before him, a woman like any other, appealing to a man. He shook his head. "I think you should go before you draw attention to yourself," he said, not unkindly. Grace stared at him in disbelief, hating her submissive aching for him, longing to be rid of her dependence. Her vision began to blur but she searched his face for signs of amusement, for surely this was a joke. Surely, this was a bloody-minded joke. But Michael's face didn't change. He looked back at her with the righteous expression of a priest. She backed away, her cheeks aflame with mortification and fury. *If Mount Melleray could cure me of you, Michael, I'd be there like a shot.*

Chapter 11

On the first Wednesday in June, Sir Digby and Lady Deverill attended the Derby, the most famous flat race in the world, at Epsom Racecourse in Surrey. Accompanied by Celia and Archie, Harry and Boysie and their insipid wives, Charlotte and Deirdre, whom the two young men would have preferred to have left at home, they were in high spirits. The women wore elegant cloche hats and coats yet Beatrice had chosen a larger, more Edwardian-style hat adorned with extravagant ostrich feathers and pearls that drew the eye as well as the comments, for many of the noble ladies considered Lady Deverill rather brassy. "Who does she think she is, the Queen?" they whispered behind their race cards. The gentlemen were dressed in the finest top hats and tails but somehow Digby's shoes and hat shone with more polish than anyone else's, the cut of his collar was slightly more flamboyant than convention dictated and his confident swagger gave the impression that he was a man of great importance. Today he felt indomitable, because, running in the race for the first time, was Digby's colt Lucky Deverill, whom he had been training up in Newmarket. "I hope he has the luck of the *London* Deverills and not the *County Cork* Deverills," Boysie whispered to Celia, who swiftly reproached him with a playful smack on the hand.

"You're wicked, Boysie!"

"One cannot be chastised for telling the truth, Celia," he replied with a sniff.

"Papa says he has a very good chance of winning."

"I think he is alone in that belief," said Boysie. "Judging by the odds."

"What do they know," Celia sniffed dismissively. "Papa says he's bred to win the Derby."

"And he came fourth in the 2000 Guineas at Newmarket, yes, I know, your father told me that too."

"You will bet on him, won't you?"

"Only for you, Celia. Though I doubt it will make me a fortune."

"If he wins, his value at stud will soar. The covering fees will be enormous. Papa will make a fortune."

"Another one," said Boysie with a smirk. "Your father's rather good at making fortunes."

Wrapped in coats and hats, sheltering beneath umbrellas, the small party who had parked their cars behind the grandstand hurried inside. It was warm and exclusive in there and they were quick to help themselves to refreshments. "Goodness, there are so many people on the hill!" Celia groaned, looking out onto the rise of common land where the fairground loomed out of the rain like a mythological sea creature. "I do so hate the great unwashed!"

"The hoi polloi," said Boysie. "I'm glad they're out *there* and we're in *here*."

"Quite," she agreed. "It's hell out there. I swear the entire East End has decamped for the day."

"Darling, the whole of London has decamped for the day," said Boysie. "You'd have thought the rain would have put people off, but no, there's nothing like a free day out for the great British public."

Due to the inclement weather the trains had been restricted and the day was soon dubbed a Petrol Derby, with makeshift parking lots being set up in the large sodden fields either side of the drive to accommodate the swollen number of vehicles. The wet and dismal conditions, however, did not deter the thousands of people who arrived in cars, double-decker buses and motor coaches. Some even arrived in stagecoaches pulled by fine horses. Piled into and *on*to the coaches, the delighted passengers waved cheerfully at the crowds as policemen in capes and helmets tried to maintain some sort of order for the arrival of the King and Queen. When they appeared at last, in the middle of a long convoy of gleaming cars, the crowd stopped what they were doing to watch. The King sat stiffly beside the Queen, who was wearing one of her typically elaborate feathered hats, raising his hand every now and again to greet his people. The girls, however, were much more interested in the dashing Prince of Wales and erupted into a clatter of applause when they saw him.

Once in the relative calm of the stands Digby and Beatrice wandered around the gallery greeting their friends and acquaintances. It was there that Digby bumped into Stanley Baldwin, the prime minister, for Parliament was always adjourned for the Derby. "Ah, Prime Minister," he exclaimed, striding up to him. The prime minister swept his eyes over Digby's flamboyant purple-and-green waistcoat and pink spotted tie and grinned. For a man of his breeding there was something rather brash about Sir Digby Deverill. Mr. Baldwin lifted his top hat in salutation. "Sir Digby, Lady Deverill, I see you have a horse racing this year," he said.

"Indeed we do," Digby replied. "He's a fine colt. Young but swift. I have high expectations of him."

"I'm sure you do, Sir Digby," said Mr. Baldwin archly. "You didn't get to where you are today without the desire to be a winner."

"Nor you, if I may be so bold."

"Indeed." Mr. Baldwin smiled, acknowledging Digby's wit with a slight nod of the head. "What are the odds?"

"Sixteen to one," Digby replied.

"A long shot." Stanley Baldwin was well known as a plain-speaking man. The prime minister chuckled. It did not seem likely that Lucky Deverill would win. "Then I wish you luck," he said. "Tell me, how is work progressing on that castle of yours?"

"My daughter is pouring money into the project. If it doesn't outshine Windsor Castle in opulence and grandeur I shall be very disappointed."

"Is she intending to live there?" Mr. Baldwin asked, incredulous, for Celia's reputation as a socialite was well documented. "I would have thought a lively girl like Mrs. Mayberry would find life in County Cork dull by comparison to London." He smiled at Beatrice, noticing the large diamonds that glittered on her ears and beneath her left shoulder in the form of an elaborately crafted flower brooch. *Those Randlords!* he thought to himself with a barely perceptible shake of the head.

"Oh, but it's beautiful in the summer," Beatrice interjected emphatically.

"But not quite so beautiful in the winter, I don't imagine," Mr. Baldwin argued.

"Then we must hope that Celia shines bright enough to bring the London glamour to Ballinakelly." Digby gave his Brigg umbrella a couple of taps on the floor and roared a belly laugh that sounded like gold in a prospector's pan. "Because, by God, no one else can."

Mr. Baldwin laughed with him. Digby's ebullience was shameless but irresistible. "Of that I have no doubt, Sir Digby. Mrs. Mayberry is the very sun itself."

Beatrice was distracted by a friend who caught her eye and Mr. Baldwin raised his hat at her departure. Digby put a hand on his shoulder and moved closer. "Do let me know if I can help the Party in any way," he said in a low voice.

"I will," said Mr. Baldwin bluffly. "Your help is much appreciated."

"I hope one day I will be rewarded," said Digby.

"You've been very well rewarded already with your baronetcy," the prime minister reminded him.

"Oh, that bauble." Digby chuckled. "A viscountcy is much more to my taste."

"Is it? Is it?" said Mr. Baldwin, embarrassed at the brashness of the Randlord. "I think you've done very well already," he added.

"Up to a point," said Digby with that golden gravel laugh. "Up to a point."

Celia threaded through the crowds with Boysie and Harry, leaving their wives discussing the weather with a tedious group of Edwardian ladies old enough to remember the Crimean War. Archie was with his mother, who had slipped her hand around his arm and thus staked her claim. There would be no getting away from her until luncheon. Celia, Boysie and Harry were only too delighted to find themselves unencumbered and wandered about in search of fun people to talk to.

As they reached the steps to the upper terrace who should be coming down, surrounded by a coterie of courtiers but the Prince of Wales himself, who had left the Royal Box to go to the paddock. He recognized Celia at once and his handsome face creased into a debonair smile. "My dear Celia," he said and Celia dropped into a deep curtsy.

"Your Royal Highness," she said. "May I present my cousin Harry Deverill and my friend Boysie Bancroft?" The Prince shook hands and the boys duly bowed.

"You know I've known Celia since she was this high," he told them, placing his hand a few feet above the step.

"And I suppose you're going to tell me that I have hardly changed." Celia laughed.

His blue eyes twinkled at her flirtatiously. "You've certainly grown taller," said the Prince. "And prettier too."

"Oh sir, you're much too kind," said Celia, blushing with pleasure. "The King looks awfully well," she added. "And the Queen . . ."

"Mama's hats are so ugly," the Prince interjected. "She looks hideous in those ridiculous toques!"

Celia giggled. "Papa has a horse running in the race."

"So I see. If he wins, he'll be insufferable."

"He's already insufferable," Celia said with a smile.

"He's a *bon viveur*," said the Prince.

Celia grinned raffishly and leaned a little closer to him. "It takes one to know one, sir."

"Celia, you're incorrigible!" He laughed. "I will go and find your papa and wish him luck."

"Oh do, sir. He's quite beside himself with nerves, though he'll never admit it." The Prince chuckled and moved on into the crowd of people who were all watching him out of the corners of their eyes and hoping he'd come their way.

"The Prince of Wales rendered me dumbstruck," said Boysie once he was gone. "He's outrageously attractive!"

"The wittiest tongue in London was silenced?" said Harry, feigning astonishment.

"I'm afraid it was, old boy," Boysie replied. "Fortunately Celia's adroit enough for the three of us."

"I've known him for years. He's a darling! Come on, let's go and find some *young* people to talk to," Celia suggested, and they headed off up the stairs.

On the common ground that was the hill, the weather had not dampened the spirits of the thousands of people who had flocked to the racecourse. The noise was overpowering: coach horns tooting, bookmakers hollering their odds, salesmen advertising their wares, car engines rattling and the general public shouting in different dialects. The refreshment tents were full to bursting, the stalls busy selling wares and the fairground full of mirth. Laughter resounded from the carousel, rose up from the game tables and was swiftly smothered in the sealed booths advertising werewolves and other monstrosities. Gypsies lured the gullible into their colorful caravans to learn their futures (and the identity of the Derby winner) in exchange for a palm crossed with silver, and artists positioned themselves beneath makeshift shelters to sketch portraits of those whose hats and hairdos had not been ruined by the rain. Double-decker buses and cars were parked as close to the running rail as possible and piled with people keen to have pole position for the races while pedlars accosted them from the ground, hawking goods. The earth grew soggy but the desire to enjoy themselves kept the spectators buoyant—as did the desire to win money, for the queues at the bookmakers' were very long indeed.

Before the Derby Celia went down to the paddock with her father to watch the horses parading. Digby's jockey was a five-foot-six Irishman of almost forty years of age called Willie Maguire, notorious for his fondness of drink. Many whispered that Willie was too unreliable and that Sir Digby had been misguided to offer him the ride, but Digby was a man wise enough to take advice from those who knew better. In this case, his trainer, Mike Newcomb, had more experience and knowledge than he did and Digby trusted him implicitly. If Newcomb had appointed a seventy-year-old jockey with arthritis he would have agreed wholeheartedly.

"Oh Papa, wouldn't it be glorious if Lucky Deverill won! Willie would most certainly win the most fetching jockey in his green and white."

Digby chuckled. "He's got more mileage under his belt than all of them put together, I suspect."

"And Lucky Deverill is a fine horse." Celia ran her eyes up and down the animal's gleaming limbs.

"He's well put together, no one can deny that. He looks like he'll get the trip as he has plenty of scope."

"Plenty," Celia agreed without understanding her father's racing jargon.

"This is *our* year," Digby said to his daughter. "If ever I am to win the Derby it will be today."

"Do you really think so?"

Digby nodded thoughtfully, remembering the day he struck lucky in the South African diamond fields. "When you're lucky, Celia, you carry that luck around with you for a while. Luck attracts more luck. That's the time to exploit it."

"Can you say the same about *bad* luck?" she asked.

"I'm afraid it works both ways. Sometimes bad luck sticks to you like mud. In that case you weather it. But we're on a lucky roll, Celia my dear, and today we're going to win." He waved at Willie as the jockey walked Lucky Deverill past.

"Oh Papa, you're wonderfully confident," she gushed, full of admiration for her daring father.

"Until my luck runs out," he added.

"But it won't, surely."

"Oh, but it will," he said with certainty. Then he grinned the grin of a gambler who is as much excited by the possibility of loss as he is of gain. What mattered to Digby was the thrill of the game. "But sometimes one can make one's own luck," he added with a wink.

The horses left the paddock and paraded in front of the grandstand where the King and Queen and the Prince of Wales observed them keenly from the Royal Box. The air grew tense as the crowd watched them canter across the downs to take their starting positions behind the rope. Celia stood beside her father at the front of the gallery at the very top of the grandstand, directly opposite the winning post. "I'm a bundle of nerves," she said, shifting her weight from one foot to the other. "But terribly excited."

Digby put his field glasses to his eyes and watched the horses arrange themselves at the start. His heart began to pound in his chest like a drum. His cheeks flushed with competitiveness and it took a great force of will to steady his hands. He could see Lucky Deverill clearly, the green-and-white silks of Willie Maguire, right in the middle of the line-up. He muttered under his breath. Then the flag fell and they were away.

Celia barely dared breathe as the horses thundered off up the long incline, contracting into a tight huddle. The crowd was pressed up against the rails either side of the track and the noise of cheering was deafening. Digby said nothing. He watched through his field glasses, perfectly still, while Celia jumped and fidgeted nervously beside him. Beatrice wrung her hands while Harry and Boysie watched Lucky Deverill fall back on the outside. "Digby might have to rename him *Un*lucky Deverill," said Boysie in a low voice and Harry chuckled. He thought of the bet he had placed in support of Celia; he might as well have just burned the money.

The horses galloped up the hill, disappearing briefly behind the copse at the top before starting their descent toward Tattenham Corner, the most famous corner in racing. The inexperienced horses, fearful of the steep slope, began to slow down while the more experienced horses advanced, creating a muddle. Lucky Deverill had not yet distinguished himself. He languished behind the first six horses. Beatrice shot a surreptitious glance at her husband, inhaling sharply through her nose at the sight of his immobile profile; there was something in the barely perceptible twitch of his lower lip that caused her heart to snag. Celia put her fingers to her mouth and began to chew her glove.

It was at that moment, when the horses slowed down just

before the home stretch, that something extraordinary began to happen. The sharp bend had flung some of the horses wide into the field and Willie Maguire, being a seasoned jockey, took advantage of this, hugging the inside. To Digby's astonishment Lucky Deverill was gaining momentum—and gaining it fast. Digby's knuckles went white. He lowered his field glasses. The horses advanced up the slope toward the winning post and all Digby could see was the bright green and white edging its way past the fourth, then the third, grabbing the rising ground. It wasn't possible! His breath stuck in his throat. The noise grew more intense but he heard nothing, just the hammering sound of blood pulsating against his temples.

Everyone was now on their feet. Celia was screaming, Beatrice gasping, Harry and Boysie mute with astonishment, mouths agape, as Lucky Deverill inched ahead of the second. With only a hundred yards to go Willie Maguire rode Sir Digby's hope as if he were riding the wind. A moment later he was parallel to the first. The two horses were now neck and neck. But Lucky Deverill was propelled by the luck of the London Deverills and with one last valiant thrust Willie Maguire rode him first past the winning post.

Digby was on his feet, punching the air. Celia was throwing her arms around him. Beatrice was dabbing her eyes with Boysie's handkerchief. Harry shook his head and wanted to throw his arms around Boysie, but he thrust his hands into his pockets and swept his eyes over the crowd now pouring onto the racecourse.

Suddenly Digby was besieged. Hands patted his back, faces smiled at him, lips congratulated him. He was swept down the grandstand like a leaf on a waterfall, carried by the hundreds of surprised spectators, both friends and strangers alike. When at last he reached the ground he hastened off to the finish to meet his horse and jockey, the victorious Willie Maguire. When he saw his triumphant horse, nostrils flaring, his coat sodden with rain and sweat, he stroked his wet nose, then took him by the reins to lead him into the winners' enclosure. He was at once surrounded by journalists asking him questions and photographers clicking their cameras, the flash bulbs momentarily blinding him. "Really, it had very little to do with me," he heard himself saying. "Willie Maguire rode with great courage and skill and Lucky Deverill proved everyone wrong. It is Newcomb, Lucky Deverill's trainer, who should be congratulated and, if you don't mind, I'd very much like to go and do that myself." And with the help of the police he extracted himself from the throng of press.

"By God, he won!" said Boysie to Celia. "He really does have the luck of the Devil!"

"Papa makes his own luck," said Celia proudly.

Beatrice had now composed herself and was graciously receiving congratulations when she was interrupted by an official-looking man with a neatly trimmed mustache and spectacles. He coughed into his hand. "Lady Deverill, may I ask you to follow me. The King would like to offer you his personal congratulations."

Beatrice beamed. "But of course. Excuse me," she said to those awaiting her attention. "I have been summoned by the King." The people stepped aside to allow her to pass and Beatrice was escorted up to the Royal Box where His Majesty was waiting in the anteroom, surrounded by courtiers. A small, bearded, gruff man in tails and top hat with a row of military medals across his chest, the King had the air of a retired military colonel.

"My dear Lady Deverill," he said when she entered. He extended his hand. Beatrice took it and allowed the King to plant a kiss on her cheek, tickling her face with his beard. She then dropped into a low curtsy. "You must be very proud," he said.

"Oh I am, sir. Very." Unlike his son, the King was a man of few words, so Beatrice found herself overcompensating to disguise any awkwardness. "I shall have a hard time keeping his feet on the ground now that he's got a Derby winner." She laughed to fill the silence that ensued.

"Oh yes, indeed," said the King finally, settling his watery blue eyes on her.

"We remember with great affection your visit to Ireland," she said, recalling his state visit to Southern Ireland fifteen years before. "Did you know that Celia is now restoring Castle Deverill?"

"Is she now?"

"Oh yes," Beatrice gushed. "It is a tragedy that some of the most beautiful houses in Ireland were razed to the ground during the Troubles. It's just wonderful to think of possibly the most beautiful of all rising once again."

"Indeed," the King muttered. "Damn good shoot at Castle Deverill." At that moment an equerry sidled over and whispered something into the King's ear. "Ah, I must go and hand Sir Digby his trophy," he said.

"Of course you must," said Beatrice, dropping once again into a low curtsy. She left his presence in high spirits in spite of the uneasiness of their conversation, because, after all, the King's the King and Beatrice was dazzled by royalty.

"ONE COULD NOT really ask for very much more," said Digby to his wife when they arrived back at Deverill House at the end of the day. He poured himself a drink while Beatrice fell into the sofa, exhausted by all the excitement.

"Where do you go from here, Digby?" she asked, sighing with the pleasure of taking the weight off her legs.

"What do you mean? I'm going to win the 2000 Guineas and the Gold Cup," he replied. Digby brought his glass to his nose and inhaled the sweet smell of whiskey. His ambition would be greatly served by entering into the public arena, but he was only too aware of the skeletons rattling about in his cupboard to risk threatening his reputation by putting his head so high above the parapet. Aware that his wife was not referring to horses he added, "I have no desire to encumber my life with politics, my dear." He sank into an armchair as a maid brought in a tray of tea.

"Rubbish," said Beatrice with a smile. "You can't resist the limelight!" The maid handed her a teacup. "Ah, thank you. Just what I need to restore my energy. What a day. What a *perfect* day. Celia is mistress of Castle Deverill and my husband has won the Derby. It's all too wonderful to be true." She watched the maid pour the tea, then dug her teeth into a short-bread biscuit. "I am aware of our blessings, Digby, and I take none of them for granted. When we lost our beloved George in the war I thought my life was over. But it's possible to rise out of the ashes and live, isn't it? One simply has to keep going in a different way. One part of me shut down, but I discovered that I am more than I believed I was. Other parts of me came to the fore. So here we are, enormously fortunate, and here am *I*, grateful and proud." She sipped her tea, dislodging the lump that had unexpectedly formed in her throat.

Digby looked steadily at his wife. "I think about George every day, Beatrice," he said quietly. "And I miss him. He would have relished today. He loved horses and he had a competitive spirit. He would have enjoyed the thrill of the race. But it was not to be. I hope he was watching from wherever he is."

They withdrew into silence as they both remembered their son, and while they both felt blessed, they knew that nothing, no accomplishment, success or triumph on any level, could make up for the devastation of so great a loss.

KITTY STRUGGLED TO live with the choice she had made. She waded through her days against an incoming tide of grief and regret, the bleeding in her heart staunched only by the burgeoning life growing inside her belly. It was as if she had prized open the very body of Ireland and ripped out its soul. Without Jack the landscape was bereft, weeping golden tears onto the damp grass as autumn stole the last vestiges of summer. She kept herself busy, looking after JP and preparing the nursery for the new baby, and she tried not to succumb to the memories of the man she loved which lingered on every hill and in every valley like mist that just won't lift. Yet, in late October, hope arrived with the first frosts as Kitty was delivered of a little girl. They called her Florence, after their honeymoon in Italy, and Kitty found, to her joy, that the overwhelming love she felt for her daughter eclipsed the longing she felt for Jack.

Robert stood at the bedside and held the tiny baby in his arms. He gazed into her face with wonder. "She is so pretty," he said to Kitty, who lay in bed propped up against the pillows.

"What do you think, JP?" she asked the little boy who was snuggled up beside her.

JP screwed up his nose. "I think she's ugly," he said. "She looks like a tomato."

Robert and Kitty laughed. "You looked like a tomato too, when you were a baby," Kitty told him. "And look what a handsome boy you are now."

"She doesn't have much hair," said JP.

"Not now, darling, but it will grow," said Kitty. "You'll have to look after her and teach her to ride."

"She'll look up to you," Robert added, handing Florence back to her mother and sitting on the edge of the bed. "You'll be her big brother."

"Although, you're really her uncle," Kitty said.

"Think of that. Uncle JP. How does that sound?" Robert asked him.

The boy grinned proudly and peered into Florence's face. The baby wriggled and began to cry. JP screwed up his nose again in distaste.

Robert put out his hand. "I think you and I should leave Kitty to feed the baby," he said.

"Is she always going to make that noise?" asked JP, jumping down from the bed.

"I hope not," said Robert.

Kitty watched them wander from the room, JP's small hand in Robert's big one, his bouncy walk full of childish vigor beside Robert, whose labored stride was slow due to his stiffened leg. Her heart buckled. As hard as it had been to make her choice, she knew she had done the right thing. She gazed into the innocent face of her child and knew that *this* was where she belonged.

Chapter 12

New York, autumn 1927

B ridie had been in New York for two years. She was now an established presence in the gossip columns, at the theater, in the elegant uptown restaurants and cafés and, of course, in the smoky underground speakeasies of Harlem. Her sorrow was a silent current beneath the hard shield that she had built around herself for protection against memory and melancholy. Like ice on a river it was beautiful to look at but cold. Her life was lived on the surface where everything was superficial and gay and without a care. Happiness was acquired in the same way that she acquired everything: with money. The moment she felt a tremor of gloom she headed out to the shops to buy more happiness in the form of expensive clothes and hats, shoes and bags, feathers and sequins, diamonds and pearls. The boutiques were full of happiness and she had the means to procure as much of it as she wanted.

There were men; plenty of men. She was never without a suitor and she took her pleasure when she wanted it. In those midnight hours when darkness wrapped its soft hands around her and lovers caressed her with tender fingers the silent current swelled and grew inside her, breaking against her heart in waves of longing. Her soul cried out to be loved and the memory she had of loving shifted into focus. For a blessed moment she could pretend that the arms holding her belonged to a man who cherished her and that the lips kissing her were devoted and true. But it was fool's gold. Reality shattered the dream every time with dawn's first light and Bridie was left fighting her desolation in the shops on Fifth Avenue.

Beaumont and Elaine Williams were her allies in her new world of fickle, fair-weather friends. Mr. Williams had known her before she had inherited her fortune, when she was a naïve and humble maid, fresh off the boat from Ireland, and she trusted him. He oversaw her investments personally and his office attended to all her bills. Bridie paid him handsomely for his cunning and wisdom. With the dreary jobs taken care of, Bridie's only responsibility was to have fun, and Elaine was her constant companion. As frivolous and acquisitive as *she* was, Bridie didn't hesitate to fund her lifestyle; after all, Elaine was as vital to her as rope to a drowning man.

Just when she believed she was forgetting her past, her past remembered *her.*

It was a hot, sticky night in Manhattan. Bridie and Elaine had been to Warners' Theater to see the movie *Don Juan*, a new "talkie" with sound effects and orchestral music starring John Barrymore as the irresistible womanizer. They were in such a high state of excitement that going home to bed was not an option. "All that kissing has got me quite shaken up," said Elaine, linking arms with Bridie as they hurried across Broadway. "What shall we do now? I'm feeling in a party kind of mood."

"Me too," Bridie agreed. "Let's go to the Cotton Club," she suggested. "There's always plenty of entertainment there." She put her hand out to hail a cab.

The Cotton Club was a fashionable nightclub in Harlem where New York's most stylish went to eat fine food, drink illegal alcohol, dance to live bands and watch shows. It was buzzing, busy and boisterous and Bridie loved it especially because in that heady, loud and crowded place she could forget who she really was.

Except on this night, sitting at a round table with a group of suited men Bridie didn't recognize and being fawned over by a couple of scantily dressed showgirls, was the only man in New York capable of making her remember: Jack O'Leary.

She stood staring at him in astonishment. He had changed. His hair was cut short, he was clean-shaven and he wore a pristine suit and tie. But he was unmistakably Jack with his deep-set pale blue eyes and crooked smile. People moved and jostled around her, but she remained as still as a rock until Elaine nudged her out of her stupor. "What's up, Bridget?" Elaine followed the line of her gaze. "Do you know those guys?" she asked, then she added huskily, "They look like they're up to no good, I'm telling you."

"I know one of them," said Bridie slowly, suddenly feeling sick.

"The handsome one?" Elaine asked with a giggle.

"He's from my past."

"Oh. Listen, if you're not happy we can go someplace else."

"No, we'll stay. I'm just surprised. He's the last person I expected to see in New York." As the two women stared at him Jack lifted his eyes. At first he didn't recognize her. He stared back, his face blank. Then his features softened and his eyes narrowed as he registered who she was. They remained a moment, gazing at each other through the smoke as if caught in a spell.

At last he pushed out his chair and began to make his way across the room toward her. "I think I'll leave you to talk about old times," said Elaine and she melted into the crowd of dancing people. Bridie waited, heart pounding, suddenly feeling small and lost and very far from home.

"Bridie?" he said, incredulous. "Is it really you?"

"Don't be so shocked. I've been back here for two years now. I'm the one who should be surprised to see *you*—and indeed I am."

He chuckled. "Fair play to you, Bridie." He gazed into her face as if searching for the way back to Ballinakelly.

"When did you get here?" she asked, unsettled by the intensity in his eyes.

"February last year—but it feels like ten years ago."

The sick feeling in Bridie's stomach grew stronger. "And Kitty?" she asked, suddenly realizing that they must have run off together.

But Jack's face darkened. "Let's go and sit down somewhere. Fancy a drink?"

"I'd kill for one!" she exclaimed and they made their way to a small round table in a quieter corner of the club. Jack summoned the waiter, who appeared to know him well, and ordered champagne for Bridie and a beer for himself. "I came on my own, Bridie, to start a new life."

Bridie's relief was immense. "Then it's fair to say that both you and I have run away."

"Indeed we have," he agreed, and the twist of his lips told Bridie that he was as tormented as she was. "When the drinks arrive, we'll raise our glasses to that."

"Did you find work, Jack?"

"It's easy for a man to find work here in New York. Half the city is Irish, it seems."

"So what are you doing?"

"This and that," he replied shiftily.

"Don't get into trouble, Jack," she warned.

"Don't worry. I've had enough trouble in my life. This time I won't get caught!" He grinned and she saw the old Jack of her childhood in his smile, but there was something different in his eyes—a hard glint, like the flash of a knife, which she didn't recognize.

"But you're a vet. You love animals."

"Not much demand for that in the city, Bridie. Let's just say I'm bringing a certain product over the Great Lakes. After all, I'm handy with a rifle in case some other fellas try to steal it off us."

"I would have thought your stint in jail would have taught you a little about breaking the law, Jack," said Bridie.

"I'm ready to make it in America, Bridie, whatever it takes. There are opportunities here and I'm not going to let them pass me by." Bridie watched him closely and wondered whether he missed the excitement and drama of the War of Independence, whether he had perhaps lived that life of rebellion for so long that it was the only life he knew. One thing was certain: he was up to no good.

The waiter brought their drinks on a tray and Bridie took a long sip of champagne. Jack put his hands around his beer glass and Bridie was at once taken back to the farmhouse in Ballinakelly where she'd return from working up at the castle to find Jack and her brothers sitting at the table plotting over their pewter mugs of Beamish stout.

"We're a long way from home, you and I," said Jack.

"What made you leave?"

"Da died," he said, but Bridie knew that wasn't the reason.

"I'm sorry, may he rest in peace," she said with compassion.

He took a swig of his beer, then stared into the glass. His face hardened and his lip curled. "I left because of Kitty." Bridie nodded. That came as no revelation. "She promised me she'd come with me, but she lied. She never intended to come." He heaved a sigh. "I don't imagine she ever really meant to leave Ballinakelly, or Robert. I was a fool to think so. She said she couldn't leave because she was expecting Robert's child." He took another swig, then grimaced. "She's as cunning as a fox, that's for sure."

Bridie's heart filled with resentment. Kitty was expecting a child of her own who would grow up alongside Little Jack. It didn't seem fair that Kitty should be so blessed when *she* had been so wronged. "Do you think she got pregnant on purpose?" asked Bridie.

"I know she did and I'll never forgive her. I've wasted my life waiting for Kitty Deverill."

"She stole my son," said Bridie and the relief of being able to say so caused her eyes to sting with tears. Jack was the only person in this city who would understand.

"Jack Deverill," he said.

"Named after *you*," Bridie reminded him.

He chuckled bitterly. "She'll be after changing his name now," he said, grinning crookedly again.

"He's my son," she repeated. "I came back for him but he thinks I'm dead. She told him I'd died, Jack. The woman has no heart. I couldn't very well tell him the truth, could I? I had to leave without him, God help me."

"I'm sorry," he said. "That's a terrible pain to carry."

"I try not to think about it. I came here to start again. A new life. A new me. I left the old Bridie behind. I'm Bridget Lockwood here, don't you know."

"Indeed and you look well on it. We both left our pasts behind in the Old Country."

She smiled and Jack thought how pretty she looked when her face was animated. Back in Ballinakelly, when he'd seen her at Mass, she had been hard and defensive, but here, even though she was smartly dressed, there was a softness and a vulnerability about her that reminded him of the grubby-faced, shoeless child who had once been frightened of hairy caterpillars and rats. He smiled too. "What a sorry pair we are," he said. "Let's drink to our good health."

She raised her glass. "And to our futures."

"Indeed. May I be touched with the hand of Midas too!"

WHEN JACK MADE love to Bridie she didn't have to pretend anymore. Here was the man she had always loved. Here was the man she had searched for in the embraces of others but never found. The hands that caressed her, the lips that kissed her and the gentle Irish vowels that took her back to a safe and familiar place belonged to the only man who really knew her. Their paths had taken years to cross but now that they had Bridie was sure that they were destined to unite forever. She believed that finally, in this faraway city, she had found home.

Jack tried to lose Kitty in Bridie's arms. He had drunk so much that every time he closed his eyes it was Kitty he was making love to and in spite of his still burning fury he couldn't bring himself to open them. His heart ached with longing and homesickness. His heart ached for Kitty. He buried his head in Bridie and willed himself home.

When they lay together, bathed in the golden glow of the city's lights, they reminisced about the old days when they had both been young and innocent and full of ambition: Bridie for a better future away from Ballinakelly, Jack for a free and independent Ireland. He lit a cigarette and lay against the pillows while Bridie propped herself up on her elbow beside him, her hair falling in dark waves over the white pillows. How Jack wished that those tresses were red.

"Tell me about Lord Deverill," he asked.

"He was *Mr.* Deverill then," she said.

"You told Michael he raped you, didn't you?"

Bridie was unrepentant. "I had to or he would have killed me."

"So he burned the castle and killed Hubert Deverill instead."

Bridie looked horrified. "Don't say that, Jack. Michael wouldn't—"

"Oh, he did much worse than that." But Jack couldn't bring himself to betray Kitty so he took a long drag of his cigarette and shook his head. "You know what he's capable of," he said instead.

"He's got a good heart, deep down," Bridie reasoned. "He

rescued my son and gave him to Kitty. He brought him home where he belongs. If he hadn't, who knows where the boy might be now? He might be lost on the other side of the world. At least this way I know where he is and I know he's safe and well cared for. Michael didn't have to do that, but he did. So you see, he's not all bad."

"No one is all bad, Bridie. But Michael is no saint either. It suited him to bring Little Jack home. Ask yourself why Michael, who is so fervently anti-British, would give his nephew to an Anglo-Irish woman for safekeeping. Why would he do that?"

"Because Little Jack is my son, that's why," Bridie repeated emphatically. "But he's not just a Doyle, he's a Deverill too. Michael couldn't very well give him to Mam, could he? She'd die of shock and Nanna too. Kitty was the only person and she's my boy's half sister."

"Indeed Little Jack is a Doyle and Michael is a family-minded man," Jack conceded ponderously. "But I figure he brought the baby to Kitty's door to allay his guilty conscience. I suppose you could say that he took the life of a Deverill with one hand, but gave another life with the other. Perhaps the baby was even a peace offering to Kitty, whom he had so wronged."

Bridie was unconvinced. "He did it for *me*, Jack. He did it for my family. Maybe he even did it to shame Mr. Deverill into facing up to his crime."

"A crime which he didn't commit," Jack reminded her.

"No, rape it wasn't," Bridie agreed, but she didn't want to accept her part in the burning of the castle and the death of Lord Deverill, so she added, "However, he shouldn't have taken advantage of me. I was the same age as his daughter and I was in no position to refuse him."

"Indeed he should not have, Bridie."

She sighed, taking her mind back to those stolen moments in the Hunting Lodge when Mr. Deverill had brought her gently to womanhood. "But I loved him, you know. He was kind to me. He made me feel special." She chuckled bitterly. "No one else did."

Jack looked at her quizzically. "How close were you?"

She smiled wistfully. "I thought we were *very* close."

"How much did you share?" he asked.

Bridie was deaf to the subtle change in his tone of voice and blind to his now steady gaze, watching her through the smoke. "I told him everything," she said carelessly. "He was my friend and confidant, or so I thought. I realized what *I* was to *him* when I told him I was carrying his child. He was brutal, Jack. He treated me like I was nothing to him. After all those intimate moments, when he had made me believe that he loved me . . ." But Jack was no longer listening. He was wondering about the brave men who had fought beside him during the War of Independence, and died. How many ambushes and raids had been scuppered due to intelligence leaked on the pillow to Mr. Deverill?

"Did you not think that Mr. Deverill might repeat your idle chat to Colonel Manley?"

"I never told him anything important."

"You didn't *think* you did."

"I didn't," she retorted.

"You were bedding the enemy, Bridie."

"When we were in bed we were simply a man and a woman who cared for each other."

"You're Michael Doyle's sister, Bridie. You were present

during many of our meetings in the farmhouse. You knew what was going on."

"But I didn't betray you."

"You were playing a dangerous game."

"I'm aware of that now," she snapped. "Would I be here, thousands of miles from home, if the game I played *hadn't* been dangerous? It cost me everything. I can never get my old life back. I tried, but the door has closed forever. Mr. Deverill might have destroyed me had it not been for my resilience and good fortune. As it is I will never get my son back and he will never know his mother. I'm aware of what I did and of what I didn't do. I slept with Mr. Deverill but I didn't betray our people. I betrayed no one."

"Every action has a consequence and yours have had more devastating consequences than most."

She stared at him with black eyes and Jack suddenly saw Michael Doyle in them. "And what consequences does *this* have, Jack?" she asked.

He stared back at her and his heart grew cold. "I hope only good ones, Bridie."

Her eyes softened and when she smiled she looked vulnerable again, like the child she'd once been with bare feet and tangled hair. "We've found each other in a city of thousands. What are the chances of that? You're the only person who really knows me in the whole of America. With you I don't have to be anyone other than myself—and you can forget about Kitty. It's not hard if you really want to. Believe me, *I know.*" She nuzzled into the crook of his arm and ran her fingers over his chest. "I've made many mistakes in my life, but this isn't one of them."

Jack stubbed out his cigarette in the ashtray on the bedside table and sighed heavily. He closed his eyes and let his hand wander over her hair that soon turned from ebony to copper in the deep longing of his imagination. Bridie slept, but Jack lay awake, for his thoughts did not allow him respite from regret. Now he was sober he realized that he wanted nothing from *this*.

When her breathing grew slow and regular and the tentative presence of the rising sun began to turn the sky from indigo to gold, he edged his way out of Bridie's limp embrace and quietly dressed. He glanced at her peacefully sleeping and felt a stab of pity. She was lost here in Manhattan, but he was not the right man to find her. They had searched for Ireland in each other and only found a false dawn.

He let himself out, closing the door gently behind him. He knew that if he was to be free of Kitty he had to be free of the past, which meant leaving Bridie too. He was sorry that he was going to cause her pain in leaving her without explanation or farewell, but she had to let go of the past too. How could they possibly find happiness otherwise?

★   ★   ★

WHEN BRIDIE AWOKE she found the bed empty. She blinked into the space where Jack had lain and smiled at the memory of their lovemaking. She felt as if she had been reborn. As if she had metamorphosed into the person she had always wanted to be. She was wealthy, independent and now she had Jack. Jack whom she had always loved. Jack whom Kitty had stolen. But now he was hers.

She rolled over and strained her ears for the sound of Jack in the bathroom next door. She heard nothing but the distant rumble of cars in the street below. She frowned. "Jack?" she called. Her voice seemed to echo through the empty room. He must be in the kitchen, she thought; men are always hungry. She slipped into her dressing gown and padded across the floor to the sitting room. The morning poured through the windows in misty shafts of light, but it only seemed to emphasize the stillness of the apartment, and the silence. Then she heard the soft scuffling of feet advancing up the corridor and her spirits gave a little leap of happiness. "Jack?" she called again.

"Good morning, madam," came the voice of Imelda, her maid. The woman walked lightly into the room, clasped her hands against her apron and smiled. Bridie put her hand on her chest and felt her head spin. She knew then that Jack had gone.

PART TWO

Barton Deverill

London, 1667

Most of the Court had arrived to attend the opening night of John Dryden's new play, *The Maiden Queen*, in the Theater Royal in Drury Lane. The richly dressed aristocrats sat in the boxes in their brightly colored silks and velvets, powdered wigs and face patches, like exotic birds of paradise, resplendent in the light of hundreds of candles. The ladies passed on the Court gossip behind their fans while the lords discussed politics, women and the King's many mistresses. Lord Deverill sat in the box beside his wife, Lady Alice, daughter of the immensely wealthy Earl of Charnwell, and his friend Sir Toby Beckwyth-Stubbs. He swept his eyes over the pit below where ladies and gentlemen sweltered in the heat and whores and orange girls squawked and flirted with the fops in the thick, heavily perfumed air, like a pen full of libidinous chickens.

The King arrived with his bastard son, the Duke of Monmouth, and his brother the Duke of York. The fops in the pit clambered onto chairs and women hung over the balconies to watch the royal party enter, and Lady Alice looked out for the King's mistress, the buxom and wanton Barbara Palmer, Countess of Castlemaine, the most fashionable lady in the country.

They muttered and chattered as the royal party settled into their seats with the rustle of taffeta and the swishing of fans. Lord Deverill found the scene distasteful. The Court of Charles II had turned out to be a sink of licentious frivolity with Catholic undercurrents and he was almost starting to miss the evil Cromwell. Deverill was only here to seek an audience with the King to procure more men and arms to keep the peace in West Cork. The construction of Castle Deverill was now completed and it stood as a formidable bastion of English supremacy, but the Irish were a riotous lot and they gnawed on their grievances like wild dogs on bitter bones. While London had staggered from the Plague to the Great Fire the year before, Lord Deverill had taken refuge at his Irish seat where the clouds that hung over him were of an entirely different kind: the haunting memory of Maggie O'Leary's curse and the threat of rebellion from the Irish over the Importation Act which prohibited them from selling their cattle to England.

As he had sworn that day on the hill above Ballinakelly he was good to his tenants. Their rent was reasonable and he was tolerant of their papist church. His wife and her ladies fed the poor and clothed their children. He was indeed a beneficent landlord. His loyalty to the Crown was unwavering, but he was furious about the act, which the King had signed. Distracted by his own domestic problems, flirting too closely with the King of France and preparing to fight the Dutch, the King hadn't wanted to upset Parliament by using his power of veto. Lord Deverill feared there would be another rebellion like the one in '41 and was determined to warn the King of danger.

Lord Deverill thought of Maggie O'Leary often. He was a religious man and he did not take curses lightly, indeed Sir Toby had insisted that her threat was an indirect threat to the King himself and was adamant that she should be burned at the stake. But Lord Deverill did not want to incite further hatred by killing a young woman—a *beautiful* young woman—be she a witch or otherwise. It was not her curse that followed him like a shadow, but her strange, unsettling beauty and her almost pungent allure.

He had only seen her twice. Once when she had publicly cursed him in the road in Ballinakelly, the second time when he had been out hunting. Accompanied by Sir Toby and a retinue of attendants, he had been galloping through the forest in pursuit of a deer. Suddenly, as the deer headed off through the thicket to his left he had spotted through the tangle of trees on his right a stag, standing on the crest of a knoll. Without time to inform his men he swerved his horse to the right and quietly trotted toward it.

Alone in the wood he pulled on the reins and drew his beast to a halt. It was quiet but for the chirruping of birds and the whispering of the wind about the branches. The stag was magnificent. It stood with the dignity of a monarch, watching him haughtily with shiny black eyes. Slowly, not to frighten the animal away, he pulled out his musket. As he loaded and aimed, the stag suddenly disappeared and in its place stood a woman.

Lord Deverill lifted his eye from the gun and stared in astonishment. She wore a cloak but beneath her hood was the unmistakable face of Maggie O'Leary. He put his gun down and gazed upon her, not knowing what to say. Her loveliness stole his words and yet he knew, even if he had managed to speak, that she would not have understood him. Her green eyes were wide and inquiring and her berry-red lips curled up at the corners in a mocking smile. At once he was overcome with lust; quite out of his mind with desire. She lifted her delicate hands and removed her hood. Her hair fell about her shoulders in thick black waves and her pale face bewitched him like the face of the full moon.

He dismounted and walked toward her. She waited until he was almost upon her and then turned and floated down the hill, moving deeper into the forest. He followed, encouraged by the coy glances she tossed him over her shoulder. The trees grew closer together. The branches were a mesh of twig and leaf, the light reduced to thin, watery beams that sliced through the dimness. Even the birds had ceased to sing. The sweet smell of decaying vegetation rose up from the earth. She stopped and turned around. Lord Deverill did not wait to be invited. He pushed her against the trunk of an oak and pressed his lips to hers. She responded hungrily, winding her arms around his neck, kissing him back. A low moan escaped her throat as he buried his face in her neck and inhaled the scent of sage that clung to her skin. His fingers tore at the laces of her bodice until her breasts were exposed, white against his brown hands, and his lust was intensified by the warmth of her naked flesh and by the intoxicating smell of her. Maddened by desire he lifted her skirts. She raised a leg and wrapped it about him so he could more easily enter her. She gasped with satisfaction and her eyelids fluttered like moth's wings as he slipped inside with a groan. They moved as one writhing beast, their faces clamped together, their breaths staggered, their heartbeats accelerating as they took their pleasure greedily.

They reached the pinnacle of their enjoyment simultaneously, then fell limp in a tangle of limbs, clothes and sweat onto the soft forest bed. At length Maggie rolled away from him and pulled down her skirts to cover herself, but she left her laces hanging loose at her waist and her breasts exposed. She fixed him with wide, brazen eyes, as feral as a wolf's, and held him in her thrall for a long moment. Then she spoke. Her voice was as silky as a spring breeze but Lord Deverill did not understand her native language. He frowned and she seemed to find his bewilderment amusing, for she burst into peals of mocking laughter. As Lord Deverill's frown deepened she turned onto her knees and crawled toward him on all fours with the speed of a cat. She climbed astride him, pinned his wrists to the ground and pressed her mouth once more to his. She took his bottom lip between her teeth and bit down hard upon it. Lord Deverill tasted the blood on his tongue and recoiled. "By God you've hurt me, woman!" he exclaimed but Maggie just laughed louder. Her black hair cascaded in thick tendrils over her exposed breasts and her bruised mouth twisted into a secretive smile, but it was her eyes, her wild green eyes, which looked at him with a coldness that froze the blood in his veins. Suddenly she was pressing a dagger to his throat. Lord Deverill's breath caught in his chest and he stared back at her in horror. A gush of bubbling laughter rose up from her belly as she leaped to her feet. She smiled at him again, this time with playfulness, then she was gone, as quickly as she had come, and he was left alone and bewildered in the middle of the forest.

He was jolted back to the theater by a sharp jab to the ribs. "Barton!" It was his wife, Alice. "The King is waving at you. Wake up!" Lord Deverill turned toward the Royal Box. Indeed the King had raised his white glove. Lord Deverill bowed in response and the King beckoned one of his attendants with a flick of his fingers. The attendant bent down and the King whispered something in his ear. "I believe you will get your meeting with the King," said Alice, smiling with satisfaction. "King Charles will always remember those who were loyal to his father." Lord Deverill turned back to the stage just as the performance was beginning, and passed a finger absent-mindedly across his lips.

Chapter 13

Ballinakelly, 1929

Celia and Kitty stood in their finest silk gowns at the top of the castle and gazed out of the window over the sea. The sun had already begun her slow descent. Her face, which had blazed a bright yellow at midday, had now mellowed into a deeper hue, transforming the sky around her into dusty pinks and rich oranges. Later she would set the horizon aflame and the soft shades would intensify into royal crimson and gold, but by then the two women would be entertaining the large number of guests who were soon to arrive from all over the county, for tonight was Celia's first Summer Ball as mistress of the newly restored and quite splendid Castle Deverill.

The rusted gates at the entrance had been replaced by an elaborate wrought-iron creation, painted black and decorated with the Deverill coat of arms, which had been incorporated into the design in an ostentatious display of family prestige. Flares had been lit on either side of the sweeping drive, which had been resurfaced in tar and shingle and covered in gravel— an extravagance that had aroused the curiosity of the locals because tar and shingle was very new and many of the roads in County Cork were still boreens made of earth or brick. The gardens had been resuscitated, the wild, overgrown areas tamed, the tennis court reinstated and the croquet lawn mown flat and even. A kaleidoscope of colorful flowers flourished in the borders, pink roses and purple clematis climbed the walls of the herbaceous border, and raised wooden beds in the vegetable garden were home to lettuces, potatoes, carrots, parsnips and radishes and rigorously weeded by the team of men Celia had employed from Ballinakelly to train under Mr Wilcox, one of the gardeners at Deverill Rising, on loan from her father. Adeline's greenhouses had been repainted, the broken panes of glass replaced, the blancmange-shaped roofs polished until they gleamed. Inside, Celia insisted on growing orchids, which required a complicated, not to mention costly, array of humidifiers and temperature regulation. The only plant that remained from Adeline's day was the now giant cannabis, which Celia had, for some reason unknown even to herself, decided to keep. Digby had paid for the old stone Mr. Leclaire had recommended and sourced from a ruined castle in Bandon in order for Castle Deverill to retain its antique flavor so only the western tower and the few surviving walls that remained from the original building hinted at its tragic past. It looked just like it had before the fire, only newer—like a battle-weary soldier whose face has been scrubbed and shaved and whose uniform has been replaced and sewn with bright gold buttons.

Inside, however, was an entirely different matter. Besides the grand hall, where the stone fireplace still stood as it always had, and the sweeping wooden staircase, which was identical to the old one, little of Adeline and Hubert's old home remained. Celia had redesigned and redecorated according to the grandiose nature of her ambition. Gone was the shabby elegance of a home that had been loved by generations of Deverills—worn thin by their affection like a child's toy bear whose fur has all but disappeared from hugging, whose ears are ragged from games, whose nose is frayed from kisses. Celia had re-created the interiors to impress her guests, not to welcome her family home from a hard day out hunting in the rain. The hall floor was checkerboard marble, the walls papered and painted and hanging with Old Master paintings, the surfaces cluttered with Romanov antiques and Roman antiquities and anything else she could find that was fashionable. Furniture had been acquired in chateau sales in France, much of it from the First French Empire of Napoleon I and wildly opulent in rich crimsons and gold. She had bought an entire library by the yard but the cozy atmosphere of Hubert's den, where he'd once sat smoking cigars in front of the fire, reading the *Irish Times* in a tatty leather armchair while Adeline painted at the table in the bay window, was gone. Everything gleamed but nothing attracted. The charm had been consumed by the fire and the opportunity to re-create it had been lost on a young woman whose inspiration was born of her shallow nature. The warm glow of love which cannot be bought had been replaced by things that can only be acquired with money.

"Do you remember when we stood here as little girls?" said Celia, her heart fuller than it had ever been.

"We were three of us then," Kitty reminded her.

"Whatever happened to Bridie?" Celia asked.

"I believe she returned to America."

"Isn't life strange," said Celia with uncharacteristic reflection. "Who would have thought that the three of us, all born in the same year, would have ended up where we are today? I am mistress of the castle with two little girls. You are married to your old tutor and have Florence and JP. Bridie is living on the other side of the world with Lord knows how many children by now. None of us had a clue what was in store for us when we stood here as girls the night of the last Summer Ball."

Kitty was aware that Celia knew little of what *she* and Bridie had been through but she wasn't about to enlighten her. "I often think of those days," she said with a sigh. "Before things went wrong."

"Before we lost people we loved in the war," said Celia quietly. She thought of her brother George, whom she rarely considered these days, and her mood took an unexpected dive. She shook her head to dispel the memories and smiled fiercely. "But everything is wonderful now, isn't it?" she said firmly. "In fact, life has never been better." She swung around and contemplated with satisfaction the splendor of her great vision brought to completion at last. "I have poured all my love into this place," she told Kitty. "Castle Deverill is like my third child. I will now spend the rest of my life embellishing her. More trips to Italy and France, more shopping. It's a never-ending project and so thrilling. I am following in the footsteps of our ancestors who went on their grand tours of Europe and brought back wonderful treasures." She sighed happily. "And tonight everyone will admire it. Everyone will appreciate all the work I have put into it. I do hope Adeline is watching, wherever she is. And I hope she approves."

Kitty knew her grandmother was watching, but doubted she really cared what Celia had done to her home, for Adeline was in a dimension now where the material world was no longer important. "Come, let's go downstairs. Your guests will be arriving shortly," she said, moving away from the window. The two women walked through the castle to the front stairs. They hesitated a moment at the top of the landing to check their reflections in the large gilt mirror that hung there. Celia, resplendent in ice blue, admired the daring cut of her dress, which exposed most of her back, while Kitty, elegant in forest-green silk, gazed upon the two faces smiling back at her and felt keenly the absence of the third. *Where are you now, Bridie, and do you miss us too?* she thought. *Because in spite of everything, I miss you.*

A long queue of cars was slowly drawing up in front of the castle. Celia's servants were in attendance to receive the ladies in long gowns and the men in white tie who climbed the few steps up to the front door to walk beneath the lintel where the Deverill family crest had survived the fire and still resonated with Barton's passion for his new home: *Castellum Deverilli est suum regnum.* The restoration of the castle had been the talk of the county for years, and the amount of money spent on it a matter of much conjecture, and they were all eager to see the results for themselves. Celia and Archie stood in front of the fireplace that had been filled with summer flowers from the gardens, shaking hands and receiving compliments. Celia enjoyed the gasps of wonder and astonishment as her guests laid eyes on the sumptuous hall for the first time. Most had been regular visitors before the fire and were quick to compare the dilapidated old building with the lavish new one. While some were delighted by the opulence there were others who found it in poor taste.

"It looks like a beautiful but impersonal hotel," Boysie whispered to Harry as they stood on the terrace overlooking the gardens. "But for God's sake keep that to yourself or I'll never be invited again."

"I'm relieved it's nothing like it was or I should suffer terrible homesickness," said Harry.

"No regrets then?" asked Boysie, who knew Harry well enough to know that he had plenty.

"None," Harry replied firmly, knocking back his champagne. "Celia has done a splendid job."

Boysie smoked languidly. "Your mama would seethe with jealousy if she were here."

"Isn't it lucky then that she isn't?"

"She'd hate to see Celia lording it about the home that should, by rights, be hers. Celia is insufferably happy and Maud hates happy people. She loves nothing more than misery because she hopes that if it's plaguing someone else it won't have its eye on *her*. Digby is more puffed up than ever. Don't you adore the way he wears his white tie? Somehow it looks brash on him. He has a talent for brash, you know. If he wasn't Sir Digby Deverill one would assume he was frightfully common. And as for your dear Charlotte, pregnant again, I see. How do you manage it, old chap? Perhaps after two daughters you'll be blessed with an heir."

Harry looked into Boysie's eyes and grinned. "You've had two so probably the same way you manage it, old boy."

Boysie chuckled and a knowing look passed between them. "Is your father aware of your mother's little friend, Arthur Arlington?" he asked, changing the subject.

"I haven't asked him. I'm sure he is. Half of London is. Mama hasn't asked for a divorce, but I'm sure Papa would give her one. The marriage is a farce and Arthur is a drip."

"A very rich drip," Boysie added.

Harry sighed resignedly. "But life is good for Papa these days." He watched his father in a small group of people who were standing on the croquet lawn looking back at the castle. Bertie was pointing at the roof, no doubt taking them through the building process. "Strange that he takes so much delight in Celia's success, isn't it?" he said softly. "One would expect him to be bitter about it, but he isn't. I truly believe he's genuinely pleased."

"Perhaps the responsibility of being Lord Deverill of Castle Deverill has secretly weighed heavily on his shoulders all these years. Who knows, maybe he's relieved to be shot of it. I know *you* are."

"I couldn't be myself here," said Harry, recalling the brief affair he'd enjoyed with Joseph, the first footman. "It would hardly have been appropriate to put you up in one of the estate cottages. I dare say you're used to finer things."

"I am indeed, old boy. Ireland is much too damp for my tastes." He took Harry's empty glass and placed it on the tray of a passing waiter. "Now, why don't we go and pay some attention to those wives of ours, eh? For better or for worse and all that . . ."

"Capital idea," said Harry, and the two men set off into the castle.

HAZEL AND LAUREL stood in the ballroom and gazed about them in wonder. Celia had decorated it in an opulent rococo style, with white walls and lavish gold stucco designed in flamboyant, asymmetrical patterns. The chandeliers no longer held candles but blazed with electricity, which was reflected in the large mirrors that embellished the room like golden stars. "But look at the flowers, Hazel," said Laurel. "I've never seen so many lilies." She inhaled through dilated nostrils. "The smell is wonderful. Really, Celia should be very proud of herself. Tonight is a triumph."

Just as Hazel was about to agree with her, they heard the familiar and nervously anticipated voice of Lord Hunt as he strode into the room, greeting them enthusiastically. They swung around, their delight at seeing him ill-concealed. "The dear Misses Swanton," he said, taking each Shrub in turn by her white-gloved hand and drawing it to his lips with a formal and slightly exaggerated bow. Both ladies shivered with pleasure, for Lord Hunt had the ability to make them feel young and beautiful and deliciously frivolous. In the three years that he had been living with his daughter, he had gained notoriety in Ballinakelly for his breezy charm, his jocular wit and his incorrigible flirting. "May I be permitted to say how radiant you both look tonight?" He ran his astute brown eyes up and down their almost identical dresses and Hazel and Laurel felt as if he had somehow got beneath the fabric and caressed with a tender finger the long-neglected skin there.

"Thank you, Ethelred," Laurel croaked when, after a short struggle, she managed to find her voice.

"I'm going to have a terrible decision to make later this evening," he said, pulling a mournful face.

"Oh dear," interjected Hazel. "What might that be, Ethelred?"

He looked from one to the other, then sighed melodramatically. "Whom to dance with first, when I want to dance with both of you." Laurel glanced at Hazel and they both tittered with shy delight. "Is there not a dance for three?" he asked.

"I'm afraid not," said Laurel. "Although Celia is very modern, so one never knows."

"I see neither of you has a glass of champagne. Let me escort you into the garden. It's the most splendid evening. Wouldn't it be nice to enjoy our drinks in the beauty of sunset?"

"Oh, it would," said Hazel.

"It certainly would," Laurel echoed.

Lord Hunt offered them each an arm. But as Laurel slipped her hand through his left she felt the first stirring of something deeply alarming and unpleasant: competitiveness. She glanced at Hazel and for a fleeting moment she wished her sister ill. With a shocked gasp she forced the feeling away. Hazel was smiling at the object of her most ardent desire, but as he turned to smile on Laurel, she too felt the beginnings of something of which she was too ashamed to even acknowledge. Both sisters turned their eyes sharply to the double doors that led into the wide corridor and through to the hall. They could never reveal to the other the degree of their passion for Ethelred, *never*. For the first time in their lives they harbored a secret they were unwilling to share.

DIGBY STOOD IN the garden and gazed upon the castle with a gratifying sense of achievement, as if he had reconstructed it from the rubble with his own hands. It was the jewel in his family's crown, the culmination of a lifelong desire. He looked back on the years he had struggled to make his fortune in South Africa and smiled with satisfaction at how far he had come and how high he had risen. A hearty pat on the back jolted him from his thoughts. He looked up to see Sir Ronald Rowan-Hampton's red face beaming at him happily. "My dear Digby," Sir Ronald exclaimed. "What a triumph the castle is. Celia and Archie have done you credit. It's a great success, a masterpiece, an example of courage in the face of adversity. You have raised it from the ashes and, my, what a palace it is. Fit for the King himself."

"I cannot take all the credit," he replied smoothly. "It is all Celia and her vision."

"Then she is a chip off the old block," said Sir Ronald. "She has your style and your sense of proportion. Isn't it true that everything you do is larger than life, Digby?" Sir Ronald gazed at the castle and shook his head. "It must have cost a small fortune."

"It cost a *great* fortune," said Digby, unabashed. "But it is worth every penny. This is Celia's now and will be her son's one day and *his* son's after that, and so it will go on. She has not only rebuilt a castle but she has created a legacy that will long outlive her. I'm mightily proud of her." He privately wondered whether, now the project was complete, his daughter would grow bored of life here and hotfoot it back to London. He was aware of her restless nature, because she had inherited it from *him*. He only hoped she was able to stifle it.

Grace stood in the French doors of the drawing room, watching her husband talking to Digby on the lawn. The guests were now beginning to make their way upstairs to dinner in the

long gallery where Adeline had always held her dinners—
except it wasn't the same long gallery because Celia had chosen
to design hers differently. For one the faces of Deverill ancestors did not watch them impassively from the walls, as many
of the paintings had been lost in the fire; Celia had bought
paintings of *other people's* ancestors, simply to fill the gaps. It
would take years to build a collection—it had taken the Deverills over two hundred.

Grace thought of Michael Doyle. She *always* thought of Michael Doyle. He plagued her thoughts, tormented her and
drove her to distraction. She thought she might go mad with
lust and longing. Never before had a man made such a fool of
her and yet, she couldn't help her foolish behavior. She had lost
her pride that day at the fair for she had later followed him
around the back of O'Donovan's public house and thrown herself at him like a mad and wanton woman, trying all the tricks
that would normally have ensured he lost control and became
putty in *her* hand. But he had shaken her off. "I have sinned,"
he had told her.

"You cannot blame yourself for things you did in the war.
Lord knows I've done my share," she had replied.

"No, you don't understand. The things I'm ashamed of have
nothing to do with war."

"Then with what?"

At that point he had turned away. "I'm sorry, Grace. I'll
speak no more about it." He had left her then, wondering what
he had done that was so terrible, that he couldn't ever speak of,
that he couldn't tell *her*. Now she gazed out onto the lawn at
her husband and Digby as Kitty walked over to tell them to
come in for dinner, and wondered again, what did he do and

how could she find out? Surely, if she could get to the root of his guilt, she could figure a way to dig him out of it.

AT THE END of dinner, when the coffee was being served, Bertie stood up and a hush fell over the guests. This was quite a different Bertie to the swaying drunkard who had announced to the family at his mother's funeral that he was not only selling the castle but legitimizing his bastard son Jack. Now he was sober, fresh-faced, groomed and slim—dashing even. "Never before have we Deverills been so united," he said, then raised his glass. "To Celia and Archie." Everyone jumped to their feet and toasted the audacious young couple, then Digby gave a speech, thanking Bertie for his generosity of spirit and repeating, once again, the family motto, which, he explained, referred not only to the castle but to their family spirit. "Which lives in all of us," he said. Beatrice wiped her eye with her napkin. Harry smiled at Celia. Kitty looked lovingly at her father and Elspeth thought how fortuitous it was that neither Maud nor her older sister, Victoria, were here to sour the sweet feeling that encompassed their family. Suddenly, a loud snort punctured the silence. Augusta glared at her husband from the other side of the table. "Do me a favor, dear," she said to the lady sitting on his left. "Give him a sharp prod in the ribs, will you?"

Archie led Celia onto the dance floor where a jazz band, brought in from London, was playing. The Shrubs restrained themselves from squabbling over who danced first with Ethelred by both pretending to give way to the other: "No really, Laurel, *you* must go first." "No, Hazel, I insist. *You* must." At length Ethelred had tossed a coin and Hazel had won, much to the chagrin of Laurel, who had to smile and act as if she didn't care, which she did, very much. Boysie and Harry danced with their spouses, secretly longing to be rid of them and free to enjoy each other in one of the flamboyantly decorated bedrooms upstairs. Kitty threw herself into the music as she danced with her father while Robert looked on longingly for his stiff leg made dancing impossible. She tried to shake herself out of her gloom—her father was happy for Celia so why couldn't *she* be? "Our daughters will grow up here as *we* did and enjoy all the things *we* enjoyed," Celia had said when Kitty had given birth to Florence. And she was right, history would indeed repeat itself and Florence would enjoy the castle just as *she* had done. So why did Kitty feel so bitter?

"This is all marvelous," said Beatrice to Grace as they watched the dancing in front of the glittering mirrors.

"Oh, it truly is," Grace agreed. "Celia said she would bring back the old days and so she has." Although both women knew that bringing back the past was never possible they were content to indulge in nostalgia and to secretly long for a time before the Great War when Ballinakelly summers had been so golden.

IT WAS WELL after midnight when Boysie and Harry found themselves alone in the hall. The grand staircase beckoned them upstairs as if the banisters were malevolent demons whispering encouragement. Their heads were light with champagne bubbles, their hearts tender with nostalgia, their longing all the more acute on account of the impossibility of their affair and their weariness of living a life of secrecy and deceit. Without a word they stepped nimbly up the stairs. The rumbling of music, thumping feet and voices receded as they made their way down the long corridors, deeper and deeper into the depths of the castle. Celia had spent a lot of money installing electricity and Harry was quite unused to bright lights where once it had only been candlelight and oil lamps. The plumbing worked too, which was miraculous considering that once the water had to be brought up in buckets by the servants. Harry was wistful for those times and, as he passed the bedroom door where Kitty had discovered him in bed with Joseph the first footman, he had to steel himself not to lose control of his emotions.

Suddenly the castle meant more to him than his lost inheritance; it also represented his failures: what had he done with his life? He had married a woman he didn't love and loved a man he couldn't have. He drifted aimlessly in London, from his club to home and home to his club, and there was no purpose to the endless round of social obligations. His job in the City was so dull and monotonous that he sometimes found himself wishing he was back in the Army where at least he had had a purpose. It seemed that the fire had taken more than his home; it seemed to have taken his rudder too. As he walked through the castle he no longer recognized, he felt a great pain expanding in his chest. A longing for what he had lost and for the man he knew he could never be.

"Boysie," he groaned.

Boysie turned around. "What is it, old boy?"

Harry couldn't put into words the sense of desolation he felt. Instead, he took Boysie's hand and retreated back the way they had come, eventually stopping outside the bedroom Celia had allocated him. Without a word he pulled his lover into the darkness inside and closed the door behind them. "This is madness," Boysie protested, but he was too giddy with champagne to resist Harry's insistent mouth kissing his.

Suddenly the light went on. They swung around in surprise to see Charlotte sitting up in the four-poster bed, her face white against the pink of her nightdress and her mouth open in a silent gasp. They stared at each other in horror. As the bubbles evaporated and Boysie and Harry were swiftly shocked into sobriety there was a part of Harry that experienced a profound sense of relief.

HIGH UP AT the top of the western tower Adeline and Hubert looked out into the starlit sky. The moon was almost full, encircled by a halo of silver mist, its eerie light throwing sharp shadows across the lawn below. "Do you remember those Summer Balls of our youth, Hubert?" Adeline asked. "Of course people came in their fine carriages back then, with men in livery driving the horses. I remember the sound of hooves on the drive as they all drew up," she reflected. "Now the guests arrive in motorcars. How times have changed." She looked at Hubert and smiled wistfully. "We lived well, didn't we?"

Hubert turned to his wife and his face was cast in shadow like the back of the moon. "But are we destined to remain here for . . ." He hesitated because he could barely utter so terrifying a word. "For eternity, Adeline? Is that what our destiny is now? Our lives were as short as a blink on the eye of time, but the eye . . . how long is the eye, Adeline?"

She put her hand against his cheek and tried to look positive. "The curse will be broken," she said firmly. "I promise you."

A voice interrupted from the armchair. "That's as likely as

them putting men on the moon." It was Barton Deverill, grumpier than ever.

Adeline ignored him. His bitterness was infectious and bringing Hubert's spirits down. "Don't listen to him, my darling. He's a sour old man with a heavy conscience."

"You know nothing of my conscience, woman," Barton growled.

"I sense it," Adeline retorted. He was really trying her patience.

"All you sense is the near two hundred and fifty years I've been rotting in this place."

"You can't rot if you don't have a body, Barton," she told him briskly, turning back to her husband. "I promise you, my darling, I'll get you out of this place. I will stay with you for as long as you are here and then we will move on, together. All of us."

Barton laughed cynically from his armchair. "So help you God."

Chapter 14

Digby sat at the breakfast table tucking into a large plate of scrambled eggs on toast, crispy bacon and fried tomatoes garnished with chives. The ball had been a great success and even though he had had little to do with the organization of the event itself, he had had a significant amount to do with the building of the castle. Having initially shied away from a project he had believed both financially suicidal and conceptually foolhardy, he had eventually succumbed to the allure of recapturing the past and inveigled his way into the plans by way of large and frequent checks. After all, hadn't those summers at Castle Deverill been the most enchanted weeks of his life? How he had envied Bertie and Rupert for growing up in this magical place. He had felt like a poor relation. Now *his* grandchildren would grow up here and he could live vicariously through them. Deverill Rising was one thing, Castle Deverill quite another: the history, the prestige, the sheer wonder of the place. He shoveled a forkful of food into his mouth and chewed with relish. Beatrice, who could read her husband's mind, smiled at him from the other end of the table.

He was enjoying his cup of tea and reading the *Irish Times* when Celia flew into the room. "Papa, last night was a triumph! I didn't sleep a wink!"

"It was a great success, my dear. You should be very proud of yourself," he said, lifting his eyes momentarily off the page to savor his daughter's beaming face. "You were the most gracious hostess."

"Everyone admired the castle!" she gushed. "Everyone complimented the decoration."

"And everyone admired *you*," her mother added with a smile.

"Oh, Mama, if I was any happier I would burst," she said. "Truly, I have never been so full of joy."

"I think you're still full of champagne," said Digby dryly, turning the page.

"In which case, you must put something else into your stomach," said Beatrice.

Celia went to the antique walnut sideboard, bought at auction at Christie's with the help of Boysie, who worked there, and helped herself to scrambled eggs and tomatoes.

A moment later Harry wandered in, ashen-faced with bloodshot eyes beneath which purple shadows shone like bruises. "Somebody had a wild night," said Celia with a chuckle, but Harry barely managed a smile.

"Good morning," he said, trying hard to be jovial. "I'm afraid I am a little worse for wear."

"Darling, come and sit down and have a cup of tea and some toast. You'll feel much better with something in your stomach," said Beatrice. "You do look pale," she added as he pulled out the chair beside her. She patted his hand with her podgy, bejeweled one and smiled sympathetically. "I suppose one must deduce that a hangover is the result of a highly successful party," she said softly.

"Quite," Harry agreed, reflecting quietly on the *un*successful way it had ended.

It wasn't long before Boysie appeared with Deirdre. The two of them looked as bright and fresh as if they had enjoyed an early night and a brisk morning walk. "What a delightful party, Celia," said Boysie, sitting beside her. "Only two bores on the guest list and I managed to avoid both!"

"Oh, do tell me who they are and I'll make sure I sit you between them next year," said Celia.

"I couldn't possibly be so indiscreet," Boysie replied with a smile. He caught Harry's eye, but swiftly turned away. "Can I help you to some breakfast, darling?" he asked Deirdre. As Boysie went to the sideboard, Charlotte wandered into the room, her face as white as a duck's egg. Beatrice looked from Charlotte to Harry and realized that their pallor had nothing to do with a hangover.

After breakfast Harry managed to talk to Boysie alone. They stood on the terrace in the warm summer sunshine while a small army of servants cleared away the debris from the night before. Boysie lit a cigarette. Harry stood with his shoulders hunched and his hands buried in his trouser pockets. "Did you want to get caught, Harry?" Boysie asked, and Harry recoiled from the hard tone of his voice.

"No . . . I mean, of course not." But he wasn't so sure.

"Damned foolish to stumble in on your wife like that. She looks none too pleased about it this morning."

"She won't say anything," he said quickly.

"She'd better not."

"She's not speaking to me, though."

"That's no surprise. It's one thing betraying your wife with another woman but quite another with a man. Poor girl. She looked as if she'd been shot in the heart."

"She had been, I suppose," said Harry. He sighed and rubbed his chin. "What a God-awful mess."

Boysie looked at him and his expression softened. "What are you going to do, old boy?"

"Nothing," said Harry.

"Nothing?"

"There's nothing I *can* do. I'll wait to see what *she* wants to do."

"See you kicked from here to eternity, I should imagine." Boysie chuckled and flicked ash onto the York stone at his feet.

"I hope not," said Harry. He swallowed nervously. "I'm hoping she'll understand."

"Celia would understand but Charlotte is not Celia. She's a sheep, Harry. Sheep follow the crowd and I'm afraid the crowd don't think very highly of homosexuality. You had better hope, no, you had better *pray* that she doesn't tell her family." He dragged on his cigarette. "Come on, let's go and find Celia." But Harry knew that Celia would be no help at all. Suddenly, he felt an overwhelming desire to talk to Kitty.

"I'm going to take a walk, old boy. I think some exercise will do me good." And he set off across the gardens in the direction of the White House.

KITTY WAS SITTING on the lawn with two-year-old Florence making daisy chains when Harry appeared at the foot of the drive, red-faced from his brisk walk. He strode through the gate and walked up the hill to meet her. "Harry!" she shouted and waved. "What a lovely surprise." Harry took off his straw hat and sat down in the shade of the apple tree that sheltered the little girl from the sun. "Splendid party last night, wasn't it," she said, but her eyes betrayed her struggle to find anything positive about the newly completed castle.

"You're finding it hard too?" he asked.

"Very," she conceded. "I feel terrible admitting that, but I know I can speak plainly to you."

"You can," he said. "My, how Florence has grown." He ran his hand down the child's flaxen hair. "She's the image of her father, isn't she?" he observed.

"Yes, she is," Kitty agreed, suffering a stab of pain as Jack O'Leary fought his way to the surface of her mind, only to be plunged back to the bottom by the superior force of her will. "She's like Robert in every way and he dotes on her."

"Where's JP?"

"Riding. He's as obsessed as I was. There's no separating him from his pony!" She laughed. "And he's a daredevil too. He's afraid of nothing. He's already riding out with the hounds. Papa is very proud. JP's a natural horseman. As for Florence . . ." She sighed and looked tenderly on her daughter. "We shall see."

"Will you walk with me, Kitty?" Harry asked suddenly.

Kitty detected the tension in her brother's voice and sat up keenly. "Of course." She called for Elsie and when the nanny appeared to look after Florence, Kitty and Harry set off down the hill toward the coastline.

"What is it, Harry?" she asked.

He replaced his hat and put his hands in his pockets. "Do

you remember that time when you found me . . ." He hesitated, unable to articulate the words.

"And Joseph," she said helpfully.

"Yes." He looked down at his feet as they paced over the grass. "I *loved* Joseph."

"I know you did," said Kitty. She glanced at him and frowned. "You don't love Charlotte, do you?"

"I'm fond of her," he conceded and Kitty sensed what he was trying so hard to say. Her heart filled with tenderness and she slipped her hand around his arm and moved closer.

"I know that Joseph loved you back. I remember the look of utter hopelessness on his face when you left to return to the Front. I saw him up at the window. He was like a ghost. I then realized that he hadn't been simply comforting you that night. At the end of the war, when you came home and you made him your valet, I knew why. I've never judged you, Harry. It's not conventional to love another man, but I love you just the way you are." Harry's throat constricted and he blinked to relieve the stinging in his eyes.

They reached the end of the path where the grass gave way to white sand and headed off up the beach. Seabirds glided on the wind and dropped out of the sky to peck at small creatures left behind by the tide. The ocean was benign beneath the clear skies, the waves breaking gently and rhythmically onto the sand. Harry placed his hand on top of Kitty's and squeezed it. "Thank you, dearest Kitty. You and I have shared many secrets over the years. I'm now going to ask you to keep another and to advise me how to proceed, because I've done a terrible thing." Kitty nodded. She dreaded what he was about to tell her. "I have been having an affair with a man for years. Ever since I came to London." He glanced anxiously at her for her reaction.

"Go on," she said encouragingly.

"I knew I had to do my duty and marry. I've given Charlotte two children and if the shock of discovering me and this man last night doesn't bring on a miscarriage, I'll have given her three."

Kitty stopped walking. "Oh Harry." She let her hands fall at her sides. "How did it happen?"

"I didn't realize she had retired early. The bedroom was dark. I pulled Boysie inside . . ."

Kitty gasped. "Boysie Bancroft?"

"Yes, didn't I say?"

Kitty shook her head. "I should have guessed. The two of you are inseparable."

"Charlotte turned on the light and saw us."

"What did she say?"

"She didn't say anything. Boysie left as fast as he could. I tried to comfort her but she just put her head under the pillow and sobbed. She sobbed all night. She still hasn't spoken to me." He raised his palms to the sky. "For the love of God tell me what I should do."

Kitty began to walk again. This time her pace quickened and her eyes focused on the ground in front of her. Harry strode beside her without speaking, hoping that she'd find the answer there in the sand. At length she stopped and turned to face him again. "Charlotte loves you, Harry, so this betrayal will have cut her very deeply. Firstly, you have to give her time to absorb it. She's made two terrible discoveries: one, that you've been having an affair, and two, that it's with a man, which as you well know is against the law and punishable by imprisonment. She will be wondering whether you ever loved her, whether you only married her to do your duty. She'll be wondering whether you hated every minute of making love to her. She'll be feeling bruised, humiliated, hurt and worried. When she comes to terms with those two discoveries, she will talk to you."

"What will she say?"

"She'll either ask for a divorce or go public and you'll have to endure a scandal that will put Bertie's scandal with JP into the shade. Mama will probably have a seizure, of course, but that'll be the least of your worries."

"God help me," he groaned.

"Or—"

"Or?" he asked eagerly. "What's the or?"

"Or she'll forgive you."

"Why on earth would she do that?"

"Because she loves you, Harry. But you must persuade her that you will give up Boysie. You'll have to convince her that it was a moment of madness. Blame it on the champagne. Tell her you love her. You love the children. You're a family man and you'll do nothing to jeopardize your family. You can do that, can't you?"

"I can't give up Boysie," he gasped, horrified.

"You'll have to. It's either Charlotte or Boysie. You can't have both, Harry."

"But I love him."

She put her hand on his arm. "I know you do. But sometimes you have to give up the person you love for the greater good." Kitty's eyes brimmed with tears. "It's hard, it's almost impossible, but it can be done."

Harry stared at her, unaware that she was speaking about herself. He hadn't anticipated having to give up Boysie when he had dragged him into his bedroom. He had willed himself to get caught only to release him from the burden of lying, not to force him to sacrifice the one person he loved above all others. What a fool he had been. He grabbed his sister by the arms and thrust his head onto her shoulder. As he wept he didn't notice that she wept also, for Jack O'Leary and her own desolate heart.

When Harry returned to the castle he found Charlotte and Deirdre playing croquet with Boysie and Celia. The Shrubs were strolling around the gardens in floral dresses and sunhats with Lord Hunt, who held his hands behind his back and was listening attentively to both. Laurel and Hazel had made a great effort with their hair and makeup and the results were surprising—they each looked far younger than their years. Digby, Archie, Bertie and Ronald were playing a men's four in long white tennis trousers and V-neck sweaters while Beatrice and Grace watched them from the bench, or at least, *pretended* to watch, sipping from tall glasses of mint and lemonade.

"Papa is leading the Shrubs a merry dance," confided Grace, watching the unlikely trio. "He's a terrible old rogue and I fear Hazel and Laurel have been totally taken in. I feel very bad about it."

"Oh, don't feel bad," Beatrice replied. "He's giving them such a lot of pleasure. I don't think they've ever had such attention from a handsome man like your father."

"He's enjoying himself immensely, but it'll be disastrous when he bores of the game, which he will. The minute it's no longer fun he'll move on to someone else. I *know* him. My mother was an exceptionally tolerant woman."

"I'm sure they take him with a pinch of salt," said Beatrice, watching Digby prepare to serve.

"They absolutely don't, Beatrice. They're smitten. They're like a pair of debutantes. I hope they don't fight over him. That would be dreadful."

"Good shot, darling!" Beatrice clapped as Digby aced his cousin. "They're grown-ups, Grace. I'm sure they're perfectly capable of looking after themselves, and each other."

"I hope you're right, but I fear the worst."

As Harry approached, Charlotte glared at him from her position beside the third hoop. Boysie watched them both warily while Celia, in a long diaphanous ivory skirt and blouse, cloche hat and pearls, lined up her ball and swung her mallet. Deirdre, who had tried and failed to find out what their fight had been about, stood beside her husband, pleased that her own marriage was free of that sort of drama. "Harry, I'm playing so badly, why don't you come and give me a hand," said Celia. "That's all right, isn't it?" she asked the others.

Charlotte dropped her mallet. "No, he can take *my* place. I've had enough." She began to stride off toward the castle, taking her sulk with her.

"Oh dear," said Celia, watching her go. "I was never that bad-tempered when I was pregnant."

"Shall I run after her?" Harry asked uncertainly, but he was afraid to hear what she might say. He glanced at Boysie and for a moment their eyes locked. How could he give him up? he thought desperately. He would rather be dead than live without Boysie.

"No, don't break up the game," said Celia, whose self-obsession had ensured that she missed the subtle tensions that coursed between certain members of the group. "Your turn, Deirdre. Leave Charlotte, Harry darling, she'll feel better after a little nap. She's probably just tired after last night, I know *I* am and I'm not carrying a child."

Harry glanced at the French doors that led from the terrace into the drawing room but his wife had disappeared. Later, when he at last plucked up the courage to talk to her, he found her lying on her bed, staring into space with a miserable, defeated look on her face. He closed the door behind him and approached her. He saw her body stiffen like a cat's, but he sat on the edge of the mattress regardless. "Darling, we have to talk about this," he began, feeling sick to the stomach with nerves. He knitted his fingers and stared into them as if working out how to *un*knit them. "I'm sorry," he said. When she didn't reply he cleared his throat and tried to remember what Kitty had told him. "I love you, Charlotte. I know that you won't believe me, after . . . after what you saw last night. I promise you, it was a moment of madness. The champagne, the excitement, the nostalgia, I wasn't in my right mind. I wasn't myself and I'm ashamed. *Deeply* ashamed and I beg for your forgiveness."

Now she turned her head and looked at him. Her face was impassive. He longed to know what she was thinking. "Do you love me, Harry?" she asked in a small voice.

"Yes, my darling, I do. I love you, I love our children, I love our family life. I'll do anything not to put in jeopardy all those things that I love so dearly."

She stared at him for a long moment. Her lips were thin and

tight, her eyes large and round and very shiny. "I cannot forgive you or Boysie. I'm ashamed on your behalf. What I saw you doing was unnatural." She turned her face the other way as her eyes filled with tears. "But I won't tell anyone. I'd rather die than tell anyone. But you won't see Boysie again, will you? You can't . . . after . . . after . . ." She began to cry hysterically.

Harry slipped off his shoes and lay on the bed beside her, putting his arm around her and drawing her close. How could he exist if Boysie was no longer part of his life? "I want you to take me back to London," she said. "I don't want to be here another minute. Say what you will, but you have to take me back to London. We'll spend the rest of the summer in Norfolk with Mama and Papa and you'll put Boysie and this shaming episode behind you." She lifted his hand off her pregnant belly. "And I don't want you to touch me."

"Charlotte," he gasped.

"I mean it, Harry. I need time. I can't easily forget what I saw. I can't pretend it didn't happen."

"It was a moment of madness."

She turned her head and her expression was hard and sharp. "And what if I hadn't been here? What then? What would you have done?" Her body shook as she began to sob again. "What would you have done, Harry?"

"Nothing. I would have done nothing. It was a kiss. That's all. A kiss." She turned away brusquely, making it clear that she didn't believe him.

Harry explained to Celia that Charlotte was suffering so much with this pregnancy that she wanted to spend the rest of the summer with her parents. "Jolly bad sport," said Celia sulkily. "She's ruined our summer. The first summer we've all been together here at Castle Deverill in nearly ten years. This was meant to be special and she's gone and ruined it." She folded her arms crossly. "Boysie won't be happy you're going. He'll be furious too. You're breaking up the party."

Harry shrugged. "I'm sorry. There's nothing I can do."

Then Celia's face brightened. "I know, she can take the children to Norfolk and you can stay here. Oh, do stay, Harry darling, it'll be just like the old days. If we could get Deirdre to go with her it really would be marvelous!"

"No," said Harry firmly. "I can't do that to her."

"Well, you're a spoilsport too and I'll find it very hard to forgive you."

"But you will, of course."

"Of course. Next time leave her at home. I don't think she likes Ireland anyway."

The car was packed and waiting on the gravel with Celia's chauffeur. Harry and Charlotte said their good-byes, managing to put on a convincing show of unity. Everyone was sorry to see them go, but none was sorrier to be going than Harry. Outside at last he helped his wife into the back seat, tucking her skirt in carefully before closing the door. Then something made him look up to the window above the front door. Boysie was standing on the landing, gazing down on him with a forlorn expression on his face. Harry's stomach gave a little flip as he remembered what Kitty had told him about Joseph. Boysie looked like a ghost too. His face was white behind the glass, his eyes like two black holes, resonating with sorrow. A lump lodged itself in Harry's throat and he remained a moment, gazing up, wanting to wave but knowing he couldn't, knowing that if he did he'd break down and cry like a boy. He wrenched his eyes away and walked slowly around to the other side of the car. As he opened the door he glanced up again. Boysie was still there. His hand was now spread on the small rectangular pane and he had dropped his forehead onto it so that his breath misted the glass in a cloudy stain. Harry inhaled deeply and forced himself onto the back seat. He slammed the door, then he put his finger in his mouth and bit down hard. If he gave in to tears Charlotte would know the truth: that he loved Boysie most of all and always would.

Chapter 15

New York

After Jack O'Leary had slipped into the dawn Bridie had plunged into a deep hole of despair out of which she had no desire, or will, to climb. She had believed that their wandering souls had at last reached the end of their searching and come to rest in each other, like a pair of blind creatures who have suddenly found the light. Yet he had gone, leaving her heart in shattered pieces about the space where he had lain, and her longing for home more acute than ever. It was as if he had taken Ireland with him and now she was completely lost, cut adrift and afraid.

She had sought solace in alcohol. Bridie discovered that a different sort of happiness could be bought in a gin bottle. She drank it on waking, when the pain of loss was at its most severe, and continued to drink it throughout the day to prevent that pain from returning. But the effects of intoxication only gave her a shallow, bitter kind of pleasure. It was like putting a ragged plaster over a seeping wound; the poison still bled through.

Elaine did everything to entice her out of her pit. She flushed the gin down the lavatory, she tempted her with shopping, new clothes and parties, but Bridie refused to be tempted and stayed at home, finding new bottles she had hidden in places that even Elaine, with her thorough searching of Bridie's apartment, had failed to find. "You're young and beautiful, Bridget," Elaine had shouted at her one afternoon, when she had found her friend still in bed with her hair matted and greasy and her eyes bloodshot and distant. "You can have any man you want."

"But I only want Jack," Bridie had replied, sobbing into her silk pillow. "I've loved him all my life, Elaine. I'll never love another. Not for as long as I live." And in her inebriated state her Irish accent was more pronounced than ever.

"You have to pull yourself together."

But Bridie had shouted back, "I'll do as I please. If you don't like it, don't come here!"

After months of steady decline Elaine was so worried about Bridie that she discussed it with her husband. "There's only one solution. You have to get rid of the bottle, Elaine," Beaumont told her firmly.

"She won't listen to me."

"She will listen to *me*," he said confidently. "*I* will talk to her."

And so it was that on a particularly windy spring morning, Elaine and Beaumont Williams rang the bell to Bridie's apartment on Park Avenue and made their way up to the top floor via the elevator. Bridie's maid opened the door and the two stepped into the immaculate hall where a large mirror seemed to open on the facing wall like a shiny silver fan. Elaine caught her anxious reflection, splintered in the various sections of the glass, but Beaumont didn't hesitate and, after giving Imelda his coat, strode straight into the airy sitting room, for he was a man who, having made a decision to get something done, was inclined not to waste time dithering. He walked over to the windows to look down onto the street below. It was a mighty fine view and he was satisfied that he had made a good decision in advising Mrs. Lockwood to rent the apartment.

At length Bridie appeared in a turquoise Japanese dressing gown, embellished with pictures of large colorful orchids, and a pair of crimson velvet slippers. For a moment Elaine thought she had been deceived, for Bridie's hair was clean and shiny and combed into a fashionable bob and her carefully applied makeup gave her face a fresh and wholesome gleam. But as she approached, Elaine noticed the unsteadiness of her step and the glassy look in her eyes that betrayed her drunkenness and her desolation, and she knew then that Bridie was simply making a great effort to disguise the truth.

"Well, this is a surprise," said Bridie, sinking into an armchair. "To what do I owe the pleasure?" But the wariness in her gaze told Elaine that she already knew.

Beaumont remained standing by the window. He turned and smiled and one could have been forgiven for thinking that this visit was simply a social one. "It's been a while since I've been here, Mrs. Lockwood. I must say, you have a very elegant home."

"Indeed I do, Mr. Williams," she replied. "Can I offer you a cup of coffee or tea? Imelda will bring it."

"No, I'm fine, thank you. Perhaps Elaine would like something."

Elaine was perching nervously on the sofa, playing with her fingers. "Coffee would be swell." She didn't dare catch eyes with her friend, in case she saw the betrayal in them.

"And I'll have a cup of tea," said Bridie.

While Imelda made the tea and coffee Beaumont chatted easily with Bridie, and Bridie, hoping that she could fool him into believing her in the very best of health, was hopeful of delaying, or even perhaps avoiding, the inevitable questions, for she knew why they had both come. After a while, which seemed interminable to Elaine, Imelda brought her a cup of coffee and her mistress a pot of tea. At that point Beaumont pulled up a chair and sat close to Bridie. As she poured from the pot her hand shook so that the top rattled noisily on the porcelain. With that simple action her poise fell apart and exposed her as surely as a mask swiped off the face of a thief. Her bottom lip trembled as she fought hard to steady her grip. Without a word Beaumont slowly and deliberately placed his hand on hers and they locked eyes. Bridie's were wild, like a cornered rabbit's, but Beaumont's were calm and full of compassion. "Allow me, Mrs. Lockwood," he said gently, and Bridie blinked at him, a child again suddenly, staring wide-eyed at a father who loved and understood her. It was that small but significant gesture that caused the tears to well. Beaumont took the pot and poured the tea and Bridie was afraid to lift the cup in case she spilled it.

"Mrs. Lockwood," he began. "Do you remember our very first meeting?" Bridie nodded. "It was in Mrs. Grimsby's parlor, was it not? You were a frightened girl, fresh off the boat from Ireland, without anyone in New York to look out for you." Two tears trickled down her cheeks, leaving wet trails in her makeup. "You've come so far from that moment and been so full of courage that if I were your father, I would burst at the seams with pride." Bridie swallowed at the mention of her dear, dead father Tomas, killed by a tinker's knife. "You have come too far to throw it all away now." Bridie dropped her gaze into her teacup. She felt uncomfortably sober. With shaking hands she lifted the cup and saucer and took a large swig of tea. "The remedy for your heartbreak is not to be found in the bottom of a gin bottle, Mrs. Lockwood, or in any other bottle, I might add. The remedy for your loss is within *you*. It is your choice to let this young man destroy you or make you stronger. You can drown your sorrow and yourself in the process or take life by the collar again, as you have done before. You are wealthy, young and beautiful. Any man would give his right arm to marry you."

"But I don't want anyone—"

Beaumont stopped her mid-sentence. "Do you remember that you once said to me that a woman without a husband has no standing in society and no protection?" Bridie nodded slowly. "You were right, but you forgot one important thing. A woman without a husband is obliged to walk life's long and often difficult road alone, and that can be a very lonely experience. We humans are not solitary creatures. We require the company of others for comfort. What you need is a husband." Bridie thought of Mr. Lockwood and for a fleeting moment she recalled the sense of security he had given her. "You have to put this Irishman out of your mind as you have so successfully done with Ireland. Heed not the voice that calls you home, but the voice that calls you forward. He's out there somewhere and we're going to find him." He gave her a reassuring smile and she put down her teacup. Elaine was so tense her shoulders ached. She sat sipping her coffee, deeply proud of her wise and articulate husband—and deeply ashamed of her *un*wise and foolish infidelity.

"Now, we're going to do this in simple steps. The first step being your commitment to giving up the booze." A shadow of anxiety passed across Bridie's face. She had been prepared to deny it, but there was no point now. Mr. Williams knew the truth. She couldn't conceal who she really was from him. "I want you to take me around your apartment and show me where it's all hidden," he said kindly. "Then we will dispose of it, bottle by bottle. It will signify the beginning of a new chapter."

With reluctance at first, then with growing enthusiasm, Bridie showed Mr. Williams the places where she had secreted her gin. Both Elaine and Beaumont were surprised by Bridie's ingenuity but neither let that show. The gin was disposed of with solemn ritual, as if they were performing an exorcism. Once again Bridie felt a sense of renewal and embraced it with both arms. Mr. Williams had thrown her a rope and she told herself that she would be foolish, suicidal even, not to take it.

Slowly and with immense effort Bridie pulled herself out of her pit. She forced herself to forget about Jack, to swallow her disappointment and regret and to focus her eyes on the future. There was a certain familiarity in her determination to leave the past behind and move forward. She had done it countless times, but it didn't get any easier; she just recognized the path for it was so well trodden. Elaine was a constant support and companion and on the various occasions that Bridie fell back, Elaine was there to encourage her without judgment.

Eventually Bridie began to take pride in herself again. She derived enjoyment from shopping and dancing, going to movie theaters and parties as she had done before, although now she was a little more subdued and a lot more cautious. She allowed a few men to court her. Her heart was still fragmented, the tears still tender, the memory of Jack still vivid. But as the months passed and the summer of 1929 blossomed into bright flowers and warm breezes, that memory dimmed and the edges of her pain were blunted. Count Cesare di Marcantonio saw her, ripe for love as a golden peach on a tree, from across the crowded garden at the Reynoldses' annual summer party in Southampton and decided to pluck.

"Who is that beautiful woman?" he asked his friend, Max Arkwright, who had brought him to the party.

"Why, that's the infamous Mrs. Lockwood," Max replied, sweeping a hand through his thick flaxen hair. "Everyone knows about *her*."

"She is married?" The Count's disappointment was palpable.

"No, widowed." This pleased the Count and Max proceeded to tell him the story, as he had read it in the newspapers and heard it in the grand dining rooms on Fifth Avenue. The Count listened intently, an eyebrow arched, his interest fanned with every enthralling detail.

Aware that she was being watched by the mysterious stranger at the other side of the garden, Bridie asked Elaine who he was. Elaine squinted in the evening sunshine and frowned. "I don't know," she confessed; she knew who most people were. "But I know the man he is with. That's Max Arkwright, a notorious womanizer. He's from a wealthy Boston family, spends most of his time in Argentina and Europe playing polo and seducing women. Unmarried scoundrel and charmer too. Birds of a feather flock together. You have been warned."

"Oh, I'm not interested in either," said Bridie dismissively, concealing her interest in *one*. "Only curious. His friend is staring at me. I can almost feel his eyes beneath my dress."

"Then you'd better move away, Bridget, before you get burned." And the two women escaped through the crowd to the wide steps that swept up to the terrace and the magnificent Italianate mansion behind. When Bridie chanced to look back over her shoulder she saw that the man was still watching her and she felt the long-forgotten frisson of excitement ripple across her skin.

Once on the terrace Bridie wandered among the vast pots of blue and white hydrangeas and mingled with friends and new acquaintances. She smiled and chatted with grace acquired over years through practice and persistence, while her dark eyes darted here and there in search of the handsome man who had caught her eye across the garden. The sun sank slowly in the western sky, bathing the lawn in a warm amber light, and the loud twittering of roosting birds died down as they settled on their positions in the branches and watched the activity below with a passive interest.

Just when she was beginning to suspect that the man had gone, she felt a light touch on her bare shoulder and turned around to see him standing before her, with an apologetic, almost sheepish look on his irresistibly attractive face. "I am sorry to interrupt," he said and his accent was so foreign that Bridie had to take a moment to understand what he was saying. "Count Cesare di Marcantonio," he said and he pronounced Cesare as "Chesaray" and the rest so smoothly that she failed to catch a single syllable. His name ran over her like warm honey and her spirits soared on the sweetness of it. "I saw you in the garden and had to come and introduce myself. It is probably not what a man should do in polite American society, but in Argentina, where I was raised, or in Italy, where I spent the first ten years of my life, it is rude not to pay homage to a beautiful woman."

Bridie blushed the color of fuchsia as his gaze swept across her face, caressing her skin. "Bridget Lockwood," she replied. "It doesn't sound as exotic as your name."

"But I'm not as beautiful as you, so there, you see, we are equal." He smiled and the lines around his mouth creased like a lion's, his big white teeth shining brightly against his brown and weathered skin. The crow's-feet were long and deep at his temples, his eyes the color of green agate, shining with mischief that at once appealed to Bridie's own sense of fun. His hair was seal-black and shone with a gloss that looked almost waxy, but the sun had caught the top of his head and bleached the hair there to a light sugar-brown and Bridie would have liked to run her fingers through it. Instead she held on to her glass of lemonade and tried not to let her nervousness show.

"So, what are you doing in Southampton?" she asked, aware that it was an inane question and wishing she could think of something better to say.

"Playing polo," he replied. "I confess, Mrs. Lockwood, I am a man of leisure." Bridie smiled, noticing how he had called her "Mrs." Lockwood when she hadn't volunteered that information. She was thrilled that he had been asking about her. "My family owns a large and highly profitable farm in Argentina so I take my pleasure where I find it. I have decided to spend the summer here, playing polo and seeing friends—one day I will take over from my father so, why not have fun before I have to take on responsibility, no?"

"Do you live in Argentina?"

He shrugged noncommittally. "I am a man of the world. I live a little in Argentina, a little in Rome, sometimes in Monte Carlo, sometimes in Paris . . . now here, in New York. Perhaps I will buy a house in Southampton; the people are certainly very charming, no?" With that he gave her a long and lingering look that made her stomach flip over like a pancake.

Impressed by his obviously moneyed and carefree existence, which was also apparent in his expensive clothes, the gleaming gold bee cuff links and matching tie pin, and in the general air of luxury and privilege that surrounded him, Bridie felt her excitement grow. She had never before met a man who exuded such mystery or had such a delightfully exotic flavor. As the conversation rattled on with ease she found herself liking him more and more. Since she had lost Jack she hadn't even tried to put back together the broken pieces of her heart, but now, suddenly, she wanted to. She wanted this stranger to have it, to hold it in his large hands and to keep it for always. Bridie allowed his gaze to consume her, and for once she didn't even think about the road home.

Curious to see that her friend had been talking to Max Arkwright's mysterious friend for longer than was decent Elaine decided to interrupt. Bridie smiled when she approached and quickly introduced her, admitting with a flirtatious smile, which Elaine hadn't seen in months, that she couldn't pronounce his name. "Cesare di Marcantonio," he repeated with a grin. "Now you say it."

"Cesare di Marc . . ." Bridie began slowly.

"Marcantonio," he repeated.

"Marcantonio," she said, then smiled triumphantly. Elaine watched with mounting unease. She might very well not have been there for these two people had eyes only for each other.

"This is my dear friend, Elaine Williams," Bridie said, putting her arm around her. "When I was new in Manhattan and had not a single friend, Elaine came to my rescue and has been by my side ever since. I don't know what I would have done without her."

Elaine looked him over coolly. "Yes, and I'm by your side right now," she said firmly. "Let's go get something to eat, Bridget. The buffet looks delicious."

"I will accompany you both," volunteered the Count to Elaine's dismay. "It will be my greatest pleasure to dine with two such charming ladies."

They made their way across the terrace and down the steps to where the tables of food were lined up on the grass. "He's certainly dishy, Bridget, but I wouldn't trust him as far as I could throw him," Elaine hissed, as they descended the steps together.

"God save me, I think I'm in love," Bridie hissed back, ignoring her friend's warning.

"Just be careful," Elaine said. "We know nothing about him."

"I know everything I want to know," said Bridie haughtily. "He's good enough for *me*."

At the bottom of the steps Beaumont appeared with two plates of dinner. "There you are, Elaine," he said. "Will you join me?"

Elaine was surprised to see her husband but she took the

plate and gave Bridie a disappointed look. "You'll be okay?" she asked.

"I'm just grand," Bridie replied and set off across the lawn with the Count.

"What's up?" Elaine asked her husband as they sat down at one of the small round tables positioned in clusters beneath lines of twinkling lights that encircled the garden.

"Bridget has found a man at last," he said with a grin.

"But is he suitable? We know nothing about him."

"Highly *un*suitable, I suspect," said Beaumont. "I doubt it will amount to much, but I think a romance is just what she needs to raise her morale."

"Is he really a count?"

"Counts are a dime a dozen in Italy," he added dismissively. "Still, he's lit her fire so we must be grateful for that. I doubt we're looking at the future Countess Cesare di Marcantonio!"

But Beaumont Williams, who was usually right about everything, was not right about *this*. The kiss that the Count stole beneath the cherry tree in the Reynoldses' garden was one of many that she would treasure. "May I see you again?" Cesare asked Bridie, taking her hand and looking into her chocolate-brown eyes as if he had discovered something precious there.

"I would like that," she replied, barely daring to believe that this beautiful man found her to his liking. "I would like that very much."

IN THE WEEKS that followed, Cesare took Bridie to watch the polo at the Meadowbrook polo club in Long Island and then to a match of his own where she sat in the stands in her summer dress and watched with her heart in her mouth as he thundered up and down the field, mallet raised. He was strong and athletic, fearless and bold, and her attraction to him intensified. She saw him as a foreign prince and her respect and admiration for him was beyond question. He told her tales of growing up in Italian palaces and then moving with his family to Argentina, where his family owned grand houses in the most elegant parts of Buenos Aires. His farm on the pampa was so large that he could travel by pony from sunrise to sunset without leaving his own land. "One day I'll take you there and show you how beautiful it is at sunset, when the plains turn red and the sky is indigo blue. You will fall in love with it."

Count Cesare seemed to relish having the infamous Mrs. Lockwood on his arm. He showed her off at fundraisers, private parties, in the dance halls of Manhattan and in the jazz clubs and speakeasies of Harlem. Wherever the fashionable people were the Count was sure to be, dressed in the most dapper suits and silk scarves with elaborate gold bees adorning the buttonholes of his shirts and jackets, stamped into the leather of his wallet and molded into the silver of his money clip. The bee emblem was everywhere. Count Cesare looked glossy and shiny with his jet-black hair as highly polished as his two-tone brogues and his dazzling white teeth matching the bright whites of his eyes. Rumor simmered and then rose in great bubbles of excitement as everyone began to predict another wedding. Flashbulbs welcomed their arrivals and journalists clamored to comment on their every move: *The ubiquitous Count Cesare di Marcantonio was once again escorting his new lady friend the socialite Mrs. Lockwood to a fundraising dinner at the Metropolitan Museum . . . She wore a gown by Jean Patou . . . Those* who despised her as an insatiable social-climber sniffed their disapproval and dismissed the Count as a "common adventurer," but those who enjoyed the colorful maid who had fulfilled the American dream and risen to be one of the richest women in the city celebrated this new chapter of her story.

Bridie let him kiss her again. And *again*. His kisses were sensual and teasing, ardent and long-lasting. He brushed his lips against hers, murmured to her in Spanish, traced his fingers beneath her blouse and dipped his tongue into the little well at her throat. He drove her to the point of madness and it was all she could do to restrain herself. And then, only a month after they'd met, he asked her to marry him.

"I love you with all my heart," he told her, bending onto one knee on the grass in Central Park where he had taken her for a picnic. "Will you do me the honor of agreeing to be my wife?"

Bridie's eyes filled with tears. She knelt in front of him and threw her arms around his neck. "I will," she replied and as he placed his lips upon hers she realized that happiness was perhaps *not* something that could be bought but something that grew out of love.

Chapter 16

London, autumn 1929

Beatrice had noticed that Digby had been somewhat subdued since the Castle Deverill Summer Ball. The event itself had been a triumph and Celia had been a radiant and gracious hostess, charming everyone with her ready smile and obvious enthusiasm for her new position as Doyenne of Ballinakelly. No one could talk of anything else for weeks afterward. The castle was awe-inspiring, the gardens the very manifestation of beauty and the guests, including the Shrubs, Bertie, Kitty and Harry, had nothing but praise for Celia and Archie's efforts. But Digby had grown morose and taciturn, which was very disconcerting for his family who knew him as flamboyant, spirited and indomitable. Beatrice wondered whether he was sinking into a mild depression on account of the castle having reached completion and his role in the project drawn to a close. A natural gambler and risk-taker, Digby had relished the undertaking, but now it was over he was back at his desk in his office speculating on the markets, plotting schemes with his solicitor and his broker and taking a keen interest as usual in his horses, but he was uncharacteristically wary and ill at ease. Beatrice noticed that he spent a lot of time standing by the window, smoking his cigars and gazing out into the road as if expecting someone or something undesirable to turn into his driveway.

Beatrice tried to distract him by filling the house with people. Her Tuesday evening Salons continued to deliver politicians, actresses, writers and socialites to her door, and she made sure that Deverill Rising was busy with Digby's racing friends at weekends. But nothing seemed to relieve him of his anxiety and restore his *joie de vivre*. When she asked him about it he simply patted her hand and smiled reassuringly. "Nothing to worry about, my dear. I've just got a lot on my mind, that's all."

Whether he had anticipated the Wall Street Crash on October 24 or his gambler's instinct sensed impending doom in the markets, she couldn't say, but the terrible fall on the London Stock Exchange a few days after Black Thursday in New York more than fulfilled his gloomy premonition. Digby locked himself in his study and remained for most of the day on the telephone, shouting. He did not emerge until very late that evening with his face red and sweating, and for the first time in their marriage Beatrice saw real fear in his eyes.

Celia had returned to London to shop for more extravagances with which to adorn her beloved castle. She had read the newspapers and listened to her mother worrying about her father but she didn't imagine that the Wall Street Crash had anything to do with *her*. When she asked Archie about the state of their finances he reassured her that they were fine, they had pots of money and no fall on the Stock Exchange could induce him to tell her to curb her expenditure. So she continued to shop in the usual way, flouncing up and down Knightsbridge and Bond Street without a care in the world, while the rest of London society trembled in their finely polished shoes and the city smog lingered in a portentous gray mist.

"It's really such a drag," she told Harry over lunch at Claridge's. "Papa's in a foul mood, which is so unlike him, and Mama is fussing around him, which makes him all the more bad-tempered. Leona and Vivien came round for tea yesterday and only made Mama worry all the more, repeating what their silly husbands have obviously told them, that we're all going to be poor and penniless and miserable. Goodness, I do dislike my sisters." She took a swig of champagne and grinned mischievously. "So, to lift my spirits, I've just bought the most gorgeous painting for the hall, to replace the one of that crusty old general with his dog that hangs at the bottom of the stairs . . ." As she rattled on Harry tried to concentrate on her words, but all he could see was her pretty red mouth moving against the roar of his thoughts, which carried in their tumultuous barrage the name Boysie Bancroft.

Celia hadn't a clue of the havoc her Summer Ball had caused, although Harry readily admitted that it was all his fault. If he hadn't taken Boysie to the room he shared with his wife . . . if he hadn't been so reckless . . . if he hadn't, in some deep and unconscious way, *wanted* to get caught. Since he had left Ballinakelly with Charlotte, he had been in a state of utter despair. Life was not worth living without Boysie. Now that he had promised his wife he wouldn't see him again the sun no longer shone, the nights were as thick as tar and his limbs were as heavy as lead. He felt as if he were walking in water and that the current was always against him. His unhappiness had engulfed him and it seemed that, while Celia was bathed in light, he dwelled in permanent shadow—and that shadow penetrated to the marrow of his bones. His misery was total and complete and yet he couldn't even begin to explain it to Celia. He had to be a master of theater, smiling in the right places, quipping as he always had, laughing in his old carefree way, while inside his heart was shriveling like a plum left on the grass at the mercy of the winter frosts.

So focused on her castle, Celia didn't even ask him about Boysie. If she had taken more notice she might have wondered why Boysie hadn't joined them for lunch. She would have questioned why he wasn't at her mother's Tuesday Salons and why, when he was such a regular visitor to Deverill House, he hadn't crossed the threshold since the summer. If she hadn't been so staunchly single-minded about herself and embellishing her new home, she might have been concerned by her cousin's pallor, by the raw pain in his eyes that no amount of dissembling could hide and by the downward twist to one corner of his mouth when his sorrow caught him off guard; but she wasn't. Celia was only too happy to tell Harry about her purchases and the fabulous plans she had for Christmas. The crowds of children they were going to have because "in a castle of that size it's only proper to fill it with family." Christmas was going to be "a riot" because they were all going to be there together instead of spending their usual fortnight at Deverill Rising.

At last she stopped motoring on about herself and put down

her empty wineglass. "Darling, I meant to ask, how is Charlotte? She was a miserable old thing at my ball. Has she cheered up?"

Harry wiped his mouth with his napkin even though it was clean. "She has," he lied. "She's had a difficult pregnancy. Spending the rest of the summer in Norfolk really cheered her up. I think she just needed to be with her family. Ours can be a little overpowering."

The truth was that Charlotte had *not* forgiven him. She had not invited him into her bedroom since they had returned from Norfolk and she had most definitely not forgotten what she had seen, nor did she intend to. She was just as unhappy as he was. Combined with the natural fatigue of pregnancy, her wretchedness was even more desperate. They existed as if in different dimensions, only coming together for the sake of the children and at social functions where their efforts went undetected and any irritability was put down to anxiety about the imminent birth on her part and the dire state of the markets on his. Most of London society felt the same about the declining economy and everyone, except Celia, was worrying about their future.

The only other person who was even more careless with money than Celia was Maud, Harry's mother. Having found a house to buy in Chester Square she had promptly set about furnishing it with the help of Mr. Kenneth Leclaire, the famous designer who had worked such magic on Castle Deverill, without a thought for her husband who had bought it for her with the proceeds of the sale of his ancestral home. Maud didn't want Bertie anywhere near her so he remained in the Hunting Lodge, courtesy of Archie and Celia, who charged him a peppercorn rent. Harry had met Maud's lover, Arthur Arlington, who was the younger brother of the Earl of Pendrith and a well-known scoundrel, twice divorced and with a notorious gambling habit. They had met at the ballet and Harry had been appalled. For a woman so desperate to be seen to be doing the right thing, Maud was very careless with Arthur, whom everyone knew was escorting her to bed as well as to the Royal Opera House. Perhaps it was because he was of aristocratic lineage, Harry mused. Nothing excited his mother more than a title.

"Perhaps you can leave Charlotte in Norfolk for Christmas," Celia continued. "She will have just had the baby. The last thing she'll want is to travel the choppy Irish Sea to Ballinakelly. Much better that she rest at home with her mama to look after her. Do you think we can persuade Boysie to leave Dreary Deirdre behind too? Perhaps he can come for New Year's. Really, why did you two have to marry? You were much more fun on your own."

"*You* married, old girl," said Harry flatly.

"That's different. Archie's such fun. Your wives are very tiresome." Her face lit up as she expressed her admiration for her husband in glowing terms: "He's denied me nothing for the castle. You should have seen the wonderful things I bought in France. We had to have it all shipped over and it took weeks—you would have thought they were sailing the Atlantic, not the English Channel! There's a sale coming up at Christie's. They're auctioning the most stunning things from Russia. After the Revolution those beastly Bolsheviks sold all the treasures. You wouldn't believe the opulence of those Russian princes. I've got my eye on a few things. I'm so excited. Would you like to come with me? I shall be bidding like crazy, waving my little hand at every opportunity. It's all so much fun. I get an enormous buzz out of it."

"I'm surprised Archie isn't reining you in, considering the present climate," said Harry, calling the waiter for the bill.

"Darling, he says there's nothing to worry about. You have to remember that I married a very clever man."

Harry wasn't convinced. "He'll have been affected by the Crash like everyone else."

"Then he must have secret reserves," she giggled. "Because I'm spending them!"

But Celia's confidence was shaken a few weeks later when her favorite couturier in Maddox Street failed to give her credit. Pale with concern she waited for Archie to return home, having enjoyed a long lunch at his club, and then she asked him.

"My darling Celia, it's simply a reflection of the times," he explained coolly. "Everyone is being extra cautious."

"So there's nothing to worry about?"

"Nothing."

Her shoulders sagged with relief. "I'm so pleased. I'd be utterly devastated if I couldn't go to the Russian sale at Christie's. I asked Harry to come with me, but he's cried off so Mama is coming instead. Really, everyone is making a fuss about nothing!" She put her arms around her husband and kissed him. "You're a wonderful man, Archie. Just wonderful. I don't know what I'd do without you."

He frowned and in her happiness she missed a certain shiftiness that made him avert his eyes. "Do you know what gives me the *most* pleasure, darling?"

"You tell me," he replied.

"Watching Papa enjoying Castle Deverill. He grew up in

the shadow of that place and he loved it and yearned to belong there as his cousins Bertie and Rupert did. All those summers in Ballinakelly made such a deep impression on him, Mama told me, that his pleasure at my ownership of it is all the more satisfying. It's as good as owning it himself, I think. You have done a wonderful thing, not only restoring the family seat, but giving it to the London Deverills. You can't imagine what that means. The prestige is enormous. I love Cousin Bertie and cherish the memories of having enjoyed the place when Hubert and Adeline were alive, but I'm happy it's fallen into *my* hands. I love it dearly and Papa does too. Thank you, my darling, for making it possible. You've made us incredibly happy."

Archie pulled her into his arms and held her close. "That's all I've ever wanted to do," he said and she felt him nuzzling his face against her hair.

AT THE END of November Charlotte Deverill was delivered of a boy who was immediately named Rupert after Harry's uncle who was killed at Gallipoli. The birth of their son mollified a little Charlotte's hostility toward her husband. After two daughters the arrival of a boy gave both parents something about which they could be truly happy. For a brief moment they could forget their resentment and celebrate the arrival of the heir to the centuries-old title and the future hope that Little Rupert would one day father a son who would secure the title for another generation. Harry loved his daughters but the arrival of his son affected him in a very different way. The child distracted him from his constant pining for Boysie and revived his withered heart. Little Rupert's innocence touched him profoundly and every wriggle he made induced smiles that came from deep inside him. But then as December brought windy nights and cold, dark mornings, the black dog of despair began to hound him once again.

Celia's busy little white hand impressed everyone at the Christie's Russian sale. With the encouragement of her mother she bid for almost everything and won all the pieces she had so desired. To celebrate, mother and daughter lunched in Mayfair and discussed Celia's plans for her grand New Year Ball. "It's going to be even more wonderful than the summer one," she told Beatrice. "I'm going to ask Maud and Victoria, even though I can't bear either. I think it's time to hold out the olive branch, don't you? I'd love Maud to see what I've done and to like it."

"Darling, I doubt very much she'll ever set foot in Ballinakelly again. I think it would be too much for her to see her husband's inheritance in your hands. But I'm sure she'll appreciate the gesture. I think your sisters might come this time. They spent Christmas with their husbands' families last year so it's our turn this year. I've told them you intend to host Christmas and they're rather curious to see what you and Archie have done to the place. I think they're the only members of the family who are yet to see it, having not been able to come in the summer." Beatrice smiled contentedly. "To think of all those children running around the castle gardens. They're going to have a wonderful time." Then her smile faded and concern furrowed her brow. She toyed with the stem of her wineglass. "I think it will be good for your father to get away from London. He's been very distracted lately. He's even told me to cut back where I can . . ."

"You mean to stop spending?" Celia asked, aghast.

"I'm afraid so. I'm doing my best. I'm sure the trouble will blow over, but until it does I'm being careful." She chuckled wistfully. "I haven't been careful since before I married. You know your father was a very wealthy man when I met him. He'd struck lucky in the diamond mines and then in the gold rush. He was such a dashing adventurer. But he's a risk-taker. I'm not sure what's going on, but I fear some of his gambles haven't paid off and that the Crash has robbed him of some of his wealth. I'm sure it's not too serious. I *hope* it's not too serious. But we'll weather it, won't we?"

"Papa will be fine," said Celia emphatically. The idea of her father being anything less than solid, rich and unshakable was an abhorrence. "He's much too clever to let something like this pull him down. But you're right, Christmas at Castle Deverill will make him feel much better. It makes us all feel better. It's that sort of place."

In the grand tradition of the Deverills who had occupied Castle Deverill before her, Celia invited the entire family to stay for two weeks over Christmas and New Year's, ending the festive period with a sumptuous ball that promised to eclipse all the previous parties ever held there.

Maud declined, as was expected. However, Victoria wrote to say that she would come, because, having done her duty by her husband's side entertaining the tenants and estate workers, followed by his mother, the dowager Countess, at Broadmere, their stately home in Kent, for the last fifteen years, she deserved to spend Christmas wheresoever she desired. Celia's grandparents, Stoke and Augusta, accepted too, which was a great surprise because Augusta had given every indication that she would be dead by Christmas. Celia's sisters agreed to come as did Harry and Charlotte, which dismayed Celia for she had hoped Harry might manage to leave his grumpy wife in England. Her biggest disappointment, however, was Boysie. He had written back in his beautiful brown calligraphy on luxuriously thick ivory paper from Mount Street that it was with great regret that he was unable to accept, for Celia Mayberry was undoubtedly unsurpassed not only in Ballinakelly but in London too as the greatest hostess of their age. Flattered though she was it saddened her that one of her dearest friends would not be present for her first Christmas at Castle Deverill and her first New Year Ball.

Kitty and Robert would come for Christmas Day with the Shrubs and Bertie, and Elspeth with her ruddy-faced, Master of the Foxhounds husband Peter, who now insisted on introducing Archie to the joys of Irish country living, thinking nothing of lending him a horse and sending him off with the hunt. The castle promised to be full of children—Deverill cousins all doing what Deverill cousins had always done: run around the grounds like wild dogs. Celia was as excited as a thoroughbred at the Derby and couldn't wait for everyone to arrive.

At last the cars swept up the drive and halted in front of the impressive entrance, which Celia had decorated with a wreath made of fir and red-berried holly. The butler was by the door to greet them and three footmen ready to carry the luggage to the bedrooms. The wet wind blew in off the sea and gray clouds gathered in heavy folds above the towers of the castle, but nothing could dampen Celia's joy at welcoming everyone into her expensively heated home.

The first to arrive were Augusta and Stoke. Augusta waited for the chauffeur to help her out of the car and then she stood a moment, gazing up at the walls, her face full of wistfulness as she remembered the days when she had come to stay with Adeline and Hubert, before the fire had done unspeakable things to the family. For a moment she thought she saw a face in the window of the western tower and she blinked to clear her vision. Perhaps it was a child playing up there, or a trick of light. Distracted by her husband, who walked around to offer her his arm, she turned her eyes to the entrance, where the open door gave a glimpse of the lavish hall and roaring fire beyond.

"SHE'S STILL ALIVE," Adeline commented to Hubert as their spirits gazed down from the tower window. "I suspect she'll outlive all of them."

"I hope not," said Hubert.

"She'll certainly outlive her husband. Stoke is more rickety in the legs than ever. Ah, there's another car. Let's see. Who's that?" She waited beside Hubert, who was getting increasingly difficult to entertain in the monotonous limbo that had been his for too many years now to count. Adeline smiled. "It's Harry and Charlotte." She sighed and dropped her head to one side. "Poor Harry, he's desperately miserable. Life is difficult."

"Life after life is worse," grumbled Hubert.

"Well, you had better get used to it," came Barton's voice from the armchair. "You have nothing to complain about."

"Don't bicker," said Adeline patiently. "You might as well get along because by the looks of things you're all here to stay for the foreseeable future. Ah, there's Digby and Beatrice. Do you remember, darling, how Digby used to bring you the finest

Cuban cigars?" Hubert grunted. "And Beatrice brought all of us the most exquisite silks. They were always so generous. Poor Digby's finding life difficult too. But these things are sent to test us, are they not? We were tested, weren't we, Hubert?"

"Wish I'd listened to you, Adeline," he said suddenly. "I just thought you were . . ." He hesitated then chuckled at the irony. "I thought you were a bit mad, but it was I who was mad. I thought your ghosts were in your imagination but now I'm one of them. How blind we human beings are and how misled. Look at them all." He stared down as another car slowly made its way over the gravel. "They're blind too. All of them. Only death can open their eyes."

There came a loud tut from behind them. "Be of good heart, Hubert. At least you're not in Hell."

Hubert turned to Barton. "I don't believe in the Hell that I was taught. Hell is on earth. That's very clear now."

"And that is Hell right now," said Adeline mischievously. Hubert smiled, for there, stepping out of the car, was Victoria, Countess of Elmrod, with her desperately dull and humorless husband, Eric. "Now that's going to set the cat among the pigeons," she said. "We're all in for a fortnight of entertainment. Isn't that fun!"

Chapter 17

Victoria had been in the castle for no more than an hour and already the servants were exasperated by her incessant demands. She wanted all her dresses ironed and her husband's shirts pressed. She insisted that her eight-year-old daughter, Lady Alexandra, have a lady's maid of her own, which meant that Bessie, one of the younger housemaids, had to be removed from her usual duties to look after her.

Victoria had arrived ready to criticize her cousin's audacious rebuilding of her father's former home, but to her surprise she found it very much to her liking. "It has proper plumbing and electricity!" she exclaimed in delight, flouncing into the bathroom. "Goodness, Celia's dragged it out of the Dark Ages and what a difference it makes. I think I'm going to be very happy here. I rather wish Mama had swallowed her pride and come because even *she* would be impressed with the comfort and luxury of the new castle."

"My dear, she'd find something to criticize, I assure you," said her husband, looking out of the window onto the manicured box garden below. "And her jealousy would make her stay intolerable."

"But she's spending Christmas alone in London."

"That's *her* choice, Victoria. She was asked and she declined."

"Well, I'm *not* going to let her make *me* feel guilty."

Eric laughed. "She'll make a fine job of trying."

HARRY AND CHARLOTTE were given the same room as they had had in the summer, which put an added strain on their already overwrought marriage. Harry hadn't laid eyes on Boysie in all those months, and now, finding himself back at the castle, he discovered that memories of his friend shone out from every corner, which only served to make him feel even more sick with misery and longing. He too looked down onto the gardens but his mother's jealousy was not the focus of *his* thoughts. No, Harry stared onto the box hedges below and contemplated the idea of hurling himself out the window. The thought of it came slowly yet steadily, creeping across his mind like an evening shadow. Death would be a release, he figured. He'd feel no more the pain of separation and the agony of guilt; he'd be free.

Charlotte left the room to go and check on the nursemaid and Little Rupert, who had been put at the other end of the house with the rest of the children. Harry lit a cigarette and allowed his memories to float before his eyes like ships on the sea. He remembered his first love, Joseph the first footman; the time Kitty had discovered them in bed together; the moment he had had to say good-bye and return to the Front. He remembered the war, the cracking sound of gunfire, the skull-shattering explosion of bombs and the yearning, the terrible *yearning*, when at night he had sat huddled in the trenches gazing up at the stars that twinkled like the distant lights of home. He felt that yearning now, for Boysie, and it was just as terrible.

That evening the Shrubs arrived with Kitty and Robert, Elspeth and Peter and all their children, and Bertie, who wandered up from the Hunting Lodge with a torch. Everyone embraced excitedly, for it had been so long since they had all been together, the London Deverills and the Ballinakelly Deverills, and they fell on each other with exclamations of joy. "I'm just grateful that I have been spared to see once again the magnificence of the castle restored to its former splendor," said Augusta in her stentorian voice, sinking into an armchair like a fat bantam. Her black dress ruffled up at her neck like feathers and the diamonds on her ears weighed so heavily that her lobes hung loose and floppy. She knitted her swollen, arthritic fingers so that the large gems she had managed to force onto them clustered together in a glittering display of bright colors. "I am ready to go, now that I have seen it one last time."

The men stood in the hall discussing the dire state of the economy while Celia showed her sisters, Vivien and Leona, around the drawing room and Kitty and Elspeth endured Augusta's self-indulgent soliloquy about death. Beatrice chatted to the Shrubs and noticed that there was something different about them. It wasn't the way they looked, although she had to admit that they were taking more trouble with their appearance. It was something intangible but distinctly noticeable. Something in the air between them that wasn't pleasant.

"I gather Archie is going to host the Boxing Day Meet," said Hazel.

"Indeed he is," Beatrice confirmed. "I dare say he'll be dragged off with the hunt. I don't think he's a very keen horseman."

"Ethelred is a mighty fine horseman." Laurel inhaled through her nostrils and pulled a face that could only be described as deeply admiring and reverential. "Have you met him?"

"Of course I have," said Beatrice, noticing the air had grown suddenly chilly between the two sisters.

"He will be at the Meet, certainly," Hazel interjected. "He's a *very* fine horseman."

Laurel smiled tensely. "He tried to persuade *me* to take it up again."

"And me," added Hazel, not to be outdone. "He tried to persuade me too. But I believe I'm too old."

"Well, *I'm not*," snapped Laurel. "I am considering it."

"You're not!" said Hazel.

"Why, do you think me incapable? I was a very competent horsewoman in my day, don't forget. Lord Hunt even told me that I would cut a dash in a riding habit." Laurel blushed and smiled smugly. "He does take liberties."

Hazel pursed her lips. "Ah, there's Charlotte," she said. "I'm longing to see Little Rupert. Do excuse me." And she stalked over to Charlotte, who was standing pale and shy in the doorway. Beatrice watched her go with a sense of helplessness. She turned back to Laurel and asked for news of Reverend Maddox— anything to draw the conversation away from Lord Hunt, who seemed to her like a fox in a henhouse.

Digby patted Archie hard on the back. "You're a good man, Archie, to host Christmas for my family. I do believe it'll be the best Christmas any of us have ever had." Archie basked in his father-in-law's admiration. "I must say," Digby continued, "I couldn't have asked for a better man for my daughter. You've made her very happy, which is no easy feat. She's flighty and easily distracted, but she's kept her eye on the castle all these years without deviation, which surprises no one more than me. You're the wind in her sails, Archie. You've got the measure of her, I daresay."

"Thank you, Digby," said Archie.

"Tell me, man to man. How are your affairs?"

"Very good," Archie replied.

Digby nodded thoughtfully, letting his eyes lose their focus in the middle distance. "Nothing I should worry about?"

"Nothing," Archie reassured him.

"These are trying times. I'm a gambling man, Archie. A speculator. I enjoy taking risks, but even I've had my fingers burned."

"I won't say we've come out of this unscathed," Archie conceded. "But I've been shrewd in my dealings."

"Good." Digby patted him on the back again, then he added, "If you were ever in financial difficulty, you wouldn't be too proud to come to me, I hope."

"Of course not," said Archie. Digby went to refill his glass and hoped he'd never be called upon; he was in no position to help anyone at the moment.

ON CHRISTMAS DAY the family attended church, then returned for lunch and the opening of gifts. The children, dressed in their very best velvet and silk, tore open the wrapping paper and ribbon with squeals of delight before being taken away by their nannies to play with their new toys in the children's wing of the castle. The grown-ups drank sherry, played charades and card games and watched the afternoon darken outside the drawing-room windows.

"Christmas should be a happy time," said Kitty to Harry as they stood together, looking out. "But it makes me feel nostalgic and a little sad for all that we have lost." She glanced at her brother, who was struggling to find the words to express his own sense of desolation. "You have done the right thing," she told him quietly. "Hard though it is. You have saved your family." He nodded, straining to hold back his emotion. His face flushed pink and his eyes sparkled but they remained locked, gazing out onto the slate-gray skies and inky gardens. "It will get better, you know," she continued. "The hurt never goes away, but the sharp pain you feel now will turn into a dull ache. Most of the time you'll be able to ignore it. Life has its many distractions, thankfully. Then, suddenly, when you least expect it, something will trigger it again and you'll be cut to the quick. But you push through those moments and they eventually pass. I think of Adeline and what she would say. These things are sent to test us, Harry. Life isn't meant to be easy." She looked at him again and his profile was so grave she wanted to take his hand and squeeze it, but she knew that, for his sake, she couldn't; her touch would only make him lose control.

The day after Christmas the Ballinakelly Foxhounds gathered on the lawn outside the castle for the Boxing Day Meet. It was a damp day, warm for December. Soft rain floated on the breeze that carried with it the scent of pine, wet soil and sea. Crows hopped on the grass, pecking the ground for grubs as the horses snorted smoke into the moist air. Women in their navy riding habits and hats sat sidesaddle, except for Kitty who had made a resolution the morning of the fire never to ride like that again. She sat astride her mare in a pair of breeches and navy jacket, a starched white stock about her neck, her fire-red hair falling in a thick plait down her back, almost reaching her waist. Beside her JP sat confidently on his pony. Almost eight years old he had the bold gray gaze of his half sister, Kitty, and the same red hair, but his face was broad and handsome like his father's, and, to Bertie's pride, he had already been blooded with his first kill. Eager to get going, JP fidgeted excitedly in the saddle while Robert looked on with their daughter, Florence, who was afraid of the horses. Peter had persuaded Archie to join the hunt and he sat awkwardly on his horse, trying not to show his fear. He pulled his silver flask out of his pocket and took a large swig of sloe gin, which didn't make him feel any better.

Lord Hunt, dashing in his black jacket and tan-topped boots, raised his hat to the Shrubs, who buzzed about his horse's head like a pair of flies. "It's a fine day for the chase," Ethelred told them jovially. "The air is mild. Those hounds will pick up a good scent. I really must find a way to persuade you both to take to the saddle again, if only to see you in your riding habits and veils." He grinned down at them as they elbowed each other to get closer.

Grace looked elegant in her black habit, her pale face half-hidden behind a diaphanous black veil. Her waist was, however, thinner than normal and her mouth, usually so full of sensuality, was drawn into a hard line. Ever since Michael Doyle had rebuffed her she had felt more keenly than ever the passing of her youth. She lamented that she was no longer the beauty she had once been, for surely, if she was, Michael would not have been able to resist her. Try as she might, Michael was rarely out of her thoughts and her body still ached for him with every memory of his touch. Dare she admit, even to herself, that Michael had stolen her heart as well as her desire? She hadn't taken a lover since and had to endure her husband strutting about with the smugness of a man who has a pretty woman in every city. She glanced at Sir Ronald, talking to Bertie, astride a horse that looked as if it was buckling beneath his great weight, and felt her irritation rise as he tossed back his head and laughed heartily.

Celia, who had thrown herself with zeal into the role of Doyenne of Ballinakelly, sat sidesaddle in her riding habit, her shiny blond hair tied into a neat chignon at the back of her neck and contained within a hairnet, a black hat set at a raffish angle on the side of her head. She walked her horse among the riders, greeting everyone with the graciousness of a queen. Bertie, distinguished in a pink hunting jacket, asked one of the servants passing around glasses of port to give one to Digby, who, he had noticed, was a little off-color. Leona and Vivien's husbands, Bruce and Tarquin, sat solidly in their saddles, for they were both accomplished riders in the Army, while their wives, who did not like horses, looked on.

Peter, as the Master of Foxhounds, blew his horn and the hunt was off. The hounds ran ahead, their noses to the ground, eager for the scent of fox. The lawn was suddenly empty but for the crows. Hazel and Laurel stood forlornly on the terrace. "Well, that's it then," said Hazel.

"Until tea," said Laurel.

"I'm going to go and sit by the fire in the drawing room."

"And suffer Augusta? Not for me."

"Then what are you going to do, Laurel?" Hazel asked, put out.

"I shall find three friends to play a rubber of bridge. I know Robert will join me at the table and I'm sure, with a little coaxing, Leona and Vivien will be game."

Hazel looked wounded. They had always played bridge together when Adeline and Hubert were alive. "Very well," she said, lifting her chin bravely. "As you wish. And, by the way, I *like* Augusta." The two women walked into the castle together, stinging from their unusual discord.

HARRY ENJOYED HUNTING because it forced him into the moment, just as it had done after the war when he had wanted to flee from the aftereffects of the brutality he had witnessed. Now he wanted to lose himself again. He had never liked hunting as a boy for he had been a coward then, but now he relished the speed and rode without a care for his safety, jumping hedges and fences and streams. The hounds picked up the scent and followed the trail excitedly. Harry galloped at the front, his veins pumping with adrenaline and his heart pounding against his chest, drowning out his longing for Boysie. In a moment he was beside Kitty, who rode with the fearlessness of a man, and she smiled at him as they took a hawthorn hedge and cleared it with a thundering of hooves. Brother and sister rode together relishing the danger that put them firmly in the moment, obliterating for a blessed day their impossible loves.

At length Grace, her face splattered with mud and her hair breaking out of the pins, came across a group of local men and boys in fancy dress, wandering slowly along the track that led from Ballinakelly to other small towns up the coast. With them was a small band and they were singing. She slowed down to a trot until she saw Michael Doyle among the faces and drew her horse to a halt. A young boy was holding a long stick covered in ribbons with a small bundle hanging off the end of it. She looked at Michael through her veil and he looked right back at her with his black and steady gaze. "Good morning, Mr. Doyle," she said. Then, dropping her eyes to the child, she asked him what it was that swung from the end of his stick.

"It's St. Stephen's Day, milady," said the boy, surprised that she didn't know. "This here's a wren."

Grace recoiled. "A wren? A *dead* wren?"

"Yes, indeed," volunteered one of the men.

"Why did you kill it?" she asked, directing her question at Michael, whose head and shoulders rose above the group with an air of authority and importance.

"There are three stories about the celebration to bury the wren," he said. "The first is that the wren drew attention to Jesus in the Garden of Gethsemane, which betrayed him to the Romans. The second is that a wren betrayed the Fenians when it landed on a drum and alerted Cromwell's army." Then the corners of his lips curled into a smile and he looked at her with more intensity. "But there is another story, a legend that tells of Cliona, a temptress, who lured men to their deaths in the sea with her wiles. A charm was discovered that protected them from her. Her only escape was to turn herself into a wren, to be hunted forever more for her skulduggery." He was staring at Grace with a knowing look on his face.

She lifted her chin. "Then you'd better be on your way," she said, giving her horse a gentle squeeze. The group wandered on down the track, but she called out to Michael.

He hung back until the other wrenboys were out of earshot. "Lady Rowan-Hampton?"

"I am that wren hanging from the stick," she said and bit her lip. "Your faith is your charm and I am that poor wren."

"Grace . . ."

She strained the muscles in her neck to hold back her emotions. "You know it is possible to be so heavenly as to be no earthly good, have you thought of that?"

"Then let it be thus," he said.

"You will come to your senses. I know you will."

He shook his head. "When one has experienced the light, Grace, there's no going back to the darkness."

She gave a furious groan, turned her horse roughly and galloped off to catch up with the hunt.

At dusk, when the weak winter sun smoldered through the latticework of trees like a blacksmith's furnace, the hunt made its way home. They had caught their fox and everyone was high on the thrill of the chase and the drama of the kill. Archie walked his horse down the hill toward the castle whose windows glowed with the welcoming lights that promised tea and cake and turf fires. As he approached, the towers and turrets of his home were silhouetted against a clear indigo sky, for the wind had blown the clouds inland and sent the drizzle with it. The sight was arresting. He wanted to stop awhile to savor it before the sun dipped below the horizon and the outline was lost to the dark, but the others were keen to get home to their baths and their tea so he continued, his shoulders suddenly heavy with the weight of responsibility. Castle Deverill was more than a castle and he knew it. It was at the heart of the Deverill spirit and it was now up to him to keep that spirit alive. Celia loved the castle but she didn't understand *why* she loved it. Archie did. He was well aware that it was more than the memory of good times; it was the Deverills' very soul.

When they reached the stables they handed their horses to the grooms and hurried into the castle to change for tea. Their breeches were splattered with mud, their faces stained with sweat and earth kicked up by the hooves. As Harry made his way across the hall toward the stairs, Celia hurried out of the sitting room, her face red and shining. "You'll never believe who's just turned up!" she hissed, grabbing his arm. For a moment Harry's heart gave a little leap. Could Boysie have changed his mind and come after all? "Maud!" Celia declared, trembling with excitement. "She says she's bored in London on her own and that Christmas is about family. Truly, I feel as if the wicked fairy has turned up to ruin the party!" But she didn't look at all unhappy about it. "What's your father going to say—and Kitty?"

Harry concealed his disappointment. "She hasn't brought Arthur Arlington with her, I trust?" he asked, trying to inject some humor into his voice.

"God no! Now *that* would be scandalous. She came on her own. She said she wanted to surprise us."

"She'll do that all right," said Harry, setting off up the stairs.

"Aren't you going to say hello?"

"And cover her immaculate dress in mud? I think not. I'll come down after my bath and relieve you."

"Ah, there's Papa!" She rushed over to Digby. "You're never going to guess who's shown up . . ."

MAUD SAT PRIMLY on the club fender in her pale tweed dress over which she wore a luxurious fur stole. Her blond hair was cut off sharply at her jawline, which accentuated the severe angles of her face. She passed her icy eyes around the room, missing nothing. Beatrice could almost hear the clicking of her mind as she calculated the cost of everything. Augusta watched her warily from the armchair while Charlotte, who had always been a little scared of her mother-in-law, remained on the sofa with Leona and Vivien hoping that she wouldn't direct any conversation her way. The Shrubs, who could think of nothing but Lord Hunt, sat on the other sofa, momentarily stunned like a pair of mice in the presence of a snake. Victoria sat beside her mother on the fender, a cigarette smoking in the holder that balanced between her fingers, enjoying the warmth of the fire on her back and the varying expressions on the faces of the ladies, which ranged from surprise to ill-concealed horror.

At last Maud spoke. "It's nice," she said tightly. Beatrice's mouth twitched.

Augusta gave a snort. "*We* were always taught that 'nice' is a most unimaginative word, Maud," she said imperiously.

"It's lovely then," Maud added. "It's certainly warm, which is a welcome change. Fortunately Adeline isn't alive to see how much it's changed."

"It *had* to change, Mama. One couldn't very well have made a replica of everything that was lost in the fire," said Victoria.

"But it's so different. The soul is missing."

"It's modern," Victoria told her. "I like it very much. In fact, it's just the way I would have done it, had *I* had the opportunity."

Beatrice smiled at Victoria. "You have always had such beautiful taste, my dear," she said, trying not to allow Maud to irritate her.

"I can see that no expense has been spared. Really, I had no idea that Archie was such a tycoon," Maud added.

Augusta snorted again. "It's very vulgar to talk about money."

"But hard to ignore in such lavish surroundings," Maud replied swiftly. "I do believe it's even more sumptuous than the days when Hubert's father lived here. It was extremely luxurious then."

Before Augusta could object the men appeared washed and dressed for tea. When Harry greeted his mother, Maud's resentment at Celia's inappropriate rebuilding of her son's inheritance evaporated like mist in sunlight. She embraced him fiercely and smiled with a rare display of warmth. "You will bring Rupert down, won't you, darling? I'm just dying to give that little baby a squeeze." Charlotte winced; Maud barely knew how to hold a baby. Digby hid his surprise and asked after her crossing. He wondered how Bertie was going to react to his wife setting foot in Ireland again, having sworn she never would.

Celia sat on the floor beside her grandmother for safety. She knew that Augusta would defend her from Maud's barbed comments. Part of her wished Maud hadn't come, but the other part found the drama of her surprise appearance thrilling.

When at last Bertie arrived for tea with Kitty and Robert a hush fell over the room. Maud had not spoken directly to her husband since Adeline's funeral over four years before, and everyone was curious to see what she would say, as well as a little anxious for Bertie, of whom they were all very fond.

Bertie saw Maud at once and his face flushed. Maud, who had prepared herself for this very moment, and loved nothing more than to draw the attention of the entire room, smiled sweetly. "Bertie," she said evenly. "How very good to see you." She believed her delivery to be gracious yet cool—the sort of delivery one might use when greeting the vicar or an old family friend of whom one is not particularly fond.

Bertie stalled in the doorway. He stared at her in amazement. Digby wanted to give him a nudge. Instead, he decided to break the awkward silence himself. "Isn't this a nice surprise," he said, hoping Bertie would agree. But Bertie cleared his throat and seemed to be searching for something to say— and failing miserably.

"Hello, Mama," said Kitty. But Maud's youngest daughter did not even pretend that she was pleased to see her.

"Hello, Kitty," said Maud. "How was the hunt?"

"Frightfully good. Fast and dangerous. Just the way I like it." She turned to her father. "Let me get you a cup of tea, Papa. After the day we've had, we both need to warm up." She laughed and Maud flinched; the affection between father and daughter was very apparent. She watched Bertie as the conversations in the room started up again and the awkwardness was lost in the murmur of voices. The last time she had seen him he had been fat and bloated and swollen with alcohol. Now he was slim, fit and clear-skinned. His hands didn't shake and his pale eyes were focused with the old intensity that had at first attracted her to him. He had been living well—and obviously very contentedly—without her.

A little while later Grace arrived with Sir Ronald and her father and the Shrubs were rescued from the snake by their gallant, who drew them away from the sofa to the window, where he was keen to show them the stars, which, he explained, were shining unusually bright this evening. "The temperature has dropped considerably," Ethelred said. "I believe it will snow."

"Oh, we love snow," said Hazel, thinking how romantic it would be to take a moonlit stroll around the gardens with Lord Hunt.

"We do indeed," Laurel agreed, wishing Hazel would entertain herself elsewhere so she and the silver wolf could gaze at the moon together. Lord Hunt sipped his tea and, in spite of their hopes, neither Shrub moved an inch.

Maud noticed how thin Grace was. She noticed too, much to her pleasure, that her old friend and rival was beginning to lose her beauty. She stood up and advanced. "My dear Grace," she said. "It's been much too long."

"Why, Maud. What a lovely surprise," said Grace with a faultless smile.

"I couldn't very well sit in London while my entire family is over here, celebrating without me."

"Of course not. You look well. London must suit you."

Maud smiled smugly. "Oh it does. But you, my dear, look a little thin. Being so terribly thin is very aging. Are you not eating?"

"I'm in fine health, thank you," Grace replied smoothly. "But this is the first time you have seen the castle since Celia bought it. Isn't it marvelous? I don't think there's a house in the whole of Ireland that can equal it. Everyone thinks so."

Maud stiffened. "I hope it doesn't all go horribly wrong," she said with an insincere frown. "Many a fortune has been wiped out due to the Crash. I hope theirs is secure. After all they've put into this place, it would be a great shame to lose it."

"You always were a positive person, Maud," said Grace.

"And you were always a dear friend, Grace," said Maud.

IT SNOWED THAT night. Thick white feathery flakes were released onto the frozen countryside by an army of cloud that advanced silently over the ocean under the cover of dark. The Deverills and their families slept undisturbed in their beds, oblivious of the flurry occurring right outside their windows. The castle was quiet, the winds had abated, the stars withdrawn; the snow fell softly and without a sound and yet, in the peaceful stillness, the spirits of Castle Deverill were restless; they sensed something terrible in the calm. And then, just as the first light of dawn glowed pink in the eastern sky, one of the men got up.

He dressed, taking care not to wake his sleeping wife. He buttoned his shirt and arranged his tie. He slipped into his jacket and shoes, making sure that his socks were pulled up beneath his trousers. His breathing was calm, his hand steady as he reached beneath the bed for the rope he had put there earlier. Without hesitation he crept to the door. He turned the knob without a squeak and stepped into the corridor. With the stealth of a cat he crept through the castle and out into the cold.

It was a beautiful dawn. The pink glow was turning golden right before his eyes as the sun heralded another day, cracking like a duck's egg onto the sky. He walked deliberately across the lawn, leaving a trail of indigo-colored footprints in the snow. The skies were clear now, the last of the stars peeping out from where the clouds had drifted away. Yet he was unmoved by it. He had a purpose and nothing would distract him from it. Neither the loveliness of the dawn nor the people he was going to leave behind. He was calm, resolute and relieved.

When he reached the tree, which was marked with a plaque that said *Planted by Barton Deverill 1662,* he climbed it with ease. He sat astride the branch that extended parallel to the ground and set about tying the rope around its girth. Making a noose was easy, he had enjoyed making knots as a boy. He pulled a flask out of his pocket and took a swig. The alcohol burned his throat and warmed his belly, giving him the last sense of pleasure he would experience on this earth. He didn't allow himself to feel sad or regretful: *that* might have prevented him from carrying out his plan. He thought of what he would have to face were he to continue living and knew, without any doubt, that death was preferable. Death was the only way out.

He put the noose around his neck and carefully rose to his feet with the slow agility of a tightrope walker. Pressing his hand against the trunk he held his balance. He lifted his eyes and gazed upon the castle one last time. The rising sun threw her rays upon the stone walls and like flames they slowly moved upward, consuming the purple shadows as they went. Soon it would be morning and the place would come to life. But now it was still and silent and ghostly somehow in the snow. He closed his eyes, lifted his hand off the tree and let himself fall. The rope gave a soft squeak as it jarred, then a rhythmic creaking as the body swayed a few feet off the ground.

A spray of crows took to the skies, their loud caws echoing through the woods with the eerie cry of the Banshee.

Chapter 18

Charlotte awoke to find Harry's side of the bed empty. She put her hand on his pillow. It was cold. He must have been up for a while. She clenched her fist. He was so distant these days, so aloof. She wondered whether their marriage would ever heal. Sometimes she thought that, after what she had witnessed, it simply couldn't. She dressed and went downstairs to the dining room where Digby, Celia, Beatrice and Maud were already having breakfast. The room smelled of fried bacon and her stomach gave a gentle rumble, although she didn't have much of an appetite nowadays.

"Ah, Charlotte," said Digby, smiling at her warmly. "I trust you slept well."

"Papa, the beds are the best money can buy. Of course she slept well," said Celia.

Charlotte glanced around the room for Harry. She had been so consumed by her own unhappiness that she hadn't given any thought to *his*. She wondered whether he'd gone out for an early walk in the snow and her heart lurched with remorse. He'd been spending a lot of time on his own lately.

"Isn't the snow marvelous!" said Beatrice.

"It's a sign of luck," said Celia with a contented sigh. "I'm feeling very lucky at the moment. This has been the best Christmas ever and the party we're going to enjoy on New Year's Eve will signal a prosperous year for all of us."

Digby raised an eyebrow. He didn't think 1930 was going to be a prosperous year for anyone, least of all himself. He shoveled a forkful of egg and toast into his mouth and chewed ponderously. Maud, who could always be relied on to be the voice of doom, added, "The country has just suffered the worst financial crisis in history. I can't imagine anyone is feeling particularly lucky right now, except you, Celia."

Celia rolled her eyes and was about to say something she'd regret when her mother thankfully came to her defense. "I think we are jolly lucky to be here, in this beautiful place, on such a lovely snowy morning. I don't know about you, but I'm going to go for a walk after breakfast to enjoy it."

There was a brief lull in the conversation as Victoria and Eric wandered in for breakfast, followed by Stoke, who looked as if he had given his sweeping white mustache a good brush. Amid the "Good mornings" and the courteous inquiries after the quality of their sleep, the butler appeared with a note on a tray. He hesitated a moment, unsure of whom to give it to. "What is it, O'Sullivan?" Celia asked.

"A letter, madam. It was on the table in the hall. But it isn't addressed to anybody."

"Well, bring it here," she instructed, waving her white fingers. She opened the envelope and pulled out a little typed card. As she read it her forehead creased in bafflement and her pretty lips pouted. "*I'm sorry.*"

"Darling?" said Beatrice.

"No, that's all it says: *I'm sorry,*" said Celia.

"Well, who's it from?" Digby demanded.

Celia turned over the note and then did the same with the envelope. "There's no name anywhere. Is this some kind of joke?" she looked from face to face crossly. "Because it isn't at all funny."

Charlotte burst into tears. "It's Harry," she choked. She pushed out her chair and stood with her hands at her throat, gasping for air. "It's Harry. I know it is. He's . . . he's . . ." She began to sob uncontrollably. Beatrice glanced uneasily at her daughter, who was staring at Charlotte in horror. Digby coughed into his napkin while Victoria looked appalled; this sort of emotional outburst simply wasn't done.

Maud blanched. "What's going on? What's happened to Harry? Charlotte, for goodness' sake, make some sense!"

Charlotte tried to pull herself together. "He . . . he wasn't in bed this morning. I don't know where he is."

"Let's not panic," said Eric, putting his plate of eggs, tomatoes and toast on the table and sitting down. "He's probably gone for a walk. It's a lovely morning."

"He's done something stupid. I can feel it," said Charlotte. "He's written the note and wandered off. I know he has."

"Then we must find him," said Digby, throwing his napkin on the table. "We must all search the grounds for Harry and no one is to resume breakfast until we find him."

Eric and Victoria sighed impatiently. "If ever there was a

storm in a teacup," said Victoria, but Maud was already making for the door. Stoke remained in his chair, watching in bewilderment as everyone left the room. In his late eighties he was hard of hearing and had consequently missed the entire conversation.

There was a terrible sense of urgency as news of Harry's disappearance and the cryptic note he'd typed spread swiftly around the castle. Digby put on his boots and coat and strode into the snow. He saw the footprints at once and set off in pursuit, a feeling of foreboding suddenly making him go quite weak in the knees. Beatrice, Maud, Celia and Charlotte ran after him, shouting for Harry at the top of their voices. The crows watched from the treetops, their black eyes shining with knowing.

"What on earth is he sorry about?" Maud asked Charlotte as they hurried after Digby. "I wish Digby wouldn't walk so fast. I'm sure this is nothing more than a false alarm. Harry's going to feel very silly when he comes back to find the entire castle looking for him."

Charlotte couldn't begin to tell Harry's mother about the night of Celia's Summer Ball. What if Harry felt his life wasn't worth living without Boysie? *Oh, God, what have I done?* She began to cry again. What if she had driven him to his death? Silently she prayed to any God who would listen to return her beloved Harry to her in one piece: *If he comes back I shall forgive him*, she promised, trudging through the snow. *He can see Boysie as much as he likes, as long as he's alive.*

Suddenly Digby spun around and began marching back toward them. His face was as red as a berry, his arms outstretched as if he was hoping to shield them from something he didn't want them to see. "Ladies, please go back to the castle," he said and his voice was fiercely commanding. Celia was suddenly assaulted by a wave of nausea. Behind her father, swinging from a tree, she could see the body of a man. She put a hand to her mouth and gasped. "Please. Beatrice, take the girls back to the castle," he repeated, more forcefully. In any other circumstance they would have done his bidding. But Celia, propelled by a sense of terror and dread, stubbornly strode past him, thrusting him out of the way with such vigor that he nearly fell over. Digby regained his balance and reached out a desperate hand to restrain her, but she was already running through the snow, her vision blinded by tears, her breathing labored and rasping. There, hanging pale and still like a sack of flour, was Archie.

Celia threw her arms around his legs in a vain attempt to lift him. A low moan escaped her throat as she struggled beneath the dead weight of her husband. At once her father was pulling at her, trying to unpeel her hands. His voice was soothing, encouraging, but all Celia could hear was the blood throbbing in her temples and the groans that rose up from her chest and were expelled in wild, unnatural sounds that were alien to her.

Beatrice was sobbing, Maud staring in shock at the dreadful scene unfolding before her, while Charlotte collapsed onto her knees in the snow and wept with relief. And then, amid the turmoil, Harry strode into view. They all turned to him in astonishment and Harry's eyes shifted to the limp body hanging from the noose and to Celia who was still clinging on to his legs, unaware that no amount of lifting could save him. He was long dead. Charlotte scrambled to her feet and fell against his chest. "Oh, Harry! I thought it was you!" she howled.

Harry wrapped his arms around his wife, but he couldn't take his eyes off Archie's blue face and broken neck. Slowly the full horror sank in.

At last Digby, with the help of Harry and Eric, who had been drawn to the scene by the commotion, managed to prize Celia off the body and take her back to the castle. Digby telephoned the Garda and the doctor, then he called the Hunting Lodge to inform Bertie of the dreadful news. "Good God!" Bertie swore. "What on earth made him do it?"

Digby sighed. "There's only one reason why a man in Archie's position would take his own life and that's money," he said. "I've got a horrible feeling that Celia is in for a rough ride."

"I'm coming right over," said Bertie, putting down the receiver.

It wasn't long before the entire family had assembled once again in the drawing room, muttering in low voices: "He had everything, why would he throw it all away?" "Did anyone notice he was unhappy?" "I don't think I'd ever seen Archie so content." "Appearances can be deceptive." "He must have been hiding something terrible." "Poor Celia, what's she going to do without him?"

Celia sat by the fire, wrapped in a blanket, drinking a glass of sherry. The glass trembled in her hand and her lips were quivering in spite of the warmth of the room. She was a pitiful sight, sobbing quietly. The woman who only moments before had been commenting on her good fortune was now grieving the loss of it. "He's ruined Christmas," she sniveled. "He's ruined my New Year's Eve party. How *could* he, Mama?"

Beatrice, who had drawn her daughter against her bosom and was stroking her hair as if she were a little girl again, turned to her older daughters and said, "She's in shock. Poor child." Leona and Vivien nodded, feeling guilty now for the animosity they had felt toward their younger sister who had appeared to have it all.

Kitty arrived with Robert. She flew to her cousin where she knelt at her feet and took her hands, squeezing them gently. "My darling Celia, I'm so sorry," she said.

Celia lifted her swollen eyes and smiled through a blur of tears. "We were so happy," she said numbly. "Archie was so happy. Castle Deverill and his family were his greatest achievements. He was so proud of it all. Why, when he was celebrating his success, did he feel the desire to run away? I don't understand. How could he do it to *me*?"

"He typed a note that said simply *I'm sorry*," Beatrice informed her. "It wasn't addressed to anybody. Isn't that an odd thing to do? Why didn't he write it in his hand and why didn't he explain himself?"

"He won't have been in his right mind," said Kitty wisely. "He won't have been thinking about you or his children. When people are that unhappy they think only of themselves."

"He didn't seem unhappy," said Leona.

"He seemed very happy," added Vivien.

"But he's left me a widow!" Celia stated sadly. She stopped crying as if the thought had only just then occurred to her. "I'm a widow. My children are fatherless. I am alone." And she was overcome by another wave of sobbing.

"You're not alone, darling," said Beatrice, pulling her deeper into her bosom. "You have all of us and we'll never leave you."

Kitty pulled a bag of green leaves out of her pocket and

thrust them in Beatrice's hand. "This is Adeline's cannabis," she told her. "Infuse it in tea. It will calm her down."

Augusta filled the doorway in her Victorian black dress and black shawl and stood for a long moment leaning on her stick and gazing around the room imperiously, searching for her granddaughter. When at last her eyes found her in her mother's arms by the fire, she waded through the throng that parted for her deferentially and ordered her husband, as she passed him, to bring her a very large glass of brandy "at once." She approached the sofa where Leona and Vivien were sitting and flicked her bejeweled fingers so that the two women vacated it at her command. Their grandmother dropped into the cushions and seemed to spread like a chocolate pudding until there was no space for anyone else on either side of her. Kitty, who was still at Celia's feet, moved herself to the club fender, where she duly sat alongside Leona and Vivien like one of a trio of birds on a perch.

"Well, my dear, this is a tragedy none of us could have foreseen," Augusta began gravely. "He was much too young to die. One never knows when the Grim Reaper is going to gather one, but to gather *oneself* is surely an act of the most selfish kind."

"Augusta," said Beatrice in a warning tone.

"I cannot hide my feelings, Beatrice. This young man has done a wicked, wicked thing. Celia does not deserve this. She has only ever been a good wife. Believe me, I have had moments in my life when I would rather not have woken up—but I would never have burdened my family with the shame or the misery. What on earth was he thinking?"

"We just don't know," said Beatrice, trying to be patient. She wished everyone would leave so that she and Celia could be alone together.

"Money," said Augusta with a snort. "A man only goes to such extremes over a woman or money. We can safely assume that it was not on account of a woman."

Celia sniffed. "He had pots of money, Grandma," she said.

"Well, we shall see," Augusta sniffed. She ran her eyes over all the expensive things in the room. "*This* just might have been his undoing," she said tactlessly, as her granddaughter dissolved once again into sobs.

The doctor arrived and Celia was taken upstairs by Kitty and her mother, where she was given valerian drops to calm her and put to bed, as Adeline had been the night Hubert was killed in the fire. "We're cursed," said Celia drowsily.

"We're not cursed," Kitty reassured her, sitting on the side of her bed and taking her hand. "Adeline used to say that I was a child of Mars and that my life would be full of conflict."

"Then I must be a child of Mars too," said Celia.

"You sleep now. Archie is all right where he is. You have to trust me on that. You are the one we need to look after now."

"Is he really all right? He's not still hanging from that tree?" Celia's eyes shone with fresh tears.

"He escaped that body before he even knew what was happening."

"But he's not going to rot in Hell . . . ?"

"God is love, Celia." She stroked the hair off her forehead. "And souls can't rot." She smiled tenderly at her cousin and remembered the long talks about life after death that she used to have with Adeline in her little sitting room that smelled of turf fire and lilac. "Archie was not a bad man. I suspect he took his life because he couldn't face the future. It is not a sin to lack courage. He'll be embraced by loving souls and shown the way home, I promise you." Celia's eyes grew heavy. She tried to speak but the words were lost on her tongue as she retreated into slumber.

Kitty returned to the drawing room. Everyone was talking in normal tones now that Celia was no longer in the room. "We will have to inform Archie's family," Bertie was saying, standing in a huddle with the other men.

"That's a responsibility I would not wish on my worst enemy," said Victoria from the sofa, where she was sitting beside her mother. She had lit a cigarette, which was placed in its elegant Bakelite holder, and was looking at Augusta, who had subsided on the sofa opposite and fallen asleep, her chins sinking into her bosom like a collapsing soufflé.

"I don't think I'll ever recover from the sight," said Maud weakly, sipping her second glass of sherry. "To think that might have been Harry."

"It wasn't Harry," said Victoria reasonably.

"But Charlotte put the fear of God into me," Maud continued. "What on earth was that all about, do you think?"

Victoria drew on her cigarette holder. "I haven't a clue. Perhaps they'd had a fight."

"Men don't write suicide notes because of a petty quarrel," said Maud. "I hope they're not in trouble. Our family can't cope with any more scandal." She looked up as Bertie took the place on the sofa beside her.

"I'm sorry you were frightened," he said softly. "Charlotte feels very bad for having scared you."

"Good," said Maud crisply. "Because she did. Silly girl, making a fuss about nothing."

"I suppose Harry's been suffering in silence," he said.

"Suffering? About what?" Maud asked.

"Losing his home. We've all had to put on a good show, but I dare say it hasn't been easy for any of us."

Maud dropped her gaze into her sherry. The sharp edges of her face softened a little as she let down her guard. Leona and Vivien had moved to the other end of the room and Augusta was still asleep, so they were alone, just the three of them. "No, I'm sure you're right," she said. "It hasn't been easy for anyone. Not even for me, who never really loved this place like you all do."

"That's what I thought." The tenderness in Bertie's voice took her by surprise.

"For all my stubbornness I mind dreadfully that Harry won't ever really be Lord Deverill of Ballinakelly as he ought to be, by right. The title's meaningless without the castle."

"I mind too, Mama," Victoria agreed. She grinned raffishly through the smoke. "We've all been very brave." She didn't feel it polite to add that, if the castle had been as comfortable before the fire as it was now, she would never have been so keen to leave it.

"I'm happy that you decided to come back," said Bertie, gazing at his wife with appreciation. "I'm only sorry that your stay has been marred by tragedy."

"We've endured a great deal of tragedy," said Maud, lifting her chin to show that she wasn't going to allow another to devastate her. "But we've survived. We'll continue as we always have. You Deverills are made of stronger stuff. I'm not, but you drag me along in your slipstream and that helps." She gave him a small smile. "Thank you, Bertie. Your concern is touching."

Bertie smiled back and Victoria wondered whether the embers of their marriage hadn't entirely been extinguished as she had thought.

Kitty's eyes strayed to one of the windows, where she could see a group of Gardai in their navy uniforms and peak caps carrying Archie's body across the lawn wrapped in a sheet. "Where's Digby?" Kitty asked as Robert joined her.

"In the library talking to the inspector. I dare say we'll find out shortly why he killed himself," said Robert. "He might have left a kinder note," he added. "Celia has no explanation, nothing."

"That's because he was too ashamed to articulate it."

"About what? Do you know something, Kitty?"

"I suspect he's lost all his money, like so many have. He couldn't bring himself to tell Celia that they have nothing left. I can't imagine why else he'd want to end his life. I'd put my money—the little I have of it—on shame."

"Good Lord. I hope she won't have to sell Castle Deverill."

"I hope not. If she does, then we're all in trouble."

Robert took her hand and smiled affectionately. "Whatever happens, Kitty, we'll be all right. We'll weather anything that's thrown at us because we're united and strong."

HARRY LATER FOUND Charlotte in their bedroom. She was sitting at the dressing table, brushing her long strawberry blond hair with a silver brush. "I was wondering where you had got to. I'm sorry. I should have been more attentive."

"Come and sit down," she said, replacing the brush on the dressing table and turning around on her stool. "I have something important I want to say."

Harry pulled up a chair and sat facing her. He dreaded that she was going to request a divorce. He didn't think his mother would survive divorce, especially after the horrors of today.

Charlotte gazed at him and he noticed that her blue eyes had softened like water in springtime. They were no longer frozen with resentment but glowing with warmth. "I thought it was *you* who had hanged yourself today," she said quietly.

"Oh my darling. Do I look so miserable?"

She smiled sadly. "Yes, you do. When I saw the empty bed and then heard what was in the note, I assumed that you had gone and done something stupid. So I made a bargain with God."

"What sort of bargain?"

"I told him that if you were alive I would forgive you and let you see Boysie again."

"Charlotte—" he began.

"Don't interrupt. I've thought about this a great deal. I love you, Harry. I wouldn't have been so hurt if I didn't love you. I'm sure that you love me too, in your own way."

"I do," he replied.

"But I know you don't love me in the way that you love Boysie. It's not conventional, but it's not for me to judge you. Love is a wonderful thing, wherever it flows." She looked down at her hands, which were folded neatly in her lap. "I don't know whether Deirdre is aware of how Boysie feels about *you*. Perhaps she knows and it is *I* who have been naïve. But I'm not going to be naïve any longer. I love Boysie too. I'm unhappy that he is not in our life anymore. I miss him."

"Oh Charlotte . . ." Harry unfolded her hands and took

them in his. "I do love you. Do you think there's room in our marriage for the three of us?"

She laughed and blinked away the tears, all except for one, which glistened in her long eyelashes. "I think there is," she said.

The irony was, that in that moment of magnanimity, Harry realized that he loved his wife more than he had known.

Chapter 19

B ridie's happiness was complete. She was engaged to the dashing Count Cesare di Marcantonio and living in a city drunk on optimism, opportunity and rising wealth. America shared her confidence. President Hoover foresaw a day when poverty would be wiped out; economists defined a "new plateau" of prosperity and predicted that the country's affluence was here to stay; ordinary people believed they couldn't go wrong buying stocks and everyone, from the shoeshine boy to the wealthiest men in the city, played the Stock Market. Bridie sang along to Irving Berlin's "Blue Skies" with the other New Yorkers who believed they had at last reached the pot of gold at the end of the rainbow, and she spent with the extravagance of someone who believes that pot to be bottomless. She ignored Beaumont Williams's warnings of an imminent crash, but Beaumont, so right about most things, was right about this.

The Crash, when it happened, was devastating, falling as it did from such a great height. Bridie listened to the wireless and read the newspapers and her first thoughts were for herself. She never wanted to return to the poverty of her youth. "How does this affect me?" she asked Mr. Williams as she settled into the familiar leather chair in his office in front of the fire, which had not been lit on account of the warm autumn weather.

"It doesn't," he replied, crossing his legs to reveal a slim ankle and a crimson sock. "I took the liberty of instructing your broker to buy you out before the panic-selling," he explained casually, as if his ingenuity were but a trifle. "You might recall that I have been expecting this for months. Stocks have been grossly overvalued for years and I decided you should take your profits. Rothschild wisely said, 'Leave the last ten percent to someone else.' You're richer than ever, Mrs. Lockwood." Indeed with unemployment rising, farms failing and automobile sales falling he wasn't the only person to sense the oncoming of disaster, but he was certainly one of the few to act in time to avoid it.

Bridie flushed with gratitude. "Why, Mr. Williams, I don't know what to say . . ."

"Your husband, Mr. Lockwood, was a shrewd man. He invested much of your fortune in gold. I predict that the gold market will recover." He opened a leather book and rested it on his knee. Then he pulled his spectacles out of his breast pocket and settled them on the bridge of his nose. "I suggest we arrange a meeting with your broker, but in the meantime I requested that he send round your portfolio to put your mind at rest. As you will see, Mrs. Lockwood, your money has been wisely invested in short-term bonds to the U.S. government, in prime property and land. I am not one to heap praise upon myself, but in this instance, I might concede that I have, indeed, been canny."

Bridie listened as Mr. Williams ran through figures and funds she barely understood. The only words that mattered to her were "gains," "interest" and "the bottom line." She watched this self-contained man, with his round belly fastened behind a pristine gray waistcoat, his clean, tidy hands and manicured nails, closely shaven face and shiny black hair and felt a flood of gratitude that she was in the care of such a sensible man. If it hadn't been for Mr. Williams, where would she be now, she wondered. What she didn't ask herself was where Mr. Williams would be without *her*—his prosperity, and he was most certainly prosperous, was more closely linked to hers than she had ever imagined.

"As you can see, Mrs. Lockwood, you have nothing to worry about. New York can crash about your ears, but you will still be one of the few people left standing."

"I am very much in your debt," she said, watching him close the book and place it on the table in front of him. She lifted her left hand and admired the diamond ring that glittered there.

"That's a very fine ring," said Mr. Williams. "May I?" He reached for her hand, drew it toward him and held it in the light. He knew a thing or two about diamonds and he could see, even without a loupe, that this one was of poor quality. "When are you going to tie the knot?"

"We haven't set a date," Bridie told him, her face glowing with happiness. "It's all happened so fast. I need to catch my breath. Cesare wants to marry as soon as possible."

"Does he indeed," said Mr. Williams, rubbing his chin thoughtfully. But Bridie was too excited to hear the concern in his voice. "Might I give you a word of advice?" he asked. Considering the amount of money he had saved her she didn't feel she was in any position to refuse.

"Of course," she replied.

"Take your time. There's no rush to marry again. Get to know the man. Meet his friends and family. After all, getting *into* marriage is much easier than getting *out* of it."

Bridie smiled and shook her head vigorously. "Oh, I know what it looks like, Mr. Williams. Of course I do. I don't know anything about him, do I? But I followed my head with Walter and look where it got me. This time I will follow my heart. Life is not worth living without love. I know that now. I can be as rich as a Rockefeller, but if I don't have love I have nothing. I do believe I have found my soulmate."

Beaumont observed her keenly. She was quite a different woman to the one she had been two years ago when she was pining for her Irishman and searching for solace in gin. Her cheeks were now flushed with the blush of a first love, her eyes shone with good health and optimism, her demeanor was both confident and satisfied, and Beaumont realized that it didn't matter whether this count was genuine or not, because Bridie loved him. After all she had been through: a life of drudgery in the service of Mrs. Grimsby, marriage to the aged Walter Lockwood, widowed at twenty-five, deserted by the Irishman she believed she loved—and those were only the facts he knew, what shadows lurked in her deeper past could only be guessed at—he realized that she deserved a taste of happiness.

"I wish you luck, Mrs. Lockwood," he said, settling back into his chair.

"Thank you, Mr. Williams," she replied and because she

was so intoxicated with infatuation, she was oblivious to Mr. Williams's reservations. However, Beaumont Williams was not a passive man. When there was something that troubled him he wasted no time in getting to the bottom of it.

Count Cesare di Marcantonio was an enigma. If Bridie knew little about him, his friends and acquaintances in New York knew even less. But Beaumont Williams had contacts in both Italy and Argentina and after a gentle digging in the right places, he was able to throw some light into the Count's murky corners. "He was born in Abruzzo, somewhere in Italy," Elaine told Bridie over lunch in Lucio's, a small restaurant on Fifth Avenue where the owner, a bearded Italian with a gift for making women feel special, always gave them the best table by the window. "But his family is really very aristocratic. His mother is a princess whose family is descended from the family of one of the popes, Barberini I think they're called, but I can't for the life of me remember which pope he was. Their names all sound the same, don't you think?"

"Go on," said Bridie, elegant in a fashionable cloche hat, olive-green dress and a string of shiny pearls that hung down to her waist.

"No one knows exactly why, but the family moved to Argentina when your count was a child. It sounds a little dubious if you ask me. They simply vanished into the night. I suspect it had something to do with owing money. Anyhow, his father is one of those men who makes a fortune, then loses it just as quickly, only to make it again. He made his first fortune in beef, then in industry, investing in railways. He bought estates and cattle, exporting the beef around the world. That's what Beaumont found out."

"And now?" Bridie asked.

Elaine shrugged. "His father, Count Benvenuto, is a notorious character in Buenos Aires. He lives the high life, takes risks investing in pipe dreams and squanders his money on his mistresses and gambling. His reputation is not entirely snow-white. Who's to say whether he's managed to hold on to his fortune or whether he's never really had one. Beaumont suspects the latter and wishes to warn you that not everything about your count is, as we say in New York, kosher." Bridie put down her knife and fork and looked thoughtful for a moment. Elaine felt bad and rushed in to soothe her doubts. "I'm not saying your Cesare is after your money, Bridget," which was exactly what she *was* saying. "But he surrounds himself with rich people who are happy to absorb him into their world. He's undoubtedly charming, entertaining and no one loves a foreign title more than the Americans." She sniffed apologetically and glanced at her friend a little fearfully. "We thought it better that you know *before* you tie the knot."

But Bridie smiled with indulgence, as if she were a parent who had just been told of her child's latest antics by a worried teacher. "I don't care about his family history, Elaine. I don't care where he comes from. God knows that *I* come from nothing. What have I got to be proud of: a farmhouse that was sinking into the mud, a few cows and barely enough food to sustain us? I didn't own a pair of shoes until I went to work at the castle. Cesare can be penniless and destitute and descended from peasants for all I care. It makes no difference to the way I feel about him. If his father's gambled all his money away, I have enough for the two of us. If he's a womanizer, I'll make him faithful. If he's an adventurer I'll give him the adventure of a lifetime. Love will carry us like the wind and our feet will never touch the ground." And there was nothing Elaine could say after that.

Bridie closed her ears and her eyes to Count Cesare's obvious faults. To her there had never lived a man more handsome and romantic and kind. Love blinded her to his arrogance and to his shameless pursuit of the rich and powerful, to his vanity and his unwavering belief in his own success. She gazed into his sea-green eyes and felt the light of his adoration reach the darkest parts of her being, reviving them like neglected gardens that are suddenly bathed in sunshine, bringing them into blossom and flower. She didn't need gifts; she needed love. And Cesare had enough of that to quench her most voracious thirst.

Cesare's charisma was so bright that it reduced to ashes any residual feelings of affection that she had for Jack O'Leary. It consumed her longing for Ireland and even quelled her yearning for her son. It raised her out of her past and carried her into a present moment where she believed that nothing and no one could ever hurt her again. Cesare would look after her now and she gladly gave him her heart. *Take it,* she told him silently as he sank his face into her neck, *and do with it what you will because I am yours and always will be.*

The wedding date was set for May, but as it was Bridie's second wedding, Marigold Reynolds had offered to host the ceremony and subsequent party in the lavish gardens of her house in Southampton. As the undisputed society queen, Marigold was only too happy to arrange another sumptuous event to which she could invite the newest stars of film, theater, media, society and sport. The Wall Street Crash might have curtailed many people's spending, but it had done little to curtail hers.

The invitations were engraved on the finest card, written in the most beautiful calligraphy and hand-delivered to the three hundred guests by one of the Reynoldses' chauffeurs.

As America descended into the most shocking economic decline in its history Bridie and Count Cesare enjoyed the happiest of engagements. They were the toast of New York and most of society welcomed a respite from the depressing news that filled the newspapers and radio waves. They began to look for a new house, which wasn't difficult as prices plummeted and those who had suddenly, from one day to the next, lost their fortunes found themselves having to sell their homes. Bridie found herself spoiled for choice.

"My darling, I need to speak with you," said Cesare, taking her hand across the dinner table in Jack and Charlie's 21 restaurant on West 52nd Street, a famous speakeasy with a secret system of levers which, in the event of a raid, tipped the shelves of the bar, sending the bottles of liquor crashing into the city's sewers.

Bridie looked concerned. "What about?"

"Money," he replied, bathing her in Latin love and shameless affection. His eyes were moist and tender, and Bridie squeezed his hand encouragingly. "My father is being difficult," he explained. "I have asked him for money but—"

In that accent, with those eyes, from those lips, money didn't sound vulgar or suspicious. It was just a gorgeous request from a gorgeous man and she wished to satisfy him immediately.

"My darling, dearest Cesare," Bridie interrupted. "I have money enough for the two of us. We don't need your father's money. I will talk to Mr. Williams, my attorney, and arrange for an account to be set up in your name and for money to be put directly into it the moment we are married. We will share everything."

Cesare tried to disguise his relief with a look of horror. "But Count Cesare di Marcantonio, descendant of the family of Pope Urban VIII, cannot accept money from a woman. It is a husband's duty to look after his wife."

Bridie held his hand tighter. "I came from nothing, Cesare. I began in Ireland as Bridie Doyle, a maid to a grand lady who lived in a castle. I came here to make a new start and worked for a wealthy old woman who died and left me a great fortune. I have been lucky. Please let me share my luck with you. I love you, Cesare. You've made me happier than I could ever have believed possible."

"It is against my nature. I cannot accept."

"Well, it is not against mine. I have suffered, God knows I have suffered, but you have restored my belief in love."

"I will write to my father again . . ."

"If you wish. But let's eat and enjoy our evening and talk no more about money."

He threaded his fingers through hers and his eyes fell heavily upon her. "I cannot wait to make love to you," he said with a smile that snatched her breath. "You are a beautiful woman and you are soon to be mine. I will take my time and explore every inch of you." He lowered his voice and leaned closer. "And when I am finished, I will do it all over again." And Bridie fell dreamily into his gaze and thought that she would buy him the world, he only had to ask.

In May the spring sunshine brought the fruit trees into blossom and warm breezes carried their pink and white petals through the streets like confetti. Yet, in spite of the change of season, the mood in the city was desperate. With growing un-employment and poverty, the atmosphere was somber, anxious and simmering with anger. However, the Great Depression hadn't reached the Reynoldses' house in Southampton. On the first Saturday of the month the road to their house was congested with chauffeur-driven Cadillacs, Chryslers and Bugattis bringing the grand and celebrated guests to the wedding. Among them were Beaumont and Elaine Williams, the only true friends Bridie had in New York. Everyone else was glitter and sparkle—people she knew would melt away at the first sign of her decline. But she didn't care, for today she was marrying the man she loved.

She wrote a brief letter to tell her family that she was marrying again but omitted to mention his aristocratic title. She didn't want them assuming that she had married him just for that. She posted the letter, then forgot all about them. She was so detached from her old life that she barely gave them a thought. Distance didn't dim her memory, infatuation did. While she was in Count Cesare's brilliance the shadows of her past could not reach her. Dressed in an ivory Chanel dress, covered in pearls and beads and sparkling in the sunlight, she walked down the aisle of white roses to where the manifestation of all her dreams stood waiting to take possession of her. Mr. Williams stood in for her father and handed her to the Count, while Elaine walked ahead as her maid of honor. Marigold sat at the front, satisfied that all the most prominent writers, actors and socialites from New York were there. But Bridie saw only Cesare. She took his outstretched hand and stepped in beside him. The priest read the vows, which they both repeated, and then it was over and the party began. Everyone drank champagne and ate from the bountiful feast and danced beneath the flower moon that rose over Long Island, pink in the light of the setting sun.

Cesare held his bride and bent his head to kiss her. The celebrations continued around them but they were a small island, rising out of the revelers who seemed to have forgotten that the party had anything to do with them. "My darling wife," he said softly. "You are now Contessa di Marcantonio, wife of Conte Cesare di Marcantonio who is descended from the family of Pope Urban VIII, Maffeo Barberini. The Barberini family coat of arms is three bees. I would like you to wear *this*, because now *you* are a Barberini too and I want the world to know it." He opened his hand to reveal a small gold bee brooch. Bridie gazed at it in awe. The magnitude of this man's ancestry made her light-headed and she swayed. Cesare slipped his fingers beneath the fabric of her dress, just beneath her collarbone, and attached the bee. "Beautiful," he said, leaving his fingers resting against her skin. Bridie saw from the way he was looking at her that he cherished her. She understood from the sleepy look in his eyes that he wanted her.

They crept away as soon as they could and closed the bedroom door behind them. The room was semi-dark, the sound of music muted by the closed windows and curtains, the air thick with the sweet smell of narcissi that Marigold had put in their room for their wedding night. Gently Cesare unhooked the back of her dress until it floated down her body, landing in a silky puddle at her feet. Bridie stood in her slip and panties, the sheen of her bare skin standing out against the silk of her lingerie. He caressed her shoulders with a light touch, then her neck, then her face, reaching behind her head to unpin her hair, scrunching it in his hands as it was released in glossy waves to fall about her body. She trembled as he lifted her slip and pulled down her panties. She stood naked before him and he admired her with lustful eyes.

Bridie had enjoyed many men, some of whom had given her satisfaction while others had been a disappointment, but Cesare took the time to pleasure her in a way that none of her lovers ever had—and he knew things that made even Bridie, with her unabashed approach to sexual gratification, blush. True to his word he explored every inch of her body, and when he was finished, he went over it once more. He brought Bridie to great heights of exultation. She moaned and murmured, sighed and finally wept as she discovered a carnal heaven made possible by her skillful and masterful lover.

If Cesare felt emasculated by Bridie's money he didn't show it. On the contrary, he lived up to his name conquering her like a sexual Julius Caesar. He was as adept in the bedroom as any man could be. The new Countess di Marcantonio relinquished control and let him take her by the hand, and *that* gave her the most exquisite pleasure of all.

Chapter 20

Connecticut

When Pam Wallace discovered that she was pregnant in the summer of 1927 she went straight to church, threw herself on her knees and thanked God for his divine intervention, for surely such a miracle, longed for and yet so elusive, had come directly from Him. She wept with joy, vowed to show her thanks with acts of charity and kindness (and never say a mean thing about anyone ever again), then hurried home to tell her husband the wonderful news.

Martha didn't know what all the fuss was about. It was as if something extraordinary had happened. Something *otherworldly.* Suddenly her mother was treated as if she was so fragile that any sudden movement might break her. She glided about the house slowly, like an invalid, but one enormously satisfied with her sickness. She moved from table to chair, chair to stair,

stair to door, making sure that her hand always had somewhere to settle in order to steady herself, just in case she tripped, and everyone did everything for her, telling her over and over again to rest "for the baby." Larry bought her flowers and jewelry in pretty red boxes, and even her father, Raymond Tobin, visited, armed with gifts, offering reconciliation. The whole house smelled like a florist's, which excited Martha far more than the thought of a baby because she adored flowers. She hovered over the petals like a bee drunk on nectar, marveling at the vibrant colors and inhaling the sweet perfume. Everyone patted her on the head and told her how lucky she was to be getting a little brother or sister and Martha secretly hoped that the baby would stay inside her mama's tummy forever, because she was very happy on her own.

The only member of the family who took the news badly, as if it were a personal affront, was Joan, who had relished the fact that Pam's child was adopted and by consequence "strange." Now that her sister-in-law was going to give birth to a genuine Wallace, Joan's competitiveness made her irritable. "I wonder if Martha will be Ma's favorite grandchild after Pam's baby is born," she said to Dorothy as they wandered around a fashionable boutique, browsing the summer dresses.

"I'm afraid I think Martha will be all but ignored once the baby arrives, poor darling," Dorothy replied. "Ted is a tribal man, for him blood is thicker than *everything*, and Diana will dote on the new arrival, because to have her own child is what Pam has wanted from the very beginning."

She has always had everything she wants, Joan thought sourly. *How galling that she's now going to get* this. Joan pulled a crimson dress off the rail and stood in front of the long mirror, holding it against her. "I have nothing against Martha. She's a child and she's very . . . sweet." It took some effort to utter the word "sweet." "I hope it's a boy. All men want sons and Larry's no different from anyone else. He'll be terribly disappointed if it's a girl." She cocked her head. "What do you think?"

"That color looks stunning," Dorothy gushed. "Why don't you try it on?"

"You don't think it clashes with my hair? I don't usually wear red."

"Oh Joan, you can get away with anything."

"That *is* true, of course. You don't think Pam will see me in it and want one too. Crimson is a better color for her and I don't want her showing me up."

"Really, Joan, you are infinitely more stylish than Pam. You know what they say about copying?"

"That it's the greatest form of flattery." She sighed. "Well, I'm not flattered, just bored. I've endured years of having her echoing my every fashion choice." She smiled with satisfaction. "At least she'll be in maternity dresses for the foreseeable future!"

Martha did not feel ignored during her mother's pregnancy because Pam was careful to include her daughter in every stage of the baby's growth. She encouraged Martha to put her hand on her belly to feel the baby moving inside. She reassured her that when babies come into the world they bring their own love with them so that there is always plenty to go around. "I won't love you less because I love this child," she told her. "I'll just have double the amount of love." Although Martha was too young to be conscious of her emotions, she began to feel secure in her mother's liking. For the first time in her life her mother's eye was not full of scrutiny and apprehension and the sucking in of her affection faded into an unpleasant memory so that, over the months before the baby was born, Martha ceased to look out for it.

Mrs. Goodwin noticed Martha's growing confidence. She was like a spring bud that had just begun to open, revealing the delicate pink and white petals inside. The atmosphere in the house became light and soft, like early evening sunshine. Pam was happy all the time. She lay on a daybed in the conservatory reading books and magazines and talking on the telephone to her friends. Ladies came to visit and drank iced tea. They shared the gossip and listened to Pam's plans for the decoration of the new baby's nursery. Martha was brought in like a little show pony and the women admired her floral frocks and commented on how much she had grown. Mrs. Goodwin was relieved that the business of Martha's imaginary friends was forgotten. It seemed that Martha had forgotten them too. She had not mentioned them since seeing the doctor and when she played in the garden on her own she no longer talked to herself or tried to catch invisible things that apparently flew about the flower beds. Fortunately, she didn't appear to suffer from their absence.

When at last the baby girl arrived in the spring of the following year the house was once again filled with flowers and gifts. Grandma Wallace, aware that Martha might be put out by all the attention her new sister was getting, brought Martha an exquisite doll's house that was the finest thing she had ever been given. It had a sweeping staircase, a grand entrance hall and nine rooms, all decorated with pretty floral wallpapers. Her mother gave her the miniature pieces of furniture, cutlery and crockery and she told Martha that the family of dolls that were to live there was a gift from the baby, who was keen to be a good friend to her sister. Martha believed her and was sure that when she was older she would make a very good friend indeed.

The baby was christened Edith and no expense was spared for this child who was so very precious to her mother. Only Pam's parents and Larry's family knew why Pam put the crib by her bed and lay on her side for hours, staring into her daughter's face. She could see Larry in Edith's features, her father about the eyes and something of her mother in the feminine pout of her lips. When Larry's family came to visit she relished pointing out the similarities to them. Especially to Joan, who bristled like a threatened cat and grudgingly handed over the gift she had bought. "She looks just like Larry," she said, peering into the crib. "I don't see you in there at all."

"Neither do I," said Pam, who didn't need to see herself in her child for she knew very well who had birthed her.

"The irony is that Martha looks more like *you*. This child is going to be fair-haired like Larry."

"She's a Tobin, Joan, as much as she's a Wallace."

Joan sniffed and sat down. "Does it feel different?"

"Does *what* feel different?"

"Having a child who is biologically yours. Do you love her more?"

Pam was affronted. "That's a horrible thing to say, Joan."

"Don't be oversensitive. It's natural to love your own child more than an adopted one, don't you think?"

"No, I *don't* think. I love Martha as much as I love Edith. It makes no difference." Joan pulled a face that suggested she didn't believe her. "You may think what you like, Joan. Perhaps *you* would love your biological child more than your adopted one were you in my position, but I'm not you. Edith has been given to me; I searched the world for Martha."

"That's a little exaggerated, even for you, Pam."

"I longed for Martha and God led me to Ireland. She was meant to belong to me from the moment she came into the world. I could not love her more."

Joan put up her hands. "All right, don't get so upset. I was only asking. Really, Pam, you're so sensitive."

"I'm not sensitive. Anyone would be offended by what you're implying."

"Trust me, it's what everyone will be thinking. Only I have the courage to say it."

"Or the lack of tact," Pam snapped. She watched Joan light a cigarette and lean back in her chair, crossing her legs. She was wearing a stunning crimson dress that clashed with her hair. Pam wondered how she could find out where she had bought it and whether they'd have another one for *her*.

MRS. GOODWIN DID not doubt that Mrs. Wallace loved her two daughters equally, but right from the very beginning Edith was indulged in a way that Martha had never been. It wasn't that Edith was more spoiled—both girls had never been denied anything on a material level—it was the way her parents responded to her behavior that was different. While Martha had always had to be mindful of her manners, aware that her every move was scrutinized by a mother so desperate for her daughter to impress and fit in, Edith could behave as she wanted and only Mrs. Goodwin ever pulled her up when she misbehaved. Things for which Martha would have been severely chastised

Edith could do with impunity. Nothing she did was ever "wrong" in her parents' eyes. She could holler and stamp her little foot, sulk, suck her thumb, spill her food, interrupt and make demands and her parents would laugh, wink at each other and make comments that they had never made about Martha: *She's so like Ma*, they would say. Or, *She's inherited her stubbornness from Grumps*. Mrs. Goodwin noticed, for the difference was stark and it saddened her, for while Martha might be too young to *see* it, she was certainly not too young to *feel* it; small children are quick to sense injustice and know things without ever being told. As little Edith grew from a toddler to a child, she was fast becoming insufferable, but her parents seemed not to notice, or chose not to care. She was their flesh and blood and their wonder at the miracle of her conception blinded them to the fact that she was growing up to be a very unpleasant child indeed.

Mrs. Goodwin tried hard to redress the balance when Mrs. Wallace was not at home. Every time Edith, now nearly three years old, took something of Martha's, she made her give it back. She was told to sit up straight, to eat with her mouth closed, not to answer back, interrupt or be rude. When she refused to share she was told she would be punished if she didn't. But Mrs. Goodwin's punishments were never severe. She'd make Edith sit on a chair in the corner or send her to her room. However, nothing seemed to correct the child's behavior because she believed herself above the laws that governed her nanny's domain. She knew she could get away with anything when her mother was around—and she was right. Mrs. Goodwin tried to keep the girls in the nursery, but Edith would escape and run through the house in search of her mama, howling her eyes out and screaming at the top of her lungs. Pam would blanch, gather her daughter into her arms and soothe her with promises and bribes and, every time she did so, Edith's belief in her preeminence grew a little stronger. Mrs. Goodwin felt a sense of helplessness. There was no doubt in the nanny's mind whom *she* loved the most.

If Martha noticed that her sister was treated differently, she made no comment. Now that she was no longer on her own she wanted very badly to find a friend in her sibling. She relished having the company of another child. Since she was six years older, she took pleasure in teaching Edith how to draw and paint and play the piano and violin. She taught her about flowers, butterflies and birds and never tired of playing games. As Edith grew she became more difficult but Martha was patient and always let her choose which character she wanted to enact and which game she wanted to play. Mrs. Goodwin tried to encourage Martha to be firm with her, not to allow her to always take the lead, but Martha was too gentle and kind and Edith's forceful character triumphed every time.

Then one afternoon at their grandmother's house, Diana Wallace took Pam aside. "My darling, don't you think Edith is becoming a little out of control?"

Pam was immediately affronted. Criticizing Edith was akin to criticizing *her*. "I don't know what you're talking about," she replied.

"Martha is so beautifully mannered and well behaved, but Edith is . . ." She hesitated. "Well, to be quite frank, she's wild." Pam didn't know what to say. In her eyes Edith was perfect. "Darling, I'm not blaming you. I'm simply suggesting that perhaps Mrs. Goodwin is not doing her job properly. If you don't enforce discipline when she's young, you'll create a monstrous adult. I fear Edith is growing up without boundaries. Bad manners are very unattractive."

Pam was hurt. "She's got character, that's all," she protested.

"Too much character, Pam," Diana replied sternly. "If she can't learn to behave you will have to leave her at home. Children who don't mind their manners should not be exposed to polite society."

Now she had Pam's attention. Having been so proud of her angelic-looking child, who was a true Tobin-Wallace, Pam worried that she wasn't fit to be seen. She was pretty, of that there was no dispute. Her heart-shaped face and cornflower-blue eyes were certainly engaging and her fair hair was long and silky like the mane of a unicorn. Her skin was as white as milk and as smooth as satin and her smile, on the rare occasions that she gave one, was enchanting. But Pam was astute enough to know that if her manners were distasteful she might as well be ugly on the outside as well.

"I will discipline her," she told her mother-in-law resolutely. "She's young and she's smart. She'll learn quickly."

"Perhaps you need a tougher nanny," Diana Wallace suggested. "Mrs. Goodwin is getting on, after all." But Pam had no intention of putting her precious child in the hands of someone she didn't know—and Mrs. Goodwin, who had come to America with them from London, was quite strict enough.

But in spite of Pam's intentions Edith still managed to have her way in everything. Having told Mrs. Goodwin to be firm, Pam then berated her for being *too* firm. Edith, although small, was an arch manipulator. She knew how to win over her mother. She was well aware of the effect her tears had and if she pushed out her bottom lip at the same time it was even more dramatic. Her mother couldn't bear her sorrow, not for a minute. As for her father, he came home late, sometimes too late to put her to bed. But on weekends she would curl up on his lap and there she was safe from Mrs. Goodwin's discipline and her grandmother's disapproving stare, because he loved her just the way she was.

Edith grew jealous of her sister's place in Grandma's heart. Diana Wallace made no secret of the fact that Martha was special to her. Joan and Dorothy could push their children forward as much as they liked, but when Diana settled her gaze on Martha it was apparent for all to see that she reserved her most tender looks for *her.* Edith was not used to being marginalized—she very much felt at the center of her parents' affection—and, as a consequence, her behavior around her grandmother only deteriorated further. Martha had every reason to be jealous of Edith but envy was not in her nature, and, in spite of their differences, Martha made every concession to be her friend.

Instead of admiring her older sister as younger siblings do, Edith was jealous of Martha. Her mother had conditioned her to believe that she was special and this only served to encourage her to resent any attention that Martha was given, from their grandmother or otherwise. Edith was only a child and her small acts of sabotage and rebellion were as ripples on the water by the feet of a gnat, but as she grew older her feet would grow bigger and the ripples would turn to great splashes of destruction.

ADELINE WAS NO longer in Martha's awareness. The child had shut her out and by the force of her will Adeline's image had receded and her voice grown distant until she was only a sensation, like a gust of wind or a ray of sunshine, which Martha chose not to feel. Yet Adeline did not desert her; Martha was a Deverill. The blood of her kin and the waters of Ireland ran in her veins. Deep in the heart of her heart Martha knew who she was. She knew where she came from. Only she had forgotten. One day, Adeline was certain, the mists of oblivion would lift and she would reconcile the longings in her soul with the land she had lost. Ireland would call to her and she would return home.

In the meantime her grandmother watched her with a keen and concerned eye. Martha loved nature, just as Adeline did, and as much as she attempted to interest her sister in the flora and fauna in the garden Edith had no sensibility for beauty. Her father bought his daughters ponies but Edith was frightened to mount. She screamed and she wriggled and she refused to be put in the saddle. But Martha found a part of herself she had left behind on the hills of Ballinakelly and felt at home with her feet in the stirrups and her hands on the reins and the feeling of the wind raking its fingers through her hair. She had no idea that her biological father had been one of the finest huntsmen in County Cork but Adeline did, and she smiled with pride as this child exhibited the Deverill spirit that was hidden in her core. Pam feared she would fall off, but Martha had never felt as safe as she did in the saddle and everyone marveled at her courage and her daring and at the speed with which she learned to master her pony.

On the outside Martha was a product of her adoptive mother. Like Pam she was dressed with polish and like Pam her movements were self-conscious and deliberate. Too much grooming had robbed her of any spontaneity and vivaciousness. She was studied, polite, gracious and always a little apprehensive. Caution was not a Deverill trait—perhaps it was a Doyle characteristic, but Adeline did not remember Bridie Doyle. However, when Martha was among nature, the magic in the trees and flowers, the twittering of birds and the buzzing of bees released something within her. She felt joy, unrestrained and profound, and Adeline knew that where Edith would only ever be aware of the superficial veneer of things, Martha was aware of the deeper mysteries inherent in the natural wonders of the world. That she had inherited from her.

"MARTHA, COME INSIDE," Mrs. Goodwin shouted from the window. "It's time for your bath." Martha, who was lying on the lawn, reading a book of poetry, sighed regretfully.

"Can't I stay out for a little longer?" she asked. "Please."

Mrs. Goodwin smiled indulgently. She looked at her watch. "Very well then," she replied. "But you must come in fifteen minutes."

"I promise." Martha rolled onto her back and gazed up at the sky. The sun was setting behind the trees and she could see it blazing like a golden ball melting into the earth. Above, the clouds were pink feathers drifting slowly on a sea of blue. She crossed her feet and put her hands behind her head and watched the pink turn to a dusty shade of indigo. The air was warm, midges hovered in clouds of gray, roosting birds sung noisily from the branches and the breeze brought with it the faint but distinct smell of the ocean. She frowned at the image that passed fleetingly through her mind, so quickly she almost missed it. She saw a coastline with high cliffs and rocks and great waves crashing against the shore. She didn't know where it had come from but it was as if a memory had been unleashed within her. Before she could dwell on it a moment longer it had dissolved, like foam, and above her the twinkling of the first star shone brightly. Reluctantly she pushed herself up and wandered inside.

Adeline watched her go. "Ireland is calling you home, my child," she said, but her voice was a whisper that was lost on the wind. "Ireland is where you belong and where you shall one day be. Love binds you to it and will eventually carry you there. I have all the time in the world to see that it is done."

Chapter 21

Ballinakelly, 1930

Mrs. Doyle sat in her usual rocking chair beside the hearth while the hunched and wizened figure of her mother, Old Mrs. Nagle, was barely noticeable in the chair opposite. Now in her late seventies and almost blind, the elderly lady toyed with her rosary beads and mumbled prayers through toothless gums while she shrank a little farther into the black dress that almost swamped her. Michael stood in the middle of the room, filling it with his physical bulk. In his hands he held a letter. He glanced at Sean and his pregnant wife, Rosetta, who sat at the table, waiting to hear Bridie's news from America, then returned his black eyes to the letter and began to read.

Dearest Mam, Nanna, Michael, Sean and Rosetta

I hope this finds you all in good health. I write with my heart full of happiness to share with you the wonderful news that I am marrying again. Soon I will no longer be a sorry widow but the wife of a gentleman with a new future to look forward to. I can't wait to bring him home so that you can all meet him and love him as I do. I hope you can share in my joy and forgive me for not informing you sooner. It has all happened so fast my feet have barely touched the ground. You are all in my thoughts and prayers.

Your loving daughter and sister, Bridie

Michael lifted his gaze from the page and swept it over the astonished faces of his family. Mrs. Doyle was dabbing her eye with a handkerchief, Old Mrs. Nagle had ceased to pray and suspended her thumb above the beads while Sean glanced at his wife and there passed between them a silent communication that is the fancy of young married couples. "Marrying for the second time. She's done well for herself," said Michael. He folded the letter and slipped it back into the envelope. "Indeed God has been gracious. We have much to be thankful for."

Mrs. Doyle pushed the handkerchief up her sleeve and smiled. "God has indeed been gracious, Michael. I never did think Bridie would amount to much, but as God is my witness, I admit I was wrong. We have much to thank her for," she said, thinking of her mangle and the other small improvements that had eased the burden of her work and worry.

To be sure Bridie had improved their lives immeasurably. In

spite of Old Mrs. Nagle's protestations, when Michael had returned from Mount Melleray he had set about using his sister's money as she had intended. He bought the land he rented from the Deverills, purchased more cows, repaired and extended the farmhouse and farm buildings and acquired a car— he even employed a few young lads to help with the business. Having repented of his sins and vowed to lead a pious life he was careful not to descend into extravagance and imprudence. He donated money to the church, which pleased Father Quinn and earned him the chairmanship of the Society of St. Vincent de Paul, which was a large Catholic charity set up to help the poor. He was careful not to flaunt his new prosperity but the townspeople mocked him behind his back for his sanctimonious vanity and nicknamed him "the Pope." The Doyles never wanted for anything, although their requirements were modest. There was always food on the table, there were always clothes on their backs and the house was sealed against the cold winter winds.

"She says she's coming home," said Rosetta quietly, edging closer to her husband. It had been five years since she had married Sean, and almost as many years since Michael had returned from Mount Melleray, but Rosetta still found her brother-in-law intimidating. His presence was enormous and, even though he had become a man of God, bent on doing good, Ballinakelly's own pope emanated a dark and powerful energy.

"And what is an American to find in Ballinakelly?" Mrs. Doyle asked, rocking gently on her chair, content now that Michael, whom she admired as much as she had admired his father, had given Bridie his blessing.

"I should like to meet him," said Sean.

"I long to see her again," agreed Rosetta. She remembered her friend "Bridget" whom she had met in New York when they were both lowly maids sharing their days off on the benches in Central Park. How far she had traveled, she mused with admiration. Rosetta looked at Bridie's grandmother and wondered whether she'd live to see her granddaughter again. She didn't think of her own family in America nor dare to speculate on the chances of ever seeing *them* again, nor did she think of her two small children who might never know their Italian grandparents. "She is the wife of a gentleman now," she added quietly. "A grand lady."

"A grand lady!" repeated Mrs. Doyle disapprovingly. "God save us."

"I should like to meet her gentleman," said Old Mrs. Nagle and they all stared at her in surprise for she didn't say much these days. The elderly lady's lips curled around her gums as she smiled. "My granddaughter married for the second time! Sacred heart of Jesus. What would Tomas have said, Mariah, about her wealth and her second marriage?" she asked her daughter. "God rest his soul."

"He'd have thought she'd got above herself, that's what," Mrs. Doyle replied, lifting her chin, but she couldn't disguise the pride that smoldered in her eyes. "The Lord looks on us all with one loving gaze, kings and peasants alike. Indeed Bridie is no better for being wealthy or for being the wife of a gentleman. In truth she would have led a more godly life if she had remained here with us. Who knows what kind of life she is living over the water." She began to snivel again and pulled the handkerchief out of her sleeve with a trembling hand.

"But she writes that she is going to come back," said Rosetta hopefully.

Michael settled his imposing gaze on his sister-in-law and watched her wince. "She will never come back," he said firmly. "There is nothing for her here."

Michael put on his cap and ducked beneath the doorframe, stepping into the sunshine. Summer had turned the grass a rich green and his cows grazed contentedly, growing fat on the wildflowers that flourished on the hillside. He put his hands in his pockets and thought of Bridie. He remembered her in Dublin, her belly swollen and her mouth full of lies about being raped by Mr. Deverill. He remembered bringing her child home from the convent, not before he had corrupted one of the nuns who aided him with his plan. He had placed the boy on Kitty's doorstep with a note and she had done what he was confident she would do: remain in Ireland. The baby had tied her to her home because he was a Deverill and he belonged in Ballinakelly, as *she* did. Michael had ensured that Jack was arrested by making a deal with the Auxiliaries—his freedom for Jack's capture—and Kitty had fled to London but she had come back as he knew she would. Now his rival had settled in America, for good. Jack had gone forever and Michael would never again have to endure the sight of the man Kitty had loved so fiercely. Kitty and JP were in Ballinakelly just as he had planned. He had counted on her indissoluble bond with Ireland and her strong maternal instinct and been proved right; Kitty was exactly where he wanted her.

His mind turned sharply to the time he had taken her in the farmhouse and the remorse came in such a powerful swell that he had to sit down. She had tempted him, *that* much was clear, and he had sinned. He had duly confessed to the rape to Father Quinn and been forgiven, and devoted himself to God's work. He had tried to keep his eye on the Lord so his thoughts didn't stray to Kitty Deverill, but despite all his efforts, that girl still had the power to touch him.

He plucked a head of purple heather and twirled it between his fingers. *Kitty Deverill.* The name was like a thorny rose: beautiful but capable of causing terrible pain. How he loved Kitty Deverill. He did his best to avoid her these days because the look on her face when she saw him was a stab to the heart. He had burned the castle because of the lie Bridie had told him and his anger and jealousy had driven him to do something unspeakable. But he had faced up to his sins at Mount Melleray and God had forgiven him. He was a different man now; a man of the Church. He wanted Kitty to know that. He wanted her forgiveness too.

GRACE, DRESSED IN a hat pulled low over her face, hurried up the path that led to the Catholic church of All Saints. The sunshine warmed the gray stone walls of the ancient building that had been at the very center of the Irish struggle for independence. She remembered the meetings held in the sacristy and the plans she had concocted with Michael Doyle and Father Quinn. She had thrived on the thrill of danger that had ultimately led to the killing of Colonel Manley on the Dunashee Road. That danger had thrown her into Michael's arms. She would never forget the violent excitement of that night, as Michael and she had torn at each other's clothes like wild animals. Now she was advancing up that familiar path but the danger she was about to face was of a very different kind.

She found Father Quinn at the back of the church, talking to a young altar boy. When he saw her he dismissed the child with a wave of his hand. "Lady Rowan-Hampton, please, come with me," he said, his feet stepping noiselessly across the flagstones. They walked through a low door and into the sacristy, which contained a wooden armoire for the priest's vestments, a small ceramic piscina, a large wooden table upon which stood elaborate silver candlesticks, fine candles, books and other sacred vessels. On the walls were religious paintings and a marble sculpture of Christ on the cross which hadn't been there the last time Grace had visited. She could see that Bridie's money had been well spent in embellishing God's house.

She sat down and folded her hands in her lap. "This is quite a different church to the one in which we used to meet during the war," she said.

"It has been furnished by the devout," Father Quinn replied. "Indeed it is their moral duty to dig deep into their pockets when the Lord has been generous enough to fill them."

"You are so right," Grace replied. She wasn't here to receive a homily about morality.

"Those days are over, thank the Lord," said Father Quinn. "Your help during those years was invaluable. In fact, without you and Miss Deverill, we would not have been as effective. The Irish people will never know how much they owe their freedom to you."

"Life is quiet and peaceful now," said Grace with a smile that hid her regret. She had never felt more alive than during the War of Independence. "It has given me time to look into my soul, Father Quinn."

He raised his badger eyebrows in surprise. "Indeed?"

"I feel a great longing . . ." She hesitated and lowered her eyelashes. "I'm ashamed to say it. My husband would divorce me. My children would be appalled. In fact, everyone I know would gasp in horror, but . . ."

"But?" Father Quinn, who had taken the chair opposite, leaned forward.

"I wish to convert to Catholicism."

His face flushed with pleasure. There was nothing more thrilling for the priest than a possible convert. "I cannot pretend that I am not astonished by your revelation, Lady Rowan-Hampton."

"I know. But I have felt this longing for many years now. Do you remember the days when I taught English to the children and plotted with their fathers?"

"I do indeed," said the priest.

"And the many times I met with Fenians in Dublin?"

"Of course."

"I became one of them, Father Quinn." Her eyes took on a feverish shimmer as she held his attention and the apples of her cheeks glowed pink. "I helped feed the poor with Lady Deverill and collected second-hand clothes and shoes for the children. I wanted to alleviate the poverty. I wanted to educate them, to give them the opportunity of a better life. I wanted to change things. But I also felt that I was one of them, Father Quinn. I can't find the words to describe what I felt in my heart. It was some sort of connection, I suppose. A deep and powerful connection. And then I knew it was more than a sense of patriotism. It was a religious conviction. I wanted to be Catholic." Father Quinn was listening with fascination, his head nodding and shaking with encouragement, not wanting her to stop. "It was like a thorn in my heart, Father. It niggled and hurt and every time I sat in church I felt out of place, as if I was an outsider. But I couldn't tell anyone. I had to keep my feelings hidden. Then the war was over and peace restored and I had time to think, to search my soul. I knew that if I didn't express my desire I would go mad."

"So you have made a decision?"

"Yes, Father Quinn. I want full Catholic communion and I want you to officiate, because I can trust you to be discreet. No one must ever find out about this."

"As you wish." He sat back in his chair. "As you are already Christian it need not take long."

There Grace interrupted him. "Father Quinn, I do not want to rush this. It is not a decision I have made lightly. I want to take my time and I want to enjoy the process. I have waited years for this moment."

"As you wish."

"And because of the delicate nature of my situation, I am unable to mix with the Catholic community here in Ballina-kelly. I am, however, in need of support and guidance within the community, am I not?"

"Is there anyone you trust, Lady Rowan-Hampton?"

She hesitated and narrowed her eyes, as if searching through names of people she knew. "Mrs. Doyle," she said at last. "Lady Deverill used to speak very highly of her when she worked at the castle. I know she is a pious woman and a discreet one too. When I think of what must have gone on in her farmhouse during those tumultuous years and she never breathed a word."

Father Quinn raised his eyebrows again. "That is a fine

choice. Mrs. Doyle is the most devout of my congregation and, as you know, Michael is a reformed man. They are an exemplary family."

"I know, which is why I thought of her. Would you ask her for me? Perhaps I can pay her a visit and we can talk."

"I'm sure she will be flattered."

She engaged him once again with her warm brown eyes, which were now filled with gratitude. "I would like to donate to the church," she said. "Perhaps we can discuss how I may help *you*, Father Quinn."

When Grace returned home she found her father sitting around the card table in the drawing room with Hazel, Laurel and Bertie, playing bridge. She unpinned her hat and put it on one of the chairs before it was quietly taken away by a maid. "Where have you been?" asked Ethelred, puffing on his cigar.

"Into town," Grace replied casually. She wandered over to the table and put her hand on her father's shoulder. She felt light of spirit and happier than she had in a very long time. "So, it's you and Hazel against Bertie and Laurel?" she said.

"They're quite serious competition, but we're doing all right, aren't we, Hazel?" he said, winking at his partner, who blushed with pleasure.

"Oh, we certainly are," she gushed, glancing at her sister, whose lips were pursed with jealousy. "We're a very good team," she added, dropping her gaze into her hand of cards.

"How is Celia?" she asked Bertie. It had been six months since Archie had killed himself. At first no one could talk of anything else but the horror of his suicide. Then the talk turned to speculation as to why he would take his own life, until finally the horrible truth emerged. He had lost all his money, and that of his family, during the financial crisis but couldn't bring himself to tell his wife, who was notoriously extravagant. Digby had spoken of his sadness that his son-in-law had been too proud to ask for help, but Grace wondered whether Digby had been in a position to help him. From what she had heard, through her husband, Sir Ronald, Digby wasn't doing very well himself.

"She's bearing up," Bertie replied.

"And the castle, dare I ask?"

Bertie sighed heavily and dropped his shoulders. They all looked up from their cards. "I'm afraid it's not looking good. But I imagine I shall be the last to know."

"You don't think she'll sell it, do you?"

"She might have to. Digby has been advising her and as far as I understand they have liquidated all of Archie's assets. But she is heavily in debt and the money must come from somewhere. She's clinging on to the castle with her fingernails, but I don't hold out much hope. It looks like I shall be at the mercy of strangers, after all."

Grace felt deeply sorry for her old friend. "I wish there was something I could do," she said.

"Besides buying the castle, I don't think there is," said Bertie.

"We'd all chip in and save it if we could," said Laurel.

"Thank you, my dear Laurel, that's very sweet of you."

The maid appeared with a tray of tea and placed it on the low table in the middle of the square of sofas and armchairs that was positioned in front of the empty fireplace. "Shall we have a break?" Ethelred asked, puffing out a cloud of sweet-smelling smoke.

"Good idea," said Hazel. "I could do with a cup of tea. How

lovely!" She got up and went to sit beside Grace, who had begun to pour from the pretty china teapot.

"Poor Celia," sighed Laurel, watching Ethelred settling into the armchair, then taking the place at the edge of the other sofa that was nearest to him.

"The whole business is simply ghastly," said Grace. "Two children without a father, Archie's parents and siblings bereft—"

"And *poor*," added Hazel bleakly.

"Oh, it's just dreadful. I can't stop thinking about it. Such a waste for a young person to throw his life away over money. Poor Archie, a long-term solution to a short-term problem."

"Folly to sink one's fortune into such an ambitious project," said Ethelred.

"Folly," repeated Laurel emphatically.

"Digby should have taken his daughter in hand," said Grace. "After all, he's a man of experience. He should have known what they were taking on."

"When I told him that Celia had bought the castle, or rather, that Archie had, he groaned and said—I remember his very words—'It'll be the ruin of them both.'" Bertie looked from face to startled face and shook his head. "Those were his very words. I don't think one can blame Digby. Celia is a very determined young lady. What she wants she usually gets."

"Goodness!" Hazel gasped.

"Indeed," Laurel agreed by default.

"I dare say Digby rather enjoyed the fact that his daughter had saved the family seat," said Grace. "He's a flamboyant, showy man. Do you remember when he won the Derby? We heard nothing else for months!"

"I'm sure he will do everything in his power to save the castle," said Bertie.

"Though I'm not sure he has the means to do it," Grace added grimly.

Ethelred puffed on his cigar and chortled. "Let's talk about something happy. Did I ever tell you of the time I bet on a winner at the Derby? It was a rather extraordinary affair . . ." He held the attention of everyone in the room except for Grace, who had heard the story a dozen times before. But no one was more enthralled by Lord Hunt's tale of adventure, deception and triumph than Laurel and Hazel, who gazed at him with doe eyes, their lips slightly parted and their breaths bated.

CELIA AND KITTY sat on the terrace as the sun set and the shadows grew longer, eating into the light on the lawn and climbing up the castle walls like demons. Wrapped in shawls they cradled mugs of Adeline's cannabis tea, which Celia had found very effective in dulling her pain. They listened to the clamor of roosting birds and the desolate cry of a lone sea gull wheeling on the wind above them.

"I thought I had had my fair share of sorrow after George was killed," said Celia quietly. "But it can come at any moment, can't it, and take everything away."

"Oh Celia, I can't stop asking myself, 'Why?'"

"Believe me, I have chewed on that word so much I'm surprised it still exists. I know *why* he did it, I just don't understand it. At no point did he tell me to stop spending. Never once did he deny me anything. I'd give it all back, all of it, if we could rewind the clock and start again. I love this place, but I could have curbed my ambition. I know that now."

"You couldn't have foreseen this," said Kitty kindly.

"That's what makes me angry. Why didn't he warn me? He didn't even try." Celia's voice cracked. She paused, giving herself time to overcome her emotions. Kitty sipped her tea and waited. The sea gull flew away, taking his sad call with him. The shadows began to blend into dusk. Soon the night would creep in, bringing Celia face-to-face with her fears, which was why Kitty now stayed with her so often; she was frightened to sleep on her own. "He didn't give me warning. We could have resolved it together, but he bailed out, leaving me alone. Leaving his children fatherless. How could he be such a coward?" Kitty didn't know what to say. Celia had never called Archie "a coward" before. "I mean, a real man would never do that to his wife and children. A real man would have sat me down and told me the situation. But Archie wasn't a real man. All the while I was blithely spending, splashing out on the castle and paintings from Italy, he was facing financial ruin. God, Kitty, it makes me so angry." She knocked back her tea and gulped. "When I think of him now I don't feel bereaved, I feel betrayed." She laughed manically. "If you see him, you can tell him how cross I am."

"You can tell him yourself, Celia. I'm sure he's watching you and wishing he hadn't caused you such pain."

"Is he in Hell?" Celia asked softly. "Reverend Maddox would tell me it's a terrible sin to take one's own life. He'd say Archie is in Hell."

"But God is forgiving, Celia."

"Well I'm not. Not yet." She sighed loudly and drained her

mug. "So I'm selling the contents of the castle. Boysie has put me in touch with a Mr. Brickworth who is coming over from London to value everything and then he's going to put it all into a big, glossy catalogue that everyone in London will see. It's embarrassing, but what can I do?"

"I'm so sorry," said Kitty. "But perhaps this way you won't have to sell the castle itself."

"I'll have to sleep on a mattress on the floor. It's ridiculous. Is it worth it?"

"No, it's not. Life is too short. Sell up and move on." Kitty smiled sorrowfully. "I could say 'it's only a castle,' but you know as well as I do that it's so much more than that."

"It's everything to me," said Celia, her eyes wide and shiny. "Everything."

"It's everything to me too," Kitty rejoined. She watched Celia pick up the teapot and refill her mug.

"Shall we just get intoxicated tonight and forget our woes?"

Kitty held out her mug. "Why not?" she said.

Chapter 22

Digby stood by the window of his study and looked furtively out onto the driveway, and beyond, to the wide avenue of leafy plane trees that ran for almost half a mile from Kensington to Notting Hill. It was, without doubt, one of the most exclusive streets in London and he was proud to live on it. He reflected on his rather less ostentatious beginnings. The youngest son of an old landed family fallen on hard times, he was always aware that his parents were more interested in climbing the social ladder than in him. Desperate to escape his mother's stifling world, he had set out to South Africa to make his own fortune in the diamond mines. There he had lived in tents, suffered the dust and heat of summer and the crippling cold of winter and yet, somehow, found in himself a strength he hadn't known he had. As he slid his eyes up and down the road, his mind wandered back to the South African diamond mines. He had been lucky, but to a certain extent he had made his own luck—after all, God only helps those who help themselves. Then a movement in the street caught his attention.

It was *him* again, standing on the opposite side of the street wearing a hat pulled low over his face, a long shabby coat and tie, a newspaper folded under his arm. He was smoking languidly, as if he had all the time in the world. Digby chuckled without mirth; if it wasn't so dire it would be funny. He looked like a comedy crook, standing there in the shadows. *Well,* Digby thought resolutely, *he's not going to intimidate me. Let him do his worst and see where it gets him.* But, underneath his bravado, he didn't feel quite as strong or confident as he appeared. There had been a time when he had felt indomitable, but as the years went by his confidence was gradually being eroded by loss: loss of the people he loved, loss of his youth, loss of his sense of invulnerability, and of immortality. In the old days a man like Aurelius Dupree would barely have rattled his cage. Now, however . . .

Digby had not only built a business, he had built a reputation. He was a pillar of the community, a contributor to the Conservative Party. He counted royalty, politicians and aristocrats among his friends. Not only did he give generously to charity but he supported the arts too. He was one of the main benefactors of the Royal Opera House, for Beatrice loved opera and ballet and attended often, frequently invited to watch from the Royal Box. He was on various committees and a member of elite clubs like White's. Of course he also had his racing commitments and since winning the Derby he was a man to be reckoned with—Lucky Deverill now commanded serious covering fees. Digby took pride in his seemingly unfaltering talent for making money. He was a gambler, a speculator, a risk-taker and most often his schemes paid off. But a man could only make so much luck. He was considering trying his hand at politics. Randlords weren't quite respectable but he was overcoming that with his charm and money. Perhaps he would buy a newspaper like his friend Lord Beaverbrook and get into politics that way. *If it wasn't for Aurelius Dupree*, he thought irritably, *nothing would hold me back.*

Digby watched him in the road. He looked like he had no intention of going anywhere—and he was watching Digby right back. Indeed, the two men were staring at each other like a pair of bulls, neither wanting to show weakness by being the first to look away. However, Digby had better things to do than compete in a stand-off, so he withdrew and called for his driver to take him to his club. It was a beautiful summer's day, but Digby didn't want to risk walking through the park to St. James's on account of Aurelius Dupree. The man could write letters to his heart's content, but Digby would never permit him an audience. Standing outside his house was the nearest he was going to get and with any luck, he'd see the futility of it and crawl back under the rock from where he'd come.

HARRY AND BOYSIE met for lunch at White's. It had been six months since Charlotte had permitted her husband to see his old friend again and the two of them met frequently, careful not to slip back into their morning trysts in Soho. Charlotte had given their friendship her blessing, but she hadn't said they could sleep together, even though she hadn't specifically prohibited it. Harry felt he owed her a deep debt of gratitude for her tolerance, a debt that would be quite wrong to repay by jumping into Boysie's bed. If this was all that was permitted, they were both accepting of it. Harry was just happy to breathe the same air as Boysie. He told himself that he didn't need to make love to him. But as the months passed the challenge to keep their distance grew ever greater.

They sat in the dining room, surrounded by familiar faces, for all the most distinguished men in London were members of White's. But Boysie and Harry only had eyes for each other. "It is better to be ignorant like Deirdre," said Boysie. "It's perfectly feasible to be happy that way."

"Charlotte is happy that we are friends again," said Harry firmly.

"But she's watching you, make no mistake. She's watching your every move. One slip and you're in serious trouble, old boy." Boysie chuckled but his eyes betrayed his sadness. "Is this all it's ever going to be?"

Harry looked into his wineglass. "I don't know."

Boysie sighed in that nonchalant way of his and pouted petulantly. "I'm not sure I can stand it."

"You *have* to stand it," Harry said in alarm. "It's all we're allowed. It's better than nothing. I couldn't live with nothing."

"After Archie did himself in I'm sure Charlotte has come to realize that." He grinned mischievously. "Would you really kill yourself for me?" he asked, leaning across the table, his pretty green eyes melting into Harry's.

"I thought about it," Harry replied quietly.

"Don't ever do it," said Boysie. "Because *I* don't have the courage and I certainly couldn't live without *you*. You won't go and leave me on my own, will you?"

Harry smiled. "No, of course not."

"Well, that's settled then. A weight off my shoulders. You

know that hotel in Soho is still there. No one would ever know. Not even Charlotte with her spying would know to look there."

"We can't," Harry hissed, glancing anxiously to his left and right for fear of being overheard.

"You know, Celia has told me that someone has made her an offer to buy the castle, lock, stock and barrel," said Boysie, changing the subject because Harry's reaction to *that* suggestion remained always the same. "News travels fast."

Harry's eyes widened. "When did she tell you?"

"This morning. She telephoned."

"Well? What did she say? Is she going to sell it?" Harry looked horrified.

"Of course she's not going to sell it. She adores it. She's just going to sell the contents. *Most* of them. I'm sure she'll keep a bed or two."

Harry shook his head. "It's desperate. I can't bear it for her. She's terribly lonely without Archie."

"Darling, she's lost more than Archie. She's lost her *joie de vivre*. Her *esprit*. I think we should persuade her to come to London for a while. She needs to get out, to see people, to remember who she really is."

"She shouldn't be a widow," Harry agreed.

"Unless she's a *merry* widow. We'll remind her of her merry side, won't we, old boy."

"God, they were good old times," Harry sighed. They began to reminisce wistfully about their lives before Deirdre and Charlotte had stepped in to complicate them.

Presently, Digby walked into the dining room with a great kerfuffle. With his flashing white teeth, his slicked-back blond hair and his diamond shirt studs, he greeted his friends loudly as he moved through the tables, finding something witty or charming to say to everyone. Harry and Boysie suspended their conversation to watch as he made his way toward them, his flamboyant attire and vibrant personality creating amusement and comment among the members of this most conventional of clubs.

"Ah, boys," Digby said when he reached their table. "At least there is one place in London where we are sure to be free of our wives." He laughed without realizing how true his words were to Boysie and Harry and moved on to where his guests awaited him.

GRACE KNOCKED ON the door of the Doyle farmhouse. It was the first time she had ever visited, for during the War of Independence she and Michael had met either at her house or Badger Hanratty's barn in the hills. As she pushed it open her heart accelerated at the thought of seeing Michael, "the Pope," whose piety repulsed her but whose physicality still thrilled her. She could feel his presence, for his energy vibrated strongly, like a strain of music permeating every inch of the farm, and her excitement mounted. She heard a voice and when her eyes adjusted to the darkness, she saw an elderly woman sitting on a chair by the hearth.

"Good day," said Grace and the elderly woman raised her hooded eyes and her cadaverous face registered surprise. Old Mrs. Nagle had not been expecting a lady to step into their humble dwelling. "My name is Lady Rowan-Hampton. I've come to see Mrs. Doyle."

A moment later Mrs. Doyle appeared at the bottom of the staircase. She stepped into the room, wringing her hands nervously. She was smaller than Grace remembered, her skin as lined as a map, her round black eyes the same color as Michael's. She nodded curtly. "Good morning, milady," she said.

"Father Quinn . . ." Grace began a little anxiously. She didn't want anyone to know that she was here, besides Michael, of course. *That* was the reason she had come, after all.

"Oh, Father Quinn, yes, he did emphasize discretion. You can be sure that Mam and I won't breathe a word, so help me God." She looked unsure of what to do next, then remembering her manners, she offered Grace a seat at the table. "Would you like tea, milady? The kettle is hot."

"Thank you. That would be lovely," said Grace, sitting down. She could smell Michael, as if he had only a moment ago stood before her, dwarfing the room with his wide shoulders and powerful authority. She wondered where he had gone and whether he'd be coming back soon. She didn't know how long she could sustain talking to his mother about God.

Mrs. Doyle placed a basin of tea and a plate of currant soda bread on the table in front of her and sat down, folding her hands in her lap. She waited for Grace to begin. Grace wrenched her thoughts away from Michael and tried to concentrate on the charade. She had no wish to convert to Catholicism, but if that's what it took to win Michael's heart she'd go the whole way and beyond.

"As Father Quinn will have told you, I would like to become a Catholic," she said. "This will be against the wishes of my family, but I feel I am being called, Mrs. Doyle, and I want to answer that call."

"So how can I help you?" Mrs. Doyle asked with a frown.

"I want to know what it means to live a Catholic life. Father

Quinn suggested *you* as a role model. You are a good Catholic, Mrs. Doyle. I would like you to set me an example."

Mrs. Doyle's face relaxed when she realized *that* was all that was expected of her. She certainly believed herself to be a good Catholic and was happy to tell Lady Rowan-Hampton how she lived a pious life. "Shall I—" Mrs. Doyle began but Grace interrupted.

"Tell me about your life from the beginning, yes, that would be most interesting. What was it like growing up a Catholic?" Mrs. Doyle began to reminisce and Grace's mind wandered through the house in search of Michael. Old Mrs. Nagle had fallen asleep in her chair and her head had slumped forward like a rag doll's. A dribble escaped one corner of her mouth and ran down the gray hairs of her chin, dropping onto the loose fabric about her scrawny chest. Mrs. Doyle warmed to her subject. She spoke of the angelus, her daily prayers, the rosary, Mass and the little things she did every day that were all part of her devotion. Grace listened with half an ear, nodding when appropriate. With one eye on the door she let Mrs. Doyle talk on, silently willing that door to open and Michael to stride in.

When Mrs. Doyle finally drew breath Grace had finished her tea. The room had grown a little darker and Old Mrs. Nagle had woken herself up with a snort. Grace realized that she couldn't stay any longer. She didn't think she could endure a minute more of Mrs. Doyle's flat voice and her piety. Then the door was flung open and she knew it was Michael even before she saw him. She pushed out her chair and jumped to her feet, forgetting for a moment that Old Mrs. Nagle and Mrs. Doyle were watching her with fascination, as if she were a rare bird that had chosen to mingle with geese.

Michael stared at her in surprise. He had seen her car parked outside and wondered what the devil she was doing in his house. Had she gone mad? "Lady Rowan-Hampton," he said and his tone demanded an explanation.

Grace smiled sweetly. "Hello, Mr. Doyle." She relished holding him in suspense for a moment.

He looked at his mother, who had now pushed herself to her feet. "Lady Rowan-Hampton and I have much to talk about," she said and, true to her word, she was careful to be discreet.

"About what?" he asked.

"Would you like tea?" she said, making for the fireplace. "I will boil the kettle."

"I must be going," said Grace. Her mood had lifted considerably. "Thank you so much, Mrs. Doyle. I really appreciate your time. Might we perhaps be able to meet again?"

"As you wish," said Mrs. Doyle, flattered. She had enjoyed talking about herself to someone who listened with such concentration.

Michael was perplexed. "I will escort you to your car, Lady Rowan-Hampton," he said, opening the door. Grace walked past him with her chin up, a gratified smile curling the corners of her lips.

Outside, the sun was on the wane. The tweeting of birds filled the air with the sound of summer. A light breeze drifted in over the cliffs. Michael turned to her, his face cast in shadow. "What's going on, Grace?"

"I'm converting to Catholicism," she stated simply.

Michael scowled. "The devil you are," he replied.

"Oh, I am," she insisted with a smile. "Your mother is helping me along my spiritual path. Father Quinn suggested I come and talk to her. She's an inspiring woman."

"You're not going to convert to Catholicism. Sir Ronald would divorce you."

"Ronald won't know," she said breezily. "As you're well aware we lead very separate lives. That suited you once."

He pulled a sympathetic face. "What's this all about, Grace?" he asked gently.

"It has nothing to do with you, Michael. I have moved on. You can rest assured that I will not be the temptress who diverts you from your path. I respect your devoutness. In fact, I admire it." She lowered her eyes demurely and hesitated, as if struggling to find the words. "I have done things in my life of which I am deeply ashamed," she said, lowering her voice. "I want to make peace with God. I want to ask forgiveness and I want to lead a better life. What we had was intense and I wouldn't go back and change it for all the world. But I've started another chapter. The old one is closed, forever." She walked to her car. "It's been nice seeing you. *Really* nice. I hope we can be friends, Michael."

He nodded, but his knitted eyebrows exposed his bewilderment. He watched her open the door and climb inside. Then she lifted her hand and gave a small wave as she set off up the track.

She looked in the rearview mirror and saw him watching her, the frown still etched on his forehead, and she smiled, satisfied with her plan and excited by the thrill of a new plot.

IT WAS HARD persuading Celia to return to London for a break, but Boysie and Harry were adamant that she should not be alone at the time she needed her friends the most. She protested that she had Kitty and Bertie on her doorstep and the Shrubs made it their business to visit her every day with cake soaked in whiskey. "That should be reason enough to bolt for the mainland," Boysie had said, and Celia had laughed and finally relented.

She arrived in London at the beginning of July and Beatrice made a great fuss of her. She put fresh flowers in her bedroom and arranged lunches with her dearest friends. She knew that her daughter would not feel up to going out into society, but the company of those she loved the most would be balm to her ailing spirit. Even Leona and Vivien were kind and no one mentioned Archie's suicide or asked whether she would have to sell Castle Deverill. Celia knew they were all burning with questions but was grateful for their tact and restraint. That is, until Augusta invited herself for tea.

Celia's grandmother arrived in a shiny black Bentley with a long thin nose and big round headlights that flared like nostrils. It drew up outside the house on Kensington Palace Gardens and came to a halt at the foot of the steps leading up to the grand entrance. Augusta waited for the chauffeur to open her door and offer her his hand, then she descended slowly, duck-ing her head sufficiently so as not to squash the feathers in her hat. The chauffeur gave her her walking stick, but knew that his mistress would not take kindly to being helped up the steps. "I'm not decrepit yet," she would say dismissively, shrugging him off.

Looking like a Victorian lady in a long black dress with a high collar buttoned tightly about her neck and her silver hair swept loosely up and fastened beneath her hat she walked past the butler without a word and found Celia waiting dutifully for her in the hall at the foot of the staircase. Augusta, who had not seen her granddaughter since Archie's death, pulled her against her vast bosom and held her in an emotional embrace. "My dear child, no one should have to suffer what you have suffered. No one. The indignity of suicide is more than I can bear." Celia was relieved when her mother appeared and the three of them went upstairs to the drawing room.

Augusta settled into the sofa and pulled off her gloves, placing them on her disappearing lap. "The whole business has been most vexing," she said, shaking her head so that the feathers quivered like a startled moorhen. "I mean, what was I to tell my friends? If it hadn't been all over the newspapers I could have made something up, but as it was, I found myself having to admit that the poor man had hanged himself. Surely, there's a way to do oneself in without drenching one's family in shame?"

Beatrice was quick to move the conversation on. They had spent enough time debating the whys and wherefores. "It is as it is," she said. "We have to look forward now and think of the future."

"The silly boy should have swallowed his pride and asked Digby for help. Digby is as rich as Croesus," Augusta said, her lips pursing into a smug smile at the thought of her son's success. "Why, out of all my chicks, Digby is the one who has flown the highest and the furthest. But pride is a terrible thing."

Beatrice handed her a teacup. "I think it was more complicated than that, Augusta," she said. Celia caught her mother's eye and pulled a face while her grandmother was dropping two sugar lumps into her tea. "How is Stoke?"

"Frail," said Augusta. "He won't last long, I'm afraid. I'm surprised when I see he's still there in the mornings. I'm as frail myself but of course I hide it."

"I thought he looked incredibly well when I saw him last," said Celia.

"That might well be. But he has his ups and downs. He must have been on an up. Sadly, the last few months have not been good. When one is as old as he is the decline is a sharp one. Still, he has had a good life." Before Beatrice could object Augusta continued stridently. "As for me, I didn't think I'd survive Archie's suicide but I'm still here. One more tragedy and I think my heart will simply pack it in. There is only so much a person can take. I've cried so much, there isn't a tear left inside me." She then proceeded to give them both a lengthy account of all her friends who were ill, dying or dead. The most gruesome tales gave her the most pleasure. "So you see, I must consider myself fortunate. When I compare myself to them I realize that shame is a small thing really. After all, no one ever died of shame."

"None of us feel at all ashamed," said Beatrice. "We just feel desperately sad for Archie and sorry for Celia. But we're not dwelling on sorrow."

"I hear from my man at Christie's that you are selling the contents of the castle." Celia flushed. "Now why would you do that? Surely Digby won't allow it."

"Digby is not in a position to help," said Beatrice, enjoying the look of surprise that took hold of Augusta's face.

"Whatever do you mean, not in a position to help? Of course he is."

"I'm afraid he is not. Most of the country has been affected by the Stock Exchange crash and Digby is no different."

"Good Lord, I don't believe it."

"I'm afraid it is true."

"I shall speak to him at once—"

"Please don't," said Beatrice swiftly. "He won't want to discuss it. You know what he's like. Like you, Augusta, he keeps everything bottled up inside. As far as anyone is concerned he is absolutely fine. But you are his mother, so you should know. Celia has to sell the contents of the castle in order to pay off Archie's debts, of which there are many." She wanted to add "and his family's debts' but she didn't want to embarrass her daughter. Celia winced at the thought of the money she had to find but hastily pushed her anxieties aside. While she sat in her mother's sumptuous drawing room she could pretend that everything was as it should be.

"And the castle?" Augusta asked in a tight voice.

Celia shrugged. "I might have to sell that too," she replied.

Augusta inhaled a gulp of air. "Then that will surely be the death of me," she said. "Shame might do me in, after all."

CELIA ESCAPED HER grandmother and the stifling heat of London and fled to Deverill Rising in Wiltshire to spend the weekend with her family. She invited Boysie and Harry, who turned up with their wives, but at least on the golf course she could be rid of them, for neither Charlotte nor Deirdre played golf. Harry and Boysie seemed just as happy to be free of them as she was.

Digby, dressed in a flamboyant pair of green checked breeches, long green socks and a bright red sleeveless sweater over a yellow shirt, was an erratic golfer. He roared with laughter when he hit his ball into the rough and punched the air when, by some miracle, he got a hole in one. His two black

Labradors headed straight into the copse like a pair of seals in search of fish, appearing a few minutes later with their mouths full of golf balls—mostly Digby's, from previous games.

Celia was a steady player while Boysie and Harry, fashionably dressed in pale, coordinating colors, were less interested in the actual sport. For them it was a way of spending a whole morning together in the company of people who didn't judge them.

"Grandma gave me a grilling," Celia told her father as they walked to the next hole. "She's incredibly tactless."

"I'm sorry to hear that, but she does like to have her say."

"She says she'll die of shame if I sell the castle."

"She'll outlive us all, mark my words," said Digby.

"She thinks Grandpa is going to pop off at any minute."

"Grandpa is not going anywhere," Digby replied firmly. "If he's survived sixty-odd years being married to her, he'll survive a few more." He chuckled. "I'm sure he's built up a strong immunity to her over the years."

Celia put her hands in her cardigan pockets. "Someone has made me an offer for the castle," she said. "A big offer. Much more than it's worth."

Digby stopped walking. "Do you know who?"

"Oh I don't know. A rich man. American."

"Are you asking my advice?"

"Yes. You know my financial situation better than I do. Really, it's such a muddle and so many noughts. I do hate all those beastly noughts."

"You don't have to sell." A shadow darkened her father's face. "At least, not yet."

"He wants to buy the castle with everything in it."

"You don't have to sell the castle," Digby said decisively, striding on. "We saved it once and we'll save it again. Now, where are those bloody dogs?"

Her father placed the ball on the tee and shuffled his feet into position. Celia noticed that his face had gone red, but she thought it was due to the exertion of walking the course. It had been a long way and the summer sun was blazing. She wondered whether he should take off his sweater. He lined up his club, patting it a few times on the green. Little beads of perspiration had started to form on his brow and his breathing had grown suddenly tight, as if he was struggling to inhale. Celia looked anxiously at the boys who had also noticed and were watching him with concern.

"Papa," said Celia. "I think perhaps we should take a break. It's very hot and even *I'm* feeling faint." But Digby was determined to take the shot. He swung his club. Just as he twisted his body, his arm went weak and he fell to his knees. Celia rushed to his side. "Papa!" she cried, not knowing where to put her hands or what to do. She felt a sickness invade her stomach. Digby was now puce. His eyes bulged and his mouth opened in a silent gasp. He pressed a hand against his chest.

Harry and Boysie helped lie him down on the grass. Harry loosened his tie and unbuttoned his shirt. His breathing was labored. He stared but seemed to see nothing. Then with a great force of will he grabbed Celia by her collar and pulled her down so that her face was an inch from his. She let out a terrified squeal. "Burn . . . my . . . letters," he wheezed. Then his hand lost its strength and fell to the ground.

PART THREE

Barton Deverill

Ballinakelly, County Cork, 1667

Charles II, six feet tall, black-eyed, black-haired, swarthy and as handsome as the Devil, was in his apartments in the rambling, ramshackle rabbit warren that was Whitehall Palace. Attended by his mistress, Countess of Castlemaine, his friend the Duke of Buckingham, and his pack of spaniels, which he referred to as his "children," he was sitting at the card table when Lord Deverill strode into the room and bowed low. "Your Majesty," he said.

"Oh join us, Deverill," said the King without looking up. "Take a hand. What's y' stake?"

The King liked winning money off his friends and Deverill tossed his into the middle of the table and sat down. "How are the girls out there in godforsaken Ireland, Deverill?"

"Bonny," Lord Deverill replied. "But my mind isn't on the girls, Your Majesty, but on the rebels . . ."

The King waved his hands and the large jewels on his fingers glittered in the candlelight and the intricate lace ruffles of his sleeves fluttered about his wrists. "We'll send you some men, of course, speak to Clarendon," he said, and that was as much business as the King wanted to discuss. Lord Deverill knew there was a strong chance that reinforcements would come too late, if at all, because the King was more concerned about the threat of invasion from the Dutch. "How considerate of you, Deverill, to marry a beautiful woman," the King continued, his lips curling into a languid smile as the Countess stuck out her bottom lip and gave a loud and irritated sigh. "We're all terribly tired of looking at the same faces and gossiping about the same people. You really must bring her to Court more often."

"She would like that very much," Lord Deverill replied. The King was unable to resist the allure of a beautiful woman and had been given the nickname "Old Rowley" after a lecherous old goat that used to roam the privy garden. Lord Deverill did not believe he would wear a pair of horns well and decided that the sooner he took his wife to Ireland the better.

However, this was not the occasion to take her to Castle Deverill. Barton left his wife in the safety of their house in London and headed for home. It was a long and arduous journey across the Irish Sea, but the weather was favorable and he reached the mainland without a hitch. With a small escort of the King's men who had met him at the port he galloped over the hills toward Ballinakelly.

The wind blew in strong gusts, propelling him on, and oppressive gray clouds gathered damp and heavy above him. Spring was but a few weeks away and yet the landscape looked wintry and cold and the buds already forming on the trees remained firmly shut. Still, in spite of the bleak light and dreary skies, Ireland's soft beauty was arresting. Her green and gently undulating fields appealed directly to his heart and Lord Deverill feared the scene of devastation that would welcome him home.

With trepidation he cantered to the crest of the hill and looked down into the valley where his castle stood, overlooking the ocean. His heart plummeted to his feet as he gazed upon the manifestation of all his ambitions, now a grisly wreck, still leaking a ribbon of smoke into the wind. Fury rose in him then like a latent beast suddenly awoken by the sharp prod of a sword. He dug his spurs into his horse's flanks and galloped down the track. His gut twisted with anguish as he approached the scene of battle. Although the castle was still standing, it had taken a terrible battering and the eastern tower had been completely lost to fire.

He recognized his friend, the Duke of Ormonde's colors at once and when the soldiers saw him they were quick to take him to their captain. "Lord Deverill," the captain said as Barton strode into the hall.

"What the devil has happened?" he asked, his feverish eyes scanning the room for damage and finding none. At least they hadn't fought their way *into* the building, he reflected.

"His Grace rushed to your aid as soon as he heard the news. We arrived just in time to secure the castle. Your men were on the back foot. Had it not been for His Grace's quick response you wouldn't have had a home to come back to."

"I cannot express my gratitude. I am forever indebted to the Duke," said Lord Deverill quietly. As loyal supporters of King Charles II during his exile in France, the Duke and

Lord Deverill had become firm friends. At the restoration Ormonde had recovered his vast estates in Ireland confiscated by Cromwell and been reinstated Lieutenant of Ireland, a position he had held under King Charles I. He was consequently the most powerful man in the country. An important ally most certainly but he was also a trusted friend; when Lord Deverill had needed him most Ormonde had not let him down.

"Who's behind this?" Lord Deverill growled. "By God I shall have their heads."

"Those who survived are imprisoned in the stables. You can be sure that the Duke will see that they are severely castigated. This is not simply a rebellion against Your Lordship, but a revolt against the King, and they shall be duly punished."

"We must make an example of them," said Lord Deverill fiercely. "Let the people of County Cork see what happens when they rise up against their English lords."

The captain rubbed his chin and frowned. "There is a woman at the heart of the plot, Lord Deverill, and she will be tried as a witch."

Lord Deverill's face drained of color. "A woman?" he said slowly, but he knew very well who she was.

"Indeed. A pagan woman called O'Leary, my lord. It is she who started the rebellion. The men are quick to accuse her of bewitching them. After all, this was her land, was it not, Lord Deverill, and it has been reported that she cursed you and your descendants. There are many who witnessed it."

Lord Deverill didn't know what to say. He could not deny the curse and any word in her favor could be counterproductive, considering what he had done to her in the woods. He pictured her face, as it appeared to him in daydreams and night terrors, and nodded sharply. "She did," he replied. His mind searched wildly for a way to help her, scurrying about his head like a rabbit in a pen, but found nothing. His jaw tensed at the thought of her inciting rebellion, at the horror of his ruined home and at her betrayal. He had no business in helping her, no business in loving her. Yet she had crawled beneath his skin and insinuated herself into his heart like an exquisite caterpillar, exploding upon his consciousness like a beautiful butterfly. Perhaps that was witchcraft too?

"What will become of her?" Lord Deverill asked.

The captain pulled a face and shrugged. "She'll most likely burn," he replied and his words made Lord Deverill wince.

"Most likely?"

"Aye, it's the decision of His Grace, His Majesty's represen-tative, and yourself."

"Very well," he replied with a shudder, knowing there was no decision to be made; no reason to save her that would not expose *him*. "I will leave it to His Grace. I have no wish to see her." He didn't want her throwing accusations at him, although he doubted anyone would believe them; he was ashamed of having taken her in the wood.

"She was pregnant, Milord, almost to term."

"Pregnant?" Lord Deverill repeated, making a great effort to keep his voice steady. But the panic that suddenly gripped his stomach was as potent as a physical blow.

"Aye, but she lost it," the captain added. "She'll be tried now and God save her soul."

Lord Deverill took his bottom lip between his teeth and ran his tongue along the soft inside part where she had bitten him.

Chapter 23

Wen Beatrice was told the news of Digby's death she was overcome with grief. Once before she had clawed herself back from the brink of hopelessness, but she knew she didn't have the inner reserves to do that again. Digby had been her sails and her rudder and the captain at the helm; now that he was gone, life was a wild and lonely ocean that threatened to consume her. She withdrew to her bedroom and took to her bed, where she remained in semi-darkness, afraid of facing the world without him. Death would be preferable to living, she thought bleakly as she lay curled up beneath the quilt, and the velvet-black allure of oblivion called to her in whispers promising sanctuary in silence.

Celia was devastated and bewildered by such a great loss, coming as it did so soon after Archie's suicide. Her father had been as solid as the ground beneath her feet; dependable, unshakable, immortal. It was impossible to imagine her world without him in it. How would she get by? She had never had to think for herself. Her husband and her father had taken care of everything. She had never looked at a bill or even spoken to her bank manager—and if she had ever had a problem one of those two capable men had sorted it out for her. To whom could she turn now? Celia had no one. She dug deep to find her inner strength and found nothing but weakness.

Boysie and Harry took their wives back to London, aware that the two women would only irritate Celia and conscious of the fact that the family needed to be together. Celia enveloped them with needy arms and copious tears, promising to let them know when the funeral would be. She waved forlornly on the steps as the taxi motored down the drive.

"Death stalks the Deverills like a relentless predator," said Boysie grimly as Celia's small figure receded and finally disappeared as they turned out into the lane.

"It certainly seems so," Harry replied.

"Do your best to elude him, old boy," Boysie added under his breath.

"If a man as indomitable as Cousin Digby yields so readily what hope is there for the rest of us?"

Celia grieved with her sisters, Leona and Vivien. Tragedy brought them closer as only tragedy can. They moved into Deverill Rising to help Celia look after their mother and Celia was grateful; her mother's collapse had been almost as shocking as her father's death and she was relieved that she didn't have to cope with it on her own. During the week that followed the sisters reminisced about the old days when they had been children, shedding tears of both joy and sorrow as they remembered their father, his ostentatious and oftentimes gaudy attire and his irrepressible spirit. Digby had been a man whose glass was always overflowing. They remembered too their brother, George, when he had been a little boy following Harry around Castle Deverill like a loyal dog, and they all longed to be transported back to those summers in Ballinakelly before the Great War and the War of Independence had swept them away. They took long walks over the Wiltshire hills, finding solace in the peaceful serenity of nature, comfort in their memories and strength in each other.

Augusta did not die then as everyone, particularly she herself, was sure she would. In the great British tradition she stiffened her jaw, lifted her chin and refused to let her son's death get the better of her. She accepted condolences with fortitude— she knew that if she gave in to sorrow she might never again recover her composure—and she clung to her religion, putting her faith in God and giving up any resistance to the way things were. "Acceptance is the only way," she told Maud, who paid her a visit as soon as she heard the terrible news. "Stoke will go now, I'm sure of it. He cannot accept that Digby is gone and therein lies the folly. It is through acceptance that one finds peace. Digby's time was up and God has gathered him into His keeping. There's no point fighting it; God won't send him back. One has to accept, *that's* the key." Maud had always found Augusta trying, but she had to admire her philosophy. She wondered, though, whether the old lady let go of her control in private. The red rims around her eyes, which one might have assumed were simply the signs of her great age, told Maud that she did.

THE FUNERAL TOOK place in the village church a few miles from Deverill Rising. It was a small, family affair. Bertie, Kitty and Robert, Elspeth and Peter and the Shrubs came from Ireland, while Augusta and Stoke, Maud and Victoria traveled down from London with Boysie and Harry and their wives. Digby's two brothers came with their spouses and some of their children, but the jealousy that had seeped poison into their hearts when Digby had made his fortune in South Africa still prevented reconciliation, even in the event of their brother's death, and they left as soon as the service was over.

Beatrice, helped by her strong sons-in-law who took an arm each, was escorted to the church, then straight back home again, where she retreated once more to her bed. She didn't feel up to speaking to anyone. One more word of condolence and she would break like a flimsy raft on a wave. Sobbing quietly into her pillow, she allowed the effects of the cannabis tea Kitty had brought from Ireland to pull her under where it was still, cool and quiet.

"Hello, Maud," said Bertie, approaching his estranged wife with caution as they gathered outside the church.

But she smiled sympathetically and he saw that her icy eyes had thawed a little more since they had met at Christmas. "Why is it that we are always brought together by tragedy?" she asked.

"I don't know," Bertie replied. "We've had rather a lot of it lately, haven't we?"

"Poor Beatrice, how she must be suffering." Bertie was astonished. For once Maud was not thinking of herself. "I remember when she lost George. I didn't think she'd ever recover, but somehow she pulled herself back from the edge. Now I fear she has toppled over it."

"It was so sudden and unexpected. He was only sixty-five."

Maud's eyes shone suddenly and a shadow of fear passed across them, or perhaps it was just the reflection of the clouds. "Death could come to us at any moment. Never before have I felt so keenly a sense of my own mortality. If Digby . . ." She caught her breath. "If Digby, so strong and powerful . . . If *he* . . ." Her voice thinned. Bertie put a hand on her arm. She didn't shrug it off, but gazed at him with a benign expression softening the chiseled contours of her face.

"One has to seize the day, Maud," he said, suddenly remembering with a jolt the time Digby had shouted to him as he was on the point of perishing in the sea, demanding that he choose between life and death. "Digby saved my life," he said quietly.

"He did?" said Maud.

"Yes. If it wasn't for Digby I would have drowned myself in a bottle of whiskey."

"Oh Bertie," she gasped.

"I chose life. I pulled myself together. I vowed never to waste my God-given existence again."

Maud wiped away a tear with her glove. "I did wonder."

"Did you?" he asked, feeling his spirits soar with something close to happiness.

She nodded. "I did, Bertie, and I was pleased to see the man I married again."

"Had he really gone so very far away?" She nodded again. "Perhaps we can reach a time in our lives when we can let bygones be bygones," he ventured.

"I don't know," she said, afraid to step back into a place that had been so dark. "Perhaps."

Kitty watched her parents talking in the sunshine and wondered what they had to say to each other. As far as she knew,

Maud was still being escorted round the London party circuit by Arthur Arlington. "We're going back to the house for a cup of tea," said Hazel, tapping Kitty on the shoulder. "Are you going to come with us?"

"I could do with something stronger than tea," said Kitty, searching the faces for Robert's. She saw him talking to Bruce and Tarquin and presumed that he would hitch a lift with them. "I'll wait for Harry and Boysie," she said. "I'll walk you to your taxi."

"Do you remember Adeline's cannabis tea?" Laurel asked as they walked down the path.

"Do I ever!" said Hazel.

"If we *all* drank it *all* of the time wouldn't we be the happier for it?" Laurel said.

"Life would pass us by," said Kitty. "As pleasant as that would sometimes be, I think we are all the better for our suffering. It drives us deeper, makes us more compassionate toward others. What selfish beings we would be if we were untouched by sorrow."

Hazel frowned. "You sound just like Adeline," she said.

Kitty smiled. "Do I?" She watched the Shrubs climb into the back of the cab. "She's here, you know," she said with certainty. "I'm sure she's seen to it that Digby has found his way home."

Celia watched the cab motor off and then swept her eyes over the somber faces of the locals who had come out to pay their respects. The men stood with their hats in their hands while the women, some with small children, looked on with sympathetic faces. Among them was an old man who caught her attention on account of the fact that he hadn't removed his hat. His cadaverous face had none of the compassion or sorrow of the others; rather it had a cold, defiant expression that offended her. The man noticed that she was watching him and narrowed his eyes with contempt. He looked right at her as if his intention was to intimidate, and Celia, shocked by his visible wrath, and bewildered by it, turned away sharply and went to find Boysie and Harry. When she found them the unpleasant man swiftly slipped from her mind.

Having made sure, even in her grief, that Charlotte and Deirdre had gone with Maud and Augusta, Celia returned to the house with Harry and Boysie. "Do you know what Papa's last words to me were?" she said, staring down at her black gloves as the car rattled up the road. The boys shook their heads. " 'Burn my letters,' " she told them solemnly. "That's the last thing he said. It's been bothering me, but do you think he had a mistress? I mean, I'd be naïve to believe he didn't entertain himself here and there, but do you think he loved somebody else?"

Harry caught Boysie's eye but Boysie knew better than to add to Celia's unhappiness by speaking his mind. "No, I don't imagine he did," said Boysie. "He loved your mama. That was very clear."

"I hope you're right."

"So are you going to burn them?" Harry asked.

"I don't know where they are." She laughed helplessly.

"You could start by looking in his study."

"If he has a safe I wouldn't have a clue of the code. I'm not about to break in, you know." She sighed. "If *you* were to keep love letters, where would *you* hide them?" She looked at Boysie and then at Harry and the world seemed to still for a long-drawn-out moment. She saw the two young men as if from a distance and from that fresh perspective she suddenly experienced a moment of clarity. Why had she never thought of it before, she wondered. It seemed so obvious now. Harry loved Boysie and, judging by the way they were always inseparable—and by the way Boysie's face lit up when he was with Harry—Boysie loved Harry back. They probably always had. Everything now made sense. Charlotte's grumpiness, the months Harry and Boysie didn't see each other, the fact that Boysie declined her invitation to Castle Deverill and stopped attending her mother's Salons. The two of them looked more of a couple than they did with their wives. She dropped her gaze, afraid that they might see the realization in it and be ashamed. But they had nothing to fear. When it came to love, she believed *she* loved *them* more than anyone else in the whole world. "Don't answer that," she said quickly, vigorously shaking her head. "It's a silly question. Where does anyone hide anything? In a bottom drawer? Behind a book in the bookcase? Really, they could be anywhere. I'll start in the obvious places and work my way through his study, inch by inch." She pressed a glove to her mouth and shut her eyes. "Oh, I do miss him." Both Harry and Boysie put an arm around her and squeezed her tightly.

"Of course you do, darling," said Harry. "But you're not alone."

"Lord no," Boysie rejoined. "You're never alone. You'll always have us."

AFTER THE FUNERAL Celia left her mother in the care of her sisters and returned to London with Boysie and Harry. Her father's last words had been delivered with urgency—it was her responsibility to see that his final wish was granted.

It felt strange to be in the house on her own. She could hear the reassuring rumble of motorcars down on Kensington High Street and the scuffling sound of the servants who inhabited the top floor of the building and the hidden recesses behind the green baize door. The streetlights bathed the road outside her father's study window in an amber glow that somehow made her feel less lonely. She closed the curtains. She could detect the sweetness of her father's cigars, the rich scent of whiskey and the musty smell of papers, ink and books. Or was she imagining it because she wanted to feel his presence so badly?

She slumped into his leather chair and ran her eyes over his desk. Digby was not a tidy man. There were books, documents, newspapers and notes strewn across it. He seemed to scrawl comments and observations on everything. She picked up a letter he had been writing and ran her fingers over the ink. He had flamboyant handwriting, like an artist's calligraphy. Dreading that it might be a love letter she held her breath, but it was only a thank-you letter to Lady Fitzherbert for a dinner party he had been to. She sighed helplessly. There were drawers, cupboards and bookcases, full of her father's life. Where was she to start looking for these incriminating letters?

Slowly and meticulously she began to rifle through his drawers. No one had tidied them, ever. She smiled as she remembered his continuous battle with her mother. He hadn't wanted the servants to invade his private room but she had been adamant that it had needed dusting at the very least. "It'll end up smelling like a hamster cage," she had said, to which he had replied, "Hamsters don't smoke cigars and drink whiskey, my dear, and I'm not opposed to a thin layer of dust." At first Celia was careful to lift everything out, piece by piece, and study it. Attached to each item must be an anecdote she'd never hear, she thought, rubbing her thumb over the surfaces, wondering how her father had come by these things and what they had meant to him. Old coins, pens, business cards, travel documents, racing cards, menus and other mementoes, all thrown in together. Eventually she lost patience and poured the contents of the drawers onto the rug.

There were no letters, or he had hidden them in a very clever place. If she couldn't find them, her mother certainly wouldn't. She was relieved; she didn't want to read love letters from a mistress. Of course she suspected that he had had mistresses, or certainly taken lovers. After all, he had been a very wealthy, attractive man who had mixed with socialites and actresses—and women of ill repute no doubt; it would have been odd if he hadn't cast his eye about. But that was a man's business. She didn't want to know anything about it. She wanted to remember him as a good husband to her mother. She didn't want anything to change the way she thought about him.

Celia went through the cupboards beneath the bookcases. She felt his presence strongly as she looked through old sepia photographs stuck into thickly bound albums. There were photographs of him in his youth: sitting on top of a camel in a panama hat, on safari in Africa, at Ascot Races in top hat and tails, standing in front of the Taj Mahal and the Pyramids of Giza. He had been dashing even then, always with a raffish smile on his face and a mischievous twinkle in his eye. There were a few photographs of his brothers, but they were strangers to Celia. Her grandmother Augusta, on the other hand, had been surprisingly beautiful then, but her grandfather hadn't changed at all. Even his sweeping mustache was the same. She dwelled on the pictures of her father. He had always been jovial, as if he had found everything in the world amusing.

With the rug almost entirely covered in her father's clutter she didn't know where to look next. She glanced at the clock on the mantelpiece. It was nearly midnight, and she was beginning to feel tired. But she was frightened to go to bed in the mansion with only the servants upstairs, sleeping like mice beneath the floorboards. The place felt uneasy, as if it understood that the master had gone and didn't know quite what to do with itself. She wished she had asked Boysie or Harry to stay with her.

Wearily she stood in the middle of the study, casting her eye about the room in search of a secret place where her father might have hidden letters he didn't want anyone to find. She hadn't even come across a safe and she had opened every drawer. Then her eyes rested on the library of books her father had never read, because it was well known in the family that her father had never read a book in his life. Why so many? For a man who never read it suddenly seemed odd. Then an idea struck her. She hurried to the shelves and began pulling out all the books and tossing them onto the floor. They clattered about her feet, releasing clouds of dust into the air. And then she found it, the safe hidden in the wall behind the row of innocent-looking books. Her excitement injected her with energy and she no longer felt tired. She didn't take long to find the key. It was sitting in an ashtray on the desk among various coins, golf tees and paperclips. Behind the door were three letters, sitting loosely on top of other documents.

With her heart thumping in her chest she took the letters to the armchair where her father used to sit and read the papers beside the fire, inhaled deeply and pulled the first out of the envelope. Just as she began to read, her father's voice came back to her on a wave of guilt. He had told her to *burn* them; he hadn't told her to *read* them. But, she reasoned, he hadn't told her *not* to read them. After a moment's hesitation her curiosity overcame any reservations and she continued to run her eyes down the page.

Her greatest fear had been love letters from a mistress but now, reading the terrible words written on the page, love letters would have been preferable to *this*. Her heart plummeted into her stomach and the blood drained from her face. The floor seemed to spin away from her as she drew the other two letters from their envelopes and hurried to read them. How she wished she had just done what her father had asked and burned them. Hadn't she been taught that curiosity killed the cat? Now she knew what these letters contained she could never *un*know it. She felt tainted by the poison contained within the words. Cursed. There was only one thing to do.

Hastily, as if the letters had a life of their own and might suddenly make off out of the house and into the public gaze, she screwed them into tight balls and threw them into the grate. She found matches on the mantelpiece and struck one. Bending down she put the flame to the paper and watched it grow into a small fire. The blaze consumed the letters until all that was left was ash, sinking into the pile of cinders left over from her father's many fires.

Aurelius Dupree. She never wanted to see or hear that name again.

Chapter 24

L *ondon has lost its brightest—and richest—light,* wrote Viscount Castlerosse in his *Express* column.

Sir Digby Deverill was one of my dearest friends and his sudden death from a heart attack has sent waves of shock through the drawing rooms of London's elite, for we all believed him immortal. It was no surprise to see his memorial service attended by the crème de la crème of British society and queens of film and theater. Earl Baldwin of Bewdley, who, it is whispered, was trying to entice the flamboyant and popular Sir Digby into politics, rubbed shoulders with Mr. Winston Churchill, the Earl of Birkenhead and Lord Beaverbrook, founder of this newspaper, and the delightful Betty Balfour and Madeleine Carroll brought the glamour of the silver screen to the somber event in Mayfair and reminded us

that Sir Digby's net was flung far and wide. The King
sent a representative, for Sir Digby was a popular
character in the racing world and I once heard that he
bought a horse from the royal stud at an inflated price, a
favor the King remembered. I was not surprised to see a
few of his fellow Randlords, among them his friend and
neighbor, Sir Abe Bailey, whom I saw chatting to the
aesthete Mr. Boysie Bancroft, one of the leading lights
at Christie's, about art no doubt; Sir Abe's collection is
said to be second to none. The black attire of mourning
did not diminish the radiant beauty of the Marchioness
of Londonderry who attended with her son, Lord
Castlereagh. But none outshone the tragic beauty of
Deverill's youngest daughter, the recently widowed
Mrs. Celia Mayberry, and the question unspoken
on everyone's lips was: Will she or won't she sell
her castle?

"Ridiculous!" Maud sniffed, closing the paper. "Nothing will induce her to sell the castle."

"She's planning on selling the contents," Harry informed her, stirring milk into his coffee.

"That's not the same as selling the castle. Viscount Castlerosse should write fiction, not fact, he'd be much better at it. Honestly, the last thing on anyone's mind yesterday was the castle."

"I'm sure Digby has left Celia enough in his will to cover any of Archie's losses," he said optimistically.

"Archie left Celia in a terrible position. Imagine doing that to one's wife. Shameful." She smiled at her son. Harry's visits did much to raise her spirits. Autumn always made her feel melancholy, with the strong winds, falling leaves and thick smog. "So what's Celia going to do now?"

"She'll sit it out here in London for a while, I think. At least until the will is read and she knows where she stands. The nanny is coming over with the children. Beatrice—"

"Beatrice," Maud interrupted, pursing her scarlet lips. "Beatrice isn't good for anything. She should remember that she has a family who needs her. I imagine Celia needs her mother very badly right now because those sisters of hers are useless, but they've never been close. You're good to her, though, aren't you, Harry? I'm sure she's taking comfort from you."

"Beatrice has returned to Deverill Rising already," Harry continued. "She doesn't want to see anyone or talk to anyone."

"She needs to eat. She's half the size she was in the summer."

"She's unhappy, Mama. I'm sure it'll pass."

"Of course it will. She'll bounce back. We Deverills are a resilient lot."

"We have to be."

"No one more than *me*, Harry. What I have been put through would have felled most normal women. But I am made of tougher stuff." Harry wondered what exactly she had been put through, besides the odd scandal and losing a castle that she never liked in the first place. He did not disagree with her, however. He knew better than to argue with his mother. "What keeps me going is my faith, my children and the certainty that I have always only ever done my best."

Harry looked around her sumptuous sitting room, which she had spared no expense in furnishing, and decided to change the subject. "You've made a fine home, Mama."

"I have, but I cannot deny that I am lonely. You are my consolation, Harry. You, Charlotte and those adorable children. I have no regrets. None." She smiled at him again and the satisfaction in it made Harry feel uncomfortable. "You have done me proud, my darling. I could not have wished for a better son."

CELIA CLOSED THE newspaper with a disdainful sniff. Her father had told her not to sell the castle. That place meant more to him than anyone could know. There was no way that she was going to give it up without a fight.

She reflected on the memorial service. What Castlerosse hadn't noticed was the strange man in the felt hat who had attended without invitation and had lurked at the back of the church, watching them all keenly—the same man as the one who had been outside the church at the funeral, staring at her with such vitriol. Celia had noticed him. She was terrible at remembering names but she never forgot a face, and his, gaunt, mottled and gray, had stuck in her memory like a thorn. She had seen him various times since, standing beneath the lamp on her street, watching the house, watching *her*. To show up at her father's funeral was one thing, but to attend the memorial service was audacious to say the least, but she didn't imagine he had many scruples. Not him. Not Aurelius Dupree.

She knew he wanted to get her attention, but she was determined not to let him. If she ignored him perhaps he would go away.

Beatrice was too unwell to attend the reading of the will. The meeting was held in a plush office in St. James's, and those present included Celia and her sisters Leona and Vivien, their husbands Bruce and Tarquin, and Harry, whom Celia had invited to stand in for Archie. The mood was somber and formal.

Mr. Riswold, Digby's solicitor, was not the usual plump, paternal solicitor, but as cadaverous and dour as an undertaker. He sat at the end of the table and opened his briefcase. After the usual pleasantries he lifted out a neat pile of papers held together by a staple and laid it carefully in front of him. "Let us begin," he said and the family waited expectantly to hear how their father had divided his great wealth.

Digby had in fact bequeathed everything to Beatrice, leaving it at her discretion to share money and property with their daughters. As Mr. Riswold explained, Sir Digby's money had been *gambled*—for that is the word he used, and he looked somewhat disapproving—on the Stock Exchange, which everyone present knew had crashed the year before. If Sir Digby had lived, Mr. Riswold was sure that he would have recuperated his losses in time; as it was—and at this point small beads of sweat began to sprout on his forehead—he had lost a great deal. He cleared his throat, avoided looking at any of them directly, and told them the grim truth. Digby's financial troubles had been far greater than any of them had imagined. The gambler's luck had finally run out.

"How are we going to tell Mama?" Leona asked, her long face ashen with shock. They had entered the room believing themselves very rich, only to discover that they had been left nothing.

"We're not going to tell Mama," said Celia decisively.

"I don't think we can keep this sort of information from her, Celia," said Vivien. "We will have to sell Papa's assets. That includes Deverill House in London and Deverill Rising in Wiltshire. Papa's greatest joys." Her eyes glittered with tears. Tarquin put his hand on hers and squeezed it encouragingly.

"Mama's in no state to hear that her homes are threatened," said Celia.

"Let's not be dramatic," Leona cut in. "The only person who will be doing any selling will be you, Celia. Mama is going to struggle to pay off Papa's debts with the little he has left, but there's certainly nothing in the pot to pay off yours."

Celia stiffened. "I am perfectly capable of paying off Archie's debts myself, thank you very much," she retorted crossly, aware that in truth she was incapable of paying off even half of them.

"Let's not fight," Harry interrupted.

"I agree," said Bruce. "We have to discuss this calmly, as one unit." His tidy brown mustache twitched as his mind, conditioned by a long career in the army, set about putting together a strategy.

"Celia is right," said Tarquin, who had enjoyed as many years in the armed forces as his brother-in-law and was as much excited by schemes, plans and tactics as *he* was. "There's no point upsetting Beatrice. She's much too fragile at the moment and it might tip her over the edge. I suggest we work out exactly how much is owed and then we can calculate how much is left to run both houses."

"I break out in a sweat just thinking about how much those houses cost," said Celia. "I know how much I spend on Castle Deverill—"

"This isn't about Castle Deverill," said Leona, her voice rising a tone. Vivien shot her a warning look, but Leona continued regardless. "If it wasn't for Papa throwing money at your stupid castle we might not be in the situation we are in."

"Leona, that's not fair," Vivien cut in. "Castle Deverill was Papa's dream."

"Well, it's turned into a nightmare, hasn't it."

"Please, let's not fight," said Harry again. If anyone should be upset about Castle Deverill it was him—and he wasn't.

"I never liked the place. It was cold and damp and much too big," said Leona. "You've made it into a palace. It was never meant to be a palace. I'm sure Adeline and Hubert are turning in their graves."

"Leona, enough," said her husband in the same tone he would use for an insubordinate officer cadet. "Let's be positive. There's no point dwelling on the past. Digby was perfectly within his rights to spend his money as he pleased. He'd earned it."

"And gambled it away," said Leona bitterly.

"We have to work out how to proceed." Bruce turned to the grim solicitor who had remained quiet and watchful as the temperature in the room had begun to rise. "Mr. Riswold, you know Sir Digby's affairs better than any of us, perhaps you can advise us."

Mr. Riswold pulled back his shoulders, licked his forefinger again and flicked through the pages of his document to the very end. "I anticipated your concern," he said in a monotone. "So I took the liberty of working out a plan for you . . ." Celia knew then why her father had chosen this meager, pedantic man to run his affairs; it was on account of his composure under pressure. "Prepare yourselves," he warned ominously. "For the worst." They all felt the vertiginous sensation of falling, falling inescapably toward poverty.

When Celia returned to Deverill House the butler handed her a letter on a tray. She recognized the handwriting at once and turned white. "A gentleman delivered it this afternoon," the butler explained when Celia asked, for there was no stamp on the envelope. The thought of Aurelius Dupree ringing her doorbell sent a chill coursing over her skin, like the march of a thousand ice-cold ants. She pulled herself together, calmly thanked the butler, then strode into her father's study, threw the letter in the grate with a trembling hand, and did what she had done with the others: burned it. She hoped that by destroying them the whole situation would go away.

There was only one thing to do, return to Castle Deverill. Perhaps Mr. Dupree wouldn't find her there. The following morning she explained to the butler that she was leaving for Ireland and, if that man was to turn up again, with or without a letter, he was to say that she had left indefinitely so there was no point in corresponding further. She hoped he wouldn't turn up at Deverill Rising and try to speak to her mother. If Beatrice knew what those letters had contained they'd most likely have another funeral to arrange.

ADELINE WATCHED CELIA'S return home with concern. She sensed Celia's fear as well as her determination to delve into her inner resources and find a strength she wasn't sure she had. Celia was alone. She might have Bertie in the Hunting Lodge and Kitty in the White House but she had never been as lonely as she was now. Adeline's heart went out to her; but there was nothing she could do to console her. Archie and Digby were gone from her sight; the fact that they were still with her in spirit meant nothing to someone who lacked the sensitivity to feel them.

"I envy the likes of Digby," said Barton, pushing himself up from the chair and joining Adeline at the window. "He's a lucky Deverill, after all."

"If you mean because he's free to come and go as he wishes, then you're right," said Adeline, who found herself losing patience with these cantankerous spirits. "But he's not very lucky to have left when he did. Much too early. He still had things to do."

"Didn't we all, Adeline," Barton rejoined. He sighed and watched Celia stride into the castle, leaving the servants to carry in her luggage and the nanny to take in the children. "This wasn't the first time the castle had to be rebuilt," he added.

"Oh?" said Adeline, her curiosity mounting.

"It has been burned down before."

"In your time?" she asked.

He nodded. "Aye. In my time. History does indeed repeat itself. The people of Ballinakelly rose up against me and set it alight. I was summoned back to Ireland to defend it. There's nothing like seeing your home blazing on the horizon. A great furnace, like God's own smithy at work, it was. Much like the great fire by the rebels that took Hubert."

"Those weren't rebels," said Adeline crossly. "That was personal."

"Love and hate are very closely intertwined," he said and his voice was heavy with regret.

Adeline looked at him. His face was contorted with pain, his mouth twisted with remorse. "What did you do, Barton?" she asked quietly.

He gazed out of the window but she knew he wasn't seeing anything but the face of a woman, for only love can do that to a man. "I did something unforgivable," he confessed. "And yet unavoidable."

"To whom?"

He shook his head and closed his eyes. For over two hundred and fifty years he had kept the secrets concealed safely in his heart. He had barely dared even face them himself. But now, with Adeline's light so dazzlingly bright, he wanted to release his burden. He wanted to free himself from the guilt, from the darkness that hung about him like a shroud, from the intolerable weight of shadow. He wanted to absorb some of her light. "I loved Maggie O'Leary," he said and his voice was so quiet Adeline wasn't sure she had heard him.

"You loved the woman who laid a curse on you and your descendants?" Adeline gasped. "The very same woman who condemned you to this limbo?"

"Aye. I loved her." The words left him like venom expelled from a wound. "I loved her to her core."

"But I don't understand. If you loved her, why did she not undo the curse?"

He turned to her, shook his head and gave a small, hopeless smile.

CELIA HAD NEVER felt so alone. In spite of the castle full of servants and the corridors full of ghosts, she felt isolated and abandoned and desperately lost. She barely dared look the servants in the eye for soon she would have to let them all go. She curled up in bed and felt ever more keenly the absence of her husband. His side of the mattress felt vast and cold and she dared not put her foot into it, for while she lay coiled like a snake she could pretend not to notice the chill beside her. Tears trickled onto the pillow until the cotton beneath her head was entirely wet. She felt like a puppet whose strings had been cut. The puppeteer had left her to her own devices, but she didn't want independence and uncertainty; she wanted security. She wanted things to be the way they were when she and Archie were in Italy, buying furniture and paintings for the castle. Before the money ran out, before Archie killed himself, before her father had died of a heart attack, before everything had gone so horribly wrong. She pressed her eyes shut and prayed to God. He was her last resort. The one person she could count on not to take offense at being the only remaining option. After all, wasn't His love unconditional?

The following day she went to see Kitty. She needed to be with someone who understood; someone who didn't criticize as Leona had done; someone who had suffered as much as *she* had. Only someone like Kitty could empathize with her predicament.

She found her in her sitting room wrapping Christmas presents at a round table by the window. It seemed like a lifetime ago that she had hosted Christmas. Her husband and father had been alive then. Everything had been wonderful, privileged, blessed. She appreciated her good fortune now as she had never done before. There was nothing like losing something to make one value its worth.

When Kitty saw her, standing diminished and forlorn in the doorway, she rose from her chair and walked over with her arms outstretched and her face full of compassion. Words were superfluous to cousins as close as they. Kitty wrapped her arms around Celia and squeezed her tightly. Celia gave in to her despair and bewilderment and sobbed loudly onto Kitty's shoulder. Kitty, who knew misery better than most, let her release her grief in gasps and hiccups and sighs, all the time murmuring words of encouragement and comfort. She knew time would dull the pain, it would no longer throb and burn, and Celia would eventually grow accustomed to the constant aching in her heart. Indeed, it would become as much part of her as the beat itself; she would barely notice it. Yet it would always be there, and in the quiet moments when she found herself left alone with her thoughts and her mind was not occupied with daily troubles, it would rise in her awareness and she would remember all over again the terrible agony of loss. Kitty shut her eyes and tried not to allow Jack's face to surface, as it so often did, when it caught her unawares. Hers was a loss she would carry to the grave.

They sat by the fire and Celia told Kitty how her father had gambled everything away on the Stock Exchange. She told her of Leona's resentment and Vivien's weak attempts to stand up for her. She divulged her thoughts about Harry and Boysie and was surprised when Kitty confessed that she had known for years, and she told her of her desolation and her pain, but she didn't tell her about Aurelius Dupree. She could never tell anyone about Aurelius Dupree, not even Kitty.

Then one day in early January Celia received another letter. Like those before, it was hand-delivered and presented on the silver tray as the afternoon sun sank into the sea. She was gripped by an icy fear. Aurelius Dupree was in Ireland. He had followed her here to Castle Deverill. He had invaded her fortress. She didn't dare open it. She couldn't bear to read any more about her father and what had happened in South Africa. She knew it was all lies. She knew her father would never hurt or deceive anyone. They were nothing more than vicious, evil lies. Once again she threw the letter into the fire, but this time she knew that however much the paper was consumed by the flames the information in it could never be destroyed, as long as Aurelius Dupree was alive.

She also knew it would only be a matter of time before Aurelius Dupree knocked on her castle door and she was obliged to let him in.

Chapter 25

To distract herself from her worries Celia spent a great deal of time with Kitty. Kitty's daughter, Florence, played with Celia's daughter Connie, just as Kitty and Celia had played together as little girls, while JP was too grown-up to be interested in small children. He was now a boisterous nine-year-old, as adept in the saddle as he was in the school room and handsome with it. He seemed to have inherited the finest Deverill qualities—the piercing gray gaze, the intelligent expression, the ready humor and easy charm—so no one seemed to give much thought to the qualities on his mother's side.

Kitty was careful to keep him away from Ballinakelly for fear of bumping into Michael Doyle, that brutal humbug known to all as "the Pope." The only time she had seen him had been through the car window on her way to church and she had deliberately turned her head so as not to catch his eye. She was determined he should never have contact with JP. The boy was a Deverill first and foremost—and secondly a Trench. Bridie had made her choice and started a new life in America. Kitty doubted she would ever come back. JP prayed for his mama who he believed to be in Heaven, but his prayers were hasty and careless; Kitty was everything a mother should be and he felt no less for the absence of a biological mother. He had two fathers, Robert, who was a constant presence around the house, and Bertie, whom he sought out in the Hunting Lodge as often as he was able. Indeed, as he grew up he and Bertie had grown close. They both loved the same things: fishing, hunting, tennis and croquet, tinkering in Bertie's shed and playing word games in front of the fire at teatime. Kitty knew there was nothing a Doyle could give him that he didn't already have.

Bertie and JP had constructed a large model railway in the attic of the Hunting Lodge. It took up a whole room, which had once been a storage room, and was spread across a quadrant of trestle tables. There were green hills with little model sheep grazing on grass, tunnels, bridges, lakes and tiny cottages and farm buildings. They had built a station complete with signals, moving tracks and a pedestrian crossing. There was even a fishing boat on the lake with a tiny man holding a rod, with a line and a gasping fish on the end of it. The more sophisticated parts that were unavailable in Dublin Bertie bought in London, but the hardware shop in Ballinakelly was well equipped with the essentials such as glue, paint, wood and card. It was on a particularly wet day in January that Bertie and JP, seizing on the idea to build a castle with a greenhouse and a stable block, decided to drive into Ballinakelly to buy what they needed for such an ambitious project.

Thick gray clouds rolled in off the ocean, propelled by a strong easterly wind that blew cold gusts over the water, whipping about the cliffs and whistling around the chimney stacks. Bertie, who drove a blue Model T Ford, sat at the wheel with his son by his side, relishing the project they were enjoying together. He was ashamed of having once rejected JP, of having all but disowned Kitty for insisting on keeping him when she had found the small baby on the doorstep of the Hunting Lodge. How ironic that the very child he had believed would bring about his demise had in fact given him a reason to live.

Father and son chatted excitedly about how they were going to design and build the castle. Bertie suggested various materials, but JP had his own ideas and was confident in voicing them. He wanted it to look exactly like Castle Deverill. "That might be beyond us, JP." Bertie chuckled.

"Nothing is beyond us, Papa," said JP cheerfully. "We can do anything, you and I." Bertie glanced admiringly at his son, for whom anything seemed possible. "We will build Castle Deverill with all its towers and windows and doors. We'll even make the trees and vegetable garden. I know exactly how to make the dome of the greenhouse using an onion, papier mâché and some green paint."

"I suppose the Hunting Lodge isn't enough of a challenge for you?" said Bertie, rather hoping JP would be inspired to build that instead.

JP looked horrified. "But that's not home, Papa. Castle Deverill is *home*." And Bertie shook his head because he knew *that* could only have come from Kitty.

Ballinakelly high street was busy. People were walking beneath umbrellas or hurrying to find shelter from the rain in the public houses and shops. Men in caps and jackets strode briskly down the sidewalk with their heads down and shoulders hunched and horses pulling carts plodded slowly up the road, too wet to care. Bertie parked the car outside the hardware shop and they dashed inside. Mr. O'Casey greeted them deferentially. An old man who remembered the days when the present Lord Deverill was a little boy, Mr. O'Casey had an innate respect for the aristocracy and counted the night the castle burned as one of the worst in living memory. He listened to JP's elaborate plan to make a model of the castle and shuffled about behind the counter, even climbing the ladder to reach the highest shelf, in order to find the right materials for the project. He piled them up on the counter. JP touched them excitedly. "We're going to make a fine castle," he said as Mr. O'Casey put on his spectacles and began to punch the prices into his cash register. Just as he was finishing the little bell rang above the door and a damp wind swept in with Michael Doyle.

Bertie put the money on the counter and turned to face the man the Royal Irish Constabulary had wanted in connection with the fire but had later set free. If Bertie felt any animosity toward Michael Doyle he was too polite to show it. "Good morning, Mr. Doyle," he said evenly.

Michael's eyes fell upon the child and his face softened. "Good morning, Lord Deverill." He took off his cap, freeing a halo of wild black curls. "And this would be young Master Jack Deverill?" he said with a smile.

JP nodded. "I'm JP," he said politely. "How do you do?"

Michael hadn't properly laid eyes on the child since he had carried him down on the train from Dublin. He had been a small baby then. Now he was a handsome boy with a twinkle in his eye. But in spite of his red hair he was a Doyle. *That* was certain. Michael could see it in the strength of his jaw and in the light sprinkling of freckles that covered his nose. He saw Bridie in his wide forehead and in the sweetness of his curved upper lip, but he recognized himself in the directness of the boy's gaze. For sure, JP was a bold, fearless child, just as *he* had been. He felt a surge of pride.

Bertie thanked Mr. O'Casey and lifted the paper bag of supplies from the counter. "Come on, JP," he said. "You and I have work to do." He nodded at Michael and Michael took off his cap again as Lord Deverill opened the door, then followed his son into the street. The little bell tinkled once more and the door shut behind them. Michael watched the boy climb into the car. He had already forgotten Michael and was chatting happily to his father. A moment later the car motored off and Michael was left with a strange sense of loss. JP was his nephew, but the boy would never know it.

Michael bought the items he had come for, then left for home in the car they had bought with Bridie's money. He wondered whether Grace would be sitting in his kitchen, praying with his mother and grandmother. He was quite used to her now. She had come enough times—and ignored him enough times—to convince him of her sincerity. At first he thought it a ruse to entice him back into her bed, but as the months passed and she received regular instruction from Father Quinn, attending Mass in the Catholic Church in Cork, he realized that her conversion to Catholicism had nothing to do with him. She genuinely wanted to find peace with herself and God. He understood that and respected her for it. Once they were together in sin; now they were together in Christ. Yet he could not quite forget her voracious passion and her burning skin.

As he drove off into the hills he thought of Kitty Deverill. Until he had her forgiveness he'd never lie with anyone again.

GRACE SAT ON the sofa in her sitting room while Father Quinn filled the armchair with his black robes, a glass of whiskey in his hand. Grace had stalked her prey like a patient snake with a cunning rat. She had always known it would take time. Father Quinn wasn't going to betray a secret so readily, but she knew him well enough to know that if it served his interests he would betray his own mother. He had to be coaxed, lured and gently persuaded—he had to believe that he was doing God's work. First and foremost he had to trust Grace. After all, they had plotted and schemed during the War of Independence so Father Quinn knew better than most that Grace could keep a secret. And he was well aware that she and Michael had been firm allies in the fight against the British in spite of the vast differences in their births. She was confident that she could use guile to wheedle out of Father Quinn the terrible crime Michael had committed in his past of which he was so ashamed.

She pushed the whiskey bottle across the table. "Please, Father Quinn, you need fortification in your job," she said, and she listened with half an ear as he railed against the young people and their lack of commitment.

"In our day we had a cause to fight. That united us and drove us," she said. "God knows, I wouldn't want another war, but the struggle for freedom was a cause I believed in with all my heart and I was willing to risk my life for it."

"You were a brave lady," Father Quinn said, refilling his glass.

"But I did terrible things," she said, lowering her voice in confidence. "I'll go to Hell for some of the things I did." She looked at him squarely.

"*Repent ye therefore, and be converted, that your sins may be blotted out,*" Father Quinn quoted from the Bible.

"I lured Colonel Manley into the farmhouse. If it hadn't been for me, Jack O'Leary would never have plunged the knife into his heart. I am as guilty of murder as he is," she said in a soft voice and her eyes welled with tears. "Can God forgive me for that?"

"If you truly repent, my dear Lady Rowan-Hampton, the Lord will forgive you and wipe clean the slate."

"I truly repent, Father, with all my heart. I regret the things I have done. The things Michael and I did." She pulled a white cotton handkerchief out of her sleeve and dabbed her eyes. "How I admire him, Father. He was the worst kind of sinner— oh, the things he did in the name of freedom—and yet he turned his life around and is as pious as any priest." *And as celibate*, she thought bitterly, but she kept that complaint to herself. "If I can be half as devout as he is I shall be happy, Father Quinn."

"Michael did indeed turn his life around. He gave up the drink, you see. It awakened the Devil in him and drove him to sin."

"He told me, Father Quinn, he told me about . . ." She began to sob. "Oh, I can't believe he could have . . ." She hesitated, barely daring to breathe, hoping he would finish the sentence for her.

"But my dear Lady Rowan-Hampton, his sins are not your sins."

She turned her face away sharply. "I know that, Father, but can God forgive such depravity?"

"Indeed he can. If Michael truly repents, then the Lord will indeed forgive him. Even for that."

She gazed at him with wide, shiny eyes. "Even for that?" she repeated, desperate to know what *that* was.

Father Quinn leaned forward and rested his elbows on his knees. He stared into his glass and shook his head. "God will forgive him, but he wants more than that. He will not rest until he receives forgiveness from Kitty Deverill."

Grace let out a controlled breath and nodded gravely. She did not show her surprise nor did she reveal her delight at having snared the rat and induced him to squeak. She kept her expression steady and unchanging. "I pray that she will find it in her heart to forgive, Father."

He looked at her and frowned. "If there is anything you can do, I would be very grateful."

"As you know Kitty is a dear friend," she said, slipping the handkerchief back up her sleeve. "She took me into her confidence many years ago. Leave it with me. Now I know that Michael is ready to beg forgiveness I will see what I can do to help. I only want the best for both of them. I ask God to give me tact. It will not be an easy task."

"Indeed not," Father Quinn agreed. "But if anyone can do it, you can, Lady Rowan-Hampton. I have great faith in your abilities." *So do I*, she thought smugly.

When Father Quinn left, weaving his way to his car, which was parked on the gravel outside the house, Grace withdrew to her bedroom. She closed the door and went and stood by the window. There, in the privacy of her room, she let out a low moan and gave in to a sudden shudder that rippled across her entire body. So Kitty Deverill was the reason Michael had rebuffed her. All these years she had imagined countless different reasons, but she had never for a second imagined this. Of course she didn't believe that Michael had violated her, which Father Quinn had implied. Kitty must have seduced him, for certain, and wracked by guilt he had taken to drink. It was all Kitty's fault. Michael was a wild and passionate man, Grace reasoned, but he wasn't a rapist.

It took her a while to quell the jealousy that rose in her like a tide of putrid water, stealing her breath. She had to use all her strength to control her movements because her instinct was to pick something up and throw it against the wall. But Grace was a woman who had spent years practicing the art of self-discipline. She focused on the garden and tried to push away the picture of Michael thrusting into Kitty, which clung to her mind as if her thoughts had got stuck on one image. At length she managed to internalize her fury by hatching a plot. There was nothing like a plan to make one feel less impotent. If Grace could persuade Kitty to forgive Michael, he might return to her bed.

THAT EVENING LAUREL returned from an afternoon hacking across the hills with Ethelred Hunt. Ever since he had suggested that she would cut a dash on a horse, she had flirted with the idea of riding again. Indeed, she had been an accomplished horsewoman in her day, brave even, out hunting, and she wasn't planning on doing anything reckless. Hazel had thought her ridiculous; after all she was only a few years off eighty. But why should her life taper toward the end? she thought defiantly. Surely, she was as young as she felt. Ethelred Hunt certainly made her feel like a girl again, and today, riding over the cliffs with the sea crashing against the rocks below and the sea gulls circling above, she had relived a moment of her youth.

Laurel was passionately in love. There was no distinguishing it from the breathless, invigorating feelings of longing that she had experienced as a twenty-year-old. She might be an old lady now but her heart was still tender, like a rosebud opening with the first gentle caress of spring. She didn't believe herself foolish; after all, why should love be the privilege of the young? If Adeline were alive she would say that it is just the physical body that grows old, the soul is eternal and therefore cannot age. Laurel might look like a grandmother, but when Ethelred Hunt had gazed into her eyes and pressed his lips to hers he was seeing a woman.

She inhaled and closed her eyes, reliving for a wonderful moment the feeling of his mouth on hers. She could still smell the spicy scent of his skin and feel the soft hair of his beard on her face. Oh, it had been like a dream, a beautiful dream. She would never forget it for as long as she lived. "We must keep this to ourselves," he had told her, unwinding his hand from around her waist, or from where her waist had been when she was young. "Or we'll upset Hazel. I think she's sweet on me," he told her. Laurel had glowed with delight. After years fighting her sister for attention from this irresistible silver wolf he had chosen *her*.

"Oh, I can keep a secret from Hazel," she had reassured him, and indeed she would.

She walked into the house, closing the door softly behind her. She hadn't seen her sister since that morning, when they had both departed, Hazel to Bertie's for a morning at the bridge table and *she* to the hairdresser. The sound of the gramophone came wafting down the corridor from the sitting room. Laurel was surprised and wondered whether Hazel had company. It wasn't usual for her to play music just for herself. She found her sister standing by the window, gazing out onto the wintry garden where they put bird food for the hardy little robins. One hand wound around the back of her neck, the other was on her hip and she was humming distractedly and swaying slightly, Laurel thought. "Hello, Hazel," said Laurel breezily, unpinning her hat.

Hazel turned, startled. "Oh Laurel, you're back."

"Yes, I am. It was such fun to be out riding again. I feel rejuvenated." She looked at her sister and realized that *she* wasn't the only one to feel rejuvenated. Hazel's cheeks were pink and her eyes sparkled.

"At least you didn't fall off," she said in a blasé tone, as if she wasn't very interested one way or the other. Hazel didn't ask her about Ethelred and Laurel was relieved; she didn't want to betray his kiss with a schoolgirl blush.

"What have you been up to?" She perched on the arm of the sofa and placed her hat on her knee.

"This and that," Hazel replied vaguely. "Bridge was entertaining as usual. This afternoon, well . . ." She sighed dismissively. "I haven't done anything this afternoon except watch the birds. Aren't they perky?"

"Who was at bridge?"

"Just the usual crowd. Bertie and Kitty and I partnered Ethelred." She went and rang the bell for the maid. "Let's have a cup of tea and finish off that porter cake." She didn't catch

Laurel's eye as she passed her. "Tell me, what is it like to be in the saddle again? Were you afraid?"

Laurel shrugged off her sister's shifty behavior and went to sit closer to the fire. "Not afraid, no," she said, smiling at the memory. "It was the most exciting thing I've done in years." And for once neither tried to outdo the other with florid tales of Ethelred Hunt. In fact, his name was not mentioned again and the cordiality with which they had always treated each other returned in eager chatter and cheerful laughter. But every now and then both women ran their fingers over their lips and smiled secretively into their hands.

As MUCH AS Celia tried to distract herself from the cold reality of her father's death and the terrible debts Archie had left her with, she was unable to ignore the fact that she had to find money somewhere, and soon. Her father was no longer around to help her and, if he had been, she now realized that he wouldn't have had the resources. She put on smiles for her children, for the friends who came calling and for the members of her family who were always popping in to check on her, but her anxiety lay in the pit of her stomach like cement. There were moments when she stood at her bedroom window, gazing up at the stars and remembering the Deverill Castle Summer Balls of her childhood, when she, Kitty and Bridie had watched the carriages arriving, bearing County Cork's finest, and wished that she could wake up as a little girl again, with no fears or worries. The skies had always been clear on those magical nights, darkening gradually as twilight receded into night with the faint glimmer of the first star.

She dreaded having to sell the castle. This was her home

now. She had placed her heart in the heart of Ballinakelly and there it would stay.

It was a particularly windy morning when her butler walked into the drawing room to find her alone at her desk, writing letters. He knocked on the door. "There is a man here to see you, Mrs. Mayberry," he said. Celia knew who it was. She had been expecting him. The cement grew heavier in the bottom of her belly and she pressed a hand to her heart. She couldn't avoid him any longer.

"Show him in please, O'Sullivan, and ask Mrs. Connell to brew us some tea." She positioned herself in the middle of the room, straightened her skirt and cardigan and took a deep breath. A moment later the man Celia had seen at the funeral and at her father's memorial service was shown into the room.

"Mrs. Mayberry," he said, and he did not smile.

"Mr. Dupree," she replied, lifting her chin. "I've been expecting you for some time. Tea?"

Chapter 26

I don't want tea," he said in a thin, reedy voice. "Whiskey." When O'Sullivan brought it, Mr. Dupree downed it in a single gulp before replacing it on the silver salver with a quivering hand. Celia noticed his nails were cracked and ingrained with dirt. He looked at her with rheumy, bloodshot eyes. "I'll have that tea now," he said and Celia nodded at the butler, who reluctantly left the room. He was uneasy about leaving his mistress alone with this menacing vagabond.

Mr. Dupree could have been a hundred years old. His white hair was so thin that his scalp could be seen pink and scabby beneath it. His skin was sheer and mottled with age spots, scars and deep, angry lines that could have been the work of a knife. Bitterness had ravaged his lips and anger blazed behind cataracts that blurred his vision and made his eyes water. A nervous twitch had taken possession of one side of his face, snatching the muscles every few minutes and pulling his mouth into an ugly grimace, and he smelled of compacted alcohol and sweat found in men who have slept rough and lived low. The energy he emitted was as sharp and prickly as his gaze, and Celia found herself struggling to conceal her utter aversion to this man who had forced himself into her life like vermin sneaking into the castle by way of the gutter. Yet there was something evasive about the manner in which he held himself, something in the slight stoop of the shoulders and the curve of the spine, that robbed him of his menace and even aroused her pity. Beneath his anger he looked desperate.

"Please take a seat," she said and her voice was cool and as- sured; she barely recognized it as her own. She watched him perch uneasily on the edge of the armchair, then took the club fender for herself, in front of the fire. "I want you to know that I have read the letters you sent my father and I don't believe a word that's in them. The letters you sent to *me* I burned without reading them. I find it outrageous that you have the audacity to prey on a grieving family in this way."

Mr. Dupree pulled a packet of cigarettes out of the inside pocket of his jacket and tapped it against his hand. "How well did you know your father, Mrs. Mayberry?" he asked in a wretched voice, popping a cigarette between his dry lips. Celia thought his accent had traces of a brogue but couldn't place it.

"I was very close to him," she replied frostily.

Mr. Dupree shook his head. "I think you'll find you didn't know him at all," he said before bursting into a fit of coughing. "Do you believe in justice?" he asked her when the coughing had passed.

"Just tell me what you want, Mr. Dupree." Celia was infu- riated that this total stranger should assume to know anything about her relationship with her father. She watched him flick his thumb against a cheap lighter and puff on the flame with his cigarette. He put away the lighter and sat back in the armchair, crossing one scrawny leg over the other, revealing threadbare socks, dusty shoes and painfully thin ankles. "Your claims are very farfetched," she said, wishing he would get up and leave, but he didn't look as if he was planning on going anywhere for some time. Mr O'Sullivan returned with a tray of tea. He poured Mr. Dupree a cup and handed it to him. The fine bone china looked incongruous in his rough and callused hands.

"Let me start at the beginning, Mrs. Mayberry. Let me tell you about the Digby Deverill *I* knew."

Celia sighed with impatience. "All right. Go on." She had no interest in hearing his story, but as he was intent on blackmailing her, she had no choice but to listen. Mr O'Sullivan poured her a cup of tea, then left them alone, closing the door softly behind him.

Aurelius Dupree exhaled a thick cloud of smoke and narrowed his eyes. In spite of the defiance in his steady gaze the hand that held the cigarette was trembling. "When Digby Deverill arrived in Cape Town in 1885 and came out to Kimberley my elder brother, Tiberius, had already been prospecting for eight years," he began. "He knew everything there was to know about diamonds. Everything. They called him 'the Brill' because he had a nose for brilliants—he could literally smell 'em—and everyone wanted him on their team. He worked for Rhodes and Barnato—all of 'em giants and they paid him well for it. *Very* well. He called me out to join him and I came on the boat from England, traveled five hundred miles up to Kimberley and learned fast." He tapped his temple with a gnarled finger. "If you had your wits about you there was always money to be made in the mines." He grinned and Celia recoiled at the black holes where teeth had once been. "When Digby arrived, Kimberley was a great piece of cheese being eaten by ten thousand mice. Rhodes and Barnato were looking to amalgamate the mines. The place was all used up. There was nothing there for Deverill. He was just a keen boy from a good family but that counted for nothing, only money and diamonds meant a thing then and he had neither. Rhodes and Barnato were as rich as Midas. They were as rich as kings. Yet Digby arrived with his ambition and his optimism and he was a man who believed in himself. I've never met a man before or since who had the self-belief that Deverill had. He put up a tent on the edge of the mines, in the dust and the midsummer heat, with the flies—and deprivations that you can't imagine and I wouldn't want to tell you, not a refined lady like you, Mrs. Mayberry. You'd never 'ave known that he was a posh boy, thrown out of Eton at seventeen for running a gambling ring and sleeping with the matron or some other boy's mother, at least that's what he told me." He chuckled joylessly, then ejected a round of coughing from lungs full of phlegm. "They say that Lord Salisbury's son lost a hundred pounds at Deverill's table. But it wasn't with the finer class that Digby mixed in Kimberley, but with the roughest of rough diamonds you ever met. Jimmy 'Mad' McManus, who'd fought in the Crimean War and disemboweled a man with his own hands, apparently. Frank 'Stone Heart' Flint and Joshua Stein, better known as 'Spleen'—and you don't want to know how he got *that* name. He was their equal. He didn't fear them. If anything, for all his manners and his Eton tricks, these cut-throats feared *him*. He had the Devil on his side. Ruffians they were but Deverill had one thing none of 'em had: luck. He was lucky at the gambling table, so lucky that he got the name 'Lucky Deverill' soon enough, and it stuck—as did his luck."

Celia thought of her father's Derby winner—the last of his luck, before it ran out for good. "Go on, Mr. Dupree. What happened then?"

Aurelius Dupree dragged on his cigarette and Celia noticed with disgust the patches on his skin where his fingers had yellowed; he looked as if he was getting jaundice. He blew out a puff of smoke, leaned forward and flicked ash into the glass tray Celia had bought at Asprey on New Bond Street. Then he cleared his fluid-clogged chest in another round of coughing, which made Celia feel quite nauseous. "So, one day, Lucky Deverill is winning at the card table," he continued. "And Stone Heart Flint has reached the seams of his pockets. All he has left is a plot of useless farmland north of Kimberley. Deverill's luck is bound to run out at some stage, right? At some stage, certainly, but not then. Not for years! Deverill reveals his winning cards and scoops up the money. And of course, he wins the land—this supposedly useless plot of dust. Now, Tiberius and Deverill had become unlikely friends. Deverill knew nothing of diamonds, but my brother knew everything. The three of us made a pact, a gentlemen's agreement, if there were diamonds up there we were going to split it two ways. Two ways, equally, you understand, and Deverill agreed. Fifty percent for him, twenty-five each for me and my brother. It was his land but he needed us, you see. He couldn't do it without us.

"At first we found nothing. The place had been left to ruin, the mine abandoned, it didn't look like it had anything besides barren land, dust and flies and an old shack where the farmhouse had once stood. Even the well was empty and full of stones. It was a dead old pile of worthless land. But we began to dig in the places that hadn't been mined. Nothing. Deverill grew despondent and talked of quitting the place altogether, but like I said, Tiberius could smell diamonds and he smelled diamonds in the earth, right there on that supposedly barren plot of land. Deverill went and lay in the shade of the only tree for miles around, put his hat over his face and went to sleep. He wasn't interested in the land anymore. He was thinking about the next game and his next hussy. But Tiberius and me, we were hard at it. Raking the ground with our bare hands and I was following Tiberius, because he smelled those brilliants like a hound sniffing for a fox. Then he found one, just sitting by the fence, or what was left of the fence. It was sitting on the earth there, like it had just dropped out of the sky. Like I said, Tiberius knew a lot about soil and this was *alluvial* soil, loose particles of silt and clay, and he came to the conclusion that there had once been water of some sort there and the diamond had been washed downstream and deposited right at the edge of the farm. We shouted to Deverill and he came running. *Now* he was interested, all right. We climbed to the top of the koppie and dug up there, and, hallelujah, we soon found the rich yellow stuff that told us one thing: diamonds. Our blood was up and even Deverill wasn't thinking about cards and girls. We were all digging like dogs, the three of us. That ground was ripe with diamonds. Lots of 'em. We couldn't believe our luck. We set about marking our claim. Deverill went off to register in the name of Deverill Dupree." At this point Aurelius's face darkened with a deep and burning regret. He grimaced. "We were so busy digging we barely looked up from the ground as we put our signatures to those papers. We trusted Deverill, you see. Biggest mistake of my life, trusting Lucky Deverill." He shook his head ruefully and stubbed out his cigarette. "He had the luck of the Devil, though, there's no disputing that."

There was a long pause as he knocked back his tea and chewed on the terrible injustice he believed Celia's father had committed. Celia remained on the fender, immobile, a sick feeling growing in her stomach. Yet she couldn't stop listening, fascinated and appalled in equal measure. A new world, a new vision of her father was opening up before her like a terrible chasm. "Now Deverill wasn't just a gambler," he went on. "He was a womanizer too. No one's wife was safe when Lucky Deverill was about. Blond and blue-eyed, you'd have thought he'd been conceived by the angels. But the Devil comes in many disguises. While Tiberius and I did all the work Deverill was . . ." He hesitated and flicked his black eyes at Celia. "Well, let's just say he kept himself busy *elsewhere*. The only thing he did, while we sweated, was put up a sign that said: *A Deverill's castle is his kingdom.* He'd written on a wooden plank in black paint and I never did understand what it meant until I saw this castle right here. We laughed at him then, but we should have known," he lamented. "We really should have known. We brought our workers, hundreds of Zulus and Xhosas, and Deverill hired his old ruffians as foremen: Stone Heart, Spleen and Mad McManus. They once caught a boy stealing a diamond and beat him to death.

"Well, we needed investment to mine the diamonds, so Deverill went to Sir Sydney Shapiro. Now Shapiro was the agent of the Rothschild family—who owned the Rothschild Bank that funded Cecil Rhodes in the development of the British South Africa Company—and Deverill was sleeping with his wife. She was a looker: fair and innocent, like butter wouldn't melt in her mouth. But those ones are often the worst sluts of the lot, if you'll forgive me, Mrs. Mayberry. As for Shapiro, he had a hand in everything, like a great big fat octopus, he was, but he didn't know his quiet little wife was sneaking into Deverill's bed. With Shapiro's money Deverill formed his own company, Deverill & Co. which was owned by Deverill Dupree, but Deverill had tricked us when he registered the company, and given himself fifty-one percent of the share to our forty-nine. So Deverill came to us with an offer to buy us out. At the time five grand each seemed good enough, with the promise of shares. But he formed the World Amalgamated Mining Company, known as WAM, and sold it to De Beers for several millions. There was nothing in the agreement about our shares. Nothing. Deverill moved down to Cape Town and bought himself a mansion, setting himself up as one of the great diamond magnates, and Tiberius saw red. We decided to sue. We wanted our share and we believed we had a very strong case."

Aurelius Dupree pulled the cigarette packet out of his jacket pocket again and his hand trembled more violently. He flicked his lighter and inhaled sharply, drawing the smoke into his wheezing lungs. When he looked at Celia his eyes were no longer black but cloudy with layers of grief. "But you lost, Mr. Dupree?" Celia asked. She knew that if he had won he wouldn't be sitting here as a human wreck. She was relieved that this was all it was, a row between diamond prospectors from years ago, one man's word against that of her beloved father.

"We would have won, I'm sure of it," Mr. Dupree continued. "We would have won something. Maybe not seven million, but everyone in Kimberley knew we was owed our share."

"So what happened? Why didn't you win?"

"That's where the Devil came in, Mrs. Mayberry," he said in a voice so quiet and ominous it made Celia shiver. "Digby—"

"If you're going to talk about my father," Celia interrupted irritably, "call him *Sir* Digby."

"Oh no, Mrs. Mayberry, he'll never be Sir Digby to me. A devil in the Devil's pay, maybe, as you will see. Back then, we used to hunt. Every day almost—gazelle, antelope, zebra, elephants and even lions. Yes, even the king of the jungle. While Deverill was in Cape Town in his new palace hobnobbing with Rhodes and Barnato, we was struggling to make ends meet. But one day, we was in the Cape, outside the city. We heard of a man-eating lion from a man called Captain Kleist, a German from German South West Africa. This white hunter invited us to join the posse. It was bad manners to refuse and besides, we needed the diversion. When we arrived with our guns on the edge of the veldt, who did we find but Mad McManus, Spleen and Stone Heart with this German captain, Kleist. I doubt he was ever a real captain, but I won't digress. Anyway, there was an awkward moment, but they greeted us like old times and we didn't blame them for Deverill. So we set off into the veldt. It was dawn. Still dark and cool. But soon it grew hot. That heat like tar you can hardly move in. On and on we went. First on horse, then on foot. We saw lions, me and Tiberius, but we never saw that man-eater, *if* he ever existed. Captain Kleist was in command. He split us into pairs. He chose Tiberius and put me with McManus. The hours passed. Nothing. Mad McManus told me stories of Deverill and his immoral ways; like they say, there's no honor among thieves. Then just as we were about to give up, it was nearly midday and too hot to continue, there came shots ringing into the air nearby. We ran across the veldt. We called out. Finally we heard Kleist's voice, shouting for help. We followed it. There we came upon a terrible scene. Tiberius was lying on the earth, but he wasn't Tiberius no more. He was beyond dead, Mrs. Mayberry. Torn apart, to pieces he was. My brother looked like an impala with his insides ripped out. Looked like the man-eating lion had got 'im, Mrs. Mayberry. Nothing else could have done that and Captain Kleist and Spleen and Stone Heart were already there just looking and saying nothing. There were no words. Nothing to say. I asked Kleist what had happened. He was with him, after all. But Kleist told me they had split up and he had left my brother alone. He claimed to have fired at the lion but it was too late." Mr. Dupree's voice trailed off and he dabbed his damp forehead with his hanky.

"A most unfortunate accident," said Celia.

"And so I thought for a while," replied Dupree. "'A tragedy' Captain Kleist called it and all the others testified to an accident. But I took the body back to camp and washed it myself. I saw what I wasn't meant to see, Mrs. Mayberry. I saw a bullet hole in his chest, hidden among the wounds, which maybe weren't even the work of a lion's jaws but of a dagger. Perhaps my brother hadn't been killed by lions, but by man, and those men were your father's henchmen. Suddenly I knew who was behind it." He narrowed his eyes and glared across the room at Celia, who sat rigidly on the fender, her tea cold in the cup. "I told the police and they made their arrest. But it wasn't Deverill they arrested; it was *me*."

"Why on earth would they think that you had murdered your own brother?" Celia asked. "You weren't even with him on the hunt."

"No, and that's what I told the police. But Captain Kleist claimed I was with him, and McManus, Stone Heart and Spleen all agreed with him. They said it was just me and Tiberius out there so I was the only one who could have killed him. It was a setup, Mrs. Mayberry. Deverill wanted us out of the way and he got what he wanted, as he always did."

"But surely there has to be a motive for killing someone?"

"Oh, don't you worry, Mrs. Mayberry, Deverill went to great lengths to find one. He dug around and discovered that we were both in love with the same girl in our hometown of Hove. We both wanted to marry her, it's true, and it was causing a rift between us, but I'd never have killed my brother for her. Some woman testified to having heard me threatening to murder him if he married her, but if I did, it was in the heat of an argument—and that was it. I thought I was done for; I thought the judge would put on the black crêpe and hang me. But there wasn't enough proof to hang me. I was charged with conspiracy to murder and sentenced to life imprisonment. While I rotted in a South African jail, forgotten, Deverill made many a fortune. But it was built on the blood of my innocent brother." Celia put down her teacup. Aurelius Dupree stubbed out his cigarette and he did not light another. "Now I'm out, I've come for my share," he said, looking at her steadily.

"Or what? You'll sell your story to some dirty rag and sully my father's reputation? He's dead, Mr. Dupree."

"Dead men still have reputations and families live off them. I only want what is mine and I *will* have my share," he said in a quiet voice. "Your father can't give me back my life, but he can make my last years as comfortable as possible. He owes me twenty grand, Mrs. Mayberry. That'll see me out. Not greedy, me. Just want some comfort before I'm gone."

Celia stood up. "I think I have heard enough fiction for one day." She walked over to the door and opened it. "O'Sullivan, please will you show Mr. Dupree out." Mr. O'Sullivan appeared in the hall, much to Celia's relief. "Mr. Dupree is just leaving," she said in a weak voice. When she turned back into the room Mr. Dupree was right beside her. She gave a small jump as he stood so close she could smell the tobacco on his breath.

"He didn't pull the trigger, Mrs. Mayberry, but he paid the piper. He should have hanged. I will be back," he said. "I will be back to claim what is mine."

Chapter 27

Celia left the castle and set off into the hills. The winter winds were cold and brisk, raking icy fingers through the long grasses and heather. The air was damp. A light drizzle began to fall. Celia strode on as fast as she could. With her head down and her gaze lost somewhere above the ground just ahead of her, she marched into the grassy nooks and valleys she had explored as a little girl with Jack O'Leary, his pet hawk and his dog. She remembered how she, Kitty and Bridie had watched the birds and Jack had taught them all the names. Loons, shearwaters, grebes and lapwings—she could recall some of them even now. They had lain in wait for badgers, their bellies flat against the earth, their whispers full of excitement and anticipation. They had played with caterpillars, which Bridie had called hairy mollies, spiders and snails and sometimes, on balmy summer nights, they had rolled onto their backs and gazed at the stars and Celia had felt the gentle stirring of something deep within her that she could not explain. She had been drawn into the velvet blackness, into the bright twinkling of stars, into the eternal vastness of space. The sweet scent of rich soil and heather had risen on the warm air and she had felt giddy with wonder. But those days were gone and innocence had gone with them. Now all she felt was fear.

Whether or not her father was guilty of murder she didn't know. But what *was* certain was Aurelius Dupree's demand for money; money she didn't have. The scandal of his story, if told in the press, would finish her mother off for sure, and she couldn't bring herself to tell her sisters, or Harry or Boysie— she couldn't share her father's shame with *anyone*. Celia was left no choice. She *had* to find the money somehow; and she had to find it alone.

Aurelius Dupree had not only made an impossible demand, he had stripped her father of his humanity and exposed him as a brutal monster whose greed had led him to take an innocent life. A monster Celia did not recognize, or want to.

She marched on, deeper into the hills, desperate to lose herself in the mist now forming in the vales in eerie pools of expanding cloud. Eventually she walked into the trees, to hide among their sturdy trunks and branches. Tears blurred her vision, but the mossy ground was soft beneath her feet and the scent of pine and damp vegetation filled the air and began to soothe her aching spirit. Blinking away her despair and looking about her she saw that the forest was beautiful—and what is beauty if not love? The mystical energy deep within the land seemed to wrap its arms around her, giving her an unexpected feeling of strength—a feeling of not being alone. She stopped thinking about Tiberius Dupree and her father, murder and money, and gazed at the wonder of the living earth she had never really taken the trouble to notice before. There were birds in the trees, creatures in the undergrowth and perhaps hundreds of pairs of eyes watching her from the bushes. As a pale beam of sunlight shone through the thicket, falling onto the path ahead of her, Celia surrendered to the effervescence of nature and let the power of this strange presence, so much bigger than herself, carry her pain away.

When she returned to the castle she felt immeasurably stronger. She went straight to the nursery to see her children. As they fought for her attention and wrapped their small arms around her, she thought of Archie and their dream of filling the castle with a large and boisterous family. *That* would never happen now. She had two daughters who would forever connect her to their father, but brothers they would never know. *Whatever happens*, she thought as she kissed their soft faces, *I will not let the troubles affecting my life ruin yours.* She'd sell the castle if she had to and make a new home somewhere else. Surely it wasn't the bricks that made the home, but the people inside it, and it was love that held them all together—and they could take that anywhere.

With this renewed sense of determination she traveled to London to meet with Mr. Riswold, the solicitor, and Archie's bank manager and stockbroker, Mr. Charters. She explored every avenue, but when she left for Ireland she realized that selling the castle was the only option. It was time to take her head out of the sand and face up to the truth: she was on the brink of bankruptcy and only selling her beloved castle could save her.

At the beginning of spring O'Sullivan appeared at the door of the sitting room, where Celia was having tea with the Shrubs.

"I'm sorry to disturb you, Mrs. Mayberry, but there is a gentleman at the door who wishes to see you." For a moment her heart plummeted at the thought of Aurelius Dupree returning for his money and she blanched, but O'Sullivan had specifically said "gentleman," which Mr. Dupree most certainly was not.

"Did he give a name?" she asked.

"He did, madam, but I'm afraid I cannot repeat it." When Celia frowned, the butler wrung his hands. "It is a foreign name, madam."

Celia smiled. "Very well. Ask him to wait in the library."

"Oh, don't make him wait on account of us," said Hazel. "We must be leaving."

"Yes, we have lots to do, don't we, Hazel?" said Laurel.

"We most certainly do," Hazel agreed. "We are going to call in on Grace, who has a horrible cold. I've made her a tincture."

"It's an old recipe of Adeline's," Laurel told her. "It works wonders."

"Oh, it does," Hazel agreed.

"Well, if you really don't mind," said Celia, watching the two women get to their feet. In their feathered hats they looked like a pair of geese. They both smiled, for they were extremely happy these days, and as compatible as they had been before the arrival of Lord Hunt.

"Not at all. Thank you for the tea and cake. Isn't it lovely that it's spring at last," said Hazel.

"It's put a spring in my step," laughed Laurel, secretly thinking that spring wasn't the *only* thing that was putting a bounce in her step.

"In mine too," Hazel agreed, and neither sister knew that Lord Hunt had put a leap in both.

The Shrubs and the mysterious foreign gentleman passed in the hall. The Shrubs chuckled like chickens as the handsome gentleman gave a low bow and smiled, revealing bright white teeth. Ballinakelly hadn't ever seen the likes of him, they thought excitedly as they set off for Grace's. They'd be sure to give her the tincture as well as an enthusiastic description of Celia's glamorous visitor.

Celia waited for the gentleman with the unpronounceable name to be shown into the room. She straightened the skirt of her blue tea dress and stood with her hands folded, not knowing what to expect. Nothing could have prepared her, however, for the arresting charms of Count Cesare di Marcantonio. The moment he stood in the doorway he filled it with his wide, infectious smile, warm eyes and honey and lime cologne. Celia was stunned; she had not expected a man such as this. He strode up to her, took her extended hand and brought it to his lips, bowing formally. When he said his name, his pale green gaze looked deeply into hers and held it firmly. Celia didn't think she had ever met a man who exuded such self-confidence.

"Please, do sit down," she said, gesticulating at the sofa. Dressed in an immaculate gray suit with a yellow waistcoat and matching silk tie, he chose the sofa, sat back against the cushions and crossed one leg over the other, revealing stripy socks and very shiny cap-toe shoes. "Can I offer you something to drink? A cup of tea perhaps, or something stronger? My husband used to drink whiskey."

"Whiskey on the rocks, please," he said, and O'Sullivan nodded and left the room.

"So, to what do I owe the pleasure?" said Celia, but she knew why he had come; there could be no other reason.

"I am interested in buying your beautiful home," he said.

Celia's cheeks flushed with emotion. She had made the decision to sell in January but a small part of her was still in denial. That small part still hoped that Aurelius Dupree's demand for money and Archie's enormous debts would just go away. But here was a wealthy foreign count who had come to realize her fears. "I see," she said, lowering her eyes.

There was a short pause that felt like minutes, and the Count's expression softened with sympathy. "I am sorry for your loss," he said quietly.

"Which one?" Celia replied with a bitter chuckle.

"It is a terrible thing to lose a father."

"And a husband. I lost both," she said.

"And now you are going to lose your home." He shook his head and his handsome face creased with compassion. "You are a beautiful young woman. If I was not married I would buy the castle and give it to you."

Celia laughed. If it wasn't for his alluring foreign accent *that* would have sounded tasteless. "Where is your wife?" she asked, hoping to curb his flirting.

"The Countess is in New York. We live there."

"Did you, by any chance, make me an offer last summer?"

"My attorney did on my behalf. Mr Beaumont L. Williams."

"Yes, I remember. You must want it very badly."

"My wife wants it very badly, Mrs. Mayberry. When she heard it was for sale she said she wanted to have it more than anything in the world. So, I will buy it for her, whatever the cost." He cast his gaze around the room. "Now I know why she wants it so much. It is very beautiful."

"Has she seen it?"

The Count frowned. "Of course she has seen it," he replied, but he didn't look very certain. "It is a famous castle, no?"

"It's been in my family since the seventeenth century. It would break my heart to lose it. After the generations of Deverills who have treasured it, I feel I am letting them down. I'm the Deverill who will be remembered as having let it go into the hands of strangers."

"We will love it, Mrs. Mayberry. You can be sure of that."

"I have no doubt that you *would*," she said softly, still reluctant to accept the fact that the castle had to go.

O'Sullivan entered with the Count's whiskey followed by Mrs. Connell with a fresh pot of tea for Celia. The Count waited for the servants to leave, then he swilled the ice in his glass and said, "I will make you an offer you cannot refuse. I will pay you more than anyone in Europe would pay. You see, the Countess has set her heart on this place and nowhere else will do. The Countess wants it exactly as it is. She will keep the servants. No one will lose their job because of the sale. Everything will continue seamlessly. She wants it so I shall buy it for her."

Celia was perplexed. What had inspired the Countess to want it so badly? "You say your wife has seen it, but has she actually *been* here?" she asked.

He shrugged. "She has always dreamed of an Irish castle and this one is special," he told her. "It has a charming history and yet it is fully modernized. I don't think that one could say the same for the vast majority of Irish castles." He swept his eyes around the room. "Irish castles are not worth much on the whole, but this one is different from the rest. You have made it beautiful, Mrs. Mayberry. You see, I am descended from the counts Montblanca and the princes Barberini, the family of Pope Urban VIII, so I know quality when I see it."

"Are you going to come and live here?"

"Eventually, yes. The Countess is expecting our first child." He grinned bashfully. "I am going to be a father. I am very happy."

"Congratulations," said Celia. She envied the Countess her vast wealth and her good fortune. There had been a time not long ago when Celia had been blessed with both those attributes, before fate had so cruelly snatched them away. "Have you undertaken the long voyage from America just to see the castle for yourself?" Celia's curiosity was aroused by this foreign man whose wife wanted the castle so badly, in spite of never having set foot in it. There was something shifty about the whole scenario.

The Count uncrossed his legs and leaned forward, placing his elbows on his knees and looking up at her from under the glossy hair that had fallen over his forehead. "I wanted to talk to you personally, Mrs. Mayberry. I also wanted to see the castle for myself, of course. I didn't want such an important purchase to be done coldly, through my attorney. I sensed that this is a home, a family home, so I felt it was only polite to talk to you face-to-face. I understand your reluctance to sell, but I can assure you that we will take good care of it."

Celia wondered whether he had somehow read the British newspapers, which had been full of her father's financial demise and the possibility that Celia was going to have to sell the castle. But there had been no photographs of the castle itself, so how had the Countess come to set her heart so firmly upon it? "Shall I show you around, Count di Marcantonio?" she asked.

"If you have the time."

"I do," she said with a sigh, pushing herself up from the fender. "I have all the time in the world."

Celia took him on a tour of the inside first. She showed him the grand rooms, lovingly restored and rebuilt after the fire, and the furniture and paintings she had bought in Italy, which he particularly loved, being of Italian origin. She told him the history, at least the parts she knew, and he nodded earnestly and listened keenly as if wanting to learn it all by heart. He praised her style, admired the splendor of the architecture and imagined himself living there, Celia thought, as she watched him running his eager eyes over everything. She thought it odd that a foreigner with no connection to Ireland should want to move here. The landscape was beautiful, of that there was no doubt, but it was cold and damp in winter and wouldn't they miss the glamour of New York? She imagined the Countess to be a flamboyant and spoiled Italian woman with a loud voice and brash taste. She saw her striding down the hall in furs and pearls and shouting at the servants. She had no reason to imagine her so, for the Count was tastefully dressed and had impeccable manners—perhaps her envy was making her mean.

The gardens were bathed in bright spring sunshine. Birds tweeted in the trees whose branches had just begun to turn green with the fresh, phosphorescent brilliance of new leaves. Apple blossom floated on the wind like snow and sea gulls wheeled and cried above them beneath fat balls of fluffy white cloud. It could not have been a more propitious day for the

Count to see the castle. It shone in all its glory and a lump lodged itself in Celia's throat, for soon it would no longer be her home. Soon, all the love and pleasure she had poured into it would belong to someone else.

The Count marveled at the neatly trimmed borders, the recently cut lawn, the flower beds where forget-me-nots and tulips interrupted the emerging green shoots with splashes of blue and red. He admired the yew hedges and ancient cedar and the giant copper beech that rose up behind the croquet lawn in a rich display of emerging red leaves. They wandered through the vegetable garden and Celia showed him the greenhouses where she had once played as a little girl. She thought of Kitty then, and her heart gave a painful lurch. No one would suffer more than Kitty at the sale of Castle Deverill. She suppressed her guilt and tried to keep her attention on the tour and the Count.

Suddenly a shout resounded across the lawn. Celia recognized the voice at once. She turned to see Grace marching across the grass toward her in a pale floral dress. Her hand was holding her hat to stop it flying off her head into the wind. The Count also turned and Grace's face flowered into a wide and enchanting smile as she reached them. "I'm so sorry, Celia, I thought your visitor would have left by now," she said, tilting her head in that coy, flirtatious way of hers, which had won many a heart, and broken just as great a number.

"I thought you had a cold," said Celia.

"Oh, those Shrubs exaggerate everything. I'm perfectly well." She looked at the Count and smiled. "I'm sorry to interrupt," she added, giving him her hand.

The Count took it and brought it to his lips and bowed. "Count Cesare di Marcantonio," he said and his words seemed to flow over her in a delicious cascade, for she shivered with delight.

"*È un grande piacere conoscerlei*," she replied and they smiled together as if they had suddenly come to a mutual understanding. Celia watched Grace's shameless flirting with admiration. The Count, who had been mildly flirting with Celia, now turned his full attention to Grace, and Celia realized, by the comparison, that he hadn't really been flirting with her at all. He had recognized a fellow epicurean in Grace.

"May I introduce Lady Rowan-Hampton," said Celia, and the Count gave her features a long caress with his heavy green eyes.

"How lovely to see Castle Deverill on such a day as this!" Grace continued, catching her breath.

"We were just saying the same thing," said the Count. He chuckled to himself as if surprised by his own luck. "Are all the women in Ireland as beautiful as you two *bellissime donne?*" he said. "Because, this is my first time here and I am wondering why no one told me. I would have come sooner."

"They are not," said Grace with a laugh. "I'm afraid you have seen the best West Cork has to offer."

They began to stroll toward the stable block. "Castle Deverill always had the best hunt meets," said Grace. "And Lord Deverill always had the best hunters. Do you ride, Count di Marcantonio?"

"Of course. I play polo. I have many horses in Southampton."

His reply was deeply satisfying to Grace. "What an exciting game polo is."

"I grew up in Argentina and there the ponies are the best in the world."

"And, as far as I understand, so are the riders," said Grace.

"You are not wrong. But I am much too polite to boast." He grinned broadly, showing off a perfect set of gleaming teeth.

"Oh, you don't need to be polite in front of us, does he, Celia? We're not opposed to a little boasting."

"Count di Marcantonio is looking to buy the castle, Grace," said Celia, hoping that Grace would modify her behavior accordingly, but she didn't. Her slanting cat's eyes widened and her chest puffed out with ill-concealed excitement that this dashing foreign count was going to come and live at Castle Deverill.

"I have to first convince Mrs. Mayberry that I am a suitable person to take over the responsibility of looking after such a historic castle. It is not only a castle but a much beloved home. Perhaps you are a good judge of character, Lady Rowan-Hampton, and can help me persuade her."

"I will do my best, for the both of you," said Grace, but she didn't once look at Celia. Her eyes lingered on the Count's. Celia continued to show the Count around, although she would have preferred to leave Grace to do it for her. The two of them chatted away like a pair of teenagers on a date. She wondered whether they realized that the other was married. She presumed they did and that they didn't care. The Countess was in America and Sir Ronald, well, Sir Ronald was anywhere but here in Ballinakelly.

At length Celia agreed to consider his offer. But on one condition.

"Yes?" he said, raising his eyebrows.

"There are two houses on the estate that are rented by my cousins, Lord Deverill and his daughter, Kitty Trench. I will only sell the castle if those houses continue to be let to them at the current rate. In fact, I will have it included in the documentation that the Hunting Lodge and the White House are always offered to Deverills first."

The Count shrugged. "I'm sure that will not be a problem," he said. "It is the castle that my countess wants so badly."

"While you think about it, why don't you come for dinner tomorrow night?" suggested Grace. "Celia, I hope you will come too. I will invite some nice people for you to meet. Do you play bridge?" she asked the Count.

"Of course," he replied with a shrug.

"Wonderful. Where are you staying and I will send an invitation round."

"Vickery's Coaching Inn in Bantry."

Grace's smile broadened. "If you are going to come and live here you might as well meet some of your neighbors."

Once again he kissed their hands and bowed. They stood on the steps and watched him climb into the back of his taxi and set off down the drive. "My goodness, what an attractive man! His countess is a very lucky lady," said Grace.

"Having seen the way he flirted with you, I'm not so sure she's very lucky! I wouldn't trust him as far as I could throw him."

"Oh, all Italian men are like that. If they can't flirt they might as well be denied oxygen too," said Grace dismissively. But her cheeks were flushed and her brown eyes shone with intent. Count Cesare di Marcantonio might be just the person to take her mind off Michael Doyle. In fact, in her mind, she was already at the royal suite in Vickery's Coaching Inn in Bantry. "I'm sorry you have to sell the castle, Celia," said Grace. "I truly am." She placed a soft hand on Celia's.

"He wants to buy it for his countess," said Celia. "I'm not sure why an Italian countess should want to come and live in Ballinakelly. They live in New York, and, as far as I understand, she's never even seen it."

"I agree, that *is* strange," said Grace, but she really didn't care. "You're very sweet to think of Bertie and Kitty."

"I feel guilty," said Celia.

"For what? Saving their castle and then losing it? If it wasn't for you it would never have been rebuilt. No one would be mad enough to do what you did."

"And look where it got me."

"It will make you rich," said Grace, turning serious. "This count will pay a fortune for it. He has more money than sense, I assure you. Don't accept his first offer. You can push him higher, *much* higher. If his countess wants it *that* badly, he'll pay you three times its value. He's a terrible old fraud." Grace laughed.

"What do you mean? I thought you were taken by him."

"Taken by him, yes, but not taken *in* by him. I have a sensitive nose. I can tell when someone is a phony. But still, he's very easy on the eye." She linked her arm through Celia's. "Let's go in and have a cup of tea and you can tell me how this count found out about the castle in the first place."

Celia sighed as they walked into the hall. "I'm afraid I don't know the answer to that question."

Grace narrowed her eyes. "Then we need to find out."

Chapter 28

Adeline stood by Stoke Deverill's bed and watched the old man's labored breath slowly enter and exit his body in a low rattle. His skin was gradually losing the color of life and turning the dull green of death. His mustache, once as majestic as the outstretched wings of a swan, now drooped and purple shadows stagnated in the holes where once his cheeks had been. Adeline knew his time was very near, for his son Digby, his grandson George, and other members of Stoke's family who had long departed, had come to take him home. Adeline smiled; if people knew they wouldn't die alone death would not frighten them so.

Augusta sat in a chair pulled up to the bedside and dabbed her eyes with a handkerchief. Maud perched on the end of the bed while Leona and Vivien stood by the window, wondering how long it was going to take because they had things to do. Beatrice was still languishing at Deverill Rising, unaware of the enormity of her late husband's debts. While she hid beneath the blankets her sons-in-law were fighting to keep her homes. There was little chance of success.

"It should be me," said Augusta with a sniff. "I have defied death at every turn. I'm bound to be waylaid by it sometime."

"You'll outlive us all," said Maud.

"He'd be a cruel God to inflict me with longevity! What's the fun of being down here if all one's friends are up there?" She raised her eyes to Heaven. "I think he's going now. He's stopped breathing." Leona and Vivien hurried to the bedside, relieved that the vigil was about to end. Then Stoke gave a splutter and inhaled sharply. "Oh no, he's back again!" Augusta cried. "I don't think he wants to go."

He would if he knew where he was going, Adeline thought. But Stoke was clinging on to life as if he were a climber digging his nails into the edge of a precipice, afraid of letting go. Adeline ran a hand across his brow. *Come now,* she whispered. *We'll catch you.*

Stoke opened his eyes. He stared in wonder at the faces surrounding him. Faces he hadn't seen for so long. "Digby, George," he gasped, reaching out his hand. Augusta caught her breath and stopped crying. Maud's mouth opened in amazement. Leona looked at Vivien and bit her bottom lip. Vivien's eyes sparkled with tears. Suddenly neither of Stoke's granddaughters wanted to be anywhere else but here.

Lost for words Augusta hiccuped loudly and pressed the handkerchief to her mouth. Stoke's face expanded into a wide smile, releasing the shadows and reviving his mustache. Adeline watched as Digby and George took his hands and lifted him from the bed. Surrounded by his loved ones he departed into the light. Adeline watched them go. Just before Digby disappeared he turned to Adeline and winked.

"He's gone," said Maud, peering into Stoke's lifeless face.

"Do you really think he saw Digby and George?" Augusta asked, the handkerchief trembling in her hand.

"I truly think he did, Grandmama," said Leona, putting a hand on her grandmother's shoulder. "I'm certain of it."

"I do hope they'll come for me when it's my turn," said Augusta. She looked at Maud and smiled sadly. "I haven't been that bad, have I?"

"No, you haven't, Augusta. No worse than the rest of us."

"Then I hope Stoke saves a place for me up there, because it won't be long." Leona rolled her eyes at her sister, who suppressed a grin.

"Augusta, you've been rehearsing your death for twenty years," said Maud, not unkindly.

"Then it's long overdue, wouldn't you say?" She pushed herself up from the chair and Vivien handed her her walking stick. "In the meantime, life goes on, such as it is without my beloved Stoke. Let's go and eat. I'm certainly not going to die of hunger!"

Back at Castle Deverill Adeline recounted Stoke's death to Hubert. "What a privilege it is to die like that," he said wistfully. "What a curse it is to die like *this*!" And there was nothing Adeline could say, because she wholly agreed with him. What a curse it was, indeed, for the poor unfortunate Lord Deverills to die like this.

CELIA SAT ON the window seat and stared out into the black night. Clouds obscured the stars and blinded the eye of the moon to her misery. She felt alone and fearful. There was no one she could confide in. No one she could turn to. No one to advise her how to proceed. She'd sell the castle, buy somewhere modest to live as close to Ballinakelly as possible and settle Archie's debts. As for Aurelius Dupree, when she thought of buying his silence something inside her recoiled into a tight, stubborn ball. She couldn't leave him to publish his outlandish claim, but allowing herself to be blackmailed went against every instinct. Her father would never have tolerated such an attack.

She pulled her knees to her chest and folded her arms on top, resting her forehead in the crook of her elbow and closing her eyes. She just wished the whole sorry business would go away. As she drifted off to sleep she found solace in her memories. She remembered so clearly the excitement of rebuilding the castle; the ebullient Mr. Leclaire with his plans and his ideas; the grand tour of Europe she and Archie had enjoyed together, choosing the pieces of furniture and the works of art to adorn their new home. She recalled Archie's pride, her father's pleasure, her mother's excitement and her sisters' jealousy, and the tears squeezed through her knitted lashes. It was then that she thought of Kitty, Harry and Bertie. If *she* was suffering at the prospect of selling the castle, how had *they* felt when she had bought it? It had never occurred to her that it might have caused them pain. She had expected them to share her joy, but how could they? Only now did she understand how hard it must have been for them and how valiantly they had dissembled, and she felt ashamed. She had been so selfish, so self-absorbed and arrogant. Maud, Victoria and Elspeth seemed to have no emotional connection to the place, but Kitty—and her heart swelled with compassion and sorrow at the thought of her—Kitty loved it more than anyone, even *her.* How had she endured it?

With these thoughts Celia fell asleep on the window seat. The clouds thinned and eventually the moon shone brightly through the openings, pouring its silver light through her bedroom window. She dreamed of her father. He was wrapping his arms around her, reassuring her that she was never alone, because he was with her, always. But when she looked at him he had the face of an ogre and she woke up with a jolt. She lifted her head off her knee and stared into the dark room in bewilderment. The impenetrable clouds blackened the sky and she felt cold and stiff in her limbs. She wiped the tears from her face with the back of her hand. She walked over to her bed, pulled back the blankets and climbed inside. She was too tired to think about Aurelius Dupree. Too tired even to think about her father. She'd think about them tomorrow. Other women would have given up, or paid up, or wept, but now the Deverill spirit began to emerge in Celia for the first time. She knew there was only one way to find out the truth—and to clear her father's name—and that was to go to South Africa. Her head fell onto the pillow and she was enveloped once again in sleep's embrace.

TEN DAYS LATER Celia was on the boat to Cape Town. "Has she gone mad?" said Boysie to Harry, as they sat at their usual table in White's, enjoying lunch.

"I believe so," Harry replied. "She's been very cagey. Wouldn't tell me what it was all about. Said there was something important that she had to do."

"Must be very important if she has to cross half the world to do it!" Boysie sipped his Sauvignon. "What the hell is going on? It's not like her to keep secrets from us."

"Kitty says some frightfully rich foreigner is buying the castle and everything in it," said Harry. "I can't say it's come as a surprise, but I'm sorry for her. That place is a curse."

Boysie shook his head. "The place isn't cursed, old boy, you and your family are."

"Nonsense, that's just a silly story Adeline made up. She believed in all sorts of ridiculous things. You know, she even believed in fairies." The two men laughed. "I promise you. She claimed to see garden spirits all the time."

"There's a damned eccentric streak running in your family."

"*Grandma's* family," Harry emphasized. "Look at the Shrubs."

"Yes, I do see. I suppose they see the dead, too, do they?"

"I think that would terrify them. They can barely cope with the living. That Lord Hunt is leading them a merry dance. Kitty says they're both going to have their hearts broken."

"I didn't think it was possible at their grand age. Aren't they a bit old for that sort of foolery?"

"One would have thought." Harry wiped his mouth with a napkin. "Apparently Celia has managed to get the foreigner to pay well over the sum that it's worth. She declined his offer and forced him to raise it. I dare say he wants it very much—or his wife does. He's buying it for her, you see."

"Since when is Celia a businesswoman?" asked Boysie with a chuckle.

"Maybe she has more of her father in her than we realized."

"Good. She deserves to get a lot for that place. She's selling her heart with it."

Harry frowned. "That's very sad."

"She's selling *all* your hearts with it," Boysie added, putting down his glass.

"Not mine," said Harry quietly. *"You* have my heart, Boysie, and you always will." They stared at each other across the table, suddenly serious.

"You have mine too, Harry," said Boysie. Then he looked away. There was no point in mentioning that little hotel in Soho. Harry wasn't going to change his mind. They just had to accept things as they were.

CELIA STOOD ON the deck of *Carnarvon Castle*, the seven-hundred-foot motor ship bound for Cape Town, and leaned on the railing and gazed out across the ocean. She had pawned jewelry to pay for the voyage to South Africa, which would take seventeen days. It was a long way indeed, but not very long in comparison to the personal journey Celia had made. She looked back at the girl she had been a year ago—that girl would never have imagined herself here on this boat, traveling across the world in search of the truth about her father's past. That girl would never have imagined even half of the events that had taken place in the last twelve months. She had lost her grandfather, her father, her husband and her home—and was being blackmailed by a man claiming her father had murdered his brother. *That* was more than most could handle, but Celia wasn't most, she was a Deverill and she was beginning to learn what that meant.

She looked down at the water, fizzing and foaming as the boat's gray hull cut through it at the speed of twenty knots, and felt a swell of exhilaration. The wind blew through her hair, and swept across her face, waking her from despondency. She

felt a strength growing inside her, like the inflating of a bal-
loon, filling her with confidence and a fresh sense of optimism.
Out of her desolation there sprouted hope. She was a Deverill
and Deverills didn't let their difficulties crush them. Tragedy
could take everything dear to her, but it couldn't take her spirit.
It couldn't take that. Hadn't Kitty said that those we love and
lose never really leave us? She lifted her face to the wind and
for the first time in months she didn't feel alone.

The elegant liner carried two hundred and sixteen first-
class passengers and double the amount of second-class passengers. Among the former was the famous Irish tenor, Rafael
O'Rourke, setting off on a world tour. In his mid-forties he
had dark, romantic looks with pale eyes the color of an Irish
morning and the heavy, soulful gaze of a matinee idol. Celia
was excited to discover that he was only too happy to sing for
the passengers in first class. In the evenings after dinner, he
sang to the accompaniment of the pianist of the ship's show
band while the gentlemen and ladies sipped champagne and
cocktails at the small round tables in the bar. Candles glowed
soft and warm and the lights were low and Celia drank just
enough alcohol to make her forget her woes. Rafael sang of
love and loss and his voice resonated with her deepest longings. She sat in the corner, alone at her table, and allowed his
music to smooth down the raw edges of her grief.

The first-class deck of the boat was large and comfortable,
with luxurious suites and tastefully decorated public rooms.
Celia spent the day in the lounge, reading quietly by herself or
playing cards with the other passengers she was slowly getting
to know. She was soon adopted by an elderly couple well acquainted with the name Deverill. "Anyone who knows any-

thing about South Africa will have heard of the name Deverill," Sir Leonard Akroyd had explained when they first met. "Edwina and I have been living in Cape Town for forty years now and Lucky Deverill is one of the great characters I remember from my past." When Celia told him that Digby Deverill was her father he had invited her to join his table every night of the voyage for dinner. "Your father once did me a great favor so I'm happy to have the opportunity to repay him by keeping an eye on his daughter." He had smiled kindly while his wife looked dutifully on. "Now let me tell you about it . . ." And he had launched into a long and rather dull anecdote that involved a stain and the lending of a fresh shirt.

Celia noticed Rafael O'Rourke whenever he came into the room, for he lit it up with his quiet charisma and easy smile. He was always surrounded by people Celia assumed to be part of his entourage. Passengers pushed themselves forward, eager to talk to him, and she imagined the only place he could be private was in his own suite. He sat smoking, reading the papers or talking to men in suits and every now and then he'd catch her looking at him from the other end of the room and she'd feel her face flush and hastily lower her eyes. She had no desire to throw herself at him like the other women did, but he did arouse her curiosity.

Soon she began to notice when he *wasn't* in the room. At those times it would feel less vibrant and strangely empty, in spite of the fact that it was full of people. Her mood would dip with disappointment until the moment he would saunter in again and inject her with a certain "aliveness" that she found confusing and slightly alarming. Was it right that a man could affect her in this way so soon after her husband's death? She felt guilty for her feelings and retreated farther into the back of the room, distracting herself with more of Sir Leonard's tedious anecdotes or the blessed relief of cards.

With only five days to go before docking in Cape Town, Celia must have been the only female in first class who hadn't introduced herself to Rafael O'Rourke. It was no surprise, therefore, when he found her on the deck one evening after dinner, and introduced himself to *her*. There is nothing as attractive for a celebrated, sought-after man like Rafael O'Rourke as a woman who holds herself back. He leaned on the railings beside her and offered her a cigarette. She looked at him in surprise but smiled and took one. "Thank you," she said, placing it between her lips.

"It's nice and quiet out here," he said and his Irish brogue caught in her chest and made her suddenly long for home. Turning out of the wind he flicked his lighter. Celia had to lean in close and cup her hands around the flame. It went out a couple of times so that on the third attempt Rafael opened his jacket wide to shield it from the gale. There was something very intimate about the way she had to bend toward his body and she was relieved it was dark so that he couldn't see her blush as she puffed on the flame. At last it lit and she stepped back and rested her elbow on the railing.

"You sing beautifully, Mr. O'Rourke, but everyone must tell you that," she said, hoping her voice sounded confident. "But what they don't tell you is that your voice has become the tonic that heals me."

"I couldn't help but notice that you're on your own," he said.

"I am," she replied.

His gaze fell softly on her face. "Might I ask why a beautiful woman like you is travelling alone?"

She laughed and wondered how many times he'd said that to strange women he met on his tours. "Because my husband is dead, Mr. O'Rourke."

He looked appalled. "I apologize. I shouldn't have asked." He turned toward the sea and looked out into the darkness.

"Please, don't apologize. It's perfectly fine. I'm getting used to being on my own."

He glanced at her and grinned. "You won't be alone for long."

"If Sir Leonard Akroyd had his way I wouldn't have a moment to myself this entire voyage. He and his wife have rather taken me under their wing."

"But you escaped out here."

"I did. They're a sweet, well-intentioned couple, but sometimes one needs a little time to oneself. I'm sure you know what I mean. From what I've noticed, you rarely have a moment's peace either."

He smiled. "So you noticed me, did you?" Before she could answer he added, "Because I noticed *you*, you see, the first day, and I've noticed you ever since. I notice when you enter a room and when you leave it." Celia blew smoke into the wind and watched the night snatch it away. "Can I show you something?" he asked.

"That depends . . ."

He laughed a deep throaty laugh. "I'm a gentleman, Mrs.—"

"My name is Celia Deverill," she said and there was something reassuring about slipping into her former identity. She almost felt as if she was regaining a little of her old self. "I'm no longer Mrs. Mayberry, you see. So you can call me Celia, if you like."

"And you can call me Rafi."

"Very well, Rafi. What is it you wish to show me?"

He walked with her along the promenade deck until they reached the end where deck chairs were lined up in rows. He stubbed out his cigarette beneath his shoe, then settled himself into one and lay back against the wood to stare up at the stars. "Aren't they grand?" he said.

Celia took the deck chair beside him and looked up at the sky. "They *are* grand," she agreed with a sigh. "They're beautiful." She remembered those stargazing evenings at Castle Deverill and the tension in her heart grew tighter.

"You see, I'm a perfect gentleman." He laughed.

"So you are," said Celia.

"Where are you from, Celia?"

"Ballinakelly in County Cork."

"I'm from Galway," he told her. "We're a long way from home."

"We are," she said quietly.

"And we have five days before we arrive in Cape Town."

"Are you married, Rafi?" she asked.

"I've been married since I was twenty-one. I have five children, all grown-up now. What would you say if I told you I'm a grandfather already?"

"That you don't look old enough. Is that what you want me to say?"

"Of course."

Celia caught her breath as he took her hand and caressed her skin with his thumb. She kept her eyes on the stars as the blood rushed to her temples. She hadn't felt a man's touch in what seemed like eons. Her heart began to pound and a warm feeling crept softly over her, reawakening the dormant buds of her sexuality. When she turned to look at him he was staring at her, his eyes shining in the moonlight. "Five days," she said, gazing back at him.

He smiled and put his hand to her face. He leaned over and pressed his lips to hers. His kiss was so tender, so sensual that it was easy to yield. *Five days*, she thought, *long enough to enjoy a delicious fantasy, short enough to walk away at the end with my heart intact. As for my virtue, isn't it time I had some fun? I'm a Deverill, after all.*

Chapter 29

The final five days on board *Carnarvon Castle* felt like another life for Celia, who threw herself into this heady adventure with the enthusiasm of someone who so badly wants to forget the world beyond the bow of the ship. On her secluded island of cabins and decks she delighted in her brief affair. Rafael O'Rourke was a sensitive and tender lover, and Celia found solace as well as a new vitality in the arms of this man who had no connection whatsoever with her family and the tragedies that had befallen it. She was able to detach from the person she really was and be someone else entirely. Someone happier, more carefree; someone closer to the untroubled girl she had once been.

In public they put on a charade of being nothing more than acquaintances. They greeted one another formally as they passed in the corridor or when they found themselves seated at next-door tables in the lounge. Rafael performed in the bar in the evenings and Celia sat at her usual table in the corner, sipping champagne and listening to the sad melodies that he sang in his rich and touching voice, only for her. In public they were strangers, but their eyes met across the room and their gazes burned, and when they found themselves alone at last in Celia's cabin they fell on each other.

At night they escaped to the deck chairs and lay in the dark, watching the stars of the Southern Cross shining brightly above them and sharing the story of their lives. As the boat gently rocked and the wind swept over the decks they lay entwined, warm from their bodies pressed together and the excitement of these stolen moments running through their veins. But five days was all they had and soon the sight of Table Mountain emerged out of the dawn mist to herald the end of their voyage and the final moments of this short chapter of their story.

Celia, so sure that she would walk away with her heart intact, found herself clinging to Rafael with a rising sense of loss. She didn't know whether her fear came from the uncertainty of where she was going and what she was going to find when she got there, from the abrupt return to real life or from the shock of their parting and the fact that they might never see each other again. He kissed her one last time, caressed her face with heavy, sorrowful eyes as if committing her features to memory and told her he would try with all his might to forget her, lest the rest of his days be dogged by longing. Then he was gone.

Celia was left with the emptiness in her heart bigger and louder than before, because, for a blissful five days, Rafael had filled it. He had made her forget who she really was and what she carried inside her. But now that she was alone again she had no alternative but to accept her position, step off the boat and face with fortitude whatever Fate threw at her. She had survived so much already, she could survive this.

IT WAS EARLY autumn in Cape Town, but for Celia it could have been midsummer because the sun was hotter than it ever was in England. The sky gleamed a bright sapphire blue and not a single cloud marred its breathtaking perfection. The light possessed a fluid quality that Celia found instantly uplifting and she turned her attention away from the shadows that preyed on her fears and squinted in the sunshine.

The city itself was tidy and clean, a sprawling mass of pale-colored Dutch-style houses simmering at the foot of the flat-topped mountain that resembled a giant's table. Having made a game of hiding from Sir Leonard and Lady Akroyd on the boat Celia was now pathetically grateful for their company as they escorted her down the gangplank and through the throng of heaving people to their chauffeur-driven car. They would deliver Celia to the Hotel Mount Nelson, where she would stay for one night, and then make sure she arrived safely at the train station and wave her on her way to Johannesburg the following morning.

Celia, who was not unacquainted with American jazz singers at her mother's Salons in London, had never seen quite so many black people all in one place before. The noise was deafening as they touted for hotels and offered to carry luggage, shouting in their eagerness to be hired in a language Celia didn't recognize. Long-legged Zulus with ebony skin in flamboyant, brightly colored costumes with vast feather-and-bone headdresses offered rides in their rickshaws and small boys scampered among the weary travelers, selling newspapers, sweets and fruit. The place smelled of humidity and dust and the salty flavor of the sea.

Celia was relieved to reach the calm seclusion of the Akroyds' plush Mercedes and sat by the window gazing out onto this famous city, which, Sir Leonard told her importantly, was "the gateway to British South Africa." She imagined her father arriving here as a boy of only seventeen and wondered at his courage and readiness for adventure. She remembered Sir Leonard's anecdote about the shirt and was confident that she would find evidence very soon to disprove Aurelius Dupree's outrageous story. She didn't doubt that the man was a liar; she simply had to prove it.

Cape Town was bustling with activity as the city awoke, stretched and set off to work. Cars weaved in and out of the double-decker trams while men in jackets and hats rode bicycles or hurried along the sidewalks on foot. Flower-sellers set up their stalls on street corners and shopkeepers opened for business. Horses and carts carried goods to sell, plodding slowly over the asphalt, and in the background Table Mountain shimmered in the morning sunshine like a large step to Heaven. As the Mercedes motored slowly up Adderley Street Sir Leonard gave Celia a brief history of the city in which he was clearly very proud to live, and Celia opened her window wide and looked out onto the main thoroughfare of grand buildings, shops and restaurants and tried to imagine what sort of place it had been when her father had first seen it.

They dropped Celia off at the very British Mount Nelson Hotel, which was positioned directly beneath Table Mountain, where she stayed for one night. The following morning Sir Leonard and Lady Akroyd saw her onto the train and insisted that she come and stay for a few days at the end of her trip. "There's so much more for you to see," said Edwina. "You can't come all this way and not see a single animal. I'm sure Leonard could persuade you to come out into the bush." Celia thought of the lion that had torn Tiberius Dupree apart and decided that she'd rather stay in the city than venture out into the bush.

The whistle blew and the Akroyds were enveloped in a cloud of steam. The train pulled out of the station and Celia set off for Johannesburg.

CELIA GAZED OUT of the window in wonder at the vast landscape. Never before had she felt so small beneath such a colossal sky. The train puffed its way through the flat and verdant plains of rich farmland, where occasional dwellings stood, bathed in sunshine. A little boy tending a herd of oxen waved as she passed, his naked torso gleaming like ebony in the early autumn light. Far away in the distance, bordering the veldt, an arresting range of mountains seemed to rise out of the earth like gigantic waves of gray rock, quivering on the horizon in the heat. Soon the veldt rose into craggy hills of low scrub and the train meandered along the valley, which eventually gave way to a wide-open landscape of dry grassland. The mountains retreated and only the sky falling softly onto the horizon shimmered in their place.

That night Celia slept fitfully in her compartment. She missed Rafael O'Rourke and wondered whether he missed her too, or whether, as she suspected, affairs were an unavoidable part of being a famous musician—a way of avoiding loneliness, which was undoubtedly also part and parcel of being on tour.

Celia feared being alone. She feared the strange rhythmic noise of the train and the unsettling sound of other passengers walking in the corridor outside her room and talking in muffled voices the other side of her wall. Yet, in spite of her fears, the movement finally rocked her into a reluctant sleep.

At last she arrived at Park Station in Johannesburg, a little stiff due to the hard mattress and raw from having slept a shallow, fretful sleep. This station was very different from the stately and immaculate station in Cape Town. It was very large and noisy and teeming with people jostling past each other impolitely. Her father's old Afrikaner foreman, Mr. Botha, was on the platform to meet her as she had arranged and because he was so tall she saw him a head above the masses, wading his way through the crowd, waving his hand in greeting. He was a large, wooly-haired man in a pair of voluminous khaki shorts with long white socks pulled up over bulging calves and scuffed brown lace-up boots on his feet. He wore a short-sleeved white shirt tucked in beneath a swollen, spherical belly and a white bush hat placed squarely above big fleshy ears. Celia imagined he must surely be in his sixties, but the thick layer of fat that covered him, as well as his bushy white beard, made him look a great deal younger. "You must be Mrs. Mayberry," he said cheerfully in a strong Afrikaans accent and extended a large, doughy hand. "It's a *murra* of a *leka dag*," he said. "A lovely day," he translated.

She shook his hand and smiled back with gratitude. "I'm so pleased to meet you," she said, feeling immediately reassured by the confidence of this exuberant man.

"I can see the family resemblance," he said, looking her over. "You have your father's eyes. The same blue. He was a great man, your father," he added, giving a meaningful nod. "I'm sorry for your loss."

"Thank you. It was all terribly sudden."

"From what I know of Digby Deverill, he wouldn't have wanted a long, drawn-out death. Too early, certainly, but it would have been the way he'd have chosen to go."

"I think you're right, Mr. Botha."

"Come, let me help you with that." He lifted her suitcase with ease, as if it were a child's toy. "Now, I'm sure you'd like to freshen up in your hotel before we get down to business. I've taken the liberty of booking you into Jo'burg's finest, the Carlton Hotel. I think you'll find it very comfortable. Then a nice lunch." He set off down the platform and Celia had to walk fast to keep up with his long strides. "This is your first time in South Africa, I believe."

"It is," she replied.

"You've come a long way, Mrs. Mayberry."

"I hope it is worth the journey."

"It is sure to be," he replied encouragingly. "You said you need to look into your father's past. Well, there is no one better than me to help you, Mrs. Mayberry, and I am at your service."

Opened in 1906 the Carlton Hotel was grand in scale and harmoniously classical in design, with shutters and iron balconies that reminded Celia of Paris. Her suite was big and comfortable and she was relieved to be back in luxurious surroundings familiar to her. She unpacked her clothes and bathed, humming happily to herself. After her bath she changed into a light summer dress and ivory-colored cardigan, which she hooked casually over her shoulders. She felt quite restored after the long train journey and stood a moment at the window gazing out onto this foreign city that had once been home to her father. Below, a double-decker tram made its way slowly along the track on Eloff Street while a few cars motored up and down in a stately fashion, their round headlights catching the sunlight and glinting. Celia's confidence increased, for Mr. Botha was sure to dismiss Aurelius Dupree's story as invention. She was certain that she would be able to return home with her head held high—for the truth would unquestionably vindicate her faith in her father. Aurelius Dupree would crawl back into the hole out of which he had slid and never trouble her again.

Mr. Botha arrived in his car to take Celia to lunch. The restaurant was an elegant, Dutch-style building designed around a wide courtyard of shady trees and pots of red bougainvillea. Autumn was already turning the leaves on the branches but the sun was still hot and the air heavy with the lingering scent of summer. They sat at a table in the garden, shielded by the yellowing leaves of a jacaranda, and Celia felt very much herself again after a large glass of South African wine. Mr. Botha was only too happy to tell her about the young Lucky Deverill and the early days before he made his great fortune. "You knew him right from the beginning?" Celia asked.

"I did and we remained in contact right up until he died, Mrs. Mayberry. Your father was never still. He was a gambler all through his life. He liked nothing better than to take a risk. He wasn't called Lucky for nothing, now, was he?"

When they had finished their main courses, Celia felt it was time to ask the question she had come all the way to South Africa to ask. "Mr. Botha, may I speak plainly?"

"Of course." He frowned and the skin on his forehead rippled into thick folds.

"I presume you know of the Dupree brothers?" she asked.

"Everyone has heard of the Dupree brothers, but I knew them well. Tiberius was killed by a lion and his brother, Aurelius, was sentenced to life for his murder." He shook his head. "They were a rum pair of losers."

"Did my father tell you about the letters Aurelius sent him, just before he died?"

"No, he didn't. What was in them?"

Celia, now utterly confident of her father's innocence, was ready to share the contents. "Aurelius accuses Papa of murdering his brother."

Mr. Botha looked satisfyingly appalled. "That's a lie. Your father wasn't a murderer."

Celia took a deep breath. "You don't know how happy I am to hear you say that. Even though I never doubted him."

"Your father wasn't an angel either," he said, digging his chins into his sunburned neck. "They were hard times back then and competition was heavy. A man had to have a certain cunning—a certain craftiness—to succeed. But murder was not something Lucky Deverill would have dirtied his hands with."

"Aurelius told me about the hunt for the man-eating lion. He said that three men were with the white hunter. Spleen, Stone Heart and McManus. I would like to talk to them."

Mr. Botha shook his head. "They are dead, Mrs. Mayberry," he said.

"Dead? They're *all* dead?"

"*Ja,* all dead," he confirmed.

"Aurelius accuses Papa of cheating them twice. Firstly, when he registered the company Deverill Dupree and took the greater share and secondly, when he bought them out and promised them shares—"

"Let me make one thing clear, Mrs. Mayberry," Mr. Botha interrupted stridently. "Yes, Mr. Deverill registered the company Deverill Dupree in his favor, but that was because *he* had won the land in a card game, so it was right that he should have fifty-one percent to their forty-nine. As for the shares, *ja,* I know all about that too. They wanted to sue, but really, they didn't have a case. They signed all the papers willingly and Mr. Deverill paid them more than he believed it was worth at the time. How was he to have known that De Beers would buy it for millions? People are greedy, Mrs. Mayberry, and those Dupree brothers were worse than most."

"So Papa didn't cheat them . . . ?"

"He certainly did not."

Celia sat back in her chair. "Can you give me evidence to prove this odious man wrong? I'm afraid he is trying to blackmail me."

"I will give you copies of the very documents they signed," said Mr. Botha. He flicked his fingers for the waiter and asked for another bottle of wine. The sun was hot, the restaurant elegant and he was enjoying reminiscing about a man whom he had held in the highest respect.

"What was Papa like as a young man, Mr. Botha?" Celia asked, light-headed with relief to have her father's innocence confirmed.

"He was a big character. When he came out here he had very little to his name. He had lived a life of privilege, but he was the youngest of three brothers so he had to make his own way. He didn't want to go into the Army or the Church, or indeed to follow in his father's footsteps and work in the financial world, *that* sort of life would have bored him. He wanted adventure. He wanted a challenge. Not only did he have a good brain, a *sharp* brain, he had guile. You should have seen him at the gambling table. I don't know how he did it, but he rarely lost and even when he did, he looked like he was winning. No one had a better poker-face than Digby Deverill."

Celia watched the waiter fill her glass. She was already feeling pleasantly tipsy. "And what of love, Mr. Botha? Did my father have love affairs? When I was going through his office I looked at old photographs of him and he was such a handsome man. I bet half the women out here fell in love with him."

"They certainly did," said Mr. Botha with a belly laugh. "But do you know who he loved the most?"

"Tell me," said Celia, smiling at him encouragingly.

"A colored woman he called Duchess."

"Colored? Isn't that black?" she asked, fascinated.

"*Half* black, Mrs. Mayberry. Your father fell in love with a beautiful colored woman."

"What happened to her?"

He shrugged. "I don't know. She lived in a township just outside Jo'burg. If she's still alive she probably lives there now. Your father was a lady's man, that's for certain, but he was Duchess's man in his heart. She was his great love for about three years. I imagine there was no secret he kept from her."

"I want to meet her," said Celia suddenly. "I want to meet this mystery woman my father loved. She'll know him better than anyone, won't she?"

Mr. Botha shook his head. "I don't think that would be a good idea," he said and there was something shifty about the way he lowered his eyes and swilled the wine about in his glass. "I'm not even sure she still lives there. We might never find her." He waved his hand dismissively. "I can find you more interesting people to meet who knew your father. Men of distinction—"

"No, I want to meet *her*," she said. "Come on, Mr. Botha."

"It was forty years ago."

"I know and of course she's married and had children and probably grandchildren, who knows, but wouldn't it be important for me to meet her? If my father loved her once, I'd very much like to see her. She must know so much about that time. I've come a long way and I'm not going home without turning over every stone."

"Your father had other women, too . . ." he added uneasily, but Celia was undeterred.

"I know about Shapiro's wife," she said.

Mr. Botha nodded. "Yes, he had her too."

"But Duchess . . ." She shook her head and drained her glass. "I'd like you to take me to see her, Mr. Botha."

"I think you should think twice about digging into your father's past," he warned. "You might discover things you wished you hadn't. They were rough times back then. You had to be tough to succeed."

"I won't take no for an answer," said Celia, standing up.

AND SO IT was with great reluctance that Mr. Botha drove Celia out of the elegant city and into the shabby, dusty township of simple wooden huts, corrugated-iron roofs, dry mud tracks and narrow shady alleyways. Celia had never seen such poverty even during the worst of times in Ireland and her exuberance evaporated in the late-afternoon heat. Skinny dogs loped over the red earth hunting for food while men in mining caps with dirty faces bounced about in the back of horse-drawn carts on their way home from the mines. Women in brightly colored headscarves chatted in the shade while half-naked, barefooted children played happily in the sunshine. A man, clearly drunk, staggered in front of the car and Mr. Botha had to stamp his foot on the brakes to avoid running him over.

As the car drove slowly over the dusty ground people emerged from their huts and stared with curiosity at the shiny vehicle. The whites of their eyes gleamed brightly against the rich color of their skin and Celia gazed back, transfixed. She remembered Adeline's passion for feeding the poor of Ballinakelly and now, on seeing for herself the desperate quality of these people's lives, she understood Adeline's need to make a difference.

Soon the car was being followed by a small group of excited children. They ran alongside, daring each other to touch the metal, shouting in a language that Celia didn't understand. "I wish I had something to give them," she said to Mr. Botha.

"If you did, you'd never have enough," he said flatly. "Besides, you feed one and you have every child in the entire township begging for food."

After a while, Mr. Botha, now sweating profusely, was clearly lost. Celia recognized a street they had already been down. Not wanting to make him nervous she decided to pretend that she hadn't noticed, but when they drove down it for the third time she knew she had to say something. "Do you know where we're going?" she asked.

"I haven't been here for years, Mrs. Mayberry. I seem to

have lost my bearings." He buried his hand in the breast pocket of his shirt and pulled out a handkerchief with which he proceeded to pat his damp brow.

"Why don't you ask someone?" she suggested. "I'm sure these children will help us." She grinned at them through the window and they smiled back with eagerness.

Mr. Botha was reluctant to speak to the locals but he knew he had no choice. Besides, if he didn't know where he was, how would he ever find his way out? He stopped the car and asked the children now crowding around where Mampuro Street was. They all pointed enthusiastically and then started running ahead of the car, shouting and laughing at each other.

Mr. Botha followed at a gentle pace, only to discover that he had been a couple of streets away all along. Recovering his bearings he put the handkerchief back in his pocket and motored down the track, pulling up outside a small brown hut with a simple wooden door and two glass windows. "Is this where she lives?" Celia asked, climbing out of the car. The children retreated, forming a semicircle around the car, watching the beautiful blond lady in the long flowing dress and T-bar shoes with large, curious eyes.

Mr. Botha knocked on the door. There came a rustling sound from within, then the door opened and an eye looked cautiously out through the crack, accompanied by the pleasant smell of smoke. A woman's voice said something that involved a string of words Celia didn't understand interspersed by sharp clicks of the tongue. Then she seemed to recognize Mr. Botha and the door opened wider. She shuffled out on her bare feet in a heavy, brightly colored *shweshwe* dress and matching turban and craned her neck to take a closer look. On her face she had painted an array of white dots. "I've brought someone to see you, Duchess," said Mr. Botha.

Duchess turned to Celia. When she saw her the woman straightened up and a curious expression took over her face. She stared for a long moment without blinking and her lips twitched with indecision. Then the shock turned to curiosity. She glanced warily at the children who quietly scampered off and lowered her voice. "You'd better come in," she said.

"I will come with you," said Mr. Botha, but Celia raised a hand.

"No, please wait in the car," she said. Mr. Botha was not happy but he did as she requested. Celia followed the older woman into the dim interior of the hut. It was cool inside and crammed with potted plants of varying colors. There was a straw mat on the floor, a wooden table and a few chairs. The walls were painted bright blue and there was a shelf, laden with objects and a few books, above an open fireplace. Celia looked through into the other room where there was a bed positioned beneath a small window that gave onto the back of another rough dwelling. On the wall above the bed was a wooden cross, which took Celia by surprise. She hadn't imagined this woman to be Christian.

She was about to introduce herself, but the woman gesticulated to a chair with long, elegant fingers. "I know who you are," she said in a heavy accent, sitting down opposite and picking up her long-handled pipe, which she had been smoking. She was a full-bodied woman with strong arms and voluptuous breasts, graying hair just visible beneath her turban and a gauntness about her cheeks that betrayed her age, but Celia could see that she had once been beautiful. Her eyes were the color of shiny brown horse chestnuts and slanted like a cat's. When she looked at Celia they possessed a certain haughtiness that Celia imagined had earned her the name Duchess. Indeed, her skin was smooth and unlined, her cheekbones high and her eyebrows gracefully arched, giving her an air of nobility. Her full lips curved in a pretty bow shape and her teeth were very big and white. "You are Digby Deverill's girl," she said, running her intense gaze over Celia's features. "I would recognize you out of a thousand women," she added. "It's the eyes. I'd know them anywhere."

"I am Digby's daughter," said Celia, smiling. "I've just arrived in South Africa and I wanted to meet you."

The woman clicked her tongue. "How is your father?" she asked.

"I'm afraid he died," said Celia quietly. The woman blinked in horror and her head fell back a little, as if she had just been slapped. "It was a terrible shock for all of us," Celia explained, suddenly questioning her wisdom in coming. "He was still young and full of life." She proceeded to tell Duchess how he had died because the woman's grief prevented her from speaking. While Celia chattered on, Duchess's long fingers played about her trembling lips.

Eventually her eyes, now heavy with sorrow, settled on Celia. "So, you want to see me because I knew your father?"

Celia was embarrassed and lowered her gaze. What right did she have to turn up uninvited and dig up this woman's past without knowing anything about it? "Yes, I want to know who he was. From what Mr. Botha tells me, you knew him better than anyone."

Duchess's eyes seemed to gather Celia into their thrall. Celia stared back, powerless to look away. It was as if the woman was a vault of secrets that was on the point of being opened. "Your father betrayed everyone around him," she said softly, blowing out a puff of blue tobacco smoke. "And he betrayed *me*. But God knows, I've never loved anyone like I loved Digby Deverill."

"He betrayed *you?*" Celia asked, astonished. The feeling of reckless happiness that had been brought on by the verification that her father wasn't the murderer of Aurelius Dupree's story now crumbled and she felt the sickening fear return as shadows swallowing the light. "I'm sorry . . . perhaps I shouldn't have come." She made to get up.

"No, perhaps you should not have. But as you are here you might as well stay." Celia remained on the chair, wishing very much that she could leave. But Duchess had waited more than forty years to tell her story and she was determined to have her say. "God has sent you to my door, Miss Deverill. I wondered whether I would ever see your father again. But the years passed and our story faded like dye in sunlight, but not for me. My heart loves now as it loved then and it has not learned otherwise. So you will not leave with nothing, Miss Deverill. You came to see me for a reason and I am glad you have come." She pressed her lips to the pipe and Celia noticed the glass-beaded bracelets around her wrists and necklaces hanging over her breasts in elaborate designs of many colors. "My name is Sisipho, which means 'gift' in Xhosa, but your father called me Duchess. He said I was beautiful and I *was* then, Miss Deverill. I was as beautiful as you are." She lifted her chin and her sultry eyes blazed with pride. "Your father was a gentleman. He always treated me with respect, not like other white men treat black women. He listened to me. He made me feel like I was worth something. He even took me around Johannesburg in a horse and buggy." She pressed her fist to her heart. "He made me feel valued." She nodded in the direction of the bookshelf. "Those books you see there. He taught me English and he taught me to read. Digby gave them to me and I have read them all a hundred times. He spoiled me. He made me feel special and I *was* special, to him." Celia wondered if anyone since had made her feel special. From the way she was now wiping her eyes with those impossibly elegant fingers Celia doubted it. "He shared all his secrets with me. I knew everything and I have kept those secrets for over forty years. But I don't want to die with them. They're a heavy burden to carry through the gates of Heaven, Miss Deverill. I'm going to give them to you."

Celia did not want to carry the burden of Duchess's secrets either, but she had no choice. Duchess was determined to relieve herself of them. She puffed on her pipe and the smoke filled the room with a sweet, persistent smell. "Digby won a farm in a game of cards. He was so good at reading people that he rarely lost. He'd come and tell me all about it. About the foolish men who lost everything they had at the gambling tables. Not Digby. He wasn't foolish like them. He was clever and he knew it. He knew he was going to make money. He wanted to go back to London a rich man. Men would do anything to make their fortunes here. Your father was no different." She chuckled and for the first time Celia saw how her face glowed like a beautiful black dahlia when she smiled. "And he did go back to London a rich man. A *very* rich man." Now she narrowed her eyes and her smile turned fiendish. "But he was ruth-

456 · SANTA MONTEFIORE

less, Miss Deverill. Your father didn't make his fortune Moses's way. No, he broke a few Commandments on the path to prosperity. After all, if he had been a virtuous man he would not have loved *me*." Celia watched in fascination as this woman enlivened in the brilliance of her memories. She laid them out before her as if they were treasures, stowed away for decades and now displayed all bright and glittering for the only person interested in looking at them. And all the while her eyes shone with zeal as the words came tumbling out.

"But Digby didn't care what other people thought and he came to see me all the same. He told me about his winnings and he spent some of it on me." Her eyes were misting now as she remembered the good times. "He'd rush in all excited, like a boy with a present for his mama, and I'd scold him for spending money on me when he should have been saving what he had for the mines he was going to build. He didn't trust his own kind. White men—they might steal his diamonds, his money, but he trusted *me*. I knew he was going to strike it rich. I could see it in his ambition. If anyone was going to make it rich it was Digby Deverill—and there were thousands of men like him, with ambition and desire, all digging in the same place, but somehow I knew Digby would make it. He had the luck of the Devil. So, having won the farm north of Kimberley, he and two others went to look for diamonds there and they found them."

"Mr. Botha told me about this," said Celia, with rising interest. "Tiberius and Aurelius Dupree."

Duchess shook her head and the beads that hung from her ears swung from side to side. "Those boys were no match for Digby," she said proudly. "Their biggest mistake was in trusting him. But he looked like an angel with those big blue eyes and that halo of golden hair. He looked as innocent as a lamb. When he no longer needed them he got rid of them the old-fashioned way."

"What do you mean?" Celia asked. The smoke suddenly seemed to turn to ice and envelop her in its chilly grip. "Tiberius was killed by a lion."

Duchess watched Celia with a steady gaze. Her voice had a stillness about it now; even the smoke seemed to stagnate. "He didn't die by a lion. He died by a bullet."

"Aurelius's bullet," said Celia firmly. Her heart was thumping so violently now against her ribs that she had to put a hand there in an attempt to quieten it.

Duchess shook her head but this time the bead earrings did not move. "Captain Kleist's bullet."

Celia stared at her, eyes wide with terror. "Captain Kleist, the white hunter?"

"He was a ruffian who fought in the Prussian army. He thought nothing of killing a man. He arranged the trip and he made sure that Tiberius's death looked like it was an accident."

"But Aurelius was accused of his brother's murder and spent four decades in prison."

"He didn't do it," said Duchess matter-of-factly. "Digby framed him."

Celia began to cough. The smoke was now choking her. She stood up and staggered to the door. Outside, the sun was setting and the air had turned grainy with dusk and dust and a cool breeze swept through the township bringing the relief of autumn. She leaned against the doorframe and gasped. Mr. Botha had fallen asleep in the car. His head was thrown back against the seat and his mouth was wide open. She could hear his snores from ten feet away.

So her father was everything Aurelius Dupree had said he was. He had cheated the brothers, had one murdered and framed the other. She wanted to vomit with the shock of it. She wanted to expel what she had heard. How she wished she had never come.

"So why did you love him?" she demanded, striding back into the room.

Duchess was still sitting on her chair. She was delving into a bright beaded bag for tobacco for her pipe. "Because he was the Devil," she said simply. "No one is more attractive than the Devil." She grinned broadly and flicked her eyes up at Celia. "And he treated me like a duchess."

Celia sat down again. She ran her knuckles across her lips in thought. "You said he betrayed you too," she said.

"One day your father stopped coming to see me. He just disappeared from my world and I never heard from him again. Because of your father I was cast out of my community and disowned by my family. But I am a Christian woman now, Miss Deverill, and I have found it in my heart to forgive. I forgive them all."

With a trembling hand Celia fumbled with the catch on her handbag. "I don't have much but what I have left I want to give to you."

Duchess put up a hand to stop her. "I don't want your money. I never asked for anything from Digby and I won't accept anything from you. I have told you my story."

"But I want to give you something. For keeping Papa's secret."

"I kept it because I love him."

"But he can't thank you himself."

Duchess narrowed her eyes and grinned. "No, but I want to thank *you* for coming, child. I want to give *you* something. It was the year 1899 and my brother was a Piccanin working for an Afrikaner gold prospector who took him down to a farm in the Orange Free State. They said there was gold there. *Lots* of gold. But it was so deep they didn't have the means to mine it. So I told Digby. You see, there was a farm for sale next door that belonged to a man named van der Merwe, and no one had thought to buy that. Digby was no fool and he knew that the land might be useless then but in years to come, he said, 'Who knows what man might have created to dig deeper into the earth.' So he bought the land for nothing and it's been sitting there, untouched, for years. Now I know that the mines around Johannesburg are going real deep now. Deeper than they ever did. Why don't you think about digging there instead of digging into your father's past, and if you find gold, *then* you can give me some."

Chapter 30

Celia left Duchess smoking on her pipe. She woke Mr. Botha with a shake. He gave one final snort and sat up. "Just dozed off for a second," he said, taking the wheel.

"Thank you for bringing me, Mr. Botha. My visit was very enlightening."

"Now back to the hotel?" he asked.

"Yes please," she said, closing the passenger door and leaning back against the leather. She needed time to digest what Duchess had told her. She needed to figure out what to do. She also wondered how much of the truth Mr. Botha knew and was concealing from her. As the car motored over the lengthening shadows the children walked out into the cloud of red dust they left behind and watched the glimmer of metal disappear around the corner. "Tell me, Mr. Botha, what do you know about van der Merwe farm?"

"I don't know what you're talking about."

Celia gave him a hard stare. "You worked for my father and yet you claim to know nothing about land my father bought?"

Mr. Botha shrugged his big shoulders. "Your father's mines have all been sold to the Anglo American Corporation, to Ernest Oppenheimer. There's nothing left but some old legal papers in the safe."

"Then I'd like to see them, please," Celia told him.

"There is nothing worth seeing, Mrs. Mayberry."

Celia gave him her most charming smile. "If you don't mind, Mr. Botha, I'd like to have a look all the same. Just in case."

"Very well," Mr. Botha replied with a weary sigh. "I will take you. But I remember nothing about van der Merwe's farm. To be frank with you, Mrs. Mayberry, Duchess is old and her memory is a little vague."

"Well, while we're being frank, do you know of a man named Captain Kleist?" she asked.

"Der Kapitän," he said. "He is an old drunk and a blaggard and I don't believe he ever fought in the Franco-Prussian War. Why? Do you want to meet him too?"

Celia did not like his tone. "Yes," she replied. "I would."

Mr. Botha shook his head disapprovingly. "He's a fraud and a phony, Mrs. Mayberry. If he remembers anything it will be through the filter of alcohol or simply invented. He's nearly ninety and losing his mind."

"Where might I find him?"

"Propping up the bar in the Rand Club," he replied with a derisory snort. "But women are not permitted."

"Then I have to see him where I *am* permitted, Mr. Botha."

He sighed. "All right, I will see what I can do, Mrs. Mayberry."

MR. BOTHA'S OFFICE was on the second floor of an elegant white building that could have been in the middle of London, yet here it was in the middle of Johannesburg. He showed her into the foyer and closed the heavy wooden door on the noisy street, where trams, motorcars, men on bicycles and women on foot went about their business with the usual urgency of city dwellers. It was quiet inside the building and the woman at the front desk in a pair of glasses and blue tailored jacket smiled at Mr. Botha. He said something to her in Afrikaans and then headed off up the stairs. He showed Celia into his office and offered her a glass of water, but Celia was anxious to find the paperwork for Mr. van der Merwe's farm. Mr. Botha filled a glass for himself and then asked her to follow him to the safe, which was in a small cupboard in a room farther down the corridor. He took a while to unlock it and Celia felt he was being slow on purpose. But it opened at last and Mr. Botha leaned in and grabbed a cardboard box with his big hand. "These are your father's papers," he told her, putting it down on the desk. "You are welcome to go through them."

The box was large and held many documents. Celia pulled out the chair and sat down. "I'll have that glass of water now," she said to Mr. Botha, lifting out a beige file and opening it. Mr. Botha left her for a few minutes as he went to find a glass and fill a jug. When he returned the desk was strewn with paper and Celia had a smug and satisfied look on her face. "You're very organized," she said and her voice showed her surprise. She hadn't thought Mr. Botha would have labeled and arranged the files so clearly. "I have found the deeds to Mr. van der Merwe's farm," she said, holding up a faded pale blue file. "Now, I would like you to arrange for me to meet Captain Kleist."

Once back at the hotel Celia sat in the lounge with a large glass of whiskey. After having feared being on her own she was relieved to have time to think without the overbearing presence of Mr. Botha. She sat on the sofa and rattled the ice about in her glass. The golden liquid burned her throat but landed warmly in her stomach, swiftly taking the edge off her disquiet. Celia could not imagine her beloved father having a heart cold enough to murder, but Duchess had left little doubt. In spite of all that, the woman still claimed to love him. In spite of everything she had learned, Celia still loved him too, although she was discovering a very different father to the one she had known. She ordered another Scotch on the rocks.

Celia slept well that night. The hotel was reassuringly comfortable. The luxury was familiar and she didn't feel afraid. However, there was a new deadness in the depths of her being, a dull feeling of non-emotion, which came from resignation. Resignation to the truth, to the *terrible* truth, that her father had built his fortune on the blood and incarceration of those Dupree brothers. No amount of money could give Aurelius back those wasted years, or Tiberius. The thought was so overwhelming that her mind simply shut down. She closed her eyes and sank into blissful oblivion.

In the morning she went down to breakfast in the dining room. There was a message for her at reception. Captain Kleist was coming to meet her at the hotel at eleven. She was surprised and a little unnerved. She thought he would be reluctant to meet her. She imagined he wouldn't want to talk about so murky a past. This gave her heart a little boost and ignited a spark of hope. Surely, if he had killed on her father's behalf, he wouldn't be so keen to come and see her.

She waited in the lounge in an elegant floral dress, narrow-brimmed hat and cloth gloves, sipping a cup of tea. As the hands of the clock slowly approached eleven o'clock Celia began to feel uneasy. Her stomach churned with nerves and she could feel herself sweating. The minute hand moved beyond the twelve and seemed to gather speed as it descended toward the six. Celia watched the door. Every time anyone appeared she expected Captain Kleist, only to be disappointed. Her nerves grew still, the churning faded away and the sweat dried. She remained on the sofa for an hour until she had to resign herself to the fact that the Captain wasn't coming.

When she telephoned Mr. Botha he didn't sound at all surprised. "He's old and infirm," he explained. "I suggest you give up, Mrs. Mayberry. He has no wish to see you."

At this point many would have given up, as Mr. Botha suggested. But Celia was discovering a steely determination inside herself that she had never had cause to find before. She had traveled thousands of miles to discover whether or not Aurelius Dupree was telling the truth. She wasn't going to return to Ireland without knowing for certain. Captain Kleist was the only one who really knew what had happened that day in the veldt and she was adamant that she was going to talk to him, one way or the other. She remained on the sofa in the lounge for a further two hours, trying to think of a way of tricking him into meeting her. And then, just when her stomach was beginning to tell her that it was lunchtime, she came up with a plan—a plan that did not include Mr. Botha.

She asked the concierge for the telephone number of the Rand Club and then asked if she could use the telephone on the desk to make a quick local call. The concierge was only too happy to oblige such a pretty young woman as Mrs. Mayberry and wandered a short distance away to give her some privacy. She dialed the number and waited. Her heart was beating so loudly she thought she'd have trouble hearing the ring tone over it. There was a brief crackle down the line, then she heard it clearly. It rang a few times before a man's voice answered.

"The Rand Club, how may I help?"

"Hello, good afternoon, my name is Mrs. Temple," she said in a calm, officious voice. "I'm telephoning from the governor general's office in Cape Town. May I speak with Captain Kleist?"

"I'm afraid he hasn't come in today," replied the man.

This was as Celia had expected. "Ah, then perhaps you can help me," she said. "His Majesty's government has a very special package to send to Captain Kleist. I think it might be a medal. Would you be able to kindly give me his address so I may send it to him? It's a matter of some urgency." The man on the other end of the telephone did not hesitate in giving her the captain's address. She thanked him and put down the receiver with a rush of triumph. Flushed with her success she thanked the concierge.

Celia took a taxi to Captain Kleist's home, which was a small, modest bungalow in a quiet suburb of Johannesburg. Armed with a bottle of gin she strode up the little path to the front door. Taking a deep breath, she rang the bell. There was a long moment of silence before she heard the rattle of a chain and then the door opened a crack. A hard-faced old man with the narrow eyes of a shrew stared at her through the gap. When he saw her, in her elegant hat and dress, his face registered his surprise. "Captain Kleist?" she said. He nodded and frowned, looking her up and down with suspicion. "I'm from the governor general's office. I have a package for you."

"What sort of package?" he asked, and his German accent was pronounced.

She looked past him to see the walls cluttered with hunting trophies mounted in rows. "I hear you're a crack shot," she said. "May I come in?" Then without waiting for his reply, she pushed past him.

Kleist swung around, his face red with indignation, and Celia saw that he was holding a gun. "You know, once I would have shot someone for doing that," he said.

"But you wouldn't shoot Digby Deverill's daughter, now would you?" He stared at her in shock, lost for words. "Shall we have a drink?"

"A drink? I'm out of drink."

"Lucky then I brought a bottle with me." She held out the gin.

He took it and looked at the label. Satisfied, he walked into the small sitting room. "How do you like yours, Fräulein?" he asked.

"With ice and water," she replied.

She followed him into the room, which was decorated with animal skins and animal heads. The air was stale with the smell of old cigarette smoke, which clung to the upholstery. She sat down and tried not to look at all the dead eyes on the wall staring at her miserably.

Kleist was unshaven and perspiring, with stains on his tie and on one lapel of his crumpled linen jacket. He did not look like he was going to remember much. He handed her a glass of gin, ran his rheumy blue eyes over her features and grinned crookedly. "You are the image of your father," he said, his German accent cutting sharply into his consonants. "You remind me of him when he was a young man. You have the same eyes."

"Everyone says that," she replied coolly, not sure whether or not it was a compliment. Did they see a sliver of ice there that had been in her father's too?

Relieved that he remembered something, Celia asked him to share his memories, which he did much like the others had, with admiration. She listened as he told banal anecdotes of Digby's daring and his cunning and his unfailing luck, digressing all the time to talk about himself. Every story about her father seemed to lead into one about him. She sat back and sipped her gin while he boasted of the Franco-Prussian War and his courage in killing "natives." Indeed, he bragged, he had been awarded a medal for valor.

Celia began to tire of his long-winded tales, which might well have been total fantasy for all she knew. She didn't believe he was going to help her either confirm or deny what Duchess had told her. Was he likely to admit murdering a white person to a woman he has only just met? "Captain Kleist," she said. "Do you remember two brothers named Dupree?"

Der Kapitän nodded thoughtfully. "Of course I do. One of them, I don't remember which, got eaten by a lion."

"Yes, he did. Is it true that you arranged the hunting trip?"

"What if I did? Possibly?" He shrugged and put his empty glass on the table in front of him.

"I think you remember that day, Captain Kleist. I think you remember it well. After all, how many times have clients of yours been eaten by lions?" She watched him with an unwavering gaze. "I imagine you made a lot of money that day. More than the usual rate."

"White hunters are paid a lot," he said, then his face seemed to narrow with cunning and one side of his mouth extended into a grin. "But, it is true, I never made as much as I made that day, and I earned every penny. Your father was a very demanding client." He nodded pensively. "And the others, Mad McManus, Stone Heart and Spleen, were all working for your father too. We all earned well that day. But Deverill was a very rich man and rich men get what they want."

"You were hunting a man-eating lion, weren't you?"

"Yes, we were."

"But you didn't get him, did you?" said Celia.

"No." He shook his head. "No, we didn't."

"But you *did* get the kill my father *wanted* you to get, didn't you?" she said with care, looking at him steadily.

Captain Kleist sobered up in a moment. He returned her stare with one of equal steadiness. The stale air in that room turned as still and silent as a tomb. The Captain's face was bereft of humanity, as flat and sharp as a stone cliff. A small smile crept across it—the smile of a man too vain to conceal his triumphs. "Let's just say, Miss Deverill, that I never missed my target."

A FEW DAYS later Celia was driven to van der Merwe's farm in Bloemfontein in the Orange Free State, a five-hour drive from Johannesburg. In the group accompanying her was a young bespectacled geologist called Mr. Gerber, a Mr. Scholtz and a Mr Daniels—two prospectors who Mr. Botha insisted were vital to the project—and Mr. Botha himself, who was now taking credit for having suggested to Celia she assess her father's farm. "It was on my mind to approach Sir Digby about it just before he died," he claimed. "It is very fortunate that you, Mrs. Mayberry, chose to come to South Africa when you did. I believe the time is right to dig." Celia didn't bother to argue with him. If they found gold she wouldn't care who had suggested it.

The farm was a small huddle of trees in the middle of a vast expanse of arid yellow veldt, with a tall water tower, a dilapidated whitewashed dwelling in the Cape Dutch style with its distinctive gable and dark green shutters, surrounded by rundown wooden fences and redundant farming equipment lying abandoned on the grass like the bones of beasts long dead. To the west of the house was a field whose red earth had been recently plowed. Beyond the house were miles and miles of flat land reaching as far as the eye could see, punctuated every now and then by clusters of trees and herds of game.

A couple of scrawny goats eyed them warily as they pulled up in their cars and climbed out. Celia was happy to stretch her legs and inhale the rich country air. As they approached the front door an elderly lady walked out to greet them, followed by a pack of mongrel dogs. She was small in stature with dovegray hair swept up into a bun pinned roughly to the top of her head and wrinkled skin browned and weathered by the harsh African summers. However, her small eyes shone brightly like two sapphires, and they settled directly on Celia. She held out her hand and smiled. "My name is Boobie van der Merwe," she said. "I am Flippy's wife, but sadly Flippy is no longer with us. I remember your father. But it was many years ago that he bought this farm. Welcome." She invited them all to freshen up in the house and then to take refreshments on the terrace. Then, while the men went off to look at the land Celia remained with Boobie in a large wicker chair that looked directly out over the veldt.

"This is a very beautiful place to live," said Celia, feeling the pull of the distant horizon tugging at her chest.

"Oh, it is," Boobie agreed with a smile. "I've lived here for seventy years."

Celia frowned. "Seventy?"

"My dear, I'm ninety-six."

"And you still farm?"

"A farmer never retires, you know. Farming is not an occupation but a way of life. Flippy died twelve years ago and I continued to farm the land with our two sons. We often wondered if your father would ever return to mine it. They're digging deep round here now. Modern technology is a wonderful thing. Perhaps Sir Digby forgot about it." *Or perhaps he had darker reasons why he never came back,* Celia thought to herself. "He certainly forgot to raise our rent," Boobie continued, her tiny eyes twinkling. "Or he *chose* to forget. He must have been a good man."

"If they mine here, Mrs van der Merwe, you have my word that you will be very well looked after. I will see that you are relocated and compensated for the loss of your home."

"You don't have to do that, my dear. We are only tenants. There is nothing to prevent you from asking us to leave, perhaps a month or two's notice. That is all. We expected to leave forty years ago." She chuckled.

"But I know what it feels like to be emotionally attached to a place. Your heart is here, Mrs van der Merwe. It will be a terrible wrench to have to leave it."

"Nothing lasts forever, Mrs. Mayberry. Everything is reduced to dust in the end. As long as I can look out over the veldt I will be happy. My boys will look after me."

"Perhaps they might consider working for *me*."

Boobie nodded thoughtfully. "Perhaps they will," she replied.

At last the men returned. They were hot and dusty but Celia could tell from Mr. Botha's face that they had reached a positive outcome. He took off his hat and fanned his sweating face. "As Sir Digby discovered forty years ago, the gold here is very deep, but it is minable. Advances in technology make it possible. If you want to persevere we will need to drill here. Or perhaps you can just sell it to Anglo American. But there's gold here. Lots of gold. This is just as large as the other deposits found in the Free State. Your father was a shrewd man, Mrs. Mayberry. What will you do?"

"I will do this myself," she said resolutely. "I will start with the men who financed my father, and their sons. They all made their fortunes with him and they will make fortunes with me. Make a list, Mr. Botha, of all his shareholders."

He replaced his hat and smiled. "I suggest you prepare to move your life to Johannesburg, Mrs. Mayberry," he said.

THE FOLLOWING DAY Celia wrote to her mother and sisters to tell them what she had discovered. There was a strong possibility that Celia would restore her family's fortune in the industry where her father had originally made it. Mr. Botha could look after her interests while she returned to England to see to the ugly business of Aurelius Dupree. Then she would return to Johannesburg with her daughters and build a new life. The castle was gone, her husband and father were gone, it was time she moved on from her losses and concentrated on rebuilding.

But there was something she had to do before she left for London.

Duchess was surprised to see her again. As the car drew up outside the humble shack she was sitting on a chair outside her front door puffing on her pipe. She looked at Celia in amazement. "I did not think I would ever see you again, Miss Deverill," she said, pushing herself up. "Will you come inside?"

Celia followed her into the dark interior of her home. She smelled the familiar scent of tobacco mixed with the herbs and spices of Duchess's cooking. "I've come to thank you for telling me about the van der Merwe farm."

Duchess chuckled and sank onto the chair. "I knew you'd find gold," she said, shaking her head. "Did I not say that you would?"

"It's very deep but, as you rightly suggested, with the machinery they have now it will be possible to dig that far into the earth."

Duchess nodded and exhaled a waft of smoke. "I'm glad. You will now be rich like your father was. Like him you are lucky."

"But unlike him my luck is not from the Devil. I will not forget the woman who made it possible, Duchess. I will not betray you as my father did."

"You have a big heart, Miss Deverill." Celia noticed that her eyes shone with emotion. "And a *good* heart, too."

Just as Celia was about to sit down the door opened, throwing light across the floor. A tall man with light brown skin stepped into the room. He was surprised to see her. The shiny car outside with the waiting driver must have aroused his curiosity and he gazed at her warily. "Miss Deverill," said Duchess, waving her long fingers. "This is my son."

Celia looked into the man's eyes and gasped. She stared at him and words failed her. It was as if she were looking into a reflection of her own eyes, for they were the same almond shape, the same pale blue, set in exactly the same way as hers. They were her father's eyes. They were Deverill eyes. She extended her hand and he took it, gazing back at her with equal wonder. "Celia Deverill," she said at last.

"Lucky," he replied, without releasing her hand. "Lucky Deverill."

Chapter 31

Grace trailed her fingers down Count Cesare's muscular chest and smiled. Her cheeks were flushed, her eyes gleamed and her greedy appetite for the gratification of the flesh was well and truly sated, for now. Indeed, the Count had not disappointed her. She had barely thought of Michael Doyle since this exotic and clearly devilish man had undone the first button of her dress. He had carried her to her bed and confirmed what she had always suspected, that Latin men know better than anyone how to pleasure a woman.

Now Michael Doyle slipped into her consciousness again. She wanted him to know what she thought of Count Cesare and she wanted him to boil with jealousy. "Now that you have bought the castle, Cesare, when are you going to move in?" she asked, propping herself up on her elbow and shaking her head so that her hair fell in tawny waves about her shoulders.

"In the fall perhaps," he replied noncommittally. "I need to sort things out in America first. Perhaps return to Buenos Aires. Play polo." He grinned and Grace devoured the beauty of it with ravenous eyes.

"I should like to watch you play polo," she said. "But I should like to see you hunt first. You cannot disappear back to America without knowing what it is like to ride a horse at full gallop over the Irish hills. There is nothing quite like it."

"I'm in no hurry to leave." He sighed and slipped his fingers through her hair to caress the back of her neck. "Now I have found entertainment here, I should like very much to enjoy a little more of what the Irish life has to offer."

She kissed his arrogant smile. "Oh, I have much more to offer and so has Ireland. You have merely scratched the surface. Stay awhile." She slid her hand beneath the covers. "I'm sure I can think of ways to keep you here."

He writhed with pleasure and groaned. "Well, the Countess is in no hurry, after all. I have bought her a castle, it is only right that I explore a little further the place where we are going to make our home."

"It most certainly is," she agreed, stroking him with deft fingers. "I shall show you everything you need to know."

KITTY RODE WITH her father up the sandy beach at Smuggler's Cove, the place where she had often walked with Jack. She gazed out across the ocean and wondered what he was doing in America and whether he ever thought of her. *Her* feelings for him had certainly not diminished with the years, but she was content with the choice she had made. She had a family of her own now and she had Ireland—always Ireland, in the heart of her heart. Only when she allowed her mind to wander freely did thoughts of Jack cut her to the quick.

News had spread fast that a handsome Italian had bought the castle and planned to bring his countess over from America to settle here. Kitty didn't imagine they would last very long. What would an Italian couple make of the gray skies and drizzle? She didn't imagine they would understand the Irish way of life. It was only a matter of time before they would move back to the glamour and sophistication of New York. A castle was a lovely fantasy for a foreigner with more money than sense but a harsh reality for strangers to this wild and unforgiving land. She didn't imagine they'd be impressed by the society here, although, from what she had witnessed at Grace's dinner parties, the Count was more than entertained by her company, in the bedroom as well as at the table.

Kitty missed Celia. She had left for South Africa without explanation, leaving her children in the care of their nanny. Kitty had kept a close eye on them, but now that Castle Deverill was no longer theirs they would surely move back to England and settle there. For all Celia's wistful reminiscences about Ballinakelly Kitty was certain that she was a Londoner at heart and would find life there very much to her liking once she'd recovered from the shock and humiliation of selling the castle. She'd be close to Boysie and Harry and her mother, of course, although Beatrice was still refusing to leave her bed and the misery of her mourning.

Celia had explained to Kitty and Bertie that the White House and the Hunting Lodge were theirs for as long as they wanted. It was even written into an agreement that Deverills should always have first refusal of those two residences, providing they didn't fall behind on their rent. The Count had promised to grant them that small concession; after all, it suited him to have the places occupied and the money coming in. It had certainly come as a relief to Bertie and Kitty to know that they could remain in their homes.

"I shall miss Celia very much," said Kitty as she rode beside her father up the wide expanse of beach.

"We have to embrace the change," said Bertie philosophically. "There's no point gnashing our teeth and wailing because that won't return things to the way they were. We have to be grateful for our memories, Kitty. We were fortunate to have lived the way we did."

"It shall grieve me very much to watch the castle inhabited by strangers."

"The Count seems a nice sort of fellow," said Bertie. "We shall probably like him very much when we get to know him."

"If he lasts long enough. I'm not sure how they are going to entertain themselves. They really are very foreign, Papa."

"They'll entertain themselves the same way we do. They'll get into the Irish way of life and it will be exciting for them because it'll be different. The spice of life is in the variety, after all."

"But surely they'll miss the glamour of New York. The society here isn't very urbane, is it?"

"Perhaps they're weary of urbane."

Kitty shrugged. "I still don't hold out much hope for them. Unless one's heart is here the mind will bore of it. The one thing that ties us to this place is love. You and I love it more than anybody and nothing can prize us from it. But the Count and his wife have no such affection, why, she has never set foot in Ireland. How can she possibly know what it is like? She must have seen a photograph in the newspapers and fancied herself living like a princess. But Ballinakelly is not a town in a fairy tale. She'll discover that as soon as she arrives and I bet you she'll be hoofing it back to New York on the next available boat with her poor count moaning behind her." She laughed. "If you and I save up all our money we might buy it when they sell."

Bertie laughed with her. "You have a fanciful imagination, my dear."

"*You* made me, Papa."

"But your imagination and your wonder at the magic of nature came directly from your grandmother."

"Which you always dismissed as rubbish," she said, smiling at him with affection.

He looked at her askance. "I have learned that it is the mark of a foolish man to scoff at things of which one knows absolutely nothing. I sense God out there, Kitty," he said, throwing his gaze across the water. "But I can't see Him with my eyes. So why not nature spirits, ghosts, goblins and leprechauns too?" He grinned at the surprised look on his daughter's face. "The idea is to grow wiser as one gets older, my dear Kitty."

"What would Grandma say?" She laughed.

"I wish I knew. I wish she were here . . ." Then he shook his head and chuckled. "But of course she *is* here, isn't she? She's always here. Didn't she insist that those we love and lose never leave us?" *Indeed I did,* said Adeline, but her voice was a sigh on the wind that only Kitty could hear.

LAUREL HAD FOUND her return to the saddle most thrilling. Hazel, on the other hand, preferred the card table. Consequently the two sisters began to find that their very different forms of entertainment took them to disparate parts of the county. In the past such regular separation would have greatly vexed them; however, now they were only too eager to be rid of each other. While Laurel stole kisses with Ethelred Hunt behind hedgerows on the windy hills above Ballinakelly, Hazel allowed him to play with her foot beneath the card table, and sometimes place his hand upon her leg when no one was looking. Kisses had to be seized in dark corridors and empty rooms and the secrecy of those moments only compounded Hazel's delight. Both women guarded their secret romances closely— until one unfortunate evening in May when a chance discovery would swipe away the veil of concealment.

Laurel had been riding, alone. She had borrowed a horse from Bertie's stable and set off on her own, for Ethelred had been summoned to the bridge table at the Hunting Lodge and it looked like he was going to be there until evening. She enjoyed riding out on her own, although she would have much preferred to have had the company of the dashing silver wolf. Little birds frolicked in the blackthorn and elder and went about building their nests while young rabbits grazed in the long grasses and heather. It was her favorite time of year and she took pleasure from spring, which had exploded onto the wintry landscape in all its glorious color.

She had stopped on the crest of the hill and gazed over the wide ocean, breathing in the bracing smells of the sea and listening to the roar of the waves breaking on the rocks below. When she set off back down the hill toward home, she was feeling light of spirit and full of joy. Everything was right with her world. She was having a delightful romance with Ethelred Hunt and she and Hazel were friends again, after months of steadily growing apart. She no longer had to feel jealous of her sister or suffer the pain of unrequited love. Ethelred Hunt loved her, of that she had no doubt. So long as Hazel never found out, everything would be fine. Poor Hazel, she thought with genuine compassion, but Ethelred had chosen *her* and she had been too weak-willed and infatuated to resist him. This was the first time in her life that she hadn't put her sister first. She wasn't proud of it, but her passion for him gave her a heady sense of carelessness and her sister's feelings were hastily and conclusively swept aside.

She walked her horse along the top of the cliff. Down below gulls and gannets pecked at sea creatures abandoned by the tide and the odd butterfly fluttered into view. Then she heard the sound of laughter that did not belong to any seabird she had ever heard. She stopped her horse and peered down onto the beach. The laughter rose on the wind and it was instantly recognizable with its distinctive warmth and flirtatiousness. The sound of a man's voice broke in then and the laughter stopped as he pulled his companion into his arms and kissed her ardently. Laurel was stunned by the vigorous passion of the man and the way the woman's knees buckled as she fell against him. So much so that she couldn't take her eyes off them. What would Sir Ronald say if he were to discover his wife in a romantic clinch with Count Cesare? Laurel thought disapprovingly—and what of the Count's wife? Laurel shook her head and tutted. Grace Rowan-Hampton should be ashamed of such licentious behavior. This wasn't the way a lady of her stature should behave. Why, anyone might stumble upon them. Laurel found it very fortunate that the only stumbling had been done by *her*. At least *she* could be trusted to keep her mouth shut.

Or could she?

Hazel didn't count, she reasoned. To gossip to one's sister

was natural and normal and Laurel knew that Hazel would ensure that it went no further. She pulled her horse away from the edge, leaving the two lovers unaware that they had just been discovered, and trotted hastily down the path toward the Hunting Lodge.

The discovery of Grace and the Count was burning on her tongue and she couldn't wait to unburden it. She hurried to the stables and, with the help of one of the grooms, dismounted and handed over the reins. She strode across the yard, removing her gloves finger by finger, impatient to find her sister. She found only Bertie and Kitty in the library. Classical music resounded from the gramophone and they were both drinking tea. "Ah, hello, Laurel. I hope you had an enjoyable ride," said Bertie from the armchair. The cards were neatly piled on the card table. The game had finished.

"Oh, I most certainly did, Bertie, thank you. It's glorious out there." She stood in the doorway, clearly not intending to join them for tea.

"I should like to go myself," said Kitty enviously. "It seems a shame to waste a lovely afternoon inside."

"There will be more," said Bertie with a chuckle.

"Has Hazel gone home?" Laurel asked, keen to find her sister.

"Not yet," Bertie replied. "She's taking a stroll around the garden with Ethelred."

"Then I shall go and find her. I have something I need to tell her," Laurel announced before leaving the room.

"I'll make sure there's a fresh pot of tea for your return," said Kitty, but Laurel had disappeared across the hall. Bertie arched his eyebrows at his daughter and Kitty shrugged. "I wonder what that's all about," she said.

"I'm sure we'll find out soon enough," Bertie replied.

The gardens at the Hunting Lodge were an assortment of lawn, vegetable garden, secret walled garden and orchard. Each was separated from the other by yew hedge, shrubs, trees or wall. These days the place had been allowed to overgrow because Bertie couldn't afford to keep on the team of gardeners who had ensured that the hedges were trimmed, the borders weeded and the annuals planted. There was a greenhouse where they used to keep cuttings and house plants during the winter months, but now it was empty, a broken pane of glass leaving an open door for rooks to enter and exit with ease along with the rain. Nothing grew in there except weeds and a small chestnut tree, which, by some miracle, had seeded itself.

Laurel set off at a brisk walk. In spite of the lack of care the gardens were full of color. Periwinkles and forget-me-nots had spread like water across the lawns and borders, and purple clematis scaled the walls with wisteria and rose. Daisies and buttercups were scattered across the grass and dandelions served as enticing landing pads for toddling bees, drunk on nectar. Monarch butterflies flew jauntily around the buddleia and swallows darted back and forth from the eaves of the house, busy nest-building. Laurel thought it all looked beautiful in a wild, overgrown kind of way. She'd like to have been young and energetic enough to have pulled out the ground elder by the roots, for it was stifling the plants and taking over the borders with bindweed and goose grass.

She marched through the secret garden, which was enclosed by yew hedge and wall. There was a bench positioned in a sun trap but the weeds had grown so tall they had almost swallowed it up. She peered around the end of the yew hedge, where a pond lay serene and quiet in the shade of a weeping willow. Pondweed grew thick and green on the surface of the water and a pair of wild ducks who had chosen to settle there were pecking at it contentedly. Laurel strained her ears for the sound of voices but heard nothing save the noisy chatter of birds. She would have called if shouting across the garden were not undignified.

She was about to give up when she saw them through the glass of the greenhouse. They were standing on the other side, in the shade, and they were holding hands—all *four* hands, Laurel noted with a jolt. And then, to her horror, she watched the man who had made her feel as if she was the only woman in the world he desired lower his head and kiss her sister on the lips. It was more than shocking, it was sickening, and she wasn't going to let him get away with it.

She strode around the greenhouse and stood a few yards away, hands on hips, scowling furiously. It took a while for them to notice her, so engrossed they were in each other. Then Hazel's eyes opened and bulged. She pushed Ethelred away with a brisk shove. "This isn't what you think," she said clumsily.

"It's *exactly* what it looks like," Laurel snapped. Ethelred swung around and stared at Laurel in surprise. *At least he has the decency to look ashamed*, she thought.

"Now, ladies," he began uncomfortably.

But Hazel interrupted him. She shook her head apologetically. "I'm sorry I didn't tell you, Laurel. I should have. Ethelred and I have been seeing each other . . ."

Laurel walked up to Lord Hunt and slapped him across the face. Hazel made to protest but Laurel turned on her. "We've been made a fool of, Hazel," she said. "I've been seeing Ethelred too!"

Hazel gazed at Lord Hunt, aghast. "Is this true?" she demanded. "Have you been seeing Laurel as well as me? You have been playing us off, one against the other?" And she pulled her hand back and slapped him on the other cheek. "How dare you."

"He's been laughing at us for months!" Laurel exclaimed, suddenly realizing the full extent of his betrayal.

"I've never felt so humiliated in all my life!" cried Hazel. "I will never get over this. Never!"

Ethelred appealed to the two sisters. "But I couldn't make a choice between the two of you," he explained, palms to the sky, face burning. "Truthfully, I fell in love with both of you."

"I've never heard anything more outrageous!" said Laurel, slipping her hand beneath Hazel's arm.

"Me neither. Outrageous!" said Hazel, glancing at her sister with tenderness. "Come, Laurel, let's leave this scoundrel to lick his wounds. I have no interest in hearing his explanations."

"But I really do love you," Ethelred pleaded, his voice cracking on the word "love." But the two sisters set off toward the house without a backwards glance.

"We mustn't tell anyone about this," said Hazel as they approached the Hunting Lodge.

"We absolutely mustn't," Laurel agreed.

"It's just too humiliating." They walked on in silence as the impact of Ethelred Hunt's dishonesty began to sink in. Then Hazel sighed sadly. "I do believe I love him, Laurel," she said in a small voice.

Laurel nodded, relieved to be able to share her pain. "So do I," she said.

"Oh, what a hopeless pair we are," lamented Hazel.

"Hopeless!"

"What would Adeline say?" said Hazel.

Laurel shook her head. "She'd have no words, Hazel," she replied. "No words at all!" In the turmoil of their anguish Laurel forgot all about Grace Rowan-Hampton and the dashing count.

Chapter 32

New York, 1931

Jack waited at the front of Trapani, an elegant Sicilian restaurant on East 116th Street in Harlem. He had been expecting this call. He had known that sometime he would be needed. There was little that daunted him and no one he feared. He dragged on his cigarette and looked around him. Trapani was a classic Italian joint, wood-paneled and smelling of fried onions and garlic. The waiters were all plump Sicilians with graying hair and brown, weathered faces. They wore black trousers and white jackets and their talk rose and fell in the musical way that Italian does. He noticed there were no diners in the main restaurant, only burly bodyguards in black suits and fedoras; Salvatore Maranzano's men. Since the killing of Joe "the Boss" Masseria, Maranzano had been *capo di tutti capi*, the Boss of Bosses. The bodyguards had been expecting Jack. They had placed him at a little round table beneath the awning in front of the restaurant, offered him a cigarette, and ordered him an Italian coffee, and Jack had sat down and waited. In his line of work he spent a lot of time waiting.

"The Boss knows you're here," said one of the bodyguards with the low brow of a Neanderthal and a squashed, broken nose. "He's eating inside. He'll be ready when he's ready."

"That's grand," said Jack. "Then I'll have another one of these." And he lifted his empty coffee cup.

Jack had never met the Boss but he knew all about him. Maranzano was famously obsessed with the Roman Empire. He devoured books on the Caesars and liked to quote Caligula and Marcus Aurelius, so that he had acquired the nickname "Little Caesar," but no one dared call him that to his face. He had recently won the war against Joe Masseria and had made an alliance with the young gangsters: Charlie "Lucky" Luciano and his Jewish allies, Meyer Lansky and Ben "Bugsy" Siegel. It was a world in which everyone had nicknames—just like Ireland—and it was a world familiar to Jack, who had fought with the rebels during Ireland's War of Independence. He knew how to handle a gun and how to use it. He'd killed Captain Manley that night on the Dunashee Road and, after you've killed once, the second time comes easier. Desperate to put his past and all its pain and disappointment behind him, he had embraced the blood-filled cauldron of New York without a backward glance. He'd resolved to look after himself, and the Devil take the rest.

The quickest way to make it in New York was to join the gangs. As an Irishman newly arrived in America it wasn't difficult; New York was full of Irish. He had contacted a friend

from the Old Country, who had made the necessary introduc-
tions, and soon he was running errands for Owen Madden,
who ran the Cotton Club. Errands that involved riding shotgun
in a truck transporting whiskey down from Canada. It wasn't
long before it got around that Jack had a streak of steel in his
heart. He had "earned his bones" shooting his first man, which
had brought him respect, and suddenly he was in demand and
earning twice the amount of money. He reflected on his meager
vet's wage back in Ballinakelly and gave a derisory sniff. He had
gained a reputation in New York as a cool hand on the trigger
and a nickname. They called him "Mad Dog" O'Leary, and in
this small, rarefied world, everyone knew who he was. He was
a man of some standing and he relished his new status. He was
unable to join the Mafia itself, for only Sicilians could become
a "made man," but Jack didn't care. The Irish had their own
gangs and rackets, and they often worked with Italians and Jews.

The Irish looked out for each other, and two and a half years
after arriving in New York and getting involved in the business
of bootlegging, Jack had married the daughter of one of Owen
Madden's henchmen at the Cotton Club, an Irish girl whose
family originated from County Wicklow. Her name was Emer
and she was freckly-skinned and pretty, gentle and submissive,
nothing like Kitty Deverill, whose love was passionate, her
fury fiery, her determination untiring. Momentarily assaulted
by the memory of her, he envisaged her running to him in the
Fairy Ring and throwing her arms around him, as she had
done so many times, the wind in her wild red hair, the sun
turning her skin to gold, her laughter rising above the roar of
waves. He pictured her face, the eagerness in her gaze, and felt

the energy in her embrace as if he were living it all over again. It took a monumental effort to dispel her image from his mind and turn his thoughts to the woman he had married.

Emer was young, sweet and straightforward and, after Kitty, it was a relief to have a love that was uncomplicated. For he *did* love Emer. It was a different kind of love, but love nonetheless, and for all his longing he was certain that Emer was good for him. She understood his business, having been brought up in the world of Irish racketeers, and she didn't question him when he returned from the Cotton Club in the early hours of the morning smelling of cheap perfume, in the same way that her mother had never questioned her father. Emer accepted what he did and the risks he ran without question, and was grateful for the money he made without asking where it came from. She knew he carried a gun and she was well aware that he had used it, to deadly effect. She had given him a daughter, Alana who was now two, and she was pregnant with their second child. Their children would never know Ireland or the part their father had played in securing its independence. Jack would see that they had a better life than the one he had known back in Ballinakelly. He would do whatever it took to earn the money to make that possible.

Just then there was a flurry of activity. Lunch was breaking up and the bodyguards were pushing out their chairs, doing up the buttons on their jackets and sidling toward the door. A young Italian in a sharp suit and fedora walked across the room with the swagger of a fighter. His face was fleshy, his coarse skin marked with a long red scar that ran the whole length of his jawline. His eyes were small, dark brown and arrogant. The bodyguards fell in behind him and the ones in front walked ahead, throwing suspicious glances up and down the street before positioning themselves beside the shiny black car. Jack knew who he was. His gait and his expression were unmistakable. He was the Boss's deputy, Lucky Luciano, the man who had arranged the killing of Masseria. Luciano looked at him circumspectly, for Jack's face was new to him. Then one of the bodyguards opened his door and he climbed inside. The car rattled up the street.

"O'Leary, the Boss will see ya now." Jack stood up and walked into the restaurant. Two men patted him down and took away his pistol and the knife he always kept in a garter around his shin. Then he was shown into the back room where Salvatore Maranzano sat at a table still stained with tomato sauce and strands of spaghetti. He was about forty-five years old, compact and sturdy, in a three-piece suit that stretched over a paunch, and a traditional string tie. His face was wide and handsome with thick black hair swept off a broad forehead. He raised his eyes when Jack entered and took a few puffs of his cigar.

"Come in, O'Leary," he said in a heavy Italian accent, gesticulating through the cloud of smoke to the chair opposite.

"Don Salvatore," said Jack, giving a small bow, for he knew the Italians, especially Little Caesar, expected this sort of flattery. Maranzano offered his hand and Jack shook it.

"Take a seat . . . Coffee? Cigarette? Cognac?"

"I'm fine," Jack replied and took the chair opposite the Boss. Maranzano nodded at his bodyguards, who left, closing the door behind them.

Jack and the Boss were now alone; the small-town Irishman

and the Boss of New York City. Jack reflected on how far he had come, but he didn't have time for wistfulness, for Maranzano was staring at him intensely, his narrowed eyes appraising him to see if he really was the Mad Dog everyone said he was.

"I heard you got balls and you can take anyone down," he said quietly.

Jack gave a nonchalant shrug. "If that's what they say."

"Well, you gotta have something to be called Mad Dog—but then again there are lots of Irish boys called mad dogs. I want a dog that's mad enough but not too mad, you get what I'm saying? I want something done right and fast."

"Then maybe I'm your man," said Jack, returning Maranzano's stare with his own fearless gaze.

"You see, it can't be an Italian and it can't be a Jew, so it's gotta be a Mick, and it's gotta to be a *new* Mick. Someone fresh in town, someone not everyone knows, and someone who can shoot straight. You know what I'm saying?"

"You called and I'm here," said Jack, sounding a great deal more confident than he felt. He had wanted a job like this, a *big* job, but a cold sensation began to creep over his skin, starting at the base of his spine and crawling slowly up, and he wondered whether it was *too* big. It was one thing bootlegging, quite another working for the Mafia. But he knew that no one walked away from Little Caesar and lived.

"You know your Roman history, boy?" Maranzano asked, puffing again on his fat cigar. *Jaysus! Here we go*, thought Jack. "Let me tell you about my favorite, Julius Caesar. He taught me how to organize my army, my centurions, my legions." Maranzano's chair scraped across the floor as he got to his feet. Then he held up his forefinger in full lecture mode. "Then there was

Marcus Aurelius. He taught me the philosophy of ruling an empire. He said, 'Don't get over-Caesarified, that's dangerous, keep sharp!' You know what I'm saying? And Augustus, *he* knew an empire needed peace after war—and that's what I gotta do right now. But he ruled with Mark Antony and in the end he knew that Mark Antony had to go. *Capisci?*"

Jack did not understand but he didn't want to guess either, because if he guessed wrong, it could cost him his neck. So he played dumb. Maranzano waved his finger again. "I'll tell you about another Caesar: Caligula. He said, 'Let them hate me as long as they fear me.' He was crazy but he was no fool either, *capisci?* So, that's why I got *you* here." He sat down again and put the cigar between his lips.

"Why *have* you got me here, Boss?" Jack asked.

"I've got a job for you. It's the biggest job of your life." He jabbed his finger at Jack. "If you fuck up, you're finished in this city, but if you do it right, you'll be my guy, my Irish centurion, *capisci?* I asked you here for a reason. You saw the guy who just came out of lunch with me?" Jack nodded. "You know who he is?" Jack nodded again. "Luciano, that's who. But that fuck is trying to kill me after I made him my deputy and gave him so much." His voice grew louder and his eyes narrowed with hatred. "He's trying to kill me with his Jewboy friends, Bugsy and Meyer. You know Bugsy with his blue eyes and his movie star looks? Well, I ain't scared of no Jewboys. I got a guy in their house, and he told me, they're already planning to get me! Well, I'm going to kill Luciano first and *you're* going to do it for me."

"That's quite a job," said Jack, but he kept his eyes steady. He didn't want the Boss to see any doubt there.

"Fifty thousand dollars. Twenty-five now. Twenty-five after. That's quite a lot of money for a Mick village boy who's new in the city. Is it enough?"

"Yeah, it's enough. I'll take the job, Don Salvatore, though I got to tell you, I don't like to be called a Mick."

Maranzano came around the table and took Jack into his arms. He smelled of garlic, chives, cigars and lemon cologne. "You're a proud man, O'Leary, and I like that. I take it back. I respect your people and I like your songs. I apologize. Are we straight?"

"Yeah, sure, no problem," said Jack.

"Good." The Boss kissed him on both cheeks and sandwiched his hand between his. "Luciano's coming to my office in a couple of days. It's nine floors up but he always takes the stairs coz he don't like being trapped in an elevator. Sensible, right? And when he comes out of the meeting, he's alone and you're going to whack him between my office and the stairs. *Capisci?*"

"Sounds like a plan," said Jack, although not a very solid one.

"Here's the first twenty-five," said Maranzano, pulling out an envelope from his pocket and thumping it down on the tablecloth in front of Jack, who had never seen so much money before. Jack folded the envelope and put it in the inside pocket of his jacket. He could do a lot with fifty grand. He could buy a house for him and Emer. He could give his children a better life than he ever had.

"No one knows about this," Maranzano continued. "None of my guys outside, you understand? No one. Just you and me. That's why I'm making you a rich man. You know I own every soldier, every block, every racket in this city, O'Leary. If you let me down, if you talk, if you miss, I will crush you, and if you run, I'll chase you back to your Irish village and I will kill everyone you love in the world, you know what I'm saying? If you succeed, I will *give* you the world. You know, Jack, I've killed many men and one thing I know for sure is that you touch the end of the gun to the guy's forehead so you can feel him, right there, and that way you know it's done. Man is the hardest animal to kill. If he gets away he will come back and kill *you*."

Chapter 33

Jack perched on the edge of a desk in a little side office near the reception of Salvatore Maranzano's office. He sipped his coffee and read the newspaper, the *New York World-Telegram*, and checked the racing scores. His thoughts drifted to the showgirl from the Cotton Club he had had the night before. He could still smell her perfume and feel the dancer's muscles beneath her skin. There were benefits to being an Irish hood in New York City. He would see her that night and have fifty thousand bucks to celebrate.

He smiled to himself and turned the page. The office buzzed around him. Pretty girls in elegant dresses passed his door without casting him so much as a glance, too busy with telegrams and letters and documents to file. Others sat at desks, heads bent, typing. The offices were elegant and sumptuous, with wood paneling, high ceilings, ornately molded cornicing and shiny marble floors adorned with crimson carpets. The walls were cluttered with paintings of Rome, and Jack read the inscriptions beneath: *the Forum, the Colosseum, Palatine Hill, the Pantheon, St Peter's Basilica,* and every couple of yards was a Roman statue of some emperor or other in his toga. Jack had heard that not everyone was so impressed with the Boss's clap-trap about Caesar but no one would dare let their lack of enthusiasm show.

This building on Forty-Fifth Street was like a palace, all shiny and new, built by the same men who had built Grand Central Station. Inside, the hall was marble, the elevators gleamed, and Jack had checked himself in the doors as they closed, and rearranged his tie on the way up. He looked good: dark suit, slim figure, his lucky trilby, seersucker shoes in black-and-white, not bad for a country boy from Ballinakelly. He still had the gap in his teeth from where he'd been punched in prison, but his blue eyes and raffish smile were hard for women to resist. He knew why he had got the job. He had no nerves. He was preternaturally calm, ice-cool, and he knew exactly what to do and when to do it. He carried a Colt Super .38 in a holster under his arm. Not many people had one yet but his was already like an extension of his hand. He had the cash for the hit in his suit pocket. He gave it a pat and took pleasure from the thick wad of it.

Everything was in place. He'd wait here in this room until Lucky was in the Boss's office, then he'd take up his position at the back by the stairs. When Lucky came out he'd pop him in the forehead, like the Boss had said, with the barrel right against his head, and then walk calmly along the corridor and take the elevator down before Luciano's bodyguards, waiting at the door to the stairs, would even have registered the two pops. All he had to do now was sit here and wait.

He had arrived on time at two thirty and Luciano had been due to arrive fifteen minutes later, but he had sent word that he was running late. Jack lit a cigarette and waited some more. He kept his eye on the long corridor, where the girls in silk stockings and tight skirts stalked back and forth from Salvatore Maranzano's office, and the antechamber, where dozens of ordinary men and women, city officials, workmen, politicians, and the odd gangster, waited to be received by Little Caesar. Time was passing and Luciano was late. *Very* late. Jack looked at his watch. It was now two forty-five. He turned his attention back to the newspaper. In this line of work patience was the greatest asset.

Just then four men came out of the elevator. They strode up to the reception desk, where the secretary greeted them with a smile. However, her smile swiftly disappeared, replaced by an anxious frown, and she shook her head. Jack's interest was aroused. The men were not with Luciano because he and his guards would have used the stairs. Then Jack noticed their uniforms. He lowered the newspaper and shifted so he could feel the snug weight of the Colt in his shoulder holster: if this was a police raid, he did not want to be caught with the gun or the cash. However, it was unlikely to be a police raid because the Boss was friends with the police, so who were they and why were they here? An unexpected courtesy call? He thought not. He began to feel an uneasiness crawling over him and his hackles rose like those of a dog sensing danger, but not quite knowing where it came from. He studied the men more closely. Two were in uniform, two in dark suits. The first in uniform showed his badge to the secretary, who looked at it, then nodded and shrugged. Jack watched and waited. A calmness settled upon him as his senses sharpened. If these were tax investigators and they were here when Luciano arrived, he'd have to do the hit another day. Everything had been planned but *this*.

Jack observed the tall man in the suit. It was a well-cut suit, he thought, for a government employee. He dropped his eyes to the patent-leather shoes and his stomach gave a sudden lurch. His gaze sprang up to the face and he recognized the dazzling blue eyes of Bugsy Siegel.

Then it all happened so quickly.

Bugsy's gun was drawn and the Boss's bodyguards were already on the floor, disarmed by the two men in uniform. Bugsy and his gang moved over them like cats. The secretaries froze where they were and no one screamed. Then Jack heard Maranzano's voice: "What the hell are you guys doing here?" followed by the instantly recognizable wet sounds of plunging knives and then the pops of gunfire. Jack was on his feet and running into the mail room farther down the corridor, near the stairs. He hid under the desk just as the assassins walked briskly out, passing the very place where only moments before he had been sitting. The men stopped and Bugsy spoke. "There was a guy sitting in there, a Mick—where is he? This broad will tell me. Hey, you, where is he? He can't have gone far!"

"I don't know," replied the terrified secretary. "I don't know . . . Please don't hurt me. I think he ran."

Bugsy slapped her hard. "Ran where?" The girl was now sobbing.

"Come on, let's get outta here," said one of the men in uniform.

"No, that was the Mick waiting for Lucky," said Bugsy. "I want to clip him right here. Right now."

"We gotta get outta here."

"Fine," Bugsy snapped. "But I offer fifty grand and a house in Westchester to anyone who kills that Mick, d'you hear me? Fifty grand and a house in Westchester." Then they were gone, their footsteps receding down the stairwell.

Jack had been holding the Colt in his hands and this time they were shaking. Slowly he climbed out from beneath the desk, keeping his pistol in front of him. People were emerging warily into the corridor, blinking in bewilderment. The place was eerily silent. He hurried into the reception area and found the secretary who had saved his life. He touched her tear-stained cheek. "Thank you," he said.

"You'd better get out of here," she replied. "And make it snappy." Jack jumped over a shattered Roman bust and made for the elevator, but virtually everyone on the floor had abandoned their offices and taken the elevator. He ran into Maranzano's office to find the Caesar of New York, the *capo di tutti capi*, lying dead in the middle of the floor. His legs were spread wide, his white shirt stained with blood and pulled out of his trousers to reveal his large belly still oozing crimson from the knife wound. His fingers were twitching and blood was streaming over his face from the shot to the head—the coup de grace, which he himself had always recommended, just to be sure.

Jack's mind stilled and shifted into sharp focus. He could not stay here a moment longer. He had to get Emer and Alana as quickly as possible and leave New York without a moment to waste. Luciano was now the Boss and Bugsy was Luciano's right hand, and somehow they knew that Jack had been here to kill Luciano. There was a bounty on his head and there was not a gangster in the city, Irish, Italian or Jew, who would see "Mad Dog" O'Leary without killing him on sight. He had to get out of New York and disappear forever. He would go down south, he decided, and start a new life. He'd done it before, he could do it again. Ireland flashed into his mind and his heart lurched with longing as those green hills and stony cliffs rose out of the mist like an emerald oasis in a vast barren desert. But he couldn't go home, for Ballinakelly was the first place they would look for him, and besides, there was nothing left but the ashes of his old life. No, he'd start again, far away, where no one from New York would find him.

As he was about to leave, he saw, on the desk beside a statue of Caesar, a large pile of crisp banknotes.

Jack made his way out of the building by way of the stairs, pulled his hat low over his head, and called Emer from a public telephone. "Don't ask questions and tell no one," he told her firmly, and she knew from the tone of his voice what he was going to say. "Get Alana, pack a small case and meet me at Penn Station. I'll find you under the clock. Come as quickly as you can. We're leaving New York forever, Emer, and we won't be coming back."

Chapter 34

As much as Bridie was thrilled about her pregnancy, she couldn't help but remember the last time and the brutality that she had endured on account of it. Back then Mr. Deverill had had the insensitivity to question whether the child was indeed his, before grudgingly accepting that it was and sending her off to Dublin to get rid of it as quickly and discreetly as possible. Lady Rowan–Hampton had treated her with equal callousness. She had made it perfectly clear that Bridie couldn't possibly keep her baby and gave her no choice in the decision to send her to the other side of the world. The nuns in the Convent of Our Lady Queen of Heaven must surely have had hearts of stone, for they had made her feel deeply ashamed and utterly worthless. They had regarded her as wanton and sinful, and her extended belly an affront to Mary, the Holy Mother of Jesus. Bridie had been robbed of her children without a word of sympathy or understanding, as if she were no better than a farm animal of little value. In spite of the years that had passed and the emotional distance Bridie had placed between that dark time and now, she still carried the guilt inside her like an indelible stain on her soul. However much her new situation glossed over the disgrace of her previous one, she still felt rotten in her core.

This time she was a married woman and her pregnancy was something to be celebrated and enjoyed. No one knew of the secrets she guarded or of the pain that came with the joy of this new life growing inside her, intertwined like threads, inseparable one from the other. Everyone bought her presents and congratulated her, and Bridie thought how wrong it was that a life should be worth less simply because of the lack of a wedding ring.

While Cesare was in Ireland she had a lot of time to think. She looked forward to having a child to love with a yearning born out of loss. She remembered Little Jack with a bitter sorrow and hoped that her new baby would fill the void in her heart, for not even Cesare, with all his love and devotion, had been able to. She lay on her bed, a hand on her stomach, and remembered her tiny daughter whom the nuns had spirited away before she had even held her. There was no grave, no headstone, nothing with which to remember her, only the memory of glimpsing her tiny face before the nuns had wrapped her in a towel and taken her away—and even *that* was faded like a photograph left too long in the sun. No one had considered Bridie and the irreparable tear in her heart. No one had felt any compassion for her as a human being or as a mother. Those babies had been stolen and yet there was no law to condemn the guilty and no aid to help her get back her son. She had been cast aside like a piece of refuse, sent off to America so she couldn't cause any trouble and, only now, as she prepared to become a mother again, did she realize the extent of the injustice.

At the beginning of summer, Cesare returned from Ireland. Bridie was overjoyed to see him, for she had missed him dreadfully and needed distraction from the turmoil in her spirit. She wrapped her arms around him and was sure that she could smell the salty wind and heather of home in his hair. Her heart lurched and a sudden jealousy arose in her for *he* had touched the green hills of Ballinakelly that had once belonged to her and she resented him for having breathed the air that she had been so cruelly denied. But it dropped as quickly as it had risen as Cesare reassured her that everything was ready for her just as soon as she was prepared to leave. Ireland was within her grasp, she only had to say the word and he would take her there.

But was she ready to go back? Was she ready to face Kitty, Celia, Lord Deverill and her son? Had she simply bought the castle so that *they* couldn't have it? Had she been motivated purely by spite? The moment Beaumont Williams had told her that his contacts in London had informed him that Castle Deverill was once again available to buy, Bridie had seized her chance and this time she had been firm. She wanted it whatever the cost, because she knew its value; she knew its value to the Deverills.

Bridie listened with growing rapture as Cesare described the lavishness of the refurbishment and the comfort of the new plumbing and electricity. She clapped her hands with glee and pressed him for more details, hanging on to his every word like a pirate queen being told of the latest stolen treasure. She wanted to know what all the rooms looked like and how lovely the gardens were and as he told her she envisaged it as it had been in her childhood days when she, Celia and Kitty had all been friends, playing in the castle grounds, before it had all unraveled—before she and Kitty had become enemies; before Kitty had stolen her son.

Bridie had told Cesare of her childhood in Ballinakelly and that her mother had cooked for Lady Deverill in the castle, but she hadn't told him about her son. She couldn't. She simply wasn't able to speak about Little Jack, not even to Cesare. *Especially* not to Cesare. He was so traditional, this Italian count, and so proud, too proud even to take money without embarrassment. What if he disapproved of her having a child out of wedlock? What if he loved her less because she had given him away? There were so many reasons *not* to tell him. So she kept the secret wrapped tightly around her heart and let him revel in the imminent birth of their first child together.

Cesare told her about his meeting with Celia and how he had kept Bridie's identity secret as she had asked him to. He told her that he had met Kitty at Lady Rowan-Hampton's dinner table and he watched his wife's face harden and her expression turn serious and severe. "I don't wish to hear of those two women," she said coldly. "We were friends once but that was long ago in the past." After that Cesare downplayed the amount of time he had spent with the Deverills and swiftly changed the subject to their future. He certainly didn't hint at the long hours he had enjoyed with Grace, nor at the other young women he had bedded in Cork. He decided he was going to enjoy living in Ireland—for a while at least.

They agreed that it would be madness to travel all the way

to Ireland while she was pregnant, so they planned to move the following summer, by which time Bridie would be strong enough to endure the journey. Their baby boy was born in the early hours of February in New York. The birth had been quick and relatively easy. Bridie sobbed when she finally held her child in her arms. She sobbed for the babies she had lost and for this one whom she was permitted to keep. She gazed into his face and fell in love as she had never done before. Nothing in her life compared to this. Nothing fulfilled her so completely. It was as if God had rewarded her suffering with a double dose of maternal love and she knew then that her heart would surely mend. This tiny baby had come into the world with enough love to heal all his mother's pain.

Cesare had waited in the study downstairs, pacing the floor as was tradition, while the doctor tended to Bridie in her bedroom. He was astonished when he was promptly informed that his son had been delivered, for he had expected his wife's labor to last for days. He climbed the stairs, two steps at a time, his heart racing with excitement. He opened the door to find Bridie sitting up in bed with their small son in her arms. Her face was glowing with happiness, her eyes soft and tender, a proud smile upon her lips. Cesare came to the bedside and sat down. He peered into the baby's face. "My son," he whispered in awe, and Bridie's heart brimmed with pleasure at the deeply satisfied tone of his voice. "You are a clever and beautiful wife to give me a son," he said, kissing her tenderly. "You cannot imagine what this means to me."

"What shall we call him?" Bridie asked.

"What would *you* like to call him?"

She gazed into her son's face and frowned. "I would like to

give him a name that has no connection to the past. A name that has no connection to my family. A name that is his alone."

"Very well," said Cesare, who had spent the last nine months thinking of names. "What about Leopoldo?"

"Leopoldo," said Bridie, smiling as she gazed upon her child.

"Leopoldo di Marcantonio," he said and the words slipped off his tongue as if they were soaked in olive oil. "*Count* Leopoldo di Marcantonio."

"Indeed it has majesty and grandeur," said Bridie.

"He might only be a count," said Cesare. "But he's a prince to me. Here, let me hold him."

WHEN THE SUMMER arrived, Bridie found that she was not ready to move to Ireland. She was afraid of returning to her past when her present was so happy. Afraid of seeing Kitty with her son, of not being able to be a mother to him, of having to carry so heavy a secret. Yet the castle called to her in whispers that woke her in the middle of the night but she resisted its allure and shut her ears to its insistent call. She dreamed of it, of running down the endless corridors, of chasing after Kitty, whose long red hair ran the length of the castle and was so thick that Bridie began to drown in it. She thought of the castle often and the shadow it cast across her soul grew dark and heavy and she began to fear it. She would go when she was ready, she resolved. She *would* be ready, eventually, she told herself, but not right now. Cesare was busy playing polo and enjoying the hectic round of social events; he was in no hurry to start a new life across the water. So they bought a grand house in Connecticut and delayed their move. Ireland would wait.

KITTY WAS ON her knees in the garden, pulling out bindweed and ground elder from the borders. She dug with her trowel but the roots lay deep and seemed to form a complex network of wiry tentacles beneath the soil that thwarted her efforts, for every time she thought she had got them all she discovered more. The sun was hot on her back but a cool wind blew in off the sea and was pleasantly refreshing. Robert was in his study, writing. His books were successful and he was earning good money, which kept the wolf from the door. Florence was now five and JP ten and both children gave her enormous pleasure. They were a tight, united family and in that respect Kitty felt complete. Yet Jack O'Leary was a constant presence, like her shadow, inseparable from her however hard she tried to run from him. And like her shadow, there were times, when the sun shone brightly, that his presence was stronger and other times, on cloudy days, when he seemed barely there at all. But he never left her, nor did the Jack-shaped hole he had left in her heart; no one else could fill it.

She sat back on her knees and wiped her forehead with her gardening glove, smearing her skin with earth. Her mind drifted then as if Jack was demanding her attention from the other side of the world. She could see his face clearly: the wintry blue eyes, the long brown fringe, his unshaven face, angular jaw, crooked smile and the incomplete set of teeth he revealed when he grinned. She smiled at the recollection and put a hand to her heart as a wave of nostalgia crashed against it. She wondered, as she so often did, how he was faring in America. Whether he had finally settled down and started a family with someone else. It wasn't fair to deny him happiness and yet she didn't want him to marry or have children—she wanted to think of him as belonging exclusively to her, even though it had been *her* choice not to run off with him. The image she treasured was of a solitary man, standing in the Fairy Ring, gazing lovingly at her. And in that gaze he promised to love her always. But she accepted that he would have made a new life for himself. She imagined him now as a simple, wholesome farmer in somewhere like Kansas, with his scythe in his hands, chewing on an ear of wheat, standing in the sunshine beside his pickup truck, thinking of her.

She was wrenched out of her reverie by the sound of a car crunching up the gravel. She turned to see Grace's shiny blue Austin slowly approaching. She stood up and pulled off her gloves. "What a lovely day!" Grace exclaimed, climbing out. She was wearing a floral tea dress with a rose-pink cardigan draped over her shoulders and ivory-colored T-bar shoes. Her soft brown hair was swept off her face and falling about her shoulders in extravagant curls, but nothing was more radiant than her smile.

"Hello, Grace," said Kitty, striding across the lawn to meet her.

"Goodness, you're gardening!" Grace exclaimed.

"After the rain the weeds have gone mad," Kitty replied. "Do you have time for a cup of tea? I could certainly do with a break."

"I'd love to," said Grace, linking her arm through Kitty's and walking with her into the house. "I haven't seen you for a while. I thought it would be nice to catch up."

They took their teacups outside and sat on the terrace out of the wind. Grace asked after the children and Kitty asked after Grace's father. "Well, I told you those silly Shrubs would have their hearts broken and I was right. My father played with them callously like a fox with a pair of hens. The trouble is now that he has neither he's pining like a pathetic dog. Really, you should see him, he's pitiful. He doesn't want to go out. He won't see anyone. He sits at home, smoking, reading and grumbling. He won't even play bridge. Bertie's four has broken up now that the three of them can't be in the same room together and he's begging me to do something about it. I wish Papa would pull himself together and stop behaving like a love-sick youth!"

"And the Shrubs? I haven't seen them in church . . ."

"That's because they're avoiding Papa. It's all so childish. You'd have thought they were in their twenties, not their seventies!"

"Oh dear. What a mess. I thought one stopped suffering that sort of heartache at their age."

"Clearly one never does! Tell me, much more interesting, what the devil is Celia doing in South Africa?"

"It seems like she's been gone for ages," said Kitty. "I miss her so much."

"Not a word then?"

"Nothing. Lord knows what she's doing. I haven't even been to the castle. I can't bear to see it inhabited by that peacock of a count. I bet his wife is frightful!"

"They haven't arrived yet," said Grace, masking her smile behind the rim of her cup. She couldn't wait for the Count to set up residence and for their afternoon trysts to resume. He was the only person she had encountered in the last decade who had the ability to take her mind off Michael. "I think we all have to accept change," Grace continued. "Time moves on and we have to move with it. Celia will find her old life in London, probably remarry, and you and I will find great entertainment in the di Marcantonios. Goodness, life would be dull without having people to laugh about. I do wish they'd hurry up and move. I can't imagine why they're taking so long. One would have thought that, having spent so much money buying the place, they'd be impatient to move in."

"I couldn't bear it when Celia bought the castle, but now that she's sold it to those silly people, I long for her to return. It was churlish of me to get so upset about it."

"Quite. It's only bricks and mortar." Kitty nodded and wanted very much to agree. "Now, my dear, I have something serious I need to talk to you about." Kitty put down her teacup. "Firstly, I have a confession."

"Oh?"

"Between us, just like old times."

"All right. Go on."

Grace put down her teacup too and folded her hands in her lap. "I have converted to Catholicism."

Kitty raised her eyebrows in surprise. "Catholicism? You?"

"Me," said Grace with a smile. "I have followed my heart, Kitty, and here I am a fully fledged member of the Catholic community."

"And Ronald doesn't know, so hence the need for secrecy," said Kitty.

"No one knows but you and the Doyles."

Kitty flushed at the mention of the Doyles. Bridie and Michael's faces appeared before her and she wasn't sure which one was worse. "Why the Doyles?"

"Because I needed a devout Catholic family to instruct me. Father Quinn insisted on it, seeing as I'm unable to attend Mass here in Ballinakelly and therefore unable to become part of the local Catholic community."

"What an extraordinary thing to do, Grace. But religion is a very personal matter, so I won't question your beliefs. You must want it very badly to take the trouble, not to mention the risk, of converting."

Grace sighed. "I feel light," she said happily. "I feel as if all the terrible things I did in the War of Independence have dissolved into nothing. I have been wiped clean like a dirty window."

"And you didn't feel that the Protestant God could forgive you?"

"The absolution I required was the Catholic sort. I am now in a state of grace and can enter Heaven. A relief considering the extent of my sins." Kitty wasn't sure whether or not Grace was joking. Her expression didn't commit to either gravity or humor but remained enigmatically somewhere in between.

"All right. The important thing is that *you* feel your conscience is clean," said Kitty, half expecting Grace to throw back her head and roar with laughter at her jest. But she didn't.

"Christianity is all about forgiveness," Grace continued. "I have been forgiven, through Christ, and I have forgiven those in my past who have wronged me." Her eyes suddenly looked at Kitty with more intensity. "I sense you carry a heaviness within *you*, Kitty, and I want to help alleviate it."

"Has Father Quinn asked you to seek a conversion from *me*?"

Grace shook her head. "Of course not, but I know now the lightness one feels after making one's peace with those who have wronged one."

"Are you suggesting I make peace with those who have wronged *me*?" Kitty asked, feeling her body stiffen like a threatened cat.

Grace's brown eyes bored deeper. "I am," she said.

"I carry no such weight, Grace. But thank you for offering to help me."

"But you do," Grace persisted. Kitty frowned. Grace's gaze made her feel cornered but she couldn't think of an excuse to get up and leave. "I know about you and Michael," she said quietly.

Kitty's breath caught in her chest. Her mind darted about for the leak of information—Robert, Jack . . . no one else knew. "Michael told me, Kitty," Grace lied. "Michael told me what happened. He has confessed before God. But not before *you*."

Kitty was so stunned she didn't know what to say. She stared mutely at Grace while the older woman watched her with a cold compassion. "You don't need to feel ashamed in front of me," she continued. "We have shared so many secrets. This is simply another one. But for your sanity, and for the peace of Michael's soul, you must forgive him."

Kitty was so outraged at this suggestion her voice came back to her in an explosion. "I *must* forgive him?" she snapped and Grace was so startled by her tone and the fire that blazed in her eyes that she blanched. "For *his* sanity? If you had any idea what Michael did you would not be seeking his soul's peace but the *burning* of his soul in the fires of Hell! How dare you even speak to me about it and how dare Michael send you in like a spy to seek my forgiveness on his behalf. If he was so desperate to be forgiven, why didn't he have the courage to come himself?"

"He would never presume to seek your invitation. He knows you wouldn't agree to see him." Grace frantically sought another tack. "He sent me in not as a spy but as a mediator. I'm flying the white flag, Kitty."

"I always knew you cared for Michael Doyle," she said, her

rage subsiding as Grace seemed to lose her footing. "You have always defended him. I should have known. Why, you were the only woman Michael listened to, the only woman he respected, and you, in turn, admired him back. *That* was plain to see, but I was too stupid to notice. All the while we were conspiring, carrying notes and guns and risking our lives for the cause, *you* were bedding Michael Doyle. How long have you known about the rape, Grace? Did he tell you the morning of the fire, after he burned down the castle and took me on his kitchen table? Did he betray Jack to the Tans and seek refuge in your home? Have you two been working together all along? Plotting like thieves and undermining us at every turn?" Kitty wasn't sure what she was saying, but the truth was beginning to seep into her consciousness like light slipping through a thin crack in a dark cave. She shook her head as the full extent of Grace's betrayal became clear. "If it wasn't for you, Jack and I might have had a chance. Why, Grace? What was it about our love that made you so obstructive? I thought you were my friend."

Grace's face had gone puce. "I am your friend. I came here today to help and this is the thanks I get? You accuse me of every wrong that's ever been done to you."

"And do you deny that you slept with Michael?"

"Absolutely," said Grace firmly. "Michael is a troubled soul and I have taken it upon myself, as a good Catholic, to help him. If you do not forgive him, Kitty, you will be condemning him to a life of misery."

"And what about *me*, Grace? What about *my* misery?" Kitty thumped her chest. "Do you think I walked away that morning and left my shame and my hurt and my anger in that kitchen?

No, I took it with me and I've been carrying it around with me for over ten years!"

Grace wanted to accuse her of lying. She wanted to force her to admit that her shame arose not out of any violation but out of the disgrace of her own conduct. Kitty had encouraged him, for Michael was no rapist, and Michael had done what any man would have done in his situation, when faced with the open legs of a beautiful woman like Kitty. But she was too astute to ruin her relationship with the only person who could restore Michael to her bed. "Kitty," she said calmly. "You're angry and you have every reason to be. But don't let your anger cloud your judgment. I am your friend and I have always been your friend. You have my loyalty and my compassion. I don't condone what Michael did but I see him as Jesus sees him—as an erring child of God. He has committed a terrible crime and has suffered through his guilt and regret. I only want your peace and his. But I see that I have greatly offended you and I'm sorry. I didn't come to fight with you. I hoped to be able to release you of this burden. I see now that the only person who can release it is you, when you are ready."

"I will *never* be ready, Grace," Kitty snarled and she watched the muscles in the older woman's jaw tense as she struggled to hide her ire. Kitty wondered why it was so important to Grace that she forgive Michael. She now knew her friend for what she really was and realized that there was only ever one ulterior motive and that was herself. The only person Grace was ever loyal to was herself. So how would Grace benefit from Kitty's forgiveness? Kitty didn't know.

Chapter 35

London

Celia returned to London to face Aurelius Dupree. The crossing was tiresome for this time there was no Rafael O'Rourke to divert her, only the truth about her father, which induced a slow hardening of the heart the more she thought of it. She resolved to keep the information she had gleaned from the rest of the family; she didn't think her mother would survive the shock of learning that Digby had a black son called Lucky! The fact that Digby was a murderer too would finish her off, if knowing about Lucky hadn't already. She would tell them instead the good news about the gold mine and watch their jaws drop when she announced that she was going back to South Africa to run it. She had called the Rothschilds, the Oppenheimers and all the other financial dynasties who had been friends with her father. Since mining companies were already investing in deep reef mining in Witwatersrand and now in the Orange Free State, and since they had known her father, she had begun to raise the money for what she had named the Free State Deep Reef Mining Company.

The mine would take many years of work, compromise and patience; she wasn't under any illusion about *that*. But it would take a special determination to raise the money and Celia would have to learn everything for herself. She'd learn about the geology of gold in the deep mines, gold that was being found not in gleaming chunks but within iron ore. She'd learn how shafts were built and cages lowered to carry the men into the mines. She'd learn how they worked in the stopes and about the chemical process of melting the iron ore to extract the gold, which was the fruit of this vast and complicated process. She'd learn how to build a small town where her workers would reside and she'd employ the technical experts to see that it was all done properly. Who would have thought that Celia, the self-proclaimed birdbrain of the family, would do all of this?

The last thing she needed was Bruce and Tarquin thinking they could do it better and coming along with her, so she would tell them that Digby's man, Mr. Botha, was going to oversee everything, although she had already resolved to find her *own* man as soon as she returned to Johannesburg.

The problem of Aurelius Dupree was not long in resurfacing. He knew she had gone and he clearly knew when she was back, because a day later he came knocking on her door in Kensington Palace Gardens. On this occasion he was invited in. Celia noticed how much he had aged in a couple of months. He seemed a little more bent, his cough had worsened and his hands shook as he steadied himself on the arms of the chair as he sat down. The fight had not gone out of his eyes, however, and he glared at her across the room as she poured the tea and handed him a cup. "I've been to South Africa," she told him. "I went to Johannesburg and met with my father's old foreman, Mr. Botha."

Aurelius Dupree nodded and his thin lips twisted with resentment. "Your father's monkey," he said. "I don't suppose he enlightened you with the truth."

"No, he didn't," said Celia.

"A long way to go to discover nothing, Mrs. Mayberry."

"I could have stopped there. That would have been very much to my satisfaction. I would have returned believing you and your brother made up a whole heap of lies and maligned my innocent father, who was an honorable man in a dirty world of cut-throats and ruffians."

Dupree raised a white eyebrow. "But you didn't?"

Celia shook her head. "I didn't. I dug deeper, Mr. Dupree, and I discovered, much to my shame, that you are right."

Aurelius Dupree put down his teacup and stared at her in bewilderment. "Sorry, Mrs. Mayberry. *What* did you say?"

"That you are right, Mr. Dupree. My father cheated you out of money and had your brother murdered and you incarcerated for a crime you did not commit." Aurelius Dupree's vision blurred as tears bled into the dry balls of his eyes and gathered there in shiny pools. "I will never speak of this again, not to anyone, and my words will never leave the four walls of this room, but I admit his crime on his behalf, and ask your forgiveness. I cannot pay you the amount you are owed and I cannot give you back the years you have lost behind bars, but I have discovered a gold mine in South Africa that my father was unable to mine because of the sheer depth of the gold. Now new machinery has made it possible and I intend to mine it. I have returned to London and have started to raise the funds. Therefore, what I can offer you, Mr. Dupree, is shares. I will also make sure you get the best medical care London has to offer. You have a shocking cough, if I may say so, and your health is in a terrible state. I would like to make the years you have left as comfortable as possible."

Aurelius Dupree pushed himself up and staggered over to where Celia was sitting and took her hands in his. The tears had now overflowed and trickled down the lines and crevices in his skin like hesitant rivulets. "You are a good woman, Mrs. Mayberry," he said huskily. "I accept your offer. When I first laid eyes on you many months ago I didn't think you were made of anything other than pretty stuffing, but you have proved me wrong. You are a woman of substance, Mrs. Mayberry. It takes courage to do what you have done. Indeed you cannot give me back the years, but you have given me something else that is almost more important: credence. I've spent thirty years protesting my innocence and my protests have been met with derision and disbelief. *You* have swept all that away with three blessed words. *You are right.* You cannot imagine what those three words mean to me." He coughed some phlegm from his lungs. "I'm undone, Mrs. Mayberry. Undone." He coughed again and Celia settled him onto the sofa. He was trembling so violently now that Celia asked one of the maids for a blanket and the butler to light the fire. She gave him a warm drink of milk and honey and some hot soup. The man who had failed to remove his hat at the funeral, who had sneaked his way into the church at the memorial service, who had terrorized her with threats and accusations, was now nothing more than a homeless old vagabond with deteriorating health and a fading heart full of gratitude. "You must stay here until you are better," she said, her own heart overflowing with compassion. "I won't take no for an answer. It is the least we can do."

"Then let me give you some advice about your mine," he said weakly. "I know a thing or two about mines and a lot about the men you're going to have to deal with." Celia listened as he shared his wisdom and for a while his pallid cheeks flushed with renewed life and his eyes flickered with forgotten pleasure, like the sudden reviving of embers in a fire that appeared to be dying. But as the day approached evening his energy waned and his eyelids drooped and he sank into a deep slumber, his breath rattling ominously in his chest.

Celia knew he wouldn't live to see his shares, nor would he require the best medical care London had to offer. She sensed that he wouldn't even survive the night. Aurelius Dupree could finally give up the fight, for he had at last found peace.

THE SECRETS OF Digby Deverill's past that threatened to devastate the family's reputation were buried with Aurelius Dupree. Only Duchess knew the truth and Celia did not doubt that she would take it to her grave. Celia informed her family of her plans to return to Johannesburg with her children and no one was more surprised than Harry and Boysie. They lunched with her at Claridge's and noticed a solemnity about her now, a depth she hadn't had before. Gone was the girl who wanted to dance at the Café de Paris and the Embassy, for whom life was "a riot," and in her place a woman who had lost so much but discovered through her loss something that she had never known was there: the Deverill spirit—the ability to overcome despair and rise beyond the limits of her own frailty. Not only had she found strength but she had found a future. She was going to restore the family fortune, and Harry and Boysie realized, as they listened to her, that she really meant to do it. "The past is gone," she told them. "And there's no point crying about it. One has to look ahead and keep one's eye on the horizon. As long as I do that, and don't look back, I'll be okay."

"But what will we do without you?" Boysie asked.

"Life won't be the same," said Harry sadly.

"You have each other," she told them with a smile. "It's always been the three of us but you've never really needed me, have you?"

"But we like to have you around," said Boysie.

"I'll come back when I'm rich and powerful."

"You're very brave, Celia," said Harry.

"Who'd have imagined it?" said Boysie.

Celia thought of Aurelius Dupree and smiled. "I didn't," she agreed. "But I've changed. There's nothing left for me here except you two and a frivolous life I no longer want. I'm going on an adventure, boys, and I'm excited. I'll write and tell you all about it and perhaps, if you both want an adventure too, you can come and join me. In the meantime, you must look after Mama and Kitty and write to me often. I want to know everything so that one day, when I come back, I won't feel I've been away."

The three of them held hands around the table and agreed to that. "Out of sight but not out of mind," said Boysie.

Harry picked up his glass. "Let's drink to that," he said.

"GOOD LORD!" HAZEL exclaimed. "Celia's off to live in South Africa. She's going to become a miner."

"A miner?" said Laurel in horror, glancing at the letter in her sister's hand.

"That's what it says. She's going to dig for gold in an old mine of Digby's."

"What, on her own?"

"That's what it looks like."

"Does she know anything about mining?"

"Of course she doesn't."

"Oh dear. It sounds very alarming," said Laurel, sipping her tea.

"She says there's nothing left for her now that the castle has gone."

"She's running away," said Laurel with certainty. "How very disastrous. Do you think someone should go and bring her back? When did she leave?"

"My dear Laurel, she left weeks ago. I'm sure that when she realizes what it is to mine for gold she will be back. It simply isn't the place for a woman."

There was a long pause as Hazel folded up the letter and replaced it in the envelope. The silence, which had been kept at bay for the duration of their short conversation, now returned to hang heavy and sad between them like a fog. In that fog was the unavoidable presence of Ethelred Hunt.

Hazel glanced at her sister. "Are you all right, Laurel?" she asked quietly.

Laurel inhaled through her nostrils and lifted her chin. "I'm all right," she said. "And you, Hazel, are *you* all right?"

"Yes," said Hazel, but her voice quivered like the string of a badly played violin.

"No you're not, I can tell."

"No, not really."

"Me neither," conceded Laurel.

"We agree on that then."

"We agree on everything these days," said Laurel with a joyless laugh.

"I love him," said Hazel. "I love the very bones of him."

"And I love him too," said Laurel. She reached out and took her sister's hand. "But we have each other."

"Thank God for that," said Hazel. "I don't know what I'd do without you."

There was a knock at the door. "Goodness, are we expecting anyone?" Laurel asked. Hazel shook her head and looked worried.

"Who could it be?" said Laurel, getting up from the sofa.

"Let's go and see," said Hazel, following her sister into the corridor. They reached the front door and took a while to release the chain and unlock it. Since the Troubles neither Shrub had been casual about the security of their home. They opened the door a crack to see the sorry face of Ethelred Hunt, who was standing with his hat in his hands. Just as Laurel was about to slam the door in his face he wedged his shoe in the gap.

"May you permit me to speak?" he asked. The Shrubs stared through the crack with wide eyes, like a pair of terrified birds. "I have come to the conclusion that I love you both and I simply can't live without you. I can't decide between you and it seems to me that you are a job-lot, that you come together and are impossible to separate. So I have an outrageous but frankly delicious suggestion. Would you like to hear it?"

The women looked at each other. "We would," said Hazel.

"Go on," said Laurel.

"What would you say to the three of us living together?" The two sisters blinked at him in amazement. "I know it's un-conventional and I'm sure my daughter will have a lot to say about it, but I can't see another way. It's all or nothing and I'm not a man to settle for nothing. It's either the three of us or . . ." He hesitated. "Or unhappiness. The last few months have been deeply unhappy. I don't regret one moment of the past; I only wish I'd had more of it. What do you say, girls? Are we on?"

There was a brief scuffle and then the door opened. "How about a cup of tea?" said Hazel happily.

"I'll put the kettle on," said Laurel, making off toward the kitchen.

"Oh, I think something stronger," said Ethelred, placing his hat on the hook in the hall, sandwiched between two pink sunhats with blue ribbons. "After all, we've got something to celebrate."

Chapter 36

Connecticut, 1938

I won't wear that dress, do you hear!" shouted Edith, stamping her foot.

"Edith dear, Grandma bought it for you and brought it all the way back from Paris so you *will* wear it," said Mrs. Goodwin patiently. "It's Christmas Day. Let's not fight on Jesus' birthday."

"I don't care who gave it to me and I don't care that it's Jesus' birthday. I hate it. I won't wear it. You can't make me!" Edith glared at her sister, who had appeared in the doorway in an elegant blue dress with grown-up shoes and stockings, her hair pinned and curled in the sophisticated fashion of the day. "What are *you* looking at, Martha?" she raged. "Why can't I have a dress like hers, Goodwin?"

"Because you're ten and Martha is almost seventeen," the

nanny replied. "When you're seventeen you will have dresses like Martha's."

Edith sat on the edge of her bed and folded her arms. "I will not wear this stupid dress." She clenched her jaw and no amount of coercing could induce her to put on the dress.

At last Mrs. Goodwin gave up. "I'll go and tell your mother."

Edith smiled. "You do that, Goodwin. Mama won't make me wear it. She'll let me wear whatever I want."

But today was not just *any* day. It was Christmas Day and lunch at Ted and Diana Wallace's house was a large family affair. Pam was mindful of her mother-in-law's warning, that if she didn't discipline Edith, the child would grow into a monstrous adult, and she was desperate for her approval—especially as Joan and Dorothy's children were considered "delightful" and "good." It was ironic that the adopted child whom she had worried might never fit into the Wallace family clan was Diana Wallace's favorite grandchild and a paragon of good manners and gentle character, while her natural child who carried the blood of the Wallaces in her veins was Diana Wallace's *least* favorite grandchild and the family nuisance. Today was the one day of the year when Edith had to do as she was told. Pam was adamant. Edith had to wear Grandma's dress, no matter what.

When Edith heard what her mother had said she could not believe it. She jumped off the bed and marched down the corridor to her mother's room, where Pam was sitting at her dressing table clipping diamond earrings onto her ears. In the mirror Pam saw the furious figure of her youngest child standing in the doorway in her underwear and turned around. "Darling, don't look at me like that. Your grandmother gifted you the dress for today so you have no choice but to wear it."

Edith started to cry. She ran to her mother and flung her arms around her. "But I hate it," she wailed.

Pam kissed the top of her head. "How about we go shopping and find you a dress you do like."

"Now?" asked Edith, cheering up.

"Of course not, darling. The shops are closed at Christmas. When they open again it's the first thing we'll do."

Edith pushed herself away and stuck out her bottom lip. "But I want a new dress now!"

"Edith, you're behaving like a spoiled child. Pull yourself together." Pam was pleased she was asserting control.

Edith stared at her mother in horror. "You don't love me anymore," she sobbed. The other two tacks hadn't worked, so perhaps self-pity would.

But Pam was having none of it. Today her girls had to be on their best behavior, come what may. Grandma Wallace had given Edith the dress, which was very pretty, and Pam was not about to offend her by bringing Edith to lunch in a different one. "Edith, go to your room and put on the dress or, I promise you, there will be no presents for you this Christmas."

"You hate me!" Edith shouted, bolting for the door. "And *I* hate *you*!"

Pam turned back to the mirror. Her face was very pale and her eyes shone. She wanted more than anything to burn the stupid dress and let Edith wear one of her own, but she couldn't. How she resented Diana Wallace. She wiped away a tear with a tremulous finger, then patted the skin around her eyes with a fluffy powder puff.

Edith wore the dress but she didn't smile and she barely spoke as she sat in the back of the car gazing out of the window at the snowy gardens and frosted houses. She wanted to punish them all for her misery, especially her mother. *You're gonna wish you hadn't made me wear it,* she thought spitefully. The fact that Martha looked so pretty and behaved so beautifully made her all the more furious.

Pam and Larry were the last to arrive. Larry's brothers, Stephen and Charles, were already there with their wives, Dorothy and Joan. Their children, all grown up now, were among them, dressed impeccably in suits and ties and tidy frocks. Pam was acutely aware of Edith, who hadn't said a word since they'd left the house. Her face was gray with fury, her lips squeezed tightly shut; she was making no secret of the fact that she was furious. Pam overcompensated, greeting everyone enthusiastically, while Larry carried in the bag of gifts to place beneath the tree. "Oh Edith, you're wearing the dress I bought you," said Diana, running her eyes up and down with approval. Edith didn't even attempt a smile.

"It's so pretty, Ma," Pam jumped in. "You're so clever to find it. Green is a lovely color for Edith."

Diana smiled at her youngest grandchild. She had registered her silent protest and chosen to ignore it. She turned her attention to Martha. "My darling child, you look beautiful. You're growing up so fast. Come and sit next to me so I can look at you properly. Is that a new dress? It's mighty grown-up, but I suppose you are about to turn seventeen. How time flies." Martha knelt on the floor beside her grandmother's armchair while Edith, encouraged by a gentle push from her mother, shuffled off to help her father put the presents under the tree. The conversation resumed and Edith's rudeness seemed all but forgotten. Joan, however, watched Edith carelessly throwing the brightly wrapped gifts onto the floor and narrowed her eyes. She had always thought that Martha would be the one to give Pam trouble but it had turned out to be Edith. She grinned into her champagne flute. Diana Wallace was a woman for whom good manners were paramount. She despised ill-disciplined people and uncivilized children. Joan looked proudly on her own children and decided that Edith's bad character had little to do with nature and everything to do with nurture. Pam had raised Martha to be a Wallace with obvious success, but she had neglected Edith because she had expected her breeding to do it for her; it hadn't.

After lunch everyone opened their gifts. The room filled with smoke as the men lit cigars and the women cigarettes. Edith seemed unhappy with all of her gifts. She was determined to ruin everyone's day, even if it meant making hers considerably worse. When Joan gave her an exquisite sewing basket with miniature cotton reels tucked into their own little slots she threw it on the floor and folded her arms. "I hate sewing," she snapped. "That's the sort of thing Martha would like."

Pam noticed her mother-in-law's appalled face and hurried to reprimand her child. "If you cannot behave you might as well leave the room," she said, although it pained her to raise her voice at Edith.

Edith, humiliated in front of the entire family, ran out of the room in tears.

"I'm sorry," said Pam with a heavy sigh. "I don't know what's got into her today."

"Come here, Pam," said Larry, patting the sofa beside him. "She'll grow out of it. She's just going through a difficult stage."

"This difficult stage has been going on for some time," said Diana drily. "I suggest you employ a strict English governess. Goodwin is much too gentle. It's time she retired, don't you think?"

"Mother has a point," said Larry, puffing on his cigar.

"Martha will be terribly upset to lose Goodwin," said Pam.

"Then why not send the two of them to London together. Martha should see a bit of the world. She should go on a tour."

"I'm not sure that's such a good idea, Mother. Europe looks like it's sliding back into another war."

"Don't be ridiculous, Larry. There's not going to be another war. No one wants a repeat of the Great War. They'll do anything they can to avoid it. Life must go on. Really, I was in Paris in the fall and I felt quite safe."

Ted, who was standing in front of the fireplace with Stephen and Charles, joined in the conversation. "The threat to peace is from dictatorships," he said emphatically, puffing on his cigar. "We Americans might be neutral but we need to be more involved in Europe in order to avoid another war . . ."

Joan wandered into the hall. She heard sniveling coming from the top of the stairs. There, sitting on the landing, was Edith. Joan carried her ashtray up the stairs and sat beside her niece. She put the cigarette between her scarlet lips and inhaled. Edith stopped crying and looked at Joan suspiciously. "I'm sorry I gave you a sewing basket. I thought it was darling." She looked down at the child's tear-stained face. "But it isn't really about the sewing basket, is it? What's it about then?"

"Mother made me wear this horrible dress."

"Don't you like it?"

"It's ugly."

"Ma gave it to you so you had to wear it whether you liked it or not. You know, when I was a child, I never had any say over what I wore. Right up until I was sixteen. My mother chose everything and I obeyed. Children were more obedient in those days."

"Mother hates me," said Edith. She started crying again.

Joan flicked ash into the little tray. Her nails were very long and painted a glossy scarlet like her lips. "Your mother doesn't hate you, Edith. That's absurd."

"She does. She prefers Martha. Martha does everything right and never gets into trouble. Martha is perfect."

"Well, she certainly behaves well."

"Mother prefers her to me."

"You know that's not true."

"It is. If she loved me she wouldn't have made me wear this horrid dress."

"Love has nothing to do with dresses, Edith. She had to make you wear it otherwise she would have upset Ma, who bought it for you."

"Mother doesn't want me. She only wants Martha," said Edith, realizing that with Aunt Joan self-pity would guarantee her lots of attention.

"Your mother wanted you so badly," said Joan. "She longed for you from the moment she married your father, but you took a long time in coming."

"She had Martha," said Edith bitterly.

"But she wanted *you*."

Edith frowned. "She didn't know me, Aunt Joan."

Joan examined her nails and considered the secret she was about to spill. She knew she shouldn't and she was well aware that if she was caught she would be in a great deal of trouble, but the child was gazing up at her with big shiny eyes and there was something inside Joan that wanted to help her—at the expense of Martha, who was so perfect and beloved and *irritating*. "Shall I tell you a secret?" she said. Edith sniffed the gravity of this secret like a hound sniffing blood and stopped crying. She gazed at her aunt, barely daring to breathe. She nodded. "But you have to promise not to tell anyone, ever. This is between you and me, Edith."

"I promise," said Edith, who at that point would have promised the world.

"Let's shake on it, then." Joan held out her hand. Edith shook it. Joan stubbed out her cigarette. The rumble of voices from the drawing room downstairs receded as Joan leaned in closer to her niece. "Martha is adopted," she said. There, it was done. Those words had been released and they could never be recovered. Edith stared up at her in amazement. "It's true. Your parents couldn't have children so they went to Ireland and bought one. You see, they wanted a baby very badly. So badly that they were willing to buy someone else's. Then, years later, by some miracle, God granted them one of their own and you were born. You see, my darling, you might think they don't love you as much as Martha, but the truth is they love you *more* than her because you belong to them in a way that she never will."

At that moment their conversation was cut short by Pam, who appeared at the bottom of the stairs. "There you are," she said, throwing her gaze onto the landing where Edith and Joan sat huddled together like a pair of conspirators. Edith, so overwhelmed by the secret, ran down the steps and into her mother's arms. "I'm sorry, Mother. I promise to be good from now on," she said and Pam frowned up at Joan. Joan shrugged and pulled a face, feigning ignorance. Relieved that Edith had cheered up, Pam mouthed a "Thank you" at Joan and took Edith back into the drawing room.

The transformation in Edith was instant. She was polite, charming and obedient. Pam was astounded and asked Joan what she had said to her at the top of the stairs, but Joan pretended that she had simply told her that life was easier if one did as one was told. For the first time since joining the Wallace family Pam felt warmly toward her sister-in-law. "You have a magic touch," she said.

"Really, it was nothing. She's a good girl at heart," Joan replied, which made Pam even more grateful. But Edith was bursting to tell the secret. She returned home at the end of the day with a smug smile on her face and a feeling of the deepest satisfaction in her heart. Every time she looked at her sister she could barely contain the information that was making her feel so superior and had to bite her tongue to stop it from slipping off. But slip off it did, because Edith was not only bad at keeping secrets, as are most ten-year-olds, but she wanted to wound. The darkness in her nature, born out of a sense of inadequacy, compelled her to continually search for the higher ground, and when it came to Martha, the only way to achieve any advantage was by pulling her sister down. Edith had no idea how far down the secret would drag her.

It didn't take long for Martha to strike the match that started the fire. Edith goaded her on purpose until Martha rolled her eyes and snapped at her, at which point Edith raised herself to her full height and out it came. Gleeful, Edith told Martha that she didn't really belong to their mother because she was adopted. At first Martha didn't believe her. "Don't be ridiculous, Edith," she said. "Why don't you go and find something to do instead of picking fights with me."

"Oh it's true," Edith insisted. "Aunt Joan told me."

That got Martha's attention. "Aunt Joan told you?" she asked, suddenly feeling less secure.

"Yes, she did, and she made me promise not to tell anyone."

"So why have you told me?"

"Because you should know. Mother and Father aren't really yours. They're mine though. Aunt Joan told me that they wanted me so badly and were so sad that they couldn't have me that they bought you. Then they had me. It was a miracle," she said with delight. "*I* was a miracle."

Martha's eyes filled with tears. "You're making all this up."

"No, I'm not. You came from a shop."

Martha shook her head and left the room, fighting tears. She ran into the snowy garden and sat on the bench beneath a cherry tree where she could cry alone. If it was true and she *was* adopted why hadn't her parents ever told her? Why did Aunt Joan decide to tell Edith? Why would anybody confide in a ten-year-old? If it *wasn't* true, why would Aunt Joan say such a spiteful thing? Martha sat on the bench and explored all the alternatives. She tried to take herself back into her childhood and remember anything that might corroborate Edith's tale but there was nothing that gave her adoption away. She knew she looked like her mother, everyone said so, and neither parent had ever made her feel less important than Edith. There was only one person she could ask.

Martha found Mrs. Goodwin in the nursery sitting room ironing a basket of clothes. When Mrs. Goodwin saw Martha's tear-stained face she put down the iron. Martha closed the door behind her. "Where's Edith?" Mrs. Goodwin asked.

"In her room I presume, where I left her."

"Are you all right, my dear? Is she being difficult again?"

Martha stood in front of the door looking uncertain. "Mrs. Goodwin, I need to ask you something and you must tell me the truth."

Mrs. Goodwin felt a sinking sensation and sat down on the arm of the chair. "All right," she replied nervously. "I will tell you the truth."

"Am I adopted?"

The old nanny's mouth opened in a silent gasp. Her skin flushed and she shook her head vigorously, not to deny the statement but to get rid of it. But the secret was out and no amount of shaking her head would expunge it. "Martha dear, come and sit down," she said, aware that her eyes were stinging with tears.

Martha began to cry. She put her hand to her mouth and choked. "I thought Edith was lying . . ."

Mrs. Goodwin did not wait for Martha to sit with her. She hurried and pulled her into her arms, holding her fiercely. "My darling child, it doesn't mean that your parents don't love you. In fact it means quite the opposite. It means they wanted you so badly they were prepared to travel the world to find you."

"But where's my real mother?"

"It doesn't matter where she is. She's irrelevant. Pam is the woman who has loved you and taken care of you since you were a tiny baby. She was so happy when she found you in that convent in Ireland, they both were. It was as if they fell in love."

"She didn't want me then? My *real* mother."

"Your biological mother is the woman who gave birth to you but she's not the woman who has loved you and—"

"But she obviously didn't want me, Goodwin. She gave me away."

"You don't know the facts. I think it's much more likely that she was a young unmarried woman who got into trouble."

Martha pulled away and searched her old friend's eyes. "Why has no one ever told me?"

"Because it's irrelevant. You're a Wallace and a Tobin, Martha." Mrs. Goodwin's face hardened. "Did Edith tell you?" Martha nodded. "How does she know? Surely your mother wouldn't have told her."

"Aunt Joan told her."

Mrs. Goodwin was horrified. "Now why would she go and do that?"

"I don't know." Martha went and sat down on the sofa and hugged herself. "I feel sick, Goodwin. I think I'm going to throw up."

Mrs. Goodwin hurried for the wash bowl. She returned a moment later and put it on Martha's lap. "Breathe, darling. Take deep breaths and you'll feel better. It's the shock." Indeed, Martha had gone very white. "Your parents didn't want you to know because they didn't want you to suffer as you are suffering now. I can't believe Joan would be so thoughtless. How can she expect a ten-year-old child to keep a secret such as this? What was she thinking? Your mother will be furious when she finds out."

"She's not going to find out," said Martha quickly. "I'm clearly not meant to know and I don't want to upset her or

Father. Edith couldn't have known what she was doing," she added and Mrs. Goodwin's heart expanded at the goodness in Martha, for even when faced with enough evidence to condemn her sister, she chose to excuse her of any blame.

"Edith knew exactly what she was doing," said Mrs. Goodwin in an uncharacteristic outburst of vitriol. "*That's* why she told you."

Chapter 37

Learning the truth about her birth had shifted something in Martha. Mrs. Goodwin noticed the change even if no one else did. She was quiet, pensive and heavy-hearted. While Edith was more buoyant than ever, grabbing her parents' attention with both hands, Martha's solemnity was barely noticeable, but Mrs. Goodwin, who knew and loved her so well, was disturbed by it. Yet unhappiness drove her deeper into herself and in that dark and silent place she found something she had lost long ago: a sense of where she came from and who she really was. She heard whispers on the wind and saw glimpses of strange lights that hovered around the snowy garden. At night when she lay crying on her pillow she had the distinct feeling that she wasn't alone. She didn't know who it was and, having been brought up in the Christian faith, she wondered whether it was God or an angel sent to reassure her. She thought of Ireland often and imagined her mother as a frightened young woman with nowhere to turn. She didn't despise her for giving her away—such negativity was not part of Martha's nature—she *pined* for her. Somewhere, in that distant land, there was a woman who was part of her. A woman who had lost her, and the frightened young woman of her imagination made her ache with pity.

Martha refused to go anywhere and stayed in her room, staring out of the window, while Mrs. Goodwin made excuses so as not to arouse Mr. and Mrs. Wallace's suspicion that something was dreadfully wrong. Martha preferred to be alone with her thoughts. She took comfort from her inner world because the outer world had so disappointed her.

Then one night in early January she had a strange thought. It seemed to come out of nowhere. She saw the image of a shoebox at the back of her mother's bathroom cupboard and heard the words *birth certificate* very clearly, as if they had been whispered into her ear. She sat up with a jolt and looked around the room. It was dark, as usual, but she sensed she was not alone. Her heartbeat accelerated and her hands grew damp with nervousness. There was somebody in her bedroom, she was sure of it. She knew, however, that if she turned on the light the being would disappear and she didn't want it to go. She wanted very badly to see it.

After a while she lay down again and closed her eyes. But her heart was racing and she felt more awake than ever. Then a memory floated into her mind. She remembered a brownstone building and the fear of going up in a lift that looked like a cage. She remembered holding her mother's hand, but she remembered also the briskness of her mother's walk—the determination in her stride to go deeper into the building. She saw a tall man with big blue eyes bending down to inspect her as if she were an insect and her stomach clamped with panic. Then she saw a strange lamp that looked like a demonic eye and she gasped with fright. Horrified, she leaned over and switched on the light. She glanced around the room. There was no one there. No sound save the thumping in her chest. She took a deep breath and tried to recall more of the memory. The man faded, taking with him the terror, but something refused to go. She couldn't discern what it was, only that it was there, just out of reach. She worked the muscle in her brain until it began to fatigue. The more she tried to recall it, the further away it drifted. Eventually she gave up. She turned off the light and lay back down on the pillow. The vision of the shoebox must surely have been a dream, she thought, but she'd take a look the following day when her mother was out, just in case. If she could find her birth certificate she'd know who to look for—because she *was* going to look. *That* she had already decided.

The following day, as soon as her mother had left the house with Edith, Martha hurried into her bathroom. She crouched down to open the cupboard beneath the sink. Inside were neat bottles lined up in rows, bags of cotton wool and packets of medication. She was astonished to see the shoebox of her vision sitting in darkness at the back, just as she had envisaged it. With a trembling hand she carefully lifted it out. Barely daring to breathe she raised the lid. Inside were papers and a piece of old blanket. Burrowing beneath the piece of blanket she pulled out the documents. There, sitting in her hand, was her birth certificate. It took a moment for her to focus because her eyes had once again blurred with tears. But she blinked and her focus returned. *Born on January 5th, 1922, at 12:20 p.m. in Dublin at the Convent of Our Lady Queen of Heaven. Name: Mary-Joseph. Sex: female. Name and surname of father: unknown. Name and surname of mother: Grace, Lady Rowan-Hampton.* She caught her breath. Her mother was an aristocrat. She presumed she had got pregnant out of wedlock and been forced to give her child away, and her heart flooded with sympathy. She wondered whether Lady Rowan-Hampton ever thought of her and wondered how she was. Wondered whether she was happy, whether she even knew that she existed. She wondered whether she regretted giving her away or whether she had simply signed the papers and moved on with her life. Was it possible to ever forget a child you gave away? She put the box back and returned to her room, where she stared at her face in the mirror and tried to imagine what Lady Rowan-Hampton looked like. Did she resemble her mother or her father? she wondered. Her father's name was unknown, but Lady Rowan-Hampton must know who he is, she thought. If she found her mother she might be able to track down her father too. Then a horrid thought occurred to her: what if Lady Rowan-Hampton *didn't want* to be found? The idea that Martha's appearance might be unwelcome was almost enough to thwart her plan, but she dismissed that as negative. There was a fifty percent chance that her mother would be grateful and she had to bank on that.

When Mrs. Goodwin told Martha that she had been dismissed in favor of a governess who was coming to look after Edith in February, and that she would shortly be leaving for England, Martha's reaction took the old nanny by surprise. She didn't sob and beg her to stay as she had expected; she gazed into the nanny's sad face and declared that she was going with her. "But, my dear, your place is here with your family," she protested.

"I will not rest until I have found my mother," Martha replied, and the determination in her voice told Mrs. Goodwin that she had made up her mind and nothing would change it.

"But what will your parents say?" Mrs. Goodwin asked anxiously.

"I will leave them a letter explaining what I plan to do. If I tell them they will try to stop me. I have thought of nothing else since our conversation in the nursery."

"But where are you going to look?

"I found my birth certificate, Goodwin, in Mother's bathroom cupboard, and discovered that my mother's name is Grace, Lady Rowan-Hampton."

Mrs. Goodwin's eyes widened. "Fancy that," she said, impressed. "You're a lady."

"I intend to travel to Dublin, to the convent where I was born. Surely they will have records."

"I'm sure they will." Mrs. Goodwin looked perplexed. "I don't have much money, Martha," she warned. "But I will help as much as I can."

"I came into some money on my sixteenth birthday," Martha explained. "And I have saved a little over the years. It will certainly pay for my passage to Ireland and, if I live modestly, it will enable me to manage once I'm there." She took Mrs. Goodwin's hands. "Will you come with me?"

"To Ireland?"

"To Dublin. Oh please, say you will. It will be an adventure. I'm afraid to go on my own. I've never been anywhere. But you, you've traveled. You're wise and experienced. I know I can do it if you come with me."

"Well, I do know a little more of the world than you do." The nanny smiled tenderly. "If you want me to, of course I will. But you have to promise me one thing."

"What?" Martha asked nervously.

"That you make it right with your parents when you get back."

"I will," she replied.

"They love you dearly, Martha. This is going to make them very unhappy."

"I cannot help that. Now I know the truth I cannot unknow it and I cannot let it go. My mother is out there somewhere. Perhaps she longs for me. Maybe she doesn't, but I have to know. I'm not the girl I thought I was, Goodwin. I have to find out who I really am."

"Very well," said Mrs. Goodwin briskly. "Leave everything to me."

AND FROM HER place in Spirit, Adeline smiled with satisfaction at a job well done.

BACK IN NEW York Bridie read the letter from Michael: Old Mrs. Nagle was dying and her mother was asking for her. As her eyes filled with tears she realized that she couldn't avoid her destiny any longer. She had bought the castle out of revenge but perhaps her deepest desire lay in the land on which it was built. In spite of her fears about confronting the people she loathed, she harbored a longing for those she loved that called her back to her roots. She put the letter on the table and gazed out of the window. The sky was a pale blue, the winter sun shining weakly onto the frozen earth. A robin hopped about on the snowy lawn, its red breast bright against the white flakes. Finding nothing for it there it spread its wings and flew away, and Bridie wished that she had wings too so she could fly away. Fly away home. This time for good.

JACK HAD SPENT the last seven and a half years in Buenos Aires. He had used some of the money Maranzano had given him to open an Irish pub in a neighborhood northeast of the city called Retiro, and bought a small apartment in a Parisian-style building close by. Both he and Emer had tried very hard to love their new home. After all, Buenos Aires was a beautiful city of tree-lined avenues, sun-dappled squares and leafy parks, but the prosperity it had enjoyed in the twenties had collapsed with the Great Depression and the atmosphere was now tense and uncertain. It was not the time to be running a new business. But Jack had had no option but to hide. He didn't think Luciano and Siegel would look for him there. However, every knock on the door gave his heart a jolt and every lingering glance in the street raised his suspicion. He slept with his gun beneath his pillow and he feared for his children every time they left the house. Emer was patient and calm but even she was beginning to tire of his constant wariness.

Alana was now ten, Liam was nearly seven and Emer had given birth to Aileen the year before. He worried for their safety and he worried about their future. He didn't see himself living out the rest of his days in this country where he struggled to speak the language and strove without success to find a sense of belonging. His pub had few customers; the Irish community in Buenos Aires was small and Argentines didn't appreciate Irish music or Irish stout. He had made a few bad investments and was losing money fast. He looked out of his bedroom window one morning and made a decision. It was time to go home.

Nearly eight years had passed since he had run from the Mafia; he didn't imagine they were looking for him now. He believed he'd feel safe in Ballinakelly. He trusted his children would have a better quality of life there and a better future. He wanted to put away his gun, dust off his veterinary bag and live a quiet life without looking over his shoulder and mistrusting every stranger. He tried not to think of Kitty. He tried to focus on what he had, not on what he had lost. He loved Emer. She was his present; he had no reason to fear the past.

Barton Deverill

Ballinakelly, County Cork, 1667

The day dawned gray and overcast. The air was cold and there was a hardness to the wind as if its edges had been sharpened like knives. Rooks and crows hopped about the castle walls where the fire had charred the stones to an ugly black, but Lord Deverill's flag flew high and defiant on the western tower so that all who saw it were reminded of his triumph over his enemies and discouraged to rise again.

Lord Deverill awoke with a sickening feeling in the pit of his stomach. He climbed out of bed with a groan and called his servant to bring him wine and bread. Maggie O'Leary had dominated his thoughts since the first time he had laid eyes on her, but today the whole sorry episode would be over once and for all. Today she would die. Burned at the stake the way many witches had gone before. He hoped that with her death so too would die her image, for it plagued him day and night and, however much he tried to distract himself, she was always present, always tormenting him with the power of her allure. He could see them now, those eerie green eyes staring at him with a mixture of insolence and wonder. Today they would close forever and he would be rid of her and rid of his guilt for having given in to his desire and taken her in the woods.

He dressed and summoned his horse. The ride into Ballinakelly seemed to take longer than normal. Accompanied by a small handful of men he made his way slowly, through dense woodland and on down the valley where a little stream meandered its way idly over glistening stones and craggy rocks. The hamlet, when he reached it, was unusually quiet. There was no one to be seen at the gates and the road was empty but for a young boy running as fast as his legs could carry him for fear of arriving late and missing the spectacle. For that's what it was, a spectacle, and the people of Ballinakelly were gathered in the square ready to be entertained.

Lord Deverill rode his horse up the road, past the modest stone cottages, the blacksmith's forge and the inn and farther into the heart of the hamlet. The closer he got the more his stomach cramped with fear. He did not want to see her. He did not want *her* to see *him*. He did not want to be reminded of his foolishness. At last he saw the crowd of people and, beyond, the pile of wood gathered to make a small hill and the stake that stuck aggressively out of it. He swallowed hard and gripped the reins to stop his hands from trembling. One or two people turned and saw him and then a ripple of whispering hissed through the crowd and a hush descended until it was so quiet that even the babes in arms were silenced by the shock of it.

Lord Deverill caught the eye of the little boy who had only a moment ago been running up the road and summoned him with a finger. The boy hurried to his horse and looked up at him with eager eyes. Lord Deverill bent down and whispered something that only the boy could hear. The child nodded and took the small bag Lord Deverill gave him and the reward of a shining coin with grubby hands. Then he disappeared into the crowd like an agile little ferret. A moment later there was a rattling noise as a cart appeared, carrying a woman dressed in a simple white robe. Her hair was long and tangled, hanging about her like a black veil, and she was kneeling on straw with her hands tied behind her back. She said nothing but she cast her eyes about the crowd and seemed to bewitch them all, for no one dared utter a sound. Even when she was on her way to her death they feared her.

She walked calmly to the stake and her hands were bound behind it. She did not try to resist. She did not fight, cry out or wail. She looked frail up there, like a child, but the nobility with which she stood was otherworldly. A priest read out her crime in a voice that echoed around the square, but Maggie seemed unmoved by it. All the while she ran her gaze over the people with her chin held high and an imperious expression on her beautiful face as if she pitied them all for their ignorance. She apparently did not fear death and the crowd sensed her bravery and were awed into a dreadful silence.

Just as the men with flares advanced to light the pyre she raised her eyes and looked directly at Lord Deverill, into his soul, and Barton's breath was frozen in his chest. He was powerless to move. It was as if she was looking deep into his very core and he didn't know whether the smile that curled her lips was of gratitude or defiance. He tried to look away but she held him steadily, like a snake with her prey, and as the sticks caught fire and gray smoke began to envelop her, her blazing eyes watched him still.

The flames lapped at her feet and grew higher but she remained silent and the crowd began to shuffle uneasily. Why didn't she cry out? Why did she not feel the burning? At last she let out a low moan. Barton stared in horror as the moan escalated into a shrill, piercing cry that threatened to shatter every eardrum in the square. And then the small bag of gunpowder she held in her hands caught light and exploded with a loud bang, thus releasing her as Barton had intended.

Lord Deverill realized that he hadn't breathed and took in a giant gulp of air. The crowd staggered back as sparks flew and the fire roared like the mouth of a mighty dragon. The people shielded their eyes and their cries rose with the crackling sound of burning wood and the stench of roasting flesh. He had seen enough. He turned his horse and galloped as fast as he could out of the village.

Chapter 38

Martha and Mrs. Goodwin arrived at the gates of the Convent of Our Lady Queen of Heaven. It was a bright February day, but the gray walls looked austere and formidable and Martha immediately felt uneasy. She imagined her mother arriving here as a young woman in trouble, as Mrs. Goodwin had said was the most likely scenario, and imagined her fear, for these walls looked more like a prison than a refuge.

They had telephoned ahead and booked an appointment to meet Mother Evangelist, who had sounded very kind and helpful, and Martha had felt greatly encouraged by her readiness to see her. Surely, if she had no information at all she would have told her on the telephone and saved her the trouble and cab fare. Now, however, faced with these high walls, Martha felt her hope draining away and she began to lose courage. Mrs. Goodwin sensed her anxiety and smiled reassuringly. "God's houses always look so forbidding, don't they? Be they churches, cathedrals or convents, they don't give one a warm welcome, do they?"

"This is the first time I've ever been to a convent," said Martha, hoping it would be the last.

At length the door opened and a nun in a dark blue habit with a sweet face and soft gray eyes introduced herself as Sister Constance and invited them in. Martha noticed the smell at once. It wasn't unpleasant; a mixture of wood polish, detergent and candle wax. They were taken to a waiting room where a fire burned in the grate and a candle flickered on the occasional table beside a large, leather-bound Bible, a jug of water and two glasses. "Please make yourselves comfortable. Mother Evangelist is expecting you. She'll only be a few minutes. Would you like a cup of tea?"

"Yes please," said Mrs. Goodwin. "We'd both love one, thank you."

Sister Constance left the room. Martha sat on the edge of the sofa and looked around. The walls were painted white and a high window gave little light. The room looked forlorn in spite of the fire. She knitted her fingers in her lap. Mrs. Goodwin sat beside her and put her hand on Martha's. "It's going to be all right. They'll have records. They must have lots of children coming to look for their mothers. I'm sure you're not the first and you won't be the last."

Sister Constance returned with two mugs of tea on a tray with a bowl of sugar, a jug of milk and a plate of Kimberley biscuits. She placed it on the occasional table beside the candle. "There," she said with a warm smile. "Have you come far?"

"From America," said Martha.

Sister Constance's eyes widened with surprise. "Goodness,

that is a long way. Well, I hope you enjoy Dublin. It's a lovely city. If you have time you must have tea at the Shelbourne. It's a very grand old hotel and quite lovely."

"Oh, we've heard of the Shelbourne," said Mrs. Goodwin.

"Of course you have, everyone's heard of the Shelbourne," said Sister Constance. Her eyes were drawn to the door where Mother Evangelist was now standing. The young nun scurried out of the room and Mother Evangelist walked in with an air of authority and sat down in the armchair.

"I'm sorry to have kept you waiting. I'm glad Sister Constance made you cups of tea. It's a bright day but a cold one. Now, you've come to find your mother," she said gently, looking at Martha.

"I have," said Martha, pressing a hand to her heart to quieten it.

"I would like to help you, Miss Wallace. Many young mothers come here when they get into trouble and adoption is the only option. We do our best to help them and find their children loving homes. However, it's natural that you should want to find the woman who gave birth to you and, if it is God's will, you will be successful. You told me you have the birth certificate."

"I don't have it," Martha explained. "I found it but my adoptive mother doesn't know so I was unable to bring it with me."

"Very well. What was the name of your mother and what was the date of your birth?"

"My birthday is January 5, 1922, and my mother's name is Grace, Lady Rowan-Hampton. My adoptive parents are Larry and Pamela Wallace of Connecticut in America."

Mother Evangelist nodded and wrote the details in a little

book. She stood up. "I won't be long. I just need to retrieve the records. Perhaps I can supply you with an address or at least something to set you on the right path. People do move around, you know, and your mother might have married and changed her name. However, let's get the records and take it from there, shall we?"

When she was gone Mrs. Goodwin patted Martha's hand. "You see, it's not so frightening after all, is it? Mother Evangelist wants to help. I'm sure they have reconciled many mothers with their children. It's the right thing to do and Mother Evangelist seems to want to do the right thing."

Martha nodded and picked up her mug. The tea was tepid and weak but she didn't mind. She wondered what Lady Rowan-Hampton would think when she discovered that her daughter had come to find her. It seemed a very long while before Mother Evangelist returned. Martha began to feel nervous again, but this time she sensed something wasn't right. "Why is she taking so long?" she whispered to Mrs. Goodwin.

"There must be drawers and drawers of files," she said. "Perhaps they're kept in a cellar somewhere. I'm sure she'll be back shortly."

At last Mother Evangelist appeared, but her expression had changed. She was no longer smiling. Martha watched her sit down and the anxiety seemed to creep up her leg and down her arms as if it were a creature with prickles. Mother Evangelist sighed. "I'm so sorry," she said, shaking her head. "It appears that your records have been mislaid. I took so long because I went to ask Sister Agatha, who was the mother superior at that time. She's old now and her memory is going. She didn't know why the records had been lost and has no recollection of a Lady

Rowan-Hampton, but then many of the girls only stayed for a short while and this was seventeen years ago. I'm sorry to disappoint you. However, you have the name, which is a very good start. Many of the children who come back don't even have that. It's an unusual name and with an aristocratic title she shouldn't be too hard to find."

Martha wanted to cry. She felt her face flush and pursed her lips to stop them trembling. Mrs. Goodwin took over the talking. She thanked Mother Evangelist, who seemed genuinely sorry not to be able to help. She showed them back down the corridor to the door. As Mother Evangelist unbolted the door Martha noticed an old nun standing in the doorway of a room farther down the corridor. She was staring at her with small, intense eyes, her hard face impassive and her thin lips drawn into a mean line. Martha knew instinctively that *she* was Sister Agatha. She shuddered and the nun closed the door with a slam. It seemed a deliberate act of rebuke.

Once out in the sunshine Martha let her tears flow freely. Mrs. Goodwin put her arms around her. "There there, dear, don't cry. We've only just started our search. We *will* find her, I have no doubt. It was never going to be easy. I know, let's go and give ourselves a treat. Let's go to the Shelbourne and have a nice cup of tea. The tea at the convent was weak and cold. I'm sure the tea at the Shelbourne will be exceptionally good."

The Shelbourne Hotel did not disappoint. It was grand and classical, with high ceilings, marble floors and tall windows looking out onto St. Stephen's Green. They made their way across the foyer to the Lord Mayor's Lounge, where a waiter showed them to a round table beside one of the windows and

Mrs. Goodwin asked for afternoon tea. "You'll feel restored once you've had some scones and jam," said Mrs. Goodwin. "We're not going to give up because we fell at the first hurdle, Martha."

"I know. I suppose I thought that, because we knew the name, the address would be easily come by. After all, if she was a grand lady she'd presumably come from a grand house that might have been in the family for a long time."

"Well, you're not wrong," said Mrs. Goodwin. "I know a little about British titles. I don't think it will be that difficult to find her."

"But where do we start?"

"We must go to London. Your mother might have traveled to Dublin from her home in England to have her child in secrecy. I'm wondering now whether she ever lived here. I have family in England who will help us. I suggest we start there."

"All right, then. Let's go to London," Martha agreed. The waiter brought the tea, which was far superior to the tea they had had at the convent, and scones, which tasted better than anything Martha had tasted in America. "Goodness, these are good," she said and the color began to return to her cheeks and the optimism to her heart. "While we're here we might as well enjoy the park and have a look around the city. I've been trying not to think of Mother and Father," she said quietly.

"The letter you left explained everything very clearly," said Mrs. Goodwin. "I imagine Edith might be in a bit of hot water, though," she added.

"I specifically told them not to blame her. She's only little."

"Your aunt Joan will be in trouble and with good reason."

"She shouldn't have told Edith," said Martha firmly. "But

I'm glad that she did. I have a right to know where I come from."

"You do, dear," Mrs. Goodwin agreed.

At that moment their attention was diverted by a couple of gentlemen who stepped into the room. The older gentleman wore a three-piece suit with a gray felt hat while the younger man, who stood a good few inches taller than the other, was equally well dressed but of a slimmer, more athletic build. Both had an air of old-fashioned grandeur and importance, for it seemed that the entire hotel staff had gathered around them to ensure their comfort. They were escorted slowly through the room in a stately fashion and the older gentleman greeted people he knew with a dashing smile and a raffish twinkle in his pale gray eyes. Those with whom he spoke seemed very happy to see him and Mrs. Goodwin noticed how the ladies put down their teacups and gave him their hands, giggling flirtatiously as he brought them to his lips with a courteous bow. Martha and Mrs. Goodwin watched them in fascination. Mrs. Goodwin was taken by the charm of the older man, with his flaxen hair and arresting eyes, and wondered who he was, for surely he was a man of some standing in this city. Martha stared at the red-headed boy, who must have been of a similar age to her, for she found his insouciance compelling. There was a jauntiness to his walk and a confidence to his smile, as if he had only ever encountered good in his life. The two men settled at their table, which was a short distance from Mrs. Goodwin and Martha's, and the waiters fussed about them with napkins and menus and pleasantries—although they placed their orders without consulting the menus.

"Well, that's an elegant pair of men if ever I saw one," gushed

Mrs. Goodwin. "Must be father and son, don't you think? Besides the color of their hair they look quite similar."

Martha did not reply. She was unable to take her eyes off the boy. He was handsome, certainly, with a mischievous curl to his smile and a lively, amused gleam in his eyes, but there was something besides. Something Martha had never found in anyone else. Then, sensing he was being watched, he raised his eyes and they locked into hers as if destiny had always meant them to be together. They stared at one another without blinking, stunned and delighted at the strange new feelings they aroused in each other.

"What are you looking at, JP?" asked Bertie, following the line of his gaze. He smiled then as he saw the pretty girl by the window. "An eye for the ladies, eh?" he commented with a chuckle. But JP was too electrified by her to reply. He gazed at her as if he had never before seen anyone more lovely. Bertie smiled at his son's enthusiasm and remembered the first time he had laid eyes on Maud. She had aroused the same excitement in *him*. He looked back at the young girl who realized she had drawn the attention of *both* men and hastily dropped her gaze to her plate, blushing profusely. But Bertie did not avert his eyes, for there was a familiarity about her that he wasn't quite able to put his finger on. It was in the way she blushed perhaps, or in the sweetness of her shy smile, he couldn't be sure, but he was certain he had seen her somewhere before. She began to nibble on a scone while her companion clucked away like a hen. He could tell that she was making a great effort not to look in their direction again and finding the task almost impossible. JP's eager gaze drew her like a magnet.

"Would you like me to ask them to join us?" Bertie asked.

JP was surprised. "Would you, Papa?"

Bertie grinned. "Leave it to me." He called over a waiter and said something in his ear. A moment later the waiter was passing the message on to Mrs. Goodwin, whose face revealed her pleasant surprise at Lord Deverill's invitation. The older woman raised her eyes and looked at Bertie, who bowed his head and smiled encouragement.

"Will they come?" asked JP impatiently.

"I do believe they will," said Bertie, and a moment later the two ladies were standing before them and Bertie and JP were on their feet, introducing themselves enthusiastically.

"How very kind of you to invite us to join you," said Mrs. Goodwin once she had sat down. "Martha and I have just arrived from America."

"Is it your first time in Ireland?" Bertie asked, noticing that the two young people were now too shy to look at each other and were equally flushed.

"It's Martha's first time," said Mrs. Goodwin.

"And how are you finding it, my dear?" asked Bertie, turning to the nervous young woman sitting on his left.

"Oh, it's charming," she replied. "Just charming."

"Will you be staying long?"

The girl glanced anxiously at Mrs. Goodwin. "I don't know. We haven't really made plans. We're just enjoying the visit."

"Quite right," said Bertie. "Ah, the tea," he added as fresh pots, jugs of milk, a little plate of sliced lemon and a five-tier cake-and-sandwich stand were placed in the center of the table.

"Goodness," said Mrs. Goodwin with a sigh. "What a wonderful display of treats." She helped herself to a cucumber sandwich.

"Which would you like?" Bertie asked Martha, who was gazing at the cakes with wide, delighted eyes.

"Oh, I don't know," she replied, moving her fingers up and down the plates indecisively before settling on an egg and watercress sandwich on the lowest level.

"That's *my* favorite," said JP, reaching out to take one for himself. The two young people grinned at each other as JP popped his sandwich into his mouth and Martha took a small bite of hers.

"Good, isn't it?" said JP, when he had finished it. Martha nodded.

"How would you like your tea, Mrs. Goodwin?" Bertie asked.

"With a slice of lemon, please," she replied. "Martha likes milk. Lots of milk. In fact, there's more milk in her tea than tea."

JP laughed. "That's just how I like it too," he said, frowning at Martha, astonished that two strangers should have so much in common.

"How extraordinary," said Mrs. Goodwin, enjoying herself immensely. "I don't know anyone who likes their tea as milky as Martha does."

Bertie poured the tea. JP and Martha filled their cups to the brim with milk, taking pleasure in this shared idiosyncrasy that immediately bonded them. The conversation continued as they drank their tea and ate their sandwiches. A while later Bertie was giving them a list of all the interesting things they should see in Dublin when JP and Martha's hands reached for the same chocolate sponge cake on the top level of the cake stand. They laughed as their fingers collided over the plate and withdrew as if scalded. "We like the same cakes too," said JP softly, gazing at Martha with tenderness.

"But there's only one left," said Mrs. Goodwin.

"Then we shall share it," said JP. He put the cake on his plate and lifted the silver knife to cut it. Martha watched him slice it in two, now dizzy with infatuation. "Half for you," he said, placing one piece on the plate in front of her. "The other half for me," he added. And they lifted the small pieces to their lips and smiled at each other as if they were conspirators, sharing in a secret plot, and popped them into their mouths.

Epilogue

Ballinakelly

The air was thick and stuffy in the backroom, arranged as it was at one end of O'Donovan's public house and partitioned by a dividing wooden wall, which didn't quite reach the ceiling. The cigarette smoke and body heat from the men next door flowed freely over the top of the partition, along with the sweet smell of stout and the sound of deep voices. Set aside for the women (for women were not permitted in the public house), this was where the six elderly members of the Legion of Mary, known as the Weeping Women of Jerusalem behind their backs, met every week, sitting in a line along the bench like a row of hens in a henhouse.

There were the Two Nellies: Nellie Clifford and Nellie Moxley, Mag Keohane, who was always accompanied by her dog, Didleen, Joan Murphy, Maureen Hurley and Kit Downey. The Legion of Mary dedicated themselves to caring for the poor. They would cook them meals, take the elderly to Mass and stay in their houses if they needed nursing. Their weekly treat was to sit in the backroom at O'Donovan's and have a glass of Bulmers Cidona or a Little Norah orange crush. Mrs. O'Donovan would put a lump of ice in each glass, as she had an icebox, and provide a plate of Mikado and Kimberley biscuits, which she couldn't sell on account of them being broken. The greatest luxury, however, was that she allowed them to use her flushing lavatory upstairs. "'Tis America at home, girl," Mag Keohane had said to Mrs. O'Donovan the first time she used it. "You're a lucky woman not to have to brave the elements to do your business and all you have to do is pull the old chain and the lot disappears. God help us, 'tis a wonder we haven't pneumonia from going out with the old chamber pot in the middle of winter." The Weeping Women of Jerusalem used it, even when they didn't need to, just for the thrill.

"Can you believe that Bridie Doyle bought the castle?" said Nellie Clifford now, nibbling her Mikado biscuit. "I remember laying out her poor dead father, God rest his soul, when she was a little thing of nine."

"She's come a long way from the streets of Ballinakelly," agreed Nellie Moxley, sipping her orange crush. "She's a countess now, which they tell me is a fine thing to be. Indeed, she's made a healthy donation to our Legion, God rain his blessings on her."

"Her new husband is eaten alive with money. A fine-looking man even if he has a foreign look about him," said Joan Murphy.

"They say that foreign cows wear long horns," said Kit Downey with a grin.

"I'm not one to say, but I hear he has an eye for the ladies,

God save us. Nonie Begley is a receptionist at the Shelbourne and says that when he stays there he has a regular lady," said Joan Murphy.

Nellie Moxley leaped to his defense. "Maybe that's a sister or a relative."

But Nellie Clifford was quick to put her straight. "You're as innocent as the suckling child, Nellie. That was no sister, girl. It's none other than Lady Rowan-Hampton." The women gasped in unison. "They were in the dining room holding hands and making sheep's eyes at each other."

"Merciful Jaysus, the maids at her place said that Michael Doyle was a regular visitor there when the master was abroad, and that he would swagger into the hall, king of all he surveyed." The women shook their heads and clicked their tongues with disapproval.

"But what does Lord Deverill make of the new mistress of the castle?" Mag Keohane asked. "She was the daughter of the cook and now she owns the place."

"Hope for us all," cackled Kit Downey.

"I heard that Kitty Deverill swore like a sailor when she heard the news."

"God save us!" muttered Nellie Moxley.

"That Michael Doyle will be above himself now. I suppose they'll all be after moving into the castle."

"I heard that Mariah won't be leaving her home for love nor money," said Kit Downey.

"She's a good woman, is Mariah. As for Old Mrs. Nagle, it won't be long now," said Nellie Moxley. There was silence for a moment as they spared their thoughts for poor Mrs. Doyle and Old Mrs. Nagle.

Then Nellie Clifford put her glass on the long shelf that ran along the partition in front of them. "It's poor Bridie Doyle we should be praying for. She might have married a rich man but, mark my words, she'll be paying for it. By Christmas he'll have a girl in every corner of the county."

A head suddenly poked through the gap at the top of the partition. "Ye are great with the prayers, girls. An example to us all. Will I walk ye home in case some blaggard tries to way-lay one of ye?"

"Get away with you, Badger, and stop codding us," said Kit Downey. "We have miraculous medals and we are like nuns, we travel in twos for safety and we have Mag's Didleen to protect us. She'd tear him limb from limb, God save the mark." Badger's chest rattled.

"That's a graveyard cough if ever I heard it," said Mag Keohane.

"I'll tell you something, girl," retorted Badger with a grin. "There's many in the graveyard who would be glad of it."

Just then a hush came over the pub as a cold wind swept in through the open door. "It's none other than the Count," Badger hissed and his wooly head disappeared behind the partition.

"The Count," said Nellie Clifford, making her mouth into an O shape as she took in a long gasp. The six women strained their ears to hear what he was saying.

"How can I help you, sir?" Mrs. O'Donovan asked from behind the bar.

"I have just arrived on the train from Dublin. I would like a cab to take me up to the castle."

There was a shuffle as the hackney cabbies looked at one another, not wanting to rush their drinks.

"Why don't ye stay for a stout and a game of cards," ventured Badger Hanratty. "You're not in a great hurry, are ye? Then one of these good men will drive you up."

The women heard the Count laugh. "A glass of stout and a game of cards? Why not? Dinner can wait. So, what are we playing?" There ensued a scraping of chairs as he made himself comfortable at one of the tables. A moment later he added in a loud, exuberant voice, "Madam, a drink for every man in the house." And a roar of appreciation rose up as the men hurried to the bar to order more stout.

"God save us, they'll be legless and good for nothing," said Nellie Moxley, shaking her head.

"He knows how to win hearts in Ballinakelly," said Joan Murphy with a smile. "I can't wait to see what happens next."

Acknowledgments

As I continue to follow the lives of Kitty, Celia and Bridie, I continue to rely on my dear friend and consultant Tim Kelly for research and guidance. Our regular meetings, over porter cake and cups of Bewley's tea, have provided me with entertainment as well as information and his wonderful stories keep me laughing long after he has left my house. I am so grateful to my books for they have given me a great friend in Tim.

I would like to thank my mother, Patty Palmer-Tomkinson, for reading the first draft and editing out all the grammatical errors and ill-chosen words, thus saving my editor at Simon & Schuster from what is probably the least interesting part of her job! My mother is patient and enthusiastic and her advice is always wise. She's also a very intuitive person and a sound judge of character, I have learned a lot from her. I'd also like to thank my father because I wouldn't be writing these books if I hadn't had the magical childhood they gave me in the most beautiful corner of England. Everything that goes into my work flows directly from them.

Writing a scene about the Derby was always going to be a challenge, but I would not have attempted it without the help of David Watt. Thank you so much, Watty, for reading it through and correcting it—and for suggesting many ways to improve it.

Thank you Emer Melody, Frank Lyons and Peter Nyhan for your warm Irish encouragement and Julia Twigg for helping me research Johannesburg.

My agent, Sheila Crowley, deserves an enormous thank you. She's the best agent a writer can have because she's there when I need a counselor, when I need a friend, when I need a strategist and when I need a warrior. Quite simply, she's always there when I need her Full Stop. Her mantra "onward and upward" reflects her positive and determined attitude and every time she says it I'm grateful that she's taking me with her!

Working with Sheila at Curtis Brown are Katie McGowan, Rebecca Ritchie, Abbie Greaves, Alice Lutyens and Luke Speed and I thank them all for working so hard on my behalf.

I'm so fortunate to be published by Simon & Schuster. I feel that it's a family and that I belong there. I'd like to thank them all for turning my career around in 2011 with my first Sunday *Times* bestseller and for continuing to put such dedication and drive into publishing my books. A massive thank you to my editor-in-chief, Suzanne Baboneau, for editing my novels with such good judgment and tact. The manuscript is always hugely improved by her appraisal and pruning and my confidence lifted by her enthusiasm and encouragement. I thank Ian Chapman for being the wind in my sails, or should I say sales! I thank him for giving me that break five years ago and for turning my books into the successes that I'd always hoped they would be. I'd also like to thank Clare Hey, my editor, and the brilliant team she works with, for putting so much energy into my books. They all do a fantastic job and I'm so grateful to every one of them: Dawn Burnett, Toby Jones, Emma Harrow, Ally Grant, Gill Richardson, Laura Hough, Dominic Brendon and Sally Wilks.

My husband, Sebag, has been key in plotting the Deverill Chronicles with me and encouraging me to challenge myself by venturing off my familiar path. He's so busy with his own books but he took the trouble to read through the manuscript and share his ideas. I'm glad I took his advice because I believe I have written something that will really entertain my readers—I have certainly entertained myself in writing it. He's my most cherished friend, my most honest critic, my most loyal ally and my greatest supporter. Thanks to Sebag I believe I am the best I can be.

And finally thank you to my daughter Lily and my son Sasha for giving me joy, laughter and love.

ALSO BY
SANTA MONTEFIORE

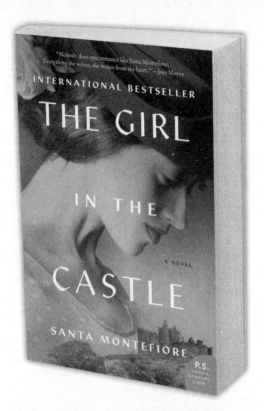

THE GIRL IN THE CASTLE
A Novel
Available in Ebook and Digital Audio

"Nobody does epic romance like Santa Montefiore.
Everything she writes, she writes from the heart."
— Jojo Moyes

Ireland. The early twentieth century.
Two girls on the cusp of womanhood. A nation on the brink of war.

A powerful story of love, loyalty, and friendship, *The Girl in the Castle* is an exquisitely written novel set against the magical, captivating landscape of Ireland—perfect for fans of *Downton Abbey* and Kate Morton.

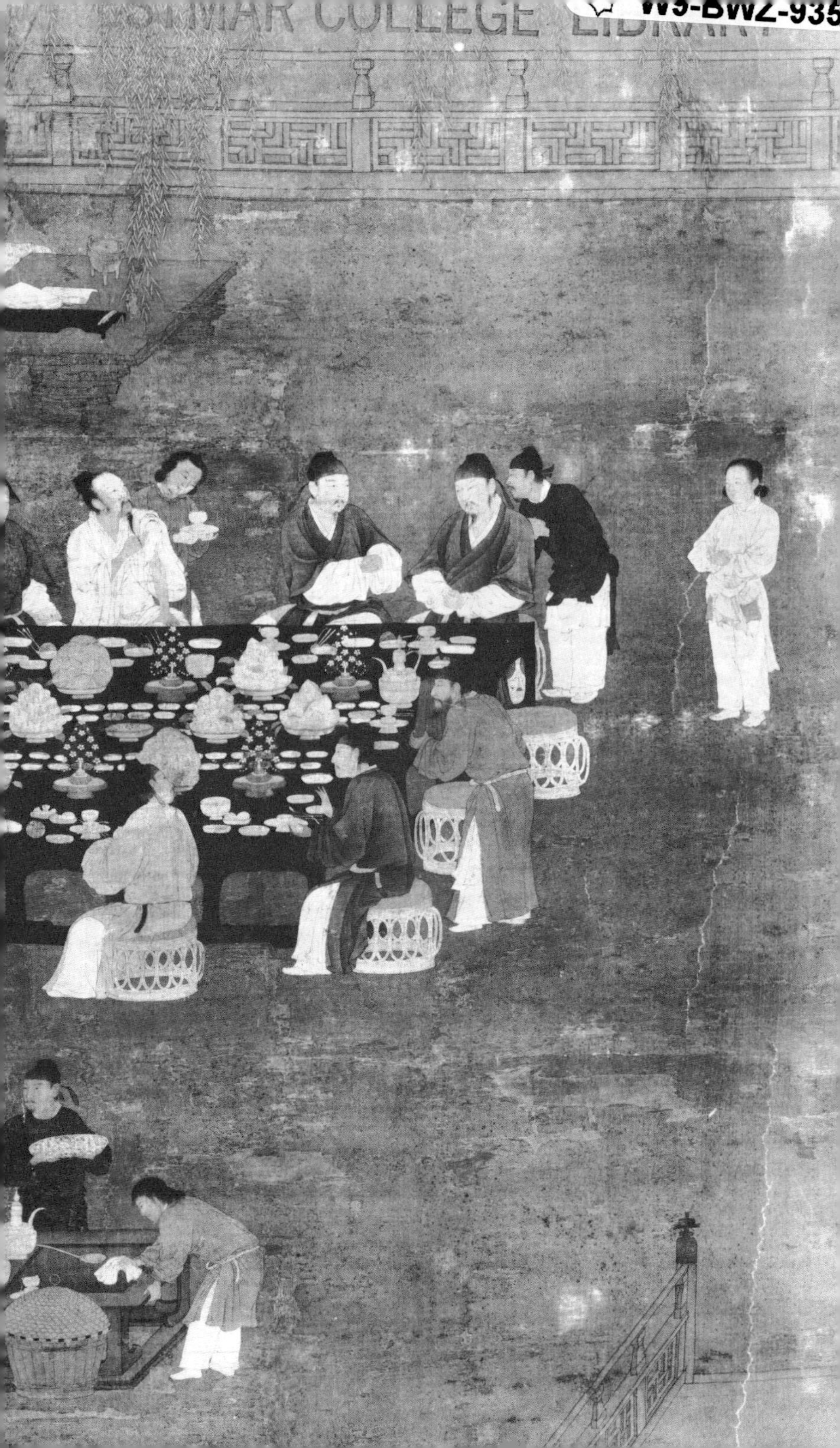

The career of Mao Tse-tung, one of the twentieth century's most influential revolutionaries, spans more than half a century of efforts to free China from the legacy of her past and to set her on the road to social and economic development. Mao's political activities began, as did the history of communism in China, in the late 1910s and early 1920s, years of social ferment known as the New Culture Movement. In the late 1960s, at the end of a career that had seen his rise to leadership of the Chinese Communist Party, Mao personally launched another "cultural revolution" designed to sustain the Party as an instrument of radical social change and to combat the resurgence of traditional social attitudes and political behavior.

Mr. Solomon's study describes Mao's struggle after the "Liberation" of 1949 to embody his political thought in the institutions of the People's Republic, and the increasing resistance from other Party leaders that led to the Cultural Revolution. Mr. Solomon begins by exploring China's traditional political culture. Basing his interpretation on interviews with mainland-born Chinese, he describes the "dependency social orientation," that is, the attitudes toward interpersonal relations, authority, and social conflict inculcated in generations of Chinese through Confucian family education and schooling.

He next discusses the development of Mao Tse-tung's conceptions of political leadership, finding a complex interplay between Mao's political ideas and traditional Chinese cultural attitudes. Whereas in the traditional era people were expected to "eat the bitterness" of life's hardships in order to ensure social harmony, Mao learned to teach China's peasants to "speak bitterness," to "vomit the bitter water" of repressed hatreds as a way of mobilizing their support for building a new world.

The final section of the book offers a detailed analysis of the intensifying conflict over policy and personal status within the leadership of the Chinese Communist Party from the mid-1950s to the Cultural Revolution of 1966. Drawing on Red Guard publications and recently disclosed secret speeches of high Party leaders, the author makes clear the continuity between Mao's pre-Liberation political thinking and his policies during two decades of Party rule. He finds that the Sino-Soviet dispute, from its inception in the mid-1950s, was related to Mao's efforts to combat "revisionism" within the Chinese Communist Party. He suggests that the opposition of long-time Party colleagues led Mao to precipitate a succession crisis in 1964 so as to ensure his continued control of Party policy. Mr. Solomon sees uncertainty surrounding Mao's ability to shape the future development of China's political culture, for this one man is struggling to transform the personalities and cultural pattern of a quarter of mankind. He suggests that Mao's particular innovation has been his concept of a political process that will motivate peasants to strive for a proletarian revolution.

MAO'S REVOLUTION AND THE CHINESE POLITICAL CULTURE

MICHIGAN STUDIES ON CHINA

*Published for the Center for Chinese Studies
of the University of Michigan*

MICHIGAN STUDIES ON CHINA

THE RESEARCH ON WHICH THIS BOOK IS BASED WAS
SUPPORTED BY THE CENTER FOR CHINESE STUDIES
AT THE UNIVERSITY OF MICHIGAN.

MAO'S REVOLUTION
AND THE CHINESE
POLITICAL CULTURE

RICHARD H. SOLOMON

UNIVERSITY OF CALIFORNIA PRESS

BERKELEY, LOS ANGELES, LONDON

FRONT ENDPAPER:
"A Literary Gathering" (detail), silk wall scroll by Emperor Hui Tsung,
Sung Dynasty (960–1279 A.D.).
Courtesy National Palace Museum, Taipei, Taiwan.

BACK ENDPAPER:
"Destroy the Four Olds."
*From a collection of Red Guard posters
of the Great Proletarian Cultural
Revolution, 1966–1969.*

UNIVERSITY OF CALIFORNIA PRESS
BERKELEY AND LOS ANGELES, CALIFORNIA
UNIVERSITY OF CALIFORNIA PRESS, LTD.
LONDON, ENGLAND
Copyright © 1971 by
The Center for Chinese Studies
University of Michigan
Second Printing 1972
ISBN: 0–520–01806–0
Library of Congress Catalog Card Number: 76–129606
Printed in the United States of America

FOR CAROL

Contents

Preface

Over the centuries of Western contact with China there seem to have been as many "Chinas" in foreign eyes 'as there have been diverse motives for involvement in this universally intriguing society. Merchant and missionary, soldier and educator each filtered the reality of China and her people through the biases of his own cultural background, personal and professional interests, and the exigencies of the age in which he lived.

The present study of China and her twentieth century revolution was initiated in the hope that through the techniques of social science analysis—interviews using controlled sampling procedures and structured questioning, psychological projective tests, content analysis of published documents, and interpretation of data on the basis of social theory—it would be possible to come to some understanding of the Chinese revolution on Chinese terms. However, given the facts that China has not been open to direct observation, and that she has presented a constantly changing face to the foreign world over the past two decades, this has been no easy task.

The research and writing of this study consumed most of the decade of the 1960s, a time when China was undergoing domestic economic crisis and political upheaval. The resources and institutions which sustained the inquiry, however, were products of the threatening Cold War era of the 1950s for the United States. Throughout the years of this enterprise there has been an ever-present contrast between early assumptions and an evolving Chinese reality which has made it difficult to be assured that one's preconceptions were correct. This constant challenge has sustained the sense of relevance of a search for a core of meaning in the kaleidoscope of China's continuing social and political revolution.

When I began formal academic training in political science and Chinese area and language studies, in the late 1950s, the People's Republic was in the most heady days of the first decade of Party rule. The nation appeared to be cast in the Soviet mold: aggressive, totalitarian, and rapidly transforming itself into a major security problem for the United States. These were years when foreign observers asked themselves nervously whether the Chinese Communist leadership just might bring about a "Great Leap Forward" in economic development, and rapidly industrialize their agrarian society through the massed application of peasant labor power. And but for a few veiled indications of Sino-Soviet tension, visible only to specialists in propaganda analysis, the People's Republic of China appeared to be a durable member of the Soviet-dominated "Socialist Camp."

By the end of the 1960s, barely a decade later, there could not have been a more drastic change in China's image abroad. The Great Leap had generated an economic crisis which took half the decade to repair; and the once monolithic Chinese Communist Party appeared decimated by a premature succession crisis precipitated by conflict over the policies of aging Party Chairman Mao Tse-tung. In addition, the Sino-Soviet alliance seemed irreparably shattered, with the two giants of the Communist world squared off in a hostile confrontation that approached open warfare during 1969.

As China enters the 1970s, our subject appears to be going through yet another incarnation. A country which only two or three years ago seemed to be virtually in a state of civil war is apparently pulling itself together and rebuilding an authoritarian political order. The economic scars of the Cultural Revolution appear to be minimal. And a state which had totally isolated itself from the international community (China recalled all but one of its ambassadors during the Cultural Revolution) is now reasserting itself with an added confidence drawn from hydrogen weapons and a ballistic missile capability. Furthermore, China's claim to be the beacon of world revolution finds surprisingly strong echoes in political turmoil on university campuses around the world, where Chairman Mao is a symbolic leader for the most alienated of a generation of political activists.

In this study we have drawn upon three analytical approaches which provide a certain stability of perspective on our constantly changing subject. The basic assumption is that China's political gyrations reflect the process of nation-building, embodying social, economic, and political facets. It is assumed that in the transformation of a peasant society into an industrializing nation-state, China's political leadership will have to confront certain universal developmental problems. The most fundamental is the process of expanding popular political participation. In China's case, the peasantry, long passive in matters of politics, must be brought into active involvement with the many problems of social and economic modernization.

A second analytical assumption, which follows from this first problem, is that these new entrants into the political process will bring with them personal traits and a cultural inheritance from the prerevolutionary era. Popular attitudes, behavioral patterns, and emotional concerns which affect society's "political culture" will be carried over from the old society into the era of revolution, and will hinder efforts to promote social change.

In China's case, the adults active in political affairs during the first two decades of Communist Party rule were educated in a time when social change had not penetrated very deeply into the educational processes of the society. Many Party leaders were schooled before the fall of the Ch'ing Dynasty in 1911. Hence as the "revolutionary vanguard" seeks to promote a new mass culture in "proletarian" values and work styles, its efforts, to some degree, will be in conflict with the traditional cultural inheritance of the adult population. The political style of the revolutionary elite itself will show the influence of the prerevolutionary culture.

As this study progressed, it became apparent that some of the most intriguing aspects of Communist rule in China relate to the endurance of the traditional culture in the revolutionary era. As is elaborated in the second half of the analysis, the conception of the leadership process of Party Chairman Mao Tse-tung embodies a complex mixture of efforts to change part of China's traditional political culture and to draw upon other elements of the tradition in order to sustain political influence. Furthermore, much of the policy conflict among Party leaders during the Cultural Revolution of the late 1960s seems to relate to how much tolerance should be given to traditions which endure in the "work-style" (*tso-feng*) of Party cadres, or how much stress should be given to Mao's "revolutionary" conceptions of political leadership.

A third set of interpretive perspectives derives from the notion of political culture. It is assumed that a basic understanding of China's political culture is to be found through analysis of the society's socialization practices, the manner in which parents educate their children and teachers instruct their students to deal with the world they will know as adults. It is further assumed that the traditional political culture can be studied by means of analysis of the socialization experiences of adults reared in the last years of the imperial era; and that one measure of change is to be found in the contrast between the learning experiences of this older generation and that of younger generations of Chinese reared under Communist Party influence.

The enduring revolutionization of a society would seem to require a congruence between altered forms of social organization and the socialization experiences of those who live and work in the

new society. If organizational changes are not supported by successful efforts to educate new values and patterns of behavior into the
new leadership, tension will result. Efforts to reduce the conflict between personal need and organizational form will be resolved in
favor of the individual's preferences. Again, as we shall stress later,
research seemed to bear out this assumption about the critical importance of educational experiences in institutionalizing the revolution. Some of the most distinctive aspects of Chinese Communist
political practice, the "thought reform" technique and "criticism–
self-criticism" meetings, were designed to exert continuing pressure
against the resurgence of traditional behavioral forms among Party
cadres reared before "Liberation."

While these three analytical perspectives helped to provide certain foci for research activities and data interpretation, our initial
interest was in trying to understand how Chinese themselves viewed
their country's social and political revolution. Hence four years of
formal study of Chinese political history, society, and language
served as the basis for an interview project with members of three
generations of adult Chinese. By means of these conversations, I
sought to explore perceptions of their country's continuing revolution, their attitudes toward politics, and the learning experiences
which underlay their social and political attitudes. This interview
project is described in detail in the introductory chapter. Altogether
more than ninety individuals participated, and the records revealed
in rich detail attitudes and personal experiences which had found
only limited expression in earlier classroom and social contacts.

As the interviewing proceeded, it became increasingly evident
that the attitudes and experiences we were exploring had considerable
inner coherence. They appeared to be integrated around several
basic cultural assumptions concerning the nature of the individual,
interpersonal relations, and the relation of the individual to society.
The first two parts of this study explore this structured set of social
attitudes—what we term the "dependency social orientation"—
and the learning process by which it was inculcated in the generations of Chinese interviewed.

After completion of a major part of the project, I began to analyze a variety of published Chinese political materials. Some derived
from the Confucian tradition, some were from the Nationalist period, but the majority were newspaper materials and documents of
the Communist era. Particular emphasis was given to study of the
leadership process of Communist Party Chairman Mao Tse-tung.

Two things became apparent in this documentary analysis. The
social and political orientation of the Chinese we had interviewed
very strongly reflected the values of the Confucian tradition—even

where the individual had not been formally schooled in classical Confucian literature. Secondly, and of greater interest for the development of this study, it was found that Mao's conception of political leadership combined a complex reaction against many traditional values even as it drew upon those behavioral patterns and emotional concerns which he deemed essential in gaining popular support. The third part of the study explores this interrelationship between the traditional political culture and Mao's conception of leadership as it evolved over the years of struggle for power.

A first draft of this analysis was completed in the spring of 1966. At that time it was uncertain just how useful it would be to carry the study into areas of policy development in the years after the Party had come to power. The period of public criticism of the Party which followed the Hungarian upheaval of 1956, the so-called "Hundred Flowers Campaign," seemed to bear many marks of Mao's style of leadership, as did the "Great Leap Forward" of 1958–1960, a program for rapid economic development. Yet to the outside observer, the Party Chairman's influence on policy during nearly two decades of Party rule appeared to be but one element in a context of collective leadership.

This view of a basic consensus among the "Long March" generation of Party leaders, widely held among foreign observers of China, was shattered in the second half of 1966 by what Mao and his supporters termed a "Great Proletarian Cultural Revolution." Bitter differences among Party leaders, previously unimagined by most foreign observers, were brought into sharp focus by this crisis within the Party leadership over policy and personal political influence. The next three years of domestic political turmoil also saw the publication, primarily in China's "Red Guard" press, of previously secret documentary materials and speeches by high Party officials. This information added greatly to our understanding of policy disputes within the Party leadership and of the manner in which Mao Tse-tung sought to influence the course of China's social revolution.

It is rare in political science analysis to be able to conduct controlled experiments in which hypotheses about the leadership style of one man, or the inner dynamic of a political system, can be tested through the actual workings of the political process. In a completely fortuitous manner, the Cultural Revolution turned out to be just such a test of the interpretation of Mao's leadership style and its relation to aspects of China's political culture which we had drawn on the eve of the Cultural Revolution. Interviews with emigrés, reinterpretation of the field observations of earlier generations of anthropologists or sociologists, and analysis of published political documents, are but crude tools in the indirect study of a society and its politics. Hence we have relied heavily on documentary disclosures of the Cultural Revolution to substantiate interpretations developed earlier on the basis of limited and indirect information.

We had made certain inferences about the personality and style of Mao Tse-tung through analysis of highly selected and edited speeches and documentation of the pre-Liberation era. Publication of his previously unpublished speeches of the 1950s and 1960s delivered behind the closed doors of Party leadership conferences reveal in this man's direct and earthy language that many inferences had been correct. Furthermore, the details of a decade of increasingly serious dispute between Mao and other Party leaders over questions of national policy which were revealed during the Cultural Revolution make quite evident the manner in which Mao has projected his personal political style into policy formulations.

In both the form which the Cultural Revolution struggle took and the content of polemical attacks on various Party leaders, the events of the late 1960s help to confirm one of the basic assumptions behind this study: that of the endurance of the traditional culture in the revolutionary era as an impediment to efforts to promote rapid social change. Mao himself evidently saw the revolution as vulnerable to the resurgence of traditional patterns of behavior and social values as they endured in the personalities of the Chinese "masses" and individual Party leaders.

In what seems likely to be the last great political battle of his career, Mao appears determined to preserve his influence on the course of China's revolution by removing from power leaders opposed to his policies, and by attempting to institutionalize his "thought" in new organizations of political power. And he is looking for support mainly from a younger generation he hopes will grow to political maturity during the protracted conflict to preserve the momentum of social change.

The final section of this book, based on a year of documentary analysis and interviewing in Hong Kong in 1969, is an effort to detail Mao's attempt to institutionalize his impact on the Chinese revolution in the years after Liberation, against increasing resistance from other Party leaders.

In preparing this study for publication we became painfully aware of the length to which the presentation had grown. Earlier inclinations to publish the first three parts separately had been resisted largely because of our desire to explore in greater detail the relationship between Mao's personality and China's political life, and we were aware that the whole story had not been told. The Cultural Revolution enabled us to detail Mao's impact on the Chinese revolution, but the documentation which became available after 1966 has added considerable length to the study. We have decided to present the analysis in its current form despite its length for two reasons: First, the four parts comprise an integrated interpretation in which the first three parts establish the premises for Part Four. Second, the detailed political analysis in Part Four has not been developed by other authors thus far using Cultural Revolution documentation. Indeed, the detailed documentation throughout is presented in the spirit of drawing together important source material. Our basic concern, however, has been to provide firm evidence on the relationship between personality and politics.

Given the length of this study, we assume that many readers will have to approach the book selectively. Thus certain interpretive themes are repeated throughout the four parts of the analysis on the assumption that a limited amount of redundancy will assist the reader who does not have the time to follow the study through from beginning to end.

Acknowledgments

The errors and shortcomings of this study must be my personal responsibility. The research and analysis which preceded the writing, however, represent a collective effort, and I would be remiss if I did not indicate my indebtedness to the many colleagues and friends who provided assistance and insight.

I wish to express a particularly deep sense of gratitude to Professor Lucian W. Pye of the Massachusetts Institute of Technology, who first encouraged me to undertake the study of Chinese society and politics. He provided much of the intellectual stimulation behind this study; and his judicious combination of guidance and toleration of my research instincts enabled me to handle the data on their own terms. The interpretations developed here, however, rely heavily on his insights into the workings of China's political culture, as elaborated in his recent study, *The Spirit of Chinese Politics*.

Professor Alexander Eckstein gave much encouragement in his dual roles as friend and Director of the Center for Chinese Studies at the University of Michigan. Dr. Tsung-yi Lin, former Director of the Taipei Children's Mental Health Center and now Professor of Psychiatry at the University of Michigan, and his wife, Mei-chen, a social worker, both contributed substantially to the advancement of this project. They made research facilities and personnel available and then provided interpretive insights which reflect their years of professional experience.

Professor David C. McClelland of Harvard University gave particularly valuable guidance in the use and interpretation of the psychological projective tests employed during the interviews.

Several pages could be filled with the names of Chinese friends and colleagues in Taiwan, Hong Kong, and the United States who in numerous ways contributed to this study and to my understanding of their society, its customs, and the revolution. I particularly wish to express my gratitude to those who assisted in the period of field research. Chen Yüeh-hsiu, Ko Chü-yi, and Lin A-mei proved to be skillful interviewers. Wei Ju-lin and Chou Mei-jung assisted with transcription of interview records and data coding. Dr. Ko Yung-ho gave generously of his time and talents in training the interviewers in the administration of the psychological tests, and in developing coding procedures and interpretations.

Additional assistance in documentary research and data processing was provided by a number of my students. Jan Berris scoured the literature for independent observations of Chinese social life and customs and assisted in administering the research procedure used here to a sample of American students as a check on our interpretations. Ronald Suleski prepared the biographical sketches contained in Appendix V from the Chinese interview records. Mary Coombs and John Deegan worked on quantitative data preparation and processing, and Joan Lustbader, Lawrence Sullivan, and Catherine Winston provided additional assistance in documentary research.

As this study progressed I received valuable criticism and suggestions from numerous colleagues and teachers. Howard Rosenthal gave generously of his time and skills in matters of data processing and interpretation, as did Sam Popkin. I also wish to acknowledge help and criticism received from A. Doak Barnett, Parris Chang, Chang Chun-shu, Chu-yuan Cheng, Dr. Chien Ching-piao, Albert Feuerwerker, Edward Friedman, John Gittings, William E. Griffith, Melvin Gurtov, Charles Hucker, Talbott Huey, Dr. Hsu Chen-chin, Harold Isaacs, Ellis Joffe, Chalmers Johnson, Lau Yee-fui, Nathan Leites, Stanley Lubman, Roderick MacFarquhar, Donald J. Munro, Ithiel deSola Pool, Stuart Schram, Franz Schurmann, Richard Sorich, Tsao Pei-lung, Ezra Vogel, Wan Wei-ying, Allen S. Whiting, Col. William Whitson, Richard W. Wilson, the late Mary C. Wright, and Dr. Yeh Eng-kung.

Mrs. Janet Eckstein and Dr. Elizabeth K. Bauer did yeoman service in the final editing of the manuscript. And Mrs. Jacqueline Evans provided important assistance in her role as Executive Secretary of the University of Michigan Center for Chinese Studies.

Financial support for this study was provided by a number of institutions. The Foreign Area Fellowship Program supported a

Preface *xix*

year of language and area studies, and the initial two-year period of field research. The Center for International Studies at M.I.T. assisted in the development of the TAT test materials. The Center for Chinese Studies at the University of Michigan supported a variety of research costs, and made it possible for me to take additional leave from teaching responsibilities in order to complete research and writing. A final year of research in Hong Kong was supported in part by grants from the Joint Committee on Contemporary China of the Social Science Research Council, and the National Science Foundation. The views and interpretations developed in this study, however, should not be attributed to any of these supporting institutions.

I also wish to express my thanks to the staff of the Universities Service Center of Hong Kong for providing research facilities and assistance, and two years of collegial atmosphere.

Finally, I wish to express filial gratitude to my own clan: to Harold and Alice Harris, and Ellen Solomon, for having generously supported so many years of study; and to my wife Carol, who in her capacities as teacher and social worker made possible many of the personal relationships which contributed so much to this study. Hopefully her forebearance during the years of research and writing has been rewarded by the many joys associated with this attempt to understand another people and their culture.

R.H.S.

Ann Arbor, Michigan
Summer, 1970

For many years we Communists have struggled for a cultural revolution as well as for a political and economic revolution, and our aim is to build a new society and a new state for the Chinese nation. That new society and new state will have not only a new politics and a new economy but a new culture.

MAO TSE-TUNG,
"On New Democracy" (1940)

The fact is, now we see that a revolution cannot change a nation—its tendencies and qualities and traits. . . . Only the form of power and of property [can be changed] but not the nation itself.

MILOVAN DJILAS (1968)*

---

* From "An Interview with Milovan Djilas," *The New York Times* (November 27, 1968), p. 10.

Worker striding past statue of Confucius
on the road to the Ming Tombs, suburbs of Peking.
René Burri, from Magnum.

Chapter I

INTRODUCTION

This is a study of one of the twentieth century's most influential political leaders in his personal struggle to adapt the weighty cultural inheritance of a quarter of mankind to the political and economic challenges of a new era.

The career of Mao Tse-tung, from his early years as a student revolutionary in Hunan Province to his rise to leadership of the Chinese Communist Party and, after 1949, Chairmanship of the People's Republic, has been intimately related to the efforts of the Chinese people to transform their ancient society into a modern nation. This book explores Mao's gradual development of a new style of politics and social organization over three decades of power-conflict, followed by the struggle to institutionalize his concepts in post-Liberation China.

Most previous studies of China's efforts to enter the modern world have focused on the evolution of the country's historical institutions, on the ferment of new ideas and social values in a society which for thousands of years has had a highly developed intellectual tradition, and on efforts to transform a peasant society into an industrializing nation-state. Here we explore a different aspect of the story. It is our basic assumption that China's difficulties in responding to the changing world of the past century have been largely cultural and psychological in quality rather than institutional or economic. Mao Tse-tung began his political career in the period of cultural challenge of the late 1910s and early 1920s known as the "May Fourth" era. He is concluding his career with a "Great Proletarian Cultural Revolution," an astounding effort which began in the mid-1960s to confront once again what he and his Red Guard supporters called China's "four olds"—her traditional customs, habits, culture, and social thought.

Thus there is an important tension between Mao Tse-tung's personal conception of how China's political and social life should be, organized in the country's search for new greatness, and the endurance of old social attitudes and political habits of millions of Chinese who embody the legacy of China's past.

1

BASIC ISSUES IN CHINA'S POLITICAL CULTURE:
AMBIVALENCE TOWARD AUTHORITY AND
AVOIDANCE OF CONFLICT

The analytical perspective adopted in this study is exploration of those Chinese social attitudes, emotional concerns, and moral norms which influence political behavior—what has been termed a society's "political culture." [1] This approach is an outgrowth of earlier research which attempted to analyze differences in "national character."

The underlying assumptions can be stated simply: Politics fundamentally involves the actions of individuals who decide how they will behave in any given political situation—even if the pressures of the social context establish clearly preferable alternatives. People are taught from early in life how to evaluate and respond to "political" situations. Basic aspects of an individual's personality include his attitudes toward those in positions of authority, and toward the use of power, and his feelings about how to handle the social conflict which is of the essence of politics.

Such attitudes are acquired within the family during childhood, are reinforced and made more explicitly "political" as the individual matures and becomes a member of adult society, and are quite stable over time. Finally, any given individual's attitudes, emotional concerns, and values concerning political behavior are not unique. He will share certain aspects of his personality with others in his society, for shared attitudes, emotions, and moral norms—culture—are essential to coordinated social action.

We began our research by trying to identify the attitudes toward politics, authority, and social conflict which are most meaningful to people reared in the Chinese cultural tradition. First, we had to identify the concepts and social values which Chinese associate most closely with politics. From students of philosophy we learned that social "harmony" and peace have long been considered basic

1. The concept of "political culture" was first suggested by Gabriel Almond in an article, "Comparative Political Systems," *Journal of Politics,* Vol. XVIII, No. 3 (August 1956), pp. 391–409. This was an attempt to bring together the systems-analysis approach to political analysis with earlier work on the study of social and cultural systems, and "national character." More elaborate discussions of this concept will be found in: Gabriel Almond and Sidney Verba, *The Civic Culture: Political Attitudes and Democracy in Five Nations* (Princeton: Princeton University Press, 1963), pp. 3–76; and Lucian Pye and Sidney Verba, *Political Culture and Political Development* (Princeton: Princeton University Press, 1965), pp. 3–26, 512–560.

and enduring political values in the Confucian tradition.[2] However, these values have contrasted with the historical reality of periods of tranquillity and social order shattered by episodes of uncompromising political conflict and unrestrained violence. Historians of Chinese society have termed this alternating pattern of peace and conflict the "dynastic cycle." [3]

The foreign observer of China is continually struck by the many ways in which the Chinese social tradition emphasizes the love of peace and interpersonal harmony as social values. China's great cities bear such names as "Southern Peace" (Nanning), "Western Tranquillity" (Sian), and "Enduring Peace" (Yenan); and the country's first great revolutionary of the twentieth century, Sun Yat-sen, stressed that commitment to "the moral quality of peace" was a "special characteristic" of the Chinese people.[4] In contrast, however, one quickly discovers that one of the most enduring symbols of Chinese political life is that of the "Warring States," an ancient period of social fragmentation and violent struggle for power. More recently we have seen the incredible destructiveness of the nineteenth century peasant insurrection known as the "Kingdom of Heavenly Peace" (T'ai-p'ing T'ien-kuo), the struggle for power of the warlords of the 1920s, and the still unresolved civil war to control a capital once named "Northern Peace" (Peiping).

One senses in this contrast between the ideal and the reality issues of great emotional concern to the Chinese about the handling of aggressive emotions and interpersonal conflict. This is hardly to say, of course, that the Chinese are in any way unique in having difficulty coming to terms with the human capacity for aggression. Rather, it suggests that through the biases of culture and personality, questions of the handling of social conflict constitute a major area of tension in the Chinese political culture.

In a similar vein, the foreign observer is struck by the determination with which Mao Tse-tung, as leader of the Chinese Communist Party, has stressed the need for "struggle" and "class conflict" in China's search for social progress even decades after the basic consolidation of state power. This concern of Mao's that his people be repeatedly prodded to "struggle for progress" or to engage in

2. *See* Derk Bodde, "Harmony and Conflict in Chinese Philosophy," in Arthur F. Wright, ed., *Studies in Chinese Thought* (Chicago: University of Chicago Press, 1953), pp. 19–80.

3. *See,* for example, John T. Meskill, ed., *The Pattern of Chinese History: Cycles, Development, or Stagnation?* (Boston: Heath, 1965).

4. Cited from a 1927 work by Sun in Arthur F. Wright, "Struggle Versus Harmony: Symbols of Competing Values in Modern China," *World Politics,* Vol. VI, No. 1 (October 1953), pp. 31–44.

mutual criticism of "backward thinking," seems to imply that the Chinese people might otherwise rest content with ancient social norms and avoid the unpleasantness of interpersonal competition. Hence, in designing research procedures for this study we gave particular emphasis to exploring Chinese attitudes and experiences concerning matters of social conflict.

Another area of particular note to the foreign observer is the emphasis which the Confucian tradition has laid on deference to those in authority. In politics, questions of authority obviously predominate. Chinese for centuries have stressed "filial piety" as the basis of superior-subordinate relations. One senses in this concern with orderly dealings between superior and subordinate some relation to the concern with social conflict. Perhaps in the highly articulated stress on filial obedience and deferential service to those in authority, we hypothesized, there was more than the desire of the peasant family head to attain security in old age. There might also be a fear that those in subordinate positions might completely reject authority.

As will be detailed in following chapters, our interview data substantiate the view that there is a notable degree of ambivalence toward authority in the attitudes of those reared in the Chinese tradition: a paradoxical combination of the desire for a strong leader; yet a concomitant resentment against the demands of this powerful authority on the individual.

As psychologists and sociologists have stressed, culture and personality are both systemic in quality: They are not unrelated collections of ideas, or attitudes and emotions. They are both structured around certain unifying themes or assumptions.[5] One of the objectives of this study is to identify the basic assumptions of life and interpersonal relations which are reflected in the dominant values of the Chinese tradition and which structure personal attitudes.

The American cultural perspective, of course, places strong emphasis on the importance of the individual in society, on personal responsibility, and on self-realization. The Chinese emphasis on social interrelatedness, on the basic importance of group life, and on submission of the individual to collective interests, stands out as a fundamental cultural difference.[6] As we will detail, Chinese

5. On this point, see in particular the analysis by Talcott Parsons, "Social Structure and the Development of Personality: Freud's Contribution to the Integration of Psychology and Sociology," *Psychiatry,* Vol. XXI, No. 4 (September 1958), pp. 321–340.

6. For a discussion of these cultural differences on the basis of interview data derived from this study, see Richard H. Solomon, "Mao's Effort to Reintegrate the Chinese Polity: Problems of Conflict and Authority in Chinese Social Processes," in A. Doak Barnett, ed., *Chinese Communist Politics in Action* (Seattle: University of Washington Press, 1969), pp. 276–297.

criticism of individualism for its "selfishness," the demand of both family head and political leader that group needs take precedence over personal interests, and the use of collective forms of punishment, are all indications of a fundamental Chinese cultural assumption that social life is *interdependent*.

In this study we characterize the individual social orientation in the Chinese tradition as one of *dependency*. The notion of a dependency social orientation as the modal personality configuration[7] seems to bring together such major aspects of Chinese social action as the attitudes toward authority and conflict, and also establishes conceptual linkages between the system of personality and the larger cultural tradition.

There are many difficulties in attempting psychological research on a society like China, which at present is largely closed to direct observation. However, interviews with emigré Chinese confirm that some of the major political changes on the mainland promoted by Mao Tse-tung and the Chinese Communist Party are closely related to themes of personality and social attitude found throughout the Chinese cultural area. For example, one sees in the Chinese Communist use of isolation forms of political punishment (described in detail later) the manipulation of strong personality needs to be accepted by the group.

In later chapters of this study we stress the ways in which Mao Tse-tung's political style at once draws on aspects of the traditional Chinese political culture and also is in part an effort to reshape the traditional style of wielding authority. We see a confirmation of our interpretation of "the power of the word" in Mao's use of his "little red book" of quotations to assert his political influence. Similarly, in the Communists' emphasis on group life, there is a line of continuity with the traditional Chinese stress on subordination of the individual to the collective.

As points of contrast, whereas the Confucian political tradition inculcated fear of authority and popular political passivity before a literate elite, Mao Tse-tung has sought to "liberate" the masses from

7. It is with some reluctance that I use the term "modal personality," developed by Daniel J. Levenson and Alex Inkeles in their article, "National Character: The Study of Modal Personality and Socio-Cultural Systems" (in Gardner Lindzey, ed., *Handbook of Social Psychology* [Cambridge, Mass.: Addison-Wesley, 1954], pp. 997–1020). At first glance it seems to suggest that Chinese tend to be "all alike." Even in the small sample of Chinese interviewed for this study we see a rich variation in personality style which thoroughly eliminates any "all alike" interpretation. What our interview data do indicate, however, is that there is a range of social attitudes and emotional concerns common to this group, and shared patterns of behavior used in coping with interpersonal situations.

their anxiety in the face of authority and to bring them into active political participation. While the traditional culture stressed avoidance of social conflict and suppression of hostility and aggression, Mao has seen conflict as the basic process of social change, and hostility as the motivating force by which politically passive peasants will struggle to build themselves a new world.

In sum, this study stresses as the "dialectic" in China's national development not the conflict of classes but the tension between established patterns of culture and personality and the new values and behavioral norms which Mao Tse-tung sees as the basis for the reconstruction of the world's largest political and economic community.

THE STRUCTURE OF THIS STUDY

This book consists of four self-contained parts linked by interpretive themes: Part One explores the way in which Chinese traditionally educated their children, both informally within the family and through formal schooling. Part Two elaborates upon themes developed in Part One and describes the attitudes of adult Chinese concerning social life and politics. Part Three is an analysis of the development of Mao Tse-tung's political attitudes and style of action during the revolutionary struggle for power. Themes developed in the first two parts of the book are found to be closely related to the evolution of Mao's political style. Part Four is a detailed analysis of Mao's efforts after the attainment of national leadership in 1949 to institutionalize the style of political life which brought him, and the Chinese Communist Party, to power. This final section of the book is a study of the growing divergence between Mao's conception of the political process and that held by other leaders whom Mao in time came to see as burdened with traditional political attitudes. Together the four parts present a picture of the weight of China's cultural inheritance and of Mao's struggle against it, a struggle to preserve the meaning of his own life in the institutions of China's social revolution.

The manner in which hypotheses were formulated for this study and research procedures developed to test them parallels rather closely the progression of sections in this book. Our preliminary hypotheses were tested during a year of intensive interviewing of mainland-born Chinese in both Taiwan and Hong Kong.[8] Interpre-

8. For a formal statement of the hypotheses which structured this study, see Richard H. Solomon, *The Chinese Political Culture and Problems of Modernization* (Cambridge, Massachusetts: Center for International Studies, M.I.T., 1964).

tations were developed and refined during several years of teaching. The final section of the book dealing with recent political history was written three years after the preliminary form of the basic interpretation had been outlined.[9] It required a further year of interviewing and documentary research in Hong Kong, during which disclosures of the Cultural Revolution were incorporated into the study.

The four sections of the book draw on differing sources of data, and the analytical procedures employed vary according to the data used. In Part One we develop an interpretation of personality formation and its relationship to Chinese social values on the basis of interview recollections of childhood and descriptions of childrearing practices gathered from a sample of ninety-one mainland-born Chinese. The reliability of these interview data was tested against independent observations of Chinese family and village life by anthropologists and sociologists, and published autobiographies of native Chinese. From these data we develop the interpretation of the "dependency social orientation," inculcated into Chinese from childhood. Our assumption is that the learning of early life prepares a child to cope with the world he will inherit as an adult, and that the form and content of the educational experience reflects the social values and patterns of interpersonal relations of both parents and educators.

In Part Two we rely upon interview data to explore adult social and political attitudes. The fact that we find major continuities between childhood experiences and adult attitudes strengthens the interpretation that childhood learning is preparation for adult life, and that attitudes and behavioral patterns acquired early in life persist in adulthood.

In Part Three we develop an interpretation of Mao Tse-tung's political style on the basis of his formally published political writings in the years of struggle for power, and from historical studies of the Chinese Communist movement. Here again, we find important linkages between cultural themes analyzed in the first two parts of the book and Mao's political style.

In Part Four we analyze the development of conflict over policy and leadership technique within the Chinese Communist Party after 1949 on the basis of newspaper articles, formally edited speeches of Party leaders, and less formally published political documents and speeches by Mao Tse-tung which have come to light as a result

9. The draft interpretation which has been expanded into this study is the author's Ph.D. dissertation, *The Chinese Revolution and the Politics of Dependency: The Struggle for Change in a Traditional Political Culture* (Massachusetts Institute of Technology, 1966).

of the Cultural Revolution. Here our analytical approach combines more familiar techniques of documentary interpretation and personnel analysis with interpretation of the China mainland press in a manner that some have characterized as "Kremlinology" or "esoteric communication" analysis.[10]

In conclusion, we summarize the interplay between the traditional political culture and Mao Tse-tung's efforts to institutionalize a new style of politics. As well, we stress what seem to be the innovative aspects of Mao's efforts to promote directed social change in a peasant society, and to prevent the reemergence of traditional social values and political practice.

THE INTERVIEW PROCEDURE

On the basis of our research assumptions that political attitudes grow from childhood socialization, and that Chinese hold distinctive attitudes toward authority and conflict, an interview procedure was developed to explore the evolution of social and political attitudes from early in life, through formal schooling, to their adult elaborations.

Interviews were carried out with the help of five standardized procedures: a set of open-ended questions about social attitudes and life experiences, a biographical schedule, an attitude survey, and two psychological "projective" tests—the standard Rorschach Test and a Thematic Apperception Test (TAT) designed especially for this study.[11]

In order to acquire a broad base of data on social attitudes and on the socialization experiences from which they had grown, a series of sixty-three questions were developed as the core of the interview procedure. These questions begin with early life experiences and attitudes toward family authority, pass on to experiences and attitudes gained through formal education, and then into general social perceptions and experience. There is a concluding section of eighteen questions which is more directly political in quality. "Political" issues had to be handled with some care while interviewing

10. For three particularly instructive statements on the problems of interpreting political communications in Communist countries, see Franz Borkenau, "Getting at the Facts Behind the Soviet Façade," *Commentary,* Vol. XVII, No. 4 (April 1954), pp. 393–400; "The Role of Esoteric Communication in Soviet Politics," in Myron Rush, *The Rise of Khrushchev* (Washington, D.C.: Public Affairs Press, 1958), pp. 88–94; and William E. Griffith, *Communist Esoteric Communications: Explication de Texte* (Cambridge, Mass.: M.I.T. Center for International Studies, 1967).

11. These materials are reproduced in Appendixes I through IV, pp. 527–540 below.

in Taiwan and Hong Kong, however, for merely the use of the word "politics" (*cheng-chih*) was sufficient to raise anxieties in some respondents. This orientation in itself is one of the things we wanted to explore in this study; and it was found in pretests that if we raised general matters of social authority and leadership indirectly, most respondents would discuss political matters at their own initiative. If, however, they were asked highly structured or explicit political questions they would "turn off." Hence, the general interview questions were designed to be as open-ended as possible.

Complementing the general questions were a seventy-three item biographical schedule, and an attitude survey of thirty-two items. The attitude survey items were created with a number of objectives in mind. They provided a standardized set of statements which could be used in group administrations to other Chinese in Taiwan and Hong Kong to test the reliability of our interview data.[12] Also, the survey could be used cross-culturally to test the degree to which attitudes found to be of particular concern to Chinese were truly "Chinese." [13]

A further objective of the attitude survey approach was to measure the degree to which social attitudes might be changing over time as a result of the Communist-promoted cultural changes. Survey responses provided data for comparing the social orientations of the different generations within the interview sample.[14] A basic assumption behind the design of the survey instrument was that as a culture changes certain types of attitudes change more rapidly than others. In particular, we anticipated that attitudes toward authority and interpersonal trust would change less readily than more superficial "value" attitudes which are only a reflection of underlying personality needs.

As an example, we found that a basic need for a strong source of authority might be met through the Confucian tradition, by participation in Christian religious activities, or through acceptance of Communist Party (or Chairman Mao's) leadership. A Chinese who accepted Christianity or Chairman Mao's leadership was a

12. The attitude survey was administered to several hundred Chinese university and high school students in Taiwan and Hong Kong. As no significant variations in attitude related to the interpretations developed here were noted in these groups, the data have not been incorporated into this study.

13. A translation of the attitude survey (modified to be suitable for American respondents) was administered to a sample of 269 American student and adult males. Data from this study have been presented in the author's article, "Mao's Effort to Reintegrate the Chinese Polity," in Barnett, ed., *Chinese Communist Politics in Action.*

14. The generational differences discovered in this study are discussed in detail in *ibid.* As they were not found to be directly relevant to the interpretations developed in this book, they have not been stressed here.

"different" man from his Confucian predecessor; yet it would be our interpretation that the manner in which he responded to authority, or utilized the authoritative writings of these religious or political movements, might be quite similar to that of a "traditional" Chinese.[15]

In order to validate attitude survey responses given by the persons interviewed, we allowed for a period of questioning as to why particular responses to individual survey items had been given. It was found that in explaining their reasons for evaluating a particular question as they had, the respondents provided rich additional information on their social attitudes. Hence, these elaborations were also recorded.

In developing the outline of the general interview, the biographical schedule, and the attitude survey instrument, items and questions were first worked up in English, then translated and pretested with the help of Chinese in both Taiwan and Hong Kong.

To explore in greater depth respondents' attitudes toward authority, their handling of feelings of aggression, and responses to situations of interpersonal conflict, two psychological projective tests were incorporated into the interview procedure: the standard Rorschach Test, and a set of nine Thematic Apperception Test (TAT) cards especially designed to analyze attitudes toward conflict and relations with authority.[16] These research techniques are designed to encourage an individual to reveal or "project" his inner thoughts and feelings. It is assumed that in interpreting the social situations described in the TAT pictures, or the highly ambiguous Rorschach ink-blots, a respondent structures his interpretations and projects his emotional concerns in a way which reveals basic aspects of his personality and world view.[17] As Henry A. Murray, the developer of the TAT technique, has suggested, the interviewee, in

15. This distinction between personality needs and manifest values is drawn from Henry A. Murray, *et al., Explorations in Personality* (New York: Oxford University Press, 1938); David C. McClelland, *The Achieving Society* (Princeton, N.J.: Van Nostrand, 1961); from the study by T. W. Adorno, *et al., The Authoritarian Personality* (New York: Harper, 1950); and from the methodological critique of the Adorno research, Richard Christie and Marie Jahoda, eds., *Studies in the Scope and Method of "The Authoritarian Personality"* (Glencoe: The Free Press, 1954). These studies, and the work by Daniel J. Lerner, *The Passing of Traditional Society* (Glencoe: The Free Press, 1958) provided much of the methodological inspiration for this research.

16. The TAT pictures designed for this study are reproduced in Appendix IV, pp. 538–540.

17. A discussion of the assumptions underlying the Rorschach Test procedure, and interpretive guidelines, will be found in Bruno Klopfer, *et al., Developments in the Rorschach Technique* (2 vols., Yonkers-on-Hudson, New York: World Book Co., 1954–1956).

creating a story in response to the test picture, "expose[s] his own personality, wishes, fears and traces of past experiences."[18] Responses to these psychological tests were analyzed by a trained psychologist who had had a decade of clinical experience.

The TAT cards were also administered to a group of American respondents to test the degree to which this technique was measuring cultural differences. Quantified analysis of these cultural differences has been presented elsewhere.[19]

The Interview Sequence. Each respondent was interviewed on three occasions, each session lasting about three hours. All three sessions, with few exceptions, were held within a period of one or two weeks.

Of the total of 91 interviews, approximately one-third were conducted by the author, without an interpreter. About half the interviews, those with the older and middle-aged respondents, were carried out on Taiwan by two Chinese female social workers, in their 20s, who had been trained to use the interview procedures. The remaining interviews, conducted in Hong Kong with young student emigrés from the mainland, were carried out by a college-educated Chinese female in her 30s, herself an emigré. Female interviewers were found to be particularly effective in gaining the confidence of the respondents.

Before coming to the first interview, each respondent had been asked by a Chinese contact person if he was willing to participate in a study of Chinese social customs and habits sponsored by an American academic. There were two refusals. Each respondent was paid a nominal fee for his time and the transportation costs of coming to the interview sessions.

The first interview began with filling in the biographical schedule and was largely taken up with open-ended questioning about early family life. The last half-hour of the session was devoted to the attitude survey. At the end of the session the interviewee was asked if he would return a second time and was told he would be given an opportunity to elaborate upon the responses he had just given to the survey.

The second session began with the survey response elaborations, and continued with the open-ended questioning on social attitudes. The concluding forty-five minutes to one hour were spent in administration of the TAT test.

By the third session a degree of rapport usually had been established between the interviewer and respondent, and most of this

18. Henry A. Murray, *et al., Explorations in Personality,* p. 531.
19. *See* Richard H. Solomon, "Mao's Effort to Reintegrate the Chinese Polity," in Barnett, ed., *Chinese Communist Politics in Action,* pp. 271–361.

final session was devoted to concluding the open-ended questioning about social and political attitudes. The last hour of the sequence was given to administering the Rorschach Test.[20] In some cases where a respondent had had experiences of particular interest to the objectives of this study, he was invited to return for an additional session.

The five basic interviewing tools developed for this study provided an effective mixture of procedures for exploring each respondent's social orientation. The variety of approaches appeared to give each individual the opportunity to put forward and elaborate upon his own personal concerns and points of view; yet his responses were sufficiently structured to enable us to test our hypotheses through aggregate data analysis.

The interview data were recorded by hand in Chinese during the interviews (except for those conducted by the author, in which responses were recorded in English translation), and later typed into a permanent record on a Chinese typewriter. The biographical and attitude survey data and responses to the open-ended questions were then coded by a team of analysts and punched on data cards for processing by computer. The TAT responses were coded by a trained psychologist according to a variety of standard and special coding systems, with the codes put on data cards for further computer analysis. These data form the base of information for the first two parts of this study.

The Interview Sample. There are obviously basic difficulties in attempting to do interview research on a society inaccessible to direct observation. Interviews with emigrés always carry the danger of biases because, for a variety of personal reasons, these people have left the society.[21] As is discussed in the next section of this

20. The Rorschach Test materials are not directly relevant to the interpretations of this study and will be handled separately in another publication.

21. In practice, our experience with emigré interviews was much like that of Soviet scholars who worked with emigrés in Europe: Despite the various —and usually very personal, not ideological—reasons why the subjects had emigrated, interviews revealed many positive attitudes toward the country the individuals had left. This seems to be a manifestation of strongly ambivalent feelings about leaving one's native society (*See* Alex Inkeles and Raymond A. Bauer, *The Soviet Citizen* [Cambridge, Massachusetts: Harvard University Press, 1959], pp. 41–64).

In the case of the Chinese emigrés interviewed for this study, the older respondents—many of whom had been closely identified with the Nationalists—were more ideological in their criticism of the Communists; yet they frequently expressed grudging admiration for the unity and national power which China had reacquired under Mao's leadership. The young students, mostly of "bourgeois" background, tended to be bitter about life on the

chapter, a number of perspectives have been adopted in interpreting the interview data in order to minimize biases. In constructing the emigré sample to begin with, however, certain procedures were used in selecting respondents to reduce biases in the data gathered.

In order to check for distortions related to place of interview, respondents were located in both Taiwan and in Hong Kong, through a variety of agencies—a Chinese cultural association, an old people's club, educational organizations, and a refugee resettlement agency. By comparing responses given in various locations, and by people referred to us by different organizations, we were able to check for biases which might be associated with the immediate political environment. In one case an interviewee appeared to have been "planted" by a government agency to test the intentions of the author. His interview has not been included in the sample. In general, the questions and procedures were not seen as politically sensitive by the persons interviewed. Indeed, in a completely unanticipated manner, several respondents to whom the author talked in Taiwan were surprisingly critical of the Nationalist government. Apparently the focus of the interviews on family life and social relations, and the physical context in which the interviews were conducted—a mental health center in a public hospital complex—were quite enough to put the respondents at ease.

The fact that a number of interviewers gathered data gave additional opportunity to check for biases which might have been introduced by the use of male and female interviewers, or by the different personalities doing the interviewing. No observable distortions were found in this regard. The respondents seemed anxious to explain their views on Chinese society and culture to an interested foreigner; and the female interviewers were found to be particularly effective in drawing out the more elderly respondents.

Four major criteria—sex, age, place of origin, and level of education—were selected in constructing the sample. Because until recently direct participation in political and social activity has been limited almost exclusively to males in Chinese society, it was decided to exclude females from the interview sample. Given the additional limitations of time and financial resources, the total sample had to be modest in size. The use of respondents of only one sex facilitated intergroup comparisons according to age, place of origin, and educational experience.

---

mainland because they had been singled out for discriminatory treatment because of their "bad" class origins. Their criticism was not so much of the system, but of the fact that they had not been allowed to participate in the process of national development in a manner commensurate with what they felt were their intellectual skills.

A major objective in this study was to acquire "baseline" data on social attitudes from Chinese who had received a traditional up-bringing before the revolutionary turmoil of the twentieth century. By comparing their attitudes with those of middle-aged and younger generational groups, we hoped to test for changes in social orientation which might have developed over more than a half-century of social change. Hence we conceived an interview sample structured into three generational groups: an older and more traditional group aged 55 and above; a middle-aged group between 30 and 54; and then a younger generational group, between the ages of 20 and 29, which had been exposed to some education under the Communists. As Table I indicates, we were largely able to meet this criterion of generational grouping.

To avoid response biases related to regional differences, we attempted to select interviewees with a broad range of provincial backgrounds, and avoid overreliance on Chinese from major urban areas who had been strongly exposed to foreign influence. In Table I we summarize the provinces of birth of the interview sample. As the data reveal, in the sample finally gathered there is particular emphasis on respondents from the coastal provinces of central and south China. Apparently people from these areas have greater social mobility, and Nationalist support is stronger in east China. Among the younger generation the preponderance were from Kwangtung Province, bordering on Hong Kong. This is largely a reflection of the difficulties Chinese face in gaining formal permission from the government of the People's Republic to emigrate. Many of the interviewees, particularly those of middle and younger years, left the mainland illegally during the crisis of food production and political control of 1961–62.

While we were able to select interviewees from a variety of provinces and native places—farming villages, county towns, and major cities—the sample does not have the geographical balance that we would have preferred. Analysis of responses according to the range of provincial origins in the sample, however, does not reveal any strong trend or bias in attitude associated with region. A respondent's generation and sibling position within the family seem to be the major variables which account for the differences in social attitude observable in this sample.

The interview techniques necessitated the adoption of a basic educational criterion of minimal literacy. Respondents had to be able to read the attitude survey and be sufficiently articulate to respond to the open-ended interview procedures. Thus all the interviewees were functionally literate. Beyond this basic criterion,

TABLE I:

INTERVIEW SAMPLE BY REGION AND PROVINCE OF BIRTH

PLACE OF BIRTH		AGE GROUP				
Region	*Province*	20–29	30–54	55–85	PROVINCIAL SUBTOTAL	REGIONAL TOTAL
NORTHEAST	Heilungkiang		1		1	
CHINA	Kirin			1	1	
	Liaoning		1	2	3	
						5
NORTH &	Hopeh		1	6	7	
NORTHWEST	Shansi			1	1	
CHINA	Shensi					
	Kansu					
						8
CENTRAL	Honan		2		2	
CHINA	Hopeh			2	2	
	Hunan	2	1	4	7	
						11
EAST CHINA	Shantung		4	3	7	
	Kiangsu	6	3	3	12	
	Anhwei		3	2	5	
	Chekiang	1	2	1	4	
	Kiangsi		1	4	5	
	Fukien	3	1	2	6	
						39
SOUTH CHINA	Kwangtung	12	8	2	22	
	Kwangsi	1	2		3	
						25
SOUTHWEST	Szechwan	1		1	2	
CHINA	Kweichow					
	Yunnan		1		1	
						3
	AGE GROUP SUBTOTALS	26	31	34		91

however, there was a range of education experiences and levels within the sample. One-third of the respondents had not graduated from high school; another third had a high school degree, or the equivalent in trade school education; and the final third had gone to college or had received military education above the high school level. We selected interviewees in the 20–29 age group from those who had had at least one year of formal education under the Communists; and respondents over the age of 54 were selected if they had had traditional education in the Confucian classics in a family or clan school.

In addition to these characteristics of the sample according to sex, age group, geographical origin, and educational background, analysis revealed that the respondents had had a variety of occupational experiences. There were few "pure" peasants; and approximately half the respondents had had some exposure to military life during the war against Japan. There was also a range of what might be termed "urban" occupations ranging from school teachers and merchants to lawyers and government employees.

In terms of economic class background, the respondents were largely from families of the middle to upper income levels of Chinese society.

The upper limit of the sample size was dictated by considerations of time and financial restrictions. The lower limit was set by our objective of selecting a group large enough to permit some statistical analyses of generational and other differences. Obviously gathering by random selection a sample large enough to represent a reliable cross-section of 700,000,000 Chinese was impossible. Yet within the limits of having to build a structured emigré sample over a year of research, it was possible to select 91 individuals who conformed rather closely to the criteria just discussed. And when interpretations developed from this moderate-sized emigré sample are tested against data derived from a variety of other independent sources, there is sufficient convergence to strengthen the major interpretive hypotheses developed in this study.

A number of general remarks should be made about this sample. This group of respondents represents the social base of semiurbanized or urbanized, literate, middle to upper income level Chinese from coastal provinces from which the Nationalist movement drew its support.[22] About one-third of the respondents had been associated with the Nationalist government either directly through participation in governmental or military activities or through family members associated with the former Nanking government. The majority of the remaining respondents' social backgrounds are similar to those with more direct ties to the Nationalists.

Given the particular characteristics of our interview sample, the social and political attitudes explored in the first two parts of this book represent the cultural orientation of that "bourgeois" element of Chinese society which Mao has struggled against most of his life.

22. An analysis of the social background characteristics of the Nationalist elite will be found in Robert C. North, *Kuomintang and Chinese Communist Elites* (Stanford, California: Hoover Institute, 1952).

During the Cultural Revolution Mao asserted that the need for another revolutionary upheaval after two decades of Communist Party rule reflected a continuation of the Party's struggle against the Kuomintang.[23] By this he meant that the style of politics which the Party had fought through long years of civil war was reasserting itself in the social values and behavior of Party and governmental cadres. In this regard, the interview sample—while not necessarily representative of Chinese society as a whole—helps to define the social orientation which Mao is seeking to overcome.

The one major group of Chinese society which this sample does not contain is the "poor and blank," illiterate, and, until recently, socially unmobilized peasantry who form the bulk of China's population. Thus we cannot make direct observations about the relationship between Mao Tse-tung's evolving style of political leadership and the attitudes of the peasants whom Mao and the Party eventually had to make the "main force" of their proletarian revolution. It is worthy of note, however, that there is a high degree of "fit" between Mao's notion of the leadership process needed to mobilize peasants into the ranks of the revolution, and the social attitudes of our "bourgeois" respondents. This finding strengthens our belief that despite differences in the level of consciousness and sophistication with which cultural attitudes are held by people of varying educational levels, and the differences in "interest" associated with economic class and social status, there is a shared core of culture and personality common to those reared within a social tradition like China's, which was stable for many generations.

SOME INTERPRETIVE PERSPECTIVES

Past efforts to interpret the relationships linking individual personality, group processes, and politics have raised as many questions as they appear to have answered. Certain authors have given evidence of a lack of conceptual clarity, or have been imprecise in delimiting the scope of their assertions. Basically, however, the precise nature of personality remains an issue of considerable debate, and the interrelationship between individual behavior and group processes is an even more elusive subject.[24] Our point of view

23. *See* one of Mao's "latest directives," translated in *Peking Review*, No. 19 (May 10, 1968), p. 2.

24. Among the literature which has attempted to develop the level of conceptual clarity in personality and politics studies, I have found particularly useful Nathan Leites, "Psycho-Cultural Hypotheses about Political Acts," *World Politics*, Vol. I (1948), pp. 102–119, and Fred I. Greenstein, *et al.*, "Personality and Politics: Theoretical and Methodological Issues," *Journal of Social Issues*, Vol. XXIV, No. 3 (July 1968).

on some of these issues might be briefly stated for the interested reader.

The Reliability of the Interview Data. The question of data reliability in this study is essentially a matter of the extent to which attitudes found in a structured sample of emigré Chinese reflect those of Chinese now on the mainland, or who lived there in generations past. The basic test of reliability used here has been whether our interview data are supported by a variety of independent sources of information about Chinese social attitudes and behavioral patterns. Thus we have drawn upon the field studies of anthropologists and sociologists, the memoirs of foreign travelers who observed life in imperial China, and a variety of Chinese documentary sources ranging from formal writings of the Confucian tradition to newspapers of the People's Republic. The interpretations advanced here, in our judgment, are supported by these varied materials.

The Validity of Attitude and Behavioral Data Gathered Through Interviews. Data validity in this analysis is a question of the relevance of attitudes expressed in the interviews to behavioral situations in the "real" context of Chinese society. Do respondents' assertions of personal value or behavioral predisposition provide a valid guide to the behavior of those who live on the mainland? Here our measure of validity relies on the same test of convergence used in estimating reliability. We assume our data to be valid when we note observations of the same value orientations and behavioral styles revealed in the interviews in mainland press materials or in the field notes of anthropologists.

One of the more gratifying aspects of this research has been the discovery of a close relationship between attitudes discussed by the interviewees and the political style which Mao Tse-tung evolved to oppose the "reactionary" aspects of China's traditional culture. As one example, interview and social data reveal weak communication linkages between superior and subordinate. Mao has attempted to institutionalize new patterns of communication between the Party and people, and among "lateral" social groupings, in order to overcome traditional weaknesses in social integration.[25]

Reducing Everything to Psychological Causes? In a study such as this which focuses on personal attitudes, there is a tendency to overstress the importance of the psychological dimensions of political action. While such an emphasis could be found equally well in a study of economics or history, some might assume that the

25. This interpretation is developed in the author's article, "Communication Patterns and the Chinese Revolution," *The China Quarterly,* No. 32 (October–December 1967), pp. 88–110.

author sees only psychological factors as relevant to understanding social processes. The environment, however, is a major factor in shaping action, for to varying degrees it "pressures" the individual to respond in certain ways regardless of his personal desires.

The second half of this book is an attempt to place the aspects of Chinese culture and personality explored in the first two parts in the context of larger historical and political events. More specifically, we try to develop a sense of the interplay between one man's personality and the development of the leadership style of a political movement. The chapters which deal with Mao Tse-tung's efforts to institutionalize his conception of a new political process for China against increasing resistance from other Party leaders, reveal with particular clarity the value of personality analysis in political research. To the extent that a man acquires power, he gains the opportunity to promote solutions to social problems which reflect his own personality. Mao's stature as leader of the Chinese Communist Party has given him this opportunity; and we would hold that the great events of Chinese domestic politics of the past two decades —the "Hundred Flowers" movement, the "Great Leap Forward," and the "Great Proletarian Cultural Revolution"—cannot be explained satisfactorily without reference to Mao's personality.

From another perspective, the increasing tensions within the Chinese Communist Party which finally burst forth into the Cultural Revolution reveal the usefulness of a culture and personality approach to political analysis. While policy differences were important factors contributing to the growing split within the Party leadership during the decade 1955–1964, Cultural Revolution documents have revealed that the ultimate breakdown within the leadership was closely related to basic differences in personal leadership style. Mao Tse-tung was unyielding in his belief that only his conception of a new Party "work style" could bring about China's modernization. Yet other leaders and the Party apparatus would not, or could not, use power in the ways that he prescribed. Mao was "fighting the system" in the sense of trying to bring about a radical change in political processes. These changes were not being sustained by the millions of Chinese who participated in the organizational life of Party and state.

One student of the organizational transformations promoted by the Chinese Communists over the past two decades has seen "the resurgence of the forces of Chinese society" in the form of pressures by China's major social groups on the Party's ideology and organization.[26] In other words, despite alterations in institutional

26. Franz Schurmann, *Ideology and Organization in Communist China* (Berkeley: University of California Press, 1968 revised edition), p. 504.

framework, even Party and governmental cadres have gradually modified China's "Communist" political system to conform more closely to their "Chinese" personalities. It was Mao's reaction to this development which led him to see the need for a "Cultural Revolution" against China's "four olds."

Unchanging China? These assertions of the endurance of China's cultural system and social orientation in a sense are "pessimistic," for they imply (and we think rightly) that efforts to bring about social change through organizational transformation will be resisted to the extent that the organizational forms conflict with widely held personal needs. Such a view is perhaps overstressed in this study, only in part because we see Mao so concerned about traditional values and patterns of behavior, and partly because in the first two sections we explore what is termed China's "traditional" social orientation.

To no small degree, however, our use of the term "traditional" is a notational convenience. How might one more easily characterize the attitudes of those elderly Chinese in our interview sample who were educated before the fall of the Ch'ing dynasty? Although these individuals in many respects are "transitional" men, living out their lives in a changing society, we find their social attitudes to be strikingly congruent with those stressed in classical Confucian texts.

Our use of the term "traditional," however, is not intended to slight the evolution of China's historical institutions, or to imply that there has been no change in recent times. "Tradition" is not necessarily an unchanging past. The question is what exactly has changed? On the basis of the limited data which would enable us to gauge the continuity of culture and personality style over the centuries, we would concur with those historians who suggest that change in China—in a society which for thousands of years has been rooted in the stable life style of a peasant social economy—has been a matter of "change within tradition." [27] Institutions have evolved, culture has been modified by the foreign influence of invading nomadic tribes. Yet the "tradition," the basic cultural logic and the personalities shaped by the learning of China's social legacy have shown remarkable continuity over time.

We do not imply that the Chinese are fated to bear the burden of an ancient way of life in a changing world. Our basic assumption of the importance of the socialization experience in shaping personality means that the focus of change will be in the new attitudes and styles of behavior developed in future generations. It should

27. John K. Fairbank, Edwin O. Reischauer, and Albert M. Craig, *East Asia: The Modern Transformation* (Boston: Houghton Mifflin, 1965), p. 5.

be recalled that the men now in positions of political leadership in China were born at the end of the imperial era. Their socialization experiences had only begun to reflect the impact of new values. And those more recent generations for whom the educational experience was significantly altered are only beginning to make their impact felt on China's political and social life.

The foreign observer cannot readily see exactly what changes have come about in the socialization process during the last twenty years of Party rule, and what alterations in social orientation have been produced by a Communist education. As the Cultural Revolution conflict has revealed, there have been strong divisions of opinion within the Party leadership about the educational process. Mao Tse-tung developed doubts that the Party was rearing a younger generation who would be "revolutionary successors," committed to realizing the goals that the Party has not yet attained. And in the Cultural Revolution conflict Mao was to find the Red Guards less than model students of his "thought."

Two points are worth stressing, however. First, when Mao Tse-tung decided to promote his Cultural Revolution, he turned for support to the student generation. Presumably they had been liberated to some degree from the cultural inheritance which Mao saw as still burdening their elders. A second and related point is that a more meaningful time framework for evaluating social change is not the passing of solar years, but rather generational time. It is only as new generations with significantly altered socialization experiences acquire political influence that enduring change will come about.

Unique China? From the stress which this analysis gives to the importance of culture and socialization experience, some may see an implication of Chinese uniqueness. Such an impression is perhaps reinforced by Chinese assertions of the distinctiveness of their own cultural tradition. Our own view is that many areas of social experience, perception, and emotional concern transcend cultural boundaries. However, a culture imparts differences in emphasis to certain emotions, attitudes, and behavioral patterns.

These conflicting perspectives seem best resolved by the view that despite the many areas of common experience and social perception which Chinese share with other people, the total configuration or "mix" of social context, cultural inheritance, and personal orientation gives China's social life a distinctiveness which has been the subject of comment by generations of foreign visitors.

There is much in China's cultural pattern which draws its meaning from the qualities of peasant life which are common to other agrarian societies. As one anthropologist has suggested, food gathering cultures tend to stress attitudes of dependency in their children in order to preserve the integrity of the family group, the organizational guarantor of individual security.[28] Despite this common cultural base which China shares with other peasant societies, however, there is a degree of elaboration to the values of rural life in her traditions which reflects the centuries of vital intellectual life sustained by the material resources of a productive peasant economy.

Any foreigner who has lived and worked in a Chinese social context knows by personal experience the cultural differences in the way conflicts are handled, authority is invoked, and emotions disciplined. For decades Westerners referred to "oriental inscrutability," which was only a way of saying that their own cultural inheritance had not prepared them to "read the signals" of interpersonal relations in Chinese society.[29] The Soviet technicians who worked in China during the 1950s described the Chinese as "vacuum bottles." Unprepared by Russian traditions, which sanction emotional expressiveness, they were unable to sense from external appearances whether "what was on the inside was hot or cold." [30]

Such expressions of cultural difference are usually damned or described as quaint from the observer's perspective. We have tried, however, to approach the distinctive structure of social values and personality configuration in Chinese political life from a Chinese or at least a neutral perspective.

All Chinese Are Alike? In contrast to the view of Chinese uniqueness, some critics of culture and personality analysis see a denial of individual differences in the effort to define that which is shared. The absurdity of such an objection is revealed in large measure by the variations in personal style which are evident in our interview data.

Such an objection is usefully confronted by turning the proposition around. "All Chinese are different." Is there nothing which they have in common? Unless one believes that all generalizations about human social life, or history, are invalid—which we do not—the question is in what respects are Chinese alike, and in what ways is

28. Eric R. Wolf, *Peasants* (Englewood Cliffs, New Jersey: Prentice-Hall, 1966), p. 69.

29. One of the more extreme interpretations of Chinese cultural patterns with a foreign bias is Arthur Smith's *Chinese Characteristics* (New York: Fleming Revell, 1894). For a discerning analysis of changing Western interpretations of the Chinese, see Harold R. Isaacs, *Scratches on Our Minds: American Images of China and India* (New York: John Day, 1958).

30. This Russian characterization of the Chinese was related to the author by Mikhail A. Klochko, a Soviet chemist who worked in China as an adviser during the 1950s. *See* his book, *Soviet Scientist in Red China* (New York: Praeger, 1964).

their individuality expressed? Such a question, it seems to us, is best answered through empirical research. The analysis in this book is an attempt to define the shared cultural dynamic of China's political life, and to examine Mao Tse-tung's efforts to reshape this ancient social tradition.

Part One

THE TRADITIONAL CHINESE SOCIALIZATION PROCESS

"Old Age," one of a collection
of twenty-four ivory carvings illustrating
the twenty-four exemplary acts of Confucian filial piety.
*Courtesy The Wellcome Institute and
Museum of the History of Medicine, London.*

Chapter II

CONFUCIANISM AND THE CHINESE LIFE CYCLE

The Confucian political order was centered on the notion that the family was the matrix of society's political relations. As is stated in one of the classic texts of this traditionally dominant social philosophy, "The filial piety with which the superior man serves his parents may be transferred as loyalty to the ruler; the fraternal duty with which he serves his elder brother may be transferred as submissive deference to elders; [and] his regulation of his family may be transferred as good government in any official position." [1] Thus, proper political leadership remained rooted in its original social context: "The ruler, without going beyond the family, completes the lessons for the state"[2]; and, "wishing to order well his state, he first regulates his family." [3]

As our analysis will elaborate, there were compelling emotional reasons why the Chinese political tradition was tenaciously linked to its familistic root—why the emperor was seen as "the Son of Heaven" and why local functionaries were termed "father-mother" officials. And for equally cogent reasons the Western political tradition has tended to ignore its roots in family life, to "forget" that an individual's conception of social authority and of the processes which mediate relations between the powerful and the subordinate were first learned within the family.

As cultural contrast can be particularly revealing of a society's habits, we begin by observing how two different social traditions have attempted to solve the difficulties of relations between the weak

1. *Hsiao Ching* [Classic of Filial Piety], trans. James Legge, in Max F. Müller, ed., *Sacred Books of the East* (50 vols., Oxford, England: Clarendon Press, 1879–1910), Vol. III, p. 483.

2. *The Great Learning,* "Commentary of the Philosopher Tsang," in *The Chinese Classics,* trans. James Legge (5 vols., Shanghai: 1935), Vol. I, p. 370.

3. Paraphrased from Section 4 of the "Text of Confucius" in *ibid.,* p. 357.

and strong through an institutional patterning of the human life cycle. Thus, while the political route to Paris may be by way of Peking, an understanding of the politics of China may begin in Greece, by a reconsideration of one of the more revealing social "myths" of Western civilization.

OEDIPUS WAS AN UNFILIAL SON

All cultural traditions express the collective hopes and concerns of their people through artistic or literary communication, thus helping to bind a society together through the sharing of life's frustrations and triumphs. Artistic works provide the social analyst with concentrated statements of a society's particular concerns and the ways in which they have been managed. One example is the Greek drama of King Oedipus, who killed his father and married his mother. In recent times the Oedipal myth has acquired connotations for understanding the emotional life of the Western family that we will consider shortly. But in keeping with our interest in relating a society's political style to roots in the training of its children, it is important to recall that the myth of Oedipus at first reading is more a story of politics than of family life or individual tragedy.

Concerned as Westerners are with the plight of the individual we may forget the problem faced by Oedipus' parents, Laius and Jocasta, who were the political rulers of Thebes: In abandoning their "fated" infant son they were trying to deal with the problem of regicide, as well as patricide and incest. Oedipus appeals to the Horatio Alger in us, for he was a "high achiever," a self-made man who, though rejected by his family, used his intelligence to outwit the Sphinx that had terrorized Thebes and thus, by his own determination, rose to great power and fame. But to the Theban people he was, until his fall, a political hero who had freed them from a community scourge.

In mythical terms, the inexorable working out of Oedipus' fate raises serious community and political problems: How is the ruler (Laius) to deal with a subordinate (Oedipus) who would destroy him and enjoy the pleasures that come with great power? How were the Theban people to deal with the paradox of having a leader whom they loved because he had saved them from the Sphinx but who also brought with him compulsions and an arrogant pride which could plague the community and destroy social order? Oedipus, the man of great courage and wisdom, was also the hot-blood who killed a traveler, his father unrecognized, in a conflict over precedence and prestige at a rural cross-road. He was the popular king who brought a plague down on his people because of a fate-driven violation of social taboo.

Consideration of the various institutional solutions developed by the ancient Greeks to deal with these problems of the relation between leader and led would take us far from our central point, which is to stress that even in the root experience of the Western political tradition family and individual problems have been intertwined with the development of political institutions. Oedipus, the tragic ruler of Thebes, was a man who became conscious of the paradoxes inherent in the human life cycle—for this was the riddle of the Sphinx which he solved. And through the solution of this riddle he was led on to conclude the tragedy of his fate. The story of the Theban king, at this individual level of insight, is a metaphorical expression of the Western life cycle, a symbolic representation of the solution worked out by our root culture to the universal "political" problem stemming from the dependent and unsocialized condition of humans at birth.

In dealing with the oracle's prediction of his son's terrible fate, Laius was facing the paradox that the dependent child must be disciplined if he is to become a participating member of society. But the process of socialization, which is the child's first exposure to "politics"—to the relation of the strong who have and the weak who want—will leave a residue of resentment of authority and a desire to "do in" the one who first forced denial or restriction of the pleasures of life. The solution to this paradox which Oedipus' parents chose, the casting out of the family of the ill-fated child, is in symbolic terms the solution worked out by Western culture: The potentially disruptive dependent is "abandoned," or more correctly, "set forth," after a period of disciplining to seek for himself in new social contexts alternative solutions to his life's most original hates and loves.

The story of Oedipus, of course, represents only one aspect of the Greek social tradition which, as with Western culture generally, had to face the concomitant social problems that arise from individuals aggressively seeking to work out their personal problems and pleasures in a world of other striving individuals. Without being diverted into a consideration of the various Western social institutions which have been developed to handle these problems, we must at least make explicit two assumptions which underlie the development of these institutions: First, the individual is the basic "actor" of society and should be trained in childhood to make do on his own, to be self-disciplining and self-directing. From this conviction have developed Western notions about moral equality and equality of social responsibility and political "rights." Second, there is the assumption that potential social conflict should be handled not by repression of the aggressive impulse so much as by providing the individual with alternative behavioral forms through which hostility can be discharged without endangering the larger society.[4]

The Chinese have since early times been concerned with the same problems of resentment of superior by subordinate and of disruptive social conflict which underlie the Oedipus myth. They have sought their own solution to such problems, as we are informed in the opening lines of the Confucian educational text *The Classic of Filial Piety*: "The ancient kings had a perfect virtue and all-embracing rule of conduct, through which they were in accord with all under heaven. By the practice of it the people were brought to live in peace and harmony, and there was no ill-will between superiors and inferiors." [5] A descriptive statement of this "all-embracing rule of conduct," and of the manner in which it shaped the Chinese life cycle, is significantly not found in a drama to stir human emotions but in an educational text to be memorized and to provide models of behavior for China's children. The "mythical" presentation of the ideal of the Confucian life is not the tragedy of one man but the triumph of twenty-four.

The first of the twenty-four models of filial piety is Yu Shun, who, like Oedipus, was rejected by his family. It is not clear what motivated Yu's father and brother to drop him down a well and

4. In this regard it is worth recalling something about the *form* in which the myth of Oedipus was presented, apart from its content. The Greek drama as an art form, Aristotle tells us in his *Poetics,* had the virtue of producing an emotional excitation or release, a catharsis, in the audience; a stimulation, "correction, and refinement" of emotions mobilized during the course of the play through such behavioral forms as laughter in response to comedy, or pity and horror at tragedy. The popularity of works of art like Sophocles' *Oedipus* was based on their ability to strike responsive emotional chords in a large audience. The performance of such plays served a function of social integration through mobilizing and then discharging in socially harmless ways widely shared emotional tensions. Each member of the audience, in "feeling" his (unconsciously held) fantasies and resentments acted out on the stage, had his own inner state of desire for the tragic act "refined" by enhancing his sense of horror or outrage—guilt—at the fantastic event. The result was that the "occurrence" of the act on the stage made the same act less likely to occur in real life.

In the Western social tradition, then, surrogate forms of emotional discharge, or self-discipline through guilt, tend to replace either the direct release of such emotions against their original objects, a total denial of the emotional impulse, or the application of external controls—group pressures or the authority of a superior individual—to regulate individual behavior. As we shall stress later, however, repression of emotional impulses and group controls over individual behavior are predominant in the Chinese social tradition.

5. *Hsiao Ching*, p. 466.

throw stones upon him, or to set fire to a granary when he was inside; we are only told that his father and brother were "stupid" and "conceited." But, unlike Oedipus, who rewarded his rejecting parents with an inexorable, fate-driven vengeance of death and violation of social taboo, Yu continued a life of toil on his family land and returned his parents' rejection with reverence for them and sincerity in his life-long social obligations as a son. His reward was the moral renovation of his family through his own example: "His parents became pleasant, and his brother more conciliatory and virtuous." [6]

A similar tale of determined filial devotion rewarded with parental abuse was the fate of Min Sun of the Chou dynasty. His mother died and his stepmother and father mistreated him, but Min's stoicism and good nature succeeded in maintaining the integrity of his family:

> In all ages men have exhibited a great love for their wives; but dutiful children have often met with unkindness. Min carefully concealed all his grievances, and refused to indulge in any complaint; even while suffering severely from cold and hunger, he maintained his affection unabated. During the long period in which he endured this oppressive treatment, his good disposition became manifest; and by his own conduct he was able to maintain the harmony of the family unimpaired. His father and mother were influenced by his filial devotion; and his brothers joined in extolling his virtues.[7]

The dutiful son thus will not accept his parents' rejection, but bears his personal pain for the greater good of family "harmony." He endures the *externally* imposed sufferings associated with dependency and subordination—as contrasted with Oedipus' *internal* sense of torment born of the terrible truth of his personal guilt—to fulfill the "fated" and life-long obligations of his social role as a son.

Other models of behavior among the twenty-four instruct us that the filial obligation is conceived as a repayment of the debt of parental nurture a son incurs during his childhood years of dependency. He reciprocates with care for his parents when they enter the dependency of old age. Chung Yu, though exhausted, traveled great distances to bring rice to his parents, and Ts'ai Shun spared his widowed mother the anxieties of years of famine and political unrest by gathering berries in distant forests. "[Ming Tsung's] mother was very ill, and one winter's day she longed to taste a soup made of bamboo shoots, but Ming could not procure any. At last he went into the bamboo grove, and clasping the bamboos with his hands, wept bitterly. His filial love moved Nature, and the ground slowly

6. *The Book of Filial Duty,* trans. Ivan Chen (New York: E. P. Dutton, 1909), p. 34.
7. *Ibid.,* p. 38.

opened, sending forth several shoots, which he gathered and carried home. He made a soup of them, which his mother tasted, and immediately recovered from her malady." [8]

More than a third of these exemplars of the Confucian life pattern are sons who endured hardships to feed their mothers and nurture them in sickness, which suggests in its own way the special relationship between mother and son which is mystically described in the tale of Tseng Ts'an: When his mother was anxious, she had only to gnaw her finger. Tseng immediately felt a pain in his heart even at a great distance and came running home to ease her discomfort.

The twenty-four models provide less frequent or vivid instruction on the relationship between father and son, although we do learn that Huang Hsiang of the Han dynasty, "in summer, when the weather was warm . . . fanned and cooled his father's pillow and bed; and in winter, when it was cold . . . warmed the bed-clothes with his body." [9] And when danger threatened, Yang Hsiang risked his life: "Once a tiger seized his father, and was slowly carrying him off, when Yang, anxious for his father and forgetting himself, although he had no iron weapon in his hand, rushed forward and seized the tiger by the neck. The beast let the prey fall from his teeth, and fled, and Yang's father was thus saved from injury and death." [10]

The nature of the relationship between father and son in the Confucian tradition is more fully revealed in the story of Hsüeh Jen-kuei, a traditional tale which is perhaps the Chinese equivalent of the Oedipus myth. (It has been incorporated in the repertory of Peking opera.) Hsüeh, a soldier of fortune of the T'ang period, had risen from humble status to become a high military officer. His martial skills attracted the attention of the emperor, who assigned him to duties on a distant frontier. The tale focuses on his return and reunion with his wife, whom he had not seen since he left her pregnant eighteen years earlier to join the imperial service.

As Hsüeh approaches his home district, he sees a youth skillfully shooting wild geese at the bank of the River Fen. He challenges the boy to a test of marksmanship, claiming that he can shoot two geese with one arrow. When the challenge is accepted, Hsüeh shoots the youthful rival instead of the geese, exclaiming, "I could have spared the boy, but a soldier like me could not let another live if he was a superior in marksmanship with the weapons in which I excel." [11]

8. *Ibid.*, pp. 54–55.
9. *Ibid.*, p. 45.
10. *Ibid.*, pp. 49–50.
11. Quoted from a synopsis of this tale entitled, "At the Bend of the River Fen," in A. C. Scott, *An Introduction to the Chinese Theater* (Singapore: Donald Moore, 1958), p. 63.

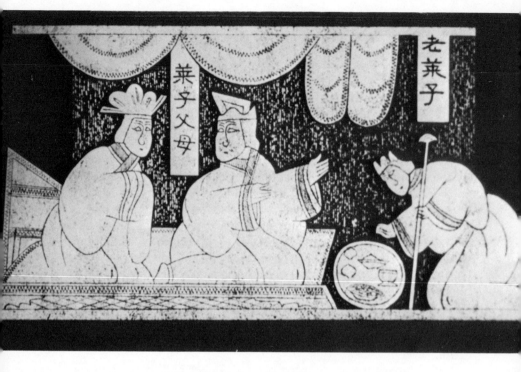

The Confucian exemplar Lao Lai-tzu,
who donned children's clothes and played games
to amuse his aged parents. Adapted from a second-century A.D. (Han
Dynasty) stone engraving.
Courtesy Houghton-Mifflin Company
and John K. Fairbank.

Hsüeh finally reaches home and is reunited with his wife, but he brings with him concern and uncertainty about her fidelity during his long absence. These doubts are increased when he discovers a pair of men's shoes under the family sleeping platform. His wife chides him for his doubts and explains that the shoes belong to his son, who was born shortly after he left home eighteen years before. Hsüeh asks his son's whereabouts, and his wife tells him that he is out hunting. The dénouement is the parents' horrified discovery that Hsüeh has killed his son.

This tale provides a revealing counterpoint to the Oedipus myth: It is Hsüeh the father, not the son, who leaves the family to make his fortune; and, of course, it is the father who kills the son unrecognized in an encounter over prestige. In mythical terms Hsüeh Jen-kuei's actions suggest the father's reluctance to let the son grow to his own maturity; his unwillingness to be challenged by him. Hsüeh's doubts about his wife's fidelity reveal a tension in the father-son relationship born of the particularly intense mother-son tie described in the twenty-four models of filial piety. But the father will not let the son challenge him "with the weapons in which he excels."

The son thus is instructed to remain a son all his life, as is explicitly symbolized in the exemplar Lao Lai-tzu, who in the fullness of his maturity donned children's clothing to amuse his seventy-year-old parents. He culminates a life of service and self-sacrifice for his parents with a vigil at their death which reciprocates the parental birth vigil. This dutiful behavior is also emphasized by Huang T'ing-chien: "When his mother was seized with illness he watched her for a whole year without leaving her bedside or even taking off his clothes; and at her death he himself fell ill and nearly lost his life." [12]

But in spite of Huang's extreme grief at the death of his beloved mother he does not die, for to do so would be unfilial; as the Confucian classic instructs, "Our bodies—to every hair and bit of skin —are received from our parents, and we must not presume to injure or wound them: this is the beginning of filial piety." [13]

Oedipus, we must conclude, by Confucian standards was a most unfilial son; not only because he unknowingly murdered his father and loved his mother, but also in that he mutilated himself. In tearing out his eyes, with which he finally saw the horror of his own guilt, he was violating that rule which Confucius tells us is the beginning of filial piety, the inviolability of the body of life which parents give the child. For by mutilating himself, Oedipus was threatening to break the cyclical Confucian life pattern, through

12. *The Book of Filial Duty*, p. 60.
13. *Hsiao Ching*, p. 466.

which life is given to the group and to its future generations rather than to the individual alone.

Here then, in the symbolic forms of cultural ideals, are expressed two polar extremes in the solution of the fundamental political problem of human life, the tie between dependent son and powerful and disciplining father: In the Western solution the parents perceive the potential for conflict born of childhood dependency and its concomitant process of disciplining. They thus set the matured child on his own to seek in adult life alternative social contexts and behavioral forms for the gratification of his hostile and pleasure-seeking impulses. The Confucian solution, however, rejects the "abandonment" of the source of generational conflict in favor of the greater ends of parental security and the integrity of the family group. The son is to realize his social identity in a life-long prolongation of his original state of dependency.[14] The original objects

14. While the son of a Chinese family was reared to remain with his parents, this was not the case with a female child. Indeed, in several respects a Chinese daughter was the "Oedipus" of her family. It will be recalled that as Oedipus was abandoned, his feet were pierced by the shepherd who was to leave him on a mountainside; hence his name, "Oedipus" or "wounded foot." The daughter of a Chinese family was quite literally, like Oedipus, sent forth from her parents with wounded feet, the painfully acquired "golden lilies" or bound feet which, according to traditional conceptions of feminine beauty, made a young girl more attractive to potential husbands and mothers-in-law. As well, female children in Chinese families, particularly in times of scarcity or famine, were sold or occasionally abandoned directly, reflecting at an extreme the generally low valuation which was placed on female children in the traditional culture.

It will also be recalled that despite his abandonment, Oedipus survived to become a great political leader, but a leader who brought tragedy to his family and a plague upon the people of Thebes. Similarly, the traditional Chinese woman was seen as not only a potentially disruptive influence in the family into which she married, but also a source of great political trouble. The Confucian classics and generations of scholar-officials explicitly warned against the influence of women in politics; and the experience of a series of assertive, powerful and often disruptive female rulers including Lady Wu of the T'ang dynasty, the Empress Dowager Tz'u-hsi of the Ch'ing, and Madame Chiang K'ai-shek and Chiang Ch'ing of the present era, indicates that the Chinese woman had the strength of character to assert herself despite (or perhaps because of) her bound feet and all that this physical mutilation symbolized. (For two very different interpretations of the strength and disruptive influence of women in Chinese society, *see* Lien-sheng Yang, "Female Rulers in Imperial China," *Harvard Journal of Asiatic Studies*, Vol. XXIII [1960–61], pp. 47–61, and Warner Muensterberger, "Orality and Dependence: Characteristics of Southern Chinese," in *Psychoanalysis and the Social Sciences*, Vol. III [1951], esp. pp. 54–65.)

Such equivalences between the mythical Oedipus and Chinese conceptions of the influence of women in their social and political life, we must stress, are meaningful because they reflect certain psychological commonalities in

of discipline and love are retained, but hostility toward the stern father is denied and love for the mother is maintained.[15]

The Confucian life pattern thus is "cyclical," for within the *inter*dependence of the family the son reciprocates the nurturance he receives in his childhood dependency by nurturing his parents in the dependency of their old age. In childhood one depends on one's parents, and in old age on one's children; thus for the filial individual, life comes full circle. The filial son in this sense remains a "son" as long as he lives; he never breaks out of his original social matrix to establish an independent life. But he bears the pain and injustice which tradition tells him is an unavoidable part of childhood because he knows that in time he will become a father while remaining a son; and he can thus look forward to a time when his own son will enable him to enjoy fully the pleasures of dependent old age.

The twenty-four models of filial piety are, of course, an ideal of hope, just as the tragedy of Oedipus is a myth of horror. Such stylized expressions of a culture's anxieties and aspirations are meaningful to the extent that they define in an explicit, if highly simplified, manner certain cultural values and conceptions of life role and social relations. By contrasting these two mythical expressions of the life cycle we have tried not only to make the Western reader more conscious of some of the distinctive aspects of Chinese social life but also to make him aware of certain biases he brings

---

the ways in which female and male children have been reared in these two very different cultural settings. Such myths and cultural stereotypes symbolize in a simplified, artistic manner, an underlying psychological reality, certain aspects of which we will explore in subsequent chapters.

15. Put in more direct terms, there was no "Oedipus complex" in traditional Chinese culture in the sense that this tradition explicitly told a son that it was both proper and morally virtuous for him to love his mother. This was not love in its sexual sense, of course, but love in the same form of oral nurturing by which the mother had loved the son as a child.

Consistent with our interpretation of the daughter as the Chinese "Oedipus" detailed in the previous footnote, the "Oedipus complex" in the Chinese family lay in the oft-observed tension between mother and daughter-in-law. The mother feared, at some level of perception, that her son's wife would detract from the affection which filiality said was her due. And the dreaded harshness of the mother-in-law represents the same rivalry for affection which can give father-son relations their tension in a Western family.

From a daughter-in-law's perspective, this competition for the affection of her husband was sufficiently intense to produce, in some instances, anxieties about her husband in fact violating the incest taboo. As is noted in the autobiography of one Chinese woman: "A girl of our village was married to a man of another village whose relationship with his mother was not a clear one. The young wife came home and wept with her mother." (Ida Pruitt, *A Daughter of Han: The Autobiography of a Chinese Working Woman* [Stanford, Calif.: Stanford University Press, 1967], p. 40.)

to the study of China given his own cultural background, which lays such stress on individual autonomy.

A Chinese viewing the Western life pattern, of course, in similar fashion reveals his own cultural biases. He notes that, "The life of a single individual is . . . incomplete. . . . Life exists in social relationships, and the family is the most fundamental of them by nature. . . . How different this is from the Western style, which makes orphans out of children and . . . lonely people out of parents by having the children live apart from their parents; how different this is from the Western style which values not companionship but separation, and condones an unstable relationship of marriage." [16]

Our task in the following chapters will be to try to go beyond interpretations of China which are based on personal judgments weighted with a Western cultural viewpoint. Rather, we shall try to evaluate, through the eyes of individuals raised in the Confucian tradition, the extent to which the myths of filiality reflect an underlying social reality, and the ways in which Chinese themselves see their society and its continuing social and political revolution.

16. C. K. Yang, *Chinese Communist Society: The Family and the Village* (Cambridge, Mass.: M.I.T. Press, 1965), Vol. I, pp. 166–167.

Chapter III

LIFE'S GOLDEN AGE (?)

The cyclical quality of the Chinese pattern of life suggested by the formal literature of the Confucian tradition finds expression in the attitudes of the Chinese we interviewed. They had few doubts that childhood and the years of youth embodied the happiest period of life. As expressed by a school teacher reared in Peking, childhood "is a golden age. You don't have to worry about anything: if you are hungry your parents give you food; if you need a haircut they give you money. You just have to study well and if there is anything you need they give it to you." [1] From the standpoint of adulthood,

1. T-9. Brief biographical sketches of the interview respondents, who are identified in the footnotes by place of interview—"T" for Taiwan, and "H" for Hong Kong—and case number, will be found in Appendix V, pp. 541–558 below.

Approximately 65 percent of our interviewees identified childhood as a happier time of life than adulthood; 15 to 20 percent saw adulthood as the happier time; and the remainder were undecided. This question about the more satisfying period of the life cycle is related to the social dislocations experienced by emigrés, who must have looked back with a degree of longing to the security of their early lives. For example, 75 percent of the thirty-one respondents in the 30–55 age group, all refugees only recently arrived from the mainland, saw childhood as the happier time of life, with few "undecided" responses. Only 56 percent of the thirty-four older refugees in the 56–85 age group, men who had been settled on Taiwan for more than a decade, saw childhood as the happier period.

It would be misleading, however, to attribute this response pattern merely to the immediate problems of being an emigré. In part the emphasis on childhood seems to reflect the bewilderments and tension of social change. Of those eighteen respondents who saw both their own social outlook and the outlook of their father as "traditional" (*shou-chiu*), 78 percent saw childhood as the happier time of life, while 91 percent of the eleven who were unable to define either their own social outlook or that of their father as either "traditional" or "modern" saw childhood as the happier time. Only 59 percent of the seventeen respondents who saw consistency between their own and their father's "modern" (*hsien-tai-hua*) outlook on life identified with childhood. This sample suggests both that these individuals had less emotional need to cling to the security of childhood and that adulthood, the attraction of the early years of life is partly the condition of having one's desire for food and other material needs effortlessly gratified. It is also a time when one is screened from the complications of life behind the high walls of the family compound and through the intercession of nurturing adults:

> Youth years are happier than adulthood because you don't know or understand anything. All you do is play; you are without worries. When you become an adult then there are problems about studying, marriage, and your working future. These all can get you bothered. I think that life up until you are twenty is a relatively happier time. After you are thirty your superiors make trouble for you; and if you do not manage interpersonal relations well you can provoke people's hatred, so it is very annoying.[2]

This idealization of childhood as a time of "tranquillity" finds expression in China's ancient philosophical traditions.[3] The reasons for this desire to find pleasure and security by being cared for by others becomes evident when seen against a complex background

---

with its greater opportunities for self-realization, is seen by those striving after modernization as life's most significant period.

Our basic interpretation, however, remains that the strong appeal of childhood for the respondents taken as a group reflects a general cultural identification with the security and forms of nurturance and pleasure known most fully in the first years of life. We find no significant variation in this attitude orientation when the sample of respondents is considered in terms of geographical origin within China, socioeconomic status, or educational level.

Cross-cultural comparison is useful here for underlining the distinctive aspect of this orientation toward the life cycle. A group of 225 male American students from two midwestern colleges, and thirty-nine male adults of white-collar occupations from a Detroit suburb, were asked whether childhood or adulthood was the happier time of life. The students were about evenly divided (45 percent "childhood"; 52 percent "adulthood"; the remainder undecided), while the adults had "shifted" in the direction of seeing adulthood as the happier time of life (74 percent). What these data suggest is that a middle-class American, after wrestling with the identity problems associated with a culture that stresses individual autonomy, is able to find a meaningful life and personal fulfillment in a professional career and through the creation of his own family. The Chinese, however, continues to see his identity linked to the life of his original family, and longs for a return to that condition where he was cared for by others. (These comparative data are discussed in more detail in the author's article, "Mao's Effort to Reintegrate the Chinese Polity: Problems of Conflict and Authority in Chinese Social Processes," in A. Doak Barnett, ed., *Chinese Communist Politics in Action* [Seattle: University of Washington Press, 1968], pp. 276–280.)

2. T-49.

3. *See* Donald J. Munro, *The Concept of Man in Early China* (Stanford: Stanford University Press, 1968), Ch. 7.

of the social maturation process experienced by a child as he develops, and the world he knows as an adult. The focus of this chapter is on a description of the way in which the Chinese reared their children, and of the basic social attitudes and patterns of interpersonal relations which they inculcated for getting along in the adult world.

THE INDULGENCE OF INFANCY

Memories of the first several years of life are, for all people, embodied in a diffuse sense of trust and well-being or mistrust and foreboding of some unforeseen calamity or evil, rather than in specific and sharply recalled incidents. Hence we must seek understanding of the events of these infant years through the field notes of the cultural anthropologist or the attitudes of adult Chinese about the proper way to rear children. In particular, some insight into how Chinese children are welcomed into life and educated to appreciate its pleasures and deal with its dangers can be gained by looking at the manner in which parents take care of an infant's bodily and emotional needs and at how adults anticipate children fitting into the social economy of their lives.

The birth of a child, especially a male, is cause for much satisfaction and celebration in a Chinese household. The mother has affirmed her generative competence and fulfilled her social role as a daughter-in-law. The father at last graduates from being a mere son to one who has added a new generation to the family line and can now face his eventual old age with a greater sense of security. Grandparents, as well, delight at the addition to the family of a new life with whom they can share the dependent leisure of their final years.

But this time of joy can also be an occasion for anxiety in a society with a high incidence of infant mortality. In rural Taiwan, when a child dies his coffin is struck in "anger" before burial. Says a villager in explanation:

> When you have a child you want him to take care of you when you are old and bury you when you die, but it is just the opposite when you have to bury him. It is because you are mad at him because he failed you [that you strike his coffin]. He wasn't really coming to be your child but just to waste your money. Also, people say that if you don't hit the child, the King of Hell will hit him as punishment for deserting his parents. If you don't hit him someone else will, so you might just as well hit him yourself.[4]

4. Reported in Margery Wolf, "Child Training in a Hokkien Village," (mimeographed; a paper prepared for a seminar on "Personality and Motiva-

Parental anxieties about survival of their offspring find expression in oral indulgence, for liberal feeding is about the only recourse beyond prayer that exists for a people with premodern notions about medicine and hygiene. In nursing, the breast is given to the child on demand by the mother or, in wealthy families, by a wet nurse. Weaning is abrupt, but takes place quite late, between one and two years according to most observations. The best morsels of food are frequently given to the youngest child, and many of our interviewees' most glowing recollection of parental love was of the mother who showed special favor through her cooking. A "proper" Chinese baby is one so plump with nourishment that there can be no doubt about his good health—or of his parents' concern that he survive infancy and grow up to take care of them when they return, in old age, to a similar state of dependency.

The considerable indulgence accorded a male child in infancy and early childhood, affection expressed above all through the giving of food, seems to be the basis of an "oral" calculus in the way that Chinese approach interpersonal relations throughout life. The reckoning of their family or population size in terms of "mouths" (*jen-k'ou*) rather than "heads," and the emphasis on eating which has produced one of the world's great culinary traditions, are only part of a view of life in which oral forms of pleasure and pain predominate.[5] Some of these forms might be noted here, not only because this oral calculus is obvious in our interview responses, but also because in important ways discussed throughout this study it colors Chinese political thinking.

A growing child finds that his society rewards achievement and success through eating. An engineer raised in a Kiangsu market town recalled as his most memorable youthful experience: "When I was about nine a little child of about four fell into a river near our house. I rescued her and carried her home. The child's parents were very thankful; and I, too, was very happy. I was given a lot of

tion in Chinese Society," Castle Harbour Hotel, Bermuda, January 26–28, 1964), p. 2. The Hokkien people of Taiwan are descendants of mainland Chinese, primarily from the coastal province of Fukien, who migrated to the island during the eighteenth century. Their language and customs have remained similar to those of the mainlanders from whom they are descended.

5. The manner in which sexual practice in China manifests an "oral" quality has been analyzed by John H. Weakland in, "Orality in Chinese Conceptions of Male Genital Sexuality," *Psychiatry*, Vol. XIX (1956), pp. 237–247. Weakland's insights seem borne out by interview and documentary data contained in a recent study of footbinding in traditional China: "When I loved a woman, I went all the way and wished that I could swallow her up. But only the tiny [bound] feet could be placed in the mouth." (Howard S. Levy, *Chinese Footbinding: The History of a Curious Erotic Custom* [New York: Walton Rawls, 1966], p. 135.)

food to eat. Even today I have not forgotten the experience." [6] But the table is also a major focus of punishments: "If my grades were not good, or if I got into fights, I would be physically punished, as by spanking, or being hit on the palm—or sometimes I would not get food to eat, and would have to sit by the side of the table and watch everyone else eat." [7]

The table is also the place where more routine social disciplines are developed; where a child acquires basic concerns about having sufficient material resources in a society traditionally faced with scarcity—anxiety about his ability to "take in" with restraint. As was recalled by an elderly lawyer from Fukien Province, "I remember that from the time we were small [my mother] always taught us to be economical about the things we ate. For example, when eating a fish you should always save a little bit; you should not eat it all at once. Hence today when I eat I am always very economical." [8]

For a Chinese the basic sense of social well-being and security remains linked throughout life to the ritual of eating. Meal-taking in a noisy, bustling setting reaffirms an individual's unity with his primary social group and recaptures the sense of being cared for that was most fully known in infancy:

(What is the thing you remember with most pleasure about your early life?) My family was a big one, and I remember that mealtimes were very bustling. When it was time to eat someone would ring a bell, and then grandmother would divide up the food. Everyone would pick up his bowl to be served his portion. Everybody crowded in and bustled around. When we were busy with the farm harvest it was even more bustling as we would hire more than seventy people. Aside from this there was nothing in particular.[9]

In present-day Taiwan the descendants of mainland Chinese who emigrated to the island in centuries past see their social identity linked to rituals of eating. "Members of a family are defined as those who share a cooking stove. . . . This identification of stove and family is so important that those who cannot afford to add a new room to house the stove of a newly created family unit [in the compound of an extended family] build a second stove in the same kitchen." [10] And the sad act of breaking up a large family because of conflict or economic difficulty is termed "dividing the stove."

6. T-40.
7. T-9.
8. T-47.
9. T-49. Questions in parentheses were addressed by the interviewer to the respondent. Brackets enclose interpolations added for greater clarity.
10. Margery Wolf, *The House of Lim: A Study of a Chinese Farm Family* (New York: Appleton-Century-Crofts, 1968), p. 28.

As a child matures he discovers that the nurturing quality of food-giving is augmented and transformed: Authority becomes associated with who eats before or better than whom, and who can speak and who must listen. As he goes to school he acquires a sense of the ritualistic qualities of language, and of the importance of using the proper words and phrases in the appropriate social contexts. He also discovers in the world beyond his family that people can "eat" people by turning the oral patterns of respect and care learned in childhood into forms of aggression.[11] Yet throughout life his basic sense of security and social self remain associated with the oral forms of nurturing and social intercourse learned while young.[12]

Although after the first year or two of life the child begins to mature physiologically, the manner in which his needs are met prolongs his dependence on adult care. The breast which was given to the infant whenever he cried is replaced by the indulgence of *amahs* in wealthy families, or grandparents and older siblings among the peasantry, who will pacify the child with food or affection whenever he is unhappy. It is quite common for *amahs* to indulge their young charges by carrying them long after they have acquired the physical capacity to walk—an aspect of the rearing of children of wealth which seems to enhance their belief that both power and pleasure are to be found in a condition of passive dependency. And even in present-day Taiwan or urban Hong Kong it is quite common to see parents or youngsters of seven or eight carrying a child or younger sibling on their backs even though these children are quite able to walk on their own.

Underlying the permissive and indulgent treatment which elders accord young children is the notion that *adults should anticipate the child's needs for him.* As one observer of Chinese family life has phrased it, "[The pre-school] child is considered incapable of learning very much, and the parents' main goal is simply to keep the child from injuring himself or others and from causing his parents too much trouble."[13] A focal activity in the growth of a young child which enables us to affirm this interpretation is bowel training. Development of sphincter control is the first bodily function around which adults might—and in some cultures determinedly do—force onto the child their own anxious concerns for cleanliness, order,

11. *See* pp. 70–71, 99–104 below.
12. As expressed by a lonely working class woman who had traveled from her home in Shantung Province to Manchuria, "I was homesick for the land to which I was accustomed. The people in Manchuria did not talk as our people talked, nor did they eat the same food." (Ida Pruitt, *A Daughter of Han,* p. 131.)
13. Wolf, "Child Training in a Hokkien Village," p. 6.

Woman carrying child,
Taipei, Taiwan, December 1970.
Richard H. Solomon.

and punctuality; their concern that an individual learn to control his own behavior. The Chinese cultural pattern, however, does *not* place undue emphasis on such traits, and the growing Chinese child is not pressured by adults to learn to regulate his bowels by himself —and through such self-control acquire a sense of personal autonomy. Chinese parents are rather permissive about toilet training.[14] "Mothers claim they 'know' when the child wants to urinate or move his bowels and hold him out so that the child soils neither himself nor his caretakers." [15] Before he can walk, a parent, grandparent, or older sibling takes care of a child's eliminative activity "for him" by anticipating his needs and encouraging movement through gentle sounds or whistling; and later on, especially in lower class households, the child is told to emulate the toilet habits of his older brothers and sisters who take him outside for relief.

The impact of this form of cleanliness training would seem to be that the child acquires neither a sense of privacy nor an exaggerated concern with self-control of bodily functions by learning to "hold in" through muscular discipline. Rather, because elimination is such a "public" function in which he moves with the help of an adult or older sibling, failures to perform properly create anxieties about his *relation* to the adult or sibling who was "helping" him. A sense of the interdependent quality of even the most personal activities is developed, and with it a basic concern for how one performs before others—a sensitivity to shame.

In sum, until a male child approaches the age of five or six, when he has become strong enough to do simple chores on the farm or has acquired sufficient intellectual skills to begin formal schooling, life is a period of indulgence and light discipline. Bodily needs are anticipated and gratified within the limits of family resources. The appeals of this "golden age" of childhood dependency remain vital to traditional Chinese throughout life; and as was suggested in the *Twenty-Four Models of Filial Piety,* the hope of the parent and obligation of the filial son or daughter was to bring life full circle to those in old age, so that the pleasures of having one's needs effortlessly fulfilled would usher life out just as the parent had in similar fashion ushered life in for the child. The pattern of infant nurture remained the model by which a true son expressed love for his aging parents:

> Father . . . had a very pure character, he was very filial to his mother. (How did he express his filiality to her?) He was very com-

14. *See* Martha Wolfenstein, "Some Variants in the Moral Training of Children," *The Psychoanalytic Study of the Child,* Vol. V (1949), pp. 313, 326.
15. Wolf, "Child Training in a Hokkien Village," p. 3.

pliant with her wishes. Anything that grandmother liked to eat, things that would help to maintain her bodily health, father would go out and buy and give to her to eat, no matter how expensive they were. Grandmother would have to go to the toilet, and even though she could take care of it herself sometimes father would even help her there.[16]

CHILDHOOD RELATIONS WITH AUTHORITY:
BASIC PATTERNS IN THE USE OF POWER

The change in treatment a traditionally educated male child encountered between the ages of five and seven was radical and painful.[17] Whereas indulgent females previously had been the dominant influence in his life, now males began to exert pressures, both directly and by way of female caretakers, for conformity to social custom. The child quickly learned that he had graduated from the years of indulgence and was confronted with stern demands that he acquire the social habits which would enable him to get along in society and in a world of material scarcity.

As we have noted, the dominant theme or mode of early childhood disciplining in a traditional Chinese family was on proper ways of "taking in" (rather than concern with "holding in," as would be the case with strict toilet training) and that mealtimes were a major focus of such disciplinary activity. In a well-to-do family it was at the table that a child acquired his first view of authority as a provider of security and as a teacher of proper forms.

> (What kind of a person was your father?) Father was a very sincere person. He thought if other people had requests to make of you, you should respond to them. For instance, in the wintertime if other people did not have enough food to eat and came to father to ask his help, he would definitely agree to help them. And he did not worry about whether they returned [the food he had given them]. (How did

16. T-33.

17. In a very helpful analysis of the periodization of the Chinese life cycle, Marion Levy notes that the youth or "*yu-nien* period of childhood ranged . . . from four years or earlier to fifteen or sixteen. During this period the real discipline of Chinese life made itself felt upon the children. . . . In the gentry family . . . the male *yu-nien* was sent to live in his father's section of the house. Nurses and servants continued to care for him, but his father took over his immediate supervision." (Marion Levy, *The Family Revolution in Modern China* [New York: Octagon Books, 1963], pp. 75–76.)

This same phenomenon of an "abrupt, bewildering, and drastic" change in the way a father treats his maturing son has been observed among lower class villagers in Taiwan. (Margery Wolf, "Child Training and the Chinese Family," in Maurice Friedman, ed., *Family and Kinship in Chinese Society* [Stanford, Calif.: Stanford University Press, 1970], p. 41.)

he treat you children?) [Father] dealt with the children very strictly: for instance, when we were eating we could not make a sound with our chopsticks, and when we lifted up food from the serving dish with chopsticks we had to do it from the table directly in front of us, otherwise we would be scolded.[18]

For China's peasant millions, however, concern with "taking in" was developed through the most basic discipline of all, an inadequate food supply. As one farmer from North China recalled:

We came to Yenan from Hengshan when I was five. That was during the great famine of 1928. . . . We went about begging. . . . We had nothing to eat. Father went to Chaochuan to gather firewood and beg food, but he didn't get any. He was carrying elm leaves and firewood when he fell by the roadside. . . . That is my earliest memory: of always being hungry, and of father there dead in the road.[19]

The handling and consuming of food thus, for Chinese of all economic levels, becomes an activity associated with considerable anxiety; anxiety about parental disapproval of one's table manners, or just the elemental concern that one is consuming scarce resources.

The frequent and often emotionally tinged recollections of our respondents about parents or a favored younger brother being given somewhat better food or a larger portion at meal-time suggest that a child's first exposure to social status relationships, to the facts that some people are more important or more highly valued than others, is also associated with table ritual. Self-respect and degree of authority become measured by the quality and amount of food one is given by one's providers:

[Parents] ought to help their children develop a sense of self-confidence and pride . . . Certainly they should see that children do not have a sense of inferiority. (How can they make sure that children do not have any sense of inferiority?) Well, for example, if a child carries a lunch box to school, we adults could eat a little less ourselves and let the child carry somewhat better food to school. In that way the child will not see his friends eating good food but he himself eating food that is not so good, and thus develop a sense of inferiority.[20]

As a child grows older and more articulate—especially in upper class families—concern with proper "taking in" becomes generalized to the more abstract give-and-take of verbal exchange:

18. T-26.
19. Jan Myrdal, *Report from a Chinese Village* (London: Heinemann, 1965), p. 135.
20. T-38.

With [father] things had to be just so; there were rules for everything. At the table we had to wait for the older people to start to eat first, we had to sit there at attention, couldn't talk with our other brothers. (What about the adults talking?) Oh, they could talk as they pleased.[21]

When father was speaking the children could not go on talking. Children were only allowed to listen to the adults speaking because they don't understand; they can only listen to people speaking and if they talk a lot then they will get hit.[22]

The giving of opinions, like the giving of food, is an activity where adults, certain adults, have precedence and take initiative. Children are made to feel that they are incompetent to develop their own opinions, that they "don't understand" and lack sufficient experience in society and hence should rely for guidance on the adults who do have the proper understanding and experience. The communication pattern which the growing Chinese child learns is thus nonreciprocal. Parents are the ones with the authority to give, whether the giving concerns food, opinions, or orders; there is no "giving back" on the child's part; he has to learn to "take in" what is given to him in proper fashion:

(When you were young did you have any differences of opinion with your parents?) Children did not have that freedom so I did not express opinions. My younger brother once had a difference of opinion with my parents. (What difference of opinion?) When we were small our parents ate food that was rather good, but we children ate food that was a bit inferior. My younger brother was rather unruly, he was dissatisfied; he argued that he wanted to eat better food. Father was unhappy, thought he was just a little troublemaker wanting to enjoy the oral pleasures of the older generation. (As a result, how was this difference of opinion resolved?) There was no use in my younger brother talking about it. Quite the contrary, father was unhappy and hence scolded him.[23]

A strong sense of social status and authority thus develops around interpersonal communications, of who may speak first, who must listen, or who is left speechless.[24]

Chinese sum up their expectations regarding relations between adult and child—as with other relationships between an authorita-

---

21. T-9.
22. T-26.
23. T-38.
24. A Chinese household servant recalls, "My master was a very tall man and well grown. . . . We were all afraid of him. . . . We were so much afraid . . . that when he gave orders we stood meekly and stuttered." (Pruitt, *A Daughter of Han*, p. 107.)

tive individual and his subordinates—in the notion of *modeling* or emulation. The superior is supposed to behave in such a way that the subordinate can "study" or imitate the superior's example. A child may occasionally be led to believe that he should receive the same treatment as an adult, as in the example above, but in most of our respondents' recollections, the superior took the initiative in communication, or gave cues as to what was acceptable behavior on the subordinate's part.

Of course emulation as an aspect of the childhood learning process is not unique to China. Children of all cultures learn from behavioral models and copy the actions of adults who are significant in their early lives. What seems distinctive about Chinese notions of model emulation is the parents' conviction that the child should sustain his deferential relationship to the "model" adult as he matures. Furthermore, this form of learning is generalized into the adult world.[25] The traditionally reared child was told to *rely upon* the greater wisdom and experience of family elders or an older sibling rather than being urged to formulate his own *internalized* set of behavioral controls. He was not encouraged to test out, within the limits of his developing physical and mental faculties, his ability as an individual to direct his own actions and to make personal judgments.

This adult expectation permeates many other aspects of the growing child's life. Interview respondents, when asked to recall the most pleasurable moments of childhood, frequently mentioned episodes of tree-climbing and swimming, or running and playing with friends. They also recalled that such activities were very likely to bring them a beating from an anxious parent, who feared that they would injure themselves or make some kind of trouble. The child yearns to test and develop his own physical and mental capabilities, but adults continually tell him that he is incompetent. He will get hurt or do something bad, and hence should either inhibit his capacity for individual activity or develop his talents in areas where adults can guide and protect him. The strength of such a point of view is, in part, a continuing expression of the parents' anxiety that their male offspring might die—as by drowning or in a fall from a tree. An adult's concern with receiving care during his own old age and his doubts about a child's competence to act apart from the guidance of more experienced elders, thus shape with great emotional force the way he trains his children.

Punishments reinforce parental pressures for reliance on adults.

25. The important place that model emulation occupies in Confucian philosophy, and in Chinese theories of learning, is discussed in Munro, *The Concept of Man in Early China,* pp. 90–96, 108–109, 167–171.

Traditionally, and particularly in lower class families, it was considered necessary and proper to beat children so that they would develop a sense of fear if they did not obey adult commands. The majority of the adults in our sample recall having been beaten with boards, whips, or rulers, or having received other forms of physical punishment.[26] Such punishments were not given *indiscriminately*, but resulted from disobeying parental orders or from failure to meet their standards of performance (especially in school). Through it all, the child can perceive a rationale and predictability behind adult power and is presented with alternatives whereby through his own behavior he can avoid punishment.[27] Yet because his parents allow him no opportunity to "talk back" or reason with them in the matter of discipline, the child learns that it is safer and less painful to ac-

26. Of the seventy-nine interviewed persons who provided information on how they had been punished in childhood, sixty-two (79 percent) recalled receiving frequent physical punishments. Twenty-one percent asserted they had received only nonphysical punishments. These data do not show any strong association with information on the respondents' economic class level. (*See* additional information on childhood punishments in Appendix VI, pp. 559–560.)

27. In an analysis of the political culture of Burma, Pye has found that a Burmese child experiences erratic and willful treatment from his parents, which establishes a sense of unpredictability, danger, and impermanence in social relationships and the expectation of a lack of congruence between personal effort and outcome in social action. (Lucian W. Pye, *Politics, Personality, and Nation Building: Burma's Search for Identity* [New Haven: Yale University Press, 1962], pp. 182–183, 195–203.) This cultural pattern contrasts with the stress on unambiguous role relationships, predictability, and a sense of purposefulness in action which Pye finds in the Chinese political culture: "Children [in China] are made to feel that in spite of constant harassment and criticism they can still demonstrate their ultimate worth by showing they are not lacking in the vital ingredient of willpower. . . . To demonstrate correct desires to act purposefully so as to reveal one's willpower is thus the most assured way that the Chinese child has of proving his worth to others. It is also the way to demonstrate dutiful compliance with authority and to receive the emotional rewards of security." (Pye, *The Spirit of Chinese Politics: A Psychocultural Study of the Authority Crisis in Political Development* [Cambridge, Mass.: M.I.T. Press, 1968], p. 141. Also see pp. 94–99, 137–143.)

These expectations of predictability and the efficacy of willpower in Chinese attitudes toward social action have an important relationship to the individual's sense of indebtedness and relationship to the family group. Having called the child's attention to his obligations to parents and family, these adults then provide a clear path by which, through his own efforts, he can repay his social "debts." Educational achievement or business success traditionally were ways in which a Chinese could "honor" his family. The compulsive work habits which give Chinese society or communities of overseas Chinese their industrious air seem the most concrete expression of the concern for fulfilling family obligations which the Chinese carry throughout their lives—even if they are separated by great physical distances.

cept parental injunctions in a passive manner. This pattern of passivity is expressed succinctly in the Chinese phrase for obedience, *t'ing-hua,* to "listen to talk." Attempts by the child to question the guidance of authoritative elders, or to reason and develop independent judgments, can only invoke parental displeasure. He learns to "take in" parental guidance without question, and is firmly discouraged from "giving out" on his own.

Certain cross-cultural research on childrearing practices has indicated that harsh physical punishment may actually increase rather than decrease a child's sense of autonomy.[28] Our interview data provide limited evidence that this may be so. Those respondents who recalled being punished physically were somewhat less likely to exhibit a dependency type of social orientation than were those who recalled nonphysical forms of punishment. In response to the interview question of whether they considered childhood or adulthood a happier time of life, those who described harsh physical punishments in early family life were somewhat less likely to look back with longing on childhood than were those who mentioned being punished primarily through emotional pressures. Because of our small number of respondents, however, this pattern must be considered suggestive only.

Our provisional interpretation, which will be elaborated in the next chapter, is that through a combination of physical and emotional sanctions Chinese parents developed in their children considerable anxiety about disobeying their instructions, and indeed fear of direct contact with a stern father. The legacy of this pattern of childhood punishments and anxiety in the face of family authority which it developed was that the child acquired an attitude of passivity toward those with power over him. He tended to follow their guidance rather than internalize their standards of behavior so that he might act independently of their control. When authority figures were not present he would feel himself "freed" of controls which he had not been encouraged to maintain on his own. From such a childhood pattern of relations with family authority seems to grow the adult Chinese concern for the presence of a strict, personalized, and unambiguous source of (political) authority who will impose order on potentially unruly peers and provide a clear source of guidance for all.[29]

28. *See* John W. M. Whiting and Irvin L. Child, *Child Training and Personality: A Cross-Cultural Study* (New Haven: Yale University Press, 1953), pp. 240–246.

29. These Chinese political attitudes are discussed in more detail in a quantitative and cross-cultural framework in the author's study, "Mao's Effort to Reintegrate the Chinese Polity," in Barnett, ed., *Chinese Communist Politics in Action,* pp. 280–285, 301–306.

The emotional pressures by which Chinese parents seek to control their children reinforce the dependency needs instilled during the first years of life. The threat of *isolation* from family approval and resources is a particularly potent parental sanction.

The recollections of our interviewees suggest that isolation can involve either being made conspicuous before the family group ("For big mistakes we would have to kneel in front of the after-dinner group and be scolded" or, as noted previously, be forced to "sit beside the dinner table and watch everyone else eat" [30]), or being cut off from family resources.

> (What kinds of punishments did you receive at home?) If I did not study well then I would be hit or isolated. (How would you be isolated?) My parents would not buy clothing for me, nor give me presents; or they would say, "All right, if your behavior is going to be that way then you won't be able to study any more. You can go out and work." [31]

The use of such sanctions to control an individual's behavior provides an important point of intersection between the sense of social interrelatedness and the dependency needs developed in a young child, the life of the family group, and paternal authority. The father invokes the solidarity of the group to shame the child, and to raise his anxieties about not fitting into group life properly; or for more serious transgressions confronts him with the ultimate horror of being cut off from family resources and having to face life alone, "like an orphan." [32]

When the child enters school such forms of control over the individual are reinforced by the teacher's invocation of group pressures. In a study of educational practices in contemporary Taiwan it was observed that, "In a first grade class . . . a child who was crying . . . was told by the teacher that he should not cry in school because it was not nice looking or sounding. Then the teacher, pointing out the weeping child, made the other students imitate the sound of crying and laughing." [33] Throughout this study we shall

30. T-9. Other observations of parents' use of family group pressures to discipline an erring son are reported in Martin C. Yang, *A Chinese Village: Taitou, Shantung Province* (New York: Columbia University Press, 1945), pp. 129–130.

31. T-11.

32. Parents' use of the threat of abandonment or adoption to control their children is reported in Wolf, *House of Lim,* p. 42.

33. This, and other examples of group shaming techniques are discussed in a discerning and well-documented study of educational practices in Taiwan by Richard W. Wilson, *Childhood Political Socialization on Taiwan* (unpublished Ph.D. dissertation, Princeton University, 1967), Ch. I.

see that to be isolated (*ku-li ti*)—in the two senses of being made to stand out in shame before one's group, or being threatened with alienation from the group and its resources—is an emotionally compelling sanction invoked widely in adult Chinese social and political life. This is most clearly seen in the use of the cangue or penal collar, a form of public shaming of social offenders which has now been institutionalized by the Chinese Communists.

While group pressures may be used to control his behavior, a growing child soon learns that his relations with other members of the family are clearly structured in hierarchical fashion and that group authority derives from the authority of the family head, usually the father. Each family member has a social role to perform, and these roles are interrelated in rank order.[34] The pattern of authority and deference the son learns in dealing with his father is primary: yet this "submission-dominance" style influences most other relations between males. There are no "brothers" in the family, only *ko-ko* and *ti-ti,* elder and younger brothers, and their relations are shaped by the pattern of father-son interaction:

> "The ruler should be a Ruler, his minister a Minister, the father a Father, and his son a Son" [a famous quote from the *Analects* of Confucius]. If a father doesn't understand the proper way to be a Father, then naturally his sons and daughters will not understand morality or the proper relationship between elder and younger brother. If the father is kindly then the son will be filial. The same kind of rationale lies behind the relationship of an older and younger brother. "The older brother should be kindly and the younger brother patient" [another Confucian quotation]. The older brother should be lenient and generous, and his younger brother should . . . accept his older brother's guidance.[35]

This response adds an important dimension to usual descriptions of the hierarchical authority of the Chinese family. In one sense the child was taught that the authority of his father was absolute and that he owed him unwavering obedience. Yet the son also learned that authority had responsibilities and that his own behavior was in some measure conditional upon the actions of those with authority over him. The formal Confucian tradition told him that while he

34. While this "role-relationship" pattern of interpersonal deference and obligation was first learned implicitly within the family, when a child began his formal education he was taught that it carried the legitimacy of the Confucian tradition. The Classics explicitly identified the *wu-lun* or five dyadic social relationships of father to son, elder to younger brother, husband to wife, friend to friend, and ruler to minister, as a reciprocal pattern of responsibility and deference which was both "natural" and morally just.

35. T-32.

Man in a penal cangue,
in a Shantung village, 1890s.
Courtesy New York Public Library.

was to give filial submission, his father or elder brother *should* be generous or kindly. In practice, our respondents recounted that fathers or elder brothers frequently did not live up to their family roles, and great resentment could grow in the gap between perform-ance and obligation. As we will see in the next chapter, grievances toward family authority were seldom translated into openly ex-pressed hostility or opposition; yet at some limit, when father or elder brother failed to perform as Father or Elder Brother should, when the dependent's minimal needs were not met, then "rebellion" had a certain legitimacy. In the sense of injustice which dependents saw in authorities who failed to fulfill the obligations of their social role lies the psychological root of the "right of rebellion" expressed in the philosophy of Mencius.

As a child approaches his teens, and the time when he will begin to have frequent contacts outside the family, his relation to paternal authority, which at the end of infancy had become stern and con-trolling, becomes more distant. His father increasingly *cuts himself off* from direct interaction with him, and the child experiences only the taking of orders, the unquestioning reliance on a more distant and unapproachable source of control.[36] He is told in deeds as well as words that his position is to *depend* on adults, who will both make decisions for him and take care of him; and he will gain their approval, if not their affection, by conforming to their demands:

> Father was very conservative; everything was old-fashioned. (In what way was he conservative?) For example, his style of life was regu-lated, he did not want to have contact with people on the outside. He was a bit selfish and rather lacking in concern for us children. . . . (What was his personality like?) Father's personality was very strong, stubborn; this was all a matter of the influence of the environment because he was a farmer and seldom had contact outside [the family]. (How did he treat you children?) He did not worry very much about us children. By temperament he liked to be alone, he did not like to

36. Of the eighty-one respondents to the question, "When you were young and had problems, with whom would you discuss them?" 46 percent replied "Mother," only 10 percent replied "Father," and 11 percent indi-cated "both Father and Mother." Fourteen percent replied "no one" or said they considered problems by themselves. The remaining respondents iden-tified siblings, friends, or other relatives, with a frequency in each case of less than 8 percent. This communication pattern suggests that the mother played a key role in relating the child to paternal authority. Responses to Thematic Apperception Test (TAT) Card III [*See* Appendix IV, p. 538 below] indicate that the mother's role was usually that of a mediator who attempted to prevent the father from venting hostility against the son. From this pattern the child learned that intermediaries were helpful in dealing with conflict-laden social relationships. (*See* pp. 128–129, 134 below.)

be together with the children; he would be annoyed with their bawling.[37]

Because father was very stern when we were small we would not dare to talk with him. . . . If you asked him something he would just say, "Children shouldn't ask so many questions!" . . . He might say, "Just you go and study!" [38]

Several important patterns in relations between superior and subordinate which find clear manifestation in Chinese political behavior seem to have their roots in the harsh and distant treatment a father accords his growing sons. First, the child learns there is a distinction between decision-making and action in his relations with authority. The father passes judgments regardless of the child's will, yet the child must obey when informed of paternal decisions. Authority becomes associated with thought and word; subordination with the need to act or execute the will of others.[39] This pattern seems to be rooted in the concept in Confucian political philosophy that "superior men" (*chün-tzu*) with "cultivated" minds are to rule over those who labor with their hands.[40]

Second, the child's contacts with authority become laden with anxiety. Chinese parents believe that the inculcation of fear is necessary in rearing filial children. The severe (*yen*) father or elder

37. T-38.

38. T-47.

39. Pye writes: "Historically the tempo of Chinese politics was lethargic and cautious. The picture one has of imperial offices and *yamen* is one of slow-moving and heavily clad officials, the only bustle of activity coming from the purposeful but anxious movements of flunkies who, however, could not be part of politics precisely because they were so active. The more important the man, the slower his pace." (*The Spirit of Chinese Politics,* p. 129.)

The Chinese inclination to rely on intermediaries in interpersonal relations, discussed elsewhere in this chapter, seems further to separate thought from action: a plan is conceived, but its execution requires the assistance of a third party. As one analysis has suggested, "Sequences of behavior directed toward aims involve a considerable differentiation of preparation and execution. The preparation is largely private or undisclosed. . . . Overt active preparations toward the protagonist's end are largely made for him by others on whom he has some claim and who react to the immediate need he reveals to them." (John H. Weakland, "The Organization of Action in Chinese Society," *Psychiatry,* Vol. XIII [1950], p. 364.)

40. ". . . there is the saying, 'Some labour with their minds, and some labour with their strength. Those who labour with their minds govern others; those who labour with their strength are governed by others. Those who are governed by others support them; those who govern others are supported by them.' This is a principle universally recognized." ("The Works of Mencius," Book III, Part I, Ch. IV, sect. 6, in *The Chinese Classics,* trans. James Legge, Vol. II, pp. 249–250.)

brother saw respect as naturally related to the anxiety his presence evoked in son or younger brother:

> (How did you get along with your older brother?) I feared him; respected him. (Why did you fear him?) Well, he had his experience, his knowledge, and could help me. He also had his power, and if my parents were not around he could direct me or punish me if I did something bad—for example, if I was reading a novel when I should have been studying.

> (What is the most important aspect of relations between brothers?) The older brother should correct the younger brother's errors and encourage his good points. The younger should respect the elder. . . . I really feared my older brother.[41]

As revealed by our interviews, most respondents sought to reduce the anxiety of dealings with authority either through avoidance or, when contact was unavoidable, by prompt obedience to authority's demands: "You can say that father never was angry with me. If I did not obey him in the least way it would just take one look from his face, a blink of his eyes, or a few words of instruction, and we would not dare [disobey him]. We just feared him and that was it. As a result we obeyed him." [42]

The reliance on intermediaries in social relations, so pronounced in adult Chinese social behavior, seems to have its roots in the child's desire to dilute or "buffer" his contact with anxiety-provoking authority. A Chinese recalls his childhood attempts to gain favorable decisions from his mother:

> We never had the courage simply to ask [her] to take us somewhere, since we felt certain that our request would be categorically refused. . . . So we sent my fourth brother, Ch'un, who was seven or eight, to act as mediator, not with full authority, but merely to report to Mother what we had said, and to bring back her answer. He was not to voice any opinion of his own, or to misreport what we had said, or to forget what Mother said in reply.[43]

A child's ability to manipulate the family social environment, of course, is in no small measure a function of the willingness of various adults to be "used" by, or to use, the child. Evidence suggests that the mother could play a particularly critical role in the constellation of family relationships in giving her son the encouragement to respond to the demands of the father. *The Twenty-four Models of Filial Piety*, discussed earlier, and interview data pre-

41. T-9.
42. T-43.
43. Chow Chang-cheng, *The Lotus Pool* (New York: Appleton-Century-Crofts, 1961), p. 59.

sented in this chapter, indicate that the relationship between mother and son could be particularly close. When a mother found that her needs for affection, respect, or security were not fulfilled by her husband—who was very likely committed to fulfilling his filial obligations to his mother—the wife would seek solace in her relationship to her son. As one analysis has put it: "The early deprivation and submissiveness which as a young girl and a young daughter-in-law, a woman has to observe, can be gradually given up after she has borne a son. . . . She has the need to establish her superiority [in her husband's family, and so she uses her son as] a highly esteemed extension of herself, a narcissistic tool." [44] Thus, the ego strength which a male child develops is in part related to the support and encouragement he acquires from his mother, who may seek to use him for her own ends.

Both the status differences within the Chinese family and the particular affection which could characterize mother-son or grandparent-grandchild relations provided emotional support and leverage which a child learned to manipulate. He found that *indirectly* he could influence the behavior of those with immediate authority over him.[45] The status and affection of a family elder could be invoked to modify the behavior of a father or elder brother: "My brother would sometimes hit me. I would get mad and say, 'You shouldn't hit me; you should help me!' I would tell mother and she would hit him." [46] Similarly, as observed in a Taiwan village, children learned to control the behavior of offensive peers, not by a direct response, but through invoking the authority of someone with superior status. "Village children . . . developed a technique for taking revenge on an attacker that is both safe and rewarding. They report the transgressor to his parent. . . . The mother of the naughty child then either beats her own child in the presence of his victim or promises to do so when she finds him." [47]

Despite the tension surrounding direct dealings with those in

44. Warner Muensterberger, "Orality and Dependence: Characteristics of Southern Chinese," p. 64.

45. It was precisely this type of family constellation which seems to have characterized Mao Tse-tung's early life. Mao told Edgar Snow in 1936 that while he hated his father, his mother was "kind, generous, and sympathetic." She formed a "united front" with Mao and his brother against the father, encouraging her sons in a strategy of "indirect attack" against the family "ruling power." (Edgar Snow, *Red Star Over China* [New York: Grove Press, 1961], p. 125.) From such indirect evidence one can infer the emotional origins of Mao's willingness to challenge established political authority as an adult.

46. T-18.

47. Wolf, "Child Training and the Chinese Family," p. 55.

authority, a child did learn that family elders were nurturant as well as severe. He knew that his physical needs would be taken care of and that he could win their implicit approval through obedience and dependence on their guidance. This experience left the child with a strong sense of ambivalence toward authority; a feeling of wanting to be protected by it, yet anxiety at approaching too near. As expressed by the son of a Ch'ing dynasty scholar-official from Chekiang:

> [Father] loved his children with all his heart, but his love was *in* his heart. He would not express it. He was concerned that we had enough to eat, that we were properly clothed, and whether we were hot or cold. Every time he would go away from home he would definitely bring back something for us to eat. But his attitude was very stern. *When you saw him you would both fear him and want to get near him.*[48]

The manner in which this ambivalence to authority is handled, both in adolescence and in adulthood, tells much about the style of Chinese political behavior, as will be elaborated in subsequent chapters.

48. T-43. Emphasis added.

Chapter IV

EMOTIONAL CONTROL

One would expect that the change in treatment from indulgence to strict control encountered by a young child as he entered the period of training for life in society would initially produce some bewilderment and frustration, if not rage. As Chinese tend to guard the intimate details of family life and personal feelings behind high walls and polite social forms, there have been few direct and systematic observations of relations between parents and children which would make possible a detailed description of the child's reaction to this change in treatment. However, a number of Western observers have noted tantrums of uncontrolled anger in young Chinese children. Rage is possibly the child's initial response to the sudden imposition of adult control.

On the basis of field observations of life in a fishing village near Hong Kong, one anthropologist has suggested that these fits of anger, in which the child will drop to the ground and kick and scream, are a reaction to fear of being abandoned by his parents, to an inability to get his way from adults (who had previously been so indulgent), and a reaction—often delayed—to teasing or bullying by older children or adults.[1] The fact that such tactics of violent loss of control are used affirms in one more dimension what we saw in the last chapter: the child finds he has little room for "talking back" or influencing the behavior of adults who control him. It appears that his *initial* reaction to this unpleasant confrontation with an unyielding source of control is to express frustration and rage in a tantrum.

What is of greater significance for the emotional development of the child than simply having tantrums is the way these and other

1. Barbara E. Ward, "Temper Tantrums in Kau Sai: Some Speculations upon Their Effects" (mimeographed; a paper prepared for a seminar on "Personality and Motivation in Chinese Society," Castle Harbour Hotel, Bermuda, January 26–28, 1964), p. 2.
Lucian Pye also notes frequent parental teasing of their children, and a general adult "fascination in observing the emotional outbursts of children who have been teased." (*The Spirit of Chinese Politics*, p. 100.)

expressions of emotionality are dealt with by adults. In the setting of the Hong Kong fishing village it was observed that, "as a general rule the child is left to cry himself out." [2] Adults neither comfort nor scold the raging youngster, with the result that after a number of ineffectual tries at influencing the offending elder, the child gives up the tactic as useless.

In describing attempts to strike back at the abuse of older siblings, respondents recalled that efforts to vent hostility at those due "respect" could only invoke greater pain: "[My brother] was five years older than I. Sometimes he would pull my hair and we would fight. I would sometimes try to hit back, but then he would only hit me harder. Mostly I had to obey him. I feared him." [3]

These observations and recollections suggest that the growing child soon learns that emotional expressiveness is dangerous because he lays himself open to manipulation by adults or older siblings. If avoidance of contact with these offending family elders is not possible, then at least a holding in of the feelings by which they seek to use him becomes the most effective way to prevent humiliation or the pain of a rage. Also, the child learns from observing the ways in which adults handle their own feelings that reserve and emotional impassiveness are appropriate ways to discipline these inner urges.

THE DANGERS OF "DROWNING A CHILD WITH LOVE" (NI-AI)

The general emotional tone of early family life that is recalled by adult Chinese suggests that there is considerable reserve in the expression of affection between parents and children. The parental models from which children learn tell them that inner feelings are not to be expressed, except in highly guarded ways, and that in public, emotions should be masked behind the forms of propriety (*li-mao*): "(How did your parents get along?) They lived off in a separate house. (Were they very natural to each other, or very courteous?) They were very mannerly; they treated each other like guests. They were very considerate to each other, and never fought or argued in front of us children." [4]

The son of a small merchant in rural Hupeh Province, when recalling his aloof father, observed, "People in the countryside very seldom expressed their love anyway. (To your mother?) Love between a Chinese husband and wife is very reserved; it is deep in one's heart. They just would not express their love in front of the

2. Ward, "Temper Tantrums in Kau Sai," p. 5.
3. T-18.
4. T-9.

children or the older generation. (Why not?) This is an old Chinese tradition." [5]

Even in matters of the "bruises and scratches" of growing up, parents seem to give children little sympathetic treatment or open emotional support. As one Hokkien mother on Taiwan told an anthropologist:

> They don't dare come crying back to me [if they hurt themselves]. I always scold them and say, "I called you to do something so why didn't you do it instead of staying here and getting yourself hurt?" Or sometimes I say, "Why don't you sit at home? Why do you have to go out and play and get hurt?" [Laughing] Really, sometimes they get a big cut, but they never tell me about it. They just go and get some medicine and put it on themselves. Besides, they shouldn't come crying to me. They are already this old [seven and nine] so they shouldn't do that any more. [6]

Adults act as if emotions are dangerous (not an unreasonable assumption in a society which traditionally has lived in dense population settlements). If expressions of affection are not restrained, once such feelings come into the open the individuals involved might lose all control. As expressed by a middle-aged teacher reared in rural Shantung, "Young people's recreation shouldn't necessarily include dancing. When I see people holding hands on the street I find it very repulsive. . . . This can lead to not maintaining order; it means that anything goes." [7]

Parental emotional reserve and "distance" communicates to the child that his expressions of feelings should be limited. If his parents are too permissive with him, his emotions might overwhelm him and disorder would follow:

> (Were you very close to your parents?) In China parents have their dignity. It is an old custom. If they are just "do as you please" (*suipien*) with the children, then probably they won't be obedient. For example, if they told me I had done something well I might get all excited and would think I could just do as I pleased, such as playing ball anywhere in the house. So for this reason they wouldn't allow any rude or disorderly behavior. [8]

Underlying the development of emotional control is the same adult attitude we encountered previously concerning the child's re-

5. T-33.

6. Margery Wolf, "Child Training in a Hokkien Village," p. 14. This attitude has also been noted by Richard Wilson in his study of socialization in Taiwan elementary schools. *Childhood Political Socialization on Taiwan,* p. 61.

7. T-26.

8. T-9.

lations with authority: A growing person is considered by family elders to be incapable of learning to discipline his own behavior, his own emotions, *by himself*. Hence parents must provide discipline for the child. In the case of controlling emotions this requires that the parents do not express their own inner feelings. If they should show their feelings to the child, his emotions might be stimulated, leading him to some "disorderly" action.

There is, of course, a circular argument here: Parents do not believe that children can learn to handle their emotions in open, if disciplined, ways; hence they educate them to reserve their feelings (and the behavior which emotions might motivate). The child thus grows up believing he can have no control of himself once these evils[9] within him come into the open—or once external controls are taken away. As a result *in fact* he may not have well-developed control over *released* emotions as an adult, both because he has not been trained for such control and because he thinks control is not possible. Logically, of course, this argument is tautological, yet it becomes a self-fulfilling prophecy when transmitted from one generation to the next through childhood socialization.

Parental concern that letting the child know he is valued will lead to loss of control and "doing as one pleases" carries with it an echo of the golden years of infancy—when the new baby was highly valued, when adults *did* openly express affection to the child, when the child obtained material satisfaction and pleasure without discipline or personal effort. That such an existence should be appealing is not strange, especially when it is followed by the imposition of stern parental controls. But yearning for such an indulgent life can appear very dangerous to people living not far above subsistence, or not far away from fallen gentry neighbors who once had been wealthy.[10] As a result traditional Chinese felt that to love a child

9. An ancient Chinese medical text asserts that, "The inner causes of diseases consist of seven types of emotion." (Cited in Pye, *The Spirit of Chinese Politics*, p. 153.) And in folk wisdom, emotions, particularly those of anger and aggression, could cause death. A Chinese working-class woman recounted to a foreign friend an incident in which a man became so "angry that he died of heat in the intestines." She also noted with sadness the death of a grandchild: "It was my daughter who destroyed the life of her own child. The foreign doctors said that she died of typhoid fever, but I knew that she had died of shame and the anger that her mother put on her." (Pruitt, *A Daughter of Han*, pp. 26, 223–224.)

10. There is much evidence in the records of clans, great families, and even popular sayings, that traditional Chinese were quite conscious of the rise and fall of family fortunes; of humble or impoverished origins and a determined advance to wealth and power, but then a decline into renewed penury within a few generations. Such "elite circulation," which has been documented in several recent studies, was often seen as related to the ma-

openly or "too much" after the years of infancy was very dangerous for both the child and his family group in a world of material scarcity and insecurity.

The Chinese expression for "spoiling" children is *ni-ai,* literally "to drown in love." Drowning is an "oral" kind of death; suffocation by taking too much in through the mouth. As we saw earlier, indulgence through the mouth was precisely the way parents expressed their love and concern for a new infant. But such "taking in" is also the form of behavior about which adults first imposed discipline on the maturing child. It is not surprising that in a world of scarcity parents should fear that if discipline is not imposed, the child (the one who is being trained to depend on his parents, and on whom parents hope to depend in old age) will "eat up" the family resources through undisciplined consumption. Therefore, since love was most fully known and expressed through eating, both eating and love must be restrained or else it could mean impoverishment, for the group if not the individual. As a result, in the rearing of Chinese children there traditionally has been a tension between "loving" the child with food so that he will survive, yet controlling him so that he will not grow up to "eat one out of house and home." This tension is clearly expressed in the following revealing comments by an elderly upper class Chinese from Shantung:

> Father's weak point was that he was excessively strict with the children. Take, for example, the son of my father's concubine: He went away to study. He was already twenty. Father gave him his tuition, but when he would return home Father would make him account for the money he had spent. If things did not tally up then Father would think that he had not used his money correctly and would beat him with a stick. Parents should be warmer than this; then you can have some emotional exchange. Being so strict is not right, the children will just fear their parents.
>
> Mother's weak point was that she "drowned her children in love." After my older sister got married her family situation turned bad; her husband gambled money. Mother would practically risk her life to give them more money, and afterwards even my sister's whole family moved in to live with us. This kind of excessive love is not good. Mother should have helped [my sister] to manage her own household properly; then she would not have been so dependent.[11]

The father expresses his anxiety that one of his offspring—significantly enough the fruit of his own pleasure—will consume family

---

terial indulgence and lack of self-discipline of the children of those who had attained wealth and status. (*See* Ho Ping-ti, *The Ladder of Success in Imperial China* [New York: John Wiley, Science Editions, 1964], Ch. IV.)

11. T-36.

resources without discipline. Yet the mother risks invoking the rage of her husband so that she can "love" her children by feeding them money to satisfy their craving for easy living (and as well her own concern that the children appreciate home life enough to remain with her?).

This type of problem was one which primarily burdened China's wealthy few. For most of the peasantry and impoverished urban dwellers the relationship between family resources and the desire to consume was not a balanced one; life in a subsistence economy imposed its own limits and offered little alternative to disciplined consumption. But the *source* of the problem was common to all those educated to depend on others. Without the responsibility for disciplining their own behavior, children were unlikely to limit their own consumption when family resources were plentiful, particularly when they saw their parental models enjoying such pleasures as concubines and good food. For the poor, dependency posed no such problem. Indeed, it was a solution to the problem of how to maintain life through family solidarity in an economy of scarcity.

The common resolution of these divergent concerns, according to our respondents, was the conviction that "too much" love, or affection too openly expressed, was bad for a child as he would become "selfish" or "lazy" and overconsume family resources. A stern parental exterior was felt to be necessary for imposing discipline on one incapable of self-discipline. Love was expressed by *implication,* indirectly from behind a strict parental "face," through concern for a child's physical well-being. As expressed in a statement noted earlier: "[Father] loved his children with all his heart, but his love was *in* his heart; he would not express it." [12]

We have traveled a circuitous route in tracing the logic behind our respondents' conviction that stern discipline is necessary for a growing child, and that "too much" love is dangerous both for the child and for the family. Inasmuch as the reasoning behind these attitudes is basic to the logic of the "dependency" social orientation, and to filial relations with authority, it is worthwhile retracing our analysis to make this cultural logic explicit: The traditional Chinese orientation to childrearing embodied a strong concern that the child grow up to provide for his parents' future security. Parents loved their young child in the manner appropriate to infancy, through oral indulgence, and they expected the same expression of love in dependent old age. Once the child had outgrown infancy, however, the concern of the parents became a matter of insuring that the maturing youngster did not grow up to leave them. To this end they imposed a strict external discipline on the child and discour-

12. T-43.

aged his explorations of autonomous behavior. The child became emotionally dependent on parental guidance and discipline. His maturation was arrested at a stage where love was expressed through oral forms, and where behavioral controls were still externally imposed by personalized sources of authority.[13]

Having educated the child to be dependent on their guidance, the parents were now caught up in the logic of the "filial" relationship: Strict discipline had to be maintained or the child would have doubts about what was appropriate behavior on his part (and parents might begin to doubt his "filial" commitment to them). Too much parental love in the sense of relaxed affection or emotional exchange would conflict with the child's need to receive external discipline and with the parents' expectation that the child could not control his own behavior once his emotions became mobilized (as indeed he had not been trained to do). Also, love in its form of feeding and material support had to be disciplined, or else—given the understandable desire of the child to recapture pleasures known in infancy—he would overconsume scarce family resources and raise doubts about his commitment to provide for his parents in what they hoped would be a return to that "golden age" of dependent security in their elderly years.

Strict authority (and guarded displays of affection) thus became the binding and guiding force of "filiality." Yet as we shall now see, this very strictness produced further reasons for seeing danger in the outward display of emotions.

THE IMPERMISSIBILITY OF HOSTILITY

In the Confucian family tradition there is no behavior which is more likely to invoke swift punishment than a child's quarreling or fighting with siblings or neighborhood peers:

13. Our interview data indicate that, in contrast to a sample of middle-class American adults, Chinese retain a personalized image of political authority, and continue to believe that their own actions in society must be guided by an external source of control to be effective. (*See* the author's "Mao's Effort to Reintegrate the Chinese Polity," pp. 280–284.)

This interpretation is supported by a recent study of the development of political attitudes in American adolescents. Through interviews it has been found that after the ages of 11, 12, or 13, children's political thinking develops beyond a conception of authority as a personalized "he" preoccupied with preventing people from doing bad things to that of a set of abstract institutions operating according to general principles intended to bring about some positive improvement in community life. (*See* Joseph Adelson and Robert O'Neil, "Growth of Political Ideas in Adolescence: The Sense of Community," *Journal of Personality and Social Psychology,* Vol. IV [1966], pp. 295–306.)

> If I fought with other children [Mother] would pull us apart and hit me, and would then apologize to the parents of the other child. (Even if the other child had started the fight?) Even then; after all I had had contact with him and so the fight started. [She would] pull me into the house by the ear, make me kneel down and then hit me with a stick.[14]

There is no right or wrong concerning the point of contention. Merely having exposed oneself to the possibility of conflict is sufficient grounds for a thrashing.[15] Among more highly educated Chinese many can recall being hit by their parents *only* for fighting with a sibling or peer. Yielding and "harmonious" behavior are presented to the child as great virtues:

> Our people have always loved peace; Chinese consider harmony valuable. From the time we are small we are taught to be yielding. . . . Harmony has a bit of the idea of yielding. For instance, if a husband and wife are not harmonious then the children will not be, and the outcome would be unthinkable. If you think ahead a little bit you can reduce trouble. Chinese also stress manners. If you are mannerly to a superior then we consider that an expression of peace. If you are mannerly then there is "harmony." [16]

Anxious parental reactions to interpersonal conflict, to expressions of hostility, work to develop in the child fears of aggressive impulses, both his own and those of other people. Such feelings should be masked behind ritualized forms of behavior, "good manners" (*li-mao*).

The reason for this uncompromising effort to inhibit expressions of aggression in children—an attitude which finds formal justification in the Confucian stress on "harmony" in interpersonal relations

14. T-18. This parental response to expressions of aggression in their children has been observed in present-day Taiwan. (*See* Wolf, "Child Training and the Chinese Family," pp. 54–55.)

15. Our interview data indicate that for our respondents as a whole, quarreling or fighting was the most frequently recalled cause of parental punishment (44.5 percent of seventy-four responding). The next most frequent causes were for doing poorly in school (33.4 percent) and disobedience of parental instructions (30.6 percent). The frequencies of other responses given were all lower than 18 percent. In some cases respondents mentioned more than one cause of punishment, which is why the percentages do not add up to 100. This punishment pattern shows some association with economic class level. (*See* Appendix VI, pp. 559–560.)

Further evidence on the importance which Chinese parents attached to inhibiting expressions of aggression in their children, based on interviews with Chinese reared on the mainland, is reported in Robert W. Scofield and Sun Chin-wan, "A Comparative Study of the Differential Effect upon Personality of Chinese and American Child Training Practices," *Journal of Social Psychology,* Vol. LII (1960), pp. 221–224.

16. T-47.

—is basic to the psychological logic of filial piety. In cultures which tolerate or encourage the development of a sense of autonomy in children, aggressive impulses play an important role in the child's efforts at self-assertion, his attempts to establish an identity for himself independent of the adults who bore and reared him.[17] But as we have stressed, self-assertion was the one thing which Chinese parents would not tolerate. Hence every indication of willful, assertive, or aggressive action on the part of the child would be severely discouraged. By inhibiting the expression of aggression in their children, Chinese parents (consciously or unconsciously) were seeking to insure the continued dependence of these guarantors of their future security. Self in the Confucian tradition was not to be considered apart from the relationships of filiality, the *wu lun*.

As is so often the case, however, the anxieties or good intentions which drive parents to attempt to develop certain behavioral patterns in their children can at times produce contradictory results. Parental efforts literally to beat the aggression out of their offspring and insure their obedience, tend to reduce the appeal of the dependent role. And they certainly teach the child that to have authority means, in part, to have the power to express aggression against inferiors. This interpretation is clearly revealed in our interview materials, where respondents indicated that they learned to repress hostility or aggressive feelings before father or elder brother, but would then release such emotions on younger siblings or weaker peers:

> (What would you say your father's weaknesses were?) When we were young we didn't think about that; we didn't know what weakness was. All I knew was that my father made me kneel every day [as a punishment]. He was very strict. As I was always being made to kneel it would get my anger up. (How did you express your anger?) How could you express it?! He is your father! You can't scold him! (Where did your anger go then?) We just wouldn't dare say anything to him. You just don't talk as you please to your father.[18]

17. An English psychoanalyst writes: "If there were no aggressive drive towards independence, children would grow up into and remain helpless adults so long as anyone could be persuaded to care for them, a fate which actually does befall some individuals who either lack the normal quota of assertiveness or else who have been subjected to regimes of childhood training which makes any kind of self-assertion seem a crime." (Anthony Storr, *Human Aggression* [New York: Atheneum, 1968], p. 44.)

The negative tone of these remarks bespeaks the deviant quality attributed to strong dependency needs in a society which values personal independence and self-reliance. In contrast, Chinese characterize strivings for autonomous behavior on the part of their children as nothing more than "selfishness."

18. T-18.

The respondent then indicated that his elder brother, who received similar treatment from the father, would turn around and play the part of a "father" with him, by hitting him or pulling his hair.

This "submission-dominance" pattern is evident in the recollections of childhood of the third son of a Kwangsi merchant. After describing how strictly his father had treated him, the respondent said that of all the people in his family he was closest to his little brother, "because he would obey me when I told him to do something." [19] The treatment received from more powerful elders provides a model of behavior which the individual, living within the Confucian social pattern of hierarchical relationships, applies to those subordinate in status. Aggression or hostile behavior is proscribed for the one dependent, but is resorted to with considerable frequency by adults anxious for the maintenance of "filiality."

"EAT BITTERNESS" (CH'IH-K'U)

The notion that feelings, especially sentiments of aggression, should not be released against authoritative individuals is expressed by Chinese in an interesting manner. As one sensitive young man explained it, "We hold things in our hearts, *in our stomachs.* . . . We hold hatred in, but we shouldn't do this." [20] Similar language was used by the son of an Anhwei peasant in recounting how a point of contention was dealt with among his brothers: "You would just put [the disagreement] in your stomach and not say anything. Everyone would try to work out a compromise. Otherwise quarreling would develop and everyone would be in a bad way." [21] The same concept is used in the peasant's interpretation of the Confucian ideal of "self-cultivation" (*hsiu-yang*):

> (How does one become a cultivated person?) You have to be patient and yielding. (When you get mad what do you do?) I very seldom get mad; *I swallow my anger, put it in my stomach.* (What is the bad point about being angry?) It never can have a good outcome. (What do you do when you try to control your anger?) Nothing in particular, just "eat a loss" (*ch'ih-k'uei*).[22]

19. T-6. Observations of this phenomenon are also reported in Wolf, *The House of Lim*, pp. 42, 130–131.

20. T-4. Emphasis added.

The same concept is used by a woman who recalls the bitterness of her first days living with her new husband's family: "I had never done much heavy work before, but after [moving in with the in-laws] I had to do all kinds of hard work, even in the fields. I cried a lot in my stomach in those days, but I didn't complain." (Wolf, *The House of Lim*, p. 54.)

21. T-27.

22. *Ibid.* Emphasis added.

This phraseology is meaningful in a number of respects. Earlier we pointed out that love and care in the Chinese tradition were above all expressed through feeding, yet from the combination of paternal harshness and nurture grew a strong sense of ambivalence toward authority. This ambivalence shapes perceptions of the act of feeding, which can become a form of aggression as well as of care: the father can make the child "eat bitterness" (*ch'ih-k'u*) as well as good food by being hostile or provoking bad feelings that the child knows must be put "in the stomach" and not expressed.

There may also be a physiological counterpart to the notion of putting hostility "in one's stomach" or "eating bitterness." The well-known phenomenon of intestinal ulceration resulting from tension indicates that feelings which must be strictly disciplined have their effects on bodily health; and unreleased rage may indeed make one's stomach tense, filled with bitterness.[23] Thus, the combined Confucian stress on filial submission, paternal unwillingness to tolerate a child's expression of hostility, and physiological mechanisms seem to work in concert to make the forced feeding of dependency an experience which combines aggression with love. The maturing child carries into his perceptions of social life the awareness that oral forms of nurturance, and the social rituals of filial deference, can be vehicles of hostility as well as of respect.[24]

This conception of dealing with hostility by holding it in one's stomach also brings to mind something pointed out earlier, that the major form of *early* childhood disciplining focuses on the develop-

---

23. Chinese speak of an individual becoming "white with rage" or "fainting with anger," which indicates that constriction of the vascular system is in some manner related to the "holding in" of aggression. (*See* Otto Kleinberg, "Emotional Expression in Chinese Literature," *Journal of Abnormal and Social Psychology,* Vol. XXXIII [1938], pp. 517–520.)

To exercise great caution or self-discipline is spoken of as being *"hsiao-hsin"* (literally, "small heart"), while to be relaxed is to *"fang-hsin,"* to "release the heart." In this culture to become "red with anger," that is, to expand one's vascular system, is viewed with great alarm, apparently because it communicates that hostile feelings are not being "held in." A Chinese servant recalls: "The master was so angry that his face became red even down his neck. If they had been ordinary people there would have been a fight. But because he was an official and because there were so many of us [servants] around he dared not beat nor revile [his offending wife]. But his anger was too great for him to bear. He jumped up, seized his whip, and began to thrash the dogs." (Pruitt, *A Daughter of Han,* p. 80.) Thus, a Chinese "signals" how aggressive impulses will be handled by becoming "white" (holding in) or "red" (mobilizing hostile feelings).

24. Interesting descriptions of how table ritual and the apparent politeness of a formal banquet can be used to offend or humiliate will be found in Wolf, *The House of Lim,* p. 53, and Pruitt, *A Daughter of Han,* pp. 15–17.

ment of proper forms of "taking in"—while little parental anxiety is expressed about the child "holding in" the products of his consumption. At the stage of development that begins at about four or five, however, it appears that "holding in" does become an important mode of discipline; but rather than being focused around a physiological or muscular "holding in," which would be the case with strict sphincter discipline, the child is taught to retain his emotions, particularly anger, hostility, and hatred. Such a pattern of discipline implies that to a Chinese an important aspect of social identity, of self-discipline and self-respect, is the control of emotions rather than of actions.[25] Self-control means restraining improper feelings more than improper behavior, especially where one has been taught to depend on external authority for guidance as to what is correct or incorrect behavior.

How does a child learn to "hold in" his emotions? The parental example of reserve in expressing feelings undoubtedly is an important factor. It also appears that teasing or bullying teaches the child the virtue of defense through emotional impassivity. Furthermore, our TAT responses suggest that an important psychological mechanism of defense in this culture involves learning to prevent the mobilization of bad feelings, to separate the perception of having been mistreated from the emotions of rage or resentment which such treatment would provoke, particularly where the offending individual is a powerful authority.[26] The oft-noted passive or indif-

25. "Holding in" conflict has its counterpart for the family group as well as the individual. Group disciplining of aggression, and its relationship to social identity, is indicated in the following recollection of childhood: "If any quarrel spread beyond our walls it was considered a blot upon the entire household. Everyone tried to curb his irritation and any inclination to quarrel." (Chiang Yee, *A Chinese Childhood* [New York: John Day, 1952], p. 302.)

26. This way of handling emotions is illustrated by one interpretation of TAT Card IV. The respondent, T-12, sees an older man directing a younger subordinate to do something improper. The younger man obeys, fails, and will evidently be punished by the authorities for his misdeed. However, he feels "nothing in particular" towards the superior who gave him the illegitimate orders. For the full story, see below, Ch. VII, p. 113.

In one effort to analyze the psychological defense mechanisms characteristic of different cultures, Francis Hsu suggests that this way of handling emotions be termed "suppression." Because Chinese parents do not force the child to internalize standards of behavior so much as to rely upon their (external) guidance, the child does not develop mechanisms of "repression" in which control can be maintained over forbidden emotions only by putting them well out of consciousness. He learns to "hold in" or to suppress sentiments which he knows will bring censure if expressed in the immediate presence of parental authority. But the forbidden feelings or thoughts remain

ferent reaction of a Chinese youth or peasant to mistreatment or misfortune is in fact such a strategy of defense. Where one has learned through painful experience that nature is beyond one's control, or that powerful individuals are beyond one's influence, emotional mobilization can at best produce personal torment and frustration and at worst the increased pain of retaliation from those who seek to keep child or peasant "in his place."

THREE "CONTRADICTIONS" IN THE FILIAL PATTERN

While Chinese recall much that is painful about the disciplining of childhood, it should be stressed that such treatment had a logic which made it meaningful within the cultural tradition. While the child undoubtedly would have preferred avoiding the pain, he came to accept it as necessary. This is clearly illustrated in the way that our respondents described their childhood dealings with authority.

> Father was very strict. If I was out playing at night and he called me to come in to study, he would hit my hand with a bamboo and make me kneel in front of President Chiang's picture if I didn't come in right away. But now I guess it was needed; I was unruly. There is a Chinese proverb: "A strict father produces a filial son." (From the point of view of personality what was your father like?) To use

---

within his consciousness. (*See* Francis L. K. Hsu, "Suppression Versus Repression," *Psychiatry,* Vol. XII [1949], pp. 223–242.)

Our data suggest that the defense termed "isolation" perhaps more aptly describes this mechanism, for what is involved is the isolation of the emotional state from the perception. Chinese, in recalling paternal mistreatment, usually do not deny that they were wronged; they just don't relate the feelings of anger which one would assume to be associated with such treatment to the recollection. (*See* Otto Fenichel, *The Psychoanalytic Theory of Neurosis* [New York: Norton, 1945], pp. 155–164.)

Whatever the best technical description of this phenomenon, it is particularly important for the present analysis because of its relation to problems of political motivation. In the traditional society, both father and political ruler sought to establish their authority by developing feelings of "awe" (anxiety, fear) in their dependents and subjects. They seem to have assumed that through the workings of such emotions they would be inviolate to expressions of hostility or aggression. As we shall see in Ch. XII, one of the problems Mao Tse-tung dealt with in developing popular support for the Communist movement was that of bringing large numbers of peasants, by tradition fearful of dealings with authority, into political participation. The techniques of political control that he helped develop to make people politically "conscious" represent, in part, efforts to reestablish the linkage between popular perceptions of authority as harsh and unjust, and the forbidden emotions of hostility and hate which tradition said must not be expressed against those in positions of power.

another common expression, he was "hard on the outside but gentle within." He was always polite to older people, and he would not just turn away the poor but would help them out with food or money. (How was he to you children?) Very strict. . . . [But] when we grew up we knew we had learned moral truth from him. We saw all parents rearing their children in that manner. And then we saw some bad children: thieves, juvenile delinquents, and bullies. It was said that their parents had loved them too much and had harmed them. They had not reared them strictly, but just let them do as they pleased. They got bad friends and learned [improper habits] from them.[27]

The pain of childhood disciplining is thus readily acknowledged, but it had a significance which the child, in time, could understand and accept. The adult, in retrospect, recalls that he was incapable of controlling himself in the face of his emotions, and affirms that strict parental authority was required to impose orderly behavior.

In addition, society was seen as rewarding with responsibility and respect those who successfully endured the pain of becoming a filial son.

When I was young I didn't like to study, to have to kneel in punishment [when my grades were poor]. I wanted to play. But when I would go out with father and see other people really respecting him [for his learning] that was really impressive! Hence if you are not strict, your children won't study. They won't grow up to be asked by others to assume responsibility for some job. They won't be respected by them.[28]

Strong authority is thus accepted as a source of personal security, particularly because the child has been told in the diverse and often indirect ways by which parents communicate with their children that an individual is incapable of managing his behavior or emotions by himself. It is also a source of security in a world where certain people have not been properly disciplined:

There are a small number of children who, no matter how strictly they are raised, will be bad—like juvenile delinquents. (Why is that?) They learn from a bad environment. (Is it easy to learn from a bad environment?) Very! Their wills are weak and they might start to steal; and then if they get excited it can lead to fighting.[29]

Because adults know that people have been trained from childhood to depend on more powerful elders for guidance, rather than to act according to a discipline within, there remains an apprehen-

27. T-19.
28. T-18.
29. T-9.

sion that others (or they themselves?) might be led astray by evil or enticing external forces: "They got bad friends and learned from them"; "They learn from a bad environment." Trusting others becomes problematical when one is uncertain about abilities for self-control and discipline. Suspicions are easily aroused that another individual is being manipulated by some unseen authority, or that his control of dangerous feelings may not be secure. Strong authority is thus a blessing, insofar as it protects against external (or internal) threats and gives clear and proper guidance.

Filiality, the relationship between strong and experienced parent and dependent child, can be conceived as a security pact, a social contract which establishes reciprocity between the generations: Parents "agree" to nurture, protect, and discipline the child when he is a vulnerable infant so that he may mature; and the child in return "agrees" to remain dependent within the family to care for those who raised him. And as the *Classic of Filial Piety* assured, "By the practise of this . . . all embracing rule of conduct . . . the people were brought to live in peace and harmony, and there was no ill-will between superiors and inferiors." [30]

In reality, of course, a child has no choice in the matter of how his parents rear him. Parents, as well, by the nature of the way cultural attitudes and values are incorporated within their personalities, do not choose, or "agree to," such a reciprocal set of life obligations. As we have seen in the recollections of adult Chinese, the filial pattern was maintained and transmitted to each new generation through the workings of such robust sentiments as anxiety and fear, feelings tempered by affection and a sense of responsibility. But it is evident that fear or anxiety within the filial tie notwithstanding, a child could come to accept the relationship in which he sacrificed a large measure of autonomy in social matters if he received a sense of security and social worth in return.

However, there is a major vulnerability in the all-embracing and self-renouncing pattern of filiality. Should the dominant member of the relationship fail in his obligations to the dependent, or should there be discipline without nurture, then feelings of having been cheated of one's proper share, or fears about being abandoned, can easily arise in the child or dependent adult and turn to great resentment or hatred for the dominant one who failed. In the world of material scarcity and insecurity known to traditional Chinese, and given the universal frailties of the human will, such failures must have been all too common.

Of the many examples we might draw upon to illustrate this vul-

30. *Hsiao Ching*, p. 465.

nerability of the filial authority pattern, it seems useful to look at a childhood recollection of the man who has now taken the lead in the Chinese social revolution, as we will in time be referring in detail to his efforts to reshape Chinese attitudes toward authority and conflict. Mao Tse-tung, in a 1936 interview with the American journalist Edgar Snow, recounted of his early family life:

> My father wanted me to begin keeping the family books as soon as I had learned a few characters. He wanted me to learn to use the abacus. As my father insisted upon this I began to work at those accounts at night. He was a severe taskmaster. He hated to see me idle, and if there were no books to be kept he put me to work at farm tasks. He was a hot-tempered man and frequently beat both me and my brothers. He gave us no money whatever, and the most meagre food.
>
> My mother was a kind woman, generous and sympathetic; and ever ready to share what she had. She pitied the poor and often gave them rice when they came to ask for it during famines. But she could not do so when my father was present. He disapproved of charity. . . . I learned to hate him.[31]

The failure of the severe taskmaster is all too clear: He hated idleness (or insecurity?) but rewarded the diligent efforts of his dependents with castigation and stinginess. The young Mao sensed no reciprocity, only exploitation: "I learned to hate him."

As was the cultural norm, Mao was discouraged by his mother from openly venting hostility toward his father or directly challenging his authority: "My mother advocated a policy of indirect attack. She criticized any overt display of emotion and attempts at open rebellion against the Ruling Power [the father]. She said it was not the Chinese way." [32] But as we indicated earlier, her support of Mao and his brother in "a policy of indirect attack" evidently developed in the boys a strength of character which in time enabled Mao to rebel against this and other harsh and unjust social authorities.

The cultural norm, however, was that family or political author-

---

31. Snow, *Red Star over China,* pp. 125–126.

To cite another example, Chu Teh, Mao's military cohort during the years of struggle for power, recalled of his early life: "I loved my mother, but I feared and hated my father. . . . I could never understand why [he] was so cruel." (Agnes Smedley, *The Great Road: The Life and Times of Chu Teh* [New York: Monthly Review Press, 1956], p. 10.)

As is probably common to all revolutionary social movements, the Communist Party, in its formative years, seems to have drawn much vital leadership from individuals with very personal "authority problems" which motivated them to challenge established social authority through violence.

32. Snow, *Red Star over China,* p. 125.

ity should be inviolate to criticism or other expressions of hostility which might weaken its "prestige" and threaten the integrity of the filial relationship. In rearing their children, Chinese parents sought to develop attitudes and emotions which would sustain a system of authority in which initiative, guidance, and responsibility to care for dependents were vested in a dominant individual, while submissive loyalty would characterize those subordinate. To allow dependents to vent hostility at authority would threaten the security of the entire family group by placing in jeopardy its source of guidance. Who could say what confusion might reign if the source of authority were removed from individuals who had been trained to depend?

Yet, in the real world of material scarcity and human frailty the reciprocal obligations of the filial bond were not always realized[33]; and the disciplines of learning to be filial were not far removed from emotions of hostility or hate. Any father or official who him-

33. It is, of course, difficult to estimate just how effective Confucian family life was in meeting the needs of individual family members. Young Chinese had been educated to believe that this family pattern was natural and morally just; and the socialization process developed in them the attitudes and emotional needs which helped to bind the individual to his family group. It is only in such phenomena as the suicide of a young girl protesting an arranged marriage, or the running away from home of a son fearful of paternal punishment that we see individual cases of the failure of this family pattern.

Of the sixty-two cases in our particular sample for whom we have sufficient data, ten (16 percent) report that they ran away from home largely because of fear of punishment or the restrictions of family life. Six respondents recall other close family relatives who ran away.

Because this is an emigré sample, we can hardly generalize this ratio to the entire population, if for no other reason than that "running away" from adversity may be a particular characteristic of this kind of a group. One important characteristic of those respondents, however, might be noted. All of the ten who ran away from home grew up in the social dislocation which characterized Chinese society between the collapse of the Ch'ing dynasty and the founding of the Communist state. Our respondents' discussions and additional biographical data suggest that the new forms of social organization which appeared in the early twentieth century—political parties, "modern" armies, new forms of schooling, and new employment opportunities in the cities—provided alternatives for discontented young men which had not existed in the old social order. In traditional times, "eating bitterness" was probably the more frequent way in which a discontented son handled his frustrations with family life.

The fact that none of these runaways were from the younger generation reared under the Communists suggests that the Party has provided outlets for youthful frustration other than running away from home, and indeed may have begun to modify in significant ways the quality of Chinese family life. Later we will suggest that the "Cultural Revolution" was one such outlet for China's youth to vent their frustrations, although the source of discontent may have been the Party itself rather than family life.

self had been reared to filiality intuitively knew all the reasons why a son or subject might not appreciate such a position. In self-protection (and to insure maintenance of the tie which was a guarantee of its own future), authority would impose discipline and restrict expressions of dissatisfaction with firm determination. In circular fashion increased dissatisfaction would only lead to greater discipline.

This was a basic contradiction in the Confucian system of authority: The very harshness which was deemed necessary to keep children and subjects in awe could produce resentment as well as anxiety, particularly when dependence on authority was not balanced by a minimal level of support and justice. And where an authority had doubts about the filial submissiveness of his dependents he was likely to resort to even harsher measures to elicit submission, thus compounding the sense of resentment. As we shall show in later chapters, it was this pattern of authority and the ways of handling the emotions of hostility and aggression which Mao Tse-tung learned to tap and utilize in the Communist Party's struggle for power.

For most individuals living within the Confucian social tradition, however, there were a variety of strategies far short of rebellion by which they might seek to avoid injustice and reduce the pain of filial subordination. As disclosed in our interviews, such strategies primarily affected the ways in which an individual related to those with authority over him, how he tied his personal interests to those of the family or peer group which was his basic social affiliation, and how he handled such emotions as anger or hostility.

By way of summarizing the analysis in Chapters II and III, we might characterize these tensions between individual needs and social values as three "contradictions" inherent in the Confucian tradition:

1. Dependence on hierarchical authority versus self-assertion.—
This first area of tension reflects the basic authoritarianism of China's social tradition. In the Confucian conception of society, order was maintained through a structuring of social relations into hierarchical dualities, the *wu-lun*. The father-son relationship was a model structural unit which, if properly realized and emulated throughout society, would insure the interdependence of the generations, social harmony, and personal security.

As we detailed in the preceding analysis, however, the paternal harshness which was seen as necessary to the rearing of filial children produced in a maturing son a strong sense of ambivalence to authority, a desire to be nurtured and protected by it, yet anxiety about approaching too near.

While he was young, a child learned a variety of strategies for dealing with anxiety-provoking authority: avoidance of contact, ready obedience, and appeals to stronger third parties for intercession. But when older, a son discovers there are situations in which he has authority over "loyal dependents." He must submit before his father, but he can play the part of a "father" to a younger brother. Thus the ambivalence of dealings with authority can find resolution by seeking out social roles in which one is the authority. The individual in this tradition seeks to affirm the potency of the self through the submission of others.

This striving for the dominant position in social relations, however, conflicts with the concern of those already in positions of leadership to insure social order and to affirm their own authority. It competes with the desires of other would-be leaders to attain positions of dominance. From such contradictions develop the uncompromising struggle for power when authority is dead or in doubt, and the concern in peer relationships that someone is always trying to put others down.

2. Social harmony and peace versus hostility and aggression.— Aggressive behavior plays an important part in a child's efforts at self-assertion. This is a phenomenon most obviously seen in the generational conflict present in many cultures when youngsters, approaching their full maturity, seek to break away from the family group to establish an independent social identity. Such conflict, however, runs counter to parental and group purposes in the Chinese tradition, and parents sternly discourage expressions of self-assertion, willfulness, or hostility in their children. According to most observations, Chinese parents quite literally attempt to beat the aggressiveness out of their youngsters through physical punishment. It is the parents' attempt to deny any legitimacy to the limited release of any aggressive emotions in their children—sentiments which are often heightened by the very harshness of parental discipline—that accounts for this second "contradiction."

What children in fact seem to learn from their parents' stern training is that sentiments of hostility must not be expressed against those in positions of authority. A sense of fear of paternal authority is developed. The child learns to "put into his stomach" the pain of parental discipline, to "eat bitterness," or prevent the mobilization of dangerous emotions even when provoked by an older member of the family. Yet he also learns from the very aggression which these family authorities invoke to insure his own filial submission that hostile feelings are appropriately released against those subordinate in status or power.

To be sure, such aggression is usually masked behind the forms of propriety (*li-mao*): the subtle twisting of good manners into an insult; the verbal abuse before a subordinate who must passively *t'ing-hua* and eat the bitterness of bad feelings he knows must be repressed. But this pattern sets up a tension between cultural ideals of peace and harmony within the (family) group, and a reality of bickering and tensions which are only masked by the social rituals of Confucian cultivation. As one Chinese expressed it: "If you look at the face of our family, it looks good, but if you look at its bones, it is not like that. In the 'bones' of the family there is ceaseless friction." [34]

This polarization of harmony and conflict is further reinforced by the contrast between the indulgence with which adults treat young children and the subsequent harshness by which parents attempt to restrict desires for pampering and to instill discipline in maturing youngsters. In the way in which parents handle their own aggressive impulses the child learns a basic social rhythm of *ho-p'ing* and *hun-luan,* the alternation between "harmony" and the "confusion" of vented aggression.

3. Self versus group.—This third area of tension reflects the way in which Chinese tradition sought to have the individual find security through group solidarity. The basic impulse which shaped the manner in which parents reared their children was the hope that, in particular, the elder male would survive the dangers of infancy to mature and remain within the family group, giving continuity to the blood-clan over the generations and providing for the security of family elders in the dependency of old age.

It is the tension between the indulgence of infancy and the subsequent harsh discipline of youth which creates the contradiction between individual and group life. Cross-cultural evidence on child-rearing practice indicates that generous breastfeeding and other forms of oral gratification develop in a child a strong sense of trust and self-esteem, a feeling of his own worth.[35] But such attitudes, if perpetuated, would run counter to parental goals of developing in their children a strong commitment to the purposes of the family group, not to the self. Thus, the subsequent harsh disciplines of youth represent the parents' effort to arrest the development of that self-esteem which is the legacy of an indulged infancy. The child matures with a "selfish" longing to recapture the oral pleasures and the sense of power known early in life. He seeks to enjoy once again

34. Wolf, *The House of Lim,* p. 35.
35. *See* Erik H. Erikson, *Childhood and Society* (New York: Norton, 1950), pp. 67–76, 219–222; and Robert Sears *et al.,* "Some Child-Rearing Antecedents of Aggression and Dependency in Young Children," *Genetic Psychology Monographs,* Vol. XLVII (1953), pp. 135–234.

the "lazy" indulgence of consuming without effort. The parents, in fear of these strivings, find that they must discipline the child's desires to consume. What had been oral nurturance now becomes oral discipline, and the child comes to see that love is mixed with aggression in those who would forcefully feed him filiality.

As we shall see in subsequent chapters, these three areas of tension between individual and society in the Chinese tradition pervade adult social relations and shape the pattern of China's politics.

Chapter V

THE PAIN AND REWARDS
OF EDUCATION

The skills of literacy, and the opportunities available to a literate individual in traditional China, were a distant goal for most of China's peasant millions. Although formal education was "available" to the rural population by virtue of the Confucian openness to class mobility, in practice a peasant's son had little opportunity for study simply because of limited family resources. The life of subsistence farming imposed disciplines which gave individuals and families little choice in career selection or education. Sons were needed on the farm for their labor. Whatever surplus family capital might have financed education was usually allocated first to savings as a hedge against the threat of flood or drought, and then to additional security through the purchase of new land. While clan schools or imperial academies provided some educational opportunity for impoverished families, the political and economic systems of landlordism, the state bureaucracy, and merchant activity concentrated the wealth sufficient for supporting the formal education of children in the hands of only a small fraction of the population.[1]

Before a peasant child entered his teens the grinding and repetitive labor pattern of rice or wheat farming would become for him a severe taskmaster, a "teacher" who would make meaningful the virtues of yielding patience and diligence which parents had stressed. A child of the gentry was fortunate to be spared this compulsion for physical labor, yet in becoming a member of the "great tradition" of Confucian scholarship, he faced disciplines and repetitive-

1. Estimates of the total literate population are necessarily approximate, and fluctuate over time with changing economic conditions and political manipulation of either examination quotas or the actual purchase of academic degrees. A rough estimate of the literate segment of the population between 1600 and 1900 puts it at between one and two percent of the total. (Statistics on population and degree holders will be found in Ho Ping-ti, *The Ladder of Success in Imperial China*, pp. 181–182 and *passim;* and Robert M. Marsh, *The Mandarins: The Circulation of Elites in China, 1600–1900* [Glencoe, Ill.: The Free Press, 1961], esp. pp. 14–15.)

ness often no less demanding.[2] There is an almost contrived equivalence between the monotony and physical discipline of agricultural life and the mental repetitiveness and unquestioning acceptance of the teacher's authority required to become literate in the Classics.

The Chinese political tradition required a rigorous and demanding period of training in language and scholarship before one could enter the political class, that small literate percentage of the population from which a large proportion of imperial administrative officials was selected. Because the Confucian educational tradition was conceived to be training for political administration, its methods and the attitudes it sought to develop give us a rather explicit picture of the behavior considered appropriate to politics and of the values and goals which Confucian government sought to attain.

Formal education in traditional China was not so much a public process which sought to bring individuals into the larger society, as a private or family function that linked the members of each generation to the Confucian great tradition. The authority of the teacher was that of the philosopher sages who extolled the virtues of family life as the pattern of the state, and more immediately of the parents who sought education and a successful career for their children. The primary institutional form of education was private instruction in a family or clan school, termed a *szu-shu*—the first character explicitly emphasizing the private nature of formal learning. The authority of the teacher reinforced parental authority, not only directly through preaching filiality, but also indirectly by maintaining for the adolescent the same image of authority as the stern and unapproachable source of control which he knew at home.

As this relationship was expressed by a respondent from the northern province of Liaoning:

> Teachers ought to take responsibility for their students and they should treat them like their own offspring. To run a school like a business is really not good. (How should students behave toward their teachers?) Students ought to respect the teacher. (How do they express this respect?) They obey the teacher; if they don't trust the teacher how can they learn things? [3]

Another, who had been the principal of a secondary school elaborated:

> The teacher . . . must be correct in his behavior. If he himself is not correct then there is no way he can teach his students. A teacher

2. Interview data concerning punishments received in childhood indicate that performance in school was the area of a child's activities on which parental anxieties focused in upper class families. (*See* Appendix VI, pp. 559–560.)

3. H-7.

A Confucian schoolroom, Hong Kong, ca. 1910.
Radio Times Hulton Picture Library.

educating his student does not mean just broadening his knowledge; at the same time moral cultivation is very important. The student must respect the teacher and the right way of doing things. But the most important thing is that the teacher's personal morality must be very good.[4]

The teacher becomes an additional source of morality for a child to emulate, a model of behavior that he must trust and obey, or else "how can he learn things?" Establishing a proper relationship with a teacher means above all expressing dependence upon him by way of submissive "respect": "You have to respect the teacher, because if you want to learn things from him but don't respect him then he won't reveal the secrets of his craft." [5]

Parents accorded a teacher the same range of authority over their children as they themselves had. After a home education which stressed dependence on adults for discipline and guidance, children were seen as requiring even more of the parental type of control to prevent them from becoming "bad":

(What attitude did your parents have to your teachers?) While I was in primary school my parents thought the stricter the teacher was with me the better. They thought they should give the school all power and responsibility over me—some children are unruly, and if teachers are too affable they will be bad. The teacher has to be strict.[6]

As in the relation of father to son, the teacher reinforced a one-way pattern of communication. The student learned to "take in" but was strongly discouraged from talking back:

The ancient relationship between a teacher and students has been the spreading of knowledge. If the teacher says something the students must definitely obey him . . . a teacher himself must explain his students' doubts. I remember once when I was a student and didn't understand a mathematics lesson I asked the teacher [for an explanation]; but the teacher just got mad at me. This is very wrong. Afterwards I wouldn't dare to ask questions of the teacher.[7]

(Did you or your fellow students ever make jokes or play tricks on the teacher?) I never did! How could I dare? That's just too much! (Why?) "The teacher has to be strict and his students must respect him" [a common aphorism]. When the teacher teaches he stands in front of the blackboard as a representative of Confucius. You just wouldn't dare make jokes. We don't even have to talk about playing tricks on him; you would get your palms slapped. However, when it comes to studying perhaps the modern type of teacher is more en-

4. T-32.
5. T-1.
6. T-14.
7. T-35.

lightened. You can joke with him and it is relatively easy to get close to him.[8]

During the first years of formal schooling, education was a painful process of blind learning through memorization of the sound patterns of classical texts. This form of instruction was primarily a course in self-restraint. For young adolescents it was an onerous business, as is described in one anthropologist's field observations of life in a Shantung village during the 1940s:

> . . . most of the boys did not like the school. They learned their lessons by rote without understanding the meaning of what they were required to read. Except for the *Jih Yung Za Tze*, all the textbooks were completely incomprehensible to them, but they were compelled to read and to remember what they had read. It was painful work. Unfortunately, neither the teacher nor the boys' parents had any interest in remedying the situation, and the boys were forced into endless memorizing and were punished severely if they failed in this dull task. Fear of punishment also made school hateful. Once a six-year-old boy, who was reading his *San Tze Ching*, fell asleep at his table. The teacher woke him with a thunderous call, scolded him harshly, and then asked him to recite his lesson. The boy was too frightened to do it well, and for this failure he was beaten. This sort of thing used to occur very frequently.[9]

Such instruction overwhelmed the child with an adult's curriculum rather than encouraging him to develop intellectual skills commensurate with his growing mental capabilities. The effect was to reinforce the sense of anxiety before authority which had been learned at home. It sustained the child's belief that he was incapable of handling adult demands without their guidance. He learned to discipline his impulses for autonomous or exploratory thinking and behavior, and his sources of authority and guidance remained external. Responsibility for discipline in the classroom remained with the teacher, and at home with the parents, for the overwhelming task of rote learning required too much self-discipline for a lively and growing child. As was observed in the Shantung village:

> The old-fashioned school offered no recreation. As a rule, a schoolboy had to sit in his seat and keep quiet all the time. When he heard the noise, the laughter, and the wild running of the boys on the street, he and all the other pupils felt a great longing to join them but did not dare. The only chance for fun was when the teacher was not in school. On these rare occasions the boys' energy, imagination, and joy broke forth immediately and simultaneously. They overturned tables and piled up benches as a stage for an impromptu "show." *They threw*

8. T-32.
9. Martin Yang, *A Chinese Village: Taitou, Shantung Province*, p. 147.

paper balls and water holders in a game of "war." They stole into the vegetable garden near the schoolhouse to pick fruits, cucumbers, or radishes. The shouting, swearing, and laughing could be heard even by distant neighbors. One or two small boys stood guard at a far corner to watch for the teacher's coming. As soon as he was sighted and the signal was given, all the boys ran wildly back into the schoolhouse and put everything in order. Occasionally they were discovered and punished.[10]

Such a scene of undisciplined adolescence is, we must stress, not unique to Chinese society. Youngsters the world over respond to the presence, or absence, of adults who are significant in their early lives. Two aspects of this traditional educational process, however, do seem of particular importance. First, the child was not presented with opportunities for testing out in *limited* ways methods for mediated control of his urges toward aggression (as in competitive sports), or for limited intellectual achievements consonant with his capabilities. It seems likely that the child developed doubts about his own abilities for self-control and achievement as a result of the demands made upon him for memorization and physical discipline. Second—and related to this point—the child continued to be taught to depend on adults, his parents or teacher, for the discipline of which he was incapable. Rather than developing abstract principles of behavior which were gradually internalized by the growing adolescent, the boy remained bound within his relationships to those specific individuals—parent or teacher—who nurtured and disciplined him to maturity.

More specifically, the child came to identify authority with "the power of the word." At home he had learned that one manifestation of paternal authority was precedence in speaking and the right to formulate opinions. In the classroom he saw that the teacher could compel the memorization of sounds and phrases which were defined as "proper" in terms of tradition and family aspirations. To exert authority came to mean having the right both to speak and to "educate" inferiors; while to be compelled to memorize and repeat the words of a teacher became a mark of subordination, a ritual of social control. As we will detail in Chapter VII, this identification of power and control with words and the process of education was given formal legitimation in the Confucian doctrine of the "rectification of names." And as will become evident in the conclusion of this study, when a Chinese political leader has doubts about his authority, the technique he instinctively selects to reaffirm his status is "education," compelling his subjects to commit to memory his words, his "thought" (*szu-hsiang*).

10. *Ibid*. Emphasis added.

While the process of formal education thus reinforced the pattern of authority first learned at home, it also provided an individual (and his family) with the opportunity to attain the most respected identity of Chinese society, that of a cultivated *literatus* or Confucian scholar-official. Parents of the gentry or would-be gentry put great demands on their children for successful scholarship, for they saw their future well-being and the prosperity of future family generations as contingent upon the achievements of their young. In the world of the traditional Chinese social elite, all prestige and potential power and wealth were concentrated in the role of the scholar-official. Merchant or militarist might come to attain power or fortune, but so potent was the appeal of literatus status that succeeding family generations would be encouraged to seek the ultimate of social achievement through scholarship and public service in the Confucian tradition. Thus parents, and to some degree teachers, transmitted their concerns for status, security, wealth, and power to their children through demands for good scholarship.

For a maturing child these adult pressures for educational achievement brought together the authority pattern of the society and the highest opportunity for self and group realization. Parents and teachers raised his anxieties about fulfilling obligations to the family through their strict demands for performance and harsh punishments for failure; yet they also provided him a clear if painful path, and distant yet appealing goal, by which he could relieve these anxieties, meet his filial obligations, and make a name for himself:

> (When you were young how did you feel about studying?) In those days I felt I would die from studying. For instance, when I was in grammar school I would memorize to death a book no matter what the ideas inside were. The teacher would not explain [what we were memorizing]. Then we were interested in studying because we always thought that it was a way to develop a name for yourself. Father and mother thought that in the future you could become an official.[11]

Earlier we suggested that control of emotions has been central to Chinese conceptions of self-identity. In the classroom the student was taught that emotional restraint was an essential part of the Confucian tradition. The "superior man" (*chün-tzu*) was one who had learned to discipline his feelings through "self-cultivation." Social order was a function of the discipline—"equilibrium" and "harmony"—of popular emotions:

> While there are no stirrings of pleasure, anger, sorrow, or joy, the mind may be said to be in the state of EQUILIBRIUM. When those

11. T-35.

feelings have been stirred, and they act in their due degree, there ensues what may be called the state of HARMONY. This EQUILIBRIUM is the great root *from which grow all the human actings* in the world, and this HARMONY is the universal path *which they all should pursue.* (Emphasis in source cited.) [12]

Where parents had indicated implicitly by their own behavior that guarded reserve was the proper way to deal with feelings (and had punished the child's failures at emotional restraint), the Sage openly condemned expressions of emotion:

> Confucius said, "There are three things which the superior man guards against. In youth, when the physical powers are not yet settled, he guards against lust. When he is strong and the physical powers are full of vigor, he guards against quarrelsomeness. When he is old, and the animal powers are decayed, he guards against covetousness. [13]

The remedies which the Confucian tradition formally developed to cope with troublesome human emotions were "cultivation" and "rectification."

> What is meant by, "The cultivation of the person depends on rectifying the mind," *may be thus illustrated:* If a man be under the influence of passion, he will be incorrect in his conduct. He will be the same, if he is under the influence of terror, or under the influence of fond regard, or under that of sorrow and distress.
>
> When the mind is not present, we look and do not see; we hear and do not understand; we eat and do not know the taste of what we eat.
>
> This is what is meant by saying that the cultivation of the person depends on the rectifying of the mind. [14]

And while attainment of knowledge was the evident purpose of education, the Classics made it clear that knowledge and learning were in the service of personal "cultivation" and "rectification," the virtues by which the wise kings of ancient China had maintained social order.

Popular interpretations of the term "cultivation" indicate more explicitly than formal philosophical works that this basic concept of the Confucian political tradition was closely related to the concern with aggression and social conflict. As a teacher reared in Peking explained the meaning of the term "cultivation":

> Well, for instance, if I am at a bus stop waiting in line, two or three people may get in front of me. If I remonstrate with them it might

12. "Doctrine of the Mean," Ch. I, in James Legge, trans., *The Chinese Classics,* Vol. I, pp. 385–386.
13. "Analects," Book XVI, Ch. VII, *ibid.,* pp. 312–313.
14. "The Great Learning," Ch. VII, *ibid.,* p. 368.

lead to a fight. They might say, "Why are you remonstrating with me? What authority have you?" If I have cultivation, then I would just say "Let's forget it." Or if you are in a group and a person is unmannerly, you just hold in your anger and in this way avoid conflict.[15]

Through the stress that "cultivation" placed on emotional restraint, formal education reinforced a student's already developed distrust of expressions of emotionality and conflict. The examples of China's history which he learned in school, the murders and factious turmoil documented in the annals of the "Spring and Autumn" period or the writings of Mencius, and the histories of the "Warring States," gave him ample proof that conflict was an ever-present possibility. But most fundamentally, a student had learned in his own early life experience that quarreling among his peers or expressions of hostility toward adults could only invoke parental wrath. Latent anxieties about conflict were thus formalized and given the legitimacy of official doctrine in the classroom.

How was a child's immature anxiety about expressing aggression developed into a "cultivated" adult restraint?

> To become cultivated requires that you read many books. This is so that you will be able to control your emotions with your intelligence. The seven emotions of man—happiness, anger, sympathy, joy, sadness, fear, and apprehension—can be controlled by cultivation. This is the so-called "middle way" (*chung-yung*). I have seen that many friends have succeeded in their work because they can control their emotions. The most capable kind of person is one who can control the seven emotions and not be used by them.[16]

> People who are cultivated have an enlightened attitude about getting along in the world; they are fair, reasonable, and not selfish. Cultivated people are not emotionally impulsive. (How does one become cultivated?) Read many books, and study the examples of cultivated ancients. You have to forgive people, and don't get angry easily.[17]

The development of personal "cultivation" is certainly related to the process of education; but is it just a matter of "reading many books"? Perhaps the ability to hold in one's emotions is acquired more as a result of the *form* of traditional teaching methods than of their content. To a certain degree, ideas were irrelevant to the training of young students; after all, the first few years of instruction were devoted to the blind memorization of sound patterns. It seems most likely that the process of subjecting students in the full physical

15. T-9.
16. T-30.
17. T-38.

vigor of adolescence to the rigorous demands of memorization of lengthy texts, or reproducing hundreds of complicated characters by brush within the squares of a copybook, was a powerful disciplinary experience in controlling impulses to take action or vent emotional frustration.[18]

In addition, as within the family, the teacher presented a model of emotional reserve which a student would fail to emulate only on pain of being "misunderstood":

> Eastern people don't like to express friendliness to others; they want the other person to express it first and then they will express it. In college, it is the same thing with the professor and his students. The students won't necessarily say hello to the teacher, they want to wait until the professor expresses himself and then they will. Probably this is because from primary and middle school experience the teacher does not pay much attention to the students. Therefore, the students do not dare to express friendship or say hello to the teacher. It's the same with your neighbors: each side wishes to maintain its dignity. Another thing is that they are afraid the other party will not understand them.[19]

The Classical books and the Confucian classroom thus gave official sanction to the logic of filiality, or the interdependence of the generations. And how striking it is to find in the enduring texts of this millennial civilization the same concerns with laziness, overindulgence, lack of concern for parents, and conflict which we find so prominent in the attitudes of Chinese interviewed in the 1960s! As Mencius tells us:

> There are five things which are said in the common practice of the age to be unfilial: The first is laziness in the use of one's four limbs, without attending to the nourishment of his parents. The second is gambling and chess playing, and being fond of wine, without attending to the nourishment of his parents. The third is being fond of goods and money, and selfishly attached to his wife and children, without attending to the nourishment of his parents. The fourth is following the desires of one's ears and eyes, so as to bring his parents

18. An interesting example of the manner in which the forms of traditional education became an integral part of an adult's equipment for emotional discipline is found in the use of calligraphy. In the diaries of Lin Tse-hsü, the famous "Commissioner Lin" sent to Canton by the emperor in 1839 to suppress the opium trade, it has been noted that during the time he was awaiting an imperial investigation of his failure to stop the British trading activity—an investigation which carried with it very serious professional consequences—he devoted days on end to calligraphic practice as a way of calming his nerves. (*See* Arthur Waley, *The Opium War through Chinese Eyes* [London: Allen and Unwin, 1958], pp. 124–127.)

19. T-37.

to disgrace. The fifth is being fond of bravery, fighting and quarreling so as to endanger his parents.[20]

The important question which remains is whether the social attitudes and emotional concerns of China's small stratum of literate elite, as expressed in the life style and ideology of the Confucian "great tradition," were shared by illiterate peasants enduring poverty and toil in the "little tradition" of the villages.

Since almost all historical materials on China have come from the "great tradition" of Confucian scholarship and public service, our view of Chinese society has tended to be filtered through the values and world-view of this elite social stratum. Students of China, in recent years, have become concerned about the possibility of biased interpretations resulting from the unrepresentative quality of their data sources.[21] Unfortunately the material on Chinese social and political attitudes gathered for this study do not provide a complete refutation of these concerns. The individuals who participated in this research project were chosen, in part, to reflect the attitudes and life experiences of "ordinary" Chinese who are not fully a part of the formal Confucian tradition. But as we mentioned in the introduction, our tools of analysis required minimal literacy and sufficient social poise to be able to respond to an interview situation. Hence we do not have direct evidence of the social attitudes of illiterate peasants.

What our data do clearly reveal, however, is that the values inculcated as part of the "great tradition," spread beyond those who received formal training in the Confucian classics. The social outlook and values of that portion of our sample who had had only elementary schooling or who were educated decades after the abolition of the Confucian educational system are very similar to those of the elderly respondents who had been educated before the turn of the last century in Confucian schools.

As we have tried to emphasize in the first part of this study, the formal values and ideology of China's traditional political elite found expression in the daily life and verbal culture of peasant villages, and in common socialization practices. Furthermore, studies of social mobility in China indicate that there was a rapid rise and fall of family fortunes associated with uncertain attainment of a scholar's status through the imperial examinations. Access to an

20. "Mencius," Book IV, Part II, Ch. XXX, in James Legge, trans., *The Chinese Classics*, Vol. II, p. 337.

21. A recent historical text by Edwin O. Reischauer and John K. Fairbank, for example, is explicitly titled, *East Asia: The Great Tradition*, perhaps to disclaim any intention of speaking for the social history of China's voiceless peasant millions.

official position within the governmental bureaucracy was equally uncertain. While this "elite circulation" was uneven throughout the society, it did promote the interpenetration of "great" and "little" traditions.

Hence while the data marshaled for this study can only be viewed as suggestive of the distribution of social attitudes across lines of economic class and educational level, the following interpretation seems justified as a working hypothesis: The general set of attitudes toward self and interpersonal relations which we have characterized as the "dependency social orientation"—in particular a hierarchical conception of authority, a strong group sense, and anxiety about aggression and conflict—had an enduring rationale in the context of China's social and economic pattern of family and village-centered agriculture. Since the elite continued to rise from and return to this social base and maintained its source of wealth in the systems of land tenure and agricultural taxation, it sustained strong links to the pattern of rural life. One senses that the formal logic of Confucianism and the life style of the scholar-official represented an *elaboration* and ideological justification of the peasant cultural pattern, rather than being divorced from it.[22] Our data reveal no significant variation in concern with social conflict or differences in conception of authority associated with socioeconomic class or educational level. Direct observations of peasant life by anthropologists support this data. China's elite seems to have used its wealth to gratify culturally developed inclinations for oral indulgence and a "tranquil" life—luxuries which an impoverished peasant could not afford.

The full extent of continuity in basic "cultural linkage" between the elite of Chinese society and the peasantry will become clearer in the next two parts of this study. First we shall explore the elaboration of our themes of childhood socialization into adult social and political attitudes. We shall then relate these adult attitudes to the strategy of revolution developed by Mao Tse-tung and the Chinese Communists in their efforts to develop a mass following in the struggle for power.

22. The notion of "great" and "little" traditions within a cultural area was developed by the anthropologist Robert Redfield, who wrote: "The two traditions are interdependent. Great tradition and little tradition have long affected each other and continue to do so . . . . The teachings of Confucius were not invented by him singlehanded; on the other hand, [such] teachings have been and are continually understood by peasants in ways not intended by the teachers. Great and little tradition can be thought of as two currents of thought and action, distinguishable, yet ever flowing into and out of each other." (*Peasant Society and Culture: An Anthropological Approach to Civilization* [Chicago: University of Chicago Press, 1956], pp. 71–72.)

Part Two

ADULT PERCEPTIONS OF SOCIAL RELATIONS: "CONFUSION" (LUAN) AND THE NEED FOR STRONG AUTHORITY

Rice merchant's wife and starving boy, 1940s.
George Silk, Life *Magazine*, © *Time, Inc.*

Chapter VI

"PEOPLE EAT PEOPLE"

The social concerns which have dominated the development of China's political institutions, and which still suffuse interpersonal relations, center about the polarity of "unity versus conflict." Historians perceive a rhythm in Chinese political life which reflects this polarity, the so-called "dynastic cycle": the alternation of periods of ordered peace and social stability with episodes of disintegration and violent conflict.[1] One of the philosophers of the Confucian tradition in centuries past saw this rhythm as elemental to human society: "A long time has elapsed since this world of men received its being, and there has been along its history now a period of good order, and now a period of confusion." [2]

Ordinary Chinese see this alternation of order and confusion in the context of conflict between the centralized authority of the emperor versus regional, clique, or clan groupings. Confucian philosophers relate this social rhythm to the moral qualities of the man who wields imperial power. Both philosopher and peasant share common ideals of peace, harmony, political unification and "The Great Togetherness" (ta-t'ung), and fear of confusion (hun-luan), social disintegration, and violence.

The historical records of the Confucian tradition amply document the civil disorder which this tradition of government has long sought to remedy. As a basis for considering the system of authority which characterized the Confucian political order, we shall first look at the attitudes toward social relations which made this pattern of political leadership meaningful to Chinese for more than two millennia.

Consonant with their perception of a tendency for political disintegration and turmoil in social life, Chinese express apprehen-

1. A useful collection of materials detailing the "dynastic cycle" concept will be found in John Meskill, ed., *The Pattern of Chinese History: Cycles, Development, or Stagnation?* (Boston: D. C. Heath, 1965).

2. "The Works of Mencius," in James Legge, trans., *The Chinese Classics* (Shanghai: 1935), Vol. II, p. 279.

sion at the ever-present possibility of conflict in interpersonal relations. One of our interviewees, a semiliterate young man of peasant
background from Kwangtung Province, expressed this anxiety in a
distinctive, and now familiar, manner in responding to one of the
TAT pictures. He saw in Card IX [3] three students threatened by a
group of ruffians. The students were undecided as to the best way
to deal with the threat:

> (Interviewer's question) So these fellows in the foreground disagree
> as to what they should do?
>
> (Respondent's reply) They are not of one opinion. The other two fel-
> lows are thinking of a way to deal with those ruffians (*liu-mang*).
> [One says], "I have my method." The other one is thinking, "I will
> have no difficulty [in dealing with this situation]. As for the govern-
> ment, although there are police, they, ah!—they want money. They
> won't deal with our problem. This small matter—they probably won't
> have anything to do with it."
>
> [This student in the foreground] feels he is not strong enough, how-
> ever. He has had no experience in dealing with such affairs of the
> world, and so he can't manage such a situation by himself. "It would
> not do *not* to have a government," the student is thinking, "because
> there is always fighting. *If there were no government, people couldn't
> live in society. People eat people, the big ones eat the small; they will
> eat them all up. Although people don't really eat people, society could
> eat you up. If there were no government, naturally people would eat
> each other; eat each other all up.*" [4]

Now it is most unlikely that this semiliterate peasant had ever
read Lu Hsün's *Diary of a Madman* (published in 1918), in which
a leading intellectual of China's "May Fourth" era, protesting the
Confucian tradition, also characterized Chinese society as one
which "ate men." This way of conceptualizing the threatening aspects of social life seems to tap common roots about the way interpersonal tensions are handled.

Lu Hsün related the "man eating" quality of Chinese society to
the demands of filiality, which consumed the life of the younger
generation in self-sacrifice for their elders: "I remember when I
was four or five years old, sitting in the cool of the hall, my brother
told me that if a man's parents were ill, he should cut off a piece of
his flesh and boil it for them if he wanted to be considered a good
son. . . . I have only just realized that I have been living all these
years in a place where for four thousand years they have been eat-

3. *See* the Thematic Apperception Test pictures in Appendix IV, pp.
538–540 below.
4. T-15. Emphasis added.

ing human flesh." [5] The Kwangtung peasant more generally relates this conception to problems of social authority and conflict; to the fact that people with power take advantage of those who have none. "The big ones eat the small."

We noted in Chapter III that Chinese are taught to hold in aggressive impulses, and to put frustrations "in the stomach." This terminology implies that interpersonal tensions, which Chinese see handled in such "oral" terms as back-biting and verbal abuse, making an adversary "lose face," and masking hostility behind the "polite" forms of *k'o-ch'i* verbal exchange and table ritual, can make an individual feel "consumed" with restrained anger. And as we shall see in Chapter IX on political perceptions, social power is conceived in the image of a tiger who quite literally devours the most precious and life-sustaining substance of all, food. Taxation, the usurious rents of the landlord, or a foraging army can, almost literally, "eat" one by consuming a limited food supply.

Whatever the psychological mechanism which lies behind the concept that "people eat people," it is clear that this is one verbal manifestation of an anxiety, widely shared in Chinese society, about conflict in interpersonal relations. Children of all social classes are taught that they must not fight with siblings or peers. Parental punishments build up in a growing child considerable anxiety about releasing hostility or being aggressive. This stress on avoiding conflict arouses in Chinese the apprehension that there is a fund of bad feelings within other people which should not be provoked, lest it lead to hostility or violence.

Our interview respondents consistently expressed the belief that it is proper to interfere in the behavior of other people to prevent them from doing bad things which would be harmful to society. This attitude, however, is in tension with the fear that in so doing resentment or hatred "held within" the offending person will be provoked into the open, leading to conflict. As expressed by the son of a shopkeeper from rural Kwangtung:

> At first I thought I should [remonstrate with a bothersome neighbor], but then I got to thinking about the Chinese sayings, "Sweep the snow in front of your own door," and "An enlightened person guards himself." Today in China you have the tradition of minding your own business. (Why is it this way?) If you don't, if you don't consider a man's power, you can bring out his resentment. (In what way?) You might get into a fight, or get beaten up in a dark alley at night. So you have to be very careful not to say anything in front of other people when it isn't your business. [6]

5. "A Madman's Diary," in *Selected Works of Lu Hsün* (Peking: Foreign Languages Press, 1956), Vol. I, p. 20.
6. T-12.

Inasmuch as children are taught to hold in their resentments and frustrations, it is not strange that they grow up *assuming* that other people are bottling up bad feelings too. Whether harmful emotional energy or hatred actually *is* pent up is less important than the belief that it is there, for the belief shapes behavior.

In the discussion of doctrines and processes of formal education in Chapter V we noted that the Confucian tradition viewed personal "cultivation" as an important method for insuring social harmony. "Cultivation" was viewed as the personal discipline which would limit social conflict.

The majority of China's peasant population, of course, had no opportunity to become "cultivated" through the long and intensive disciplinary process of traditional education. Probably part of the aloofness with which the "cultivated" literati held themselves apart from the peasantry, and their stern use of authority in dealing with the common people, was based on the apprehension that these uneducated souls lacked self-discipline. Just as a child required stern paternal authority to keep him from becoming bad, so the common people required the harshness of "father-mother officials" (*fu-mu kuan*) to keep them from being unruly.

Activities which would tend to foster aggressiveness or conflict, such as athletic competition or militarism, were viewed by the literati as threatening to social order—perhaps because such stimulation tended to draw out an individual's capacity for aggression. Thus competition in most of its forms was discouraged in the traditional society. Competitiveness came to be closely identified with the unrestrained aggressiveness of interpersonal violence and war. A law professor from Hunan Province answered the question, "What is the effect of interpersonal competition on society?" thus: "Initially competition between people is not bad. For instance, two people may cooperate in doing something, but in the middle of things they may get to fighting over their personal interests, and then it's 'I'll kill you or you'll kill me.' " [7]

This notion that conflicts of personal interest can easily lead to deadly violence, even in the context of cooperation, seems to reflect an idea we saw earlier regarding childrearing: Human emotions are considered dangerous and uncontrollable once mobilized. Hence, interpersonal relations are laden with anxiety for they always contain the possibility of serious conflict.

Then too, in a subsistence agricultural economy, the insecurities of life undoubtedly contributed to the serious consequences of conflict. Avoidance of conflict became a matter of survival in a situa-

7. T-31.

tion where family energies were fully committed to the basic task of producing enough to eat.

Given this set of perceptions and emotional concerns, China's difficulty in becoming a well integrated national society is understandable. Reluctance to face up to points of dispute and avoidance of contact out of fear of aggression fragment the society into suspicious family groupings. This phenomenon was described by a respondent from a well-to-do rural family of Anhwei Province:

> (What kind of a relationship did your family have with the neighbors?) Most of our neighbors were farmers. Those who got along well had contact rather often, and those who didn't get along too well usually understood [what the situation was] and went out of their way to avoid having contact. (Why didn't some get along?) For instance, because their children fought. *Everyone in general avoided contact so as to avoid quarrelsome situations.*[8]

There is an all-or-nothing quality about this style of social relations: either the full trust and reliance characteristic of "dependency," or apprehension and avoidance of outsiders. Extending the range of social transactions beyond a close circle of known and trusted individuals is unlikely when there is an expectation that one will be cheated, or where the striving for personal interests seems to lead to violent conflict.

With such a view of social relations, it is not surprising that the world of childhood seems a safe and tranquil "golden age":

> Youth is a relatively happy period of life because you have no responsibility. In those times society was relatively simple, not so complicated (*fu-tza*) as today. Now if people seek to make friends they have some [ulterior] motive. Relations between friends usually have some political or economic flavor. There are many people who are not so talented but who have bad motives creating a lot of confusion (*luan*) for their own selfish interests.[9]

The particular vocabulary which this young man from Kwangtung uses to express the difficulties of interpersonal relations, of "complications" and of conflict leading to social "confusion," is encountered again and again in the responses of our interviewees. It suggests that Chinese conceptualize social conflict within a formula of *"complicated"* (*fu-tza*) *interpersonal relationships leading to competition, producing conflict and violence which creates social chaos or "confusion"* (*hun-luan*).

"Complications" imply emotional tension, conflicting desires,

8. T-27. Emphasis added.
9. H-7.

unresolved issues of great importance, and interpersonal hostility. It can be said of an individual, "That man is complicated." A relationship with another person, or a social situation, can be characterized as "complicated," all with the implication that conflict is a likely possibility just behind the face of social custom.

In this second part of the study, which focuses on adult Chinese attitudes toward authority, social relations, and politics, we will explore the roots of the social tension between unity and conflict in basic Chinese cultural patterns, some of which were identified in Part One as growing from childhood educational experiences. More specifically, we will suggest that Chinese hold a paradoxical orientation to social authority which draws its inspiration from this tension between unity and conflict. On the one hand, they look to authority for security against conflict and material deprivation, and willingly accept as "natural" a unitary, dominant, and personalized political leadership. On the other hand, however, they express concern with the manipulative and harsh qualities of that same authority, and seek to avoid contact with what is seen as the "tiger" of governmental power.

Chapter VII

INSTITUTIONAL PATTERNS
OF AUTHORITY

> The philosopher Yu said, "They are few who, being filial and fraternal, are fond of offending against their superiors. There have been none, who, not liking to offend against their superiors, have been fond of stirring up confusion (*luan*)." [1]

A pervasive concern with social disorganization and interpersonal conflict gave enduring meaning to the authoritative institutions of Chinese society, and an individual's early-life experiences with family authority prepared him for commitment to these social institutions as an adult. The major patterns of relations with authority which we found in our investigation of childhood recollections—dependence, emulation, and the power of the word—are encountered again in the more elaborate dress of Confucian political concepts. Thus early life experiences and political orthodoxy combined to give coherence to what has been one of the world's most enduring political systems.

THE IMPORTANCE OF NAMES

The structure of interpersonal relations was embodied in society's five moral or natural relationships (*wu-lun*): the pattern of deference and obligation linking ruler and minister, father and son, husband and wife, brothers, and friends. This concept differs significantly from the Western notion of an individual's social "role," because unlike a role, which is defined in terms of the action of the *individual*, the Chinese emphasis is on the *relationship*. In the Confucian tradition an individual's social identity was defined not so

---

1. From "The Analects," in *The Chinese Classics,* Vol. I, p. 138.

much by what he had achieved, as by those to whom he was related through ties of kinship or personal loyalty.[2]

This social structure is reflected in the Chinese language—in its highly differentiated terminology for identifying social, and specifically family, relationships.[3] More importantly, it is revealed in the way that Chinese *use* language. In any society there are rituals for mediating interpersonal relations, particularly power relationships, the interaction between the superior and subordinate. The Chinese language, with its mystical origins in bone divination, carries great weight in this regard, as is expressed in the Confucian doctrine of the "rectification of names":

> Tsze-lu said, "The ruler of Wei has been waiting for you, in order with you to administer the government. What will you consider the first thing to be done?"
>
> The Master replied, "What is necessary is to rectify names (*cheng-ming*).
>
> "If names be not correct, language is not in accordance with the truth of things. If language be not in accordance with the truth of things, affairs cannot be carried on to success. . . .
>
> "Therefore a superior man considers it necessary that the names he uses may be spoken [appropriately], and also that what he speaks may be carried out [appropriately]. What the superior man requires is just that in his words there may be nothing incorrect." [4]

In the life of an individual, the importance of words was impressed upon him early in his dealings with paternal authority. Words were further invested with considerations of status in the learning of kinship nomenclature. This was no small task:

> [The] *Ta Ch'ing Lü Li* (Laws and Regulations of the Ch'ing Dynasty) distinguished forty-one different groups of kinship members, each group designated by distinct kinship terms. Within a group, each member was designated by an individual term based on sex and age, age being arranged numerically by the order of birth, such as "first

2. The anthropologist Hsu suggests the term "situation-centered" to describe this type of social structure. It would seem that the term "relation-centered" is a more accurate description, primarily because the word "situation" has a strong spatial connotation. The essence of the Confucian system was the set of interpersonal relationships, and more specifically the blood relations, which defined an individual's social identity. *See* Francis L. K. Hsu, *Americans and Chinese, Two Ways of Life* (New York: Henry Schuman, 1953), p. 10.

3. A thorough analysis of Chinese kinship terminology will be found in Han-yi Feng, "The Chinese Kinship System," *Harvard Journal of Asiatic Studies*, Vol. II, No. 2 (July 1937), pp. 141–275.

4. From "The Analects," in *The Chinese Classics*, Vol. I, pp. 263–264.

elder sister" or "third elder brother." These terms were used by kinship members in addressing one another.[5]

The sociologist C. K. Yang observed in a study of life in a south China village,

> Learning the complete system of kinship terms constituted an important part of a peasant's training to fit him for social life in a kinship oriented community. . . . The effective operation of this complicated system . . . enabled each individual in the kinship group to identify his own status, to assert his authority or to offer his obedience, to exercise his privilege or to fulfill his obligations.[6]

The concept behind this stress on nomenclature seems to have been that if people acted according to the obligations of the social relationships into which they had been born or matured (a "Son" or a "Father") or of which they had been named a part (a "Prince" or his "Minister"), then society would be properly ordered, each individual would be cared for, and there would be no "confusion." The development of an elaborately differentiated set of status "names" is basic to this conception, for it would make unmistakably clear to everyone who was to show filial deference to whom, and who was to depend on whom.

The practical problem, however, is to insure that a person behaves in accordance with the requirements of his "name." This problem finds expression in the concern shown by both Chinese philosophers and political leaders for "rectification," for insuring that people behave as their status names say they should. Of course, humans have a well-developed ability for maintaining the form of an ideal in the absence of its reality: a minister calls himself a loyal Minister just as he is trying to unseat his prince; or a father does things to his son that no proper Father would do. And the classical literature of Confucianism amply documented the social disruption that resulted when individuals did not act as their status names required.

What then was the reality which developed from Confucius' doctrine that, "There is government when the prince is a Prince, and the minister a Minister, when the father is a Father, and the son a Son"?[7] First, it is clear that political philosopher and official alike, ruling in times when the state was unable to maintain a pervasive presence in society, looked to such basic social organizations as the

---

5. C. K. Yang, *Chinese Communist Society: The Family and the Village* (Cambridge, Mass.: M.I.T. Press, 1965), Vol. II, pp. 86–87.
6. *Ibid.*
7. From "The Analects," in *The Chinese Classics*, Vol. I, p. 256.

family and clan to assume much of the burden of insuring social order. The sense of respect for authority which Confucian family life sought to instill was seen as basic to the stability of the dynasty; and in times of increasing disorder imperial officials sought to strengthen family and clan life:

> Without the *tsung-tzu* as the clan head, the imperial court has no hereditary official to depend on. If the system of *tsung-tzu* is revived, people will learn to respect their ancestors and value their origins, and then the court will naturally command more respect. In ancient times, young people looked up to their fathers and elder brothers. Now the reverse is true, because people no longer respect their origins. . . . Only recognition of the relationship between superior and subordinate, between high and low, can insure order and obedience without confusion. How can people live properly without some means of control? [8]

If children were reared to respect the system of authority embodied in strict adherence to the nomenclature, imperial officials assumed, then the emperor's subjects would know their places in society. "This is what is meant by the saying, 'The government of his kingdom depends on his regulation of the family.' " [9]

RITUALS OF CONTROL

Deference rituals played an important part in maintaining the hierarchical system of authority ideally defined by the *wu-lun*. An individual used status names in addressing other people, and practiced the rituals of filiality—the *k'ou-t'ou* before parents at New Year's time and the ceremonies of ancestor worship—as a way of indicating his continuing commitment to the social order.[10] Saying the name became a way of reaffirming the authority hierarchy. As one respondent's almost unconscious use of family nomenclature indicates, if the proper verbal symbol has not been invoked the defer-

8. A quote from the Northern Sung philosopher Ch'eng I, cited in Hui-chen Wang Liu, "An Analysis of Chinese Clan Rules: Confucian Theories in Action," in David S. Nivison and Arthur F. Wright, eds., *Confucianism in Action* (Stanford: Stanford University Press, 1959), pp. 64–65.

9. From "The Great Learning," in *The Chinese Classics*, Vol. I, p. 372.

10. The subversive impact on the legitimacy of authority that would result from refusals to perform deference rituals is illustrated with particular clarity in the tensions and drama surrounding early Sino-British diplomatic contact. British unwillingness to perform the kowtow ceremony before the emperor raised anxieties among Ch'ing imperial officials, who feared the effect on the Chinese of this demonstration of lack of respect for the Manchu court. For interesting documentation on Ch'ing official reactions to one of the first English refusals to abide by the tribute system see John L. Cranmer-Byng, *Lord Macartney's Embassy to Peking in 1793 from Official Chinese Documents* (Hong Kong: University of Hong Kong Press, 1961).

ential relationship has been left in doubt: "(How did your father teach you to behave toward family elders?) Naturally we had to respect them. If father's brothers—we called them *shu-shu,* and we were very mannerly (*li-mao*) to them—if they came to visit we couldn't sit down unless they asked us to." [11]

Words thus acquire great "political" weight, for failure to use them properly signals to the individuals involved a person's unwillingness to accept the prescribed power relationships. Conversely, an authority will go to great lengths to make certain that the proper words are spoken before the right people, for it is in the *act* of speaking the name that acceptance of the deference pattern is affirmed.

Family rituals provided the basic model for an individual's efforts to establish relationships with other people. When a parent introduced an acquaintance to his child as "auntie" or "uncle" he indicated the desire to have the individual treated with the same respect and intimacy due those who more accurately bore such titles. And in political life, attempts to establish alliances or stabilize relationships of power frequently took the form of family ritual:

> After his defeat at Kiangsi, Sun Ch'uan-fang went to Tientsin to ask the northern warlords for assistance. He begged Marshal Chang Tso-lin to forgive his previous revolt against the Fengtien Clique. Sun even went through the rites of kowtow and made Chang his adoptive father and Chang Hsueh-liang, son of the Marshal, his sworn brother.[12]

This affirmation of authority relationships through ritualized deference is reinforced by the form of social sanction most characteristic of Chinese society. In Part One we noted how children were educated to acquire great sensitivity to shaming as a form of punishment. They learned to fear "sticking out" from their proper relationships to others. The adult expression of this sensitivity is embodied in the complex calculus of "face," of social approbation for successful management of life's interpersonal responsibilities and ridicule for failures.[13] One could "lose face" by not observing properly the rituals of deference to others and by not fulfilling the obligations which were implied by the social pattern of authority and dependence. If he feared "losing face" before relatives or peers or was anxious to "acquire face," an individual could observe with

11. T-18.
12. From *The Reminiscences of General Li Tsung-jen* (unpublished manuscript of the Columbia University East Asian Institute, Chinese Oral History Project, n.d.), Ch. XXI, p. 1.
13. The most thorough exploration of the meanings of "face" will be found in Hsu Hsien-chin, "The Chinese Concepts of 'Face,'" *American Anthropologist,* Vol. XLVI (January–March 1944), pp. 45–65.

exaggerated correctness those ritualized forms of behavior which would publicly indicate his desire to assume his social obligations.[14]

Students of animal life have observed that ritualized forms of behavior play an important part in the control of conflict among members of a given species, and the affirmation of status relationships within an animal group.[15] Social ritual, the *li,* seems to have played a similar role in Confucian efforts to end social violence and maintain the integrity of authority. As expressed by the philosopher Hsün Tzu: "*Li* is that whereby . . . love and hatred are tempered, whereby joy and anger keep their proper place. It causes the lower orders [of society] to obey, and the upper orders to be illustrious."[16]

The Chinese conception *ch'eng,* usually translated as "sincerity," is closely related to the effort to control troublesome human emotions through social ritual. In the West "sincerity" implies that an individual acts on the "outside" in congruence with his inner feelings. The Chinese, as we saw in Chapter III, have considerable distrust of what is being held inside, of what has been "put in the stomach." The last thing they want is to have inner feelings find public expression. Their conception of "sincerity" is exactly the opposite of the Western meaning. One demonstrates "sincerity" by commitment to one's interpersonal obligations, to society, and not to one's inner feelings. Indeed, one is perhaps most sincere when doing the socially correct thing at precisely the time that inner feelings are urging a different course of action. Sincerity in the Confucian context means bringing social behavior into accord with an external truth of moral or social principles, *not* inner feelings: "[The man] who possesses sincerity is he who, without an effort, hits what is right, and apprehends without the exercise of thought —he is the sage who naturally and easily embodies the right way. He who attains to sincerity is he who chooses what is good, and firmly holds it fast."[17]

14. Western observers of corruption and nepotism in Chinese bureaucratic behavior have tended to overemphasize the element of individual consumption in such practice, without seeing its basic relationship to the interdependent quality of Chinese social life. Such behavior was usually motivated by an individual's desire not to "lose face" before those members of his family and clan who had supported him in his rise to public office. Similarly, conspicuous consumption by Chinese in positions of social leadership represented efforts to "increase face," to obtain the loyalty and respect of dependents by indicating a willingness to care for their needs.

15. *See* Konrad Lorenz, *On Aggression* (New York: Harcourt, Brace, and World, 1966), Ch. V.

16. Cited in Donald J. Munro, *The Concept of Man in Early China* (Stanford, Calif.: Stanford University Press, 1968), p. 33.

17. From "The Doctrine of the Mean," in *The Chinese Classics,* Vol. I, p. 413.

To be sincere is to be socially trustworthy, to demonstrate self-discipline, to conform to the proper pattern of human relationships and thus to contribute to social order.

MODELING

How were individuals raised in this tradition taught to be "sincere," to fit their behavior within the social "box" whose boundaries were formed by familial and social relationships? An important aspect of the development of this form of social discipline seems to have been embodied in the techniques of formal education. Acquiring the self-control for rote memorization of lengthy texts and repetitive copying of characters into the squares of a copybook would seem to develop the discipline for "holding in" emotional impulses and adapting one's behavior to approved social forms. Also, the constant use of models—characters to copy, approved texts to commit to memory—and punishments which made obedience the most painless course of action, must have reinforced the perception gained from family life of the importance of emulating those in authority.

The notion that superiors in status are models of behavior to be emulated is, as was discussed in Part One, quite basic to a child's image of parental authority. The teacher was also presented as one who would make an example of his behavior (*i-shen-tso-tse*) for the child to follow. This conception of authority and leadership applied as well to political life:

> Let the ruler discharge his duties to his elder and younger brothers, and then he may teach the people of the state.
>
> In the Book of Poetry, it is said, "In his deportment there is nothing wrong; he rectifies all the people of the state." Yes; when the ruler, as a father, a son, and a brother, is a model, then the people imitate him.[18]

This image of authority brings to mind subordinates within the cardinal social relationships—ministers, sons, wives, and younger brothers—attentively searching the actions of their superiors for guides to proper behavior. One can see a series of influence hierarchies in which the man at the top carries out a proper action which is then imitated down the line. But in practice how did this idealized conception of leadership function? Our interview materials indicate that people do, in fact, look to superiors for guidance and initiative. Indeed, an important aspect of this system of authority relations is that initiative and precedence in communication are vested in those with power. To describe such a relationship as one

18. From "The Great Learning," in *The Chinese Classics*, Vol. I, p. 372.

of "modeling," however, would be inaccurate, for *within* the tie there is no equivalence or reciprocity; the subordinate does not copy or emulate his superior's action in response. The subordinate, rather, looks to the superior for cues or instruction as to what will be appropriate or permissible behavior on his part. Filiality requires that deference in judgment and decision-making, and communication precedence, be given to the superior within the relationship.

Modeling or imitation of the superior's behavior does seem to occur, however, through the subordinate's adopting his superior's style and judgments of what is proper or permissible behavior *in those other relationships in which he himself is a superior*. In so many of our respondents' descriptions of family life an elder brother is a Son with his father, but a Father with his younger brother. In this sense, the behavior of a prince or a father is transmitted down the hierarchy of social authority. This tendency gave the Confucian tradition its hope that if only a proper leader could be found, his influence would pervade the entire society. But this system of authority also embodied the fear that if the top leader were *not* a "superior man," then the entire society would be vulnerable to the pervasive imitation of a bad model:

> From the loving example of one family a whole state becomes loving, and from its courtesies the whole state becomes courteous, while, from the ambition and perverseness of the One man, the whole state may be led to rebellious disorder—such is the nature of the influence. This verifies the saying, "Affairs may be ruined by a single sentence; a kingdom may be settled by its One man." [19]

ANXIETY IN THE FACE OF AUTHORITY

In terms of the functioning of personality how does this system of leadership seem to have worked? Our findings concerning adult attitudes toward authority follow from the descriptions of how authority was first experienced in childhood. In Part One we emphasized the "dependency" theme in family relations. The traditionally educated male child was taught that he was to depend on his parents, and especially his father, for guidance, initiative, and security. To give emotional force to this conception, parental punishments developed in the child anxieties about either acting independently or contravening parental guidance. Adults reared in this tradition carry with them the legacy of this early-life experience: an anxiety before social authority which produces such behavior as indirection in dealings with superiors, great reluctance to criticize, and an over-willingness to please those in power.

19. *Ibid.*, pp. 370–371.

Perhaps the best way to describe this orientation is a sense of passive impotence before power. The TAT interpretations of our respondents were particularly helpful in exploring this attitude. A typical interpretation of the relation between superior and subordinate was given by a 28-year-old factory worker from Kwangtung Province:

> This [older] person is rather experienced in social matters; an understanding person. This other fellow is relatively young and inexperienced. They have some kind of a relationship. (What kind?) Like commercial people, but yet not like that; like landlords, but yet not. In any case, rather low level in society.
>
> The older man is telling the younger to do something. (What kind of thing?) Not too enlightened a thing. (Why?) You can tell just from their appearances. The younger fellow is fearful; he is unwilling to do it. (What kind of thing might it be?) Just not proper. That could include many things [laughs].
>
> (What does the older man feel about the younger?) He is just telling him to do the job and not to worry about it as the responsibility is all on his shoulders. (How does the younger feel about the older?) He is afraid; he doesn't dare to do the thing.
>
> (What is the result of this situation?) He goes and does it. (Does he succeed?) From his expression he does it and fails, because he is afraid. (Afterwards what is the relationship between the two men?) The older one feels the younger is of no use. (What about the younger?) He thought it could not be avoided, doing that thing, so he did it. (How does he feel toward the elder man?) Nothing in particular; he just had to do the thing. (Then what is their relationship?) The younger man is arrested. (By whom?) The police, another organization, or intelligence group. Then the older man runs away. The younger is very straightforward in telling [his captors] about the thing.[20]

This interpretation is interesting in a number of respects: The initially favorable characterization of the more powerful man—"an understanding person"—changes to one who is manipulating the innocent young man for malevolent purposes. The initial "face" of benevolent authority is quickly dropped, and the respondent reads into the situation his own fears of being manipulated by those with power.[21]

Second, the respondent is unable to face up to the nature of the young man's misdeed. Many of the people we interviewed refused

20. T-12. This interpretation was given in response to TAT Card IV.
21. Other TAT interpretations alter the characterization of authority in the opposite direction: A powerful individual initially is described as being evil or manipulative, but then the respondent "covers over" this disturbing face of authority by making the man benevolent, as if to deny the existence of such exploitation.

to identify improper acts. This "covering over" implies either that whatever the young man in the picture is contemplating is too terrible to articulate or that simply naming the evil deed is tantamount to its execution. Both these factors may be at work, although the second interpretation has particular importance in this tradition. As was observed earlier, Chinese feel that to let people see improper behavior even in the fantasy world of movies or novels brings the act closer to reality, because it may incite others to its performance.

The respondent reveals, as well, an unwillingness to discuss openly the emotional reaction of the young man to such manipulation: "(How does he feel toward the older man?) Nothing in particular. . . ." As we suggested in Chapter III, an individual seems to learn to protect himself against manipulation by divorcing bad feelings from the unavoidable perception that he has been mistreated. By preventing anger from welling up the manipulation may not be avoided, but at least one does not feel so bad about it or become provoked into a rash response against implacable and dangerous power.

Finally, there is described an effortless submission to a new source of authority after the "bad" man has fled. The young man shows no guilt at having done something improper, precisely because in the face of authority he was powerless to do otherwise. The subordinate seeks protection by investing as little of himself in the relationship as possible. There is no sense of personal responsibility; indeed he may have failed deliberately so as to "get back at" the one who promised to bear the responsibility, and who manipulated him into doing something improper.

Now in theory the Confucian tradition did not sanction this passive and uncritical obedience of a subordinate to his superiors. As the *Classic of Filial Piety* instructs:

> . . . when a case of unrighteous conduct is concerned, a son must by no means keep from remonstrating with his father, nor a minister from remonstrating with his ruler. Hence, since remonstrance is required in the case of unrighteous conduct, how can [simple] obedience to the orders of a father be accounted filial piety? [22]

But the formally articulated social ideal runs afoul of the workings of personality. The legacy of learning to be filial carries with it a basic anxiety about dealings with authority, which seems to dominate the behavior of those in subordinate positions.

Interview responses indicate a number of other emotional factors which tend to reinforce a sense of anxiety and impotence be-

22. *Hsiao Ching,* in Max F. Müller, ed., *Sacred Books of the East* (Oxford, England: Clarendon Press, 1879–1910), Vol. III, p. 484.

fore power. The fear of conflict, of provoking aggression in the superior, is a theme frequently encountered:

> (Why did you agree a little bit with the notion that subordinates should avoid criticizing their superiors?) It's difficult to explain. . . . You don't want to criticize your superiors too directly. The boss might misunderstand, he might think we were opposing him or not obeying his orders. He might get angry and then conflict would develop; and possibly the outcome would be bad for you. Therefore I approve of criticism, but it has to be agreeable. You have to understand the superior's degree of cultivation. If he is insufficiently cultivated, if his personality is too strong, then he will have no way of accepting criticism, and it is just best for you to leave him of your own accord. Don't get near him.[23]

In addition to anxieties about aggression, the complex of emotional concerns we have termed "dependency," of wanting to be cared for and a fear of being "cut off" from a powerful individual who will provide guidance and security, further limit a subordinate's critical ability:

> If a subordinate is very polite, very mannerly, and unconditionally obeys his superior [in tasks he is given], the superior will rely upon him and will let him do anything. . . . A subordinate should not express his own opinions in front of a superior; he cannot contradict or contend with him. If you should say that the leader has made some error you will destroy his position. He definitely will be angry with you, will hate you; he will not want to use you again.[24]

There is no dishonor attached to wanting to be used by a more powerful individual, for "being used" (as opposed to "being cheated") implies security—that one has found a relationship within which one gains responsibility and power. And where one's security is intimately related to the status and success of an authoritative individual, criticism comes to be self-destructive, if not directly through rejection by the superior, then indirectly as a result of the superior's loss of position.

Interview data indicate that fear of rejection by authority is predominantly of an economic nature—losing a job or a position of subordinate responsibility—rather than fear of loss of affection or respect. Consonant with the way in which authority was learned in childhood, there is no expectation of such positive emotional sentiments as affection, humor, or warmth in dealings with authority. The subordinate looks only for material security or the status and

23. T-40.
24. T-49.

responsibility that will come to him indirectly through association with a more powerful man.

This tradition of filial or loyal dependence on those with power develops in a subordinate the sense that neither authority nor responsibility can be shared; they are only delegated or acquired indirectly within a superior-subordinate relationship. Hence a passivity, a reluctance to take initiative or to be critical—what the historian Balazs has termed a "panicky fear of assuming responsibility" [25]—becomes the safest course for avoiding the harshness of authority.

DEPENDENCY AND SOCIAL INTEGRATION

The fear that "talking back" to authority, or even airing differences of opinion among family members, will lead to conflict and "confusion" has serious implications for social integration. Respondents' expectations about the manner in which disputes are dealt with both within and beyond the family were revealed in their interpretations of the TAT pictures. The general impression they give is that interpersonal problems are resolved only with considerable difficulty.

The following description of a dispute within the family was given by a 32-year-old government clerk from Kwangtung, responding to TAT Card III:

> This looks like a family. The mother and father are rather conservative from the looks of their clothing. The son is pleading with his father about something. (What kind of circumstance is this?) From their faces *it looks as if they have already split apart. The problem can't be solved.* The father has already decided. The mother is very fearful. (What kind of an affair would this be about?) According to the present situation, it probably is about money. (How does the son feel?) He is very pitiable. You can see it from his face. (What attitude does he have toward his father?) He is beseeching him. (And what attitude does the father have toward the son?) He is trembling with rage. The mother is very much afraid. (What about the father?) He hates the son because he has done some bad thing. (What kind of a thing?) It is about money [laughs].

25. Etienne Balazs, *Chinese Civilization and Bureaucracy*, trans. H. M. Wright, ed. Arthur F. Wright (New Haven: Yale University Press, 1964), p. 18.

Students of Chinese bureaucratic behavior have amply documented the paralysis of initiative and creativity that resulted from the traditional system of authority. *See,* for example, Albert Feuerwerker, *China's Early Industrialization* (Cambridge, Massachusetts: Harvard University Press, 1958), pp. 23–24.

(Afterwards what will be the relation of the father to the son?) The son, for a short period won't have anything to do with the father, as they can't solve the problem. (Ultimately?) *They will get together as before. After all, it is a family.* (How will the father then feel toward the son?) *He will think the son shouldn't bring up money problems.* (What will the son feel toward the father?) The son thinks the father is too conservative, too stubborn. (What about the mother?) She feels very unhappy, out of sorts, but she will try to be good to both of them.[26]

There are two striking aspects of this interpretation: First, there is no meaningful dialogue between the father and son, no attempt to discuss the problem or the son's supposed misdeed. In many TAT characterizations of conflict with authority there is a very ambiguous interpretation of the responsibility for a bad situation. It is seldom *directly* attributed to the authoritative person; yet the implication of responsibility for the problem being with the subordinate is usually ambiguous, almost phrased as, "Yes, the young man did something wrong, but he really isn't to blame." Persons without power or in weaker positions are felt to be blameless; authority is not shared. The subordinate was only following the orders of some powerful individual. In the above story, the father has made a decision, and the relationship has already "split up." The father is about to explode with hostility toward the son, and mother and son fearfully beseech calm and understanding.

Second, there is no meaningful resolution of the problem. For a time the two disputants have nothing to do with one another, as they can't resolve the difficulty; and while they later resume contact, apparently they do so for normative reasons alone. ("After all, it is a family.") The emotional implication of the unresolved dispute is covered over: The father does not want the son to bring up money problems (that is, no attribution of feelings at all, just a desire to cut off communication about the dispute), and the son has only bad *thoughts* about the father.

This set of expectations about the way problems are handled within a family makes more comprehensible the Chinese concern that if differences of opinion are brought into the open it will lead to "confusion" or conflict. Problems really don't get solved; they remain, along with bad feelings, behind the face of filial deference as sources of conflict which might "split up" the family group and hence are better not discussed.

In relations with authority beyond the family the same conception of limited meaningful communication or compromise between superior and subordinate is revealed in TAT responses; and the outcome of differences of opinion frequently is a separation:

26. T-7. Emphasis added.

Here is a superior criticizing this young man's work; he doesn't like the work of his underling. (What is the superior's attitude toward him?) He feels that his technical level isn't high. (What does he *feel* about the young man?) He feels he isn't smart, isn't clever enough. (What does the young man feel toward his superior?) He is expressing his difficulties. (But what does he *feel*, or think, about the superior?) From his facial expression he indicates that the work can't be done. (In the future what will be their relationship, or the situation?) In the future they could split apart. (Why?) He is trying to teach the younger fellow; but he thinks it can't be done. (So what happens in the future?) They split apart.[27]

There is no attempt to come to a meeting of minds, and there is a strong inclination on the part of the respondent to cover over the emotional implications of the conflict. In spite of the interviewer's urgings that he attribute feelings to the characters in the story, the respondent keeps his interpretation at a safe distance from potentially troublesome emotions.

To gauge the extent to which these perceptions of social conflict were shared by the various respondents in our interview sample, interpretations of the three TAT stories dealing with conflict within the family, in superior-subordinate relations, and in dealings among peers, were coded for the entire group. The coding procedure was designed simply to see if the respondent perceived conflict as the immediate outcome of the situation he was describing; and then whether he thought cooperative relations among the major figures in the story would be maintained in the future. For purposes of contrast, responses to these same TAT cards (modified only for dress and facial appearance) given by an American student sample were coded according to the same procedure. The results are summarized in Table II.

The overall pattern one sees in the data from the Chinese respondents is of a level of conflict in family and peer relations approximately twice as high as that in dealings between nonfamily superiors and subordinates. Evidently considerations of career or job security help to dampen down conflict in such situations (although TAT Card IV is somewhat less likely to evoke conflict fantasy than Cards I and III). The most suggestive interpretation, however, is indicated by comparison with the American responses. Not only did the American students see somewhat less conflict in these cards than did the Chinese; they also anticipated that cooperative relations were much more likely to be maintained in the future.

Comparison between the American students and the Chinese emigrés must be handled with care, for reasons of age difference

27. T-10. This interpretation was given in response to TAT Card IV.

TABLE II

PERCEPTION OF CONFLICT AND COOPERATIVE OUTCOMES IN TAT
RESPONSES GIVEN AS A PERCENTAGE OF TOTAL RESPONDING*

Group Tested	FAMILY RELATIONS (TAT III)		SUPERIOR-SUBORDINATE RELATIONS (TAT IV)		PEER RELATIONS (TAT I)	
	Present Conflict†	Future Coop-eration‡	Present Conflict	Future Coop-eration	Present Conflict	Future Coop-eration
Chinese emigré males, total sample, N = 88	76.3	25.0	34.5	57.7	79.5	27.4
"Traditional" Chinese adult males,§ N = 29	72.4	30.8	41.3	57.7	75.0	29.4
"Communist" Chinese student males,# N = 30	80.0	18.5	30.8	60.0	75.0	32.0
American student males, ‖ N = 30	64.3	64.3	15.4	76.9	55.2	55.2

* Because of variations in the number of respondents in each sample who did not directly describe either immediate outcomes or future relationships, we have used only those responses which include an interpretation which could be coded in making these calculations. This means there are some minor fluctuations in sample size for the various figures.

† This figure is calculated on the basis of those who attributed conflict, hostile, or "splitting-up" outcomes to the *immediate* social situation they described.

‡ This figure is calculated on the basis of those who attributed cooperative or non-hostile competitive *future* relationships to the people in the social situations they described.

These two columns († and ‡) should not be added together (to obtain 100) as they represent separate calculations. The key to the analysis is the distinction between the respondents' perception of *immediate outcome* and *future relationship*. Americans could see *both* present conflict and future cooperation. Chinese could not.

§ This sample consists of Chinese emigrés who had attended a traditional Confucian-style "home school" (*szu-shu*) when young. Their average age is 60.9 years.

This sample consists of emigré Chinese, mostly from southern and coastal provinces, who had received secondary education in Communist-run schools, or who were in the Communist Party or Youth League. Their average age is 25.3 years.

‖ This sample consists of graduate students from the University of Michigan selected to represent a broad distribution of places of geographical origin and areas of academic interest. They are about evenly divided between urban and small town or rural backgrounds, and come from a range of socioeconomic status families. Their average age is 25.5 years, very close to that of the Communist-trained Chinese student group.

119

if nothing else; yet even when their responses are compared with those of the student element of the Chinese sample, the pattern of less immediate conflict and greater future cooperation is maintained. These data seem to reaffirm our conclusion that Chinese are not taught to see conflict as a legitimate aspect of social life; hence when conflict does develop it becomes most difficult to maintain functioning personal relationships. Indeed, the generally higher level of conflict in the Chinese stories as compared to the American interpretations suggests that the effort to "gloss over" points of dispute makes their disruptive impact on interpersonal relations that much greater.

While the meaning of these data for peer relations and generational change will be discussed in later chapters, we can say at this point that the TAT interpretations, seen in conjunction with material discussed earlier on communication with authority, indicate tensions in the superior-subordinate relationship which tend to weaken "vertical" social integration: The subordinate is reluctant to initiate communication or raise criticism in dealings with his superior.[28] Hence problems are not directly faced, and sources of discontent are not exposed and worked out. The superior may find himself cut off from the reality of problems and popular morale that are his responsibility because of his harshness and the concomitant reserve of subordinates. His effectiveness may be further eroded by passive resistance on the part of subordinates who are unwilling to confront him directly with difficulties or sources of discontent. Finally, he may be "abandoned" by his subordinates, or even subjected to direct retaliation by those who were allowed no moderated redress of grievances.

These disintegrative effects of the dependency orientation toward authority were ameliorated by the Confucian stress on personal "cultivation." To the extent that an individual in an authoritative position could moderate his dealings with subordinates and treat them with "human-heartedness" (*jen*), he could enlist their more active cooperation. As one of our respondents, a governmental official, observed:

> If you are not happy with [the performance of] a subordinate then sometimes you will get angry at him or give him a lecture. But I do not get angry very much any more. I go out of my way to avoid it. (Why?)

28. The weak communication linkages between different levels of Chinese industrial bureaucracies has been noted by Franz Schurmann in *Ideology and Organization in Communist China* (Berkeley: University of California Press, 1968), pp. 230–231. This author's interpretation lays particular stress on the wide "policy-operations" gap created by authority's role conception that he must not involve himself with matters of practical management.

Because no matter at whom you get angry, there always will remain an irritant to keep you apart, and afterwards it will not be easy to cooperate with that person. He will think you are not sufficiently cultivated.[29]

In addition, subordinates could appeal to the "emotions" (*kan-ch'ing*) of those on whom they depended for moderation in treatment. This notion of *kan-ch'ing* reflects the degree to which the relationship between superior and subordinate was personalized and diffuse in content, not mediated by legal norms or considerations of some specified technical function, as tends to be the case in industrial societies. The subordinate would appeal for sympathy or fair treatment on the basis of his past loyalty; and an authority could ignore such requests only at the risk of degrading the cooperation and commitment he might receive in the future. An anthropologist has written of such appeals to emotion:

> *Kan-ch'ing* differs from friendship in that it presumes a much more specific common interest, much less warmth and more formality of contact, and includes a recognized degree of exploitation. It is the common property of all classes. . . . *Kan-ch'ing* operates in the absence of kin ties which can bridge important gaps in status.[30]

Considerate treatment of subordinates not only might make an authority more effective through their active support; it could also enhance his social status through respect and the desire of other individuals to establish relations with him. The willing submission or dependence of people on a powerful individual could increase his power through the skills or resources they might bring to the relationship, and by increasing his prestige, his social "face," in the eyes of others. (This, of course, was the logic behind China's traditional tributary system of international relations.)

The only problem with this approach to wielding authority, from a superior's point of view, was the tendency of subordinates to "eat him up" through claims on his resources, or their tendency to become "unruly" if not under stern control. Weak authority was thus as problematical in its social effects as authority too harshly applied, as is indicated in one respondent's rueful recollection of his mild-mannered father: "He was very honest; and many people in the countryside took advantage of him. When I was small and saw this happen I really felt very upset."[31]

29. T-33.
30. Morton Fried, *Fabric of Chinese Society* (New York: Praeger, 1953), pp. 226–227.
31. T-45.

THE ENDURING AMBIVALENCE TOWARD AUTHORITY

The sum of these institutional aspects of authority embodies the same sense of ambivalence which we noted in Part One. Individuals in the Confucian tradition had come to expect guidance and initiative from superiors early in life, and they looked to the wealthy and powerful to provide for their material well-being and security from social conflict. Uncertain application of power would lead to squabbling among subordinates or "unruly" demands for support. Superior and subordinate alike saw the necessity for strong authority.

The harshness with which authority was applied, however, reflected the concern of those in positions of leadership that their subordinates might show insufficient filial respect and loyalty. Dependents needed to be told what was expected of them, or else they would become demanding, lazy, and hard to control.

Given these contradictions in the orientation toward authority, it is not surprising that we find Chinese seeking an idealized, nonhierarchical brotherhood of friendship as a solution to their problems. As we shall see in the next chapter, however, the idealization of the bond of friendship contrasts with a more somber set of expectations about dealings with peers. In the final chapter in this section, an analysis of Chinese attitudes toward politics, we find that the concern with peer conflict gives renewed meaning to strong political authority, and the sense of ambivalence remains unresolved.

Chapter VIII

FRIENDS AND PEERS

THE HOPE OF FRIENDSHIP . . .

Chinese pride themselves on the degree to which their traditions have developed the bond of friendship to a high art. "We *really* know how to be friends," is a comment frequently addressed to foreigners. Within the society there is a glorification of friendship ties that in quality is not unlike the American idealized conception of romantic love.

Relations among friends constitute one of the five Confucian natural or moral human relationships (*wu-lun*), and is the only one which is nonhierarchical. In expounding on the meaning of friendship, our interview respondents indicated that, in part, the appeals of this relationship represent a breaking away from the harsh controls and emotional restrictions of their society's rigid structure:

> Relations between friends are without restrictions, very free and casual. They are without limits and tend to stress emotions. You can say anything to your friends. For example, if you have some problem with another person you can talk about it with a friend, get his help; he may help you deal with the situation. But superior and subordinate relations are not that way. You do not dare to say many things to a superior. If you talk a lot then your superior will easily be dissatisfied with you.[1]

Unlike dealings with authority which are laden with anxiety, among friends there is relaxation, a "stress on emotions" and an openness in communication. In recalling the learning of authority within the family, respondents repeatedly used the expression, "You can't be just 'do as you please' (*sui-pien*) in relations with Father." The same phrase, to act "as one pleases," occurs repeatedly in descriptions of the appeals of friendship.

Chinese novels reveal a strong element of escapism in the conception of friendship. Note, for example, the bravado of the three sworn brothers in *The Romance of the Three Kingdoms* and the escape from the oppressions of harsh official power into the world

1. H-7.

of banditry recounted in *All Men Are Brothers*. Here, urges for revenge and revelry can find uninhibited expression, and seem to be outlets in fantasy from authority's strict or unjust control. But such novels were read in concealment behind a copy of the Classics, much as the unrestrained behavior they described was intended to be covered over by the social rituals of the Confucian tradition.[2]

Another aspect of the idealization of friendship is its fulfillment of the dependency needs which we have described thus far as central to relations with authority. As one respondent phrased it, "We rely on parents at home, and on friends in society."[3] The belief that a person is not a social individual apart from those to whom he is related, and cannot exist in isolation of the human ties which define his life obligations, is also a part of the conception of friendship:

> (What is the most important thing a person obtains from friends?) [Their] sympathy and support. (Why is that so important?) A person can't take care of things all by himself. If he has friends who come and help him, encourage him, and support him, then things can be dealt with effectively.[4]

This sense of interrelatedness, the belief that the support and encouragement of others is necessary to effectiveness in social life, is expressed most often in the hope of mutual assistance among friends and of cooperation in dealings with one's peers.

. . . AND THE REALITY

Between the idealization of friendship and the manner in which our respondents had experienced dealings with friends in daily life, however, there existed a wide divergence which grew from the excessive hopes they placed in such relations. Almost to a man they agreed that it was most difficult to establish really close friend-

---

2. Mao Tse-tung recalled of his early school days: "I was the family 'scholar.' I knew the Classics, but disliked them. What I enjoyed were the romances of Old China, and especially stories of rebellions. I read the *Yo Fei Chuan* (*Chin Chung Chuan*), *Shui Hu Chuan*, *Fan T'ang*, *San Kuo*, and *Hsi Yu Chi*, while still very young, and despite the vigilance of my old teacher, who hated these outlawed books and called them wicked. I used to read them in school, covering them up with a Classic when the teacher walked past. So also did most of my schoolmates. We learned many of the stories almost by heart, and discussed and rediscussed them many times. (Edgar Snow, *Red Star Over China* [New York: Grove Press, 1961], p. 127.)

3. T-18.

4. T-36.

ships.[5] Part of the difficulty is in releasing the controls over expression of emotions and thoughts that had been developed from a lifetime of "holding in":

(Why did you agree [that it is difficult to have friends to whom you can express your innermost thoughts and feelings]?) I think it is very difficult to express [such things]. (Why?) Because they are deep in people's hearts. They can't mutually express them. Isn't that unfortunate? From my experience, of the male or female friends I have had there hasn't been a complete expression of emotions. You have had a common life for several decades but cannot completely have a mutual opening up of what is in your hearts. I think this is very sad.[6]

The most frequent explanation given to the difficulty in having true friends, however, is closely related to the need to rely or depend upon other people, to the hope that one will gain advancement in one's career through the help of a friend or acquire financial assistance when in trouble. As expressed by a university graduate from Hupeh Province:

It is very difficult to have friends who really understand you, just too difficult. (Why is it so difficult?) It is not easy to explain. For instance, when you both are poor you are good friends. But once your friend makes big money, becomes a big official, he just forgets his old friends. I once had a close friend. Then he became wealthy and the friendship gradually lost its flavor. (Why?) Because he had money. He was afraid that people would go and ask him for money—but I wouldn't do that.[7]

Because in this cultural tradition the obligations of friendship are so intensive, potential friends may shy away from establishing or maintaining a relationship when there is a low expectation of reciprocity. Such a tie strongly implies the acquisition of a dependent who will make demands on one's resources. Thus, as with authority relations, the social implications of dependency work to limit the establishment of interpersonal relationships through fear of being "eaten" by impoverished or demanding friends.

DISTRUST OF PEERS

The conception of friendship is in a sense a special case of contact among peers. Actually, social transactions between people of equal

5. Quantified interview data on this point, and comparative information on American attitudes towards friendship, are presented in the author's article, "Mao's Effort to Reintegrate the Chinese Polity: Problems of Conflict and Authority in Chinese Social Processes," in A. Doak Barnett, ed., *Chinese Communist Politics in Action* (Seattle: University of Washington Press, 1969), pp. 298–301, 360.

6. T-52.

7. T-33.

or near-equal social status were relatively "underdeveloped" in the Chinese tradition. The concern with conflict in social life gave particular emphasis to the hierarchical conception of interpersonal relationships. And much of the effort in dealings among peers was either to place the relationship within a nexus of kin or friendship ties or to "buffer" the transaction, to keep it at a distance through the "politeness" (*k'o-ch'i*) forms of social ceremony or the mediation of a third party.[8]

From the time children begin to have contact with nonfamily peers, they are led to acquire a distrust of other people's motives or of their own ability to deal effectively with interpersonal disputes. We previously noted how anxieties about conflict develop out of parental reactions to quarreling among children. In addition, our respondents frequently observed how important it was that parents choose "proper" friends for their children to play with; for "bad" friends would provoke fighting or lead the child astray into sensual indulgence (a "wine and meat friend" [*chiu-jou p'eng-yu*] or "wine and women friend" [*chiu-se p'eng-yu*]). Again, the basic assumption is that since children cannot discipline their own behavior, parents must limit their social contacts in ways to give them proper guidance:

> (Why do you think it is relatively easy for a child to be influenced by a bad environment?) The attraction of external material things is just too great. This is the same both for children and adults. The Western way of doing things is to try to satisfy your desires, but there is no way completely to satisfy a person's desires. . . . Some people, if they have not had a good upbringing, will just do as they please—even until they are old. They will be muddleheaded and there will be no way for them to correct themselves. You have to give children a good educational environment. This is the idea behind the story of Mencius' mother moving three times: children have a strong sense of modeling [themselves on] the behavior of other people; they imitate the actions of those around them.[9]

The legacy of these early life images of social relations beyond the family is a limited sense of interpersonal trust. One has been led to believe that self-control and guidance of one's own behavior are difficult to achieve, and hence one comes to doubt other people's ability for self-control. As one has been taught to rely upon family elders for guidance, there remains the assumption that peers are not independent social actors, but represent the interests of superiors

8. For an interesting analysis of the Chinese tendency to use intermediaries in social transactions, *see* John H. Weakland, "The Organization of Action in Chinese Society," *Psychiatry,* Vol. XIII (1950), pp. 361–370.

9. T-31.

whose interests may be at variance with those of one's own group. Consequently adults feel that social transactions with peers are safest when they can be placed within the hierarchical framework of mutual obligations and restraints, the "human feelings" (*jen-ch'ing*) characteristic of family life.

Chinese describe the attempt to fit nonfamilial peer relations within the nexus of family or friendship obligations as literally to "speak of human feelings" (*chiang jen-ch'ing*), which might be more formally translated as to "speak on behalf of another":

> (What does it mean to *chiang jen-ch'ing?*) On many occasions Chinese worry about "face." For example, if someone is having a building constructed and the work is going slowly, if the owner of the new building has a friend who knows the contractor, and this friend asks the contractor to help him [the friend] by finishing the building a bit faster for the owner, the contractor will do his best to help. That is *jen-ch'ing* [human feelings]. (What if the owner doesn't have a mutual friend?) Then the contractor may just use talk to rebuff his request.
>
> If you know a person, and he is a friend, then feelings are real. If you don't know him then feelings are false. (How is that?) If you don't know the person, then you don't know the relevance of his requests [for your relationship]. But if you know him then you know the implications of reputation and self-interest.
>
> (What is the importance of *jen-ch'ing* for Chinese society?) Chinese society is based on the inculcation of etiquette (*li-mao*). In interpersonal relations there are certain requirements of etiquette, and these requirements contain *jen-ch'ing*. For instance, we think that the English have no *jen-ch'ing-wei* [sensitivity to other people's feelings]. They are proud, and think China is vulgar and backward. They look down on us. This lacks *jen-ch'ing*.[10]

There are two major points that might be made on the basis of this involved but revealing response. The first is that "human feelings" (*jen-ch'ing*) are the dynamic element in interpersonal transactions; they are the primary test of whether the mutual expectations and obligations of a "face to face" relationship have been met. To accede to that deference which an individual expects to be accorded because of his social "face" or status is to respect him and his social position, and thus give him good feelings. Conversely, to fail to meet these expectations of status deference is to provoke bad feelings. Thus, in the example given by the above respondent, the British are criticized for not according China that respect which she considers appropriate to her proper place in the world. And hence, as the expression goes, the British can no longer properly "face up to" (*tui-pu-ch'i*) China because of British failure (in

10. T-9.

China's eyes) to meet their part of what would be considered appropriate deference. Thus bad feelings are provoked, and the relationship will disintegrate or become hostile unless some "face-saving" solution to the offense can be found.

THE IMPORTANCE OF INTERMEDIARIES

Given the importance which Chinese attach to status deference in social contact, in instances of dealings with unknown individuals they tend to seek out a mutually known third party who understands the "face" expectations of all involved to mediate the relationship. The intermediary who "speaks of human feelings" (*chiang jen-ch'ing*) is thus one who tries to reconcile differences in status by linking the deference hierarchies which are the basic component of the Chinese social structure. If the intermediary is mutually known he understands the expectations of "face" of each party, and hopefully, he can effectively bridge the gap of trust, reconcile differences in status, and prevent bad feelings from being provoked.

In the absence of an intermediary, relations with unknown individuals become problematical, for each party must try to make certain that both the requirements of his own status or "face" and those of his opposite are properly recognized. Failures through mutual ignorance or ill-intention can lead to bad feelings and potential conflict.[11] Such are the difficulties resulting from teaching individuals that their self-respect is based above all on their status relationships to other people, rather than on their personal accomplishments.

Relations with peers thus become caught up in the complex of

11. The ritualized forms of self-deprecation which a Chinese might practice in dealings with peers can thus be viewed as an effort to convince someone of equal status that he has no intention of putting himself "one up"; indeed, he is willing to accept a position of lower status to demonstrate his respect and the desire to maintain a friendly relationship.

An English traveler in China in the early nineteenth century described such ritualized deference at a banquet held in the residence of a literatus: "When all was ready we were led in with great ceremony and placed in the principal seats of honour. We now had the opportunity of seeing the extent to which the Chinese carry their ceremony and politeness amongst themselves when they are about to be seated at table. Our host and his friends were nearly a quarter of an hour before the whole of them were seated. Each one was pressing the most honorable seat upon his neighbor, who, in his turn, could not think of occupying such a distinguished place at the board. However, after a great deal of bowing and flattery, all was apparently arranged satisfactorily and the dinner commenced." (Robert Fortune, *Three Years' Wanderings in the Northern Provinces of China* [London, John Murray, 1847], p. 140.)

feelings and social forms intended to provide security from conflict. One has been taught that there is "order" when everyone knows who is to defer to whom, but the effort to impose this hierarchical calculus on peer relations is beset by the ambiguities of dealing with unknown individuals and the natural tendency to prefer a dominant to a subordinate status. The intercession of a mutually known third party can thus help to fit a transaction within the web of interpersonal status relations and obligations that help to insure "peace."

In addition, the personal obligations and group controls that come with relations of kin or friendship are seen as making people trustworthy, for an individual would make trouble only at the risk of jeopardizing his "face" and place in life's basic social groupings.[12] Thus an intermediary known to friends and kin can insure that an unknown individual becomes subject to these basic sources of social control, and will not create "disorder":

> *"Chiang jen-ch'ing"* means, for example, if you want to find a tenant to live in your house but you don't dare carelessly to let anyone come to live with you, you definitely should find a third party who knows you both, to "speak on both of your behalves," to introduce you. . . . In this way things will be peaceful. You won't have any disorder and no difficulties will develop. If there is someone to introduce you then you won't have any bad people coming in to create confusion (*kao-luan*).[13]

PEER CONFLICT AND CONTROL

The lack of trust and directness in dealings among peers is compounded by fears of conflict; and the social forms of Confucian cultivation—politeness in talk (*k'o-ch'i hua*) and good manners (*li-mao*)—are seen as essential to avoiding conflict. Personal reserve is necessary if one is not to provoke hostility or obstructive behavior in others:

> If a person's cultivation is good it is easy for him to get along with other people, to cooperate with other people. He seldom will develop friction with them, and he will have many friends. If a person's cultivation is not good he will not be easy to cooperate with, he will get into

---

12. Studies of group life and shaming have indicated that an important aspect of "losing face" is embarrassing one's primary group, and not just oneself, through some personal misbehavior, again indicating the extent to which Chinese social identity is relational, not individual. *See* Richard W. Wilson, *Childhood Political Socialization on Taiwan* (unpublished Ph.D. dissertation, Princeton University, 1967), p. 54; and Hsu Hsien-chin, "The Chinese Concepts of 'Face,'" p. 50.

13. T-38.

conflicts, and because he can't get along with others he will not succeed in his work.

(How does a person become cultivated?) When he runs into some worldly problem he should not be too impulsive, he must be mannerly to people, kindly. He can't just do as he might like to do in some situation, be so aggressive with other people that he turns their faces all red. When speaking to other people he should not be so assertive that he hurts their self-respect.[14]

In evaluating problem-solving situations among peers (through TAT interpretations), our respondents generally indicated that they expected a breakdown in interpersonal communication or cooperative relationships to follow differences of opinion.[15] A typical response to TAT Card I, which deals specifically with peer relations, was given by a former government official from Fukien Province:

> These five people are holding a meeting to discuss something. This fellow on the side disagrees with the proposal supported by most of the others, and so he is unhappy. He has stood up and is preparing to leave the group, or is thinking of opposing them. He is not the leader of the group. Probably he just has his own proposal.
>
> (How do these people in the group feel?) Because of the fellow on the side getting up to leave, they have been provoked into feeling tense. Consequently they have put their heads together to discuss the situation and there are many opinions: Some are saying let the fellow go and be done with it; some think that his opinion is not bad and should be reconsidered.
>
> (How does the fellow on the side feel about the others?) He feels that their opinion is nonsense. He wants to support his own proposal but the others won't listen to him. Hence he is unhappy. He is pacing up and down considering whether to participate in the discussion or to leave the group.
>
> (What is the outcome?) This fellow is very unhappy; and so he withdraws from the group—indicates his disapproval and goes.
>
> (In the future what relationship do these people have with the fellow who left?) They have no mutual concern: "You take care of yours, and I'll take care of mine." [16]

Differences of opinion among peers result in a breakdown of cooperative relations, obviously limiting social integration and opening the door to the "bad feelings" which usually accompany

14. T-33.

15. As summarized in Table II, p. 119 above, the full sample of persons interviewed saw conflict outcomes in 79.5 percent of their interpretations of TAT Card I, with future cooperation being maintained in only 27.4 percent of the cases.

16. T-28.

such disputes. As this was phrased in one interview record: "(What happens when, as you have described it, two people 'split apart?') They have resentment (*fan-kan*). (Why do they have resentment?) Because in their basic positions they are not alike." [17] Thus to problems of resolving differences of opinion is added the possibility of conflict based on emotional resentment.

Competition among peers is seen to be as troublesome for social unity as differences of opinion, for the expectation is that rivalry will bring out bad feelings and lead to unrestrained conflict:

> (What is the greatest effect of interpersonal competition on society?) If it is aggressive or emotional then it is not good. It can lead to hatred or jealousy, and the outcome would be too bad! (What would the outcome be?) It can lead to bad emotions on both sides. In lower class society this kind of competitive struggle leads to killing, and so the outcome is not peaceful.[18]

The pattern of peer conflict which our respondents saw resulting from differences of opinion has the same polarized quality of either apparent "peace" or unrestrained violence which we have noted earlier. If a neighbor is troublesome it is best to avoid a confrontation and maintain a "face" of harmony, for the outcome of a critical interchange could only be bad feelings and open conflict:

> If you try to correct the neighbor and are too assertive, you may not succeed. You may create strife. For example, if the neighbor plays mahjong, and you ask him to be quiet, it can develop into conflict. It can lead to a fight [laughs]. Another way of handling this situation would be just to move away—that would be a bit better. If you talk to him about it and he does not accept your point of view, there is nothing you can do.[19]

One can hope that one's neighbors are "cultivated" and can accept criticism; but the concern always remains that even if the "face" reaction is not hostile, underneath there will be hatred to poison the relationship:

> If the neighbor is so objectionable he must have a low educational level. If he was cultivated he wouldn't act that way. If his educational level is low, if you try to correct him it won't have any good effect. He'll just be more objectionable. If he is really bad he might on the surface say, "Good," and then [underneath] he'll hate you. But a cultivated person would thank you for helping him out.[20]

17. T-10.
18. T-47.
19. H-2.
20. T-14.

Observers of daily life in China have consistently reported the unrestrained, "confused" quality of conflict which occasionally breaks through the "face" of cultivated reserve:

> While Chinese in their normal intercourse with each other observe the greatest courtesy, they go to the other extreme once the restraints of polite behavior are thrown aside. Then the foulness of the language, the depths of the insults hurled back and forth can find few parallels. . . . A couple of women who have had a disagreement over some trivial matter will entertain the neighborhood for hours with the picturesque but unprintable phrases that they fling at each other. Each accuses the other of every moral depravity which comes in mind. . . . This often continues until one or both are physically exhausted.[21]

In a society that teaches its children that avoidance of a dispute is preferable to moderated resolution of interpersonal differences, there is little between the poles of "harmony" and "confusion," *ho-p'ing* and *hun-luan*.

The effort to control conflict among peers often includes the disputants' involvement of neighbors and friends. Foreign observers have frequently noted that "quarrels in China take place by preference before an audience, and the attention of the combatants is directed as much to the effect of their words on the observers as upon each other." [22] The practice of "cursing the street" (*ma-chieh*),[23] of airing one's grievances in a public place or initiating a conflict where friends will be forced to intervene will, it is hoped, bring down on one's opponent the sense of shame and group pressures which will right the wrong.

Fears of conflict and distrust of the unruly behavior of peers, however, lead many to see the only hope of maintaining social order in the external controls of social organization, in which the individual will be "boxed in" by the combined forces of group obligations and ties, and the authority of strong leaders:

> (Please explain what it means to have *chih an hao* [good peace and order]). . . . *Everything has to be well organized.* For example, if a person wants to steal, if you know his motivation you can prevent it. (What kind of organization?) *It is not a special, it cannot be a simple*

21. Carl Crow, *The Chinese Are Like That* (New York: Harper, 1939), pp. 281–282. A more scholarly analysis of the peaceful, docile, yet violent qualities of China's peasants will be found in Hsiao Kung-chuan, *Rural China: Imperial Control in the Nineteenth Century* (Seattle: University of Washington Press, 1960), esp. Chapter 10.

22. Margery Wolf, *The House of Lim: A Study of a Chinese Farm Family* (New York: Appleton-Century-Crofts, 1968), p. 105.

23. *See* Arthur Smith, *Chinese Characteristics* (New York: Fleming Revell, 1894), pp. 219–221.

organization. It has to be united with others. You have to know what a person is doing from the time he is small. . . . *A person cannot be isolated (ku-li ti); he cannot live alone. You have to have 4, 5, 6, 6,000 people around him.* For example, if he gets sick you have to take him to a hospital to get cured—so you have to have things well united. . . . *They ought to have a file on every person from the age of eight,* so if, for example, he comes for a job we will know just what he has done. Also, you have to use good people to implement the plan. For example, Wang Mang in the Han dynasty era, or Wang An-shih: Their methods were good but they failed because they did not have good people to support them.[24]

Interestingly enough, this assertion of the need for organizational control ends with a reaffirmation of the need for highly personalized leadership. The concept of authority remains personified. Social harmony requires the potency of "men of talent" (*jen-t'sai*) who will impose order and control those who in their dependency lack the self-discipline to order their own affairs.

PEER RELATIONS AND PROBLEMS OF LATERAL SOCIAL INTEGRATION

Our argument has come full circle. We began this section of the study by discussing the concern with "confusion" (*luan*)—the ever-present expectation of conflict and disorder—that is the diffuse undertone of Chinese perceptions of social relations. The Confucian concept of social authority attempted to deal with this problem through a hierarchical organization of society in which individuals would submit to the guidance of their elders. Perhaps the most important aspect of the analysis was the implication that this system of authority seemed to trap Chinese society in a vicious circle, where the strength of authority and the dependent submission to it which were designed to prevent confusion actually generated conditions which could produce it: The "holding in" of resentments and hatred of oppressive authority might explode into unrestrained conflict, particularly when individuals were made to feel that they were incapable of acting without guidance. If the necessary superior authority were removed, "confusion" would indeed reign until another powerful individual could institute a new hierarchical ordering of social relationships.

To this analysis we now have added peer relations. The Chinese tradition did not inculcate expectations of trust or rituals of cooperation in dealings among status equals which might have facilitated lateral social transactions. The intense expectations of friend-

24. H-7. Emphasis is added.

ship were such as to limit even that relationship's frequency, in part because it embodied the gratification of dependency needs—for a more powerful "friend" to be a provider in times of difficulty. Thus even friendship took on something of the flavor of hierarchical obligations.

Relations among peers were felt to be most effective if they could be brought within the web of kin or friendship ties and obligations. Intermediaries were seen as necessary for such transactions because they helped to resolve expectations of status or social "face" and overcome distrust by involving primary group ties.

Where intermediaries were lacking, relations among peers tended to be drawn into a competition for dominance: Individuals within this social tradition were made to feel that their self-respect was intimately related to the acquisition of interpersonal authority, and security and stability were felt to reside only within a hierarchical ordering of social relations. This pattern of peer contact reinforced the tendency for unrestrained conflict in the absence of a strong authority, because status equals were not educated to settle disputes effectively on their own.

Dependency needs and anxieties about conflict thus worked to make strong authority a personal necessity; yet strong authority generated its own resentments—in others if not in oneself—which made conflict a continuing possibility. Here is a cultural tautology, a vicious circle rooted in the socialization process which worked to insure the endurance of the Confucian pattern. Nowhere does this circularity of cultural logic find more vivid expression than in perceptions of politics, of the society's highest level of authority, to which we now turn.

Chapter IX

THE TIGER WORLD OF POLITICS:
WILL ONE EAT OR BE EATEN?

> Ever since ancient times China has had too
> much war. When the confusion (*luan*) gets
> extreme people yearn for government. There
> has been just too much war. The people
> really despise war and long for peace.[1]

Chinese attitudes toward political authority and personal involvement in politics betray the same strong ambivalence which we have
traced from roots in childhood to general social perceptions: a paradoxical combination of the desire to depend on those with power
for material support and security from conflict, yet great anxiety
about dealing directly with authoritative individuals because of
their capacity for manipulation and aggressiveness.

Any society's intellectuals tend to articulate through formal, rationalized doctrines attitudes and emotional concerns they share
with less educated compatriots. A good example is the Confucian
concept of "the Mandate of Heaven" (*t'ien-ming*) as the basis of a
ruler's political legitimacy. Simply stated, this doctrine held that
the emperor's claim to be Emperor was *conditional* upon his fulfilling "Heaven's will" in ruling the people. The test of whether Heaven
accorded the emperor its mandate to rule was the reaction of the
people themselves to governmental authority. Social tranquillity
and interpersonal harmony indicated that Heaven was smiling at
the rule of an emperor through his people, while *luan* and rebellion
reflected improper policies and morally degenerate leadership—
and perhaps the need for a new imperial house.

Now it seems true, as historians have argued, that this doctrine
is in part an expression of differences in interest and political objectives among three groups: the scholar officials who directly ad-

1. T-26.

"Wu Sung Wrestles the Tiger," an episode
from the classical novel *Shui Hu Chuan* [All Men Are Brothers].
*From a Ming Dynasty (1368–1644 A.D.) collection
of illustrations for the novel.*

ministered the empire for the imperial house; the Confucian gentry who represented the provincial, agrarian life style of China's rural elite; and a central policy-making group (often tied to the "foreign" interests of a militarily powerful border society) who were concerned with maintaining full control of administration and the wealth of the empire.[2]

At another level of perception, however, the doctrine reflects the influence of a culturally normative orientation toward authority: a willingness of the people to be orderly and politically passive under the control of those with power, provided that their material well-being and security were not endangered; but their tendency to withdraw into a potentially explosive hostility when they thought their dependency had been unreciprocated or abused. The actual bursting forth of *luan,* of the unrestrained violence and destruction characteristic of peasant rebellions, was the ultimate expression of popular rejection of existing political authority—and the final judgment of the political lives of numerous officials and dynasties.

The Mandate of Heaven doctrine thus was an expression of the *conditional* nature of the relationship between China's unenfranchised majority and the elite who exercised power, either formally within the state administration or informally through local social leadership roles. The passive deference which China's peasants accorded their leaders provided considerable leeway in policy-making and in the demands which could be made on the population's energies and resources. Yet the Mandate doctrine was a reminder to those with imperial power (from the scholar-officials who administered imperial policy) that there were limits to the demands that could be made on the common people. Those dependent on the powerful expected reciprocity. Even if their methods tended to be passive and indirect, they had ways of influencing the behavior of those in authority.

As we shall now see, political authority was perceived as having two very different faces. There was an ambivalence related to this dual perception which made filial submission conditional upon obligations fulfilled, just as dynastic legitimacy was said to depend upon fulfillment of Heaven's Mandate.

POWER AND THE HOPE OF SECURITY

The hopeful face of political power is viewed through that lens of our respondents' social perception which seeks economic security

2. This point has been developed by Joseph R. Levenson, among others. *See* his *Confucian China and Its Modern Fate: The Problem of Monarchical Decay* (Berkeley: University of California Press, 1964), pp. 97–98.

through reliance on authority in a world of material scarcity and uncertain employment. A respondent from Hopeh Province replied to the question, "What is the most important thing a nation's leaders should do for their people?" as follows:

> They have to be all for the people; like a father, all for the younger generation. The nation is like a family, so the highest leaders have to take responsibility for doing things for the benefit of the people, work things out well for them. (What kinds of problems should they pay attention to?) Problems of the people's livelihood: education, jobs, science. All these things have an effect on the people's livelihood.[3]

This typical attitude is meaningful in two respects. First, the respondent develops his interpretation of political leadership on the basis of an analogy with the family. Social authority has not been generalized to a set of universal principles or laws; the image of state power is still personified and paternal. Just as Confucius instructed, the family is the basic referent of all other social and political relations. Second, the domain of social authority is seen to be as all-inclusive as that of the family. A teacher from Liaoning Province expressed it this way:

> [If] you have enlightened government then you will have good social order. Everyone will have clothing to wear and enough food to eat. Everyone will be able to receive education and you will not have to lock your outer doors. There will be no fear or any more violence. (What methods does the society have to use to maintain this kind of a situation?) You have to use political methods: Raise the level of the people's daily livelihood, extend the period of public education, cultivate public morality. From the time a person is small you have to start educating him, training him. And you might put up slogans in public places stressing public morality.[4]

This willing acceptance of the intrusion of public power into all areas of social activity seems in part a legacy of childhood's teaching that there are few private corners of an individual's life,[5] combined with well-developed needs to be taken care of by a strong external authority.

3. T-19.
4. T-32.
5. A frequent Chinese reaction to American life is discomfort at the strong emphasis on privacy. A recent emigré from the mainland has written, "I am aware that my American hosts, motivated by kindness, ensure that I have privacy and that my social life leaves me regular periods of solitude. Just as they cannot understand *not* needing privacy, I cannot understand the need for it. I suppose one never learns to want what one has never had. In any case I suffer as much from too much privacy as most Americans do from the lack of it." (Tung Chi-ping and Humphrey Evans, *The Thought Revolution* [New York: Coward McCann, 1966], pp. 252–253.)

The positive or constructive image of what public authority can accomplish seems to be overshadowed, however, by the need to control "bad" or destructive tendencies among the people themselves. Concerning the ease with which children are believed to emulate the behavior of their parents, one respondent was asked, "What if a child's parents are bad; what should society do about this kind of a situation?" He replied, "In a well-founded society there ought to be a good leader, an organization which would know what is going on in every house, to help guide children in their weak points." [6]

The notion that the government should intrude even into family life, to "know what is going on in every house," is acceptable when there is a threat to the proper ordering of society. Our respondents frequently used the phrase, "The government must have intimate relations (*mi-ch'ieh kuan-hsi*) with the people"—apparently a popular elaboration of the Confucian idea that social order can be maintained only by "boxing in" people's antisocial potentialities through a hierarchical pattern of deference and obligation:

> If the government and people have intimate relations, if the people have vigilance and mutually involve themselves in each other's affairs, then it would not be easy for people to do bad things. If people are uninterested [in social life]; if they just "sweep the snow in front of their own doors," if they don't obstruct the bad behavior of others and don't think about its long-term effects, then it will not be good for the nation. [7]

The notion that organization is above all a technique for controlling potentially troublesome individuals is shared by leaders and led alike. Just as Sun Yat-sen felt the Kuomintang party organization would enable him to control the activities of the Communists, [8] so one of our respondents felt that the People's Republic could be controlled through the U.N. organization:

> You [Americans] should let China enter the United Nations. (Why?) Because if China is rejected and remains on the outside then she can do bad things. Then there will be no way to control her. If you let her into the United Nations then you can, according to the rules of the organization, give the Communists a kind of education and control. [9]

6. T-9.
7. T-15.
8. *See* Conrad Brandt, Benjamin Schwartz, and John K. Fairbank, *A Documentary History of Chinese Communism* (New York: Atheneum, 1966), p. 68.
9. T-21.

For all the appreciation of the security that can come with strong and intrusive power, however, there is a marked inclination to deny the need for such control in relation to one's own behavior. Apprehensions about dealings with authority combine with fears of conflict to produce an orientation where government is wanted for its ability to impose interpersonal harmony and social tranquillity, yet not for one's self—only for "bad" people:

> (What does *chih-an hao* [good peace and order] mean?) It is a matter of dealing with bad situations: once they break out, immediately doing away with them. (What kinds of things?) Stealing; just excessive incidents—cheating, male-female questions. (How can this kind of a situation be maintained?) There are two aspects: you have to strengthen the moral aspect of life; and then there are a minority of bad social elements—you have to rely on the government to control them.

> (How is it that every now and then a society becomes confused [*hun-luan*]?) What kind of *hun-luan* do you mean? (Whatever you think.) Well let's look at it the opposite way: If there is good governmental power then you can control things—I don't mean like the Communists, they have no morals, no limits. You have to have democracy —but if you don't have [a strong government] then everyone is just out for himself. There will be no limits on people's behavior. (Why do you need a strong government?) *A small group in society is not mannerly (li-mao). They do not abide by social custom, and the government has to use methods to control them—but not for most ordinary people who are mannerly.*[10]

There remains the hope that public morality and merely the distant example of outstanding governmental leaders will make social order and peace a reality. The intrusion of state power is reserved for those individuals who will only submit to the harsh controls of law—a popular attitude that gives continuing meaning in daily life to the philosopher's distinction between Confucianism and Legalism as contrasting approaches to social control in the Chinese tradition.

Government's benign face is thus to a large degree its ability to control society's potential for conflict, to prevent *luan*. And as is indicated in the remark of a peasant's son from Hopeh Province, both the potential for social confusion and the political authority to prevent it are rooted in family life:

> (Why in the early years of the Republic were there warlords?) The central government had no strength. It could not concentrate its power, and the local powers could give orders separately. You see, it is the same thing with a family: If the head of the family cannot manage

10. T-14. Emphasis added.

family affairs, unify family management, then every child will himself think of some way to do things and the family will be split into several cliques. When everyone has his own way of administering affairs then divergencies develop and things become *luan*. Things are the same way with the nation. . . . You have to concentrate power.[11]

THE TIGER OF GOVERNMENTAL POWER

In passing by the side of Mount Thai, Confucius came on a woman who was wailing bitterly by a grave. The Master . . . sent Tze-lu to question her. "Your wailing," said he, "is altogether like that of one who has suffered sorrow upon sorrow." She replied, "It is so. Formerly, my husband's father was killed here by a tiger. My husband was also killed [by another], and now my son has died in the same way." The Master said, "Why do you not leave the place?" The answer was, "There is no oppressive government here." The Master then said [to the disciples], "Remember this, my little children. Oppressive government is more terrible than tigers." [12]

The second face of public authority is perceived in the glaring image of a rapacious tiger, stirring all those concerns about the harshly punitive and manipulative use of power which were acquired early in life. The well-known Confucian anecdote from the *Book of Rites* cited above brings to mind our earlier encounter with the Kwangtung peasant who felt that, "People eat people; the big ones eat the small, will eat them all up."

This perception of authority as "tigerish," as capable of "eating people," we suggested earlier, seems to reflect the way Chinese are taught to control their personal fears and tensions. At a much more obvious level of perception, however, there is good reason why ordinary people saw official power as capable of devouring them and why they characterized entering the local magistrate's *yamen* as walking into "the tiger's mouth." [13] When one's life is spent in neverending toil for subsistence in an insecure world of natural disasters and material scarcity, to have landlords or officials take large parts of a precious and hard-earned food supply can indeed make one feel "eaten." The harsh application of official justice to those unfortunate enough to "disturb the tranquillity of the Empire" (for whatever reason)—examination through torture, punishment by beating and whipping, and execution by the

11. T-38.

12. From "Li Ki" (Book of Rites) in Max F. Müller, ed., *Sacred Books of the East*, Vol. XXVII, pp. 190–191.

13. *See* Jerome Alan Cohen, "Chinese Mediation on the Eve of Modernization," *California Law Review*, Vol. LIV (August 1966), pp. 1213 and *passim*.

thousand cuts or strangulation—can easily consume one with the same fear that might be expected should one encounter a tiger.

For the peasantry, however, direct contacts with governmental officials were rather infrequent. For them the full force of the tiger of power was known through the ravagings of bandit groups or official "pacifying" troops who lived off the land. A Shensi peasant recalls a "bandit suppression" campaign of the 1930s:

> When Hu Tsung-nan [a warlord, and his troops] came, almost every-one left Liu Ling. We went up into the hills. I was in the people's militia then. We had buried all our possessions and all our corn. Hu Tsung-nan destroyed everything, and *his troops ate and ate. They discovered our grain stores, and they stole our cattle.*[14]

Another peasant of the same area describes his enforced service in the warlord's army:

> Our platoon commander was called Liu. He was a bad-tempered man; he hit people when he was angry. I was often beaten. Sometimes he hit me with a stick, and sometimes he took my rifle and hit me with that. I was hit the most of us eleven new ones. Then we began to march. *We marched and marched and everywhere we ate up all the villagers' pigs and poultry. After all, we were hungry too.*[15]

We suggested earlier that within the Chinese tradition there is no expectation of compromise in matters of authority. This perception finds its fullest expression in political conflict, where, as our respondents had known it through the last century of social instability and war, power presents its ugliest visage:

> In the last hundred years China has had so many changes of government, so many changes in political programs, that ordinary people really are disgusted with politics. Each party says that it is the best, it is the only one, and suppresses all others. The people are really fed up with all that confusion (*hun-luan*). It is not surprising that the common people are disgusted with politics.[16]

> [During the 1910s and 1920s, the warlords] held power in their own hands, and so they could do anything they wanted to. . . . These powerful men thought of uniting China—although some, like Tuan Ch'i-jui and Feng Kuo-chang, also thought of competing for the position of emperor. The result was that there were many wars. (Why couldn't the warlords peacefully coexist?) If I want to eat your piece of meat, naturally you won't want to give it to me! [Respondent laughs.] Their fighting was pure avariciousness. Powerful men can

14. Jan Myrdal, *Report from a Chinese Village* (London: Heinemann, 1965), p. 140. Emphasis added.
15. *Ibid.,* pp. 88–89. Emphasis added.
16. H-4.

grab people as they please. They can kill people. This was just competition for power.[17]

When power is unified in the hands of one leader, he can impose a structure of political authority which will control the potential for social "confusion." Personal relations can then be mediated by the customs of civilized society. But the struggle for power, the striving for that dominance which will make a new order possible, causes great disorder. The forms of interpersonal relations appropriate to a peaceful society, such as deference rituals (*li-mao*) and intermediation, must await the creation of the new order.

> (Why is it that some people are interested in politics and others are not?) Those people who are interested have great ambition. People without ambition are not interested in politics. The ambitious ones hope to attain some position through politics, to become an official and get rich. (What do you think should be done about this difference?) This is very difficult; everyone is different; a "third party" [intermediary] can't reconcile this difference.[18]

The competition for power is seen as provoking a hatred which compounds the tendency for violent "confusion," even where there is the appearance of an ordered set of political processes:

> (How is it that a society becomes "confused"?) Everyone is out for status or profit. Take for example competing to be a political representative: If a person is defeated then he will have hate; he will want to destroy the person who defeated him. Now on Taiwan governmental organizations are relatively numerous [and can prevent violence], but before on the mainland this kind of a situation developed just too frequently: If you had been defeated then you would organize some local bandits to go out and kill the person who had won.[19]

But paradoxically, where order and "unity" have finally been imposed, the process of their attainment is seen as having laid the groundwork for further "confusion," as one respondent affirmed in this recollection of China's first political unification:

> Progress [in the Chou dynasty] was very great. Many different kinds of thinking sprang up. (What was the outcome of this situation?) Chin Shih Huang absorbed all of their good thinking. He used talented men and was able to unite China. (But were not all of the books of the famous men burned by Li Ssu?) A part of them. Those that he did not want. (Why didn't he want some of them?) He feared that they would influence people's thinking. (What do you mean by

17. T-26.
18. T-45.
19. T-26.

that?) He feared that people under his control would not obey him, would oppose him and create *luan*. (Why did he fear that?) He had destroyed all those other countries. He feared their people. He thought that by burning all those books he could cause them to forget or not understand what had happened in the past.[20]

What is the way out of this dilemma, the longing for harmony and order, yet realization that the political methods used to impose order themselves produce the "bad feelings" which make *luan* an enduring problem?

> I don't think laws have any usefulness, the only thing you can do is to have a highest leader. Having a [good] government includes [the leader] making an example of his own action, and having very strict punishments. If the highest leader can promote good government then the subordinates below him would not dare but do the same thing.[21]

The imposition of a still stronger authority, a "highest leader" who can maintain control over the dangerous world of politics, is the solution most often envisaged by our respondents. Yet for themselves, for their personal relation to the world of politics, avoidance of those in authority is usually seen as the most desirable course to follow.

THE GAP BETWEEN LEADERS AND LED

We have seen avoidance of dealings with the powerful in a variety of contexts, from family life and educational experiences to perceptions of social relations. The growing son fears contacts with a harsh, demanding, and potentially explosive father; a student runs away from school because of the overbearing treatment he receives from a teacher; and in relations with authority an adult uneasily balances the expectation of loyalty with anxious concern that he might be "cheated" or led into trouble by a superior. In the world of politics, maintaining a physical distance has been a time-honored defense for China's rural population. And where avoidance is not possible, creating an "emotional distance" becomes a strategy to guard oneself against the sting of manipulation or of being made to "eat a loss" (*ch'ih-k'uei*) in dealings with the powerful.

The tiger of governmental power was sufficiently distant from the lives of most peasants that even the revolutionary changes of the early twentieth century did not significantly touch their lives.

20. H-7.
21. T-45.

As an elderly peasant from China's northwest province of Shensi recalled:

> When I was nineteen, I got myself sheep and goats of my own and two years after that we heard that there was a revolution. I ran off to the hills. Then we were told that now we were called the Republic of China, and that the Ching dynasty was at an end. That was all. We were old country people, and we seldom went into the town and never talked about such things as the emperor or government. Nobody would have dared do that. And we never saw them either. The officials in the nearest yamen watched over us, and they were the same after the revolution as before it.
>
> Ordinary people did not like going to see the officials. That was a thing one did only if compelled. If one met them, one had to kneel before them. It was exactly the same after the revolution. I could not see that there was any difference at all.[22]

Imperial politics and the "great tradition" of the scholar-officials for the most part were known to the peasantry only indirectly, through contacts with agents of the local gentry who taxed their harvest and the activities of yamen officials who made known the word of the district magistrate. Yet even when a peasant sought to establish more intimate relations with the powerful, so that he might receive some special consideration, authority presented itself in all the harshness first known in childhood and asserted its influence through "the power of the word." As a peasant recalled of dealings with his landlord:

> Any small mistake and he blew up. I had to carry water through the gate. There was a threshold there and a sharp turn. If I spilled some water on the ground, he cursed me for messing up the courtyard. Once I tore the horse's collar. *He cursed me and my ancestors. I didn't dare answer back. I think that was worse than the [bad] food and the filthy quarters—not being able to talk back. In those days the landlord's word was law.* They had their way. When it was

22. Myrdal, *Report from a Chinese Village*, pp. 286–287.
One study has found that there were somewhere between 100,000 and 250,000 people "under the control of" each imperial official during the Ch'ing dynasty. (*See* Hsiao Kung-chuan, *Rural China: Imperial Control in the Nineteenth Century*, p. 5.)
Under such circumstances intimate contact between officials and the population was hardly possible. Indeed, evidence suggests that popular attitudes of fear and avoidance of governmental power were purposefully encouraged by dynastic officials so as to keep the people "in their places," to discourage them from making demands on state resources or causing trouble which would require direct official involvement. (This point is explored in the author's article "On Activism and Activists," *The China Quarterly*, No. 39 [July–September 1969], pp. 77–86.)

really hot and they said it was not, we dared not say it was hot; when it really was cold and they said it wasn't we dared not say it was cold. *Whatever happened we had to listen to them.*[23]

It is not surprising to find the peasantry alienated from those with power, from what was in many respects another world of education, leisure from physical toil, and a degree of material security and comfort. One of the more striking findings revealed by our interview data, however, is that educated and "socially mobilized" Chinese viewed political power with a similar degree of aloofness and anxiety. From early in life they, too, had learned that to show respect and obedience was to *t'ing-hua*, to "listen to talk," and not give out personal opinions.

We find a similar pattern of communication in our interview respondents' contacts with the world of political power. Judging from their newspaper reading habits, political events are of considerable interest to them. Of the sixty-one who were asked how often they read a newspaper, 95 percent indicated daily attention to the news. One respondent said he read a newspaper once a week; and only two said they did not follow the news at all. When asked, "Do you read the national political news?" 86 percent replied they did, and 90 percent indicated that they read news of the international political situation. However, when asked, "With whom do you discuss politics?" only 43 percent of a total of seventy-five admitted that they discussed political matters. The remaining 57 percent denied discussing politics. "Taking in" information is a well-developed habit, but "giving out" opinions about politics is another matter. The respondents showed a strong tendency to deny this minimal level of political involvement.

The reasons given for this apparent lack of interest in political discussion are varied. The feeling that "you can't reach a conclusion" was frequently voiced, recalling the expectation we encountered in nonpolitical social contexts that differences of opinion cannot be resolved. Some respondents emphasized the notion that society is "complicated" (*fu-tza*), that there are important and emotionally explosive issues unresolved behind society's orderly "face," and that talking about them will needlessly provoke hostility and trouble:

> I very seldom discuss [political questions]. (Why?) Because society today is very complicated. Each person's thinking, point of view, and opinions are different. If you discuss these differences you won't be able to reach any conclusion. Possibly it would lead to some trouble.

23. William Hinton, *Fanshen: A Documentary of Revolution in a Chinese Village* (New York: Monthly Review Press, 1966), p. 39. Emphasis added.

(What kind of trouble?) People will not understand your thinking. Possibly they will think it is not correct. They might pay special attention to your behavior, or even lock you up.[24]

Of course Chinese society today *does* embody great unresolved political issues related to the civil war and social revolution. But this reluctance to discuss politics cannot be explained merely by the immediate social context in which some of our interviews took place. Respondents interviewed in Hong Kong held attitudes quite similar to those in Taiwan; and the behavior of Chinese who have migrated to more distant cultural areas indicates that they regard open personal involvement in politics as dangerous. The attitudes recalled by our respondents are well *internalized* on the basis of early life experience, in addition to being reinforced by the immediate social context.

Furthermore, it should be stressed that we merely asked respondents whether they *discussed* political issues, and not specific questions about personal political preference. It is also striking that similar attitudes were frequently expressed by elderly mainlanders in Taiwan whose professional careers and political loyalties had at one time placed them in positions of public responsibility. At most we got an admission that political issues were discussed

> with fellow workers or with friends with a similar disposition, or at Party meetings. We discuss these things if our thinking is similar. We don't discuss them with people we don't know, because if you do then you may confuse what is right and wrong. Everyone must be in basic agreement; then you can secretly discuss [politics]. You shouldn't indiscriminately go around [discussing political matters].[25]

Respondents' disclaimers of *any* discussion of politics should not be taken too literally, for when pressed many would admit that current issues were discussed with friends or coworkers in the privacy of home or a trusted group setting. Rather, their responses to the word "politics" (*cheng-chih*) give a further indication of the sense of anxiety about contact with authority. They manifest a fear that if political questions are discussed with people whose thinking is not similar it will lead to conflict or some ill-defined "trouble." Where one's relation to authority is expected to be above all a matter of the personal loyalty characteristic of dependence, rather than social involvement on the basis of specific public issues, the expression of political opinions means submitting one's commitment to a man and group to public scrutiny. Where everyone's "thinking," or political loyalty, is similar, discussion can pro-

24. T-32.
25. T-49.

ceed within a framework of common cause. But where commitment may be uncertain, or where issues threaten to divide, then discussion may "confuse right and wrong" (i.e., loyalties may be called into question), and issues may be evaluated on their own merits rather than in terms of the "truth" of expected deference to the "highest leader." In such circumstances the safest course to follow is outward acceptance of the official view; or better yet, avoidance of trouble through withdrawal and silence.[26]

The sum of these popular attitudes toward politics compounds the problems of vertical and lateral social integration discussed earlier. There was a "gap" in relations between leader and led based on fear of authority. During the dynastic era, the imperial bureaucracy could be paralyzed when local officials feared the consequences of accurate reporting of local conditions to their superiors. In telling the emperor and his ministers what they wanted to hear, local officials literally "cut the emperor off from reality." [27]

In times of political turmoil, when those in official power sought to insure commitment to the public good through deference to established institutions, the harshness of authority would only compound "selfish" popular desires to withdraw into private con-

26. Avenues of political avoidance and withdrawal were well institutionalized in traditional China, not only in "bandit" life and the activities of clan associations and professional guilds which sought to protect their members from official power, but also in the appeals of the Taoist and Buddhist traditions. (*See* Charles O. Hucker, "Confucianism and the Chinese Censorial System," in Nivison and Wright, eds., *Confucianism in Action*, p. 198.) Successful members of the rural gentry often warned their offspring that social success lay in avoiding politics (Ho Ping-ti, *The Ladder of Success in Imperial China* [New York: John Wiley, Science Editions, 1964], pp. 129–130); and within the Confucian tradition itself there was recognition of the legitimacy of withdrawal from society in times of *luan*. (*See* Fredrick W. Mote, "Confucian Eremitism in the Yüan Period," in Arthur F. Wright, ed., *The Confucian Persuasion* [Stanford, Calif.: Stanford University Press, 1960], pp. 202–240.)

27. The famous Ch'ing official, Tseng Kuo-fan, "regarded the lack of communication between official and emperor as the chief cause of the administrative paralysis of his time." He was writing of the period of near collapse of the dynasty in the mid-nineteenth century. (Liu Kwang-ching, "Nineteenth-Century China: The Disintegration of the Old Order and the Impact of the West," in Ho Ping-ti and Tang Tsou, eds., *China in Crisis* [Chicago: University of Chicago Press, 1968], Vol. I, Book 1, pp. 123–124.)

An emperor's concern with being cut off from reality by the distorted reporting of servile or ambitious ministers is revealed in the memoirs of the Ch'ien-lung Emperor. (*See* Harold L. Kahn, "The Education of a Prince: the Emperor Learns His Roles," in Albert Feuerwerker, Rhoads Murphey, and Mary C. Wright, eds., *Approaches to Modern Chinese History* [Berkeley: University of California Press, 1967], pp. 37–40.)

cerns. As Chiang K'ai-shek complained in the difficult year of 1943:

> In the past our adult citizens have been unable to unite on a large scale or for a long period. They have been derisively compared to "a heap of loose sand" or spoken of as having "only five-minutes' enthusiasm." Now incapacity to unite is a result of selfishness, and the best antidote for selfishness is public spirit.[28]

Among peers, the expectation of loyal support for a leader worked to produce a strong "in-group, out-group" orientation, an exclusiveness based on clique affiliation. And as interview data concerning communication habits reveal, there tends to be meager interaction between various factions out of fear of provoking conflict. Differences of opinion can hardly be resolved as they are rooted in exclusive personal loyalties which cause society to fragment along the lines of narrow hierarchies.

The traditional Chinese political culture, as is true of most traditional polities, was nonparticipant for the majority of the people. Involvement in public issues was discouraged by authority's appeals to those elements of personality—anxiety in the face of authority and a willingness to depend on the powerful—which had been developed through childhood socialization. An individual sought security not through his personal efforts, but by adjustment to group norms and interests, and through "obedient respect" for those with authority. The world of political power, for most people, was far away, embodying that sense of "distance" which was acquired in early life relations with authority: "An ordinary person wouldn't see a leader harming the people's welfare";[29] "He would be afraid to do anything [about it]"; "There is nothing he can do to influence politics" (*mei-yu pan-fa*).[30]

This "gap" between leader and led, formally recognized in the Mencian notion that those who use their minds govern those who labor with their muscle, gave reality to the concern of philosopher and political leader about the troublesome distinction between knowledge and action, theory and practice.[31] Those with power

---

28. Chiang K'ai-shek, *China's Destiny*, trans. in William Theodore de Bary, ed., *Sources of the Chinese Tradition* (New York: Columbia University Press, 1960), pp. 810–811.

29. T-18.

30. T-22.

31. The distinction between "knowledge" and "action" has been an enduring theme in Chinese social thinking. (*See* David S. Nivison, "The Problem of 'Knowledge' and 'Action' in Chinese Thought since Wang Yangming," in Arthur F. Wright, ed., *Studies in Chinese Thought* [Chicago: University of Chicago Press, 1953], pp. 112–141.) This philosophical dis-

asserted their authority through the word, while those who were dependent manifested their loyalty by translating word into action. Where the words of the ruler were "rectified," where there was justice with authority, this relationship could insure social order. But where there was a sense of exploitation or resentment, the conviction of having been cheated or misused could transform anxious dependents into hate-filled rebels. And in the vengeful violence which characterized China's periods of disorder, society's authoritative relationships would be swept away.

THE DREAM OF UNITY

In order to resolve their contradictory feelings about authority, strangely enough the Chinese begin by dreaming about the invocation of a still stronger authority. Even the revolutionary accomplishments of the revered Sun Yat-sen are called into question by the aftermath of *luan* which characterized the warlord period!

> I have a rather strange point of view. It was not too correct for the father of our country [Sun Yat-sen] to have overthrown the Ch'ing Emperor. The people must have a symbol. We have had a dictatorial country for several thousand years, and then in a moment the Em-

tinction had its social basis in the relational quality of authority in Chinese society; in the pattern of a superior who in his wisdom was to guide dependents in implementing his will.

As long as those in positions of authority are secure in their values and world-view, "It is not the knowing that is difficult, but the doing," as the Ch'ien-lung Emperor observed. (*See* Harold Kahn, "The Education of a Prince," in Feuerwerker *et al.*, eds., *Approaches to Modern Chinese History*, pp. 34–35.) The literati knew their place in the world; the only problem was to make certain that the people acted as Confucian morality said was proper.

Once the Confucian tradition had lost its aura of efficacy, however, under the combined impact of Western intervention and domestic social change, the "thought" vs. "action" distinction was turned upside down. Sun Yat-sen now phrased it, "Action is easy and knowledge is difficult." (*See* Nivison, "The Problem of 'Knowledge' and 'Action,' " p. 137; and Lyon Sharmon, *Sun Yat-sen: His Life and Its Meaning* [Stanford, Calif.: Stanford University Press, 1966], pp. 232–233.) And a generation of Chinese revolutionaries searched for a new political world-view which would orient their actions—some finding answers in Marxism-Leninism, and others in a resurrected version of Confucianism.

As we will suggest in the second half of this study, one of the aspects of change in China's political culture that has been promoted by Mao Tse-tung has been the effort to resolve the troublesome distinction between thought and action, "theory and practice," by eliminating the gap between a ruling elite that formulates policy, and a dependent population that merely carries out orders.

peror was overthrown and everyone became confused (*luan-le*). If there had been an Emperor in those days then we would not have had the warlords.[32]

While there is a respected leader to impose order, society's divisive forces are kept in check. But once he is gone, competitors for power rise up in a selfish scramble for full control. Such confusion can only be overcome through the action of powerful leaders who establish organizational control over those who would compete for power or make trouble:

> A nation does not develop from tranquillity. You have to govern it, make it peaceful. Therefore the leaders have to have great power and courage. To see if laws and orders agree with the wishes of the people, to manage things well so that there will be peace—these are questions of control. To maintain "peace and order" requires strong political organization.[33]

Our respondents manifest a great distrust of the harshness and impersonality of laws in maintaining an organization, however, for throughout Chinese history imperial Legalism (*fa-chia*) has been associated with oppressiveness. A personalized "highest leader" of talent and moral integrity is seen as society's only way to deal with the possibility of violence and unrestrained competition for power.

How do Chinese see social unity developing from the tension between the hope of a leader whose moral example will be emulated by subordinates, and the belief that only strict controls and punishments will maintain social order? Education as it is related to social control is the usual answer to this problem. Society requires

> a great leader stronger than anyone else to prevent competition for power—like President Chiang. Nowadays there are only a few who will compete for power. They do it in secret. (Why does having President Chiang do away with competition?) It is a matter of education. The leaders pay attention to the thinking of [potential competitors for power]. They make them study "The Three People's Principles," as if President Chiang were their teacher. You don't go against your teacher—after he dies maybe, but not before.[34]

Such an interpretation states clearly the control function of political ideology, the importance of "studying the thoughts of (the

32. T-37.
33. T-49.
34. T-18.

highest leader)." But it also reveals the fragile quality of such ideological unity: "You don't go against your teacher—after he dies maybe, but not before."

Thus, in the popular mind there is no resolution to the problem of how to insure social order without the use of strict authority. A strong leader can prevent *luan* for a time, but the harshness of his rule generates resentment. "Education" can help, but loyal commitment to a teacher must be ended by his death. The argument always comes full circle: When an external authority is removed there will be *luan*.

The longing for social unity remains, however. And the gap between fears of *luan* and the ideal of social harmony ultimately is bridged only by hope. There is hope that somehow all that is painful and threatening in daily life will give way to a condition of "great togetherness" (*ta-t'ung*).

Ta-t'ung is as enduring a concept in the Chinese world-view as the polarity between harmony and conflict from which it draws its inspiration. Taoist recluses read into this idealized condition of the world their search for the ultimate tranquillity, while Confucius saw *ta-t'ung* as China's perfected communal society once known in an early "golden age"—a state of social harmony he sought to reestablish through the political rituals of the Chou dynasty.[35] When the nineteenth-century philosopher K'ang Yu-wei sought to adapt Confucianism to a developmental concept of history, he described Chinese society as evolving from origins of disorder (*shuai-luan*) through "approaching peace" to a utopia of "the great unity" (*ta-t'ung*).[36] Each imperial official hoped to realize *ta-t'ung* in his area of administrative responsibility.[37] The revolutionary Sun Yat-sen impressed foreigners and countrymen alike with his deep desire to make China "an integral part of a world order," and with his devotion to "the Confucian ideal of a world in which men will really get together for the common good."[38]

A variety of translations have been given to the conception of *ta-t'ung* or *shih-chieh ta-t'ung*, "the universal harmony" and "the world commonwealth" among them. From our respondents' elaborations of this term, however, "the great togetherness" seems to

---

35. *See* Munro, *The Concept of Man in Early China,* Ch. 7.

36. Derk Bodde, "Harmony and Conflict in Chinese Philosophy," in Arthur F. Wright, ed., *Studies in Chinese Thought,* pp. 34–36.

37. *See* C. K. Yang, "Some Characteristics of Chinese Bureaucratic Behavior," in Nivison and Wright, eds., *Confucianism in Action,* p. 138.

38. Sharman, *Sun Yat-sen,* p. 269.

be a rendering which catches its essentially a-political quality:[39] the yearning for social harmony and security, and the desire for an end to interpersonal distinctions. As one respondent put it:

> *"Ta-t'ung"* means mutual assistance; everyone has a spirit of mutual assistance and this means that there will be no conflict among the common people and no war between one nation and another. Everyone has enough food to eat, has clothing to wear, and there can be unity in thinking among everyone. (How can *ta-t'ung* be attained?) Mankind can create this. If everyone has received an education and everyone's point of view is the same, then there will be no disorder, there will be no war. . . . Education must be universal, then everyone's knowledge will be about the same and then you can do away with much nonsensical bother. . . . If everyone's opinions are not the same it can lead to quarreling and confusion (*luan*).[40]

The longing is for an end to all interpersonal conflict, a "togetherness" in which there will be mutual assistance and, as some respondents phrased it, "there will be no difference between you and me." [41] The human condition of conflict based on distinctions of material wealth or differences in status and thinking will, it is hoped, evolve to a tranquil state of interpersonal unity that in quality can only be compared to that "golden age" of early life where, within the unbroken unity of the family, one knew only gratification without conflict.

39. The appeal of group life as "the great togetherness" has also been suggested by Robert J. Lifton in his study, *Thought Reform and the Psychology of Totalism* (New York: Norton, 1963), p. 254.
40. T-28.
41. T-16.

Part Three

THE MAOIST
POLITICAL REVOLUTION

Communist Party Chairman Mao Tse-tung and
Kuomintang General Director Chiang K'ai-shek
toast the beginning of peace negotiations
in Chungking, August 1945.
Jack Wilkes, Life *Magazine,* © *Time, Inc.*

[Political] synthesis is a matter of eating one's enemy. How did we synthesize the Kuomintang? Didn't we take in things captured from the enemy and transform them! We didn't just kill captured enemy soldiers. Some of them we let go, but the large part we absorbed into our ranks. Weapons, provisions, and all kinds of things were taken in. What was of no use we eliminated, to use a philosophical term. . . . Eating is both analysis and synthesis. Take eating crabs for example. You eat the meat and not the shell. One's stomach absorbs the nourishment and expels the waste. . . . Synthesizing the Kuomintang was a matter of eating it up, absorbing most of it and expelling a smaller part.

MAO TSE-TUNG
(*from a speech to*
Party leaders at Hangchow,
December 1965)

Chapter X

POLITICS IS AN
EMOTIONAL STORM

Why does a society have a revolution? This is the kind of broad question which might be approached from an historical perspective, in terms of the sociological or economic dimensions of social change, or at the attitudinal level. One might explore the reasons for the breakdown in acceptability of social traditions for those living in a given society. In this third part of our study we will look at China's twentieth century revolution through the eyes of Communist Party Chairman Mao Tse-tung. This man was to emerge as the most influential political leader of China's search for modern statehood, economic development, and social transformation. How did he mobilize a peasant population to gain political power and bring about a social revolution? As we shall see in the following chapters, there is a complex interplay between the traditional attitudes toward politics and social relations explored in the first two parts of this study, and the institutions of leadership developed by Mao and the Chinese Communists over three decades of struggle for power.

How does Mao Tse-tung account for the success of the Chinese Communist Party after years of bitter conflict with the Nationalists? Some indication of his views on this question is contained in an official Party statement of September 1949, published as the People's Liberation Army was completing its rout of Nationalist military forces and just a few days before the founding of the People's Republic. Mao's statement, entitled "The Bankruptcy of the Idealist Conception of History," began with an attack on Secretary of State Dean Acheson's attempt to explain to the people of the United States the reasons for the impending collapse of the Nationalist government and with it, the failure of America's China policy. Mao cited a passage by Acheson from the State Department's widely publicized "White Paper," distributed earlier in the year. Acheson wrote:

The population of China during the eighteenth and nineteenth centuries doubled, thereby creating an unbearable pressure upon the land. The first problem which every Chinese Government has had to face is that of feeding this population. So far none has succeeded. The Kuomintang attempted to solve it by putting many land-reform laws on the statute books. Some of these laws have failed, others have been ignored. In no small measure, the predicament in which the National Government finds itself today is due to its failure to provide China with enough to eat. A large part of the Chinese Communists' propaganda consists of promises that they will solve the land problem.[1]

Mao's response to this American interpretation of the Chinese revolution was addressed to Chinese, and particularly to those of his countrymen who may have found in Acheson's remarks hope for eventual Communist failure: "To those Chinese who do not reason clearly the above sounds plausible. Too many mouths, too little food, hence revolution. The Kuomintang has failed to solve this problem and it is unlikely that the Communist Party will be able to solve it either. 'So far none has succeeded.' "[2] Mao then added with a characteristic irony:

Do revolutions arise from overpopulation? There have been many revolutions, ancient and modern, in China and abroad; were they all due to overpopulation? Were China's many revolutions in the past few thousand years also due to overpopulation? Was the American Revolution against Britain 174 years ago also due to overpopulation? Acheson's knowledge of history is nil. He has not even read the American Declaration of Independence. Washington, Jefferson and others made the revolution against Britain because of British oppression and exploitation of the Americans, and not because of any overpopulation in America. Each time the Chinese people overthrew a feudal dynasty it was because of the oppression and exploitation of the people by that feudal dynasty, and not because of any overpopulation.[3]

These remarks carry with them the emotional triumph of a revolutionary at his hour of success; the sense of power and purpose of one who has guided to victory the storm of a people's resentments, frustrated hopes, and threatened security. Yet they also evince the concern of one who knows that destruction is about

1. Mao Tse-tung, "The Bankruptcy of the Idealist Conception of History" (1949), *SW*, English, IV, p. 452.
The notational system used in citing Mao's works is discussed in the bibliography, p. 584 below. "*SW*" stands for *The Selected Works of Mao Tse-tung.*
2. *Ibid.*
3. *Ibid.*

to end and the more demanding trials of rebuilding are soon to begin. And there is a certain pique at the awareness that there are many who do not wish him well, but who look on in hope of his eventual failure:

> The serious task of economic construction lies before us. We shall soon put aside some of the things we know well and be compelled to do things we don't know well. This means difficulties. The imperialists reckon that we will not be able to manage our economy; they are standing by and looking on, awaiting our failure.[4]

At his moment of triumph Mao thus looked forward to the coming period of national reconstruction in terms of a past built on popular resentment of "oppression and exploitation" by established authority. Despite his biting rejection of the interpretation that his success lay in the failure of others to feed the Chinese people, however, he knew well that the legitimacy of authority was in large measure based on fulfilling the needs of its dependents. His own career as a revolutionary had begun in student days nearly half a century earlier when he witnessed the popular outrage that resulted when a governor of the Ch'ing dynasty failed to feed the people in a year of starvation:

> There had been a severe famine . . . , and in Changsha thousands were without food. The starving sent a delegation to the civil governor, to beg for relief, but he replied to them haughtily, "Why haven't you food? There is plenty in the city. I always have enough." When the people were told the governor's reply, they became very angry. They held mass meetings and organized a demonstration. They attacked the Manchu yamen, cut down the flagpole, the symbol of office, and drove out the governor. . . . A new governor arrived, and at once ordered the arrest of the leaders of the uprising. Many of them were beheaded and their heads displayed on poles as a warning to future "rebels." [5]

Such an event becomes a catalyst in the process of revolution, rapidly eroding the aura of legitimacy surrounding established institutions of government. And a revolutionary sees in it the promise of a new era as much as the failure of the old. The people look to constituted authority as a legitimate source of security. It is the responsibility of those with power to provide for those who depend on them. But the starving citizens obtain no redress. As they see it, authority, in well-provided and ignorant isolation, denies

4. Mao, "On the People's Democratic Dictatorship" (1949), *SW*, English, IV, p. 422.

5. Edgar Snow, *Red Star Over China* (New York: Grove Press, 1961), p. 129.

Citizens of Changsha reaching out
for relief grain during the famine of the spring of 1910.
Courtesy of the Bain Collection, Library of Congress.

them their due, and unjustly labels them as "rebels." Indeed the regime in power cuts itself off more irrevocably than ever from the people's problems; reciprocity and communication are fully severed, all too literally in the chopping off of heads.

At such a point the dependent's attitude toward those in power goes through a qualitative change: His sense of acceptability which ultimately is based on the hope that obligations will be fulfilled breaks down into hostility. And for those who have known such use of power in the intimacy of family life, and have the strength of character to rebel, the *public* injustice becomes a *personal* call to action:

> This incident was discussed in my school for many days. It made a deep impression on me. Most of the other students sympathized with the "insurrectionists," but only from an observer's point of view. They did not understand that it had any relation to their own lives. They were merely interested in it as an exciting incident. I never forgot it. *I felt that there with the rebels were ordinary people like my own family and I deeply resented the injustice of the treatment given to them.*[6]

Mao's ability to relate injustice suffered by others to his own experience indeed seems to reflect his early family life, for he recalled similar treatment at the hands of his father.[7]

HOSTILITY: THE EMOTIONAL FUEL OF REVOLUTION

The route traveled by Mao Tse-tung in becoming the leader of the Chinese Communist Party has been told elsewhere by biographers and students of Party history.[8] What is of particular concern to us here is Mao's conception of the political process and the manner in which his style of leadership grew in response to the political attitudes of those the Party has sought to lead. This conception is most clearly revealed in Mao's early political tracts, written before the ideological filters of the Marxist-Leninist dialectic dimmed the clarity of his native style of expression.

In 1926, writing under the pen name of Jun-chih, Mao described a peasant uprising in Chekiang Province:

6. *Ibid.,* p. 130. Emphasis added.
7. *Ibid.,* pp. 125–126.
8. Of particular help in this study have been Jerome Ch'en, *Mao and the Chinese Revolution* (Cambridge, England: Oxford University Press, 1965); Stuart R. Schram, *Mao Tse-tung* (Baltimore: Penguin Books, 1967); and Benjamin I. Schwartz, *Chinese Communism and the Rise of Mao* (Cambridge, Massachusetts: Harvard University Press, 1964).

In recent months there occurred a great insurrection in the Shanpei area of [Tz'u Hsi County]. The peasants of this Shanpei area are violent by nature, and frequently indulge in armed combat. On top of this, in recent years the officials and police have been unreasonably oppressive and the bad landlords have stepped up their exploitation. So *the accumulated exasperation of the peasants was already deep.* By chance the climate this year was unstable, and as a result the rice and cotton crops failed, but the landlords refused to make any reduction whatever in their harsh rents. The peasants' insurrection against famine thereupon *exploded.* . . .

They burned down the police station, and distributed the arms of the police among themselves. They then turned to go to the homes of the village gentry landlords to *"eat up powerful families."* After eating them up, and out of anger at the evils of the village gentry landlords, they destroyed the landlords' screens, paintings, and sculptured ancient doors and windows. They did this every day; they did not listen much to others' exhortation, but *let off their steam* in this manner.[9]

Mao's reaction to such events was elation at injustice meeting its due: "If you are a person of determined revolutionary viewpoint, and if you have been to the villages and looked around, you will undoubtedly feel a joy never before known. Countless masses of slaves—the peasants, are there striking down their man-eating enemies." [10] The accumulated exasperation of years of holding in forbidden feelings and frustration at last explodes; the "man-eaters" are devoured by those consumed with rage.

The energies that are released as a result of these grievances and resentments can be likened only to the elemental violence of nature:

Within a very short time, several hundred million peasants from the provinces of China's central, southern, and northern sections will rise up, and their power will be like a blasting wind and cloudburst so extraordinarily swift and violent that no force however large will be able to suppress it. They will burst through all trammels that restrain them, and rush toward the road of liberation.[11]

9. Mao (under the pen name Jun-chih), "The Bitter Sufferings of the Peasants in Kiangsu and Chekiang, and Their Movements of Resistance" (1926), cited and translated in Stuart R. Schram, *The Political Thought of Mao Tse-tung* (New York: Praeger, 1963), p. 179. Emphasis added. Hereafter this source will be cited as "Schram, *PTMTT.*"

10. Mao, "Report on an Investigation of the Peasant Movement in Hunan" (1927), *SW,* I, Chinese, p. 17. Hereafter this article will be cited as "Hunan Report."

11. *Ibid.,* p. 13.

Mao's basic conception of political motivation is thus that of an emotional storm, in which hatreds, resentment, and a sense of hopeless desperation burst through social restraints in an overwhelming surge. The progress of the revolution has the stormy rhythm of "advancing waves," "upsurges," and "high tides" as the emotions that fuel political involvement rise to crests and then diminish through action.

"MUTUALLY RELATED AND MUTUALLY ANTAGONISTIC"

The calculus of such political action draws its logic from the authority relations of the traditional society, where initiative was fully vested with the powerful, where a subordinate had to discipline himself against the expression of frustrations and resentment, and where personal security was felt to be ultimately in other hands. When any hope of just treatment has vanished, dependent "respect" becomes a fused explosive; the greater the sense of resentment at injustice or failure of obligation, the greater the accumulated charge. One small added injustice may be the "single spark" that will "liberate" great intrinsic energy.

> At the slightest provocation [the peasants] make arrests, crown the arrested with tall paper hats, and parade them through the villages, saying, "You dirty landlords, now you know who we are!" Doing whatever they like and turning everything upside down, they have created a kind of terror in the countryside. . . . The local tyrants, evil gentry, and lawless landlords have themselves driven the peasants to this. For ages they have used their power to tyrannize over the peasants and trample them underfoot; that is why the peasants have reacted so strongly. The most violent revolts and the most serious disorders have invariably occurred in places where the local tyrants, evil gentry and lawless landlords perpetrated the worst outrages.[12]

Mao thus looks for the energy of revolution in the sense of injustice and resentment separating various social groups:

> . . . the industrial proletariat . . . is the most progressive class in modern China and has become the leading force in the revolutionary movement. . . . They have been deprived of all means of production, have nothing left but their hands, have no hope of ever becoming rich *and, moreover, are subjected to the most ruthless treatment by the imperialists, the warlords and the bourgeoisie. That is why they are particularly good fighters.*
>
> The third section [of the petty bourgeoisie] consists of those whose standard of living is falling. . . . As such people have seen better days and are now going downhill with every passing year, their debts

12. Mao, "Hunan Report" (1927), *SW,* English, I, p. 28.

mounting and their life becoming more and more miserable, they "shudder at the thought of the future." They are in great mental distress because there is such a contrast between their past and their present. Such people are quite important for the revolutionary movement. . . .

The semi-owner peasants are worse off than the owner-peasants because every year they are short of about half the food they need, and have to make up this deficit by renting land from others, selling part of their labour power, or engaging in petty trading. [They] are therefore more revolutionary than the owner-peasants, but less revolutionary than the poor peasants . . . who are exploited by the landlords. . . .

The shop assistants are employees of shops and stores, supporting their families on meagre pay and getting an increase perhaps only once in several years while prices rise every year. If by chance you get into intimate conversation with them, *they invariably pour out their endless grievances (chiao-k'u)*.[13]

Mao gave the following revealing perception of class conflict in 1939 as he surveyed the progress of the revolution: "The Chinese bourgeoisie and proletariat, seen as two specific social classes, are newly born; they have been born from the womb of feudal society, and have matured into new social classes. They are two *mutually related and mutually antagonistic* classes; they are twins born of old Chinese [feudal] society." [14]

Such family imagery in the context of an analysis of the relationship between economic classes reveals the linkage in Mao's mind between the relational quality of Confucian social authority, the *wu-lun,* and the hostility which will drive the revolution. His own life had sensitized him to the humiliation and sense of injustice that could come with dependence on those in power, and this sensitivity shaped his perceptions of social action. The notion of "mutually related and mutually antagonistic" was raised to the level of a philosophy of politics and social change in his theory of "contradictions" (*mao-tun*): the belief that "there is internal contradiction in every single thing. . ."; that "contradictoriness within a thing is the fundamental cause of its development. . ."; and that hatred, "antagonism" (*tui-k'ang*) is the motive force behind political action.[15]

13. Mao, "Analysis of the Classes in Chinese Society" (1926), *SW,* English, I, pp. 16–18. Emphasis added.
14. This passage from Mao's 1939 essay, "The Chinese Revolution and the Chinese Communist Party," has been analyzed in a provocative article by John Weakland, "Family Imagery in a Passage by Mao Tse-tung," *World Politics,* Vol. X (1958), pp. 387–407. Emphasis added.
15. Mao, "On Contradiction" (1937), *SW,* English, I, p. 313 and *passim.*

ON BEING "CONSCIOUS"

In 1919, after the impact of World War One had provoked in China the political ferment of "May Fourth," Mao wrote with obvious elation in a popular journal:

> Within the area enclosed by the Great Wall and the China Sea, the May 4th movement has arisen. Its banner has advanced southward . . . the tide is rising. Heaven and earth are aroused, the traitors and the wicked are put to flight. Ha! We know it! We are awakened! The world is ours, the nation is ours, society is ours. If we do not speak, who will speak? If we do not act, who will act? If we do not rise up and fight, who will rise up and fight?[16]

"The tide is rising"; "we are awakened." The notion that the storm of revolution wakes people up, makes them "conscious" was expressed by Mao with greater reservation in 1945 at the conclusion of the anti-Japanese war, when he looked back on the Party's historical development:

> The condition of our Party today is vastly different from what it was in 1927. In those days our Party was still in its infancy and did not have a clear head or experience in armed struggle or the policy of opposing weapons with weapons. Today the level of political consciousness in our Party is very much higher.
>
> Apart from our own political consciousness, the political consciousness of the vanguard of the proletariat, there is the question of the political consciousness of the masses of the people. When the people are not yet politically conscious, it is entirely possible that their revolutionary gains may be handed over to others. This happened in the past. Today the level of political consciousness of the Chinese people is likewise very much higher.[17]

As this passage indicates, political "consciousness" is seen as crucial to the success of the revolution. The objective of the revolution, of course, is "liberation" (*chieh-fang*), as the Chinese Communists characterize life under their leadership. Thus development of the revolution is symbolized as a process of awakening, becoming conscious, and then achieving liberation through struggle. But what does "awakening" really mean? What does "consciousness" bring into mind? And what is "liberated" through revolution?

16. Mao, "Toward a New Golden Age" (1919), cited and translated in Schram, *PTMTT*, p. 105.
17. Mao, "The Situation and Our Policy after the Victory in the War of Resistance against Japan" (1945), *SW*, English, IV, p. 19. Translation revised slightly on the basis of the Chinese text.

In the quotation on p. 168, Mao directly links "consciousness" to the capacity for promoting conflict. As we have seen in preceding chapters, however, the traditional culture taught the individual to deny even mediated expressions of hostility against those in authority and viewed conflict as illegitimate to "proper" social relations. Hostile feelings were supposed to be covered over with the social forms of filial respectfulness; they were to be put "in one's stomach." Thus becoming politically "awake" and "conscious," at one level of analysis, means mobilizing *feelings* which the old society said it was impermissible to express.

"Liberation" (a term which could also be translated as "get rid of" or "release") in the Maoist vocabulary means working up all the bitterness that society has made one swallow and releasing or liberating it through revolutionary struggle with "man-eating" enemies. And as Mao wrote with impatience shortly before the founding of the Chinese Communist Party, if only this emotional fuel of revolution could be tapped, organized, and directed for political ends, the Chinese people could create for themselves a new world:

> We must act energetically to carry out the great union of the popular masses, which will not brook a moment's delay. . . . Our Chinese people have great intrinsic energy; the deeper their oppression the greater will be their resistance, and as their sense of grievance has accumulated for a long time it will burst forth quickly. The great union of the Chinese people must be achieved. Gentlemen! We must all exert ourselves, we must all advance with the greatest effort. Our golden age, our age of brilliance and splendor, lies ahead.[18]

Life's golden age no longer lies in an idealized past, but in a yet-to-be attained future.

In the five chapters of Part Three which follow, we will explore in detail Mao's conception of politics as an emotional storm. In Chapter XI we will see the ways in which traditional attitudes toward leadership and social action influenced the political style of the Party in its formative years, producing what Mao saw to be "deviations" from an effective leadership line. Chapters XII through XIV explore the uses of ideology and organization as tools of leadership: their ability to structure the mobilization of popular support for the Party; their capacity to impose political discipline in the revolutionary struggle, to prevent the "confusion" which Chinese have long associated with conflict over power; and the

18. Mao, "Toward a New Golden Age" (1919), cited in Schram, *PTMTT*, p. 105. Translation revised slightly on the basis of the Chinese text.

importance of organization in giving the peasantry the confidence to oppose those in established authority. In Chapter XV we will look at Mao's tactical strategy for gaining power, a conception which draws on traditional Chinese notions of "divide and rule" as well as popular fears of isolation and the divisiveness which is so much a part of the struggle for power.

Chapter XI

REVOLUTIONARY LEADERSHIP AND
THE DEVIATIONS OF TRADITION

Outbursts of violence by China's peasantry held for an enthusiastic young Mao the promise of mass revolutionary energy. But he knew that for centuries a small but organized rural gentry and imperial bureaucracy had exercised effective control over the fragmented rural population. Mass hostility had to be organized and subject to political direction if revolutionary goals were to be attained. As Mao himself wrote after he had acquired greater experience, "If the masses alone are active without a strong leading group to organize their activity properly, such activity cannot be sustained for long, or carried forward in the right direction, or raised to a high level." [1]

One of the most interesting facets of the history of the Chinese Communist movement has been the development of an effective strategy of leadership: the evolution of organizational forms and a Party "line" appropriate to historical circumstances which could be used to coalesce and direct mass energies for political ends. From Mao's own perspective, in the course of the revolution the Party has had to wage a continuing struggle with tendencies to "deviate" from a proper leadership line in order to remain in the vanguard of the revolution. These deviations have roots in the traditional political culture.

THE PARTY MUST NOT
"CUT ITSELF OFF FROM THE MASSES"

Mao, the son of a Hunan peasant, was an aspiring young intellectual in the years of confusion surrounding the collapse of the Ch'ing dynasty. In his late teens he volunteered for eighteen months of service in a provincial army in order to "help complete the revolution" against the Manchus, but with the establishment of

1. Mao, "Some Questions Concerning Methods of Leadership" (1943), *SW*, English, III, p. 118.

the Republic he returned to an uncertain search for a career. Between 1913 and 1918 he studied to be a teacher at the First Normal School in the provincial capital of Changsha; and for a short time in 1918–19 he worked as a librarian's assistant at Peking University.[2]

In China intellectuals have always been close to the world of power. The Confucian imperial examinations were a major channel for the recruitment of public officials until the system was abolished in 1904. Hence a young man like Mao, seeking to make some personal contribution to the revitalization of China, almost instinctively turned to the world of education and the life of the cities, where "new learning" influenced by Western ideas seemed to hold promise for China's renaissance.

Of the many lessons Mao learned in his student days, one of the most enduring was of the gap between the social status of the intellectuals and the poverty and injustice which were his birthright as a provincial peasant. In part this gap reflected differences in life style between those reared in the cities and their rural compatriots. More fundamentally, however, the intellectuals' arrogant aloofness from those engaged in physical labor reflected a desire to rise above the bitter life of toil and insecurity endured by China's peasant millions. Mao himself recalled for Edgar Snow his own seduction by the Mencian notion of the superiority of mental over manual labor while a student serving in the anti-Ch'ing army: "I . . . had to buy water. The [ordinary] soldiers had to carry [it] from outside the city, but I, being a student, could not condescend to carrying, and bought it from the water peddlars." [3]

Mao's personal response to this time-honored aloofness of the intellectual was shaped by a sense of resentment which came from his own rejection by intellectual leaders who inspired many of his generation. While a library worker at Peking University he sought to question the philosopher Hu Shih after a lecture, only to be ignored because he did not have regular student status.[4] And his efforts to establish contact with other intellectual heroes of the hour met with hardly greater success:

> My office [in the library] was so low that people avoided me. One of my tasks was to register the names of people who came to read

2. Mao's recollections of his early life were recounted to Edgar Snow in a series of interviews held in Paoan, Shensi Province, during 1936. This document remains the basic source of information on Mao's early life and a valuable expression of his personal attitudes rendered in a relatively non-Marxist vocabulary. *See Red Star Over China*, pp. 121–156.

3. *Ibid.*, p. 138.

4. Stuart R. Schram, *Mao Tse-tung*, p. 48.

newspapers, but to most of them I didn't exist as a human being. Among those who came to read I recognized the names of famous leaders of the renaissance movement, men like Fu Ssu-nien, Lo Chia-lung, and others, in whom I was intensely interested. I tried to begin conversations with them on political and cultural subjects, but they were very busy men. They had no time to listen to an assistant librarian speaking southern dialect.[5]

From such incidents grew a bitter distrust of intellectuals as a group which has been a constant theme in Mao's social outlook. This orientation has remained in tension with the needs of a political movement for the leadership skills that traditionally have been the exclusive preserve of China's educated few. Mao has sought to resolve this tension through ridicule of intellectual pretentiousness and the remolding of traditional attitudes toward the use of power.

After the Party's near destruction in 1927, Mao found a number of disgraced intellectuals among the leadership who could be held up for ridicule as "negative examples" to educate Party cadres. Mao told Edgar Snow that Ch'en Tu-hsiu, the Party's General Secretary, suffered from "wavering opportunism [which] deprived the Party of decisive leadership"; and he ridiculed the Comintern representative, M. N. Roy, by noting that "he talked too much without offering any method of realization [of Party goals]." [6] But this tendency of the intellectual to use words, without direct involvement in practical problems, was hardly unique to these early Party notables. In a 1930 essay, "Oppose Book Worship," Mao complained of comrades "who like to make political pronouncements the moment they arrive at a place and who strut about, criticizing this and condemning that when they have only seen the surface of things or minor details. Such purely subjective nonsensical talk is indeed detestable." [7] Others, he noted, "eat their fill and sit dozing in their offices all day long without ever moving a step and going out among the masses to investigate. Whenever they open their mouths, their platitudes make people sick." [8]

In the Kiangsi days Mao sought institutional ways of bringing together power and practice: "No investigation, no right to speak." [9] Yet he seemed mocked in his efforts by the legacy of China's political culture, shared by leader and led alike: "What-

5. Snow, *Red Star Over China*, p. 150.
6. *Ibid.*, p. 165.
7. Mao, "Oppose Book Worship" (1930), *Selected Readings from the Works of Mao Tse-tung* (Peking: Foreign Languages Press, 1967), p. 34.
8. *Ibid.*, p. 39.
9. *Ibid.*, p. 33.

ever is written in a book is right—such is still the mentality of culturally backward Chinese peasants." [10] With the influx of disaffected intellectuals into Communist-controlled Yenan during the war with Japan, Mao attempted to reform through ridicule "those who regard Marxism-Leninism as religious dogma":

> We must tell [such people] openly, "Your dogma is of no use," or to use an impolite formulation, "Your dogma is less useful than shit." Dog shit can fertilize the fields. . . . And dogmas? They can't fertilize the fields. . . . Of what use are they? (Laughter) Comrades! You know that the object of such talk is to ridicule those who regard Marxism-Leninism as dogma, to frighten and awaken them. . . . Marx, Engels, Lenin, and Stalin have repeatedly said, "Our doctrine is not dogma; it is a guide to action." Of all things, these people forget this most important sentence.[11]

Throughout his career this peasant revolutionary has reserved his most bitter, scatological irony for those who threaten to transform the ideology of China's future greatness into a new language of control which would heighten the distinction between an order-issuing elite and a peasant mass that only dumbly obeys—a division of function and status that would lead to the Party's "cutting itself off from the masses" (*t'o-li ch'ün-chung*). Mao expressed his determination to bring together word and action in a philosophy of "Practise," [12] and instructed intellectual cadres that they must not write Marxist analyses of Chinese society in the formalistic style of the Confucian "eight-legged essay." [13]

By Yenan days this concern with insuring communication and contact between Party cadres and the people was institutionalized in the leadership concept of the "mass line" (*ch'ün-chung lu-hsien*):

> All correct leadership is necessarily "from the masses; to the masses." This means: take the ideas of the masses (scattered and unsystematic ideas) and concentrate them (through study turn them into concen-

10. *Ibid.,* p. 34.
11. Mao, "Reform in Learning, the Party, and Literature" (1942), in Schram, *PTMTT,* p. 120.
12. *See* Mao's 1937 essay "On Practise," *SW,* English, I, pp. 295–309.
13. *See* "Oppose Stereotyped Party Writing" (1942), *SW,* English, III, pp. 53–68. This and other essays from the 1942 Party "rectification" campaign deal primarily with problems of maintaining effective communications between the leadership and led. *See also* "Preface and Postscript to *Rural Surveys*" (1941), "Reform Our Study" (1941), "Rectify the Party's Style of Work" (1942), and "Talks at the Yenan Forum on Literature and Art" (1942), all in Volume III of the *Selected Works.*

trated and systematic ideas), then go to the masses and propagate and explain these ideas until the masses embrace them as their own.[14]

But this effort to develop a dialogue between Party and people has been in constant tension with enduring traditional attitudes about the relation of superior to subordinate. Various approaches have been tried. In the post-Liberation development of the periodic *hsia-fang* or "transfer downwards" campaigns, students and government workers have been sent out to labor with peasants in the fields. Another educational innovation is the "half-work—half-study" schools, designed to raise new generations of intellectuals who would know through personal experience a relationship between labor and leadership.[15]

It is perhaps because of his perception of the ability of the intellectual to stifle action with words that Mao has placed such emphasis in his style of leadership on the manipulation of emotions; on the rationale of injustice, not on the rhetoric of scholasticism used so long in China as an instrument of political control.

DARE (KAN)!

While Mao's bugbear among early Party leaders was Ch'en Tu-hsiu, his hero was Ch'en's coequal in founding the Communist movement, the intellectual Li Ta-chao. Li was Mao's mentor in Peking, the man who placed him on the staff of the University library, and who headed the Marxist study group in which Mao received his first exposure to the ideology of the Bolshevik revolution. This personal relationship cemented a common social outlook: a shared commitment to activism; concern about the isolation of China's intellectuals from the practical problems of their society; and acceptance of the direct political action approach that had been rejected by men like Hu Shih and Ch'en.[16] But where Li's career was cut short through strangulation during the nation-wide anti-Communist suppression of 1927, Mao had the opportunity, and the commitment, to transform Li's ideals into a technique of leadership.

14. Mao, "Some Questions Concerning Methods of Leadership" (1943), *SW*, English, III, p. 119.

15. *See* Donald J. Munro, "Maxims and Realities in China's Educational Policy: The Half-Work, Half-Study Model," *Asian Survey*, Vol. VII, No. 4 (April 1967), pp. 254–272.

16. These aspects of Li Ta-chao's social outlook are documented and analyzed in Maurice Meisner, *Li Ta-chao and the Origins of Chinese Marxism* (Cambridge, Massachusetts: Harvard University Press, 1967).

The problems Mao faced in creating an activist cadre of leaders were based on more than just the intellectuals' aloofness from the problems of China's peasant masses. Common Chinese attitudes toward authority and conflict continued to bind individuals into the structure of a society which endured beyond the destruction of the Ch'ing state apparatus. For Mao and many of his generation the binding effects of Confucian social relations were symbolized in the matter of marriage choice. The selection of a mate, a problem confronted personally by most young radicals, brought to a focus the clash between the wishes of the individual and family interests. When he was twenty-six, Mao wrote an article about the suicide of a young girl who was unwilling to submit to an arranged marriage. In it he expressed many of the frustrations of his generation, and revealed some of the concepts of social action that later evolved into institutionalized techniques of leadership:

> A person's suicide is entirely determined by circumstances. . . . The circumstances in which Miss Chao found herself were the following: (1) Chinese society; (2) the Chao family of Nanyang Street in Changsha; (3) the Wu family of Kantzuyuan Street in Changsha, the family of the husband she did not want. *These three factors constituted three iron nets, composing a kind of triangular cage.* . . . [But] if in society there had been a powerful group of public opinion to support her, if there were an entirely new world where the fact of running away from one's parents' home and finding refuge elsewhere were considered honorable and not dishonorable, in this case, too, Miss Chao would certainly not have died.
>
> Since there are factors in our society that have brought about the death of Miss Chao, *this society is an extremely dangerous thing.* . . . All of us, the potential victims, must be on our guard before this dangerous thing that could inflict a fatal blow on us. *We should protest loudly,* warn the other human beings who are not yet dead, and condemn the countless evils of our society. . . .[17]

For Mao and others of the "May Fourth" era the "five human relationships" which had bound together Confucian society seemed as cold and restrictive as "iron nets." But as Miss Chao's suicide indicated, old custom still had the potency to force the individual to direct life's frustrations inward as aggression against the self. Unlike Miss Chao, however, who withdrew to a private escape, Mao generalized the problem to a public issue in which he saw everyone threatened. He longed for some organized force to counter the source of danger: ". . . if in society there had been a powerful group of public opinion to support her. . . ." This passage reveals another dimension of Mao's personal style

17. Cited in Schram, *PTMTT*, pp. 226–227. Emphasis added.

which, in combination with his ability to generalize personal difficulties in terms of social ills, seems to account for his effectiveness as a revolutionary leader: his ability to "protest loudly." Mao's assertiveness is a quality he revealed early in life, in a number of youthful rebellions through which he came to perceive that his father was really dependent on him. At the age of ten Mao ran away from school in fear of the beatings administered by a teacher of the "stern treatment school." Afraid of receiving a beating at home as well, he wandered lost for three days before he was finally located by his family. He recalled with satisfaction, however: "After my return . . . to my surprise conditions somewhat improved. My father was slightly more considerate, and the teacher was more inclined to moderation. The result of my action of protest impressed me very much. It was a successful 'strike.' " [18]

A more serious incident occurred a few years later, revealing to Mao the way that authority could be manipulated through the logic of filial dependence:

> When I was about thirteen my father invited many guests to his home, and while they were present a dispute arose between the two of us. My father denounced me before the whole group, calling me lazy and useless. This infuriated me. I cursed him and left the house. My mother ran after me and tried to persuade me to return. My father also pursued me, cursing at the same time that he demanded me to come back. *I reached the edge of a pond and threatened to jump in if he came any nearer.* In this situation demands and counterdemands were presented for cessation of the civil war. My father insisted that I apologize and *k'ou-t'ou* as a sign of submission. I agreed to give a one-knee *k'ou-t'ou* if he would promise not to beat me. Thus the war ended, and from it *I learned that when I defended my rights by open rebellion my father relented, but when I remained meek and submissive he only cursed and beat me the more.*[19]

The notable aspect of this incident, which Mao characterized as "open rebellion," is that the physical threat still was self-directed; the adolescent was capable of attacking his father only *indirectly* by threatening to drown himself (thus "abandoning" his father by leaving him without a son to depend on) and by making his father "lose face" before the guests. Yet Mao saw that if authority were "dared" its harshness could be mitigated, while "meek and submissive" behavior would only invoke greater pain.

In his personal development, the pond before which Mao had defied his father was transformed into one of this revolutionary's most powerful symbols of opposition to dependence on authority.

18. Snow, *Red Star Over China*, p. 125.
19. *Ibid.*, p. 126. Emphasis added.

In Part One we noted how Chinese parents sought to restrict their children's physical activity, such as swimming, out of fear that they would harm themselves. Aggressive impulses and actions which threatened to break the filial bond were to be held in through physical reserve. But where Mao the child had to "dare" authority through the threat of self-destruction because of his inability to swim, as a young man he expressed his determination to turn aggression outwards by learning how to swim. His self-assertiveness found expression in a keen interest in physical culture:

> In the winter holidays we [student friends] tramped through the fields, up and down mountains, along city walls, and across the streams and rivers. If it rained we took off our shirts and called it a rain bath. . . . We slept in the open when frost was already falling and even in November swam in the cold rivers. All this went on under the title of "body training." [20]

The relationship between such physical disciplining and political assertiveness was first articulated by Mao in an essay written in 1917, "A Study of Physical Education." He saw his nation "wanting in strength. The military spirit has not been encouraged." In seeking to remedy this situation he drew on his personal experience:

> Physical education . . . strengthens the will. The great utility of physical education lies precisely in this. . . . Let me explain with an example. To wash our feet in ice water makes us acquire courage and dauntlessness, as well as audacity. In general, any form of exercise, if pursued continuously, will help train us in perseverance. . . . *Exercise over a long time can produce great results and give rise to a feeling of personal value.*" [21]

Within a decade this youthful preoccupation with developing a "feeling of personal value" and the martial spirit through body-building was to be transformed into Mao's first effort to build a peasant military force, an act of personal assertiveness which "dared" the Comintern-backed Party Central Committee and the orthodox, urban-oriented strategy of revolution which was then the official Party line.

In later years the link between Mao's willingness to "dare" authority through swimming and military action became central to the mythology of the revolution:

> To make a revolution and wage a war is often not a matter of learning before doing, but of doing and then learning, for doing is learn-

20. *Ibid.*, p. 146.
21. Mao, "A Study of Physical Education" (1917), in Schram, *PTMTT,* pp. 99, 101.

ing. Only by following Chairman Mao's instructions and putting "daring" and "doing" above everything else, and courageously plunging into the practice of war—tempering ourselves in the teeth of storms and learning to swim by swimming—can we acquaint ourselves with the laws of war and master them." [22]

On the eve of perhaps his last great political battle, Mao was to symbolize his determination to "dare" the Party which had passed beyond his control by swimming in the Yangtze. He called on a new generation to share his own youthful experience of learning to challenge authority by "advancing with Chairman Mao amidst great winds and waves" [23] in the Great Proletarian Cultural Revolution.

While the strength of his own self-assertiveness enabled the young Mao to seek ways of dealing with the harshness of authority, his early writings reveal that he was sensitive to the forms of psychological support which an individual needed to oppose the established social order. He found that an ideology could provide an alternative source of authority to answer the criticisms of those in control: "I discovered a powerful argument of my own for debating with my father on his own ground, by quoting the Classics." [24] He also saw that an organized group could back an individual in protest, overcoming fears of acting in isolation and providing an alternative source of support (". . . if in society there had been a powerful group of public opinion to support [Miss Chao]. . . .")

Perhaps the most important aspect of such incidents is that *even* for a man who in time had the audacity to challenge a social order weighted with "five thousand years of history," attacking authority directly was an extremely difficult thing to do: It invoked those aspects of personality—anxiety in the face of authority, and fears of isolation and conflict—which gave the Confucian social pattern its durability.

THE "RIGHTIST" DEVIATION: AVOIDANCE OF CONFLICT

Mao's personal capacity to accept direct conflict and his distrust of a position of passive dependence find expression in his reading,

22. From a *Liberation Army Daily* editorial, "Study 'Problems of Strategy in China's Revolutionary War,' " trans. in *Peking Review,* No. 3 (December 29, 1966), p. 18.

23. *See* the photographs and news release of Mao's swim in the Yangtze, and the editorial "Advance with Chairman Mao Amidst Great Winds and Waves," in the *People's Daily* issues of July 25 and 26, 1966. *See also* pp. 476–477 below.

24. Snow, *Red Star Over China,* p. 125.

and rewriting of Party history, through which he has used past defeats to criticize deviations from his interpretation of the proper leadership line.

During the first six years of its existence, the Party's Central Committee, under General Secretary Ch'en Tu-hsiu, accepted Comintern pressures to work as a "bloc within" the more powerful Kuomintang. Ch'en's personal attitudes toward this Party dependence on "bourgeois" (and Comintern) leadership are obscured by the complexity of events, but in the most detailed study to date of this period, Benjamin Schwartz has concluded: "In the face of what was considered to be the formidable power of the enemy, [the Ch'en leadership group] wished to conserve its strength for the future"; and, "in the implementation of policy they bowed to the superior wisdom of the Kremlin." [25] In spite of the warning of the vulnerability of the masses implicit in the "February Seventh" 1923 slaughter of organized but unarmed workers by Wu P'ei-fu's army, or the promise of mass energies revealed in the "May Thirtieth" [1925] anti-Japanese outbursts, the Ch'en leadership refrained from developing independent armed power. Even Chiang K'ai-shek's arrest of Party and Comintern leaders in March of 1926 produced no basic change in policy, with the result that the Party organization was nearly annihilated in the 1927 anti-Communist suppression carried out by Nationalist military forces.

The most notable aspect of Ch'en's handling of this situation is that despite his doubts, he was unwilling or unable to translate the perception of a bad Party line into a change in policy. He continued to submit to Comintern pressures rather than organize support for a more effective strategy. The basis for Ch'en's lack of assertiveness, or what Mao once termed his "wavering opportunism," was suggested by Mao in 1936:

> Ch'en was really frightened of the workers and especially of the armed peasants. Confronted at last with the reality of armed insurrection he completely lost his senses. He could no longer see clearly what was happening, and his petty-bourgeois instincts betrayed him into panic and defeat.[26]

Mao characterized Ch'en as an "unconscious traitor," [27] and as we have seen previously, "consciousness" in Mao's political vocabulary is directly linked to the capacity for mobilizing hatreds that will fire revolutionary violence. Like other political leaders, Mao has used history to justify present policy rather than to affirm past

25. Schwartz, *Chinese Communism and the Rise of Mao*, p. 64.
26. Snow, *Red Star Over China*, p. 165.
27. *Ibid.*

fact. His criticism of Ch'en can thus be read as an indication that even within the Party leadership, traditional Chinese fears of conflict and anxieties about challenging established authority require constant criticism lest they undermine the momentum of the revolution.[28] Such attitudes were particularly notable in the early, "urban" days of the Party. For example, the Central Committee, meeting in Shanghai in 1926, expressed its distrust of armed peasants and concern about the "destructive tendencies" of such quasi-military rural secret societies as the Red Spears.[29]

It is noteworthy that these two traditional attitudes, fear of conflict and passivity before the power of established authority, are threads which run through the history of Mao's attempt to develop and maintain a successful revolutionary leadership. One of his criticisms of "bourgeois" parties and leaders is that they fear the conflict of revolution:

> . . . the national bourgeoisie cannot be the leader of the revolution, nor should it have the chief role in state power. The reason it cannot be the leader . . . is that the social and economic position of the national bourgeoisie determines its weakness; *it lacks foresight and sufficient courage and many of its members are afraid of the masses.*[30]

The "bourgeois" tendency to fear conflict and mass upheaval, however, manifests itself even within the Party. The "opportunism" which led Ch'en Tu-hsiu to become passive before Nationalist power becomes evident in "liberalism" (*tzu-yu-chu-yi*):

> Liberalism is one expression of opportunism, [and] is fundamentally in conflict with Marxism. *It is a passive thing, and subjectively serves to aid the enemy.* . . . *We must use the active spirit of Marxism to overcome passive liberalism. A Communist should . . .*

28. The autobiographical writings of Ch'ü Ch'iu-pai, a leader of the Party for a short period in late 1927 and early 1928—and, ironically, a man removed from leadership because of a "left" or adventurist deviation in leadership—reveal a strong sense of discomfort about interpersonal conflict. *See* T. A. Hsia, "Ch'ü Ch'iu-pai's Autobiographical Writings: The Making and Destruction of a 'Tender-hearted' Communist," *The China Quarterly*, No. 25 (January–March 1966), pp. 176–212.

This perceptive article reveals a number of other aspects of one Party leader's emotional life which bear out several of the themes of the traditional political culture explored above: a man's dependence on family assistance even when he detested family life (pp. 184–185); a strong desire to return to childhood (p. 194); and a longing for social unity (p. 193).

29. Cited in Meisner, *Li Ta-chao and the Origins of Chinese Marxism*, p. 244.

30. Mao, "On the People's Democratic Dictatorship" (1949), *SW*, English, IV, p. 421. Emphasis added.

be active . . . and wage a tireless struggle against all incorrect ideas and actions, so as to consolidate the collective life of the Party and consolidate the relationship between the Party and the people.[31]

These culture-enhanced impediments to the "revolutionary" use of power—passivity, and fear of conflict—found particular manifestation in the development of Mao's strategy of guerrilla warfare. To become "conscious" of one's potential for violent combat was not sufficient; one had to gain initiative in action and force the enemy into a passive position:

> Freedom of action is the very life of an army and, once it is lost, the army is close to defeat or destruction. *The disarming of a soldier is the result of his losing freedom of action through being forced into a passive position. . . . For this reason both sides in war do all they can to gain the initiative and avoid passivity.* . . . Initiative is inseparable from superiority in capacity to wage war, while *passivity is inseparable from inferiority.*[32]

Mao sensed that although the invading Japanese possessed superiority in firepower and certain types of communication and transport, there were a number of objective circumstances—insufficient troops, lack of knowledge of China and contacts with her people, and a rigid leadership—which would limit their initiative. Hence if the Party could overcome Chinese tendencies to be passive before power, Japan could be defeated through the "activism" of superior initiative:

> Japan's general position has become one of only relative superiority, and her ability to exercise and maintain the initiative, which is thereby restricted, has likewise become relative. As for China, though placed in a somewhat passive position strategically because of her inferior strength, she is nevertheless quantitatively superior in territory, population and troops, and also superior in the morale of her people and army and their patriotic hatred of the enemy; this superiority . . . reduces the degree of China's passivity so that her strategic position is one of only relative passivity. *Any passivity, however, is a disadvantage, and one must strive to shake it off. . . .* Through . . . local superiority and local initiative in many campaigns, we can gradually create strategic superiority and strategic initiative and extricate ourselves from strategic inferiority and passivity. Such is the interrelation between initiative and passivity, between superiority and inferiority.[33]

31. Mao, "Combat Liberalism" (1937), *SW*, Chinese, II, p. 347. Emphasis added.

32. Mao, "On Protracted War" (1938), *SW*, English, II, pp. 161–162. Emphasis added.

33. *Ibid.*, p. 163.

While the Party's promotion of guerrilla warfare was hardly a decisive factor in the defeat of Japan, it did serve to build up Communist military strength and create a leadership with skill and experience. After 1945 these weapons of revolution were turned against the Nationalist government in civil war. Yet here again, according to Mao, individuals within the Party manifested the "rightist" deviation of fear of conflict before apparently superior forces, and a reluctance to stimulate to full fury the "political consciousness" of the masses.[34] Yet after more than two decades of military trial and growth, the strength of such a deviation had been eroded:

> The Right deviations consist chiefly in *over-estimating the strength of the enemy, being afraid of large-scale U.S. aid to Chiang Kai-shek,* being somewhat weary of the long war, having certain doubts about the strength of the world democratic forces, *not daring to arouse the masses fully* in order to abolish feudalism, and being indifferent to impurities in the Party's class composition and style of work. Such Right deviations, however, are not the main ones at present; they are not too difficult to correct.[35]

Even in victory, when nationwide power was within grasp, Mao's fear of passivity before power did not vanish: "Just because we have won victory, we must never relax our vigilance against the frenzied plots for revenge by the imperialists and their running dogs. *Whoever relaxes vigilance will disarm himself politically and land himself in a passive position.*"[36]

This enduring, anxious concern with activism in the use of power and fear of passivity in the face of strong enemies seems to reflect Mao's personal reaction to the pain and injustice he had known in the dependent period of his own life. Also, from the vantage point of a leader who wants to revolutionize a tradition-bound society, Mao's preoccupation with passivity reveals a concern that those around him, other leaders and followers, will give in to those anxieties about criticizing established authority and custom that are the legacy of China's traditional political culture. In such circumstances, the revolution would become mired down in enduring social patterns characteristic of a discredited way of life.

34. In 1967 this deviation was attributed to Mao's long-time cohort Liu Shao-ch'i as part of a general attack on Liu for his "passive" approach to leadership. *See* pp. 396, 400–404 below.

35. Mao, "A Circular on the Situation" (1948), *SW*, English, IV, p. 220. Emphasis added.

36. Mao, "Address to the Preparatory Committee of the New Political Consultative Conference" (1949), *SW*, English, IV, p. 407. Emphasis added.

"LEFT OPPORTUNISM" AND LUAN

There is a dialectical partner to the "rightist" deviation of passivity in the face of superior power: a tendency to promote conflict without caution. Such "left opportunism" has manifested itself in Party history in such incidents as the Nanchang uprising of August 1927, the precipitate formation and failure of the Canton Commune in December of that same year, and the abortive attacks on Changsha by military forces from the Soviet areas in September 1927 and again in the summer of 1930. Such tactical failures resulting from the impetuous promotion of conflict have been associated with the early Party leaders Ch'ü Ch'iu-pai, Li Li-san, and Wang Ming.

Mao himself, in student days, had toyed with the anarchist's glorification of violence largely for its own sake.[37] Indeed, in later years he was to affirm the legitimacy of conflict with the slogan, "There cannot be construction without destruction." However, since his 1921 acceptance of the need for a Leninist party organization, and the caution with which he committed to battle the meager military forces under his control in the Kiangsi Soviet areas, one can conclude that early in his career Mao had placed revolutionary violence under the discipline of larger political goals.

An inability to express aggression with control, what Marxist-Leninists term adventuristic "left opportunism" in the use of power, seems closely related to Chinese fears of *luan*. As was elaborated in Part Two, traditionally there has been an expectation that once hostile emotions come into the open a person becomes overwhelmed with his own aggressive impulses, his mind becomes "complicated" (*fu-tza*), and he gets carried away into a "confusion" of interpersonal conflict. In the Confucian tradition "cultivation" was conceived as a way of keeping a "clear head," of holding in the bad feelings which, if mobilized, could destroy social order. In looking back on the Party's political adventures of the 1920s Mao once remarked: "In those days our Party was still in its infancy and did not have a clear head or experience in armed struggle. . . ."[38] Early Party history seems to confirm that learning discipline in the use of violence was almost as much of a leadership problem as overcoming the reluctance to mobilize the hatreds that make revolutionary violence possible.

37. Mao recalled that while in Peking he "often discussed anarchism and its possibilities in China. At that time I favored many of its proposals." (Snow, *Red Star Over China*, p. 151.) On this point *see also* Schram, *Mao Tse-tung*, p. 49.

38. Mao, "The Situation and Our Policy after the Victory in the War of Resistance against Japan" (1945), *SW*, English, IV, p. 19.

The first major manifestation of "adventurism," or the undisciplined promotion of conflict, followed the Party's near annihilation in the urban areas in the spring and summer of 1927. An emergency conference of the Central Committee held on August seventh replaced the "right opportunist" Ch'en Tu-hsiu with Ch'ü Ch'iu-pai as Party leader. Thereafter, under prodding from the Comintern, the new leadership initiated planning for the immediate establishment of urban Soviets through provoking uprisings in provincial cities. A Party investigation team surveying preparations for this precipitate insurrection in Hunan found that "Those who are sufficiently angry to want to overthrow the government are in the minority. Most of them would prefer to be passive and inert." [39] But despite such intimations of incipient defeat, the Central Committee pressed on with its plans. The failure of the uprising was to be repeated in the equally hasty Canton insurrection of December 1927.

As with Ch'en's earlier defeat resulting from submission to Comintern pressure, Ch'ü's misjudgment held for Mao the lesson of the dangers of blind dependence on a "superior" authority divorced from China's immediate social conditions. Yet Mao himself was singled out for criticism by his Party superiors as a "rightist" because of "having done too little killing and burning. . . ." [40]

While the urban-based Central Committee bore most of the blame for the adventures of the latter half of 1927, Mao found that his efforts to build a military force in the mountains of the Hunan-Kiangsi border region were also hindered by "leftist" deviations. In an analysis of 1929 he criticized "the ideology of roving guerilla bands" and those elements of the Red Army who resorted to violence as a form of personal indulgence, who "only want to go to the big cities to eat and drink." And perhaps with the increasingly influential Li Li-san in mind, he attacked those who urged "blind action regardless of subjective and objective conditions." [41]

Where Ch'en Tu-hsiu symbolized for Mao "rightist" revolutionary reticence, Li Li-san came to be the personification of "leftist" impetuosity. Mao's first contacts with the impulsive Li had not gone well,[42] and with Li's rise to major prominence in the Party in

39. Cited in Roy Mark Hofheinz, *The Peasant Movement and Rural Revolution: Chinese Communists in the Countryside, 1923–1927* (unpublished Ph.D. dissertation, Harvard University, 1966), pp. 281–282.
40. Cited from Mao's own recollection of this period in Schram, *Mao Tse-tung*, p. 131.
41. Mao, "On Correcting Mistaken Ideas in the Party" (1929), *SW*, English, I, pp. 114–115.
42. Mao recalled that in student days he once put an advertisement in a Changsha paper, "inviting young men interested in patriotic work to make

1928–29 their differences in personal style found expression in conflict over revolutionary strategy. Li criticized Mao's efforts to create a peasant military force as un-Marxist, and asserted that without urban working class leadership (that is, leadership exercised from the urban areas under Central Committee control) there likely would be "a complete destruction of the revolution and of the Party." [43]

In fact, it was Li's own precipitate commitment of the Chu-Mao military forces to urban insurrection which cost the Party dearly, and seriously threatened Mao's growing power base in the rural Soviet areas. A Comintern directive of October 1929 talked vaguely of an approaching "upsurge" in China's revolutionary situation. Li overinterpreted the language to call for a new round of urban insurrections and ordered attacks on major cities in South-Central China during the summer of 1930. [44] Changsha was held for ten days, but attacks on Nanchang and Wuhan encountered superior Kuomintang forces, and within three weeks the unsuccessful venture was abandoned.

While Mao's reading of the uncertainties of the situation had been accurate, Li's failure only led to a new, Comintern-oriented Party leadership headed by the young Wang Ming (Ch'en Shao-yü), recently returned from studies in Moscow. From Mao's perspective this new leadership once again engaged in "leftist" tactical deviations which nearly led to the total destruction of the Red Army during the fifth Kuomintang "Encirclement and Extermination" campaign of 1934. It was only the "Long March," and Mao's rise to Party leadership after the January 1935 Central Committee conference held in the Kweichow market town of Tsunyi which finally gave Mao the opportunity to assert his own political style.

THE IMPORTANCE OF DISCIPLINED STRUGGLE

Mao's reading of these early deviations in leadership was not that they were solved simply by removing the responsible leaders; rather, these twin dangers of indiscriminate conflict or fear of revolution-

---

contact with me." He received "three and one-half replies. The 'half' reply came from a noncommittal youth named Li Li-san. Li listened to all I had to say, and then went away without making any definite proposals himself, and our friendship never developed." (Snow, *Red Star Over China*, p. 145.)

43. Cited in Schram, *Mao Tse-tung*, p. 139.

44. Evidence that Li Li-san overinterpreted a Comintern directive to suit his personal inclinations is discussed in James P. Harrison, "The Li Li-san Line and the CCP in 1930" (Part I), *The China Quarterly*, No. 14 (April–June 1963), pp. 188–189; and the "Comment" by Richard Thornton, *ibid.*, No. 18 (April–June 1964), pp. 208–211.

ary struggle were widespread and enduring dangers within the Party. Indeed, in a revealing statement of 1928 he indicated that manifestations of "right" and "left" opportunism could be found even in the behavior of one individual:

> . . . in the last twelve months [of 1927–28] manifestations of opportunism continued to be widespread. On the approach of the enemy, some members, lacking the will to fight, hid in remote hills, which they called "lying in ambush." Other members, though very active, resorted to blind insurrection. . . . *On the approach of the enemy, either reckless battle or precipitate flight would be proposed. Often both ideas emanated from the same individual in the course of the discussions on what military action to take. This opportunist ideology has been gradually corrected through prolonged inner-Party struggle* and through lessons learned from actual events.[45]

In his early efforts to build an effective and politicized military force out of uprooted peasants, "bandit" groups, and defectors from Kuomintang military units, Mao had discovered that ideological education could serve to mobilize and discipline otherwise aimless military action. One of his points of conflict with Li Li-san was his conviction that the peasantry, through education, could serve China's "proletarian" revolution.[46] And by 1938 he asserted that, "in the last seventeen years our Party has learned to use the Marxist-Leninist weapon of ideological struggle against incorrect ideas within the Party on two fronts—against Right opportunism and against 'Left' opportunism." [47]

Mao's stress on ideological struggle seems to be a composite of his belief that without efforts to overcome the traditional reluctance to criticize or engage in conflict China will never complete her social revolution, and the concomitant concern that without some form of discipline such conflict will degenerate into *luan*. Criticism of the behavior of Party members in terms of standards of conduct defined by ideology could increase Party discipline and unity.[48]

45. Mao, "Struggle in the Chingkang Mountains" (1928), *SW*, English, I, pp. 92–93. Emphasis added.

46. *See* Schram, *Mao Tse-tung*, pp. 127, 141.

47. Mao, "The Role of the Chinese Communist Party in the National War" (1938), *SW*, English, II, p. 205.

In Chinese Communist ideological notation, "Left" with quotation marks indicates false or extreme revolutionary views, while Left without quotes is a true revolutionary position.

48. Mao's belief that unity can come through ideological struggle is explored in more detail in the author's analysis, "Mao's Effort to Reintegrate the Chinese Polity: Problems of Conflict and Authority in Chinese Social Processes," in A. Doak Barnett, ed., *Chinese Communist Politics in Action* (Seattle: University of Washington Press, 1969), pp. 322–337.

Yet as he noted with concern in 1929, "Inner-Party criticism . . . sometimes turns into personal attack. As a result it damages the Party organization as well as individuals." [49] Above all, Mao saw that ideology could be used to dilute the personalized quality of authority which had contributed to the fragmentation of the traditional polity into hostile cliques. In 1944 he admitted, however, that change was not easily brought about:

> In the history of our Party there were great struggles against the erroneous lines of Ch'en Tu-hsiu and Li Li-san, and they were absolutely necessary. But there were defects in the methods employed. . . . *Too much stress was placed on the responsibility of individuals,* so that we failed to unite as many people as we could have done for our common endeavour. We should take warning from these two defects. This time, *in dealing with questions of Party history we should lay the stress not on the responsibility of certain individual comrades but on the analysis of the circumstances in which errors were committed, on the content of the errors and on their social, historical and ideological roots,* and this should be done in a spirit of "learning from past mistakes to avoid future ones" and "curing the sickness to save the patient." [50]

Mao's belief in the importance of "ideological struggle" was given its most complete institutional expression in the "Party rectification" (*cheng-feng*) movement of 1942–1944, when the leadership attempted to transmit two decades of Party experience in political struggle to a new generation of peasant and intellectual cadres recruited for the continuing struggle against Japan and the Kuomintang. The key to the rectification mechanism is the "criticism–self-criticism" meeting of approximately a dozen Party members, in which each individual's past behavior and attitudes are subject to group and personal attack in terms of Party policy and the ideological inheritance of Marxism-Leninism. Documents from the first great rectification movement reveal, however, that the basic social rhythm of *ho-p'ing* and *hun-luan* manifests itself within the ranks of the Party, threatening either to stifle corrective criticism or to split Party ranks through vicious personal attack. As expressed by Party Vice Chairman Liu Shao-ch'i, who a little more than two decades later was to be purged for the deviations he criticized in 1941:

> A formal kind of peace and unity have been manifest in the Party, for many comrades ordinarily do not dare to speak or criticize. But

49. Mao, "On Correcting Mistaken Ideas in the Party" (1929), *SW*, English, I, p. 110.

50. Mao, "Our Study and the Current Situation" (1944), *SW*, English, III, pp. 163–164. Emphasis added.

once the continued concealment of contradictions becomes impossible, once the situation becomes serious and the mistakes are exposed, they criticize and fight recklessly; opposition, schism, and organizational confusion develop in the Party, and it is difficult to reestablish order.

Some comrades think that the more savage the intra-Party struggle, the better. . . . If the words are louder, the expressions more violent, and the fangs longer . . . they consider this better and the "most revolutionary thing possible." In the intra-Party struggle and self-criticism, they do not endeavor to do what is proper, do not weigh their opinions, or stop when they have gone far enough; they struggle on with no limit.[51]

Such deviations from what Mao saw to be an effective style of leadership only stressed the degree to which patterns of the traditional political culture continued to manifest themselves in the behavior of those the Party sought to recruit into positions of leadership. For Mao, the promotion of "ideological struggle" to keep Party ranks pure became all the more meaningful. And if such deviations continued to exist within the revolution's "vanguard" organization, it is hardly surprising that we find the major techniques of leadership promoted for dealings with the masses also reflecting concern with the endurance of similar cultural patterns.

51. From Liu Shao-ch'i, "On the Intra-Party Struggle," trans. in Boyd Compton, ed., *Mao's China: Party Reform Documents, 1942–1944* (Seattle: University of Washington Press, 1952), p. 208.

Chapter XII

IDEOLOGY AND ORGANIZATION, I:
THE POWER TO MOBILIZE

If political deviations rooted in the traditional cultural orientations toward authority and conflict created tensions within the Party leadership, these same factors have been of even greater significance in the Party's dealings with the masses, those who are to be "liberated." Success in political revolution for the Chinese Communists, from one point of view, has meant the effective implementation of Leninist principles of organization and political struggle. But as is indicated by the failures of several leadership "lines" during the early years of the movement, simple adoption of foreign organizational techniques and policies has been no guarantee of success. Organization and the ideology of the revolution have had to be used in ways peculiar to Chinese society: Social groups other than the working class have been appealed to for support, and techniques of leadership often at great variance with the experience of Soviet Marxism have been developed in the struggle for state power.

THE IMPORTANCE OF IDEOLOGY:
TRANSFORMING ANXIETY INTO ANGER

The period of the "Great Revolution," when in alliance with the Kuomintang the Communists pressed for revolution in China's urban areas, ended in the bloodshed of 1927. The Communist defeat did more than precipitate a change in Party leadership and policy line. Nationalist armies destroyed the organizational linkages—primarily the labor unions—by which the Party had sought to draw support from the working class. This organizational catastrophe was paralleled by changes in mass attitudes which further deprived the Party of proletarian support, as many recoiled from the "tiger" of Nationalist power.

The reluctance of China's workers to involve themselves in the dangerous world of domestic politics was a constant concern to early Party leaders. After the bloody suppression of the Peking-

Hankow railroad workers' strike in 1923 by troops of the warlord Wu P'ei-fu, General Secretary Ch'en Tu-hsiu had complained:

> The Chinese proletariat is immature both quantitatively and qualitatively. Most of the workers are still imbued with patriarchal notions and their family ties and regional patriotism are extremely strong. These former handicraft workers carry over the habits of their previous existence even when they become industrial workers. They do not feel the need for political action and are still full of ancient superstitions.[1]

If this early incident produced political reticence on the part of the workers, the widespread anti-Communist violence of 1927 shocked them into a full withdrawal. As the historian Benjamin Schwartz has written: "Once again that strain of political cynicism which seems such a deep-rooted Chinese tendency asserted itself. The Chinese workers again became immersed in their own private trials and tribulations."[2] This tendency to "privatize," to withdraw from political involvement to a concern with the details of daily existence, seems more than just "political cynicism," for the harshness of politics stimulated all those anxieties about authority and conflict which were the legacy of a Chinese upbringing. The "ancient superstitions" of which Ch'en complained indicate that the "tiger" of political power was still a vital symbol for China's young proletariat. The social class which Marxist ideology assured Party members was the foundation of the revolution was burdened with its own cultural heritage.

Mao Tse-tung's efforts to enlist the peasantry in the ranks of the revolution encountered similar difficulties. Avoidance of landlord and governmental authority was a time-honored technique by which the agricultural population sought to mitigate the harshness of power in the countryside. While Mao, the enthusiastic young provincial Party leader, appealed for support of his organizational activities with promises of the "storm" of power that was to be found in the peasantry, he himself knew well of the peasants' traditional resistance to political involvement.

Mao's political activities during the period of Kuomintang-Communist collaboration initially had been centered in urban organizational work.[3] It was only after he retired to his native village of Shao Shan in 1925, ill and under attack from Li Li-san and other Party members who opposed excessive reliance on the United Front, that Mao grasped the peasants' revolutionary possibilities.

1. Cited in Benjamin I. Schwartz, *Chinese Communism and the Rise of Mao*, p. 48.
2. *Ibid.*, p. 98.
3. *See* Schram, *Mao Tse-tung*, p. 77.

Formerly I had not fully realized the degree of class struggle among the peasantry, but after the May 30 [1925] Incident, and during the great wave of political activity which followed it, the Hunanese peasantry became very militant. I left my home, where I had been resting, and began a rural organizational campaign. In a few months we had formed more than twenty peasant unions.[4]

The very success of these efforts provoked the opposition of local landlords and the provincial military leader Chao Heng-t'i, who forced Mao to flee to Canton. There during 1926–27 he became affiliated with the Peasant Movement Training Institute, which had been established under the reorganized Kuomintang in 1924.

The first Communist efforts to bring the peasantry into the revolution had been carried out at the initiative of P'eng Pai, a landlord's son from Kwangtung Province. P'eng was the first director of the Peasant Movement Training Institute, and his own experiences in organizing peasants reflect problems of which Mao undoubtedly was aware. Anxiety in the face of authority was a major element in the "political enslavement" of the rural population. As P'eng wrote: "The peasants fear the landlords, literati, and government officials just as a rat fears a cat, daily groaning out their lives under the blows of the landlord's grain-measure, the scholar's fan, and the chains of the official." [5] P'eng saw that the peasants' political passivity was not based simply on the grinding material poverty of their lives; the old culture reinforced their sense of hopeless apathy.

P'eng's initial efforts to propagandize the peasants encountered deeply rooted attitudes that rationalized passive acceptance of a miserable life and justified the turning of aggression against a politically ineffectual self:

> We talked to the peasants about the political problems of national calamity and popular harm that China had suffered at the hands of imperialism and the warlords. We asked their opinions, but most of them held to their millennial old concepts: "Until a true son of heaven comes, the world cannot be peaceful. When a son of heaven with a true mandate comes, then even guns will not be able to fire. . . ." Concerning economics, if we talked about all the bitterness and oppression of the poor, they would mostly say: "This is fated by heaven," or, "We did not have good *feng-shui* [geomantic influences]." [6]

4. Snow, *Red Star Over China*, p. 160.
5. P'eng Pai, *"Hai-feng nung-min yün-tung"* [The Hai-feng Peasant Movement], in *Ti-yi-t'zu Kuo-nei Ko-ming Chan-cheng Shih-ch'i ti Nung-min Yün-tung* [The Peasant Movement during the First Period of Domestic Revolutionary War] (Peking: *Jen-min ch'u-pan-she,* 1953), p. 40.
6. *Ibid.,* p. 49.

P'eng recalled that merely the differences in attire and physical mien of a young intellectual seeking to propagandize in the countryside were barriers to communication, for such outward characteristics stimulated the peasants' anxiety to avoid contact with those who seemed to represent state power. After days of ineffective efforts to make contact with peasants in his native Kwangtung district of Hai-feng, P'eng analyzed:

> I suddenly began thinking about what we had been saying to the peasants: first, it was much too cultured; much of what we had been saying the peasants didn't understand . . . much of the bookish terminology had to be translated into plain talk. Secondly, my face, body, and dress were not the same as the peasants, and as [they] had long been cheated and oppressed by those with different faces and clothing, once they caught sight of me they assumed I was their enemy; and then when they saw the difference in class, the difference in style, they always were reluctant to get close to me. . . .[7]

Eventually, to P'eng's delight, several younger peasants responded to his verbal appeals at a rural crossroad. The peasants explained to this landlord's son the ways of rural life, and suggested methods by which he might reach those who labored in the countryside. P'eng observed of these few men who responded to his revolutionary agitation: "They were all youthful peasants, less than thirty years of age; they spoke with animation, and were all very lively." [8] Here one sees in its most primitive form the archetype of the political activist: the member of the younger generation not fully socialized by career, not fully bound into society by the responsibilities of family life and occupation, who out of his own "liveliness" responds to the Party's propaganda.

P'eng Pai's efforts to enlist the peasants of coastal Kwangtung Province into the ranks of the revolution bore modest fruit during Chiang K'ai-shek's "Eastern Expedition" of 1925 against the regional warlord Ch'en Ch'iung-ming, when peasants assisted Nationalist military movements. And during the turmoil of 1927, Party-organized rural uprisings in Hai-lu-feng during May and September culminated in the formation of China's first, if short-lived, Soviet government in November.[9] But P'eng's efforts were cut short by his death in 1929 at the hands of the Nationalists, who now feared the mass power that was gravitating into Communist hands as a result

7. *Ibid.*, p. 54.
8. *Ibid.*, p. 56.
9. A detailed analysis of this early effort at peasant mobilization will be found in Shinkichi Eto, "Hai-lu-feng—The First Chinese Soviet Government," *The China Quarterly,* Nos. 8, 9 (October–December 1961; January–March 1962), pp. 161–183, 149–181

of their organizing activities among the workers and peasants. Here again, Mao was to carry on the work that others had begun.

The clearest statement of the lessons of leadership which Mao derived from his own efforts at peasant organization is his "Report on an Investigation of the Peasant Movement in Hunan," written in the spring of 1927, on the eve of the Party's flight to the mountains of South China. Combining ridicule of formal education with a recital of the power of slogans to focus peasant anger, Mao revealed that he had grasped what is perhaps his most basic insight into the process of politicizing peasants:

> Even if ten thousand schools of law and political science had been opened, could they have brought as much political education to the people, men and women, young and old, all the way into the remotest corners of the countryside, as the peasant associations have done in so short a time? I don't think they could. "Down with imperialism!" "Down with the warlords!" "Down with the corrupt officials!" "Down with the local tyrants and evil gentry!"—these political slogans have grown wings, they have found their way to the young, the middle-aged and the old, to the women and children in countless villages, they have penetrated into their minds and are on their lips. For instance, *watch a group of children at play. If one gets angry with another, if he glares, stamps his foot and shakes his fist, you will then immediately hear from the other the shrill cry of "Down with imperialism!"*
>
> In the Hsiangtan area, when the children who pasture the cattle get into a fight, one will act as Tang Sheng-chih, and the other Yeh Kai-hsin [two warlords notable for their respective support of, and opposition to, the "Northern Expedition" of 1926–27]; when one is defeated and runs away, with the other chasing him, it is the pursuer who is Tang Sheng-chih and the pursued, Yeh Kai-hsin. As to the song, "Down with Imperialist Powers!" of course almost every child in the towns can sing it, and now many village children can sing it too.[10]

This description of the interplay between Party slogans and children's play indicates that Mao had come to see that *private and apolitical emotions of aggression could be projected into public issues to serve as the driving force of revolution.* What is "political" about the aggressiveness of a child's game? Nothing, until the slogan of "Down with imperialism!" has linked it to a public issue.

Furthermore, Mao perceived that *the anxiety before authority which underlay the millennial political passivity of China's peasants could be overcome if it were transformed into anger and directed*

---

10. Mao, "Hunan Report" (1927), *SW,* English, I, pp. 47–48. Emphasis added.

outward through the force of ideology expressed in a political slo-gan:

> Some of the peasants can also recite Dr. Sun Yat-sen's Testament. They pick out the terms "freedom," "equality," "the Three People's Principles" and "unequal treaties" and apply them, if rather crudely, in their daily life. When somebody who looks like one of the gentry encounters a peasant and stands on his dignity, refusing to make way along a pathway, the peasant will say angrily, "Hey, you local tyrant, don't you know the Three People's Principles?" Formerly when the peasants from the vegetable farms on the outskirts of Changsha en-tered the city to sell their produce, they used to be pushed around by the police. Now they have found a weapon, which is none other than the Three People's Principles. When a policeman strikes or swears at a peasant selling vegetables, the peasant immediately answers back by invoking the Three People's Principles and that shuts the police-man up. Once in Hsiangtan when a district peasant association and a township peasant association could not see eye to eye, the chairman of the township association declared, "Down with the district peasant association's unequal treaties!" [11]

Ideology thus had the power to fuse passion and political pur-pose. A revolutionary slogan could give a voice to those who by tradition had shown submissive obedience by "listening to talk" (*t'ing-hua*). And as Mao once asserted with all the enthusiasm of the May Fourth era: "As soon as we arise and let out a shout, [our enemies] will get up and tremble and flee for their lives." [12]

"SPEAK BITTERNESS" (SU-K'U)

For a leadership anxious to maintain the momentum of a peasant revolution, the problem is how to transform sporadic outbursts of violence into sustained political involvement. In a 1965 interview with André Malraux, Mao recalled, "You know I've proclaimed for a long time: we must teach the masses *clearly* what we have re-ceived from them *confusedly*. What was it that won over most vil-lages to us? The expositions of bitterness [*su-k'u*]. . . . We or-ganized these expositions in every village . . . but we didn't in-vent them." [13]

The emotions which Mao came to see as the motive force of peasant political involvement were "received from them confus-

11. *Ibid.*, p. 48.
12. Mao, "The Great Union of the Popular Masses" (1919), in Schram, *PTMTT*, p. 171.
13. André Malraux, *Anti-Memoirs* (New York: Holt, Rinehart and Winston, 1968), p. 362. Emphasis added.

edly," with all the *luan* which Chinese have traditionally associated with feelings of aggression. But Mao conceived the Party's job as using its ideological "consciousness" to clarify, discipline, and direct this energy of revolution, and to organize what would otherwise be sporadic and dispersed action. This task became institutionalized in the various forms of political agitation and ideological "study" developed during the struggle for power.

According to Mao the most basic of these techniques, which he asserted "won over most villages to us," was the *su-k'u* or "speak bitterness" meeting, first used during the period of civil war and then adapted to the struggles of land reform. The terminology of this ritual of political mobilization reveals its links to the traditional political culture. In encouraging peasants to "speak of the bitterness" of rural life, and to "vomit the bitter water" (*t'u k'u-shui*) of injustice suffered at the hands of the rural gentry, local bullies, and warlord troops, the Party urged "the masses" to work up all the rage and resentment that by tradition was "put in the stomach." This combination of ideological study and organized class struggle makes people politically "conscious" in the sense of bringing together the *perception* of mistreatment and injustice with the repressed *emotion*. The separation of thought and feeling which Confucian culture had made the basis of "cultivated" behavior was brought to an end.

In developing this form of political mobilization, Mao began with the belief that simply redistributing land to poor peasants was insufficient for destroying the power of the landlords and rural gentry. The status of this elite derived in part from economic wealth, but even more from the prestige of "the word" of the old culture in the ears of the peasants: "It is they [the gentry] who know how to speak, it is they who know how to write." [14] The peasants could sustain their commitment to the revolution only if they participated directly in the humiliation of those who represented the traditional system of authority. The "land verification movement" of the early 1930s was one of the first efforts to apply such political tactics on a large scale.[15] Mao thus institutionalized his belief that only the tension of conflict between those "mutually related and mutually antagonistic" could sustain a peasant revolution.

14. From a 1933 article by Mao on the land verification movement; cited in Schram, *Mao Tse-tung*, p. 167.

15. This movement is discussed in *ibid.*, pp. 166–168; and in Ilpyong J. Kim, "Mass Mobilization Policies and Techniques Developed in the Period of the Chinese Soviet Republic," in A. Doak Barnett, ed., *Chinese Communist Politics in Action* (Seattle: University of Washington Press, 1969), pp. 78–98.

A P.L.A. *su-k'u* [accusation meeting
for "speaking bitterness" against the old society]
during the civil war of the late 1940s.
From China Pictorial, *October 1967.*

The cultural logic behind this form of political mobilization is hardly obscure, yet its full meaning is difficult to communicate through an abstract analysis. It is basically an experience of participation, not perception. William Hinton's description of the humiliation of a Shansi village leader in 1948 by peasants organized by Party cadres gives a clearer sense of the use of hostility to overcome anxiety before power, and the importance of an organized confrontation in destroying the established authority of a rural society:[16]

> T'ien-ming [a Party cadre] called all the active young cadres and the militiamen of Long Bow [village] together and announced to them the policy of the county government, which was to confront all enemy collaborators and their backers at public meetings, expose their crimes, and turn them over to the county authorities for punishment. He proposed that they start with Kuo Te-yu, the puppet village head. *Having moved the group to anger with a description of Te-yu's crimes,* T'ien-ming reviewed the painful life led by the poor peasants during the occupation and recalled how hard they had all worked and how as soon as they harvested all the grain the puppet officials, backed by army bayonets, took what they wanted, turned over huge quantities to the Japanese devils, forced the peasants to haul it away, and flogged those who refused.
>
> As the silent crowd contracted toward the spot where the accused man stood, T'ien-ming stepped forward . . . "This is our chance. Remember how we were oppressed. The traitors seized our property. They beat us and kicked us. . . .
>
> *Let us speak out the bitter memories.* Let us see that the blood debt is repaid. . . ."
>
> He paused for a moment. *The peasants were listening to every word but gave no sign as to how they felt.*
>
> He spoke plainly. His language and his accent were well understood by the people among whom he had been raised, but *no one moved and no one spoke.*
>
> "Come now, who has evidence against this man?"
>
> Again there was silence.
>
> Kuei-ts'ai, the new vice-chairman of the village, found it intolerable. He jumped up, struck Kuo Te-yu on the jaw with the back of his hand, "Tell the meeting how much you stole," he demanded.
>
> *The blow jarred the ragged crowd.* It was as if an electric spark had tensed every muscle. Not in living memory had any peasant ever struck an official. . . .

16. The following quotes are drawn from Hinton, *Fanshen: A Documentary of Revolution in a Chinese Village* (New York: Monthly Review Press, 1966), pp. 112–116. Emphasis added.

The people in the square waited fascinated as if watching a play. They did not realize that in order for the plot to unfold they themselves had to mount the stage and speak out what was on their minds. *No one moved to carry forward what Kuei-ts'ai had begun.*

Despite the agitator's effort to manipulate mass emotions, and the role of the violent act in breaking the prestige of established authority, the peasants still required some further stimulus to step over the awesome line of passivity into direct, violent action. That stimulus was provided by social pressures focused through organization, and the direct incitement of Party activists:

That evening T'ien-ming and Kuei-ts'ai called together the small groups of poor peasants from various parts of the village and sought to learn what it was that was really holding them back. *They soon found the root of the trouble was fear* of the old established political forces, and their military backers. The old reluctance to move against the power of the gentry, the fear of ultimate defeat and terrible reprisal that had been seared into the consciousness of so many generations lay like a cloud over the peasants' minds and hearts.

. . . The mobilization of the population could spread only slowly and in concentric circles like the waves on the surface of a pond when a stone is thrown in. The stone in this case was a small group of *chi-chi-fen-tzu* or "activists," as the cadres of the new administration and the core of its militia were called.

Evidently the activists in the village which Hinton describes did their work of mobilization well, for he observed:

Emboldened by T'ien-ming's words other peasants began to speak out. They recalled what Te-yu had done to them personally. Several vowed to speak up and accuse him the next morning. After the meeting broke up, the passage of time worked its own leaven. In many a hovel and tumbledown house talk continued well past midnight. Some people were so excited they did not sleep at all. . . .

On the following day the meeting was livelier by far. It began with a sharp argument as to who would make the first accusation and *T'ien-ming found it difficult to keep order.* Before Te-yu had a chance to reply to any questions, a crowd of young men, among whom were several militiamen, surged forward ready to beat him.

Thus the peasants' fear-based passivity finally is overcome through the agitator's mobilization of their resentments and hostilities. Political participation in the revolution is no rational consideration of issues, no "dinner party, or writing an essay, painting a picture, or doing embroidery." The cadre finds it difficult to maintain order over the mobilized peasants. But the masses have been "liberated"; the old order is under attack; the Party has its active followers.

THE VIRTUES OF AN ENEMY

In application, this form of political mobilization had to be meshed with the historical rhythm of China's revolution; that is, the Party leadership had to adapt the content of its appeals for popular support to shifting social and political issues. In the period of the Kiangsi Soviet (1927–1934), issues of land distribution and the evil activities of landlords and counterrevolutionary "big tigers" were used to mobilize peasant support; while appeals to warlord troops based on the harshness of discipline within military units were used to gain recruits. In the effort to rebuild the Party and army after the Long March, social grievances deriving from the system of land tenure, usurious taxation and loan interest, the brutality of warlord troops, and the threat of famine were all issues invoked by the Party in its mobilization efforts.[17]

While the Marxist commitment of the Chinese Communists orients them toward the exploitation of economic issues in appeals for support, underlying their stress on "class" interest is the more basic striving to reach an individual's sense of personal grievance and resentment toward established authority. The landlords are not evil simply because they control greater economic wealth, but because they use their power and social position with cruelty and injustice. The "class struggle" of land reform focuses on personal misuses of power—a landlord's raping of a peasant girl, a rich peasant's refusal to reduce or delay the payment of rent in a year of famine, or the violence with which a "local bully" (*t'u-hao*) treats a tenant farmer—rather than on the injustice of the economic relationship *per se*. Activist "tiger beater" cadres in a factory question workers and foremen for instances of personal abuse or injustice suffered at the hands of the manager,[18] for such willful

17. Detailed analyses of Party appeals during the Yenan period will be found in Donald G. Gillin, "Peasant Nationalism in the History of Chinese Communism," *Journal of Asian Studies*, Vol. XXIII, No. 2 (February 1964), pp. 269–289; and Mark Selden, "The Guerilla Movement in Northwest China: The Origins of the Shensi-Kansu-Ninghsia Border Region," *The China Quarterly*, Nos. 28, 29 (October–December 1966; January–March 1967), pp. 63–81, 61–81.

18. One personal account of the way cadres attempted to exploit worker grievances during the *"wu-fan"* movement of 1952 will be found in Robert Loh and Humphrey Evans, *Escape From Red China* (New York: Coward McCann, 1963), pp. 84–94. A scholarly analysis of this process is contained in John Gardner, "The *Wu Fan* Campaign in Shanghai: A Study in the Consolidation of Urban Control," in Barnett, ed., *Chinese Communist Politics in Action*, pp. 495–523.

misuses of authority communicate most effectively to those long dependent on power. Mao believes that the intense sentiment of aggression is the only motive force powerful enough to sustain the involvement of China's peasants and workers in the tasks of social revolution.

It is from this perspective that we may view the Party's most significant period of growth and institutionalization which came during the war of resistance against Japan. The importance of the Japanese invasion of China for the Communist rise to power can scarcely be doubted. After the "Mukden" incident of late September 1931, when Japanese troops moved to establish direct control over Manchuria, Chiang K'ai-shek was forced to call an uncertain conclusion to the third "Encirclement and Suppression" campaign against the Kiangsi Soviet. The diversion and division of Nationalist military resources remained a constant factor in Chiang's efforts to deal a final death-blow to the Communists up to the final defeat of Japan in 1945.

The war against Japan provided a political context which the Communists were able to use effectively to establish the legitimacy of their politico-military insurgency. While they did not take the initiative in kidnapping Chiang K'ai-shek at Sian in December of 1936, their response to this incident enabled them to acquire a measure of formal recognition as a patriotic political movement in the wartime "united front" with the Nationalists.[19]

Perhaps most basically, however, the impact of the Japanese invasion of China proper after the summer of 1937 created the social conditions that the Party had learned to exploit effectively in recruiting and motivating supporters for its cause. In the early days of the peasant movement, Party activities had been most successful in those rural areas where established authority—in the form of clan organizations, secret societies, and gentry-led local militia— was weak or disrupted.[20] Similarly, during the Japanese occupation, the undermining of established political relationships "freed" people for new commitments. And the Party provided one well-organized alternative to submission to the foreigner's political order.

The impact of Japanese military operations in North China was

19. The most recent effort to evaluate the Sian Incident is Lyman P. Van Slyke, *Enemies and Friends: The United Front in Chinese Communist History* (Stanford: Stanford University Press, 1967), pp. 75–91. This analysis stresses the interpretation that the Chinese Communists decided to press for Chiang K'ai-shek's release *before* they received similar instructions from Stalin, because they saw the United Front as essential to their own survival.

20. These findings are presented in Roy Mark Hofheinz, *The Peasant Movement and Rural Revolution: Chinese Communists in the Countryside, 1923–1927* (unpublished Ph.D. dissertation, Harvard University, 1966).

another basic aspect of the period of the War of Resistance which enabled the Party to consolidate its new base in the Shensi-Kansu-Ningsia border region. In the most detailed study of this period of Party history, Chalmers Johnson indicates that it was the cruelty of the Japanese, their inability or unwillingness to apply military force with discrimination and establish that degree of security and order which was the limited expectation of China's peasants toward political authority, which mobilized those who traditionally had been passive before power:

> . . . Japan had earned the hatred of the Chinese people. This hatred derived from Japanese attempts to subjugate the countryside by force. . . . The threat of terror and devastation was a constant ingredient in Chinese rural life for seven years; the party that met this challenge with an effective policy and the organizational ability to make this policy work won the support of the peasant population as no other political group has done in recent times.[21]

It is clear from the extent of direct Chinese collaboration with the invading Japanese, and the passive resistance policy which Chiang K'ai-shek adopted in a situation of indigenous political fragmentation and military weakness, that the traditional attitude of accommodation to a superior power remained a durable political tactic even in the China of the 1940s. One can only speculate as to what would have happened had the Japanese been more discriminating in their use of power, or had they not involved themselves at the same time in a multi-front war in the Pacific and Southeast Asia. Chinese history provides the precedents of Mongolian and Manchurian invaders successfully allying themselves with indigenous Chinese to establish durable "alien" dynasties.

To the Communists at the time, the prospect of such accommodation had all the reality of Wang Ching-wei's collaborationist regime at Nanking; and the strategic threat to themselves inherent in further Chinese concessions to the Japanese was very great. As Mao wrote in 1938:

> The enemy will go all out to wreck China's united front, and the traitor organizations in all the occupied areas will merge into a so-called "unified government." Owing to the loss of big cities and the hardships of war, vacillating elements within our ranks will clamour for compromise, and pessimism will grow to a serious extent.[22]

21. Chalmers A. Johnson, *Peasant Nationalism and Communist Power: The Emergence of Revolutionary China, 1937–1945* (London: Oxford University Press, 1963), p. 49.
22. Mao, "On Protracted War," (1938), *SW*, English, II, p. 139.

By mid-1940 the increasing isolation of the limited forces of active resistance within China compounded these tendencies toward political accommodation with the Japanese. The United States was still sixteen months away from Pearl Harbor, and in Europe resistance to German expansion had nearly collapsed, diminishing prospects for outside assistance and making even further isolation an almost certain prospect. To oppose the tendency to "compromise" and to reduce the threat of increased Japanese and Nationalist military pressure on their own base area, the Communists launched what was called the "Hundred Regiments Offensive," forcing the war to a more active level where political accommodation became more difficult for wavering "patriotic" forces within the United Front.[23] As a result of this initiative, Japanese military operations against Communist areas in the Northwest increased sharply, producing serious difficulties in material existence and even a flagging of determination within the Party itself.

It is some measure of the effectiveness of the Party's organizational forms of indoctrination and control—most obvious in the "rectification" or *cheng-feng* procedure developed during this period —that discipline was maintained and economic self-sufficiency made a near-reality through the stress on self-reliance (*tzu-li keng-sheng*) in which even the military was committed to tasks of production. And as Johnson's analysis concludes, in maintaining its own discipline, the Party was able to gain substantial popular support:

23. During the Cultural Revolution supporters of Mao alleged that P'eng Teh-huai had, "without the knowledge of the Party Central Committee . . . waged on his own authority 'the big battle of a hundred regiments,' thereby causing serious setbacks to the development of the North China base areas and of our army." (*See* "Principal Crimes of P'eng Teh-huai, Big Ambitionist and Schemer," Canton *Chingkangshan* and *Kwang-tung Wen-i Chan-Pao* [September 5, 1967]; translated in *Survey of the China Mainland Press* [Hong Kong], No. 4047 [October 25, 1967], p. 9.)

While the allegation is absurd taken at face value, there is additional—if largely indirect—evidence that Mao may not have approved of the Hundred Regiments Offensive. He evidently feared the risks of seriously degrading the Party's military capability, but he was not in full control of military policy in 1940. Semiofficial histories of this period, such as Hu Chiao-mu's *Thirty Years of the Communist Party of China* do not mention the offensive, a strange omission in view of the Party's claim of its leading role in the anti-Japanese war. Mao's own writings of this time criticize "the ultra-Left military policy" of "decisive battles" and those who would "deny the basic role of guerilla warfare" in the resistance. (*See* "On Policy" [December 1940], *SW*, English, II, pp. 441–442.) Mao may not have approved of the conventional military offensive of the summer of 1940, but was probably "outvoted" by collective Party leadership.

In spite of the shrinkage of the guerilla areas and the severe losses suffered in them, the Communists reaped certain advantages from the fact that there was now hardly a village left in Hopei or Shansi that was not half-burned or worse. The revolution spread and became irreversible in the years 1941–42. Instead of breaking the tie between the Eighth Route Army and the peasantry, the Japanese policy drove the two together into closer alliance. This alliance derived partly from nationalism (hatred of the invader), but to a large extent it was purely a matter of survival.[24]

As this passage only parenthetically concludes, it was at base "hatred of the invader" and fear for survival which mobilized the peasants, rather than a more abstract sentiment of Nationalism. Mao has made the same point himself:

> . . . after occupying northern China . . . the enemy everywhere pursued a barbarous policy and practised naked plunder. Had China capitulated, every Chinese would have become a slave without a country. . . . Under the flag of the "Rising Sun" all Chinese are forced to be docile subjects, beasts of burden forbidden to show the slightest trace of Chinese national spirit. This barbarous enemy policy will be carried deeper into the interior of China. . . . [It] has enraged all strata of the Chinese people. *This rage is engendered by the reactionary and barbarous character of Japan's war—"there is no escape from fate," and hence an absolute hostility has crystallized.*[25]

Some scholars have appropriately questioned Johnson's analysis for its stress on the Japanese invasion as the *antecedent* of Party and Red Army expansion,[26] when important periods of growth in these organizations occurred well before the actual invasion. The fact remains, however, that the Party had learned to use effectively issues like the threat of foreign invasion and the injustices of rural life, and to take advantage of social dislocation, in tapping those personal motives of resentment, fear, and hatred which Mao saw to be the driving force of revolution. Party appeals to a sense of "Nationalism," like the earlier stress on issues of class struggle, were important because they helped to give political orientation to an uprooted and threatened rural population and rationalized their commitment to larger political objectives.

For Mao himself, the war against Japan strengthened his earlier belief in the need to involve peasants personally in "struggle" with

24. Johnson, *Peasant Nationalism and Communist Power*, pp. 58–59.
25. Mao, "On Protracted War" (1938), *SW*, English, II, p. 129. Emphasis added.
26. *See*, in particular, Gillin, "Peasant Nationalism in the History of Chinese Communism," pp. 269–289.

[class] enemies, for it was once again the tension between those who were "mutually related and mutually antagonistic" which enabled the Party and army to expand and discipline their ranks. As he phrased it himself in a public statement in 1939: "To be attacked by the enemy is not a bad thing, but a good thing." [27] Enemies are good because they help the Party to sustain popular involvement in the process of social revolution.

DOWN WITH POLITICAL DEPENDENCE!

The years of resistance against the Japanese occupation were a time of major institutional growth and consolidation for the Party, largely because the political context of war against a foreign invader produced a more complete convergence of interests between the Party and people. Where earlier appeals for support of the revolutionary cause had been based on socially divisive issues of class conflict, the Japanese aggression enabled appeals to be phrased on the basis of national unity. Yet Mao's underlying concern was with the unacceptability of a position of passive accommodation to one more cruel and humiliating power. The Japanese effectively dramatized to the Chinese population Mao's personal striving: the desire to eliminate political dependency.

This way of looking at the wartime intersection of interests between Mao and China's millions, however, abstracts the leader's personal objectives from the broad popular appeals for heroic resistance in the face of a foreign threat. It is important not to obscure the very significant differences in perception and motivation with which various people "read" the Party's wartime slogans. Such differences are the basis for understanding why popular support of the Party was to a certain degree partial and temporary and why "con-

27. Mao, "To Be Attacked by the Enemy is not a Bad Thing but a Good Thing" (1939), in *Selected Readings from the Works of Mao Tse-tung*, pp. 130–132.

In a 1964 interview with visiting Frenchmen, Mao told an anecdote which underscores his perception of the positive role which the Japanese enemy played in the Party's rise to power: "Recently a Japanese merchant came to see me and said, 'I very much regret that Japan invaded China.' I replied to him: 'You are not being fair. Of course, the aggression wasn't fair either, but there is no need to apologize. If the Japanese had not occupied half of China, it would have been impossible for the entire Chinese population to rise and fight the Japanese invader. And that resulted in our army strengthening itself by a million men, and in the liberated bases the population increased to 100 millions.'

"That is why I said to him (pause and smile): 'Should I thank you?' "

tradictions" continue to exist to this day within the Communist Party and between the Party and the people. The danger of political passivity was presented to the people by Communist propaganda in a specific manner: "Being passive before *Japanese* power is dangerous; the invading imperialists are cruel and will kill you and destroy your property. You had better stand up and fight." And when the killing and destruction occurred, the Party helped the people to fight. But Mao and certain of his followers read the problem in more general terms: "The condition of being passive and dependent on any power is dangerous and should be destroyed through a revolution in favor of self-reliance."

For most Chinese, the Japanese occupation represented a specific problem of a harsh and humiliating foreign presence, a context in which the security and status of a dependency relationship could not be established. But the normative cultural pattern was to see dependency as the most natural of conditions in relation to authority. The problem was, as it always had been, that the relationship, far from being worthy of destruction, was just not properly implemented. (As was expressed so often in our interview characterizations of dealings with authoritative individuals: "The elder brother *should* be polite and yielding; the younger brother *should* respect the elder." "Teachers *ought* to take responsibility for their students, they *should* treat them like their own offspring. . . . Students *ought* to respect the teacher." "A good leader *should* be just; he *should* solve all the people's problems.") And if the ideals of life's authoritative relationships were not lived up to in practice, at least the dependent individual could bide his time in *hopes* of justice or of one day himself gaining the authoritative position. In sum, many of those who supported the Party did so in order to save a China in which all that their traditional experience told them could be good and proper might be realized. But Mao and certain of his followers sought popular support in the striving for a "new China," a new social order to be realized by a fundamental revolution against the authority system of the old.

During the War of Resistance this discrepancy in objective was obscured behind the symbols of Nationalism. In recruiting people to its wartime cause, the Party created a politico-military organization which was subsequently turned against the Nationalists in the final contest of the unresolved civil war. But as we shall see in Part Four, with the attainment of full power, Mao and his close colleagues faced another series of struggles between their own revolutionary goals and the personal inclinations of the Chinese people—a test of political style and social objective that culminated in the Cultural Revolution of the mid-1960s.

ORGANIZATION: A FRAMEWORK FOR PARTICIPATION

While social injustice and the cruelty of a foreign invader provided the motivational context of Party growth, Mao also found that the organizational forms which the Party had developed to harness this mass energy could be used to heighten popular involvement in the tasks of revolution. His personal rejection of political dependency found expression in efforts to develop a new "work style" (*tso-feng*) in the way Party cadres asserted their authority over "the masses."

In his 1964 recollections to André Malraux, Mao stressed: "You must realize that before us, among the masses, no one had addressed themselves to women or to the young. Nor, of course, to the peasants. For the first time in their lives, every one of them felt *involved*." [28] The capacity of a political organization to involve, and not just to control, was revealed to Mao in the way that members of the traditional "protective" forms of social association found they could express their resentments against the old society through Party-organized peasant associations:

> . . . members of the secret societies have joined the peasant associations, in which they can openly and legally play the hero and vent their grievances, so that there is no further need for the secret "mountain," "lodge," "shrine," and "river" forms of organization. *In killing the pigs and sheep of the local tyrants and evil gentry and imposing heavy levies and fines, they have adequate outlets for their feelings against those who oppressed them.*[29]

A more revolutionary insight into the mobilizing capacity of organizational life was that by altering the traditional dependency relationship—by delegating some responsibility to the individual and by eliminating the physical brutality of traditional military life—the Party could produce a "spiritual liberation" and gain the active commitment of those who had long been politically passive:

> Apart from the role played by the Party, the reason why the Red Army has been able to carry on in spite of such poor material conditions and such frequent engagements is its practise of democracy. The officers do not beat the men; officers and men receive equal treatment; soldiers are free to hold meetings and to speak out; trivial formalities have been done away with; and the accounts are open for all to inspect. The soldiers handle the mess arrangements. . . . All this gives great satisfaction to the soldiers. The newly captured soldiers in particular feel that our army and the Kuomintang army are

28. André Malraux, *Anti-Memoirs*, p. 361.
29. Mao, "Hunan Report" (1927), *SW*, English, I, pp. 52–53. Emphasis added.

worlds apart. *They feel spiritually liberated,* even though material conditions in the Red Army are not equal to those in the White [Kuomintang] Army. The very soldiers who had no courage in the White Army yesterday are very brave in the Red Army today; such is the effect of democracy. The Red Army is like a furnace in which all captured soldiers are transmuted the moment they come over. In China the army needs democracy as much as the people do. Democracy in our army is an important weapon for undermining the feudal mercenary army.[30]

That Mao labels this system "democracy" when it lacks the checks on the use of power basic to Western interpretations of that term seems irrelevant within the social context of China, and in a period of violent revolution. Simply the contrast with the traditional use of power was quite enough to produce a "spiritual liberation" and gain the active commitment of those who by cultural inheritance assumed there was no alternative to the harshness of dependency.

Mao's *insight* into the heightened popular commitment which would come with a new style of authority, however, was far from sufficient for realizing a new Party "work-style," for his perception conflicted with deeply rooted attitudes held by those who joined the movement. As Mao complained:

> People's political power has been established everywhere at county, district and township levels, but more in name than in reality. . . . Authority is monopolized by the Party committees. . . . Not that there are no councils of workers, peasants and soldiers worthy of the name, but they are very few. The reason is the lack of propaganda and education concerning this new political system. *The evil feudal practise of arbitrary dictation is so deeply rooted in the minds of the people and even of the ordinary Party members that it cannot be swept away at once;* when anything crops up, they choose the easy way and have no liking for the bothersome democratic system. Democratic centralism can be widely and effectively practised in mass organizations only when its efficacy is demonstrated in revolutionary struggle and the masses understand that it is the best means of mobilizing their forces and is of the utmost help in their struggle.[31]

While the pattern of authority exercising a monopoly of power and initiative remained rooted in the personalities of Party members, the Maoist leadership was, and continues to be, conscious of the political energies that could be released by altering the traditional relationship to authority, by giving the individual the opportunity

30. Mao, "Struggle in the Chingkang Mountains" (1928), *SW,* English, I, p. 83. Emphasis added.
31. *Ibid.,* pp. 90–91. Emphasis added.

to liberate the grievances that tradition forced him to "hold in," and by delegating certain personal responsibility. The Party has tried to face directly the abuses of power characteristic of the politics of dependency:

> The ugly evil of bureaucracy, which no comrade likes, must be thrown into the cesspit. The methods which all comrades should prefer are those that appeal to the masses, i.e., those which are welcomed by all workers and peasants. . . . Commandism is another manifestation. To all appearances, persons given to commandism are not slackers; they give the impression of being hard workers. But in fact cooperatives set up by commandist methods will not succeed, and even if they appear to grow for a time, they cannot be consolidated. In the end the masses will lose faith in them, which will hamper their development. . . . We must reject commandism; what we need is energetic propaganda to convince the masses . . . and do all work . . . in accordance with the actual conditions and the real feelings of the masses.[32]

To work with the "real feelings" of a people is not easy when their traditions have stressed the holding in of emotions; and to mobilize their active involvement in politics is problematical when traditional attitudes toward authority endure in the personalities of leaders and led alike. The skills of leadership which were the legacy of nearly three decades of political struggle, however, enabled the Party to use its ideology and organization to mobilize popular "consciousness." On the eve of victory in the civil war Mao wrote with satisfaction of the effectiveness of the *su-k'u* and political indoctrination in motivating the People's Liberation Army:

> The correct unfolding of the movement for pouring out grievances (the wrongs done to the labouring people by the old society and by the reactionaries) and the three check-ups (on class origin, performance of duty, and will to fight) has greatly heightened the political consciousness of commanders and fighters throughout the army in the fight for the emancipation of the exploited working masses for nationwide land reform and for the destruction of the common enemy of the people, the Chiang K'ai-shek bandit gang.[33]

32. Mao, "Pay Attention to Economic Work" (1933), *SW*, English, I, p. 135.
33. Mao, "On the Great Victory in the Northwest and on the New Type of Ideological Education Movement in the Liberation Army" (1948), *SW*, English, IV, p. 214.

Chapter XIII

IDEOLOGY AND ORGANIZATION, II: THE POWER TO DISCIPLINE

Given the burden of passivity before power which was the legacy of China's traditional political culture, problems of mobilization predominated in Party efforts to gain support. Yet maintaining discipline over those mobilized was also a problem, largely because tradition provided no cultural framework for the purposeful, politicized promotion of conflict or for limited ways of challenging established authority.

In earlier chapters we saw that the Confucian social ethic placed all expressions of aggression beyond the pale of respectability. Unlike the Samurai warriors of Japan or the knights of feudal Europe, whose skills in violence became wedded to a moral ethic or code of the established social order, the military in China was an illegitimate element of society in the eyes of the imperial literati. The universal human capacity for aggression remained unallied to any set of abstract social principles which might have tempered or channeled conflict into relatively harmless, if not constructive, social activity. The Confucianists sought no "war" with nature, only accommodation; and China's scientific insights never became translated into attempts to control a threatening physical environment. Commercial activity remained bound within a state-controlled framework of monopoly enterprise, stunting the growth of entrepreneurship which in other societies (and in Chinese communities overseas) developed through the stimulus of competition. And in the realm of politics, the pattern of dependence on the moral wisdom of an elite class of "cultivated" scholar-administrators preempted the development of forms of controlled competition for power which might have checked abuses of authority.

To be sure, the Confucian polity required the application of military power to "pacify" those who disturbed the tranquillity of the empire; but, beyond the scholar-generals who directed such activity, there developed no respected officer corps and military tradition which merited prestige and social meaning among the institutions of imperial China. For the uneducated lower leadership ranks and the peasant boys dragooned into imperial or warlord armies, the military life had little rationale beyond a brotherhood of violence and the security of power.

The only meaning of armed force for the farming population was the apparently aimless foraging and destruction by the "pacification" troops who lived off the land. The military was a tiger which ate up their source of livelihood, turning the world into *luan*. Even the marginal life of banditry was nothing more than the last recourse of desperate men run afoul of the standards of Confucian justice—a tradition of escape in which violence had only the most elemental meaning of self-protection and survival. In traditional Chinese society conflict thus acquired no significance short of "confusion," the breaking away from all social restraints of impulses for hostility. Aggression had no meaning beyond security or self-assertion, no tie to moral values or constructive social tasks.

VIOLENCE FOR THE REVOLUTION

During the early years of Red Army growth this cultural tradition of self-serving, undisciplined violence was manifest in warlordism and the activities of local protective associations which had long provided some relief from the harshness of imperial power. From the perspective of its long-term objectives, a major Party goal was to eliminate the warlords and their undisciplined armies and to make the defensive secret societies unnecessary within a framework of national political unity. But the immediate need to recruit a military force which could be used to attain these goals required that the Party, now isolated from a "proletarian base" in the mountains of south China, draw on these very groups for manpower.[1] And as Mao wrote in 1926, a major problem was how to instill in the new recruits the discipline required to fight for long-term Party goals:

> . . . there is the fairly large lumpen-proletariat, made up of peasants who have lost their land and handicraftsmen who cannot get work. They lead the most precarious existence of all. In every part of the country they have their mutual-aid organizations for political and economic struggle, for instance, the Triad Society in Fukien and

1. *See* Stuart R. Schram, "Mao Tse-tung and Secret Societies," *The China Quarterly,* No. 27 (July–September 1966), pp. 1–13.

One estimate has given the "class" composition of the Red Army in the early 1930s as 57.5 percent peasant, 28 percent soldier, 8.75 percent "bandit," and 5.75 percent worker. Cited in James P. Harrison, "The Li Li-san Line and the CCP in 1930, Part I," *The China Quarterly,* No. 14 (April–June 1963), p. 184.

Kwangtung, the Society of Brothers in Hunan, Hupeh, Kweichow and Szechuan, . . . and the Green Band in Shanghai and elsewhere. *One of China's difficult problems is how to handle these people. Brave fighters but apt to be destructive, they can become a revolutionary force if given proper guidance.*[2]

Organization and the Party's ideology came to be seen as sources of discipline, even as they were used as instruments of mobilization. In his "Hunan Report," Mao listed as one of the fourteen great accomplishments of the peasant associations the elimination of banditry, for the growth of these rural political organizations provided a framework within which indiscriminate violence found social meaning: ". . . [our] armies are recruiting large numbers of soldiers and many of the 'unruly' have joined up. Thus the evil of banditry has ended with the rise of the peasant movement." [3]

A more revolutionary innovation was to seek to discipline these peasant and "bandit" troops through political indoctrination. Mao's military cohort in building the Red Army, Chu Teh, recalled that even the "modern" armies that had helped to overthrow the Ch'ing dynasty sustained the tradition of brutal treatment of the enlisted ranks, an approach to "discipline" that only encouraged the *in*discipline with which the common soldiers treated the rural population:

> . . . the soldiers of the Reform Army [of Yunnan] had been given modern military training, weapons, and uniforms, but nothing had been done to change their minds. No changes had been made in their treatment as men, and they were still subjected to the same brutalizing humiliating beatings and cursings as in past ages. Not even the revolutionary intellectuals could think of the common soldier as anything but a ruffian who had to be treated like an animal.[4]

In developing an organizational style in which officers were not allowed to beat their men, the Party taught a lesson in the disciplining of aggression; and in allowing enlisted ranks to criticize the errors of their officers, conflict found control within the rationale of military effectiveness and the goals of a revolutionary organization:

> Always after each campaign, we held two conferences: the first of commanders and the second of commanders and men together where the battle or campaign was analyzed. . . . Each fighter and each com-

2. Mao, "Analysis of the Classes in Chinese Society (1926), *SW*, English, I, p. 19. Emphasis added.

3. Mao, "Hunan Report" (1927), *SW*, English, I, p. 53.

4. Quoted in Agnes Smedley, *The Great Road: The Life and Times of Chu Teh* (New York: Monthly Review Press, 1956), p. 87.

mander had complete freedom of speech in these joint conferences. They could criticize one another or any aspect of the general plan or the way it had been carried out. . . . Any commander who cursed or struck a fighter or otherwise violated army rules had to answer before this court of public opinion.[5]

Marxist orthodoxy held that industrial workers constituted the only class which was disciplined and politically conscious enough to lead the struggle for Socialism. But this article of revolutionary faith was largely academic after the 1927 rout from the urban areas. Survival required the recruitment of available manpower regardless of class origin. Under the force of these circumstances, Mao came to believe that an army constituted of declassed peasants and defectors from "White" or warlord military units could be "proletarianized" through political indoctrination. As he asserted in a 1928 defense of his unorthodox army-building efforts:

> . . . the Red Army consists partly of workers and peasants and partly of lumpen-proletariat. Of course, it is inadvisable to have too many of the latter. But they are able to fight, and as fighting is going on every day with mounting casualties, it is already no easy matter to get replacements even from among them. *In these circumstances the only solution is to intensify political training.*
>
> The majority of the Red Army soldiers come from the mercenary armies, but their character changes once they are in the Red Army. . . . After receiving political education, the Red Army soldiers have become class-conscious, learned the essentials of distributing land, setting up political power, arming the workers and peasants, etc., and they know they are fighting for themselves, for the working class and the peasantry. Hence they can endure the hardships of the bitter struggle without complaint.[6]

These efforts at political indoctrination were inherently limited, however, by a combination of the cultural background of such recruits and the high casualty rates in Red Army units, which saw the loss of many of those whose attitudes might have undergone real change. The army of the Kiangsi era continued to reflect the traditions of its social environment. As a Party Central Committee report of 1930 complained: "In many of the partisan bands, lumpen-proletarian ideas exist, often expressing themselves in unorganized burning, plundering and killing." [7] In this situation, a political

5. *Ibid.*, p. 292.
6. Mao, "The Struggle in the Chingkang Mountains" (1928), *SW*, English, I, p. 81.
7. Cited in Harrison, "The Li Li-san Line and the CCP in 1930, Part I," p. 184.

commissar system provided an organizational solution to a cultural problem. A cadre of specialists in indoctrination were diffused through the military organization to sustain the discipline and political orientation lacking in the enlisted ranks:

> Experience has proved that the system of Party representatives must not be abolished. The Party representative is particularly important at company level, since Party branches are organized on a company basis. He has to see that the soldiers' committee carries out political training, to guide the work of the mass movements, and to serve concurrently as the secretary of the Party branch. Facts have shown that the better the company Party representative, the sounder the company, and that the company commander can hardly play this important political role.[8]

It is a measure of both the strength of purpose and the organizational skills of the Party leadership that under such adverse circumstances the successes of the Kiangsi period were attained. A group of several hundred would-be revolutionaries was able to build an effective military organization up to a strength of nearly half a million men between 1928 and 1934. Out of this force less than 20,000 survived the Long March; yet these "refugees" remained a cadre of organizational skills and political commitment capable of reconstituting itself. In the thirteen years of Resistance War and civil conflict between 1936 and 1948 this leadership core expanded itself into a force nearly two-and-a-half million men strong.[9]

DISCIPLINE THROUGH ORGANIZED CRITICISM

As was discussed earlier in Chapter XI on "deviations" in leadership, Mao came to believe that the controlled conflict of "rectification"—in which Party members underwent group and self-criticism on the basis of ideological norms and operational performance—provided a way of institutionalizing the discipline necessary to promote revolutionary social change. This organizational innovation was in tension, however, with the traditional image of authority as immune to criticism and the enduring use of aggression as a form of self-assertion. In his 1937 attack on "liberalism" (*tzu-yu chu-yi*)—a concept more accurately translated as "self-ism" or just plain "selfishness"—Mao indicated that the basic impulse behind this "deviation" was

8. Mao, "The Struggle in the Chingkang Mountains" (1928), *SW*, English, I, pp. 81–82.

9. These figures are from Edgar Snow, *Red Star Over China*, pp. 189–191, 215; and Mao, "A Circular on the Situation" (1948), *SW*, English, IV, p. 223.

to let things slide for the sake of peace and friendship . . . and to refrain from principled argument because [a person] is an old acquaintance, a fellow townsman, a schoolmate, a close friend, a loved one, an old colleague, or old subordinate. Or to touch on the matter lightly instead of going into it thoroughly, so as to keep on good terms.[10]

Once such reluctance to engage in "principled argument" was overcome, however, the problem became one of *luan*, the undisciplined release of personal hostility:

To indulge in irresponsible criticism in private instead of actively putting forward one's suggestions to the organization. To say nothing to people to their faces but to gossip behind their backs, or to say nothing at a meeting but to gossip afterwards. To show no regard at all for the principles of collective life but to follow one's own inclinations. This is a second type [of liberalism].[11]

At its worst, the indiscriminate use of criticism worked to fragment the organization into hostile cliques, for such conflict had no significance beyond the venting of personal grievance or an effort at self-assertion:

. . . in order to enforce their will, the exponents of the third "Left" line invariably and indiscriminately branded all Party comrades who found the wrong line impracticable and who therefore expressed doubt, disagreement or dissatisfaction, or did not actively support the wrong line or firmly carry it out; they stigmatized these comrades with such labels as "Right opportunism," "the rich peasant line," "the Lo Ming line," "the line of conciliation" and "double-dealing," *waged "ruthless struggle" against them and dealt them "merciless blows," and even conducted these "inner-Party struggles" as if they were dealing with criminals and enemies.* This wrong kind of inner-Party struggle . . . eliminated the democratic spirit of criticism and self-criticism, turned Party discipline into mechanical discipline and fostered tendencies to blind obedience and docility. . . . Such factionalist errors very greatly weakened the Party, causing dislocation between higher and lower organizations and many other anomalies in the Party.[12]

What information is available on the post-Liberation promotion of "criticism–self-criticism" indicates that reluctance to give and accept criticism endures, as does the "left" inclination to criticize irresponsibly or to retaliate against those who have exposed one's

10. Mao, "Combat Liberalism" (1937), *SW*, English, II, p. 31.
11. *Ibid.*
12. Mao, "Our Study and the Current Situation: Appendix: Resolution on Certain Questions in the History of Our Party" (1945), *SW*, English, III, pp. 209–210. Emphasis added.

shortcomings.[13] Yet for all the difficulties in institutionalizing this form of mediated political combat, its persistence represents Mao's conviction that the traditional personalized and family-centered concept of authority can only acquire a larger social meaning if wedded to an ideology, and that social change will endure only in a critical dialogue between those who wield Party power and the creative, yet conservative, "masses."

THE "LUAN" OF LAND REFORM

During the war years of the second United Front with the Nationalists, the problem of maintaining discipline over mass energies was inconsequential in relation to the basic problem of sustaining resistance to the foreign invader. The Japanese provided a clear target for the promotion of conflict. With the defeat of Japan, however, the civil conflict again became China's main "contradiction"; and the problem of *luan* acquired a new reality.

In resuming attacks on its domestic enemies the Party faced the problem of disciplining the struggle so that its political objective of destroying the power of the Nationalists did not degenerate into a confusion of personalized aggression. After years of decentralized partisan warfare, Mao called for the establishment of a system of centralized political reporting which would tie scattered political and military units to Central Committee control and "overcome any conditions of indiscipline or anarchy existing in the Party and the army." [14]

A more basic problem of maintaining discipline in conflict was presented by the process of land reform, promoted concurrently with the civil war to gain peasant support for the Party and to eliminate Nationalist influence in the rural areas. The personalized hatreds which Party cadres stimulated in the village "speak bitterness" struggles were difficult to control. The peasants, lacking the discipline of political "consciousness," tended to be indiscriminate in using the violence of land reform to settle old personal grudges or to embark on an orgy of "eating up" the material possessions of

13. *See* the study based on Party documents and emigré interviews by Martin K. Whyte, *Small Groups and Political Rituals in Communist China* (unpublished Ph.D. dissertation, Harvard University, 1970), esp. Ch. I. Additional material on this subject will be found in the author's "Mao's Effort to Reintegrate the Chinese Polity," in Barnett, ed., *Chinese Communist Politics in Action*, pp. 322–337, and "On Activism and Activists," *The China Quarterly*, No. 39 (July–September 1969), pp. 92–114.

14. Introductory footnote to Mao, "On Setting Up a System of Reports" (1948), *SW*, English, IV, p. 178.

their class enemies. The Party faced the danger of "tailism"—of becoming a mere appendage manipulated by the peasant violence it sought to use:

> . . . on the question of identifying class status [the Party organization in the Shansi-Suiyuan Liberated Area] adopted an ultra-Left policy; . . . on the question of how to destroy the feudal system it laid too much stress on unearthing the landlords' hidden property; and . . . on the question of dealing with the demands of the masses it failed to make a sober analysis and raised the sweeping slogan, "Do everything as the masses want it done." With respect to the latter point, which is a question of the Party's relationship with the masses, the Party must lead the masses to carry out all their correct ideas in the light of the circumstances and educate them to correct any wrong ideas they may entertain.[15]

A second source of "leftist" *luan* resided within the Party itself. Cadres tended to get carried away with their own revolutionary enthusiasm in the land reform process, leaving the masses behind and excessively broadening the "scope of attack" on rural enemies. The danger inherent in over-enthusiastic or aggressive cadres "broadening the scope of attack" was that the Party would be led into *luan,* into attacking "the People" and not their enemies, thus provoking popular hatred against itself rather than just helping to vent old hatreds derived from "feudal exploitation":

> . . . in the fierce struggles in the land reform of the past year, the Shansi-Suiyuan Party organization failed to adhere unequivocally to the Party's policy of strictly forbidding beating and killing without discrimination [*luan-sha, luan-ta*]. As a result, in certain places some landlords and rich peasants were needlessly put to death, and the bad elements in the rural areas were able to exploit the situation to take revenge and foully murdered a number of working people.[16]

Throughout his career Mao has tended to take the position that revolutionary excesses are better than no revolution at all and that injustices done to individuals in the promotion of class conflict can be corrected at a later date. Nevertheless, it can be said that Mao reveals no personal fascination with violence for its own sake or a compulsive need to assert political control by doing violence to opposition elements. He has seen the Party's task as one of disciplining physical violence, depersonalizing political conflict, and getting people concerned with questions of social change:

15. Mao, "Speech at a Conference of Cadres in the Shansi-Suiyuan Liberated Area" (1948), *SW*, English, IV, p. 232.
16. *Ibid.,* p. 229.

The aim of the land reform is to abolish the system of feudal exploitation, that is, to *eliminate the feudal landlords as a class, not as individuals.* Therefore a landlord· must receive the same allotment of land and property as does a peasant and must be made to learn productive labour and join the ranks of the nation's economic life. *Except for the most heinous counterrevolutionaries and local tyrants, who have incurred the bitter hatred of the broad masses, who have been proved guilty and who therefore may and ought to be punished, a policy of leniency must be applied to all, and any beating or killing without discrimination must be forbidden.* The system of feudal exploitation should be abolished step by step, that is, in a tactical way. In launching the struggle *we must determine our tactics according to the circumstances and the degree to which the peasant masses are awakened and organized.* We must not attempt to wipe out overnight the whole system of feudal exploitation.[17]

The Party, in rousing the mass hatreds which give life to the revolution, thus creates for itself a very delicate task of control: If it fails fully to mobilize the masses it may lack the strength to survive the counterattacks of "armed reaction," or it may not be "thorough" in destroying the economic and social roots of the traditional system of authority. But if it is too vigorous in its use of power, it will attack "enemies" where the people do not see them, thus creating new hatreds. This dilemma presents what is probably an impossible task of discernment because of the indiscriminate qualities of power and mobilized emotions. What the Party has chosen to do in the face of this problem is to attempt to drain off any newly generated hatreds by exposing *its cadres* to attack ("criticism") by "the People" for the errors they have made in implementing what are assumed to be inherently correct Party policies:

> We must criticize and struggle with certain cadres and Party members who have committed serious mistakes and certain bad elements among the masses of workers and peasants. In such criticism and struggle we should persuade the masses to adopt correct methods and forms and to refrain from rough actions. This is one side of the matter. The other side is that these cadres, Party members and bad elements should be made to pledge that they will not retaliate against the masses. It should be announced that the masses not only have the right to criticize them freely but also have the right to dismiss them from their posts when necessary or to propose their dismissal, or to propose their expulsion from the Party and even to hand the worst elements over to the people's courts for trial and punishment.[18]

17. *Ibid.*, p. 236. Emphasis added.
18. Mao, "Important Problems of the Party's Present Policy" (1948), *SW*, English, IV, pp. 185–186.

As the Party advanced toward the attainment of state power Mao could only hope that it would maintain its "clear head" concerning the use of power and not let Chinese society degenerate into further *luan* because of failures of political control—a weakness in leadership which would generate a new storm of political hatred against the revolutionary vanguard itself.

Chapter XIV

IDEOLOGY AND ORGANIZATION, III:
THE POWER TO OPPOSE

A third major aspect of the significance of Party skills at organization and ideological exhortation is the power to aggregate those who have been mobilized and committed to the revolutionary cause. In a society where for centuries the fragmentation of rural life enabled a proportionately small gentry and imperial elite to exercise effective political control, the ability to concentrate an aroused peasantry represents the power to oppose the traditional social order.

We have already detailed how Mao and other Party leaders found both workers and peasants reluctant to oppose established political authority, especially where it continued to exhibit great strength. The continuing acceptance by those in positions of official leadership of the political culture of dependency meant that opposition in terms other than humble supplication for redress of grievance was viewed as a basic challenge to authority. With little middle ground allowed for criticism, and with all contenders for leadership of one mind in the expectation that power was not to be shared, opposition tended to polarize rapidly at the extremes of either full submission to the established order or total rejection of it.

From Mao's perspective this polarization was in the Party's interest because it eliminated alternatives to the revolutionary cause. The uncommitted were thus forced to choose between support of the Communists and submission to the Nationalists. And in Mao's mind, given the harshness of Kuomintang power, there was no question as to the justice and appeal of the Party's cause. As he wrote after the apparent destruction of the Party's urban base in 1927:

> The masses will certainly come over to us. The Kuomintang's policy of massacre only serves to "drive the fish into deep waters," as the saying goes, and reformism no longer has any mass appeal. It is certain that the masses will soon shed their illusions about the Kuomintang.

In the emerging situation, no other party will be able to compete with the Communist Party in winning over the masses.[1]

END ISOLATION THROUGH ORGANIZATION

While Mao, the contender for Party leadership, revealed little doubt about his ability to win over the masses, in earlier days he had candidly expressed the difficulties confronting those who were forced to choose between submission and rebellion. Previously we noted how he found the authority of the Classics helpful in opposing his father, and how he longed for "a powerful group of public opinion" to support those like Miss Chao who could reject the norms of tradition only through self-destruction. In 1926 Mao expressed a similar lament about the inability of the peasants to sustain opposition to the landlords because of their lack of organization:

> The day after [a peasant outburst], the landlord in question ran to the city to report, and soldiers and police came down to the village and turned everything upside down, but the leaders of the peasants had already mostly escaped. There was widespread propaganda about "Violation of the law" and "Crimes," the farmers became fearful, and thus the movement was suppressed. The reason for the failure of this movement is that the masses did not fully organize themselves, and did not have leadership, so that the movement barely got started and then failed.[2]

The basic problem in promoting an opposition political movement in a society where established authority permits no "talking back" or accepts no open, even if limited, challenges to its policies is that opposition is pushed to totality. The ability to press for limited adjustments of position has been ruled out, and hence full destruction of the position of either opposer or opposed becomes a likely prospect. In this context, to oppose alone, to stand in isolation, becomes little more than self-destruction. In encouraging impoverished peasants to challenge the established authority of the countryside, Mao thus forced them into a most vulnerable position. As a Shansi peasant recalled of his village's early opposition to landlord power:

1. Mao, "A Single Spark Can Start a Prairie Fire" (1930), *SW*, English, I, p. 122.
2. Mao (under the pen name Jun-chih), "The Bitter Sufferings of the Peasants in Kiangsu and Chekiang, and Their Movements of Resistance" (1926), in Schram, *PTMTT*, p. 179.

There were eight households in Liu Ling then, and we made a distribution of the land. Many people were worried and anxious. *They wondered if the communists would be able to stay in power.* "If we take the land and later the Red Army is beaten, we shall have to bear the blame," they said. *They didn't think the Red Army looked strong enough.* One old man called Ai Shen-you said: "I won't touch anyone's land. I have always been a day labourer and farmhand and I intend to go on being one. That's the safest." An old woman called Hsiu said: "I don't want to take any land. I have only one grandson left. He is the last of my family. If I take any of the land, the landowner will kill him when he comes back. And if they cut my grandson's head off, my family will be dead." Stepfather and Mother discussed the question a great deal. Stepfather thought that we ought not to take part in dividing up the land; that that would be dangerous and that it was unnecessary to run such a risk. *The landowners were strong and they always used to win in the long run. . . .* The communists had people making propaganda here, and they talked with people and in the end persuaded them. They said: "We are strong enough to deal with the landowners. If we hadn't been strong enough we should not have begun the revolution. You are all poor and how are you going to be able to live if you don't have any land?" [3]

In the early years of the agrarian revolution, however, the strength of the Red Army *was* uncertain; it was weak in comparison with Nationalist forces and the power of provincial and local authorities. In this context, peasants and wavering Party supporters in rural market towns, feeling themselves isolated and weak, retreated before the *luan* of counterrevolutionary "White terror":

In this period the poor peasants, having long been trampled down and feeling that the victory of the revolution was uncertain, frequently yielded to the intermediate class and dared not take vigorous action. [Action] is taken against the intermediate class in the villages only when the revolution is on the upsurge, for instance, when political power has been seized in one or more counties, the reactionary army has suffered several defeats and the prowess of the Red Army has been repeatedly demonstrated. . . .

When the revolution is at a low ebb in the country as a whole, the most difficult problem in our areas is to keep a firm hold on the intermediate class. . . . *When there is a revolutionary upsurge in the country as a whole, the poor peasant class has something to rely on and becomes bolder, while the intermediate class has something to fear and dare not get out of hand.* . . . Now that there is a nationwide tide of counterrevolution, the intermediate class in the White areas, having suffered heavy blows, has attached itself almost wholly to the

3. Jan Myrdal, *Report from a Chinese Village* (London: Heinemann, 1965), pp. 136–137. Emphasis added.

big landlord class, and *the poor peasant class has become isolated.* This is indeed a very serious problem.[4]

In developing a solution to this elemental problem of the reluctance of potentially "revolutionary" individuals and groups to oppose the established order when faced with a sense of isolation, Mao found himself in opposition both to other Party leaders and to elements of the Red Army on basic questions of strategy.[5] His effort to strengthen peasant involvement in the revolution raised fears among the Central Committee, which was still operating from an urban base, that the proletarian revolution would be swamped in a peasant society; and his concern with the sporadic quality of rural insurrection conflicted with those within the Red Army who tended to see the revolution as only a *luan* of unorganized destructiveness, an attitude which found expression in the apparently random violence of "roving guerilla actions." Mao's contention was that only if the Party established stable and visible centers of revolutionary power on which wavering supporters could depend for strength could people acquire the "self-confidence" for action:

> . . . the policy which merely calls for roving guerilla actions cannot accomplish the task of accelerating [the] nationwide revolutionary high tide, while the kind of policy adopted by Chu Teh and Mao Tse-tung and also by Fang Chih-min is undoubtedly correct—that is, the policy of *establishing base areas;* of systematically setting up political power; of deepening the agrarian revolution; of expanding the people's armed forces by a comprehensive process of building up first the township Red Guards, then the district Red Guards, then the county Red Guards, then the local Red Army troops, all the way up to the regular Red Army troops; of spreading political power by advancing in a series of waves, etc., etc. *Only thus is it possible to build the confidence of the revolutionary masses throughout the country, as the Soviet Union has built it throughout the world* . . . only thus is it possible to hasten the revolutionary high tide.[6]

4. Mao, "Struggle in the Chingkang Mountains" (1928), *SW*, English, I, pp. 88–89. Emphasis added.

This type of failure to sustain popular support of the Party's insurgency was repeated shortly after the Long March in the Wei Pei area of the Shensi-Kansu border region. Nationalist forces, having access to areas where the Party promoted land reform from their base at Sian, attacked peasants who cooperated with the Communists, and the reform movement failed. *See* Mark Selden, "The Guerilla Movement in Northwest China: The Origins of the Shensi-Kansu-Ninghsia Border Region, Part II," *The China Quarterly*, No. 29 (January–March 1967), p. 64.

5. *See* Schram, *Mao Tse-tung*, pp. 135–143.

6. Mao, "A Single Spark Can Start a Prairie Fire" (1930), *SW*, English, I, p. 118. Emphasis added.

Mao's reference here to the "confidence-building" importance of the Soviet Union carries into the realm of international politics an attitude toward dealings with power which has its roots in childhood: Fears about challenging established authority are most easily overcome when there exists a strong alternative power, an authority on whom a new dependency tie can be established in replacement of the old and a source of support to allay fears of acting in isolation.

We find this calculus in dealings with power affirmed by one of China's peasants, who described to Jan Myrdal how he faced the potentially fatal choice of commitment to either "revolution" or "reaction." As his recollection makes clear, it was at base the issue of power, of which side held the promise of being more effective in providing security from violence and alleviating economic hardship, which determined the direction of choice:

> [The Communists] had their government at Lochuan [in 1935] and the Red Army was commanded by Liu Chih-tan. To begin with, people were afraid of them and said that communists were murderers, but when they came here they were ordinary people and they always said: "Divide up the land and fight against landowners and despots." They talked a lot and held lots of meetings, and *at the meetings we used to stand up and shout "Yes, yes!" but we did not really believe in them or that they had any real power.*
>
> But in April 1935 the Red Army defeated an armed counterrevolutionary landowners' corps ten *li* from here. They killed the leader of the Southern District, Mu Hsin-tsai, and took lots of booty. After that they came more often. They also killed other counterrevolutionaries. *Then the people saw that the Red Army did have power, and so we stopped driving into the town with our taxes and goods. Instead, we organized ourselves into guerilla bands. . . .*
>
> We no longer went to the town and we no longer sold grain to the town and we paid no taxes, and *those who were K.M.T. no longer dared live out in the country, but began to run away. The town was isolated.*[7]

This peasant's use of the term "isolation" is worth noting, for he means by it that the local Kuomintang backers became "cut off" from support, and hence weakened, by Communist military power. With no organized source of strength to rely upon they ran away, isolating the town from Nationalist power.

This notion that in politics, as in society at large, people do not act as self-reliant individuals but only in relation to a source of power on which they can rely is in the most basic sense what we mean by characterizing the main theme of China's political culture

7. Myrdal, *Report from a Chinese Village*, p. 67. Emphasis added.

as "dependency." The expectation is that once you have "cut off" or isolated an individual or group from its external source of power it will lose the strength which gives it political life. No one acts independently; personal integrity is a matter of one's commitment to a *relationship*—"loyalty". This fundamental orientation toward social action is the basis of Mao's strategy for gaining power, which is explored in detail in the next chapter. Here, however, we want to emphasize one aspect of this orientation: the importance of taking political action only when there is an aggregated source of strength which will sustain the confidence to oppose.

The importance of organized and concentrated peasant support as the basis for opposing the established social order was recognized by Mao in his "Hunan Report" of March 1927:

> Almost half the peasants in Hunan have now been organized. . . . *It is on the strength of their extensive organization that the peasants have gone into action* and within four months they have brought about a great revolution in the countryside, a revolution without parallel in history. . . . *This astonishing and accelerating rate of expansion explains why the local tyrants, evil gentry and corrupt officials have been isolated.* . . .[8]

Effectiveness in political action thus depends on a favorable balance between the organizational unity of those in opposition and the concurrent fragmentation of their enemies, who can be isolated and neutralized. As Mao described the problem in the tactics of land reform:

> The main and immediate task of the land reform is to satisfy the demands of the masses of poor peasants and farm laborers. In the land-reform program it is necessary to unite with the middle peasants; the poor peasants and the farm laborers must form a solid united front with the middle peasants, who account for about 20 percent of the rural population. Otherwise the poor peasants and farm laborers will find themselves isolated and the land reform will fail.[9]

Failure to sustain organizational unity exposes one to manipulation: "It is mainly because of the unorganized state of the Chinese masses that Japan dares to bully us." [10] But where that unity has been attained, the mere power of a word shouted in unison will overcome one's enemies: "When this defect [of national fragmentation] is remedied, then the Japanese aggressor. . . will be surrounded by

8. Mao, "Hunan Report" (1927), *SW*, Chinese, I, pp. 15, 24. Emphasis added.

9. Mao, "The General Line of Land Reform: Unite Ninety Percent of the Population" (1948), cited in Schram, *PTMTT*, p. 246.

10. Mao, "On Protracted War" (1938), *SW*, English, II, p. 186.

hundreds of millions of our people standing upright, [and] the mere sound of their voices will strike terror into him. . . ." [11]

From this conviction of the power that comes with unity derives the Party's endless concern with "consolidation" (*t'uan-chieh*) and the belief that the unitary voice of millions of people shouting common political slogans or reciting the words of one great leader represents real political power. And conversely, this belief sustains the notion that all enemies can be controlled if they are made to "stick out" in isolation, whether they be landlords paraded past jeering villagers, tethered with ropes and crowned with tall paper hats,[12] or opponents of a more recent day decked out with signs around their necks revealing their political errors and subjected to angry denunciations before shouting masses.[13]

11. *Ibid.*
12. *See* Mao, "Hunan Report" (1927), *SW*, English, I, p. 37
13. *See* p. 483 below.

Chapter XV

STRATEGY FOR VICTORY:
FOR THE PARTY AND PEOPLE—UNITY;
FOR THEIR ENEMIES—DISINTEGRATION,
ISOLATION, AND DEFEAT

> When [the enemy] is united, divide him. . . .
> Sometimes drive a wedge between a sovereign and his ministers; on other occasions separate his allies from him. Make them mutually suspicious so that they drift apart. Then you can plot against them.
>
> SUN TZU,
> *The Art of War*[1]

The basic strategic concept which Mao brought to the revolutionary struggle merges his personal assertiveness with the dynamic of the Chinese political culture. A social tradition which prepared people for a life of dependence on those with authority provided strategies by which the weak could defend themselves against more powerful superiors—just as fears of isolation and conflict enabled those in authority to control their subordinates. Throughout the struggle for state power the Communists operated from a position of relative weakness: in the early years of alliance with the Kuomintang, during the wartime struggle against the Japanese, and in the final period of conflict with the Nationalists. Reality imposed on the Party a strategic ratio of "one against ten"; yet Mao and other leaders rejected abandonment of the struggle and developed a tactical style enabling them to pit "ten against one." This technique involved the use of initiative, superior organizational discipline, and

1. Sun Tzu, *The Art of War,* trans. Samuel B. Griffith (Oxford: Oxford University Press, 1963), p. 69.

manipulation of the vulnerabilities and internal divisions of Party enemies. The weaknesses in social integration which were the legacy of a tradition of personalized, hierarchical authority provided lines of cleavage which could be struck to divide and disorganize opposition forces.

FOR THE ENEMY: DISINTEGRATION AND ISOLATION

In orienting Party members to the difficulties of the war against superior Japanese forces, Mao encouraged doubters to take heart from "the record of defeats suffered by big and powerful armies and of victories won by small and weak armies." [2] In each of a series of foreign and Chinese cases cited, Mao asserted,

> the weaker force, pitting local superiority and initiative against the enemy's local inferiority and passivity, *first inflicted one sharp defeat on the enemy and then turned on the rest of his forces and smashed them one by one,* thus transforming the over-all situation into one of superiority and initiative. The reverse was the case with the enemy who originally had superiority and held the initiative; owing to subjective errors and internal contradictions, it sometimes happened that he completely lost an excellent or fairly good position in which he enjoyed superiority and initiative, and became a general without an army or a king without a kingdom. . . . The fact that every ruling dynasty was defeated by revolutionary armies shows that mere superiority in certain respects does not guarantee the initiative, much less the final victory.[3]

This conception of the strength which could be derived from a position of relative weakness reflects in part Mao's own political style—his fear of passivity and a sensitivity to the "subjective errors and internal contradictions" dividing those holding and competing for power; but also it is a conception which drew reality from the political fragmentation of the era in which the Party struggled for growth. As Mao wrote in an analysis of 1928:

> . . . since the first year of the Republic [1912], the various cliques of old and new warlords have waged incessant wars against one another, supported by imperialism from abroad and by the comprador and landlord classes at home. . . . These prolonged splits and wars within the White regime provide a condition for the emergence and persistence of one or more small Red areas under the leadership of the Communist Party amidst the encirclement of the White regime. . . . In difficult or critical times some comrades often have doubts about the survival of Red political power and become pessimistic. The reason is that they have not found the correct explanation for its emergence and survival.

2. Mao, "On Protracted War" (1938), *SW*, English, II, p. 164.
3. *Ibid.*, p. 165.

If only we realize that splits and wars will never cease within the White regime in China, we shall have no doubts about the emergence, survival and daily growth of Red political power.[4]

The "contradictions" among China's warlords fragmented the Party's opponents, limiting their ability to take concerted action against Red Army forces operating in the political and geographical interstices of the Hunan-Kiangsi border region. Their mutual contention for regional power restricted their willingness to commit troops against Party forces if it would mean a gain in position for some provincial rival. And their common belief that Chiang K'ai-shek sought to destroy unattached units not fully under his control by pitting them against the Red Army further limited initiative within the loose central government coalition.[5]

Within this political context Mao came to see "correct" (successful) leadership as the ability to make an accurate evaluation of the enemy's "contradictions" and to act in accordance with his state of internal unity or disunity:

> The sole reason for the August [1928] defeat was that, failing to realize that the period was one of temporary stability for the ruling classes, some comrades adopted a policy suited to a period of splits within the ruling classes and divided our forces for an adventurous advance on southern Hunan, thus causing defeat both in the border area and in southern Hunan.[6]

And in dialectical fashion, the early military successes of the Chu-Mao forces taught that unity of command and concentration of superior force were needed in the face of the enemy, "so as to avoid being destroyed one by one."[7]

4. Mao, "Why Is It that Red Political Power Can Exist in China?" (1928), *SW*, English, I, p. 65. Emphasis added.

5. Li Tsung-jen recalled in his memoirs: ". . . The Communist suppression policy of the central government was to use the Communist army to eliminate the "unattached units." The major task of the so-called "central armies" was to supervise the "unattached units." . . . Thus, whenever fighting with the Communists began, all armies avoided concrete action and busied themselves with abstract tasks in order to preserve their strength. Meanwhile the Communist Party exploited the situation and became more powerful." (*The Reminiscences of General Li Tsung-jen* [unpublished manuscript of the Columbia University East Asian Institute, Chinese Oral History Project, n.d.], Ch. 44, p. 14.)

A similar evaluation of Chiang's style of political control will be found in Ch'ien Tuan-sheng, *The Government and Politics of China* (Cambridge, Massachusetts: Harvard University Press, 1961), pp. 128–132.

6. Mao, "Struggle in the Chingkang Mountains" (1928), *SW*, English, I, p. 76.

7. *Ibid.*

As was pointed out earlier, Mao analyzed the revolutionary potential of various social classes on the basis of their degree of exploitation. In the same spirit, his "contradiction analysis" of political combat involves a detailed search for those resentments, competitive conflicts, deprivations, and differences in objective which can be used against Party enemies. Such divisive tactics either provoke dissension and thus neutralize one's opponents in mutual conflict, or identify sources of temporary common interest which can be used to gain allies for the Party's cause:

> *The question whether there will soon be a revolutionary high tide in China can be decided only by making a detailed examination to ascertain whether the contradictions leading to a revolutionary high tide are really developing.* Since contradictions are developing in the world between the imperialist countries, between the imperialist countries and their colonies, and between the imperialists and the proletariat in their own countries, there is an intensified need for the imperialists to contend for the domination of China. While the imperialist contention over China becomes more intense, both the contradiction between imperialism and the whole Chinese nation and the contradictions among the imperialists themselves develop simultaneously on Chinese soil, thereby creating the tangled warfare which is expanding and intensifying daily and giving rise to the continuous development of the contradictions among the different cliques of China's reactionary rulers. In the wake of the contradictions among the reactionary ruling cliques— the tangled warfare among the warlords—comes heavier taxation, which steadily sharpens the contradiction between the broad masses of taxpayers and the reactionary rulers. . . . *Once we understand all these contradictions, we shall see in what a desperate situation, in what a chaotic state, China finds herself. We shall also see that the high tide of revolution against the imperialists, the warlords and the landlords is inevitable and will come very soon.*[8]

For Mao the tactician, China's "chaotic state" (*hun-luan chuang-t'ai*) was a condition of promise, for in the tensions among those who were "mutually related and mutually antagonistic" lay the contradictions which weakened opposition unity. An effective revolutionary strategy would use these "contradictions" to disintegrate the forces of the enemy and to increase the unity of "progressive forces" through the polarization of political conflict. As a Central Committee resolution of 1945 put it:

> An important basis for determining our varying tactics is the different impact of the revolution on the interests of different enemies. Consequently Comrade Mao Tse-tung has always advocated that we "*utilize*

8. Mao, "A Single Spark Can Start a Prairie Fire" (1930), *SW,* English, I, pp. 120–121. Emphasis added.

every conflict within the counterrevolution and take active measures to widen the cleavages within it," and "oppose the policy of isolation, and affirm the policy of winning over all possible allies." The application of the tactical principles, *"make use of contradictions, win over the many, oppose the few and crush our enemies one by one,"* was brilliantly developed in the campaigns Comrade Mao Tse-tung led against "encirclement and suppression" and especially, after the Tsunyi Meeting, in the Long March and in the work of the Anti-Japanese National United Front.[9]

Mao's various writings reveal that he conceives the problem of utilizing "contradictions" in two different dimensions. The first is "horizontal"—creating dissension among competitive leadership groups so as to prevent the formation of coalitions against the Party. As he wrote in an analysis of political tactics during the anti-Japanese war:

> Most of the leaders of the regional power groups belong to the big landlord class and the big bourgeoisie and, therefore, progressive as they may appear at certain times during the war, they soon turn reactionary again; nevertheless, because of their contradictions with the Kuomintang central authorities, the possibility exists of their remaining neutral in our struggle with the die-hards, provided we pursue a correct policy.
> . . . We must [also] know how to exploit the contradictions among the die-hards and must not take on too many of them at a single time, but must direct our blows at the most reactionary of them first. Herein lies the limited nature of the struggle.[10]

And during the final phase of civil war he warned Party members not to forget that the Kuomintang was a "complicated" (*fu-tza*) political party, embodying potentially hostile factions which could be manipulated so as to disintegrate enemy unity.[11]

The second dimension is the "vertical" one of relations between a leadership group and its base of popular support. Through mass agitation, "contradictions" between leaders and followers can be

9. Mao, "Our Study and the Current Situation: Appendix: Resolution on Certain Questions in the History of Our Party" (1945), *SW*, English, III, p. 202. Emphasis added.
A secret Party directive of 1940 which discloses the difficulty of implementing this tactic is presented in Van Slyke, *Enemies and Friends*, pp. 263–265.
10. Mao, "Current Problems of Tactics in the Anti-Japanese United Front" (1940), *SW*, English, II, pp. 424, 426.
11. *See* Mao, "On Coalition Government" (1945), *SW*, English, III, pp. 271–272. The Chinese version of this passage uses the word "complicated" (*fu-tza*) to describe the Kuomintang. The English translation renders *fu-tza* as "not homogeneous."

stimulated into open hostility, thus isolating the elite from the people who might provide them support:

> . . . the Kuomintang's resumption of conscription and grain levies has aroused popular discontent and created a situation favourable for the development of mass struggles. The whole Party must strengthen its leadership of the mass struggles in the Kuomintang areas and intensify the work of disintegrating the Kuomintang army.[12]

The aim of disintegrating enemy forces, whether "horizontally" through stimulating disruptive conflict among leadership factions or "vertically" by encouraging popular resentments against authority, is to induce paralysis in action through mutual antagonism, or to isolate (*ku-li*) elements of the enemy for destruction in piecemeal fashion. Such a tactic can be applied in either military or political action:

> When you are attacking Chinchow, be prepared also to wipe out the enemy forces that may come to its rescue from Changchun and Shenyang. *Because the enemy forces in and near Chinchow, Shanhaikuan and Tangshan are isolated from each other, success in attacking and wiping them out is pretty certain.*[13]

> In order to reduce the number of hostile elements and to consolidate the Liberated Areas, we should help all those landlords who have difficulty in making a living and induce runaway landlords to return and give them an opportunity to earn a living. In the cities, besides uniting with the working class, the petty bourgeoisie and all progressives, *we should take care to unite with all the middle elements and isolate the reactionaries. Among the Kuomintang troops, we should win over all the possible opponents of civil war and isolate the bellicose elements.*[14]

Mao's offensive political strategy, in its simplest terms, is thus a formula of correctly identifying and stimulating contradictions (*mao-tun*) among opponents so as to produce division and *disintegration* (*wa-chieh, fen-san, fen-sui, p'o-lieh*) in which individual elements of the enemy can be *isolated* (*ku-li ti*) and destroyed one by one.

This tactical conception is hardly unique to Mao. As is indicated in the opening quote of this chapter, drawn from the writings of Sun Tzu, a military strategist of the Warring States period (453–221 B.C.), the effort to establish and maintain power through the disunity of one's opponents has been a long-standing approach in

---

12. Mao, "A Three Months' Summary" (1946), *SW*, English, IV, p. 117.
13. Mao, "The Concept of Operations for the Liaohsi-Shenyang Campaign" (1948), *SW*, English, IV, p. 262. Emphasis added.
14. Mao, "Smash Chiang K'ai-shek's Offensive by a War of·Self-Defence" (1946), *SW*, English, IV, p. 90. Emphasis added.

the Chinese tradition. "Divide and rule" was a basic tactic used to control the nomadic tribes who threatened China's security from her northern frontier; and the playing off of one local power group against another seems to have been the conception which underlay the *pao-chia* system of local security and political control.[15] The enduring reliance placed upon this approach to political rule seems related to its effectiveness within the traditional political culture. Such tactics as playing off various opponents against each other through manipulating their "contradictions," "splitting them up," and "disintegrating" their unity will only work where there are basic conflicts of purpose among opposition leaders (compounded by the belief that power is not to be shared), and where capacities for cooperation and compromise are severely limited. "Isolating" an enemy, or threatening to "cut him off" from a relationship on which he depends, will be an effective tactic only where the sense of dependency or fear of isolation is shared by that enemy, where he, too, finds such a sanction threatening.

We need only recall here in summary that such images as these, which Mao has incorporated into a strategy of power, are precisely the major themes we discovered in our respondents' expectations of dealings with peers and authority. In the Chinese tradition, authority's domain was seen as all-inclusive; its proper function was to establish a noncompetitive and hierarchical social order. There was little sense of cooperation among peers in the resolution of specific issues of mutual interest. Such conflicts were to be resolved through loyal reliance on the initiative of a superior leader. The personalized quality of authority fostered the creation of narrow cliques of loyal subordinates; and equals in power tended to be drawn into competition for full dominance because unitary, personalized leadership was seen as the only effective way to realize an ordered and peaceful society. We found that our respondents had limited expectation of the ability of peers to resolve differences of opinion. Thus Mao shares with those of his countrymen who comprised our interview sample the expectation that with conflict will come a "splitting up."

Furthermore, the effort to cut off a leadership group from its followers can be an effective strategy where there already exists an exploitable gap in communication and sentiment between leaders and led. In our study we have already discussed the early development of this gap in the life of the Chinese child. This problem is further reinforced by anxieties about dealings with potentially aggressive and manipulating power. The limited reciprocity of supe-

15. *See* Hsiao Kung-chuan, *Rural China, Imperial Control in the Nineteenth Century* (Seattle: University of Washington Press, 1960), pp. 72–83.

rior-subordinate relations works to cut off an individual in a position of leadership from his subordinates; and the Communists have been quick to exploit this gap to undermine the mass base of their enemies and to win converts to their own cause.

Finally, we suggested that traditional attitudes toward authority were strongly ambivalent, embodying a paradoxical hatred of its harshness and tendency to be manipulative, yet a longing to find security and guidance under its control. Mao's perception of the importance of stable centers of power from which to oppose forces of "reaction" seems based on an intuitive awareness of the workings of this ambivalence: the desire to strike out at hated power, yet a fear that in so doing one will be cut off from security and subject to an intensely hostile reaction. In a very practical way the Party, by establishing "revolutionary bases" of military and political strength, helped people to resolve this ambivalence, for such centers of power provided an alternative authority on which to depend. From the "liberated areas" hated authority could be attacked: The Party provided ideological justification for the attack and physical security from its consequences.

Mao's revolutionary strategy, derived from this calculus of the Chinese political culture, was succinctly and forcefully summed up on the eve of the civil war:

> . . . we must at all times firmly adhere to, and never forget, these principles: unity, struggle, unity through struggle; to wage struggles with good reason, with advantage and with restraint; and to make use of contradictions, win over the many, oppose the few and crush our enemies one by one.[16]

FOR THE PARTY AND PEOPLE: UNITY

> If we study history, we find that all the movements that have occurred in the course of history, of whatever type they may be, have all without exception resulted from the union of a certain number of people. A greater movement naturally requires a greater union, and the greatest movement requires the greatest union. All such unions are more likely to appear in a time of reform and resistance. . . .

> That which decides between victory and defeat is the solidity or weakness of the union and whether the ideology that serves as its basis is new or old, true or false.[17]

If the first major goal of Mao's strategy is "divide and rule," the second centers around the maintenance of Party and coalition unity

16. Mao, "On Peace Negotiations with the Kuomintang" (1945), *SW*, English, IV, p. 49.

17. Mao, "The Great Union of the Popular Masses" (1919), in Schram, *PTMTT*, p. 170.

while enemies are being "disintegrated." Much of the concern for unity shown by Mao and other leaders has the quality of a reaction against the strategy of disintegration which they seek to impose on their enemies. Seeing their own political action within a calculus of unity opposed to disintegration and isolation, it is but a short step from there to the assumption that the enemy's objectives are similar to those of the Party: ". . . the [Japanese] enemy will not relax his divisive tricks to break China's united front, hence the task of maintaining internal unity in China will become still more important, and we shall have to ensure that the strategic counteroffensive does not collapse halfway through internal dissension." [18]

This perception was fully reinforced by the political fragmentation which had characterized the first decade of the Republic. Sun Yat-sen—who in 1924 was to turn to the Soviet Union for assistance in organization-building—lamented that the post-1911 Kuomintang "was split to pieces and could not agree upon orders." [19] He saw his movement's failure deriving from this fragmentation, and the concomitant unity of his opposition: "Yuan Shih-kai had a firm organization while we in the Revolutionary Party were a sheet of loose sand, and so Yuan Shih-kai defeated the party." [20] This recent history was a powerful lesson to Mao; and it is hardly surprising that he came to gauge success or failure in tactical operations within a framework of isolation versus being isolated:

> The illegal and divisive "National Assembly," which was convened by Chiang K'ai-shek, in order to isolate our Party and other democratic forces, and the bogus constitution fabricated by the body enjoy no prestige at all among the people. Instead of isolating our Party and other democratic forces, they have isolated the reactionary Chiang K'ai-shek ruling clique itself. Our Party and other democratic forces adopted the policy of refusing to participate in the bogus National Assembly; this was perfectly correct. [21]

In Party writings one frequently encounters reassuring little reminders that the "progressive forces" are not really isolated (are they?):

> The broad masses of people in foreign countries are dissatisfied with the reactionary forces in China and sympathize with the Chinese people's forces. They also disapprove of Chiang K'ai-shek's policies. *We*

18. Mao, "On Protracted War" (1938), *SW,* English, II, p. 143.
19. Sun Yat-sen, *San Min Chu I*; cited in Sharman, *Sun Yat-sen,* p. 169.
20. *Ibid.*
21. Mao, "Greet the New High Tide of the Chinese Revolution" (1947), *SW,* English, IV, p. 122.

have many friends in all parts of the country and of the world; we are not isolated.[22]

This concern with "isolation"—with being cut off from one's group or a source of authority and power—as we have seen in both social and political contexts, strikes at the Chinese sense of social inter-relatedness. Its strength is based on emotional needs, shared by subordinate and superior alike, to depend on the support of group life for assistance and security. The preoccupation that Mao has shown throughout his career about the Party becoming "cut off from the masses" betrays the fear of isolation, of standing alone in rebellion apart from popular support. As he wrote in the bleak days of 1928:

> Wherever the Red Army goes, the masses are cold and aloof, and only after our propaganda do they slowly move into action. Whatever enemy units we face, there are hardly any cases of mutiny or desertion to our side and we have to fight it out. . . . *We have an acute sense of our isolation which we keep hoping will end.*[23]

In a similar vein the editors of Mao's *Selected Works,* in an introductory footnote to the "Hunan Report," attacked the "Right opportunist" Ch'en Tu-hsiu leadership for its policy of alliance with the Kuomintang: "They preferred to desert the peasantry, the chief ally in the revolution, and thus left the working class and the Communist Party isolated and without help." [24] The unwavering commitment to mass mobilization which Mao was to display in the years after Liberation reveals, in part, the continuity of his concern with finding himself and the Party alone, without popular support in the process of promoting social change.

An additional reason for the preoccupation with unity lies in the divisive social loyalties which were such an elemental aspect of China's traditional society. The exclusive commitments to family and clan, school class, region, and work group fostered much of the fragmentation of Chinese political life; and in student days Mao had personally known the sting of social isolation which came from such narrow loyalties. As he told Edgar Snow:

> I was disliked because I was not a native of Hsiang Hsiang. It was very important to be a native of Hsiang Hsiang and also important to be from a certain district of Hsiang Hsiang. There was an upper, lower and middle district, and lower and upper were continually fighting,

22. Mao, "On the Chungking Negotiations" (1945), *SW,* English, IV, p. 55. Emphasis added.

23. Mao, "The Struggle in the Chingkang Mountains" (1928), *SW,* English, I, pp. 98–99. Emphasis added.

24. Mao, "Report on an Investigation of the Peasant Movement in Hunan" (1927), *SW,* English, I, fn. pp. 23–24.

purely on a regional basis. Neither could be reconciled to the existence of the other. I took a neutral position in this war, because I was not a native at all. Consequently all three factions despised me. I felt spiritually very depressed.[25]

The political impact of such regional loyalties was brought home to Mao in the early days of army building. In 1928 he wrote with exasperation of the blood feuds which hindered development of a unified base of popular support: "A very wide rift has long existed between the native inhabitants [of the Kiangsi border regions] and the settlers whose forefathers came from the north several hundred years ago; their traditional feuds are deep-seated and they sometimes erupt in violent clashes." [26]

The sum of these varied factors fostering social divisiveness accounts for the determination of Party efforts to maintain internal discipline. Such factors account for the seeming paradox that just as victory in the civil war was approaching, Mao evinced even greater concern with tendencies within the Party and military which threatened to create "indiscipline, anarchy, and localism":

> Because our Party and our army were long in a position in which we were cut apart by the enemy, were waging guerilla warfare and were in the rural areas, we allowed very considerable autonomy to the leading organs of the Party and army in the different areas. This enabled the Party organizations and armed forces to bring their initiative and enthusiasm into play and to come through long periods of grave difficulties, but at the same time *it gave rise to certain phenomena of indiscipline and anarchy, localism and guerilla-ism which were harmful to the cause of the revolution. The present situation demands that our Party should do its utmost to centralize all the powers that can and must be concentrated in the hands of the Central Committee and its agencies,* so as to bring about the transition in the form of the war from guerilla to regular warfare.[27]

Concentration of power thus acquires the weighty justification of overcoming the divisive tendencies inherent in Chinese society. And it seems likely that for a long time to come rational justifications for decentralization of Party, governmental, and economic bureaucracies will be in "contradiction" with fears of *luan* based on anticipated loyalties to family, region, or clique lying below a social face of commitment to nation and Party.

25. Edgar Snow, *Red Star Over China*, p. 132.
26. Mao, "The Struggle in the Chingkang Mountains" (1928), *SW*, English, I, p. 93.
27. Mao, "On the September Meeting" (1948), *SW*, English, IV, p. 273. Emphasis added.

THE UNITY OF RESENTMENT

The approach to maintaining political unity which became most meaningful to Mao apparently is based on the organizational core of the Party:

> Unity within the Chinese Communist Party is the fundamental pre-requisite for uniting the whole nation to win the War of Resistance and build a new China. Seventeen years of tempering have taught the Chinese Communist Party many ways of attaining internal unity, and ours is a much more seasoned Party. Thus we are able to form a powerful nucleus for the whole people in the struggle to win victory. . . . Comrades, so long as we are united, we can certainly reach this goal.[28]

This stress on the Party is in part a legacy of the political fragmentation of the period in which the Communist movement had its early growth, and of the influence of Comintern advisers who brought to China the Leninist experience in building a combat organization. If China's "progressive forces" could only maintain their unity, they could make a revolution on the "confusion" which characterized their opponents.[29] A disciplined party came to be seen as the core of this unity.

Yet (as was to become clear only in the days after Liberation) the elite Party institution was less sacred to Mao than the "many ways of attaining internal unity" which were the product of "seventeen years of tempering" in the struggle of domestic revolution. The forms of mobilization and control which comprise Mao's approach to political integration are closely related to his basic concept of political motivation. Unity grows from a shared sense of outrage at exploitation and injustice. Mao told Edgar Snow that the family "United Front" of his childhood grew from hatred of oppressive paternal authority;[30] and in a later day he asserted that the wartime United Front against the Japanese, in similar fashion, drew its cohesiveness from a shared hatred of the aggressor: "We can rally the overwhelming majority of the people to fight with one heart and one mind because we are the oppressed and the victims of aggression."[31]

28. Mao, "The Role of the Chinese Communist Party in the National War" (1938), *SW*, English, II, p. 210.

29. Sun Tzu, too, had seen "unity versus confusion" as a tactical dimension of combat: ". . . if one wishes to feign disorder to entice an enemy he must himself be well-disciplined. Only then can he feign confusion . . . order or disorder depends on organization." (Sun Tzu, *The Art of War*, p. 93.)

30. Snow, *Red Star Over China*, p. 126.

31. Mao, "Problems of Strategy in China's Revolutionary War" (1936), *SW*, English, I, p. 207.

The organizational forms developed by the Party to mobilize resentment at such treatment (discussed in Chapter XII) and the techniques of political study used to rationalize opposition to the common enemy gave structure and control to this basic concept of the unity of resentment. And as Mao asserted on the eve of victory, these forms and techniques accounted for the sharp contrast between the disciplined forces of "revolution" and the disintegration of the "counterrevolutionary" camp:

> In the last few months almost all the People's Liberation Army has made use of the intervals between battles for large-scale training and consolidation. This has been carried out in a fully guided, orderly and democratic way. ["Speak bitterness" meetings and political study have] aroused the revolutionary fervour of the great masses of commanders and fighters, enabled them clearly to comprehend the aim of the war, eliminated certain incorrect ideological tendencies and undesirable manifestations in the army, educated the cadres and fighters and greatly enhanced the combat effectiveness of the army. . . . . You can see clearly that neither the Party consolidation, nor the ideological education in the army, nor the land reform, all of which we have accomplished and all of which have great historic significance, could be undertaken by our enemy, the Kuomintang. On our part, we have been very earnest in correcting our own shortcomings; we have united the Party and army virtually as one man and forged close ties between them and the masses of the people. . . . *With our enemy, everything is just the opposite. They are so corrupt, so torn by ever-increasing and irreconcilable internal quarrels, so spurned by the people and utterly isolated and so frequently defeated in battle that their doom is inevitable.* This is the whole situation of revolution versus counterrevolution in China.[32]

The dynamic aspect of Mao's approach to building a unity of revolutionary forces derives from his belief that people are sustained in their political involvement through the tension of conflict with their oppressors: "Struggle is the means to unity and unity is the aim of struggle. If unity is sought through struggle it will live; if unity is sought through yielding, it will perish." [33] The tactical problem confronting the leadership in implementing this conception is first to identify the proper enemy and then to invoke his "contradictions" with uncommitted social groups in order to mobilize and build a base of popular support. As Mao asserted in 1926:

> Who are our enemies? Who are our friends? This is a question of the first importance for the revolution. The basic reason why all pre-

32. Mao, "Speech at a Conference of Cadres in the Shansi-Suiyuan Liberated Area" (1948), *SW*, English, IV, p. 234. Emphasis added.
33. Mao, "Current Problems of Tactics in the Anti-Japanese United Front" (1940), *SW*, English, II, p. 422.

vious revolutionary struggles in China achieved so little was their failure to unite with real friends in order to attack real enemies.[34]

The creative edge of leadership is the ability to perceive the social issues which can be used to mobilize different social groups and separate them from the Party's enemies in creating the broadest base of popular support. This calculus of coalition-building, however, embodies the "deviational" dangers of either excessive exclusiveness ("sectarianism") in mobilizing support—leading to the isolation of the Party on a narrow base of support—or appealing for popular backing with such broad and uncontroversial issues that the revolution flags in moderate "reformism." In Party history the sectarian deviation was most fully developed in the Kiangsi era:

> Our experience teaches us that the main blow of the revolution should be directed at the chief enemy and to isolate him, whereas with the middle forces, a policy of both uniting with them and struggling against them should be adopted, so that they are at least neutralized; and, as circumstances permit, efforts should be made to shift them from their position of neutrality to one of alliance with us in order to facilitate the development of the revolution. But there was a time—the ten years of civil war from 1927 to 1936—when some of our comrades crudely applied [Stalin's formula of isolating middle-of-the-road elements] to China's revolution by turning their main attack on the middle forces, singling them out as the most dangerous enemy; the result was that, instead of isolating the real enemy, we isolated ourselves and suffered losses to the advantage of the real enemy.[35]

The dangers of working with too broad a base of support were experienced in 1927, when Chiang K'ai-shek, taking advantage of the first United Front, seized leadership of the military forces of the revolutionary coalition and turned them against the Party: "It was all alliance and no struggle in the latter period of the First Great Revolution, and all struggle and no alliance . . . in the latter period of the Agrarian Revolution—truly striking demonstrations of the two extremist policies. Both . . . caused great losses to the Party and the Revolution." [36]

According to Mao, it was only under his "correct" leadership that the proper balance of coalition and struggle was attained during the conflict with Japan and in the ensuing civil war. While an impartial evaluation of the many reasons for the Party's spectacular

34. Mao, "Analysis of the Classes in Chinese Society" (1926), *SW*, English, I, p. 13.

35. *People's Daily* editorial, "On the Historical Experience of the Dictatorship of the Proletariat" (April 5, 1956), cited in Schram, *PTMTT*, p. 298.

36. Mao, "On Policy" (1940), *SW*, English, II, p. 442.

rise to power must be found in the works of students of Party history, it is at least clear that Mao has sought to present the image of unity versus disintegration as the tactical reality of the Party's rise to power. As he proclaimed in early 1949, when victory was in sight:

> Total power is in the hands of the Chinese people, the Chinese People's Liberation Army, the Communist Party of China and the other democratic parties, not in the hands of the badly split and disintegrating Kuomintang. *One side wields total power, while the other is hopelessly split and disintegrated,* and this is the result of the prolonged struggle of the Chinese people and the prolonged evil-doing of the Kuomintang. No serious person can ignore this basic fact of the political situation in China today.[37]

The unambiguous military successes of the Red Army in the civil war gave weighty support to Mao's assertion, and more sharply defined the polarity between justice and evil, unity and disintegration. As Nanking fell in late April of 1949 and the Liberation Army prepared to cross into south China, Mao brushed a poem which summed the symbols of his revolution, and revealed his elation in *luan:*

> Around Mount Chung a sudden storm has arisen,
> A million courageous warriors cross the great river . . .
> The universe is in turmoil, we are all exhaulted and resolute.
> Let us gather up our courage and pursue the broken foe. . . .[38]

As the Party's "broken foe" prepared to withdraw to an island retreat, Mao taunted the Kuomintang in a farewell of elated satisfaction that nearly leaps from the page: "You are defeated. You have enraged the people. And the people have all risen against you in a life-and-death struggle. The people do not like you, the people condemn you, *the people have risen, and you are isolated; that is why you have been defeated."* [39]

ENDING AN ERA AND "RECTIFYING NAMES"

By early 1949 it had become clear that "Heaven's Mandate" of political leadership was no longer in the hands of the Kuomintang.

37. Mao, "Why Do the Badly Split Reactionaries Still Idly Clamour for 'Total Peace'?" (1949), *SW,* English, IV, p. 344. Emphasis added.

38. Extracted from Mao's poem, "The People's Liberation Army Gains Nanking," of April 1949; translated in Schram, *Mao Tse-tung,* p. 244.

39. Mao, "On Ordering the Reactionary Kuomintang Government to Re-arrest Yasuji Okamura, Former Commander-in-Chief of the Japanese Forces of Aggression in China, and to Arrest the Kuomintang Civil War Criminals —Statement by the Spokesman for the Communist Party of China" (1949), *SW,* English, IV, p. 328. Emphasis added.

And as is the long established tradition in this political culture, the old set of "names" which had represented the underlying realities of power required "rectification."

For the Communists' part, in reacting to the repatriation to Japan of General Yasuji Okamura, Mao declared:

> Gentlemen of the reactionary traitorous Kuomintang government, this action of yours is too unreasonable and is too gross a violation of the people's will. *We have now deliberately added the word "traitorous" to your title, and you ought to accept it.* Your government has long been traitorous, and it was only for the sake of brevity that we sometimes omitted the word: now we can omit it no longer.[40]

In noting a change in the "name" used by the Kuomintang in describing the Communists, Mao rhetorically inquired: "Why has the term 'Communist bandits' been changed into 'Communist Party' in all Kuomintang public documents issued since January 1, 1949?" [41] And in response to an evaluation of responsibility for China's changing political circumstances by the Kuomintang's new acting president, Mao noted with satisfaction:

> If there is nothing else good about Li Tsung-jen, at least it is good that he has made . . . one honest statement. What is more, instead of speaking about "putting down the rebellion" or "suppressing the bandits" he calls the war a "civil war," and this, for the Kuomintang, may be said to be quite novel.[42]

"Names" were being "rectified"; China was about to enter a new political era. And Mao could only hope that with the Party's rise to power it would be possible to "heal the wounds of war and build a new, powerful and prosperous People's Republic *whose reality will be worthy of its name.*" [43]

40. Mao, "Peace Terms Must Include the Punishment of Japanese War Criminals—Statement by a Spokesman for the Chinese Communist Party" (1949), *SW*, English, IV, p. 335.

41. Mao, "On the Kuomintang's Different Answers to the Question of Responsibility for the War" (1949), *SW*, English, IV, p. 352.

42. *Ibid.*, p. 354.

43. Mao, "Address to the Preparatory Committee of the New Political Consultative Conference" (1949), *SW*, Chinese, IV, p. 1471. Emphasis added.

Part Four

THE MAOIST
POLITICAL RECONSTRUCTION

Peasants in a People's Commune Production Brigade
eat lunch between militia drill and the afternoon's labor
during the Great Leap Forward, 1958.
Black Star Agency.

Comrade Mao Tse-tung has said that our direction must be the step by step and systematic organization of industry, agriculture, commerce, education, and the military (militia, that is an armed population) into big communes, thereby forming the basic units of our society. . . . The flag of Mao Tse-tung is the red flag held high by the Chinese people. Under the leadership of this great red flag, the Chinese people, in the not-distant future, will steadily and victoriously advance to the great Communist society.

Red Flag,
July 1958

Chapter XVI

AN END TO THE
POLITICS OF DEPENDENCY?

Since they learned Marxism-Leninism, the
Chinese people have ceased to be passive in
spirit and gained the initiative. The period of
modern world history in which the Chinese
and Chinese culture were looked down upon
should have ended from that moment. The
great, victorious Chinese People's War of
Liberation and the great people's revolution
have rejuvenated and are rejuvenating the
great culture of the Chinese people.[1]

For Mao the attainment of state power was both fulfillment and
promise. He saw in the Party's military and political triumph over
the Nationalists the "liberation" of the Chinese people from a discredited political order and the conclusion of an era of social turmoil and foreign intervention. Yet he expressed awareness that
"countrywide victory is only the first step in a long march of ten
thousand *li*,"[2] in which the Party would have to learn the skills of
social reconstruction. Unlike the founders of past dynasties, however, he did not see China's "golden age" in an idealized past but
in an unrealized future. As the political spokesman for a generation
which had rejected the Confucian heritage, he sought to replace the

1. Mao Tse-tung, "The Bankruptcy of the Idealist Conception of History" (1949), *Selected Works of Mao Tse-tung* (4 vols., Peking: Foreign
Languages Press, 1961–1965), Vol. IV, p. 458. Hereinafter cited as *SW*,
English.
2. Mao, "Report to the Second Plenary Session of the Seventh Central
Committee of the Communist Party of China" (1949), *SW*, English, IV, p.
374.

cyclical historical pattern of China's "feudal" era with the Marxian notion of unilinear social development.[3]

The exact form of China's Communist future was hardly certain in 1949, however. The unexpectedly swift victory in the civil war seems to have caught Party leaders almost unprepared for the constructive dimension of their revolution.[4] The instruments of political and military combat which had brought them to power and the precedent of "socialist transformation" in the Soviet Union, enabled the Party to destroy rapidly the organizational remnants of Nationalist political and economic control. By late 1955, "the socialist transformation of the ownership of the means of production in agriculture, handicrafts and capitalist industry and commerce was in the main completed!"[5] It was only as this period of consolidation of power drew to a close that the attention of Party leaders turned fully to the question of the form of China's future social institutions.

The leadership shared a commitment to realize "communism" in China, but the vagueness of that distant goal was such that on the eve of victory Mao could even compare it to the traditional Chinese utopia of *ta-t'ung*.[6] Between the fact of political and military conquest and the millennium lay an undefined middle range of policies and institutions which would have to implement the transition to China's future greatness.

From the perspective of hindsight, it is now clear that the decade 1955–1964 was a period of experimentation and debate among

3. Mao's mentor, Li Ta-chao, had explicitly opposed the notion of a "golden age" in China's past, and criticized the cyclical view of history, "for it causes men to lose their faith and hope." (Maurice Meisner, *Li Ta-chao and the Origins of Chinese Marxism* [Cambridge, Mass.: Harvard University Press, 1967], p. 167.) Mao shared Li's concern with subjective views of the world which would hinder social progress. He wrote in 1940, "as far as the masses and young students are concerned, the essential thing is to guide them to look forward and not backward." (Mao, "On New Democracy" [1940], *SW*, English, II, p. 381.)

4. It was only gradually during 1947 that the Communists began to sense victory in the civil war. The decisive battle of the Huai-Hai came in November–December 1948, less than a year before country-wide victory. *See* F. F. Liu, *A Military History of Modern China* (Princeton: Princeton University Press, 1956), pp. 252, 263.

5. Lin Piao, "Report to the Ninth National Congress of the Communist Party of China," in *Survey of the China Mainland Press* (Hong Kong: United States Consulate General), No. 4406 (May 1, 1969), p. 15. Hereinafter cited as *SCMP*.

6. *See* Mao, "On the People's Democratic Dictatorship" (1949), *SW*, English, IV, p. 414.

Party leaders over the most appropriate way to transform Chinese society. Many assumed that the basic question of political control had been solved. They saw China's problems of modernization largely in technical and economic terms. Mao, however, increasingly came to see the cultural and political difficulties of the country's development. As we shall stress in this final part of the study, Mao had a personal sensitivity to the authority pattern of the traditional society and believed that only through controlled conflict could China sustain social change. He sensed in the consolidation of Party, governmental, and army organizations the slow reemergence of old, exploitative political relationships in "bourgeois" or "revisionist" guise.

These personal concerns were heightened by challenges to Mao's policies from the Party and state apparatus which came in part as a result of "de-Stalinization" in the Soviet Union. Mao had been Party Chairman since the 1935 Tsunyi Conference and in 1949 he was elected Chairman of the newly established People's Republic, but his dual role as leader of both Party and state hardly gave him total power. In an altered context of political reconstruction, power diffused to the economic and political organizations of "socialist construction". During the 1950s, Mao became increasingly distrustful of China's new bureaucratic and technical elite. He read into their resistance to his concepts for modernizing a peasant society an attempt to restore the pattern of dependent submission by "the People" to the initiative of a small ruling class. To the degree that Mao's colleagues within the Party leadership did not share his personal concerns, and actively resisted his efforts to institutionalize forms of mass political participation, Mao came to see them as "counterrevolutionaries."

At the end of this decade of experimentation and debate, differences of opinion within the Party leadership—compounded by the economic crisis which followed the Great Leap Forward—had become strong enough to hinder cooperative relations and collective decision-making. Mao, feeling his political influence slipping away, asserted himself by initiating a "cultural revolution" designed to remove from power those long-time comrades whom he now saw as bringing about "a restoration of capitalism." And with the help of China's younger generation, the Party Chairman sought to create new forms of mass political participation which would embody his own strategy of social change.

At another level of perception, the experience of this decade seems to have made it increasingly clear to Mao that simply the destruction of the organizational forms of old China—the governing institutions and the "relations of production" which were their base—and their replacement by new "socialist" institutions, were insufficient to guarantee social change. In time he saw that the "four olds" of China's traditional ideas, culture, customs, and habits were the main obstacles to development. In one sense Mao came to reject the Marxist stress on class conflict as the basis of social development in favor of a stress on cultural conflict. He increasingly emphasized the need to transform people's thinking and not just their social organization. In the Great Proletarian Cultural Revolution of 1966 "the thought of Chairman Mao" was to replace Marxism-Leninism as the major source of ideological guidance in China's political life.

In an indirect way, however, the need for a "cultural revolution" affirmed Marxism in that it emphasized that a society would have to pass through a set of discrete stages of social, economic, and political development to realize "communism." The road to utopia was not to be shortened by organizational short-cuts.

The events of 1966–1969 are in part an admission that in cultural terms China remains largely a traditional peasant society. The organization and ideology have changed; yet the Confucian heritage endures in the personalities of the Chinese people. Mao, however, in his unwavering belief that his own revolutionary experience embodies a way to transform a peasant society—and driven by his intolerance of the traditional political culture—has sought ways of institutionalizing "continuous revolution" (*chi-hsü ko-ming*). Without this effort to sustain the process of social change in a peasant society, Mao came to feel, the revolution would succumb to the burden of the Confucian political heritage. China would see the reemergence of a social polarization between an elite leadership group and an exploited, dependent population; an increasingly antagonistic "contradiction" between modern, urban China, and a majority of the population which remained mired in rural poverty.

In the following sections of this chapter we will emphasize the personal values and political style which Mao brought to the process of defining a strategy for China's national development, and then summarize the main lines of leadership debate during the decade 1955–1964. In the next three chapters, we explore in detail the major events by means of which Mao has attempted to transform his conception of China's modernization process into functioning political institutions.

TOWARD THE AUTONOMY OF THE GROUP

As we saw in Part Three, Mao's personal involvement in the revolution and the resistance against Japan revealed his rejection of the passive and dependent quality of the traditional political order. His own aggressiveness merged with that of an age in which the Chinese people, as a society, were attempting to reassert themselves as a major center of world civilization. In this process, shocked into life by a series of military clashes with commercially ambitious foreigners and a great peasant rebellion, Chinese intellectuals slowly came to question the basic assumptions of Confucian culture.

The literati who led the "self strengthening" movement of the late nineteenth century had initially concluded that China's "spiritual essence" could be defended through the selective use of Western technology. More conservative Confucianists, however, saw with greater clarity the manner in which the adoption of this foreign material culture would begin to undermine established bases of power, and the social values that supported them. And from the treaty ports, missionary participants in the ferment of these times pointed out through Chinese language periodicals some of the basic cultural differences which hindered the adaptation of Western technology to established Chinese purposes. They stressed that "the Western peoples looked to the future for fulfillment while the Chinese wished to return to the past," and asserted that "the Confucian moral culture was defective in that it did not emphasize the autonomy (*tzu-chu,* literally 'being one's own master') of each individual." [7]

It was only in the deepening unrest of the May Fourth era after 1919, however—a period of cultural challenge which followed the failures of "self-strengthening" and efforts to establish parliamentary democracy in China—that there developed a vague awareness among the intellectuals that China's difficulties in adjusting to a new era in some way were related to the social orientation of dependency. The spokesmen for this perception were the angered students who saw in the failures of their elders the corruption and weakness of the Confucian cultural heritage. Writing in the influential radical magazine *New Youth* in 1916, Ch'en Tu-hsiu, who five years later was to be a founder of the Chinese Communist Party, revealed the degree to which rejection of Confucian dependence and self-assertion had become the strivings of a revolutionary generation:

> There are three sacred virtues under this Confucian doctrine: *chung* (loyalty), *hsiao* (filiality), and *chieh* (chastity), which are the morals of a slave and not of an independent person. The conduct of a man

7. Cited in Kwang-ching Liu, "Nineteenth-Century China: The Disintegration of the Old Order and the Impact of the West," in Ping-ti Ho and Tang Tsou, eds., *China in Crisis* (Chicago: University of Chicago Press), Vol. I, p. 140.

should be self-centered. Without this self-centeredness, other acts are meaningless. The morals of a slave are not self-centered, therefore every act of a slave is dependent on someone else. Those who proudly regard themselves as the youth of 1916 should struggle to get rid of this dependency and to restore their independent personalities.[8]

Whatever appeals may have existed for a "Western solution" to these strivings for a new cultural orientation—as in the valuation of individualism—were undermined largely by the Westerners themselves. The first Great European War of 1914–1918, and the sense of grievance which Chinese derived from the Versailles peace settlement—in which German concessions in Shantung Province were turned over to Japanese control—seriously degraded the stature of the West in the eyes of China's intellectuals. And in the Bolshevik Revolution of 1917 some began to see an alternative road to national resurgence.

The 1920s and '30s were decades in which China's social leadership became increasingly divided in the search for a world outlook. The Nationalists, under Chiang K'ai-shek, attempted a Confucian revival;[9] and the first leaders of the Chinese Communist movement adhered closely to the Russian revolutionary precedent. In Mao Tse-tung's political career one begins to see an uncertain but persistent effort to define a Chinese way of national development, combining both rejection and innovation within China's own social traditions.

The assertiveness which Mao has displayed throughout his life underscores the degree to which he personally rejects the tradition of dependence on authority. During the Party rectification movement of the early 1940s Mao urged an end to the tradition of uncritical obedience to those in authority: "In order to get rid of the practise of acting blindly which is so common in our Party, we must encourage our comrades to think, to learn the method of analysis and to cultivate the habit of analysis. There is all too little of this habit in our Party."[10] In his policy planning, Mao has revealed a sensitivity to the dependency needs of the population, and to the possibility of the Party being "eaten up" by those who look to authority for security:

In the big cities, food and fuel are now [1948] the central prob-

8. Ch'en Tu-hsiu, "1916," in *New Youth (Hsin Ch'ing Nien)*, Vol. I, No. 5 (January 1916), p. 3.

9. *See* Mary C. Wright, *The Last Stand of Chinese Conservatism: The T'ung Chih Restoration, 1862–1874* (New York: Atheneum, 1966), Ch. XII.

10. Mao, "Our Study and the Current Situation" (1944), *SW*, English, III, p. 175.

lems; they must be handled in a planned way. Once a city comes under our administration, the problem of the livelihood of the city poor must be solved step by step and in a planned way. Do not raise the slogan, "Open the granaries to relieve the poor." Do not foster among them the psychology of depending on the government for relief.[11]

In an earlier day, however, Mao evinced the politician's awareness that only by fulfilling the broad popular expectations toward government characteristic of the politics of dependency could the Party gain active support for its cause:

> We must lead the peasants' struggle for land and distribute the land to them, heighten their labour enthusiasm and increase agricultural production, safeguard the interests of the workers, establish co-operatives, develop trade with outside areas, and solve the problems facing the masses—food, shelter and clothing, fuel, rice, cooking oil and salt, sickness and hygiene, and marriage. In short, all the practical problems in the masses' everyday life should claim our attention. If we attend to these problems, solve them and satisfy the needs of the masses, we shall really become organizers of the well-being of the masses, and they will truly rally round us and give us their warm support. Comrades, will we then be able to arouse them to take part in the revolutionary war? Yes, indeed we will.[12]

Mao's writings thus reveal a paradoxical orientation toward the dependency theme in Chinese culture which is based on the demands of power: The leader seeking revolutionary change finds a valuable goal in the strength and dignity of critical self-integrity; yet the practical politician perceives that dealing effectively with the needs and habits of the people must be the Party's role if power is to be attained.

Mao's resolution of this "contradiction" between his own valuation of self-reliance and the legacy of a culture which stressed dependence on authority has been to stress the autonomy of the group —to have the individual find self-realization in a mutually supporting community of equals, rather than through submissive reliance on hierarchical authority. Like his cultural forebears Mao rejects as "selfishness" the assertion of the individual apart from collective purposes; yet his personal sensitivity to the oppressiveness of authority has led him to seek ways of shifting power away from one dominant individual to the group.

---

11. Mao, "Telegram to the Headquarters of the Loyang Front after the Recapture of the City" (1948), *SW*, English, IV, p. 248.

12. Mao, "Be Concerned with the Well-Being of the Masses, Pay Attention to Methods of Work" (1934), *SW*, English, I, pp. 147–148.

This stress on the self-reliant group has been most obvious to foreign observers in Mao's assertion of national independence. As he wrote in 1945, when even the Soviet Union had proven itself to be an uncertain ally through its declaration of continuing recognition and support for Chiang K'ai-shek's Nationalist government:

> On what basis should our policy rest? It should rest on our own strength, and that means regeneration through one's own efforts (*tzu-li keng-sheng*). We are not alone (*pu ku-li,* not isolated), all the countries and people in the world opposed to imperialism are our friends. Nevertheless, we stress regeneration through our own efforts. Relying on the forces we ourselves organize, we can defeat all Chinese and foreign reactionaries. Chiang K'ai-shek, on the contrary, relies entirely on the aid of U.S. imperialism, which he looks upon as his mainstay.[13]

And in an attempt to destroy with his pen whatever hopes educated and Western-oriented Chinese might have had of depending on United States intervention in the final phase of the civil war, Mao contemptuously wrote of the "belly ache" that would come from eating foreign fish:

> The Americans have sprinkled some relief flour in Peiping, Tientsin and Shanghai to see who will stoop to pick it up. Like Chiang Tai Kung fishing, they have cast the line for the fish who want to be caught. But he who swallows food handed out in contempt will get a belly ache.[14]

Mao's stress on the autonomy of the group was to find varied expression in the years after Liberation: in the domestic effort to build self-reliant agricultural communities through mass mobilization; in the full assertion of independence from the Soviet Union; and in the attempt to maintain the People's Liberation Army as a mass fighting and production organization, in which hierarchical authority would be played down through abolition of the symbols of rank and promotion of regular social contact between officers and enlisted ranks.

THE LEGACY OF THE REVOLUTION

Mao provided a combination of personal values and institutional forms in defining a strategy of national development which has characterized his leadership of the revolution. Three aspects of his conception of the political process seem to define the areas where

13. Mao, "The Situation and Our Policy after the Victory in the War of Resistance against Japan" (1945), *SW*, English, IV, p. 20.
14. Mao, "Farewell, Leighton Stuart!" (1949), *SW*, English, IV, p. 437.

he departs from or merges with China's traditional political culture, and where he has put himself in conflict with other Party leaders.

1) *The Importance of Struggle.* The area where Mao most notably departs from Chinese tradition—and where he brushes aside Confucian fears of *luan*—concerns his stress on mobilization and struggle. As was explored in Part Three, Mao saw political conflict as "awakening" people out of that passivity which characterized political dependency. He came to believe that if the Party forced confrontations with sources of social resentment and discontent even peasants could become "conscious" and mobilized to the revolutionary cause. Grievance-telling and study were institutionalized during the Yenan period and were designed to enhance people's awareness of their social enemies. The criticism and struggle meetings which were a product of both Party rectification and land reform formalized conflict with opponents of the revolution.

Military action, of course, most fully expressed Mao's commitment to struggle; yet the martial spirit has been no end in itself. By merging military organization with the tasks of economic production—another Yenan development which was to be reapplied during the Great Leap Forward—Mao has sought to institutionalize the "liberation" of those aggressive emotions which, denied legitimate expression in Confucian society, could promote social change.[15]

In the post-Liberation period, the continuing series of political and economic campaigns (*yün-tung*) express most fully Mao's commitment to struggle. By mobilizing the resentments and energies of an entire population for concerted action in periodic surges of activity, and by requiring individuals to criticize the erroneous thinking and behavior of themselves and their cohorts, Mao has attempted to sustain the momentum of social revolution.

2) *The Authority of the Group.* A second dimension of Mao's political style is his effort to shift authority away from its personalized, hierarchical form to group processes. Where Confucian culture placed authority beyond criticism, Mao merged his commitment to struggle with a belief that authority was generated from group life, and he sought to institutionalize forms which would subject even Party authorities to group pressures.

In student days Mao revealed a belief that those in power should be criticized for their errors, but on the basis of principles, not per-

15. Franz Schurmann has suggested that the merging of "war and production" through organization was one of the great innovations of Chinese Communist leadership. *See Ideology and Organization in Communist China* (Berkeley: University of California Press, 1968), p. 425.

sonal attack.[16] And as a Party member he came to see that an ideology could further depersonalize authority, by providing standards for criticism. The experience of the revolution, however, revealed how difficult it was both to sustain criticism and to keep it depersonalized; and in the post-Liberation era Mao eventually came into conflict with other Party leaders who resisted his efforts to subject the Party to criticism from "outside" groups.

When his own control over China's political institutions began to slip away after the failure of the Great Leap Forward, Mao saw that he had to repersonalize authority in order to maintain his impact on the shaping of China's new social institutions. But as we shall see in Chapter XIX, even in this effort he was seeking ways of subjecting those in authority to group criticism. The image of the Paris Commune has remained for Mao and other radical Chinese leaders a vital symbol of the people creating and criticizing their own leadership, just as the People's Commune became an ideal of group self-reliance in economic productivity. The problem has been, and remains, how to institutionalize these ideals in a society with enduring traditions of hierarchical leadership.

Group processes have provided some of the most potent forms of social control in post-Liberation China; and they further merge Mao's commitment to struggle with collective authority. In Part Three we saw that Mao's basic strategy of political conflict has been to unite as large a group as possible against a handful of isolated enemies. In terms of the workings of personality, the effectiveness of this approach is based on individual fears of being isolated from group support and standing alone before the angered "masses." In this process, Mao draws on the traditional dependence of the individual on group life, and anxieties about aggression, as bases of political integration.

Group processes also provided a way of generating the authority which traditionally had stood above those in subordination. The search for individual models of revolutionary behavior in group activities who can be used as objects of mass emulation, in Mao's view, enables the people to produce leaders from their own midst. And in post-1949 China there has been a constant search for and propagation of model citizens and workers—individuals used by the Party as authoritative examples of how the people in new China are to build a modern society.

Model production experiences have also played a key role in the leadership process by providing lower-level cadres with examples

16. This incident is recounted in Jerome Chen, *Mao and the Chinese Revolution*, p. 43.

to follow in the promotion of their work. And as we shall see, it was in terms of competing models of the development process that China's leaders came to express their increasingly divisive conflict in the 1960s.

The stress on learning through model emulation draws on traditional forms of education, just as the stress on group life adapts enduring themes in China's political culture to contemporary political tasks. As we shall stress in the conclusion, the need for those in authority to be increasingly manipulative in the use of model experiences and "thinking" reveals the distance between Mao's objective of well-institutionalized group processes which will give genuine authority to the people, and the increasing reliance which, in fact, has been placed on traditional forms of political control. The dividing line between innovation and restoration is often very thin, and at the end of his career Mao has had to make increasingly greater adjustments to the fact that for all his revolutionary insights, China's traditional culture persists in the personalities of his people.

3) *The Need for Study.* A third major aspect of Mao's political style which was institutionalized during the period of revolution is his stress on mass political education. Unlike the traditional deference and loyalty to an individual teacher, Mao has sought to make ideology a more impersonal basis for "rectifying" the social outlook of the Chinese people. One senses that his conviction is that if only China's seven hundred millions would learn the insights about society and politics which were central to his own political awakening, they would be able to build a new society based on coordinated group life. Hence, he has sought to propagate his "thought," his own social experience, as a model worthy of emulation.

Ideological unity, moreover, serves as the basis of group solidarity and provides the people with standards of behavior by which they can criticize those leaders who "deviate" in their use of authority. As was true in traditional China, there is no legitimacy given to divergence of opinion; and Mao, like imperial leaders of an earlier time, assumes that social unity is possible only on the basis of unified thinking. Here again, the dividing line between ideological study as a foundation for personal initiative and the traditional assertion of authority through memorization of the word is very thin. In the early 1960s conflict between Mao and Liu Shao-ch'i was to develop over whose "word"—whose book and thought—was to serve as the basis for China's new socialist unity and national development. And in the turmoil which followed the first months of the Cultural Revolution Mao was increasingly to use study of his little red book of quotations as a method of reimposing social order and discipline.

TOWARD A STRATEGY OF NATIONAL
DEVELOPMENT: A DECADE OF DEBATE

The major dimensions of Mao's political style are continually visible throughout the increasingly divisive debate among Party leaders during the decade 1955–1964. The question first at issue was the most appropriate strategy for China's national development; but by the end of this decade, the Party leadership was to be rent by an uncompromising struggle for control of the decision-making process in the People's Republic, and conflict over who was to be Mao's "revolutionary successor" to Party leadership.

The initial differences among Party leaders concerned whether China's problems in national development were primarily political and social in nature, or whether a major emphasis on economic reconstruction would produce a nation-state of power and wealth. Many of the leaders apparently felt that the question of "who will win" in the revolutionary struggle had been solved by the mid-1950s, and that primary emphasis should be given to economic development through technical change. The Party, through its army, the public security forces, and the newly created governmental system and mass organizations, seemed successfully to have replaced the structures of Nationalist control in both the urban and rural areas. Mao, however, increasingly came to define the problems of development in political and cultural terms. As his chosen successor Lin Piao recalled, Mao had asserted in 1956 that "the question of which will win out, socialism or capitalism, is still not really settled." [17]

Mao's personal sensitivities made him ever aware of those traditional misuses of authority which he had spent a lifetime opposing. With the creation of the Party's own political system, he increasingly came to see the danger of the emergence of a new exploitative ruling elite which would resort to the old traditional abuses—material self-indulgence, suppression of criticism, and bureaucratic entrenchment—forms of asserting authority which would "cut the Party off from the masses." To the degree that his life-time colleagues did not share this sensitivity to misuses of power—as he was to discover in the Hundred Flowers episode of 1957—Mao came to question their commitment to revolution. And as they resisted those of his policies which were designed to eliminate such problems, he came to see them as "right opportunists" or "revisionists" and eventually as active "counterrevolutionaries."

17. Lin Piao, "Report to the Ninth Party Congress of the Communist Party of China," *SCMP*, No. 4406 (May 1, 1969), p. 15.

This polarization of good and evil reflects the sharpening of the leadership conflict that emerged from the failure of the Great Leap Forward; but in the mid-1950s differences among Party leaders were still "non-antagonistic." Documents from this period indicate that different individuals and groups within the leadership looked to different social problems as the focal areas of national reconstruction. They tended to define their strategies in terms of which social class was to be the Party's main ally during the period of transition to socialism. And in a striking manner, the evolution of Party policy during this period replays the pattern of class coalition and leadership "deviation" which characterized the decades of struggle for power.

The years from the Liberation to mid-1957 were a period of reliance on China's intellectuals, the "bourgeoisie" (in the sense of an urbanized, technical elite educated before the revolution), in an attempt to build the economy on the Soviet Union's pattern of modernization. "Heavy industry received the bulk of investment funds (including Soviet aid) and made notable advances, while agriculture and consumer goods were relatively neglected." [18] Like the revolutionary period of 1921–1927—when Comintern advisers played a key role in Party construction, in formulating the alliance with the "bourgeois" Kuomintang, and in the urban focus of the revolution—Soviet advisers exercised a heavy influence over China's post-Liberation economic, military, and social policies.

Mao was leader of both Party and state during this period, but evidence indicates that he was only first among equals in his influence over policy-making. Furthermore, his leadership may have come under serious challenge. In 1955 it was revealed that Kao Kang, head of the Party's Northeast Bureau and Chairman of the State Planning Commission, had formed an "anti-Party" clique with Jao Shu-shih of the Shanghai Party apparatus, and had attempted an "unprincipled" takeover of the leadership from their "independent kingdoms." [19] Mao seems to have drawn two lessons from this challenge which later expressed themselves in coherent policies:

18. Audrey Donnithorne, *China's Economic System* (London: George Allen and Unwin, 1967), p. 17.

19. The exact nature of the Kao-Jao affair has remained obscure, and what little evidence is available suggests that Mao was not directly challenged but that Kao and Jao directed their activities at men like Liu Shao-ch'i and Chou En-lai. There has been speculation that Mao was sick at this time, and that the factional struggle in late 1953 and early 1954, culminating in the Fourth Plenum of the Seventh Central Committee, was on the order of a premature succession crisis. *See* Frederick Teiwes, "The Evolution of Leadership Purges in Communist China," *The China Quarterly*, No. 41 (January–March 1970), pp. 122–126.

First, it was clear that the modernized sectors of Chinese society—in this case the relatively small centers of industrial economy in Manchuria and Shanghai—could make powerful claims on limited state resources. The highly organized nature of these sectors (as was also to be the case with the army and Party) enabled them to serve as influential bases from which the political leadership could be challenged. Second, one may speculate that Mao saw in Kao's challenge one more indication of Russian interference in China's domestic leadership struggles. At least he had another example of Chinese leaders being "misled" by Soviet policy precedents.[20]

In any event, it is clear that by mid-1955 Mao began to express concern publicly about the stress on industrialization at the expense of the agricultural sector and about the tendency of Party members blindly to emulate the Soviet development experience. In his first major post-Liberation statement on agricultural policy he warned, "on no account should we allow . . . comrades to use the Soviet experience as a cover for their idea of moving at a snail's pace." [21] As with his earlier reaction to Ch'en Tu-hsiu's "rightist" deviation, Mao saw some of his colleagues endangering the progress of the revolution by adhering too closely to the Russian precedent. In this case the stress on industrial development conflicted with his own evaluation of the agricultural sector as the focal area of China's development problems. And in response to those who dragged their feet in finding a radical solution to problems of production in the countryside, Mao invoked his characteristic irony by observing

20. There has been speculation that Stalin, distrustful of the assertive Mao, attempted to encourage Kao Kang as an alternative Party leader. Kao emerged as the dominant figure in the "Northeast People's Government" established in Manchuria in 1948, and went to Moscow several months before the founding of the People's Republic to sign a trade agreement with the Soviet Government on behalf of the Manchurian regime.

After Liberation, almost all of his public appearances were associated with official Russian visitors. There has been no direct evidence, however, that Stalin actively interfered in leadership struggles within the Chinese Party through Kao, as he had done earlier in the case of Wang Ming—and as Khrushchev encouraged P'eng Teh-huai in 1959 (*see* pp. 390–392 below). The most detailed examination of evidence on this subject to date is Frederick C. Teiwes, *Rectification Campaigns and Purges in Communist China* (unpublished Ph.D. dissertation, Columbia University, New York, 1970), Ch. X.

Franz Schurmann has documented the relationship between the rise of the "one man management" system of industrial organization in Manchuria and the career of Kao Kang. See *Ideology and Organization in Communist China,* pp. 266–287.

21. Mao, "On the Question of Agricultural Co-operation" (1955), in *Selected Readings from the Works of Mao Tse-tung* (Peking: Foreign Languages Press, 1967), p. 331.

that, "some of our comrades are tottering along like a woman with bound feet and constantly complaining, 'You're going too fast.' " [22]

Mao's estimation was that this major problem area in development required a "vertical" alliance between the Party ("the working class") and those who constituted a majority of the population, the peasantry. He asserted that without a radical effort to attain "socialist" ownership in China's countryside, a capitalist, rich-peasant economy would soon emerge and bring about a new polarization between rich and poor in the villages. Only by creating "common prosperity"—that is, by eliminating wide disparities in income among the rural population—could the Party hold the loyalty and gain the active support of the poor and lower-middle peasants. ". . . this is the only way to consolidate the worker-peasant alliance. Otherwise, this alliance will be in real danger of breaking up." [23]

Mao's position, formally expressed in a twelve-year program for agricultural development which was presented in draft form in January 1956, apparently was overruled by a majority of those in the Party leadership who saw the key to China's progress in industrialization. These "economic" developers held that the major problem lay in encouraging China's precious few intellectuals to lend their skills to the Party's cause. Stress on the technical aspects of economic progress called for a "horizontal" alliance with the urban intellectuals who held such skills. These "economic" leaders saw the major deviational danger as "leftist" in the sense of sectarianism or exclusive attitudes toward non-Party intellectuals by those within the Party (like Mao) who tended to look with suspicion or contempt on this "bourgeoisie."

When Soviet Party First Secretary Nikita Khrushchev unexpectedly attacked Stalin and the "personality cult" in February 1956, opponents of Mao's "worker-peasant" alliance acquired the issue of an overly-assertive Party leader whose abandonment of collective leadership had brought great harm to a Party. This event in the Soviet Union apparently strengthened the collective decision-making process in China and led to the overruling of Mao's agricultural development plan in April of 1956.[24] The impact of Khrushchev's anti-Stalin attack on leadership conflict within the Chinese Communist Party can hardly be overstressed. In fact, Mao has dated the inception of the Sino-Soviet dispute from this event.

22. *Ibid.*, p. 316.
23. *Ibid.*, p. 334.
24. *See* Schurmann, *Ideology and Organization in Communist China,* pp. 142–143.

The upheavals in Poland and Hungary in the fall of 1956 (events also triggered by de-Stalinization) appear to have shifted the coalition of power within the Party leadership more in Mao's favor in the development debate. While the public Party interpretation of these events was that "counterrevolutionary" elements had taken advantage of domestic problems in Hungary, Mao drew the conclusion that even in a country which was in the process of "building socialism," the Party and governmental systems were vulnerable to "degeneration." [25] And he stressed to Chinese Party members that, "in order to get rid of the root cause of disturbances, we must stamp out bureaucracy." [26]

With his hand thus strengthened by the events in Eastern Europe, Mao sought to apply his conception of controlled struggle between those social groups still "mutually related and mutually antagonistic." His aim was to check "conservatism" and abuses of authority by lower-level Party and government cadres and to criticize "antisocialist" attitudes held by people both within and outside the Party. He apparently felt that if the intellectuals were given a constructive role in China's new socialist political process, their energies would be "liberated" in the service of Party rectification and national development. In the Hundred Flowers period of public "blooming and contending" during the spring of 1957, Mao sought to establish a critical dialogue between the Party and the intellectuals.

The criticism encouraged by Mao and his supporters, however, came to exceed the bounds of attack on lower-level cadres. Many intellectuals and students challenged the Communist Party's basic monopoly of decision-making power and the appropriateness of

25. This perception was eventually expressed formally in public polemics with the Soviet Union. (*See* "On Khrushchev's Phoney Communism and Its Historical Lessons for the World" [1964], *Polemic on the General Line of the International Communist Movement* [Peking: Foreign Languages Press, 1965], p. 468.) And when "revisionism" had revealed itself even within the leadership ranks of the Chinese Party, Mao was to claim that through the Great Proletarian Cultural Revolution "a new era in the history of the international Communist movement" had opened. Through this mass movement he had found a solution to the problem of leadership degeneration—a danger not perceived before in the history of the movement. (*See* the *People's Daily* and *Red Flag* joint editorial, "Carry the Great Proletarian Cultural Revolution through to the End"; trans. in *Peking Review* [Peking], No. 1 [January 1, 1967], p. 8.)

26. Mao, "On the Correct Handling of Contradictions among the People" (1957); trans. in *Communist China, 1955–1959* (Cambridge, Mass.: Harvard University Press, 1962), p. 291. Hereafter, this collection of documents will be cited as *CC 1955–59*.

some of the Party's most fundamental policies. Party leaders characterized the events of the spring of 1957 as the "betrayal" of April 1927 all over again:[27] The "bourgeoisie" were unreliable allies in the development process; and an urban-centered strategy which stressed their skills would only put responsibility and resources in disloyal hands and undermine Party leadership. In the "anti-rightist" reaction to the events of the spring the Party reasserted its leading role, and Mao "retreated" to a rural-centered strategy of development.

While Mao's personal sponsorship of the Hundred Flowers policy may have temporarily diluted his political influence among those leaders who questioned his approach to Party rectification through criticism from the "outside," the events of the spring (and continuing problems of agricultural production) strengthened his assertion that development could not proceed through a strategy which placed primary reliance on the skills of disloyal "bourgeois" intellectuals. His earlier call for a twelve-year program of agricultural development, which placed primary reliance on the mass energies of China's majority rural population, was revived in October 1957; and in the years of 1958–1960, Mao sought to convince those colleagues who were tottering along with "bound feet" that through mobilization of the peasantry the country could make a "great leap forward." This was a new "Kiangsi" era in its stress on rural action: The peasants were organized into military units for production, and on all fronts there was a "leftist" effort to wage an adventuresome war with the forces hindering social and economic change in the countryside.

Through the "three red flag" policies of the Great Leap period, Mao attempted to adapt the methods of political mobilization and control developed during the struggle for power to the tasks of economic development. In effect, he was saying that where the Soviet experience was inappropriate to China's specific conditions and problems, the precedent of China's (Mao's) own revolutionary experience provided the shortest road to national greatness. In suggesting that the People's Communes had placed China on the verge of realizing communism[28]—and by implication ahead of the Soviet Union—Mao was trying to reassert the legitimacy of his revolution

27. This characterization was explicitly drawn by P'eng Chen, First Secretary of the Peking Party Committee. (*See SCMP,* No. 1588 [August 12, 1957], p. 2.)

28. The most detailed analysis of Chinese claims that the communes would enable the country to realize communism in the near future—and the impact of these claims on Sino-Soviet relations—will be found in Donald S. Zagoria, *The Sino-Soviet Conflict, 1956–1961* (Princeton: Princeton University Press, 1962), Ch. III.

in the wake of the attack on Stalin, with whom he had so closely identified himself.

The production crisis which resulted from the overly-ambitious and ill-planned Great Leap effort produced, however, a new "long march," both in the sense of a seven-year period of recovery to the level of production which had been reached in 1958,[29] and in Mao's loss of influence among his top Party colleagues. The failures of the Great Leap revealed that there were new critics like Wang Ming among the Party leadership, men who continued to see the Soviet experience as an appropriate developmental model.

Evidence suggests that as with Stalin's earlier sponsorship of Chinese Party members as a way of gaining influence in a potentially rival Party, the Russians probably encouraged first P'eng Teh-huai, and then other "revisionists" within the Chinese Party, to criticize Mao's leadership. Mao was beginning to present a major challenge to their own national policies and their primacy within the International Communist Movement. The period 1959–1966 was a time of increasing conflict among Chinese Party leaders. The escalation in Sino-Soviet tensions during this period seems intimately related to Mao's effort to undercut the arguments of his domestic critics who may have sought to justify less radical approaches to China's national development in terms of "socialist" precedents in Yugoslavia and the Soviet Union.

At the 1959 Lushan Central Committee Plenum Mao successfully met P'eng Teh-huai's challenge to his development policies; but in the deepening leadership crisis Mao apparently was compelled to repeat the earlier pattern of his rise to Party control. He turned to the army to rebuild a power base as his influence over Party and governmental organizations slipped away. Under the leadership of the ever-loyal Lin Piao, who replaced P'eng as Defense Minister, the People's Liberation Army became a new source of support for the aging leader and a testing ground for new approaches to political indoctrination and control which would institutionalize Mao's conceptions of political action and social organization.

During the "three difficult years" of food shortage and natural disasters which forced a pullback from the Great Leap effort, Party control was relaxed in the villages. Mao apparently watched with growing concern as the peasants asserted their own approaches to restoring production in the countryside. Many sought to withdraw

29. *See* Alexander Eckstein, "Economic Planning, Organization and Control in Communist China: A Review Article," *Current Scene* (Hong Kong: United States Consulate General), Vol. IV, No. 21 (November 25, 1966), p. 1.

from collective farming, and resumed traditional social practices. Local cadres took advantage of their positions to increase their own incomes while others were verging on starvation.

At the Tenth Central Committee Plenum in September 1962, Mao called for renewed promotion of "socialist education" in the countryside to combat the reemergence of "capitalist tendencies" and stated forcefully that the Party must continue to wage "class struggle" with traditional practices still evident among its cadres and the population at large.

The ensuing years of the Socialist Education Campaign were a time of qualitative change in relations among Party leaders. Some who disagreed with Mao's policies on Party rectification and leadership in the rural areas apparently expressed their disagreement by applying the Chairman's line in such an extreme way that support would be lost. Even though Mao remained the symbol of national resurgence, he complained that his opponents' practices were "left in form but right in essence"; they "waved red flags" of deference to him even as they "opposed the red flag" of his policies.

In the summer of 1964 which apparently was *the* critical period of change in relations among Party leaders, Mao publicly raised the issue of "cultivating revolutionary successors." He thus reopened the question of who was to follow him in the leadership of Party and nation. The army was put forward as a model organization in a national campaign that by implication slighted the leading role of the Party. Organizationally, political departments patterned on army practice appeared in the Party and in governmental agencies; and in the next two years army personnel were increasingly to fill these supervisory roles. In retrospect it is clear that Mao, through Lin Piao and the army, was explicitly challenging the power base of those whom he now considered to be his opponents.

The precise reasons for the timing of the breakdown in relations among Party leaders and the opening of public conflict during 1966 —a period when the war in Viet-Nam seemed to involve serious threats to China's security—remain obscure. However, from the vantage point of 1970 it seems clear that Mao's objectives in the Cultural Revolution were to remove from power those leaders whom he saw opposing his development and foreign policies and to reestablish his "thought" as the guide to China's national development. Now in his seventies, and reportedly in uncertain health, Mao saw this effort as requiring both the aid of the loyal and more youthful—if scarcely more healthy—Lin Piao, and the support of China's younger generation.

In the Cultural Revolution of 1966–1969 Mao vicariously relived his own political career in the struggles of the student Red

Guards whom he set against "revisionists" within the Party. In declaring to the young intellectuals that Marxism's essence was the notion that "to rebel is justified," Mao was trying to transmit to a new generation the spirit of his own youthful rebellion against established authority. But now the "establishment" was a Party and governmental system which had proven itself increasingly resistant to his influence.

The Eleventh Central Committee Plenum of August 1966 was for Mao another Tsunyi meeting in that it reaffirmed his control over Chinese political life. And the Ninth Party Congress of April 1969 was a new Seventh Congress, reestablishing the guiding role of "the thought of Mao Tse-tung" in the life of the Chinese Communist Party.

*   *   *

The emphasis in this overview on the parallel political rhythms of the periods of revolution and post-Liberation reconstruction is a way of stressing the continuity that Mao has revealed in his personal political style. Also, many of the social issues which Mao confronted as he sought ways of transforming Chinese society have shown remarkable endurance. The conflict over a development strategy which characterized Party leadership relations from the mid-1950s also emphasizes that Mao has remained determined to prevent what he sees as the "restoration" of China's traditional political culture in either elite abuses of authority, a new class polarization in the villages, or an increasing disparity between urban and rural life. The Hundred Flowers period of 1957, the Great Leap Forward of 1958–1960, and the Cultural Revolution of 1966–1969 are the three post-Liberation periods when Mao's personal style has had its greatest impact on China's political life. In the following chapters, we will explore in greater detail aspects of these periods which reveal Mao's efforts to institutionalize the political legacy of the revolution.

Chapter XVII

ONE PARTY AND
"ONE HUNDRED SCHOOLS":
LEADERSHIP, LETHARGY, OR *LUAN?*

> Bourgeois reactionary thinking has invaded
> the militant [Chinese] Communist Party!
> Certain Communist Party members claim to
> have learned Marxism. Where has it gone?
>
> MAO TSE-TUNG.
> May 1951.[1]

With consolidation of basic military and political control of the China mainland the Communist Party leadership faced a problem that had confronted the founders of past dynasties: how to "dismount from the horse" of military conquest and administer a vast peasant empire. Traditionally this problem had embodied a great paradox, especially for those dynasties established by nomadic invaders committed to a martial style of life. If control of this extensive, decentralized society were to be achieved, the dynasty had to gain the active cooperation of the Confucian-oriented rural gentry who provided the major source of literate imperial administrators. Yet in gaining the cooperation of this indigenous elite, concessions had to be made to their style of life and control of local resources, thus perpetuating a life style which was an appealing—and "corrupting"—alternative to the martial virtues of a conquest genera-

---

1. *People's Daily* editorial, "We Must Give Attention to Discussing the Film 'The Life of Wu Hsün' " (May 20, 1951).

During the Cultural Revolution of 1966–1969 it was revealed that this editorial was one of several written personally by Mao Tse-tung in the early 1950s criticizing the "bourgeois reactionary thinking" of Party intellectuals. This fact emphasizes the continuity of Mao's concern with the problem of intellectuals "corrupting" the Party's revolutionary commitment because of their "backward" or "antisocialist" attitudes.

tion. If given sufficient time, the Confucian gentry could "absorb" —or more accurately, "convert"—their conquerors.

For the Chinese Communists this old paradox was sharpened with a new and double edge. Basically, the Party leadership was committed to a program of national resurgence through social change and economic modernization, yet the necessary political commitment and technical skills were in exceedingly short supply. Party membership in 1956 represented less than 3 percent of China's total population, more than 80 percent of which still eked out a living by ancient agricultural techniques in the rural districts. The "vanguard of the proletariat" was more than 70 percent a peasant organization, and workers comprised only 15 percent of total Party membership.[2] Hence, in the modernization effort there was a basic danger that the revolution might become submerged in the habits and life style of China's peasant majority.

The other edge of this problem was that only a small fraction of China's intellectuals, her small but highly-trained technical, administrative, educational, and artistic elite, appeared committed to the Party's cause. Hardly more than 10 percent of all Party members in 1956 were classified as intellectuals; and less than half of the country's total of approximately four million "high" and ordinary intellectuals were considered to be politically "progressive."[3] If development efforts were to proceed, considerable reliance would have to be placed on their skills; yet such reliance would give political influence and control of scarce resources to this small, urban, and largely foreign-trained "bourgeoisie."

In short, a small political elite committed to social and economic change saw its revolution threatened from both peasant conservatism and the life style of a small urban skill group. As Mao Tse-tung and his supporters phrased it in the mid-1950s, "Rightist conservative ideology . . . presents a most serious threat to our Party."[4]

There was significant divergence of opinion within the Party leadership, however, as to the actual strength of this threat, and

2. These figures are drawn from Franz Schurmann, *Ideology and Organization in Communist China,* pp. 128–139.

3. This evaluation was presented by Chou En-lai in his report, "On the Question of Intellectuals" (January 14, 1956); trans. in *CC 1955–59,* pp. 130–131.

4. *Ibid.,* p. 128.

Mao had stressed the dangers of "right opportunism" and "rightist conservatism" in his report of late July 1955, "On the Question of Agricultural Co-operation" (*see* the text in *Selected Readings from the Works of Mao Tse-tung,* esp. pp. 322, 330), and in his editorial notes of December of that same year in *Socialist Upsurge in China's Countryside* [Peking: Foreign Languages Press, 1957], esp. pp. 10, 12).

whether the greater danger was the "conservatism" of the peasantry or that of the intellectuals. Furthermore, there was disagreement as to the best method for dealing with these challenges to the primacy of "proletarian" values and goals. During the period of the First Five Year Plan (1953–1957) majority opinion within the Party leadership held that China's social revolution could best be promoted on the basis of a program which placed primary emphasis on rapid industrialization.[5] As a consequence, most Party leaders were willing to subordinate any sense of threat of "corruption" by the intellectuals to the need to gain their precious skills for the development effort. Hence, in contrast to Mao's emphasis on the danger from the "right," a number of important documents published during 1956 stressed the "leftist" danger of sectarianism on the part of Party members which would hinder cooperation with non-Party intellectuals.

An attitude of tolerance toward the intellectuals was most obvious at the Chinese Communist Party's Eighth Congress of September 1956. The Party's Vice Chairman Liu Shao-ch'i, in the main political report to the Congress, asserted: "The question of who will win in the struggle between socialism and capitalism in our country has now been decided," and he criticized "some members of our Party who hold that everything should absolutely be 'of one colour.' "[6] Perhaps the clearest expression of a conciliatory attitude toward "class" differences was contained in the report of the Party's Secretary-General, Teng Hsiao-p'ing, on the revision of the Party Constitution. In justifying less stringent standards for admission to Party membership Teng stressed:

> The difference between workers and office employees is now only a matter of division of labor within the same class. . . . The vast majority of our intellectuals have now come over politically to the side of the working class. . . . What is the point, then, of classifying these social strata into two different categories? And even if we were

5. This point of view was detailed in Li Fu-ch'un's report on the First Five Year Plan, delivered in July 1955, and reiterated in Liu Shao-ch'i's political report to the Party's Eighth Congress held in September of 1956.

6. Liu Shao-ch'i, "The Political Report of the Central Committee of the Communist Party of China to the Eighth National Congress of the Party" (September 15, 1956), in *Eighth National Congress of the Communist Party of China* (Peking: Foreign Languages Press, 1956), Vol. I, pp. 37, 74.

Liu was to be attacked for these words of tolerance toward class differences during the Cultural Revolution. *See* "The Third Confession of Liu Shao-ch'i," in *Chinese Law and Government*, Vol. I, No. 1 (Spring 1968), pp. 77–78.

to try and devise a classification, how could we make it neat and clear-cut? [7]

Teng's rhetorical question was very likely addressed to Mao who continued to hold different views. Within six months, the Party Chairman was to assert, "There can be no development without differentiation and struggle." [8] Such conflicting evaluations of the Party's relationship to the intellectual skill group which it sought to use in national development were the basis of leadership debates over the question of Party rectification during the years 1956–57. With the perspective of more than a decade of hindsight, this conflict can be seen to be part of a larger debate over the issue of the most appropriate "road" to China's national resurgence. Should there be moderately paced development, emphasizing economic construction in the urban areas, or should there be an intensely paced, politicized effort aimed primarily at bringing China's rural majority into the modern world through socialist forms of collective work organization?

In the following pages we will trace the evolution of leadership conflict over the question of Party rectification, and the effect on the mobilization of China's intellectuals in support of the development effort during the years 1956–57.

Mao's personal position in this period of debate seems to have been shaped by his enduring distrust of the intellectuals, although his major concern was a matter of the Party's "alliance" with this technical and administrative "bourgeoisie." He saw the stress on Soviet-style industrialization as giving excessive influence to "bourgeois" values *within* the Party and leading to a slighting of development in the rural areas.

In its simplest terms, the argument explored in this chapter is that in late 1955 Mao was persuaded of the need to win greater support from intellectuals in order to develop the economy, but that he was unwilling to accept passively their "rightist conservatism." Their working conditions should be improved, but they also should be expected to "remold" their bourgeois world outlook. This policy was considerably liberalized in application, however, as a result of "de-Stalinization" in the Soviet Union. Other Party leaders, some of whom were opposed to Mao's policies for developing the rural

7. Teng Hsiao-p'ing, "Report on the Revision of the Constitution of the Communist Party of China" (September 16, 1956), in *Eighth National Congress of the Communist Party of China,* Vol. I, pp. 213–214.

8. Mao Tse-tung, "Speech at the Chinese Communist Party's National Conference on Propaganda Work" (March 12, 1957), in *Selected Readings from the Works of Mao Tse-tung,* p. 399.

economy, used Khrushchev's February 1956 attack on Stalin to restrict Mao's influence over policy in the spring of 1956; and they diluted the struggle against "rightist conservatism" as they pressed their own conservative economic line. It was only after the upheaval in Hungary in late 1956 that Mao was able to reassert a policy of "unity and struggle" in the Party's relationship with the intellectuals. Then, however, as a result of the thwarting of his agricultural policies and the lesson of Hungary, the Party Chairman turned his attention to "right opportunism" within the Party itself.

The essence of Mao's "Hundred Flowers" policy, as he sought to apply it in the spring of 1957, was the effort to set intellectuals and Party cadres against each other in a critical debate which would expose and "rectify" improper behavior and attitudes held by each group. What at the time appeared to be an unprecedented move toward liberalization was really Mao's first major effort since the 1949 Liberation to combat "bourgeois" influences within the Party. This was a strategy—to use a phrase of the Cultural Revolution— which was "right in form but left in essence."

Mao's strategy of "unity and struggle" was resisted, however, by the Party apparatus, by cadres who objected to criticism "from the outside," and by other Party leaders who did not want to jeopardize the active support of non-Party intellectuals in the industrialization effort. Thus during 1956–57 there developed a shifting interplay between events in the Soviet Union and Eastern Europe, the balance of political influence within the Chinese Communist Party leadership, and the Party's relationship to the intellectuals.

"DE-STALINIZATION" AND DEVELOPMENT

In late 1955, as part of the promotion of the revised First Five Year Plan for the economy, the Party began efforts to improve relations with non-Party intellectuals. Apparently the initiative lay with such men as Li Fu-ch'un, Chairman of the State Planning Commission, and State Premier Chou En-lai. After several years of "thought re-form" and recently concluded national campaigns to discredit as "counterrevolutionaries" the writer Hu Feng and philosopher Hu Shih, the intellectual community showed signs of serious demoralization and a tendency to withdraw from active social involvement.[9]

9. Mao's close personal involvement in these campaigns has been revealed in Cultural Revolution materials. He is now identified as the author of editorial critiques on the Hu Feng affair which appeared in the *People's Daily* on May 20th, 24th, and June 10th, 1955. (*See* the pamphlet, *Mao Tse-tung Szu-hsiang Wan-sui!* [Long Live the Thought of Mao Tse-tung!] [n.p., April 1967], pp. 11–12, hereinafter cited as *Long Live the Thought of*

The Party's united front organizations, the National People's Congress and the Chinese People's Political Consultative Conference, made a survey of the nation's intellectuals and their working conditions. On January 14th, 1956, Chou En-lai addressed a select group of Party and non-Party intellectuals in an effort to improve the utilization of the country's scant technical, educational, and artistic resources.

Chou's report was a "Maoist" document to the extent that it stressed "opposition to rightist conservative ideology" as the Party's major task. He emphasized that the intellectuals needed to be given "political and professional leadership" by the Party. A policy of "unity and struggle" was evident in his presentation, for while he called for improved working conditions and a rationalization of the job assignments of non-Party intellectuals, he made it clear that their incorporation into the ranks of the revolution, "was a process that cannot possibly be free from certain struggle." [10]

Chou admitted that a major aspect of the problem of Party relations with the intellectuals was a matter of "sectarianism" on the part of Party cadres: "Some comrades easily get themselves estranged from intellectuals outside the Party, and even adopt the attitude of respecting them but keeping them at a distance. In this way, there is a lack of mutual understanding, and estrangement becomes the easier." [11] But he also emphasized "a tendency of passivity and an inclination towards compromise" with the intellectuals' political defects. And in a curious example of ideological juggling which seems to reveal Mao's hand in a compromise policy, the State Premier observed of "sectarianism" (a "left" deviation) and "rightist" tolerance: "The two tendencies are opposite to each other in form, but both of them in practise lead to a kind of rightist conservatism." [12]

Chou went on to note with indignation that some non-Party intellectuals

> refuse to study Marxism-Leninism, and even slander Marxism-Leninism. They belittle labor, belittle the laboring people, belittle the cadres who grew from the ranks of laborers, and are not willing to get together with workers, peasants, and worker and peasant cadres. . . .

Mao Tse-tung!) Analysis of these campaigns will be found in Merle Goldman, *Literary Dissent in Communist China* (Cambridge, Massachusetts: Harvard University Press, 1967), pp. 129–157.

10. Chou En-lai, "On the Question of Intellectuals," in *CC 1955–59*, p. 138.

11. *Ibid.*, p. 134.

12. *Ibid.*, p. 132.

They are vainglorious and look upon themselves as the best in the world, and will not accept the leadership and criticism of any other.[13]

Chou's report concluded with an attack on the "baseless view" that "the Party is not capable of leading intellectuals in scientific and cultural construction." [14]

In short, as of January 1956 the Party sought to combine political pressures and strengthened Party leadership with improvements in working facilities in an effort to "use" more effectively the nation's scanty scientific, intellectual and administrative resources in the process of "socialist construction."

Chou En-lai's encouraging, yet patronizing air was to receive three sharp jolts during the next eighteen months: Khrushchev's criticism of Stalin, the Polish and Hungarian uprisings, and the outspokenness of China's intellectuals against Communist Party rule. The first of these shocks came within six weeks when the Russian Communist Party leader Nikita Khrushchev, at the Twentieth Congress of the Soviet Communist Party, launched his unanticipated and officially secret attack on Stalin and the "cult of personality."

The Chinese Party's reaction to this Russian attack on Stalin's abuses of power was defensive, for in both organizational form and personal commitment it had closely identified itself with the man and his system of authority. In a major editorial on April 5th, 1956, the Party paper *People's Daily* summarized discussions held by the top leaders who admitted that,

> After the victory of the revolution . . . the leading personnel of the Party and state, beset by bureaucratism from many sides, face the great danger of using the machinery of state to take arbitrary action, alienating themselves from the masses and collective leadership, resorting to commandism, and violating Party and state democracy.[15]

The editorial went on to reaffirm the Party's commitment to the style of leadership which had brought it to power:

> . . . if we want to avoid falling into such a [Stalinist] quagmire, we must pay fullest attention to the use of the mass line method of leadership, not permitting the slightest negligence. To this end, *it is necessary for us to establish certain systems,* so as to ensure the thorough implementation of the mass line and collective leadership, to avoid elevation of oneself and individualist heroism.[16]

13. *Ibid.,* p. 136.
14. *Ibid.,* p. 143.
15. *People's Daily* editorial, "On the Historical Experience of the Dictatorship of the Proletariat" (April 5, 1956); trans. in *CC 1955–59,* p. 149.
16. *Ibid.* Emphasis added.

Mao Tse-tung was "ducking his head"—or having it ducked. His name was not mentioned once in the long editorial; and a quotation from his 1943 article "Some Questions Concerning Methods of Leadership," in which he had first spelled out the "mass line" concept, was cited only as "a Central Committee Resolution." The question in the minds of Party leaders was how serious would be the tendency of people within China to develop doubts about the Party and Mao as a result of Khrushchev's revelation of Stalin's errors.

The response of the Party "center" to this threat to its own legitimacy was two-fold: First, collective leadership was strengthened so as to avoid as much as possible the tendency to compare the "cult" of Stalin with the glorification of Mao.[17] And second, the

17. The Party's shift to collective leadership was emphasized by Teng Hsiao-p'ing in his report on the revision of the Party constitution delivered to the Eighth Party Congress in September 1956. Teng observed that, "It has become a long-established tradition in our Party to make decisions on important questions by a collective body of the Party, and not by any individual. Although violations of this principle of collective leadership have been frequent in our Party, yet once discovered, they have been criticized and rectified by the Central Committee." Teng then went on to quote from a Central Committee decision of late 1948 [only in 1960 identified as having been drafted by Mao—*see* pp. 398–399 below] which stresses the importance of the Party committee system in strengthening collective leadership. (*See* Teng's report in *Eighth National Congress of the Communist Party of China,* Vol. I, esp. pp. 192–195.)

It is open to interpretation whether Teng's remarks were intended to exonerate Mao of any "personality cult," or whether they were purposefully ironic. That the 1956 stress on collective leadership was "anti-Mao" in quality is suggested by other indications of opposition to the Chairman in that year: in the blocking of his twelve-year program for agricultural development in April; in the elimination of "Mao Tse-tung's thought" from the revised Party Constitution passed at the Eighth Party Congress; and more generally in Liu Shao-ch'i's dominant role at this Congress. Liu placed notable emphasis on collective leadership in his lengthy political report. (*See Eighth National Congress of the Communist Party of China,* Vol. I, pp. 103–104.)

Furthermore, during the Cultural Revolution, several leaders prominent at this time, such as Teng Hsiao-p'ing, were attacked for "parroting Khrushchev and in the name of 'opposing the personality cult,' [directing] the spearhead straight at Chairman Mao." (From a Red Guard pamphlet, "Thirty-three Leading Counterrevolutionary Revisionists," reprinted for circulation in the Canton area in March 1968; trans. in *Current Background* [Hong Kong: United States Consulate General], No. 874 [March 17, 1969], p. 5.) P'eng Teh-huai, the Defense Minister and a man who was to criticize Mao's "Great Leap" policies in 1959, was said to have been the one who suggested that "the thought of Mao Tse-tung" be deleted from the Eighth Party Constitution.

leadership tried to modify its relations with non-Party people so as to reduce tensions resulting from "sectarian" or "dogmatic" behavior on the part of Party cadres.

This latter effort merged with the leadership's earlier desire to enlist the support of the intellectuals in the development process. The key operative passage in the *People's Daily* editorial of April 5th sustained Chou En-lai's earlier call for an attitude of "unity and struggle" with the bourgeois intellectuals, but the emphasis was modified to the need for efforts to "shift them from their position of neutrality to one of alliance with us, for the purpose of facilitating the development of the revolution." [18]

The editorial's most obvious point of disagreement with Mao's position was its stress on the danger of Stalin's "leftist" error of directing the main blow of political struggle against "the middle-of-the-road social and political forces of the time." [19] The political implication in 1956 of this reevaluation of Stalin's policies seems to have been that a majority within the leadership feared that Mao's line of continuing to oppose "rightist conservatism" among the intellectuals would only create added problems for the Party in its relations with non-Party people.[20] These relations were already tense in the wake of the campaigns against Hu Feng and Hu Shih and now were given the added strain of Khrushchev's attack on Stalin with all that it implied for popular questioning of a Communist Party's right to a monopoly of political leadership.

The passage in the editorial which hinted that in order to sustain the "mass line" style of leadership it was "necessary for us to establish certain systems" does not appear to have reflected a clear conception or consensus within the leadership. Indeed, much of the

18. "On the Historical Experience of the Dictatorship of the Proletariat," in *CC 1955–59*, p. 149.

19. *Ibid.*

20. While I do not interpret this editorial as unequivocally "anti-Mao," it appears to be a collectively produced document—written on the basis of an enlarged meeting of the Politbureau—which checks Mao's influence on Party policies. The evidence for this interpretation is based on the opposition to Mao's "leftist" agricultural line, which built up as the "high tide" of co-operativization was pressed in the winter and spring of 1955–56. This opposition is documented in Ch. XVIII, pp. 351–356 below.

Furthermore, the eventual bitterness of Chinese attacks on Khrushchev for having "subverted" the leaderships of other Parties indicates that Mao came to see the Soviet leader's attack on Stalin as having undermined his personal authority within China after the Soviet Twentieth Party Congress. (*See* the *People's Daily* and *Red Flag* joint editorial, "On the Origin and Development of the Differences between the Leadership of the CPSU and Ourselves" [September 6, 1963], in *Polemic on the General Line of the International Communist Movement*, p. 63.)

debate within the Party over the next twelve months as related to the organization of Party power, policy toward the intellectuals, and Party rectification seems to represent an effort to evolve such a conception and consensus.[21]

Mao himself appeared to take the first step in this process, perhaps as a way of trying to regain the initiative. On May 2nd, Mao delivered a speech to a meeting of the Supreme State Conference in which he apparently spelled out his own views on how to deal with the intellectuals. In this speech, which has never been published, Mao first invoked the full slogan, "Let a hundred flowers bloom, let a hundred schools of thought contend." We do not know all the arguments which Mao presented at this time, but the main lines of his speech[22] apparently served as the basis for an address

21. Six months after publication of the editorial, the Eighth Party Congress made certain structural changes in the formal Party organization. A Standing Committee was created within the Politbureau, a separate post of General Secretary of the Central Committee was established, and a General Political Department set up. Very little is known about the thinking, or politicking, which underlay the promotion of these changes, and whether proposals for reorganization were advanced before or after the onset of "de-Stalinization."

The main argument advanced here, however, is that the major pressure for strengthening "collective leadership" came from Party leaders who objected to Mao's economic initiatives of 1955. As Mao sought to regain the political initiative in late 1956, he had to utilize a variety of non-Party organizational forums—the Supreme State Conference, a national conference on propaganda work, and criticism of the Party from the intellectual community—to implement his own notion of "mass line" politics. In these policy differences of 1955–1957 lie conflicting conceptions of the leadership process, and of cadre rectification, which in the 1960s were to grow into the open political conflict of the Cultural Revolution.

22. Given the fact that Mao's May 1956 speech has never been published —while his February 1957 "contradictions" analysis has been given wide publicity—it seems that his views on the intellectuals and on "class struggle" in a socialist society were going through a process of evolution under the impact of events during 1956. My own reading of Lu's speech is that it represents a very liberal interpretation of Mao's views. And if one assumes that Mao was increasingly "boxed in" during 1956 as a result of "de-Stalinization," the fact that Lu spoke for Mao could be read as an indication that Party leaders with primary influence at this time were pulling Mao's line on the intellectuals "to the right," that the Chairman could not "speak for himself" publicly on this issue, but had to accept a collective interpretation of his views.

In any event, Lu's speech is clearly more liberal than Chou's report on the intellectuals of the preceding January. Gone is the stress on opposition to "rightist conservatism." Where Chou had stressed Party leadership over intellectual matters, Lu goes to great pains to separate them from politics. ("We cannot fail to notice that although art, literature and scientific research have a close bearing on the class struggle, they are not, after all, the

by the Director of the Central Committee's Propaganda Department, Lu Ting-yi, delivered three weeks later in Peking to a selected group of intellectuals.

Lu's speech, which emphasizes the Party's commitment to the encouragement of scientific and artistic innovation, began by invoking the image of a new "golden age" in Chinese intellectual life:

> During the epoch of the Spring and Autumn Annals and the Warring States two thousand years ago, there emerged in China the phase of "letting all schools contend in airing their views" in the academic field. It became the golden era of academic development in the history of our country. The history of our country has proved that if there were no encouragement of independent thinking and if there were no free discussion, then academic development would stagnate. The epoch of the Spring and Autumn Annals and the Warring States was very different from the situation we are facing today. At that time, society was in a chaotic state (*tung-luan ti*). The contention of all schools in airing their views in the academic field was spontaneous and had no conscious, unified leadership.[23]

This striking introduction reveals all too clearly the bind in which the Party felt itself to be: There had to be unfettered intellectual creativity if China was to develop, yet Chinese history confirmed that intellectual diversity was associated with war and social chaos, with *luan*. And both Party members and non-Party intellectuals must have wondered whether the encouragement of intellectual freedom would lead to a new golden age or to another fearful era of "confusion." [24]

---

same thing as politics.") And where Chou had observed rather sourly that "intellectuals in many units . . . have been slow in making changes," Lu warmly observed: ". . . in the course of [the struggle against bourgeois idealism] most intellectuals have given a very good account of themselves and made remarkable progress." (*See CC 1955–59*, pp. 131, 153–154.)

From such differences in attitude toward the intellectuals apparently grew the Cultural Revolution charge that Lu Ting-yi, among others, had "prettified the bourgeoisie."

23. Lu Ting-yi, "Let a Hundred Flowers Bloom, a Hundred Schools of Thought Contend," *People's Daily* (June 13, 1956); trans in *Current Background*, No. 406 (August 15, 1956), p. 3.

24. The intimate association between intellectual diversity—differences in "thinking" or opinion—and *luan* in the Chinese social orientation is amply revealed in our interviews. Most notable is the following interpretation of the question, "Why since the time of Confucius has Chinese society placed such emphasis on 'Peace'?" by a 50-year-old shop-keeper and former soldier from the North China province of Liaoning: "In that era you had the Warring States period: there were seven or eight countries; they were all scattered, all split up; society was all confused (*luan*). But that was also a very enlightened period, very vigorous. You had all of those "*tzu*"; Confucius (*Kung-fu-tzu*), Mencius (*Meng-tzu*), Han Fei-tzu, etc." (Why, if

Lu's speech tried to answer this implicit question by stressing that intellectual freedom was limited by the bounds of the revolution and permitted only for those who accepted the leadership of the Communist Party and its objective of "socialist transformation":

> We advocate that the counterrevolutionaries should be denied freedom. We hold that we must practice dictatorship over counterrevolutionaries. But among the people we take the stand that there must be democracy and freedom. This is a political line. In politics, we must distinguish ourselves from the enemy.
>
> The line of "letting all flowers bloom together and all schools contend in airing their views" which we advocate stands for freedom inside the camp of the people. We advocate the broadening of this freedom in accordance with the consolidation of the people's regime.[25]

Lu also made it clear that the Party's objective was the elimination of "bourgeois idealism" and acceptance by all of Marxism-Leninism and dialectical materialism as the bases of a new and "correct" social orientation. These were the conditions under which "intellectual freedom" would be prevented from degenerating into *luan*. For those who accepted these conditions there would be free-

---

that was an enlightened period, was there also the *luan*, the warring?) "It is like when a person is about to die, he will have a last period of great spirit. The Chou dynasty was dying, and in its last years all those men came out; and then, like a man, the dynasty died." (H-7)

25. Lu Ting-yi, "Let a Hundred Flowers Bloom, a Hundred Schools of Thought Contend"; trans. in *Current Background*, No. 406, p. 6.

Lu's use of the term "the People" indicates how vital remains the old Confucian notion that social order can be maintained by "naming" or defining a "proper" relationship between authority and its subordinates. To accept or be worthy of one's "name" means to accept the relationship of power, to play one's social role as authority has defined it. Mao has updated the "naming" conception of political control by indicating that the term "the People" is a variable conception which should be defined or "rectified" under given historical circumstances. As he wrote in 1949, at the conclusion of the "bourgeois-democratic" stage of the revolution: "Who are the people? At the present stage in China, they are the working class, the peasantry, the urban petty bourgeoisie and the national bourgeoisie. These classes, led by the working class and the Communist Party, unite to form their own state and elect their own government; they enforce their dictatorship over the running dogs of imperialism—the landlord class and bureaucrat-bourgeoisie, as well as the representatives of those classes, the Kuomintang reactionaries and their accomplices—suppress them, allow them only to behave themselves and not to be unruly in word or deed. . . . The right to vote belongs only to the people, not to the reactionaries. The combination of these two aspects, democracy for the people and dictatorship over the reactionaries, is the people's democratic dictatorship. (Mao, "On the People's Democratic Dictatorship" (1949), *SW*, English, IV, pp. 417–418.)

dom of inquiry, discussion, and criticism—and freedom to be coun-
tercriticized as well.

To a foreign observer this paradoxical point of view—in which
"intellectual freedom" is permitted only with the prior acceptance
of the truth of an exclusive doctrine—is difficult to see as much
more than arrogant hypocrisy. The prior condition negates the objective. Seen within the context of Chinese society, however, the
willingness of the Party to advance this apparently cynical point of
view drew meaning from the experience of the Party's rise to power:
The recently concluded century of internal chaos undoubtedly
seemed sufficient justification for placing social order at the top of
the Party's list of political priorities. Popular fears of *luan,* amply
documented in our interviews with Chinese of all present generations, would have strengthened the Party's conviction that by maintaining social order it would win wide approval from "the People."

In addition, there was the still vivid contrast of Party discipline
with the corruption and demoralization of the Nationalist regime;
the phenomenal attainment of power from the low ebb following
near destruction in south China; the grueling Long March; and
expansion in the face of powerful Japanese invaders—feats which
the Party associated with its ideological commitment. It would have
taken extremely powerful counterarguments to convince a Party
member that his position was not "correct." Hence there was little
trace of self-consciousness in Lu's speech at the paradox which
underlay the Party's call for "open debates" in the struggle to overcome "idealist thinking."

Apparently the Party leadership believed that the intellectuals
would become willingly committed to the Party's cause, to its inherently "correct" policies, if given a constructive professional role
in China's national development and the opportunity to criticize
unthinking, doctrinaire attitudes on the part of Party members.
Lu's speech thus went on to elaborate Mao's conviction that political unity and social development, not *luan,* would grow from a
critical dialogue between Party and non-Party intellectuals within
the general framework of commitment to the "socialist" path of
national resurgence.

Lu's discussion picked up themes raised by Chou En-lai in his
January report on the intellectuals. Like Chou, he noted that some
non-Party intellectuals adopted "the lordly attitude of the bourgeoisie to oppress the young Marxist academic workers"; but his
stress was clearly on

> the habit of certain Party members to look upon themselves as the
> "authority," their intolerance of criticisms made against them and their

abstention from practicing self-criticism; the practice of restraint by certain Party members in criticizing others for fear of wrecking the united front and unity; the habit of certain Party members to refrain from criticizing or even to shelter the mistakes of other people on account of personal friendship.[26]

Where Chou's report had stressed "rightist conservatism" as the Party's main problem, Lu—in line with the *People's Daily* editorial of early April—stressed that "the main defect is a tendency toward doctrinairism" on the part of Party members. In short, in the wake of Khrushchev's attack on Stalin there was a clear shift of responsibility onto the shoulders of Party members to encourage the co-operation of non-Party intellectuals. They were to raise their own ideological standards and level of professionalism so as to be able to win, on intellectual grounds, the "struggle" against "idealism."

Lu's speech also revealed a new degree of Party toleration for intellectual diversity. He asserted that, "As everyone knows, the natural sciences, including medicine, have no class character." [27] Such an official line, repudiated in the "anti-rightist" reaction of the summer of 1957 and then revived briefly in 1961–62, was to be scathingly denounced by the Maoists during the Cultural Revolution.

Lu's speech concluded with a discussion of how to promote criticism, giving added emphasis to the contention of the Party leadership that it intended to subject its own cadres to the test of open debate with non-Party colleagues. The promotion of such a dialogue, however, was seen to be no easy matter. Lu rhetorically raised the question, "The present forms of criticism make people afraid. If they do not make people afraid they are banal. How is this problem to be solved?" [28] His answer was that there were two kinds of criticism, one directed at the enemy and, "meant to kill with one stroke or attacking criticism. The other kind is directed against good people which is constructive criticism based on comradeship." [29] Lu indicated that the problem was that among "the People" there still existed "the wrong belief that criticism means attack." And he made a plea for the proper distinction between hostile criticism to be directed at enemies, and rational criticism to be used for constructive and unifying purposes among "the People":

> It is common for good men to commit mistakes. Nobody in the world can be completely free from mistakes. Such mistakes should

26. Lu Ting-yi, "Let a Hundred Flowers Bloom," in *Current Background,* No. 406, p. 10.
27. *Ibid.,* pp. 7–8.
28. *Ibid.,* p. 11.
29. *Ibid.,* p. 14.

be distinguished rigidly from counterrevolutionary utterances. Criticism of such mistakes should be well-intended, calm and cool-headed reasoning by taking the whole matter into consideration, and should only proceed from unity with a view to reaching unity. . . . The criticized people have basically nothing to fear.

It is easy to commit mistakes, but such mistakes should be corrected as fast as possible. Persistence in such mistakes would lead to heavy loss. Those who are subject to criticism should stick firmly to truth. They should voice their disagreement if they feel that the criticisms directed against them are wrong. But they should rectify their mistakes and should humbly accept the criticisms rightly made by other people. . . . This can have only advantages but no disadvantages to ourselves and the development of our cause of science and literature and the arts.[30]

This speech is notable for its indication of the groping efforts being made within the Party to deal with the most basic problems of innovation, social integration, and interpersonal cooperation, and with control of abuses of authority—issues all tinged with a concern about *luan*. The Party's strategy of calling for active political participation and controlled criticism of abuses of authority bore the stamp of Mao's personal leadership. He had learned in the mountains of south China that people would actively commit themselves to the movement if given some personal responsibility instead of being told to remain passive and obedient before authority. The opportunity to criticize abuses of power could "liberate" great reserves of popular emotional energy which, through Party direction, could propel history forward.[31]

To make this strategy work in the new context of peaceful reconstruction, and in relations between people both within and outside the Party, however, required some radical changes of attitude. As our interviews revealed, and as Lu's speech confirms, authority does not expect to be criticized and those in subordinate status do not tend to criticize—except when resentments can no longer be held in and burst forth in a "confusion" of emotional attack. Thus there would appear to have been some wishful thinking behind Lu's call for rational, "well-intentioned, calm and cool-headed reasoning . . ." in criticism within the ranks of "the People."

Lu's speech of late May set one of the main themes for speeches delivered to the Third Session of the First National People's Congress which met during the month of June. Li Wei-han, Director of the Party's United Front Work Department, spoke of continuing class conflict, but he diluted the form of this "struggle" by stressing

30. *Ibid.*, p. 15.
31. *See* pp. 207–209 above.

that it was now a matter of "reasoning, emulating, of criticism and self-criticism and encouragement coupled with criticism." [32] And he invoked words of Mao on the need to "unite all possible forces" for the tasks of "socialist construction." The relation of "blooming and contending" to scientific advancement was given particular emphasis by Kuo Mo-jo, President of the Chinese Academy of Sciences. Kuo observed that, "the 'let diverse schools of thought contend' policy is really the best way of encouraging scientific workers to unleash a high degree of activeness and creativity." [33]

Despite this concentrated effort on the part of the Party leadership to overcome lethargy in the intellectual community, doubts persisted. Non-Party people were confused about the intentions of the campaign, coming as it did after several years of struggle with "counterrevolutionaries" in their midst. How far could open "contending" proceed if the Marxist point of view, by Party precondition, was destined to triumph in the end?

Shortly after the adjournment of the National People's Congress, Kuo Mo-jo attempted to air these doubts about the limits of intellectual freedom, and fear of *luan* resulting from genuine expression of opinion, by affirming that the "symphony" of contending schools was to play under the Party's unified direction:

> The present "contending of a hundred schools" is different from the wasp-like swarming of all kinds of schools during our country's Warring States era. The "hundred contending schools" of that period concerned the change from slave society to feudal society. . . . The "contending of a hundred schools" today is based on the motive of establishing a socialist society, and, with progress, the establishment of communism. We want to safeguard this motive in organizing our "symphony orchestra," and play historically unprecedented powerful symphonies. Let there be ten thousand different kinds of instruments playing together, but they should always play according to a definite score. We want "contention" (*cheng-ming*); we don't want "confused cackling" (*luan-ming*).
>
> . . . If there is some confused blowing and striking of instruments (*luan-chiao luan-ta*) other people may cover up their ears, or even ask you to leave the stage.[34]

Some within the Party leadership, however, were evidently displeased with the reticence of the intellectuals to voice opinions and

32. Li Wei-han, "The Democratic United Front in China"; trans. in *Current Background,* No. 402 (July 24, 1957), p. 3.

33. Kuo Mo-jo, "Development of Scientific Research in China"; trans. in *ibid.,* No. 400 (July 17, 1956), p. 3.

34. Kuo Mo-jo, "Play Powerful Symphonies," *People's Daily* (July 1, 1956), p. 7.

to strike out on new paths of investigative research, for an authoritative "Commentator," writing in the Party paper only a few weeks later, on July 23rd, indirectly challenged Kuo's cautious interpretation of the "contention" policy:

> All the various schools ought to create their own music, and not just play according to the music indicated by the conductor. As long as the melodies they play are not counterrevolutionary they will have freedom to contend. We have only one expectation of the contenders, and that is that they genuinely do academic research. . . . Many people have suggested that contention is not "confused cackling." But what is "confused cackling?" No one's understanding about this is the same. Of course, if there is to be "contention" it cannot be guaranteed there will be "no confusion." If "confused cackling" is a matter of, "the masses say it is confusing," or "establishing theories of the new and unusual," this kind of "confused cackling" isn't necessarily bad.[35]

"Commentator" then concluded with the hopeful assertion that "the condition of Marxism as the leading thought of the academic and cultural world has already been established." [36]

The manner in which these contrasting interpretations of the "blooming and contending" policy were expressed in the press suggests that strong differences of opinion were unresolved within the Party leadership.[37] During the remainder of the summer of 1956, and into the fall, the effort of the first months of the year to mobilize the intellectuals into the national development effort remained a low key operation devoid of political content. At the Eighth Party Congress held in September, Mao—in a brief opening speech which, in contrast to Liu Shao-ch'i's lengthy political report, only seemed to emphasize the degree to which the Chairman's power remained circumscribed—stressed the need for "determined action to get rid of any unhealthy manifestations in any part of our work that are detrimental to the unity between the Party and the people." [38]

Liu's political report, however, gave scant attention to the call for

35. Commentator, "An Interpretive Discussion of 'Let a Hundred Schools of Thought Contend,' " *ibid.*, (July 21, 1956), p. 7.

36. *Ibid.*

37. Kuo Mo-jo is one of the few intellectuals of national prominence in China who over the years has maintained close personal ties with Mao. During the 1960s his public statements and writings were to be the precursor of Mao's political initiatives (*see* pp. 418, 484 below). Hence, one senses that Kuo's 1956 exchange with "Commentator" may be a veiled debate between Mao and other Party leaders.

38. Mao Tse-tung, "Opening Address at the Eighth National Congress of the Communist Party of China" (September 15, 1956), in *Eighth National Congress of the Communist Party of China*, Vol. I, p. 8.

"blooming and contending," mentioning it only once in the context of the need to foster the development of science and the arts. His discussion of Party rectification stressed the strengthening of Party leadership over state organs, and "supervision over subordinates by superiors." "Criticism and exposures from below" was ranked last in his discussion; and the need for "supervision" by the "democratic parties" was brushed aside.[39] Similarly, the report by Teng Hsiao-p'ing on the revision of the Party Constitution mentioned only the need to "greatly intensify criticism and self-criticism *within the Party*." [40]

In his January report on the intellectuals, Chou En-lai had revealed that "the Central Committee of our Party has decided to make opposition to rightist conservative ideology the central question for the Eighth National Congress of the Party. . . ." [41] Documents from the Congress, in striking contrast, hardly mention this danger on the "right." Liu Shao-ch'i repeatedly called attention to the "leftist" errors of doctrinairism, impetuosity, and rashness; and he recalled with emphasis the great harm that had been done to the Party's revolutionary cause by the various "leftist" lines of the 1930s.[42] Similarly, the final resolution of the Congress stressed the "mistake of adventurism" in China's development effort.[43] And just as "the thought of Mao Tse-tung" was no longer mentioned in the revised Party Constitution, an open, critical debate between Party members and non-Party intellectuals was no longer part of the content of "blooming and contending."

THE MEANING OF "HUNGARY"

The second shock to the Party and its effort to establish better relations with the intellectuals came in October and November of 1956, and again came from within the Communist world. The riots and liberalizing ferment in Poland and the upheaval of the Hungarian

39. Liu Shao-ch'i, "Political Report of the Central Committee of the Communist Party of China to the Eighth National Congress of the Party," *ibid.,* pp. 76–77.

40. Teng Hsiao-p'ing, "Report on the Revision of the Constitution of the Communist Party of China," *ibid.,* p. 207. Emphasis added.

41. Chou En-lai, "On the Question of Intellectuals," in *CC 1955–59,* p. 129.

42. Liu Shao-ch'i, "The Political Report of the Central Committee of the Communist Party of China to the Eighth National Congress of the Party," in *Eighth National Congress of the Communist Party of China,* Vol. I, pp. 98–102.

43. "Resolution of the Eighth National Congress of the Communist Party of China on the Political Report of the Central Committee," *ibid.,* p. 124.

"counterrevolution" exposed to Party contemplation outbursts of *luan,* fears of which had dampened reaction to Mao's call for "blooming and contending." Did these events prove that a policy of encouraging "intellectual freedom" and criticism was foolish, or that it had become necessary?

The Party leadership's initial reaction to these events was largely in the realm of international relations. The Chinese were clearly concerned about the erosion of cohesion in the "socialist camp," which continued to provide them both international security and a sense of legitimacy at home. Hence China continued to support the leading role of the Soviet Union in the International Communist Movement, and warned of the need to "overcome nationalist tendencies in smaller countries [i.e., Hungary]." [44] But at the same time, the Chinese, who were well acquainted with Russian interference in their own domestic political life, supported Poland's desire for greater independence within the bloc—to the exasperation of the Russians. [45] This Chinese position of walking between the dangers of bloc disintegration and oppressive Russian control was manifest in Chou En-lai's mediation trip through Eastern Europe in January 1957, an initiative which heightened Soviet sensitivities to China's role in the International Communist Movement and set the stage for subsequent escalation in Sino-Soviet tensions.

The significance of "Hungary" for China's domestic political life took some time to become apparent. The initial impact of the events of the autumn in Eastern Europe was to strengthen Mao's contention that deviations to the "right"—"rightist conservatism" and "revisionism"—were the main dangers to China's revolution. His earlier exasperation with those who blindly followed the Soviet precedent (expressed in his mid-1955 report on agricultural cooperation) seemed justified by events. The first official Party editorial in response to the developments of the fall warned that "indiscriminate and mechanical copying of experience that has been successful in the Soviet Union—let alone that which was unsuccessful there—may lead to failures in another country." [46] Mao's earlier

44. *People's Daily* editorial, "More on the Historical Experience of the Dictatorship of the Proletariat" (December 29, 1956), in *CC 1955–59,* p. 270.

45. Chinese initiatives within the "socialist camp" in reaction to the developments in Poland and Hungary, and Soviet responses to them, are analyzed in Zagoria, *The Sino-Soviet Conflict, 1956–1961,* pp. 54–65.

46. "More on the Historical Experience of the Dictatorship of the Proletariat," in *CC 1955–59,* p. 266.

My basic interpretation of this editorial is that it is a "compromise" document, reflecting uncertainties within the Party leadership as to the full relevance of the events of the fall in Eastern Europe for China's domestic

belief that toleration of non-Marxist views held by the "bourgeois" intellectuals would weaken Party leadership, and should be the object of struggle, seems also to have been strengthened.[47] Whereas earlier in the year his desire to promote ideological struggle had been characterized as "leftist" sectarianism which would isolate the Party from the intellectuals, Mao now could stress that "opposition to doctrinairism has nothing in common with tolerance of revisionism"; and he warned that "in the present antidoctrinaire tide" the Party must not compromise with those who would "attempt to weaken or renounce the . . . leading role of the Party." [48]

The key issue which divided Party leaders in the wake of the events in Poland and Hungary concerned the most appropriate way to strengthen the "leading role of the Party." As events of the winter and spring of 1957 unfolded, one group of Party leaders, apparently centered around Liu Shao-ch'i and P'eng Chen, continued to adhere to the position that "class struggle should not continue to be stressed as though it was being intensified, as was done by Stalin." [49] Mao, on the other hand, increasingly saw the events in Eastern Europe, and their reflection in China, as basically a product of Party misuses of power which required correction. Against increasing resistance from within the Party he continued to stress that

> we need a rectification movement. Will it undermine our Party's prestige if we criticize our own subjectivism, bureaucracy and sectarianism? I think not. . . . Even great storms are not to be feared. It is amid great storms that human society progresses.[50]

---

political life. No clear line on internal policy is expressed, in contrast to the detailed evaluation of international developments. Indeed, most of the subsequent analysis in this chapter concerns the attempt of the leadership to reach consensus on a domestic political line in the wake of "Hungary."

47. In the 1960s Mao was to make repeated references to the Hungarian "Petofi Circles"—groups of Party and non-Party intellectuals who had provided much of the leadership in the 1956 "de-Stalinization" movement in Hungary—as an example of the corruption of a Party organization by "revisionists" (*see* p. 450 below). The major lesson which Mao evidently drew from the Hungarian upheaval was of the danger for a revolutionary party of close ties with non-Marxist intellectuals. Or perhaps more precisely, Mao may have used the Hungarian example to assert to other Party leaders the correctness of his earlier concern about "bourgeois reactionary thinking" within the Chinese Communist Party.

48. "More on the Historical Experience of the Dictatorship of the Proletariat," in *CC 1955–59*, p. 266.

49. *Ibid.*, p. 267.

50. Mao, "Speech at the Chinese Communist Party's National Conference on Propaganda Work," in *Selected Readings from the Works of Mao Tse-tung*, pp. 394, 400.

The playing out of these differing interpretations of the meaning of the Hungarian events for the Chinese revolution provides much of the tension and drama of domestic Chinese politics in the spring of 1957. From a retrospective evaluation of press materials published during this year we can reconstruct the main lines of leadership conflict which were only dimly revealed in official editorials, postponed meetings, and the public appearances and statements of various Party leaders.

AN EARLY COMPROMISE

Early January 1957 apparently was the first point of decision at which Mao attempted to turn the "blooming and contending" policy into a rectification movement which would stress criticism of the Party from *outside* groups—particularly the intellectuals. This effort, however, met with determined resistance within the Party leadership. On January 7 an article was published in the *People's Daily* by Ch'en Ch'i-t'ung, a Vice Director of the Cultural Section of the General Political Department of the People's Liberation Army, and three other senior army political workers. In view of the criticism which this otherwise obscure piece received in subsequent weeks, it evidently reflected the leadership debate of the moment.[51]

51. Following Mao Tse-tung's "contradictions" speech to the Supreme State Conference on February 27th, Ch'en and his colleagues were to be criticized by name no less than five times in the *People's Daily*: on March 1st by one Ch'en Liao (perhaps a pseudonym); on March 18th by Mao Tun, Minister of Culture; on April 4th in an article compiled from readers' letters; on April 10th in an official editorial (*see* p. 302 below); and on April 11th in a published interview with Chou Yang, Deputy Director of the Party Propaganda Department.

In the inner-Party rectification which followed public "blooming and contending," Ch'en Ch'i-t'ung was relieved of his duties and sent to his home village for "self-reform."

In a note of political irony, Mao Tse-tung himself praised Ch'en and the three other PLA critics of "blooming and contending" for "commendable courage" in expressing criticism of his policy. This was in early 1958 when Mao had reasserted his influence in matters of Party leadership, and hence his remarks have the air of a graceful winner. His speech, moreover, continues to stress the virtue of public criticism of the cadres as a way of mobilizing popular support for the Party leadership's cause. Ch'en's error was probably in opposing the Chairman's *method* of leadership. He and Mao may not have had differing views on the intellectuals. (*See* "Chairman Mao's Speech at the Ch'eng-tu Conference" [March 22nd, 1958], in Joint Publications Research Service, *Translations on Communist China*, No. 90 [Washington, D.C.: 1970], pp. 48–52.)

By 1959 Ch'en was back at work in army cultural and political affairs, where he remained active and increasingly influential until the Cultural Rev-

Opening with one of those expressions of humility which usually signals that someone in higher authority is being challenged, Ch'en and his colleagues observed that, "our views are immature because we have no time to delve deep into theories." [52] Nevertheless, they went on to attack in detail Mao's "blooming and contending" policy, arguing that non-Party intellectuals still were not loyal to the socialist cause. They noted that among the intellectuals there were those who "tried to avoid the word 'socialist' and used 'realistic' only, or replaced the term with the obscure concept of 'realism of the socialist era.'" And in an effort to shift the focus of political struggle onto the intellectuals (and away from the Party) they asserted: "We should not keep silent in front of certain sceptics and countermandists, nor should we play the sycophant; instead, we should raise our bright colors high, be steady in our battle array, and proceed with the struggle." [53]

The immediate outcome of the leadership debate reflected in this article, however, seems to have been a compromise decision in favor of a mild rectification. The need for a Party *cheng-feng* was affirmed in a Central Committee directive, but it was to be an *internal* Party matter which would proceed at a slow pace. The year 1957 was to be devoted to the study of materials based on the Party's Eighth Congress documents (not a meeting at which Mao was influential), with rectification to proceed only in 1958.[54]

Mao, however, had the "time to delve deep into theories," and in the face of this resistance to a rectification movement which would confront both Party abuses of power and "revisionism" among the intellectuals, he wrote one of his major theoretical statements on the relationship between political struggle and social change. He affirmed that Marxism-Leninism provided the guiding

olution. He was one of the first army leaders purged in 1966. One can only wonder who had been his protectors within the PLA and/or Party, for by all appearances he had served as a "mouthpiece" for those in positions of greater authority who were opposed to "blooming and contending."

52. Ch'en Ch'i-t'ung, *et al.*, "Some of Our Opinions on Current Literary and Art Work," *People's Daily* (January 7, 1957); trans. in *Union Research Service* (Hong Kong), Vol. VII, No.7 (April 23, 1957), p. 84.

53. *Ibid.*, p. 85.

54. As is the case with much of the limited information available to foreign observers about important policy developments within China, the rectification campaign directive was revealed initially by references to its implementation gleaned from relatively obscure press materials. (*See* Chi Lu, "Some Questions on the Work Style Rectification Movement," *China Youth*, No. 2 [January 16, 1957]; trans. in *Extracts from China Mainland Magazines* [*ECMM*] [Hong Kong: United States Consulate General], No. 70 [February 18, 1957], p. 1.) This publication is currently titled *Selections from China Mainland Magazines*.

theory and political structure of China's development effort, and tried to convince Party members that encouragement of popular criticism of cadre abuses of authority was the best way to prevent "contradictions" between Party and people from going unresolved. *Suppression* of criticism, Mao held, would lead to "confusion"; while a critical dialogue between Party members and "the People" would resolve points of tension, promote social change, and prevent the Party from "cutting itself off from the masses."

Mao formally presented his position on China's proper political course to another session of the Supreme State Conference held on February 27, 1957, developing those ideas which had found indirect public expression in Lu Ting-yi's speech of the preceding May. He began his discussion "On the Correct Handling of Contradictions among the People" with what must have seemed, in the face of events in Hungary, a note of uncertain reassurance: "Never before has our country been as united as it is today. . . . The days of national disunity and chaos (*hun-luan*) which the people detested have gone, never to return." [55]

The major import of this highly revealing speech—even in its edited form[56]—was Mao's conviction of the error in equating po-

55. Mao Tse-tung, "On the Correct Handling of Contradictions among the People" (February 27, 1957), in *Selected Readings from the Works of Mao Tse-tung,* p. 350.

A basic question affecting efforts to interpret Mao's speech is an evaluation of whether he was "optimistic" or "pessimistic" in calling for criticism of the Party from non-Party people. Did he fear a Chinese "Hungary," or did he call for public criticism with an air of confidence over the solidarity of the People's Republic? My personal interpretation straddles both extremes: Mao most likely did not expect the degree of criticism which was to be expressed by the intellectuals in May and early June; yet he was very concerned about the significance of the Hungarian rebellion for other ruling Communist Parties. Mao probably had few illusions about either the commitment to "socialism" of the *older* intellectuals, or of the effects of bureaucratism and "sectarianism" on Party relations with "the People." Yet he apparently felt that patriotism and the power of the state were both strong enough to bind the Party and intellectuals together in "unity and struggle." Mao evidently underestimated the degree of resentment toward Party authority which was latent in the intellectual community—especially among the younger generation—and the strength of resistance to "blooming and contending" which the Party apparatus was to display throughout the spring.

56. The official version of the "contradictions" speech must be handled with some care, for it was published only on June 18th, 1957, and then with "certain additions" by the author.

What was reported as a summary and extracts from a transcript of the original speech—which apparently Mao delivered as a rambling verbal presentation, several hours in length—was published in the *New York Times* on June 13th, 1957 on the basis of a version "leaked" to American correspondent Sidney Gruson by sources in Poland. And a recollection of the major

litical unity with the absence of all social conflict. He saw China's political danger as one of falling into the traditional trap of stagnation and disunity out of fear of conflict. Many people still carried with them anxieties about *luan,* which in the past had hindered progress and had actually contributed to social divisiveness and political passivity through fear of resolving outstanding problems:

> Many dare not openly admit that contradictions still exist among the people of our country, although it is these very contradictions that are pushing our society forward. Many do not admit that contradictions continue to exist in a socialist society, with the result that they are handicapped and passive when confronted with social contradictions; they do not understand that socialist society will grow

points of the original speech, which were noted by a Chinese industrialist who heard a tape-recording of the February 27th presentation, was published in 1962. (*See* Robert Loh and Humphrey Evans, *Escape from Red China* [New York: Coward McCann, 1962], pp. 289–293.)

A comparison of these accounts of the "original" version of the speech and the authoritative version published in June—after attacks on the non-Party critics had begun—suggests that two major types of editorial changes had been made: First, it appears that the official version contains six additional criteria which define more explicitly the limits of acceptable criticism of the Party. Secondly, certain specific information about Party mistakes, and the intention to rectify them, apparently was omitted.

It would seem that Mao's original speech was designed to justify to Party members the need for public criticism in the light of their past errors and of the effects which failure to rectify such errors could have on domestic political life—as illustrated by events in Hungary. Furthermore, the speech seems to have given added encouragement to non-Party people to voice criticism; even against the weight of a political tradition which did not sanction criticism of authority. In these respects the original version of the speech seems to have been more "liberal" in its admission of Party errors and in the encouragement of public criticism.

There has been considerable speculation as to the motivation behind publication of the edited version in mid-June. The most plausible explanation, suggested by Michel Oksenberg, is that the Party leadership had by now reached a decision to initiate attacks on "anti-Party rightists" and would use the immanent session of the National People's Congress as a forum for these attacks. Hence publication of Mao's revised speech was a way of reshaping the "blooming and contending" so as to focus on the critics of the Party. (*See* Michel C. Oksenberg, *Policy Formulation in Communist China: The Case of the Mass Irrigation Campaign, 1957–58* [unpublished Ph.D. dissertation, Columbia University, New York, 1969], pp. 423–439.)

A further factor which may have affected the timing of publication of the speech was the "leaking" of an unofficial version through Eastern Europe (perhaps by the Russians, who later were said to have been upset by Mao's "blooming and contending" line). An "official" version of the speech would tend to supplant the one which was circulating in the Bloc and which had been extracted in the *New York Times* only five days before release of the "official" version.

more united and consolidated through the ceaseless process of the correct handling and resolving of contradictions. For this reason, we need to explain things to our people, and to our cadres in the first place, in order to help them understand the contradictions in a socialist society and learn to use correct methods for handling these contradictions.[57]

Mao's personal orientation had long been that conflict could be a force for progress, and not simply the cause of *luan*. But in this new era of "socialist unity," with military conflict at an end, could he convince the many doubters of the importance of *controlled* conflict? His speech went on to outline the way in which conflict could be kept within bounds, and how it could help to unite China and promote her progress.

Essentially, Mao asserted, the "storm" of revolution "has basically concluded." And while "class struggle is by no means entirely over," the Party need not fear that "counterrevolutionaries" will unleash a new storm against it, for class enemies have been effectively destroyed. Even the provocative influence of events in Hungary had caused only minor restlessness among a portion of the intellectuals; they had not been able to raise anything approaching "winds and waves."

In these conditions of basic Party control, Mao seemed to be saying, the Party could only blame itself for any new condition of *luan:* If it continued to see enemies everywhere and used only methods appropriate for dealing with enemies, then trouble would be *created:*

> The fact is, there still are counterrevolutionaries (of course, that is not to say you'll find them everywhere and in every organization), and we must continue to fight them. . . . If we drop our guard, we shall be badly fooled and shall suffer severely. Counterrevolutionaries must be rooted out with a firm hand wherever they are found making trouble. But, *taking the country as a whole, there are certainly not many counterrevolutionaries. It would be wrong to say that there are still large numbers of counterrevolutionaries in China. Acceptance of that view would also end us up in a mess (kao-luan).*[58]

There also remained the old tendency of those in positions of authority to use their power exploitatively for personal advancement, consumption, and a life of ease:

> A dangerous tendency has shown itself of late among many of our personnel—an unwillingness to share the joys and hardships of the

57. Mao, "On the Correct Handling of Contradictions among the People," in *Selected Readings from the Works of Mao Tse-tung,* pp. 358–359.
58. *Ibid.,* pp. 364–365. Emphasis added.

masses, a concern for personal fame and gain. . . . We must see to it that all our cadres and all our people constantly bear in mind that ours is a big socialist country but an economically backward and poor one, and that this is a very great contradiction. To make China rich and strong needs several decades of intense effort, which will include, among other things, the . . . policy of building up our country through diligence and frugality.[59]

Mao's basic problem was to convince the Party that manifestations of popular discontent, "disturbances," should not be anxiously suppressed as in the past, but should be openly accepted and dealt with in order to solve problems stemming from abuses of power on the part of Party cadres: "In a large country like ours, there is nothing to get alarmed about if small numbers of people create disturbances; on the contrary such disturbances will help us get rid of bureaucracy." [60]

Party members must learn to wield their power with discipline, to accept popular criticism, and to criticize both "the People" and Party comrades with reason and restraint, not with the hostility which in the past had produced resentments and generated *luan*. Mao emphasized that in the rectification campaign of 1942 the Party had developed ways of preventing criticism from leading to *luan*:

> The "Left" dogmatists [of the revolutionary period] had resorted to the method of "ruthless struggle and merciless blows" in inner-Party struggle. This method was incorrect. In criticizing "Left" dogmatism, we discarded this old method and adopted a new one, that is, one of starting from the desire for unity, distinguishing between right and wrong through criticism or struggle and arriving at a new unity on a new basis. . . . *The essential thing is to start from the desire for unity. For without this desire for unity, the struggle is certain to get out of hand (tou-luan).* Wouldn't this be the same as "ruthless struggle and merciless blows?" And what Party unity would there be left? It was this very experience that led us to the formula: "unity, criticism, unity." [61]

Unity, however, Mao made clear, was reserved for "the People," for those who accepted Party leadership and socialism. Hostile criticism could and should be expressed against enemies, but within the ranks of "the People" criticism should be divorced from antagonism. This approach is perhaps the essence of Mao's strategy for institutionalizing progress by bringing conflict into the open.

59. *Ibid.,* p. 384.
60. *Ibid.,* p. 381.
61. *Ibid.,* p. 356. Emphasis added.

By divorcing bad feelings from criticism in dealings with people who accept the larger order and goals of Chinese society (recognizing contradictions among "the People" as "non-antagonistic"), *but sanctioning the release of bad feelings in dealings with "the enemy"* ("antagonistic contradictions") Mao hopes to make criticism less fearful by preserving society's order. At the same time an outlet is provided for the hostility which, "held in" by tradition, had been one of the sources of *luan*.

One of the problems associated with this approach, of course, is to "distinguish clearly between self and enemy." As Mao admitted:

> Quite a few people fail to make a clear distinction between these two different types of contradictions—those between ourselves and the enemy and those among the people—and are prone to confuse the two. It must be admitted that it is sometimes quite easy to do so. We have had instances of such confusion in our work in the past. In the course of suppressing counterrevolutionaries, good people were sometimes mistaken for bad, and such things still happen today. We are able to keep our mistakes within bounds because it has been our policy to draw a sharp line between ourselves and the enemy and to rectify mistakes whenever discovered.[62]

Despite such past mistakes, Mao seemed genuinely convinced of the correctness of his approach, of the importance of allowing hostility to be vented in a disciplined manner, of airing popular grievances against abuses of power by lower-level cadres, and of doing away with the "holding in" of bad feelings, which in the past had provided the motive force of *luan*.[63] He undoubtedly sensed that

62. *Ibid.,* p. 358.
63. To gain some idea of how people felt about the compulsory and highly institutionalized system of criticism which Mao and the Party have developed, we asked those of our interview respondents who had experienced this system about their reactions to it. One of the more revealing responses, affirming how criticism can help to overcome the disunity of the past, was given by a man who had been a member of the Kuomintang and a Nationalist military officer before Liberation, and subsequently had served as an instructor in the PLA: (I have heard that the Communists use the people to criticize the cadres. What is this about?) "They use the ordinary people to oversee the cadres; and also use the cadres to oversee the ordinary people. This is a political method; [both these groups] are equal, and [their mutual criticism] can prevent problems from developing." (But can the ordinary people criticize high level cadres?) "They have criticism meetings among themselves; they talk about their problems and develop a sense of unity. The Communists are always encouraging people to talk, to express their opinions. Originally there is no enmity among people, and if you talk about problems you can prevent misunderstandings and can maintain unity in work. During the Nationalist era things were not this way; you would hold back your

any such feelings which now were held in would in time burst forth —as in Hungary—to threaten the Party itself. And above all Mao seemed convinced of the justice of his cause. He could slide over the basic paradox that "Marxism is accepted as the guiding ideology by the majority of the people in our country . . ." while at the same time noting that "Marxists are still a minority among the entire population as well as among the intellectuals." [64] His conviction was born of the irrefutable argument that the Party had attained power. Obviously the methods used to attain that power had been both correct and the cause of its success. Hence he affirmed:

> Marxism is scientific truth and fears no criticism. If it did, and if it could be overthrown by criticism, it would be worthless. . . . Marxists should not be afraid of criticism from any quarter. Quite the contrary, they need to temper and develop themselves and win new positions in the teeth of criticism and in the storm and stress of struggle. Fighting against wrong ideas is like being vaccinated—a man develops greater immunity from disease as a result of vaccination. Plants raised in hot-houses are unlikely to be sturdy. Carrying out the policy of letting a hundred flowers bloom and a hundred schools of thought contend will not weaken but strengthen the leading position of Marxism in the ideological field. [65]

Mao's determination to press for a policy of public "blooming and contending" can be interpreted as a summation of both immediate political objectives and personal political style. In terms of basic political approach, the struggle to resolve "contradictions" could be the vehicle for confronting "rightist conservative" ideas held by people both within and outside the Party. Mao's emphasis on a policy of "unity and struggle" in the Party's "alliance" with the intellectuals could serve as a way of incorporating non-Party people, in particular the intellectuals, into the revolution on the Party's own terms. It could also expose errors on the part of Party cadres. Mao's personal commitment to "struggle" thus seemed to find expression at this time in an attempt to set the Party and the intellectuals against each other in a controlled conflict which would

---

opinions and they would continuously get greater. The distance between you would get greater and eventually you would become enemies." (Does criticism lead to hating the other person?) "People would not dare to develop hatred, or they would not dare to express it. If they did, they would just receive more criticism or eventually be punished." (Which do you think is a better method, the Communist or the Nationalist method?) "During the last hundred years China has been very *luan,* people didn't obey the laws. This method enables everybody to understand the law and obey it." (H-7)

64. Mao, "On the Correct Handling of Contradictions among the People," in *Selected Readings from the Works of Mao Tse-tung,* p. 376.

65. *Ibid.,* p. 375.

expose and "rectify" errors or "incorrect" attitudes held by people within each social group. Mao was to use this technique of provoking a confrontation in order to test or expose a political situation again in the Taiwan Straits crisis of 1958, and most notably in the Cultural Revolution of the mid-1960s.

In the area of immediate policy objectives, it seems likely that Mao was trying to use the events of the fall of 1956 in Poland and Hungary to reassert his leading role within the Party. Whereas opponents of his economic and social policies had earlier used the attack on Stalin to restrict his influence within the context of collective decision-making processes, Mao could now point to the events in Eastern Europe as justification for the view that Party errors were more a function of "bureaucratism, subjectivism and sectarianism" on the part of a Party-governmental apparatus than the result of one leader's mistakes. And by invoking the danger of "revisionist" attacks on a Party leadership (as had occurred in Hungary) Mao could restrict the influence of more conservative Party leaders within the context of an "anti-rightist" struggle, and in this way reassert the legitimacy of his previous plans for a more rapidly-paced, rural-centered development strategy.

Finally, Mao's resolve to press for a public rectification movement seemed to carry the conviction born of earlier successes in the revolutionary struggle that a leadership style of merely trying to suppress criticism of those in authority would only lead to the holding in of resentments and the lack of resolution of the social tensions that were the cause of *luan*. Only now if the mass hostility on which the Party had risen to power were generated anew, the emotional storm of politics would be turned against the Party itself.

TO OVERCOME PARTY RESISTANCE

Given these varied concerns, Mao and his supporters within the Party leadership resorted to a variety of organizational means to make public "blooming and contending" an institutional reality. The intellectuals continued to be reticent, and there was increasingly determined resistance within the Party. During the two months of March and April 1957, support for this policy was pressed through the numerous united front organizations of "the new democracy." Members of the Chinese People's Political Consultative Conference who had heard Mao's February speech to the Supreme State Conference discussed implementation of the policy at a National Committee meeting held between March 5th and 20th. The Central Committees of the various "democratic parties" were convened from March 11th to the 26th to discuss promotion of the policy of "long-term coexistence and mutual supervision." And between March 6th and 13th the Propaganda Department of the Party Central Committee convened a national conference on propaganda work, attended by almost 500 Party and non-Party intellectuals, to discuss promotion of "blooming and contending." On March 12th Mao addressed the conference, elaborating on his "contradictions" speech of the previous month.

Coming as it did at the end of this meeting of propaganda workers, Mao's speech seems to reveal major points of concern which he felt had to be overcome if public rectification was to become a reality. His analysis balances concern about the prospect of "antisocialist" attacks on Party rule by non-Party intellectuals with an effort to overcome resistance to the policy within Party ranks.

Mao observed that a majority of the intellectuals still "wavered" in their attitudes toward Marxism-Leninism. While many had studied the new ideology, they still were "very conceited, and having learned some book-phrases think themselves terrific and are very cocky; but whenever a storm blows up, they take a stand very different from that of the workers and the majority of the peasants." [66] Hence he warned that in the coming period of public criticism "the basic principles of Marxism [i.e., Party leadership] must never be violated, or otherwise [political] mistakes will be made." And he reiterated that, "in present circumstances, revisionism [a "rightist" deviation] is more pernicious than dogmatism." [67]

Mao went on to point out that the Party itself resisted public exposure of its errors. He concluded by emphasizing that, "In many places, the Party committees have not yet tackled the question of [incorrect] ideology, or have done very little in this respect. . . . The first secretaries of the Party committees in all localities should personally tackle this question." And Mao conspicuously noted that, "The Central Committee of the Party is of the opinion that we must 'open wide' (*fang*), not 'restrict' (*shou*)" in promoting criticism of both Party errors and non-Marxist ways of thinking.[68]

This assertion of the unity of the Central Committee in support of public "blooming and contending" seems more a statement of Mao's hopes than of political fact, for there is considerable indirect evidence that the leadership was divided over the wisdom of Party

66. Mao, "Speech at the Chinese Communist Party's National Conference on Propaganda Work" (March 12, 1957), in *Selected Readings from the Works of Mao Tse-tung*, p. 391.
67. *Ibid.*, pp. 400, 401
68. *Ibid.*, pp. 401, 398.

rectification through criticism from outside groups.[69] These differences of opinion were so strong as to become obvious to cadres beyond the Party "center" and to certain leaders in the intellectual community. And as the movement progressed, appeals were made to Party leaders who favored either "opening wide" or "restricting" the public criticism by opponents and proponents of the rectification.

For many of the intellectuals, the lack of leadership unanimity over the rectification issue was highly unsettling. What would happen to non-Party critics if Mao's protection of their "opening wide" were removed by the opposition of other Party leaders? The vulnerable position in which the intellectuals felt themselves was expressed in late March by the American-trained sociologist Fei Hsiao-t'ung. In an article published by the *People's Daily,* Fei invoked the imagery of the intellectual ferment of the preceding year in Eastern Europe. He asserted that as far as the older intellectuals were concerned, there was only a feeling of "early spring" in the air. In fact, he noted, "The weather of early spring, when there are still sudden changes between warmth and cold, is actually the most difficult season in which to relax." [70]

Fei asserted that following Chou En-lai's report on the intellectuals of the previous year there had been some improvement in the material condition of the intellectuals, "but this only had made them too obvious [because of their relative advantages], made others feel uncomfortable, and even had produced resentments among the masses." [71] There had been a heightening of their professional activism, but they feared that without unified and explicit leadership by the Party, their enthusiasm for work would be without direction and they would become "confused." Finally, Fei asserted that while the activism of the intellectuals had been stimulated,

> depressing factors are numerous. Their anxieties about a hundred schools contending are heavy; they don't dare to contend or struggle,

69. Some measure of Party opposition to Mao's policy is found in the Cultural Revolution assertion that Lu Ting-yi and Hu Ch'iao-mu suppressed publication of Mao's talk at the national conference on propaganda work, which revealed resistance to "blooming and contending." (*See* "Liu Shao-ch'i Is Guilty of Heinous Crimes in Staging Counter-Revolutionary Seizures of Power on Three Occasions in Our Country's Journalistic Circles," in *Jen-ta San-hung* [People's University Three Reds, Peking], May 11, 1967.)

This speech was finally published in 1963 when, after the Tenth Plenum of the Eighth Central Committee, Mao began to press his "thought" as a test of the loyalty of long-time colleagues within the leadership.

70. Fei Hsiao-t'ung, "The Intellectuals' Early Spring Weather," *People's Daily* (March 24, 1957), p. 7.

71. *Ibid.*

even to the point that many of them clam up about questions having a relatively close relationship to politics.[72]

Fei observed that he had encountered no great stirring among higher level intellectuals in response to the events in Poland and Hungary; and while in one respect this was good as an indication of the firmness of their political standpoint, in another sense it only revealed their alienation from matters of politics. They kept silent through fear of being "capped" or labeled as rightists for their "idealism," and attacked as "anti-Party" elements for raising criticisms of Party leadership. In short, Fei and other non-Party intellectuals sensed that they were pawns in a game whose rules they did not fully understand, and in which they were powerless to protect themselves against being used.[73]

Apprehension among the intellectuals was paralleled by growing resistance to the rectification from within Party ranks at all levels. Much had transpired during the early months of 1957 to indicate to a Party member that he was to be a major target of "blooming and contending." At about the same time that the Central Committee announced a rectification campaign for 1958 it also issued a directive temporarily halting the recruitment of new Party members during 1957.[74] Further tension followed another article by Propaganda Director Lu Ting-yi, released just after Mao's February "contradictions" speech. In commemoration of the fifteenth anniversary of the first inner-Party rectification, Lu noted that more than 60 percent of the Party membership had joined Party ranks after Liberation. While these new cadres constituted fresh blood,

> they have not been ideologically transformed by the Party's work style rectification movement of 1942. . . . Many of them still preserve the undesirable ideologies of the old society and have not given up the

72. *Ibid.*

73. As with the articles critical of "blooming and contending" written by Ch'en Ch'i-t'ung and the other PLA officers, the intriguing but unanswerable question is who may have "encouraged" Fei Hsiao-t'ung to write his article for the *People's Daily,* and who on the editorial staff of the paper allowed it to be published?!

74. The existence of this Central Committee directive was revealed in scattered reports in the provincial press during the spring. These reports were published as local Party organizations tried to prevent demoralization among non-Party "activists" by explaining to them the reasons for the policy. *See,* for example, Li Shen-sheng, "Clearly Explain to Activists the Reason Why Temporarily No New Party Members Are Being Accepted this Year," *Kung-jen Sheng-huo* (Wuhsi, Kiangsu Province), March 21, 1957; trans. in *SCMP,* No. 1521 (May 2, 1957), p. 20.

stand of the petty bourgeoisie to make way for the stand of the proletariat.[75]

Even veteran Party cadres were warned that they "were liable to be contaminated by bureaucratism. Among our veteran Party members, some have become vain because of their meritorious feats and some have forgotten the historical experiences of the Party." [76] It would not have taken a particularly devious mind to sense that Mao was trying to use the intellectuals to hit at what he saw to be "rightist conservatism" and the three evils of "bureaucratism, sectarianism, and subjectivism" within Party ranks.

While we do not know precisely the forms which inner-Party debates and opposition to public rectification took at this time, press materials do reveal something of the nature and evolution of Party resistance to "blooming and contending." In late March an article appeared in the Peking *Ta Kung Pao* by Chang Chih-yi, Deputy Director of the United Front Work Department of the Central Committee and the Party's delegate to the meeting of the Chinese People's Political Consultative Conference, then in session.

Like the army officers who had criticized "blooming and contending" in January, Chang began a discussion of united front work with an expression of humility—"my understanding of the people's democratic united front not being deep, I can only set forth some immature views" [77]—which only seems to emphasize that he was challenging Mao's policy line. He then invoked words which Mao had delivered to the Eighth Party Congress almost a year earlier (as if nothing had happened in the meantime to strengthen the position of the Party Chairman). Mao had talked then of the primary importance of uniting all possible forces in order to strengthen the Party's worker-peasant alliance.

Chang's basic contention was that given the country's immediate development problems, the Party's most pressing need was to win the active support of the "bourgeois" intellectuals. He stressed the necessity of maintaining the Party's *two* class "alliances"—with both the peasantry and the bourgeoisie. He contradicted Mao's assertion of the primary importance of the worker–peasant alliance by noting that

75. Lu Ting-yi, "In Commemoration of the Fifteenth Anniversary of the Party's Work Style Rectification Movement," *People's Daily* (March 5, 1957); trans. in *ibid.*, No. 1511 (April 16, 1957), p. 36.

76. *Ibid.*

77. Chang Chih-yi, "Problems Concerning the People's Democratic United Front," *Ta Kung Pao* [Peking] (March 31, 1957); trans. in *ibid.*, No. 1522 (May 3, 1957), p. 1.

at a certain period or in a certain locality where the masses have not gained a predominance it is necessary to establish the second alliance [with the bourgeoisie] in order to gain gradually the predominance of the masses under the cover of the second alliance.[78]

In a line that expresses the heart of his challenge, Chang asserted, "It goes without saying that, if the second alliance is established because of strategic demand, such an alliance should not be lightly broken." [79] This was evidently Chang's way of stressing that if the "blooming and contending" policy were pressed, it would bring into the open differences in political "standpoint" which would force the Party to break the worker-bourgeoisie alliance through attacks on the "idealist" or "anti-Party" views of the intellectuals. Instead he called for attention to "the legitimate interests and reasonable aims" of these class allies, and asserted that such concessions "genuinely accord with the interests of the working class [i.e., the Party]." [80] Finally, Chang urged moderation in the political struggle, and in a contradiction of Mao's view that the main danger was on the "right," he noted that in past periods of stress on the united front, "the 'leftist' dangers were the main ones," and that "if we [now] commit gross errors in these respects [Party] leadership will not be stable and may even be lost." [81]

Chang, like his immediate superior in United Front work, Li Wei-han, and many other Party notables of this period, was to fall from power during the Cultural Revolution under charges of having advocated a "dying out of class struggle" and for "glorifying the bourgeoisie";[82] but his article of late March 1957 seems to reflect a widely held sentiment within the Party that the promotion of open criticism would endanger Party interests. We can only speculate as to whether Chang perceived these interests narrowly as the security of incumbent Party members, or more broadly as the need to encourage the cooperation of the intellectuals in the development effort.

In any event, the month following publication of Chang's article was apparently a period of increasing effort by Mao and his supporters to push through the "blooming and contending" policy against a most resistant Party apparatus.

78. *Ibid.*, p. 2.
79. *Ibid.*, p. 3.
80. *Ibid.*, p. 4.
81. *Ibid.*, p. 9.
82. *See* "Towering Crimes of Enrolling Capitulationists and Renegades by Li Wei-han and Hsü Ping," in *Pursue the Desperate Foe* [Peking], No. 4 (May 20, 1967); trans in *SCMP*, No. 3970 (June 29, 1967), pp. 1–2; and "Thirty-three Leading Counterrevolutionary Revisionists" (March 1968); trans. in *Current Background*, No. 874 (March 17, 1969), pp. 32–33.

On April 10th the *People's Daily* once again attacked the anti-"blooming and contending" line of Ch'en Ch'i-t'ung and the other army political workers by noting that "their criticism could only cause ideological confusion, and in fact certain confusion in thinking [has] indeed been brought about." [83] In an unusual self-criticism that apparently reflects the resistance to "blooming and contending" which had come from those engaged in propaganda work, the Party paper observed, "We should admit that the fact that this paper has delayed in commenting on their article after its publication is one of the major reasons for this confusion." [84]

The next day these army critics again were criticized in the Party paper through the device of an interview with Chou Yang, Deputy Director of the Central Committee's Propaganda Department. Since Chou had previously opposed expressions of liberalism among the intellectuals, his conspicuous support of the "blooming and contending" line, and his criticism of the army opponents, appears to represent the "winning over" of one source of opposition to Mao's cause. [85]

On April 13th the *People's Daily* published a major editorial urging the vigorous promotion of measures to resolve "contradictions among the people." Beginning with a detailed review of all the meetings since late February at which "blooming and contending" had been *discussed*, the paper went on to stress the need for active Party support in *implementing* the policy. The editorial observed that, "if it is claimed that no contradictions exist inside a thing, that will be the strangest of tales"; [86] and in a clear identification of the form which inner-Party resistance to the rectification was taking, it was stressed that

> Party committees of all levels, especially the first secretaries of Party committees, must take up this task earnestly. . . . We must urge the

83. *People's Daily* editorial, "Continue to Implement Thoroughly and with a Free Hand the Policy of 'Letting All Flowers Bloom and All Schools of Thought Contend'" (April 10, 1957); trans. in *Union Research Service*, Vol. VII, No. 7 (April 23, 1957), p. 79.

84. *Ibid.*

85. *See* "Comrade Chou Yang Replies to Questions of a *Wen Hui Pao* Correspondent about 'A Hundred Flowers Blooming and a Hundred Schools Contending,'" *People's Daily* (April 11, 1957), p. 7.

Chou Yang's shifting position with respect to the "blooming and contending" policy during 1956–57 is discussed in the larger context of literary and artistic policy during this period in Merle Goldman, *Literary Dissent in Communist China*, esp. pp. 162–166, 190–193.

86. *People's Daily* editorial, "How to Deal with Contradictions among the People" (April 13, 1957); trans. in *SCMP*, No. 1512 (April 17, 1957), p. 1.

leadership personnel of the various departments of the Party and the government to act in this manner, and not merely entrust this task to the propaganda departments of the Party and the educational departments of the government.[87]

Since Mao's policy during this period had been articulated by Lu Ting-yi, the Central Committee's Director of Propaganda, it seems likely that resistance to the policy was taking the form of an effort to slough off implementation by entrusting it to those within the Party who had been its primary advocates.

Increasing pressure on the Party organization to implement "blooming and contending" was revealed in two further *People's Daily* editorials. On April 17th, the Party was urged to encourage criticism "based on the wish for unity." The paper admitted that as a result of criticism from outside the Party, "the prestige of certain Party organizations and state organs may possibly suffer." [88] But it stressed that failure to air complaints would hold even more serious consequences:

> If no support is given to the masses in carrying out criticism of bureaucracy and the masses are prevented by long suppression from presenting their correct views and just demands, once such a bureaucratic tendency becomes intolerable to them, they may take extreme actions to oppose bureaucracy, and may even demand the solution of certain questions which cannot for the moment be solved. By this time the contradictions will really become acute and complicated.[89]

In the April 23rd editorial, the heat was fully turned on continuing resistance within the Party. The *People's Daily* asserted that present difficulties lie "in the fact that the leadership personnel of many Party organizations have during the past few years buried themselves in the busy duties connected with socialist construction." [90] It was stressed that "The first secretaries and other responsible cadres of Party committees of all levels must *personally* lead in the discussion of this question, must *personally* lead in ideological work." [91] "When you say that there are no contradictions, it means your sense of detection is wanting, and you have not yet discovered them." And in a direct warning, the paper asserted: "People in leading positions

87. *Ibid.*, p. 5.
88. *People's Daily* editorial, "Criticism Based on the Wish for Unity" (April 17, 1957); trans. in *ibid.*, No. 1516 (April 25, 1957), p. 2.
89. *Ibid.*
90. *People's Daily* editorial, "The Whole Party Must Seriously Study How to Solve Contradictions within the Ranks of the People Correctly" (April 23, 1957); trans. in *SCMP*, No. 1518 (April 29, 1957), p. 2.
91. *Ibid.* Emphasis added.

who fail to see or are unable to solve correctly the internal contradictions within the ranks of the people undoubtedly are in danger
politically." [92]

A COMPROMISE DECISION
IN FAVOR OF PUBLIC CRITICISM

By all evidence, the two weeks of late April and early May constituted the period both of greatest conflict and of compromise in pushing ahead with "blooming and contending." Differences within the
Party leadership became so apparent, even to leading non-Party
intellectuals, that both those who supported and those who opposed
involvement in the Party rectification invoked the names of top
Party leaders in support of their positions at public meetings.

Ch'ien Wei-chang, a member of the Central Committee of the
China Democratic League, a leading natural scientist, and a Vice
President of Tsinghua University, later was reported to have said at
a criticism meeting that " 'blooming and contending' is not good
because it is not supported by the line of Liu Shao-ch'i through P'eng
Chen." [93] Party member Hsü Liang-ying, a research scholar in the
Philosophy Institute of the Chinese Academy of Sciences, was accused of asserting: " 'The Party center has split,' 'Chairman Mao is
under the sectarian opposition of high-level cadres. These high-level
cadres want to retaliate against him. It's too immoral.' 'Chairman
Mao has had to compromise.' " [94] And in support of greater strengthening of the policy of "long-term coexistence and mutual supervision," Chang Po-chün, Vice Chairman of the Democratic League
and Minister of Communications, was said to have "twisted" words
of Mao delivered to another (and unannounced) meeting of the
Supreme State Conference on April 30th. Chang's aim was apparently to promote a policy of eliminating Party committees in the

92. *Ibid.*, p. 4.
93. "Firmly Support the Leading Power of the Party in Scientific Work,"
People's Daily (July 17, 1957), p. 2.

As discussed later in the chapter, it is our basic assumption that this information on the policy positions of various Party leaders was published in
the Party press at this time (mid-July) for several reasons: in part to justify
attacks on non-Party "rightists" who were said to have tried to play on such
leadership divisions; partly to make clear to both Party and non-Party people
which leaders had been opposed to public "blooming and contending"; and
perhaps also as an indirect way of other Party leaders expressing subtle
criticism of Mao for his having pressed for a policy which exposed the
Party to public criticism and threatened China's political stability.

94. "Hsü Liang-ying and Li Teh-chi Are Traitors to the Party," *People's
Daily* (August 3, 1957), p. 2.

universities and reducing Party controls over the "democratic parties." [95]

Additional, indirect evidence supports the interpretation that Mao was opposed by Liu Shao-ch'i and P'eng Chen in his advocacy of public "blooming and contending," and that the Chairman had to invoke the authority of his leadership of Party and State in order to gain active implementation of the policy. Mao was said to have been so angered at Party resistance to the rectification that he told friends in Shanghai that "he would prefer not to be chairman in order to get involved [personally] in 'a hundred flowers blooming and a hundred schools contending.' " [96]

Material published between April 26th and May 11th suggests that Mao finally reached a compromise with Liu and P'eng (perhaps "ratified" by a vote of the Politbureau) in which the public rectification would be pressed and leading cadres would engage in physical labor to overcome bureaucratic isolation from the masses, but that those Party leaders who were criticized or found to have committed errors would not be subject to harsh punishment.

This shift to unanimity within the leadership is revealed first in a *People's Daily* editorial of April 26th which explicitly sides with the "democratic parties" in support of the policy of "long-term co-existence and mutual supervision." Party members were criticized for "showing no due respect for the independent and equal position of the democratic parties." [97] Criticisms of the Party raised by these parties were "welcomed" and considered to be "basically correct"; and the Party paper asserted, "we are elated with the success of these meetings [of the democratic parties to foster long-term coexistence and mutual supervision]." [98]

The following day, the 27th, Liu Shao-ch'i delivered an unpublicized address to cadres of the Shanghai Party organization in which he gave rather modest support to Mao's policy of public criticism. Liu's emphasis was on restraining "dogmatists" within the Party "who would compare [their authority] to that of the leadership" and promote an ideological struggle in the style of "striking deadly blows" as had been done by "leftists" in control of the Party in the early 1930s. He asserted that the objective of "blooming and contending" was not to "create a tense situation" and that the Party

95. Ma Che-min, "I Want to Renew Myself," *People's Daily* (July 18, 1957), p. 10.

96. *Ibid.*

97. *People's Daily* editorial, " 'Long-Term Co-Existence and Mutual Supervision' Discussed at Meetings of Democratic Parties" (April 26, 1957); trans. in *SCMP*, No. 1524 (May 7, 1957), p. 1.

98. *Ibid.*, p. 2.

Communist Party Chairman Mao Tse-tung
and Shanghai Municipal Party Committee First Secretary K'o Ch'ing-shih
inspect *ta-tzu-pao* [big character posters] during
the Hundred Flowers campaign of 1957.
From China Reconstructs, *December 1957.*

leadership "does not love struggle." However, because the Party "represented the entire nation" it should "adopt the method of gentle breezes and light rain" as a way of dealing with contradictions "among the People."[99]

On this same day the Central Committee made public a directive instructing Party organizations above the county level to initiate implementation of the rectification and affirming that "first secretaries of Party committees must assume personal responsibility and grasp leadership" of the movement.[100] After publication of this directive provincial Party organizations began to fall into line. New China News Agency reported on May 1st that upon receiving the directive, the Shensi Provincial Committee "immediately called an emergency meeting of the secretariat the same evening, to study the implementation of the directive."[101] At 8 o'clock the next morning there was another emergency meeting of the Provincial Party Standing Committee to discuss further promotion of the directive.

In the weeks that followed, other provincial Party Committees, and organizations under the direct control of the Central Government, began to implement public rectification. The United Front Work Department of the Party Central Committee convened forums of the democratic parties to solicit criticisms of the work style of Party cadres; and their remarks were published throughout the month in the *People's Daily*.

As this Party-sponsored criticism proceeded, resistance continued to be manifest from within Party ranks. And in an effort to strengthen the assertion of unanimity within the leadership in support of "blooming and contending," information was released in the press which seems to reveal the nature of the compromise which top leaders had reached. On May 7th the *People's Daily* published a notable editorial entitled, "Why Must We Carry Out the Rectification Movement 'As Gently as a Breeze or a Mild Rain'?" Invoking

99. "Liu Shao-ch'i's Speech to a Meeting of Cadres of the Shanghai Municipal Party Organization" (April 27, 1957), in *Ta-tao Tang-nei Tsui-ta ti Tsou Tzu-pen-chu-yi Tao-lu Tang-ch'uan-p'ai—Liu Shao-ch'i* [Strike Down the Biggest Person in Authority within the Party Taking the Capitalist Road—Liu Shao-ch'i] (Peking: Peking Chemical Engineering Institute, Mao Tse-tung's Thought Propaganda Personnel, April 10, 1967), Vol. IV, pp. 63–71.

100. "Directive of the Central Committee of the Chinese Communist Party Concerning the Rectification Movement" (April 27, 1957), in *Chung-hua Jen-min Kung-ho-kuo Fa-lü Hui-pien* [Legal Compendium of the People's Republic of China], (Peking: Legal Publishing House, 1957), p. 38.

101. New China News Agency, hereinafter cited as NCNA, "CCP Shensi Committee Calls Emergency Sessions to Discuss Rectification of Work Style" (May 1, 1957); trans. in *SCMP*, No. 1527 (May 10, 1957), p. 14.

phrases from the Central Committee Directive of April 27th, the editorial threatened Party resisters even as it sought to provide them "a way out." The paper sternly warned that, "In our Party there do not exist, and there will not be permitted, sects and groups with different interests and opposed to one another." [102] It threatened:

> In dealing with counterrevolutionaries who have infiltrated into the ranks of the Party, class dissidents who persist in acts of disintegration within the Party, and other decadent and depraved elements who are beyond salvation, the Party has always adopted a resolute attitude and expelled them from its ranks.[103]

Finally, the editorial invoked the name of Liu Shao-ch'i—the only personal reference to him in official documents of this period related to the rectification campaign—in a quote from his lengthy political report to the Eighth Party Congress. His words sounded the only conciliatory note in an otherwise stern editorial: ". . . severe punishment will not guarantee that . . . mistakes will not recur in the Party, and it may even lead to greater mistakes." [104] And on these words the editorial concluded with a stress that, "as long as [Party members] are willing to correct their mistakes, they will generally be exempted from disciplinary measures, particularly disciplinary measures of a grave nature." [105]

102. *People's Daily* editorial, "Why Must We Carry Out the Rectification Movement 'As Gently as a Breeze or a Mild Rain'?" (May 7, 1957); trans. in *SCMP*, No. 1529 (May 14, 1957), p. 2.

103. *Ibid.*

104. *Ibid.*, pp. 2–3.

It might be added that Liu's stress on a policy of leniency towards erring Party cadres—coming as it did in a context of his own increasing influence at the Eighth Party Congress, and in the wake of the revelations about Stalin's purges in the Soviet Party—conveys the air of an attempt to strengthen his personal position within the Party organization at Mao's expense. Liu seemed to be appealing to the Party for support on the grounds that he would be no Stalin by promoting a purge of the Party. This may be one of a number of reasons why Mao, in time, was to call Liu Shao-ch'i "China's Khrushchev"; for like Russia's Khrushchev, Liu apparently was attempting to consolidate his position by appealing to the Party organization for support.

In any event, it seems that many Party members tended to equate Mao with Stalin during 1957 for his determination to press for a Party rectification (*see* pp. 322–323 below).

105. *Ibid.*, p. 3.

On the day this editorial was published Liu Shao-ch'i addressed the Higher Party School in Peking on questions of the rectification movement. There is nothing particularly notable about his remarks as they pertain to the rectification. What is remarkable is his discussion of economic matters. Liu called for China to adopt measures which were "more varied and flexible" than the Soviet approach to economic management. He suggested that

Three days later the *People's Daily* carried a report of a meeting of the Peking Municipal Party Committee held on May 8th, at which P'eng Chen also identified himself personally with the policy of rectification in the style of "a gentle breeze and light rain." [106] And on May 9th P'eng was photographed carrying stones at a road-building project in Peking. Other top Party leaders also participated in this demonstration of personal involvement in that aspect of the Central Committee-endorsed rectification movement which called for participation in physical labor; but the fact that P'eng's photograph was the only one of a major Party figure circulated nationally in the *People's Daily* seems to have been intended to emphasize to resistant Party members that the conflict at the "center" had been resolved, that those within the inner circle of power who had resisted "blooming and contending" were now personally involved in the rectification. [107]

Furthermore, the information about P'eng and Liu's support for the policy of leniency toward erring cadres—an aspect of the Central Committee directive not explicitly associated with the names of any other Party leaders—seems intended to make it clear to opponents of the rectification that those within the leadership who had resisted the public campaign were responsible for protecting Party interests in the context of a compromise decision.

THE BREAKDOWN OF THE
COMPROMISE DECISION

The compromise among Party leaders, embodied in the April 27th Central Committee directive, was to prove fragile and short-lived. "Blooming and contending" was promoted by lower level Party organizations; but the evidence suggests that many Party cadres implemented the directive in a grudging spirit. Some may even have hoped to elicit such extreme criticisms of the Party that the move-

---

the Party permit "controlled free markets" and "assent to a certain number of capitalist commercial enterprises, industries, and underground factories." Within four months such economic "flexibility" and toleration of vestiges of "capitalism" were to go by the board as Mao and his supporters began to press for a politicization of the economy that led to the Great Leap Forward. (*See* "A Record of Liu Shao-ch'i's Talk to Personnel of the Higher Party School on Questions of the Rectification" (May 7, 1957), in *Strike Down the Biggest Person in Authority within the Party Taking the Capitalist Road—Liu Shao-ch'i*, Vol. IV, pp. 94–98.

106. *See* "Comrade P'eng Chen Speaks in Support of the Gentle Breeze Mild Rain Method," *People's Daily* (May 10, 1957), p. 1.

107. *See* "Leading Personnel and the Masses Participate Together in Physical Labor," *People's Daily* (May 10, 1957), p. 4.

人 民 日 報

5月9日，中共北京市委第一書記、北京市市長彭眞（中）在豬市大街同築路工人一起劳动。　　　　新华社記者　顧德华攝

"May 9 [1957], Communist Party Peking Municipal
Committee First Secretary, Peking City Mayor,
P'eng Chen (center) Labors with Construction Workers
at *Chu-shih* Boulevard."
From Jen-min Jih-pao [People's Daily], *May 10, 1957.*

ment would be wrecked by the "antisocialist" intemperance of the non-Party critics. At all "blooming and contending" meetings criticisms of the Party given either verbally or in "big character posters" (*ta-tzu-pao*) were recorded by special work teams, ostensibly so that the Party would be able to learn from the "supervision" of its non-Party critics. This material, however, was soon to be used both in confidential Party reports and in the press to convince those Party leaders who had had doubts about the public rectification campaign that it was not working, and then later as incriminating evidence to justify counterattacks on the non-Party critics.

Some analysts have seen in this encouragement of criticism from non-Party intellectuals a "trap" designed by Mao to expose and discredit "anti-Party" elements in the intellectual community.[108] Aside from the fact that this interpretation ignores all the evidence that "blooming and contending" was directed above all at the "bourgeoisification" of the Party itself, there are also indications that Mao

108. The "trap" interpretation of the "blooming and contending" policy in part derives from a statement in a *People's Daily* editorial of June 22, 1957 which asserted that "the Party decided not to deal immediate counterblows [to its critics], so that the masses might fully recognize the faces of the bourgeois rightists. . . ." (*See* "Unusual Spring," *People's Daily* [June 22, 1957], p. 1.)

This statement is accurate to the extent that Party opponents of "blooming and contending" may have encouraged, or gone along with, the criticism in the expectation that they could use attacks on Party leadership and "socialism" as a basis for terminating the movement. But it would be an error to assume that the only target of the rectification was the intellectual community. If Mao was out to "trap" anyone, it apparently was those Party members who had "allied" themselves with the "bourgeoisie" in the development effort, or who had manifested an interest in "bourgeois rightist" values and ways of asserting Party authority.

A more intriguing question, given the various warnings which had been made by Mao and other official sources that Party leadership should not be challenged in the criticism, is why did many critics nonetheless fall into the "trap" of excessive criticism? Aside from the fact that most non-Party critics *did* seem to sense the limits of acceptable criticism, some may not have had the political sensitivity or experience to "read" properly the context in which criticism was being promoted, and others apparently "got carried away" once criticism began, motivated by personal resentments which they carried as a result of past Party injustices.

At base, however, our interpretation is that except in the highly unlikely circumstance that the non-Party critics would have observed nearly perfect political discipline (that is, no attacks on Marxism or the Party's leading role), the Party apparatus would have used just about any "anti-Party" criticism as an excuse to terminate the movement. In short, lack of Party leadership unanimity in support of "blooming and contending" was a major political factor behind the termination of public rectification and in the "trapping" of non-Party critics.

personally had gambled that the intellectuals were sufficiently disciplined to limit their criticisms to Party abuses of power, and would not resort to fundamental attacks on Party rule and the socialist path of development. This severe criticism of the Party from the intellectual community constituted the third major shock to Party efforts to incorporate intellectuals into the development effort.

Documents published before June 1957 amply reveal that the intellectuals had been warned to keep their criticisms within the bounds of acceptance of Party leadership. Mao had stressed this limitation in his speech to the national conference on propaganda work in early March. On April 6th an editorial in the *People's Daily* again warned the intellectuals that they must diligently study China's new political ideology: "Only by using the standpoint, outlook, and methods of Marxism-Leninism in viewing affairs and in dealing with problems can you avoid committing [political] errors; only then can you overcome the influence of capitalism, individualism and idealism on your thinking." [109] And again in late May, when the intellectuals' criticism had already begun to undermine his position, Mao gave public warning that "words and actions which deviate from the cause of socialism are utterly wrong." [110] Where Mao apparently miscalculated was in overestimating the "socialist discipline" of the intellectuals, and above all in underestimating the resistance within the Party.

That resistance had revealed itself only days after publication of the Central Committee's April 27th directive. In a May 9th interview published in the Peking *Daily Worker,* Lai Jo-yü, Secretary-General of the All-China Federation of Trade Unions and a Party member active in the leadership of the National People's Congress (of which P'eng Chen was Secretary General), disparaged the "blooming and contending." He repeatedly observed that "the views of the masses are, of course, not always or completely correct"; and he stressed that in trade union work it was not possible to "form one's own school of thought" as was being done in the academic field.[111]

This challenge to the rectification movement received a quick and uncompromising reply in the form of a *People's Daily* editorial

109. *People's Daily* editorial, "The Educators Must Receive Education: A Discussion of the Remoulding of Intellectuals" (April 6, 1957), p. 1.

110. These remarks were made to a meeting of Youth League delegates, and subsequently given national publicity. See *SCMP,* No. 1549 (June 13, 1957), p. 20.

111. "How Contradictions within the Ranks of the People Are Handled by the Trade Unions," *Daily Worker* [Peking] (May 9, 1957); trans. in *SCMP,* No. 1535 (May 22, 1957), pp. 8–11.

entitled "On Labor Trouble." "Why," the paper asked, "are there strikes and petitions?" [112] According to the editorial, the cause lay in the bureaucracy of leading cadres. And in remarks apparently addressed to comrade Lai and those for whom he spoke, it was observed:

> A number of leading comrades have their "difficulties." When things are difficult and undoubtedly impossible, you dare not say so. Without a doubt things are impossible, but you choose to make promises. Without a doubt things are difficult, but you choose to say "everything is satisfactory." When a mess is made of things, the masses accuse you of cheating them; and as a matter of fact, you do cheat them.[113]

The editorial then concluded with a reaffirmation that encouragement of criticism and "contrary opinions" was necessary to help the Party resolve "contradictions" in a timely manner and eliminate mistakes in leadership.

A further *People's Daily* editorial on May 19th entitled "Continue to Contend, Aid the Rectification Movement," stressed that although "some comrades . . . feel uneasy and panic-stricken" in the face of criticism, it was all the more necessary to pursue the uncovering and solution of "contradictions," for "they can no more be covered up than a fire can be wrapped in a sheet of paper." [114]

After barely three weeks of public "blooming and contending," pressures began to build within the Party leadership to quash the open criticism. Hints of this pressure were revealed on May 20th and again on the 23rd in New China News Agency reports from Shanghai and Canton: "Old workers" were said to have complained that the press was filled only with accounts of the "defects" of the Party. The "blooming and contending," they implied, had produced poisonous weeds, not fragrant flowers.[115] Within three weeks of these reports the period of encouragement of criticism from non-Party groups was to be brought to an end with a counterattack on the critics entitled "The Workers Start to Speak Up." [116] The Party was reasserting "proletarian" leadership.

The reversal of the compromise decision to promote public criticism occurred sometime between May 25th and June 8th; and the process of this reversal can be approximated from materials

112. *People's Daily* editorial, "On Labor Trouble" (May 13, 1957); trans. in *ibid.*, No. 1536 (May 23, 1957), p. 1.

113. *Ibid.*, p. 3.

114. *People's Daily* editorial, "Continue to Contend, Aid the Rectification Campaign" (May 19, 1957); trans. in *ibid.*, No. 1537 (May 24, 1957), p. 3.

115. *See ibid.*, No. 1546 (June 7, 1957), pp. 4–7.

116. *See* the *People's Daily* editorial, "The Workers Start to Speak Up" (June 12, 1957); trans. in *ibid.*, No. 1553 (June 19, 1957), pp. 6–7.

published in the open press. On the 25th Mao had given his public warning at the Youth League Conference that criticism should not weaken the leading role of the Party. On the same day it was announced that a session of the National People's Congress originally scheduled to open on June 3rd was postponed until June 20th. (On June 19th the meeting was again postponed. It finally convened on the 26th.) [117] Given the fact that this meeting was to be a forum for the public humiliation of anti-Party "rightists" in July, and that P'eng Chen as Secretary-General of the National People's Congress and Liu Shao-ch'i as Chairman of the Congress Standing Committee were directly involved in the planning of the Congress session, it seems most likely that those who opposed public "blooming and contending" were delaying the meeting in order to bring about a reversal of policy.

It was also on May 25th—as the *People's Daily* revealed in its editorial of June 8th signaling a halt to public criticism—that a member of one of the "Democratic Parties" closely identified with the government was sent "an anonymous letter intimidating him" for his support of the Party.[118] Whether this confluence of events on May 25th indicates that it was *the* date on which the Party leadership decided to cut off the public criticism is uncertain. If it was, it confirms the subsequent official line that once the "rightists" publicly exposed their basic opposition to Party rule, the Party held its hand for another two weeks to allow the "poisonous weeds" to sprout fully before turning them into "fertilizer." [119]

In any event, it seems clear that the Party allowed increasingly drastic criticism to be published in the public media in late May and early June in order to mobilize opposition to "blooming and contending" by stimulating fears of *luan*. The most obvious example

117. These reports are translated in *SCMP,* No. 1540 (May 29, 1957), p. 1; and No. 1556 (June 24, 1957), p. 1.

118. *People's Daily* editorial, "What Is This For?" (June 8, 1957); trans. in *SCMP,* No. 1553 (June 19, 1957), p. 3.

Another bit of evidence indicating that May 25th was probably *the* day in which the "blooming and contending" line was reversed is the fact that in 1966 the public phase of the Cultural Revolution began on May 25th with publication of a "big character poster" attacking "bourgeois intellectuals" in control of China's educational system (*see* p. 492 below). The Cultural Revolution seems to have represented for Mao a resumption and carrying to conclusion of attacks on "bourgeois rightist" intellectuals within the Party which was begun, and then thwarted, in 1957.

Roderick MacFarquhar and Michel Oksenberg are to be credited with this interpretation of the significance of May 25th. *See* Oksenberg, *Policy Formulation in Communist China,* pp. 423–428.

119. *See* footnote 108 above. Mao made the same assertion himself, in a *People's* Daily editorial of July 1st, 1957. *See* pp. 319–320 below.

of this purposeful manipulation of criticism in the press to build Party and public opposition to the rectification is found in the case of Ko P'ei-ch'i, a young lecturer in the Department of Industrial Economics at Peking University. On May 31st Ko was quoted in the *People's Daily* as having said:

> China belongs to 600,000,000 people including the counterrevolutionaries. It does not belong to the Communist Party alone. . . . If you [Communists] carry on satisfactorily, well and good. If not, the masses may knock you down, kill the Communists, overthrow you. This cannot be described as unpatriotic, for the Communists no longer serve the people. The downfall of the Communist Party does not mean the downfall of China.[120]

Again on June 8th, the very day that the first official *People's Daily* editorial attacking critics of the Party was issued, Ko was quoted once more: "I want to reiterate once again that the masses want to overthrow the Communist Party and kill the Communists." [121] This verbal violence seems to have been given wide and repeated publicity in order to bring about a reversal of the decision on public "blooming and contending," and then to justify counterattacks on "rightist" critics.

The precise reasoning adopted by the Party leadership in reversing the policy can only be approximated: An unexpected restiveness among university students,[122] scattered acts of physical violence, and the basic criticisms of Party rule by older intellectuals helped to justify fears that "a fire was being lighted" which might indeed produce a Chinese "Hungary." It was revealed later that certain leaders feared that if Party critics gained the forum of the imminent session of the National People's Congress, Party rule would be seriously undermined.[123] Finally, it seems evident that opposition to this form of public rectification continued to remain

120. Cited in Roderick MacFarquhar, *The Hundred Flowers Campaign and the Chinese Intellectuals* (New York: Praeger, 1960), pp. 87–88.

121. *Ibid.,* p. 88.

122. This aspect of the events of the spring of 1957 is documented in René Goldman, "Peking University Today," *The China Quarterly,* No. 7 (July–September 1961); the same author's "The Rectification Campaign at Peking University: May–June 1957," *ibid.,* No. 12 (October–December 1962); and in Dennis J. Doolin, *Communist China: The Politics of Student Opposition* (Stanford: The Hoover Institution on War, Revolution, and Peace, 1964).

123. This reasoning, said to have come from "reliable sources," also appears to have been purposely "leaked" in the Party press during the period of "anti-rightist" attacks in July. *See* "Attempting to Transform the Ministry of Timber Industry into an Independent Kingdom of the Rightists," *People's Daily* (July 22, 1957), p. 2.

active within the Party leadership. Hence resistant Party cadres encouraged the "poisonous weeds" to expose themselves in the expectation that a reversal of Mao's policy could be brought about by an inner-Party opposition mobilized through fears of erosion of the Party's leading role.

This opposition can be said to represent in part the desire to maintain the institutional interests which came with Party membership. Such an interpretation, while necessary, seems hardly sufficient, however, for in other political systems such institutional interests endure amidst public criticism of abuses of power. It seems evident that underlying the formal justifications for terminating open rectification were strong emotional responses, rooted in attitudes toward authority and conflict, which made such public criticism intolerable to most Party members. The old notions were still there—that those in authority were beyond criticism by their subordinates, that criticism would quickly erode the legitimacy of the Party, and that out of this combination of criticism and lack of respect for authority would come *luan.*

Such emotional responses were effectively used by opponents of Mao's policy within the leadership; and some time before the 8th of June, opinion within the Party "center"—perhaps expressed through a vote of the Politbureau—reversed the compromise decision of late April, bringing to a halt public "blooming and contending." As one "rightist" Party member was reported to have said: "Chairman Mao was under very great pressure, and in this domestic crisis the telegrams [from Party opponents of this form of rectification] flew like snowflakes, all demanding restriction." [124]

In the *People's Daily* editorial of June 8th signaling the end of the period of "blooming and contending" and raising the curtain on the "anti-rightist" campaign, some familiar images from China's political past found expression in a new context. The Party paper indignantly declared that some people had sought to characterize the Party as a "fearful man-eating 'tiger.' " And then the editorial noted with predictive satisfaction that "while these rightist elements want to use the rectification campaign for isolating the Communist Party and isolating those who support socialism, the result is that only they themselves are isolated." [125] The subsequent weeks of "struggle" with non-Party critics were to give all too much reality to the "tiger" of Party power, and to the "isolation" of its enemies. Criticism was ended, but the Party was trapped in that old dilemma

124. "The Treachery of Yüan Yung-hsi Being a Rightist and Promoting Attacks on the Party," *People's Daily* (July 22, 1957), p. 2.

125. *People's Daily* editorial, "What Is This For?" (June 8,1957); trans. in *SCMP,* No. 1553 (June 19, 1957), pp. 2–3.

of knowing that behind an apparently docile popular face lay resentments which might burst forth into *luan* if an occasion ever presented itself.

In the weeks following this editorial inquiry into "What is this for?" Party organizations turned on their non-Party critics in an attempt to reaffirm the inviolability of Party authority. Criticisms expressed in May were republished in the public press as demonstrations of the "antisocialist" perfidy of those now under attack and to define clearly the types of criticism which went beyond the limits of political acceptability.

Even in this reversal of policy, however, there apparently was lack of unity within the leadership, and a very mixed outcome as far as Mao's personal position and his political objectives were concerned.

A documentary revelation of the Cultural Revolution suggests that as the Party leadership debated its response to the public criticism of Party rule, Mao sought to emphasize that the main danger exposed by "blooming and contending" was "right opportunism" *within* the Party. He is reported to have said:

> Within the Communist Party there are various kinds of people. Marxists, they are in the majority. They have their faults, but not serious ones. There is another section of people with dogmatic thinking. The majority of these people are loyal and honest; they are for the Party and nation, but their way of dealing with things suffers from the "left" prejudice. If they overcome this prejudice, they will make a great step forward. *There also is a section of people with the erroneous thinking of revisionism, or right opportunism. These people are rather dangerous, because their thinking is a reflection of bourgeois thought within the Party. They lean toward bourgeois liberalism; they are negative about everything. They have a thousand and one connections with the bourgeois intellectuals in society.*[126]

126. Mao, "Things Are Beginning to Change" (May 1957), in *Long Live the Thought of Mao Tse-tung!* p. 15. Emphasis added.

Unfortunately this pamphlet gives no more specific information as to the exact date on which Mao made this statement, or the audience he was addressing. From its content it appears to have been made late in the month, when the criticism of May had exposed both the intellectuals' opposition to the Party, and "bourgeois liberalism" among Party members. One would assume that such a statement would have been made to other Party leaders, which is why we suggest that it represents Mao's attempt to convince the leadership that the main target of the "anti-rightist" struggle should be the "rightists" within the Party.

Mao then went on to reveal his concern with the manner in which the press had been used by the Party in the "blooming and contending" campaign:

> Our Party has a large group of new members who are intellectuals (they are even more numerous in the Youth League). Among them one portion really has quite serious revisionist thinking. They deny the party and class nature of the newspapers. They confuse the differences in principle between proletarian journalism and bourgeois journalism. They confuse the journalism which reflects the collective economy of a socialist country and that which reflects the anarchy and group competition of a capitalist country. *They admire bourgeois liberalism, and oppose the leadership of the Party. They approve of democracy, but oppose centralism. . . . They echo the rightist intellectuals in society, and are united with them as closely as elder and younger brothers.*[127]

While the setting in which Mao made these remarks is uncertain, it appears that he was responding to the direct criticisms of Party rule which had appeared in the national press as "blooming and contending" proceeded during the month of May. What is clear, however, is that Mao's concern was with the influence of "bourgeois liberalism" *within* the Party. And while no doubt he would have approved of efforts to arrest open attacks on the Party from the intellectual community, he sought to focus the emphasis of the ideological struggle on revisionism within the Party. As he phrased it: "Over the past several months people have been criticizing dogmatism. Dogmatism ought to be criticized . . . but at present we must start to pay attention to criticizing revisionism." And he played down the importance of "leftist" errors by asserting that, "Some of what has been attacked as 'dogmatism' actually is a matter of certain errors in work. Some of what has been attacked as 'dogmatism' actually is Marxism." [128]

As the Party organization turned to cut off the attacks of the intellectuals after June 8th, however, there was a period of several months when it appeared uncertain as to whether "right opportunism" within Party ranks in fact would be the major target of struggle.

After an additional delay for planning sessions, the meeting of the National People's Congress originally scheduled for June 2nd opened on the 26th. Three days after Chou En-lai's opening speech —a defensive document that sought to detail the achievements of "socialist transformation" even as it affirmed that "we still have a severe class struggle" [129]—Mao left Peking for Shanghai. It was at

127. *Ibid.* Emphasis added.
128. *Ibid.*
129. Chou En-lai, "Report on the Work of the Government" (June 26, 1957); trans. in *Current Background,* No. 463 (July 2, 1957), p. 6.

this point that public humiliation of leading non-Party intellectuals like Chang Po-chün and Fei Hsiao-t'ung began, as the meeting turned into a forum for attacks on non-Party "rightists."

Why did Mao go to Shanghai? There does not appear to be a certain answer to this question, but a number of interpretations may be advanced on the basis of the limited evidence available.

On July 1st an editorial entitled "The Bourgeois Trend of the *Wen Hui Pao* Should be Subject to Criticism" appeared in the *People's Daily*. During the Cultural Revolution this editorial was identified as having been written personally by Mao;[130] and in a larger sense this criticism of the Shanghai non-Party paper presages Cultural Revolution developments inasmuch as it was the final blast in an attack which had been launched on June 14th in the *People's Daily* by a young literary critic from Shanghai—Yao Wen-yuan.[131] Mao's editorial makes it unmistakably clear that the non-Party press would not be permitted to serve as a platform for "anticommunist and antisocialist" attacks on the Party, or to become the mouthpiece of non-Party politicians like the soon-to-be humiliated Vice Chairman of the China Democratic League, Lo Lung-chi.

Again presaging a theme of the Cultural Revolution, Mao stressed that the "freaks and monsters" who had appeared during "blooming and contending" would be criticized as negative examples in order to educate the Party through struggle. Yet the Chairman asserted that these non-Party critics "may be leniently dealt with without punishment" as long as they recant their errors and mend their ways. At the same time, however, he observed that "blooming and contending" had exposed "bourgeois rightists" within the Communist Party and Youth League; and he concluded by emphasizing

130. *See* "Outline of the Struggle between the Two Lines from the Eve of the Founding of the People's Republic of China through the Eleventh Plenum of the Eighth CCP Central Committee"; trans. in *Current Background*, No. 884 (July 18, 1969), p. 14.

131. *See* Yao's article, "Noted for the Record," and an accompanying *People's Daily* editorial of June 14, 1957 which also has been attributed to Mao, in *SCMP*, No. 1567 (July 11, 1957), pp. 14–16.

Yao was to fire the opening shot of the Cultural Revolution with an article published in the Shanghai *Wen Hui Pao* on November 10, 1965 attacking Wu Han, a literary figure closely associated with P'eng Chen and the Peking Party organization (*see* pp. 478–479 below). During 1966 Yao was to rise to the heights of power as a member of the Small Group of the Central Committee in charge of the Cultural Revolution. He has remained as the youngest member of the Mao-Lin "inner circle" following the Ninth Party Congress of April 1969. The unusual mobility of this otherwise undistinguished young man has led to unconfirmed speculation that Yao is Mao's son-in-law. (*See* Ting Wang, "Yao Wen-yuan: Newcomer in China's Politburo," *Current Scene*, Vol. VII, No. 14 [July 15, 1969], p. 6.)

that the Party would proceed with rectification after it had dealt with the intellectuals.

Given this personal attack on the Shanghai paper, Mao may have gone to the city to investigate the situation there for himself, and to consult with his earlier-mentioned "friends"[132]—perhaps his close supporters K'o Ch'ing-shih, Chang Ch'un-ch'iao, Yao Wen-yuan, and others[133]—about the current state of affairs.

Confusing this straightforward interpretation, however, was the publication of two brief news items on the front page of the *People's Daily* early in July. On the 9th the Party paper carried a notice that Mao had met with a group of non-Party intellectuals for a meal, and had had two hours of "intimate exchanges" with them.[134] And two days later on the 11th a photograph of this meeting— showing Mao seated informally with these intellectuals, at the extreme left edge of the picture—was published on page one of the Party paper without further explanation.[135]

Why should the Party Chairman publicly identify himself with non-Party intellectuals in Shanghai at a time when intellectuals were being publicly humiliated at the National People's Congress meeting in Peking? Was Mao trying to show that he *did* have supporters within the intellectual community? Or was he trying to prove that he was not really "anti-intellectual," only "anti-rightist"? Given the evidence discussed earlier that the Party organization had strongly resisted public "blooming and contending," and that Mao all along had seen his major target in the movement as "rightist conservatism" and "revisionism" within the Party itself, another plausible explanation is that Mao left Peking to disassociate himself from a situation in which the Party organization, under the leadership of Liu Shao-ch'i and P'eng Chen, was trying to "direct the spearpoint" of the struggle at the intellectuals alone. Thus Mao appeared in public with these intellectuals as a subtle expression of

132. *See* p. 305 above.

133. K'o Ch'ing-shih rose to influence in the East China Bureau of the Party in 1954, following the purge of Kao Kang and Jao Shu-shih. He was Chairman of the Shanghai Party Municipal Committee during the Hundred Flowers period. During the Great Leap he was one of Mao's most active supporters. In November 1958 he became Mayor of Shanghai, a post he held until his death in 1965.

Chang Ch'un-ch'iao, like Yao Wen-yuan, was active in artistic and propaganda work as a member of the Shanghai Municipal Party Committee until his rise to national political prominence after 1966 as a Maoist spokesman and influential member of the Cultural Revolution leadership.

134. *See* "Chairman Mao Receives Shanghai Representative Personages of All Walks of Life," *People's Daily* (July 9, 1957), p. 1.

135. *See* the *People's Daily* (July 11, 1957), p. 1.

毛主席接見上海各界代表人士

毛主席7月7日在上海中苏友好大厦接見上海科学、教育、文学、艺术和工商界代表 圖为毛主席和他們亲切交談。　新华社記者　侯　波攝（無綫电傳眞）

"Chairman Mao Holds Meeting with Representative Personages
of Shanghai's Scientific, Educational, Literary, Artistic
and Industrial and Commercial Circles on July 7 [1957] at Shanghai's
Sino-Soviet Friendship Building. The Photograph Shows Chairman Mao
Having Intimate Exchanges with Them."
From Jen-min Jih-pao, *July 11, 1957.*

protest over the course of events in which the Party was trying to protect itself against an "anti-rightist" rectification.

A former Party cadre viewing the photograph of Mao with the Shanghai intellectuals observed that whoever had selected this picture with Mao seated at the extreme left—rather than in the center, where the Chairman of both Party and State normally appears—may have been engaging in a subtle ridicule of Mao for his "leftism" of having pressed the struggle with "right opportunism." The image of Mao seated at the extreme left of a group of intellectuals does seem to convey the message "right in form but left in essence," and this perhaps is the most accurate characterization of Mao's "blooming and contending" policy: establishing a temporary relationship with the intellectuals by encouraging them to criticize "rightist" errors of Party cadres who apply the policies of the leadership.

Assuming that such a tactic was Mao's original intention in promoting "blooming and contending," the excessive "anti-Party" criticism of the intellectuals in May undermined the Chairman's position and justified the opposition of those Party leaders who had resisted the movement. This interpretation only stresses that Mao may have left Peking "in defeat," and gone to Shanghai to mobilize support from like-minded comrades in the provincial Party organizations for initiatives which the Chairman was to press at the Tsingtao Conference of Party leaders in mid-July.

These additional developments in July, and the above interpretation of the *People's Daily* photograph, are given added support by critical material that appeared in the Party paper during the ensuing weeks. As attacks on the intellectuals progressed in Peking, information was published in the *People's Daily* documenting the "anti-Party" perfidy of the "rightists." Some of this material appears to represent an effort by the Party organization to criticize Mao subtly by exposing him to public ridicule (as they felt he had tried to do to them). An article recounting the "crimes" of Chang Po-chün quotes this leader of the Chinese Peasants' and Workers' Democratic Party and Minister of Communications as having said, "Socialist democracy ought to exceed capitalist democracy. The president of a capitalist country has a term of three or four years; and how many years had Stalin? And who knows how many years Chairman Mao will want?" [136]

A "rightist" Party member and journalist, Tai Huang, was reported to have "madly attacked the Chinese People's respected and beloved great leader Chairman Mao, saying that he 'early had had

136. "The Viciousness and Intrigues of the Chang-Lo Alliance," *People's Daily* (July 22, 1957), p. 6.

his doubts' about Chairman Mao, and that after the Twentieth Party Congress of the Soviet Union he had 'begun to suspect that Chairman Mao had committed errors.' "[137] And Ch'en Ming-shu, a member of the dissident Revolutionary Committee of the Kuomintang, was quoted as having said that Chairman Mao was "hot tempered," "impetuous," and "reckless," and that "these characteristics . . . have often affected his decisions in matters of policy, causing unnecessary deviations in the implementation of governmental policy." [138] Ch'en was said to have added that Mao "lets his temper get the best of him, and is apt to hurt the feelings of ranking cadres despite their high positions."

These and other remarks critical of Mao, placed in the mouths of "anti-Party rightists," seem to convey with biting irony the resentment felt by many within the Party toward Mao for his impulsive policy interventions. Some of these men felt that Mao had betrayed the Party organization by fostering public criticism of cadre errors by disloyal intellectuals. Similarly, the "leak" published at this time about the opposition of Liu Shao-ch'i and P'eng Chen toward "blooming and contending," and the other information about inner-Party decision-making processes discussed earlier in this analysis, seems intended to reveal to all with political awareness the division of responsibility for the decisions of the spring. Party rule had been threatened and those who were willing to tolerate "bourgeois" interests in the development effort were now being forced to promote the public humiliation of the intellectuals.

This interpretation of the political uses of the press is reinforced by later developments. Liu, P'eng and other leaders were to use the writings of intellectuals as voices of veiled criticism of Mao in the wake of the Great Leap Forward;[139] and many of the major actors of the period of "blooming and contending"—Hu Ch'iao-mu, a man long associated with the press and propaganda work, Teng T'o, editor of the *People's Daily,* and Propaganda Director Lu Ting-yi—were to fall from power during the Cultural Revolution under such charges as having used their power over the press to "facilitate attacks by bourgeois rightists." [140] Lu Ting-yi, in par-

137. "New China News Agency Besieges Tai Huang on Successive Days," *People's Daily* (August 8, 1957), p. 2.

138. "Kuomintang Revolutionary Committee Holds Symposium Exposing Ch'en Ming-shu and the Rightists on July 14th," *NCNA* (Peking), in *Current Background,* No. 475 (August 28, 1957), p. 45.

139. *See* pp. 415–418 below.

140. Red Guards alleged in 1967 that, "When bourgeois rightists launched rabid attacks against the Party in 1957, Hu Ch'iao-mu, . . . taking advantage of the power of supervising Party newspapers he had usurped, . . . on

ticular, was accused of having "used stealthy means to castrate the revolutionary soul of Chairman Mao's policy of 'letting a·hundred flowers bloom and a hundred schools of thought contend.' " [141]

What is most notable in documentation from the Cultural Revolution, however, is the almost complete absence of specific charges against leaders such as Liu Shao-ch'i and P'eng Chen related to the 1956–57 period of "blooming and contending." The above vague references to Lu Ting-yi and Hu Ch'iao-mu are two of the infrequent Red Guard allegations of attempts by Party leaders to distort Mao's policy line during this period.

There seem to be a number of reasons for this silence which can be advanced on the assumption that our basic interpretation of the late April 1957 compromise decision between Mao and Liu-P'eng is correct. First, the evidence would indicate that while there was disagreement within the top leadership, it was kept within the bounds of open institutional procedures and processes of decision-making. Unlike the earlier charges against Kao Kang, or those to be made against P'eng Teh-huai in 1959 and later against P'eng Chen and Lu Ting-yi during the Cultural Revolution, there has been no indication that Liu and P'eng resorted to "conspiratorial" methods at this time to resist Mao.[142] Indeed, one should add that they probably had no need to, inasmuch as Party resistance to public "blooming and contending" at all levels was evidently strong and persistent. Mao had been on the political defensive ever since Khrushchev's attack on Stalin, and if anyone would have had to resort to conspiratorial methods to oppose majority opinion within the Party, most likely it would have been Mao himself. In this sense, Mao "lost" an open debate within the Party leadership.

Furthermore, Mao's policy of using the intellectuals to help

---

numerous occasions resisted and defied Chairman Mao's directives and criticisms in a futile attempt to stop propagating the Party's general and specific policies in Party newspapers and to facilitate attacks by bourgeois rightists." (The Revolutionary Rebel Detachment of the Union of Chinese Writers, "Liu Shao-ch'i's Black Hand in the Realm of Literature and Art: The Assorted Crimes of Hu Ch'iao-mu," *Literary Combat Journal* [Peking], No. 4 [April 14, 1967]; trans. in *SCMP*, No. 3942 [May 19, 1967], p. 8.)

141. "Thirty-three Leading Counterrevolutionary Revisionists"; trans. in *Current Background*, No. 874 (March 17, 1969), p. 40.

142. Indeed, Red Guard materials cite Mao as having explicitly stated that, "Liu [Shao-ch'i] and Teng [Hsiao-p'ing] have always done their work in the open," in contrast to the "double-dealers" like Kao Kang, Jao Shu-shih, P'eng Teh-huai, and later P'eng Chen and Lu Ting-yi, who conspired in secret. (Cited from the transcript of a talk which Mao gave in October 1966, in the Red Guard pamphlet, *Long Live the Thought of Mao Tse-tung!* p. 45.

rectify Party errors had been proved wrong, for the non-Party critics had not limited their attacks to individual abuses of authority but had criticized the very basis of Party rule. It seems unlikely that Mao and his supporters would want to recall these events in 1957 at a time when Liu and P'eng were under bitter attack for their past errors.

In several very important respects, however, Mao can be said to have "won" even though his public rectification program was cut off—which perhaps most fully explains the lack of rancor during the Cultural Revolution concerning the events of 1957. Seen in terms of both the larger Party debate on a strategy of national development and policy decisions made before and after 1957, Mao gained in two important policy areas: Party rectification, and the basic approach of the development effort.[143]

Even as the public humiliation of non-Party "rightists" proceeded during the July session of the National People's Congress, Mao was pressing for a continuation of the "anti-rightist" struggle within the Party. A *People's Daily* editorial of July 28th emphasized that rectification was only in the process of expanding at all levels and all places in the country. As a result of the events of the spring, "it cannot be denied that the [political] standpoint of a portion of Party members was neither clear or firm." [144] Another editorial of early September entitled "Handle Inner-Party Rightists Sternly" asserted that, "There are also many 'rightists' who are veteran Party members of ten or twelve years," and that, "If the existence of rightists within our Party is tolerated, these rightists will collude with rightists outside the Party to attack and oppose us from within." [145]

Thus Mao apparently had been able to use the public criticism of the spring—and Party resistance to it—to convince his colleagues

143. Mao has made this assertion himself. In remarks to Chinese students in Moscow in November 1957 he observed; "Some people say that the real victory of the socialist revolution in our country was achieved in 1956, but as I see it this actually took place in 1957. The system of ownership was transformed in 1956, and this was relatively easy to carry out. But in 1957 the socialist revolution was victorious in the political and ideological spheres. Now the rightists have been toppled, although there are still shortcomings in our work. The current rectification campaign is an important event and we must truly reform ourselves." ("Talk at a Meeting with Students and Trainees of Our Country in Moscow" [November 17, 1957], in *ibid.*, p. 16.)

144. *People's Daily* editorial, "The Anti-Rightist Struggle Is a Weighty Test for Every Party Member," (July 28, 1957), p. 1.

145. *People's Daily* editorial, "Handle Inner-Party Rightists Sternly" (September 11, 1957); trans. in *SCMP,* No. 1616 (September 24, 1957), p. 2.

that "rightist conservatism" *was* the main danger, and that the Party had to be disciplined. This shift towards consensus within the Party leadership in Mao's favor appears to have developed between mid-July and September of 1957, culminating in the Third Plenary Session of the Eighth Central Committee. This Plenum agreed to promote a vigorous rectification within the Party and also revived Mao's twelve-year program for agricultural development which had been shelved in April 1956.

Hence, with increasing scope after Teng Hsiao-p'ing's report on the rectification movement delivered to the Central Committee Plenum in late September, the rectification was pressed within the Party.[146] In part this process involved attacks on those Party intellectuals who had opposed the strengthening of ideological controls over artistic life,[147] but it also took a toll of more than seventy-five leadership cadres of ranks as high as alternate Central Committee member, provincial Party secretary, and provincial vice-governor.[148]

One analyst has concluded that in almost every one of these provincial purges rural policy was an issue,[149] which stresses the second respect in which Mao was able to turn the events of the spring to his advantage. To the degree that the "blooming and contending" policy had been conceived by Mao as a way of confronting "bourgeois rightist" ideas within the Party, the criticisms of the spring provided further support for his contention that the "alliance" with the intellectuals in a heavy-industry-oriented approach to development created a threat to the Party's revolutionary goals: Mao had stressed in his 1955 writings on agricultural cooperation the fundamental importance for China's development of increasing agricultural productivity; and this position had been reiterated in his April 1956 analysis, "On the Ten Great Relationships" and again in the "contradictions" speech of February 1957.[150] The

146. *See* Teng Hsiao-p'ing, "Report on the Rectification Campaign" (September 23, 1957), in *CC 1955–59*, pp. 343–363. This document affirms Mao's evaluation of the state of the Party and Chinese society which had been the basis of the public rectification campaign policy, and is notable for its striking contrast in tone with Teng's speech to the Eighth Party Congress of the previous year.

147. *See* Goldman, *Literary Dissent in Communist China*, Ch. IX.

148. The organizational positions and policy errors of the major "objects" of the inner-Party "anti-Rightist" purge of the fall and winter of 1957–58 are analyzed in Frederick C. Teiwes, "The Purge of Provincial Leaders, 1957–1958," *The China Quarterly*, No. 27 (July–September 1966), pp. 14–32.

149. *Ibid.*, p. 17.

150. Mao phrased it, "As China is a large agricultural country, with over 80 percent of her population in the rural areas, industry must

"betrayal" of the intellectuals enabled him to stress that a development strategy which placed reliance on their skills held great dangers for the Party.

This argument, combined with continuing problems of agricultural production, appears to have enabled Mao to bring about a major reorientation in China's development effort beginning with the Third Central Committee Plenum of September 1957. Within a year of this meeting China's entire rural population had been reorganized into township or county-wide amalgamations of Agricultural Producers Cooperatives called People's Communes. In this respect, the two-year debate over "blooming and contending" prepared the way for the policies of the Great Leap Forward by breaking the Party's "alliance" with the intellectuals and the development strategy which that "alliance" implied.

In this analysis we have stressed the impact of events in the Soviet Union and Eastern Europe in shaping the leadership debate and coalition of forces within the Chinese Communist Party. Mao's "blooming and contending" policy in large measure was a reaction to "de-Stalinization" and to events in Hungary as they held meaning for China. In a notable way Chinese responses to these developments within the Bloc produced their own counterresponses in the U.S.S.R. and Eastern Europe.

Mao's encouragement of public criticism of the Chinese Communist Party set a disturbing precedent for other Bloc Parties (as initially had been the case with Khrushchev's criticism of Stalin). At the Fortieth Anniversary celebrations of the October Revolution in November 1957, both Mao (in Moscow) and Liu Shao-ch'i (in Peking) gave speeches which *inter alia* attempted to explain and justify to other "fraternal Parties" the policy of public "blooming and contending." [151] It was later revealed that Khrushchev had

---

develop together with agriculture. . . . Without agriculture there can be no light industry. But it is not yet so clearly understood that agriculture provides heavy industry with an important market." And then he noted cryptically that there was a "contradiction between the objective laws of economic development of a socialist society and our subjective understanding of them—which needs to be resolved ·in the course of practise. *This contradiction also manifests itself as a contradiction between different people,* that is, a contradiction between those with a relatively accurate understanding of these objective laws and those with a relatively inaccurate understanding of them." However, as of early 1957, Mao was able to add that this "contradiction" was one among "the People." (Mao, "On the Correct Handling of Contradictions among the People," in *Selected Readings from the Works of Mao Tse-tung,* pp. 385–386. Emphasis added.)

151. These speeches are reproduced in *CC 1955–1959. See* esp. pp. 392, 397–398.

been upset by the Chinese Party's rectification line,[152] and his displeasure with Mao was to be increased by Chinese claims made during the fall of 1958 that the People's Communes had placed China on the verge of realizing communism (and by implication ahead of the Russians).[153]

Khrushchev's attack on Stalin had undermined the legitimacy of the Soviet experience for other Communist Parties, and the People's Commune experiment can be seen as an effort by Mao and other Chinese leaders to evolve an approach to national development adapted to local circumstances and derived from their own revolutionary traditions. This effort was further to erode Soviet leadership of the Bloc, and heighten Sino-Soviet tensions. In dialectical fashion, political developments within the International Communist Movement in the wake of Stalin's death produced reactions and counterreactions which have continued to disintegrate Stalin's empire.

In the matter of differing approaches to Party rectification, the Chinese "blooming and contending" of 1957 was to have a disturbing influence within the Bloc; yet one that was mild relative to Soviet horror in reaction to Mao's greatest Party "rectification," the Great Proletarian Cultural Revolution of 1966–1969. The full impact of these most recent events in China on other ruling Communist Parties has yet to be felt fully.

In terms of domestic Chinese political developments of the next decade, the Hundred Flowers period of 1956–57 reveals in muted outline some of the key issues which were to grow into the Cultural Revolution. Liu Shao-ch'i's attenuated appeal at the first session of the Eighth Party Congress—and again in the spring of 1957—for support on the basis of his protection of the Party apparatus against a Maoist public rectification was to be repeated in the "four clean-ups" movement after 1962. Thus resistance within the Party to another rectification was to be a major stimulus to the Cultural Revolution.[154] The public "blooming and contending" of 1957 presaged the Cultural Revolution in the sense that in 1966

152. *See* Edward Crankshaw's summary of Khrushchev's attack on Mao at the Bucharest Party Congress of June 1960, in Jerome Ch'en, ed., *Mao* (Englewood Cliffs, N.J.: Prentice-Hall, 1969), p. 148.

153. Soviet displeasure with the Chinese Commune experiment is analyzed in Zagoria, *The Sino-Soviet Conflict, 1956–1961*, Ch. III.

154. *See* Charles Neuhauser, "The Chinese Communist Party in the 1960s: Prelude to the Cultural Revolution," *The China Quarterly*, No. 32 (October–December 1967); Richard Baum and Frederick C. Teiwes, "Liu Shao-ch'i and the Cadre Question," *Asian Survey*, Vol. VIII, No. 4 (April 1968); and the "Comment" and "Reply" by Neuhauser in *The China Quarterly*, No. 34 (April–June 1968), pp. 133–144.

Mao was to turn again to groups outside the Party to force a large-scale attack on those who resisted rectification.

The efforts of P'eng Chen and other leaders to shield the intellectuals from Mao's policies of "unity and struggle" and opposition to "rightist conservatism" was to be another major theme in leadership conflict after the Tenth Central Committee Plenum of September 1962. And the indirect use of the press to snipe at Mao was to grow into encouragement of but lightly-veiled ridicule following the failure of the Great Leap Forward. But in the dialectic of inner-Party politics, the Great Leap would have to run its course before opponents of the Chairman's policies would have an issue of sufficient strength to enable them to attempt, once again, to limit Mao's influence on the course of China's revolution.

Chapter XVIII

TO LEAP FORWARD:
THE RELATIONSHIP OF
POLITICAL CONFLICT
TO SOCIAL CHANGE

The struggle in the socialist countries between the road of socialism and the road of
capitalism—between the forces of capitalism
attempting a comeback and the forces opposing it—is unavoidable. But the restoration of
capitalism in the socialist countries and their
degeneration into capitalist countries are certainly not unavoidable. We can prevent the
restoration of capitalism so long as [we] . . .
wage a prolonged, unremitting struggle. *The
struggle between the socialist and capitalist
roads can become a driving force for social
advance.*[1]

In one of his earliest philosophical writings, "On Contradiction,"
Mao stressed the relationship between conflict and social change:

The fundamental cause of the development of a thing is not external
but internal; it lies in the contradictoriness within the thing. . . .
Changes in society are due chiefly to the development of internal contradictions. . . . [It] is the development of these contradictions

1. Editorial Departments of *People's Daily* and *Red Flag*, "On Khrushchev's Phoney Communism and Its Historical Lessons for the World," in
Polemic on the General Line of the International Communist Movement, p.
470. Emphasis added.

[through struggle] that pushes society forward and gives the impetus for the supersession of the old society by the new.[2]

One of the major aspects of Mao's impact on the course of the Chinese revolution has been the effort to institutionalize forms of conflict—methods for resolving "contradictions"—in a society where traditional attitudes toward authority inhibit criticism of the old and established, retard innovation, and slow the pace of social and economic advance.

In the previous chapter we explored Mao's attempt to establish a critical relationship between "the People" and the Party as a way of subjecting conservative ideas to "rectification." Here we shall examine the period of recent political history which most clearly manifests the Maoist approach to promoting controlled social conflict as a way of changing the organization of work and of forcing people to clarify their political "standpoint." The policies of the Great Leap Forward—formulated in the fall and winter of 1957–58 and applied through 1960—are a particularly concentrated expression of Mao's political values and methods of operation: The People's Commune system of rural social and economic organization which was instituted during these years embodies Mao's belief in the virtues of self-reliance and popular "activism." In the Taiwan Straits crisis of 1958, the Party Chairman resorted to another political confrontation in order to test the international balance of power and to force China's major ally to clarify its stand in relation to the revolution and China's national defense. And in the combined policies of the Great Leap Forward, as they were promoted in the fall of 1958, Mao revealed his continuing commitment to that style of political action which intertwines war, social change, and economic production.

As with the Hundred Flowers period preceding these developments, the Party leadership was not in agreement as to whether the rapid effort to establish the People's Communes was the most appropriate way to promote the country's social and economic advance. The conflict over a proper strategy of national development had found increasingly sharp expression after Liberation over questions of land reform, industrial organization, and agricultural collectivization. By 1958 Mao and other leaders had become conscious of a temporal rhythm in the evolution of Party policy and the process of social change. Mao appears to have used the outcome of the 1957 "blooming and contending" (the discrediting of the intellectuals, and the inner-Party rectification), as well as the uncertain state of the

2. Mao, "On Contradiction," *SW*, English, I, pp. 313, 314.

economy in the fall of 1957, to play consciously on what the Party leadership characterized as a "saddle shaped" pattern of social advance. The Chairman sought to mobilize support for policies designed to organize the Chinese people into self-reliant economic and political communities which would see them through the transition to communism.

Also in common with the events of 1956–57, Sino-Soviet relations were an important element in the evolution of Chinese domestic policy during the period of the Great Leap Forward. Now, however, Mao was on the offensive. He was searching for a *Chinese* solution to the problems of social change in an underdeveloped peasant society. He conceptualized organizational solutions for rural reconstruction which the Soviets saw as a deliberate challenge to their preeminent position in the International Communist Movement. During the years 1958–59 Mao does not seem to have challenged Soviet leadership of the Bloc directly; rather, he seems to have gone his own way in domestic policy and to have promoted international policies which would force the Russians to take a more militant stand in dealings with "imperialism."

In the Taiwan Straits crisis of 1958 Mao was apparently deliberately testing what the Soviet Union's new intercontinental ballistic missile capability implied for China's national defense. From the outcome of this confrontation, as well as from Russian reactions to the Sino-Indian border conflict of the following year, Mao was to find Khrushchev sorely lacking in "proletarian internationalism." When the Russian Party leader came to Peking in October 1959—just after a tour of the United States—to attend celebrations marking the Tenth Anniversary of the People's Republic, Mao became fully convinced of the necessity of promoting struggle with "revisionism" within the International Communist Movement. He saw that China's national interests and her social revolution needed to be safeguarded against external political pressures and ideological subversion.

Foreign and domestic developments during the period of the Great Leap were most clearly linked in the actions of the Chinese Defense Minister, P'eng Teh-huai. It may have been with Khrushchev's encouragement that P'eng challenged Mao's economic and defense policies in the wake of the unsuccessful Taiwan Straits venture and the increasingly serious economic difficulties resulting from the Great Leap Forward. Mao weathered P'eng's challenge at the Eighth Central Committee Plenum in the summer of 1959, and brought the Chinese Communist Party to the point of open conflict with Soviet "revisionism." Yet in the context of increasingly serious difficulties for China in both her domestic economy and international relations, Mao's political authority was to become seriously eroded—thus setting the stage for a more serious leadership conflict in the 1960s.

As with other agricultural societies seeking to become industrial states, China's problems in economic modernization are basically related to the transformation of the peasants' productive capabilities. Increased agricultural output is the key to economic development, as products of the rural economy provide almost 80 percent of the raw materials for light industry. Increases in food production are necessary to support urbanization and to feed a growing rural population. And the sale of food grains is a major source of foreign exchange.

Conversely, stagnation in the rural economy will inhibit the importation of certain foreign products necessary to promote industrialization, slow down domestic industry because of the lack of raw materials, restrict the rural market for industrial products, and aggravate all the social problems associated with population growth under conditions of decreasing standards of living. But until the late 1940s, China's peasants still followed ancient social and technical patterns. *How* should the country proceed to increase agricultural productivity? This issue is still one of the most contentious facing the Party leadership.

During the first years after Liberation the Soviet experience in economic development exercised a major influence over the thinking of the Chinese leadership on the question of the relationship between agricultural growth and industrialization. Specifically, while industrial expansion was seen as closely related to agricultural productivity the full development of agriculture's productive potential was assumed to be dependent upon mechanization—itself a function of industrialization. In Maoist terms, here was a "sharp contradiction."

In the Soviet Union socialization of the rural economy into large-scale, collectivized production units had occurred on the basis of the technical reform of agriculture. Increases in labor productivity and per-acre yields were brought about through the introduction onto state farms of the tractors, pumps and irrigation equipment, chemical fertilizers, and so on, which are the products of an established industrial economy. Industrialization had *preceded* the social transformation of rural life.

It was this experience which shaped Chinese thinking during the early stages of social change in the rural areas: land reform between 1947 and 1952; the formation of mutual aid teams during

1952–53; and then the establishment of "primary stage" Agricultural Producers' Cooperatives (APCs) in 1954–55 (in which the peasants pooled their land for management by the cooperative, but retained private ownership and the right to withdraw). A powerful element within the Party leadership assumed that the "socialist transformation of agriculture"—the elimination of private ownership and management by individual peasant families—would occur *after* China's industrial capacity had grown to the point of making possible the mechanization of agricultural production.

This view of the relationship between industrialization and agricultural growth was challenged during 1954–55, in part as a result of two years of poor harvests. The agricultural sector was not meeting its targeted contributions to the First Five Year Plan (1953–1957), with the result that industrial goals could not be attained. In the now apparent contradiction between the rural and urban economies, agriculture increasingly came to be seen as the bottleneck in China's overall economic modernization.

Beginning in 1954 there was an attempt to rethink China's strategy of economic development.[3] In contrast to the Soviet experience, China's industrial base was small relative to the size of her agricultural sector. There was little unused land which could be brought into production (unlike the vast tracts of "virgin land" in the Soviet Union). And China's rural population density and her underemployed agricultural labor force were both high, in contrast to Soviet labor scarcity. The process of reconsidering the relevance of the Soviet precedent for China's economic and social conditions began with a rethinking of the relationship between mechanization of the rural economy and the social transformation of peasant life.

According to Mao's one-time personal secretary Ch'en Po-ta, it was Mao himself who challenged "the old concept originally held by some comrades that without the mechanization of agriculture it would be very difficult to realize the large-scale cooperativization of agriculture."[4] Mao evidently came to believe that the "contradiction" between China's industrialization and her agricultural growth could be resolved by bringing about the social transformation of rural life *before* its mechanical revolution. Agricultural

3. In this discussion I have found particularly helpful Kenneth R. Walker, "Collectivization in Retrospect: The 'Socialist High Tide' of Autumn 1955–Spring 1956," in *The China Quarterly,* No. 26 (April–June 1966), pp. 1–43; and Alexander Eckstein, *Communist China's Economic Growth and Foreign Trade* (New York: McGraw-Hill, 1966), esp. Chs. I–III.

4. Ch'en Po-ta, "Under the Flag of Comrade Mao Tse-tung," *Red Flag,* No. 4 (July 16, 1958), p. 4.

productivity could be increased through the intensive application of peasant labor power, mobilized through socialist (collective) forms of work organization and political control. Mao's program thus implicitly challenged the Soviet development precedent, and the thinking of many colleagues within the Party leadership. In the second half of 1955 the Chairman began to press for rapid completion of "primary stage" collectivization, the immediate socialization of these larger production units into "advanced stage" cooperatives, and the promotion of a basic form of technical change through the widespread introduction of a double-wheel double-shared plow.

Mao's initial efforts to rethink a development strategy suited to Chinese conditions—expressed, in part, in a twelve-year program for agricultural development drafted in late 1955—generated strong resistance within the Party leadership. His efforts in the first months of 1956 to follow on cooperativization with measures to bring about a "leap forward" in production under the slogan of "more, better, faster, and more economically" were blocked by those who saw this continuous pressure for progress as the promotion of "reckless advance." They saw his policies for "continuous revolution" as not allowing sufficient time to consolidate the organizational changes brought about by collectivization, producing economic imbalances, and shifting emphasis away from the high-priority industrialization effort. And as we suggested previously, this opposition to Mao's policies was strengthened by the process of "de-Stalinization" in the Soviet Union.

The outcome of the Hundred Flowers experiment, and disappointing harvests in 1956 and 1957, however, gave Mao and his supporters the added political influence needed to reinvoke these thwarted plans of 1956 for increasing agricultural production. With the convening of the Third Plenum of the Eighth Central Committee in September 1957, the "reds" within the leadership began to reestablish their control over China's pattern of economic development. This reassertion of Mao's influence was promoted through the "anti-rightist" Party rectification which was intensified in the fall of 1957 and continued well into the fall of 1958, when the movement to establish People's Communes throughout China was fully under way.

The details of the process by which Mao came to the full conception of the Great Leap Forward and the People's Communes as the basis for China's national development are not fully known by foreign observers, but the concept and its relationship to an altered strategy of economic development are not difficult to describe.

In its simplest terms, the policy of "developing industry and

毛主席观看新式农具——双轮双铧犁　　　侯　波摄（新华社稿）

"Chairman Mao Inspects a New Type
of Agricultural Tool—a Double-Wheel, Double-Shared Plow."
From Jen-min Jih-pao, *October 25, 1955.*

agriculture simultaneously on the basis of priority to heavy industry" which was advanced following the Third Central Committee Plenum in September 1957 represented an effort to promote China's economic growth without paying the price of a slowdown in the rate of industrialization.[5] Heavy industry was to continue to receive priority in the investment of capital, while agricultural productivity was to be increased through more intensive application of the "capital" of peasant labor. The State was not to provide investment funds. Rather, there was to be local financing of capital construction through the accumulation and investment of local production surpluses. What was to become known as the policy of "walking on two legs" in economic development represented an effort to rely on local resources to increase productivity in the rural areas, while using China's scarce "hard" capital and technically advanced manpower in the urban economy to promote rapid industrialization. One senses that this policy may have reflected a compromise within the Party leadership: Mao was given support for his "political" policies in the countryside in return for his continued acceptance of such "economic" considerations as priority in capital investment for the development of heavy industry.

In any event, the "three red flags" of policy during the period of the Great Leap Forward (1956–1960)—the "general line" for socialist construction of "more, better, faster, and more economically"; the effort to achieve a "great leap" in production; and the formation of People's Communes—were presented as an integrated set of policies designed to promote the pace of China's development fast enough to overtake Britain's level of economic productivity within fifteen years.

The organizational core of these policies was the People's Commune, which was to be the instrument for mobilizing peasant labor and capital in order to create self-reliant rural communities and to

5. This new economic line was formally promoted after a two-week National Economic Planning Conference held in early December 1957. It replaced the formula of "step by step, to bring about socialist industrialization of the country, and step by step, to accomplish the socialist transformation of agriculture, handicrafts and capitalist industry and commerce" which was stressed by Li Fu-ch'un in his mid-1955 report on the First Five Year Plan, and reiterated by Liu Shao-ch'i in his political report to the first session of the Eighth Party Congress.

The "simultaneous development" line of 1958–1960 was replaced at the Ninth Central Committee Plenum of January 1961 with a formula of "agriculture as the foundation of the national economy, and industry as the leading factor," in which still greater efforts and resources were concentrated on development of the rural economy in the context of the Great Leap production crisis.

strengthen economic and political leadership over the peasants. The Commune concept reflects both Mao's values of self-reliance and activism and his continued commitment to the successful experience of the revolutionary period.[6] As early as 1956 Mao had asserted the continuing relevance of the Party's pre-Liberation experience for the period of economic construction:

> To mobilize all the active factors and all the available strength has always been our principle. Formerly, this principle was applied to winning the people's democratic revolution and terminating the imperialist, feudalist, and bureaucratic-capitalist domination. Now it is [to be] applied to a new revolution—the socialist revolution and the construction of a socialist country.[7]

Self-reliance and local initiative are the two dominant themes that run through the rationale advanced by the Party for the Communes. In line with the "walking on two legs" concept, the cadre journal *Study* (*Hsüeh-hsi*) stressed, "it is impossible for the State to provide all the capital required for agricultural development and we must depend primarily on the cooperatives [later to be renamed Communes] for the accumulation of such capital."[8] The rural economy was thus to "pay its own way" in the purchase of machinery and fertilizer from its own production surpluses (after paying taxes to the State). The farmers were also to pay the costs of any destruction of farm machinery and animals, such as had occurred on a limited scale in 1955–56 as a result of peasant resistance to the "high tide" of collectivization.

This approach to mechanization was also seen as a way of encouraging the development of initiative and of managerial and technical skills at the local level. In 1956 Mao had complained about the increasing bureaucratization of economic planning:

> Now there are dozens of hands interfering with local administration, making things difficult for the region[s]. Although neither the Center nor the State Council knows anything about it, the Departments [of the Central Government] issue orders to the offices of the provincial

6. A detailed analysis of the experiments in political and economic organization of the "Yenan" period which were reapplied during the Great Leap Forward will be found in Mark Selden, "The Yenan Legacy: The Mass Line," in A. Doak Barnett, ed., *Chinese Communist Politics in Action* (Seattle: University of Washington Press, 1969), pp. 99–151.

7. Mao, "On the Ten Great Relationships" (April 1956), in Jerome Ch'en, ed., *Mao*, p. 66.

8. Yüeh Wei, "Capital Accumulation in the Agricultural Producer Cooperatives," *Hsüeh-hsi* [Study], No. 7 (April 3, 1958); trans. in *Extracts from China Mainland Magazines* (hereinafter cited as *ECMM*), No. 132 (June 16, 1958), p. 32.

and municipal governments. . . . Forms and reports are like floods. This situation must change and we must find a way to deal with it.[9]

Mao's "way to deal with it," as policy evolved in the fall and winter of 1957–58, came to embody fundamental changes in the pattern of work and administration in the rural areas. In 1956 the Party Chairman had (unsuccessfully) called for a "cut of two-thirds of our party and government organizations." [10] In 1958 this call was manifest in a large-scale *hsia-fang* or "down to the country-side" campaign which involved millions of Party and government office workers in rural labor.[11] Mao seemed determined to prevent the formation of a huge bureaucratic superstructure with such a vested interest in centralized economic planning that all initiative in the rural areas would be quashed under a weight of departmental directives. And as with his 1955–56 effort to prevent a reemergence of class polarization in the villages by forming fully socialized collectives, his decentralization of economic decision-making to the provinces and communes seemed designed to prevent polarization between town and countryside. He could see the dangers of the entrenchment of a small, urbanized political and economic elite, increasingly "cut off from the masses" by physical distance and bureaucratic routine.

Mao's effort to strengthen local economic leadership also manifested itself in rejection of Soviet agricultural institutions. In Russia the Machine Tractor Stations had been a major vehicle by which the State had taxed the collective farms. Mao sought to dilute the "contradictions" in taxation and technical skill between state and society by giving the rural producers direct control over agricultural machinery, and by allowing them greater choice in the investment of their own production surpluses.[12]

To be successful as an experiment in economic self-reliance, the rural management and production organizations had to be large enough to include sufficient labor, capital (chiefly land, agricultural tools, animals, and machinery), and raw materials to enable them to be self-supporting economic units. Thus, the essential

9. Mao, "On the Ten Great Relationships," in Ch'en, ed., *Mao*, p. 75.

10. *Ibid.*, p. 77.

11. *See* Rensselaer W. Lee III, "The *Hsia Fang* System: Marxism and Modernization," *The China Quarterly*, No. 28 (October–December 1966), esp. p. 47.

12. *See* the excellent analysis of the extended leadership debate over state control versus local initiative in agricultural mechanization in, The Editor, "The Conflict between Mao Tse-tung and Liu Shao-ch'i over Agricultural Mechanization in Communist China," *Current Scene* (Hong Kong: United States Information Service), Vol. VI, No. 7 (October 1, 1968), esp. pp. 8–12.

institutional transformation of the Communization drive was the amalgamation of "primary stage" APCs (approximately 30–40 households; roughly comprising a small "natural agricultural village") and the "advanced stage" APCs (approximately 300 households) into Commune units of somewhere between 5,000 and 8,000 households.[13]

This basic pattern of amalgamation in rural organization was seen as one of the great strengths of Communization. In practice, however, it embodied some of the major weaknesses of the movement. Theoretically, this larger scale of production activity would overcome the fragmentation which traditionally had accounted for the low level of China's agricultural productivity, and break down the strong sense of local interest in opposition to that of the political "center." As Franz Schurmann has phrased it, Communization was seen as a way of penetrating to the "inaccessible core of Chinese social organization," the kinship groups and small villages, and of establishing an institutional "bridge on which state and society would meet and merge." [14]

In application, however, the Communes were to alienate the peasant from his most basic social ties and remove from him both initiative in the making of production decisions and economic reward commensurate with personal effort. Thus the human relationships which integrate a society were seriously weakened, and some of the most basic motives for work and innovation—personal responsibility and remuneration according to effort—were eliminated. Similarly, while the objective in forming Communes was to replace a centralized economic bureaucracy with local decision-making units, in fact the reorganization was brought about by a political command structure which was as insensitive to local conditions as any metropolitan economic ministry. Thus, ironically, what Mao saw from the "center" as an effort to promote greater local initiative in fact took initiative out of the hands of the primary producers, the peasants. Power passed "up" from the villages to the Communes and regional Party organizations.

From a social perspective, the Commune concept was seen by its advocates as a way of eliminating enduring sources of social

13. The best discussions of what the amalgamation of APCs into Communes implied for agricultural planning, management and commodity exchange will be found in Kenneth R. Walker, *Planning in Chinese Agriculture: Socialization and the Private Sector, 1956–1962* (Chicago: Aldine Publishing Co., 1965); and G. William Skinner, "Marketing and Social Structure in Rural China, Part III," *Journal of Asian Studies,* Vol. XXIV, No. 3 (May 1965), pp. 363–399.

14. Schurmann, *Ideology and Organization in Communist China,* pp. 471, 496.

inequality. By decentralizing industrial activity—most notably in the mass campaign for the smelting of iron and steel and in the creation of local light industry—the Communes would moderate the social distinctions separating industrial and agricultural workers, urban and rural residents. And by involving governmental bureaucrats and Party cadres directly in economic production several months each year, the Communes would help to bridge the gap between mental and manual labor which traditionally had reinforced the "contradiction" between state and society.

Furthermore, the Communes were supposed to foster popular socialist consciousness through a restructuring of the pattern of property ownership and daily living. Class distinctions in the countryside, already weakened by land reform, were to be reduced further by eliminating all major forms of private ownership of the means of production (private plots, small farm animals, and agricultural tools). As one writer observed, Communization was intended "thoroughly to overcome the desire for private property and private interest on the part of the upper-middle peasants." [15]

The "liberation" of women from household activities for productive labor, and the concomitant formation of communal mess halls, nurseries, kindergartens and boarding schools, and "homes of respect for the aged," were seen as weakening male-female distinctions and aiding in "obliterating the role of family head and the bourgeois authoritarian ideology in respect to family relations." [16]

Mobilization of labor for production was one of the major economic objectives of Commune formation; and here the links of the movement to the Party's revolutionary past, as well as to its hopes for the future, become most apparent. As we have noted, one of the basic characteristics of Chinese Communist political organization during the Yenan period was the intertwining of war, production, and social change. Peasants in the Liberated areas were both producers and guerrilla fighters, mobilized by Party cadres for both war and production through Party control of the peasant associations and militia, and through the manipulation of land rent and interest rates—and later the system of land ownership.

This close linkage between Party leadership, local defense, and the organization of production had weakened after land reform. On the eve of the 1955–56 "high tide" of collectivization, Mao had

15. Wang Yen-li, *et al.*, "An Investigation and Study of the Problems of Transition from Higher Stage Cooperatives to People's Communes," *New Construction*, No. 9 (September 3, 1958); trans. in *ECMM*, No. 145 (October 13, 1958), p. 8.

16. T'ien Sheng, "The Outlook of Communism as Seen from the People's Communes," *Political Study*, No. 10 (October 13, 1958); trans. in *ECMM*, No. 151 (December 22, 1958), p. 10.

attacked local Party organizations for showing "a spineless attitude toward agricultural cooperation," and for not exercising active leadership in promoting social change in the villages.[17] It was such a situation which Mao sought to correct through the varied policies of the Great Leap Forward.

The institutional forms by which Mao sought to have the Party reassert leadership over rural life embody the two major organizational innovations of the Commune movement. First, Party control over operational economic decisions was effected through the merging of township (*hsiang*) government and Commune economic unit—an amalgamation which placed the organs of local government under the control of Party committees directed by the provincial Party organization. In this way Mao sought to shift power away from the bureaucrats and "experts" discredited in the "blooming and contending" of 1957, and place it in the hands of a politically mobilized Party organization. Thus power moved "down" from the central government ministries to the provincial Party organizations. At the same time power was being pulled "up" from the primary producers, the peasant families and villages, to the levels of township/Commune and province.

Second, the Party sought to exercise control over peasant labor power through the militarization of the labor force. Drawing on the wartime experience of embattled Yenan, when the Party successfully rebuilt its strength in a poor agricultural region under conditions of economic blockade by Nationalist and Japanese troops, the Party now sought to organize the rural population into "regiments," "battalions," "companies," and "squads." The peasants, "who have for several thousand years lived in a scattered state, [were thus to be transformed] into a highly organized and disciplined group of new people with an increasingly high degree of Communist awareness."[18]

While the public press gave partial justification for the militarization of work and the expansion of the People's Militia (*min-ping*) in terms of the strengthening of national defense,[19] the primary

17. See Mao, *Socialist Upsurge in China's Countryside*, pp. 136–139, 206–207.

18. "Countless Advantages of Militarization: An Account of the Militarization of Hsü-Shui People's Commune," in *Double Collection of Works on the National Defense of China*, Vol. IV, trans. in Joint Publications Research Service, *Strengthening of National Defense and Socialist Construction and Advantages of Militarization*, No. 22,800 (January 20, 1964), p. 86.

19. Prior to mid-September of 1958 the formation of militia units had been carried out without fanfare in selected areas of China. It was only after the Taiwan Straits crisis had passed its peak of military danger and entered a diplomatic phase that a nationwide campaign for "everyone a soldier" was launched, and a national conference on militia work convened.

rationale advanced for this change in the organization of production was the more effective mobilization of labor. As the newly published Party journal *Red Flag* stressed:

> To "get organized along military lines" of course does not mean that [peasants] are really organized into military barracks, nor does it mean that they give themselves the titles of generals, colonels, and lieutenants. It simply means that the swift expansion of agriculture demands that they should greatly strengthen their organization, act more quickly and with greater discipline and efficiency, so that like factory workers and army men they can be deployed with greater freedom and on a larger scale.[20]

In China's "war" on her poverty, Mao sought to invoke the heroic spirit and work style of pre-Liberation military actions which had brought the Party to power. A *People's Daily* editorial exhorted "Secretaries of Party committees regularly [to] mobilize the masses to examine their thinking, energy, working style, plans, measures, and coordination. Like fighting a war, we must win one battle after another and must, on the completion of one target, immediately put forward another." [21]

The "blooming and contending" of 1957 had exposed conservative or antisocialist attitudes in the cities, and now Mao sought to invoke the same technique of public debate to reshape the peasants' attitudes toward their involvement in the development process. He revealed his belief in "the power of the word" in a celebrated statement of April 1958 in which he referred to China's people as "poor and blank":

> On a blank sheet of paper free from any mark, the freshest and most beautiful characters can be written, the freshest and most beautiful pictures can be painted. The big character poster is a very useful weapon, which can be used . . . wherever the masses are to be found. It has already been widely used and should always be used. A poem by Kung Tzu-chen of the Ching Dynasty reads:
>
> *Only in wind and thunder can the country show its vitality;*
> *Alas, the ten thousand horses are all muted!*

20. *Red Flag* editorial, "Greet the Upsurge in Forming People's Communes," No. 7 (September 1, 1958); trans. in *Current Background*, No. 517 (September 5, 1958), p. 3.
There is perhaps no clearer symbolic indication of Mao's effort to shift China's development pattern away from one of bureaucratic administration to an emphasis on "mass line" popular mobilization than the change in title of the cadre theoretical journal in the summer of 1958 from *Study* to *Red Flag*.
21. *People's Daily* editorial, "Push Forward Steel Production by Every Means" (August 27, 1958); trans. in *SCMP*, No. 1855 (September 17, 1958), p. 6.

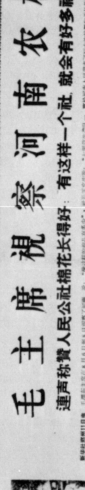

毛主席視察河南農村

連聲稱贊人民公社棉花得好：有這樣一個社，就會有好多社

"CHAIRMAN MAO INSPECTS HONAN FARM VILLAGES
Repeatedly Praises the Good Growth of Cotton in a People's Commune:
'If There Is This Kind of a Commune, Then There Can Be Many Communes.'"
From Jen-min Jih-pao, August 12, 1958.

O Heaven! Bestir yourself, I beseech you,
And send down men of all the talents.

Big-character posters have dispelled the dullness in which "ten thousand horses are all muted." [22]

The "word" which was to bestir China's people was Mao's conception of the People's Commune, which was put forward during the summer of 1958 with propaganda rather than planning. The cadres drew their policy guidance from the national press. In August, Mao made a widely publicized tour of the provinces during which he asserted, "It is best to form People's Communes." [23] And he was quoted as having told Wu Chih-p'u, his supporter in the Honan Party organization, "If there is this kind of a Commune [in Honan], then there can be many Communes." [24] From such assertions of oracular simplicity, Party cadres learned of the major objectives of institutional reform which they were expected to adapt to their local conditions, and the production targets which they would be required to meet in the coming year.

In the air of tension which surrounded the convening of the enlarged Politbureau meeting at Peitaiho in August of 1958—as gunfire was breaking over the offshore islands—it was claimed that Mao's conception would be the basic unit of society to take China rapidly through the transition to Communism. A *Red Flag* editorial declared with incautious elation that "people can easily see the budding sprouts of Communism," [25] thus strengthening Ch'en Po-ta's earlier assertion:

> It is very obvious that under the guidance of Mao Tse-tung's thought, under the flag of Comrade Mao Tse-tung, in this time of a universal high tide when the nation's economy and culture are developing as if "one day equals twenty years," people already can see a future in which the step-by-step transition from socialism to communism will not be long.[26]

Mao's spokesman, Wu Chih-p'u, stated in the national press that the People's Communes would be "not very different from" the old Marxist ideal of the Paris Commune; and he asserted that with hard work China's people could create the material conditions

22. Mao, "Introducing a Co-Operative" (April 1958), in *Selected Readings from the Works of Mao Tse-tung,* pp. 403–404.
23. *People's Daily* (August 13, 1958), p. 1.
24. *Ibid.* (August 12, 1958), p. 1.
25. *Red Flag* editorial, "Greet the Upsurge in Forming People's Communes" (September 1, 1958); trans. in *Current Background,* No. 517 (September 5, 1958), p. 2.
26. Ch'en Po-ta, "Under the Flag of Comrade Mao Tse-tung," *Red Flag,* No. 4 (July 16, 1958), p. 9.

which would enable them to be remunerated according to the Communist principle of "to each according to his need," in "six or seven years, or somewhat longer." [27]

The inflated rhetoric and exaggerated claims which accompanied the movement to form People's Communes in the fall of 1958 seem to have been advanced purposefully by the leadership to raise the enthusiasm of Party cadres and "the People" for one more great organizational transformation of Chinese society. Yet the process by which Mao attained the power to implement his conception of the People's Commune was hardly without conflict or opposition. Indeed, as the Great Leap increased in momentum, official Party documents revealed a consciousness among the leaders of a temporal pattern in policy formation. This pattern was commented upon by Liu Shao-ch'i in his political report to the second session of the Party's Eighth National Congress held in May of 1958:

> The development [of the economy] is U-shaped [literally, "horse-saddle shaped," *ma-an-hsing*], i.e., high at the beginning and end, but low in the middle. Didn't we see clearly how things developed on the production front in 1956—1957—1958 in the form of an upsurge, then an ebb, and then an even bigger upsurge or, in other words, a leap forward, then a conservative phase, and then another big leap forward?
>
> The Party and the masses have learned a lesson from this U-shaped development.[29]

27. Wu Chih-p'u, "On People's Communes," *China Youth Daily* (September 16, 1958); trans. in *Current Background*, No. 524 (October 21, 1958), pp. 5, 14–15.
It was such statements as this, and earlier ones by Ch'en Po-ta—issued by highly authoritative Party spokesmen—which stimulated Khrushchev's ire by intimating that the Chinese expected to attain "Communism" before the Soviets. *See* Chinese and Soviet differences on this point documented in Zagoria, *The Sino-Soviet Conflict, 1956–1961*, Ch. III.
28. The analysis in this section draws much inspiration from two earlier studies of cyclical patterns in Communist Chinese political and economic life: G. William Skinner and Edwin A. Winckler, "Compliance Succession in Rural Communist China: A Cyclical Theory," in Amitai Etzioni, ed., *Complex Organizations: A Sociological Reader*, pp. 410–438; and Alexander Eckstein, "Economic Fluctuations in Communist China's Domestic Development," in Ping-ti Ho and Tang Tsou, eds., *China in Crisis*, Vol. I, Book 2, pp. 691–729.
29. Liu Shao-ch'i, "Report on the Work of the Central Committee of the Communist Party of China to the Second Session of the Eighth National Congress," trans. in *CC 1955–59*, p. 427.

The nature of the "lesson" to which Liu referred, however, seems more political than economic in quality.[30] Liu himself had been a major spokesman for the "go slow" approach to agricultural development which had predominated in the spring of 1956, shaped the policies of the first session of the Eighth Party Congress, and persisted as a "conservative phase" through the first half of 1957.[31] The second session of the Eighth Party Congress of May 1958 must be seen as a new start for Mao, a reassertion of the economic line which had been thwarted by more cautious leaders after the "high tide" of collectivization. Liu's report to the Congress represents the *mea culpa* of those leaders who had opposed Mao's mass mobilization approach to breaking the agricultural bottleneck to China's economic development.

The "saddle-shaped" pattern to which Liu referred is more political than economic also because underlying the economic policies of these years (1955–1958) is a sequence of leadership debates and policy shifts which shaped the Party's approach to promoting social change. This repetitive pattern can be described simply as follows: First there is a phase of conflict between radical and conservative

30. *See* Liu Kuo-tung, "How May We Understand the 'U-Shaped' Curve?" in *Study*, No. 12 (August 3, 1958); trans. in *ECMM*, No. 145 (October 13, 1958), pp. 38–39.

31. At the Lushan Central Committee Plenum in the summer of 1959 Mao referred back to "those people who opposed venturesome advance" in 1956. He noted that, "The wavering of 1956 and 1957 was not given a dunce cap but was described as a question of method of thinking." He ridiculed their conservatism as "representing the dreary, tragic disappointment and pessimism of the petty bourgeoisie," but made light of their opposition by noting that, "They merely had no experience, and once there were signs of trouble, they were unable to stand firm and turned to oppose venturesome advance."
These opponents of 1956–57, while on Mao's side during the Great Leap, evidently again became the focus of growing resistance as the Commune movement ran into trouble. Perhaps referring to former Minister of Commerce Ch'en Yün, and to Liu Shao-ch'i, Mao warned at Lushan: "The road taken by the comrades who made mistakes in the second half of 1956 and the first half of 1957 has been repeated [in 1959]. They are not rightists, but they have cast themselves toward the brink of rightism. . . . It will be strange indeed if the tune of these comrades is not welcomed by the rightists. Comrades of this kind adopt the policy of brinkmanship. This is rather dangerous, and for those who have any doubts about this, the future will be my witness. My saying these things in public will hurt some people, but it will be [more] harmful to these comrades if I do not speak out now." (Mao Tse-tung, "Speech at the Lushan Conference" [July 23, 1959], in *Mao Chu-hsi tui P'eng, Huang, Chang, Chou Fan-tang Chi-t'uan ti P'i-p'an* [*Chairman Mao's Criticism and Repudiation of the P'eng, Huang, Chang, and Chou Anti-Party Clique*] [n.p., n.d.], pp. 8–9.) This publication is hereinafter cited by its English title.

groups ("reds" and "experts") within the Party leadership over proper policies for social advance—a debate in which several years of poor economic performance enable the radicals to build support for a basic institutional restructuring of society. The radical claim is that they will "liberate the productive forces" (popular energies) through a rearrangement of the "relations of production" (the pattern of property ownership and work organization).

This change in policy line within the leading councils of the Party is followed by an inner-Party rectification campaign, in which lower level opponents of a more radical line are criticized or purged, and the Party organization is mobilized for the leadership tasks of a new mass campaign. A period of public "study" and discussion ensues, in which the objectives of the campaign are propagated to "the masses" and objections are refuted. On the basis of these preparations, a period of intense institutional change or labor mobilization then takes place.

In the period of "upsurge" in organizational change or work activity, excesses are committed by over-zealous Party cadres. These excesses produce economic or organizational difficulties which more conservative leaders invoke in order to shift opinion within the Party "center" toward a period of consolidation. The radicals thus begin to lose their influence in policy-making. "Expert" considerations reemerge and a more moderate orientation persists until further economic or social problems once again enable the "reds" to reassert their influence over Party policy. Thus another round of the pattern or cycle begins.

To grasp fully this "saddle-shaped" pattern, as it led to the Great Leap Forward of 1958, it is necessary to retrace the major agricultural policy decisions since mid-1955. As noted previously, Mao's July 1955 speech on agricultural collectivization came at a time of increasingly uncertain Party leadership over the rural economy. As Marshal of the Army Ch'en Yi recalled in late 1955, this speech "settled the arguments on the question of cooperativization of agriculture during the past three years, [overcame] the rightist vacillating ideology, and enabled certain comrades to turn from their mistaken paths to the correct road of Marxism-Leninism." [32] More exactly, Mao's speech—in combination with decisions of the Sixth Plenum of the Seventh Central Committee which followed in October—reversed a trend toward dissolution of those coopera-

32. Ch'en Yi, "Comrade Mao Tse-tung's Report on Agricultural Cooperativization Is a Classic Example of Combining Theory and Practise," *People's Daily* (November 13, 1955); trans. in *SCMP*, No. 1177 (November 24–25, 1955), p. 45.

tives which already had been formed. Mao derided the fact that "some comrades" had disbanded cooperatives "in a state of panic," and he observed that continuing problems in the rural areas derived from the fact that certain Party leaders had "become scared of the several hundred thousand small cooperatives." [33]

In this state of uncertainty in Party leadership, and in what Mao saw to be a situation of the increasing reemergence of class polarization in village life, the problem was how to mobilize the Party into an effective instrument of leadership in the rural areas. This process began with the creation of consensus within the leadership over plans for a period of rapid formation of "primary stage" APCs. Mao personally exercised direction over the collection of reports from regional areas where cooperativization had already progressed in the early months of 1955, and "advance copies of these articles were printed and distributed to responsible comrades from provincial, municipal, autonomous regional, and regional Party committees" who attended the October enlarged Central Committee Plenum.[34] This documentary summation of "advanced experience," and a revised version of the collection which was published in December of 1955, was to serve as the "model" for study by those who would be guiding the "upsurge" in cooperativization.

Mao's effort to disseminate the experiences of selected regions in organizing APCs, however, trailed behind the actual formation of cooperatives, for political pressures now far outweighed practical concerns. The level of political tension within the Party was substantially heightened at the October enlarged Central Committee Plenum. A resolution on cooperativization, based on Mao's July report, stressed that in the new stage of the revolution the Party had to deal forcefully with "the struggle of the peasants against the rich peasants and other capitalist elements," and that the essence of cooperativization was "a struggle over the choice between two roads—the development of socialism or of capitalism." The resolution also reaffirmed that "the criticism made by the Political Bureau of the Central Committee against Right opportunism is absolutely correct and necessary." [35]

Such remarks, coming as they did in the last stages of a nationwide campaign for the "liquidation of counterrevolutionaries" (*su-*

33. Mao, "On the Question of Agricultural Co-Operation," in *Selected Readings from the Works of Mao Tse-tung,* p. 322.

34. *See* Mao's "Preface" in *Socialist Upsurge in China's Countryside,* p. 7.

35. "Decisions on Agricultural Cooperation," adopted at the Sixth Plenary Session (Enlarged) of the Seventh Central Committee of the Chinese Communist Party; trans. in *CC 1955–59,* pp. 106–107.

fan), made it clear to Party cadres that failure to press for the formation of APCs would hold the very serious consequences of "right opportunism." Or still worse, a laggard might be accused of being one of the "landlord, rich peasant, or counterrevolutionary elements" who were alleged to "have already wormed their way in various guises into cooperatives." [36]

The shift within the Party leadership from economic to political considerations was further emphasized by the temporary eclipse of the cautious Director of the Party's Rural Work Department, Teng Tzu-hui. In pre-1955 statements on agriculture, Teng had revealed a concern about not repeating the errors of collectivization which had occurred in the Soviet Union in the early 1930s.[37] Mao, in his report on cooperativization, conspicuously downplayed the significance of the Soviet difficulties by noting that they had been "quickly corrected." And it seems likely that he had Teng in mind when he noted that "on no account should we allow . . . comrades to use the Soviet experience as a cover for their idea of moving at a snail's pace." [38] Teng's eclipse was made obvious to Party members by the fact that explanations on the draft of the Plenum resolution on cooperativization were presented to the Central Committee not by Teng, but by Mao's close associate Ch'en Po-ta.

Finally, it appears that determination within the Party leadership to press for rapid formation of APCs was enhanced by reports of a bountiful summer harvest (a 9 percent increase over the 1954 level, in contrast to the meager increases of 1.6 percent and 2.1 percent for the two previous years).[39] The harvest provided a resource margin which would help to cushion any temporary dislocations which might result from disruptions in the organization of rural life.

This combination of a mobilized Party organization and a population tense in the wake of efforts to root out "counterrevolutionaries" in the rural areas established the political context for the first big surge in the "high tide" of cooperativization. At the October Plenum it was estimated that about 15 percent of all peasant households in China were already in APCs. By December Mao observed with satisfaction that this figure had swelled to more than 60 percent, making the planning of the summer and fall already out of

36. *Ibid.*, p. 114.

37. *See* the "General Introduction" to *CC 1955–59,* p. 3.

38. Mao, "On the Question of Agricultural Co-Operation," in *Selected Readings from the Works of Mao Tse-tung,* p. 331.

39. Alexander Eckstein, "Economic Fluctuations in Communist China's Domestic Development," *China in Crisis,* Vol. I, Book 2, p. 716.

date. The Party Chairman stressed: "All must be appropriately expanded and accelerated." [40]

A second surge in the formation of cooperatives was initiated with a meeting of the Supreme State Conference in late January 1956. Mao now pressed for a "leap forward" in production which would bring about early completion of the First Five Year Plan. It was also at this meeting that his twelve-year program for agricultural development was first presented—and elaborated upon by Minister of Agriculture Liao Lu-yen. The fact that the press release of this session of the Supreme State Conference identified Liao by his Party position as Deputy Director of the Central Committee's Rural Work Department seems intended to emphasize the continuing eclipse of the Director of that Department, Teng Tzu-hui, who was thus all the more conspicuous by his absence from among those leaders identified as having attended the meeting. Teng was to resume his public role as Party spokesman on agricultural matters only after the meetings of the Politbureau in April of 1956, at which Mao's influence over economic policy was restricted.[41]

Between January and April of 1956, however, a mobilized Party and peasantry raised the socialist organization in the Chinese countryside one further level. In December of 1955 only 4 percent of all rural households had been organized into the "higher stage" cooperatives. By the time the Politbureau met in enlarged session in late April 1956 this figure had risen to 58 percent, where it temporarily stabilized.

While the rapidity of this expansion can be accounted for in part by the harvest cycle—the effort to complete organizational changes before the spring planting season—it would also appear that Mao, sensing opposition within the Party leadership to rapid change in the rural areas, pressed ahead to present his more cautious colleagues with a *fait accompli*. And by all evidence the late April meeting of the Politbureau, which was not publicly disclosed until Liu Shao-ch'i and Wu Chih-p'u made passing references to the session in subsequent publications,[42] represented the culmination of

40. Mao's "Preface" to *Socialist Upsurge in China's Countryside*, p. 8.

41. The role of the cautious Teng Tzu-hui in formulation of agricultural policy, and the waning of his influence in times of political radicalization, is documented in Michel Oksenberg, *Policy Formulation in Communist China*, pp. 145–155, 578–580.

42. Wu Chih-p'u has indicated that April 25th, 1956 was the date on which Mao delivered his economic analysis, "On the Ten Great Relationships." (*See* "Contradictions Are the Force that Moves a Socialist Society Forward," *People's Daily* [June 14, 1960]; trans. in *SCMP*, No. 2285 [June 27, 1960].)

a period of decision during which Mao's influence over the Party's political and economic policies was temporarily restricted.[43]

The particular significance of the April 25th meeting as a point of major conflict and opposition to Mao is further reinforced by the disclosure—as a result of the Cultural Revolution—of the full text of an analysis of the economy which Mao presented to his Party colleagues at this time. Entitled "On the Ten Great Relationships," Mao spelled out the contradictory choices which faced the Party in its efforts rapidly to modernize China's economy. He also gave his judgments as to how those contradictions should be resolved.

Most notable is his analysis of the "contradiction between industry and agriculture." The phrasing of his discussion suggests that the Party Chairman faced strong opposition from those leaders who were determined to prevent a reallocation of capital away from investment in heavy industry. As he called for a rise in the proportion of capital invested in agriculture and light industry Mao stressed: "Does this mean that heavy industries are no longer important? They are still important. Is this to shift our focus of attention from them? Let me put it this way: most of our investment will continue to go to heavy industries." [44]

In the wake of the Hungarian uprising a year later when he was in a stronger political position, Mao more forthrightly stressed the paradox that by giving greater investment priority to agriculture and light industry in the short run, "what may seem to be a slower pace of industrialization will actually not be so slow, and indeed may even be faster." [45]

In the spring and summer of 1956, however, opposition to Mao's economic line seems to have been a composite of economic consid-

43. As noted earlier (*see* pp. 275–276 above) this period of restriction in influence began in the wake of Khrushchev's "de-Stalinization" effort. The Party leadership met at the end of March or early April, and issued the editorial interpretation of Stalin's errors on April 5th. At the same time, a Central Committee and State Council joint directive was published attacking "extravagance and waste" in the new APCs, and criticizing local cadres for "making a show of their work." (*See* "CCP Central Committee and State Council Issue Joint Directive on Running of Cooperatives," NCNA [April 4, 1956]; trans. in *SCMP*, No. 1268 [April 16, 1956], p. 3.) In late April Mao presented his comprehensive analysis of China's economic problems, "On the Ten Great Relationships." One infers from the lack of publicity given to this speech at the time, and the silence on references to the twelve-year agricultural plan which Mao had presented in January, that the Chairman's influence had been restricted.

44. Mao, "On the Ten Great Relationships," in Jerome Ch'en, ed., *Mao*, p. 67.

45. Mao, "On the Correct Handling of Contradictions among the People," in *Selected Readings from the Works of Mao Tse-tung*, p. 385.

erations cemented together by institutional interests and the impact of "de-Stalinization." Mao's critics stressed the dangers of "disequilibrium" and "weak links" in the overall pattern of development, together with the existence of supply shortages in certain construction materials, especially steel. The fiasco of the 1955–56 program for wide application of the double-wheel double-share plow, which had proven to be unusable in the soft mud of south China's paddy fields, had wasted large quantities of steel. And even as stalwart a Maoist spokesman as Chou En-lai subjected this early experiment in the technical reform of agriculture to criticism at the Eighth Party Congress as being an example of "reckless zeal." [46]

Peasant opposition to the formation of "advanced stage" APCs, while mild in comparison to the violence and dislocation of rural life which had occurred during the similar period of Soviet collectivization,[47] prompted some Party leaders to characterize the "high tide" of the fall and spring as "reckless advance." They were able to mobilize sufficient support to throw "doubts" and "misgivings" on Mao's plans,[48] and on his general line of "more, better, faster, and more economical" increases in production.[49]

The determination of more conservative leaders to thwart Mao's political pressures, to consolidate the changes brought about by the

46. Noted in "The Conflict between Mao Tse-tung and Liu Shao-ch'i Over Agricultural Mechanization in Communist China," *Current Scene*, Vol. VI, No. 17 (October 1, 1968), p. 8. *See also* Roy Hofheinz, "Rural Administration in Communist China," *The China Quarterly*, No. 11 (July–September 1962), p. 148.

47. Thomas P. Bernstein, "Leadership and Mass Mobilization in the Soviet and Chinese Collectivization Campaigns of 1929–30 and 1955–56: A Comparison," in *The China Quarterly*, No. 31 (July–September 1967), pp. 1–47.

48. Noted by Liu Shao-ch'i in his political report to the Second Session of the Eighth Party Congress. *See CC 1955–59*, pp. 426–427.

In view of the evidence that Liu himself had had "misgivings" about Mao's policies of "reckless advance" in 1956, his remarks of 1958 have the ironical quality of a public self-criticism.

49. Given the particular significance which swimming has had for Mao (*see* p. 178 above, and p. 476 below), it may be some reflection of the frustration which the Chairman apparently felt during the late spring and summer of 1956 at his inability to sustain the drive to form APCs that he swam in the Yangtze several times in May and June. After these occasions he wrote a poem on "Swimming" which seems to express his impatient "pacing" outside the room of political influence:

Heedless of boisterous winds and buffeting waves,
Better this seemed than leisurely pacing home courtyards,
Today I have obtained my release.

(Extracted from Mao's June 1956 poem, "Swimming," in Wong Man, trans., *Poems of Mao Tse-tung* [Hong Kong: Eastern Horizon Press, 1966], p. 50.)

drive to form agricultural cooperatives, and to sustain the primary emphasis on industrialization, gained political momentum with the publication of a *People's Daily* editorial on June 20th, 1956, entitled "Oppose Both Conservatism and Hastiness." Subsequently identified as the work of Teng T'o, Hu Ch'iao-mu, and Lu Ting-yi writing under Liu Shao-ch'i's direction,[50] the editorial gives an ironical twist to words taken from Mao's preface to *Socialist Upsurge in China's Countryside*: ". . . one should not indulge in idle fantasies unrelated to reality, plan one's actions beyond the conditions dictated by the objective situation or force oneself to do the impossible." [51] It observed that, "The forty articles of the National Program for the Development of Agriculture are supposed to be put into effect separately in five, seven and twelve years, but some comrades, being hasty, try to do all things in two or three years." [52] And in a nearly direct identification of those "some comrades," the editorial noted:

> That hastiness is a serious question is due to the fact that it exists not only among the cadres of the lower levels but *primarily among the cadres of the higher levels,* and that in many cases the hastiness manifest at the lower levels is the result of pressure applied by the higher levels.[53]

The phrasing of this editorial and subsequent political and economic developments suggest, however, that there was a significant discrepancy between the efforts of certain leaders at the Party "center" to bring about a period of consolidation in the rural areas and the determination of Mao and his supporters within the regional Party apparatus to complete the work of organizing "advanced stage" APCs.[54] Between May and December of 1956 the percentage

50. *See* "Outline of the Struggle between the Two Lines from the Eve of the Founding of the People's Republic of China through the Eleventh Plenum of the Eighth CCP Central Committee," *Liberation Daily* (Shanghai); trans. in *Current Background*, No. 884 (July 18, 1969), p. 11. Also, "Confession by Counter-Revolutionist Wu Leng-hsi," *Worker's Review*, No. 5 (June 1968); trans. in *SCMM*, No. 662 (July 28, 1969), p. 5.

51. *People's Daily* editorial, "Oppose Both Conservatism and Hastiness" (June 20, 1956); trans. in *SCMP*, No. 1321 (July 3, 1956), p. 11.

52. *Ibid.*

53. *Ibid.*, p. 12. Emphasis added.

54. This division within the leadership influenced many areas of economic activity. For instance, Minister of Water Conservancy Fu Tso-yi, complained in early 1957 of the lack of clear policy guidelines during the spring and summer of 1956: "Some people [within the leadership] spoke of blind advance and others did not speak of blind advance. There was much confusing discussion." (Cited in Oksenberg, *Policy Formulation in Communist China*, p. 270.)

of rural households in the fully socialized cooperatives increased from 62 percent to 88 percent.[55]

In contrast to this completion of cooperativization after the harvest season, documents from the Party's Eighth Congress of September 1956 reveal continuing disagreement with Mao's economic policies, and they deprecate through silence his contributions to Party leadership. Liu Shao-ch'i's political report began by recalling the Party's accomplishments since the Seventh Congress held at the end of the War of Resistance against Japan. In line with the stress on collective leadership, Liu gave hardly a mention to Mao's leading role in formulating the Party's policies which had led to a successful prosecution of the Civil War against the Nationalists, and to the recently concluded "socialist transformation" of the rural economy.[56]

Liu referred to the continuing movement to form APCs, but he phrased his comments in a manner that obscured the impact of Mao's July 1955 intervention on the question of agricultural policy. He noted that the recent formation of the cooperatives had "followed on the correction by the Party's Central Committee and Comrade Mao Tse-tung of the rightist conservative ideas within the Party which had tended to stifle the peasant masses' enthusiasm for agricultural cooperation." [57] And as if there had been no "upsurge" in the formation of APCs in the fall and winter/spring of 1955–56, he noted ironically that the Party's policy of "step-by-step" advance in the socialization of rural life had enabled the peasants "gradually [to] accustom themselves to the ways of collective production." Such a policy, he asserted, meant that "losses

55. These figures, based on Chinese sources, are drawn from Kenneth R. Walker, "Collectivization in Retrospect," *The China Quarterly,* No. 26 (April–June 1966), p. 35; and the same author's *Planning in Chinese Agriculture,* p. 14.

56. This slighting of Mao in 1956 contrasts with Liu's political report to the Party's Seventh Congress in 1945, where he had invoked Mao's name and policies more than one hundred times. In his Eighth Congress report Liu cited Mao by name on only four occasions. (Noted in Roderick MacFarquhar, "Communist China's Intra-Party Dispute," *Pacific Affairs,* Vol. XXXI, No. 4 [December 1958], fn. 21, p. 333.)

57. Liu Shao-ch'i, "Political Report of the Central Committee of the Communist Party of China to the Eighth National Congress of the Party," in *Eighth National Congress of the Communist Party of China,* Vol. I, pp. 25–26.

This phrasing contrasts with Liu's use of the formulation "the great Chinese Communist Party and its leader Comrade Mao Tse-tung," as well as his repeated references to the leading role of "the thought of Mao Tse-tung" and Mao's "guiding principles" in his political reports of 1945 and 1958. (*See* p. 359 below.)

which might have resulted from sudden changes could be averted, or greatly reduced." [58] And even as Party cadres in the provinces were continuing to press for completion of the movement to form the "advanced stage" APCs, Liu stressed,

> we have to win over, on the basis of the policy of voluntariness and mutual benefit, a small number of peasant households still outside cooperatives to join the cooperatives, and give guidance to the transformation of elementary cooperatives into cooperatives of the advanced type. But we have to be patient and give them time; coercion or commands in any form will not be allowed. The most urgent problem awaiting solution now is that all possible efforts must be made to ensure an increase in the output of about a million cooperatives now existing and in the income of their members.[59]

Concerning the contentious issue of competing investment priorities between industry and agriculture, Liu bluntly stated,

> Some comrades want to lower the rate of development of heavy industry. This line of thinking is wrong. We put this question to them: If we do not very quickly establish our own indispensable machine-building industry, metallurgical industry and other related branches of heavy industry, how are we going to equip our light industry, transport, building industry and agriculture? [60]

Mao gave a public reply to this rhetorical challenge five months later in his "Contradictions" speech:

> Without agriculture there can be no light industry. But it is not yet so clearly understood that agriculture [also] provides heavy industry with an important market. This fact, however, will be more readily appreciated as gradual progress in the technical improvement and modernization of agriculture calls for more and more machinery, fertilizer, water conservancy and electric power projects and transport facilities for the farms, as well as fuel and building materials for the rural consumers.[61]

Then Mao observed:

We must realize that there is a contradiction here—the contradiction between the objective laws of economic development of a socialist society and our subjective understanding of them—which needs to be resolved in the course of practise. *This contradiction also manifests itself as a contradiction between different people,* that is, a contradic-

58. *Ibid.*
59. *Ibid.,* p. 37.
60. *Ibid.,* pp. 49–50.
61. Mao, "On the Correct Handling of Contradictions among the People," in *Selected Readings from the Works of Mao Tse-tung,* p. 385.

tion between those with a relatively accurate understanding of these objective laws and those with a relatively inaccurate understanding of them.[62]

Mao added in conclusion, however, that this conflict in understanding "between different people" was still "a contradiction among the people"—that is, "nonantagonistic" in quality.

Mao's opportunity to resolve this leadership conflict over economic policy "in the course of practise" grew from the political and economic developments of the spring and summer of 1957: the "anti-Party, anti-Socialist" attacks of the "bourgeois rightists," and the second year of meager growth in agricultural productivity following the bumper harvest of 1955. All evidence indicates that the Third Plenum of the Eighth Central Committee, held in late September of 1957, was the major turning point in several months of effort on Mao's part to reverse the "conservative phase" which since the spring of 1956 had thwarted his plans for agricultural development.[63] Less than a week before the Third Plenum a Central Committee directive was issued strengthening the trend toward a scaling-down and consolidation of the "advanced stage" APCs. In contrast to Mao's long insistence on the superiority of large-scale cooperatives, this directive observed that "large collectives and large [production] teams are generally not adaptable to the present production conditions"; and it called for a rationalization of their size, which in most cases would mean that they should "be divided into smaller units in accordance with the wishes of the members." [64] In conclusion, the directive stressed: "After the size of the collectives and production teams has been decided upon, it should be publicly announced that this organization will remain unchanged in the next ten years." [65]

This trend toward division of the "advanced stage" APCs and stabilization of the pattern of work and administration in the countryside was sharply reversed by the Plenum. Mao's twelve-year plan for agriculture was revived by Tĕng Hsiao-p'ing in his report

62. *Ibid.*, p. 386. Emphasis added.

63. The influence of harvest estimates on policy debate, and Mao's efforts to radicalize agricultural policy in mid-1957 beginning at a leadership conference held in Tsingtao in July and running through the Third Central Committee Plenum in September, is discussed in Oksenberg, *Policy Formulation in Communist China*, pp. 442–446, 635–636.

64. "Directive of the Central Committee of the Chinese Communist Party Concerning Doing Well the Work of Managing Production in Agricultural Cooperatives" (September 14, 1957); cited in Choh-ming Li, "The First Decade: Economic Development," *The China Quarterly*, No. 1 (January–March 1960), p. 43.

65. *Ibid.*

on the rectification movement;[66] and the Plenum agreed to press the "anti-rightist" purge within the Party, while at the same time promoting a nationwide campaign of popular "socialist education."

The People's Commune, both as an organizational solution to the strengthening of Party leadership in the rural areas and an instrument for mobilizing peasant labor power, hardly came full blown from the meeting of the Third Plenum. Indeed, the Plenum communiqué indicated that Mao's agricultural plan had only been "basically adopted" and would be brought up again before a Party Congress for discussion and adoption, and then sent to the National People's Congress for final approval. Between October 1957 and the enlarged meeting of the Politbureau at Peitaiho in late August of 1958—at which time a Party resolution launching Commune formation on a nationwide scale was passed—there was a constant series of meetings between high Party officials and regional leaders which seems to reveal a "feedback" process in which Mao's evolving ideas on a reorganization of the pattern of rural work and administration were put into operation and tested in selected areas in a winter mass water conservancy campaign and later in the spring planting and summer harvest.[67]

66. As Franz Schurmann has suggested, the fact that the Party's General Secretary should have reinvoked this agricultural plan—seen in conjunction with the fact that the Plenum speeches of such "economic" leaders as Minister of Commerce Ch'en Yün and Premier Chou En-lai, who reported to the Plenum on wages and welfare, were never made public—indicates that a line of "political economy" won out over strictly economic considerations during the course of the Plenum. See *Ideology and Organization in Communist China,* pp. 195–199.

67. The most important of these meetings were: a secret leadership conference at Hangchow in December–January 1957–58 which dealt with the mass water conservancy campaign and other economic policies designed to bring about a "great leap" in production in 1958; a meeting to consider similar issues held at Nanning in late January; and a conference on agricultural mechanization and amalgamation of APCs convened at Chengtu in March.

Two months later came the second session of the Eighth Party Congress which formally presented Mao's economic line to the Party (although without its organizational form specified). From late May through July there was a continuous series of meetings of the Central Committee's Military Affairs Committee which apparently dealt with issues of militia formation and the role of amalgamated APCs in a new strategy of national defense—as well as China's defense relationship to the Soviet Union and ways of developing an independent nuclear weapons capability.

The term "commune" was first used authoritatively in Ch'en Po-ta's *Red Flag* article of mid-July (*see* p. 247 above). The full phrase "People's Commune" was invoked by Mao for the first time in the national press on August 13th.

Here was the "mass line" approach to leadership embodying a combination of centralized direction and local initiative in its most developed form.[68] From this period of experimentation evolved the concept of the People's Commune which Mao presented to the August meeting of the Politbureau, and shortly thereafter published nationally as the "Tentative Regulations (Draft) of the *Weihsing* [Sputnik] People's Commune"—a model for nationwide emulation.[69]

This period of experimentation in rural organization evidently proceeded on the basis of some form of compromise or understanding among top Party leaders. Such a development was stressed by Liu Shao-ch'i in his political report to the second session of the Eighth Party Congress which met in May of 1958. In striking contrast to his silence on Mao's contributions to Party leadership which had marked his report to the first session of this Congress in 1956, Liu made repeated reference to "guiding principles laid down by Comrade Mao Tse-tung," and revealed in detail speeches and policy guidelines advanced by Mao that had not been given previous publication (or implementation).[70]

In view of Liu's opposition to Mao's economic and social policies during 1956–57, in which the question of investment priorities had been prominent, it can be hypothesized that Liu's renewed support for Mao reflects, in part, a compromise among Party leaders in which Mao was backed in his plans for organizational changes in the countryside inasmuch as his "general line for socialist construction" continued to give investment priority to the development of heavy industry. One does not know if Mao would have preferred to see more State-supplied capital invested in agriculture and light industry in the short run (as he had suggested in his February 1957 "Contradictions" speech)—and hence had evolved the "walking on two legs" approach as a way of compromising with his op-

68. Mao's repeated use of the provincial Party organization to promote policies which had limited support from other leaders, or were actively resisted by them, is documented in Parris H. Chang, *Patterns and Processes of Policy Making in Communist China, 1955–1962* (unpublished Ph.D. dissertation, Columbia University, New York, 1969).

69. These regulations had been issued without publicity in early August, and were published in the *People's Daily* on September 4th, after the Politbureau meeting at Peitaiho. *See CC 1955–59,* pp. 463–470.

70. Most notable was his revelation of aspects of Mao's comprehensive analysis of the "contradictions" in China's economic development, the April 1956 speech, "On the Ten Great Relationships." *See* Liu's speech in *CC 1955–59,* esp. p. 426. This emphasizes that the second session of the Eighth Party Congress was for Mao a reassertion of his authority and influence over policy which had been restricted in the spring of 1956.

ponents within the leadership. Or did he genuinely believe that a policy of social mobilization in the rural areas would be sufficient to enable agricultural production to keep pace with the development of industry?

In any event, the process of translating this new consensus within the Party leadership into operational policies which would bring about an upswing from the "conservative phase" of 1956–57 repeats the mobilization pattern of the "high tide" of cooperativization of the fall and winter of 1955–56. The "anti-rightist" purge within the Party mounted in intensity during the late fall of 1957, heightening tension among the cadres and removing certain leaders who had opposed the implementation of Mao's agricultural policies.[71] This Party rectification was advanced in conjunction with a mass "socialist education campaign," in which "landlord" and "capitalist" elements in the villages were subjected to public criticism. Political tension was thus heightened nationwide.

On the basis of these developments, the first large-scale mobilization of peasant labor occurred during the winter of 1957–58 in a mass campaign to build irrigation and water-control facilities with local labor and capital resources. During this campaign the first experiments in the running of public mess-halls were carried out, as women were "liberated" from family kitchens to make up for farm labor shortages. And the virtues of militarizing the rural work force were perceived in the need to direct the activities of large numbers of laborers in the winter-spring campaign.

With spring came the first efforts to amalgamate APCs into township-scale production and administrative units. One of the most widely publicized of the early Commune experiments took place in Honan, where Mao's close supporter in the provincial Party apparatus, Wu Chih-p'u—with power enhanced as a result of the provincial "anti-rightist" purge—was promoting "advanced experience" which would be used as a model in the late summer and fall when the People's Communes were organized throughout rural China.[72]

As the summer progressed political tension within the country was further heightened. There were massive public demonstrations to protest American and British interventions in the Middle East.

71. The workings of this rectification campaign, and its removal of Party leaders who had opposed Mao's agricultural policies, are detailed in Frederick Teiwes, *Rectification Campaigns and Purges in Communist China*, Ch. XV.

72. *See* Chang, *Patterns and Processes of Policy Making in Communist China*, pp. 180–185, and Oksenberg, *Policy Formulation in Communist China*, pp. 409–422.

And as air clashes and artillery bombardments escalated in the Taiwan Straits the Politbureau held an enlarged meeting at Peitaiho which—with the assurances of a bumper harvest for 1958—agreed to press ahead with the country-wide formation of People's Communes.

By all evidence, in coming to this decision Mao had presented reluctant colleagues within the Party leadership with another *fait accompli*. In mid-September Wu Chih-p'u disclosed that sometime prior to the late August meeting of the Politbureau Mao had issued a "directive" on Commune formation.[73] It is unclear whether this was anything more than an assertion of the Chairman's personal authority; yet this "directive," combined with Mao's public approbation of People's Communes in the national press in mid-August, served as the political basis for local initiative in Commune formation. By late August virtually the entire province of Honan had been reorganized into township and county-wide amalgamations of APCs.[74] And a year later the State Statistical Bureau revealed that by the end of August 1958, 30 percent of all peasant households throughout China had already been Communized.[75]

The fact that this momentous restructuring of rural life proceeded with no more official direction than a cautiously worded Politbureau resolution—no Central Committee decision, no plan approved by the National People's Congress, legally the highest national political authority—strongly suggests that Mao was pressing against continuing resistance within the upper levels of the Party and government, and forged ahead through the support of the provincial Party organization. Furthermore, it would appear from the context of these times that Mao used the political climate of the Taiwan Straits confrontation to make open opposition to Commune formation and militarization of the peasant labor force—developments closely related to his new national defense line—appear to be virtually an act of treason. The Chairman apparently mobilized all the political weapons at his disposal to push Communization through to completion and to prevent the reemergence of a conservative opposition which would thwart his plans—as *had* occurred in the spring of 1956.

73. Wu Chih-p'u, "On People's Communes," *China Youth Daily* (September 16, 1958); trans. in *Current Background*, No. 524 (October 21, 1958), p. 4.

74. "Questions and Answers on People's Communes," *Daily Worker* [Peking] (September 8, 1958); trans. in *SCMP*, No. 1860 (September 24, 1958), p. 7.

75. From *Ten Great Years*. Cited in Kenneth R. Walker, *Planning in Chinese Agriculture*, p. 14.

Massed peasant laborers at the

In the late summer and fall of 1958, war, production, and social change thus merged once again. And as the Party journal *Red Flag* observed in an editorial of mid-September, the emotions of hatred and aggression released in the military confrontation with "American imperialism" provided the motive power for China's "war" with her own poverty:

> *The [Dulles] policy of hostility toward the Chinese people . . . has constantly aroused in them a swelling tide of anger* against the United States and an ever greater will to rise energetically and become strong themselves. On this count alone, *it can be said that Dulles has done something useful indirectly for the Chinese revolution* and the revolution of other countries of the world. He ought to be given a medal.

> The U.S. policy of hostility toward the Chinese people has failed to prevent the gigantic advance of new China. On the contrary, *it has proved advantageous to China's economic construction* which is based on its own resources.[76]

An important question concerning these events of 1958 is whether Mao had been purposefully manipulative in creating the Taiwan Straits crisis (in part) as a context for Commune formation, or whether the Chairman had used a situation largely beyond his control to his own domestic political advantage. The evidence now available on the offshore island events most strongly suggests that Mao took the initiative in escalating the existing confrontation between Communist and Nationalist forces in the Straits (*see* pp. 386–388 below). And while Mao appears to have had a number of political goals in mind when pressing the confrontation, one important objective seems to have been the creation of a motivational climate in which resistance to Commune formation from both Party leaders and peasants would be minimized. In April 1956 Mao had told a meeting of the Politbureau, "We must do something to raise the self-confidence of our people. We must do what Mencius said: 'When talking about a big man, belittle him.' We must develop the kind of contempt of American imperialism shown during the anti-American war in aid of Korea." [77]

In the spring of 1956 Mao's plans for developing this national confidence and bringing about a "leap forward" had been cut short by resistant Party leaders. In 1958 the Chairman was determined

---

76. *Red Flag* editorial, "The U.S. Aggressors Have Put Nooses around Their Own Necks" (September 14, 1958); trans. in *SCMP*, No. 1856 (September 18, 1958), pp. 2–3. Emphasis added.

77. Mao, "On the Ten Great Relationships," in Ch'en, ed., *Mao*, p. 84.

that a "conservative phase" should not reemerge and thwart Communization. The Straits confrontation appears to have been one important phase of his strategy for pressing ahead with his plans.

In these events of 1955 through 1958 one sees the outline of a pattern which seems to embody the essential elements by which Mao has promoted "struggle" in the process of leadership and social change. In both 1955 and 1957 Mao's personal inclination to promote collective forms of social organization and to raise the "activism" of China's population was given political weight by poor harvests in two preceding years.[78]

With more conservative "experts" within the leadership thus on the defensive, the Party organization is prepared for an upsurge in social transformation through a rectification campaign. Tension increases as "objects" (*tui-hsiang*) are singled out for criticism, struggle, or purge. The actual removal of leadership cadres, however, is usually restricted in scope, for the basic objective of the rectification is to mobilize the majority of Party members: to increase their understanding of the goals of the new campaign by criticizing the "objects" and their own errors in attitude and to raise anxieties about committing "rightist" errors, thus motivating them for the tasks of leadership.

This air of tension within the leadership is transmitted to "the masses" through a public criticism campaign, which subjects "objects" or targets of past error to public criticism. With both leadership and population thus oriented and emotionally "primed," the movement proceeds.

In Part Three we suggested that one of the major characteristics of the leadership process which Mao evolved during his years in the countryside was the transformation of peasant anxieties in the face of established authority into hatred, thus motivating the rural population for involvement in the revolution. One senses that the post-Liberation use of Party rectification campaigns and mass movements is an effort to sustain this motivational basis of past Party successes. We do not know, however, just how conscious and purposefully manipulative the leadership has been in relying upon this procedure in mobilizing people for political involvement. It is a

78. Ironically, however, it was good harvests in 1955 and 1958 (the result, in part, of more conservative economic policy), which enabled the radicalized leadership to press ahead with organizational changes designed to cope with the poor agricultural performances of the two preceding years (1953–54, and 1956–57). A good harvest on the eve of a period of change provides a margin of security in resources which can limit opposition and make up for disruptions in production stemming from organizational changes.

process which over the years seems to have become second nature to Mao and other leaders.

Mao observed to comrades at a Central Committee Plenum in 1959, "When one is not anxious, one has not the spirit and enthusiasm, and cannot do a good job." [79] And it seems evident enough that in post-Liberation years Mao has shown a determination to sustain a style of leadership which will make people anxious and "active"; a political climate in which popular anxieties about committing errors (*fan tso-wu*) before authority are transformed into anger or indignation over some social evil or enemy, thus creating the motivational basis for change through political struggle.

The intimate relationship between motives of aggression and social change in the development of China's social revolution is nowhere more clearly revealed than in the association of major periods of social upheaval with the violence of war. With only one major exception—the "high tide" of cooperativization of 1955–56—the periods of major institutional change promoted by the Chinese Communists also have been times of war or threatening foreign intervention: The first periods of land redistribution occurred during the War of Resistance against Japan (also a time of continuing civil conflict with the Nationalists). Land reform was promoted during the final phase of the Civil War and completed during the Korean War. The socialization of industry and commerce proceeded in the context of the patriotic movement to "Resist America and Aid Korea." Communization was carried out during the Taiwan Straits crisis of 1958. And the Great Proletarian Cultural Revolution has run its uncertain course while the Viet-Nam War and border clashes on the Sino-Soviet frontier have held the possibility of involving China in a foreign conflict.

With the exceptions of the Civil War, the Taiwan Straits crisis of 1958, and the Sino-Soviet border incidents, these periods of military violence have been the result of developments almost completely beyond Chinese control; hence, the major pattern one sees is how the Communist Party leadership has learned to *respond to* and cope with a war environment. The one sure conclusion that can be reached is that the leadership has not viewed such situations as occasions for inaction. On the contrary, the tension of a violent confrontation is a context which they have learned to use to further their social and political goals. Consistent with interpretations developed at various points throughout this study, we would observe

79. Mao, "Speech at the Lushan Meeting," in *Chairman Mao's Criticism and Repudiation of the P'eng, Huang, Chang and Chou Anti-Party Clique*, p. 10.

that a political or military confrontation with an enemy provides the Party with the most appropriate context for promoting the natural translation of anxiety about conflict with a powerful authority into aggressive emotions and legitimated "struggle."

For Mao the problem of leadership in post-Liberation China has been how to sustain the momentum of social change in a non-wartime environment. The Party Chairman's policy preferences in the period of "socialist transformation" reveal an enduring commitment to the forms of political action which were evolved during the years of struggle for power. One must ask (as did other Party leaders), however, whether the techniques of "struggle" and mass movement which are the legacy of the revolution remain appropriate after the assumption of state power, after foreign military intervention has been eliminated from the mainland and the most blatant forms of social injustice have been reduced through the Party's social reforms?

From the mid-1950s on, Mao himself was to assert with ever greater vehemence that the Party's organizational transformation of Chinese society was in danger of subversion by "bourgeois reactionary" attitudes and patterns of behavior as they endured in the life style of the population, and even in the behavior of Party cadres. This, of course, was the meaning for Mao of the "blooming and contending" experiment; and from the summer of 1957 on, the Chairman was to assert the continuing relevance of struggle politics as a way of sustaining China's revolution in the political and ideological spheres. It was the eventual resistance of other Party leaders to this effort which was to lead to a breakdown in the unity of the leadership. The increasingly divisive factional conflict within the Party during the 1960s grew from Mao's efforts of the late 1950s to speed the pace of China's social advance by sustaining the interrelationship between war and political conflict, production, and institutional change.

One notable aspect of the post-Liberation periods of institutional change within China, particularly those directly promoted by Mao, is their intensity and brief duration in time. In the 1955–56 cooperativization drive it took just six months to organize 45 percent of all rural households into the "primary stage" APCs; and just over four months in the spring of 1956 to bring almost 50 percent of these households into the "advanced stage" organizations. During the Great Leap Forward of 1958 it took only a month to raise the proportion of rural households in People's Communes from 30 percent to 98 percent.[80]

80. The figures are from Walker, *Planning in Chinese Agriculture*, p. 14.

There seem to be two interrelated reasons for the intense quality of these periods of institutional change: First, Mao's belief that it is necessary to "strike while the iron is hot";[81] to move while the "activism" of the masses and political tensions within the Party are high. A second reason is the determination of more radical leaders to bring about change before opposition within the Party can be mobilized to block the movement. As we have detailed previously, Mao has faced strong resistance from within the Party to his major proposals for Party rectification and social and economic reorganization in the rural areas. It is a measure of both his determination as a revolutionary and his skill as a political tactician that he has pressed his proposals despite the opposition. One can only speculate as to whether China's social revolution would be less characterized by periods of intense upheaval if the Party leadership were fully united behind Mao's policies; yet it does seem clear that as a result of this opposition Mao has had to "move fast" to bring about change.

It is the very rapidity of the periods of institutional transformation, however, which produces the excesses and dislocations which strengthen the conservative opposition within the Party leadership. The period of Communization was no exception. There was a notable discrepancy between public Party directives which called for earnest efforts by the local cadres to adhere to the principle of voluntariness in reorganizing society, to avoid "commandism" and overcome popular doubts and resistance through "patient reasoning," and a reality marred by coercion and the rapid and indiscriminate application of "model experiences" propagated by the "Center" when local conditions required variations in approach. The politicized quality of the periods of revolutionary change makes any cadre determined to be "red," not "right"; "left," not a laggard. And in the excesses and disruptions which follow, more conservative leaders acquire the political leverage to bring about a period of "consolidation of gains."

Thus the political balance within the Party leadership swings back to the "right." "Expert" considerations replace those of the "reds," and there is a shift away from calls to the heroic, or coer-

81. As Mao was reported to have told a meeting of the Supreme State Conference in January 1958: "There are two methods of leadership and two styles of work. On the question of [agricultural] cooperation, some advocate that it should be carried out at a faster rate and some at a slower pace. I think the former one is better. It is better to strike while the iron is hot. It is better to accomplish something at one stroke than to resort to procrastination." (From *Chairman Mao's Criticism and Repudiation of the P'eng, Huang, Chang, and Chou Anti-Party Clique*, p. 2.)

cive threats, to renewed appeals to the material interests of the population—wage incentives, increases in living standards—combined with greater toleration of such "capitalist" and "bourgeois" social remnants as private plots, free markets, family life, and choice in job. These moderations of policy, in time, correct the excesses of the period of upheaval, yet set the stage for the renewed emergence of "rightist conservatism" in its many guises. Thus the political context evolves toward a new round in the cycle of leadership debate over the need for radical social change as "spontaneous tendencies toward capitalism" emerge once more, again strengthening the cause of the radicals.

The two cycles of this "saddle-shaped" pattern of leadership debate and policy change which began in 1955 and were played out with the purge of "leftists" in the period of recovery from the Great Leap Forward during 1961–62,[82] should not be viewed as either a highly stable or easily manipulable political process. The pattern described above is not a consciously fabricated rhythm of policy change controlled by one man or a small group of Party leaders. It is the natural result of political conflict within a party whose ideology enhances the tension between "right" and "left," and the effect of techniques for asserting political influence which have become part of the Chinese Communists' methods of operation. How long this pattern will endure seems largely a function of how long the Party leadership will sustain the ideological and institutional legacy of the revolution. And this question itself was raised by the excesses of the Great Leap Forward.

THE "RIGHTIST" REACTION TO THE GREAT LEAP

Within the ranks of the Party there is a small group of right opportunists antagonistic to the Party and the people. They are opposed to the Party's general line and are waging a frantic attack on it. . . . The attack which the bourgeois rightist elements launched against the Party from without in 1957 and the present attack which the right opportunists are waging from within have this in common: To oust the proletarian class and place the bourgeois class in political command.[83]

82. *See* Frederick C. Teiwes, *Provincial Party Personnel in Mainland China, 1956–1966* (New York: Columbia University, East Asian Institute Occasional Paper, 1967), Ch. IV.

83. Shang Chen, "Who Is Supposed to Take Command?" *People's Daily* (November 30, 1959); trans. in *SCMP*, No. 2155 (December 14, 1959), pp. 1–2.

The author's name, which does not appear in other mainland publications, apparently is a pseudonym. In translation its meaning is "On the Truth" or "Toward the Truth"; and as with more frequently encountered pseudonyms it probably masks the identity of a key political leader, or leaders.

In promoting the policies of the Great Leap Forward, Party spokesmen made it clear from the very beginning that doubters and opposition persisted within the leadership. In his May political report to the second session of the Eighth Party Congress Liu Shaoch'i made this direct assertion:

> Many of those comrades who expressed misgivings about the principle of building socialism by achieving "greater, faster, better and more economical results," have learned a lesson [from political and economic developments since the Third Plenum of 1957]. But some of them have not yet learned anything. They say: "We'll settle accounts with you after the autumn harvest." Well, let them wait to settle accounts. They will lose out in the end! [84]

It is uncertain whom Liu had in mind when he used such threatening language. It may not have been the opposition which eventually emerged at the Lushan Central Committee Plenum of July and August 1959. To some degree Liu may have been raising the spectre of a strong opposition in order to silence doubters within the Party. Yet the evidence of the "anti-rightist" struggle, as it continued through 1958, indicates that opposition remained active at all levels of the Party apparatus. During his tour of the countryside in September 1958 Mao himself was said to have encountered criticism of the mass movement and the militarization of work by local Party officials, who disparaged the drive with epithets of "rural work style" and "the guerrilla habit." [85]

In order to counter such attitudes, the formal termination of the "anti-rightist" rectification in August of 1958 was followed by publication of a Central Committee directive launching a winter and spring campaign of "socialist and communist education." [86] The directive stressed:

> We must lead the masses to recall the historical lessons of the "U-shaped" development of the situation in the past three years, and thoroughly criticize the "Theory of Conditions" which places reliance on nature for existence, and the "Theory of Custom" which calls on the people to walk in the footsteps of those who have gone before. We must break down rightist conservatism, which leaves us satisfied with remaining at the half way point, and promote the ideology of exerting the utmost effort to press forward consistently. The "tide-watching

84. Cited in *CC 1955–59*, p. 427.

85. Fan Jung-k'ang, " 'Rural Work Style' and 'Guerilla Habit' Are Orthodox Marxism," *Political Study,* No. 10 (October 13, 1958); trans. in *ECMM,* No. 150 (December 8, 1958), pp. 1–3.

86. *People's Daily* editorial, "For a Still Bigger Leap Forward in Agriculture Next Year" (September 13, 1958); trans. in *SCMP,* No. 1857 (September 19, 1958), p. 12.

group" and the "post-autumn-account-settlement group" must not only be made to remain silent before the facts of the big harvest, but also become thoroughly bankrupt ideologically.[87]

This effort to sustain mass enthusiasm for the Commune drive through another "education" movement was accompanied by continued warnings to leadership cadres that "rightist conservative ideology" must not again emerge and thwart the pace of social advance. In the *People's Daily* editorial which initiated the "summing up" phase of the rectification movement, it was stressed that inasmuch as the Party was an advocate of the theory of "continuous revolution," cadres should look forward to further revolutionary struggles and rectifications—and conduct themselves accordingly. And there were somber references to "problems concerning some of the leadership cadres that have not yet been solved." [88]

While the exact composition of leadership groups which opposed Mao's policies remains obscure—as well as their procedures for urging caution in forming Communes, and modifying Great Leap policies—hints of their resistance are evident in public press materials.

Pressures for a period of consolidation increased in the fall of 1958 as the political excesses of the drive to form Communes became apparent. The radicalized Party leadership in late August and September had not only stimulated a furious pace in the formation of Communes (over 90 percent of all rural households were reported to be in Communes by the end of September),[89] it also loaded political rewards in favor of the creation of enormous organizations. The Peitaiho Politbureau resolution on the formation of Communes of late August had suggested that, "at present it is better to establish one commune to a township with the commune comprising about two thousand peasant households"; and while the resolution noted that the creation of larger organizations "need not be opposed," it was urged that "for the present we should not take the initiative to encourage them." [90] This caution was thrown

87. "Directive of the CCP Central Committee on the Universal Development of a Socialist and Communist Education Movement in the Rural Areas in the Coming Winter and Next Spring" (August 29, 1958); trans. in *ibid.*, p. 2.

88. *People's Daily* Commentator, "The Rectification Movement Must Be Properly Wound Up" (August 15, 1958); trans. in *SCMP*, No. 1851 (September 11, 1958), p. 10.

89. *See* the NCNA dispatch, "Nearly All Peasant Households in People's Communes" (September 30, 1958); in *SCMP*, No. 1872 (October 16, 1958), pp. 14–15.

90. "Resolution of the Central Committee of the Chinese Communist Party on the Establishment of People's Communes in the Rural Areas" (August 29, 1958); trans. in *CC 1955–59*, pp. 454–455.

to the winds by Mao's more enthusiastic supporters in the regional Party apparatus; and in a *Red Flag* article of mid-September, Honan's Governor and Party First Secretary, Wu Chih-p'u, repeatedly invoked Mao's name in support of huge cooperatives. He boasted that in his province the People's Communes contained an average of 7,500 households.[91]

After a tour of Honan and other provincial areas in late September, the more cautious Minister of Finance and Central Committee member Li Hsien-nien gingerly criticized the Honan Communes. They had grown well beyond the bounds of the township (*hsiang*) to include entire counties (*hsien*); and radicalized cadres had pressed for the more advanced level of property ownership "by the whole people." Management decisions thus went well beyond the control of the local Party and government organizations—not to mention taking them out of the hands of the peasants. Li observed: ". . . all the communes will follow this road *in the future*. But I think that this category of communes may, at present, involve problems which require careful consideration." [92] Li then attempted to rein in Wu's "advanced" initiatives by citing him personally as having stressed the need "to strengthen management and step up planning." In his conclusion, he appealed for more thoughtfulness and caution in the emulation of Honan's experience: "As the situation differs in various places, the concrete practices may also be different, and not necessarily unified." [93]

In fact, however, political considerations outweighed those of economics. As G. William Skinner has shown, it was the indiscriminate application of a few model experiences to areas of China where they were inappropriate, and the creation of very large Commune organizations, which produced much of the dislocation of rural economic activity during the Great Leap. Communes larger than the township (*hsiang*) disrupted the "natural" pattern of rural administration and commodity exchange.[94]

Political momentum for a period of consolidation of the organizational changes of the early fall increased as examples of excess and mismanagement became more apparent. The pressures on basic level cadres to bring about huge increases in grain production had

91. Cited in G. William Skinner, "Marketing and Social Structure in Rural China, Part III," *Journal of Asian Studies,* Vol. XXIV, No. 3 (May 1965), p. 392.

92. Li Hsien-nien, "A Glance at the People's Communes," *Red Flag,* No. 10 (October 16, 1958); trans. in *ECMM,* No. 149 (December 1, 1958), p. 34. Emphasis added.

93. *Ibid.,* pp. 38, 39.

94. Skinner, "Marketing and Social Structure in Rural China, Part III," pp. 383–392.

led them to ignore vegetable growing and the raising of pigs and chickens (activities now socialized as a result of the abolition of private plots and the free market system). Thus there developed a serious drop in the production of the peasants' major sources of protein and carbohydrates; and social tensions increased as the quality of food and service in the public mess-halls succumbed to cadre concern with meeting production quotas in those crops for which they would be held politically accountable. In a fall editorial urging that Party secretaries personally take charge of the running of public mess-halls, the *People's Daily* stressed: "If we do not properly run the public mess-halls and nurseries, then we shall not be able to consolidate the collectivization of daily living." [95]

A related set of problems came from the mass campaign to smelt iron and steel. In their determination to meet Mao's production quotas, cadres had commandeered all available sources of "scrap" metal, including cooking pots, iron doors, and in one North China Commune even the heating pipes of a secondary school. The popular resentments generated by such measures were intensified by the fact that with poor quality food and service in the public mess-halls, many who would have preferred to eat at home now were unable to do so for lack of cooking implements. Furthermore, the quality of the "native" steel was so low because of its high sulphur content that it was virtually unusable for fabrication into new products.

A further cause for social discontent was generated by the cadres' determination to establish the most "communistic" forms of food supply and wage payment possible. Being more "progressive," such developments would win greater support from radical Party leaders. "Free food" was provided in some Communes, although with limited grain supply and vegetable shortages this tended to mean a poorer diet for those who worked harder. Privately-owned farm animals and family-grown vegetables were commandeered for community consumption; and in some areas the total abolition of wage payments further reduced labor incentives. This was what Mao himself was to criticize in 1959 as "blowing the wind of communism," a "left-opportunist" deviation that he attributed to the excessive political enthusiasm of Commune and county-level cadres.[96]

It was such excesses which the Sixth Central Committee Plenum

95. *People's Daily* editorial, "Run Public Mess Halls Properly" (October 25, 1958); trans. in *Current Background*, No. 538 (December 12, 1958), p. 1.

96. "Mao Tse-tung's Speech at the Eighth Plenary Session of the CCP Eighth Central Committee" (July 1959); in *The Case of P'eng Teh-huai* (Hong Kong: Union Research Institute, 1968), pp. 17–18.

of November–December 1958 sought to correct. Its resolution calling for a consolidation of the changes of the fall did not yet shift the level of management and accounting back "down" to the natural villages,[97] but it did stress the need for the Communes to "plan their production, exchange, consumption and accumulation," and emphasized the importance of maintaining wage incentives, an eight-hour working day, and a high level of social services.[98] Furthermore, cadres were urged to accept the fact that the process of increasing production to a level at which everyone could be remunerated "according to his needs" and where ownership would be by "the whole people" was one which would "take fifteen, twenty or more years to complete, starting from now." [99] In the interim, however, cadres were "reminded" that the peasants should not be overworked and that "exaggeration" in setting production targets and reporting harvest yields to superiors was not permissible.

An important question which is not yet answered concerns the amount of political pressure on Mao at the end of 1958. While the resolution of the Sixth Plenum calling for consolidation of the People's Communes sought to eliminate the air of politicized euphoria prevalent during the summer and fall, it was not hostile to "good-hearted" but "over-eager" comrades who wanted to push the revolution faster than objective circumstances would permit. With the entire rural population now organized into Communes, there is no reason to believe that Mao would not have been in favor of a period of consolidation in order to "even up" the advances of the fall.

On the other hand, the Plenum approved "the proposal of Chairman Mao that he not stand as candidate for Chairman of the People's Republic for the next term of office." [100] During the Cultural Revolution Mao was reported to have remarked that he "was not satisfied with the [results of the] Wuchang Conference" at which the decision that he step aside as State Chairman had been made.[101] Some have interpreted this statement to mean that he had been forced to relinquish the post.

In conflict with this interpretation, however, is a Central Committee document drafted by Mao in January of 1958 in which he

97. This was to come about only in late 1960. *See* Schurmann, *Ideology and Organization in Communist China,* pp. 490–492.

98. "Resolution on Some Questions Concerning the People's Communes" (December 10, 1959); trans. in *CC 1955–59,* pp. 490–503.

99. *Ibid.,* p. 492.

100. *See* the Sixth Plenum resolution of this title in *CC 1955–59,* pp. 487–488.

101. Mao, "Speech at a Report Meeting" (October 24, 1966), in *Long Live the Thought of Mao Tse-tung!* p. 45.

raised the issue of giving up the chairmanship in terms almost identical to those of the Plenum communiqué of December of that same year.[102] In addition, there is one report that in the original presentation of his 1957 "Contradictions" speech Mao had hinted that he might step aside for other leaders.[103] Mao apparently had raised this issue a number of times, perhaps for tactical political reasons: to deflate the argument that he was another Stalin, or to "remind" the Party of his authority when there was opposition to his policies.

Also in support of the interpretation that Mao was not "forced aside" in 1958 are statements attributed to the Party Chairman in October of 1966, in which he reveals that sometime in the 1950s he had conceived of "two lines" of leadership—one at the operational level, and a second "policy" line—as a way of training other top leaders and avoiding a succession struggle, as well as of diminishing the security problems which would come with overly centralized leadership.[104] Furthermore, with the basic social organization which was to see the Chinese people through the transition to communism now created on a nationwide scale, Mao—in his mid-sixties—might indeed have thought of giving greater day-to-day responsibility to other leaders.

From the context of events prior to the Great Leap Forward and developments thereafter, however, one senses that Mao's decision was not so politically innocent. If nothing else, the experiences of 1956–57 (in which Liu Shao-ch'i, Teng Hsiao-p'ing, and P'eng Chen had differed with Mao on important issues of economics, Party rectification, and the treatment of intellectuals) meant that Mao was well aware of disagreements over policy and personal commitment. The Party Chairman may have been anticipating coming political battles in making a "voluntary" withdrawal. Mao may have sensed the likely scope of opposition to his leadership as

102. *See* "Sixty Work Methods (Draft)," issued by the General Office of the Central Committee of the Communist Party of China (February 19, 1958); trans. in *Current Background,* No. 892 (October 21, 1969), p. 13.

103. *See* Loh and Evans, *Escape from Red China,* p. 292.

104. *See* the remarks attributed to Mao from two political conferences of October 24 and 25, 1966; published in the Cultural Revolution pamphlet *Long Live the Thought of Mao Tse-tung!* pp. 40–42, 44–46.

The phrasing of Mao's remarks suggests that the division of the leadership into "two lines" grew from the separation of the Party "center" into two groups in mid-March 1947 for reasons that seem basically related to the security of the leadership during the final phase of the Civil War. (*See* Mao, *SW,* IV, English, footnote 3 on page 132 for a description of this separation.) Yet the exact timing of the creation of the "two lines" after 1949 remains obscure.

a result of communization and the outcome of the Quemoy confrontation (to be discussed below), and hence stepped aside as State Chairman as a way of deflating his opposition. Perhaps he wanted to strengthen his support from Liu Shao-ch'i, who was to succeed him as State Chairman in April of 1959. The exact meaning of this development remains uncertain.

There is no doubt, however, that the "rightist" reaction to the Great Leap Forward did emerge during the spring and summer of 1959, when it was already apparent that a combination of natural disasters, mismanagement, and the disruption of rural life brought about by the changes of the preceding year had led to a drastic drop in grain production. It also had become evident that the production figures for the bumper harvest of 1958 had been highly inflated as a result of "exaggerations" by the cadres reporting local yields. At the Central Committee Plenum held at Lushan, Kiangsi Province, in July and August of 1959, Mao was to see an attempt to unseat him from the "saddle" of influence over China's social development.

At the time the public press gave only indirect indication of the seriousness which Mao attached to the challenge to his policies which was launched at Lushan by a group led by Defense Minister P'eng Teh-huai. On August 6th the *People's Daily* carried an editorial exhorting cadres to fulfill their production targets for the year, and urgently requiring them to "take a determined stand against the rightist-inclined sentiment which has found its way into some of the cadres." [105] At the end of this month an article entitled "The 'Chronic Disease of Right Deviation' and Its 'Remedy' " appeared in the Party paper and stated more forcefully that

> It is a downright crime to ridicule, attack or slander this great, new thing [the Communes], to raise the charge that the commune movement has been "too early," "too quick" and that it has "ended in a mess," or to say that the commune movement is "a fanatical movement of the petty bourgeoisie." [106]

105. *People's Daily* editorial, "Overcome Rightist-Inclined Sentiment and Endeavor to Increase Production and Practise Economy" (August 6, 1959); trans. in *CC 1955–59*, p. 531.

106. Wu Ch'uan-ch'i, "The 'Chronic Disease of Right Deviation' and Its 'Remedy,' " *People's Daily* (August 30, 1959); trans. in *SCMP*, No. 2108 (October 2, 1959), p. 5.

The curious phrasing "chronic disease" reflects Mao's successful defense at Lushan: He has tended to describe political errors as "diseases," and has stressed the necessity of "curing the disease to save the patient" through the method of "criticism–self-criticism" (*see* Mao, "Rectify the Party's Style of Work," *SW*, English, III, p. 50). Also, and more specifically, Mao, in a bit-

Exactly who had "slandered" the Leap policies in this manner remained unstated, although there were several exceedingly sharp references to "frantic attacks" on the Party and the "general line of socialist construction," and the need to obey Chairman Mao. One astute yet cautious observer suggested shortly afterwards that the "rightist opposition within the Chinese Communist Party had been a considerable force, with growing grievances against the leadership." [107]

It was only a year or two later that sufficient information had "leaked" from China (perhaps by way of the Soviet Union) to enable government analysts to begin to piece together the linkage between the dismissal of Defense Minister P'eng Teh-huai—announced in a government proclamation of September 17th, 1959, over the signature of the new State Chairman Liu Shao-ch'i—and the emergence of a new national "anti-rightist" campaign after the Lushan Plenum of the summer.[108] And only during the Cultural Revolution, when documentation on the affair was published by the Maoists for reasons of contemporary political need, did inner-Party information begin to add detail to this incident.

On the basis of the version of P'eng's "Letter of Opinion" to Mao of mid-July 1959 which was made public in 1967, it appears that the Defense Minister criticized the policies of the Great Leap in a way that would draw maximum political leverage from the now apparent economic consequences of Mao's "general line." P'eng's attack, assuming that the letter is an authentic revelation of his arguments, is a detailed *economic* critique of the results of the first year of the Great Leap. But why should the Defense Minister be the one to promote such an attack, and not one of the more conservative economists within the leadership?

A number of interpretations might be advanced. Assuming that P'eng spoke on his own initiative,[109] that his critique had not been

---

ingly ironic letter to Chang Wen-t'ien, one of P'eng Teh-huai's co-conspirators, in early August 1959, told him: "In my opinion, you have relapsed into your old illness" (*The Case of P'eng Teh-huai*, p. 315). Ostensibly this referred to malaria, which Chang had contracted during the Long March; yet Mao's political meaning was a reference to the old "disease" of Chang's policy deviations which were part of his association with the "Internationalist" or pro-Soviet Party faction during the 1930s.

107. From *CC 1955–59*, p. 36.

108. *See* David A. Charles, "The Dismissal of P'eng Teh-huai," *The China Quarterly*, No. 8 (October–December 1961), pp. 63–76.

109. The one shred of direct evidence that P'eng may have been a spokesman for other Party leaders—P'eng Chen and Liu Shao-ch'i in particular—is the revelation of 1965 that on June 16, 1959 (three days after P'eng's

"ghost-written" by other Party leaders more familiar with economic matters, one can see an attempt by P'eng to appeal for support from the Central Committee in terms which were meaningful to all, and hence would gain wide backing. But even assuming that P'eng's letter was not fully his own creation, why should the Defense Minister be the spokesman for such an attack? Conflicting personal styles or political rivalry may have been an element in the confrontation,[110] yet policy issues were clearly a major factor in P'eng's challenge. In particular, it was changes in Mao's military policy in 1958 and the increasingly strained defense relationship between China and the Soviet Union which seems to account for the Defense Minister's actions.

To explore this dimension of the "rightist reaction" to the Great Leap Forward it is necessary to retrace one aspect of the events of 1958–59 which in its own way reveals how Mao has used "struggle" and confrontation politics to further his own policies and position.

---

return from Eastern Europe and the Soviet Union) the *People's Daily* published an article "Hai Jui Scolds the Emperor." The ostensible author of this piece, Liu Mien-chih, in fact was Wu Han, a close associate of P'eng Chen in the Peking Municipal Government. It could be that this article was intended to "prepare opinion" for the Lushan confrontation; yet one does not know whether at this early date it was known that "Hai Jui" would be P'eng Teh-huai. (*See* the *People's Daily* editor's note to Yao Wen-yuan's article "On the New Historical Play *The Dismissal of Hai Jui*" [November 30, 1965]; trans. in *Current Background,* No. 783 [March 21, 1966], p. 1.)

Shortly after P'eng Teh-huai's removal, Wu Han wrote another article "On Hai Jui," published in the *People's Daily* on September 21, 1959, which indirectly defended P'eng's action. And in 1961 Wu Han wrote a play in the style of Peking Opera, "The Dismissal of Hai Jui," which more directly criticized "the emperor's" action against P'eng.

As is discussed throughout the next chapter, the issue of P'eng's dismissal runs through leadership debates leading right up to the Cultural Revolution (*see* esp. pp. 417–421, 425–429 below). P'eng's criticism of Mao was a major factor in the transformation of leadership conflict from matters of policy to that of Mao's personal authority after 1959. Yet at present there is only slim evidence that at Lushan P'eng spoke with the direct backing of leaders other than those who were purged with him at the time.

110. Personal rivalry between Mao and P'eng during the late 1920s was rumored repeatedly in the context of conflict over military policy. (*See* Benjamin Schwartz, *Chinese Communism and the Rise of Mao* [Cambridge, Mass.: Harvard University Press, 1964], pp. 174, 176, 182); and in his confession before Party leaders in 1959, P'eng admitted that he had long adopted a "quarrelsome attitude" towards Mao and had a "prejudice" against him. ("P'eng Teh-huai's Speech at the Eighth Plenum of the Eighth CCP Central Committee" [Excerpts], in *Current Background,* No. 851 [April 26, 1968], p. 28.)

TESTING THE WIND

> Either the east wind overpowers the west wind or the west wind over-powers the east wind; on the question of line there is no room for compromise.[111]

> We hold that to defend world peace it is necessary constantly to expose imperialism and to arouse and organize the people in struggle against the imperialists headed by the United States, and it is necessary to place reliance on the growth of the strength of the socialist camp.[112]

The Soviet Twentieth Party Congress of 1956 was a major watershed in Sino-Soviet relations. Not only did Khrushchev's attack on Stalin produce reactions in China which tended to undermine Mao's personal authority, but the Russian leader also put forward basic policy guidelines which conflicted with Mao's own policy positions —"peaceful coexistence" and "peaceful competition" with non-Socialist states, and the possibility of "peaceful transition" to socialism. The Chinese Party leader and his supporters watched with increasing distress as Khrushchev's "peace" line went through a process of "emergence, formation, growth and systematization" during the years 1956–1959.[113] Here was an authoritative alternative to Mao's view of the importance of sustaining political struggle, put forward by the leading Party of the International Communist Movement. And by all evidence, Khrushchev's line found sympathetic response within the Chinese Party leadership, for in time Mao was to charge that there were "Chinese Khrushchevs."

Even from Mao's perspective, however, there were many positive dimensions to the Chinese relationship with the Soviet Union, not the least of which was the degree of national security which came from membership in the "Socialist Camp" defended by Soviet nuclear weapons. Furthermore, the strength of the "Camp" appeared to have increased substantially over that of its "imperialist" adversaries in 1957 with the Soviet development of an intercontinental ballistic missile capability for its nuclear weapons. The launching of the Russian Sputniks in October and November, on the eve of

111. *People's Daily* editorial, "The Bourgeois Trend of the *Wen Hui Pao* Should Be Subjected to Criticism" (July 1, 1957). As noted in footnote 130, p. 319 above, this editorial has been identified as written by Mao himself.
112. *People's Daily* and *Red Flag* joint editorial, "Two Different Lines on the Question of War and Peace" (November 19, 1963), in *Polemic on the General Line of the International Communist Movement,* p. 254.
113. *People's Daily* and *Red Flag* joint editorial, "The Origin and Development of the Differences between the Leadership of the CPSU and Ourselves" (September 6, 1963), in *ibid.,* p. 59.

the Fortieth Anniversary of the Bolshevik Revolution, seemed to imply greater security for China, and to prove the correctness of the socialist path of national development with its now demonstrated superiority in scientific achievement. As Mao proclaimed to representatives of Communist and Workers' Parties assembled in Moscow in November 1957:

> I consider that the present world situation has reached a new turning point. There are now two winds in the world: the east wind and the west wind. . . . I think the characteristic of the current situation is that the east wind prevails over the west wind; that is, the strength of socialism exceeds the strength of imperialism.[114]

Behind this public expression of faith in the socialist system, however, was Mao's uncertainty about how Khrushchev might use this Russian scientific and military superiority, for Sputnik had been preceded by the launching of the "peace" line. Did "peaceful coexistence" now mean that the hand of "imperialist aggressors" could be stayed by Soviet defense superiority? Or were the Russians preparing to take a less militant line in resolving outstanding issues of great importance for the "Camp" like Berlin and—at least for the Chinese—Taiwan? Did the increased possibilities of "peaceful transition" to socialism as a result of the Soviet scientific breakthrough mean that Communist Parties around the world would gain greater prestige through association with the Socialist system, or that the Russians would back off from aiding struggling revolutionary movements? It was such questions which Mao sought to test during the years 1957–1959.

Mao headed a delegation to Moscow in early November of 1957 —only his second trip abroad—to attend celebrations marking the Fortieth Anniversary of the October Revolution, and to participate in an historic meeting of representatives of Communist and Workers' Parties from all over the world. Mao made the trip with renewed political strength. His period of defensiveness after the "de-Stalinization" drive had ended only weeks earlier with the Third Central Committee Plenum of September–October. Khrushchev, as well, was in a strengthened position. He had recently defeated an "anti-Party" group which included Stalin's old associate Molotov, and had ousted the popular army leader, Marshal Zhukov. The triumph of Sputnik, moreover, appeared to have diverted attention away from the difficulties in Poland and the Hungarian intervention of the preceding fall.

114. From the collection of Mao's statements, "Imperialism and All Reactionaries Are Paper Tigers," *People's Daily* (October 31, 1958); trans. in *Current Background,* No. 534 (November 12, 1958), p. 8.

By all evidence the meetings between Mao and Khrushchev in November of 1957 embodied discussion of political and military issues of primary importance to both countries. Only two weeks before Mao's arrival in Moscow, the Chinese later revealed, the Russians had signed an agreement with the People's Republic to aid in the development of "new technology for national defense." [115] The Chinese also implied that they had requested (unsuccessfully) that the Soviets supply them with "a sample of an atomic bomb and technical data concerning its manufacture." [116] Whether such a request had been made at the time of the October negotiations on the agreement for aid in developing "national defense technology," when Mao met Khrushchev in early November, or at some point subsequent to the world meeting of Communist Parties, is unclear. Yet only two days after Khrushchev's first meeting with Mao and P'eng Teh-huai, a high-level Chinese military delegation suddenly went to Moscow at the invitation of the Soviet Defense Ministry. Evidently defense matters of the highest importance were under discussion.[117]

Whether these Sino-Soviet military contacts involved joint defense planning, the sharing of military and technical information, or bargaining over aspects of either or both issues, cannot be estimated from the public record. Yet it seems evident that both countries were trying to make adjustments in military strategy and defense liaison in the wake of the Soviet ICBM breakthrough. In addition, Khrushchev appeared anxious to be more generous to the Chinese as a way of gaining political backing from Mao. Khrushchev wanted to consolidate his domestic political position and shore up Russia's leading role within the Bloc in the wake of "de-Stalinization" and Hungary.[118]

At the November meeting of representatives of Communist and Workers' Parties, Mao apparently "did a great deal of work" to cor-

---

115. *People's Daily* and *Red Flag* joint editorial, "The Origin and Development of the Differences between the Leadership of the CPSU and Ourselves" (September 6, 1963), in *Polemic on the General Line of the International Communist Movement*, p. 77.

116. *Ibid.*

117. This delegation was composed of fourteen of China's top generals, including Chief of the General Staff Su Yü. It was headed by Defense Minister P'eng Teh-huai, who was already in Moscow. The delegation remained in the Soviet Union for nearly a month. The long duration of this visit suggests that detailed planning discussions were held.

118. This point is discussed and documented in Ellis Joffe, *Party and Army: Professionalism and Political Control in the Chinese Officer Corps, 1949–1964* (Cambridge, Massachusetts: Harvard University, East Asian Monographs, 1965), pp. 94–95.

rect what he considered to be the erroneous views of the Soviet leadership on the questions of "peaceful transition" and their attitude toward capitalist countries. He is said to have "waged struggles" against the Khrushchev leadership, successfully pressed the world meeting to adopt the thesis that "U.S. imperialism is the center of world reaction and the sworn enemy of the people," and urged other more militant changes in the Soviet draft of the conference document. The Chinese delegation was said to have desisted from pressing their viewpoint only "out of consideration for the difficult position of the leadership of the CPSU at the time." [119]

This belated Chinese admission of a policy of "unity and struggle" with the Soviets in 1957–58 is borne out by documentation published at the time. The "stalking horse" in Chinese efforts to resist the reconciliation themes in Khrushchev's evolving political line was the issue of Yugoslav "revisionism." In mid-1955 Khrushchev had partially repaired Stalin's 1948 open break with the Tito government; and one of the key issues surrounding the 1957 Moscow meeting was whether the Yugoslavs would return to the Socialist Camp on terms acceptable to the Russians. On the eve of the world conference Tito developed, as one analyst has put it, a "diplomatic illness." [120] He apparently feared that if he attended the conference he would either be pressured into signing a conference declaration which would go against his domestic and foreign policies, or be subject to public attack from more militant Parties.

Tito's decision to send to the meeting a lower-level delegation (which was, in fact, subjected to threats and pressures, even from the Russians) meant that Khrushchev's reconciliation efforts within the Bloc had met a serious setback; and following the November conference a partial break in Soviet-Yugoslav relations reappeared. The evidence indicates, however, that at the beginning of the winter of 1957–58 the Russians limited public attacks on the Yugoslavs in hopes of eventually reaching some accommodation with Tito.[121]

It was in this context of political uncertainty that the Chinese intervened in early May of 1958 by launching a blistering public attack on Yugoslav "revisionism"—ostensibly in response to the April publication of the Yugoslavs' "Draft Program" discussed at their Seventh Party Congress. The Chinese termed this political

119. *People's Daily* and *Red Flag* joint editorial, "The Origin and Development of the Differences between the Leadership of the CPSU and Ourselves," in *Polemic on the General Line of the International Communist Movement*, pp. 72–74.
120. Zagoria, *The Sino-Soviet Conflict, 1956–1961*, p. 178.
121. *Ibid.*, pp. 178–184.

program "out-and-out revisionist," and of such danger to the International Movement that the new "sacred task" before all Parties was to "wage an irreconcilable struggle against modern revisionism." [122]

The second *People's Daily* editorial in this attack, however, noted that "some people" thought such a struggle might be "going too far," and would bring harm to the International Movement.[123] In response to this objection, the Chinese detailed the extent of American efforts to split the Socialist Camp—in part by giving military and economic aid to the Yugoslavs—and stressed that, "Those who do not see the danger of Yugoslav revisionism should give careful consideration to this." [124] In conclusion the editorial asserted: "We hold that modern revisionism must be fought to the end and there can be no room for concession here." [125]

The third article in this series came from the pen of Ch'en Po-ta, over the years Mao's closest political spokesman. Ch'en detailed the degree to which the Yugoslavs had blurred the lines of struggle between "imperialism" and "socialism," and had given in to bureaucratism and capitalist tendencies within their own country. His conclusion was that, "It is impossible to cease this struggle [against revisionism]." [126] Ch'en then rhetorically asked: "Is this struggle good for Marxism-Leninism?" His answer was that a continuing political confrontation would "enable people to distinguish still more clearly between Marxism-Leninism and anti-Marxism-Leninism. Marxism-Leninism has always grown and developed by combating opportunism of every description." [127]

To readers of this polemic in Moscow there would have been little doubt that Chinese references to "some comrades" and to the need to struggle against "opportunism" were directed above all at the Soviet Party leadership. Indeed, at a later date the Chinese were to admit publicly that during this period, "for the sake of the larger interest, we refrained from publicly criticizing the comrades of the CPSU and directed the spearhead of struggle against the imperialists

122. *People's Daily* editorial, "Modern Revisionism Must Be Repudiated" (May 5, 1958); trans. in *Peking Review,* No. 11 (May 13, 1958), p. 6.

123. *People's Daily* editorial, "Modern Revisionism Must Be Fought to the End" (June 4, 1958); trans. in *Peking Review,* No. 15 (June 10, 1958), p. 7.

124. *Ibid.,* p. 9.

125. *Ibid.*

126. Ch'en Po-ta, "Yugoslav Revisionism—Product of Imperialist Policy," *Red Flag,* No. 1 (June 1, 1958); trans. in *Peking Review,* No. 16 (June 17, 1958), p. 12.

127. *Ibid.*

and Yugoslav revisionists." [128] But in 1958, in a period of increasingly uncertain Soviet militancy, the Chinese were trying to force the Russian Party leadership to "distinguish clearly between friend and enemy," and to assume those obligations of active aid to "fraternal Parties" which were implied by their leadership of the International Movement (at least in Chinese eyes).

The declining militancy of the Soviet Party's domestic and foreign policies created great problems for Mao, and as he saw it, for the future of China's revolution and state interests. If the Russians were willing to accept as true socialism such modifications of the "dictatorship of the proletariat" as the Yugoslav experiments in economic and political reform and their acceptance of aid from "the sworn enemy of the people," "U.S. imperialism," what would be the impact within China in leadership debates?

We have noted above that there had been strong opposition to Mao's policy of combating "rightist conservatism" in the intellectual community and within the Party, and to his progam of social mobilization in developing the rural economy. Would Soviet toleration of Yugoslav "revisionism" enhance the legitimacy of less radical approaches to social change and strengthen the political position of Mao's domestic opponents? At a time when American support for the Nationalists on Taiwan and the offshore islands of Quemoy and Matsu continued to hold China's revolutionary struggle in abeyance, and when American diplomatic efforts tended to strengthen the reality of "two Chinas," would Soviet nuclear superiority help to solve this basic political and defense problem, or would it lead to an easing of Soviet-American tensions?

Mao's response was a characteristic promotion of open confrontation with the issues. Politically, he launched an ideological polemic against "modern revisionism"—initially personified in the Yugoslav Party leadership—in order to "draw a line" between acceptable and unacceptable forms of social organization and political policies. At best he could force the Russians to draw a similar line; but at least he could make it very difficult for "revisionist" sentiments within the Chinese leadership to be expressed as policy alternatives to his own political line.

In the matter of national defense policy Mao also chose to promote a confrontation, both with domestic military leaders and with the Soviets. Military developments of 1958 reflect several goals: to

128. *People's Daily* and *Red Flag* joint editorial, "The Origin and Development of the Differences between the Leadership of the CPSU and Ourselves," in *Polemic on the General Line of the International Communist Movement,* p. 78.

encourage greater Russian militancy in the international struggle; to test the limits of both Soviet and American power as it affected China; and to invoke the temporary Soviet missile advantage in resolving the Taiwan issue.

Such objectives, intimately related to China's national defense, provoked an intense debate within the Party leadership in the spring and summer of 1958 and were the subject of an extraordinary meeting of the Military Affairs Committee of the Party Central Committee between May 27th and July 22nd. The final communiqué of this exceptionally lengthy convocation—attended by more than a thousand officers, and addressed by the highest political and military leaders—revealed little more than that the sessions had "decided on the principle for future development" of the People's Liberation Army [PLA].[129]

From later developments, however, it seems evident that after debating the price which the Soviets expected the Chinese to pay for a strengthened defense relationship, Mao was able to establish the "principle" of complete Chinese independence of the Soviet Union in matters of both military organization and national defense strategy. As Mao is reported to have said to high-ranking military officials during the meetings: "We cannot feed on meals cooked for us, otherwise, defeat will be our lot. This point must be clearly explained to the Soviet comrades." [130]

The Russians evidently had pressed the Chinese for a strategy of "united action," [131] which in practical terms meant a proposal for a joint Sino-Soviet naval command in the Far East,[132] more closely

129. NCNA, "CCP Military Committee Holds Enlarged Conference" (July 25, 1958); in *SCMP*, No. 1822 (July 30, 1958), p. 1.

130. Mao, "Speech at the Symposium of Group Leaders of the Enlarged Meeting of the Military Commission (Excerpts)" (June 28, 1958), in *Chairman Mao's Criticism and Repudiation of the P'eng, Huang, Chang, and Chou Anti-Party Clique*, p. 4.

131. "The Criminal History of Big Conspirator, Big Ambitionist, Big Warlord P'eng Teh-huai," in *The Case of P'eng Teh-huai*, p. 202.

132. *See* Alice Langley Hsieh, *Communist China's Strategy in the Nuclear Era* (Englewood Cliffs, New Jersey: Prentice-Hall, 1962), p. 117.

According to Cultural Revolution disclosures, the Soviets made the proposal for a joint naval command in "the second half of 1958," which apparently means while the Military Commission was in mid-session. Mao is reported to have denounced this proposal at the Tenth Plenum in 1962 as having been an attempt "to dominate the coastal area, and to blockade us." And in an apparent reference to Khrushchev's hasty and secretive visit to Peking of late July and early August 1958, Mao noted: "Khrushchev came to China because of this problem [of China's rejection of the plan]." (From Mao's "Speech at the Tenth Plenary Session of the Eighth Central Committee" [September 24, 1962], in the pamphlet *Chairman Mao's Criticism and Repudiation of the P'eng, Huang, Chang, Chou Anti-Party Clique*, p. 25.)

integrated air defenses, and perhaps base agreements and control arrangements for stationing Soviet rockets and nuclear weapons on Chinese territory.[133] The Chinese later indignantly recalled that "these unreasonable demands designed to bring China under Soviet military control" had been "rightly and firmly rejected by the Chinese Government." [134]

In the face of Soviet conditions which in Mao's eyes would have made China a military dependency of the Russians, the Party Chairman urged his colleagues to make the most of a difficult situation through self-reliance. It was during this period that Mao stressed the importance of China developing an independent nuclear weapons capability based on her own resources.[135] Conversely, he apparently proposed rejection of an attempt to keep up with China's enemies in the development of conventional weaponry (aircraft, tanks, a naval fleet, etc.)—which would tax her limited industrial capacity to the extreme—in favor of reliance on the guerrilla warfare defense strategy which was the Party's revolutionary legacy. The formation of a decentralized political and economic system— the Communes—and the strengthening of popular military organization through expansion of the People's Militia were central to this new defense strategy of nuclear weapons to deter attack and "people's war" to resist invasion.

As with his efforts of the preceding three years to break China's dependence on the Soviet experience in economic development, the assertive and independent-minded Mao thus resisted Russian proposals which would have increased China's dependence in matters of national defense.

This shift in defense policy had hardly proceeded without struggle, however. As the communiqué of the Military Affairs Committee meetings disclosed, the sessions had been carried out "using the method of the rectification campaign." [136] The meaning of this cryp-

---

133. *See* Raymond L. Garthoff, "Sino-Soviet Military Relations, 1945–66," in Raymond L. Garthoff, ed., *Sino-Soviet Military Relations* (New York: Praeger, 1966), p. 90.

134. *People's Daily* and *Red Flag* joint editorial, "The Origin and Development of the Differences between the Leadership of the CPSU and Ourselves," in *Polemic on the General Line of the International Communist Movement*, p. 77.

135. On the occasion of China's first successful hydrogen bomb test in June of 1967 an official press communiqué crowed: "Chairman Mao Tsetung pointed out as far back as June 1958: 'I think it is entirely possible for some atom bombs and hydrogen bombs to be made in ten years' time.' " (*People's Daily*, June 18, 1967, p. 1.)

136. NCNA, "CCP Military Committee Holds Enlarged Conference," in *SCMP*, No. 1822 (July 30, 1958), p. 1.

tic remark was first suggested in a speech by Chu Teh on Army Day, August 1st. After stressing that the army "absolutely follows the leadership of the Communist Party," and that the Party "has established a complete set of systems whereby the Party exercises leadership over the army," Chu revealed: "There are people who advocate an exclusively military viewpoint, who have a one-sided high regard for military affairs and who look down upon politics." [137]

The identity of the people to whom Chu Teh alluded would have been suggested to a careful observer by personnel movements and changes at this time. The political significance of the unexplained disappearance from public view of Chief of the General Staff Su Yü and senior generals Liu Po-ch'eng and Yeh Chien-ying—men "who over the years had been identified with professional [military] thinking" [138]—became clear when Su Yü was removed from office in October. Whether these changes in personnel reflected opposition to Mao's military "principle" of independence from the Soviets or conflicting judgments over the feasibility of events which were shortly to take place in the Taiwan Straits is difficult to estimate. The reemergence of all three men as Mao's supporters during the Cultural Revolution suggests that their opposition had been related to tactical considerations.

In any event, it seems certain that the issue of Taiwan and the offshore islands (Quemoy and Matsu), still occupied by Nationalist forces, was discussed in detail by the Military Affairs Committee during its long deliberations. A week after the meeting concluded, on July 29th, Communist and Nationalist aircraft clashed over the Taiwan Straits; and two days later Khrushchev, accompanied by his Defense Minister, Malinovsky, secretly arrived in Peking for three days of talks. It seems unlikely that such a visit would have taken place had not the Soviet leaders had some idea of Chinese plans for an attempt to "solve" the offshore island problem through military action.

The press communiqué which was issued at the end of Khrushchev's hasty and initially undisclosed visit made no mention of the Taiwan Straits situation, but instead focused on the current Middle East crisis. Events there were hardly of such importance to Sino-Soviet relations that they would account for the Khrushchev-Malinovsky visit. It seems most likely that the Soviet leaders came to define the limits of their support for the Chinese, if not to cool Mao's ardor for a test in the Straits.

137. Chu Teh, "People's Army, People's War," NCNA (July 31, 1958); in *Current Background*, No. 514 (August 6, 1958), pp. 1–2.
138. *See* Hsieh, *Communist China's Strategy in the Nuclear Era*, p. 122.

The fact that the Mao-Khrushchev communiqué eventually was issued—publicly revealing the Russian leader's presence in Peking —can be explained in terms which would account for conflicting interests on both sides: The failure to mention Taiwan in the communiqué would have made it clear that the Soviets were unwilling to give Mao direct backing in the coming confrontation over the offshore islands; yet the fact that the Soviet visit was revealed probably helped to sustain in American minds the air of uncertainty as to whether the Russians, in fact, might become involved—which is possibly all that Mao felt he needed in the coming test.[139]

One suspects that Mao tried to convince Khrushchev and Malinovsky that the confrontation could be localized and that artillery fire directed at the offshore islands would run only a limited risk of involving the Americans directly. Yet one cannot rule out the possibility of a major political confrontation between Mao and Khrushchev at this time. It may be that the real "test" of Soviet reliability in aid of China's national defense concluded with this meeting.

Whatever the exact explanation for the visit, it is clear from subsequent developments that Mao was determined to act. He probably estimated that the United States, beset by an economic recession at home,[140] and distracted by its current intervention in the Middle East, would find it difficult to respond to a limited and indirect action in a distant theater. Further, merely the knowledge of Soviet missile superiority and the possibility of Russian intervention would have seemed enough to give the Americans additional cause for inaction. Hence, as Cultural Revolution materials later revealed:

> After bald-headed Khrushchev left [Peking on August 3rd], Chairman Mao ordered the shelling of Quemoy. This was a forceful reply to Soviet revisionism, and traitor P'eng Teh-huai was very dissatisfied over this. Chairman Mao personally directed this important military action, but traitor P'eng Teh-huai stealthily slipped away on the grounds of making an inspection tour.[141]

In the event, of course, the military aspect of Mao's calculated gamble failed, initially because the Americans deployed a military

139. Shortly after Khrushchev's August visit to Peking, rumors began circulating in Warsaw that the Russians had granted the Chinese nuclear weapons and missiles. These reports, which have never been substantiated, are thought to have been planted by Chinese agents. *Ibid.,* p. 123.

140. The first issue of *Red Flag* (June 1, 1958) carried a lengthy analysis of the deteriorating state of the American economy by Chang Wen-t'ien entitled, "On the Economic Crisis of the United States."

141. "The Criminal History of Big Conspirator, Big Ambitionist, Big Warlord P'eng Teh-huai," in *The Case of P'eng Teh-huai,* p. 202.

task force to the area and showed themselves willing to take the risks of convoying Nationalist supply vessels to the offshore islands. A further factor in the playing out of this challenge, however, was the demonstrated Soviet unwillingness to invoke their nuclear weapons in support of the Chinese initiative. The shelling of Quemoy began on August 23rd, and by the last days of the month it was clear that the United States was actively mobilizing naval strength for the confrontation. On September 6th Premier Chou En-lai issued a statement asserting that the Government of the People's Republic was willing to discuss the dispute with the United States through the ambassadorial talks at Warsaw; and the next day the *People's Daily* carried a defensive editorial asserting that the "U.S. imperialists' attempt to impose war on the Chinese people comes at a time when they are making a big leap on the road to socialist construction" (i.e., they are not interested in a military confrontation), and that the Chinese people "have every right to liberate their own territory by all suitable means at a suitable time" (that is, not at present).[142]

It was only after this public expression of Peking's willingness to seek a political solution to the crisis that Khrushchev sent a message to President Eisenhower warning that "an attack against China is tantamount to an attack against the Soviet Union"—a tardy and ambiguous response in its military implications that was nonetheless given wide publicity in the Chinese press.

As the Straits crisis thus entered a diplomatic phase, Mao emphasized the turning of this confrontation with "U.S. imperialism" into a context for motivating still greater "leaps" in the areas of production and social reorganization by promoting a nationwide campaign to make "everyone a soldier." [143] Mao thus speeded the militarization of the rural work force and the implementation of his new national defense line which called for large militia units. His personal support for these developments was emphasized by a publicized tour in late September of production facilities in newly communized areas of central China.

Whether or not one assumes that Mao had consciously exacerbated the confrontation in the Taiwan Straits in part as a test of Soviet and American responses, it seems evident that as a result of the demonstrated Soviet reluctance to back a "fraternal Party" in a confrontation with the "imperialists and their lackeys," Mao could

142. *People's Daily* editorial, "Six Hundred Million People Mobilize to Crush the U.S. Aggressors' Military Threats and War Provocations!" (September 7, 1958); trans. in *SCMP*, No. 1851 (September 11, 1958), pp. 3, 6.

143. National publicity was given to this movement beginning on September 11th. *See* NCNA dispatches in *SCMP*, No. 1856 (September 18, 1958), pp. 17–19.

affirm the correctness of his earlier judgment that China should be independent of the Soviets in matters of defense. Yet as with the "blooming and contending" confrontation with the intellectuals of the preceding year, one cannot be certain that Mao had manipulated a "struggle" situation to make a political point clear to resistant colleagues within the Party leadership.

While in a strategic sense Mao could claim his judgment vindicated by these developments, tactically the Russians had seriously let him down by requiring a retreat before a "paper tiger." Mao's rage at Khrushchev for this further betrayal of "proletarian internationalism" was hinted at after the crisis had passed into its political phase. A *Red Flag* editorial of September 16th, entitled "The U.S. Aggressors Have Put Nooses around Their Own Necks," stressed that the "tense situations" created by the Americans around the world only helped to mobilize "the People" to make revolution. But the editorial went on to observe that

> up to now there are still some people who have failed to understand this reality. They often overestimate the strength of the enemy and underestimate the strength of the people. . . . They often only see the fact that some ice-bound rivers are not yet thawing as a whole, but fail to see the torrential streams underneath which will soon break up the ice completely and rise in mighty waves.[144] ʼ

The unusual imagery of the "ice-bound rivers" would seem to have been intended to evoke in Chinese minds the picture of the "allies" to the north across the frozen Amur and Ussuri rivers, and to make it clear to politically sensitized minds that those "some people" who failed to understand the weakness of "imperialism" included Khrushchev. This theme was to be repeated in late October with the republication of Mao's 1945 work, "Imperialists and All Reactionaries Are Paper Tigers." The introductory editorial again observed that, "At present there are quite a few people who still fail to see [that the United States is a paper tiger], and still remain in a state of passivity." [145]

The full extent of Mao's rage at the now lengthy record of Soviet failures to assist their "fraternal allies" in China—a record that Mao, with no little justice, could contrast with evidence of repeated Chinese sacrifices on behalf of Soviet security going back to the 1920s—erupted publicly in the open polemics of 1963. The

144. *Red Flag* editorial, "The U.S. Aggressors Have Put Nooses around Their Own Necks" (September 14, 1958); trans. in *SCMP*, No. 1856 (September 18, 1958), p. 4.

145. "Comrade Mao Tse-tung on 'Imperialists and All Reactionaries Are Paper Tigers,'" *People's Daily* (October 31, 1958); trans. in *Current Background*, No. 534 (November 12, 1958), p. 1.

Chinese gave a blistering reply to Soviet charges that in the Straits crisis they had tried to provoke a "head-on clash" between Russia and the United States:

> Our answer is: No, friends. You had better cut out your sensation-mongering calumny. The Chinese Communist Party is firmly opposed to a "head-on clash" between the Soviet Union and the United States, and not in words only. In deeds too it has worked hard to avert direct armed conflict between them. Examples of this are the Korean War against U.S. aggression in which we fought side by side with the Korean comrades and our struggle against the United States in the Taiwan Straits. We ourselves preferred to shoulder the heavy sacrifices necessary and stood in the first line of defense of the socialist camp so that the Soviet Union might stay in the second line.[146]

The clear implication of this expression of controlled rage was that the Soviets had not "shouldered heavy sacrifices" on behalf of the socialist camp, but had repeatedly hidden themselves behind Chinese skirts. And in a direct refutation of Soviet assertions that they had invoked their nuclear weapons in behalf of Chinese security during the off-shore island confrontation, the Chinese detailed:

> What are the facts? In August and September of 1958, the situation in the Taiwan Straits was indeed very tense as a result of the aggression and provocations by the U.S. imperialists. The Soviet leaders expressed their support for China on September 7 and 19 respectively. Although at that time the situation . . . was tense, there was no possibility that a nuclear war would break out and no need for the Soviet Union to support China with its nuclear weapons. It was only when it was clear that this was the situation that the Soviet leaders expressed their support for China.[147]

Mao had thus "tested the wind" and found the Russians unwilling to translate their temporary superiority in a nuclear weapon delivery system into efforts to resolve an outstanding political-military issue of great importance to the Chinese. Yet the initiative in the events of the fall had been with Mao, and there were both domestic and international prices which would have to be paid for this exposure of Soviet reticence.

The meaning of the fall confrontation for the Sino-Soviet defense relationship almost certainly was one of the issues which Defense Minister P'eng Teh-huai had to deal with in a tour of the

146. *People's Daily* and *Red Flag* joint editorial, "Two Different Lines on the Question of War and Peace," in *Polemic on the General Line of the International Communist Movement*, p. 246.

147. "Statement of the Spokesman of the Chinese Government" (September 1, 1963), in Garthoff, ed., *Sino-Soviet Military Relations*, p. 233.

Soviet Union and Eastern Europe between April 24th and June 13th, 1959. P'eng was in Albania during Khrushchev's visit to what within a few years was to become China's lonely "fraternal ally"; and the Defense Minister's critics were later to charge that, "He informed baldheaded Khrushchev of the shortcomings of the Great Leap Forward, and the latter encouraged the former to go home and oppose Chairman Mao." [148]

The Chinese later revealed that one week after P'eng's return from his trip to Eastern Europe, on June 20th, the Soviets "unilaterally tore up the agreement on new technology for national defense." [149] It seems likely that this development was somehow related to P'eng's trip, although it is not yet known whether the Defense Minister had engaged in secret negotiations with the Soviets concerning the now strained defense relationship between the two countries. Perhaps the Russians presented the Chinese Party leadership with certain demands through P'eng which they refused to accept, and then broke the agreement. It seems likely, however, that the Russians timed the breaking of the agreement to try to strengthen the hands of those within the Chinese leadership who might oppose Mao on economic and military issues at the coming Central Committee Plenum.

Such was the political climate after P'eng returned to China, and within a month he circulated his "Letter of Opinion" to the Party leaders at Lushan. What has been reported as P'eng's letter of self-criticism to Mao contains no reference to his dealings with Khrushchev, and the excerpt from the Central Committee Resolution condemning P'eng's "anti-Party clique" suggests that the "Party should continue to adopt an attitude of great sincerity and warmth" toward P'eng.[150] Furthermore, the Defense Minister—in contrast to Kao Kang—was given lenient personal treatment after his dismissal. Hence, it seems most likely that P'eng's errors had

148. "The Criminal History of Big Conspirator, Big Ambitionist, Big Warlord P'eng Teh-huai," in *The Case of P'eng Teh-huai,* p. 204.

The 1961 study of the P'eng case by David A. Charles indicates that P'eng had been charged with giving a "letter" of criticism of Mao's policies to Khrushchev during their meeting in Tirana. (*See* "The Dismissal of P'eng Teh-huai," *The China Quarterly,* No. 8 [October–December 1961], pp. 67, 74.) This "letter" was not mentioned in Cultural Revolution documents on the P'eng affair.

149. "Statement by the Spokesman of the Chinese Government" (August 15, 1963), in *SCMP,* No. 3043 (August 20, 1963), p. 36.

150. "Resolution of the Eighth Plenary Session of the Eighth Central Committee of the Communist Party of China Concerning the Anti-Party Clique Headed by P'eng Teh-huai (Excerpts)," in *The Case of P'eng Teh-huai,* p. 44.

been to engage in excessively critical or indiscreet discussions with the detested Khrushchev and Russian military leaders concerning China's internal affairs, and to present criticisms to the Eighth Plenum which "objectively" placed him on the same political ground as the increasingly "revisionist" Soviets.[151]

Behind Mao's uncompromising response to P'eng's critique of the Great Leap Forward was the complex set of issues of personal authority, development strategy, and national defense line which Khrushchev had raised beginning with the Soviet Twentieth Party Congress. P'eng was said to have *"depended entirely on the Khrushchev revisionist clique* for the improvement of our army's equipment and the development of up-to-date military science and technology, in a futile attempt to *turn our army into a dependency of that clique."* [152] The Defense Minister's actions had tapped the intense emotionalism of a leader rebelling against a political culture of dependency:

> . . . the attitude Comrade Khrushchev has adopted is patriarchal, arbitrary and tyrannical. He has in fact treated the relationship between the great Communist Party of the Soviet Union and our Party not as one between brothers, but as one between patriarchal father and son.[153]

The assertive Mao, for his part, had now alienated Khrushchev through the exaggerated claims which had been made for the People's Communes, and his initiative in the Taiwan Straits. Following the Lushan Plenum it was little more than a matter of time before the strains between the two leaderships became public. The Chinese claimed that the Russians brought the dispute "right into the open before the whole world" by verbally siding with the Indians in Sino-Indian border clashes which grew from the rebellion in Tibet in the spring of 1959.[154] And when Khrushchev came to China to

151. The lenient treatment accorded P'eng may also reflect the efforts of his supporters within the Party leadership to mitigate Mao's counterattack. As we shall stress in the next chapter, evidence strongly supports the interpretation that during the 1960s there was continuing pressure from within the leadership to "reverse the verdict" on P'eng once the aftermath of the Great Leap Forward had more fully vindicated his criticism of Mao's policy.

152. "Settle Accounts with P'eng Teh-huai for His Crimes of Usurping Army Leadership and Opposing the Party," in *The Case of P'eng Teh-huai*, p. 165. Emphasis added.

153. "Statement of the Delegation of the Communist Party of China at the Bucharest Meeting of Fraternal Parties" (June 26, 1960), in *Polemic on the General Line of the International Communist Movement*, p. 110.

154. *People's Daily* and *Red Flag* editorial, "The Origin and Development of the Differences between the Leadership of the CPSU and Ourselves," in *ibid.*, p. 77.

attend celebrations marking the Tenth Anniversary of the founding of the People's Republic—just after his September meeting with Eisenhower at Camp David—he is said to have "read China a lecture against 'testing by force the stability of the capitalist system.' " [155]

Before long, the "unbreakable" Sino-Soviet alliance was sundered by these fully developed strains over defense and development strategies, leadership, and political line. The Chinese escalated the dispute to the level of ideological polemics with publication of the April 1960 theoretical challenge "Long Live Leninism!" and three months later the Soviets suddenly began to remove from China all their scientific and technical experts working on aid projects.

Thus Mao had pushed his differences with Khrushchev to the point of an open break between the two countries rather than compromise on issues which he felt would sacrifice China's interests and the future of the revolution. And while this confrontation brought with it great costs in the areas of economic assistance and national defense, Mao sought to turn even these losses to advantage by mobilizing hatred for the "revisionist" Soviets in order to build China's "revolutionary vigor." The *People's Daily* observed as the Soviet advisers were being withdrawn:

> Where does revolutionary vigor come from? . . . Only when you are conscious of having been oppressed and cheated, and don't want to be placed in this kind of a position, and because of this suppress a stomach full of anger—get angry enough to want to go and change the situation —only then can you produce a lot of revolutionary vigor. To use a Chinese proverb, this is "drawing strength from anger" (*fa-fen t'u-ch'iang*), this is revolutionary spirit.[156]

THE DEEPENING CRISIS OF LEADERSHIP

Mao was able to mobilize sufficient support at the Lushan Central Committee Plenum in the summer of 1959 to turn P'eng Teh-huai's criticisms of his "general line" for modernizing China into an attack on "right opportunism," and to have the Defense Minister replaced by the loyal Lin Piao.[157] Yet the deepening economic

155. *Ibid.,* p. 78.
156. "If You Want to Make Revolution You Must Have Revolutionary Spirit," *People's Daily* (August 13, 1960), p. 7. This article is an abridgment of the original version which appeared in the Shanghai periodical *Liberation,* No. 15 (1960).
157. The circumstances under which Mao was able to bring about P'eng's replacement as Defense Minister by Lin Piao remain one of the most obscure, yet important, aspects of political developments in the late 1950s leading to the Cultural Revolution. The fact that within three years after

Communist Party Chairman Mao Tse-tung Welcomes
Soviet Premier and Party First Secretary Nikita Khrushchev
at Peking Airport, September 30, 1959.
Brian Brake, from Rapho Guillumette.

crisis which grew from the Great Leap Forward was to serve as a powerful defense of P'eng's critique. By 1962, when the crisis reached its depth, the coalition of power which had enabled Mao to weather the Lushan challenge began to disintegrate.

Mao made a self-criticism before his Central Committee colleagues at Lushan. He observed: "Now I should be attacked because I have not exercised supervision over many things." [158] And he expressed awareness of how, in practice, the power of the word and popular activism had not justified "the abandonment of planning":

> Diseases enter by the mouth and all disasters come through the tongue. I'm in great trouble today. . . . I decided upon and promoted the target of 10,700,000 tons of steel, and as a result 90 million people were thrown into battle. . . . Next, the People's Communes. I did not invent the People's Communes, but I promoted them. When I was in Shantung a correspondent asked me: "Are the People's Communes good?" I said, "Good"; and on the basis of this he published a report in a newspaper. From now on, I must avoid reporters.[159]

The tension of the Plenum had been very great, and not all of Mao's comrades had, in Chinese fashion, put the bitterness "in their stomachs." Using his characteristic scatology, Mao revealed a hope that the "disasters of the tongue" would—like some evil air—pass away. He concluded: "This trouble I have brought on is a great one, and I hold myself responsible for it. Comrades, you also should analyze your own responsibilities, and you will all feel better after you have broken wind and emptied your bowels." [160]

Despite Mao's candor before his colleagues within the leadership, the question remained just how the Party organization and "the People" would assign responsibility for the deepening economic crisis. It was perhaps in response to this nagging question that the fourth volume of Mao's *Selected Works* was published in Septem-

---

Lin's rise an attempt was made to "reverse the verdict" on P'eng suggests that by 1962 other Party leaders were quite concerned about Mao's increasing reliance on the army as his base of power. Yet whether this possibility had been foreseen at Lushan is uncertain. At the same time that Liu was promoted, Lo Jui-ch'ing—who was to be purged in the early stages of the Cultural Revolution—was advanced to the position of Vice Minister of National Defense; but whether he had been elevated as part of a "deal" to balance off Lin's new power remains uncertain.

158. Mao Tse-tung, "Speech at the Lushan Conference" (July 23, 1959), in *Chairman Mao's Criticism and Repudiation of the P'eng, Huang, Chang and Chou Anti-Party Clique*, p. 10.

159. *Ibid.*

160. *Ibid.*, p. 11.

ber of 1960.[161] As a contemporary political document this book appears to be an attempt to reaffirm Mao's preeminent contribution to the Party's attainment of power. It contains the veiled assertion that leaders other than Mao had been responsible for "leftist" errors in the application of Party policy in the rural areas, and reaffirms the collective responsibility of the Party "center" for leadership decisions. Such an interpretation of Volume Four is most clearly seen if the editorial footnotes elaborating each article are taken as the main text, with the historical materials serving as documentation to affirm the continuity of accurate judgment or political error on the part of various Party leaders.[162]

Earlier we noted that Liu Shao-ch'i's political report to the Eighth Party Congress of 1956 had been notably silent on Mao's role in shaping Party policies which led to final victory over the Nationalists. The first twenty-three articles in Volume Four give clear emphasis to the position that only Mao's correct assessment of the balance of forces within China in 1945–46 led to the Party's successful prosecution of the Civil War.

The editorial notes stress that it was Mao, in August of 1945, who "unmask[ed] the counterrevolutionary face of Chiang K'ai-shek [in order to] teach the whole people to be on guard against his civil war plot." [163] "Some comrades [had] overestimated the strength of imperialism . . . [and] showed weakness in the face of the armed attacks of the U.S.-Chiang K'ai-shek gang and dared not resolutely oppose counterrevolutionary war with revolutionary war." [164] But

161. Publication of this volume may also have been timed to coincide with the November meeting of eighty-one Communist Party delegations in Moscow, as a way of emphasizing Mao's stature as a leader and theoretician.

162. I am indebted to Mr. John Gittings for having called my attention to the contemporary political relevance of the editorial footnotes in the fourth volume of Mao's *Selected Works*.

163. Introductory note to "Two Telegrams from the Commander-in-Chief of the Eighteenth Group Army to Chiang K'ai-shek" (August 1945), in *SW*, English, IV, p. 34.

164. Introductory note to "Some Points in Appraisal of the Present International Situation" (April 1946), in *ibid.*, p. 88.

The "some comrades" apparently include Stalin, for as Mao recalled to Party leaders in 1962, "Stalin tried to prevent the Chinese revolution by saying that there should not be any civil war." (Mao, "Speech at the Tenth Plenum of the Eighth CCP Central Committee" [September 24, 1962], in *Chairman Mao's Criticism and Repudiation of the P'eng, Huang, Chang, and Chou Anti-Party Clique*, p. 25.) Liu Shao-ch'i may have supported Stalin's position by claiming in 1945–46 that China was about to enter "a new era of peace and democracy" in which the Communist Party would challenge the Nationalists for power through political rather than military means. (*See* the *Red Flag* and *People's Daily* editorial, "Along the Socialist or Capitalist Road?" [August 17, 1967]; trans. in *Peking Review*, No. 34 [August 18, 1967], p. 13.)

"in accordance with the strategic plan laid down by Comrade Mao Tse-tung, the People's Liberation Army went over to the offensive" in the fall of 1947. And finally, as if to emphasize that it was Mao's sole responsibility to have mobilized the PLA for the Civil War, the notes reveal that it was after the Central Committee had divided into two groups—with Mao heading the Party Secretariat which went to northern Shensi Province, while a "working party" of the Central Committee headed by Liu Shao-ch'i went south to Hopei[165] —that Mao drafted the "Manifesto" of the PLA's victory offensive.[166]

The contemporary political purpose of this historical analysis seems to have been to recall to Party members in the strained situation of 1960 that the Party owed its power to Mao's correct judgments of the late 1940s. It also seems intended to recall the heroic contributions of various comrades at the Party and army's hour of triumph, and thus to reevoke a spirit of collective unity.

A second group of articles and editorial notes in Volume Four appears to express the view that a share of the blame for the "left opportunist" deviations of the Great Leap Forward was the responsibility of those Party members on the "first line" of leadership who held the authority for implementing policy. This is done through historical analogy, by revealing that in the past Liu Shao-ch'i had committed adventurist mistakes when promoting the Party's land reform policies. According to the editorial notes, Mao's December 1947 article, "The Present Situation and Our Tasks," had been described by the Central Committee at the time of its adoption as "a programmatic document . . . for the entire period of the overthrow of the reactionary Chiang K'ai-shek ruling clique and of the founding of a new-democratic China." [167] Party members were exhorted to apply this Party resolution strictly in practice.

Then with a series of personal references which make it clear that Liu Shao-ch'i was responsible for implementing Party policy in the Shansi-Suiyuan Liberated Area,[168] the articles reveal that serious "leftist" errors had occurred in areas under Liu's jurisdic-

165. "On the Temporary Abandonment of Yenan and the Defense of the Shensi-Kansu-Ningsia Border Region—Two Documents Issued by the Central Committee of the Communist Party of China" (November 1946, and April 1947), in *SW*, English, IV, p. 132, fn. 3.

166. Introductory note, "Manifesto of the Chinese People's Liberation Army" (October 1947), in *ibid.*, p. 148.

167. Introductory note to "The Present Situation and Our Tasks" (December 1947), *ibid.*, p. 158.

168. *See* especially the introductory note to "Different Tactics for Carrying Out the Land Law in Different Areas" (February 1948), p. 194; and the passage from "Speech at a Conference of Cadres in the Shansi-Suiyuan Liberated Area" (April 1948), *ibid.*, pp. 231–232.

tion. A telegram which Mao sent to Liu in February 1948 warns that, "Haste will certainly do no good" in promoting the Party's Land Law.[169] And an inner-Party directive instructs unnamed cadres: "Do not be impetuous" in carrying out land reform; "Do not start the work in all places at the same time, but choose strong cadres to carry it out first in certain places to gain experience, then spread the experience step by step and expand the work in waves." [170] The inference which Party members might draw, reading these documents in the wake of the communization drive, would have been that Liu, Mao's enthusiastic supporter on the "first line" of leadership, had been responsible once again for "leftist" errors —for the breakneck speed in Commune formation, and the indiscriminate application of a few model experiences throughout the country.

Finally, an article of April 1948 stresses:

> . . . while many comrades remember our Party's specific line for work and specific policies, they often forget its general line and general policy. If we actually forget the Party's general line and general policy, then we shall be blind, half-baked, muddle-headed revolutionaries, and when we carry out a specific line for work and a specific policy, we shall lose our bearings and vacillate now to the left and now to the right, and the work will suffer.[171]

It is clear that at the Lushan Plenum in the year before republication of these words of 1948, Mao's "general line" of 1958 had been challenged. Hence, this document seems to be significant as a warning to comrades that they must not abandon Mao's policy or else serious problems will arise on the economic front. And unless the Party learns to manage the nation's productive enterprises effectively, Mao asserted through this old article, "you cannot be called good Marxists." [172]

Whatever the justice of these historical insinuations that Liu Shao-ch'i bore much of the responsibility for the "leftist" errors of the Great Leap, it seems evident that Mao was concerned about being held responsible in isolation for the difficulties which resulted from implementation of the policies of 1958. Accordingly, a third group of articles in Volume Four deals with problems of consolidating Party unity on the eve of nationwide victory. Beginning

169. "Different Tactics for Carrying Out the Land Law in Different Areas," *ibid.*, p. 194.

170. "Essential Points in Land Reform in the New Liberated Areas" (February 1948), *ibid.*, p. 202.

171. "Speech at a Conference of Cadres in the Shansi-Suiyuan Liberated Area," *ibid.*, p. 238.

172. *Ibid.*, p. 33.

with a gratuitous editorial identification of Teng Hsiao-p'ing's responsibilities in this area of work,[173] Mao republished an article of May 1948 which noted with concern:

> There are people who, without authorization, modify the policies and tactics adopted by the Central Committee. . . . There are also people who, on the pretext of pressure of work, adopt the wrong attitude of neither asking for instructions before an action is taken nor submitting a report afterwards and who regard the area they administer as an independent realm.[174]

The republication of these words would have had doubtful political significance in 1960 were it not for the fact that during the Cultural Revolution Teng Hsiao-p'ing was to be attacked for precisely this error: After 1959 "he took arbitrary action in all things, and never made reports to or asked for instructions from Chairman Mao, who once criticized him for acting 'like the emperor.' " [175] Mao himself is reported to have complained at a meeting of the Party leadership in the fall of 1966, "Teng Hsiao-p'ing never consulted with me. He has never consulted with me about anything since 1959. In 1962 four vice premiers . . . came to Nanking to consult me. Later they went to Tientsin [to consult with me again]. I forthwith gave them my approval. . . . But Teng Hsiao-p'ing never came." [176]

Finally, the editorial notes reveal that in 1956 Teng Hsiao-p'ing had invoked a Party decision of 1948 which had been drafted by Mao as justification for the stress on collective leadership which Party leaders had used to restrict Mao's influence at the Eighth Party Congress.[177] In 1960, when Mao apparently feared that he alone would be blamed for the deepening economic crisis, the Party Chairman turned this argument of 1956 back on his critics. In an introductory note to the republished Central Committee resolution of 1948, the editors of Volume Four cite Teng Hsiao-p'ing by name and quote his words of 1956 on the need for "conscientious practice of collective leadership." [178] "The meaning of this citation for 1960

173. *See* the introductory note to "Tactical Problems of Rural Work in the New Liberated Areas" (May 1948), *ibid.*, p. 252.

174. "The Work of Land Reform and of Party Consolidation in 1948" (May 1948), *ibid.*, p. 258.

175. "Thirty-three Leading Counterrevolutionary Revisionists," trans. in *Current Background*, No. 874 (March 17, 1969), p. 5.

176. Mao, "Speech at a Report Meeting" (October 24, 1966), in *Long Live the Thought of Mao Tse-tung!* p. 45.

177. *See* p. 275 above.

178. Introductory note, "On Strengthening the Party Committee System" (September 1948), *SW*, English, IV, p. 268.

was that the Party leadership had to take collective responsibility for the Great Leap Forward, and that no one leader should be singled out as a scapegoat.

Mao's effort to sustain the unity of the leadership through collective responsibility, however, was to fail for two major reasons. First, Mao had been too obvious as the primary formulator and promoter of the "three red flags" of the Great Leap Forward, the People's Communes, and the "general line" of socialist construction. Second, the food and production crisis of the winter of 1961–62 was a powerful spokesman in support of P'eng Teh-huai's defeated Lushan critique. And according to later Maoist revelations, it was Liu Shao-ch'i himself who in early 1962 at a Central Committee work conference defended P'eng by observing of his 1959 "Letter of Opinion": "much is in conformity with the facts." [179] Liu was also accused of having encouraged P'eng to write "a document running into a full 80,000 words aimed at reversing the verdict passed on him." [180]

Such charges suggest that the P'eng issue contributed substantially to the eventual breakdown in the Mao-Liu coalition. The Party Chairman was able, once again, to defend his position at the Tenth Central Committee Plenum of September 1962—as is indicated by the Plenum communiqué's assertion that the "great historic significance" of the Lushan Plenum of 1959 had been that it "victoriously smashed attacks by right opportunism." [181] Nevertheless the increasing strains within the Party leadership were revealed by new assertions of the inevitability of class struggle, which was said to be "very sharp" at times, finding expression even "within the Party." [182] Thus the "saddle-shaped" rhythm of policy swing from "right" to "left" and back which Mao had tried to "ride" in pushing China's social advance began to fall apart as the Party leadership became increasingly polarized over basic questions of personal authority and social vision.

THE SEARCH FOR A CONFLICT MANAGER

One of the major themes in Parts Three and Four of this study has been Mao's effort to institutionalize forms of disciplined political

179. *Red Flag* editorial, "From the Defeat of P'eng Teh-huai to the Bankruptcy of China's Khrushchev," No. 13 (1967); trans. in *Peking Review,* No. 34 (August 18, 1967), p. 20.

180. *Ibid.*

181. "Communiqué of the Tenth Plenary Session of the Eighth Central Committee of the Chinese Communist Party," NCNA (September 28, 1962) in *Current Background,* No. 691 (October 5, 1962), p. 4.

182. *Ibid.,* pp. 3–4.

conflict in order to attain power and promote social change. This effort was to become a central issue in the deepening leadership crisis which grew out of the Great Leap Forward.

In 1960 Mao had republished an article of 1948 which seems to express his view of the pattern of Party leadership over the preceding five years:

> The history of our Party shows that Right deviations are likely to occur in periods when our Party has formed a united front with the Kuomintang and that "Left" deviations are likely to occur in periods when our Party has broken with the Kuomintang.[183]

Mao was apparently drawing a parallel between this earlier era and his perception of the two periods we have been describing in these last two chapters: In 1956–57 the Party had "allied" itself with the bourgeois intellectuals in a manner which he felt was producing "right opportunism" within the Party; and in 1958, after the "break" with the intellectuals in June of 1957, the Party had committed "leftist" deviations in promoting the "three red flag" policies for economic development.

Who was responsible for these deviations? In the largest sense perhaps the Party as a whole, for as we have tried to show, it was resistance to Mao's political initiatives by other Party leaders or by lower level cadres which produced the abrupt swings in policy between "right" and "left." Mao apparently found that the political tensions of rectification campaigns and mass movements were needed to goad cadres and the population as a whole into institutionalizing the "transition to socialism." Yet as he revealed in his editorial observations in *Socialist Upsurge in China's Countryside,* Mao saw the deviations of lower-level cadres as resulting from "opportunism" within the Party leadership.[184] In Volume Four he sought to stress that deviations in leadership were the responsibility of those on the "first line" who were charged with implementing Party decisions.

In regard to these policy swings between "right" and "left" there remains one important matter of interpretation which we have not yet confronted: How was it that Liu Shao-ch'i, who had had "misgivings" about Mao's economic policies and the "blooming and contending" line in 1956–57, also could have been one of the Chairman's most vocal supporters during the Great Leap Forward? This question evidently bothered Mao, too. Possibly a major issue in the breakdown of relations between these two leaders—which

183. "A Circular on the Situation" (March 1948), *SW,* English, IV, p. 219.

184. Mao, ed., *Socialist Upsurge in China's Countryside,* p. 138.

was to become apparent only during the Cultural Revolution—was Mao's feeling that Liu was not an effective "conflict manager," and that over the years he had not promoted the social conflict necessary to sustain the revolution.

Previously we noted that Mao reserved his most biting criticism for those Party leaders who had not dealt successfully with conflict situations: He disparaged Ch'en Tu-hsiu for his fear of armed struggle, and criticized Li Li-san for impulsively pressing conflict where it led only to defeat.[185] In one of his writings from the late 1920s Mao had observed that "right" and "left" opportunism sometimes were evident in the behavior of one individual.[186] This pattern was personified first in the policy lines of Wang Ming, and later in the behavior of P'eng Teh-huai[187] and Khrushchev.[188] Liu Shao-ch'i drew Mao's ire for a similar pattern of policy misjudgment: a "wavering" between avoidance of conflict when it was opportune, and the inability to promote struggle with discipline when it was necessary.

The Maoist critique of Liu's errors in leadership, as it came to be expressed publicly in 1967, stresses his misjudgment of the situation in 1945 as "a new phase of peace and democracy" in which the Party would limit itself to a "parliamentary" struggle against the Kuomintang.[189] Subsequently Liu is said to have been responsible for "leftist" errors during the period of civil war land reform: for permitting "excessive burning and killing" in the struggles against the landlords, and for allowing undue strictness to be used in assigning class status in the rural areas, thus disrupting agri-

185. *See* pp. 180, 185 above.

186. *See* p. 187 above.

187. In a denunciation of P'eng in 1959, Lin Piao is reported to have told unspecified Party members: ". . . Comrade Mao Tse-tung cannot tolerate his [P'eng's] Right opportunism, nor his 'Left' opportunism." ("Vice Chairman Lin's Talk about P'eng Teh-huai [Excerpts]" [October 12, 1959], in *Ko-ming Tsao-fan Pao* [Revolutionary Rebellion Journal] [November 25, 1967].) Examples of rightist tendencies were said to be his support of Kao Kang in 1953 and his activities at Lushan; while his leftism was illustrated by his initiative in promoting the "Battle of a Hundred Regiments" in the winter of 1940. (*See* additional documentation on these charges in *The Case of P'eng Teh-huai,* pp. 136, 160.)

188. After Khrushchev fell from power the Chinese jeered: "Pursuing an adventurist policy at one moment, he transported missiles to Cuba, and pursuing a capitulationist policy at another, he docilely withdrew the missiles and bombers from Cuba on the order of the U.S. pirates. . . . In so doing, Khrushchev brought a humiliating disgrace upon the great Soviet people unheard of in the forty years and more since the October Revolution." (*Red Flag* editorial, "Why Khrushchev Fell" [November 21, 1964], in *Polemic on the General Line of the International Communist Movement,* pp. 485–486.)

189. *See* note 164 above.

cultural production through excessive restriction of the rich and middle peasant economy.[190]

During the land reform after Liberation, Liu apparently swung well to the "right" in handling class struggle—perhaps overreacting to Mao's criticism of his errors of the late 1940s. In his 1950 report on land reform Liu stressed that

> chaotic conditions (*hun-luan hsien-hsiang*) must not be allowed to occur, and no deviation or confusion may be allowed to remain uncorrected for long in our agrarian reform work in the future. Agrarian reform must be carried out under guidance, in a planned and orderly way.[191]

Liu's "rightist" stress on guidance and order—and the playing down of class struggle—was to endure through mid-1957. He was lenient toward the "national capitalists," [192] failed to support socialization of the rural economy when Mao thought the moment ripe, and resisted the struggle with "rightist conservatism" among the intellectuals and within the Party in 1956–57.

Liu's public support for the Great Leap Forward in the fall of 1957 suggests his renewed conversion to the Left; yet as our interpretation of Volume Four indicates, Mao apparently held Liu responsible for failure to guide the mass movement properly. He was "Left," not Left,[193] and incurred Mao's disfavor for his lack of skill in promoting the "mass line" style of leadership.

Liu's willingness to "reverse verdicts" on Great Leap critics in 1962 reveals his swing back to the "right." During the Cultural Revolution he was to be attacked for promoting policies in the rural areas between 1963 and 1965 which were characterized as "left in form but right in essence." [194]

This latter charge suggests the difficulty of relying on categories of "right" and "left" in analyzing Liu's policy positions. Rather, Mao seems to be responding to something much more basic in Liu's style of leadership—his inability to promote conflict with judgment

190. These charges, which Mao revealed in the fourth volume of his *Selected Works* as discussed earlier, were admitted by Liu in his second self-criticism. (*See* "The Confession of Liu Shao-ch'i," *Atlas* [April 1967], p. 15.)

191. Liu Shao-ch'i, "Report on the Question of Agrarian Reform" (June 1950), in *The Agrarian Reform Law of the People's Republic of China* (Peking: Foreign Languages Press, 1959), p. 62.

192. *See* the *Red Flag* and *People's Daily* editorial, "Along the Socialist or the Capitalist Road?"; trans. in *Peking Review*, No. 34 (August 18, 1967), p. 13.

193. *See* above, Chapter X, fn. 47, for "left" vs. left.

194. *See* Richard Baum and Frederick C. Teiwes, "Liu Shao-ch'i and the Cadre Question," *Asian Survey*, Vol. VIII, No. 4 (April 1968), pp. 323–345.

and skill. The attacks on Liu during the Cultural Revolution thus reveal Mao's fear that the style of leadership which he has evolved over a lifetime of struggle, and which he feels is still essential to sustaining China's social advance, will go with his passing. The polemical charges hurled at Liu as "China's Khrushchev" likewise reveal Mao's concern about the continuing appeal for certain Party leaders of "revisionist" policies advocated by Russia's Khrushchev—policies which Mao bitterly rejected as unsuited to China's development needs and likely to sustain the political culture of dependency.

Attacks on Liu in 1967 accuse him of propagating a theory of "cultivation" of Party members which would have turned cadres into "docile tools," "blindly obedient" to their organizational superiors,[195] of advocating a "dying out of class struggle,"[196] and of advising other Communist Parties to lay down their arms and give up the struggle against imperialism and its lackies.[197] These charges reflect Mao's personal assertiveness and his determination to find a "revolutionary successor" committed to sustaining his life-long effort to institutionalize a revolutionary political culture after his death. It is this determination which was to lead Mao in the early 1960s to the Great Proletarian Cultural Revolution, a mass political upheaval directed against "revisionism" in the Chinese Communist Party out of which was to emerge a leader with demonstrated skills as a political "conflict manager"—Chou En-lai.[198] The development and course of the Cultural Revolution is the subject of the next chapter in this study.

195. *See* Red Guards' Regiment of the Philosophy and Social Sciences Department of Mao Tse-tung's Thought under the Chinese Academy of Sciences, "Bury the Slave Mentality Advocated by China's Khrushchev," *People's Daily* (April 6, 1967); trans. in *SCMP*, No. 3920 (April 17, 1967), pp. 1–7; and *People's Daily* editorial, "Refuting the Reactionary Theory of 'Docile Tools'" (April 10, 1967); trans. in *SCMP*, No. 3922 (April 19, 1967), pp. 8–11.

196. *See Liberation Army Daily* editorial, "Fight for the Thorough Criticism and Repudiation of the Number One Person in Authority Taking the Capitalist Road" (April 11, 1967); trans. in *SCMP*, No. 3918 (April 13, 1967), pp. 1–4.

197. *See* Cheng Li-chia, "Down with the Capitulationism of China's Khrushchev!" *People's Daily* (July 6, 1967); trans. in *Peking Review*, No. 31 (July 28, 1967), pp. 19–22.

198. *See* the analysis by Thomas W. Robinson, "Chou En-lai and the Cultural Revolution in China," in Thomas W. Robinson, ed., *The Cultural Revolution in China* (Berkeley and Los Angeles: University of California Press, 1971), pp. 165–293.

Chapter XIX

A CULTURAL REVOLUTION? THE RECAPITULATION OF A POLITICAL CAREER

A revolution probably ends only when opportunists join the ranks and undermine it from within.

LU HSÜN, 1928[1]

Thought, culture, customs must be born of struggle, and the struggle must continue for as long as there is still a danger of a return to the past. Fifty years is not a long time; barely a lifetime—our customs must become as different from the traditional customs as yours [in France] are from feudal customs.

MAO TSE-TUNG,
TO ANDRÉ MALRAUX, 1965[2]

A great revolutionary rebellion must be launched against the old ideas, old culture, old customs and old habits and all things opposed to the thought of Mao Tse-tung!

RED GUARDS OF PEKING,
July 1966[3]

---

1. Lu Hsün, "Wiping Out the Reds—A Great Spectacle," in *Selected Works of Lu Hsün* (Peking: Foreign Languages Press, 1959), Vol. III, p. 42.
2. André Malraux, *Anti-Memoirs* (New York: Holt, Rinehart and Winston, 1968), p. 374.
3. The Red Guards of Tsinghua University Middle School, "Third Comment on Long Live the Rebellious Revolutionary Spirit of the Proletariat," *Red Flag*, No. 11 (August 21, 1966), p. 2.

The years of crisis brought on by the Great Leap Forward heightened the social and political tensions which we have explored in the two preceding chapters. Most basic were the problems in the rural areas. The collective organization of agriculture weakened as peasants sought to "go it alone" either by engaging in "sideline" production on their private plots or by seeking nonagricultural employment—thus swelling the numbers of uprooted rural workers in China's major cities.

This diffusion of economic discipline was heightened by a general relaxation of political controls as the social discontent surrounding the production crisis increased in intensity. As a result of unpopular Party policies, peasants were reluctant to assume the responsibilities of basic Party and governmental leadership in the rural areas. Former cadres complained that to bear the burdens of local leadership was to "eat a loss" (*ch'ih-k'uei*); and in Lien-chiang County, Fukien, almost 10 percent of the basic level cadres expressed the desire to resign from their posts.[4]

This erosion of leadership was compounded by abuses of authority on the part of many of the cadres who remained. They used the power of their offices to weather the hardships of the "three bitter years." Gambling, economic speculation, religious frauds, and a return to the practice of money marriages, were varied manifestations of the deep anxiety generated by the production crisis.[5] As one production team Party branch secretary reported to the county Party committee:

> At present [early 1963], production and standards of living are not good and difficulties remain, even though some persons are demanding and extravagant with everything. The problem of excessive eating and drinking is also very severe and is also prominent among cadre members. As a result, a number of those among the masses have said that if we do not oppose these evil tendencies, it will be difficult to strengthen and expand the collective economy of the people's communes. . . . This is especially so in regard to the problems of excessive eating and drinking, taking of special privileges and conveniences, and excessive spending and borrowing by the cadres.[6]

4. Richard Baum and Frederick C. Teiwes, *Ssu-ch'ing: The Socialist Education Movement of 1962–1966* (Berkeley: Center for Chinese Studies, University of California Research Monograph No. 2, 1968), p. 12, note 4. *See also* Appendix A.

5. Such phenomena stemming from the Great Leap crisis are revealed throughout the "Lien-chiang" documentary collection. *See* C. S. Chen, ed., *Rural People's Communes in Lien-Chiang* (Stanford, Calif.: Hoover Institution Press, 1969).

6. "Report of the Expanded Cadre Meeting of the Ch'ang-sha Brigade" (February 20, 1963), in *ibid.*, pp. 213–214.

The Party was finding itself "cut off from the masses." And that natural political authority which is sustained by success became seriously eroded—for the Party at large and for Mao personally within the Party. It was Mao's own conception of the manner in which Chinese society should be organized during the period of socialist construction which seemed to carry much of the responsibility for the hardships.

This crisis of authority within the Chinese Communist Party was manifest during the years 1961–62 by veiled yet sharp criticism of Mao's policies and his style of leadership. There developed strong pressure to reverse the condemnation of the Lushan critics of 1959, for the reality of events seemed to have proven them right. Mao, however, remained unyielding in his commitment to the conception of the Communes and to the importance of waging struggles against the "right opportunism" of his domestic critics, and the now open political attacks and economic difficulties created by the Soviet "revisionists." During the Party debates in the wake of the Great Leap crisis, Mao increasingly defended the correctness of his "three red flag" policies as a matter of his personal authority. His uncompromising stress at the Tenth Central Committee Plenum in September of 1962 on the need to press "class struggle" at home and to wage an unyielding polemic with the Soviet Party was in part a manifestation of the deepening challenge from within the Chinese Party to his own position of leadership.

In earlier chapters we noted that during the 1950s, Mao had repeatedly challenged the Party to remain true to its revolutionary goals—to prevent a new polarization of class relationships in the villages, to promote the development of a collectivized economy, and to discipline Party ranks against the insidious influence of "bourgeois conservatism" among the intellectuals. In the early 1960s, as his own position within the Party weakened, Mao phrased his concern about the Party's commitment to promote social revolution in more somber terms: He warned that unless a determined effort were made to resist the reemergence of old social habits and patterns of leadership new China would "change color" from revolutionary red to the white of a bourgeois revisionist party. There was the increasing danger, he asserted, of "a restoration of capitalism." [7]

The endurance of the basic social problems the Party had con-

7. This evaluation was given its most developed expression in the programmatic *People's Daily* and *Red Flag* joint editorial, "On Khrushchev's Phoney Communism and Its Historical Lessons for the World" (July 14, 1964), in *Polemic on the General Line of the International Communist Movement*.

fronted during the 1950s seems to have brought home to Mao the fact that although more than a decade of effort had been devoted to smashing the state machinery of China's prerevolutionary political order, the old political culture continued to endure. It was rooted in the personalities and "work style" (*tso-feng*) of the millions of Chinese who participated in the organizational life of the Party, state, and economic system. Hence, he concluded, "class struggle" had to be sustained. As this idea was expressed in the communiqué of the Party's Tenth Plenum which met in September 1962:

> Throughout the historical period of transition from capitalism to communism (which will last scores of years or even longer), there is class struggle between the proletariat and the bourgeoisie and struggle between the socialist road and the capitalist road. The reactionary ruling classes which have been overthrown are not reconciled to their doom. They always attempt to stage a come-back. Meanwhile, there still exists in society bourgeois influence, the force of habit of the old society and the spontaneous tendency towards capitalism among a part of the small producers [peasants]. . . . Class struggle is inevitable under these circumstances. This class struggle inevitably finds expression within the Party. . . . [We] must remain vigilant and resolutely oppose in good time various opportunistic ideological tendencies within the Party.[8]

This gnawing perception that, despite the great organizational changes of the 1950s, the forces of habit of the old society were constantly trying to "stage a come-back," pervades Maoist pronouncements of the 1960s with increasing pessimism. In the rural areas Party cadres warned of "the power of old customs":

> The peasants have gone through several thousand years of feudal control and more than a hundred years of semifeudal semicolonial control. . . . Although they have received ten years of education in socialist ideology since the liberation, the peasants fall back on the old customs when the opportunity occurs.[9]

By 1964 this concern with the reemergence of old cultural patterns was more formally stressed to the entire Party and the International Movement:

> The socialist revolution on the economic front (in the ownership of the means of production) is insufficient by itself and cannot be con-

8. Cited from the NCNA English translation of the Plenum communiqué; in *Current Background*, No. 691 (October 5, 1962), pp. 3–4.

9. Wang Hung-chih, "Implementation of the Resolution of the Tenth Plenum of the Eighth Central Committee on Strengthening the Collective Economy and Expanding Agricultural Production," in Chen, ed., *Rural People's Communes in Lien-Chiang*, p. 97.

solidated. There must also be a thorough socialist revolution on the political and ideological fronts. Here *a very long period of time is needed to decide "who will win" in the struggle between socialism and capitalism. Several decades won't do it; success requires anywhere from one to several centuries.* On the question of duration, it is better to prepare for a longer rather than a shorter period of time. On the question of effort, it is better to regard the task as difficult rather than easy. It will be more advantageous and less harmful to think and act in this way. Anyone who fails to see this or appreciate it fully will make tremendous mistakes.[10]

It was the combined perception of the erosion of his authority within the Party and a preoccupation with the fact that despite more than a decade of Party rule traditional customs and habits, culture and thinking continued to endure in the social practice of the Chinese people that shaped Mao's determination in the 1960s to press for a "class struggle" against these backward influences. This struggle was first to be promoted through a new "Socialist Education Movement"; but in time it led to the upheaval of the "Great Proletarian Cultural Revolution."

That Mao came to feel the need for a "Cultural Revolution" is perhaps the most basic reassurance that the underlying assumption of this study—that culture and personality are enduring influences shaping political behavior—is well founded. Although Party leaders continued to use Marxist rhetoric to articulate policy, many had come to question Marxism's basic assumption, that man's economic life determines his social behavior. Mao's stress on the need to "remold" people's thinking reveals his awareness that the basic factor shaping social action is the human personality. To be sure, the economic base in some measure shapes cultural superstructure, and culture, in turn, shapes personality. Yet a revolutionary alteration in economic relationships and the pattern of property ownership—in the short run—is likely to have but limited effect on the way people relate to each other, or on the assertion and response to authority.

While it would be too much to say that Mao and his close supporters have come to reject their commitment to Marxism, it is nonetheless noteworthy that as the 1960s progressed the Chairman's closest comrades talked more of the "thought of Mao Tse-tung" and less of the relevance of Marxism-Leninism as a theoretical guide for coping with the problems of China's social development.

10. *People's Daily* and *Red Flag* joint editorial, "On Khrushchev's Phoney Communism and Its Historical Lessons for the World," in *Polemic on the General Line of the International Communist Movement*, pp. 471–472. Emphasis added.

As we will detail, however, an important element within the Party leadership continued to see Marxism-Leninism rather than Mao's "thought" as their guide in charting China's path to Communism. Their policy disagreements with Mao were now considerably intensified as a result of the experiences of the Hundred Flowers episode and the crisis aftermath of the Great Leap Forward. Much of the drama of Chinese domestic politics after 1960 thus reflects the increasingly sharp divergence between those Party leaders who continued to see the social development of their country as but one part of a world revolutionary movement which drew its inspiration from the Soviet Marxist experience and those who "waved the red flag of the thought of Mao Tse-tung" as the guiding standard of China's revolution.

This divergence within the leadership, rooted in earlier disputes over policy, increasingly passed into questions of personal authority: Had justice been done to those who had been branded as "rightists" in the 1959 purge of P'eng Teh-huai? Who would succeed Mao in his position of leadership of both Party and nation? The question of succession ties together many of the political issues explored in earlier chapters of this study. By the Tenth Plenum, Mao came to question the revolutionary commitment of long-time comrades who had become increasingly resistant to maintaining the struggle with "bourgeois rightism" among the intellectuals, "revisionism" within the International Communist Movement, the peasants' "spontaneous tendencies toward capitalism," and deviations in both political orientation and practice by lower-level Party cadres.

The first half of the decade of the 1960s thus replays the major themes of the period 1955–1959 in the sense of reconfronting Mao and other Party leaders with the issues which had been dealt with in the great movements of the preceding decade. Yet there were significant new dimensions to these problems, and to the leadership's response to them. Mao was now in his seventies, and at one time during this period he was reported to be in poor health. In addition, the generation of leaders who had brought the revolution to the attainment of state power was increasingly divided over basic issues of policy for promoting the long period of "socialist construction." Further, for Mao there were disturbing signs that the younger generation was not firm in its commitment to the goals which its elders had struggled for through force of arms.

For Mao the 1960s was the reliving of his career: He had to face again many of the social and political problems of earlier years—a fact that was to be emphasized by the republication of many of his earlier writings, which he felt to be of continuing relevance. In a more direct way, however, as the Chairman lost influence over the

Party in the wake of the Great Leap Forward, he turned once again to the Army as the base of his power. In the period from Lin Piao's appointment as Defense Minister to the Eleventh Plenum of August 1966 he repeated the pattern of his rise to Party leadership from the Chingkang Mountains to the Tsunyi Conference by relying upon the People's Liberation Army as the instrument for insuring his influence over Chinese political life.

Mao's advancing age constituted an important limit on the reassertion of his authority, however. And his determination to institutionalize his own conception of a new political life for China led him to seek a way of passing on the lessons of the revolution to a new generation. He was seeking a way to combine theory with practice without relying on bookish recitations alone. At some point before the summer of 1966 Mao conceptualized a way of confronting in "unity and struggle" both the opposition of long-time Party leaders and the political immaturity of the younger generation. In the Cultural Revolution of 1966 Mao was to relive his political career vicariously by stimulating a new student generation to rebel against a Party organization which the Chairman had come to see as hopelessly compromised by "revisionist" thinking and habits in the use of power. In the "rebellion" of the student Red Guards, the aging Mao was to seek to father a new generation of student revolutionaries and bring them into a place of influence within China's political life.

In terms of this study, the events of the 1960s are also a recapitulation of the major issues we have explored, bringing together in sharp focus the major analytical themes developed in earlier chapters. In Mao's concern with the problems of cadres "overeating," in their vulnerability to "sugar-coated bullets," we see enduring problems with the discipline of power in a society with dominant oral traditions. Mao was to see the Party as increasingly "cut off" from the masses, again exposing that gap between superior and subordinate, state and society, which has been an enduring theme in Chinese political life. In the Party Chairman's isolation atop the Party bureaucracy we see one of the key psychological vulnerabilities of a culture which has laid such stress on interdependence. Mao was to turn his own isolation back upon those Party leaders who opposed his solutions to China's national resurgence by having them dragged out for isolated exposure and humiliation before the angered masses.

The manner in which Mao came to reassert his authority during the 1960s reflects the enduring Confucian concept of the "power of the word." It was through his writings, the "little red book" of *Quotations from Chairman Mao,* and emulation of model students of his "thought," that the Party Chairman sought to sustain his influence over the course of the Chinese revolution. And then, when such measures had proven ineffective, the man who throughout his career had attempted to convince his colleagues that controlled conflict should endure as a vital aspect of Chinese political life, purposefully provoked the "confusion" of a rebellion of youth to disorganize a Party and governmental apparatus that had become impervious to his will.

WILL GHOSTS AND DEMONS STAY BURIED?

Speaking of the internal conditions of . . . a socialist society . . . it has just grown from the old society, and in many areas the scars of the old society are still preserved. Lenin stated well, the corpse of the bourgeois society "cannot be put into a coffin and buried underground." In a socialist society, "the beaten capitalist society will corrupt and decompose in our midst, contaminate the air, and poison our life. From all sides, the corrupt and dead things will encircle the fresh, young and vital things." . . . In addition to remaining in the minds of the people, bourgeois ideology also through various forms (such as certain cultural heritages) is ingeniously and somewhat attractively preserved, and over a very long historical period, will continue to spread its influence.[11]

The initial reaction of the Party organization to the Great Leap crisis was much the same as its response to the shock of Khrushchev's attack on Stalin: Collective ranks were closed, and the Party sought to affirm the correctness of its policies. Study of Volume Four of Mao's works was promoted nationwide by provincial Party organizations. Liu Shao-ch'i was quoted as deferring to Mao as "the greatest revolutionary and statesman in the history of China, and also the greatest theorist and scientist in the history of China." [12] The Chairman was said to be the Party's "best model" in "educating us not only in applying successful experiences but also in seizing the mistakes in our work and summing up the lessons of mistakes." [13]

11. Commentator, "Put Ideological Work in the Primary Position," *Red Flag,* No. 5 (March 17, 1964); trans. in *SCMM,* No. 412 (April 13, 1964), p. 3.

12. *Ch'ün-chung* [The Masses] editorial, "Build a Powerful Army of Marxist-Leninist Theoreticians," No. 3 (February 1, 1960); trans. in *SCMM,* No. 212 (May 23, 1960), p. 10. This publication is the theoretical magazine of the Kiangsu Provincial Party Committee, equivalent in function to the national publication *Red Flag.*

13. Hsiao Shu and Yang Fu, "The Party's Policy Is a Guarantee for Victory in Revolution," *Red Flag,* No. 22 (November 16, 1960); trans. in *SCMM,* No. 238 (December 5, 1960), p. 20.

Despite these assertions of solidarity and deference to Mao, the Party "center" was faced with very real problems of political discipline in its regional and local organizations. In a situation where the Chairman's policies seemed to be responsible for the difficulties of the Great Leap, regional leaders were proving to be increasingly unresponsive to guidance from the center, prompting the national Party to reaffirm the principle of "democratic centralism":

> In the case of questions which should and must be decided upon and made public by the Central Committee, the local Party organizations must not override their commissions and state their views in advance of the Central Committee. In regard to problems of a national nature, all spokesmen of the Party, including members of the Central Committee, may not state their views without the consent of the Central Committee.[14]

These words of Liu Shao-ch'i were strengthened in organizational terms by the creation, in the late fall of 1960, of six regional Party bureaus under the direct control of the Secretariat of the Party's Central Committee.[15] In one respect this development reflected the desire of the national Party leadership to maintain organizational discipline in the Great Leap crisis. Yet in another sense, it seemed to reflect the desire of certain Party leaders to build channels of political control which would render the provincial Party organizations less susceptible to the pressures of the Chairman.

One affirmation of this interpretation was to be the pattern of political purge during the Cultural Revolution: Mao found himself increasingly isolated by the Secretariat after 1960; and seeing his policies blocked or distorted in their implementation by the Party organization, he was to turn to the Army for political backing in an effort to remove from power those national Party leaders who continued to thwart his political initiatives.

In the immediate context of the Great Leap crisis, however, it appears that many within the Party attempted through subtle criticism to induce Mao to moderate his struggle against the many forms of "right opportunism" within the Party, among the intel-

14. Li Chien-chen, "Strengthen the Organization and Discipline and Consolidate the Solidarity and Unity of the Party," *Nan-fang Jih-pao* [Southern Daily, Canton] (November 26, 1960); trans. in *SCMP*, No 2416 (January 13, 1961), p. 2.

15. The creation of six regional Party bureaus was formally approved by the Ninth Central Committee Plenum in January 1961, along with the promotion of a new Party rectification campaign. (*See* "Communiqué of the Ninth Plenary Session of the Eighth Central Committee of the Chinese Communist Party" [January 20, 1961]; in *Current Background*, No. 644 [January 27, 1961], p. 4.)

lectuals, in rural life, and in the International Communist Movement, while continuing to express deference to the man and to his
contributions to the revolution. The Chairman was still a powerful
symbol of national unity and political authority, and the Party
organization could repudiate him only at the cost of calling into
question its assertion of being China's only source of "correct"
political leadership. The Party was in large measure a prisoner of
the Chairman's prestige and the unity which he gave the organization.

In early 1961 a slim book of ancient fables entitled *Stories about
Not Fearing Ghosts* was published under the sponsorship of the
Literary Research Institute of the Chinese Academy of Sciences
and the All-China Federation of Literary and Artistic Circles. As
the noted writer Ho Ch'i-fang indicated in the preface to this
volume, the objective of republishing these ancient ghost stories
was to publicize Mao's assertion that "all reactionaries are paper
tigers" and awaken people to the fact that like ghosts, "imperialism,
reactionaries, revisionism and all kinds of calamities" are not to be
feared. "As far as Marxist-Leninists are concerned, all these can be
beaten and overcome." [16] Ho noted that even China's ancient sage
Confucius, in the *Analects,* had shown a progressive social attitude
by disparaging the existence of ghosts; and he added that Mao himself, as a revolutionary student, had expressed the same view. Ho
applauded this "scientific attitude," and he cited Mao's words on
the importance of winning over all possible allies and avoiding
"leftist" errors in the continuing struggle against contemporary
political "ghosts."

Was Ho's preface actually in praise of Mao, or was it a sly way
of turning the Party Chairman's own arguments back on him? Did
the words imply, "True, revisionists and reactionaries continue to
give us trouble, but let us not overestimate their strength and push
the struggle to the point at which it causes us great loss?" As a
wealth of Cultural Revolution materials were to affirm, this publication was part of a widespread yet subtle expression of protest from
the intellectual community against Mao's policies—sentiments expressed within the context of a limited revival of the "Hundred
Flowers" spirit of 1956.[17]

16. Ho Ch'i-fang, "Preface to *Stories about Not Fearing Ghosts," Red
Flag,* No. 3–4 (February 1, 1961); trans. in *SCMM,* No. 252 (March 13,
1961), p. 1.

17. The theory that "ghosts are harmless" was said to have been proposed
in 1961 by the writer Liao Mo-sha, Director of the United Front Work Department of the Peking Municipal Party Committee, in order to "oppose the
thought of Mao Tse-tung and vilify revolutionaries." (*See "Notes on Sanchia Village* and *Night Causerie at Yenshan* Criticized by *Ch'ien Hsien* and

The 1956–57 slogan of "Let a hundred flowers bloom" was raised again in January 1961 by a *Red Flag* article which stressed the importance of a pragmatic and scientific approach to dealing with China's current problems: "Being Marxist-Leninists, we hold that questions of right and wrong in science are not decided by subjective 'convincing arguments,' but by their conformity or nonconformity to reality." [18] This was but one manifestation of a widespread distrust of revolutionary "spontaneity" brought on by the Great Leap Forward; one indication that certain Party leaders wanted to enforce "democratic centralism" and to have cadres be "docile tools" of the organization.[19]

By all evidence, the Hundred Flowers theme was reasserted at the initiative of Liu Shao-ch'i and other leaders who bore the "first line" burdens of seeing the country through the Great Leap crisis.[20] As had been true before the Great Leap Forward, many high-ranking officials continued to see the intellectuals and their skills as a major national resource in the development effort: The intellectuals should be protected from undue political pressure as long as they gave their services in support of the Party's economic and social policies.

This attitude was restated in early September 1961 by Foreign

Peking Jih-pao," *Yang-ch'eng Wan-pao* [Canton] [April 16, 1966]; trans. in *SCMP,* No. 3686 [April 28, 1966], p. 2.)

Chiang Ch'ing is said to have organized the publication of articles criticizing this viewpoint after the Tenth Plenum. (*See* Chung Hua-min and Arthur C. Miller, *Madame Mao: A Profile of Chiang Ch'ing* [Hong Kong: Union Research Institute, 1968], p. 95); and it became the subject of public attack during the "Cultural Revolution." (*See* the Red Guard publication, "Chiang Ch'ing's Outstanding Contributions to the Cultural Revolution," in *Hsin Pei-ta* [New Peking University], May 30, 1967.)

18. *Red Flag* editorial, "Stand Firm on the Policy of Letting a Hundred Flowers Bloom and a Hundred Schools of Thought Contend in Academic Research," No. 5 (February 28, 1961); trans. in *SCMP,* No. 2451 (March 8, 1961), p. 2.

19. *See,* for example, T'ao Teh-lin, "Be a Docile Tool of the Party," *People's Daily* (January 14, 1960); trans. in *SCMP,* No. 2184 (January 26, 1960), pp. 3–6.

This particular article observes that "some Party members imbued with serious bourgeois individualism are opposed to being docile tools of the Party," while wanting the Party to be their "docile tool" (p. 4). During the Cultural Revolution Mao was to attack Liu Shao-ch'i for having propagated the "docile tool" concept. (*See* p. 404 above.)

20. Liu publicly identified himself with the revival of the "Hundred Flowers" policy (which Mao did not) in a speech marking the Fortieth Anniversary of the founding of the Chinese Communist Party delivered at a rally in Peking on June 30th, 1961. *See* the NCNA translation of this speech in *Current Background,* No. 655 (July 12, 1961), p. 6.

Minister Ch'en Yi, in a commencement address to university graduates in Peking. Ch'en told the students that "The Party and State need you," and he stressed the importance of specialized knowledge and professional expertise for "the work of building up our country as a great socialist power with modern industry, modern agriculture, and modern science and culture." He also asserted that "there is, in my opinion, nothing wrong about [advanced students] taking part in political activities less frequently." [21] As we shall see, such an attitude was a direct challenge to Mao's concurrent effort to politicize the People's Liberation Army through the study of his writings. [22]

The Party's encouragement of pragmatism and professionalism in 1961 was accompanied by a general political relaxation in artistic and cultural life. During this year there appeared in the public media historical commentaries, anecdotal columns, poems, and plays on historical themes which were veiled yet biting criticisms of Mao for having led the Party and people into the Great Leap crisis. In the first months of the Cultural Revolution in 1966 attacks were to be focused on the authors of this material, with the "spear point" of the conflict eventually turning against those Party leaders who had given them encouragement and political protection.

One of the most notable of these critics of 1961–62 was the former editor of the *People's Daily,* and Cultural Director of the Peking Municipal Party Committee, Teng T'o. In newspapers and magazines under the direct control of the Peking Party Committee —of which P'eng Chen was First Secretary—Teng subjected the Party Chairman to veiled ridicule and political threats in the context of commentaries on historical topics. In a discussion of social difficulties during the Sung dynasty, he quoted an imperial magistrate who exhorted the powerful official Ssu-ma Kuang to heed the suggestions of lower-level officials. And in an oblique reference to Mao, Teng invoked the magistrate's complaint that there are

> some persons . . . who always want to assert their own ideas, attempt to win by surprise and refuse to accept the good ideas of the masses under them. If persons with such shortcomings do not wake up and rectify their shortcomings themselves, they will pay dearly one day. [23]

21. *See* this speech as published in *China Youth Journal* [*Chung-kuo Ch'ing-nien Pao*] (September 2, 1961); trans. in *SCMP*, No. 2581 (September 19, 1961), pp. 1–7.

22. *See* esp. pp. 437–442 below.

23. Cited in Merle Goldman, "The Unique 'Blooming and Contending' of 1961–62," *The China Quarterly,* No. 37 (January–March 1969), p. 77.

In an essay entitled "Talking Nonsense," Teng criticized those who rejected the work of China's scholars and scientific research workers, or who manifested a continuing distrust of the intellectual community. He complained of the Sung reformer Wang An-shih: "[Wang] considered everyone else inferior to himself and used to criticize them vehemently on no grounds at all. His major shortcoming was his lack of humility" [24]—apparently a veiled reference to Mao's attack on P'eng Teh-huai. In a column entitled, "How to Make Friends," Teng criticized Mao's obduracy in pressing the Sino-Soviet conflict to the point of an open break. In the article, "Who Were the Earliest Discoverers of America," he lauded the "long tradition of Chinese-American friendship." And in an essay, "Great Empty Talk," published in *Front Line* (*Ch'ien-hsien*), the theoretical magazine of the Peking Party Committee, he disparaged Mao's dictum that the "East wind" was now prevailing over the "West wind" as being clever words lacking in reality.[25]

In a society where words have been the touchstone of political power, such ridicule of the Chairman for "Talking Nonsense" and "Great Empty Talk" could not be a clearer expression of the erosion of his authority—and a challenge to which Mao was to respond in kind, by reasserting his influence through the "word" of his writings.

Political focus was given to these expressions of discontent through criticism of the programs which had generated the present social crisis, and also through pressures to rehabilitate those who had criticized Mao's policies at the Lushan Plenum. Teng T'o ridiculed the Great Leap Forward as having "substituted an illusion for reality";[26] and he criticized Mao in a published poem for his ignorance of the plight of the peasantry.[27]

These issues were more sharply drawn in the play *The Dismissal of Hai Jui,* written in 1961 by Wu Han, Deputy Mayor of Peking (P'eng Chen was Mayor), former professor of history, and a leading non-Party intellectual.[28] Wu described the suffering of Soochow peasants exploited by rapacious Ming dynasty officials who had confiscated their land. Hai Jui was an upright imperial governor who dared to intervene against the officials on the peasants' behalf

24. *Ibid.,* p. 79.
25. *Ibid.,* pp. 78–82.
26. *Ibid.,* p. 80.
27. *See* Chung and Miller, *Madame Mao,* pp. 50–52.
28. "Cultural Revolution" attacks on Wu Han and his play and various articles related to Hai Jui are contained in the documentary collection, "The Press Campaign against Wu Han," *Current Background,* No. 783 (March 21, 1966).

by appealing to the emperor for the return of their land. For his directness the emperor removed him from office. The analogy of this historical episode to the plight of the peasants under the Commune system and to the intervention and dismissal of P'eng Teh-huai is apparent. Such artistic works, Mao was to contend during the Cultural Revolution, were intended to "prepare public opinion" for a reversal of the judgment against P'eng Teh-huai and abandonment of the Great Leap policies.

In the years 1961–62, however, Mao confined his open response to these expressions of discontent among the intellectuals to poetic assertions of his own determination to press the struggle against political "revisionism." He also resisted, within the framework of Party decision-making procedures, any efforts to bring about a reconsideration of the treatment accorded P'eng Teh-huai and other "anti-Party rightists." In late 1961 Mao's friend among the intellectuals Kuo Mo-jo commiserated with the Chairman over the increasingly bitter and public dispute with "the monk" Khrushchev:

> Confounding humans and demons, right and wrong,
> The monk was kind to foes and mean to friends.
> Endlessly he intoned the "Incantation of the Golden Hoop,"
> And thrice he let the demon escape.[29]

Mao replied that despite the now public "storm" of the Sino-Soviet dispute, the "demon" (*kuei*, ghost) of "revisionism" was so dangerous that the Party's only course was to wage a continuing struggle against its "malignant" influence:

> A thunderstorm burst over the earth,
> And the demon rose from a heap of white bones.
> The deluded monk was not beyond the light,
> But the malignant demon must wreak havoc.

He added:

> The Golden Monkey wrathfully swung his massive cudgel,
> And the jade-like firmament was cleared of dust.[30]

Mao's determination to wield the "cudgel" of class struggle against the influence of revisionism among the intellectuals and within the Party was expressed more directly in a *Red Flag* editorial of mid-May 1962 in commemoration of the twentieth anniversary of his "Talks at the Yenan Forum on Literature and Art." The

29. From Kuo's poem to Mao, "On Seeing *The Monkey Subdues the Demon*"; trans. in *Ten More Poems of Mao Tse-tung* (Hong Kong: Eastern Horizon Press, 1967), p. 29.

30. From Mao's poem, "Reply to Comrade Kuo Mo-jo" (November 17, 1961), *ibid.*, p. 14.

editorial asserted, "It is impossible to fulfill the tasks of socialist construction if we do not persist in carrying out the socialist revolution in the fields of ideology and culture and if we neglect ideological work among the intellectuals." [31] It emphasized that the "Talks" showed "how completely friendly was Comrade Mao Tsetung's attitude in conducting intimate talks, consultations and discussions" with intellectuals. Yet it affirmed that this did not mean toleration of their anti-socialist attitudes. The editorial bluntly stated: "On the question of whether the world should be transformed according to the proletarian or bourgeois outlook, a question of principle, Marxist-Leninists are unequivocal and will never make any compromise." [32]

No doubt responding to the veiled ridicule of his person and the increasingly serious criticism of his policies, Mao thus expressed his determination to press the conflict. And apparently in response to this pressure, Teng T'o's critical columns terminated in the late summer of 1962, on the eve of the Party's Tenth Plenum.

Revelations of the Cultural Revolution suggest that in 1962, as the leadership debated how to modify its policies in the lingering economic crisis, certain Party leaders attempted to resurrect P'eng Teh-huai—with obvious implications for the "burial" of Mao's policies and political stature within the Party.

In January of 1962 the Party Central Committee convened an enlarged work conference, apparently to review the policies which had been adjusted at the Ninth Central Committee Plenum held a year earlier. In this period permissive policy alternatives to Mao's "three red flag" guidelines were said to have been formulated and discussed within the Party. Domestically, a line of "three privates and one guarantee" (*san-tzu yi-pao*) was suggested, extending the peasants' private plots, encouraging rural free markets, and tolerating small scale private business and manufacturing enterprises, while fixing agricultural production quotas on the basis of the labor of individual households. Internationally, a line of "three reconciliations and one reduction" (*san-ho yi-shao*) was proposed in order to moderate China's conflicts with "imperialists, reactionaries, and revisionists," and to reduce the amount of support given to "national liberation" insurgency movements.[33]

31. *Red Flag* editorial, "The Intellectuals' Way Forward," No. 10 (May 16, 1962); trans. in *SCMM,* No. 317 (June 12, 1962), p. 2.

32. *Ibid.,* p. 3.

33. The exact manner in which these policy alternatives to Mao's "three red flags" were formulated and discussed within the Party remains obscure. In a work report to the First Session of the Third National People's Congress in late 1964, Chou En-lai asserted that these policy lines had been put forward between 1959 and 1962, and had been actively advocated by "quite

During the Cultural Revolution Mao's supporters were to charge that at this work conference Liu Shao-ch'i had "openly tried to reverse the verdict on P'eng Teh-huai." [34] Other Red Guard pamphlets of early 1967 more plausibly quote Liu as having said at the meeting: "In respect to persons who share P'eng Teh-huai's views, cases may be reopened provided they are not cases of collusion with a foreign country";[35] and, "Provided the persons concerned lodge an appeal, cases may be reopened if the leading body and other comrades consider it necessary to do so." [36]

It would appear that where P'eng's critique of the Great Leap seemed to have been vindicated by subsequent events, there was strong sentiment within the Party for a rehabilitation of those who had previously been denounced as "rightists." Whether Liu actually made an open appeal directly on P'eng's behalf is much more problematical. Mao's sensitivity on this issue had been clearly revealed at Lushan in 1959; and his poetic exchange with Kuo Mo-jo shortly before the January 1962 meeting reiterated his determination to face up to the storm of criticism whether from the Soviets or from domestic "demons." [37] Liu may have raised the issue of "reversal

a number of people." (*See* Chou's speech in *SCMP*, No. 3370 [January 5, 1965], p. 9.) In his third Cultural Revolution confession, Liu Shao-ch'i implied that the *san-tzu yi-pao* line on agriculture had been formulated by Teng Tzu-hui, and that he personally had only "not refuted him." The "three reconciliations and one reduction" in international relations, Liu revealed, "was put forward by [an unnamed] comrade in a rough draft and was not brought up at any Central Committee meeting. At the time I did not know about this proposal. Afterwards, it was removed from the comrade's safe." (*See* "The Third Confession of Liu Shao-ch'i, in *Chinese Law and Government*, Vol. I, No. 1 [Spring 1968], pp. 78–79.) The fact that Chou En-lai made mention of these policies of 1959–1961 as late as 1964 suggests that certain Party leaders were being warned not to continue to press for alternatives to Mao's "three red flags."

34. *Red Flag* and *People's Daily* joint editorial, "Along the Socialist or the Capitalist Road?" (August 17, 1967); trans. in *Peking Review*, No. 34 (August 18, 1967), p. 20.

35. From an article in the Peking Red Guard publication, *Chingkangshan* [Chingkang Mountains], (January 1, 1967) entitled "Look at Liu Shao-ch'i's Sinister Features!"

36. From the Red Guard pamphlet, *Selected Edition of Liu Shao-ch'i's Counter-Revolutionary Revisionist Crimes* (April 1967); trans. in *SCMM*, No. 652 (April 28, 1969), p. 30.

37. Mao revealed his use of poetry to express political sentiments in a letter to the editors of the poetry publication *Shih-k'an* in January 1959. Commenting on the two poems "Shaoshan Revisited" and "Ascent of Lushan," which he had written at the time of the P'eng Teh-huai challenge, he asserted with a peasant's asperity: "These two poems of mine are replies to those bastards [*wang-pa-tan*]." Translated from *Ko-ming Tsao-fan Pao* [Revolutionary Rebellion Journal] (November 25, 1967). The poems may be found in *Ten More Poems of Mao Tse-tung*, pp. 4, 6.

of verdicts" on "rightists" in general terms, perhaps hoping to prepare the political climate for a further appeal by P'eng himself. It was later claimed that P'eng did issue a long document in June of 1962 aimed at vindicating his actions of 1959.[38]

A more speculative interpretation of these Cultural Revolution charges is that the Party organization—well aware by this time of Mao's increasing reliance upon the People's Liberation Army and Lin Piao for political support (to be commented upon below)—was anxious to dilute Mao's influence within the Army. Party leaders may have hoped for a vindication of P'eng and subsequent personnel changes within the Army which would check Mao's increasing influence.

Whatever the actions and motives related to "reversing verdicts" in January of 1962, later developments reveal increasing conflict over whose influence was to prevail at the Tenth Plenum to be held in September. There was a sharpening of debate in a press campaign on the question of how to strengthen the Party's "democratic centralism."

Mao's own position in this debate had been expressed to Party leaders at the January work conference. Consistent with his views on how to resolve "contradictions" between the Party and "People" as expressed in his writings of 1957, the Chairman held that genuinely centralized leadership could be attained only by allowing "the masses" to air their criticisms of the Party for the difficulties of the preceding years:

> Without democracy, there can be no correct centralism because when people have differing opinions and no unified thinking, it is impossible to establish centralism. . . . If there is no democracy, the conditions of the lower levels are not understood, things are not clear, the views of different quarters are not gathered together to the fullest extent, the higher and the lower levels cannot air their views to each other, and the leading organs at the higher level depend only on one-sided or untrue materials to make decisions on questions. Then it is difficult to avoid subjectivism, it is not possible to achieve unified thinking and action, and genuine centralism cannot be attained.[39]

There must have been strong resistance to this view of how to handle popular discontent, for Mao observed that some "veteran revolutionaries" within the Party leadership

38. *See* the *Red Flag* and *People's Daily* joint editorial, "Along the Socialist or the Capitalist Roads?" trans. in *Peking Review,* No. 34 (August 18, 1967), p. 20.

39. Mao, "Talk on Problems of Democratic Centralism" (January 30, 1962), in *Long Live the Thought of Mao Tse-tung!* pp. 23–24.

still do not understand this question [of how to promote democratic centralism]. . . . Some comrades fear mass discussion very much; they fear that the masses may put forward views different from those of the leading organs and leaders. When problems are discussed, they suppress the enthusiasm of the masses and forbid them to speak out. This attitude is extremely bad. Democratic centralism is incorporated into our Party Rules and our Constitution, but they do not carry it out.[40]

As with the "blooming and contending" policy of 1957, many within the Party evidently feared that to allow public grievances to be expressed in the context of the Great Leap crisis would only bring to the surface great popular resentment and seriously erode the authority of the Party. Yet Mao adhered to his conviction that only by allowing problems to be "talked out" and bad feelings vented through open discussion of how "correct" policies had been misapplied, could a genuine political consensus be achieved.

Was Mao blind to his own responsibility in formulating policies which might not be practicable in application through the Party system? Was he so convinced of the correctness of his conception of how Chinese society should be organized that he assumed "the People"—those who accepted the Commune system and "extensive democracy" under Party guidance—were in the majority? Did he really feel that a new period of "opinion airing" in a time of great social tension could be kept within the bounds of acceptance of Party rule? Such questions remain imponderables. Yet Mao's stature as Party leader and symbol of national unity continued to accord him protection from political attack outside the inner circle of Party leadership. This fact provided much of the tension between the Party and its leader in Mao's call for "extensive democracy."

Mao may have felt that his policies had been correct, while China's current problems were in fact the result of errors on the part of those who had implemented them—compounded by three years of natural disasters and the economic sabotage of the Soviet "revisionists."

The Party organization, however, did not want to be subject to mass criticism for operational errors in implementing policy; the "democracy" wanted by the cadre was the right to criticize plans they had been pressured to implement.

The "centralism" demanded by other Party leaders was the discipline of organizational channels which would protect those on the "first line" of operational responsibility against Mao's lobbying for support within the Party's provincial organizations.

Throughout the spring and summer of 1962 a flood of articles

40. *Ibid.,* p. 23.

appeared in the daily press and in magazines under the control of the Party apparatus giving the organization's interpretation of how "democratic centralism" should be implemented and the unity and authority of the Party sustained. *China Youth* (*Chung-kuo Ch'ing-nien*), the monthly magazine of the Youth League, published an article in early March which called on unnamed comrades to "treat others as equals." [41] It asserted,

> If one, having assumed the tasks of leadership, feels that he is better than others and is always right while the masses and lower levels are not good, and consequently takes arbitrary actions and monopolizes things without consulting the masses or convincing others in democratic ways, and uses certain "authority" to humiliate others, then democracy cannot but be damaged.[42]

The article then invoked words of Liu Shao-ch'i delivered to the Eighth Party Congress in 1956:

> Each leader must know how to hear patiently and consider dispassionately opposing views and resolutely accept those opposing views which are rational. . . . [He] must not assume an exclusive attitude toward any comrade who, out of a correct motive, puts forward any opposing views according to normal procedures.

The author then asserted that "these words are applicable to our leading body at all times." [43]

An article of April 1 was pointedly entitled "On Modesty." The author, one Yü Chin (apparently a pseudonym) observed that Stalin had praised Lenin because he "always placed himself in the midst of the masses and never behaved as if he were special." [44] Yü Chin urged that those who had made distinctive contributions to the revolution take a broad historical perspective of their accomplishments:

> A man may have done many things, and in his own view, in the opinion of his friends, or even in the opinion of his contemporaries, his contributions may be enormous. But if such contributions are observed in the light of the long river of history, their importance will be relatively limited. The modest [leader], by anticipating objective judgments and by making allowance for them in advance, is able instead to win the admiration of others.[45]

41. *See* Wu Ch'iang, "Centralism Based on Democracy," *China Youth,* No. 5 (March 1, 1962); trans. in *SCMM,* No. 307 (April 2, 1962), p. 2.
42. *Ibid.*
43. *Ibid.,* p. 3.
44. Yü Chin, "On Modesty," *China Youth,* No. 7 (April 1, 1962); trans. in *SCMM,* No. 312 (May 7, 1962), p. 15.
45. *Ibid.,* p. 14.

An article by one Pai Yeh pleaded that "Listening to Divergent Opinions Is Essential to Fostering the Democratic Work Style." The author tried to explain just how complicated social problems could be; and how different people, in all honesty, could analyze them quite differently from their varying social perspectives. His illustrative example was the politically loaded image of the Sung dynasty poet Su Tung-po describing Mount Lushan as resembling either a sharp peak or a whole range of mountains, depending on the vantage point from which it was viewed. And he exhorted "some people" with the observation: "If you listen to the opinions of the masses, your own knowledge will become more comprehensive and will get nearer to the truth, and this will give you more prestige"; while, "If you cling to your own one-sided or even erroneous ideas and the truth is not on your side, how can you have prestige?" [46]

Finally, a June article in *Red Flag* entitled "On Whipping and Spurring," observed that such treatment was "meant for horses"; intended to encourage them to go at a fast pace. But "even good horses sometimes slow down." [47] The author then went on to imply that Mao's criticisms of "the horse" of the Party had their usefulness if not taken too far, while Mao himself might benefit from a bit of the "whipping and spurring." "We must make a mirror out of people's criticisms of us and encouragements to us, other people's strong points and foibles, their successes and mistakes, and spur ourselves onward." [48]

Such articles, in retrospect, seem all too obviously to represent the Party organization pleading with Mao to accept well-intentioned criticism of his policies, to show greater personal modesty, and to limit his "whipping and spurring" of critical comrades. Were these articles published at the instigation of high Party leaders in order to prepare the climate of opinion within the Party for P'eng Teh-huai's appeal of the summer and for a sharp reconsideration of Mao's policies at the Tenth Plenum? We don't know.

A Maoist response to these appeals seemed to be expressed in a *Red Flag* article of mid-May entitled "Combine Exacting Demand with Painstaking Persuasion." Author T'ang P'ing-chu called attention to the high ideological standards of the People's Liberation Army in handling "contradictions" within its organizational life.

46. Pai Yeh, "Listening to Divergent Opinions Is Essential to Fostering the Democratic Work Style," *China Youth*, No. 7 (April 16, 1962); trans. in *ibid.*, p. 4.

47. Wu Chieh-min, "On Whipping and Spurring," *Red Flag*, No. 12 (June 16, 1962); trans. in *ibid.*, No. 321 (July 9, 1962), p. 38.

48. *Ibid.*, p. 39.

Such standards, it was asserted, "cannot be lowered, and no make-shift or indulgence can be allowed." [49] Then after stressing that this attitude was good for the work of "other departments and units," the author observed:

> Sometimes the subjection of some persons to disciplinary repression and necessary disciplinary punishment of a coercive nature is also an essential and correct means by which to make the demand [for high ideological standards] exacting, but this is still based upon persuasion and education.[50]

This veiled debate on the justice of the Lushan Plenum decision against P'eng Teh-huai also proceeded throughout the spring of 1962 in the press of provincial Party organizations. On April 4th the *Southern Daily* (*Nan-fang Jih-pao*), organ of the Party's Central-South Bureau, initiated a series of eight articles intended to implement Vice Chairman Liu Shao-ch'i's call to strengthen Party members' knowledge of democratic centralism. The series asserted the right of Party members to raise criticisms of their superiors, even as it criticized "dispersionism"—"a lack of organization and discipline, characterized by free action in the field of politics and disrespect for the leadership *of the Party Central Committee.*" [51] In what again appears to be a lightly veiled reference to the P'eng Teh-huai case, the third of these articles observed:

> Some leadership personnel at the higher levels like to put on airs and look dignified. They only criticize others and teach others lessons and cannot persuade themselves to consult those below them, to listen to their criticisms, or to criticize themselves before them. . . . [The] responsible persons of some Party organizations do not protect such just actions by Party members as the airing of opinions at meetings, criticisms of the leadership, and the making of representations to organizations at higher levels in accordance with proper procedures, but criticize such actions as erroneous or even consider them as anti-Party acts or acts of insubordination; and when they take disciplinary actions

49. T'ang P'ing-chu, "Combine Exacting Demand with Painstaking Persuasion," *Red Flag,* No. 10 (May 16, 1962); trans. in *ibid.,* No. 317 (June 12, 1962), p. 17.

50. *Ibid.,* p. 22.

51. "Strengthen the System of Democratic Centralism: Lectures on Basic Knowledge about the Party," *Southern Daily*; trans. in *ibid.,* No. 2750 (June 1, 1962), p. 2. Emphasis added.

The consistent identification of Teng and Liu in these various articles of the period 1960–1962 as advocates of strengthened Party organizational discipline seems one more affirmation that the Party Secretariat was the organizational focus of efforts within the leadership to restrict Mao's influence over policy implementation.

or pass sentences on a Party member, they will not allow him to appear in a tribunal to make representations in person.[52]

A response to this plea for toleration of criticism from subordinates within the Party organization appeared in the same provincial paper in early July—shortly after P'eng Teh-huai is said to have presented a lengthy document to the Party leadership in his own defense. The article was entitled "Distinguish Well-Meant Criticisms from Reactionary Opinions"; and the author Ch'en Yi-yen began, rather curiously, by invoking a quote from a *People's Daily* editorial of 1955 on the Hu Feng affair which asserted that in the case of "reactionaries" it was both right and necessary to "restrain them from carrying out their restoration activities and stop all counterrevolutionaries from utilizing freedom of speech to attain their objective of counterrevolution."[53] During the Cultural Revolution these words of 1955 were attributed directly to Mao. Hence, one senses that in 1962 the Chairman's authority was close to the assertion that

> those who raise questions as to restraint on reactionary opinions have forgotten the viewpoint on the class struggle and the viewpoint on dictatorship over the enemy. They have blurred their vision on what are questions of right and wrong among the people and what are questions concerning relations between the enemy and ourselves.[54]

Finally, this article reveals something of the nature of the appeals which some Party leaders may have been making on P'eng Teh-huai's behalf. Observers of international affairs reported during the spring of 1962 (when the Great Leap crisis was at its peak) that the Nationalists on Taiwan initiated active planning for a possible invasion of the South China coast.[55] Furthermore, the question of possible American support for a Nationalist attack became the subject of a diplomatic exchange between American and Chinese Communist officials at the Warsaw ambassadorial talks.[56] Within China, concern over a possible Nationalist military action seems to account for a reduction in Maoist political pressures on the Party apparatus

52. "Strengthen Democratic Centralism: Lectures on Basic Knowledge about the Party: III. Fully Develop Democracy," *Southern Daily* (April 18, 1962); trans. in *SCMP*, No. 2738 (May 15, 1962), p. 2.

53. Ch'en Yi-yen, "Distinguish Well-Meant Criticisms from Reactionary Opinions," *Southern Daily* (July 6, 1962); trans. in *SCMP*, No. 2789 (July 13, 1962), p. 5.

54. *Ibid.*

55. *See* "Chiang Wants Ban Lifted: Said to Ask for Right to Invade China if Revolt Erupts," *New York Times* (March 16, 1962), p. 14.

56. *See* "U.S. Tells Peiping It Will Not Support Nationalist Attempt to Attack the Mainland," *New York Times* (June 27, 1962), p. 1.

in the spring and summer of 1962 (*see* pp. 443–444 below). One also may speculate that P'eng Teh-huai's supporters within the Party were attempting to gain the rehabilitation of the former Defense Minister in the interests of political unity, if not in order to strengthen Army leadership.

The *Southern Daily* article, however, reaffirmed the necessity of distinguishing "well-meant criticism" from "reactionary opinions" (". . . words uttered against the Party and government and against socialism and the fundamental systems of the state [the Communes]" [57]). In more direct terms it stated:

> It is true that due to Chiang K'ai-shek's reckless planning for an invasion of the mainland, counterrevolutionary sabotage activities have been intensified, and the contradictions between the enemy and ourselves have become more prominent. Despite the confrontation of such contradictions, we will not relax our efforts to resolve the contradictions among the people.[58]

Whether behind such phrases lay the specific issue of reconsideration of P'eng Teh-huai's dismissal is uncertain; yet it was in the context of this active debate in both the national and provincial presses over the question of how to sustain organizational discipline while strengthening Party "democracy" that preparatory meetings for the Central Committee's Tenth Plenum began in late July with a meeting of the leadership at Peitaiho.

The lines of debate at these meetings must have been sharply drawn. The plea of the Party organization for moderation in the policies which had produced the "three bitter years," and for open Party debate on the issues, culminated on August 1st with the republication in the *People's Daily* and in *Red Flag* of a newly edited version of Liu Shao-ch'i's 1939 work, "How to Be a Good Communist" [literally, "On the Cultivation of a Communist Party Member" (*Lun Kung-ch'an-tang Yüan ti Hsiu-yang*)]. During the Cultural Revolution, Mao's supporters were to charge that Liu's work had been edited to delete references to "class struggle," and to negate the importance of the "dictatorship of the proletariat"— which in Mao's eyes meant eliminating the importance of mobilizing "the masses" for active participation in the political life of the state.[59] After the "blooming and contending" of 1957, and the mas-

57. Ch'en Yi-yen, "Distinguish Well-Meant Criticisms from Reactionary Opinions," *Southern Daily*; trans. in *SCMP*, No. 2789 (July 31, 1962), p. 6.
   58. *Ibid.*
   59. *See* the *People's Daily* and *Red Flag* joint editorial "Betrayal of Proletarian Dictatorship Is the Essential Element in the Book on 'Self-Cultivation'" (May 8, 1967); trans. in *Peking Review*, No. 22 (May 12, 1967), pp. 7–11.

sive mobilization of the Great Leap, Liu was likely to find readers within the Party who would be responsive to a leadership approach which down-played mass campaigns and public criticism of Party errors.

Cultural Revolution charges also indicate that the preparatory sessions for the Tenth Plenum were only the culmination of earlier meetings convened by regional Party leaders during 1961–62 at which—the Maoists alleged—"black material" was gathered to negate the achievements of the Great Leap Forward.[60] Other attacks on Party leaders after 1966 also indicate that there was strong sentiment at the Plenum's preparatory meetings further to ease economic pressures on the peasantry.[61]

The full dimensions of this two-month-long period of reconsideration of the Party's basic economic, social, and political policies which culminated in the brief four-day Plenum have yet to be analyzed in detail in the light of Cultural Revolution disclosures. Yet it is notable that the final Plenum communiqué appears to be an across-the-board approval of Mao's analysis of China's domestic and international situation.

Given all the resistance to Mao's policies and assertive leadership style revealed in the Party press during the years 1961–62, one can only wonder by what process he had been able to mobilize such political support in a time of great economic difficulty. Given the Party's call of the spring for an end to "dispersionism" and the strengthening of "democratic centralism," one can only speculate that, as had been the case in past periods of the Chairman's policy initiatives, Mao and his supporters in "the center" had successfully

60. Such meetings were said to have been convened in the fall of 1961 by P'eng Chen in Peking Municipality, and by T'ao Chu in the Central-South region. (*See* "Events Surrounding the 'Changkuanlou' Counter-Revolutionary Incident," *Tung-Fang Hung* [The East is Red, Peking], April 20, 1967; "Tao Chu Is a Loyal Knave of the Bourgeoisie: The Real Facts Exposed at a Black Meeting," *Hung-wei-ping Ko-ming Tsao-fan Ping-t'uan Ch'uan-tan* [Handbill of the Red Guard Revolutionary Rebel Corps, Canton], No. 1, January 16, 1967.)

In early 1962, Liu Shao-ch'i, Teng Hsiao-p'ing, and Ch'en Yün convened what was said to have been a "black conference" at the "Hsi-lou" (West building) in Peking to discuss financial work in the light of the Great Leap crisis. (*See* "Down with Counter-Revolutionary Revisionist Ch'en Yün," *Tung-fang-hung* [January 27, 1967].)

61. These charges are associated with the names of Liu Shao-ch'i, Ch'en Yün, Teng Tzu-hui, Po Yi-po, and Chu Teh, in a number of Red Guard publications. (*See* the pamphlet, *Selected Edition of Liu Shao-ch'i's Counter-Revolutionary Revisionist Crimes* [April 1967]; trans. in *SCMM*, No. 652 [April 28, 1969], esp. p. 23; and "Down with Old Swine Chu Teh, *Tung-fang-hung* [February 11, 1967].)

mobilized backing from provincial members of the Central Committee by going around the newly formed regional bureaus under the control of the Party Secretariat.[62] The force of Mao's personality and his ability successfully to invoke the authority of his Chairmanship—factors which may have been strengthened by such political issues as the threat of a Nationalist attack, and the need for Party unity in the face of an imminent military confrontation with India —must have helped Mao to carry the day on issues where he indicated a determination not to compromise.

The Plenum communiqué forcefully asserted the necessity of struggling against "revisionism" both domestically and in China's international relations, thus confirming Mao's assertion of the first day of the Plenum that it was necessary to "rename right opportunism as revisionism in China." [63] Mao was ever more directly linking his conflict with the Soviets with domestic leadership debates. The communiqué reaffirms the "great historic significance" of the Lushan decision against P'eng Teh-huai. In his speech to the opening session of the Plenum, Mao reveals his continuing resistance to the political rehabilitation of his critics of 1959: "My advice to you comrades [apparently P'eng Teh-huai and his co-'conspirators'] is that although you have worked hand-in-glove with a foreign country and formed a secret faction against the Party, provided you make a clean breast of yourselves in a down-to-earth manner, we will welcome you and give you work." [64] Yet he continued to stress:

> Recently there has been a tendency to vindicate and rehabilitate people. This is wrong. Only those who have been wrongfully charged can be vindicated and rehabilitated, but those who have been correctly dealt with cannot be so vindicated.[65]

While continuing to be inflexible on the P'eng issue, Mao apparently took a soft line toward those leaders who had continued to

62. The Plenum communiqué notes that in addition to the eighty-two regular and eighty-eight alternate members of the Central Committee who attended the Plenum, "thirty-three other comrades from the departments concerned of the Central Committee and from the provincial, municipal and autonomous region Party committees were also present." (*See Current Background*, No. 691 [October 5, 1962], p. 1.) One does not know, however, if these additional "members present" represented Mao's having "packed the court"—as he appears to have done at the Eleventh Plenum in the summer of 1966.

63. Mao, "Speech Delivered to the Tenth Plenum of the Eighth Central Committee" (September 24, 1962), in *Chairman Mao's Criticism and Repudiation of the P'eng, Huang, Chang, and Chou Anti-Party Clique*, p. 26.

64. *Ibid.*

65. *Ibid.*

raise the matter of "reversing verdicts." Inasmuch as during the Cultural Revolution Mao was to allude cryptically to Liu Shao-ch'i's "right deviation" of 1962,[66] Liu may have been among those whom Mao addressed at the Tenth Plenum with the observation:

> Comrades who have made mistakes must think hard. Provided you admit your mistakes and return to the Marxist side, we will unite with you. I welcome a number of comrades now present. Don't feel shy just because you have made mistakes. We tolerate mistakes. Since you have made mistakes, you also are allowed to rectify them. . . . Many comrades have successfully transformed themselves. This is good! XXX's speech is a confession. Since XXX has rectified his mistakes, we trust him! [67]

The Chairman went on to stress that in leadership conflict it was still necessary to "reason people into compliance"; to adhere to the policy of avoiding forced confessions while emphasizing the method of "curing the disease to save the patient." And he stressed that even in the case of "anti-Party" factions, the "taboo against killing must not be violated." [68]

For all this leniency within the leading council of the Party, the Chairman came down hard on the intellectuals who had sniped at him during the two preceding years:

> Isn't the writing of novels the fashion of the day now? The use of novels to carry out anti-Party activities is quite an invention. To overthrow a political power, it is always necessary first of all to create public opinion, to do work in the ideological sphere.[69]

This intolerance of criticism of his policies or person in the open press, and his determination to propagate the "universal truth" of Marxism in opposition to the "malignant" influence of "revisionism," was to be the focus of Mao's political pressures on the Party in the months following the Tenth Plenum—and the source of increasing leadership conflict.

The Plenum, in retrospect, appears to have been largely a paper victory for Mao; an assertion in words rather than in functioning Party policies of the necessity of sustaining "class struggle." Following the Plenum there was to be an increasing divergence between expressions of deference to the Chairman and his policies,

66. Mao, "Bombard the Headquarters! My Big-Character Poster" (August 5, 1966); trans. in *Peking Review*, No. 33 (August 11, 1967), p. 5.
67. Mao, "Speech Delivered to the Tenth Plenum of the Eighth Central Committee," p. 26.
68. *Ibid.*
69. *Ibid.*, pp. 26–27.

and attempts, by the Party organization to restrict his personal influence and dilute the impact of his policies in practice.

Ever since he assumed charge of the work of the Military Commission [in 1959], Comrade Lin Piao has called for holding high the great red banner of Mao Tse-tung's thought. . . . On the other hand, Liu Shao-ch'i came out [in 1962] with his talks about *How to Be a Good Communist,* in which he shunned any mention of Mao Tse-tung's thought. Instead, for ulterior motives, he spoke lavishly of the need to become good pupils of the "creators" of Marxism-Leninism. . . .

Comrade Lin Piao pointed out as early as 1959: "Comrade Mao Tse-tung has comprehensively and creatively developed Marxism-Leninism. . . ." He further pointed out in 1960: "Mao Tse-tung's thought is the apex of Marxism-Leninism." Liu Shao-ch'i has openly opposed Comrade Lin Piao's view. In order to oppose Mao Tse-tung's thought, he even went so far as to invoke help from feudalism and capitalism to "replenish" his revisionist thinking. In *How to Be a Good Communist,* he quoted no fewer than ten times the "maxims" of such dead ancients as Confucius and Mencius down to Fang Chung-yen. On the other hand, it is very difficult to find in his book truisms uttered by Chairman Mao, which are so succinct that one sentence packs in it the import of ten thousand sentences! [70]

Analysis of the evolution of Chinese Communist leadership relations and policy disputes following the Tenth Central Committee Plenum on the basis of published press materials is an increasingly difficult task. There is a growing divergence between words and actions, between assertions of policy and their implementation, and between apparent expressions of deference to Mao and his programs and covert opposition to them. Mao himself during the Cultural Revolution was to express exasperation at this widening gap between appearance and reality by observing that long-time comrades had begun to "wave red flags" of apparent support for his leadership, while in fact "opposing the red flag" by distorting his policies in application.

The years 1962–1964 following the Plenum were a period of rapid polarization within the leadership between those who remained loyal to Mao and his Great Leap concept, and those whose

70. "Thoroughly Smash Liu Shao-ch'i's Counter-Revolutionary Conspiracy: A Brief Commentary on the 1962 Revised and Expanded Edition of *How to Be a Good Communist,*" in *Chingkangshan* (Peking), February 8, 1967; trans. in *Chinese Law and Government,* Vol. I, No. 1 (Spring 1968), pp. 63–64.

commitment was to the Party organization and to the Marxist-Leninist tradition as they understood it. This polarization found expression in the press in the split between those leaders committed to "the thought of Mao Tse-tung," and those who upheld the importance of "Marxism-Leninism" as the Party's guiding ideology. Terminological differences, however, were but the outward expression of an increasingly divisive conflict within the leadership over whose conception of the Party, mass political life, and economic construction would shape the revolution. In Chinese fashion this was a political conflict fought with "words" and "models": Did one promote "ideological remolding" (*szu-hsiang kai-tsao*) through the study of Mao's writings; or the "cultivation" (*hsiu-yang*) of Party members by reading Vice-Chairman Liu's work, *How to Be a Good Communist?* Did one strive to build post-Liberation China's political and economic institutions on the model of wartime Yenan or in terms of the Soviet experience in Party-building and "socialist construction"?

The polarization between Mao's conception of the revolutionary process and Party interests was no more clearly revealed than in the uncertain progress of efforts to rebuild the collective rural economy and peasant political discipline in the wake of the Great Leap crisis. Not long after the Tenth Plenum Mao called a conference which was designed to launch a large-scale Socialist Education Movement in the rural areas. It was a more elaborate development of the effort of 1957–58 to prepare the peasantry for the formation of Communes and to "clean up" cadre abuses of authority. In what was to become known as the "First Ten Points" of policy for Party work in the countryside, Mao stressed that it was necessary to wage an unremitting class struggle in the villages against "landlords and rich peasants who . . . are employing all kinds of schemes in an attempt to corrupt our cadres in order to usurp the leadership and power." [71]

71. "Draft Resolution of the Central Committee of the Chinese Communist Party on Some Problems in Current Rural Work" (The "First Ten Points," May 20, 1963); trans. in Baum and Teiwes, *Ssu-Ch'ing,* p. 61.

During the Cultural Revolution, the "First Ten Points" and the "Twenty-three Article Charter" on rural work of January 1965 were said to have been drawn up under Mao's "personal leadership." They were affirmed by the Eleventh Central Committee Plenum of August 1966 as the Party's authoritative guides to rural work, in contrast to the distortions in policy introduced by Liu Shao-ch'i and others in the "Later Ten Points" (September 1963) and its revision of September 1964. (*See* "Communiqué of the Eleventh Plenary Session of the Eighth Central Committee of the Communist Party of China" [August 12, 1966], in *CCP Documents of the Great Proletarian Cultural Revolution, 1966–1967* [Hong Kong: Union Research Institute, 1968], p. 64.)

Mao's strategy for coping with what he described as a fundamental threat to the socialist economy in the rural areas was to resharpen class lines and set poor and lower-middle peasants against the rich, and the erring cadres, in renewed class struggle.

> To assure this movement [of socialist education and Party rectification] of strong leadership, *we must rely on the organizations of the poor and lower-middle peasants;* we must do the job well in conducting investigation and research on the masses; and *we must set the masses in motion.* Decisions for and disposition of all important problems must be made through *full discussions among the masses.* During the course of the movement, *the masses must be given the opportunity fully to express their views,* to make criticism of errors and shortcomings, to expose bad people and evil deeds.[72]

As in the case of Party resistance to criticism from the intellectuals in 1957, however, cadres were to show themselves highly resistant to this effort at rectification "from below." Some complained, "if the masses criticize the cadres, the cadres will not be able to lead them at all. It's all right for the higher levels to criticize cadres, but if the masses do it, things will become chaotic (*luan*)." [73]

The next major document concerning this combined movement to instill popular "socialist consciousness" and rectify cadre errors has been termed the "Later Ten Points" of September 1963. It reveals the Party's effort to control the development of the movement "from above," and to direct the brunt of mass criticism against non-Party class enemies. This document stressed that the "key to the question of whether [or not] the Socialist Education Movement can be carried out smoothly . . . lies in the leadership. Leading organizations at provincial, district and county levels must pay close attention [to the movement]." [74] These "Later Ten Points" emphasized that while poor and lower-middle peasants should be mobilized, it would be wrong "to brush aside the basic organizations [of the Party] and existing cadres, instead of carrying out work by relying upon them." Furthermore, it was asserted that "we should see that the great majority of basic-level rural cadres are good." [75]

The Party's "class allies," however, were deprecated for their political immaturity. Some of the masses were said to have been

72. *Ibid.,* pp. 66–67. Emphasis added.
73. Cited from a Radio Tientsin broadcast of December 19, 1964 in *ibid.,* p. 33.
74. "Some Concrete Policy Formulations of the Central Committee of the Chinese Communist Party in the Rural Socialist Education Movement" (The "Later Ten Points," September 1963), in *ibid.,* p. 75.
75. *Ibid.,* pp. 76, 85.

utilized by the enemy out of temporary foolishness. Among the peasant masses, there is a small part, including a very few poor and lower-middle peasants, who are backward ideologically and are unable to draw a clear line between classes. Under the enticement of the [class] enemy, they have either committed some crimes which are detrimental to the state or collective interests, or have taken part in some feudalistic or superstitious activities.[76]

This effort of the Party to control the rectification and the reestablishment of discipline in rural life persisted in the movement of mid-1964 to form Poor and Lower-Middle Peasant Associations, which Mao intended to be an organizational counterweight to the Party in the countryside and a concentration of "proletarian" strength in the continuing struggle against rural class polarization. Yet the draft charter of the Associations stresses that these organizations were to be "led by the Party" and were intended to become "a powerful arm of the Party" in raising the class consciousness of the rural population.[77]

The Party's relentless attempt to co-opt the rectification of the "four uncleans" in rural administration (ideological deviations, lack of political discipline, deviations in organizational life, mismanagement of economic affairs) and to lead rather than mobilize the peasants apparently stimulated behind-the-scenes pressures from Mao to open up the movement. A September 1964 revision of the "Later Ten Points," published just three months after the draft rules on Poor and Lower-Middle Peasant Associations had been issued, stressed that "Only by freely mobilizing the masses can this movement achieve complete victory." [78] "The key and prerequisite for correctly launching and leading the Socialist Education Movement is to study the thought of Comrade Mao Tse-tung concerning such questions as classes, class contradictions, and class struggle in a socialist society." [79]

Despite these introductory expressions of deference to Mao and the "mass line," the revision of the "Later Ten Points" continued to stress leadership "from above": "To launch the Socialist Education Movement at any point requires the sending of a work team from the higher level. The whole Movement should be led by work

---

76. *Ibid.*, p. 78.

77. "Organizational Rules of Poor and Lower-Middle Peasant Associations" (Draft, June 1964), in *ibid.*, p. 95.

78. "Some Concrete Policy Formulations of the Central Committee of the Chinese Communist Party in the Rural Socialist Education Movement" (The "Revised Later Ten Points," September 10, 1964), in *ibid.*, p. 102.

79. *Ibid.*, p. 103.

teams." [80] And while there was a call for "stern" treatment of erring cadres, this was still a matter of "education by persuasion":

> We may also adopt such measures as "recollection" and "comparison" [of how life was in the past] to enlighten them, improve their understanding, and make them repent of their own accord. [But] in dealing with them, no struggle rallies, false accusations, and especially no beatings are allowed.[81]

During the Cultural Revolution, Liu Shao-ch'i was to be attacked for these distortions of Mao's effort to sustain "class struggle" in the countryside. He was said to have promoted policies which were "left in form but right in essence" for their failure to arouse the masses. He was charged with having taken measures to protect "revisionists" within the Party leadership by directing the peasants to struggle against the basic-level cadres, rather than their erring superiors at higher levels of the Party administration. This was said to be a line of "hitting at the many [local cadres] to protect the few [higher leaders]." [82] In a "confession" of October 1966, Liu sidestepped responsibility for these policies. He said he "did not know" how the "Later Ten Points" had been formulated; but he vaguely associated them with the work of P'eng Chen. He asserted that it was only in September 1964 that he "came to discover that the Later Ten Points contained elements which hampered efforts to arouse the masses." [83]

Whatever the justice of these charges and efforts at a defense, within four months after publication of the "Revised Later Ten Points," in January of 1965, a new document on rural rectification termed the "Twenty-Three Articles" was issued. It superseded all previous directives and sharply redefined the objectives of the Socialist Education Movement as an effort to confront the fundamental "contradiction between socialism and capitalism" in China's countryside. The "spear-point" of the rectification was now directed at "those people in authority within the Party who take the capitalist road." [84] Above all, this reformulation of the "Four

80. *Ibid.*, p. 105.
81. *Ibid.*, p. 109.
82. Policy conflict between Mao and Liu on the matter of cadre rectification is discussed in detail in Richard Baum and Frederick C. Teiwes, "Liu Shao-ch'i and the Cadre Question," *Asian Survey*, Vol. VIII, No. 4 (April 1968), pp. 323–345.
83. "The Confession of Liu Shao-ch'i," *Atlas* (April 1967), p. 16.
84. "Some Problems Currently Arising in the Course of the Rural Socialist Education Movement" (The "Twenty-Three Articles" [January 1965], in Baum and Teiwes, *Ssu-Ch'ing*, p. 120.)

Clean-Ups" and "Socialist Education" campaigns stressed the need for a genuine release of mass criticism "from below": "We must let people fully express themselves"; "The most important supervision [of Party cadres] is that which comes from the masses"; ". . . we must boldly unleash the masses, we must not be like women with bound feet—we must not bind our hands and feet." [85] Yet even in this reorientation of the effort to "clean up" the rural Party organization, Mao was to find that there were long-time comrades who continued to block a real "mobilization" of mass resentments against the Party organization.[86]

In contrast to this resistance by the Party, the People's Liberation Army after 1963 became increasingly conspicuous in the public media as an organization embodying Mao's political principles. The center of gravity of Chinese domestic politics after the Tenth Plenum shifted to the steady polarization between Mao and the Army on the one side, and Liu and the Party organization on the other. This conflict was to bloom during the Cultural Revolution of 1966, but its seeds were planted in the years 1959–1962.

Mao's increasing reliance on the PLA grew in the context of efforts to confront the major issues in Chinese political life in the years following the Lushan Plenum: First was the increasing resistance of the Party organization to the Chairman's policy prescriptions; second, Mao's concern—obviously raised by P'eng Teh-huai's challenge—with what would happen should "the Party" (Mao) lose the support of "the gun"; third, the necessity of sustaining Army

85. *Ibid.,* p. 121.

86. Cultural Revolution charges have linked resistance to implementation of the "Twenty-Three Articles" in particular to P'eng Chen's administration of the Socialist Education Movement in Peking Municipality. (*See* the Red Guard pamphlet, *Counter-Revolutionary Revisionist P'eng Chen's Towering Crimes of Opposing the Party, Socialism, and the Thought of Mao Tsetung* [June 10, 1967]; trans. in *SCMM,* No. 639 [January 6, 1969], pp. 18–22.)

In a cryptic remark to Party leaders at a work conference of October 1966, Mao observed of resistance to his policies by the Peking Party Committee: "The time our vigilance was aroused was when the Twenty-Three Articles were drafted." (Mao, "Speech at a Work Conference of the Central Committee" [October 25, 1966], in *Long Live the Thought of Mao Tsetung!* p. 40.)

The exact meaning of this remark, and its relationship to the timing of Mao's personal decision to "get (*kao*) the Party Secretariat" (*ibid.*) is obscure. As is detailed below, there is strong evidence that Mao had decided to challenge the power of other top Party leaders by mid-1964, more than six months before the drafting of the "Twenty-Three Articles." (A recent revelation by Edgar Snow of resistance to Mao at a Party leadership meeting of January 25, 1965 [*see* p. 460, and fn. 185, p. 469 below] adds a bit of light to this question.)

discipline through the social crisis generated by the Great Leap Forward;[87] and fourth, the particular problems of morale which were raised for the military by the dispute with the Soviets—the breaking off of Russian nuclear protection and military and economic assistance, and the increasingly hostile confrontation with a formidable power sharing a long common frontier.[88] Lin Piao was to oversee the handling of these problems; and in Mao's eyes he must have done a successful job, for after the Tenth Plenum the Chairman drew upon the Army's experience in coping with more extensive political difficulties, and on Lin's support in his deepening conflict with the Party organization.

The task of rebuilding the loyalty of the PLA to Mao personally commenced only months after Lin Piao succeeded P'eng Teh-huai as Defense Minister. In the spring of 1960 the Army initiated a "ten year plan" for the cultural development of its troops which stressed inculcation of the old Red Army's "three-eight" work style[89] —one of the legacies of the revolutionary years—and the study of Mao's writings. On National Day, October 1st, 1960, Lin Piao stressed that the victory of the Chinese revolution had been a victory for "the thought of Mao Tse-tung"; and he asserted that the forms of political life which had enabled the Party to attain its power were needed to sustain political discipline in the face of China's present difficulties.[90]

To give organizational life to these assertions, an enlarged meeting of the Party's Military Affairs Committee was convened between September 14 and October 20, 1960 (at the time of publica-

87. Problems of military discipline during the Great Leap crisis are revealed in the secret military "Work Bulletins." *See* J. Chester Cheng, ed., *The Politics of the Chinese Red Army: A Translation of the Bulletin of Activities of the People's Liberation Army* (Stanford, Calif.: The Hoover Institution, 1966).

88. Sino-Soviet border clashes, according to the Chinese, are said to have begun in 1960, initially leading to a serious popular uprising in the Ili region of Sinkiang Province in 1962. The Chinese attributed this uprising to the efforts of Russian agents to undermine the political loyalty of minority groups living in China's Northwest frontier region.

89. "Chairman Mao condensed this working style to three phrases and eight words [characters]. The three phrases are: A steadfast and correct political direction; an industrious and thrifty working style; and a flexible and mobile strategy and tactics. The eight words are: unity; earnestness; seriousness; and liveliness [eight Chinese characters]." (Cited in Hsiao Hua, "Cultivation of the 'Three-Eight' Working Style Is an Important Task in the Building of Our Army [Excerpts]," NCNA [May 22, 1960]; in *SCMP*, No. 2270 [June 2, 1960], p. 1.)

90. Lin Piao, "The Victory of the Chinese People's Revolutionary War Is the Victory of the Thought of Mao Tse-tung," *Red Flag*, No. 19 (October 1, 1960); trans. in *SCMM*, No. 231 (October 18, 1960), pp. 7–20.

tion of Volume Four of Mao's works) to discuss ways of "strengthening political and ideological work in the Army." This conference reaffirmed the line on army-building which Mao had formulated at the Kut'ien conference of 1929 and stressed the need to study and apply "the thought of Mao Tse-tung." With the greatest import for later political developments, the "Central Authorities" of the Party stressed that this directive was

> not only . . . for the work of building up the Army and conducting political activities in the Army. . . . [It] is [also] useful to the Party organizations, government organs, schools, and enterprises at various levels, and accordingly should be distributed to organizations of the local [Party] committee level and above for reference.[91]

While this resolution on military work of late 1960 was only "for reference" by the Party and other organizations, the question which was to be posed with increasing sharpness after the Tenth Plenum was whether the Army was to be a model organization for emulation by the Party, or whether the Party still exercised political predominance over "the gun."

The lines between Party and Army, in retrospect, appear to have been drawn with surprising clarity even in the fall of 1960, as each organization apparently sought to define and defend its areas of operation. While the Party's national media the *People's Daily* and *Red Flag*, as well as the press of the regional Party apparatus, waged a campaign which stressed the need to obey and follow the "Party's policy"[92] (not the "thought of Mao Tse-tung"), the Army launched campaigns to study Mao's works and to strengthen its influence among China's youth. A *Liberation Army Daily* editorial of mid-November 1960, republished in the paper of the Youth League, initiated a movement to develop the "five goods."[93] No-

91. "Endorsement by the Central Authorities of the Chinese Communist Party of the 'Resolution on Strengthening Political and Ideological Work in the Army Made by the Enlarged Meeting of the Military Affairs Commission" (December 21, 1960); trans. in Cheng, *et al., The Politics of the Chinese Red Army,* p. 65.

92. *See* the collection of national and regional press materials, "Emphasis on Party Policy," *Current Background,* No. 646 (February 17, 1961).

93. "Five good" fighters of the PLA, models for Youth League members to emulate, were characterized as good at political ideology, good at military technique, good at the "three-eight" work style, good at fulfilling tasks assigned to them, and good at physical training. (*See* "Conditions for 'Five Good' Fighters," *China Youth Daily* [November 18, 1960]; trans. in *SCMP,* No. 2433 [February 7, 1961], p. 5. *See also* the *Liberation Army Daily* editorial, "Let the Entire Armed Forces Do Youth Work and Further Develop the 'Five Good' Campaign," *China Youth Daily* [November 17, 1960]; trans. in *ibid.,* pp. 1–3.)

tably emphasized as the first "good" was the need to "read assidu-ously Chairman Mao's works"—a prerequisite to accepting the Party's political guidance. The republication of *Liberation Army Daily* editorials in the press organs of the Party and Youth League was to become one of the more visible signs of the increasing polit-ical pressure which Mao was placing on the Party organization through the Army.

In 1961, as the production crisis of the Great Leap deepened, the differing responses of the two organizations to the social and economic difficulties revealed basic differences in leadership tech-nique. The Party called for a new period of "blooming and contend-ing" to encourage the intellectuals to lend their skills to the Party in coping with China's production problems. In direct opposition to this line, the Army stressed that "we must have positive education and not 'blooming and contending' and debating" in stimulating people to greater production efforts.[94] This "positive education," as implemented by the Army, sought to reinstate the form of political motivation which had characterized Mao's leadership from the early days of the revolution—the effort to draw upon people's resent-ments, indignation, and feelings of hatred.

Beginning after the October 1960 meeting of the Military Af-fairs Commission, a new "education" movement termed "the two remembrances and the three investigations" was initiated within the PLA.[95] Essentially this was the old technique of "speaking bit-terness" adapted to the problems of the 1960s. In order to hold the discipline of the Army, to help officers and men rationalize (emo-tionalize) their present economic and political difficulties, meetings were organized to enable them to "recall the bitterness of the past and compare it with the sweetness of the present." They were urged to think of "taking revenge" for [Soviet] economic exploita-tion and imperialist aggression, to express their hatred for the per-sonal hardships and exploitation suffered in "feudal" China, and to compare the old life with the new socialist political order.

In 1963 this same technique was applied throughout China in the context of the Socialist Education Movement. Meetings were held in factories and schools, communes and workshops, to have old peasants and workers recall for the younger generation the bit-terness of pre-Liberation life, in order to develop that sense of in-

94. "Several Notable Problems in the Current Educational Movement of the 'Two Remembrances and the Three Investigations'—Summary of a Talk Given by Deputy Director Liu Chih-chien in a Telephone Conference on January 7, 1961," *Kung-tso T'ung-hsün* (January 11, 1961); trans. in Cheng, *et al., The Politics of the Chinese Red Army,* p. 104.

95. Ibid., pp. 97–115.

dignation and hatred which would motivate people to struggle to overcome their present hardships, and to define by contrast the virtues of China under Party rule. "The more one hates the old society, the more will one love the Party and the new society." [96]

Combined with this effort to motivate the Army and people to weather present problems was the commitment of military units to tasks of economic production. Under the Yenan slogan of "regeneration through one's own efforts" (*tzu-li keng-sheng*), the production activities of Red Army military units in the Nanniwan district of the Shen-Kan-Ning border region were held up as a model of economic self-reliance.[97] The PLA was turned out to the fields to cope with the new "blockade" of the Soviet "revisionists" and China's continuing production difficulties.

Mao's increasing personal identification with the PLA was indicated during the summer of 1961 by the publication of an article in the *China Youth Daily* entitled "The Good Traditions of a Certain Company of the Red Army." The author was Chiang Ch'ing— Mao's wife. In terms that from the perspective of Cultural Revolution developments seem laden with political weight, Chiang Ch'ing praised a PLA company because

> on three occasions it had shouldered the most honorable task of safeguarding our great leader Chairman Mao, and was also on guard duty during the Kut'ien Conference [of 1929] which had great historical significance [because of Mao's assertion at the Conference that political indoctrination could establish discipline over insurgent military units].[98]

She added that in the past "this company [also] guarded Marshal Lin Piao and his headquarters, and directly received Marshal Lin Piao's personal instructions and concern."

That Mao's wife should "recall" the glories of the Army in protecting her husband—at a time when Mao was under veiled personal attack in the public media by intellectuals backed by other Party leaders—would almost certainly indicate to politically astute readers in the Party and Army that Mao and Lin were invoking the "protection" of the PLA as their base of political power. The degree of political polarization implied by Chiang Ch'ing's article

96. *Daily Worker* (Peking) editorial, "Never Forget the Past" (September 8, 1963); trans. in *SCMP*, No. 3072 (October 3, 1963), pp. 3–6.

97. *See* Wang Chen, "Self-Sufficiency in Production in Nanniwan Today and in the Past," *China Youth Daily* (September 23, 1960); trans. in *ibid.*, No. 2366 (October 27, 1960), pp. 6–9.

98. Chiang Ch'ing, "The Good Traditions of a Certain Company of the Red Army," *China Youth Daily* (August 26, 1961); trans. in *SCMP*, No. 2581 (September 19, 1961), p. 8.

A peasant describes the sufferings of life
in pre-Liberation China to members of the younger generation
during a "recall bitterness" meeting of the
Socialist Education Campaign, 1963–1966.
From China Pictorial, *November 1967.*

is further manifest in the publication by the same *China Youth Daily* one week later of Marshal Ch'en Yi's permissive graduation address to Peking's young intellectuals.[99] The lines were drawn between a Party adhering to "Marxism-Leninism" and an Army waving the flag of "Mao's thought."

The sudden emergence into political activity of Chiang Ch'ing, who ever since her marriage to Mao in 1940 had been as politically withdrawn as the wives of other Party leaders, was—in Chinese terms—an ominous sign.[100] It indicates the degree of the breakdown in trust and communication between top Party leaders which was to lead to the open conflict of the late 1960s. During the Cultural Revolution Chiang Ch'ing was to reveal that for some time she had acted as a "roving sentinel" for Mao, observing developments in culture and education, and in international affairs.[101] The Chairman evidently did not trust the information which reached him through Party channels.

Chiang Ch'ing's emergence was matched after 1962 by the increasingly frequent public appearances of the wife of Liu Shao-ch'i. Wang Kuang-mei was an attractive and sophisticated younger woman educated at a famous Peking missionary college. As the wife of China's State Chairman she was to assume the role of "first lady" when she hosted the wife of Indonesian President Sukarno during a visit to Peking in the fall of 1962, when she accompanied her husband on a diplomatic excursion through Southeast Asia in 1963, and through frequent contacts with foreigners in the Chinese capital between 1964 and 1966. Also, she was to be Liu Shao-ch'i's "eyes" in observing, and then commenting upon, the progress of the Socialist Education Movement during 1964.

Wang Kuang-mei's public activity contrasts with Chiang Ch'ing's behind-the-scenes efforts on Mao's behalf to bring an end to the public sniping of the intellectuals, and to inject a "proletarian" spirit into Army and civilian artistic life. Madame Mao's activities seemed to culminate in the summer of 1964 with a festival of Peking Opera on revolutionary themes. Yet as Cultural Revolution developments were to confirm, the public appearances of these once politically inactive women marked the beginning of a period of breakdown in cohesion within the Party leadership. During the open political conflict after 1966 the previously muted rivalry be-

99. *See* pp. 415–416 above.
100. *See* the comment on the traditionally disruptive influence of women in Chinese politics on p. 36, fn. 14 above.
101. Chiang Ch'ing, "Do New Services for the People" (a speech of April 13, 1967 delivered to an enlarged meeting of the Military Affairs Committee), in *Tung-fang-hung* (June 3, 1967).

tween these two women was to inject a very bitter and personal note into the Cultural Revolution struggle.[102]

The subtle public indications of political tension between the Army and Party in 1961 were followed by a year in which Lin Piao was inconspicuous in the public "waving of the red flag" of support for Mao. In contrast to his National Day speeches of 1959 and 1960, in which he lavishly praised Mao's contributions to the revolution, and his political activity in the fall of 1961, Lin was notably silent during 1962.

On Army Day, August 1st, Lin was conspicuous by his absence from a reception presided over by Chief of Staff Lo Jui-ch'ing and Foreign Minister and Army Marshal Ch'en Yi. In his reception speech Lo made no mention of "the thought of Mao Tse-tung," while recalling with emphasis the military successes of the PLA in the Korean War.[103] A *Liberation Army Daily* editorial of the day bore the curious title, "Be Ruthless to the Enemy, and Be Kind to Ourselves." In an apparent reference to the P'eng affair, it stressed that "we must unite ourselves properly." [104] And while deference was given to the importance of political indoctrination, the editorial added with the loaded "however" (*tan-shih*): "to strike hard and accurately [at the enemy], and to win a big victory at a small price, we must also learn to use the weapons in our hands skillfully and master flexible tactics." [105] A *China Youth Daily* Army Day editorial, in recalling military heroes of the Long March, stressed that their heroism was due to the fact that "they had in their hearts fervent love for the Party" [106]—not for Chairman Mao.

These signs of an easing of Party-Army political tensions in 1962 seem to be a composite of the domestic political pressures generated by the Great Leap crisis: the issue of "reversing verdicts" which appears to have been actively pressed in the spring and summer, the threat of a Nationalist invasion, and tensions on the Sino-Indian

102. *See,* for example, the transcript of the struggle meeting of April 1967 at which Wang Kuang-mei was humiliated for her "bourgeois" behavior during the diplomatic trip to Indonesia in 1963, "How to Wage 'Revolutionary Struggle': 'Teaching Material' Provided by Red Guards of Tsinghua University, Peking," *Current Scene,* Vol. VI, No. 6 (April 15, 1968).

103. *See,* "Text of General Lo Jui-ch'ing's Speech at [Army Day] Reception," *People's Daily* (August 2, 1962); trans. in *SCMP,* No. 2801 (August 17, 1962), pp. 2–4.

104. *Liberation Army Daily* editorial, "Be Ruthless to the Enemy, and Be Kind to Ourselves" (August 1, 1962; as excerpted in the *People's Daily*); trans. in *ibid.,* p. 5.

105. *Ibid.,* p. 6.

106. *China Youth Daily* editorial, "Show Fervent Love for the PLA and Learn from It" (July 31, 1962); trans. in *ibid.,* p. 8.

frontier which were to explode in the Chinese military initiative of October. Political conflict thus submerged below the level of press visibility in a context where the economic, political, and military issues of the hour were loaded in favor of Party unity and military professionalism. It was the successful Maoist defense at the Tenth Plenum, and the devastating attack on the Indians, which put political initiative back in the hands of Mao and Lin.

That initiative was revealed during 1963 and 1964 over an increasingly wide range of activities with ever greater intensity, as Mao attempted to translate his Plenum victory into major modifications of Party policy. He used the Army as a prod to push the Party in a more revolutionary direction by publicizing "models" of Army practice which the Party was to emulate. Another Army political work conference was held in February 1963; and it issued a set of regulations which stressed that even "a slight deviation from the thought of Mao Tse-tung and we shall lose our direction and experience defeat." [107]

To make fully explicit just how people were to apply "the thought of Mao Tse-tung" in practice, national campaigns were initiated in 1963 to hold up for public approbation exemplary individuals who embodied Mao's political principles in their daily lives. The most widely publicized of these models in the application of Mao's "thought" was the "great ordinary soldier," the young martyr Lei Feng, who in his selfless devotion to the people wanted to be "a rust-proof screw" in the machinery of the revolution.[108] Lei's selflessness and service to the people were attributed to the fact that he never forgot his past sufferings. Through the study of Chairman Mao's words he "knew how to love the people ardently and hate the enemy. He never forgot the class hatred of the old society where people perished and families fell apart." [109] He constantly remained on political alert, "never forgetting the pain [of the old society] when the scars [of exploitation] were healed." [110]

107. *Liberation Army Daily* editorial, "Raise Aloft the Great Red Banner of the Thought of Mao Tse-tung, Resolutely Implement Regulations Governing PLA Political Work!" (May 8, 1963); trans. in *SCMP*, No. 2984 (May 22, 1963), p. 2.

108. Liu Chih-chien, "A Great Soldier with a Noble Character," *China Youth Daily* (February 5, 1963); trans. in *ibid.*, No. 2927 (February 27, 1963), p. 5.

109. *China Youth Daily* editorial, "Fight and Live as Lei Feng Has Done" (February 5, 1963); trans. in *ibid.*, p. 6.

110. *People's Daily* commentator, "A Great Ordinary Soldier" (February 7, 1963); trans. in *ibid.*, p. 3.

A more extended discussion of the manner in which the model hero Lei Feng embodied Mao's notion of political motivation through cultivation of sentiments of hatred is in the author's article, "On Activism and Activists:

A major organizational model propagated at this time was "the Good Eighth Company of Nanking Road." "Armed with the thought of Mao Tse-tung," it had maintained its revolutionary discipline despite the corrupting surroundings of urban life: "Billeted in a big, bustling city for the past fourteen years, warriors of this company have steered clear of all sorts of temptations and have more than once repelled the sugar coated cannon ball attacks unleashed by the bourgeois class, and have stood firm on Nanking Road." [111]

These emulation campaigns reveal Mao's concern that the years of peace following the attainment of victory in 1949 were steadily eroding the legacy of the revolutionary period—a commitment to group life, a willingness to endure material hardships, and a determination to promote social change. In the spring of 1963 authoritative spokesmen began to stress a theme which finally was to express itself in the Cultural Revolution upheaval: "What is really to be feared is political degeneration, separation from the masses of the people, ideological disarmament, and the weakening or the loss of the determination to fight." [112]

How to prevent such political "degeneration," however, was a matter of dispute among Party leaders. Where Mao and Lin Piao, through the Army, gave increasing stress to political indoctrination through the study of Mao's works and emulation of those who incorporated his ideas in their daily activities, Party spokesmen cited Liu Shao-ch'i's writings on the need to stress "cultivation" of Communist morality and submission to the Party's organizational discipline.[113] Even within the Army itself, alternative models to Lei

Maoist Conceptions of Motivation and Political Role Linking State to Society," *The China Quarterly*, No. 39 (July–September 1969), pp. 98–99.

111. A *Liberation Army Daily* correspondent, "An Austere and Hardship-Defying Work Style Passed on from Generation to Generation: An Account of 'The Good Eighth Company of Nanking Road,'" *China Youth Daily* (March 30, 1963); trans. in *SCMP*, No. 2965 (April 24, 1963), p. 1.

112. Hsiao Hua, "Basic Experiences of the Past Two Years Concerning the Creation of 'Four-Good' Companies in the Army" (excerpted in *People's Daily*, April 1, 1963); trans. in *SCMP*, No. 2971 (May 3, 1963), pp. 2–3.

Hsiao Hua at this time was Deputy Director of the PLA's General Political Department. It was through this department that Mao and Lin Piao asserted their influence over military affairs after 1959. A detailed analysis of the political rivalries and associations within the PLA which contributed to the Cultural Revolution struggle will be found in William W. Whitson, with Huang Chen-hsia, *The Chinese Communist High Command: A History of Military Politics, 1927–1969* (New York: Praeger, 1971).

113. *See*, for example, Ching Ch'ien, "What Is Communist Morality?" *Southern Daily* (April 20, 1963); trans. in *SCMP*, No. 2982 (May 20, 1963), pp. 5–6.

Feng began to appear: An Yeh-min, glorified as a combat soldier on the Taiwan front (rather than as a student of Mao's writings, skilled at production tasks); and Kuo Hsing-fu, a model in the teaching of military technique.[114]

In early 1964 the "advanced experience" of the PLA was propagated even more broadly. Following another lengthy PLA conference on political work which ended in mid-January, a national campaign to "learn from the People's Liberation Army" was initiated, "in the hope that the entire country will study the valuable experience of the PLA in political-ideological work in a more penetrating and extensive manner and obtain a high proletarian and combat character just like the PLA." [115]

In contrast to the stress on study and emulation of the previous year's campaigns, however, the 1964 activity was transformed into direct organizational pressures in areas that had long been the exclusive preserve of the Party and government ministries. In late February a *People's Daily* editorial declared that the government's commercial departments should "humbly and sincerely try to learn from other departments, other localities and other units, in particular from the PLA, which has armed itself with Mao Tse-tung's thinking and is highly vigilant, well organized and disciplined." [116] This "vigilance" and organizational discipline were now not just a matter of something to "study," for the editorial revealed that "since last year" [1963] "a considerable number of military cadres" had been transferred to work in basic-level commercial departments.[117]

This development was reinforced by the creation of political departments, patterned on Army practice, in Central Committee organizations concerned with work in finance, trade, industry, and transportation. By June of 1964 more than twenty ministries of the government were reported to have established such political departments, which subsequently expanded their influence down to pro-

114. "Officers and Men of Naval Units Unfold Activities of Learning the Excellent Character of An Yeh-min, a Great Communist Soldier," NCNA (September 11, 1963); trans. in *SCMP,* No. 3069 (September 27, 1963), p. 10. *People's Daily* editorial, "Inspiration from Kuo Hsing-fu's Teaching Method" (February 10, 1964); trans. in *SCMP,* No. 3175 (March 10, 1964), pp. 1–4.

For comments on the "anti-Maoist" character of these models, *see* pp. 447–449 below.

115. *People's Daily* editorial, "The Whole Country Must Learn from the PLA" (February 1, 1964); trans. in *SCMP,* No. 3164 (February 24, 1964), p. 1.

116. *People's Daily* editorial, "Commercial Departments Should also Learn from the PLA" (February 20, 1964); trans. in *SCMP,* No. 3177 (March 12, 1964), pp. 1–2.

117. *Ibid.,* p. 4.

vincial and local levels. These political departments were staffed, in part, by demobilized Army men, and by Party cadres who received political indoctrination at PLA training centers.[118] Through such developments Mao expressed his determination to inject political discipline into a Party-governmental system which he saw as increasingly unwilling to confront its own bureaucratic "revisionism."

Further propagating the Chairman's political pressures into areas of economic activity was the publicizing of model industrial and agricultural units which had successfully applied "the thought of Mao Tse-tung." Early in February of 1964 the press began to laud the achievements of a production brigade of the Tachai People's Commune, a model of hard work and self-reliance in a barren county of the Northwest province of Shansi. The Secretary of the Party branch of this production brigade, Ch'en Yung-kuei, was to become a major spokesman for Mao's conception of politicized rural administration and production leadership.[119] Similarly, the Taching Oil Field received national press attention beginning in the spring of 1964 as a model of the Maoist virtues of self-reliance and struggle in industrial development.[120]

This pressure, while overwhelming in its press impact, apparently met with continuing, though veiled, efforts by the Party apparatus and Party supporters within the Army to divert or dilute the Maoist initiatives. Only on the basis of Cultural Revolution attacks on leaders of this time do we know that certain "model" experiences publicized in the national press—and others which never received attention in the public media—were advanced by Party and Army leaders as alternatives to those which embodied "the thought of Mao Tse-tung." Other Maoist models were "co-opted" by leaders who sought to dilute the impact of the Chairman's policies by distorting the content of his advanced experiences.

In opposition to the stress of Mao and Lin on the primary im-

---

118. *See* John Gittings, *The Role of the Chinese Army* (London: Oxford University Press, 1967), pp. 254–258. I am also indebted to Professor Ellis Joffe for his guidance in interpreting the expanding political influence of the PLA during this period. He has gathered additional documentaton on these organizational changes in an unpublished paper, "The Chinese Army on the Eve of the Cultural Revolution: Prelude to Intervention" (prepared for a conference on Government in China: The Management of a Revolutionary Society, August 1969), pp. 26–28.

119. *See* Ch'en Yung-kuei, "Self Reliance Is a Magic Wand," *Red Flag,* No. 1 (January 6, 1965); trans. in *SCMM,* No. 454 (February 1, 1965), pp. 25–29.

120. Commentator, "On Man as the Primary Factor," *Red Flag,* No. 10 (May 23, 1964); trans. in *SCMM,* No. 422 (June 22, 1964), pp. 5–6.

portance of political study, Chief of Staff Lo Jui-ch'ing was said to have organized weapons competitions within the PLA in January of 1964 in order to emphasize military technique.[121] As noted earlier, Lo's public statements of the 1960s seem to give primary emphasis to combat heroes, rather than to model soldiers in politics and production like Mao's good student Lei Feng. Lo was said to have "borrowed" the Maoist model Kuo Hsing-fu and turned him into a technician in the context of the All-PLA Great Tournament of military skills in the beginning of 1964.[122]

P'eng Chen and Organization Department Director An Tzu-wen were to be attacked for advancing the Tatuho and Nanliu Party branch organizations as model alternatives to "The Good Eighth Company" and the Tachai production brigade.[123] P'eng Chen and Liu Shao-ch'i were criticized for formulating a "hundred key counties" scheme in opposition to Mao's plans for local initiative in advancing agricultural mechanization; while Liu is said to have obstructed publication of the story of the Chinhsing production brigade as a model of self-financed mechanization.[124]

Other provincial Party leaders were accused of having channeled scarce financial resources into local industrial models in order to compete with Taching.[125] Liu and Wang Kuang-mei were to be attacked for publicizing throughout the Party the "Peach Garden Experience" of the "Four Clean-Ups" campaign in a Hopei production brigade as an alternative to Mao's effort to promote "class struggle" in rural rectification.[126] And in the arts, P'eng Chen was said to have promoted certain theatrical productions in oppo-

---

121. *See* the Cultural Revolution pamphlet, *Chairman Mao's Successor— Deputy Supreme Commander Lin Piao;* trans. in *Current Background,* No. 894 (October 27, 1969), p. 22. Also, "Counter-Revolutionary Revisionist Lo Jui-ch'ing Is Loaded with Crimes," *Chan-pao* [Combat News], January 30, 1967.

122. "Counter-Revolutionary Revisionist Lo Jui-ch'ing Is Loaded with Crimes," *Chan-pao,* January 30, 1967.

A detailed analysis of Lo's opposition to the Mao-Lin military policies, leading to his purge in 1965, will be found in Harry Harding and Melvin Gurtov, *The Purge of Lo Jui-ch'ing: The Politics of Chinese Strategic Planning* (Santa Monica, Calif.: The Rand Corporation, 1970).

123. *See* "Events Surrounding the 'Ch'angkuanlou' Counter-Revolutionary Incident," in *Tung-fang-hung* (April 20, 1967).

124. *See* "The Conflict between Mao Tse-tung and Liu Chao-ch'i over Agricultural Mechanization in Communist China," *Current Scene,* Vol. VI, No. 17 (October 1, 1968), pp. 12–16.

125. *See* "China's Taching Oilfield: Eclipse of an Industrial Model," *Current Scene,* Vol. VI, No. 16 (September 17, 1968), p. 8.

126. "Sham Four Clean-Ups, Real Restoration," *People's Daily* (September 6, 1967); trans. in *SCMP,* No. 4024 (September 20, 1967), pp. 1–20.

sition to Chiang Ch'ing's models of revolutionary Peking Opera.[127] "Model" experiences thus became weapons in the war of words over whose conception of the development process was to shape national social and economic policies.

In addition to the developments of early 1964 in the areas of Party and military life, political indoctrination, and economic activity, there also was a sharpening of issues within the intellectual community, most notably in theatrical work and press debates on apparently obscure issues of philosophy and historical interpretation. As seems to be the case in Communist countries, where the combination of ideologically-oriented politics and the need for the skills of a small, highly educated group charges academic life with political tension, intellectual developments in China during 1963–64 were to be a bellwether for far-reaching changes in Party and Army political alignments. As in 1957 and 1961–62, the intellectuals were pawns in a political conflict; a surrogate for those leaders who did not want to confront Mao directly on issues which would have split the Party "center."

Party use of the intellectuals to resist Mao's Tenth Plenum call for renewed "class struggle" was said to lie behind a "Forum on Confucius" convened by the Shantung Historical Society in November 1962 to commemorate the 2,440th anniversary of the death of China's ancient philosopher-sage. According to Cultural Revolution documents, this forum was encouraged by Chou Yang, Deputy Director of the Party's Propaganda Department and Vice-Chairman of the All-China Federation of Literary and Artistic Circles. His purpose was to reaffirm the ancient Confucian virtues of "human-heartedness" (*jen*) and benevolent government in order to dilute Mao's effort to sharpen political confrontation.[128]

In May of 1963 a national conference of writers and artists was convened to enable China's intellectuals to "play their full militant role" in the intensifying struggle against "modern revisionism" and to help them "identify themselves with the broad masses of the laboring people, with the workers, peasants and soldiers." They were exhorted "not to dodge or cover up the struggle between [political]

127. *See* "Comrade Chiang Ch'ing Leads Us to Struggle," *Hsin Pei-ta,* (May 30, 1967).

Other indications of opposition to Chiang Ch'ing's efforts to create "model" Peking operas by P'eng Chen and other leaders, based on Red Guard materials, will be found in Chung and Miller, *Madame Mao,* pp. 111, 127.

128. " 'The Forum on Confucius'—A Black Session of Monsters and Demons for Attacking the Party," *People's Daily* (January 10, 1967); trans. in *SCMP,* No. 3863 (January 19, 1967), pp. 4–13.

contradictions" in their work. "Works devoid of conflict are liked by nobody." [129] This conference was but one of a continuing series of measures initiated by Mao and his supporters to confront the political "revisionism" which they saw propagated by intellectuals backed by Party leaders.

Chiang Ch'ing became increasingly active in artistic matters at this time. She is said to have carried out investigations into the background and intent of the Wu Han play, "The Dismissal of Hai Jui." She found it to have "serious political problems," and initiated a behind-the-scenes campaign to have it banned from the stage.[130]

And with the help of Mao's supporters in Shanghai—K'o Ch'ing-shih, Chang Ch'un-ch'iao, and Yao Wen-yuan—Chiang Ch'ing promoted the publication of an article in the local press attacking the notion that "ghosts are harmless." [131] Her pre-Cultural Revolution influence was to culminate in the summer of 1964 with sponsorship of a national festival of Peking Opera on revolutionary themes.

Such activities reflected Mao's total disaffection with the political orientation of China's intellectuals. As he commented in late 1963 upon reading a report by K'o Ch'ing-shih on artistic matters:

> Problems abound in all forms of art . . . and the people involved are numerous; in many departments very little has been achieved so far in socialist transformation. The "dead" still predominate in many departments. . . .
>
> Isn't it absurd that many communists are enthusiastic about promoting feudal and capitalist art, but not socialist art?[132]

It was such a concern which lay behind the promotion of a rectification campaign in the All-China Federation of Literary and Artistic Circles beginning in June of 1964. In a statement on the campaign, Mao warned: "Unless [these intellectuals] remold themselves in real earnest, at some future date they are bound to become groups like the Hungarian Petöfi Club." [133]

Mao's disgust with what fifteen years of Party rule had wrought in China's intellectual life was also evident in his evaluation of the

129. See "National Conference of China's Writers and Artists," NCNA (May 21, 1963); trans. in *SCMP*, No. 2986 (May 24, 1963), pp. 2–5.

130. "Comrade Chiang Ch'ing's Outstanding Contributions to the Cultural Revolution," *Hsin Pei-ta* (May 30, 1967).

131. Chiang Ch'ing, "Do New Services for the People," in *Tung-fang-hung* (June 3, 1967).

132. Mao, "Comment on Comrade K'o Ch'ing-shih's Report" (December 12, 1963), in *Long Live the Thought of Mao Tse-tung!* p. 25.

133. Mao, "Instructions Concerning Literature and Art" (June 1964), *ibid.*, p. 26.

educational system. In an almost exact repetition of words he had used in an essay on educational methods written in 1917, Mao attacked contemporary teaching practices: "The current method tramples men of talent and young people underfoot. I do not approve of it. So many books have to be read and the examination method is one for tackling enemies. This is harmful and must be put to an end." [134] And in a phrase which reveals how contemporary Chinese life had begun to strike the old anti-dependency themes in his character, the Chairman observed to foreign visitors, "The [teaching] method now used is the forced feeding type, and is not spontaneous." [135]

Mao was to be increasingly negative in his evaluation of the educational system and its influence on China's youth in remarks to foreign visitors after 1964. In January 1965 he told his old acquaintance Edgar Snow that for all anyone knew the younger generation in time might "make peace with imperialism, bring the remnants of the Chiang K'ai-shek clique back to the mainland, and take a stand beside the small percentage of counterrevolutionaries still in the country." [136] In August of the same year he denounced Peking University before a visiting French delegation, adding that "this youth is showing dangerous tendencies"; "youth must be put to the test." [137]

That Mao should express such negative remarks to foreign visitors is only one of a number of indications that the Chairman felt his words were no longer being heeded within the Party. Realizing that his voice was being muffled by an unresponsive bureaucracy, he began to think of ways of giving a political voice to others (and to himself) who would be concerned with the social problems he saw but could not confront. In a comment on educational reform written in the summer of 1965, Mao stressed:

134. Mao, "Instructions Given at the Spring Festival Concerning Educational Work (Excerpts)" (February 13, 1964), in *ibid.*, p. 27.

In his essay "A Study of Physical Education" (*New Youth,* 1917) Mao had written: "In the educational system of our country, required courses are as thick as the hairs on a cow. Even an adult with a tough, strong body could not stand it, let alone those who have not reached adulthood, or those who are weak. Speculating on the intentions of the educators, one is led to wonder whether they did not design such an unwieldy curriculum in order to exhaust the students, to trample on their bodies and ruin their lives." (Cited in Stuart R. Schram, *The Political Thought of Mao Tse-tung* [New York: Praeger, 1963], p. 96.)

135. Mao, "Talk with the Nepalese Educational Delegation on Educational Problems" (1964), *ibid.*, p. 28.

136. Edgar Snow, "Interview with Mao," *The New Republic* (February 27, 1965), p. 23.

137. André Malraux, *Anti-Memoirs,* pp. 375, 366.

Political work must take the mass line. It won't do to rely merely on the leaders alone. . . . [It] is necessary to mobilize everybody to assume responsibility, to speak out, to give encouragement and make criticism. Everybody has a pair of eyes and a mouth. They should be allowed to use their eyes and mouths. It is democracy to let the masses handle their own affairs. . . . Since everybody has a mouth, they must bear two kinds of responsibilities—to feed and to speak. They should speak out and take up the responsibility of fighting against bad deeds and bad styles of work.[138]

It was in the summer of 1965 that Mao remarked to André Malraux: "I am alone with the masses, waiting." [139] The Chairman thus contrasted his own isolation atop the Party bureaucracy with the need to find a political voice through the actions of others. It was such a sentiment that led Lin Piao to exclaim, in a later day when the muffling Party organization had been destroyed:

. . . as Liu Shao-ch'i and his gang of counterrevolutionary revisionists blocked Chairman Mao's instructions, the broad revolutionary masses could hardly hear Chairman Mao's voice directly. The storm [of the Cultural Revolution] made it possible for Mao Tse-tung's thought to reach the broad revolutionary masses directly. This is a great victory.[140]

But before a new Party leadership purged of (some of) Mao's opponents could pass a resolution on the mass distribution of the Chairman's writings,[141] there were decisive political battles to be fought.

THE MATTER OF SUCCESSION

Is our society today thoroughly clean? No, it is not. Classes and class struggle remain, the activities of the overthrown reactionary classes plotting a comeback still continue, and we still have speculative activities by old and new bourgeois elements and desperate forays by embezzlers, grafters and degenerates. *There are also cases of degeneration in a few primary organizations; what is more, these degenerates do their utmost to find protectors and agents in the higher leading*

138. Mao, "Comment on Peking Normal College's Investigation Material Report" (July 3, 1965), in *Long Live the Thought of Mao Tse-tung!* p. 30.
139. André Malraux, *Anti-Memoirs*, p. 375.
140. Lin Piao, "Report to the Ninth National Congress of the Communist Party of China" (April 1, 1969); trans. in *Current Background*, No. 880 (May 9, 1969), p. 31.
141. *See* "Chinese Communist Party Central Committee Decides to Speed Up the Mass Publication of Mao Tse-tung's Works" (August 7, 1966); trans. in *SCMP*, No. 3759 (August 12, 1969), p. 11.

bodies. We should not in the least slacken our vigilance against such phenomena but must keep fully alert.

PEOPLE'S DAILY and RED FLAG, 1964[142]

. . . the question of cultivating successors [to lead the revolution] has become increasingly urgent and important. Internationally, imperialism headed by the United States has placed its hope of realizing "peaceful evolution" in China on the corruption of our third and fourth generations. *Who can say that this way of thinking of theirs is not without a certain foundation?*

RED FLAG, 1964[143]

So many deeds cry out to be done,   Times presses.
And always urgently;   Ten thousand years are too long,
The world rolls on,   Seize the day, seize the hour!

MAO TSE-TUNG, 1963[144]

Following the Tenth Plenum in the fall of 1962 more than three years were to elapse before Mao's voice was heard in national political matters with anything like the assertiveness of the years 1955 through 1958. And even when his influence was reasserted, "the thought of Mao Tse-tung" was to be invoked by other voices, Lin Piao and Yao Wen-yuan. A key question in the interpretation of Chinese domestic politics during the 1960s is the point at which Mao came to realize that if his influence on the Chinese revolution was to endure, basic issues related to the control of the policy-implementing process would have to be raised.

According to Lin Piao, it was as early as 1962 that Mao was "first to perceive the danger of the counterrevolutionary plots of Liu Shao-ch'i and his gang." [145] As we suggested earlier, it may have been Liu's unwillingness to sustain his support of Mao on the P'eng Teh-huai issue which undermined the political relationship between the two men.

A second poetic exchange between Mao and Kuo Mo-jo in early 1963 suggests that shortly after the Tenth Plenum the Chairman

142. *People's Daily* and *Red Flag* joint editorial, "On Khrushchev's Phoney Communism and Its Historical Lessons for the World" (July 14, 1964); in *Polemic on the General Line of the International Communist Movement*, p. 470. Emphasis added.

143. *Red Flag* editorial, "The Cultivation of Successors Is an Unending Great Task of Revolution," No. 14 (July 31, 1964), p. 34. Emphasis added.

144. Mao, "Reply to Comrade Kuo Mo-jo" (January 9, 1963), in *Ten More Poems of Mao Tse-tung*, p. 20.

145. Lin Piao, "Report to the Ninth National Congress of the Communist Party of China" (April 1, 1969); trans. in *Current Background*, No. 880 (May 9, 1969), p. 24.

was quite conscious of a coming political "storm." Kuo wrote to Mao in what seems almost a spirit of optimism, given the nation's economic problems and the Sino-Soviet conflict:

When the seas are in turmoil,
Heroes are on their mettle.
Six hundred million people,
Strong in unity,
Firm in principle,
Can keep the falling heavens suspended,
And create order out of the reign of chaos.
. . .
Four great volumes
Show us the way.[146]

Mao, however, was not so certain of the "firmness in principle" of the people or Party. He certainly had doubts about the willingness of certain Party leaders to follow the "four great volumes" of his political thought. Mao replied to Kuo that "shrilling, moaning" insects were plotting "to topple the giant tree"; that it was necessary to "seize the day, seize the hour!" of confrontation.[147] And he concluded impatiently:

The Four Seas are rising, clouds and waters raging,
The Five Continents are rocking, wind and thunder roaring.
Away with all pests!
Our force is irresistible.[148]

Just how much of this poetic imagery of early 1963 reflects Mao's sentiments about domestic leadership conflicts, as opposed to the Sino-Soviet dispute, is uncertain. As we have tried to document, however, Mao's domestic political influence in the wake of the Great Leap Forward hardly justified the assertion that "Our force is irresistible." On the basis of evidence in the public record, it appears that it was not until the summer of 1964 that Mao felt he had sufficient organizational power—based on his strengthened influence within the Army—to raise political issues related to the erosion of his control over Party policy. The present section is an effort to document the timing and manner of Mao's confrontation with those who resisted his leadership within the Party.

In late May of 1964 an obscure article on philosophical concepts appeared in the Peking paper of the intellectuals, the *Kuang-ming*

146. Kuo's poem, untitled and undated, is translated in *Ten More Poems of Mao Tse-tung*, p. 31.
147. Mao, "Reply to Comrade Kuo Mo-jo" (January 9, 1963), in *ibid.*, p. 20.
148. *Ibid.*, p. 22.

Daily. The apparently esoteric assertion of the two authors, Ai Heng-wu and Lin Ch'ing-shan, was that "two combining into one" —or "the unity of opposites"—was the universal law of materialist dialectics, whereas "one dividing into two" was a matter of the analytical approach used by Marxists in comprehending the natural world and man's social life.

Among the examples they gave to illustrate their interpretation was the matter of evaluating the contributions and errors of Party members: The best comrades were bound to have their flaws; and those with defects still had their good points. "Some comrades," however, made the "metaphysical" mistake of seeing only the bad points in other people's work.

> They see only the contradictory aspect of the problem, but fail to see the other aspect. When things are observed, they often tend to be absolute, holding that good things are absolutely good, and bad things absolutely bad. . . . When this method is used to size up other comrades, units, sectors, or localities, only the shortcomings, mistakes, and bad points will be noticed. The driving force for development and progress is thus missing in one's work, and harmful feelings of self-importance, arrogance, self-satisfaction and conservatism are bound to be engendered.[149]

This article drew indignant replies from other writers who reminded Comrades Ai and Lin that according to Chairman Mao the struggle between opposites, "dividing one into two," was the fundamental law of human progress.

By the end of the summer more than ninety published articles in the national press had carried this debate to a furious pitch; and the editorial department of the Party's theoretical journal *Red Flag* had convened a special two-day forum on the issue, so that students and cadres of the Higher Party School could debate the relative merits of "two combining into one" or "one dividing into two."

After three months of exchanges in the press, *Red Flag* gave some inkling of what the debate was all about in an article which attacked by name the Director of the Higher Party School, Yang Hsien-chen. Yang was said to have deliberately provoked the controversy by disseminating the idea among his students that the reconciliation of "contradictions"—"two combining into one"—was the fundamental law of Marxist dialectics. After invoking threatening phrases and historical images from the era of Stalin's purges, *Red Flag* asserted:

149. Ai Heng-wu and Lin Ch'ing-shan, " 'Dividing One into Two' and 'Combining Two into One,' " *Kuang-ming Daily* (May 29, 1964); trans. in *Current Background,* No. 745 (December 2, 1964), p. 3.

It is no accident that Comrade Yang Hsien-chen should at this time have made public the concept of "two combining into one." He has done this with the aim and plan of pitting the reactionary bourgeois world outlook against the proletarian world outlook of materialist dialectics.[150]

Yang and his cohorts were said to have been "actuated by ulterior motives" in asserting that "an academic question should not be turned into a political question." The manner in which this debate on philosophical concepts was related to political matters was left unstated; but *Red Flag* asserted that "whenever a sharp class struggle develops in the political and economic fields, there is bound to be acute class struggle in the ideological field as well." [151] It was recalled that during the 1920s in the Soviet Union, during the political struggle against the "anti-Party" faction of Trotsky and Bukharin, "antidialectical philosophical views became the ideological weapon of the anti-Party group." *Red Flag* observed that this debate was "still far from being concluded. Step by step it is deepening. Truth always develops in struggle." [152]

Only from the perspective of Cultural Revolution developments can one infer that behind these veiled assertions of the emergence of an "anti-Party" group, and a debate over the question of whether "contradictions" would lead to division or reconciliation, was the question of whether the leadership of the Chinese Communist Party would be split. Would the unitary Party "divide into two," or could underlying conflicts over policy and leadership approach be resolved?

It remains obscure why the lines of conflict within the Party leadership became so tightly drawn in the early summer of 1964. In part it must have been a reflection of the organizational pressures which Mao and Lin Piao were putting on the Party through the "learn from the PLA" campaign. The key question seems to be why Mao had come to feel the press of time, the need to "seize the day, seize the hour." Why did he now choose to press issues related to personnel and political organization to the point of "dividing one into two"?

150. *Red Flag* correspondent, "New Polemic on the Philosophical Front," *Red Flag*, No. 16 (August 31, 1964); trans. in *ibid.*, p. 29.
151. *Ibid.*, p. 31.
During the Cultural Revolution one Red Guard publication hinted that a *coup* attempt against Mao and Lin Piao had its origins in the Peking Higher Party School in June of 1964. (*See* "The February [1966] Coup," *Chan Pao* [Combat Bulletin], April 17, 1967.) This document, however, has not been supported by additional evidence.
152. *Ibid.*

In 1964 the Chairman was in his seventy-first year; and beginning in the fall, rumors began to circulate that he had had a stroke, was suffering from Parkinson's disease, or had some other serious health problem.[153] Edgar Snow was struck by Mao's repeated observation that "he was soon going to see God," and his musing on how, in a career filled with the violence of revolution, he had so long escaped death.[154] In August 1965 André Malraux observed a nurse at the Chairman's side.[155]

While Mao's subsequent political vigor tends to belie these rumors of ill health and indications of a personal awareness of imminent death, it nonetheless may be that medical problems heightened for Mao the sense that he had only limited time in which to insure that his style of leadership would endure in the institutions of new China. For almost a decade, Khrushchev's denunciation of Stalin and the "personality cult," had been one source of the erosion of his authority. It was now compounded by the direct experience of P'eng Teh-huai's challenge and continuing pressures from within the Party leadership for "reversing verdicts" and reconsideration of the policies of the Great Leap Forward.

In short, Mao's faith in his "claim to immortality" [156] through the permanence of policies and political institutions which were the sum of a life of struggle was being undermined. Perhaps burdened with what Robert Lifton has termed "death anxiety," the Chairman was seeking to sustain the meaning of his life in the support of those who would survive his passing.[157]

It is not known whether the debate over "two into one" or "one into two" reflects a confrontation within the leadership in the spring of 1964 which raised basic questions of policy or personal status. Perhaps Mao invoked his authority in an uncompromising way in order to reassert influence over developments now beyond his con-

153. A French delegation which visited Mao at his Hangchow retreat in September 1964 observed him shaking in a manner which reminded one of the observers of his own father's Parkinson's disease. (*See* Edward Behr, "Red China Face to Face," *Saturday Evening Post* [November 14, 1964], pp. 21–28.) Other reports from China reaching Hong Kong during late 1964 and 1965 rumored that Mao was recuperating from a mild stroke, or had high blood pressure and a heart condition. (*See* Stanley Karnow, "Status of Vanished Mao—Dead, Ill, or Lively—Stumps Experts," *Washington Post* [May 8, 1966], p. 1.)

154. Edgar Snow, "Interview with Mao," *The New Republic* (February 27, 1965), p. 23.

155. André Malraux, *Anti-Memoirs*, p. 372.

156. *See* the suggestive essay by Robert Jay Lifton, *Revolutionary Immortality: Mao Tse-tung and the Chinese Cultural Revolution* (New York: Random House, 1968), p. 93.

157. *Ibid.*, pp. 19–20.

trol. The polemic over Yang Hsien-chen's philosophical concepts, however, does convey the sense of a Party organization appealing for reconciliation, with Maoist spokesmen responding with an uncompromising determination to "divide one into two." Other developments which followed in late May also strongly suggest that the Chairman had invoked the one issue on which his own attenuated authority within the Party still carried considerable influence: the matter of his public approbation of a successor to his leadership of the Party. Mao apparently decided that the test of who was to receive that approbation was to be a matter of unquestioned loyalty to his person and unwavering commitment to his conception of the revolution, his "thought."

Ten days after the *Kuang-ming Daily* published the first article supporting Yang Hsien-chen's thesis of the fundamental importance of "two combining into one," the same paper republished a *Liberation Army Daily* editorial of June 6th. This editorial was apparently a veiled warning to Liu Shao-ch'i and his supporters that the basic issue of loyalty to the "thought of Mao Tse-tung," was now at stake. The editorial quoted from Liu's *How to Be a Good Communist* on the need to hold firm to political principles "at a time when the [political] situation is complex, the environment is beset with sharp changes, and there is need to follow a zigzagging road." [158] Yet which political principles were to guide one through such a complicated environment, Marxism-Leninism or "the thought of Mao Tse-tung"?

To study Chairman Mao's works is a shortcut to the study of Marxism-Leninism. Chairman Mao is a great standard bearer of Marxism-Leninism in the contemporary era, and Mao Tse-tung's thought is an important development of Marxism-Leninism. Now, many revolutionary people are studying Chairman Mao's works.[159]

The editorial then pointedly observed:

158. *Liberation Army Daily* editorial, "Study Chairman Mao's Works with a Profound Class Feeling," *Kuang-ming Daily* (June 8, 1964); trans. in *Current Background*, No. 739 (August 24, 1964), p. 60.
This passage cited from Liu's book appears to be a politically "loaded" addition to the 1962 revision. During the Cultural Revolution this particular passage was to be singled out for criticism as an example of Liu's political deviousness. (*See* "*How to Be a Good Communist* Is a Revisionist Program Opposed to the Thought of Mao Tse-tung," *Ching-kang-shan*, reprinted in *Kuang-ming Daily* [April 8, 1967]; trans. in *Current Background*, No. 827 [June 1, 1967], pp. 1–16.) Hence, one senses that in 1964 Liu was indirectly being called to account for his opposition to Mao.
159. *Liberation Army Daily* editorial, "Study Chairman Mao's Works with a Profound Class Feeling." Emphasis added.

. . . not every comrade understands clearly what must be done before a success can be made of the study [of Chairman Mao's works]. Some comrades hold that the mentality of a person and his ideological cultivation (*hsiu-yang*) have something to do with whether or not he is able to study Chairman Mao's works well. This view is incorrect.[160]

The implication of these assertions of the PLA paper was that Mao's writings and his emphasis on "thought reform" (*szu-hsiang kai-tsao*) took precedence over Liu's efforts to establish the "cultivation" (*hsiu-yang*) of Party members as the basis for their "rectification." The test of political commitment in the coming period of trial was to be whether one deferred to Mao's "thought" or to Marxism-Leninism as the basis of one's political life.

Later in June, the Party's Youth League held its Ninth National Congress. Mao used the Congress to raise publicly the issue of "cultivating" (*p'ei-yang,* not *hsiu-yang*) a new generation of "revolutionary successors" (*chieh-pan jen*).

The "important directive" in which the Party Chairman discussed the succession problem has never been made public; yet its major arguments appear to be included in the ninth of a year-long series of polemical exchanges with the Soviet Party leadership which was published in mid-July. In an evaluation of the lessons for China of "Khrushchev's Phoney Communism," Mao revealed his concern with "careerists and conspirators like Khrushchev" "usurping the leadership of the Party and government at any level." The article hinted that political degenerates with influence at high levels within the Chinese Party were violating the "mass line" style of leadership, were "despotic like Khrushchev," and were likely to "make surprise attacks" on their comrades—"like Khrushchev." [161]

By raising the issue of succession within the Chinese Party in the context of a public polemic with the Soviets, Mao thus revealed just how interwoven in his own mind had become the erosion of his authority which followed Khrushchev's "surprise attack" on Stalin, P'eng Teh-huai's "surprise attack" on his Great Leap policies at Lushan, and continuing conflicts within the Chinese Party leadership over policy and personal status. One also infers from the Cultural Revolution characterization of Liu Shao-ch'i as "China's Khrushchev" that by mid-1964 Mao had developed strong doubts about Liu's status as his successor. The Chairman saw his

160. *Ibid.,* p. 61.
161. *People's Daily* and *Red Flag* joint editorial, "On Khrushchev's Phoney Communism and Its Historical Lessons for the World" (July 14, 1964), in *Polemic on the General Line of the International Communist Movement,* pp. 478–479.

life's work as vulnerable to repudiation by disloyal comrades; and he was trying to preempt their attacks, to avoid Stalin's posthumous degradation, by selecting new and loyal successors.

How directly did the Chairman challenge Liu Shao-ch'i's authority within the councils of the Party at this time? As reported by Edgar Snow, it was not until a meeting of the Party leadership on January 25th, 1965, that Mao finally "decided Liu had to go" (see fn. 185, p. 469 below). Given all the indications of policy differences between the two leaders explored in these last three chapters, however, it seems most unlikely that this meeting was anything more than a final, explicit confrontation between the two men; an exchange on the question of how to rectify a "revisionist" Party in which Mao found Liu fully beyond his influence. It seems more likely that by raising in mid-1964 the general problem of succession, Mao was giving Liu a last chance to "stand on his side," and using the succession issue to drive a wedge between opponents within the Party leadership.

At the Youth League Congress in June 1964, although Mao had intimated that there were political degenerates "at all levels" of the Party, he had raised the issue of cultivating "revolutionary successors" in very general terms. From the point of view of political tactics, for Mao to have drawn the succession issue too explicitly would have provoked a showdown at a time and in a manner in which he was hardly certain to win. Since his earliest days in politics, Mao has shown great discipline in biding his time when out of influence, and an ability to "disintegrate" enemies and "crush opponents one by one." [162] The Chairman apparently was now playing his one remaining source of strength—his ability to confer legitimacy on a successor—for all it was worth. By keeping silent on his choice of a successor, even as he publicly raised the issue, he acquired the political leverage to divide those within the Party leadership who opposed his "thought," and to build a new coalition of supporters for a confrontation with diehard "revisionists."

Such an interpretation is one way of accounting for the pattern of conflict during 1965 and 1966, in which second rank leaders like P'eng Chen, Teng Hsiao-p'ing, and T'ao Chu appeared to rise in political influence. Then with other leaders Lo Jui-ch'ing and Liu Shao-ch'i, they were sequentially purged over the period of a year.

Whatever the accuracy of this interpretation, one sees in editorial reactions to Mao's June initiative on the question of cultivating "revolutionary successors" an effort by the Party and Youth League

162. *See* pp. 228–234 above.

to incorporate the Chairman's pressure into their regular pattern of organizational activity. They either ignored or did not dare to grasp the full implication of the range of issues which Mao and the Army had raised on all fronts since the winter of 1964. An editorial in *China Youth Daily* at the conclusion of the aforementioned Youth League Congress in June asserted that "our socialist new China has all the favorable conditions for turning the youth into proletarian successors of the revolution." [163] Yet a *Red Flag* article of this time spoke with concern of the influence of modern revisionism on youth, "causing them to become pampered little gentry who will only know how to seek after personal pleasure, who will only know how to eat, drink, and play." [164] And within a year Mao was repeatedly to call into question before foreign visitors the political maturity of the younger generation.[165]

A *People's Daily* editorial of early August stressed that the purpose of cultivating "revolutionary successors" was "to strengthen constantly the nucleus of Party leadership at all levels so that the correct line and correct policies of the Party are adhered to at all times." [166] By the end of the year, however, Mao had intervened twice in an attempt to correct what he considered to be the erroneous policy orientation of the Socialist Education Movement, which, under Liu Shao-ch'i's "first line" guidance, was giving stress to Party leadership "from above."

As had happened with so many of Mao's policies since the inception of the Great Leap crisis, the Party took the Chairman's initiative and tried to turn it back on him. The *People's Daily* editorialized on Mao's assertion that "revolutionary successors" must be good at uniting with their colleagues, even those with whom they disagreed:

> Members of the nucleus of leadership must make the best use of collective wisdom and be good at listening to all useful opinions and working with people of differing views, be good at creating an atmosphere of earnestly discussing and studying problems so that comrades with differing views can freely express their opinions, undertake debates and make right and wrong clear, and through such dis-

163. *China Youth Daily* editorial, "Forever Be Firm Revolutionaries" (July 8, 1964); trans. in *SCMP*, No. 3278 (August 13, 1964), p. 2.

164. *Red Flag* editorial, "The Cultivation of Successors Is an Unending Great Task of Revolution," No. 14 (July 1964), p. 35.

165. *See* Mao's comments to Edgar Snow and André Malraux, on p. 451 above.

166. *People's Daily* editorial, "Cultivate and Train Millions of Successors Who Will Carry on the Cause of Proletarian Revolution" (August 3, 1964); trans. in *SCMP,* No. 3274 (August 7, 1964), p. 1.

cussions to raise comrades' ideological level of Marxism-Leninism, raise their ability to discover errors and strengthen unity among them on Marxist-Leninist principles.[167]

The Party paper then pointedly added:

> It is necessary resolutely to oppose the arbitrary style of "do as I say," resolutely oppose the rude style of not treating others as equals, and resolutely oppose the style of those who welcome flattery and turn like a wounded tiger on those who raise criticism.[168]

A further response to Mao's initiative on the succession issue which more completely reveals a fear of the growing political polarization between Party and Army was expressed in an article of late September by An Tzu-wen, Director of the Party's Organization Department. In contrast to Mao's insistence on pressing "class struggle," An Tzu-wen declared that

> during the socialist period, building socialism is the highest criterion of our unity. All the comrades building socialism should be seriously united with thorough criticism–self-criticism even if they hold different views which conflict with ours over certain concrete problems or when they show certain shortcomings or even make mistakes.[169]

In contrast to Mao's assertion of mid-July that it was "essential to test and know cadres and choose and train succeessors in the long course of mass struggle," [170] An Tzu-wen talked about cultivating successors "on a business-like basis":

> . . . with workers and peasants gradually acquiring knowledge and with intellectuals performing labor, fine and cultured workers and peasants and revolutionary intellectuals having close connections [with each other] will be brought up in large numbers. This is a safe and dependable road to bringing up newborn forces of revolution and training revolutionary successors.[171]

Mao evidently had made clear to Party leaders his determination to press for "mass struggle" as the way to rear a successor genera-

167. *People's Daily* editorial, "Educate the Younger Generation to Be Revolutionaries Forever" (July 8, 1964); trans. in *Current Background,* No. 738 (July 30, 1964), pp. 41–43.

168. *Ibid.*

169. An Tzu-wen, "Cultivating and Training Revolutionary Successors Is a Strategic Task of the Party," *Red Flag,* Nos. 17–18 (September 23, 1964); trans. in *SCMM,* No. 438 (October 12, 1964), p. 7.

170. *People's Daily* and *Red Flag* joint editorial, "On Khrushchev's Phoney Communism and Its Historical Lessons for the World," in *Polemic on the General Line of the International Communist Movement,* p. 479.

171. An Tzu-wen, "Cultivating and Training Revolutionary Successors Is a Strategic Task of the Party," p. 11.

tion, and it was increasingly apparent that the Army was to be the guarantor of this intention. An Tzu-wen, however, tried to reinterpret Mao's assertion of the need to confront modern revisionism by reformulating the current conflict as a contest between the "true Marxist-Leninists" (of the Party) and "phoney Marxist-Leninists" (in the Army). In what perhaps is an indirect reference to Lin Piao, Mao's chosen successor to PLA leadership, An Tzu-wen stressed the importance of being able to distinguish those

> who are true Marxist-Leninists and [those] who are phoney Marxist-Leninists. [We] must very carefully select and train revolutionary successors, place the responsibility for leading the revolution in the hands of true Marxist-Leninists, and prevent phoney Marxist-Leninists from usurping the political leadership. It is not easy to distinguish true Marxist-Leninists from phoney Marxist-Leninists. Frequently, a wrong view is taken of a person.[172]

An Tzu-wen then recalled with concern the Kronstadt mutiny of 1921 in Russia, in which a rebellious naval unit had attempted to overthrow Communist Party leadership: "It will be remembered that when the White Guards of Russia staged a counterrevolutionary mutiny in Kronstadt, they raised this pernicious cry: 'Soviets without Communists!' "[173]

Who were the real, and who the phoney "Marxist-Leninists?" The Party organization clearly saw Mao's political reliance upon the Army as creating the danger of "Soviets without Communists." Yet one can only wonder whether as early as the summer of 1964 Mao knew how far his determination to press the conflict with Party opponents was to take him; and whether the Party had any inkling that Mao's "White Guards" of the Army were to be but the protectors of his "Red Guard" rebels among China's younger generation.

VIET-NAM!

On Army Day, August 1st of 1964, a *Liberation Army Daily* editorial seemed to express the degree to which Mao's disenchantment with the course of the revolution had led him back to the earliest

---

172. *Ibid.*, p. 3.

According to Cultural Revolution charges, Lo Jui-ch'ing (and presumably others) attempted at this time to get Lin Piao to step aside as Defense Minister, in the context of new decisions on State personnel which would be taken at the approaching first session of the Third National People's Congress. (*See* "Counter-Revolutionary Revisionist Lo Jui-ch'ing Is Loaded with Crimes," *Chan Pao* [January 30, 1967].)

173. *Ibid.*, p. 4.

battles of his political career. Entitled "Long Live the Firm and Complete Revolutionary Spirit of Chingkang Mountain," the editorial revealed that despite China's isolation within the International Communist Movement, military tensions on the country's southern border, and domestic political opposition, the Chairman remained determined to press the revolution through to the end.[174] Lines were invoked from a 1928 poem by Mao:

> Flags and banners flared at the mountain's foot
> While drums and bugles sounded from the peaks.
> The enemy army encircled us in countless cordons,
> But like the peaks I remained unmoved.[175]

The Chairman thus drew inspiration from early successes against great odds in the revolutionary struggle—and confidence from his renewed political support from the PLA.

In this context where Mao had pushed his differences with life-long Party cohorts to the point of "dividing one into two," the escalation of the war in Viet-Nam—sharply emphasized by the Tonkin Gulf clash between North Vietnamese and American naval vessels on August 5th—must have produced a political explosion within the Chinese Party leadership.

As the Viet-Nam conflict continued to expand over the next year, Mao and his supporters faced two related dangers: If the war enlarged in scope as a result of American participation to the point of directly threatening China's national security, the PLA—the Chairman's base of power in the recently escalated domestic political confrontation—might very well be dragged from his hands as a political instrument into military action against the United States. Concurrently, if pressures from within the "socialist camp" for "united action" in support of the North Vietnamese in their conflict with the Americans intensified, China might be forced to abandon the political confrontation with Soviet "revisionism." Renewed Sino-Soviet military and political cooperation in aid of the Vietnamese was likely to bring with it further Russian efforts to strengthen the hands of Mao's domestic rivals and new Soviet influence in Chinese military affairs.

The impact of the American escalation on China's internal politics was revealed in the months following the Tonkin Gulf incident in a predictable shift to military preparedness by the PLA, and

174. *Liberation Army Daily* editorial, "Long Live the Firm and Complete Revolutionary Spirit of Chingkang Mountain," *People's Daily* (August 1, 1964), p. 1.
175. *Ibid.*

a blurring of the lines of conflict between Party and Army. On September 8th a *People's Daily* "short comment" noted apprehensively: "We must brighten our eyes and keep a close watch against all conspiracies of the U.S. imperialists and class enemies at home and abroad. We must prepare for the worst and make all kinds of preparations." [176] The New Year's Day editorial of the *Liberation Army Daily* more explicitly revealed the shift to war preparations and collective Party (versus Maoist) influence in Army policy by its dominant emphasis on "training for combat." [177] It was stressed that the PLA was "able to fulfill any tasks assigned to it by the Party and the state" (not Chairman Mao). In a clear indication of the degree to which the war threat had forced "two to combine into one," the editorial exhorted Party cadres to "study energetically Marxism-Leninism *and* the thought of Mao Tse-tung, particularly Chairman Mao's philosophical works *and* Chairman Liu's book, *How to Be a Good Communist.*" [178] Further emphasizing a shift to collective leadership, the editorial stressed that in the work of Party branches within the Army, "decisions [must not] be made by a single person, and no individuals should be permitted to change at will the decisions of the Party branch."

The degree to which the war context had forced a (temporary) reconciliation of domestic political differences was revealed in a *People's Daily* editorial and article of late 1964. Entitled "The Interests of the Party above Everything Else," the editorial commented on an article which described how a Party branch leader of a certain PLA platoon—"vexed by family problems"—had carried out his work assignments poorly. The editorial then revealed that by studying Liu Shao-ch'i's *How to Be a Good Communist* he had learned that "the Party's interests are above all else," and was able to subordinate his personal difficulties to the collective interests of the Party.[179]

The accompanying article also described a quarrel between the

176. *People's Daily* short comment, "Persevere in Struggle to the End" (September 8, 1964); trans. in *SCMP*, No. 3307 (September 29, 1964), p. 5.

177. From a *People's Daily* summary of a *Liberation Army Daily* editorial, "Hold Even Higher the Great Red Banner of the Thought of Mao Tse-tung and Carry through in an Even More Thorough-going Manner the Movement of Creating More 'Four Good' Companies" (January 1, 1965); trans. in *SCMP*, No. 3376 (January 13, 1965), p. 3.

178. *Ibid.*, p. 4. Emphasis added.

179. *People's Daily* editorial, "The Interests of the Party above Everything Else" (December 20, 1964); trans. in *SCMP*, No. 3369 (January 4, 1965), pp. 4–5.

leader of a certain PLA company and a member of the company's Party branch committee—apparently an indirect reference to the tensions between Army and Party leaderships—and how the two had resolved their differences through the study of Mao's writings on criticism–self-criticism and the relevant chapters of Liu's *How to Be a Good Communist*. After the argumentative Party member had read a passage from Liu's book on the harmfulness of excessive criticism of other people's errors, "his face turned red with shame and he felt that Comrade Liu Shao-ch'i's criticism had hit his vulnerable spot." [180] Through their combined political study, the two quarreling comrades "united with each other more closely than before."

This indirect revelation of efforts by the Party leadership to bring about a solution of political differences on the basis of the larger interests of Party unity and national security were contrasted in the press by continuing attacks on Yang Hsien-chen for his advocacy of reconciliation in dealing with political "contradictions." Conflicting "signals" in the press through 1965 suggest that despite Party efforts to depoliticize the confrontation within the leadership, Mao persisted in his determination to resolve the issues raised in 1964.

This unwillingness to compromise was reflected in the evolution of China's policy toward the Viet-Nam war. A remarkable public debate in the national press during 1965 on national defense policy revealed that the Viet-Nam situation, far from healing differences, actually increased the political differentiation within the leadership which had begun in the summer of 1964 over the issue of succession.

The question of China's relations with the Soviet Union was a major and highly divisive factor in this debate. The Sino-Soviet conflict had worsened steadily following the 1959 events centered about P'eng Teh-huai and the Chinese ideological challenge to the Russians in the spring of 1960. In June of that year, first at the General Council meeting of the World Federation of Trade Unions in Peking and then at the Rumanian Party Congress in Bucharest, there was public political conflict between Soviet and Chinese Party delegates. And in July and August Soviet technicians and economic aid were suddenly withdrawn from China. A world meeting of eighty-one Communist Parties in Moscow in November of 1960 only papered over the fundamental differences in political strategy

180. "The Party Branch of a Nanking Armed Forces Unit Studies *How to Be a Good Communist* in the Light of Reality," *People's Daily* (December 20, 1964); trans. in *ibid.*, p. 3.

and personal authority which had developed following Khrushchev's initiatives of 1956.[181]

In November of 1961, at the Soviet Party's Twenty-second Congress, Khrushchev had read the Albanians out of the International Movement, an action which the Chinese interpreted as "killing the chicken to warn the monkey." In protest, Chou En-lai, the Chinese delegate to the Congress, staged a walk-out and demonstratively laid a wreath at Stalin's inconspicuous new grave before returning to Peking. The Chinese and Albanians were now staunch, if lonely, fraternal allies in the International Movement.

The collapse of the Soviet-Cuban missile adventure in the fall of 1962, a striking contrast to the Chinese success in their border war with India (toward which the Russians adopted a stand of "positive neutrality" in favor of the Indians), only increased Chinese hostility and Russian vulnerability to Chinese attacks. The years 1963 and 1964 saw further unsuccessful efforts to limit the conflict, and a subsequent expansion into direct public polemics.

There was an abortive bilateral meeting between Soviet and Chinese Party representatives in Moscow in July of 1963, followed by a series of press attacks in which both Parties exposed many previously unknown developments that had led to a deepening of the confrontation.[182] Beginning in 1963 the Chinese initiated a year-long series of scathing articles which challenged Soviet leadership of the International Movement. Khrushchev responded with (unsuccessful) efforts to convene another international conference of Communist Parties in a "collective mobilization" of opinion against Chinese factional agitation within the Movement and in other Party organizations.

Khrushchev's fall from power in October of 1964—on the very day that the Chinese exploded their first atomic device—must have occasioned considerable debate within the Chinese Party leadership. A Chinese delegation—with what appears to be a careful political balance between Chou En-lai and K'ang Sheng as representatives of Mao, and Ho Lung and Wu Hsiu-ch'uan as representatives of Army-Party interests—was dispatched to Moscow within three weeks of Khrushchev's ouster. But the resumption of public

181. In addition to the study by Zagoria, *The Sino-Soviet Conflict, 1956–1961*, this brief survey of the major developments in Sino-Soviet relations after Lushan draws major guidance from the two analytical works on this period by William E. Griffith, *The Sino-Soviet Rift* (Cambridge, Massachusetts: M.I.T. Press, 1964), and *Sino-Soviet Relations, 1964–1965* (Cambridge, Massachusetts: M.I.T. Press, 1967).

182. *See*, for example, the information on Sino-Soviet military relations discussed on pp. 378–393 above.

Chinese attacks on the new Soviet leadership shortly after the return of this delegation indicates that the differences between the two Parties had passed well beyond Mao's personalized opposition to Khrushchev.

A *Red Flag* editorial of late November 1964 smugly declared that the Chinese Party, with its true Marxist-Leninist orientation, had "long foreseen" Khrushchev's political demise. It listed twelve policies promoted by the fallen Soviet leader which assertedly had led to the ouster of "this buffoon on the contemporary political stage." [183] The scope of these twelve points embodied a complete defense of Mao's domestic and international policies. For the new Soviet leadership to have accepted the correctness of these alternatives would have meant subordinating their Party and country to Chinese leadership in both domestic and international affairs. Obviously no Soviet leaders would or could accept such a position.

A further intensification of the threat to China's—and Mao's—interests came with the initiation of American air attacks on North Viet-Nam in early February of 1965 and the introduction of large numbers of American ground forces into the south. The bombings began as the new Soviet Premier Alexei Kosygin arrived in Hanoi to negotiate defense arrangements with the North Vietnamese leaders. The combined effect of these developments was to heighten the danger of a Sino-American confrontation as the air war neared China's southern border, to increase Soviet influence within North Viet-Nam through the military and economic aid which they could provide Hanoi, and to strengthen pressures from within the "socialist camp" for "united action" with the Soviets in aid of the Vietnamese.

The following months of debate among Chinese leaders over how to respond to this situation revealed both the diffusion of authority within the Party and the heightening conflict within the leadership. Between February and September of 1965, on a variety of occasions, Party and Army spokesmen revealed through subtle yet significant variations in their evaluation of the Viet-Nam situation, their conflicting views on policy toward the Soviet Union, the United States, and to China's national defense.[184] Chief of the

183. *Red Flag* editorial, "Why Khrushchev Fell" (November 21, 1964), in *Polemic on the General Line of the International Communist Movement,* pp. 483–492.

184. This discussion of the position of various Chinese leaders in evaluating the meaning of the Viet-Nam conflict for China's national security draws much inspiration from the detailed analysis by Uri Ra'anan, "Peking's Foreign Policy 'Debate,' 1965–1966," in Tang Tsou, ed., *China in Crisis* (Chicago: University of Chicago Press, 1968), Vol. II, pp. 23–71; and Donald S. Zagoria, *Viet-Nam Triangle* (New York: Pegasus, 1967).

General Staff Lo Jui-ch'ing appeared to stress the need for an "active defense" against what he characterized as an almost certain American extension of the war to China—a threat that required China to reach some accommodation with the Soviets.[185]

Liu Shao-ch'i, Teng Hsiao-p'ing, and their spokesmen in the Party seemed to call for a relaxation of tension with the Russians for economic as well as military reasons. And P'eng Chen—in a manner which apparently reflected his current domestic political defense of vigorously "waving the red flag"—assumed a virulent anti-Soviet line which foreclosed any possibility of "united action." P'eng may have been seeking to eradicate any doubts in Mao's mind about his own "revisionism" through demonstrative opposition to the Russians. His call for great caution before American strength, however, was to lead to criticism by Mao that he was cowering before "imperialism" just like the Soviet "revisionists."

The position of Mao and Lin Piao in this debate was not formally expressed until early September. In the article "Long Live the Victory of People's War," Lin Piao finally attempted to reassert the correctness of Mao's strategy of national defense which had been evolved in 1958, and the validity of the form of military struggle against superior forces which had brought the Party to power.

Basically, Lin asserted that if the Vietnamese adopted a strategy of "people's war" they would be able to cope with the American intervention without direct Chinese or Soviet assistance (other than the supply of light arms and economic assistance). He revealed an unremitting hostility toward the United States, but stressed that "revolution or people's war in any country is the business of the masses in that country." [186] Similarly he expressed an uncompromising attitude against "united action" with the Soviets by emphasizing that Khrushchev's successors continued to collude with the United States in attempting to "extinguish the flames of revolution."

Thus Mao and Lin tried to establish a policy line which would avoid both confrontation with the Americans and collusion with the Soviets, while encouraging a prosecution of the war in Viet-Nam in such a way that the Vietnamese could slowly drive out American influence through their own efforts. Such a strategy also enabled

185. While this book was in press, Edgar Snow reported that Liu Shao-ch'i himself, during 1965, sought "to reactivate the Sino-Soviet alliance" because of the Viet-Nam situation (if not for domestic political reasons). *See* Edgar Snow, "Mao Tse-tung and the Cost of Living: Aftermath of the Cultural Revolution," *The New Republic* (April 10, 1971), p. 19.

186. Lin Piao, "Long Live the Victory of People's War" (September 3, 1965), as cited in Uri Ra'anan, "Peking's Foreign Policy 'Debate,'" in Tang Tsou, ed., *China in Crisis*, Vol. II, pp. 57–58.

Mao and Lin to sustain the Army's domestic political role and to continue to exclude Soviet influence from China.

Why did it take so many months for Mao and Lin to formulate this alternative to the conflicting evaluations expressed by other leaders during the spring and summer? And why was a debate on matters directly related to China's national security so publicly revealed? In part the policy debate must have reflected uncertainty about the course of events which were largely beyond Chinese control. In this sense the September statement by Lin Piao reflects an evaluation of the impact of the Viet-Nam conflict on China's security after more than six months of watching to see what, in fact, would be the extent of the American escalation and the concomitant ability of the Vietnamese to cope with it.

Given the context of Party leadership conflict in which these differing policies were expressed, however, we would suggest that there were important domestic reasons for both the timing of the debate and the conflicting positions expressed by various leaders. First, Mao and Lin were probably not in a position to impose their view on other Party leaders—as was emphasized by continuing opposition to Lin's policy statement after its publication. The full implications of the war were hardly certain in the spring and summer of 1965, and Mao and Lin would probably have wanted to avoid a showdown on the defense issue when they could not make a strong case for their position through regular Party decision-making procedures. And for obvious reasons, they would not have wanted to force the issue to a point at which Army power would have to be invoked in a domestic confrontation while it was still uncertain whether the PLA might have to assume a direct military role in the war situation.

The fact that the policy debate proceeded in such public fashion is one further indication that power had diffused considerably within the Party. No one leadership group could control the public media, much less set a common defense line. And given all the signs of a heightening of leadership conflict in the early summer of 1964, it is reasonable to assume that the policy alternatives expressed by various leaders reflected their awareness that the defense position eventually adopted would have a major influence on the course of Mao's effort to press the domestic conflict. Thus, the persistent call for a policy of "active defense" by Lo Jui-ch'ing can be seen as a defense against Mao and Lin as well as a position directed against the United States.[187]

187. One Cultural Revolution publication implied that Lo and other leaders who fell from power in 1966 had created a "war scare" over the Viet-Nam situation "from May 1965 to the beginning of 1966" in order

By the late summer of 1965 Mao evidently felt that the Viet-Nam situation had stabilized sufficiently so that he could return to the issues he had raised a year earlier. How did he come to believe that he could divert his own attention, and that of the PLA, to a major domestic political battle with a potential war situation on China's southern frontier? He probably concluded that the Vietnamese could cope with the American ground forces, and that Hanoi would not be pressured into a negotiated settlement of the conflict by the air bombardment. In addition, one suspects that Mao came to see the limits of American escalation. Whether such limits had been communicated to the Chinese through the 126th meeting of the Warsaw ambassadorial talks on June 30th, through some other channel, or simply as a result of a tacit understanding of the situation is not known.

It is telling, however, that after the publication of Lin Piao's September 3rd analysis of the war, official Chinese spokesmen seemed to be at pains to stress the mutual concern shared by both the United States and China about a direct military confrontation. In an exchange with Japanese parliamentarians on September 6th, Foreign Minister Ch'en Yi remarked, "To tell the truth, America is afraid of China and China is somewhat afraid of America. I do not believe that the United States would invade present-day China." [188] And as if appealing to the United States to go no further than her present level of involvement in the war, official Chinese spokesmen continued to reiterate through the end of 1965 and into 1966 that China would not attack unless her territory were directly invaded or the existence of the Hanoi regime were threatened.

On the very day that Lin Piao articulated Mao's position on the war, however, Chief of Staff Lo Jui-ch'ing gave a public statement on the Viet-Nam situation—in the presence of Liu Shao-ch'i and Teng Hsiao-p'ing—which contradicted the Mao-Lin analysis by continuing to stress the danger of a war with the United States and the necessity of relying upon the strength of the "socialist camp" and Soviet nuclear weapons as a deterrent to an American attack.[189]

Punctuating Lo's assertion of the dangers of a Sino-American

---

to divert attention from their efforts to stage an anti-Mao and Lin *coup* and to involve the PLA in matters of national defense rather than Maoist politics. (*See* "The February Coup," *Chan Pao* [April 17, 1967], and as noted in Franz Schurmann, *Ideology and Organization in Communist China*, p. 555.)

188. These remarks were given wide circulation by Communist publications in Eastern Europe. Cited here from Donald S. Zagoria, "The Strategic Debate in Peking," in Tang Tsou, ed., *China in Crisis*, Vol. II, p. 267.

189. *See* Uri Ra'anan, "Peking's Foreign Policy 'Debate,' 1965–1966," in *ibid.*, Vol. II, pp. 54–56.

war were two clashes between Communist and Nationalist shore patrol craft, first on August 6th and again on November 14th. During the Cultural Revolution, criticism of Lo Jui-ch'ing in a Red Guard publication implied that the Deputy Defense Minister was responsible for provoking these clashes, perhaps as a way of mobilizing support for his assertion of the need for war preparedness against the United States:

> On a certain date in 196x, without consulting Chairman Mao, the Party Central Committee and the Military Commission, Lo Jui-ch'ing acted on his own by giving instructions to the Foochow Military District to the effect that in future sea battles the military region might "actively attack the enemy on its own initiative" according to the situation, and "in order not to lose the initiative in battle, it may go into battle and file a report at the same time." In many other important affairs, Lo Jui-ch'ing often took reckless action without asking the Military Commission for instructions.[190]

Given his public contention with Lin Piao on September 3rd, and this veiled charge of having instituted "active defense" in contravention of Mao's authority, it seems likely that Lo's fall from power after his last public appearance on November 26th was related in some manner to insubordination in matters of defense policy.[191]

That the Viet-Nam issue continued to divide the leadership into 1966—and may have given Mao grounds for taking action against his opponents—is suggested by the final political hours of P'eng Chen and Liu Shao-ch'i. P'eng's last month of public activity, March 1966, was spent in constant contact with a Japanese Communist Party delegation which arrived in Peking on March 3rd for a first round of talks. It went to Korea, and then returned to Peking for further discussions, expanded to include a top-ranking North Vietnamese political delegation which was also in the Chinese capital, between the 22nd and the 30th. P'eng was last seen in public on the 30th, sending off the Japanese group. Subsequent dip-

190. "Counter-Revolutionary Revisionist Lo Jui-ch'ing Is Loaded with Crimes," *Chan Pao* (January 30, 1967).

191. It may be significant that Lo's last appearance was at a reception for the naval men responsible for sinking a Nationalist patrol vessel in the November 14th clash. (*See* "Premier Chou En-lai Receives Naval Men," NCNA [Shanghai], [November 26, 1965]; in *SCMP,* No. 3588 [December 1, 1965], p. 22.)

A Cultural Revolution pamphlet asserts that "Comrade Lin Piao decisively exposed Lo Jui-ch'ing's plot to oppose the Party and usurp power in the army at the Shanghai Conference held in December 1965." (*Chairman Mao's Successor—Deputy Supreme Commander Lin Piao,* trans. in *Current Background,* No. 894 [October 27, 1969], p. 22.)

lomatic reports that these discussions may have attempted to work out a compromise formula for "united action" on the war which Mao angrily rejected suggest that the precipitating event in P'eng's fall may have been his "switching sides" on the issues of opposition to the Soviets and Chinese aloofness from the Viet-Nam situation.[192]

Liu Shao-ch'i's last political initiative was a government statement issued during a massive Peking rally in support of Viet-Nam on July 22nd. In language which had not been used in official Chinese statements on the war for over a year, Liu reasserted "proletarian internationalism" as the supreme principle of China's foreign policy, and the importance of condemning "national chauvinism and national egoism which betray the interests of the revolutionary people of the world."[193] He asserted that "the Chinese people are

192. The exact position which P'eng Chen took in these talks, however, remains uncertain. An account of the talks released by the Japanese Communist Party through its journal *Akahata* on January 24, 1967, only adds to the uncertainty about the positions of various Chinese leaders on foreign policy issues.

A further political element in P'eng Chen's fall, as well as that of Lo Jui-ch'ing, may have been responsibility for Chinese policy related to the "September 30" *coup* attempt, and subsequent anti-Communist suppression, in Indonesia in the autumn of 1965. Both men had been actively involved in China's relations with the Sukarno government. There is indirect evidence that Mao may have opposed the policy promoted by Liu and others of working through the "bourgeois-nationalist" Sukarno government. He appears to have favored the Indonesian Communist Party taking power by building its own armed mass base of popular support.

For obvious reasons of national security, the exact manner in which Viet-Nam policy, Sino-Soviet relations, and the Indonesian affair may relate to the fall of Lo, P'eng, and Liu, and other Party leaders, has not been disclosed through Cultural Revolution documents. The interpretation advanced here remains inferential and tentative. It should be emphasized, however, that while these foreign affairs issues may have been important, or precipitating, elements in the leadership conflict, the domestic policy disputes of the preceding decade had established the basic context for the Cultural Revolution.

193. "Chairman Liu Shao-ch'i Issues Statement in Support of President Ho Chi Minh's Appeal," NCNA [Peking, July 22, 1966]; in *SCMP*, No. 3747 (July 27, 1966), p. 27.

A revealing and contrasting Chinese policy statement on the Viet-Nam situation is a *People's Daily* editorial of February 15, 1966 which asserts that "The South Vietnamese people are sure to win and the U.S. aggressor forces and their lackeys will certainly lose. This is now a foregone conclusion." With such an evaluation of the war, China obviously had no need to "undertake the greatest national sacrifices" or to make preparations for direct action, as Liu implied needed to be done in July. (*See* "*People's Daily* Celebrates South Vietnamese Liberation Forces' Anniversary," NCNA [Peking, February 15, 1966]; in *SCMP*, No. 3641 [February 18, 1966], p. 32.)

ready to undertake the greatest national sacrifices" in aid of the Vietnamese, that China was "the reliable rear area of the Vietnamese people," and that "the Chinese people have made up their minds and have made every preparation to take . . . actions at any time and in any place that the Chinese and Vietnamese people deem necessary." [194]

Four days after this statement was issued, Mao publicly reasserted his authority over Chinese political life. The "golden monkey" was not to have his "massive cudgel," the People's Liberation Army, pulled from his hands. It was to be his weapon in the imminent battle with "freaks and monsters."

THE POLITICS OF LUAN

In the last analysis, all the truths of Marxism can be summed up in one sentence: "To rebel is justified."

MAO TSE-TUNG, 1939, 1966[195]

Trust the masses, rely on them and respect their initiative. Cast out fear. Don't be afraid of disorder (*luan-tzu*).

CENTRAL COMMITTEE DECISION ON THE GREAT
PROLETARIAN CULTURAL REVOLUTION, August 8, 1966[196]

I feared confusion (*luan*) and extensive democracy. I feared the rising up of the masses and their rebelling against us.

LIU SHAO-CH'I, 1967[197]

Revolution means rebellion, and rebellion is the soul of the thought of Mao Tse-tung. . . . We want to wield the massive cudgel [of the thought of Mao Tse-tung], express our spirit, invoke our magic influence and turn the old world upside-down, smash things into chaos, into smithereens, smash things *luan-luan-ti*, the more *luan* the better!

STUDENT RED GUARDS OF PEKING, June 1966[198]

194. The communiqué of the Eleventh Plenum, issued on August 12th, reaffirmed the correctness of Lin Piao's analysis, "Long Live the Victory of People's War," obviously a repudiation of the Liu statement.

195. Cited in the *People's Daily* editorial, "It Is Fine!" (August 23, 1966). Mao had first invoked this phrase in 1939, at a celebration in Yenan marking Stalin's sixtieth birthday.

196. "Decision of the Central Committee of the Chinese Communist Party Concerning the Great Proletarian Cultural Revolution" (August 8, 1966); in *CCP Documents of the Great Proletarian Cultural Revolution, 1966–1967*, p. 45.

197. "The Confession of Liu Shao-ch'i" (October 23, 1966), *Atlas* (April 1967), p. 17.

198. Red Guards of Tsinghua Middle School, Peking, "Long Live the Revolutionary Rebel Spirit of the Proletariat" (June 24, 1966), in *Red Flag*, No. 11 (August 21, 1966), p. 27.

The year 1966 began in China as one would expect for a country "building socialism." The *People's Daily* January 1st editorial bore the businesslike title "Usher in 1966, the First Year of China's Third Five-Year Plan." It stated that the continuing campaign for Socialist Education would help to establish the conditions for increasing agricultural output and strengthen the foundation for China's continued industrial development.[199]

A few days later the paper of P'eng Chen's Peking Municipal Party Committee published an editorial on Party building. The editorial stressed the need to expand membership in order to strengthen Party leadership in "first-line basic-level" organizations for the tasks of economic construction set by the new Five-Year Plan.[200] Perhaps the one note of testiness in this otherwise "business-as-usual" expression of policy was the assertion that in recruiting Party members

> we should not impose additional conditions that depart from the established standards specified in the Party Constitution. Rather, we should accept new members strictly according to the provisions laid down in the Party Constitution.[201]

The Party Constitution of 1956 contained no reference to the "thought of Mao Tse-tung"; neither did the editorial.

By the summer of 1966 this air of routine had been shattered by "The Great Proletarian Cultural Revolution." P'eng Chen had disappeared from political view, and his Peking Party Committee and its paper the *Peking Daily* and magazine *Front Line* had been reorganized. High-school and university students of Peking, wearing the red armbands of "Red Guard" units, surged through the capital streets searching for manifestations of "the four olds" and dragging out "freaks and monsters" for public denunciation. In early August a Party Central Committee Plenum, packed with representatives of the new Red Guard organizations, approved a restructuring of the Party leadership that demoted Vice-Chairman Liu Shao-ch'i and affirmed Lin Piao as Chairman Mao's "closest comrade in arms." Even greater reorganization and disorganization followed.

How much of the momentous political conflict that exploded in 1966 had Mao anticipated, or planned? How spontaneous were the

199. *People's Daily* editorial, "Usher in 1966, the First Year of China's Third Five-Year Plan" (January 1, 1966); trans. in *SCMP,* No. 3610 (January 5, 1966), p. 10.
200. *Peking Daily* editorial, "Seriously and Successfully Expanding Party Membership Is an Important Task of Party Organizations" (January 8, 1966); trans. in *SCMP,* No. 3661 (March 21, 1966), p. 1.
201. *Ibid.,* p. 3.

student uprisings? At a leadership work conference in late October, Mao discussed the great changes of the spring and summer months:

> It was I who started the fire. . . . As I see it, shocking people (*ch'ung-yi-hsia*) has its good points. For many years I thought about how to administer [the Party] a shock, and finally conceived [this shock of the Cultural Revolution].[202]

Mao's imagery was telling. His phrase "to shock" (which used the character *ch'ung* with the two-stroke ice radical) implied shock in the way that an individual would react to having a bucket of ice water thrown on him. The man who from youth had seen discipline developed through swimming in icy rivers, who had spent more than a decade trying to find a way to discipline the Party organization, finally decided to rebel against it.[203] In July of 1966, as he moved to reassert his control over China's political life, Mao swam in the Yangtze, and appealed to China's younger generation to relive with him his own rebellion by "following Chairman Mao and advancing in the teeth of great storms and waves." [204] Thus Mao's career came full circle, as his earliest symbol of rebellion against paternal authority was reenacted in an attack on Party authorities.

The events of 1966 replay, in short compass and great intensity, the major themes of policy conflict and personal political style which have been explored throughout this study. Mao was reliving his lifelong conflict with the "bourgeois intellectuals" and his opposition to a system of authority which expected people to be "docile tools." Yet he was also trying to find a way to pass on his own political experience to a new generation through a ritualized "class struggle," so that his unfinished life struggle against the "four olds" of China's cultural heritage would not die with his passing.

The Cultural Revolution, in its initial conception, was a massive ritual of initiation. It was an attempt to institutionalize "class conflict" so as to temper a younger generation untested in political combat. And through the struggle of the young people, those long-time leaders who Mao felt had substituted "revisionism" for revolution, routine for "remolding," were to be removed from positions of Party authority.

The drama of the Cultural Revolution raises as many questions as it answers. Did Mao see how far the conflict would go? Did he consciously plan to oust long-time comrades in revolution from their leading posts in the Party and state? As a general interpretive

202. Mao, "Talk at a Central Work Conference" (October 25, 1966), in *Long Live the Thought of Mao Tse-tung!* pp. 41–42.

203. *See* p. 178 above.

204. *See* the *People's Daily* editorial, "Follow Chairman Mao and Advance in the Teeth of Great Storms and Waves" (July 26, 1966).

人民日报

"我们敬爱的领袖毛主席这样健康，这是全中国人民的最大幸福！是全世界革命人民的最大幸福！"

毛主席畅游长江

毛主席乘风破浪畅游长江

毛主席在快艇甲板上检阅正在同江水搏斗的游泳大军。（本报记者摄）

十四日电 我们伟大的领袖……七月十六日，再一次乘风破……万里，长江两岸万众欢腾……主席曾经三次在武汉横渡长江……诗篇《水调歌头·游泳》，十年……大江中遨游，历时一时零五……不管风吹浪打，胜似闲庭信步多……

们的心。人们想着，是毛主席为我们在长江上开劈了平坦大道，今天，毛主席又是怎样来看我们横渡长江，那末多行？

毛主席是我们心中的红太阳，毛主席永远和我们在一起。……在比赛渤湘开始的一刹那，这时，不知是游泳健儿中的哪一个，第一眼看见了快艇上的毛主席，立即情不自禁地高呼："毛主席来了！毛主席万岁！"紧接着……

"CHAIRMAN MAO JOYOUSLY SWIMS IN THE YANGTZE."

From Jen-min Jih-pao, *July 25, 1966.*

guideline we would suggest that Mao knew very well the policy changes he wanted to bring about, and that from years of daily contact and conflict, he knew the leadership styles and points of opposition of other leaders. His approach seems to have been to press once more for long-advocated changes in China's educational system, in Party propaganda work, and in rectification, but now to press to the end. If high Party leaders continued to resist his plans—as they had in the past—this time they would be removed from positions of influence.

Backed by the PLA, the Chairman was trying to make certain that his conception of a new China, his "thought" and life-experience, would prevail in the continuing struggle with the old way of life.

The escalation of this conflict into the full-blown Red Guard rebellion of the summer carries certain remarkable echoes of the events of the "blooming and contending" of 1957 and the Lushan Plenum. The beginning of this process was a working conference of the Party leadership held in September and October of 1965— just after Mao and Lin had published their position on China's relation to the Viet-Nam War. At this meeting Mao raised the issue of continuing criticism of his dismissal of P'eng Teh-huai by "giving instructions" that Wu Han, author of *The Dismissal of Hai Jui,* be attacked for his political errors in opposing the Lushan judgment and the Great Leap Forward.[205]

Mao was now forcing those Party leaders, particularly P'eng Chen, who had supported the veiled criticism of the intellectuals either to admit their own political error and repudiate the critics, or themselves become the objects of attack. By all evidence, P'eng Chen and others continued to resist this pressure.

On November 10, 1965 an article "On the New Historical Play *The Dismissal of Hai Jui*" appeared in the Shanghai paper *Wen Hui Pao.* The author of this public criticism of Wu Han for his political error of "making veiled criticism of contemporary people with ancient people" was Yao Wen-yuan. In 1957 Yao had been Mao's public spokesman for a *People's Daily* attack on the *Wen Hui Pao* for its publication of "bourgeois rightist" criticism of Party rule.[206] In 1965, however, Mao had few political supporters in the Party and capital city. The *People's Daily* and the papers of the Peking Party Committee initially refused to publish this attack. As Mao later told Party leaders:

205. *See* "Circular of the Central Committee of the Chinese Communist Party" (May 16, 1966), in *CCP Documents of the Great Proletarian Cultural Revolution,* p. 20.
206. *See* p. 319 above.

Nothing could be done about either Peking or the Center. In September and October of last year [1965] it was asked: If revisionism emerged at the Center, what would the local [Party organizations] do about it? At that time I thought that my suggestions could not be implemented in Peking. Why was the criticism of Wu Han started not in Peking but in Shanghai? Because Peking had no people who would do it.[207]

The Chairman was isolated by the Party leadership at "the Center."

Yao's article was published by the *People's Daily*, apparently after arm-twisting, on November 30th; but the editor's note prefacing the attack on Wu Han stressed that the matter at issue was an academic question of "how to deal with historical characters and plays." [208] Pointed quotes from Mao were invoked: "Our regime is a people's democratic regime which provides advantageous circumstances for writing for the people"; "Our guideline is that both the freedom of criticism and the freedom of countercriticism should be allowed. In regard to erroneous views, we also adopt the methods of reasoning and seeking truth from facts to convince people with reason."

Ten days after this effort to negate the political relevance of the Wu Han play the *Peking Daily* published a defense of the author and his work entitled, *"The Dismissal of Hai Jui* Is a Good Play." [209]

Mao, however, continued to press for politicization of the criticism, to raise this issue to one of political "principle" and personal loyalty. At a meeting of the leadership in Shanghai on December 21, the Chairman stressed: "The crux [of the play is] the question of dismissal from office. . . . In 1959 we dismissed P'eng Teh-huai from office. And P'eng Teh-huai is 'Hai Jui' too." [210]

On December 30th Wu Han published a self-criticism for his political errors in the play; but he avoided the issue of "dismissal from office," and asserted that he was not "beyond remedy" for his mistakes.[211]

Thus by the end of 1965 the issues had been raised and the lines

207. Mao, "Talk at a Central Work Conference" (October 25, 1966), in *Long Live the Thought of Mao Tse-tung!* pp. 40–41.

208. *People's Daily* editor's note to the article by Yao Wen-yuan, "On the New Historical Play *The Dismissal of Hai Jui*" (November 30, 1965); trans. in *Current Background*, No. 783 (March 21, 1966), p. 1.

209. *See* the *Peking Daily* article by Li Chen-yü translated in *SCMP*, No. 3669 (March 31, 1966), pp. 1–5.

210. *Red Flag* editorial, "Two Diametrically Opposed Documents," No. 9 (May 27, 1967); trans. in *SCMM*, No. 581 (June 26, 1967), pp. 11–12.

211. Wu Han, "Self-Criticism on *The Dismissal of Hai Jui*," *People's Daily* (December 30, 1965); trans. in *Current Background*, No. 783 (March 21, 1966), pp. 28–51.

of conflict which had been established in 1964 were redrawn. The struggle intensified throughout 1966, with Mao ever more directly intruding the authority of the PLA into remaining areas of Party defense.

During the last days of 1965 the Army convened another conference on political work which continued until January 18th. It may have been at this conference that the case of Lo Jui-ch'ing was formally dealt with. His name was not among the conference participants; and the fact that the Deputy Chief of the General Staff, Yang Ch'eng-wu, delivered a speech was the first public hint that Lo was no longer politically active. Furthermore, excerpts of a speech by Hsiao Hua, Director of the Army's General Political Department, published on January 24th, included telling criticisms that whereas "some people say 'Military affairs are politics,' . . . such views are absolutely wrong"; and "One must fight for the military authority of the Party, for the military authority of the people, and not for individual military authority." [212]

This conference apparently represented the consolidation of control over the PLA by the Mao-Lin forces; the final politicization of the Army for the domestic confrontation. Hsiao Hua's speech stressed that a five-point principle put forward by Lin Piao in late November of 1965 on the matter of "bringing politics to the fore" had been adopted by the conference as the guideline for its work in 1966.

With the Army thus oriented, and with a major opponent of Mao's policies removed from influence within the PLA, political pressures were not long in coming. As in 1957, a low-key Party rectification campaign was launched in early February with the propagation of a new model in the study of "the thought of Mao Tse-tung"—the county Party secretary Chiao Yü-lu.[213] And on February 2nd, PLA influence in intellectual matters was heightened

212. Hsiao Hua, "Hold High the Great Red Banner of the Thought of Mao Tse-tung and Resolutely Implement the 5-Point Principle of Bringing Politics to the Fore" (Extracts), NCNA (January 24, 1966); trans. in *SCMP*, No. 3627 (January 31, 1966), pp. 6–20.

Following his detention, Lo Jui-ch'ing evidently was investigated and interrogated for more than two months. On March 12 he completed a self-examination; and on the 18th he attempted to commit suicide by jumping from the upper floors of the building in which he was detained. (*See* "Comment of the CCP Central Committee on the Transmission of the Report of the Work Group of the Central Committee Concerning the Problem of Lo Jui-ch'ing's Mistakes" [May 16, 1966], in *CCP Documents of the Great Proletarian Cultural Revolution*, pp. 31–32.)

213. *See* the *People's Daily* editorial, "Carry on the Study in the Spirit of Rectification" (February 14, 1966); trans. in *SCMP*, No. 3645 (February 25, 1966), pp. 10–13.

with a "Forum on the Work in Literature and Art in the Armed Forces" convened in Shanghai. Chiang Ch'ing directed the work of the conference.[214]

This meeting appears to have been part of the increasingly direct challenge to P'eng Chen. Its work on artistic matters proceeded at the same time that P'eng, head of a "group of five" which since late 1964 had been deputized by the Party leadership to direct the work of a "Cultural Revolution," [215] was preparing a report on guidelines for implementing Mao's Tenth Plenum call for "class struggle" against revisionism within the intellectual community.[216]

Public expression of the increasing political pressure being exerted by the Army was contained in a remarkable series of *Liberation Army Daily* editorials which received nationwide publicity through their republication in the *People's Daily* beginning on February 4th. The very title of the first editorial, "Forever Bring Politics to the Fore," was a clear indication of the way in which Mao was trying to "push" the Party organization through PLA activities. The second editorial stressed that everyone was going to be forced to take a stand in the intensifying "class struggle," that "sectarian" interests were a dangerous expression of "individualism," and that people would have to choose between their own immediate interests and some undefined "common good." (". . . this turbulent conflict [between "the common good" and "self-interest"] will suck everyone into its vortex. There is no escape.")[217]

The third editorial appeared to be a refutation of continuing pressures to divert the Army into a more active defense role in relation to the Viet-Nam War. It stressed that ideological preparation was the most fundamental basis of war-preparedness. Apparently responding to those who continued to press for "united action" with the Soviets, or acceptance of a negotiated understanding with the United States on the limits of the war, it asked incredulously: "Can it be that we should bend our knees and surrender to the imperialists as the modern revisionists have done? . . . Oh no! We say no

214. *See* "Summary of the Forum on the Work in Literature and Art in the Armed Forces with Which Comrade Lin Piao Entrusted Comrade Chiang Ch'ing," in *Peking Review*, No. 23 (June 2, 1967), p. 10.

215. Cultural Revolution material which indicates that P'eng Chen had been placed in charge of the "group of five" probably as early as the latter half of 1964 is discussed in Chung and Miller, *Madame Mao*, p. 127.

216. Mao's use of the Army conference to pressure P'eng is asserted in the *Red Flag* editorial, "Two Diametrically Opposed Documents," No. 9 (May 27, 1967); trans. in *SCMM*, No. 581 (June 26, 1967), p. 10.

217. *Liberation Army Daily* editorial, "Promoting Civic-Mindedness: Again on Bringing Politics to the Fore" (as republished in the Peking *Ta Kung Pao*, February 10, 1966); trans. in *SCMP*, No. 3645 (February 25, 1966), p. 2.

a thousand times, ten thousand times." "We shall not succumb to panic." [218]

The fifth editorial in the series was an uncompromising assertion of Mao's personal authority in China's political life. It directly stated that "the thought of Mao Tse-tung is the peak of contemporary Marxism-Leninism," that Mao's writings were "the highest directive for all our work," and that "the thought of Mao Tse-tung alone is our invincible banner." [219]

Finally, the eighth and last editorial of April 5th threw down the gauntlet to P'eng Chen. It cited Mao's words that "leadership by a Party committee is collective leadership, not personal dictatorship by the first secretary." [220] A further quote from Mao all but directly called on P'eng, the first secretary of the Peking Municipal Party Committee, to accept his responsibilities for having shielded the critics of the early 1960s, Wu Han and Teng T'o:

> When a man assumes the post of first secretary, he must also assume responsibility for any shortcomings or errors in the work of his committee. All those who refuse to assume, or who are afraid of assuming responsibility, who will not allow others to speak, and who, like the tiger's backside, cannot be touched, will fail.[221]

Mao was about to grab the "tiger" P'eng Chen by his "tail," and to do it in true Maoist style. One of the series of *Liberation Army Daily* editorials had asserted:

> If we are mentally lazy, do not seek progress, rely on our "rich store of experience," have blind faith in foreign rules, and are so afraid of being hurt and embarrassed that we will not take off our pants and have our tails removed, our mind will not be properly reformed and the thought of Mao Tse-tung will not take root in our heads.[222]

By year's end P'eng and other Party leaders who proved to be too "embarrassed" to have their "tails" exposed through voluntary confession were to be dragged out in isolation before the masses to have their disloyalty to the "thought of Mao Tse-tung" publicly exposed.

218. *Liberation Army Daily* editorial, "The Most Important and Fundamental War Preparation" (from extracts published by NCNA on February 14, 1966); trans. in *SCMP*, No. 3641 (February 18, 1966), pp. 14, 15.

219. *Liberation Army Daily* editorial, "Regard Chairman Mao's Books as the Highest Directive for All Work Throughout the PLA," NCNA (March 2, 1966); trans. in *SCMP*, No. 3652 (March 8, 1966), p. 2.

220. *Liberation Army Daily* editorial, "The Key Lies in Leadership by the Party Committee," NCNA (April 5, 1966); trans. in *SCMP*, No. 3676 (April 13, 1966), p. 8.

221. *Ibid.*

222. *Liberation Army Daily* editorial, "Regard Chairman Mao's Works as the Highest Directive for all Work Throughout the PLA," p. 5.

PLA cadres jeering at dunce-capped
Party "revisionists" as they are paraded through the streets of Peking
during the Great Proletarian Cultural Revolution, 1966.
United Press International.

P'eng Chen made his last public appearance on March 30th; and the month of April saw a rapid escalation in the political confrontation. P'eng's absence from the meeting of the Standing Committee of the National People's Congress on April 14th was contrasted with a report by the Vice Minister of Culture Shih Hsi-min entitled, "Raise High the Great Red Banner of Mao Tse-tung's Thought, Carry the Socialist Cultural Revolution through to the End." At the same meeting Mao's friend among the intellectuals, Kuo Mo-jo, made a self-abasing speech in which he asserted that all he had written in the past should "be burned to ashes, for it has not the slightest value." [223] If a friend of the Chairman would make such a public self-criticism, what would others be expected to do?

The answer was not long in coming. On April 16th New China News Agency released an article carried by the major national and provincial papers in which the publications of the Peking Party Committee attacked by name "anti-Party" elements Wu Han and Teng T'o for their critical writings of the early 1960s.[224]

These developments took place in the absence of Liu Shao-ch'i and Foreign Minister Ch'en Yi. The two had left the country on March 26 on a curious diplomatic expedition of more than three weeks that took them to countries on China's western and southern borders—Pakistan, Afghanistan, and Burma. During the month of April they returned twice to China's western provinces for stops lasting several days before continuing on to new destinations in Afghanistan and then Burma. Whether this extended diplomatic absence was a convenient way for Liu to disassociate himself from the purge of P'eng Chen—which apparently occurred at the end of the first week of April [225]—or whether the Mao-Lin forces took advantage of the trip for their own purposes, is not known.

223. Kuo Mo-jo, "Learn from the Masses of Workers, Peasants and Soldiers and Serve Them," *Kuang-ming Daily* (April 28, 1966); trans. in *SCMP*, No. 3691 (May 5, 1966), p. 7.

224. *Notes on Sanchia Village* and *Night Causerie at Yenshan* Criticized by *Ch'ien Hsien* and *Peking Daily:* Works by Wu Han, Liao Mo-sha and Teng T'o Are Representative of an Undercurrent against the Party and Socialism" (April 16, 1966); trans. in *SCMP*, No. 3686 (April 28, 1966), pp. 1–3.

225. According to one Cultural Revolution report of the circumstances surrounding P'eng's fall, Chou En-lai convened a meeting of the Secretariat of the Party Central Committee between April 9 to 12 so that K'ang Sheng could "convey Chairman Mao's instructions to the meeting and make a systematic critical review of the many crimes committed by P'eng Chen in the Cultural Revolution." Mao himself is said to have convened an expanded meeting of the Politbureau's Standing Committee on April 16 "to deliberate on the question of P'eng Chen's anti-Party activities." This indicates that

Conflicting political signals continued to be evident in the national press during this time. In late March *Red Flag* published an article commemorating the ninety-fifth anniversary of the Paris Commune, describing it as a "great lesson" in how to seize the machinery of state by way of a mass uprising and establish "proletarian dictatorship" through revolutionary violence.[226] In retrospect, this commemorative article is a remarkable blueprint—by historical analogy—of political events which were to unfold in China beginning in late May.

Early in April, however, the *People's Daily* initiated an interpretive series of articles on "bringing politics to the fore" which appears to represent a last-ditch effort by the Party organization to reply to the nearly concluded *Liberation Army Daily* series on this same subject. The first article by the Party paper tried to emphasize the fundamental importance for China of economic development ("Economy is the foundation and politics is the concentrated expression of economy." "Politics is in the service of the economic base."[227]) It stated that elimination of the social distinctions between town and countryside, workers and peasants, and mental and manual labor was a process that necessarily was gradual, but was being carried out on the basis of existing Party policies.

The second article in the series was a defensive assertion that the Party *was* putting politics to the fore, even while it stressed the concomitant necessity of developing technical skills for "socialist construction." ("Redness must lead expertness, but Redness and expertness must be achieved at the same time."[228]) The third article made a valiant attempt to express deference to Mao even as it contradicted Lin Piao's assertion that the "thought of Mao Tse-tung" was the "peak" of contemporary Marxism: "Comrade Mao Tse-tung has made great contributions to enriching and developing the philosophy and economics of Marxism-Leninism . . ."; "Under the leadership of the Central Committee of the Chinese Communist Party headed by Comrade Mao Tse-tung, the Chinese people are

P'eng was "detained" some time between the 1st of April and the 9th. The pamphlet notes that April 5 was "the eve" of P'eng's collapse. (*See* "Preparation, Release, and Collapse of the Counter-Revolutionary 'February Outline Report,' " *Chingkangshan* [Peking], May 27, 1967.)

226. *See* Cheng Chih-szu, "The Great Lessons of the Paris Commune," *Red Flag*, No. 4 (March 24, 1966), pp. 4–18.

227. *People's Daily* editorial, "Placing Politics in a Prominent Position Is the Root of All Work: On Bringing Politics to the Fore, I" (April 6, 1966)· trans. in *SCMP*, No. 3680 (April 19, 1966), p. 2.

228. *People's Daily* editorial, "Politics Commands Functional Work: On Bringing Politics to the Fore, II" (April 14, 1966); trans. in *SCMP*, No. 3682 (April 22, 1966), p. 5.

holding aloft the banner of Marxism-Leninism . . ." [229]—not the "banner of the thought of Mao Tse-tung."

This continuing Party effort to counterpose Marxism-Leninism against Mao's "thought" was cut short by a *Liberation Army Daily* editorial signaling direct Army intervention into domestic politics. It asserted that the Army "has consistently played a vital role in the proletarian revolutionary cause and will also play an important part in the great socialist cultural revolution." [230] It reiterated that Mao's "thought" was the "highest peak" of contemporary Marxism, and that Mao's writings "will be useful for a long time." It stressed that the Army must rid itself of the influence of the "black line" on the cultural front (a reference to the recently commenced public attacks on P'eng Chen's subordinates Teng T'o and Wu Han) and that "after this black line has been eliminated, there will still be another black line in the future and further struggle will be inevitable."

Finally, anticipating developments of the early summer, the editorial asserted:

> There has been an upsurge in the great socialist cultural revolution and a mass movement is rising in this revolution. The great revolutionary waves will wash away all the filth of the bourgeois trends in art and literature and open up a new epoch of socialist proletarian art and literature. . . . Something must be destroyed and something must be set up in the course of the socialist cultural revolution. Without destruction there can be no construction.

Liu Shao-ch'i returned to Peking sometime after April 19th to a radically altered political scene. Lo Jui-ch'ing, P'eng Chen, and Director of Propaganda Lu Ting-yi had been politically neutralized.[231] Liu's own isolation seemed emphasized by the fact that there was no official reception committee to welcome him at Peking Airport on his return from the diplomatic mission. It appears that Mao was now implementing his assertion of mid-1964 that, "It is essential to test and know cadres and choose and train successors in the long course of mass struggle."

229. *People's Daily* editorial, "To Put Politics in the Forefront It Is Necessary to Put the Thought of Mao Tse-tung Firmly in Command: On Bringing Politics to the Fore, III" (April 22, 1966); trans. in *SCMP,* No. 3688 (May 2, 1966), pp. 2–3.

230. *Liberation Army Daily* editorial, "Hold High the Great Red Banner of the Thought of Mao Tse-tung and Take an Active Part in the Great Socialist Cultural Revolution" (as reprinted in the *People's Daily* on April 19, 1966); trans. in *SCMP,* No. 3687 (April 29, 1966), pp. 5–13.

231. It appears from a Cultural Revolution pamphlet that Lu Ting-yi was not actually detained until the end of April. (*See* "Preparation, Release, and Collapse of the Counter-Revolutionary 'February Outline Report,' " *Chingkangshan,* May 27, 1967.)

The "test" for Liu and Party Secretary-General Teng Hsiao-p'ing was their handling of the Cultural Revolution in the schools of Peking during the late spring and summer months. In mid-May a Central Committee document was circulated throughout the Party organization officially removing P'eng Chen from his position as head of the "group of five" in charge of the Cultural Revolution. The remarkable thing about this circular is the warning it contained to Liu Shao-ch'i that the manner in which he implemented the work of the Cultural Revolution would be the test of his political future:

> Above all, we must not entrust [representatives of the bourgeoisie who have sneaked into the Party] with the work of leading the Cultural Revolution. In fact many of them have done and *are still doing such work,* and this is extremely dangerous. . . . *Some are still trusted by us and are being trained as our successors, Khrushchev-type persons, for example, who are still nestling beside us.* Party committees at all levels must pay full attention to this matter.[232]

A *Red Flag* and *People's Daily* editorial commemorating the first anniversary of this document observed, "The Circular unmasked the P'eng Chen counterrevolutionary revisionist clique. . . . This forced a break in the counterrevolutionary revisionist front headed by the Khrushchev of China, and threw it into confusion (*luan-le hsien-chiao*)." [233]

In essence what Mao was doing was forcing an isolated Liu Shao-ch'i to make a Hobson's Choice: Either he must genuinely "mobilize the masses"—who would criticize him for his past errors against "the thought of Mao Tse-tung," even though he might sustain his political life through an expression of submission to Mao—or continue to play the "revisionist" game and thus suffer the fate of P'eng Chen and Lu Ting-yi. It was a choice which Mao was to force on the entire Party organization. As he told a meeting of Central Committee leaders in mid-July of 1966, when Liu and Teng had failed their "test":

> When you are told to set a fire to burn yourselves, will you do it? After all, you yourselves will be burned. . . . It won't do just to sit in an office and listen to reports. We should rely on and have faith in the masses, and make trouble to the end. Be prepared for the revolution to come down on your own heads. Leaders of the Party and the

232. "Circular of the Central Committee of the Communist Party of China" (May 16, 1966); trans. in *SCMP,* No. 3942 (May 19, 1967), p. 5. Emphasis added.

233. *Red Flag* and *People's Daily* joint editorial, "A Great Historic Document" (May 16, 1967); trans. in *SCMM,* No. 578 (June 5, 1967), p. 6.

government and responsible comrades of the Party must all be prepared.[234]

With the orientation of the confrontation sharpened by the May 16th Circular, and with the national press in Maoist hands,[235] the Chairman retired to his customary retreat near Hangchow to watch the course of events.[236]

As viewed through the national press, the unfolding of the mass struggle phase of the Cultural Revolution, marked by the formation of the first Red Guard units in Peking schools in late May,[237] carried with it all the tension and drama of the early revolutionary years. In a remarkable series of editorials beginning on June 1, the *People's Daily* invoked all the symbols of the revolution for a new student generation. The editorial "Sweep Away All Freaks and Monsters" was a powerful echo of Mao's "Hunan Report":

> With the tremendous and impetuous force of a raging storm, [the revolutionary masses] have smashed the shackles imposed on their minds by the exploiting classes for so long in the past, routing the bourgeois "specialists," "scholars," "authorities," and "venerable masters" and sweeping every bit of their prestige into the dust.[238]

234. Mao, "Talk to Central Committee Leaders" (July 21, 1966), in *Long Live the Thought of Mao Tse-tung!* p. 37.

235. In a speech of early 1967 Mao revealed that the series of *People's Daily* editorials which began on June 1, 1966 to "prepare public opinion" for the Cultural Revolution had been published only after a Maoist faction had "seized power" from the Party-dominated editorial board of the paper. *See* Mao, "Speech at a Meeting of the Cultural Revolution Group of the Central Committee" (January 9, 1967), in an untitled collection of statements by Mao Tse-tung, trans. in *Current Background*, No. 892 (October 21, 1969), p. 47.

236. Mao had been conspicuous by his political absence since the fall of 1965, stimulating rumors that he was seriously ill. After attending a series of receptions for foreign visitors which concluded on November 26, 1965, Mao's presence was not reported in the national press until May 11, 1966, when he received an Albanian delegation at his Hangchow retreat. After more than two further months of public silence, Mao returned to Peking (on July 18th) to launch the Cultural Revolution, as was publicized on July 25th through the reporting of his swim in the Yangtze nine days before.

237. In a description of the evolution of the Red Guard movement designed for foreign audiences, Mao's American friend Anna Louise Strong revealed that the first Red Guard unit had been formed "under cover" at the middle school attached to Peking's Tsinghua University in "late May" of 1966. This student organization came into the open on June 6th, after the Peking Municipal Party Committee had been reorganized and the Maoists had reasserted control over the *People's Daily*. (*See* Anna Louise Strong, *Letters from China*, No. 41 [September 20, 1966].)

238. *People's Daily* editorial, "Sweep Away All Freaks and Monsters" (June 1, 1966); trans. in *SCMP*, No. 3712 (June 6, 1966), p. 2.

The "storm" of this new political struggle was to be an assault on the "four olds" (*szu-chiu*) of China's traditional culture, thinking, customs, and habits as they endured in the minds of a quarter of mankind. The meaning of Marxism, in Mao's words, was reduced to the battle-cry: "To rebel is justified." [239] As the *People's Daily* asserted, "This great task of transforming customs and habits is without any precedent in human history." [240] Mao was calling on seven hundred million Chinese to be "critics of the old world." [241]

All of Mao's hatred of the intellectuals spewed forth in the editorial "Tear Aside the Bourgeois Mask of 'Liberty, Equality, and Fraternity.'" The "scholar-tyrants" who had slighted the Hunanese peasant in the Peking University library, who had ridiculed his conception of China's "leap forward," were pushed to the wall: "We have torn aside your filthy curtain of counterrevolution and caught you red-handed. We shall strip you of your disguises and expose you in all your ugliness." [242]

The lingering spectre of the Hungarian uprising, in Mao's eyes the result of bourgeois intellectuals' corruption of a once-revolutionary Party, found renewed expression:

> We must never regard our struggle against [the bourgeois intellectuals] as mere polemics on paper. . . . It was a number of revisionist literary men of the Petöfi Club who acted as the shock brigade in the Hungarian events. The turbulent wind precedes the mountain storm. [China's bourgeois intellectuals] have worked hard to let emperors and kings, generals and prime ministers, scholars and beauties, foreign idols and dead men dominate the stage. This is the prelude to the vain attempt of the revisionists at a counterrevolutionary restoration.[243]

In the initial phase of the Cultural Revolution—the period of public criticism of Wu Han beginning in November 1965—Mao evidently had found the political dialogue still too muted, as Party

239. *See* fn. 195, p. 474 above.

As the Cultural Revolution struggle became increasingly undisciplined, this slogan was modified to read, "Rebellion *against All Counterrevolutionaries* Is Justified."

240. *People's Daily* editorial, "Sweep Away All Freaks and Monsters" (June 1, 1966); trans. in *SCMP*, No. 3712 (June 6, 1966), p. 3.

241. *See* the *People's Daily* editorial, "We Are Critics of the Old World" (June 8, 1966); trans. in *SCMP*, No. 3717 (June 13, 1966), pp. 1–3.

242. *People's Daily* editorial, "Tear Aside the Bourgeois Mask of 'Liberty, Equality, and Fraternity'" (June 4, 1966); trans. in *SCMP*, No. 3714 (June 8, 1966), p. 3.

243. *People's Daily* editorial, "A Great Revolution that Touches People to Their Very Souls" (June 2, 1966); trans. in *SCMP*, No. 3713 (June 7, 1966), p. 2. These quotations have been transposed at the elipsis for the sake of continuity.

leaders sought to ignore the full implications of the Chairman's political initiative. He told Party leaders in the fall of 1966:

> . . . in January, February, March, April, and May [of 1966] many articles were written and circulars were issued by the Central Committee, but they did not draw widespread attention. Attention was aroused only by the big character posters and the Red Guard movement; you would have been in trouble if you had not paid attention to them.[244]

As in 1957, those Party members and their protectors who resisted public criticism sought to fend off Mao's attack: "When the movement was barely initiated and before the masses were mobilized, [the resisters] raised a blast of evil wind, spread rumors, created chaos, shifted the targets, laid one obstacle after another, thus binding the hands and feet of the masses." [245]

But Mao had permitted his voice to be muffled by a bureaucratic political structure long enough. Through the *ta-tzu-pao,* the large-character wall posters which were to be produced in millions by the newly mobilized Red Guards, Mao's "thought" was amplified. The big-character posters were Mao's weapon for rousing the younger generation to political involvement, and for exposing his opposition within the Party.

> Revolutionary big-character posters are a mirror reflecting all freaks and monsters. They constitute the most effective means of mobilizing the masses freely to launch the most powerful attack on the enemy. All anti-Party and antisocialist counterrevolutionary elements are most afraid of big-character posters.[246]

How were the masses to decide who were "freaks and monsters," and who were the remaining revolutionaries within the Party? The standard was a man's past loyalty and present commitment to Mao's "thought":

> Mao Tse-tung's thought is our political orientation, the highest instruction for our actions; it is our ideological and political telescope and microscope for observing all things. . . . The attitude toward Mao Tse-tung's thinking, whether to accept it or resist it, to support it or oppose it, to love it warmly or be hostile to it, this is the watershed between true revolution and sham revolution, between

244. Mao, "Speech at a Central Committee Work Conference" (October 25, 1966), in *Long Live the Thought of Mao Tse-tung!* p. 41.

245. *People's Daily* editorial, "Mobilize the Masses Freely, Knock Down the Counter-Revolutionary Black Gang Completely" (June 16, 1966); trans. in *SCMP,* No. 3726 (June 27, 1966), p. 6.

246. *Ibid.*

Student Red Guards posting *ta-tzu-pao*
[big character posters] at Peking University
attacking University President Lu P'ing and
other "scholar tyrants" and "revisionists,"
June 1966.
From China Pictorial, *November 1967.*

revolution and counterrevolution, between Marxism-Leninism and revisionism, and the touchstone to test them.[247]

Such was the political orientation established in early June as the Party organization, prodded by Mao and the Army, moved to rouse the students of Peking to rise up in criticism of the "scholar-tyrants" who controlled the educational system.

While the student "rebellion" itself must be the subject of other studies, Cultural Revolution documents make it clear that the point of difference between Mao and Liu since the "blooming and con-tending" of 1957—whether or not to release (*fang*) the masses in unrestrained criticism of the errors of those with Party authority—endured, and became the issue on which the Chairman finally sought to settle accounts with "China's Khrushchev."

The initial weeks of the student uprising in Peking were directly supervised by Liu Shao-Ch'i and Teng Hsiao-p'ing. Mao was elated by the spirit of a big-character poster, published on the significant date of May 25th, denouncing Party rule at Peking University. The Chairman later described this poster as "a declaration of the Chi-nese Paris Commune of the sixties of the Twentieth Century [whose] significance surpasses that of the Paris Commune [of 1871]." [248] Yet Mao was to see this expression of revolutionary spontaneity thwarted by continuing Party efforts to impose control on the stu-dent movement "from above."

As had been the case with Liu's direction of the Socialist Educa-tion Movement and the Four Clean-Ups Campaign after 1963, the Party Vice Chairman sought to control the release of mass criti-cism of those in authority through the dispatch of Party work teams. But Mao wanted uprising "from below"; and by mid-July he had confirmed that Liu was unwilling or unable to implement the spirit of "the thought of Mao Tse-tung." As Liu himself was reported to have stated in a confession of October 1966: "If we had been able to understand the Chairman's thoughts, we naturally would have suspended these activities [of the work teams], and we would not have committed a mistake in policy line and direc-tion." [249]

Probably during the first two weeks of July Mao decided to es-tablish direct control over the course of the Cultural Revolution, and to remove from positions of leadership that "small handful of

247. *Liberation Army Daily* editorial, "Mao Tse-tung's Thought Is the Telescope and Microscope of Our Revolutionary Cause" (June 7, 1966); trans. in *SCMP*, No. 3716 (June 10, 1966), pp. 2–3.
248. Mao, "Talk to Central Committee Leaders" (July 21, 1966), in *Long Live the Thought of Mao Tse-tung!* p. 36.
249. "The Confession of Liu Shao-ch'i," *Atlas* (April 1967), p. 3.

people in authority within the Party taking the capitalist road." On July 16th the Chairman swam in the Yangtze as a sign of his good health and a symbol of his determination to press his rebellion against Party authority to the end. On the 18th he returned to Peking, and a leadership conference was convened to reestablish a more permissive policy line on the student rebellion and prepare for a Central Committee Plenum. At the July meeting Mao forcefully declared his determination to let the students "lay seige" to the old educational system and manifestations of Party "revisionism" by siding with the masses against the Party organization (as he had only threatened to do in 1957). He challenged other Party leaders:

> Since you do not show your face [to the masses], I'll show mine. It all comes down to your putting fear above everything else, your fear of counterrevolutionaries, your fear of knives and guns. How can there be so many counterrevolutionaries? [250]

The Eleventh Central Committee Plenum opened on August 1st, Army Day. It was a fitting occasion for the formal inception of this assault on the Party and the civilian "superstructure" of government by Mao and his supporters within the PLA. Press photographs of the Chairman attending the first Red Guard rallies at this time show Mao in simple army fatigues with an armband bearing the single character "soldier." There could not be a clearer statement of the manner in which Mao was seeking to recapture the heroic era of his revolution. A *People's Daily* editorial of the day entitled "The Whole Country Should Become a Great School in Mao Tse-tung's Thought," stressed the bankruptcy of the old educational system in Mao's eyes, and the fact that the Army, not the Party, was the only organization which sustained the legacy of the revolution.[251]

Whereas in 1964 Mao had called on the Party to "learn from the PLA," he now was relying on the Army and the "whole country" to attack through criticism those within the Party who were not loyal to his "thought." As the Plenum decision on the Cultural Revolution stressed: "The main target of the present movement is those within the Party who are in authority and are taking the capitalist road." [252]

250. Mao, "Speech to Regional Secretaries and Members of the Cultural Revolution Group under the Central Committee" (July 22, 1966), in *Long Live the Thought of Mao Tse-tung!* p. 43.

251. *See* the *People's Daily* editorial, "The Whole Country Should Become a Great School in Mao Tse-tung's Thought" (August 1, 1966); trans. in *SCMP*, No. 3754 (August 5, 1966), pp. 6–8.

252. "Decision of the Central Committee of the CCP Concerning the Great Proletarian Cultural Revolution" (August 8, 1966), in *CCP Documents of the Great Proletarian Cultural Revolution,* p. 46.

Communist Party Chairman Mao Tse-tung,
in PLA fatigues and wearing a red armband
with the character *"ping"* [soldier], salutes Red Guards
attending a massive rally at *Tien-an Men*
[The Gate of Heavenly Peace] in Peking,
August 18, 1966.
From Hung Chi [Red Flag], *October 1966.*

The Plenum moved to resolve for Mao the remaining political issues of the 1950s concerning the Party's relations with the intellectuals. If the Great Leap Forward was Mao's effort to complete the work of social transformation in rural life that had been blocked by the Party in 1956, the Cultural Revolution can be seen as the Chairman's effort to destroy the Party–urban intellectual relationship which had been unsuccessfully confronted in 1957:

> At present, our objective is to struggle against and crush those persons in authority who are taking the capitalist road, to criticize and repudiate the reactionary bourgeois academic "authorities" and the ideology of the bourgeoisie and all other exploiting classes and to transform education, literature and art and all other parts of the superstructure that do not correspond to the socialist economic base, so as to facilitate the consolidation and development of the socialist system.[253]

In promoting what seems likely to be the last great confrontation of his political career, the Chairman was determined to disorganize the resistant Party organization "beneath him." The Plenum itself was an affirmation of the split with the Party leadership. The demotion of Liu Shao-ch'i from second to eighth place in the order of Party precedence[254] and Lin Piao's rise to second position as Mao's "closest comrade in arms" were probably but the formalization of decisions reached at the leadership meetings which were held after Mao's July 18th return to Peking.

The Eleventh Plenum passed a sixteen-point decision to guide the mass struggle phase of the Cultural Revolution. This document provided the political orientation for the more than twelve million young people who were to make their own "long marches" to Peking between August 18th and late November to participate in a series of eight gigantic rallies. At these meetings, Mao and his supporters within the Party leadership received and encouraged the "revolutionary masses." Mao was isolated no more.[255]

The mobilized millions were to be the embodiment of Mao's effort to generate a new revolutionary generation committed to his "thought" in an incredible "revolution from above and below." Mao was unshakable in his belief that only by "learning swimming

253. *Ibid.*, pp. 42–43.
254. Liu's demotion in the order of Party precedence was made public at the first mass Red Guard rally held in Peking on August 18th. *See* "Peking Mass Rally Celebrates the Great Proletarian Cultural Revolution," NCNA (August 18, 1966), in *SCMP*, No. 3766 (August 23, 1966), p. 1. Compare this listing of Party precedence with the one published on National Day in 1962, just after the Tenth Plenum, in *Current Background*, No. 692 (October 12, 1962), p. 1.
255. *See* the *People's Daily* editorial, "Chairman Mao Is with the Masses" (August 20, 1966); trans. in *SCMP*, No. 3767 (August 24, 1966), pp. 6–7.

Communist Party Chairman Mao Tse-tung
and other Party leaders mingle with the masses
during a massive rally at *Tien-an Men*
[The Gate of Heavenly Peace],
August 18, 1966.
From China Pictorial, *September 1966.*

through swimming," by setting the younger generation against Party "revisionists," would his life-experience survive his passing in the political mobilization of China's youth who were to "grow up in the great storm." [256] Mao was convinced that from such a struggle would emerge consensus, not "confusion":

> I firmly believe that a few months of *luan* will be mostly for the good, and that little harm will result from this confusion. It doesn't matter if there are no provincial Party committees, we still have the district and county committees.[257]

Initiative was being passed to the people. How would they use it?

LUAN FOR THE REVOLUTION?

> In his recent instruction Chairman Mao has said: There is no fundamental clash of interests within the working class. Under the dictatorship of the proletariat, there is no reason whatsoever for the working class to split into two big irreconcilable organizations.
> RED FLAG, September 17, 1967 [258]

> *Luan* has a class nature. Before the establishment of the revolutionary committees, *luan* meant causing confusion among the enemy and steeling the masses. For [the class enemy] to propose *luan* after the establishment of revolutionary committees means creating confusion among ourselves and the newborn revolutionary committees.
> KWEIYANG RADIO, August 2, 1968 [259]

The Eleventh Plenum of August 1966 reestablished Mao's control over the Party center, but the larger problem of "revisionism" within the regional apparatus remained as a source of resistance to the full reassertion of the authority of "the thought of Mao Tsetung." Shortly after National Day a Central Committee work conference was convened to promote Party rectification on a nation-wide scale. Against an uncertain degree of resistance from remaining Party leaders, and limited signs that in the growing political upheaval local Party and governmental officials were attempting to protect themselves by encouraging factional conflicts among the Red Guards or by setting workers and peasants against

256. *See* the speech by Ch'en Po-ta, "Grow Up in the Great Storm" (August 16, 1966), *Red Flag*, No. 11 (August 21, 1966); trans. in *SCMM*, No. 540 (September 6, 1966), pp. 12–13.

257. Mao, "Speech at a Central Committee Work Conference" (August 23, 1966), in *Long Live the Thought of Mao Tse-tung!* p. 40.

258. *Red Flag* editorial, "In the High Tide of Revolutionary Criticism, Attain a Revolutionary Great Alliance," No. 14 (September 17, 1967), p. 18.

259. From a transmission by Kweiyang Radio (Kweichow Province), August 2, 1968.

the students,[260] Mao and Lin Piao sought to press the confrontation to its conclusion.

With doubtful candor the Chairman told the leaders attending the October work conference:

> I did something disastrously wrong in the Cultural Revolution. I approved the big-character poster by Nieh Yuan-tzu of Peking University, wrote a letter to the middle school of Tsinghua University, and myself wrote a big-character poster. . . . The time was very brief, but the impact [of these things] was quite violent. It was beyond my expectation that the publication of the big-character poster of Peking University would stir up the whole country. Before the letter to the Red Guards was sent out [on August 1st] Red Guards of the whole country were mobilized and went on charging—charging with such force as to amaze you. I myself caused this big trouble, and I cannot blame you if you have complaints against me.[261]

In a manner reminiscent of his self-criticism at the Lushan Plenum, Mao commiserated with still-loyal comrades over their difficulties and distraction, even as he held firm to the determination to press the policy of disorganizing the regional Party apparatus. In a statement on the last day of the conference, Lin Piao revealed Mao's unwavering belief·that controlled political conflict was the answer to China's continuing struggle with "revisionism" and the "four olds." He characterized the Chairman's "concept of chaos" (*luan-tzu kuan*) as follows:

> Chaos (*luan-tzu*) has a dual character. This was said early on by Chairman Mao. It has a good aspect, and a bad aspect. Don't only look at the bad aspect without seeing the good. The bad aspect [also] can be turned to the good.
>
> The general [political] situation cannot become one of great chaos. Our military forces are very consolidated, and our production is steadily increasing. What kind of chaos was produced by a few students and young people promoting the Cultural Revolution struggle? They can't produce any great chaos. This is our attitude toward the question of *luan-tzu,* this is our "concept of chaos." [262]

260. Mao's awareness that the "class enemy" was likely to "incite the masses to struggle against each other" and to "shift the targets" of the Cultural Revolution struggle was clearly revealed in the Central Committee decision on the Cultural Revolution of August 1966. *See CCP Documents of the Great Proletarian Cultural Revolution,* pp. 45, 48.

261. Mao, "Speech at a Central Committee Work Conference" (October 25, 1966), in *Long Live the Thought of Mao Tse-tung!* p. 41.

262. Lin Piao, "Speech at a Central Committee Work Conference" (October 25, 1966), in *Tzu-kuo* [China Monthly, Hong Kong], No. 65 (August 1, 1969), p. 45.

Such was the attitude of Mao and his chosen successor in late 1966 as they prepared to press the Cultural Revolution throughout the provinces. And with the coming of the new year they called on China's "proletarian revolutionaries" to rise up and seize power from "revisionists" in the regional Party apparatus for Chairman Mao and his "thought." A *People's Daily* editorial of the hour explicitly stated what must have been all too obvious to those within the existing structure of political power, that Mao was intent on seizing direct control of the organization which had become increasingly resistant to his initiatives and had distorted his policies in application:

> Right from the beginning, the Great Proletarian Cultural Revolution has been a struggle for the seizure of power. . . . The revolutionary masses, with a deep hatred for the class enemy, grind their teeth and, with steel-like determination, make up their minds to unite, form a great alliance, and seize power! Power!! And more power!!! [263]

Less certain to all concerned, however, was the extent of conflict and the degree of destruction of two decades of Party-built political order which was to be generated by Mao's country-wide assault. A *Red Flag* article of early February gave some indication of how far Mao felt he might have to go when it stressed the continuing relevance of the Paris Commune experience of smashing the existing state machinery for the Cultural Revolution struggle:

> Since a number of units, in which a handful of Party people in authority taking the capitalist road have entrenched themselves, have been turned into organs of bourgeois dictatorship, we cannot of course take them over ready-made, we cannot accept reformism, cannot combine two into one and cannot effect peaceful transition. We must smash them thoroughly.[264]

A full analysis of the incredible turmoil of 1967 and 1968 which appears to have nearly undermined the ability of Mao and Lin Piao to ride out the *luan* of their effort to wrest political control from the Party organization is beyond the scope of this study. Perhaps the passage of time will give a better perspective to the factional conflict and violence which appears to have brought China to the verge of civil war.

In terms of the interpretations developed throughout this study,

263. *People's Daily* editorial, "Proletarian Revolutionaries, Form a Great Alliance to Seize Power from Those in Authority Who Are Taking the Capitalist Road!" (January 22, 1967); trans. in *SCMP,* No. 3868 (January 26, 1967), pp. 1–2.

264. *Red Flag* editorial, "On the Struggle to Seize Power by the Proletarian Revolutionaries," No. 3 (February 1, 1967); trans. in *SCMM,* No. 563 (February 13, 1967), p. 5.

however, three characteristics of this period of turmoil deserve special comment: the unwillingness of those in authority to tolerate "mass criticism"; the inability of China's younger generation to promote political struggle with discipline; and the eventual disillusionment of Mao and his supporters with the young intellectual Red Guards. These characteristics of the Cultural Revolution struggle became manifest in the great difficulty the Maoists encountered in keeping the political conflict within the bounds of nonviolent struggle and in rebuilding a new political order consonant with their stated goal of a Paris Commune-type of mass organization of "proletarian dictatorship."

It is hardly surprising that as the political purge was pressed throughout the country those in positions of authority resisted. Notably little of this resistance took the form of open opposition to Mao Tse-tung, however. As with so much of the resistance to the Chairman's policies in preceding years, the regional Party apparatus sought to divert or dilute Mao's attack, to turn official policy back on its maker, to discredit it by pushing it to its ultimate extreme, or to co-opt it into their own sphere of authority. Those who suspected that they would be the targets of Mao's *luan* attempted to create a counter-*luan* to disorganize the Chairman's controlled chaos.[265]

Regional Party leaders who were the targets of Red Guard attacks organized their own "Red Guard" units to counterattack Mao's student supporters, or mobilized workers and peasants to attack the young "rebels." In urban areas Party and government authorities granted workers wage increases and other material benefits —what the Maoists came to term "counterrevolutionary economism"—in order to win the support of the local "proletariat" and to force Mao and Lin into the difficult position of having to rescind the workers' economic gains. Union leaders urged laborers to travel to Peking to present demands for further improvements in their working conditions, thus "turning the spearpoint of struggle" away from the regional apparatus of government and clogging a transportation network already burdened with millions of "long-marching" student Red Guards.

Party personnel attempted to control local communication channels so as to prevent the mobilization of opinion against local lead-

265. The numerous ways in which leaders of the regional Party apparatus attempted to resist the purge are revealed in the series of leadership directives. Most of these directives were issued under the name of the Central Committee, the State Council, and the Party's Military Affairs Commission, and were republished in *CCP Documents of the Great Proletarian Cultural Revolution, 1966–67.*

ers. Radio stations and newspapers had to be "seized" from Mao's opponents, and secret personnel files and other political information had to be placed under direct PLA control. The "targets" of attack further resisted by spreading false information about who were the local "revisionists," by fabricating false dossier information, and even by painting city walls with Mao's quotations so that the Red Guards would have to desist from "defacing" the walls with big-character posters attacking local leaders.[266]

In time "fake power-seizures" were attempted, as local leaders sought to limit the struggle by claiming that "revolutionaries" (they themselves) were now in power—having "seized" authority from themselves. They attempted to turn student and worker opinion against the PLA in order to force the basic instrument of Mao's power to struggle against "the masses." In certain areas of China, arms (some stolen from military shipments bound for Viet-Nam) were "made available" to Red Guard units in order to stimulate armed violence against other Red Guard factions, and to force the Army to intervene and fire on the "revolutionary left."[267] In their determination to resist public "struggle" and removal from power, there were few distortions of Mao's policies not invoked by regional "revisionists."

From Mao's point of view a much more serious problem than the resistance of entrenched Party cadres was the degree of political indiscipline shown by the younger generation. The students displayed an inability—for which they can hardly be blamed—to distinguish between Mao's supporters in the now-decimated Party organization, and "the small handful taking the capitalist road." The Red Guards proved to be vulnerable to the political deceptions and provocations of local "revisionists," and uncertain of the objectives of the struggle.

As the Cultural Revolution progressed, the young students came to manifest that age-old Chinese ambivalence toward authority in their combined "fervent love" for Chairman Mao and a growing mistrust of any concrete authority and organizational discipline. As the struggle deepened during 1967, a *People's Daily* editorial complained of a trend toward "counterrevolutionary anarchy":

266. *See* "Circular of the CCP Central Committee and the State Council Concerning Prohibition of the Extensive Promotion of the So-Called 'Red Ocean,'" in *CCP Documents of the Great Proletarian Cultural Revolution,* p. 146.

267. On this point, *see* in particular, "Important Talk Given by Comrade Chiang Ch'ing on September 5 [1967] at a Conference of Representatives of Anhwei Who Have Come to Peking," in *CCP Documents of the Great Proletarian Cultural Revolution,* pp. 529–533.

It is completely wrong to regard all persons in authority as untrustworthy and overthrow all of them indiscriminately. This idea of opposing, excluding, and overthrowing all indiscriminately and its implementation run completely counter to Marxism-Leninism, Mao Tse-tung's thought.[268]

An article attacking anarchism in the same paper during this period observed of some of the "revolutionary rebels":

What [they] want is democracy and freedom, not democratic centralism and discipline. They put the masses in opposition to the leadership. They take advantage of supreme directives and the Party's general and specific policies, applying only those which suit their purposes and not enforcing them to the letter. This tendency is absolutely dangerous.[269]

Such disregard for Mao's authority was compounded by the factional conflict among Red Guard units that intensified throughout 1967. With the old Youth League and Party organizations "smashed" or in poor repute, the student groups and "rebel" organizations in factories, Communes, and government organizations struggled with each other for the position of *the* leading "center" of Maoist authority.[270] These factions often fragmented within a given organizational unit on the basis of leadership "centers" formed at different times and around conflicting individuals. They fought what were termed "civil wars" (*nei-chan*) with varying degrees of violence, destruction of property, and loss of life throughout 1967 and 1968.

Mao's "thought" seemed to provide a fragile basis for political discipline, perhaps because from the perspective of the provinces the conflict which had erupted at the Party center was highly personal, and because Mao's "thought" was so generalized that it provided little concrete guidance in the context of an intense and complicated conflict for power. As Mao's Shanghai supporter, Chang Ch'un-ch'iao, told a meeting of factious university students in early 1968: "The reading of quotations [from Mao's "little red book"] has become nothing but a war of words. I will only read passages

268. *People's Daily* editorial, "A Good Example in the Struggle by Proletarian Revolutionaries to Seize Power" (February 10, 1967); trans. in *Peking Review*, No. 8 (February 17, 1967), p. 19.

269. Hung Yung-ping and Wei Tung-piao, "Down With Anarchism!" *People's Daily* (March 1, 1967); trans. in *SCMP*, No. 3889 (March 15, 1967), p. 14.

270. For analyses of the origins and conflict among student and various "adult" factions, *see:* "Mass Factionalism in Communist China, *Current Scene*, Vol. VI, No. 8 (May 15, 1968), pp. 1–13; Michel Oksenberg, "Occupational Groups in Chinese Society and the Cultural Revolution," in *The Cultural Revolution: 1967 in Review* (Ann Arbor: Michigan Papers in Chinese Studies No. 2, 1968), pp. 1–44.

from the quotations which are favorable to me, but will not read anything which is unfavorable to me." [271]

The factional rivalry and erosion of political authority reached a peak of violence during the spring and summer months of 1967,[272] culminating in a July military insurrection at Wuhan in which Maoist mediators from Peking were kidnapped for a time by rebellious Army authorities. Despite such signs of growing divisiveness within the PLA in reaction to the expanded scope of the purge and the breakdown in public order, Mao and Lin had sufficient control over the Army to ride out the chaos they had provoked. By September enough calm had returned to enable Mao to make a mediating trip through provinces in north, central-south, and east China.[273] And in the wake of this test of Mao's "concept of chaos," Lin Piao reasserted the correctness of the Chairman's political strategy:

> The victory of this Cultural Revolution is very great. The costs are the smallest, smallest, smallest, the victories the greatest, greatest, greatest. Superficially things are *luan,* but this chaos is created by the reactionary line, by reactionary classes, it has burst forth from their actions, [it has been] created by the small handful in authority within the Party taking the capitalist road. This *luan* is necessary, correct. If things were not thrown into chaos reactionary elements would not be exposed. The reason we dare to do things in this way is precisely because we have Chairman Mao's supreme prestige and the power of the Liberation Army. Given these conditions, if we did not let [the opposition] expose itself, when might it then reveal itself [and attack us]? *Luan,* under Chairman Mao's leadership, is nothing to be feared.[274]

Despite such expressions of self-confidence, the available evidence indicates that Mao and Lin have been less than successful in their efforts to balance off the destruction of the Cultural Revolution with the construction of new forms of political organization consonant with Maoist goals and under Mao-Lin control. In early

271. "Comrade Chang Ch'un-ch'iao's Speech at Chiaot'ung University of Shanghai" (January 18, 1968), *Tzu-liào Chuan-chi* [Special Collection of Information Material] (Canton, February 10, 1968); trans. in *SCMP,* No. 4146 (March 26, 1968), p. 3.

272. *See* the *People's Daily* editorial, "Immediately Restrain Armed Struggle" (May 22, 1967).

273. *See* the NCNA press release of September 25, 1967, "Chairman Mao Inspects North, Central-South, and East China, in the Unprecedentedly Fine Situation in China's Great Proletarian Cultural Revolution."

274. "Deputy Supreme Commander Lin's Important Directive" (August 9, 1967), as republished in the Red Guard publication *Chu-ying Tung-fang-hung* (Canton, September 13, 1967); reproduced in *Tzu-kuo* [China Monthly], No. 44 (November 1, 1967), p. 29.

1967 Chiang Ch'ing and Ch'en Po-ta called for the formation of a "Paris Commune" type of political organization in Peking to implement Mao's objective of realizing true "proletarian dictatorship" in China. The sixteen-point decision on the Cultural Revolution of August 1966 had declared that it "is necessary to institute a system of general elections, like that of the Paris Commune, for electing members to the cultural revolutionary groups and committees and delegates to the cultural revolutionary congress." [275] Soon afterwards "Commune" governments were proclaimed in Taiyuan, Peking, and Shanghai. [276] These organizational expressions of faith in the "revolutionary masses," however, appear to have succumbed quickly to factional turmoil and mass violence. In their place appeared "three-way alliances" of PLA representatives, "revolutionary" mass organizations, and trusted Party cadres. Later, "revolutionary committees" of trusted Maoist supporters became the core of organizational efforts to rebuild a new political order in China which would be impervious to "revisionist degeneration." [277]

The first revolutionary committee was established in Heilungkiang Province in late January of 1967. The twenty-one months it took to create loyal leadership cores in all of China's twenty-nine other provinces, municipalities, and autonomous regions is some measure of the difficulty the Maoists faced—and continue to face —in reasserting their authority. [278] In September 1967 Chiang Ch'ing told the feuding "Good Faction" and "Fart Faction" of Anhwei Province,

> At present, a gust of foul wind is blowing. Apart from being directed at the Party Central Committee headed by Chairman Mao and at the People's Liberation Army, it is [also] directed at the revolutionary committee—a newborn thing. . . . A wind is being stirred up with the object of dissolving all revolutionary committees set up with the approval of the Central Committee. [279]

275. "Decision of the Central Committee of the CCP Concerning the Great Proletarian Cultural Revolution" (August 8, 1966), in *CCP Documents of the Great Proletarian Cultural Revolution,* p. 50.

276. See "China's Revolutionary Committees," *Current Scene,* Vol. VI, No. 21 (December 6, 1968), pp. 2–3.

277. The authoritative editorial of support for the revolutionary committees is the joint *People's Daily, Red Flag,* and *Liberation Army Daily* editorial, "Revolutionary Committees Are Fine" (March 30, 1968); trans. in *Peking Review,* No. 14 (April 5, 1968), pp. 6–7.

278. For preliminary analyses of efforts to establish revolutionary committees, *see* Parris H. Chang, "The Revolutionary Committee in China: Two Case Studies, Heilungkiang and Honan," *Current Scene,* Vol. VI, No. 9 (June 1, 1968); "Mao Fails to Build His Utopia: A Political Assessment of Communist China," *ibid.,* Vol. VI, No. 15 (September 3, 1968).

279. "Important Talk Given by Comrade Chiang Ch'ing on September

In their efforts to block the reassertion of the authority of Mao and Lin, purged or threatened members of the now-decimated Party organization evidently played on resentments against those who had risen to prominence within Mao's "small group" in the Cultural Revolution. They also stirred up the bitter rivalry for power among student groups, in order to stimulate a diffusion of power away from Mao-Lin's "center." What the Maoists came to attack in the national press as the "theory of many centers" and renewed manifestations of the divisive forces of "departmentalism," "small group mentality," "ultra-democracy," "mountain-top-ism," and "selfishness," were pressures for local political autonomy grown from resentments against more than a decade of Mao's manipulative interventions in domestic political life.[280] Those who had tasted a period of genuine political initiative in Cultural Revolution struggles appeared determined to attain or consolidate a position of local dominance in the new "anti-revisionist" order; while those purged still struggled to make a comeback.

As the trend toward "selfishness" in matters of authority reasserted itself,[281] Mao directed his frustration over this diffusion of authority at the intellectuals. In late 1967 he attacked what he termed an "outpouring of petty-bourgeois and bourgeois ideology from the intellectuals and young students," describing them as "vacillating and amorphous, . . . [and] opportunistic to a certain extent." [282] And in the summer of 1968 he bitterly criticized still-feuding Red Guard leaders. "You have let me down," the Chairman was reported to have told them, "and what is more, you have disappointed the workers, peasants, and Army men of China." [283] Within a month the official political line had shifted away from sup-

---

5 at a Conference of Representatives of Anhwei Who Have Come to Peking," in *CCP Documents of the Great Proletarian Cultural Revolution*, p. 531.

280. See, for example, the *People's Daily* editorial, "Unite under the Leadership of the Proletarian Headquarters Headed by Chairman Mao" (August 4, 1968); trans. in *SCMP*, No. 4236 (August 12, 1968), pp. 13–16; and the *Wen Hui Pao* editorial, "Comment on the 'Theory of Many Centers' " (August 6, 1968), in *ibid.*, No. 4253 (September 9, 1968), pp. 11–12.

281. See the Red Guard article, "Get Rid of 'Self-Interest,' Forge a Great Alliance of Revolutionary Rebels," and the accompanying *Red Flag* editorial note; trans. in *Peking Review*, No. 7 (February 10, 1967), pp. 20–21, 31.

282. Mao, "Our Strategy" (September 1967); trans. in *Chinese Law and Government*, Vol. II, No. 1 (Spring 1969), p. 6.

283. Cited in Parris H. Chang, "Mao's Great Purge: A Political Balance Sheet," *Problems of Communism*, Vol. XVIII, No. 2 (March–April 1969), p. 3.

port for China's student "rebels." The "working class" was to exercise dominant political leadership, with the Red Guards relegated to the background and subject to PLA and "proletarian" political discipline.[284]

Such indications of the difficulty Mao encountered in propagating his "thought" as the basis for more spontaneous political initiative from "the masses" have also been revealed in an increasing tendency by the Maoists to resort to traditional forms of asserting authority in their attempt to consolidate a new political order. Whereas in the post-Civil War years of Party rule the Army had been relegated to the background as an instrument of social control, in the anarchy of the Cultural Revolution this most basic form of political discipline was reinvoked to support the rebellion of "the left" and then to dampen the conflict among contending Maoist factions.

As we have stressed in previous chapters, in earlier years Mao attempted to depersonalize political authority and make ideology the basis for a more decentralized, self-initiating political order. Yet with the diffusion of authority in the Cultural Revolution, the Chairman has resorted to an ever more direct repersonalization of his power to sustain his influence over Chinese political life. Within the PLA, oath-taking rallies are held in which soldiers swear their personal loyalty to Mao and his "thought." And the renewed use of the traditional character *chung* for loyalty in civilian propaganda themes bespeaks Mao's inability to sustain political discipline solely on the basis of his "thought."

Over the centuries in China, education has been a basic means of asserting authority, and as noted earlier, Mao has attempted to make the study of Marxism and his own writings the basis for mass political initiative. Yet one sees in the Cultural Revolution the subtle transformation of the study of Mao's quotations from an act of creative learning to a new ritual of political control. The establishment of "Mao's thought propaganda teams" under the direction of the PLA has become one of the basic instruments for the reestablishment of political discipline.[285] Although earlier Mao had hoped that ideological education would produce new generations of Chinese able to take initiative in self-conscious political action, now the controlled recitation of Mao's quotations has become a new ritual

284. *See* the authoritative article by Yao Wen-yuan, "The Working Class Must Exercise Leadership in Everything," trans. in *Peking Review,* No. 35 (August 30, 1968), pp. 3–6.

285. *See People's Daily* editorial, "Organize Classes for the Study of Mao Tse-tung's Thought Throughout the Country" (October 12, 1967); trans. in *SCMP,* No. 4045 (October 23, 1967), pp. 1–3.

A PLA cadre leads a study group
in discussing Party Chairman Mao Tse-tung's political writings.
From China Pictorial, *February 1968.*

A "Mao's Thought Propaganda Team"
leads peasants of a People's Commune Production Brigade
in chanting slogans from the "little red book" of
Quotations from Chairman Mao.
From China Pictorial, *February 1968.*

of deference. As the Shanghai paper *Wen Hui Pao* baldly stated after the violent summer of 1967, "We must carry out Chairman Mao's instructions whether we understand them or not." [286]

These indications that the purposeful *luan* of the Cultural Revolution passed beyond Mao's control raise basic questions about his ability to reshape China's political order. In dynasties past a ruler of Mao's stature would have been content to see the establishment of civil order after a period of domestic political strife. In the historical pattern, the *luan* of a time of troubles would give way to *ho-p'ing;* and in the tranquillity of a new dynastic cycle China's rural population would build the material basis of another period of prosperity. Mao's objective, however, has been to transform a peasant society; and he has remained convinced that *ho-p'ing,* in its traditional sense of a period of political amelioration and bureaucratic rule, will hinder China's social transformation through the uncritical acceptance of traditional social values and rule by a small, educated, and paternalistic elite group.

China's problem has certainly not been one of trying to reestablish a period of political tranquillity. As we have shown, it has been Mao himself—in the 1956–57 period of "blooming and contending," in the Great Leap Forward, and in the Cultural Revolution—who has resisted the trend toward reconsolidation of domestic political order out of his fears that the momentum of social change would die. The Cultural Revolution is not a manifestation of the failure of Party rule; quite the contrary, it is a result of Mao's objection to the Party's success.

In Mao's terms the problem has been to institute a new style of politics somewhere between the poles of Cultural Revolution *luan* and Party *ho-p'ing,* in which criticism of the old way of life and those who wield Party authority becomes part of the political life of the Chinese people in their struggle to become a modern nation. The violence and social fragmentation of the Cultural Revolution indicates how difficult it is to institutionalize limited and disciplined political conflict in a society where for centuries interpersonal "harmony" has been stressed as a basic social value. Conversely, the rapid consolidation of bureaucratic Party rule, and the resistance of the Party apparatus to public criticism, bespeaks the ease with which traditional forms of political paternalism reemerge. Only time will tell whether out of the destruction of the Cultural Revolution Mao and his supporters will be able to build a new political order in which controlled "struggle" will become an accepted part of China's political life, and the basis for her social advance.

286. *Wen Hui Pao* editorial (September 30, 1967), p. 1.

Chapter XX

CONCLUSION:
THE ROLE OF AGGRESSION
IN SOCIAL CHANGE

The Ninth National Congress of the Chinese Communist Party, which convened in April of 1969, represented for Mao Tse-tung both the conclusion of more than a decade of struggle with "revisionist" Party leaders and the beginning of a period of efforts to rebuild a national political structure shattered by the Cultural Revolution. The new Party Constitution adopted by the Congress reaffirmed "the thought of Mao Tse-tung" as the theoretical guide to China's national development, *the* expression of Marxism-Leninism in "the era in which imperialism is heading for total collapse and socialism is advancing to world-wide victory."[1] Thus, on the eve of the twentieth anniversary of the People's Republic of China, Mao was able formally to break the influence of the Soviet precedent of national development within the Chinese Communist Party and initiate a new beginning in the long march to free the country of foreign influence and the burden of her past.

This formal development, however, does not warrant the conclusion that Mao has finally established his conception of a new political order for China. Indeed, during the three years following the conclusion of the Cultural Revolution there have been developments which only increase the uncertainty surrounding Mao's influence on China's future. While the Chinese people, by all accounts, have restored daily patterns of disciplined collective labor, rote learning, and directed political participation characteristic of the traditional culture, the Party leadership around Mao has displayed an instability which reflects personal rivalries and resentments exacerbated by the Cultural Revolution struggle.

1. "The [Ninth] Constitution of the Communist Party of China" (April 14, 1969), in *Current Background,* No. 880 (May 9, 1969), p. 51.

In the early fall of 1970 the Chairman's long-time comrade and exponent of "the thought of Mao Tse-tung" Ch'en Po-ta was purged at a Party Plenum that shifted China's political line away from the "left" orientation that had characterized policy during the preceding decade[2]; and in September of 1971 Mao's own chosen successor Lin Piao disappeared from view, apparently the loser in a struggle for power between the Army's political leadership and those who would reestablish the preeminent role of the Communist Party. Mao, speaking through the symbol of his old hero Lu Hsün, denounced the "betrayal" of Lin Piao in terms that implied that the Defense Minister— like his predecessor P'eng Teh-huai—had had "illicit relations" with the Soviet Union[3]—perhaps in an effort to moderate the Sino-Soviet dispute, which in 1969 had escalated to near warfare. By late 1971 it was evident that day-to-day leadership in China had passed to the man who had emerged from the Cultural Revolution as Mao's "conflict manager"—Chou En-lai.

Exactly what these developments imply for the succession to Mao Tse-tung's leadership remains uncertain. In terms of domestic policies, the political pendulum has taken at least a temporary swing to the "right," as is evident in the rebuilding of a Party apparatus and renewed stress on relatively non-politicized approaches to economic development. While Mao's opposition to Soviet "revisionism" endures, this "leftist" line became "right in essence" in 1972 as Mao and Chou En-lai promoted a major reorientation of China's foreign policy that included receiving an American President in the People's Republic. Thus the legacy of the *luan* of the Cultural Revolution is an uncertain set of leadership relations, an unresolved succession to the aging but still influential Mao, and shifts in China's domestic policies and foreign relations which give no clear indication of implementing the development concepts which Mao evolved in the mass campaigns of the 1950s and '60s.

Thus, this study concludes on a major note of uncertainty. As an exercise in the still imperfect science of political analysis, our conclusions must focus on Mao Tse-tung's life-long effort to reshape China's traditional political life, on his approach to promoting social change in a peasant society, and on the areas of tension that are likely

2. *See* "Communiqué of the Second Plenary Session of the Ninth Central Committee of the Communist Party of China," in *SCMP,* No. 4741 (September 21, 1970), pp. 18–21.

3. *See* Lo Szu-ting, "Learn the Thoroughgoing Revolutionary Spirit With Which Lu Hsün Criticized the Confucius Shop—In Memory of the 90th Anniversary of the Birth of the Great Revolutionary, Thinker, and Litterateur Lu Hsün," *People's Daily* (September 25, 1971); trans. in *SCMP,* No. 4989 (October 6, 1971), pp. 44–53.

to endure in a country still trying to find its road to renewed greatness.

THE INTERPLAY BETWEEN
REVOLUTIONARY LEADER AND CULTURAL LEGACY

In overview, one has a sense of the complex interplay among China's social and political traditions, popular social attitudes, and Mao Tse-tung's personal political style. In part this complexity reflects the endurance of cultural norms in the personalities of millions of Chinese reared before Liberation, and in part, Mao's adaptation of old behavioral patterns and social values to the demands of leading a quarter of mankind to cope with the challenges of a new era. For all that endures, however, there is also the revolutionary leader's personal determination to overcome what he sees as backward in the national tradition.

The one theme in Mao's personality which stands in sharpest contrast to China's traditional cultural pattern is his strong element of self-assertiveness, in a society which for millennia has stressed social interdependence and personal dependence. Mao's youthful opposition to the role of a filial son, his rebellion against the pain and manipulation suffered while dependent on paternal authority, however, acquired meaning beyond personal assertiveness. Mao's individual struggle merged with that of an age in which millions of Chinese witnessed the increasing ineffectiveness of the Confucian social tradition and suffered humiliation at the hands of exploitative foreign powers. Thus, one unique individual's efforts to break the bonds of personal subordination found larger meaning in a nation's struggle to overcome political subordination. Mao's call for a confrontation with Japanese invaders and rejection of a position of dependence on Comintern and Soviet political guidance were powerful appeals for China to "stand up" against manipulative authority.

Mao's personal style seems to have been a major factor shaping the evolution of the Chinese Communist Party's policies and leadership methods. While other leaders advocated withdrawal from confrontation with the Japanese, acceptance of Soviet political authority, and reliance on non-Chinese models in national development, Mao's policies, with few exceptions, have stressed confrontation and self-assertiveness.

From a psychological perspective, there is no little irony in the fact that in contrast to the unfilial Mao, the ancient philosophers of China's political tradition, Confucius and Mencius, were men who lost their fathers early in life. One is tempted to see in their system of filial deference to authority an effort by these ancient sages to construct a source of authority which was lacking in their personal lives. Mao, however, was a man who knew a harsh reality of filial subordination; and in his political life he has tried to pass on to the Chinese people a system of political participation in which subordinate opinion becomes a powerful element in checking abuses of authority. Whether it be criticism of Party cadres from the intellectuals or from members of the Associations of Poor and Lower-Middle Peasants, or the uprising of the student Red Guards against erring Party leaders, Mao has sought to institutionalize his own rebellion against manipulative authority in the political life of new China—even as he has sought to control the "struggle" and use it as a technique for asserting political discipline.

Rejection of the dependency social orientation finds varied expression in the Maoist political style. Where Confucianism lauded the virtues of tranquillity and interpersonal harmony, Mao has made activism the key to the behavior of the ideal Party cadre. Where fear and avoidance of conflict characterized the "cultivated" response to social tension in the traditional society, Mao has stressed the importance of criticism and controlled struggle in resolving those issues which block China's social advance.

Perhaps Mao's most innovative reaction against tradition has been his effort to liberate in disciplined, politicized fashion the aggressive emotions which were denied legitimate expression in the political culture of dependency.[4] Where the Confucian order stressed emotional restraint as the basis of personal discipline, and "eating bitterness" as the only appropriate response of the subordinate, Mao,

4. While this study has not been cast in comparative terms, we would suggest that the emphasis which Mao has placed on drawing forth emotions of resentment, anger, and hatred as the motivational basis of the revolution is one of the distinguishing characteristics of China's struggle for national development in contrast to other great revolutions of the twentieth century. In the case of Japan, the Samurai tradition apparently provided a basis of value congruence for incorporating the military challenge of the West. And as is readily attested by Japan's aggressiveness during the first half of the century, that country readily emulated the combative expansionism of the European nations. In India, a strong tradition of pacifism has found expression not only in Gandhi's politics, but also in Indian foreign policy in the years after independence. And as Nathan Leites has concluded in his study of Soviet Bolshevism, Lenin's stress on the need for a highly disciplined revolutionary party in part represents a reaction against the emotional "spontaneity" of the Russian character. (*A Study of Bolshevism* [Glencoe: The Free Press, 1953], Ch. V.)

early in his career, saw resentment and hatred as the motivational basis of mass political participation.[5]

Hence among the institutional forms which were evolved in the years of struggle for power, Mao developed the "speak bitterness" meetings, in which the peasants were encouraged to "vomit the bitter water" of repressed hatreds which tradition said should be "put in the stomach." Mobilization of such sentiments of aggression thus constitute a powerful tool of social change, both motivating people to seek change and overpowering that anxiety which is the emotional support of authority and precedent.

A concomitant of the traditional orientation toward authority was Confucian rejection of open social conflict. Conflict, when it did occur, tended to pass beyond the bounds of dispute over specific issues into a "confusion" (*luan*) of personal animosity. Aggression, once released, knew few limits.[6] Mao sought to "liberate" aggressive emotions in the service of political ends by subjecting them to disciplined release. In contrast to the unrestrained violence of a traditional peasant rebellion, Mao has stressed the need for political education as a way of both making men "conscious" of their rage at exploitation *and* disciplining the aggression into purposeful political action. Emotional manipulation and political "education" thus constitute complimentary dimensions of the Maoist approach to mass mobilization.

One of the most profound contradictions facing a political leadership seeking to institutionalize change in a peasant society, however, is centered around this basic motivational mechanism of the Maoist political style. As was revealed in the resistance of certain Communist Party leaders to the "mass movement" approach to political mobilization in post-Liberation China, and in Party opposition to criticism from non-Party groups, there are those who

5. Inhibitions against expressing aggression in limited ways against established authority may very well be a universal aspect of peasant life. (*See,* for example, Frantz Fanon, *The Wretched of the Earth* [New York: Evergreen, 1968], p. 54.) One of the appeals of Maoism to revolutionary groups in other parts of the "underdeveloped" world thus may be Mao's solution to the motivational problem of mobilizing people long accustomed to turning aggression inward into conscious political participants willing to attack established authority.

6. Apparently identifying another universal quality of peasant life, Fanon speaks of "waves of uncontrollable rage" among Algeria's peasants, which a revolutionary leader finds to be "objectively reactionary." (*Ibid.,* p. 111.) Here again, the concomitant aspect of Mao's mobilization technique, the disciplining of aggression through heightening political "consciousness" of the need for limit and purpose in "struggle," may constitute another important dimension of the appeal of Mao's "thought" to revolutionaries in peasant societies.

have questioned the appropriateness of emotional mobilization in the years of "socialist construction." Should a highly emotionalized style of politics be sustained in a period where the Party's goals seem to require a rationalized approach to leadership and the promotion of technical innovation? How relevant is emotional manipulation in an era when the Party has eliminated many of the worst abuses of authority and the sources of social injustice which genuinely fueled the mass mobilizations of the revolutionary years?

In addition, one senses that there endures in the political orientation of many Party cadres attitudes that reject even the limited conflict and tension of political "struggle," and criticism of authority by subordinates. As was indicated in earlier chapters, the question of whether or not to sustain "class struggle" after the consolidation of Party rule was one of the central issues which came to divide the leadership. During the Cultural Revolution Mao managed to remove from power those Party leaders who resisted "struggle" politics. But will the leaders and institutions which emerge from the current efforts to rebuild a national political order sustain Mao's approach to mass mobilization and "class struggle?"

From another perspective, Mao's conception of an emotional mechanism for ensuring political participation in a peasant society is self-defeating, for as the Party moves toward the attainment of its social goals, it eliminates many of the sources of discontent which previously generated popular support for Party programs. One sees a reflection of this contradiction in the Hundred Flowers Campaign, the Socialist Education Movement, and the Cultural Revolution, as strained efforts to make the most of existing social discontent in order to eliminate cadre abuses of authority—even as this criticism is intended to sustain popular support for "correct" leadership.

In the eyes of Party cadres, however, there was little justice in holding them responsible for difficulties in implementing overambitious policies formulated at the Party "center." In addition, one senses that there is likely to be limited effectiveness in encouraging peasants to "recall the bitterness of the past" as the basis for their allegiance to the Party. The landlords were eliminated as a political and economic force two decades ago and the hardships created by the Great Leap Forward are much more immediate—and Party-created—sources of discontent. Such emotional manipulation, in time, can only produce dissimulative responses and political cynicism.

It is in this light that Mao's repeated warnings about the dangers of a "restoration of capitalism" and his calls for "class struggle" reveal a fear that there is insufficient popular commitment to the Party's radical social goals for the revolution to be sustained through a rationalized approach to leadership and stress on economic growth. In post-Cultural Revolution developments, the most significant point to watch is the *manner* in which Mao and his supporters seek to restructure China's political life so as to sustain popular participation and prevent a return to bureaucratic rule by an elite administrative class.

Whatever the contradictions in this approach to political mobilization, however, a major point of departure from traditional Chinese political values has been Mao's effort to institutionalize "the unity of opposites." He has sought to substitute controlled political conflict between the Party's operative cadres and those they lead, as well as between different social and economic groups, for the traditional ideal of "the great unity" (*ta-t'ung*) in which social conflict was denied legitimate expression.

Although Maoist politics are a "dialectical" departure from China's traditional political culture, many of the institutions of the People's Republic continue to bear the stamp of the social traditions from which the revolution has grown. "The power of the word" was a major expression of authority in Confucian China, and Mao has sought to give the long-unenfranchised masses a sense of political efficacy both by popularizing literacy and by institutionalizing the (controlled) mass expression of political opinion. The "big character poster" (*ta-tzu-pao*) is both a sign of efforts to diffuse political authority to the people and a symbol of greater popular political participation. Mao departs from imperial forms in trying to use the critical voice of the people to discipline his officials, even as he merges with Chinese tradition in attempting to assert his authority through the study of his own writings. This contradictory combination of tradition and innovation is no more clearly symbolized than in "the little red book" of Mao's quotations. His words are used to attack established Party authority even as their recitation has now become a ritual of discipline for unruly Red Guards and factious cadres.

The one Maoist political value which fully merges with tradition is an uncompromising stress on the collective good above the interests of the individual; the damning of individualism as "selfishness." The Cultural Revolution call to "destroy self and establish the collective" (*p'o-szu, li-kung*) in part reflects the leadership's response to the indiscipline manifested by Mao's youthful supporters during a period of political combat. Yet it also reveals a paradox which brings our analysis full circle. While Mao calls for China's people to "stand up" and reject the dependency social orientation, he must cope with the need for social order and political discipline in a society where traditions have not prepared people for a critical and participatory role in the affairs of state. The Party Chairman wants to encourage popular innovation in economic matters and mass criticism of cadre abuses of authority, even as he seeks to sustain policy control and initiative from a revolutionary center of national political leadership. The resolution of this contradiction, as with other points of divergence between Maoist ideals and enduring Chinese realities, is in large measure a matter of the extent to which "the masses" come to absorb Mao's "thought" as the basis for social action.

Throughout this study we have been impressed by the close correspondence between the requirements for survival in a social economy of subsistence agriculture, the "eating" themes which predominate in Chinese social imagery, and the dependency style most characteristic of the "oral" stage of personality formation.[7] Apparently all the anxieties associated with having enough to eat in an economy of extreme scarcity had an enduring influence on the manner in which Chinese organized their social relations and reared their children to cope with life's hardships. The great stress on family interdependence is a clear response to the needs of production and security in this type of society. Adults had to rely on the lifelong commitment of their children to the family group for both labor power and, eventually, for their material needs in old age. Love was thus suffused with the "oral" qualities of feeding and being fed, while discipline was associated with the "taking in" of scarce resources and the "eating" of emotions which would disrupt the interdependent group. Aggression was conceptualized in terms of "being eaten" by others, or "putting in one's stomach" frustrations and rage which would threaten group solidarity if given free expression.

The dominant forms of authority and social sanction which characterized traditional Chinese society reflect this basic logic of social interdependence. Authority mirrored the harshness of the natural environment; it was hierarchical and had all the sternness of submission-dominance. Social authority remained external to the individual—in the superior experience of family elders and what Max Weber has termed the tradition-based authority of the "eternal yesterday."[8] One might characterize such an authority pattern as one of the "external superego." The major form of social sanction, furthermore, reinforced external controls over an individual's be-

7. Erik H. Erikson, *Childhood and Society* (New York: Norton, 1950), pp. 67–72, 222–224.
8. Max Weber, "Politics as a Vocation," in Hans H. Gerth and C. Wright Mills, *From Max Weber: Essays in Sociology* (New York: Oxford University Press, 1958), p. 78.

havior. The punishments of shame, of "loss of face" and social isolation, reflected the predominance of the interdependent group as well as manipulation of the individual's dependency needs.

While the natural environment sustained for generations of Chinese rural dwellers the relevance of this pattern of social relations, it is clear from our interviews with Chinese of middle and upper-income levels—many of whom had lived in urban areas—that this cultural pattern was not restricted to the countryside. The social logic of an agrarian society became elaborated into a "great tradition" of culture which celebrated the virtues of peasant life and rationalized the status of those who lived off the peasant's produce.

Given the manner in which culture is incorporated within the developing personality through socialization experiences, however, the dependency orientation acquired something of a life of its own apart from the environment which gave it meaning. Chinese sustained this pattern of social relations even when they migrated to distant societies with very different social systems and economic patterns.

It is the endurance of this cultural pattern in the personalities of millions of Chinese that Mao Tse-tung has sought to confront, in part through changes in organizational pattern and "work style," and in part through efforts to promote the "thought reform" of adults socialized before Liberation. The difficulty of changing mature personalities, and the endurance of traditional Chinese social values and behavioral patterns, however, ultimately led Mao to resort to the upheaval of the Cultural Revolution. Between 1966 and 1968, he sought to remove from positions of political authority "revisionist" adult Chinese and replace them either with adults whose behavioral style was consonant with Maoist ideals or with members of the younger generation schooled in Mao's "thought."

There are, of course, a variety of levels at which one might analyze Mao's political style: the organizational forms developed during his leadership of the Party; the economic or political policies he has promoted; or his social and political philosophy. In addition, if one assumes, as we have throughout this study, that a single personality is critical both as a carrier of culture and as an organizer of individual social action, then personal style becomes another major factor in the analysis of societies and social change.

How might one characterize Mao's style of political leadership? In summarizing themes that are only implicitly developed in the preceding analysis, let us begin in proper Chinese fashion by invoking a series of quotations from the Chairman concerning matters of leadership:

It seems that right up to the present quite a few have regarded Marxism-Leninism as a ready-made panacea: Once you have it, you can cure your ills with little effort. This is a type of childish blindness and we must start a movement to enlighten these people. . . . We must tell them openly, "Your dogma is of no use," or to use an impolite formulation, "Your dogma is less useful than shit." We see that dog shit can fertilize the fields and man's can feed the dog. And dogmas? They can't fertilize the fields, nor can they feed the dog. Of what use are they? (Laughter) Comrades! You know the object of such talk is to ridicule those who regard Marxism-Leninism as dogma, to frighten and awaken them, to foster a correct attitude toward Marxism-Leninism. Marx, Engels, Lenin, and Stalin have repeatedly said, "Our doctrine is not dogma; it is a guide to action." [9]

Subjectivism, sectarianism and stereotyped Party writing are . . . gusts of contrary wind, ill winds from the air-raid tunnels. (Laughter) It is bad . . . that such winds should still be blowing in the Party. We must seal off the passages which produce them. Our whole Party should undertake the job of sealing off these passages, and so should the Party School.[10]

With victory, certain moods may grow within the Party—arrogance, the airs of a self-styled hero, inertia and unwillingness to make progress, love of pleasure and distaste for continued hard living. With victory the people will be grateful to us and the bourgeoisie will come forward to flatter us. It has been proved that the enemy cannot conquer us by force of arms. However, the flattery of the bourgeoisie may conquer the weak-willed in our ranks. There may be some Communists, who were not conquered by enemies with guns and were worthy of the name of heroes for standing up to these enemies, but who cannot withstand sugar-coated bullets; they will be defeated by sugar-coated bullets. We must guard against such a situation.[11]

Conscientious practise of self-criticism is a hallmark distinguishing our Party from all other political parties. As we say, dust will accumulate if a room is not cleaned regularly, our faces will get dirty if they are not washed regularly. Our comrades' minds and our Party's work may also collect dust, and also need sweeping and washing. The proverb "Running water is never stale and a doorhinge is never worm-eaten" means that constant motion prevents the inroads of germs and other organisms. . . . Fear neither criticism or self-criticism . . .

9. Mao Tse-tung, "Reform in Learning, the Party, and Literature" (February 1942), in Stuart R. Schram, *The Political Thought of Mao Tse-tung* (New York: Praeger, 1963), p. 120.

10. Mao Tse-tung, "Rectify the Party's Style of Work" (February 1942), *SW*, English, III, p. 36.

11. Mao, "Report to the Second Plenary Session of the Seventh Central Committee of the Communist Party of China" (March 1949), *SW*, English, IV, p. 374.

—this is the only effective way to prevent all kinds of political dust and germs from contaminating the minds of our comrades and the body of our Party.[12]

. . . [Our] aim in exposing errors and criticizing shortcomings, like that of a doctor curing a sickness, is solely to save the patient and not to doctor him to death. . . . So long as a person who has made mistakes does not hide his sickness for fear of treatment or persist in his mistakes until he is beyond cure . . . we should welcome him and cure his sickness so that he can become a good comrade. . . . In treating an ideological or a political malady, one must never be rough and rash but must adopt the approach of "curing the sickness to save the patient," which is the only correct and effective method.[13]

Diseases enter by the mouth and all disasters come through the tongue. I'm in great trouble today. . . . I decided upon and promoted the target of 10,700,000 tons of steel, and as a result 90 million people were thrown into battle. . . . Next, the People's Communes. I did not invent the People's Communes, but I promoted them. When I was in Shantung a correspondent asked me: "Are the People's Communes good?" I said, "Good"; and on the basis of this he published a report in a newspaper. From now on I must avoid reporters. . . . This trouble [of the Great Leap Forward] I have brought on is a great one, and I hold myself responsible for it. Comrades, you should also analyze your own responsibilities, and you will all feel better after you have broken wind and emptied your bowels.[14]

It is evident from the predominantly scatological tone of Mao's humor—ridicule of those who would assert their authority in the time-honored Confucian manner through "the power of the word" as but issuing faeces and "ill winds,"—that "anal" themes have a particular emotional weight in his perception of the world.[15] In his efforts to evolve a new style of political leadership he seems to be reacting against the "oral" characteristics of the traditional political culture, which he symbolizes most vividly in the dangers for the Party of "sugar-coated bullets."

These clues to the organizing emotional theme of Mao's personal style are strengthened when we consider the common dimensions

12. Mao, "On Coalition Government" (April 1945), SW, English, III pp. 316–317.

13. Mao, "Rectify the Party's Style of Work" (February 1942), CW, English, III, p. 50.

14. Mao Tse-tung, "Speech at the Lushan Conference" (July 23, 1959), in *Chairman Mao's Criticism and Repudiation of the P'eng, Huang, Chang, and Chou Anti-Party Clique*, in *Chinese Law and Government*, Vol. I, No. 4 (Winter 1968/69), p. 11.

15. A description of the character traits that psychoanalysts identify as "anal" and "oral" will be found in Otto Fenichel, *The Psychoanalytic Theory of Neurosis* (New York: Norton, 1945), pp. 278–284, 488–492.

of political policies he has promoted, and the manner in which they contrast with themes of the traditional culture and with policies promoted by other Party leaders.

Perhaps the strongest theme in Mao's politics is the stress on "self-reliance," the need for the Chinese people to "stand on their own feet"—a self-assertiveness which contrasts so strongly with the traditional dependency. Mao's glorification of "activism" similarly seems to be a reaction against the passivity inherent in relying on others. His stress on struggle, on "liberating" with political discipline bad feelings which have been "swallowed" and "put in the stomach," indicates that his major mode of self-discipline is associated with "letting go" or "releasing" (*fang*, as in *chieh-fang* "to liberate," or *fang-p'i* "to break wind") rather than the traditional concern with proper "taking in."

In contrast to the oral omnipotence inherent in the traditional style of asserting authority, in which skill in the use of words was the measure of a man's right to assert power over others, Mao has stressed the need to bring together thought and action, theory and practice. Party cadres are no longer to derive their status from skill in manipulating an official ideology, but through effective involvement in the tasks of economic production. Only thus, says Mao, can the Party avoid the traditional "gap" between leaders and led.

Finally, Mao's opposition to the use of material incentives in motivating people for national development, his general concern with the loss of revolutionary vitality that will come with increased consumption on the part of both Party cadres and population, and his stress on the need to develop self-discipline through such physical "struggle" as swimming in the teeth of winds and waves, indicate a determination to overcome the "oral" characteristics of the traditional political culture. Mao might be said to be an "anal" leader seeking to transform an "oral" society.

THE ROLE OF AGGRESSION IN SOCIAL CHANGE

In the Western experience of social change, leadership in the development of new economic and social patterns has been taken by distinctive social subgroups whose culture and personality characteristics provided the motivational basis for innovative activity.[16] In China, efforts to promote economic and social innovation during the late nineteenth century were thwarted by a political elite which

16. This is the central thesis explored in David McClelland's *The Achieving Society* (Princeton, N.J.: Van Nostrand, 1961), and Everett E. Hagen's *On the Theory of Social Change: How Economic Growth Begins* (Homewood, Illinois: Dorsey Press, 1962).

sought to sustain a life style antithetical to commercial and techno-
logical activity and the agrarian social basis of its power.[17] Leadership in social change eventually fell to a revolutionary party committed to the Marxist conception of political and economic development.

In conclusion, what does this study suggest about the motivational basis upon which the Chinese Communists have attempted
rapidly to transform a relatively homogeneous peasant culture
through centralized political leadership? In the first two parts, we
found that individuals reared in the Chinese tradition responded to
authority with a strong sense of anxiety. Such a sentiment helped
to sustain filial dependence, and suppressed challenges to those in
positions of leadership and to the traditions from which they drew
authority. In positive terms, moreover, China's people had been
taught for centuries to draw a sense of security from traditional productive processes and the interpersonal patterns which were the
time-tested cultural distillation of this ancient and enduring society.
The motivational problem of China's revolution at base has been a
matter of how to overcome these emotional roots of tradition and
established authority.

In the West the profit motive, a need to achieve or to attain personal salvation, or the determination to reattain a status denied by
a dominant culture have provided the personal motivation behind
innovative activity. China's traditions, however, gave scant legitimacy to commercial pursuits. The strong emphasis on the group
above the individual and the primacy of ancient traditions dampened that self-assertiveness which might have spurred innovation
and social change.

In the case of Mao's revolution we found sentiments of aggression
to be the distinguishing motivational quality of political activity.
This characteristic reflects, in part, the fact that because of foreign
aggression the development of Chinese society has been a defensive and highly politicized process. The difficulty with which the
Chinese responded to the pressures of assertive Western nation-
states (in contrast to the rapidity with which the Japanese, for example, absorbed foreign military and commercial technology and
social practice), however, is in itself a reflection of the incompati-
bilities of cultural pattern. And finally, the *persistence* of Mao's

17. This interpretation is developed at a philosophical level in Joseph R.
Levenson's *Confucian China and Its Modern Fate: The Problem of Monar-
chical Decay* (Berkeley: University of California Press, 1964), and in terms
of difficulties in promoting new economic patterns in Albert Feuerwerker's
China's Early Industrialization (Cambridge, Mass.: Harvard University
Press, 1958).

stress on political techniques which emphasize emotions of resentment and hatred, his determination to sustain "class struggle" more than two decades after the attainment of state power, leads to the conclusion that Mao sees great motivational problems associated with sustaining social change in a peasant society.

Students of the functions of violence and conflict in social processes have stressed the role of such aggressive behavior in modifying the actions of those in established authority, in signaling the depth of commitment of those who seek change, and—in the extreme—in destroying by force the organizational power of "the establishment." [18] China's revolution suggests, however, that the expression of aggression may be just as important in modifying the behavior *of those who are struggling for change* as it is in influencing, or destroying, the existing order of things.

In the land reform process, Party writings indicate, it was not enough simply to redistribute land to the peasantry to gain their support for the revolutionary cause. If the authority of social traditions and interpersonal relationships which sustained the "feudal" pattern of landholding and agricultural production was to be destroyed, the peasants had to become active participants in attacking the landlords who personified the rural social order. Through the "speak bitterness" meetings, Party cadres worked up the rage of the peasantry over past injustices and economic inequities. It was only through the mobilization of such aggression that the peasants dared to attack those who carried the authority of tradition, and acquired new perceptions of their altered political status and of possibilities for social change.

Mao's particular contribution to the process of promoting social change would seem to be his conception of an institutionalized motivational mechanism for mobilizing a basically conservative and politically reticent peasantry. Sentiments of aggression, when disciplined in their expression through organizational controls and given purposeful direction through a social ideology, become a powerful tool for promoting change where established authority and custom are rooted in personal anxieties. Such emotions apparently are the only motive force powerful enough to overcome rapidly the inhibitions which sustained tradition in the personalities of China's peasants.

In the fourth part of this study we found, however, that Mao's stress on emotionally charged mass campaigns and controlled "class conflict" came to be resisted by other Party leaders. This suggested

18. See H. L. Nieburg, "The Threat of Violence and Social Change," *The American Political Science Review*, Vol. XVI, No. 4 (December 1962), pp. 865–873.

that tradition-based fears of social conflict and the expression of aggression—anxieties about *luan*—were at work in many Party members, inhibiting their acceptance of the Maoist approach to promoting social change. Given his "dialectical" view of social processes, Mao has attempted to sustain his influence over Party policies by playing upon the same aggressive emotions which have been used to break the rural population out of their traditional social patterns. By mobilizing popular resentments against Party cadres, as was first done in the 1957 "Hundred Flowers" period of mass criticism, later in the post-1962 "Four Clean-ups" Campaign, and most fully in the Cultural Revolution, Mao has sought to subject to public criticism those Party members who manifest in their leadership style the "four olds" of the traditional political culture. Such criticism was intended to reshape the attitudes of the critics as much as those criticized, by giving them a participant role in the political process, and by propagating new social norms and standards of behavior.

SPEEDING UP THE PACE OF SOCIAL CHANGE

> Perhaps there are still children who have
> not eaten men? Save the children . . .
>
> LU HSÜN[19]

In the first draft of this analysis, completed on the eve of the Cultural Revolution, we concluded with some speculative observations about the likely psychological impact of a totalitarian political order on Chinese society. We suggested that a political party which sought to exercise total social control by penetrating into all areas of a society, down into the basic social unit of the family, sowed in its striving for total influence the seeds of its own psychological self-destruction. We based this conclusion on the assumption that the roots of a population's submissive acceptance of an authoritarian political order were the anxieties before the powerful which were the product of the traditional family socialization process. By diluting the authority of the stern family head, the totalitarian state would foster the rearing of new generations which would not have in their personalities the emotional inhibitions which were the basis of political submissiveness. And in time, as these new generations entered the political process, they would show greater willingness to challenge established authority than would their elders. In such a

---

19. Lu Hsün, "A Madman's Diary," in *Selected Works of Lu Hsün* (Peking: Foreign Languages Press, 1959), p. 21.

pattern of generational change, we suggested, lay the long-term possibilities for the erosion of a totalistic state.[20]

The Cultural Revolution, in an unexpected way, would lead us to conclude that not only does this interpretation have certain validity, but that Mao Tse-tung himself has attempted to play upon such a mechanism of social change in order to speed up the pace of China's revolution.

After 1962 Mao repeatedly expressed to other Party leaders his concern about the "restoration" of old social practices in the Communist Party and in Chinese society at large. In essence he was affirming Max Weber's observation that revolutionary leadership eventually becomes routinized into bureaucratic administration, or reverts to traditional forms of authoritarian control.[21] In his struggle against domestic "revisionism" Mao was asserting that the Chinese Communist Party was not sustaining its commitment to social change, but was giving in to the influence of old cultural patterns and a leadership style which in time would stifle the revolution.

In the Cultural Revolution Mao resisted this trend by speeding up the process by which new generations—with new personal styles —are socialized and brought into positions of social influence. The Red Guard movement was in one sense a contrived *rite de passage,* a political ritual of initiation for cultivating "revolutionary successors" by which Mao sought to recreate his own socialization experience for millions of Chinese youngsters. In its initial conception the Red Guard movement, as common to the mass campaign pattern, was to generate new "activists" committed to the Maoist political style; and these bearers of a revolutionary leadership style would be incorporated into a reconstituted Party organization.

At present it appears uncertain whether Mao's effort to speed up the socialization and recruitment processes of Chinese society have worked. What scanty evidence exists indicates that the Red Guards were not simply "little Maos"; that under the influence of their families and the social context they had acquired many traditional or nonrevolutionary behavioral inclinations, and were not the disciplined and selfless fighters for the revolution that Mao had hoped they would be. Moreover, it appears that Mao and his close comrades are hardly in full control of the process of reconstituting the Party and state.

The social composition and leadership style of those who emerge

20. *See* "On the Psychological Self-Destruction of a Totalitarian Society," in Richard H. Solomon, *The Chinese Revolution and the Politics of Dependency* (unpublished Ph.D. dissertation, M.I.T., 1966), pp. 388–397.

21. Max Weber, "The Meaning of Discipline," in Gerth and Mills, *From Max Weber,* p. 253.

from the Cultural Revolution struggle, and the policy commitments of Mao's successors, are uncertain quantities which the foreign observer can only wait to see evolve. Mao sought to use the Cultural Revolution to accelerate the institutionalization of his version of a new Chinese political culture. In practice, however, the endurance of the thought and word of the revolutionary innovator will depend on a myriad future small decisions by millions of Chinese as to whether they will sustain Mao's political legacy in the actions of their daily lives.

Appendix I

INTERVIEW SCHEDULE
(Translation)

I. EARLY FAMILY LIFE

A. RELATIONS BETWEEN PARENTS AND CHILDREN

1. What kind of person was your father/mother?
   How did he/she treat you children?
2. What did you admire most about your father/mother?
3. Naturally, no one is without faults. What would you say were your father's/mother's weak points?
4. What should parents pay closest attention to in rearing a child?
5. What was the most important thing you obtained from your parents?
6. Did your father often take you to play? (In what way?)
7. Naturally there are times when parents and children will have differences of opinion. What kinds of things did you and your parents have differences of opinion about? How did you resolve the problem?
8. a. When you were young, when you made some mistake what would your parents do? For what kinds of mistakes would they punish you in that way?
   b. Who ordinarily punished you at home? What kinds of punishment did you ordinarily receive? For what kinds of mistakes were you punished? Which kind of punishment did you think was the worst?
9. Whom is your personality most like? In what ways?
10. At home to whom were you closest? Why?
11. When you were small, what caused you the most bother?
12. When you had problems, with whom would you discuss them? Why (with that person)?
13. Many people, when they are small, have bad dreams. Do you remember any bad dreams you had when you were small?
14. What kinds of dreams have you had recently?

B. RELATIONS BETWEEN PARENTS

15. How did your parents get along?
16. Who ordinarily made decisions about family affairs?
    How were differences of opinion resolved?
17. Naturally at times in every family there will be differences of
    opinion. What differences of opinion were there in your family?
    How were they resolved?

C. SIBLING RELATIONS

18. How did you and your brothers and sisters get along together?
19. With whom were you closest? Why?
20. When you would get mad at each other, what would you do?
21. What is the most important thing in the relationship between
    an elder and a younger brother?

D. RELATIVES AND NEIGHBORS

22. How many relatives lived near your house? Did they often
    come to your house?
23. What kind of relationship did your family have with the neigh-
    bors? What kind of people were they?

E. GENERAL QUESTIONS ABOUT FAMILY LIFE

24. a. How many rooms were there in your family house?
       How many people lived together?
    b. Did you all sleep together in one room? Where did your
       parents sleep?
    c. What was the approximate population of the village/town/
       city where you grew up?
    d. When members of your family would go out, what kind of
       transportation would they use?
    e. When your parents would go out during the cold time of
       the year, what kind of clothing would they wear?
    f. When you were small, who in the house cooked food for
       you?
    g. Ordinarily at meal time how many dishes and soups were
       there?
    h. Was there a high wall around your family house? Why?
    i. In your home, when you wanted to go into another person's
       room, would you first knock on the door? Why (not)?
25. From the point of view of personality, what is the difference
    between a child and an adult? From the point of view of emo-
    tions?

26. a. Why do you think it is relatively easy for a child to be influenced by a bad environment?
    b. At what age can a child distinguish between right and wrong?
27. What is the thing you remember with most pleasure about your early life at home?
28. Which is a relatively happier period of life, childhood or adulthood? Why?
29. What changes have occurred in family life today? Are these changes for better or for worse? Why?

II. ADOLESCENCE

A. RELATIONS BETWEEN TEACHER AND STUDENT

30. What is the most important aspect of relations between a teacher and his student?
31. What attitude did your parents have toward your teacher?
32. In elementary and middle school, what teaching methods did your teachers use?
33. At that time how did you feel about studying?
34. Did you or your fellow students ever play tricks on the teacher? Did you ever play such tricks on your father? (If "no":) Why? (If "yes":) What was the outcome?
35. a. What is the effect of "cultivation" (*hsiu-yang*) on the way a person gets along in the world?
    b. How does a person become "cultivated"?
    c. What do you do when you get angry?
    d. When you try hard to overcome your anger, what do you do?
    e. What was your father like when he would get angry? What would you children do?

B. IMPORTANT LIFE CHOICES

Career:

36. When you were young, what did you hope to become in the future?
37. What did your parents hope you would do? (If there was a difference of opinion:) How did you resolve this difference?

Marriage:

38. a. How did you and your wife become engaged?
    b. Did your parents object to your choice? (If "yes":) How did you resolve this difference?
39. If a housewife goes out and works, what influence will it have on family life?

III. ADULTHOOD

40. How is it that some people succeed in their careers and others do not? Other people's help?

Friendship:

41. What is the most important thing a person obtains from friends?
42. What is the best kind of friend?
43. What is the difference between the relation of a superior to his subordinate and relations among friends?
44. What is the source of conflict between people?
45. Why is *chiang jen-ch'ing* ("speaking on behalf of another") so important in Chinese society? Could you give me a specific example of what it means to *"chiang jen-ch'ing"*?

IV. GENERAL SOCIAL ATTITUDES

Order:

46. Please explain what *ta-t'ung* ("the great harmony," or social unity) means. How can *ta-t'ung* be realized?
47. Why, in the early years of the Republic, were there warlords? Why couldn't they peacefully coexist? What method can prevent such a situation from developing?
48. Please explain what *chih-an hao* ("law and order") means. What method can a society use to maintain *chih-an*?
49. Why has Chinese society especially emphasized *ho-p'ing* ("peace")?
50. What is the greatest effect of interpersonal competition on society? Are there others?
51. How is it that society becomes *hun-luan* ("confused")? What are conditions like in a *hun-luan* society? In what way can *hun-luan* be avoided?
52. a. Why is everyone at present so concerned about the *t'ai-pao* and *liu-mang* (juvenile delinquents and ruffians)?
    b. Why is their influence on society so great?
    c. How should they be dealt with?

International Order:

53. Please name, in decreasing order of importance, the four most important countries in Asia. How can they maintain peace in Asia?
54. What is your point of view on China having the atomic bomb?
55. What could enable the United Nations to become a more effective organization for world peace?

Leadership:

56. Why is it that some people have an interest in politics and others do not? How do you feel about this difference?
57. Of the things a country's leaders can do for their country, which is the most important?
58. a. If you were mayor of this city, what would be the first policy you would like to promote?
    b. If you were president (a leader of China)?
59. If a newspaper asked you to write an article, one concerning some especially important contemporary social problem, what problem would you select to write about?
60. Under what conditions should the people support their leaders?
61. a. What is the best way of preventing a political leader from engaging in activities that endanger the people's welfare?
    b. If a political leader engages in some activities that endanger the people, what should an ordinary person do?
62. a. With whom do you ordinarily discuss political problems? (If the respondent says he does not discuss them with anyone:) Why not?
    b. With family members? (If not:) Why not?
    c. With co-workers? (If not:) Why not?
    d. With friends? (If not:) Why not?
63. a. When you hear the word "politics" what feeling do you have?
    b. Which problems belong to the sphere of politics?

Appendix II

BIOGRAPHICAL SCHEDULE

Interview Case Number _____
(T—interviewed in Taiwan
H—interviewed in Hong Kong)

Date_____   Interviewer_____
Language used_____   Interpreter_____

===

1. Sex: male/female
2. Marital status: single/married/divorced/widow/widower
3. Number of children:_____
4. Birth date:_____; Age:_____
5. Province of birth:_____(county, city, or village also may be given)
6. Place where parents lived after marriage:_____ (Province, county, city, or village)
7. Place where paternal grandparents lived after marriage:_____ (Province, county, city, or village)
8. Place where maternal grandparents lived after marriage:_____ (Province, county, city, or village)
9. Province where you grew up:_____
10. Reared by: parents/relatives (which)_____/other_____
11. Province where spent adult life:_____
12. Date arrived in Hong Kong_____and/or Taiwan_____
13. Father: alive/deceased, at what age of R.?_____
13a. Father's educational level:_____
14. Mother: alive/deceased, at what age of R.?_____
14a. Mother's educational level:_____
15. Siblings: Number of older brothers_____
16. Number of younger brothers_____
17. Number of older sisters_____
18. Number of younger sisters_____
19. Primary education: Private family school/home tutor/parents/ church/public/other_____
20. Secondary education: Public/church/private/tutor/other_____

21. Highest grade attained ————
22. Activity after leaving school————
23. College: which————; where———— type: public/private/church————
24. Major subject studied————
25. Chinese dialects spoken:————
26. Foreign languages studied in school:————
    Middle School: which:————; amount of time devoted to each:———— College: which:————; amount of time devoted to each————; Could you read an article in this language? no/with difficulty/could
27. Radio listening: none/entertainment programs/news programs/other————
28. Movie attendance; frequency: every week/every month/several times per year/never
29. Percentage of all movies seen which are foreign (estimate):——
30. Newspaper reading: never/daily/several times each week/occasionally
31. First part of a newspaper read: entertainment/sports/business/local social situation/national situation/international situation/editorial
32. Part of a newspaper most likes to read: entertainment/sports/business/local social situation/national situation/international situation/editorial
33. Do you read national political news? Yes/no
34. Do you read news of the international situation? Yes/no
35. Do you read news about the international political situation? Yes/no
36. Travel abroad: Where:————
37. Travel for: pleasure/work/other reason————
38. How much time have you spent abroad?————
39. Occupation————
40. Father's occupation————
41. Religion————
42. Do you actively participate in religious activities? Yes/no
43. Number of times per month goes to church:————
44. Would you consider your childhood and adolescence to have been: traditional/relatively modern?
45. Would you consider childhood and adolescence to be basically a happy/unhappy time of life?
46. Would you consider your personal attitude to be: traditional/modern?
47. Would you consider your father's attitude to have been: traditional/modern?

Appendix III

ATTITUDE SURVEY

(Translation)

A SURVEY OF PEOPLE'S OUTLOOK
ON CONTEMPORARY LIFE
INTRODUCTION

During the past several decades all our lives have changed very much. Some changes are for the better; some are not so good. Some people approve of recent developments; some object to various aspects of life today.

We are interested in your point of view concerning various aspects of contemporary life. This will give us a better understanding of those recent developments which people in general think are good, as well as those which perhaps are not so popular.

We will appreciate your help and cooperation in this survey of popular opinion. It should be emphasized that in asking for your point of view there are no "right" or "wrong" answers. The best answer is your personal opinion. You can be sure that, whatever your own opinion, some people may disagree, and others are sure to agree with you.

In this survey we have tried to include many aspects of contemporary life as well as various different points of view. You will probably find yourself agreeing strongly with some statements, disagreeing with others, and perhaps agreeing only slightly with still others.

If you are willing to help us in this survey, please answer the questions as follows:

(1) Read each statement carefully, and mark it according to your first reaction. It isn't necessary to consider any one statement too long; each one should take you about a minute. Or in other words, to complete the entire survey should take you not much more than 30 minutes.

(2) Answer every question.

(3) Try your best to give your true and accurate point of view.

(4) Respond to the statements as follows. If you:

534

Strongly agree, mark +3
Agree somewhat, mark +2
Agree a *little,* mark +1

Strongly disagree, mark −3
Disagree somewhat, mark −2
Disagree a *little,* mark −1

For example, if you strongly disagree with the statement, "The style of the most recently constructed buildings in the city is ugly," mark −3 in the answer box □. If you *slightly agree* with the statement, mark +1; if you agree, but not strongly, mark +2; etc.

This survey, like any study of popular opinion, works just like an election: your answers are private, and you need not write down your name.

1. It is basically a good thing that young people can have more fun these days, such as by going out dancing or walking hand in hand in the park.   □

2. The nation naturally has its importance; but family life is more important.   □

3. Schools today put too much emphasis on mathematics, physics, and chemistry, and not enough on such worthwhile subjects as classical literature and calligraphy.   □

4. In the long run it is a good thing that a young man select his own career for himself.   □

5. A large part of the crime and immorality around here these days is due to so many strangers and travelers from abroad.   □

6. Although laws and political programs have their place, what our country needs even more is a few courageous, firm and dedicated leaders in whom the people can put their trust.   □

7. Although many people think that fortune-telling is nonsense, in the future it just may be proved that it really can explain many things.   □

8. It is an unfortunate thing that today there are many young women who prefer having a career to remaining at home and having a simple, happy family life.   □

9. Although the theories of Confucius and Mencius in the past had their value, their works cannot explain the many problems of interpersonal relations in society today.   □

10. Just as foreigners have come to appreciate many Chinese things, we also ought to adopt various good customs and habits of foreign countries.   □

11. Obedience and respect for their elders are the most important virtues children should develop.   □

12. Nowadays a young man can make a valuable and interesting career for himself in commerce.   □

13. It is more important to prove you are right in a discussion than to take an attitude of "why bother" or "forget it" just for the sake of friendliness or out of a desire not to hurt the other person's feelings.   □

14. There are few things more enjoyable for entertainment than China's traditional songs and regional operas. ☐

15. It is better, in these modern times, if parents are not so strict in expecting their children to do things just the way they do them. ☐

16. If a neighbor is making a public nuisance of himself, it is best just to try and ignore him or avoid the trouble of involvement than to attempt to correct the situation. ☐

17. If China would place greater emphasis on putting into practice her time-tested customs, habits, and social virtues, then many problems of contemporary society could be solved. ☐

18. Although criticizing the thoughts and suggestions of our superiors is useful for improving our work, it can lead to much trouble, and hence is best avoided. ☐

19. Although Chinese history possibly can provide some good experience, there are many important things we need to learn from modern economics, science, and social research. ☐

20. While it might not be bad for a son to live with his parents after marriage, it is basically better for a young couple to set up their own household. ☐

21. If there were not so many foreigners attempting to help other people deal with their own problems, then the world would be a much more peaceful place. ☐

22. In contemporary society, the professions of a scientist or engineer are particularly interesting and valuable. ☐

23. It is essential for effectiveness in study or work that our teachers or superiors give us detailed explanations and directives. ☐

24. For understanding different social customs and ways of interpersonal relations, as well as various foreign things, foreign movies are worthwhile to see. ☐

25. Human nature being what it is, unfortunately there will probably always be interpersonal disputes, conflicts, or war. ☐

26. History will probably prove that the contribution of the scholar or artist has been more important for society than that of the scientist or manufacturer. ☐

27. It is annoying to hear people always stressing the virtues of patience, compromise, and restraint. We should be bold enough to work for great change and seek to improve things now, even though some people may be opposed. ☐

28. If someone is lying hurt in the street, it is best not to rush right up and help, and thus avoid bringing on a lot of trouble, as someone whose proper job it is will always come along quickly to take charge. ☐

29. It is an unfortunate thing that during one's life it is so difficult to find true friends with whom one can share the thoughts and feelings deep in one's heart. ☐

30. Although sciences like chemistry, physics and medicine have helped in the advancement of mankind, there are many important things which can never be understood by human intelligence. ☐

31. When the national situation gets a bit difficult, it is only natural and proper that people be expected to make a greater contribution, such as by extending the time of military service, controlling consumption, or directing people in their work and study, etc. ☐

32. If two people really love each other but both their parents object, it is better for their long run happiness that they not marry. ☐

Appendix IV

THEMATIC APPERCEPTION TEST
(TAT) PICTURES

I

II

III

IV

V

VI

VII

VIII

IX

Appendix V

RESPONDENTS' BIOGRAPHICAL
SKETCHES

These biographical sketches are designed to provide the reader with a general description of each respondent's social background and life history. They have been written on the basis of detailed biographical information contained in the respondent's interview record. A standard biographical data schedule, reproduced in Appendix II above, served as the basis for collecting this information, although supplemental material, gathered during the course of the interview, was also utilized in preparing the sketches.

The interviews were carried out during the year 1965. The fifty-six respondents in the "T" series were interviewed in Taipei City, Taiwan. The thirty-six "H" series interviews were done in Hong Kong. In general, the respondents in the 55–84 age group emigrated to Taiwan during the late 1940s. Those in the 20–29 age group emigrated from the mainland during or subsequent to the large exodus into Hong Kong of 1962, the period of crisis following the Great Leap Forward. The respondents in the 30–54 year old group have mixed times of emigration. Some left the mainland in the late 1940s, and others have come out since 1962.

* * *

T-1: 32 years old at the time of interview; reared in a well-to-do rural family of Heng-hsien, Kwangsi Province. As a young adult the respondent moved to Canton. He taught in an elementary school on the mainland for three years. He now holds a clerical position with the Nationalist government on Taiwan.

His father was trained at the Paoting Military Academy, eventually rising to the rank of major-general in the Nationalist army. He commanded the military district which included the family's old home at Heng-hsien, Kwangsi. The Communists classified this family as "landlord." The father was executed as a class enemy in 1951.

T-2: A 36-year-old former soldier; born at Hoyuan, Kwangtung Province and reared in the market town of Chacheng, Kwangtung. He received a high school education and worked on the mainland as a mechanic. He now works as a mechanic in Taiwan.

His father was a small merchant who owned about 20 *mou* of land in Kwangtung.

T-3: 33 years old; grew up in Shantung Province, but returned to his home province of Kiangsu at the age of 15 where he was tutored in the Confucian classics. He taught at a private elementary school on the mainland for five years, and now works as a clerk for the Nationalist government on Taiwan.

His father, who was singled out for criticism by the Communists, was a wealthy salt merchant whose business was in Shantung.

T-4: 26 years old; born and raised in Shanghai City. The son of a landlord family, he studied public health in high school and worked for one year in a public health clinic on the mainland. He is now a library worker in Taiwan.

His father was a college graduate who later became captain of a ship engaged in international trade.

T-5: 26 years old; reared in Liuchou, Kwangsi Province. From a well-to-do family. He attended a college in South China for two years under the Communists, but the experience consisted primarily of manual labor. He taught himself to read and write music, and now writes music for a broadcasting station in Taiwan.

His father, whose home was in Heng-hsien, Kwangsi, was trained at the Paoting Military Academy and became a lieutenant-general in the Nationalist army. His father was stationed at Liuchou, and was killed by the Communists in the early 1950s.

T-6: 53 years old; from Kueip'ing, Kwangsi Province. He served 19 years in the Nationalist army as a communications specialist. After the Communists attained power he was unable to find a regular job and so supported himself in Canton City by working as a street secretary for three years, and then by running a noodle stand. He now works as a research aide for a cultural organization in Taiwan.

His grandfather had been a classical scholar of some reputation. His father had operated a successful wholesale food business in Kueip'ing.

T-7: 32 years old; born and raised in Canton City, Kwangtung. He had been a cadre in the Communist Party during the land reform period (1950–1953) and up through the failure of the Great Leap Forward (1962). He now works in Taiwan as a statistical clerk.

His father had been the leader of a religious sect in Canton, and died in prison in 1959 after six years of internment by the Communists.

T-8: 53 years old; born in Loting-hsien, Kwangtung, but moved to Canton City as a young man. He spent many years in the Nationalist military. After World War II he began police work, first in Kwangtung and now in Taiwan.

His family was classified as "landlord" by the Communists. His father had been principal of an elementary school for many years in Loting-hsien. He was killed during a "struggle" meeting in 1951.

T-9: A 49-year-old college graduate from a large and wealthy family; born and raised in Peking. He directed the family's private school in Peking for many years. After the Communists attained power he worked as a laborer and spent one year in jail. He now teaches high school in Taiwan.

His father, who was an official at the close of the Ch'ing dynasty, owned many pawn shops in Peking.

T-10: A 63-year-old intellectual and teacher; born and raised in Tientsin City, Hopeh Province. He graduated from Yenching University and spent three years in Japan studying law at Meiji University.

His father, who was a colonel in the Manchu army during the last days of the Ch'ing dynasty, died when the respondent was very young. He was reared by an uncle, also a military man.

T-11: A 38-year-old high school teacher from Mei-hsien, Kwangtung Province. He graduated from Chuhai University in Canton and taught high school biology on the mainland before coming to Taiwan.

His father owned shops in Mei-hsien and Canton which sold rice, tea, and other staples. The father died of a disease shortly after being classified as a landlord and subjected to criticism by the Communists.

T-12: 29 years old at the time of interview, the respondent came from a poor family living in Huiyang-hsien, Kwangtung. After graduating from high school he had five years of training at a trade school on the mainland, and now works as an electrical technician in Taiwan.

His father was a small merchant in Huiyang-hsien.

T-13: Born into a well-to-do family from Sui-hsien, a town of some 200 families in Hupeh Province. The respondent was 63 years old when interviewed. He had worked for many years in a county-level governmental office under the Nationalists on the mainland. After reaching Hong Kong he supported himself for a time by begging. Since arriving in Taiwan he has sold beancake and is now a fortune teller in a public park.

T-14: 26 years old; born in Ningpo-hsien, Chekiang Province and grew up in Shanghai City. He received five years of architectural training in Shanghai and now works as an architect in Taiwan.

His father was a small merchant in Shanghai who now works as an accountant in Taiwan. From the ages of nine to twenty-three the interviewee was separated from his parents as they had been in Taiwan when the Communists gained control of Shanghai and had not returned. During these years the interviewee and his brother were reared by an aunt in Shanghai.

T-15: 35 years old; from Wuhua-hsien, Kwangtung. Although he had had a high school education, the interviewee worked as a farmer and general laborer on the mainland. He now works as a clerk in Taiwan.

His father had been a local official (*hsiang-chang*) in Wuhua-hsien under the Nationalists. The father died of a disease while in jail during the Communist period.

T-16: 26 years old; reared in a farming village of about 2,000 people in Kwangtung Province. After graduating from high school he worked as an accountant in a factory in Canton. In 1957 he was sentenced to two years of labor reform for criticizing the Communist government during the Hundred Flowers Movement. He now works as a clerk in a government bureau in Taiwan.

His father, who was classified as a landlord by the Communists, died when the interviewee was very young. He was reared by his mother who managed to support the family by opening a small provisions store.

T-17: 33 years old; from Ilan-hsien, Heilungkiang Province. He moved to Peking at the age of 18 and spent seven years (during the 1950s) in the People's Liberation Army. He now drives a truck in Taiwan.

His father ran a small inn, and also had served as a superintendent over several thousand forestry workers.

T-18: 36 years old, from a scholarly and respected family in Hokou-chen, a market town of about 300 families, in Loshan-hsien, Honan Province. He served in the Nationalist army during the last days of World War II. After 1949 he ran a wine shop and worked as a manual laborer for several years. He was sentenced to a period of political reform in a labor camp by the Communists in 1955 for having urged his fellow workers to demand higher wages. He escaped from the labor camp which was in

Szechwan Province, and spent three years wandering about China, often working as a truck driver. He managed to reach India via Tibet, and eventually was brought to Taiwan.

His grandfather and father had been teachers of the Confucian classics and occasionally were called upon to settle local disputes.

T-19: 26 years old; born in the small village of Chofang, Wuchiao-hsien, Hopeh Province, and later raised in the town of Kiangtien-lan, Changlo-hsien, Fukien. He graduated from high school in 1957 and worked in administrative jobs until he was selected to receive two years of training at a technical school in Inner Mongolia. Accused of being uncooperative with Party personnel, the Communists sentenced him to two years of labor reform on a farm. After serving his sentence, he escaped to Taiwan.

His father had been an officer in a local unit of the Nationalist security forces near their village in Fukien. The father was killed during a "struggle" meeting in 1950. His mother was a nurse who operated a small clinic.

T-20: 39 years old at the time of interview; born in the village of Koko-chuangtsun (population about 2,000 persons), in Tsaiyang-hsien, Shantung. He was reared in Dairen, Liaoning Province. He received one year of trade school education under the Japanese during their occupation of North China, and later worked as a repairman of electrical machinery for the Communist government. He joined a guerrilla band in Tibet during the middle 1950s to fight the Communists. He escaped to India and then came to Taiwan.

His father was a housing contractor with about 50 employees, whose business was in Dairen.

T-21: A 26-year-old medical student born in Shanghai. His family moved to Kansu Province when he was 12. His parents had separated when he was two years old, and he was reared by his mother's relatives—a grandmother and an uncle. He studied medicine for eighteen months under the Communists at the Changyi Medical School in Kansu, and at the time of interview had continued his medical studies in Taiwan for three years.

His father worked as a hired sailor on a commercial ship. His mother's relatives were also of moderate means.

T-22: A 35-year-old overseas Chinese, born in Singapore and raised both in Yungch'un-hsien, Fukien Province, and Ampenan, Indonesia. In 1948 he decided to join the Communist movement on the mainland after being influenced by an overseas Chinese high school teacher who was a Party member. He traveled from Djakarta to Hong Kong and joined a guerrilla band in Kwangtung Province. He spent three years during the 1950s studying physics at Chungshan University in Canton, but was assigned to labor reform in 1957 for having criticized the secret police system. He succeeded in escaping from the mainland in 1962 after one earlier failure, for which he served a one-year prison sentence. He is now studying physics at a Taiwan university.

His father had worked in a small import-export store in Yungch'un-hsien, Fukien, and later opened a grocery store in Indonesia. The father returned to the mainland in the early 1950s to search for his son, but died there without finding him.

T-23: 46 years old; born and raised in Chinchiang-hsien, Kiangsu Province. As the only male child in his generation, he was eligible to inherit much land that belonged to his family's clan. He was disgusted by the family quarrels over this matter and ran away from home at the age of 20 to join the Nationalist navy. He later returned to his home village and served as village chief for eight years, until the Communists came. He now works as a clerk in the town office of a market center in Taiwan, where he has lived since 1951.

The interviewee's father was a wealthy land owner who concerned himself mainly with his land's agricultural production.

T-24: 54 years old; from a wealthy family in Nanchang-hsien, Hupeh Province. He served in the Nationalist army during World War II and the civil war, after graduation from a military school. He retired in the early 1950s on Taiwan as a lieutenant-colonel.

His father was a college professor on the mainland.

T-25: 46 years old; born in Leishang-hsien, Anhwei. He graduated from the Anhwei Provincial Agricultural College just before World War II. Although his parents hoped he would become a school teacher in the local district, the interviewee left home to join the Nationalist army. Since the early 1950s he has been a special member of the Nationalists' Committee on Tibetan-Mongolian Affairs.

His father was an elementary school teacher in Leishang-hsien and also served for six years as a local official (*hsiang-chang*).

T-26: 44 years old; born in T'anch'eng-hsien, Shantung Province. He taught school for several years, then joined the Nationalist army during World War II. He retired from the army in 1959 and now runs a small grocery store in Taiwan.

His father was a well-to-do farmer.

T-27: 47 years old; born and raised in Hsühsüan-hsien, Anhwei. He grew up in an extended family of 31 persons who lived together in a large house. At the age of 14 he was appointed a minor official (*li-chang*) by his uncle and later was a township functionary (*hsiang-chang*) for three years. He joined the Nationalist army at the age of 24, at the beginning of World War II. He is now a policeman in Taiwan.

His father was a poor farmer, although his grandparents and uncle had some wealth.

T-28: 68 years old; born and raised at Hohsing-cheng, a town of some 10,000 people, in Ch'anglo-hsien, Fukien. He majored in political science at the Foochow Political Science College. After graduation in the early 1920s he served the central government as a secretary in the National Assembly in Peking and in the Judicial Yuan at Hankow. From 1928 to 1935 he was an administrator for the Nationalist government, serving at Shanghai and Foochow. Before retiring on Taiwan in 1952, he was a propagandist for the Central News Bureau.

His father, although poor, became a Ch'ing dynasty scholar (*hsiu-ts'ai*) and taught the classics in a private school. The father died when the respondent was three years old.

T-29: 76 years old; from a gentry family in Hsuanhsing-hsien, Kiangsu Province. After receiving a traditional education from his father, and some additional study in Nanking, the respondent received an M.A. in Western history from the University of Wisconsin and later a Ph.D. from the University of Heidelberg in Germany. He is now a professor of history in a Taiwan university.

His father was a Ch'ing dynasty scholar (*chü-jen*). His mother died when he was eight years old and his father remarried.

T-30: 72 years old; born into a poor family in Chiangtu-hsien, Kiangsu Province. He received a traditional education from his father, and later graduated from the Kiangsu Law College. He then worked as a newspaper editor, a high school teacher, and was general secretary of the Nationalist Party's Central Political Council. He is today a popular writer in Taiwan.

His father ran a dry goods store.

T-31: 56 years old; born to a well-to-do family in Hengshan-hsien, Hunan. He spent eight years in Japan and graduated from Kyoto University where he majored in law. He later worked as a newspaper manager and is now a college professor.

The respondent's father was a "revolutionary" and a member of the *Tung Meng Hui*. Because he spent so much time in political work, the respondent claimed, the father devoted too little attention to his children and was not adequately concerned about their welfare.

T-32: 64 years old; reared by a wealthy family in Kaier-hsien, Liaoning Province. After an early career as a teacher and secondary school principal, the interviewee taught in government police academies. During World War II he joined the Nationalist army and became an officer.

The interviewee had been given by his natural parents to a wealthy family to be brought up. His foster father, who owned much land, also served as a district chief (*ch'ü-chang*) for several years. The interviewee said his foster parents treated him very well.

T-33: 57 years old; born and raised in Hanchou-hsien, Hupeh. He graduated from Chunghua University in Wuchang, majoring in political science. He is now a staff adviser in the Ministry of National Defense in Taiwan.

His father ran a small dry goods shop and was often away from home on business.

T-34: 54 years old; born and raised in Ihuang-hsien, Kiangsi Province. Encouraged by his older brother who was studying in the United States, the respondent worked part time to earn money for his own schooling. He graduated from Facheng University in Nanking, majoring in law. He worked for the Nationalist government as a principal of secondary schools, and now teaches at a political cadre training school in Taiwan.

His father was a small merchant who was often away from home buying cloth in Shanghai. His mother died when the respondent was very young, and he was reared by his maternal grandmother. His father later remarried, but the respondent continued to live with his grandmother.

T-35: 66 years old; raised in Nanch'ang, Kiangsi Province. He majored in law at Facheng College in Nanchang. He has spent many years as the head of various departments of the Nationalist government, and is a member of the National Assembly in Taiwan.

His father was a Ch'ing dynasty scholar (*hsiu-ts'ai*). The respondent described his family's financial situation as difficult. His mother managed family affairs.

T-36: 72 years old at the time of interview; from a wealthy family in the small village of Kaoai-chen in Anch'iu-hsien, Shantung Province. He graduated from Shanghai T'ungchi University. He has worked for most of his life as a civil engineer.

His father was the largest land owner in the area and also ran a small business buying and selling brass.

T-37: 58 years old; from a wealthy family in Nanch'ang, Kiangsi. He majored in education at National Tungnan University in Nanking. He taught high school after graduation and later became supervisor of a Nationalist government educational bureau. He is now a professor in Taiwan.

His father was a financial administrator for the Nationalist government. The respondent said his father was usually working at the office and spent little time at home.

T-38: 56 years old; born in the small village of Shih-chuang in Yung-p'ing-fu, Hopeh Province. The respondent left home to study in Peking at the age of 12. He spent three years in a military training academy and is now an administrative officer for the Nationalist army.

His father was a peasant who owned some land.

T-39: 56 years old; born and raised in a village in Chungchiang-hsien, Szechuan. After finishing high school he graduated from a military school in Nanking, spent one year at the Whampoa Military Academy, and then served as a career officer in the Nationalist army. He retired with the rank of captain.

His parents were peasants who owned some land. The respondent and his parents lived in an extended family which included three paternal uncles and their families.

T-40: 71 years old when interviewed; reared in the city of Wuhsi, Kiangsu Province. He graduated from a high school in Tokyo and then attended Tokyo Industrial University. He was a mechanical engineer.

His father was a Ch'ing dynasty scholar (*chü-jen*) who later became a judge and a lawyer.

T-41: 52 years old; raised in a family of wealth in a village in Shenyang-hsien, Liaoning Province. He graduated from Tungpei University, where he majored in political science. During World War II he followed the Nationalist government to Szechuan. He now teaches mathematics at a government school in Taiwan, and also runs a night school.

His father, who was a grand nephew to the Hsuan-t'ung emperor, was also a Ch'ing dynasty scholar (*chü-jen*).

T-42: 55 years old when interviewed; raised in Kut'ang-chen, Chiu-chiang-hsien, Kiangsi Province. He graduated from an accounting school in Kiangsi Province. Most of his adult life was spent as an officer in the quartermaster corps of the Nationalist army. He was retired in 1962 and now runs a small business in Taiwan.

For thirty years his father operated a soap factory in Kiangsi.

T-43: 69 years old; born in a village in Ch'anghsing-hsien, Chekiang. He graduated from the Facheng Academy in Hengchou, majoring in political science and economics. He worked for the Chinese Customs Bureau for several years, then spent fifteen years in the Nationalist army. He retired in 1949 with the rank of lieutenant.

His father was a Ch'ing dynasty scholar (*hsiu-ts'ai*).

T-44: 63 years old; reared in the small village of Hsich'i-lits'un Hsia-hsien, Shansi Province. He graduated from Shansi University in T'ai-yuan, where he majored in law. He spent many years studying in Germany and became a translator after his return to China. Five years later he began working for the Nationalist government and is now a specialist in legal and administrative work.

His father was a peasant who owned and farmed his own land.

T-45: 69 years old; raised in Chungshan-hsien, Kwangtung Province. He completed high school in Japan and then graduated from the Imperial University, majoring in law. He spent 40 years working as a specialist in the Railroad Bureau of the Ministry of Transportation for the Nationalist government. Although now retired from government service he works as a secretary in a high school in Taiwan.

His father ran a small tea store in Chungshan-hsien.

T-46: 74 years old; from a gentry family in Pailien-ts'un (population about 100), in Huoshan-hsien, Anhwei Province. He taught for ten years in a traditional private school (*szu-shu*) then entered the Provincial Fak'o University in Hupeh Province where he majored in law. Since graduating he has operated Chinese medicine shops.

His father was a Ch'ing dynasty scholar (*hsiu-ts'ai*), who served as a county official (*hsien-chang*) for four years and owned much land.

T-47: 65 years old; born and raised in Foochow City, Fukien Province. He graduated from the private Facheng Academy in Foochow where he majored in law. After spending many years as a judge he became a lawyer. He is now a lawyer in Taiwan.

His father was also a lawyer in Foochow.

T-48: 54 years old at the time of interview; reared in Chiahsing-fu, Chekiang Province. During the course of twenty-two years he served for a time in the Nationalist army, ran a stationery store, and opened an elementary school. Later he rejoined the army and came to Taiwan. He retired in 1963.

His father was an official in the Shanghai municipal government.

T-49: 57 years old; raised in a village in Linglu-hsien, Hopeh Province. He ran away from home at the age of 14. An uncle in Hankow helped him attend high school. He graduated from a private military academy in Nanking and for several years worked in a provincial office of the Nationalist Party. He then spent twelve years as a military instructor. In 1949 he retired and now runs a small food store in Taiwan.

His father was a peasant who owned his own land.

T-50: 56 years old; raised in a poor family from the small village of Wuchia-han Mop'ing-hsien, Shantung Province. For over 20 years he worked in records and administration for the Nationalist Party, first at Party headquarters and later in the Fukien provincial government. He is now a political officer in the Nationalist army in Taiwan.

His father was a peasant who owned and farmed his own land.

T-51: 66 years old; reared in the village of Hsiang-ts'un, Tach'eng-hsien, Hopeh Province. He helped his father farm the land until the age of 20, when he left home to join the Nationalist army. After twenty-five years in the army he retired as a lieutenant colonel.

His father was a peasant who farmed his own land.

T-52: 72 years old when interviewed; raised in Fengyang-hsien, Anhwei Province. After graduating from a naval academy, he spent over twenty years in the Chinese navy. He participated in the 1911 revolution, and eventually became a staff officer in the Nationalist armed forces. He also served as a police official. He retired in 1965.

His father was a Ch'ing dynasty scholar (*chü-jen*), who operated a traditional style school for ten years and then opened a "western style" elementary school.

T-53: 57 years old; raised in Ch'angli-hsien, Hopeh Province. He served in the Nationalist army for seventeen years, then worked for five years as a secretary in a police department. He is now a missionary for the Protestant Church in Taiwan.

His father was a carpenter.

T-54: 55 years old at the time of interview; raised in the village of Tali-chuang, Kirin Province. He spent many years working on various railroads in North China as a dispatcher and in railroad administration. He then worked as an accountant in a friend's business for four years. He retired in 1959.

His father was a poor peasant who farmed his own land.

T-55: 83 years old; of a gentry family from a village in Ts'ailing-hsien, Hunan Province. He passed the imperial examinations to become a Ch'ing dynasty scholar (*hsiu-ts'ai*), and also graduated from the Facheng Academy in Ch'angsha, where he majored in law. After serving in the army, he spent the next eleven years at home at the request of his father. He later worked for three years as a secretary in the provincial government of Honan. He has been living in retirement since coming to Taiwan.

His father was a Ch'ing dynasty *chin-shih* scholar.

T-56: 63 years old; reared in Shant'ou (Swatow) City, Kwangtung Province. He spent some years in government service, as chief of the Financial Bureau of the Fukien provincial government and as a police official in Hsiamen (Amoy) City. He entered the import-export business in 1934. Since coming to Taiwan in 1947 he has been a teacher.

His father ran an import-export business.

H-1: 24 years old; from a wealthy family living in Shanghai. After high school he entered Hsiamen (Amoy) University to major in chemistry. After two years of study, upon the death of both parents, he went to Hong Kong. He is now working as a tailor's assistant.

His father was a chemical and electrical engineer who was trained at universities in the United States.

H-2: 30 years old when interviewed; from a former gentry family of the city of Foshan (Fatshan), Kwangtung Province. He received five years of architectural training at Chungshan University in Canton under the Communists, and worked in Canton for a time. He is now a draftsman with a Hong Kong architectural firm.

Both of the interviewee's grandfathers had been officials in the Ch'ing dynasty. His father was an officer in the Nationalist army who attained the rank of major.

H-3: 25 years old; reared in Hsiamen (Amoy) City, Fukien Province. After graduating from middle school he received two years of training in chemical engineering at the Chekiang Chemical Engineering School in Hangchow. After a serious illness he was unable to find work. He arrived in Hong Kong shortly before the interview.

His father was an accountant in a Hong Kong soy sauce factory.

H-4: 38 years old; raised in Shant'ou (Swatow) City, Kwangtung. During World War II he aided his parents in supplying information about Japanese forces to Chinese Communist guerrilla units. He served in the People's Liberation Army, fought in the Korean War, and later became a bodyguard for some of China's highest officials.

His father, who originally ran a boxing school in Shant'ou joined the Chinese Communist Party in the 1930s. Because of the father's activities against the Japanese, he was executed by them in 1942.

H-5: 23 years old; raised in Shanghai. He spent one year studying medicine under the Communists at the Second Medical School in Shanghai. He then came to Hong Kong.

His father, who had studied law in Japan, was at one time president of the Judicial Yuan in the Nationalists' Nanking government.

H-6: 23 years old at the time of interview; reared in Meilung-chen (population about 300), Haifeng-hsien, Kwangtung Province. After graduating from high school under the Communists he worked for one year as a farmer, then came to Hong Kong. At present he is an assistant in a library of classical Chinese materials.

His father was a school teacher and also a county level secretary for the Nationalist Party. He was executed by the Communists in 1951.

H-7: 49 years old; reared in the city of Yingk'ou, Liaoning Province. During World War II he joined the Nationalist army and rose to the rank of colonel. After the Communists gained control of the mainland he joined the People's Liberation Army and served as an instructor, teaching former guerrilla units the tactics of regular warfare. He came to live in Hong Kong in 1957 and now runs a small store.

His father ran a small shipping business along the North China coast, and later opened a jewelry store.

H-8: 25 years old; raised in the cities of Shant'ou (Swatow) and Nanking. He spent one year studying at the Nanking Theological Seminary. In 1958, as a result of having criticized the Communist government during the Hundred Flowers movement of the previous year he was sentenced to four years of labor reform. In 1961 he spent one year studying Chinese art at Nanking Normal University. He is now a student in Hong Kong.

His father was a Baptist missionary who spent sixteen years preaching in Singapore.

H-9: 31 years old; born and raised in Shanghai. He worked as a laborer in a nationalized Shanghai factory producing industrial stoves. He now is employed in a Hong Kong cotton mill as a machinery maintenance worker.

His father was a cook on an American-owned ship.

H-10: 25 years old; from a gentry family of Yangchiang-hsien, Kwangtung. He entered Shant'ou (Swatow) Normal University to study Chinese, but because of his athletic abilities became a prominent track star in China. He later became a track instructor in the Foshan (Fatshan) special district, Kwangtung Province. He also served eight years as a branch secretary in the Communist Youth League. He is now a student in Hong Kong.

His grandfather was a Ch'ing dynasty scholar (*hsiu-ts'ai*) and a man of some wealth. His father was an officer in the Nationalist army.

H-11: 23 years old at the time of interview; born in a market town in Shih-hsing-hsien, Kwangtung Province and moved to Canton City at the age of seven. After graduating from high school he spent one year studying Chinese medicine at the Canton Medical College. He then left China and is at present a student in Hong Kong.

His father was a medical doctor. The interviewee was reared by his mother, a nurse, after his father's death.

H-12: 39 years old; born and raised in the market town of Ch'eng-chen, Yu-hsien, Honan Province. During World War II he fought the Japanese in the Nationalist army. After returning home he eventually obtained a responsible position under the Communists in a local government office handling documents. In 1958 he took an administrative position with a local coal mine. Since coming to Hong Kong in 1961 he has worked as a laborer on construction crews.

His father had been in the Ch'ing dynasty military forces, and later worked at a relative's restaurant.

H-13: 25 years old; from a well-to-do business family of Amoy City, Fukien Province. He received two years of technical training at the Anhwei Mining College in Huainan City. After graduation he worked at the college for two years. He is now studying civil engineering in Hong Kong.

For many years his father operated private food companies. Under the Communists he became an adviser at a food products company.

H-14: 21 years old; reared in Hong Kong and in Suchow City, Kiangsu Province. After graduating from high school on the mainland he returned to Hong Kong. He is now studying civil engineering.

His father works in a thermos bottle factory in Hong Kong.

H-15: 20 years old when interviewed; born and raised in a well-to-do business family in Shanghai. In 1963 he began studying chemistry in Hong Kong.

His father, a graduate of St. John's University in Shanghai, was director of a Shanghai insurance company and later opened an import-export business.

H-16: 64 years old; from a poor peasant family in Liaoning Province. He left his home village at the age of 18 and later studied sociology for two years at Chungshan University in Hankow. He has since worked as a foreman in various factories.

His father farmed his own land. The respondent said he himself was the only member of his family who left home to work away from the family.

H-17: 21 years old; from a wealthy family of Tayung-hsien, Hunan Province. After the death of their father, the interviewee and his older brother moved to Canton where they were reared by an aunt. After graduating from high school he came to Hong Kong, where he works in a wine house.

His father was an officer in the Nationalist army and was executed by the Communists in 1951.

H-18: 22 years old; the older brother of H-17. After graduating from high school he failed to gain admittance to a university. He then worked as a farmer in Anhwei Province. At present he is working at a gas station in Hong Kong.

H-19: 22 years old; reared in Huan-hsien, Kwangtung. He graduated from high school and then worked as a farm laborer for a year. He is now studying civil engineering in Hong Kong.

His father was an officer in the Nationalist army who escaped to Hong Kong just before the Communists gained control of the mainland. He is currently a foreman with a heavy construction firm in Hong Kong.

H-20: 21 years old; from a rich and well-known family in Hsinhsing-hsien, Kwangtung Province. Because of his family's wealth and former association with the Nationalist government, the respondent and his family were under observation by the Communists after 1949. He was brought up in a family from another district of Kwangtung. After graduating from middle school he taught elementary school for a short time, then came to Hong Kong.

His grandfather participated in the 1911 revolution under Sun Yat-sen and was a military officer during China's warlord period. Because of the family's wealth, the respondent's father never had to work.

H-21: 23 years old at the time of interview; born and raised in Yang-chiang-hsien, Kwangtung. In 1960, after graduating from high school, he entered the Kwangtung Chiaot'ung Academy in Canton where he studied water conservancy and dam construction for two years. Since arriving in Hong Kong he has been studying social science topics at a private academy.

His father formerly was a printer for a Nationalist newspaper. He moved to Hong Kong in 1949 and has worked since as an electrical repairman for the British military.

H-22: 28 years old; of a poor family from Lingshan-hsien, Kwangtung. Two years after graduating from high school, in 1959, he entered the Kansu Province Railway Academy in Lanchou where he studied transportation. In 1960 he was unable to obtain food and was reduced to eating weeds and tree bark. He became sick and went to Canton, but was unable to support himself. He then worked as a farm laborer in Paoan-hsien, Kwangtung. In 1962 he came to Hong Kong and now works in a toy factory.

His father was an officer in the Nationalist army during World War II. After 1949 he was accused by the Communists of being a reactionary and spent two years in prison. Since his release he has worked as a factory laborer in China.

H-23: 21 years old; from a wealthy Shanghai family. After graduating from high school he tried unsuccessfully for three years to enter a university. Since coming to Hong Kong he has worked part time while studying chemistry at a local college.

His father had studied in the United States and became an airline pilot in China. After the Communists gained power he opened his own factory but later decided to come to Hong Kong, where he is manager of a factory.

H-24: 31 years old; from a wealthy Canton family. In 1950 he entered Peking Industrial University where he studied civil engineering for six years. He then began working for the Central Chemical Engineering Planning Bureau in a job that required travel to many parts of China. Accused in 1963 of being a rightist, he left his job and returned to Canton. He later came to Hong Kong.

His father was an overseas Chinese from Panama who came to study civil engineering in Canton. Shortly after marrying, the father returned to Panama. The respondent has never seen his father.

H-25: 21 years old at the time of interview; reared in a village in Hai-feng-hsien, Kwangtung. He graduated from high school in 1961 but failed to pass the college entrance examinations. He came to Hong Kong in 1962 and is now studying the humanities at a local academy.

His father was a peasant who later worked as a school janitor.

H-26: 60 years old; raised in a peasant family from P'u-hsien, Shantung Province. After finishing primary school his father put him to work on the family farm. He left home at age 15 to become a soldier, and spent his adult life in the Nationalist military.

His father was a poor peasant.

H-27: 57 years old; from a wealthy landowning family of Hangchow City, Chekiang. He entered Chihchiang University in Hangchow to study literature, but because World War II was in progress left school to do political work for the Nationalist government. After the war he continued to work for the Nationalist Party. Before the Communists gained control of the mainland he escaped to Hong Kong, leaving his wife and children in China.

His father, a Ch'ing dynasty scholar (*chü-jen*), died when the respondent was six years old.

H-28: 20 years old; reared in Canton City. After graduating from high school he tried unsuccessfully for three years to enter a university. He then came to Hong Kong and is at present a student.

His father was a businessman in Hong Kong who occasionally visited the interviewee and his mother in Canton.

H-29: 75 years old; brought up in a wealthy land-owning family from Hengshan-hsien, Hunan Province. He graduated from Hunan University in Ch'angsha, where he studied law and government. He began working for the Nationalist government at the county level and eventually became a judge. He came to Hong Kong in 1949 and is now living alone.

His father was a high level county official during the last days of the Ch'ing dynasty.

H-30: 22 years old; from a wealthy family of Haifeng-hsien, Kwangtung. Because he had been classified by the Communists as coming from a landlord family, he was unable to gain admission to a university after graduating from high school. He came to Hong Kong in 1962 along with his mother and younger brother. He is now studying literature and history.

His father, who was a landlord, died when the interviewee was four.

H-31: 49 years old; born and raised in Ch'ingtao (Tsingtao) City, Shantung Province. After receiving an elementary education he became an apprentice in a metal fabricating shop. He later operated his own small plumbing and electrical repair shop and still runs such a business in Hong Kong.

His father ran a small business in Ch'ingtao, but after becoming addicted to opium he left home and moved to Dairen City, Liaoning Province, where he worked in a mine. He returned home after overcoming his addiction.

H-32: 76 years old when interviewed; from a land-owning family in P'ingchiang-hsien, Hunan Province. He was educated at home until the age of 17, when he entered the Hunan First Normal School in Ch'angsha (where he was a few classes ahead of Mao Tse-tung). After six years of study he returned home to become principal of a local school. He left home when the Communists came to power and went to Hong Kong.

His father was a landlord.

H-33: 69 years old; raised in Kanchou City, Kiangsi Province. He graduated from Wuhan Normal University, where he studied history. He participated in the Northern Expedition of 1927–28, and later did administrative work in the Nationalist government. He also taught school for a time.

His family had formerly been wealthy, but his father had both to farm and run a small business to provide for his dependents.

H-34: 51 years old; reared in Wuhu City, Anhwei Province. He studied economics at Futan University in Shanghai and graduated from Nanking's Chengchih University. During World War II he worked for the Nationalist government in Chungking. After the war he sold motor vehicles in Nanking. Since coming to Hong Kong in 1949 he has taught school.

His father had been in charge of a Nationalist government bureau concerned with strategic resources. He later opened a coal mine.

H-35: 54 years old; raised in Chinan City, Shantung Province. He never received a formal education. He left home in his teens and joined the warlord army of Wu P'ei-fu. He now operates a shoe repair stand in Hong Kong.

His father was a poor peasant.

Appendix VI

CHILDHOOD PUNISHMENTS AND
CHINESE SOCIAL VALUES

The pattern of punishments characteristic of a culture is an important indicator of social values, for the pain which parents purposefully inflict on their children reflects both their own social values and personal anxieties, and the areas of concern they develop in their children. As Talcott Parsons has observed, punishments and rewards in the childrearing process play a particularly important role in organizing a maturing personality.[1] Pleasure and pain as administered by parents establish an important link between the generations, providing continuity of value systems. Such sanctions and rewards also help to establish a (partial) congruence between the individual's personality system and the values of the culture and society he will enter when mature.

As is discussed in the first part of this study, our interview data indicate that expressions of aggression were the primary cause of parental punishment in Chinese society, revealing a pervasive concern with social conflict.[2] By way of contrast, the punishment pattern of American culture accepts (disciplined) aggressive behavior, while failures to be self-disciplining or to assume personal responsibility violate the American concern with developing self-reliance in children.[3]

The interview data suggest several variations in the way that parents of different socioeconomic status (S.E.S.) levels in Chinese society punish their children.[4] As the following table suggests, a child's failure to

1. Talcott Parsons, "Social Structure and the Development of Personality," *Psychiatry*, Vol. XXI (1958), pp. 321–340.
2. *See* pp. 67–73 above.
3. Comparative data is presented in the author's, "Mao's Effort to Reintegrate the Chinese Polity," in A. Doak Barnett, ed., *Chinese Communist Politics in Action*, p. 286.
4. Socioeconomic status differences were estimated for the interview sample on the basis of responses to questions 24a–i of the interview schedule. (*See* Appendix I, p. 528.) Because of missing data we were not able to develop a measure of S.E.S. for all respondents, which is why there is only a total sample of 62 in the table.

perform well in school was evidently the focus of parental anxieties in upper class families.

MAJOR CAUSE OF PARENTAL PUNISHMENT,
AS RECALLED IN ADULTHOOD

		Fighting	Doing poorly in school	Disobeying parental instructions	Being lazy	N
	Low	33% (5)	7% (1)	40% (6)	20% (3)	15
FAMILY	Medium	52% (12)	9% (2)	30% (7)	9% (2)	23
S.E.S.	High	29% (7)	38% (9)	25% (6)	8% (2)	24
	Total %	39% (24)	19% (12)	31% (19)	11% (7)	62

This distribution of responses indicates relatively constant parental concern with displays of aggression across lines of socioeconomic status, and slightly higher concern at lower S.E.S. levels with maintaining obedience and overcoming laziness. The low number of cases in several of these categories, however, makes the percentage differences of uncertain stability. It is in the area of performance in school that the major difference seems to lie.

Inasmuch as all these respondents had received at least some secondary-level education, the following interpretation seems justified: At lower S.E.S. levels students probably were highly conscious of the sacrifices parents were making for their education, and the family hopes which resided in their performance. They were probably highly motivated students, striving for the previously unattainable goals of economic security and social status that would come with educational achievement. Their parents, coming from lower social and literacy levels, probably had a certain sense of awe concerning the educational experience.

In well-to-do families, however, students grew up in surroundings where wealth and education were familiar attainments. They lacked that sense of urgency, both for their family and their personal security and status, which motivated students of lower S.E.S. levels. Their parents, however, well aware of the ease with which family fortune and status could be lost, pressured their children for performance in the one area where status and security could be *maintained*—successful scholarship. And as is corroborated by interview recollections of childhood, the educational process was a painful experience, apparently particularly so for the children of well-to-do families where parents and children did not share a common sense of urgency about successful scholarship.

A Glossary
of Chinese Terms and Phrases

amah 阿媽

A female servant.

ch'eng 誠

Sincerity; to act according to the obligations of one's social role and society's moral norms.

cheng-chih 政治

Politics.

cheng-feng 整風 [整风]*

"Party rectification"; an abbreviated form of *cheng-tun tang ti tso-feng* (整頓黨的作風) [整頻党的作风], to rectify the Party's work style.

cheng-ming 正名

To rectify names. The Confucian concept that if people acted according to the moral obligations of their social status or "name" then society would be well ordered and secure. A ruler was to "rectify names" by clearly defining what was proper or improper behavior for each social status, and by making a model of his own actions for others in authority to emulate.

ch'i 氣 [气]

Anger; hostile or aggressive feelings. (See *p'i-ch'i.*)

chi-chi fen-tzu 積極份子 [积极分子]

An activist; one who is motivated to promote Party policy.

chi-hsü ko-ming 繼續革命 [继续革命]

Continuous revolution. A Maoist alternative to Trotsky's heretical theory of "Permanent revolution" (trans. as *pu-tuan ko-ming* 不斷革命 [不断革命]).

* The character forms in brackets are the simplified characters now in common use in the People's Republic of China.

561

chiang jen-ch'ing 講人情
[讲人情]

To speak on behalf of another; to intercede for a friend in difficulty, invoking one's status or personal associations to help solve his problem.

chiao-k'u 叫苦

To pour or shout out one's grievances.

chieh 潔 [洁]

Chastity.

chieh-fang 解放 [解放]

Liberation, as from an oppressive political order. To liberate, to let go or to release, as to release hostile feelings that have been denied expression by being "put in the stomach."

chieh-pan jen 接班人

Revolutionary successors.

Ch'ien-hsien 前綫 [前线]

Front Line. Theoretical magazine of the CCP's Peking Municipal Party Committee.

chih-an hao 治安好

Good peace and order.

ch'ih-k'u 吃苦

To "eat bitterness," to put frustration or hostility "in one's stomach" rather than express such socially improper feelings.

ch'ih-k'uei 吃虧 [吃亏]

To "eat a loss," to suffer some failure or to be mistreated by a more powerful individual.

chin-shih 進士 [进士]

An advanced degree conferred by the imperial examination system (lit. "advanced scholar"). Roughly equivalent to the doctor's degree in the West.

chiu-jou p'eng-yu 酒肉朋友

A "wine and meat friend," a friend who leads one astray into sensual indulgence.

chiu-se p'eng-yu 酒色朋友

A "wine and women friend," a friend who leads one astray into sensual indulgence.

ch'ü-chang 區長 [区长]

A district chief.

chü-jen 舉人 [举人]

An advanced degree conferred by the imperial examination system (lit. "an elevated man"). Roughly equivalent to a master's degree in the West.

ch'ün-chung lu-hsien 群眾路綫 [群众路线] The Mass Line, the Maoist leadership concept that the Party should stimulate active popular participation in discussing and applying policies.

chün-tzu 君子 The Confucian concept of a morally cultivated "superior man."

chung 忠 Loyalty, the Confucian concept of personal commitment to one's superior as required by the virtue of filial piety.

Chung-kuo Ch'ing-nien 中國青年 [中国青年] *China Youth,* the magazine of the CCP's Youth Corps.

ch'ung-tung 衝動 [冲动] To be impulsive or assertive, implying lack of proper reserve or control of aggressive feelings.

ch'ung-yi-hsia 衝一下 [冲一下] To shock or startle; to dash against, as to throw cold water against someone or something.

chung-yung 中庸 The Confucian concept of the "Middle Way," implying lack of extremism or aggressiveness in personal behavior.

fa-fen t'u-ch'iang 發奮圖強 [发奋图强] To draw strength from anger.

fan-kan 反感 Bad feelings, resentment.

fan tso-wu 犯錯誤 [犯错误] To commit an error; in CCP parlance, to make a political mistake.

fang 放 To release, to let go, implying an easing of control. (See *chieh-fang.*)

fen-san 分散 To scatter or disperse, in political terms implying the breakdown of an organization's unity, as in Sun Yat-sen's lament during the early years of the Republic that the Chinese nation was just "a sheet of scattered sand" (*yi-p'an sha-tzu* 一盤沙子 [一盘沙子]).

fen-sui 粉碎

To disintegrate, to fragment; in political parlance implying the disintegration of the cohesiveness of an organization or coalition.

feng-shui 風水 [风水]

The geomantic forces of the natural environment. If one adjusts one's behavior to these forces they can provide assistance, while to violate them is to bring on trouble.

fu-mu kuan 父母官

"Father-mother officials." An informal designation for local magistrates during the imperial era.

fu-tza 複雜 [复杂]

To be complicated, as of a social relationship. The term implies tension or clashing interests which might lead to open conflict.

han-hsü 含蓄

To be reserved. The opposite of impulsiveness. (See *ch'ung-tung*).

ho-ch'i 和氣 [和气]

To be affable, considerate.

ho-p'ing 和平

Harmony, peace, the absence of social conflict. The opposite of *hun-luan.*

ho-tso 合作

To cooperate.

hsia-fang 下放

To "transfer downward," as to transfer administrative cadres "down" to the countryside to engage in physical labor.

hsiang 鄉 [乡]

The township level of political organization in China.

hsiang-chang 鄉長 [乡长]

A township's chief administrative official.

hsiang-yüeh 鄉約 [乡约]

Lectures on Confucianism delivered to the common people by imperial scholar officials. The title of the local official in charge of such lectures.

hsiao 孝

The Confucian virtue of filial piety.

hsiao-chi ti-k'ang 消極抵抗 [消极抵抗] Passive resistance.

Hsiao Ching 孝經[孝经] *The Classic of Filial Piety.*

hsien 縣 [县] The county level of administrative organization in China.

hsien-chang 縣長[县长] The chief administrative official of a county.

hsiu-t'sai 秀才 A popular term for holders of the lowest scholarly degree conferred by the imperial examination system (lit., "cultivated talent"). Roughly equivalent to a bachelor's degree in the West. (See *sheng-yüan.*)

hsiu-yang 修養 [修养] The Confucian concept of moral self-cultivation through study.

hsüeh 學 [学] To study, with the implication of emulating the object of one's attention, as to "study" a person in order to learn his good points and imitate them.

Hsüeh-hsi 學習[学习] *Study,* the theoretical journal of the CCP from 1949 to 1958. At the time of the Great Leap Forward it was superseded by *Hung Ch'i* (紅旗), *Red Flag.*

hua-ch'iao 華僑[华侨] An "overseas Chinese," one who has migrated to a country beyond China.

hun-luan 混亂[混乱] Confusion, chaos, a breakdown in social order implying conflict and the unrestrained release of aggression.

hun-luan chuang-t'ai, 混亂狀態 [混乱状态] or *hun-luan hsien-hsiang* 混亂 現象 [混乱现象] Chaotic (social) conditions, implying a breakdown of authority and unrestrained conflict.

je-nao 熱鬧 [热闹] To be bustling, busy, as of an environment; a positive term implying a warm and active group atmosphere, giving the individual a sense of security.

jen 仁 — The Confucian virtue of human-heartedness, compassion, a lack of selfishness. A subordinate hopes that *jen* will mitigate the harshness of authority and give him security in job and material amenities.

jen-ch'ing 人情 — Human feelings, the emotional sensitivities involved in one's social relations and obligations to others. (See *chiang jen-ch'ing.*)

jen-k'ou 人口 — Population (lit. "human mouths").

jen-min kung-she 人民公社 — People's Commune.

jen-t'sai 人才 — Men of talent and ability, a concept that reflects the personalized image of political authority in the Confucian tradition.

ju-chia 儒家 — The Chinese term for the Confucian school of political philosophy.

kan 敢 — To dare, to challenge the existing order of things.

kan-ch'ing 感情 — Emotions, feelings, particularly as they enter into one's relationship with another person. It can be said, "I have good *kan-ch'ing* with that man," implying that he will be sympathetic and provide both emotional and material support.

k'ang 坑 — A clay sleeping platform used in North China. A fire can be built under it to provide warmth during the winter months.

kao-luan 攪亂 [搅乱] — To make trouble, to stir up confusion. (See *hun-luan.*)

k'o-ch'i 客氣 [客气] — To be polite, mannerly, implying lack of aggressiveness or quarrelsome behavior.

k'o-ch'i-hua 客氣話 [客气话] — Polite or mannerly talk.

ko-ko 哥哥 — An elder brother.

k'ou-t'ou 叩頭 [叩头] — To kneel and knock one's head on the floor before a person in authority as an expression of filial submission and loyalty.

ku-li 孤立 — To isolate.

ku-li ti 孤立的 — To be isolated, implying either to be surrounded and exposed to group hostility, or to be rejected and cut off from group support.

kuei 鬼 — Ghost, spirit, implying something grotesque, as in the Cultural Revolution phrase used to ridicule Party "revisionists," *niu-kuei she-shen* (牛鬼蛇神) "freaks and monsters" (lit. "ox ghosts and snake spirits").

kung-she 公社 — Commune, as in the Paris Commune of 1871. (See also *jen-min kung-she*.)

li 禮 [礼] — The Confucian concept of social ritual used to express deference to those in authority and acceptance of one's social obligations.

li-chang 里長 [里长] — The chief official of a *li,* an administrative subdivision of approximately 100 households used to collect revenue for the central political authorities.

li-mao 禮貌 [礼貌] — Good manners, etiquette, propriety in one's social relations.

luan 亂 [乱] — Confusion, chaos, implying conflict and unrestrained release of aggression. (See *hun-luan*.)

luan-sha, luan-ta 亂殺亂打 [乱杀乱打] — To beat and kill indiscriminately.

luan-tzu 亂子 [乱子] — A disturbance; disorder.

luan-tzu kuan 亂子觀 [乱子观] — The Maoist "Concept of Chaos," expressed during the Cultural Revolution, which held that the disturbances and confusion caused by the Red Guards would be a positive test of the revolutionary commitment of Party cadres.

Lun Kung-ch'an-tang Yüan ti Hsiu-yang 論共產黨員的修養 [論共产党员的修养]

On the Cultivation of a Communist Party Member; also translated as *How to Be a Good Communist.* Written in 1939 by Liu Shao-ch'i, Vice Chairman of the CCP, in the form of three lectures delivered to Party cadres. First published as a book in 1949. Revised versions, published in 1962 and 1964, were attacked by Maoists during the Cultural Revolution as being Confucian in spirit and for playing down the importance of class struggle.

ma 罵 [骂]

To scold, criticize, or curse.

ma-an-hsing 馬鞍形 [马鞍形]

Horse-saddle shaped, "U-shaped."

ma-chieh 罵街 [骂街]

To "curse the street," to air one's grievances in public so as to expose to public ridicule the individual who caused one difficulties.

mao-tun 矛盾

Contradiction, in Maoist usage implying conflicting economic interests and/or personal grievances and resentment toward an individual or group.

mei-yu pan-fa 没有辦法 [没有办法]

"There is nothing that can be done" (about a situation). A popular expression implying lack of personal ability to deal with a problem or to influence a (more powerful) individual.

mi-ch'ieh kuan-hsi 窋切關係 [窋切关係]

To have intimate relations (with someone or a group), implying involvement in their affairs as a way of either assisting or controlling them.

ming-che pao-shen 明哲保身 — "An enlightened man protects himself."

mou 畝 [亩] — A measure of land area. One acre equals 6.6 *mou*.

Nan-fang Jih-pao 南方日報 [南方日报] — *The Southern Daily*. The press organ of the Kwangtung Province Party Committee, published in Canton since 1949.

nei-chan 內戰 [內战] — Civil war.

ni-ai 溺愛 [溺爱] — To spoil a child with too much love; lit. "to drown with love."

pao-chia 保甲 — A form of village political organization used in the imperial era to establish dynastic control at the lowest levels of society through group responsibility for individual misdeeds. One hundred households were organized into *chia* units, with ten *chia* comprising a *pao*.

p'ei-yang 培養 [培养] — To rear or nurture, as a child.

p'i-ch'i 脾氣 [脾气] — Temperament. An irascible individual would be said to be *p'i-ch'i pu-hao* (脾氣不好).

pi-tzu pang-mang 彼此幫忙 [彼此帮忙] — To render mutual assistance; reciprocal support.

p'o-szu li-kung 破私立公 — "Destroy selfishness, establish the collective spirit." A Maoist slogan propagated during the Cultural Revolution when factional conflict among Red Guards threatened to undermine all political discipline.

san-ho yi-shao 三和一少 — "Three reconciliations and one reduction." A foreign policy line which Maoists attacked during the Cultural Revolution as having been formulated by "revisionist" Party leaders in the early 1960s. It called for reconciliation rather than struggle with Soviet "revisionism," U.S. "imperialism," and all for-

	eign "reactionaries," and reduction of aid to "revolutionary" insurgency movements.
san-tzu yi-pao 三自一包	"The three privates and the one guarantee." An economic policy line attacked by the Maoists during the Cultural Revolution. It was said to have been formulated by "revisionist" Party leaders in the early 1960s, during the period of recovery from the Great Leap Forward. It advocated extension of the peasants' private plots, private enterprise, and the free market system, while guaranteeing the peasants that grain production targets would be fixed at the household level of planning.
sheng-yüan 生員 [生员]	The first level imperial examination degree, which qualified the recipient as a candidate for the higher degrees of *chü-jen* and *chin-shih*. Roughly equivalent to a bachelor's degree in the West. (See also *hsiu-ts'ai*.)
shih-chieh ta-t'ung 世界大同	The Confucian concept of a human utopia, a world commonwealth or universal society without political divisions, conflict, or material insecurity. (See *ta-t'ung*.)
Shih-k'an 詩刊 [诗刊]	*Poetry*. A magazine published in Peking since 1957.
shou 收	To restrict or restrain, as to restrict criticism.
shu-shu 叔叔	Paternal uncle, i.e., father's younger brother.
su-fan 蕭反 [蕭反]	"Liquidation of Counterrevolutionaries." The short form of *Su-ch'ing fan-ko-ming fen-tzu* 蕭清反革命份子 [蕭清反革命分子]. A political campaign of 1955 by which the Party sought to elimi-

nate "counterrevolutionaries" in governmental organizations. (Not to be confused with the *chen-fan* 鎮反 [镇反] or *chen-ya fan-ko-ming fen-tzu* 鎮壓反革命份子 [镇压反革命分子] ["Suppression of Counterrevolutionaries"] movement of 1951.

su-k'u 訴苦 [诉苦] — To speak bitterness, to express one's resentment at personal mistreatment or social injustice.

sui-pien 隨便 [随便] — To do as one pleases.

szu-chiu 四舊 [四旧] — "The four olds," a Cultural Revolution slogan by which the Maoists called for criticism of China's "old customs, habits, culture, and social thought" as they continued to be manifest in the behavior of Party cadres and the population.

szu-hsiang 思想 — Thought, in the sense of relatively formal or systematic ideas about something based on personal experience. A term used in common parlance in the sense of "ideology," *yi-shih hsing-t'ai* 意識形態 [意识形态].

szu-hsiang hun-luan 思想混亂 [思想混乱] — Ideological confusion.

szu-hsiang kai-tsao 思想改造 — Ideological remolding, or thought reform.

szu-shu 私塾 — A traditional Confucian home-school which educated children in the classical literature.

Ta Kung Pao 大公報 [大公报] — A newspaper published in Shanghai before Liberation which since 1949 has been published in Peking. It specializes in economic news.

ta-t'ung 大同 — "The great togetherness," a concept that in popular usage implies social unity, security, lack of divisive conflict, and no distinctions of hierarchy, wealth, or loyalty that would divide people. In Confucian thinking, an idealized state of society in which there is universal brotherhood, mutual assistance, and tranquillity.

ta-tzu-pao 大字報[大字报] Big character posters.

tan-shih 但是   However. An adverb used in political discourse to link two clauses of a sentence expressing conflicting policy positions. The clause modified by the "however" usually contains the speaker's criticism of "some comrades," his preferred policy alternative, or a refutation of the argument contained in the first clause.

ti-ti 弟弟   A younger brother.

ti-tui ti 敵對的 [敌对的]   Hostile, antagonistic, as of a relationship or a political contradiction.

t'ien-ming 天命   The Mandate of Heaven. The Confucian political doctrine that a ruler's right to legitimate power is based upon heaven's will, as expressed through popular confidence in the justice of his rule.

t'ing-hua 聽話 [听话]   To obey; lit. "to listen to talk."

t'o-li ch'ün-chung 脫離群眾 [脫离群众]   To be cut off from the masses. A ruling group's alienation from popular support because of bureaucratic procedures and/or unpopular policies.

tou-luan 鬥亂 [斗乱]   To "struggle to confusion." To promote political criticism without limit, producing organizational fragmentation.

tso-feng 作風 [作风]   Work style, as of a Party cadre's manner of applying policy and dealing with the masses.

tsung-tzu 宗族   A clan.

t'u k'u-shui 吐苦水   To "vomit bitter water." A phrase used to describe the release of hostility in "speak bitterness" meetings. (See *su-k'u*.)

t'uan-chieh 團結 [团结]   To unite, to consolidate, as an organization.

tui-k'ang 對抗 [对抗]   An antagonism.

tui-pu-ch'i 對不起 [对不起] To be embarrassed or ashamed; lit., to be unable to face someone (because of a sense of shame).

tung-luan ti 動亂的 [动乱的] To be confused, chaotic. (See *luan*.)

tzu-chu 自主   Autonomy, self-direction in behavior.

tzu-li keng-sheng 自力更生   Self-reliance; regeneration through one's own efforts.

tzu-szu 自私   To be selfish; selfishness.

tzu-yu-chu-yi 自由主義 [自由主义]   Liberalism; lit., self-ism. (See *tzu-szu*, selfishness.)

wa-chieh 瓦解 [瓦解]   To fragment, to disintegrate, as a political organization or coalition.

wang-pa-tan 王八蛋   A bastard.

Wen Hui Pao 文匯報 [文汇报]   A paper published since before Liberation in Shanghai. It specializes in intellectual affairs.

wen-nuan 温暖   To be warm, nurturing.

wu-fan 五反   "The Five Antis." A political campaign of 1952 used to gain control of commerce and industry by attacking the "five poisons" of bribery, tax evasion, theft of state property, cheating on government contracts, and stealing of state economic information by members of the business community.

wu-lun 五倫 [五伦]   The five cardinal social relationships—prince and minister, father and son, elder and younger brother, husband and wife, friend and friend—which according to the Confucian conception of society would sustain order and security if each member of the relationship would act according to the obligations of his status.

yamen 衙門 [衙门]　A government office.

yen 嚴 [严]　To be strict, stern.

yi-hsiao-ts'o 一小撮　"A small handful," as of a political faction, implying lack of strength and isolation from popular support.

yi-shen-tso-tse 以身作則　To make a model or example of one's own behavior for others to emulate. Said especially of those in authority, as a ruler, teacher, or father.

yün-tung 運動 [运动]　A political campaign or mass movement.

Selected Bibliography

I. PERSONALITY FORMATION, SOCIALIZATION, AND SOCIAL CHANGE: GENERAL WORKS

Adelson, Joseph, and Robert O'Neil. "Growth of Political Ideas in Adolescence: The Sense of Community," *Journal of Personality and Social Psychology,* Vol. IV (1966), pp. 295–306.

Adorno, T. W., *et al. The Authoritarian Personality* (New York: Harper, 1950).

Almond, Gabriel. "Comparative Political Systems," *Journal of Politics,* Vol. XVIII, No. 3 (August 1956), pp. 391–409.

———, and Sidney Verba. *The Civic Culture: Political Attitudes and Democracy in Five Nations* (Princeton, N.J.: Princeton University Press, 1963).

Atkinson, John W., ed. *Motives in Fantasy, Action and Society* (Princeton: Van Nostrand, 1958).

Atlas (New York: 1961–   ).

Bandura, Albert, and Richard H. Walters. *Social Learning and Personality Development* (New York: Holt, Rinehart and Winston, 1963).

Berkowitz, Leonard. *Aggression: A Social Psychological Analysis* (New York: McGraw-Hill, 1962).

Christie, Richard, and Marie Jahoda, eds. *Studies in the Scope and Method of "The Authoritarian Personality"* (Glencoe, Ill.: The Free Press, 1954).

Coser, Lewis A. *The Functions of Social Conflict* (Glencoe, Ill.: The Free Press, 1956).

Dawson, Richard E., and Kenneth Prewitt. *Political Socialization* (Boston: Little, Brown, 1969).

Erikson, Erik H. *Childhood and Society* (New York: Norton, 1950).

———. "Ego Development and Historical Change," *Psychoanalytic Study of the Child,* Vol. II (1946), pp. 359–396.

———. *Young Man Luther* (New York: Norton, 1958).

Fenichel, Otto. *The Psychoanalytic Theory of Neurosis* (New York: Norton, 1945).

Gerth, Hans H., and C. Wright Mills. *From Max Weber: Essays in Sociology* (New York: Oxford University Press, Galaxy, 1958).

Goode, William J. *World Revolutions and Family Patterns* (New York: Free Press, 1963).

Greenstein, Fred I. *Children and Politics* (New Haven: Yale University Press, 1965).

———, *et al.* "Personality and Politics: Theoretical and Methodological Issues," *Journal of Social Issues,* Vol. XXIV, No. 3 (July 1968).

Hagen, Everett E. *On the Theory of Social Change: How Economic Growth Begins* (Homewood, Ill.: Dorsey Press, 1962).

Hsu, Francis L. K. *Psychological Anthropology* (Homewood, Ill.: Dorsey Press, 1961).

Klopfer, Bruno, *et al. Developments in the Rorschach Technique* (2 vols., Yonkers-on-Hudson, New York: World Book Company, 1954–1956).

Kluckhohn, Clyde, and Henry A. Murray, eds. *Personality in Nature, Society, and Culture* (New York: Knopf, 1956).

Leites, Nathan. "Psycho-Cultural Hypotheses about Political Acts," *World Politics,* Vol. I (1948), pp. 102–119.

Lerner, Daniel J. *The Passing of Traditional Society* (Glencoe, Ill.: The Free Press, 1958).

Levenson, Daniel J., and Alex Inkeles. "National Character: The Study of Modal Personality and Socio-Cultural Systems," in Gardner Lindzey, ed., *Handbook of Social Psychology* (Cambridge, Mass.: Addison-Wesley, 1954), pp. 997–1020.

Lorenz, Konrad. *On Aggression* (New York: Harcourt, Brace, and World, 1966).

McClelland, David C. *The Achieving Society* (Princeton, N.J.: Van Nostrand, 1961).

Mead, Margaret, and Martha Wolfenstein, eds. *Childhood in Contemporary Cultures* (Chicago: University of Chicago Press, 1955).

———. *Soviet Attitudes toward Authority* (New York: McGraw-Hill, 1951).

———, and Rhoda Metraux. *The Study of Culture at a Distance* (Chicago: University of Chicago Press, 1953).

Montagu, M. F. Ashley, ed. *Man and Aggression* (New York: Oxford University Press, 1968).

Moore, Barrington. *Social Origins of Dictatorship and Democracy* (Boston: Beacon, 1967).

Murray, Henry A., *et al. Explorations in Personality* (New York: Oxford University Press, 1938).

Nieburg, H. L. "The Threat of Violence and Social Change," *American Political Science Review,* Vol. XVI, No. 4 (December 1962), pp. 865–873.

Parsons, Talcott. "Social Structure and the Development of Personality: Freud's Contribution to the Integration of Psychology and Sociology," *Psychiatry,* Vol. XXI, No. 4 (September 1958), pp. 321–340.

———, and Winston White. "The Link Between Character and Society," in S. M. Lipset and Leo Lowenthal, eds., *Culture and Social Character* (Glencoe, Ill.: The Free Press, 1961).

Pye, Lucian W. *Aspects of Political Development* (Boston: Little, Brown, 1966).

————. *Politics, Personality, and Nation Building: Burma's Search for Identity* (New Haven, Conn.: Yale University Press, 1962).

————, and Sidney Verba. *Political Culture and Political Development* (Princeton, N.J.: Princeton University Press, 1965).

Redfield, Robert. *Peasant Society and Culture: An Anthropological Approach to Civilization* (Chicago: University of Chicago Press, 1956).

Sears, Robert, *et al.* "Some Child-Rearing Antecedents of Aggression and Dependency in Young Children," *Genetic Psychology Monographs,* Vol. XLVII (1953), pp. 135–234.

Storr, Anthony. *Human Aggression* (New York: Atheneum, 1968).

Whiting, John W. M., and Irvin L. Child. *Child Training and Personality: A Cross-Cultural Study* (New Haven, Conn.: Yale University Press, 1953).

Wolf, Eric R. *Peasants* (Englewood Cliffs, N.J.: Prentice-Hall, 1966).

Wolfenstein, Martha. "Some Variants in the Moral Training of Children," in *Psychoanalytic Study of the Child,* Vol. V (1949), pp. 310–328.

II. CHINESE CULTURE AND SOCIAL RELATIONS

Balazs, Etienne. *Chinese Civilization and Bureaucracy,* trans. H. M. Wright, ed. Arthur F. Wright (New Haven, Conn.: Yale University Press, 1964).

The Book of Filial Duty, trans. Ivan Chen (New York: Dutton, 1909).

Bunzel, Ruth. *Explorations in Chinese Culture* (mimeographed; Columbia University, Research in Contemporary Cultures, 1950).

————, and John H. Weakland. *An Anthropological Approach to Chinese Communism* (mimeographed; Columbia University, Research in Contemporary Cultures, 1952).

Chai Ch'u. "Chinese Humanism: A Study of Chinese Mentality and Temperament," *Social Research,* Vol. XXVI (1959), pp. 31–46.

Chiang Yee. *A Chinese Childhood* (New York: John Day, 1952).

The Chinese Classics, trans. James Legge (5 vols., Shanghai: 1935).

Chow Chang-cheng. *The Lotus Pool* (New York: Appleton-Century-Crofts, 1961).

Crow, Carl. *The Chinese Are Like That* (New York: Harper, 1939).

Dai, Bingham. "Personality Problems in Chinese Culture," *American Sociological Review,* Vol. VI (1941), pp. 688–696.

de Bary, William Theodore, ed. *Sources of Chinese Tradition* (New York: Columbia University Press, 1960).

Fairbank, John K. *Chinese Thought and Institutions* (Chicago: University of Chicago Press, 1957).

————, Edwin O. Reischauer, and Albert M. Craig. *A History of East Asian Civilization:* Vol. II, *East Asia–The Modern Transformation* (Boston: Houghton Mifflin, 1965).

Feng, Han-yi. "The Chinese Kinship System," *Harvard Journal of Asiatic Studies,* Vol. II, No. 2 (July 1937), pp. 141–275.

Feuerwerker, Albert, Rhoads Murphey, and Mary C. Wright, eds. *Ap-*

proaches to Modern Chinese History (Berkeley: University of California Press, 1967).

———. *China's Early Industrialization* (Cambridge, Mass.: Harvard University Press, 1958).

Fortune, Robert. *Three Years' Wanderings in the Northern Provinces of China* (London: John Murray, 1847).

Fried, Morton H. *Fabric of Chinese Society* (New York: Praeger, 1953).

Friedman, Maurice, ed. *Family and Kinship in Chinese Society* (Stanford, Calif.: Stanford University Press, 1970).

Headland, Isaac Taylor. *Home Life in China* (London: Methuen, 1914).

Ho Ping-ti. *The Ladder of Success in Imperial China* (New York: John Wiley, Science Editions, 1964).

Hsiao Ching [Classic of Filial Piety], trans. James Legge, in Max F. Müller, ed., *Sacred Books of the East* (50 vols., Oxford, England: Clarendon Press, 1879–1910), Vol. III.

Hsu, Francis L. K. *Americans and Chinese: Two Ways of Life* (New York: Henry Schuman, 1953).

———. "Suppression Versus Repression," *Psychiatry,* Vol. XII (1949), pp. 223–242.

Hsu Hsien-chin. "The Chinese Concepts of 'Face'," *American Anthropologist,* Vol. XLVI (January–March 1944), pp. 45–65.

Isaacs, Harold R. *Scratches on Our Minds: American Images of China and India* (New York: John Day, 1958).

Kleinberg, Otto. "Emotional Expression in Chinese Literature," *Journal of Abnormal and Social Psychology,* Vol. XXXIII (1938), pp. 517–520.

LaBarre, Weston. "Some Observations on Character Structure in the Orient: II, The Chinese," *Psychiatry,* Vol. IX (1946), pp. 215–237, 375–395.

Lang, Olga. *Pa Chin and His Writings: Chinese Youth between the Two Revolutions* (Cambridge, Mass.: Harvard University Press, 1967).

Levenson, Joseph R. *Confucian China and Its Modern Fate: The Problem of Monarchical Decay* (Berkeley: University of California Press, 1964).

Levy, Howard S. *Chinese Footbinding: The History of a Curious Erotic Custom* (New York: Walton Rawls, 1966).

Levy, Marion J., Jr. *The Family Revolution in Modern China* (New York: Octagon Books, 1963).

Lin Mousheng Hsi-tien. "Confucius on Inter-personal Relations," *Psychiatry,* Vol. II (1939), pp. 475–481.

Lin Tsung-yi. "Tai-pau and Liu-mang: Two Types of Delinquent Youths in Chinese Society," *British Journal of Delinquency,* Vol. VIII, No. 4 (April 1958), pp. 244–256.

Muensterberger, Warner. "Orality and Dependence: Characteristics of

Southern Chinese," *Psychoanalysis and the Social Sciences,* Vol. III (1951), pp. 37–69.

Müller, Max F., ed. *Sacred Books of the East* (50 vols., Oxford, England: Clarendon Press, 1879–1910).

Nivison, David S., and Arthur F. Wright, eds. *Confucianism in Action* (Stanford, Calif.: Stanford University Press, 1959).

Pruitt, Ida. *A Daughter of Han: The Autobiography of a Chinese Working Woman* (Stanford, Calif.: Stanford University Press, 1967).

Reischauer, Edwin O., and John K. Fairbank. *A History of East Asian Civilization:* Vol. I, *East Asia—The Great Tradition* (Boston: Houghton Mifflin, 1960).

Scofield, Robert W., and Sun Chin-wan. "A Comparative Study of the Differential Effect upon Personality of Chinese and American Child Training Practices," *Journal of Social Psychology,* Vol. LII (1960), pp. 221–224.

Scott, A. C. *An Introduction to the Chinese Theater* (Singapore: Donald Moore, 1958).

Smith, Arthur H. *Chinese Characteristics* (New York: Fleming Revell, 1894).

————. *Village Life in China* (New York: Fleming Revell, 1899).

Ward, Barbara E. "Temper Tantrums in Kau Sai: Some Speculations upon Their Effects" (mimeographed; prepared for a seminar on "Personality and Motivation in Chinese Society," Castle Harbour Hotel, Bermuda, January 26–28, 1964).

Weakland, John H. "Orality in Chinese Conceptions of Male Genital Sexuality," *Psychiatry,* Vol. XIX (1956), pp. 237–247.

————. "The Organization of Action in Chinese Society," *Psychiatry,* Vol. XIII (1950), pp. 361–370.

Wilson, Richard W. *Childhood Political Socialization on Taiwan* (unpublished Ph.D. dissertation, Princeton University, 1967).

————. *Learning to Be Chinese: The Political Socialization of Children in Taiwan* (Cambridge, Mass.: M.I.T. Press, 1970).

Wolf, Margery. "Child Training in a Hokkien Village" (mimeographed; a paper prepared for a seminar on "Personality and Motivation in Chinese Society," Castle Harbour Hotel, Bermuda, January 26–28, 1964).

————. *The House of Lim: A Study of a Chinese Farm Family* (New York: Appleton-Century-Crofts, 1968).

Wright, Arthur F., ed. *The Confucian Persuasion* (Stanford, Calif.: Stanford University Press, 1960).

————. "Struggle *vs.* Harmony: Symbols of Competing Values in Modern China," *World Politics,* Vol. VI, No. 1 (October 1953), pp. 31–44.

————, ed. *Studies in Chinese Thought* (Chicago: University of Chicago Press, 1953).

Wright, Mary C. *The Last Stand of Chinese Conservatism: The T'ung Chih Restoration, 1862–1874* (New York: Atheneum, 1966).

Yang, C. K. *Chinese Communist Society: The Family and the Village* (Cambridge, Mass.: M.I.T. Press, 1965).

Yang, Lien-sheng. "Female Rulers in Imperial China," *Harvard Journal of Asiatic Studies,* Vol. XXIII (1960–1961), pp. 47–61.

Yang, Martin C. *A Chinese Village: Taitou, Shantung Province* (New York: Columbia University Press, 1945).

III. CHINESE POLITICS

The Agrarian Reform Law of the People's Republic of China (Peking: Foreign Languages Press, 1959).

Asian Survey (Berkeley, California: 1961–   ).

Barnett, A. Doak, with a contribution by Ezra Vogel. *Cadres, Bureaucracy and Political Power in Communist China* (New York: Columbia University Press, 1967).

————, ed. *Chinese Communist Politics in Action* (Seattle: University of Washington Press, 1969).

Baum, Richard, and Frederick C. Teiwes. "Liu Shao-ch'i and the Cadre Question," *Asian Survey,* Vol. VIII, No. 4(April 1968), pp. 323–345.

————. *Ssu-Ch'ing: The Socialist Education Movement of 1962–1966* (Berkeley: Center for Chinese Studies, University of California Research Monograph No. 2, 1968).

Belden, Jack. *China Shakes the World* (New York: Harper and Brothers, 1949).

Borkenau, Franz. "Getting at the Facts behind the Soviet Façade," *Commentary,* Vol. XVII, No. 4 (April 1954), pp. 393–400.

Brandt, Conrad. *Stalin's Failure in China, 1924–1927* (New York: Norton, 1966).

————, Benjamin Schwartz, and John K. Fairbank. *A Documentary History of Chinese Communism* (New York: Atheneum, 1966).

Bridgham, Philip. "Mao's Cultural Revolution: Origins and Development," *The China Quarterly,* No. 29 (January–March 1967), pp. 1–35.

The Case of P'eng Teh-huai: 1959–1968 (Hong Kong: Union Research Institute, 1968).

CCP Documents of the Great Proletarian Cultural Revolution, 1966–1967 (Hong Kong: Union Research Institute, 1968).

Chang, Parris H. *Patterns and Processes of Policy Making in Communist China, 1955–1962* (unpublished Ph.D. dissertation, Columbia University, 1969).

Charles, David A. "The Dismissal of P'eng Teh-huai," *The China Quarterly,* No. 8 (October–December 1961), pp. 63–76.

Ch'en, Jerome. *Mao and the Chinese Revolution* (London: Oxford University Press, 1965).

————, ed. *Mao* (Englewood Cliffs, N.J.: Prentice-Hall, 1969).

Ch'en Po-ta. *Notes on Ten Years of Civil War, 1927–1936* (Peking: Foreign Languages Press, 1954).

Chen, S. C., ed. *Rural People's Communes in Lien-Chiang* (Stanford, Calif.: Hoover Institution Press, 1969).

Cheng, J. Chester, ed. *The Politics of the Chinese Red Army: A Translation of the Bulletin of Activities of the People's Liberation Army* (Stanford, Calif.: The Hoover Institution, 1966).

Ch'ien Tuan-sheng. *The Government and Politics of China* (Cambridge, Mass.: Harvard University Press, 1961).

China Monthly [Tzu-kuo Yueh-K'an] (Hong Kong: 1965–   ).

China Pictorial (Peking: 1951–   ).

The China Quarterly (London, 1960–   ).

China Reconstructs (Peking, 1952–   ).

Chinese Law and Government (White Plains, N.Y., 1968–   ).

Chung-hua Jen-min Kung-ho-kuo Fa-lü Hui-pien [Legal Compendium of the People's Republic of China] (Peking: Legal Publishing House, 1957).

Chung Hua-min, and Arthur C. Miller. *Madame Mao: A Profile of Chiang Ch'ing* (Hong Kong: Union Research Institute, 1968).

Cohen, Jerome Alan. "Chinese Mediation on the Eve of Modernization," *California Law Review,* Vol. LIV, No. 2 (August 1966), pp. 1201–1226.

Communist China, 1955–1959: Policy Documents with Analysis (Cambridge, Mass.: Harvard University Press, 1962).

Compton, Boyd, ed. *Mao's China: Party Reform Documents, 1942–1944* (Seattle: University of Washington Press, 1952).

Cranmer-Byng, John L. *Lord Macartney's Embassy to Peking in 1793 from Official Chinese Documents* (Hong Kong: University of Hong Kong Press, 1961).

Current Background (Hong Kong: United States Consulate General, 1950–   ).

Current Scene (Hong Kong: United States Information Service, 1961–   ).

Donnithorne, Audrey. *China's Economic System* (London: George Allen and Unwin, 1967).

Doolin, Dennis J. *Communist China: The Politics of Student Opposition* (Stanford, Calif.: The Hoover Institution, 1964).

Eckstein, Alexander. *Communist China's Economic Growth and Foreign Trade* (New York: McGraw-Hill, 1966).

———. "Economic Fluctuations in Communist China's Domestic Development," in Ping-ti Ho and Tang Tsou, eds., *China in Crisis,* Vol. I, Book 2, pp. 691–729.

———. "Economic Planning, Organization and Control in Communist China: A Review Article," *Current Scene,* Vol. IV, No. 21 (November 25, 1966).

Eighth National Congress of the Communist Party of China (3 vols., Peking: Foreign Languages Press, 1956).

Eto, Shinkichi. "Hai-lu-feng—The First Chinese Soviet Government," *The China Quarterly,* Nos. 8, 9 (October–December 1961; January–March 1962), pp. 161–183, 149–181.

Extracts from China Mainland Magazines (Hong Kong: United States Consulate General, 1955–1960).

Fanon, Frantz. *The Wretched of the Earth* (New York: Evergreen, 1968).

Garthoff, Raymond L., ed. *Sino-Soviet Military Relations* (New York: Praeger, 1966).

George, Alexander. *The Chinese Communist Army in Action* (New York: Columbia University Press, 1967).

Gillin, Donald G. "Peasant Nationalism in the History of Chinese Communism," *Journal of Asian Studies,* Vol. XXIII, No. 2 (February 1964), pp. 269–289.

Gittings, John. *The Role of the Chinese Army* (London: Oxford University Press, 1967).

Goldman, Merle. *Literary Dissent in Communist China* (Cambridge, Mass.: Harvard University Press, 1967).

———. "The Unique 'Blooming and Contending' of 1961–62," *The China Quarterly,* No. 37 (January–March 1969), pp. 54–83.

Griffith, William E. *Communist Esoteric Communications: Explication de Texte* (Cambridge, Mass.: M.I.T. Center for International Studies, 1967).

———. *Sino-Soviet Relations, 1964–1965* (Cambridge, Mass.: M.I.T. Press, 1967).

———. *The Sino-Soviet Rift* (Cambridge, Mass.: M.I.T. Press, 1964).

Harding, Harry, and Melvin Gurtov. *The Purge of Lo Jui-ch'ing: The Politics of Chinese Strategic Planning* (Santa Monica, Calif.: The Rand Corporation, 1970).

Harrison, James P. "The Li Li-san Line and the CCP in 1930, Part I," *The China Quarterly,* No. 14 (April–June 1963), pp. 178–194.

Hinton, William. *Fanshen: A Documentary of Revolution in a Chinese Village* (New York: Monthly Review Press, 1966).

Ho, Ping-ti and Tang Tsou, eds. *China in Crisis:* Vol. I, *China's Heritage and the Communist Political System* (2 vols., Chicago: University of Chicago Press, 1968).

Hofheinz, Roy Mark. *The Peasant Movement and Rural Revolution: Chinese Communists in the Countryside, 1923–1927* (unpublished Ph.D. dissertation, Harvard University, 1966).

Hsia, T. A. "Ch'ü Ch'iu-pai's Autobiographical Writings: The Making and Destruction of a 'Tender-hearted' Communist," *The China Quarterly,* No. 25 (January–March 1966), pp. 176–212.

Hsiao Kung-chuan. *Rural China: Imperial Control in the Nineteenth Century* (Seattle: University of Washington Press, 1960).

Hsieh, Alice Langley. *Communist China's Strategy in the Nuclear Era* (Englewood Cliffs, N.J.: Prentice-Hall, 1962).

Hsin Ch'ing-nien [New Youth] (Peking: 1915–1926).

Hsin-hua Pan-yüeh-k'an [New China Semi-Monthly] (Peking: 1956–).

Hsu, Kai-yu. *Chou En-lai: China's Gray Eminence* (Garden City, New York: Doubleday, 1968).

Hsüeh-hsi [Study] (Peking: 1949–1958).

Hu Chiao-mu. *Thirty Years of the Communist Party of China* (Peking: Foreign Languages Press, 1951).

Hung-ch'i [Red Flag] (Peking: 1958–   ).

Inkeles, Alex, and Raymond A. Bauer. *The Soviet Citizen* (Cambridge, Mass.: Harvard University Press, 1959).

Isaacs, Harold R. *The Tragedy of the Chinese Revolution* (New York: Atheneum, 1966).

Jen-min Jih-pao [The People's Daily] (Peking: 1948–   ).

Joffe, Ellis. "The Chinese Army on the Eve of the Cultural Revolution: Prelude to Intervention" (a paper prepared for a conference on "Government in China: The Management of a Revolutionary Society" held in Cuernavaca, Mexico, August 1969).

———. *Party and Army: Professionalism and Political Control in the Chinese Officer Corps, 1949–1964* (Cambridge, Mass.: Harvard University, East Asian Monographs, 1965).

Johnson, Chalmers A. "Lin Piao's Army and Its Role in Chinese Society," *Current Scene,* Vol. IV, No. 14 (July 14, 1966).

———. *Peasant Nationalism and Communist Power: The Emergence of Revolutionary China, 1937–1945* (London: Oxford University Press, 1963).

Joint Publications Research Service, Translations on Communist China (Washington, D.C.: 1960–   ).

Journal of Asian Studies (Ann Arbor: 1956–   ).

Klochko, Mikhail A. *Soviet Scientist in Red China* (New York: Praeger, 1964).

Lee, Rensselaer W. "The *Hsia Fang* System: Marxism and Modernization," *The China Quarterly,* No. 28 (October–December 1966), pp. 40–62.

Leites, Nathan. "Panic and Defenses against Panic in the Bolshevik View of Politics," *Psychoanalysis and the Social Sciences,* Vol. IV (1955), pp. 135–144.

———. *A Study of Bolshevism* (Glencoe, Ill.: The Free Press, 1953).

Lewis, John Wilson. *Leadership in Communist China* (Ithaca, New York: Cornell University Press, 1963).

Li Choh-ming, "The First Decade: Economic Development," *The China Quarterly,* No. 1 (January–March 1960), pp. 35–50.

Li Tsung-jen. *The Reminiscences of General Li Tsung-jen* (unpublished manuscript of the Columbia University East Asian Institute, Chinese Oral History Project, n.d.).

Lifton, Robert Jay. *Revolutionary Immortality: Mao Tse-tung and the Chinese Cultural Revolution* (New York: Random House, 1968).

———. "Thought Reform of Chinese Intellectuals: A Psychiatric Evaluation," *Journal of Social Issues,* Vol. XIII (1957), pp. 5–20.

———. *Thought Reform and the Psychology of Totalism* (New York: Norton, 1963).

Liu, F. F. *A Military History of Modern China* (Princeton, N.J.: Princeton University Press, 1956).

Liu Shao-chi. *Collected Works of Liu Shao-chi* (3 vols., Hong Kong: Union Research Institute, 1969).

Loh, Robert, and Humphrey Evans. *Escape from Red China* (New York: Coward McCann, 1962).

London, Kurt, ed. *Unity and Contradiction* (New York: Praeger, 1962).

Lu Hsün. *Selected Works of Lu Hsün* (3 vols., Peking: Foreign Languages Press, 1956).

MacFarquhar, Roderick. "Communist China's Intra-Party Dispute," *Pacific Affairs,* Vol. XXXI, No. 4 (December 1958), pp. 323–335.

―――. *The Hundred Flowers Campaign and the Chinese Intellectuals* (New York: Praeger, 1960).

Malraux, André. *Anti-Memoirs* (New York: Holt, Rinehart and Winston, 1968).

Mao Chu-hsi tui P'eng, Huang, Chang, Chou Fan-tang Chi-t'uan ti P'i-p'an [Chairman Mao's Criticism and Repudiation of the P'eng (Teh-huai), Huang (K'o-ch'eng), Chang (Wen-t'ien), and Chou (Hsiao-chou) Anti-Party Clique] (n.p., n.d.). This pamphlet has been translated in *Chinese Law and Government,* Vol. I, No. 4 (Winter 1968/69).

Mao Tse-tung Hsüan-chi [The Selected Works of Mao Tse-tung] (4 vols., Peking: People's Publishing House, 1960–1964).*

Mao Tse-tung. "Chairman Mao's Selected Writings," *Joint Publications Research Service, Translations on Communist China,* No. 90 (February 12, 1970).

―――. *Poems of Mao Tse-tung,* trans. Wong Man (Hong Kong: Eastern Horizon Press, 1966).

―――. *Selected Readings from the Works of Mao Tse-tung* (Peking: Foreign Languages Press, 1967).

―――. *Selected Works of Mao Tse-tung* (4 vols., Peking: Foreign Languages Press, 1961–1965).*

―――, ed. *Socialist Upsurge in China's Countryside* (Peking: Foreign Languages Press, 1957).

* In Parts Three and Four of this study we make numerous citations from official political statements by Mao Tse-tung. Most of these citations have been drawn from Mao's *Selected Works.* We have relied upon two versions of this collection of political statements. The first one, in Chinese, was published between 1960 and 1964 by the *Jen-min Ch'u-pan She* (The People's Publishing House) in Peking in an edition of four volumes. The English language version of the *Selected Works,* published in four matching volumes, was released by the Foreign Languages Press in Peking between 1961 and 1965.

Our general procedure in using these materials has been to compare the English translation of a passage with the Chinese "original" (an edited "original" of the first versions of these statements in some cases), and to cite the English translation where no significant alterations in meaning or tone were found. Where the official translation seems to obscure an important point, we have made a direct translation from the Chinese edition. The language of the version used in any particular citation is indicated in the footnote.

————. *Ten More Poems of Mao Tse-tung* (Hong Kong: Eastern Horizon Press, 1967).

Mao Tse-tung Szu-hsiang Wan-sui! [Long Live the Thought of Mao Tse-tung!] (n.p.: April 1967). This pamphlet has been translated, along with an untitled collection of Mao Tse-tung's speeches and statements from the years 1956–1967, in *Current Background* (Hong Kong: United States Consulate General), Nos. 891, 892 (October 1969).

Marsh, Robert M. *The Mandarins: The Circulation of Elites in China, 1600–1900* (Glencoe, Ill.: The Free Press, 1961).

Meisner, Maurice. *Li Ta-chao and the Origins of Chinese Marxism* (Cambridge, Mass.: Harvard University Press, 1967).

Meskill, Jonathan, ed. *The Pattern of Chinese History: Cycles, Development, or Stagnation?* (Boston: Heath, 1965).

Munro, Donald J. *The Concept of Man in Early China* (Stanford, Calif.: Stanford University Press, 1968).

————. "Maxims and Realities in China's Educational Policy: The Half-Work, Half-Study Model," *Asian Survey,* Vol. VII, No. 4 (April 1967), pp. 254–272.

Myrdal, Jan. *Report from a Chinese Village* (London: Heinemann, 1965).

Nan-fang Jih-pao [Southern Daily] (Canton: 1949–   ).

Neuhauser, Charles. "The Chinese Communist Party in the 1960s: Prelude to the Cultural Revolution," *The China Quarterly,* No. 32 (October–December 1967), pp. 3–36.

New Youth [*Hsin Ch'ing-nien*] (Peking: 1915–1926).

North, Robert C. *Kuomintang and Chinese Communist Elites* (Stanford, Calif.: Hoover Institution, 1952).

Oksenberg, Michel Charles. "Occupational Groups in Chinese Society and the Cultural Revolution," in *The Cultural Revolution: 1967 in Review* (Ann Arbor: University of Michigan Center for Chinese Studies, Papers in Chinese Studies No. 2, 1968).

————. *Policy Formulation in Communist China: The Case of the Mass Irrigation Campaign, 1957–58* (unpublished Ph.D. dissertation, Columbia University, 1969).

Payne, Robert. *Mao Tse-tung, Ruler of Red China* (New York: Henry Schuman, 1950).

Peking Review (Peking: 1958–   ).

Polemic on the General Line of the International Communist Movement (Peking: Foreign Languages Press, 1965).

The People's Daily [*Jen-min Jih-pao*] (Peking: 1948–   ).

Problems of Communism (Washington, D.C.: United States Information Agency, 1951–   ).

Pye, Lucian W. *The Dynamics of Hostility and Hate in the Chinese Political Culture* (mimeographed; Cambridge, Mass.: Center for International Studies, M.I.T., 1964).

————. *The Spirit of Chinese Politics: A Psychocultural Study of the Authority Crisis in Political Development* (Cambridge, Mass.: M.I.T. Press, 1968).

Red Flag [*Hung-ch'i*] (Peking: 1958–   ).

Rush, Myron. *The Rise of Khrushchev* (Washington, D.C.: Public Affairs Press, 1958).

Schein, Edgar H., *et al. Coercive Persuasion* (New York: W. W. Norton, 1961).

Schram, Stuart. *Mao Tse-tung* (Baltimore, Md.: Penguin Books, 1967).

———. "Mao Tse-tung and Secret Societies," *The China Quarterly*, No. 27 (July–September 1966), pp. 1–13.

———. *The Political Thought of Mao Tse-tung* (New York: Praeger, 1963).

Schurmann, Franz. *Ideology and Organization in Communist China* (Berkeley: University of California Press, 1968).

Schwartz, Benjamin I. *Chinese Communism and the Rise of Mao* (Cambridge, Mass.: Harvard University Press, 1964).

Selden, Mark. "The Guerilla Movement in Northwest China: The Origins of the Shensi-Kansu-Ningsia Border Region," *The China Quarterly*, Nos. 28, 29 (October–December 1966; January–March 1967), pp. 63–81, 61–81.

Selections from China Mainland Magazines (Hong Kong: United States Consulate General, 1960–   ).

Sharman, Lyon. *Sun Yat-sen: His Life and Its Meaning* (Stanford, Calif.: Stanford University Press, 1968).

Sheridan, James E. *Chinese Warlord: The Career of Feng Yü-hsiang* (Stanford, Calif.: Stanford University Press, 1966).

Siao, Emi. *Mao Tse-tung, His Childhood and Youth* (Bombay: People's Publishing House, 1955).

Siao Yü. *Mao Tse-tung and I Were Beggars* (London: Hutchinson, 1961).

Simmonds, J. D. "P'eng Teh-huai: A Chronological Re-examination," *The China Quarterly*, No. 37 (January–March 1969), pp. 120–138.

Skinner, G. William, and Edwin A. Winckler. "Compliance and Succession in Rural China: A Cyclical Theory," in Amitai Etzioni, ed., *Complex Organizations: A Sociological Reader* (New York: Holt, Rinehart and Winston, 1969).

———. "Marketing and Social Structure in Rural China, Part III," *Journal of Asian Studies*, Vol. XXIV, No. 3 (May 1965), pp. 363–399).

Smedley, Agnes. *The Great Road: The Life and Times of Chu Teh* (New York: Monthly Review Press, 1956).

Snow, Edgar. "Interview with Mao," *The New Republic* (February 27, 1965), pp. 23–27.

———. *Red Star Over China* (New York: Grove Press, Black Cat Edition, 1961).

Solomon, Richard. "America's Revolutionary Alliance with Communist China: Parochialism and Paradox in Sino-American Relations," *Asian Survey*, Vol. VII, No. 12 (December 1967), pp. 831–850.

———. *The Chinese Political Culture and Problems of Modernization* (mimeographed; Cambridge, Mass.: Center for International Studies, M.I.T., 1964).

————. *The Chinese Revolution and the Politics of Dependency* (unpublished Ph.D. dissertation, M.I.T., 1966).

————. "Communication Patterns and the Chinese Revolution," *The China Quarterly,* No. 32 (October–December 1967), pp. 88–110.

————. "Mao's Effort to Reintegrate the Chinese Polity: Problems of Conflict and Authority in Chinese Social Processes," in A. Doak Barnett, ed., *Chinese Communist Politics in Action* (Seattle: University of Washington Press, 1968), pp. 271–361.

————. "On Activism and Activists: Maoist Conceptions of Motivation and Political Role Linking State to Society," *The China Quarterly,* No. 39 (July–September 1969), pp. 76–114.

Southern Daily [Nan-fang Jih-pao] (Canton: 1949–   ).

Strong, Anna Louise. *Letters from China* (Peking: New World Press, 1963–1970).

Study [Hsüeh-hsi] (Peking: 1949–1958).

Sun Tzu. *The Art of War,* trans. Samuel B. Griffith (Oxford, England: Oxford University Press, 1963).

Survey of the China Mainland Press (Hong Kong: United States Consulate General, 1950–   ).

Ta-tao Tang-nei Tsui-ta ti Tsou Tzu-pen-chu-yi Tao-lu Tang-ch'uan-p'ai –Liu Shao-ch'i [Strike Down the Biggest Person in Authority Taking the Capitalist Road–Liu Shao-ch'i] (Peking: Peking Chemical Engineering Institute, Mao Tse-tung's Thought Propaganda Personnel, April 10, 1967), Vol. IV.

Teiwes, Frederick C. *Provincial Party Personnel in Mainland China, 1956–1966* (New York: Columbia University, East Asian Institute, 1967).

————. "The Purge of Provincial Leaders, 1957–1958," *The China Quarterly,* No. 27 (July–September 1966), pp. 14–32.

————. *Rectification Campaigns and Purges in Communist China* (unpublished Ph.D. dissertation, Columbia University, 1970).

Ten Great Years: Statistics of the Economic and Cultural Achievements of the People's Republic of China (Peking: Foreign Languages Press, 1960).

Ti-yi-t'zu Kuo-nei Ko-ming Chan-cheng Shih-ch'i ti Nung-min Yün-tung [The Peasant Movement During the First Period of Domestic Revolutionary War] (Peking: People's Publishing House, 1953).

Townsend, James R. *Political Participation in Communist China* (Berkeley: University of California Press, 1967).

Tsou, Tang, ed. *China in Crisis:* Vol. II, *China, The United States, and Asia* (Chicago: University of Chicago Press, 1968).

Tung Chi-ping, and Humphrey Evans. *The Thought Revolution* (New York: Coward McCann, 1966).

Tzu-kuo Yueh-k'an [China Monthly] (Hong Kong: 1965–   ).

Union Research Service (Hong Kong: 1955–   ).

Van Slyke, Lyman P. *Enemies and Friends: The United Front in Chinese Communist History* (Stanford, Calif.: Stanford University Press, 1967).

Vogel, Ezra F. *Canton under Communism: Programs and Politics in a Provincial Capital, 1949–1968* (Cambridge, Mass.: Harvard University Press, 1969).

Waley, Arthur. *The Opium War through Chinese Eyes* (London: George Allen and Unwin, 1958).

Walker, Kenneth R. "Collectivization in Retrospect: The 'Socialist High Tide' of Autumn 1955–Spring 1956," *The China Quarterly*, No. 26 (April–June 1966), pp. 1–43.

———. *Planning in Chinese Agriculture: Socialization and the Private Sector, 1956–1962* (Chicago: Aldine Publishing Co., 1965).

Weakland, John. "Family Imagery in a Passage by Mao Tse-tung," *World Politics*, Vol. X (1958), pp. 387–407.

Whitson, William W., with Huang Chen-hsia. *The Chinese Communist High Command: A History of Military Politics, 1927–1969* (New York: Praeger, 1971).

Who's Who in Communist China (2 vols., Hong Kong: Union Research Institute, 1969–1970).

Whyte, Martin K. *Small Groups and Political Rituals in Communist China* (unpublished Ph.D. dissertation, Harvard University, 1970).

Wright, Mary C. "From Revolution to Restoration: The Transformation of Kuomintang Ideology," *Far Eastern Quarterly*, Vol. XIV, No. 4 (1955), pp. 515–532.

Zagoria, Donald S. *The Sino-Soviet Conflict, 1956–1961* (Princeton, N.J.: Princeton University Press, 1962).

———. *Viet-Nam Triangle* (New York: Pegasus, 1967).

INDEX

Acheson, Dean, 161
Activist (*chi-chi fen-tzu*), activism, 561
  emerges from the younger generation, 193, 525
  as a political mobilizer, 198–200
  as sign of subordination, 57
  See also Mao Tse-tung: Political Attitudes, on activism
"Adventurism," 184–185
Aggression, emotions of
  cause illness, 64n
  childhood disciplining of, 67–70, 79, 559–560
  controlled through ritual, 68, 79–80, 110, 124
  expressed only to inferiors, 69, 79
  and organizational unity, 238–239
  overcome anxiety, 194–196
  as political motivation, 6, 73n, 194–196, 204, 363, 364, 393, 439, 444, 499, 513–514, 522–523
  and social change, 514, 522–523
  suppression of, 70–73, 101, 559–560
  turned against the self, 176, 192
  See also: Eating, as aggression; Emotions
Agriculture, and economic development, 333ff.
Agricultural Producers' Cooperatives (APCs), 327, 334, 340, 348–349
  amalgamated to form People's Communes, 327, 340, 358n, 360
  transition from "primary stage" to "advanced stage," 353, 354–356, 357, 366
All-China Federation of Literary and Artistic Circles, 414, 450
All Men Are Brothers, 124
American culture, compared with Chinese, 4, 11, 40n, 67n, 118–120, 123, 125n, 138n, 559; *see also* Western culture, compared with Chinese
An Tzu-wen, Director CCP Organization Dept.

attacked in the Cultural Revolution, 448
disagrees with Mao on training successors, 462–463
Authority
  ambivalence toward, 4, 60, 71, 104, 135, 150, 234, 501
  anxiety in the face of, 5–6, 52, 57–58, 86, 112–116, 147, 192, 522
  depersonalized, 179, 188, 257, 506
  of group, 257
  not to be criticized, 114–115, 316, 421–422
  not internalized, 152, 517
  personalized, 138, 144, 151
  and security, 74–75, 104, 133–134, 139
  sustained through deference rituals, 108
  See also: Confucianism, filial piety; Communications, interpersonal
Autonomy, 52, 69, 86, 252, 522
  as "selfishness," 4–5, 80, 254, 516

Balazs, Etienne, 116
Barnett, A. Doak, xviii
Bauer, Elizabeth K., xviii
Berris, Jan, xviii
Big character posters (*ta-tzu-pao*), 343–344, 490, 491, 498, 516, 572
"Blooming and contending." *See* Hundred Flowers Campaign
Bolshevik ["October"] Revolution (1917), 253
  fortieth anniversary celebration of, 327, 379
Bureaucratic behavior, 116n, 120n, 148
  Mao's opposition to, 173, 208–209, 263, 287, 292–293, 338–339, 342
Burmese culture, compared with Chinese, 51n

Calligraphy, 91n, 111
Campaigns (*yün-tung*), 256, 574; *see also:* Great Leap Forward; Hundred Flowers Campaign; Socialist Education Movement

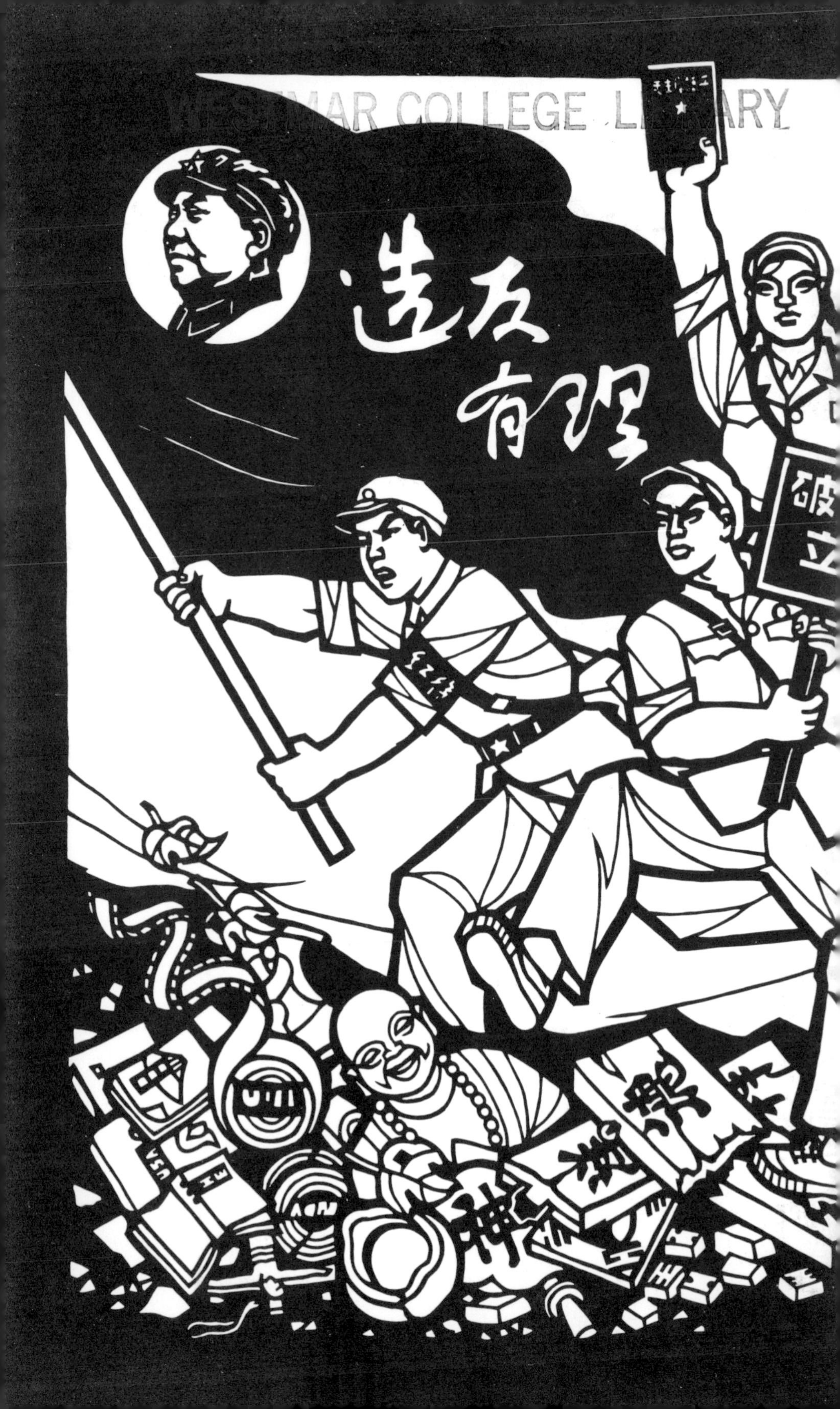
造反
有理
破
立